The Heart of the Matter

Stamboul Train
Orient Express

A Burnt-out Case

The Third Man

The Quiet American

Loser Takes All

The Power and the Glory

GRAHAM GREENE

Heinemann/Octopus

Graham Greene: Title Verso Page

The Heart of the Matter was first published in Great Britain by
William Heinemann Ltd in 1948; in the United States by The Viking Press in 1948.
Stamboul Train was first published in Great Britain by
William Heinemann Ltd in 1932; in the United States (as *Orient Express*)
by Doubleday, Doran in 1933.
A Burnt-out Case was first published in Great Britain by
William Heinemann Ltd in 1961; in the United States by The Viking Press in 1961.
The Third Man was first published in Great Britain by
William Heinemann Ltd in 1950; in the United States by The Viking Press in 1950.
The Quiet American was first published in Great Britain by
William Heinemann Ltd in 1955; in the United States by The Viking Press in 1956.
Loser Takes All was first published in Great Britain by
William Heinemann Ltd in 1955; in the United States by The Viking Press in 1957.
The Power and the Glory was first published in Great Britain by
William Heinemann Ltd in 1940; in the United States by The Viking Press in 1940.

This edition first published in the United States of America
in 1979 jointly by

William Heinemann Inc
450 Park Avenue, New York, NY 10022

and

Octopus Books Inc
The Olympic Towers, 645 Fifth Avenue,
New York, NY 10022

Published by arrangement with The Viking Press

ISBN 0 905712 01 3

This edition first published in Great Britain in 1977

The Heart of the Matter Copyright 1948,
Copyright © renewed 1976 by Graham Greene
Stamboul Train, (Orient Express) Copyright 1932,
Copyright © renewed 1960 by Graham Greene
A Burnt-out Case Copyright © 1960,
1961 by Graham Greene
The Third Man Copyright 1949,
Copyright © renewed 1977 by Graham Greene
The Quiet American Copyright 1955 by Graham Greene
Loser Takes All Copyright 1954,
1955 by Graham Greene
The Power and the Glory Copyright 1940,
Copyright © renewed 1968 by Graham Greene

Printed in the United States of America
by R. R. Donnelley and Sons Company

CONTENTS

THE HEART OF
THE MATTER

THE HEART OF THE MATTER

To V.G., L.C.G. and F.C.G.

Le pécheur est au coeur même de chrétienté . . .
Nul n'est aussi competent que le pécheur en matière
de chrétienté.
Nul, si ce n'est le saint.

Péguy

The poem quoted on page 189 is from
Selected Poems of Rainer Maria Rilke
translated by J. D. Leishmann
(Hogarth Press, 1941).

BOOK ONE

PART I

I/i

Wilson sat on the balcony of the Bedford Hotel with his bald pink knees thrust against the ironwork. It was Sunday and the Cathedral bell clanged for matins. On the other side of Bond Street, in the windows of the High School, sat the young negresses in dark-blue gym smocks engaged on the interminable task of trying to wave their wirespring hair. Wilson stroked his very young moustache and dreamed, waiting for his gin-and-bitters.

Sitting there, facing Bond Street, he had his face turned to the sea. His pallor showed how recently he had emerged from it into the port: so did his lack of interest in the schoolgirls opposite. He was like the lagging finger of the barometer, still pointing to Fair long after its companion has moved to Stormy. Below him the black clerks moved churchward, but their wives in brilliant afternoon dresses of blue and cerise aroused no interest in Wilson. He was alone on the balcony except for one bearded Indian in a turban who had already tried to tell his fortune: this was not the hour or the day for white men–they would be at the beach five miles away, but Wilson had no car. He felt almost intolerably lonely. On either side of the school the tin roofs sloped towards the sea, and the corrugated iron above his head clanged and clattered as a vulture alighted.

Three merchant officers from the convoy in the harbour came into view, walking up from the quay. They were surrounded immediately by small boys wearing school caps. The boys' refrain came faintly up to Wilson like a nursery rhyme: 'Captain want jig jig, my sister pretty girl school-teacher, captain want jig jig.' The bearded Indian frowned over intricate calculations on the back of an envelope–a horoscope, the cost of living? When Wilson looked down into the street again the officers had fought their way free, and the schoolboys had swarmed again round a single able-seaman; they led him triumphantly away towards the brothel near the police station, as though to the nursery.

A black boy brought Wilson's gin and he sipped it very slowly because he had nothing else to do except to return to his hot and squalid room and read a novel–or a poem. Wilson liked poetry, but he absorbed it secretly, like a drug. *The Golden Treasury* accompanied him wherever he went, but it was taken at night in small doses–a finger of Longfellow, Macaulay, Mangan: 'Go on to tell how, with genius wasted, Betrayed in friendship, befooled in love. . . .' His taste was romantic. For public exhibition he had his Wallace. He wanted passionately to be indistinguishable on the surface from other men: he wore his moustache like a club tie–it was his highest common factor, but his eyes betrayed him–brown dog's eyes, a setter's eyes, pointing mournfully towards Bond Street.

'Excuse me,' a voice said, 'aren't you Wilson?'

He looked up at a middle-aged man in the inevitable khaki shorts with a drawn face the colour of hay.

'Yes, that's me.'

'May I join you? My name's Harris.'

'Delighted, Mr Harris.'

'You're the new accountant at the U.A.C.?'

'That's me. Have a drink?'

'I'll have a lemon squash if you don't mind. Can't drink in the middle of the day.'

The Indian rose from his table and approached with deference, 'You remember me, Mr Harris. Perhaps you would tell your friend, Mr Harris, of my talents. Perhaps he would like to read my letters of recommendation . . .' The grubby sheaf of envelopes was always in his hand. 'The leaders of society.'

'Be off. Beat it, you old scoundrel,' Harris said.

'How did you know my name?' Wilson asked.

'Saw it on a cable. I'm a cable censor,' Harris said. 'What a job! What a place!'

'I can see from here, Mr Harris, that your fortune has changed considerably. If you would step with me for a moment into the bathroom . . .'

'Beat it, Gunga Din.'

'Why the bathroom?' Wilson asked.

'He always tells fortunes there. I suppose it's the only private room available. I never thought of asking why.'

'Been here long?'

'Eighteen bloody months.'

'Going home soon?'

Harris stared over the tin roofs towards the harbour. He said, 'The ships all go the wrong way. But when I do get home you'll never see me here again.' He lowered his voice and said with venom over his lemon squash, 'I hate the place. I hate the people. I hate the bloody niggers. Mustn't call 'em that you know.'

'My boy seems all right.'

'A man's boy's always all right. He's a real nigger—but these, look at 'em, look at that one with a feather boa down there. They aren't even real niggers. Just West Indians and they rule the coast. Clerks in the stores, city council, magistrates, lawyers—my God. It's all right up in the Protectorate. I haven't anything to say against a real nigger. God made our colours. But these—my God! The Government's afraid of them. The police are afraid of them. Look down there,' Harris said, 'look at Scobie.'

A vulture flapped and shifted on the iron roof and Wilson looked at Scobie. He looked without interest in obedience to a stranger's direction, and it seemed to him that no particular interest attached to the squat grey-haired man walking alone up Bond Street. He couldn't tell that this was one of those occasions a man never forgets: a small cicatrice had been made on the memory, a wound that would ache whenever certain things combined—the taste of gin at mid-day, the smell of flowers under a balcony, the clang of corrugated iron, an ugly bird flopping from perch to perch.

'He loves 'em so much,' Harris said, 'he sleeps with 'em.'

'Is that the police uniform?'

'It is. Our great police force. A lost thing will they never find—you know the poem.'

'I don't read poetry,' Wilson said. His eyes followed Scobie up the sun-drowned street. Scobie stopped and had a word with a black man in a white panama: a black policeman passed by, saluting smartly. Scobie went on.

'Probably in the pay of the Syrians too if the truth were known.'

'The Syrians?'

'This is the original Tower of Babel,' Harris said. 'West Indians, Africans, real Indians, Syrians, Englishmen, Scotsmen in the Office of Works, Irish priests, French priests, Alsatian priests.'

'What do the Syrians do?'

'Make money. They run all the stores up country and most of the stores here. Run diamonds too.'

'I suppose there's a lot of that.'

'The Germans pay a high price.'

'Hasn't he got a wife here?'

'Who? Oh, Scobie. Rather. He's got a wife. Perhaps if I had a wife like that, I'd sleep with niggers too. You'll meet her soon. She's the city intellectual. She likes art, poetry. Got up an exhibition of arts for the shipwrecked seamen. You know the kind of thing—poems on exile by aircraftsmen, water-colours by stokers, pokerwork from the mission schools. Poor old Scobie. Have another gin?'

'I think I will,' said Wilson.

I / ii

Scobie turned up James Street past the Secretariat. With its long balconies it had always reminded him of a hospital. For fifteen years he had watched the arrival of a succession of patients; periodically at the end of eighteen months certain patients were sent home, yellow and nervy, and others took their place—Colonial Secretaries, Secretaries of Agriculture, Treasurers and Directors of Public Works. He watched their temperature charts every one—the first outbreak of unreasonable temper, the drink too many, the sudden stand for principle after a year of acquiescence. The black clerks carried their bedside manner like doctors down the corridors; cheerful and respectful they put up with any insult. The patient was always right.

Round the corner, in front of the old cotton tree, where the earliest settlers had gathered their first day on the unfriendly shore, stood the law courts and police station, a great stone building like the grandiloquent boast of weak men. Inside that massive frame the human being rattled in the corridors like a dry kernel. No one could have been adequate to so rhetorical a conception. But the idea in any case was only one room deep. In the dark narrow passage behind, in the charge-room and the cells, Scobie could always detect the odour of human meanness and injustice—it was the smell of a zoo, of sawdust, excrement, ammonia, and lack of liberty. The place was scrubbed daily, but you could never eliminate the smell. Prisoners and policemen carried it in their clothing like cigarette smoke.

Scobie climbed the great steps and turned to his right along the shaded outside corridor to his room: a table, two kitchen chairs, a cupboard, some rusty handcuffs hanging on a nail like an old hat, a filing cabinet: to a stranger it would have appeared a bare uncomfortable room but to Scobie it was home. Other men slowly build up the sense of home by accumulation—a new picture, more and more books, an odd-shaped paper-weight, the ash-tray bought for a forgotten reason on a forgotten holiday; Scobie built his home by a process of reduction. He had started out fifteen years ago with far more than this. There had been a photograph of his wife, bright leather cushions from the market, an easy-chair, a large coloured map of the port on the wall. The map had been borrowed by younger men: it was of no more use to him; he carried the whole coastline of the colony in his mind's eye: from Kufa Bay to Medley was his beat. As for the cushions and the easy-chair, he had soon discovered how comfort of that kind down in the airless town meant heat. Where the body was touched or enclosed it sweated. Last of all his wife's photograph had been made unnecessary by her presence. She had joined him the first year of the phoney war and now she couldn't get away: the danger of submarines had made her as much a fixture as the handcuffs on the nail. Besides, it had been a very early photograph, and he no longer cared to be reminded of the unformed face, the expression calm and gentle with lack of knowledge, the lips parted obediently in the smile the photographer had demanded. Fifteen years form a face, gentleness ebbs with experience, and he was always aware of his own responsibility. He had led the way: the experience that had come to her was the experience selected by himself. He had formed her face.

He sat down at his bare table and almost immediately his Mende sergeant clicked his heels in the doorway. 'Sah?'

'Anything to report?'

'The Commissioner want to see you, sah.'

'Anything on the charge sheet?'

'Two black men fight in the market, sah.'

'Mammy trouble?'

'Yes, sah.'

'Anything else?'

'Miss Wilberforce want to see you, sah. I tell her you was at church and she got to come back by-and-by, but she stick. She say she no budge.'

'Which Miss Wilberforce is that, sergeant?'

'I don't know, sah. She come from Sharp Town, sah.'

'Well, I'll see her after the Commissioner. But no one else, mind.'

'Very good, sah.'

Scobie, passing down the passage to the Commissioner's room, saw the girl sitting alone on a bench against the wall: he didn't look twice: he caught only the vague impression of a young black African face, a bright cotton frock, and then she was already out of his mind, and he was wondering what he should say to the Commissioner. It had been on his mind all that week.

'Sit down, Scobie.' The Commissioner was an old man of fifty-three—one counted age by the years a man had served in the colony. The Commissioner with twenty-two years' service was the oldest man there, just as the

Governor was a stripling of sixty compared with any district officer who had five years' knowledge behind him.

'I'm retiring, Scobie,' the Commissioner said, 'after this tour.'

'I know.'

'I suppose everyone knows.'

'I've heard the men talking about it.'

'And yet you are the second man I've told. Do they say who's taking my place?'

Scobie said, 'They know who isn't.'

'It's damned unfair,' the Commissioner said. 'I can do nothing more than I have done, Scobie. You are a wonderful man for picking up enemies. Like Aristides the Just.'

'I don't think I'm as just as all that.'

'The question is what do you want to do? They are sending a man called Baker from Gambia. He's younger than you are. Do you want to resign, retire, transfer, Scobie?'

'I want to stay,' Scobie said.

'Your wife won't like it.'

'I've been here too long to go.' He thought to himself, poor Louise, if I had left it to her, where should we be now? and he admitted straight away that they wouldn't be here—somewhere far better, better climate, better pay, better position. She would have taken every opening for improvement: she would have steered agilely up the ladders and left the snakes alone. I've landed her here, he thought, with the odd premonitory sense of guilt he always felt as though he were responsible for something in the future he couldn't even foresee. He said aloud, 'You know I like the place.'

'I believe you do. I wonder why.'

'It's pretty in the evening,' Scobie said vaguely.

'Do you know the latest story they are using against you at the Secretariat?'

'I suppose I'm in the Syrians' pay?'

'They haven't got that far yet. That's the next stage. No, you sleep with black girls. You know what it is, Scobie, you ought to have flirted with one of their wives. They feel insulted.'

'Perhaps I ought to sleep with a black girl. Then they won't have to think up anything else.'

'The man before you slept with dozens,' the Commissioner said, 'but it never bothered anyone. They thought up something different for him. They said he drank secretly. It made them feel better drinking publicly. What a lot of swine they are, Scobie.'

'The Chief Assistant Colonial Secretary's not a bad chap.'

'No, the Chief Assistant Colonial Secretary's all right.' The Commissioner laughed. 'You're a terrible fellow, Scobie. Scobie the Just.'

Scobie returned down the passage; the girl sat in the dusk. Her feet were bare: they stood side by side like casts in a museum: they didn't belong to the bright smart cotton frock. 'Are you Miss Wilberforce?' Scobie asked.

'Yes, sir.'

'You don't live here, do you?'

'No! I live in Sharp Town, sir.'

'Well, come in.' He led the way into his office and sat down at his desk. There was no pencil laid out and he opened his drawer. Here and here only had objects accumulated: letters, india-rubbers, a broken rosary—no pencil. 'What's the trouble, Miss Wilberforce?' His eye caught a snapshot of a bathing party at Medley Beach: his wife, the Colonial Secretary's wife, the Director of Education holding up what looked like a dead fish, the Colonial Treasurer's wife. The expanse of white flesh made them look like a gathering of albinos, and all the mouths gaped with laughter.

The girl said, 'My landlady—she broke up my home last night. She come in when it was dark, and she pull down all the partition, an' she thieve my chest with all my belongings.'

'You got plenty lodgers?'

'Only three, sir.'

He knew exactly how it all was: a lodger would take a one-roomed shack for five shillings a week, stick up a few thin partitions and let the so-called rooms for half a crown a piece—a horizontal tenement. Each room would be furnished with a box containing a little china and glass 'dashed' by an employer or stolen from an employer, a bed made out of old packing-cases, and a hurricane lamp. The glass of these lamps did not long survive, and the little open flames were always ready to catch some spilt paraffin; they licked at the plywood partitions and caused innumerable fires. Sometimes a landlady would thrust her way into her house and pull down the dangerous partitions, sometimes she would steal the lamps of her tenants, and the ripple of her theft would go out in widening rings of lamp thefts until they touched the European quarter and became a subject of gossip at the club. 'Can't keep a lamp for love or money.'

'Your landlady,' Scobie told the girl sharply, 'she say you make plenty trouble: too many lodgers: too many lamps.'

'No, sir. No lamp palaver.'

'Mammy palaver, eh? You bad girl?'

'No, sir.'

'Why you come here? Why you not call Corporal Laminah in Sharp Town?'

'He my landlady's brother, sir.'

'He is, is he? Same father same mother?'

'No, sir. Same father.'

The interview was like a ritual between priest and server. He knew exactly what would happen when one of his men investigated the affair. The landlady would say that she had told her tenant to pull down the partitions and when that failed she had taken action herself. She would deny that there had ever been a chest of china. The corporal would confirm this. He would turn out not to be the landlady's brother, but some other unspecified relation—probably disreputable. Bribes—which were known respectably as dashes—would pass to and fro, the storm of indignation and anger that had sounded so genuine would subside, the partitions would go up again, nobody would hear any more about the chest, and several policemen would be a shilling or two the richer. At the beginning of his service Scobie had flung himself into these investigations; he had found himself over and over again in the position of a partisan, supporting as he believed the poor and innocent tenant against the wealthy and guilty house-owner. But he soon discovered that the guilt and innocence were as relative as the wealth. The wronged tenant turned out to be also the wealthy capitalist, making a profit of five shillings a week on a single room, living rent free herself. After that he had tried to kill these cases at birth: he would reason with the complainant and point out that the investigation would do no good and undoubtedly cost her time and money; he would sometimes even refuse to investigate. The result of that inaction had been stones flung at his car window, slashed tyres, the nickname of the Bad Man that had stuck to him through all one long sad tour – it worried him unreasonably in the heat and damp; he couldn't take it lightly. Already he had begun to desire these people's trust and affection. That year he had blackwater fever and was nearly invalided from the service altogether.

The girl waited patiently for his decision. They had an infinite capacity for patience when patience was required – just as their impatience knew no bounds of propriety when they had anything to gain by it. They would sit quietly all day in a white man's backyard in order to beg for something he hadn't the power to grant, or they would shriek and fight and abuse to get served in a store before their neighbour. He thought: how beautiful she is. It was strange to think that fifteen years ago he would not have noticed her beauty – the small high breasts, the tiny wrists, the thrust of the young buttocks, she would have been indistinguishable from her fellows – a black. In those days he had thought his wife beautiful. A white skin had not then reminded him of an albino. Poor Louise. He said, 'Give this chit to the sergeant at the desk.'

'Thank you, sir.'

'That's all right.' He smiled. 'Try to tell him the truth.'

He watched her go out of the dark office like fifteen wasted years.

I /iii

Scobie had been out-manoeuvred in the interminable war over housing. During his last leave he had lost his bungalow in Cape Station, the main European quarter, to a senior sanitary inspector called Fellowes, and had found himself relegated to a square two-storeyed house built originally for a Syrian trader on the flats below – a piece of reclaimed swamp which would return to swamp as soon as the rains set in. From the windows he looked directly out to sea over a line of Creole houses; on the other side of the road lorries backed and churned in a military transport camp and vultures strolled like domestic turkeys in the regimental refuse. On the low ridge of hills behind him the bungalows of the station lay among the low clouds; lamps burned all day in the cupboards, mould gathered on the boots – nevertheless these were the houses for men of his rank. Women depended so much on pride, pride in themselves, their husbands, their surroundings. They were seldom proud, it seemed to him, of the invisible.

'Louise,' he called, 'Louise.' There was no reason to call: if she wasn't in the living-room there was nowhere else for her to be but the bedroom (the kitchen was simply a shed in the yard opposite the back door), yet it was his habit to cry her name, a habit he had formed in the days of anxiety and love. The less he needed Louise the more conscious he became of his responsibility for her happiness. When he called her name he was crying like Canute against a tide—the tide of her melancholy and disappointment.

In the old days she had replied, but she was not such a creature of habit as he was—nor so false, he sometimes told himself. Kindness and pity had no power with her; she would never have pretended an emotion she didn't feel, and like an animal she gave way completely to the momentary sickness and recovered as suddenly. When he found her in the bedroom under the mosquito-net she reminded him of a dog or a cat, she was so completely 'out'. Her hair was matted, her eyes closed. He stood very still like a spy in foreign territory, and indeed he was in foreign territory now. If home for him meant the reduction of things to a friendly unchanging minimum, home to her was accumulation. The dressing-table was crammed with pots and photographs—himself as a young man in the curiously dated officer's uniform of the last war: the Chief Justice's wife whom for the moment she counted as her friend: their only child who had died at school in England three years ago—a little pious nine-year-old girl's face in the white muslin of first communion: innumerable photographs of Louise herself, in groups with nursing sisters, with the Admiral's party at Medley Beach, on a Yorkshire moor with Teddy Bromley and his wife. It was as if she were accumulating evidence that she had friends like other people. He watched her through the muslin net. Her face had the ivory tinge of atabrine: her hair which had once been the colour of bottled honey was dark and stringy with sweat. These were the times of ugliness when he loved her, when pity and responsibility reached the intensity of a passion. It was pity that told him to go: he wouldn't have woken his worst enemy from sleep, leave alone Louise. He tiptoed out and down the stairs. (The inside stairs could be found nowhere else in this bungalow city except in Government House, and she had tried to make them an object of pride with stair-carpets and pictures on the wall.) In the living-room there was a bookcase full of her books, rugs on the floor, a native mask from Nigeria, more photographs. The books had to be wiped daily to remove the damp, and she had not succeeded very well in disguising with flowery curtains the food safe which stood with each foot in a little enamel basin of water to keep the ants out. The boy was laying a single place for lunch.

The boy was short and squat with the broad ugly pleasant face of a Temne. His bare feet flapped like empty gloves across the floor.

'What's wrong with Missus?' Scobie asked.

'Belly humbug,' Ali said.

Scobie took a Mende grammar from the bookcase: it was tucked away in the bottom shelf where its old untidy cover was least conspicuous. In the upper shelves were the flimsy rows of Louise's authors—not so young modern poets and the novels of Virginia Woolf. He couldn't concentrate: it was too hot and his wife's absence was like a garrulous companion in the room reminding him of his responsibility. A fork fell on the floor and he watched Ali surreptitiously wipe it on his sleeve, watched him with affection. They had been together fifteen years—a year longer than his marriage—a long time to keep a servant. He had been 'small boy' first, then assistant steward in the days when one kept four servants, now he was plain steward. After each leave Ali would be on the landing-stage waiting to organise his luggage with three or four ragged carriers. In the intervals of leave many people tried to steal Ali's services, but he had never yet failed to be waiting—except once when he had been in prison. There was no disgrace about prison; it was an obstacle that no one could avoid for ever.

'Ticki,' a voice wailed, and Scobie rose at once. 'Ticki.' He went upstairs.

His wife was sitting up under the mosquito-net, and for a moment he had the impression of a joint under a meat-cover. But pity trod on the heels of the cruel image and hustled it away. 'Are you feeling better, darling?'

Louise said, 'Mrs Castle's been in.'

'Enough to make anyone ill,' Scobie said.

'She's been telling me about you.'

'What about me?' He gave her a bright fake smile; so much of life was a putting off of unhappiness for another time. Nothing was ever lost by delay. He had a dim idea that perhaps if one delayed long enough, things were taken out of one's hands altogether by death.

'She says the Commissioner's retiring, and they've passed you over.'

'Her husband talks too much in his sleep.'

'Is it true?'

'Yes. I've known it for weeks. It doesn't matter, dear, really.'

Louise said, 'I'll never be able to show my face at the club again.'

'It's not as bad as that. These things happen, you know.'

'You'll resign, won't you, Ticki?'

'I don't think I can do that, dear.'

'Mrs Castle's on our side. She's furious. She says everyone's talking about it and saying things. Darling, you aren't in the pay of the Syrians, are you?'

'No, dear.'

'I was so upset I came out of Mass before the end. It's so mean of them, Ticki. You can't take it lying down. You've got to think of me.'

'Yes, I do. All the time.' He sat down on the bed and put his hand under the net and touched hers. Little beads of sweat started where their skins touched. He said, 'I do think of you, dear. But I've been fifteen years in this place. I'd be lost anywhere else, even if they gave me another job. It isn't much of a recommendation, you know, being passed over.'

'We could retire.'

'The pension isn't much to live on.'

'I'm sure I could make a little money writing. Mrs Castle says I ought to be a professional. With all this experience,' Louise said, gazing through the white muslin tent as far as her dressing-table: there another face in white muslin stared back and she looked away. She said, 'If only we could go to South Africa. I can't bear the people here.'

'Perhaps I could arrange a passage for you. There haven't been many sinkings that way lately. You ought to have a holiday.'

'There was a time when you wanted to retire too. You used to count the years. You made plans—for all of us.'

'Oh well, one changes,' he said.

She said mercilessly, 'You didn't think you'd be alone with me then.'

He pressed his sweating hand against hers. 'What nonsense you talk, dear. You must get up and have some food. . . .'

'Do you love anyone, Ticki, except yourself?'

'No, I just love myself, that's all. And Ali. I forgot Ali. Of course I love him too. But not you,' he ran on with worn mechanical raillery, stroking her hand, smiling, soothing. . . .

'And Ali's sister?'

'Has he got a sister?'

'They've all got sisters, haven't they? Why didn't you go to Mass to-day?'

'It was my morning on duty, dear. You know that.'

'You could have changed it. You haven't got much faith, have you, Ticki?'

'You've got enough for both of us, dear. Come and have some food.'

'Ticki, I sometimes think you just became a Catholic to marry me. It doesn't mean a thing to you, does it?'

'Listen, darling, you want to come down and eat a bit. Then you want to take the car along to the beach and have some fresh air.'

'How different the whole day would have been,' she said, staring out of her net, 'if you'd come home and said, "Darling, I'm going to be the Commissioner."'

Scobie said slowly, 'You know, dear, in a place like this in war-time—an important harbour—the Vichy French just across the border—all this diamond smuggling from the Protectorate, they need a younger man.' He didn't believe a word he was saying.

'I hadn't thought of that.'

'That's the only reason. You can't blame anyone. It's the war.'

'The war does spoil everything, doesn't it?'

'It gives the younger men a chance.'

'Darling, perhaps I'll come down and just pick at a little cold meat.'

'That's right, dear.' He withdrew his hand: it was dripping with sweat. 'I'll tell Ali.'

Downstairs he shouted 'Ali' out of the back door.

'Massa?'

'Lay two places. Missus better.'

The first faint breeze of the day came off the sea, blowing up over the bushes and between the Creole huts. A vulture flapped heavily upwards from the iron roof and down again in the yard next door. Scobie drew a deep breath; he felt exhausted and victorious: he had persuaded Louise to pick a little meat. It had always been his responsibility to maintain happiness in those he loved. One was safe now, for ever, and the other was going to eat her lunch.

I / iv

In the evening the port became beautiful for perhaps five minutes. The laterite roads that were so ugly and clay-heavy by day became a delicate flower-like pink. It was the hour of content. Men who had left the port for ever would sometimes remember on a grey wet London evening the bloom and glow that faded as soon as it was seen: they would wonder why they had hated the coast and for a space of a drink they would long to return.

Scobie stopped his Morris at one of the great loops of the climbing road and looked back. He was just too late. The flower had withered upwards from the town; the white stones that marked the edge of the precipitous hill shone like candles in the new dusk.

'I wonder if anybody will be there, Ticki.'

'Sure to be. It's library night.'

'Do hurry up, dear. It's so hot in the car. I'll be glad when the rains come.'

'Will you?'

'If only they just went on for a month or two and then stopped.'

Scobie made the right reply. He never listened while his wife talked. He worked steadily to the even current of sound, but if a note of distress were struck he was aware of it at once. Like a wireless operator with a novel open in front of him, he could disregard every signal except the ship's symbol and the S.O.S. He could even work better while she talked than when she was silent, for so long as his ear-drum registered those tranquil sounds—the gossip of the club, comments on the sermons preached by Father Rank, the plot of a new novel, even complaints about the weather—he knew that all was well. It was silence that stopped him working—silence in which he might look up and see tears waiting in the eyes for his attention.

'There's a rumour going round that the refrigerators were all sunk last week.'

He considered, while she talked, his line of action with the Portuguese ship that was due in as soon as the boom opened in the morning. The fortnightly arrival of a neutral ship provided an outing for the junior officers: a change of food, a few glasses of real wine, even the opportunity of buying some small decorative object in the ship's store for a girl. In return they had only to help the Field Security Police in the examination of passports, the searching of the suspects' cabins: all the hard and disagreeable work was done by the F.S.P., in the hold, sifting sacks of rice for commercial diamonds, or in the heat of the kitchen, plunging the hand into tins of lard, disembowelling the stuffed turkeys. To try to find a few diamonds in a liner of fifteen thousand tons was absurd: no malign tyrant in a fairy-story had ever set a goose girl a more impossible task, and yet as regularly as the ships called the cypher telegrams came in—'So and so travelling first class suspected of carrying diamonds. The following members of the ship's crew suspected. . . .' Nobody ever found anything. He thought: it's Harris's turn to go on board, and Fraser can go with him. I'm too old for these excursions. Let the boys have a little fun.

'Last time half the books arrived damaged.'

'Did they?'

Judging from the number of cars, he thought, there were not many people at the club yet. He switched off his lights and waited for Louise to move, but she just sat there with a clenched fist showing in the switchboard light. 'Well, dear, here we are,' he said in the hearty voice that strangers took as a mark of stupidity. Louise said, 'Do you think they all know by this time?'

'Know what?'

'That you've been passed over.'

'My dear, I thought we'd finished with all that. Look at all the generals who've been passed over since 1940. They won't bother about a deputy-commissioner.'

She said, 'But they don't like me.'

Poor Louise, he thought, it is terrible not to be liked, and his mind went back to his own experience in that early tour when the blacks had slashed his tyres and written insults on his car. 'Dear, how absurd you are. I've never known anyone with so many friends.' He ran unconvincingly on. 'Mrs Halifax, Mrs Castle . . .' and then decided it was better after all not to list them.

'They'll all be waiting there,' she said, 'just waiting for me to walk in. . . . I never wanted to come to the club to-night. Let's go home.'

'We can't. Here's Mrs Castle's car arriving.' He tried to laugh. 'We're trapped, Louise.' He saw the fist open and close, the damp inefficient powder lying like snow in the ridges of the knuckles. 'Oh, Ticki, Ticki,' she said, 'you won't leave me ever, will you? I haven't got any friends—not since the Tom Barlows went away.' He lifted the moist hand and kissed the palm: he was bound by the pathos of her unattractiveness.

They walked side by side like a couple of policemen on duty into the lounge where Mrs Halifax was dealing out the library books. It is seldom that anything is quite so bad as one fears: there was no reason to believe that they had been the subject of conversation. 'Goody, goody,' Mrs Halifax called to them, 'the new Clemence Dane's arrived.' She was the most inoffensive woman in the station; she had long untidy hair, and one found hairpins inside the library books where she had marked her place. Scobie felt it quite safe to leave his wife in her company, for Mrs Halifax had no malice and no capacity for gossip; her memory was too bad for anything to lodge there for long: she read the same novels over and over again without knowing it.

Scobie joined a group on the verandah. Fellowes, the sanitary inspector, was talking fiercely to Reith, the Chief Assistant Colonial Secretary, and a naval officer called Brigstock. 'After all this is a club,' he was saying, 'not a railway refreshment-room.' Ever since Fellowes had snatched his house, Scobie had done his best to like the man—it was one of the rules by which he set his life, to be a good loser. But sometimes he found it very hard to like Fellowes. The hot evening had not been good to him: the thin damp ginger hair, the small prickly moustache, the goosegog eyes, the scarlet cheeks, and the old Lancing tie. 'Quite,' said Brigstock, swaying slightly.

'What's the trouble?' Scobie asked.

Reith said, 'He thinks we are not exclusive enough.' He spoke with the comfortable irony of a man who had in his time been completely exclusive, who had in fact excluded from his solitary table in the Protectorate everyone but himself. Fellowes said hotly, 'There are limits,' fingering for confidence the Lancing tie.

'Tha's so,' said Brigstock.

'I knew it would happen,' Fellowes said, 'as soon as we made every officer in the place an honorary member. Sooner or later they would begin to bring in undesirables. I'm not a snob, but in a place like this you've got to draw lines—for the sake of the women. It's not like it is at home.'

'But what's the trouble?' Scobie asked.

'Honorary members,' Fellowes said, 'should not be allowed to introduce guests. Only the other day we had a private brought in. The army can be democratic if it likes, but not at our expense. That's another thing, there's not enough drink to go round as it is without these fellows.'

'Tha's a point,' Brigstock said, swaying more violently.

'I wish I knew what it was all about,' Scobie said.

'The dentist from the 49th has brought in a civilian called Wilson, and this man Wilson wants to join the club. It puts everybody in a very embarrassing position.'

'What's wrong with him?'

'He's one of the U.A.C. clerks. He can join the club in Sharp Town. What does he want to come up here for?'

'That club's not functioning,' Reith said.

'Well, that's their fault, isn't it?' Over the sanitary inspector's shoulder Scobie could see the enormous range of the night. The fireflies signalled to and fro along the edge of the hill and the lamp of a patrol-boat moving on the bay could be distinguished only by its steadiness. 'Black-out time,' Reith said. 'We'd better go in.'

'Which is Wilson?' Scobie asked him.

'That's him over there. The poor devil looks lonely. He's only been out a few days.'

Wilson stood uncomfortably alone in a wilderness of arm-chairs, pretending to look at a map on the wall. His pale face shone and trickled like plaster. He had obviously bought his tropical suit from a shipper who had worked off on him an unwanted line: it was oddly striped and liverish in colour. 'You're Wilson, aren't you?' Reith said. 'I saw your name in Col. Sec.'s book to-day.'

'Yes, that's me,' Wilson said.

'My name's Reith. I'm Chief Assistant Col. Sec. This is Scobie, the deputy-commissioner.'

'I saw you this morning outside the Bedford Hotel, sir,' Wilson said. There was something defenceless, it seemed to Scobie, in his whole attitude: he stood there waiting for people to be friendly or unfriendly—he didn't seem to expect one reaction more than another. He was like a dog. Nobody had yet drawn on his face the lines that make a human being.

'Have a drink, Wilson.'

'I don't mind if I do, sir.'

'Here's my wife,' Scobie said. 'Louise, this is Mr Wilson.'

'I've heard a lot about Mr Wilson already,' Louise said stiffly.

'You see, you're famous, Wilson,' Scobie said. 'You're a man from the town and you've gate-crashed Cape Station Club.'

'I didn't know I was doing anything wrong. Major Cooper invited me.'

'That reminds me,' Reith said, 'I must make an appointment with Cooper. I think I've got an abscess.' He slid away.

'Cooper was telling me about the library,' Wilson said, 'and I thought perhaps . . .'

'Do you like reading?' Louise asked, and Scobie realised with relief that she was going to be kind to the poor devil. It was always a bit of a toss-up with Louise. Sometimes she could be the worst snob in the station, and it occurred to him with pity that perhaps now she believed she couldn't afford to be snobbish. Any new face that didn't 'know' was welcome.

'Well,' Wilson said, and fingered desperately at his thin moustache, 'well . . .' It was as if he were gathering strength for a great confession or a great evasion.

'Detective stories?' Louise asked.

'I don't mind detective stories,' Wilson said uneasily. 'Some detective stories.'

'Personally,' Louise said, 'I like poetry.'

'Poetry,' Wilson said, 'yes.' He took his fingers reluctantly away from his moustache, and something in his dog-like look of gratitude and hope made Scobie think with happiness: have I really found her a friend?

'I like poetry myself,' Wilson said.

Scobie moved away towards the bar: once again a load was lifted from his mind. The evening was not spoilt: she would come home happy, go to bed happy. During one night a mood did not change, and happiness would survive until he left to go on duty. He could sleep. . . .

He saw a gathering of his junior officers in the bar. Fraser was there and Tod and a new man from Palestine with the extraordinary name of Thimblerigg. Scobie hesitated to go in. They were enjoying themselves, and they would not want a senior officer with them. 'Infernal cheek,' Tod was saying. They were probably talking about poor Wilson. Then before he could move away he heard Fraser's voice. 'He's punished for it. Literary Louise has got him.' Thimblerigg gave a small gurgling laugh, a bubble of gin forming on a plump lip.

Scobie walked rapidly back into the lounge. He went full tilt into an arm-chair and came to a halt. His vision moved jerkily back into focus, but sweat dripped into his right eye. The fingers that wiped it free shook like a drunkard's. He told himself: Be careful. This isn't a climate for emotion. It's a climate for meanness, malice, snobbery, but anything like hate or love drives a man off his head. He remembered Bowers sent home for punching the Governor's A.D.C. at a party, Makin the missionary who ended in an asylum at Chislehurst.

'It's damned hot,' he said to someone who loomed vaguely beside him.

'You look bad, Scobie. Have a drink.'

'No, thank you. Got to drive round on inspection.'

Beside the bookshelves Louise was talking happily to Wilson, but he could feel the malice and snobbery of the world padding up like wolves around her. They wouldn't even let her enjoy her books, he thought, and his hand began to shake again. Approaching, he heard her say in her kindly Lady Bountiful manner, 'You must come and have dinner with us one day. I've got a lot of books that might interest you.'

'I'd love to,' Wilson said.

'Just ring us up and take pot luck.'

Scobie thought: What are those others worth that they have the nerve to sneer at any human being? He knew every one of her faults. How often he had winced at her patronage of strangers. He knew each phrase, each intonation that alienated others. Sometimes he longed to warn her—don't wear that dress, don't say that again, as a mother might teach a daughter, but he had to remain silent, aching with the foreknowledge of *her* loss of friends. The worst was when he detected in his colleagues an extra warmth of friendliness towards himself, as though they pitied him. What right have you, he longed to exclaim, to criticise her? This is my doing. This is what I've made of her. She wasn't always like this.

He came abruptly up to them and said, 'My dear, I've got to go round the beats.'

'Already?'

'I'm sorry.'

'I'll stay, dear. Mrs Halifax will run me home.'

'I wish you'd come with me.'

'What? Round the beats? It's ages since I've been.'

'That's why I'd like you to come.' He lifted her hand and kissed it: it was a challenge. He proclaimed to the whole club that he was not to be pitied, that he loved his wife, that they were happy. But nobody that mattered saw—Mrs Halifax was busy with the books, Reith had gone long ago, Brigstock was in the bar, Fellowes talked too busily to Mrs Castle to notice anything—nobody saw except Wilson.

Louise said, 'I'll come another time, dear. But Mrs Halifax has just promised to run Mr Wilson home by our house. There's a book I want to lend him.'

Scobie felt an immense gratitude to Wilson. 'That's fine,' he said, 'fine. But stay and have a drink till I get back. I'll run you home to the Bedford. I shan't be late.' He put a hand on Wilson's shoulder and prayed silently: Don't let her patronise him too far: don't let her be absurd: let her keep this friend at least. 'I won't say good night,' he said, 'I'll expect to see you when I get back.'

'It's very kind of you, sir.'

'You mustn't sir me. You're not a policeman, Wilson. Thank your stars for that.'

I / V

Scobie was later than he expected. It was the encounter with Yusef that delayed him. Half-way down the hill he found Yusef's car stuck by the roadside, with Yusef sleeping quietly in the back: the light from Scobie's car lit up the large pasty face, the lick of his white hair falling over the forehead, and just touched the beginning of the huge thighs in their tight white drill. Yusef's shirt was open at the neck and tendrils of black breast-hair coiled around the buttons.

'Can I help you?' Scobie unwillingly asked, and Yusef opened his eyes: the gold teeth fitted by his brother, the dentist, flashed instantaneously like a torch. If Fellowes drives by now, what a story, Scobie thought. The deputy-commissioner meeting Yusef, the store-keeper, clandestinely at night. To give help to a Syrian was only a degree less dangerous than to receive help.

'Ah, Major Scobie,' Yusef said, 'a friend in need is a friend indeed.'

'Can I do anything for you?'

'We have been stranded a half hour,' Yusef said. 'The cars have gone by, and I have thought—when will a Good Samaritan appear?'

'I haven't any spare oil to pour into your wounds, Yusef.'

'Ha, ha, Major Scobie. That is very good. But if you would just give me a lift into town . . .'

Yusef settled himself into the Morris, easing a large thigh against the brakes.

'Your boy had better come in at the back.'

'Let him stay here,' Yusef said. 'He will mend the car if he knows it is the only way he can get to bed.' He folded his large fat hands over his knee and said, 'You have a very fine car, Major Scobie. You must have paid four hundred pounds for it.'

'One hundred and fifty,' Scobie said.

'I would pay you four hundred.'

'It isn't for sale, Yusef. Where would I get another?'

'Not now, but maybe when you leave.'

'I'm not leaving.'

'Oh, I had heard that you were resigning, Major Scobie.'

'No.'

'We shopkeepers hear so much—but all of it is unreliable gossip.'

'How's business?'

'Oh, not bad. Not good.'

'What I hear is that you've made several fortunes since the war. Unreliable gossip, of course.'

'Well, Major Scobie, you know how it is. My store in Sharp Town, that does fine because I am there to keep an eye on it. My store in Macaulay Street—that does not bad because my sister is there. But my stores in Durban Street and Bond Street they do badly. I am cheated all the time. Like all my countrymen, I cannot read or write, and everyone cheats me.'

'Gossip says you can keep all your stocks in all your stores in your head.'

Yusef chuckled and beamed. 'My memory is not bad. But it keeps me awake at night, Major Scobie. Unless I take a lot of whisky I keep thinking about Durban Street and Bond Street and Macaulay Street.'

'Which shall I drop you at now?'

'Oh, now I go home to bed, Major Scobie. My house in Sharp Town, if you please. Won't you come in and have a little whisky?'

'Sorry. I'm on duty, Yusef.'

'It is very kind of you, Major Scobie, to give me this lift. Would you let me show my gratitude by sending Mrs Scobie a roll of silk?'

'Just what I wouldn't like, Yusef.'

'Yes, yes, I know. It's very hard, all this gossip. Just because there are some Syrians like Tallit.'

'You would like Tallit out of your way, wouldn't you, Yusef?'

'Yes, Major Scobie. It would be for my good, but it would also be for your good.'

'You sold him some of those fake diamonds last year, didn't you?'

'Oh, Major Scobie, you don't really believe I'd get the better of anyone like that. Some of the poor Syrians suffered a great deal over those diamonds, Major Scobie. It would be a shame to deceive your own people like that.'

'They shouldn't have broken the law by buying diamonds. Some of them even had the nerve to complain to the police.'

'They are very ignorant, poor fellows.'

'You weren't as ignorant as all that, were you, Yusef?'

'If you ask me, Major Scobie, it was Tallit. Otherwise, why does he pretend I sold him the diamonds?'

Scobie drove slowly. The rough street was crowded. Thin black bodies weaved like daddy-long-legs in the dimmed headlights. 'How long will the rice shortage go on, Yusef?'

'You know as much about that as I do, Major Scobie.'

'I know these poor devils can't get rice at the controlled price.'

'I've heard, Major Scobie, that they can't get their share of the free distribution unless they tip the policeman at the gate.'

It was quite true. There was a retort in this colony to every accusation. There was always a blacker corruption elsewhere to be pointed at. The scandalmongers of the secretariat fulfilled a useful purpose—they kept alive the idea that no one was to be trusted. That was better than complacence. Why, he wondered, swerving the car to avoid a dead pye-dog, do I love this place so much? Is it because here human nature hasn't had time to disguise itself? Nobody here could ever talk about a heaven on earth. Heaven remained rigidly in its proper place on the other side of death, and on this side flourished the injustices, the cruelties, the meanness that elsewhere people so cleverly hushed up. Here you could love human beings nearly as God loved them, knowing the worst: you didn't love a pose, a pretty dress, a sentiment artfully assumed. He felt a sudden affection for Yusef. He said, 'Two wrongs don't make a right. One day, Yusef, you'll find my foot under your fat arse.'

'Maybe, Major Scobie, or maybe we'll be friends together. That is what I should like more than anything in the world.'

They drew up outside the Sharp Town house and Yusef's steward ran out with a torch to light him in. 'Major Scobie,' Yusef said, 'it would give me such pleasure to give you a glass of whisky. I think I could help you a lot. I am very patriotic, Major Scobie.'

'That's why you are hoarding your cottons against a Vichy invasion, isn't it? They will be worth more than English pounds.'

'The *Esperança* is in to-morrow, isn't she?'

'Probably.'

'What a waste of time it is searching a big ship like that for diamonds. Unless you know beforehand exactly where they are. You know that when the ship returns to Angola a seaman reports where you looked. You will sift all the sugar in the hold. You will search the lard in the kitchens because someone once told Captain Druce that a diamond can be heated and dropped in the middle of a tin of lard. Of course the cabins and the ventilators and the lockers. Tubes of toothpaste. Do you think one day you will find one little diamond?'

'No.'

'I don't either.'

I / vi

A hurricane-lamp burned at each corner of the wooden pyramids of crates. Across the black slow water he could just make out the naval depôt ship, a disused liner, where she lay, so it was believed, on a reef of empty whisky bottles. He stood quietly for a while breathing in the heavy smell of the sea. Within half a mile of him a whole convoy lay at anchor, but all he could detect were the long shadow of the depôt ship and a scatter of small red lights as though a street were up: he could hear nothing from the water but the water itself, slapping against the jetties. The magic of this place never failed him: here he kept his foothold on the very edge of a strange continent.

Somewhere in the darkness two rats scuffled. These water-side rats were the size of rabbits. The natives called them pigs and ate them roasted; the name helped to distinguish them from the wharf rats, who were a human breed. Walking along a light railway Scobie made in the direction of the markets. At the corner of a warehouse he came on two policemen.

'Anything to report?'

'No, sah.'

'Been along this way?'

'Oh yes, sah, we just come from there.'

He knew that they were lying: they would never go alone to that end of the wharf, the playground of the human rats, unless they had a white officer to guard them. The rats were cowards but dangerous—boys of sixteen or so, armed with razors or bits of broken bottle, they swarmed in groups around the warehouses, pilfering if they found an easily-opened case, settling like flies around any drunken sailor who stumbled their way, occasionally slashing a policeman who had made himself unpopular with one of their innumerable relatives. Gates couldn't keep them off the wharf: they swam round from Kru Town or the fishing beaches.

'Come on,' Scobie said, 'we'll have another look.'

With weary patience the policemen trailed behind him, half a mile one way, half a mile the other. Only the pigs moved on the wharf, and the water slapped. One of the policemen said self-righteously, 'Quiet night, sah.' They shone their torches with self-conscious assiduity from one side to another, lighting the abandoned chassis of a car, an empty truck, the corner of a tarpaulin, a bottle standing at the corner of a warehouse with palm leaves stuffed in for a cork. Scobie said, 'What's that?' One of his official nightmares was an incendiary bomb: it was so easy to prepare: every day men from Vichy territory came into town with smuggled cattle—they were encouraged to come in for the sake of the meat supply. On this side of the border native saboteurs were being trained in case of invasion: why not on the other side?

'Let me see it,' he said, but neither of the policemen moved to touch it.

'Only native medicine, sah,' one of them said with a skin-deep sneer.

Scobie picked the bottle up. It was a dimpled Haig, and when he drew out the palm leaves the stench of dog's pizzle and nameless decay blew out like a gas escape. A nerve in his head beat with sudden irritation. For no reason at all he remembered Fraser's flushed face and Thimblerigg's giggle. The stench from the bottle moved him with nausea, and he felt his fingers polluted by the palm leaves. He threw the bottle over the wharf, and the hungry mouth of the water received it with a single belch, but the contents were scattered on the air, and the whole windless place smelt sour and ammoniac. The policemen were silent: Scobie was aware of their mute disapproval. He should have left the bottle where it stood: it had been placed there for one purpose, directed at one person, but now that its contents had been released, it was as if the evil thought were left to wander blindly through the air, to settle maybe on the innocent.

'Good night,' Scobie said and turned abruptly on his heel. He had not gone twenty yards before he heard their boots scuffling rapidly away from the dangerous area.

Scobie drove up to the police station by way of Pitt Street. Outside the brothel on the left-hand side the girls were sitting along the pavement taking a bit of air. Within the police station behind the black-out blinds the scent of a monkey house thickened for the night. The sergeant on duty took his legs off the table in the charge-room and stood to attention.

'Anything to report?'

'Five drunk and disorderly, sah. I lock them in the big cell.'

'Anything else?'

'Two Frenchmen, sah, with no passes.'

'Black?'

'Yes, sah.'

'Where were they found?'

'In Pitt Street, sah.'

'I'll see them in the morning. What about the launch? Is it running all right? I shall want to go out to the *Esperança*.'

'It's broken, sah. Mr Fraser he try to mend it, sah, but it humbug all the time.'

'What time does Mr Fraser come on duty?'

'Seven, sah.'

'Tell him I shan't want him to go out to the *Esperança*. I'm going out myself. If the launch isn't ready, I'll go with F.S.P.'

'Yes, sah.'

Climbing again into his car, pushing at the sluggish starter, Scobie thought that a man was surely entitled to that much revenge. Revenge was good for the character: out of revenge grew forgiveness. He began to whistle, driving back through Kru Town. He was almost happy: he only needed to be quite certain that nothing had happened at the club after he left, that at this moment, 10.55 p.m., Louise was at ease, content. He could face the next hour when the next hour arrived.

I /vii

Before he went indoors he walked round to the seaward side of the house to check the black-out. He could hear the murmur of Louise's voice inside: she was probably reading poetry. He thought: by God, what right has that young fool Fraser to despise her for that? and then his anger moved away again, like a shabby man, when he thought of Fraser's disappointment in the morning–no Portuguese visit, no present for his best girl, only the hot humdrum office day. Feeling for the handle of the back door to avoid flashing his torch, he tore his right hand on a splinter.

He came into the lighted room and saw that his hand was dripping with blood. 'Oh, darling,' Louise said, 'what have you done?' and covered her face. She couldn't bear the sight of blood. 'Can I help you, sir?' Wilson asked. He tried to rise, but he was sitting in a low chair at Louise's feet and his knees were piled with books.

'It's all right,' Scobie said. 'It's only a scratch. I can see to it myself. Just tell Ali to bring a bottle of water.' Half-way upstairs he heard the voice resume. Louise said, 'A lovely poem about a pylon.' Scobie walked into the bathroom, disturbing a rat that had been couched on the cool rim of the bath, like a cat on a gravestone.

Scobie sat down on the edge of the bath and let his hand drip into the lavatory pail among the wood shavings. Just as in his own office the sense of home surrounded him. Louise's ingenuity had been able to do little with this room: the bath of scratched enamel with a single tap which always ceased to work before the end of the dry season: the tin bucket under the lavatory seat emptied once a day: the fixed basin with another useless tap: bare floorboards: drab green black-out curtains. The only improvements Louise had been able to impose were the cork mat by the bath, the bright white medicine cabinet.

The rest of the room was all his own. It was like a relic of his youth carried from house to house. It had been like this years ago in his first house before he married. This was the room in which he had always been alone.

Ali came in, his pink soles flapping on the floorboards, carrying a bottle of water from the filter. 'The back door humbug me,' Scobie explained. He held his hand out over the washbasin, while Ali poured the water over the wound. The boy made gentle clucking sounds of commiseration: his hands were as gentle as a girl's. When Scobie said impatiently, 'That's enough,' Ali paid him no attention. 'Too much dirt,' he said.

'Now iodine.' The smallest scratch in this country turned green if it were neglected for an hour. 'Again,' he said, 'pour it over,' wincing at the sting. Down below out of the swing of voices the word 'beauty' detached itself and sank back into the trough. 'Now the elastoplast.'

'No,' Ali said, 'no. Bandage better.'

'All right. Bandage then.' Years ago he had taught Ali to bandage: now he could tie one as expertly as a doctor.

'Good night, Ali. Go to bed. I shan't want you again.'

'Missus want drinks.'

'No. I'll attend to the drinks. You can go to bed.' Alone he sat down again on the edge of the bath. The wound had jarred him a little and anyway he was unwilling to join the two downstairs, for his presence would embarrass Wilson. A man couldn't listen to a woman reading poetry in the presence of an outsider. 'I had rather be a kitten and cry mew . . .' but that wasn't really his attitude. He did not despise: he just couldn't understand such bare relations of intimate feeling. And besides he was happy here, sitting where the rat had sat, in his own world. He began to think of the *Esperança* and of the next day's work.

'Darling,' Louise called up the stairs, 'are you all right? Can you drive Mr Wilson home?'

'I can walk, Mrs Scobie.'

'Nonsense.'

'Yes, really.'

'Coming,' Scobie called. 'Of course I'll drive you back.' When he joined them Louise took the bandaged hand tenderly in hers. 'Oh the poor hand,' she said. 'Does it hurt?' She was not afraid of the clean white bandage: it was like a patient in a hospital with the sheets drawn tidily up to the chin. One could bring grapes and never know the details of the scalpel wound out of sight. She put her lips to the bandage and left a little smear of orange lipstick.

'It's quite all right,' Scobie said.

'Really, sir. I can walk.'

'Of course you won't walk. Come along, get in.'

The light from the dashboard lit up a patch of Wilson's extraordinary suit. He leant out of the car and cried, 'Good night, Mrs Scobie. It's been lovely. I can't thank you enough.' The words vibrated with sincerity: it gave them the sound of a foreign language—the sound of English spoken in England. Here intonations changed in the course of a few months, became high-pitched and insincere, or flat and guarded. You could tell that Wilson was fresh from home.

'You must come again soon,' Scobie said, as they drove down the Burnside road towards the Bedford Hotel, remembering Louise's happy face.

I / viii

The smart of his wounded hand woke Scobie at two in the morning. He lay coiled like a watch-spring on the outside of the bed, trying to keep his body away from Louise's: wherever they touched—if it were only a finger lying against a finger—sweat started. Even when they were separated the heat trembled between them. The moonlight lay on the dressing-table like coolness and lit the bottles of lotion, the little pots of cream, the edge of a photograph frame. At once he began to listen for Louise's breathing.

It came irregularly in jerks. She was awake. He put his hand up and touched the hot moist hair: she lay stiffly, as though she were guarding a secret. Sick at heart, knowing what he would find, he moved his fingers down until they touched her lids. She was crying. He felt an enormous tiredness, bracing himself to comfort her. 'Darling,' he said, 'I love you.' It was how he always began. Comfort, like the act of sex, developed a routine.

'I know,' she said, 'I know.' It was how she always answered. He blamed himself for being heartless because the idea occurred to him that it was two o'clock: this might go on for hours, and at six the day's work began. He moved the hair away from her forehead and said, 'The rains will soon be here. You'll feel better then.'

'I feel all right,' she said and began to sob.

'What is it, darling? Tell me.' He swallowed. 'Tell Ticki.' He hated the name she had given him, but it always worked. She said, 'Oh Ticki, Ticki. I can't go on.'

'I thought you were happy to-night.'

'I was—but think of being happy because a U.A.C. clerk was nice to me. Ticki, why won't they like me?'

'Don't be silly, darling. It's just the heat: it makes you fancy things. They all like you.'

'Only Wilson,' she repeated with despair and shame and began to sob again.

'Wilson's all right.'

'They won't have him at the club. He gate-crashed with the dentist. They'll be laughing about him and me. Oh Ticki, Ticki, please let me go away and begin again.'

'Of course, darling,' he said, 'of course,' staring out through the net and through the window to the quiet flat infested sea. 'Where to?'

'I could go to South Africa and wait until you have leave. Ticki, you'll be retiring soon. I'll get a home ready for you, Ticki.'

He flinched a little away from her, and then hurriedly in case she had noticed, lifted her damp hand and kissed the palm. 'It will cost a lot, darling.' The thought of retirement set his nerves twitching and straining: he always prayed that death would come first. He had prepared his life insurance in that hope: it was payable only on death. He thought of a home, a permanent home: the gay artistic curtains, the bookshelves full of Louise's books, a pretty tiled bathroom, no office anywhere—a home for two until death, no change any more before eternity settled in.

'Ticki, I can't bear it any longer here.'

'I'll have to figure it out, darling.'

'Ethel Maybury's in South Africa, and the Collinses. We've got friends in South Africa.'

'Prices are high.'

'You could drop some of your silly old life insurances, Ticki. And, Ticki, you could economise here without me. You could have your meals at the mess and do without the cook.'

'He doesn't cost much.'

'Every little helps, Ticki.'

'I'd miss you,' he said.

'No, Ticki, you wouldn't,' she said, and surprised him by the range of her sad spasmodic understanding. 'After all,' she said, 'there's nobody to save for.'

He said gently, 'I'll try and work something out. You know if it's possible I'd do anything for you–anything.'

'This isn't just two in the morning comfort, Ticki, is it? You will do something?'

'Yes, dear. I'll manage somehow.' He was surprised how quickly she went to sleep: she was like a tired carrier who has slipped his load. She was asleep before he had finished his sentence, clutching one of his fingers like a child, breathing as easily. The load lay beside him now, and he prepared to lift it.

2/i

At eight in the morning on his way to the jetty Scobie called at the bank. The manager's office was shaded and cool: a glass of iced water stood on top of a safe. 'Good morning, Robinson.'

Robinson was tall and hollow-chested and bitter because he hadn't been posted to Nigeria. He said, 'When will this filthy weather break? The rains are late.'

'They've started in the Protectorate.'

'In Nigeria,' Robinson said, 'one always knew where one was. What can I do for you, Scobie?'

'Do you mind if I sit down?'

'Of course. I never sit down before ten myself. Standing up keeps the digestion in order.' He rambled restlessly across his office on legs like stilts: he took a sip of the iced water with distaste as though it were medicine. On his desk Scobie saw a book called *Diseases of the Urinary Tract* open at a coloured illustration. 'What can I do for you?' Robinson repeated.

'Give me two hundred and fifty pounds,' Scobie said with a nervous attempt at jocularity.

'You people always think a bank's made of money,' Robinson mechanically jested. 'How much do you really want?'

'Three fifty.'

'What's your balance at the moment?'

'I think about thirty pounds. It's the end of the month.'

'We'd better check up on that.' He called a clerk and while they waited Robinson paced the little room–six paces to the wall and round again. 'There and back a hundred and seventy-six times,' he said, 'makes a mile. I try and put in three miles before lunch. It keeps one healthy. In Nigeria I used to walk a mile and a half to breakfast at the club, and then a mile and a half back to the office. Nowhere fit to walk here,' he said, pivoting on the carpet. A clerk laid a slip of paper on the desk. Robinson held it close to his eyes, as though he wanted to smell it. 'Twenty-eight pounds fifteen and sevenpence,' he said.

'I want to send my wife to South Africa.'

'Oh yes. Yes.'

'I daresay,' Scobie said, 'I might do it on a bit less. I shan't be able to allow her very much on my salary though.'

'I really don't see how . . .'

'I thought perhaps I could get an overdraft,' he said vaguely. 'Lots of people have them, don't they? Do you know I believe I only had one once–for a few weeks–for about fifteen pounds. I didn't like it. It scared me. I always felt I owed the bank manager the money.'

'The trouble is, Scobie,' Robinson said, 'we've had orders to be very strict about overdrafts. It's the war, you know. There's one valuable security nobody can offer now, his life.'

'Yes, I see that of course. But my life's pretty good and I'm not stirring from here. No submarines for me. And the job's secure, Robinson,' he went on with the same ineffectual attempt at flippancy.

'The Commissioner's retiring, isn't he?' Robinson said, reaching the safe at the end of the room and turning.

'Yes, but I'm not.'

'I'm glad to hear that, Scobie. There've been rumours. . . .'

'I suppose I'll have to retire one day, but that's a long way off. I'd much rather die in my boots. There's always my life insurance policy, Robinson. What about that for security?'

'You know you dropped one insurance three years ago.'

'That was the year Louise went home for an operation.'

'I don't think the paid-up value of the other two amounts to much, Scobie.'

'Still they protect you in case of death, don't they?'

'If you go on paying the premiums. We haven't any guarantee, you know.'

'Of course not,' Scobie said, 'I see that.'

'I'm very sorry, Scobie. This isn't personal. It's the policy of the bank. If you'd wanted fifty pounds, I'd have lent it you myself.'

'Forget it, Robinson,' Scobie said. 'It's not important.' He gave his embarrassed laugh. 'The boys at the Secretariat would say I can always pick it up in bribes. How's Molly?'

'She's very well, thank you. Wish I were the same.'

'You read too many of those medical books, Robinson.'

'A man's got to know what's wrong with him. Going to be at the club to-night?'

'I don't think so. Louise is tired. You know how it is before the rains. Sorry to have kept you, Robinson. I must be getting along to the wharf.'

He walked rapidly down-hill from the bank with his head bent. He felt as though he had been detected in a mean action–he had asked for money and had been refused. Louise had deserved better of him. It seemed to him that he must have failed in some way in manhood.

2/ii

Druce had come out himself to the *Esperança* with his squad of F.S.P. men. At the gangway a steward awaited them with an invitation to join the captain for drinks in his cabin. The officer in charge of the naval guard was already there before them. This was a regular part of the fortnightly routine—the establishment of friendly relations. By accepting his hospitality they tried to ease down for the neutral the bitter pill of search; below the bridge the search party would proceed smoothly without them. While the first-class passengers had their passports examined, their cabins would be ransacked by a squad of the F.S.P. Already others were going through the hold—the dreary hopeless business of sifting rice. What had Yusef said, 'Have you ever found one little diamond? Do you think you ever will?' In a few minutes when relations had become sufficiently smooth after the drinks Scobie would have the unpleasant task of searching the captain's own cabin. The stiff disjointed conversation was carried on mainly by the naval lieutenant.

The captain wiped his fat yellow face and said, 'Of course for the English I feel in the heart an enormous admiration.'

'We don't like doing it, you know,' the lieutenant said. 'Hard luck being a neutral.'

'My heart,' the Portuguese captain said, 'is full of admiration for your great struggle. There is no room for resentment. Some of my people feel resentment. Me none.' The face streamed with sweat, and the eyeballs were contused. The man kept on speaking of his heart, but it seemed to Scobie that a long deep surgical operation would have been required to find it.

'Very good of you,' the lieutenant said. 'Appreciate your attitude.'

'Another glass of port, gentlemen?'

'Don't mind if I do. Nothing like this on shore you know. You, Scobie?'

'No, thanks.'

'I hope you won't find it necessary to keep us here tonight, major?'

Scobie said, 'I don't think there's any possibility of your getting away before midday to-morrow.'

'Will do our best, of course,' the lieutenant said.

'On my honour, gentlemen, my hand upon my heart, you will find no bad hats among my passengers. And the crew—I know them all.'

Druce said, 'It's a formality, captain, which we have to go through.'

'Have a cigar,' the captain said. 'Throw away that cigarette. Here is a very special box.'

Druce lit the cigar, which began to spark and crackle. The captain giggled. 'Only my joke, gentlemen. Quite harmless. I keep the box for my friends. The English have a wonderful sense of humour. I know you will not be angry. A German yes, an Englishman no. It is quite cricket, eh?'

'Very funny,' Druce said sourly, laying the cigar down on the ash-tray the captain held out to him. The ash-tray, presumably set off by the captain's finger, began to play a little tinkly tune. Druce jerked again: he was overdue for leave and his nerves were unsteady. The captain smiled and sweated. 'Swiss,' he said. 'A wonderful people. Neutral too.'

One of the Field Security men came in and gave Druce a note. He passed it to Scobie to read. *Steward, who is under notice of dismissal, says the captain has letters concealed in his bathroom.*

Druce said, 'I think I'd better go and make them hustle down below. Coming, Evans? Many thanks for the port, captain.'

Scobie was left alone with the captain. This was the part of the job he always hated. These men were not criminals: they were merely breaking regulations enforced on the shipping companies by the navicert system. You never knew in a search what you would find. A man's bedroom was his private life. Prying in drawers you came on humiliations; little petty vices were tucked out of sight like a soiled handkerchief. Under a pile of linen you might come on a grief he was trying to forget. Scobie said gently, 'I'm afraid, captain, I'll have to look around. You know it's a formality.'

'You must do your duty, major,' the Portuguese said.

Scobie went quickly and neatly through the cabin: he never moved a thing without replacing it exactly: he was like a careful housewife. The captain stood with his back to Scobie looking out on to the bridge; it was as if he preferred not to embarrass his guest in the odious task. Scobie came to an end, closing the box of French letters and putting them carefully back in the top drawer of the locker with the handkerchiefs, the gaudy ties and the little bundle of dirty handkerchiefs. 'All finished?' the captain asked politely, turning his head.

'That door,' Scobie said, 'what would be through there?'

'That is only the bathroom, the w.c.'

'I think I'd better take a look.'

'Of course, major, but there is not much cover there to conceal anything.'

'If you don't mind. . . .'

'Of course not. It is your duty.'

The bathroom was bare and extraordinarily dirty. The bath was rimmed with dry grey soap, and the tiles slopped under his feet. The problem was to find the right place quickly. He couldn't linger here without disclosing the fact that he had special information. The search had got to have all the appearances of formality—neither too lax nor too thorough. 'This won't take long,' he said cheerily and caught sight of the fat calm face in the shaving-mirror. The information, of course, might be false, given by the steward simply in order to cause trouble.

Scobie opened the medicine-cabinet and went rapidly through the contents: unscrewing the toothpaste, opening the razor box, dipping his finger into the shaving-cream. He did not expect to find anything there. But the search gave him time to think. He went next to the taps, turned the water on, felt up each funnel with his finger. The floor engaged his attention: there were no possibilities of concealment there. The porthole: he examined the big screws and swung the inner mask to and fro. Every time he turned he caught sight of the captain's face in the mirror, calm, patient, complacent. It said 'cold, cold' to him all the while, as in a children's game.

Finally, the lavatory: he lifted up the wooden seat: nothing had been laid between the porcelain and the wood. He put his hand on the lavatory chain, and in the mirror became aware for the first time of a tension: the brown eyes were no longer on his face, they were fixed on something else, and following that gaze home, he saw his own hand tighten on the chain.

Is the cistern empty of water? he wondered, and pulled. Gurgling and pounding in the pipes, the water flushed down. He turned away and the Portuguese said with a smugness he was unable to conceal, 'You see, major.' And at that moment Scobie did see. I'm becoming careless, he thought. He lifted the cap of the cistern. Fixed in the cap with adhesive tape and clear of the water lay a letter.

He looked at the address—a Frau Groener in Friedrichstrasse, Leipzig. He repeated, 'I'm sorry, captain,' and because the man didn't answer, he looked up and saw the tears beginning to pursue the sweat down the hot fat cheeks. 'I'll have to take it away,' Scobie said, 'and report. . . .'

'Oh, this war,' the captain burst out, 'how I hate this war.'

'We've got cause to hate it too, you know,' Scobie said.

'A man is ruined because he writes to his daughter.'

'Daughter?'

'Yes. She is Frau Groener. Open it and read. You will see.'

'I can't do that. I must leave it to the censorship. Why didn't you wait to write till you got to Lisbon, captain?'

The man had lowered his bulk on to the edge of the bath as though it were a heavy sack his shoulders could no longer bear. He kept on wiping his eyes with the back of his hand like a child—an unattractive child, the fat boy of the school. Against the beautiful and the clever and the successful, one can wage a pitiless war, but not against the unattractive: then the millstone weighs on the breast. Scobie knew he should have taken the letter and gone; he could do no good with his sympathy.

The captain moaned, 'If you had a daughter you'd understand. You haven't got one,' he accused, as though there were a crime in sterility.

'No.'

'She is anxious about me. She loves me,' he said, raising his tear-drenched face as though he must drive the unlikely statement home. 'She loves *me*,' he repeated mournfully.

'But why not write from Lisbon?' Scobie asked again. 'Why run this risk?'

'I am alone. I have no wife,' the captain said. 'One cannot always wait to speak. And in Lisbon—you know how things go—friends, wine. I have a little woman there too who is jealous even of my daughter. There are rows, the time passes. In a week I must be off again. It was always so easy before this voyage.'

Scobie believed him. The story was sufficiently irrational to be true. Even in war-time one must sometimes exercise the faculty of belief if it is not to atrophy. He said, 'I'm sorry. There's nothing I can do about it. Perhaps nothing will happen.'

'Your authorities,' the captain said, 'will blacklist me. You know what that means. The consul will not give a navicert to any ship with me as captain. I shall starve on shore.'

'There are so many slips,' Scobie said, 'in these matters. Files get mislaid. You may hear no more about it.'

'I shall pray,' the man said without hope.

'Why not?' Scobie said.

'You are an Englishman. You wouldn't believe in prayer.'

'I'm a Catholic, too,' Scobie said.

The fat face looked quickly up at him. 'A Catholic?' he exclaimed with hope. For the first time he began to plead. He was like a man who meets a fellow countryman in a strange continent. He began to talk rapidly of his daughter in Leipzig; he produced a battered pocket-book and a yellowing snap-shot of a stout young Portuguese woman as graceless as himself. The little bathroom was stiflingly hot and the captain repeated again and again,

'You will understand.' He had discovered suddenly how much they had in common: the plaster statues with the swords in the bleeding heart: the whisper behind the confessional curtains: the holy coats and the liquefaction of blood: the dark side chapels and the intricate movements, and somewhere behind it all the love of God. 'And in Lisbon,' he said, 'she will be waiting, she will take me home, she will take away my trousers so that I cannot go out alone: every day it will be drink and quarrels until we go to bed. You will understand. I cannot write to my daughter from Lisbon. She loves me so much and she waits.' He shifted his fat thigh and said, 'The pureness of that love,' and wept. They had in common all the wide region of repentance and longing.

Their kinship gave the captain courage to try another angle. He said, 'I am a poor man, but I have enough money to spare. . . .' He would never have attempted to bribe an Englishman: it was the most sincere compliment he could pay to their common religion.

'I'm sorry,' Scobie said.

'I have English pounds. I will give you twenty English pounds . . . fifty.' He implored. 'A hundred . . . that is all I have saved.'

'It can't be done,' Scobie said. He put the letter quickly in his pocket and turned away. The last time he saw the captain as he looked back from the door of the cabin, he was beating his head against the cistern, the tears catching in the folds of his cheeks. As he went down to join Druce in the saloon he could feel the millstone weighing on his breast. How I hate this war, he thought, in the very words the captain had used.

2/iii

The letter to the daughter in Leipzig, and a small bundle of correspondence found in the kitchens, was the sole result of eight hours' search by fifteen men. It could be counted an average day. When Scobie reached the police station he looked in to see the Commissioner, but his office was empty, so he sat down in his own room under the handcuffs and began to write his report. 'A special search was made of the cabins and effects of the passengers named in your telegrams . . . with no result.' The letter to the daughter in Leipzig lay on the desk beside him. Outside it was dark. The smell of the cells seeped in under the door, and in the next office Fraser was singing to himself the same tune he had sung every evening since his last leave:

> '*What will we care for*
> *The why and the wherefore,*
> *When you and I*
> *Are pushing up the daisies?*'

It seemed to Scobie that life was immeasurably long. Couldn't the test of man have been carried out in fewer years? Couldn't we have committed our first major sin at seven, have ruined ourselves for love or hate at ten, have clutched at redemption on a fifteen-year-old death-bed? He wrote:

A steward who had been dismissed for incompetence reported that the captain had correspondence concealed in his bathroom. I made a search and found the enclosed letter addressed to Frau Groener in Leipzig concealed in the lid of the lavatory cistern. An instruction on this hiding-place might well be circulated, as it has not been encountered before at this station. The letter was fixed by tape above the water-line . . .

He sat there staring at the paper, his brain confused with the conflict that had really been decided hours ago when Druce said to him in the saloon, 'Anything?' and he had shrugged his shoulders in a gesture he left Druce to interpret. Had he ever intended it to mean: 'The usual private correspondence we are always finding.' Druce had taken it for 'No'. Scobie put his hand against his forehead and shivered: the sweat seeped between his fingers, and he thought, Am I in for a touch of fever? Perhaps it was because his temperature had risen that it seemed to him he was on the verge of a new life. One felt this way before a proposal of marriage or a first crime.

Scobie took the letter and opened it. The act was irrevocable, for no one in this city had the right to open clandestine mail. A microphotograph might be concealed in the gum of an envelope. Even a simple word code would be beyond him; his knowledge of Portuguese would take him no farther than the most surface meaning. Every letter found—however obviously innocent—must be sent to the London censors unopened. Scobie against the strictest orders was exercising his own imperfect judgment. He thought to himself: If the letter is suspicious, I will send my report. I can explain the torn envelope. The captain insisted on opening the letter to show me the contents. But if he wrote that, he would be unjustly blackening the case against the captain, for what better way could he have found for destroying a microphotograph? There must be some lie to be told, Scobie thought, but he was unaccustomed to lies. With the letter in his hand, held carefully over the white blotting-pad, so that he could detect anything that might fall from between the leaves, he decided that he would write a full report on all the circumstances, including his own act.

Dear little money spider, *the letter began,* your father who loves you more than anything upon earth will try to send you a little more money this time. I know how hard things are for you, and my heart bleeds. Little money spider, if only I could feel your fingers running across my cheek. How is it that a great fat father like I am should have so tiny and beautiful a daughter? Now, little money spider, I will tell you everything that has happened to me. We left Lobito a week ago after only four days in port. I stayed one night with Senor Aranjuez and I drank more wine than was good for me, but all my talk was of you. I was good all the time I was in port because I had promised my little money spider, and I went to Confession and Communion, so that if anything should happen to me on the way to Lisbon—for who knows in these terrible days?—I should not have to live my eternity away from my little spider. Since we left Lobito we have had good weather. Even the passengers are not seasick. To-morrow night, because Africa will be at last behind us, we shall have a ship's concert, and I shall perform on my whistle. All the time I perform I shall remember the days when my little money spider sat on my knee and listened. My dear, I am growing old, and after every voyage I am fatter: I am not a good man, and sometimes I fear that my soul in all this hulk of flesh is no larger than a pea. You do not know how easy it is for a man like me to commit the unforgivable despair. Then I think of my daughter.

There was just enough good in me once for you to be fashioned. A wife shares too much of a man's sin for perfect love. But a daughter may save him at the last. Pray for me, little spider. Your father who loves you more than life.

Mais que a vida. Scobie felt no doubt at all of the sincerity of this letter. This was not written to conceal a photograph of the Cape Town defences or a microphotograph report on troop movements at Durban. It should, he knew, be tested for secret ink, examined under a microscope, and the inner lining of the envelope exposed. Nothing should be left to chance with a clandestine letter. But he had committed himself to a belief. He tore the letter up, and his own report with it, and carried the scraps out to the incinerator in the yard—a petrol-tin standing upon two bricks with its sides punctured to make a draught. As he struck a match to light the papers, Fraser joined him in the yard. '*What will we care for the why and the wherefore?*' On the top of the scraps lay unmistakably half a foreign envelope: one could even read part of the address—Friedrichstrasse. He quickly held the match to the uppermost scrap as Fraser crossed the yard, striding with unbearable youth. The scrap went up in flame, and in the heat of the fire another scrap uncurled the name of Groener. Fraser said cheerfully, 'Burning the evidence?' and looked down into the tin. The name had blackened: there was nothing there surely that Fraser could see—except a brown triangle of envelope that seemed to Scobie obviously foreign. He ground it out of existence with a stick and looked up at Fraser to see whether he could detect any surprise or suspicion. There was nothing to be read in the vacuous face, blank as a school notice-board out of term. Only his own heart-beats told him he was guilty—that he had joined the ranks of the corrupt police officers—Bailey who had kept a safe deposit in another city, Crayshaw who had been found with diamonds, Boyston against whom nothing had been definitely proved and who had been invalided out. They had been corrupted by money, and he had been corrupted by sentiment. Sentiment was the more dangerous, because you couldn't name its price. A man open to bribes was to be relied upon below a certain figure, but sentiment might uncoil in the heart at a name, a photograph, even a smell remembered.

'What sort of day, sir?' Fraser asked, staring at the small pile of ash. Perhaps he was thinking that it should have been his day.

'The usual kind of a day,' Scobie said.

'How about the captain?' Fraser asked, looking down into the petrol-tin, beginning to hum again his languid tune.

'The captain?' Scobie said.

'Oh, Druce told me some fellow informed on him.'

'Just the usual thing,' Scobie said. 'A dismissed steward with a grudge. Didn't Druce tell you we found nothing?'

'No,' Fraser said, 'he didn't seem to be sure. Goodnight, sir. I must be pushing off to the mess.'

'Thimblerigg on duty?'

'Yes, sir.'

Scobie watched him go. The back was as vacuous as the face: one could read nothing there. Scobie thought, what a fool I have been. What a fool. He owed his duty to Louise, not to a fat sentimental Portuguese skipper who had broken the rules of his own company for the sake of a daughter equally unattractive. That had been the turning point, the daughter. And now, Scobie thought, I must return home: I shall put the car away in the garage, and Ali will come forward with his torch to light me to the door. She will be sitting there between two draughts for coolness, and I shall read on her face the story of what she has been thinking all day. She will have been hoping that everything is fixed, that I shall say, 'I've put your name down at the agent's for South Africa,' but she'll be afraid that nothing so good as that will ever happen to us. She'll wait for me to speak, and I shall try to talk about anything under the sun to postpone seeing her misery (it would be waiting at the corners of her mouth to take possession of her whole face). He knew exactly how things would go: it had happened so often before. He rehearsed every word, going back into his office, locking his desk, going down to his car. People talk about the courage of condemned men walking to the place of execution: sometimes it needs as much courage to walk with any kind of bearing towards another person's habitual misery. He forgot Fraser: he forgot everything but the scene ahead: I shall go in and say, 'Good evening, sweetheart,' and she'll say, 'Good evening, darling. What kind of a day?' and I'll talk and talk, but all the time I shall know I'm coming nearer to the moment when I shall say, 'What about you, darling?' and let the misery in.

2 / iv

'What about you, darling?' He turned quickly away from her and began to fix two more pink gins. There was a tacit understanding between them that 'liquor helped'; growing more miserable with every glass one hoped for the moment of relief.

'You don't really want to know about *me*.'

'Of course I do, darling. What sort of a day have you had?'

'Ticki, why are you such a coward? Why don't you tell me it's all off?'

'All off?'

'You know what I mean—the passage. You've been talking and talking since you came in about the *Esperança*. There's a Portuguese ship in once a fortnight. You don't talk that way every time. I'm not a child, Ticki. Why don't you say straight out—"you can't go"?'

He grinned miserably at his glass, twisting it round and round to let the angostura cling along the curve. He said, 'That wouldn't be true. I'll find some way.' Reluctantly he had recourse to the hated nickname. If that failed, the misery would deepen and go right on through the short night he needed for sleep. 'Trust Ticki,' he said. It was as if a ligament tightened in his brain with the suspense. If only I could postpone the misery, he thought, until daylight. Misery is worse in the darkness: there's nothing to look at except the green black-out curtains, the Government furniture, the flying ants scattering their wings over the table: a hundred yards away the Creoles' pye-dogs yapped and wailed. 'Look at that little beggar,' he said, pointing at the house lizard that always came out upon the wall about this time to hunt for moths and cockroaches. He said, 'We only got the idea last night. These things take time to fix. Ways and means, ways and means,' he said with strained humour.

'Have you been to the bank?'

'Yes,' he admitted.

'And you couldn't get the money?'

'No. They couldn't manage it. Have another gin and bitters, darling?'

She held her glass out to him, crying dumbly; her face reddened when she cried–she looked ten years older, a middle-aged and abandoned woman–it was like the terrible breath of the future on his cheek. He went down on one knee beside her and held the pink gin to her lips as though it were medicine. 'My dear,' he said, 'I'll find a way. Have a drink.'

'Ticki, I can't bear this place any longer. I know I've said it before, but I mean it this time. I shall go mad. Ticki, I'm so lonely. I haven't a friend, Ticki.'

'Let's have Wilson up to-morrow.'

'Ticki, for God's sake don't always mention Wilson. Please, please do something.'

'Of course I will. Just be patient a while, dear. These things take time.'

'What will you do, Ticki?'

'I'm full of ideas, darling,' he said wearily. (What a day it had been.) 'Just let them simmer for a little while.'

'Tell me one idea. Just one.'

His eyes followed the lizard as it pounced; then he picked an ant wing out of his gin and drank again. He thought to himself: what a fool I really was not to take the hundred pounds. I destroyed the letter for nothing. I took the risk. I might just as well . . . Louise said, 'I've known it for years. You don't love me.' She spoke with calm. He knew that calm–it meant they had reached the quiet centre of the storm: always in this region at about this time they began to speak the truth at each other. The truth, he thought, has never been of any real value to any human being–it is a symbol for mathematicians and philosophers to pursue. In human relations kindness and lies are worth a thousand truths. He involved himself in what he always knew was a vain struggle to retain the lies. 'Don't be absurd, darling. Who do you think I love if I don't love you?'

'You don't love anybody.'

'Is that why I treat you so badly?' He tried to hit a light note, and it sounded hollowly back at him.

'That's your conscience,' she said, 'your sense of duty. You've never loved anyone since Catherine died.'

'Except myself, of course. You always say I love myself.'

'No, I don't think you do.'

He defended himself by evasions. In this cyclonic centre he was powerless to give the comforting lie. 'I try all the time to keep you happy. I work hard for that.'

'Ticki, you won't even say you love me. Go on. Say it once.'

He eyed her bitterly over the pink gin, the visible sign of his failure: the skin a little yellow with atabrine, the eyes bloodshot with tears. No man could guarantee love for ever, but he had sworn fourteen years ago, at Ealing, silently, during the horrible little elegant ceremony among the lace and candles, that he would at least always see to it that she was happy. 'Ticki, I've got nothing except you, and you've got—nearly everything.' The lizard flicked across the wall and came to rest again, the wings of a moth in his small crocodile jaws. The ants struck tiny muffled blows at the electric globe.

'And yet you want to go away from me,' he said.

'Yes,' she said, 'I know you aren't happy either. Without me you'll have peace.'

This was what he always left out of account—the accuracy of her observation. He had nearly everything, and all he needed was peace. Everything meant work, the daily regular routine in the little bare office, the change of seasons in a place he loved. How often he had been pitied for the austerity of the work, the bareness of the rewards. But Louise knew him better than that. If he had become young again this was the life he would have chosen to live; only this time he would not have expected any other person to share it with him, the rat upon the bath, the lizard on the wall, the tornado blowing open the windows at one in the morning, and the last pink light upon the laterite roads at sundown.

'You are talking nonsense, dear,' he said, and went through the doomed motions of mixing another gin and bitters. Again the nerve in his head tightened; unhappiness had uncoiled with its inevitable routine—first her misery and his strained attempts to leave everything unsaid: then her own calm statement of truths much better lied about, and finally the snapping of his own control—truths flung back at her as though she were his enemy. As he embarked on this last stage, crying suddenly and truthfully out at her while the angostura trembled in his hand, '*You* can't give me peace,' he already knew what would succeed it, the reconciliation and the easy lies again until the next scene.

'That's what I say,' she said, 'if I go away, you'll have your peace.'

'You haven't any conception,' he accused her, 'of what peace means.' It was as if she had spoken slightingly of a woman he loved. For he dreamed of peace by day and night. Once in sleep it had appeared to him as the great glowing shoulder of the moon heaving across his window like an iceberg, Arctic and destructive in the moment before the world was struck: by day he tried to win a few moments of its company, crouched under the rusting handcuffs in the locked office, reading the reports from the sub-stations. Peace seemed to him the most beautiful word in the language: My peace I give you, my peace I leave with you: O Lamb of God, who takest away the sins of the world, grant us thy peace. In the Mass he pressed his fingers against his eyes to keep the tears of longing in.

Louise said with the old tenderness, 'Poor dear, you wish I were dead like Catherine. You want to be alone.'

He replied obstinately, 'I want you to be happy.'

She said wearily, 'Just tell me you love me. That helps a little.' They were through again, on the other side of the scene: he thought coolly and collectedly, this one wasn't so bad: we shall be able to sleep to-night. He said, 'Of course I love you, darling. And I'll fix that passage. You'll see.'

He would still have made the promise even if he could have foreseen all that would come of it. He had always been prepared to accept the responsibility for his actions, and he had always been half aware too, from the time he made his terrible private vow that she would be happy, how far *this* action might carry him. Despair is the price one pays for setting oneself an impossible aim. It is, one is told, the unforgivable sin, but it is a sin the corrupt or evil man never practises. He always has hope. He never reaches the freezing-point of knowing absolute failure. Only the man of goodwill carries always in his heart this capacity for damnation.

PART II

I / i

Wilson stood gloomily by his bed in the Bedford Hotel and contemplated his cummerbund, which lay ruffled like an angry snake; the small room was hot with the conflict between them. Through the wall he could hear Harris cleaning his teeth for the fifth time that day. Harris believed in dental hygiene. 'It's cleaning my teeth before and after every meal that's kept me so well in this bloody climate,' he would say, raising his pale exhausted face over an orange squash. Now he was gargling: it sounded like a noise in the pipes.

Wilson sat down on the edge of his bed and rested. He had left his door open for coolness, and across the passage he could see into the bathroom. The Indian with the turban was sitting on the side of the bath fully dressed. He stared inscrutably back at Wilson and bowed. 'Just a moment, sir,' he called. 'If you would care to step in here . . .' Wilson angrily shut the door. Then he had another try with the cummerbund.

He had once seen a film—was it *Bengal Lancer?*—in which the cummerbund was superbly disciplined. A native held the coil and an immaculate officer spun like a top, so that the cummerbund encircled him smoothly, tightly. Another servant stood by with iced drinks, and a punkah swayed in the background. Apparently these things were better managed in India. However, with one more effort, Wilson did get the wretched thing wrapped around him. It was too tight and it was badly creased, and the tuck-in came too near the front, so that it was not hidden by the jacket. He contemplated his image with melancholy in what was left of the mirror. Somebody tapped on the door.

'Who is it?' Wilson shouted, imagining for a moment that the Indian had had the cool impertinence to pursue . . . but when the door opened, it was only Harris: the Indian was still sitting on the bath across the passage shuffling his testimonials.

'Going out, old man?' Harris asked, with disappointment.

'Yes.'

'Everybody seems to be going out this evening. I shall have the table all to myself.' He added with gloom, 'It's the curry evening too.'

'So it is. I'm sorry to miss it.'

'You haven't been having it for two years, old man, every Thursday night.' He looked at the cummerbund. 'That's not right, old man.'

'I know it isn't. It's the best I can do.'

'I never wear one. It stands to reason that it's bad for the stomach. They tell you it absorbs sweat, but that's not where I sweat, old man. I'd rather wear braces, only the elastic perishes, so a leather belt's good enough for me. I'm no snob. Where are you dining, old man?'

'At Tallit's.'

'How did you meet him?'

'He came into the office yesterday to pay his account and asked me to dinner.'

'You don't have to dress for a Syrian, old man. Take it all off again.'

'Are you sure?'

'Of course I am. It wouldn't do at all. Quite wrong.' He added, 'You'll get a good dinner, but be careful of the sweets. The price of life is eternal vigilance. I wonder what he wants out of you.' Wilson began to undress again while Harris talked. He was a good listener. His brain was like a sieve through which the rubbish fell all day long. Sitting on the bed in his pants he heard Harris–'you have to be careful of the fish: I never touch it'–but the words left no impression. Drawing up his white drill trousers over his hairless knees he said to himself:

> *the poor sprite is*
> *Imprisoned for some fault of his*
> *In a body like a grave.*

His belly rumbled and tumbled as it always did a little before the hour of dinner.

> *From you he only dares to crave,*
> *For his service and his sorrow,*
> *A smile to-day, a song to-morrow.*

Wilson stared into the mirror and passed his fingers over the smooth, too smooth skin. The face looked back at him, pink and healthy, plump and hopeless. Harris went happily on, 'I said once to Scobie,' and immediately the clot of words lodged in Wilson's sieve. He pondered aloud, 'I wonder how he ever came to marry her.'

'It's what we all wonder, old man. Scobie's not a bad sort.'

'She's too good for him.'

'Louise?' Harris exclaimed.

'Of course. Who else?'

'There's no accounting for tastes. Go in and win, old man.'

'I must be off.'

'Be careful of the sweets.' Harris went on with a small spurt of energy, 'God knows I wouldn't mind something to be careful of instead of Thursday's curry. It is Thursday, isn't it?'

'Yes.'

They came out into the passage and into the focus of the Indian eyes. 'You'll have to be done sooner or later, old man,' Harris said. 'He does everybody once. You'll never have peace till he does you.'

'I don't believe in fortune-telling,' Wilson lied.

'Nor do I, but he's pretty good. He did me the first week I was here. Told me I'd stay here for more than two and a half years. I thought then I was going to have leave after eighteen months. I know better now.' The Indian watched triumphantly from the bath. He said, 'I have a letter from the Director of Agriculture. And one from D.C. Parkes.'

'All right,' Wilson said. 'Do me, but be quick about it.'

'I'd better push off, old man, before the revelations begin.'

'I'm not afraid,' Wilson said.

'Will you sit on the bath, sir?' the Indian invited him courteously. He took Wilson's hand in his. 'It is a very interesting hand, sir,' he said unconvincingly, weighing it up and down.

'What are your charges?'

'According to rank, sir. One like yourself, sir, I should charge ten shillings.'

'That's a bit steep.'

'Junior officers are five shillings.'

'I'm in the five-shilling class,' Wilson said.

'Oh no, sir. The Director of Agriculture gave me a pound.'

'I'm only an accountant.'

'That's as you say, sir. A.D.C. and Major Scobie gave me ten shillings.'

'Oh well,' Wilson said. 'Here's ten bob. Go ahead.'

'You have been here one, two weeks,' the Indian said. 'You are sometimes at night an impatient man. You think you do not make enough progress.'

'Who with?' Harris asked, lolling in the doorway.

'You are very ambitious. You are a dreamer. You read much poetry.'

Harris giggled and Wilson, raising his eyes from the finger which traced the lines upon his palm, watched the fortune-teller with apprehension.

The Indian went inflexibly on. His turban was bowed under Wilson's nose and bore the smell of stale food—he probably secreted stray pieces from the larder in its folds. He said, 'You are a secret man. You do not tell your friends about your poetry—except one. One,' he repeated. 'You are very shy. You should take courage. You have a great line of success.'

'Go in and win, old man,' Harris repeated.

Of course the whole thing was Couéism: if one believed in it enough, it would come true. Diffidence would be conquered. The mistake in a reading would be covered up.

'You haven't told me ten bob's worth,' Wilson said. 'This is a five-bob fortune. Tell me something definite, something that's going to happen.' He shifted his seat uncomfortably on the sharp edge of the bath and watched a cockroach like a large blood blister flattened on the wall. The Indian bent forward over the two hands. He said, 'I see great success. The Government will be very pleased with you.'

Harris said, '*Il pense* that you are *un bureaucrat.*'

'Why will the Government be pleased with me?' Wilson asked.

'You will capture your man.'

'Why,' Harris said, 'I believe he thinks you are a new policeman.'

'It looks like it,' Wilson said. 'Not much use wasting more time.'

'And your private life, that will be a great success too. You will win the lady of your heart. You will sail away. Everything is going to be fine. For you,' he added.

'A real ten-bob fortune.'

'Good night,' Wilson said. 'I won't write you a recommendation on that.' He got up from the bath, and the cockroach flashed into hiding. 'I can't bear those things,' Wilson said, sidling through the door. He turned in the passage and repeated, 'Good night.'

'I couldn't when I first came, old man. But I evolved a system. Just step into my room and I'll show you.'

'I ought to be off.'

'Nobody will be punctual at Tallit's.' Harris opened his door and Wilson turned his eyes with a kind of shame from the first sight of its disorder. In his own room he would never have exposed himself quite like this—the dirty tooth-glass, the towel on the bed.

'Look here, old man.'

With relief he fixed his eyes on some symbols pencilled on the wall inside: the letter H, and under it a row of figures lined against dates as in a cash-book. Then the letters D.D., and under them more figures. 'It's my score in cockroaches, old man. Yesterday was an average day—four. My record's nine. It makes you welcome the little brutes.'

'What does D.D. stand for?'

'Down the drain, old man. That's when I knock them into the wash-basin and they go down the waste-pipe. It wouldn't be fair to count them as dead, would it?'

'No.'

'And it wouldn't do to cheat yourself either. You'd lose interest at once. The only thing is, it gets dull sometimes, playing against yourself. Why shouldn't we make a match of it, old man? It needs skill, you know. They positively hear you coming, and they move like greased lightning. I do a stalk every evening with a torch.'

'I wouldn't mind having a try, but I've got to be off now.'

'I tell you what—I won't start hunting till you come back from Tallit's. We'll have five minutes before bed. Just five minutes.'

'If you like.'

'I'll come down with you, old man. I can smell the curry. You know I could have laughed when the old fool mixed you up with the new police officer.'

'He got most of it wrong, didn't he?' Wilson said. 'I mean the poetry.'

I /ii

Tallit's living-room to Wilson, who saw it for the first time, had the appearance of a country dance hall. The furniture all lined the walls: hard chairs with tall uncomfortable backs, and in the corners the chaperons sitting out: old women in black silk dresses, yards and yards of silk, and a very old man in a smoking-cap. They watched him intently in complete silence, and evading their gaze he saw only bare walls except that at each corner sentimental French postcards were nailed up in *a montage* of ribbons and bows: young men smelling mauve flowers, a glossy cherry shoulder, an impassioned kiss.

Wilson found there was only one other guest besides himself, Father Rank, a Catholic priest, wearing his long soutane. They sat in opposite corners of the room among the chaperons whom Father Rank explained were Tallit's grandparents and parents, two uncles, what might have been a great-great-aunt, a cousin. Somewhere out of sight Tallit's wife was preparing little dishes which were handed to the two guests by his younger brother and his sister. None of them spoke English except Tallit, and Wilson was embarrassed by the way Father Rank discussed his host and his host's family resoundingly across the room. 'Thank you, no,' Father Rank would say, declining a sweet by shaking his grey tousled head. 'I'd advise you to be careful of those, Mr Wilson. Tallit's a good fellow, but he won't learn what a western stomach will take. These old people have stomachs like ostriches.'

'This is very interesting to me,' Wilson said, catching the eye of a grandmother across the room and nodding and smiling at her. The grandmother obviously thought he wanted more sweets, and called angrily out for her granddaughter. 'No, no,' Wilson said vainly, shaking his head and smiling at the centenarian. The centenarian lifted his lip from a toothless gum and signalled with ferocity to Tallit's younger brother, who hurried forward with yet another dish. 'That's quite safe,' Father Rank shouted. 'Just sugar and glycerine and a little flour.' All the time their glasses were charged and recharged with whisky.

'Wish you'd confess to me where you get this whisky from, Tallit,' Father Rank called out, and Tallit beamed and slid agilely from end to end of the room, a word to Wilson, a word to Father Rank. He reminded Wilson of a young ballet dancer in his white trousers, his plaster of black hair and his grey polished alien face, and one glass eye like a puppet's.

'So the *Esperança*'s gone out,' Father Rank shouted across the room. 'Did they find anything, do you think?'

'There was a rumour in the office,' Wilson said, 'about some diamonds.'

'Diamonds, my eye,' Father Rank said. 'They'll never find any diamonds. They don't know where to look, do they, Tallit?' He explained to Wilson, 'Diamonds are a sore subject with Tallit. He was taken in by the false ones last year. Yusef humbugged you, eh, Tallit, you young rogue? Not so smart, eh? You a Catholic humbugged by a Mahomedan. I could have wrung your neck.'

'It was a bad thing to do,' Tallit said, standing midway between Wilson and the priest.

'I've only been here a few weeks,' Wilson said, 'and everyone talks to me about Yusef. They say he passes false diamonds, smuggles real ones, sells bad liquor, hoards cottons against a French invasion, seduces the nursing sisters from the military hospital.'

'He's a dirty dog,' Father Rank said with a kind of relish. 'Not that you can believe a single thing you hear in this place. Otherwise everybody would be living with someone else's wife, every police officer who wasn't in Yusef's pay would be bribed by Tallit here.'

Tallit said, 'Yusef is a very bad man.'

'Why don't the authorities run him in?'

'I've been here for twenty-two years,' Father Rank said, 'and I've never known anything proved against a Syrian yet. Oh, often I've seen the police as pleased as Punch carrying their happy morning faces around, just going to pounce–and I think to myself, why bother to ask them what it's about? they'll just pounce on air.'

'You ought to have been a policeman, Father.'

'Ah,' Father Rank said, 'who knows? There are more policemen in this town than meet the eye–or so they say.'

'Who say?'

'Careful of those sweets,' Father Rank said, 'they are harmless in moderation, but you've taken four already. Look here, Tallit, Mr Wilson looks hungry. Can't you bring on the bakemeats?'

'Bakemeats?'

'The feast,' Father Rank said. His joviality filled the room with hollow sound. For twenty-two years that voice had been laughing, joking, urging people humorously on through the rainy and the dry months. Could its cheeriness ever have comforted a single soul? Wilson wondered: had it even comforted itself? It was like the noise one heard rebounding from the tiles in a public baths: the laughs and the splashes of strangers in the steam-heating.

'Of course, Father Rank. Immediately, Father Rank.' Father Rank, without being invited, rose from his chair and sat himself down at a table which like the chairs hugged the wall. There were only a few places laid and Wilson hesitated. 'Come on. Sit down, Mr Wilson. Only the old folks will be eating with us–and Tallit of course.'

'You were saying something about a rumour?' Wilson asked.

'My head is a hive of rumours,' Father Rank said, making a humorous hopeless gesture. 'If a man tells me anything I assume he wants me to pass it on. It's a useful function, you know, at a time like this, when everything is an official secret, to remind people that their tongues were made to talk with and that the truth is meant to be spoken about. Look at Tallit now,' Father Rank went on. Tallit was raising the corner of his black-out curtain and gazing into the dark street. 'How's Yusef, you young rogue?' he asked. 'Yusef's got a big house across the street and Tallit wants it, don't you, Tallit? What about dinner, Tallit, we're hungry?'

'It is here, Father, it is here,' he said, coming away from the window. He sat down silently beside the centenarian, and his sister served the dishes. 'You always get a good meal in Tallit's house,' Father Rank said.

'Yusef too is entertaining to-night.'

'It doesn't do for a priest to be choosy,' Father Rank said, 'but I find your dinner more digestible.' His hollow laugh swung through the room.

'Is it as bad as all that being seen at Yusef's?'

'It is, Mr Wilson. If I saw you there, I'd say to myself, "Yusef wants some information badly about cottons–what the imports are going to be next month, say– what's on the way by sea, and he'll pay for his information." If I saw a girl go in, I'd think it was a pity, a great pity.' He took a stab at his plate and laughed again. 'But if Tallit went in I'd wait to hear the screams for help.'

'If you saw a police officer?' Tallit asked.

'I wouldn't believe my eyes,' the priest said. 'None of them are such fools after what happened to Bailey.'

'The other night a police car brought Yusef home,' Tallit said. 'I saw it from here plainly.'

'One of the drivers earning a bit on the side,' Father Rank said.

'I thought I saw Major Scobie. He was careful not to get out. Of course I am not perfectly sure. It *looked* like Major Scobie.'

'My tongue runs away with me,' the priest said. 'What a garrulous fool I am. Why, if it was Scobie, I wouldn't think twice about it.' His eyes roamed the room. 'Not twice,' he said. 'I'd lay next Sunday's collection that everything was all right, absolutely all right,' and he swung his great empty-sounding bell to and fro, Ho, ho, ho, like a leper proclaiming his misery.

I /iii

The light was still on in Harris's room when Wilson returned to the hotel. He was tired and worried and he tried to tiptoe by, but Harris heard him. 'I've been listening for you, old man,' he said, waving an electric torch. He wore his mosquito-boots outside his pyjamas and looked like a harassed air-raid warden.

'It's late. I thought you'd be asleep.'

'I couldn't sleep until we'd had our hunt. The idea's grown on me, old man. We might have a monthly prize. I can see the time coming when other people will want to join in.'

Wilson said with irony, 'There might be a silver cup.'

'Stranger things have happened, old man. The Cockroach Championship.'

He led the way, walking softly on the boards to the middle of his room: the iron bed stood under its greying net, the arm-chair with collapsible back, the dressing-table littered with old *Picture Posts*. It shocked Wilson once again to realise that a room could be a degree more cheerless than his own.

'We'll draw our rooms alternate nights, old man.'

'What weapon shall I use?'

'You can borrow one of my slippers.' A board squeaked under Wilson's feet and Harris turned warningly. 'They have ears like rats,' he said.

'I'm a bit tired. Don't you think that tonight . . . ?'

'Just five minutes, old man. I couldn't sleep without a hunt. Look, there's one—over the dressing-table. You can have first shot,' but as the shadow of the slipper fell upon the plaster wall, the insect shot away.

'No use doing it like that, old man. Watch *me*.' Harris stalked his prey. The cockroach was half-way up the wall, and Harris, as he moved on tiptoe across the creaking floor, began to weave the light of his torch backwards and forwards over the cockroach. Then suddenly he struck and left a smear of blood. 'One up,' he said. 'You have to mesmerise them.'

To and fro across the room they padded, weaving their lights, smashing down their shoes, occasionally losing their heads and pursuing wildly into corners: the lust of the hunt touched Wilson's imagination. At first their manner to each other was 'sporting'; they would call out, 'Good shot' or 'Hard luck', but once they met together against the wainscot over the same cockroach when the score was even, and their tempers became frayed.

'No point in going after the same bird, old man,' Harris said.

'I started him.'

'You lost your one, old man. This was mine.'

'It was the same. He did a double turn.'

'Oh no.'

'Anyway, there's no reason why I shouldn't go for the same one. You drove it towards me. Bad play on your part.'

'Not allowed in the rules,' Harris said shortly.

'Perhaps not in your rules.'

'Damn it all,' Harris said, 'I invented the game.'

A cockroach sat upon the brown cake of soap in the washbasin. Wilson spied it and took a long shot with the shoe from six feet away. The shoe landed smartly on the soap and the cockroach span into the basin: Harris turned on the tap and washed it down. 'Good shot, old man,' he said placatingly. 'One D.D.'

'D.D. be damned,' Wilson said. 'It was dead when you turned on the tap.'

'You couldn't be sure of that. It might have been just unconscious–concussion. It's D.D. according to the rules.'

'Your rules again.'

'My rules are the Queensberry rules in this town.'

'They won't be for long,' Wilson threatened. He slammed the door hard behind him and the walls of his own room vibrated round him from the shock. His heart beat with rage and the hot night: the sweat drained from his armpits. But as he stood there beside his own bed, seeing the replica of Harris's room around him, the washbasin, the table, the grey mosquito-net, even the cockroach fastened on the wall, anger trickled out of him and loneliness took its place. It was like quarrelling with one's own image in the glass. I was crazy, he thought. What made me fly out like that? I've lost a friend.

That night it took him a long while to sleep, and when he slept at last he dreamed that he had committed a crime, so that he woke with the sense of guilt still heavy upon him. On his way down to breakfast he paused outside Harris's door. There was no sound. He knocked, but there was no answer. He opened the door a little way and saw obscurely through the grey net Harris's damp bed. He asked softly, 'Are you awake?'

'What is it?'

'I'm sorry, Harris, about last night.'

'My fault, old man. I've got a touch of fever. I was sickening for it. Touchy.'

'No, it's my fault. You are quite right. It *was* D.D.'

'We'll toss up for it, old man.'

'I'll come in to-night.'

'That's fine.'

But after breakfast something took his mind right away from Harris. He had been in to the Commissioner's office on his way down town and coming out he ran into Scobie.

'Hallo,' Scobie said, 'what are you doing here?'

'Been in to see the Commissioner about a pass. There are so many passes one has to have in this town, sir. I wanted one for the wharf.'

'When are you going to call on us again, Wilson?'

'You don't want to be bothered with strangers, sir.'

'Nonsense. Louise would like another chat about books. I don't read them myself, you know, Wilson.'

'I don't suppose you have much time.'

'Oh, there's an awful lot of time around,' Scobie said, 'in a country like this. I just don't have a taste for reading, that's all. Come into my office a moment while I ring up Louise. She'll be glad to see you. Wish you'd call in and take her for a walk. She doesn't get enough exercise.'

'I'd love to,' Wilson said, and blushed hurriedly in the shadows. He looked around him: this was Scobie's office. He examined it as a general might examine a battle-ground, and yet it was difficult to regard Scobie as an enemy. The rusty handcuffs jangled on the wall as Scobie leant back from his desk and dialled.

'Free this evening?'

He brought his mind sharply back, aware that Scobie was watching him: the slightly protruding, slightly reddened eyes dwelt on him with a kind of speculation. 'I wonder why you came out here,' Scobie said. 'You aren't the type.'

'One drifts into things,' Wilson lied.

'I don't,' Scobie said, 'I've always been a planner. You see, I even plan for other people.' He began to talk into the telephone. His intonation changed: it was as if he were reading a part—a part which called for tenderness and patience, a part which had been read so often that the eyes were blank above the mouth. Putting down the receiver, he said, 'That's fine. That's settled then.'

'It seems a very good plan to me,' Wilson said.

'My plans always start out well,' Scobie said. 'You two go for a walk, and when you get back I'll have a drink ready for you. Stay to dinner,' he went on with a hint of anxiety. 'We'll be glad of your company.'

When Wilson had gone, Scobie went in to the Commissioner. He said, 'I was just coming along to see you, sir, when I ran into Wilson.'

'Oh yes, Wilson,' the Commissioner said. 'He came in to have a word with me about one of their lightermen.'

'I see.' The shutters were down in the office to cut out the morning sun. A sergeant passed through carrying with him, as well as his file, a breath of the Zoo behind. The day was heavy with unshed rain: already at 8.30 in the morning the body ran with sweat. Scobie said, 'He told me he'd come about a pass.'

'Oh yes,' the Commissioner said, 'that too.' He put a piece of blotting-paper under his wrist to absorb the sweat as he wrote. 'Yes, there was something about a pass too, Scobie.'

Mrs Scobie led the way, scrambling down towards the bridge over the river that still carried the sleepers of an abandoned railway.

'I'd never have found this path by myself,' Wilson said, panting a little with the burden of his plumpness.

Louise Scobie said, 'It's my favourite walk.'

On the dry dusty slope above the path an old man sat in the doorway of a hut doing nothing. A girl with small crescent breasts climbed down towards them balancing a pail of water on her head; a child naked except for a red bead necklace round the waist played in a little dust-paved yard among the chickens; labourers carrying hatchets came across the bridge at the end of their day. It was the hour of comparative coolness, the hour of peace.

'You wouldn't guess, would you, that the city's just behind us?' Mrs Scobie said. 'And a few hundred yards up there over the hill the boys are bringing in the drinks.'

The path wound along the slope of the hill. Down below him Wilson could see the huge harbour spread out. A convoy was gathering inside the boom; tiny boats moved like flies between the ships; above them the ashy trees and the burnt scrubs hid the summit of the ridge. Wilson stumbled once or twice as his toes caught in the ledges left by the sleepers.

Louise Scobie said, 'That is what I thought it was all going to be like.'

'Your husband loves the place, doesn't he?'

'Oh, I think sometimes he's got a kind of selective eyesight. He sees what he likes to see. He doesn't seem to see the snobbery, and he doesn't hear the gossip.'

'He sees you,' Wilson said.

'Thank God he doesn't, because I've caught the disease.'

'You aren't a snob.'

'Oh yes, I am.'

'You took *me* up,' Wilson said, blushing and contorting his face into a careful careless whistle. But he couldn't whistle. The plump lips blew empty air, like a fish.

'For God's sake,' Louise said, 'don't be humble.'

'I'm not really humble,' Wilson said. He stood aside to let a labourer go by. He explained, 'I've got inordinate ambitions.'

'In two minutes,' Louise said, 'we get to the best point of all–where you can't see a single house.'

'It's good of you to show me . . .' Wilson muttered, stumbling on again along the ridge track. He had no small talk: with a woman he could be romantic, but nothing else.

'There,' Louise said, but he had hardly time to take the view in–the harsh green slopes falling down towards the great flat glaring bay–when she wanted to be off again, back the way they had come. 'Henry will be in soon,' she said.

'Who's Henry?'

'My husband.'

'I didn't know his name. I'd heard you call him something else—something like Ticki.'

'Poor Henry,' she said. 'How he hates it. I try not to when other people are there, but I forget. Let's go.'

'Can't we go just a little further—to the railway station?'

'I'd like to change,' Louise said, 'before dark. The rats begin to come in after dark.'

'Going back will be downhill all the way.'

'Let's hurry then,' Louise said. He followed her. Thin and ungainly, she seemed to him to possess a sort of Undine beauty. She had been kind to him, she bore his company, and automatically at any first kindness from a woman love stirred. He had no capacity for friendship or for equality. In his romantic, humble, ambitious mind he could conceive only a relationship with a waitress, a cinema usherette, a landlady's daughter in Battersea or with a queen—this was queen. He began to mutter again at her heels—'so good'—between pants, his plump knees knocking together on the stony path. Quite suddenly the light changed: the laterite soil turned a translucent pink sloping down the hill to the wide flat water of the bay. There was something happily accidental in the evening light as though it hadn't been planned.

'This is it,' Louise said, and they leant and got their breath again against the wooden wall of the small abandoned station, watching the light fade out as quickly as it came.

Through an open door—had it been the waiting room or the station master's office?—the hens passed in and out. The dust on the windows was like the steam left only a moment ago by a passing train. On the forever-closed guichet somebody had chalked a crude phallic figure. Wilson could see it over her left shoulder as she leant back to get her breath. 'I used to come here every day,' Louise said, 'until they spoilt it for me.'

'They?'

She said, 'Thank God, I shall be out of here soon.'

'Why? You are not going away?'

'Henry's sending me to South Africa.'

'Oh God,' Wilson exclaimed. The news was so unexpected that it was like a twinge of pain. His face twisted with it.

He tried to cover up the absurd exposure. No one knew better than he did that his face was not made to express agony or passion. He said, 'What will he do without you?'

'He'll manage.'

'He'll be terribly lonely,' Wilson said—he, he, he chiming back in his inner ear like a misleading echo I, I, I.

'He'll be happier without me.'

'He couldn't be.'

'Henry doesn't love me,' she said gently, as though she were teaching a child, using the simplest words to explain a difficult subject, simplifying . . . She leant her head back against the guichet and smiled at him as much as to say, it's quite easy really when you get the hang of it. 'He'll be happier without me,' she repeated. An ant moved from the woodwork on to her neck and he leant close to flick it away. He had no other motive. When he took his mouth away from hers the ant was still there. He let it run on to his finger. The taste of the lipstick was like something he'd never tasted before and that he would always remember. It seemed to him that an act had been committed which altered the whole world.

'I hate him,' she said, carrying on the conversation exactly where it had been left.

'You mustn't go,' he implored her. A bead of sweat ran down into his right eye and he brushed it away; on the guichet by her shoulder his eyes took in again the phallic scrawl.

'I'd have gone before this if it hadn't been for the money, poor dear. He has to find it.'

'Where?'

'That's man's business,' she said like a provocation, and he kissed her again; their mouths clung like bivalves, and then she pulled away and he heard the sad to-and-fro of Father Rank's laugh coming up along the path. 'Good evening, good evening,' Father Rank called. His stride lengthened and he caught a foot in his soutane and stumbled as he went by. 'A storm's coming up,' he said. 'Got to hurry,' and his 'ho, ho, ho' diminished mournfully along the railway track, bringing no comfort to anyone.

'He didn't see who we were,' Wilson said.

'Of course he did. What does it matter?'

'He's the biggest gossip in the town.'

'Only about things that matter,' she said.

'This doesn't matter?'

'Of course it doesn't,' she said. 'Why should it?'

'I'm in love with you, Louise,' Wilson said sadly.

'This is the second time we've met.'

'I don't see that that makes any difference. Do you like me, Louise?'

'Of course I like you, Wilson.'

'I wish you wouldn't call me Wilson.'

'Have you got another name?'

'Edward.'

'Do you want me to call you Teddy? Or Bear? These things creep on you before you know where you are. Suddenly you are calling someone Bear or Ticki, and the real name seems bald and formal, and the next you know they hate you for it. I'll stick to Wilson.'

'Why don't you leave him?'

'I am leaving him. I told you. I'm going to South Africa.'

'I love you, Louise,' he said again.

'How old are you, Wilson?'

'Thirty-two.'

'A very young thirty-two, and I am an old thirty-eight.'

'It doesn't matter.'

'The poetry you read, Wilson, is too romantic. It does matter. It matters much more than love. Love isn't a fact like age and religion . . .'

Across the bay the clouds came up: they massed blackly over Bullom and then tore up the sky, climbing vertically: the wind pressed the two of them back against the station. 'Too late,' Louise said, 'we're caught.'

'How long will this last?'

'Half an hour.'

A handful of rain was flung in their faces, and then the water came down. They stood inside the station and heard the water hurled upon the roof. They were in darkness, and the chickens moved at their feet.

'This is grim,' Louise said.

He made a motion towards her hand and touched her shoulder. 'Oh, for God's sake, Wilson,' she said, 'don't let's have a petting party.' She had to speak loud for her voice to carry above the thunder on the iron roof.

'I'm sorry . . . I didn't mean . . .'

He could hear her shifting further away, and he was glad of the darkness which hid his humiliation. 'I like you, Wilson,' she said, 'but I'm not a nursing sister who expects to be taken whenever she finds herself in the dark with a man. You have no responsibilities towards me, Wilson. I don't want you.'

'I love you, Louise.'

'Yes, yes, Wilson. You've told me. Do you think there are snakes in here—or rats?'

'I've no idea. When are you going to South Africa, Louise?'

'When Ticki can raise the money.'

'It will cost a lot. Perhaps you won't be able to go.'

'He'll manage somehow. He said he would.'

'Life insurance?'

'No, he's tried that.'

'I wish I could lend it to you myself. But I'm poor as a church-mouse.'

'Don't talk about mice in here. Ticki will manage somehow.'

He began to see her face through the darkness, thin, grey, attenuated—it was like trying to remember the features of someone he had once known who had gone away. One would build them up in just this way—the nose and then if one concentrated enough the brow; the eyes would escape him.

'He'll do anything for me.'

He said bitterly, 'A moment ago you said he didn't love you.'

'Oh,' she said, 'but he has a terrible sense of responsibility.'

He made a movement and she cried furiously out, 'Keep still. I don't love you. I love Ticki.'

'I was only shifting my weight,' he said. She began to laugh. 'How funny this is,' she said. 'It's a long time since anything funny happened to me. I'll remember this for months, for months.' But it seemed to Wilson that he would remember her laughter all his life. His shorts flapped in the draught of the storm and he thought, 'In a body like a grave.'

When Louise and Wilson crossed the river and came into Burnside it was quite dark. The headlamps of a police van lit an open door, and figures moved to and fro carrying packages. 'What's up now?' Louise exclaimed, and began to run down the road. Wilson panted after her. Ali came from the house carrying on his head a tin bath, a folding chair, and a bundle tied up in an old towel. 'What on earth's happened, Ali?'

'Massa go on trek,' he said, and grinned happily in the headlamps.

In the sitting-room Scobie sat with a drink in his hand. 'I'm glad you are back,' he said. 'I thought I'd have to write a note,' and Wilson saw that in fact he had already begun one. He had torn a leaf out of his notebook, and his large awkward writing covered a couple of lines.

'What on earth's happening, Henry?'

'I've got to get off to Bamba.'

'Can't you wait for the train on Thursday?'

'No.'

'Can I come with you?'

'Not this time. I'm sorry, dear. I'll have to take Ali and leave you the small boy.'

'What's happened?'

'There's trouble over young Pemberton.'

'Serious?'

'Yes.'

'He's such a fool. It was madness to leave him there as D.C.'

Scobie drank his whisky and said, 'I'm sorry, Wilson. Help yourself. Get a bottle of soda out of the ice-box. The boys are busy packing.'

'How long will you be, darling?'

'Oh, I'll be back the day after to-morrow, with any luck. Why don't you go and stay with Mrs Halifax?'

'I shall be all right here, darling.'

'I'd take the small boy and leave you Ali, but the small boy can't cook.'

'You'll be happier with Ali, dear. It will be like the old days before I came out.'

'I think I'll be off, sir,' Wilson said. 'I'm sorry I kept Mrs Scobie out so late.'

'Oh, I didn't worry, Wilson. Father Rank came by and told me you were sheltering in the old station. Very sensible of you. He got a drenching. He should have stayed too–he doesn't want a dose of fever at his age.'

'Can I fill your glass, sir? Then I'll be off.'

'Henry never takes more than one.'

'All the same, I think I will. But don't go, Wilson. Stay and keep Louise company for a bit. I've got to be off after this glass. I shan't get any sleep to-night.'

'Why can't one of the young men go? You're too old, Ticki, for this. Driving all night. Why don't you send Fraser?'

'The Commissioner asked me to go. It's just one of those cases—carefulness, tact, you can't let a young man handle it.' He took another drink of whisky and his eyes moved gloomily away as Wilson watched him. 'I must be off.'

'I'll never forgive Pemberton for this.'

Scobie said sharply, 'Don't talk nonsense, dear. We'd forgive most things if we knew the facts.' He smiled unwillingly at Wilson. 'A policeman should be the most forgiving person in the world if he gets the facts right.'

'I wish I could be of help, sir.'

'You can. Stay and have a few more drinks with Louise and cheer her up. She doesn't often get a chance to talk about books.' At the word books Wilson saw her mouth tighten just as a moment ago he had seen Scobie flinch at the name of Ticki, and for the first time he realised the pain inevitable in any human relationship—pain suffered and pain inflicted. How foolish one was to be afraid of loneliness.

'Good-bye, darling.'

'Good-bye, Ticki.'

'Look after Wilson. See he has enough to drink. Don't mope.'

When she kissed Scobie, Wilson stood near the door with a glass in his hand and remembered the disused station on the hill above and the taste of lipstick. For exactly an hour and a half the mark of his mouth had been the last on hers. He felt no jealousy, only the dreariness of a man who tries to write an important letter on a damp sheet and finds the characters blur.

Side by side they watched Scobie cross the road to the police van. He had taken more whisky than he was accustomed to, and perhaps that was what made him stumble. 'They should have sent a younger man,' Wilson said.

'They never do. He's the only one the Commissioner trusts.' They watched him climb laboriously in, and she went sadly on, 'Isn't he the typical second man? The man who always does the work.'

The black policeman at the wheel started his engine and began to grind into gear before releasing the clutch. 'They don't even give him a good driver,' she said. 'The good driver will have taken Fraser and the rest to the dance at the Club.' The van bumped and heaved out of the yard. Louise said, 'Well, that's that, Wilson.'

She picked up the note Scobie had intended to leave for her and read it aloud. *My dear, I have had to leave for Bamba. Keep this to yourself. A terrible thing has happened. Poor Pemberton . . .*

'Poor Pemberton,' she repeated furiously.

'Who's Pemberton?'

'A little puppy of twenty-five. All spots and bounce. He was assistant D.C. at Bamba, but when Butterworth went sick, they left him in charge. Anybody could have told them there'd be trouble. And when trouble comes it's Henry, of course, who has to drive all night. . . .'

'I'd better leave now, hadn't I?' Wilson said. 'You'll want to change.'

'Oh yes, you'd better go—before everybody knows he's gone and that we've been alone five minutes in a house with a bed in it. Alone, of course, except for the small boy and the cook and their relations and friends.'

'I wish I could be of some use.'

'You could be,' she said. 'Would you go upstairs and see whether there's a rat in the bedroom? I don't want the small boy to know I'm nervous. And shut the window. They come in that way.'

'It will be very hot for you.'

'I don't mind.'

He stood just inside the door and clapped his hands softly, but no rat moved. Then quickly, surreptitiously, as though he had no right to be there, he crossed to the window and closed it. There was a faint smell of face-powder in the room—it seemed to him the most memorable scent he had ever known. He stood again by the door taking the whole room in—the child's photograph, the pots of cream, the dress laid out by Ali for the evening. He had been instructed at home how to memorise, pick out the important detail, collect the right evidence, but his employers had never taught him that he would find himself in a country so strange to him as this.

PART III

I / i

The police van took its place in the long line of army lorries waiting for the ferry. Their headlamps were like a little village in the night. The trees came down on either side smelling of heat and rain, and somewhere at the end of the column a driver sang—the wailing, toneless voice rose and fell like a wind through a keyhole. Scobie slept and woke, slept and woke. When he woke he thought of Pemberton and wondered how he would feel if he were his father—that elderly, retired bank manager whose wife had died in giving birth to Pemberton—but when he slept he went smoothly back into a dream of perfect happiness and freedom. He was walking through a wide cool meadow with Ali at his heels: there was nobody else anywhere in his dream, and Ali never spoke. Birds went by far overhead, and once when he sat down the grass was parted by a small green snake which passed on to his hand and up his arm without fear, and before it slid down into the grass again touched his cheek with a cold, friendly, remote tongue.

Once when he opened his eyes Ali was standing beside him waiting for him to awake. 'Massa like bed,' he stated gently, firmly, pointing to the camp-bed he had made up at the edge of the path with the mosquito-net tied from the branches overhead. 'Two three hours,' Ali said. 'Plenty lorries.' Scobie obeyed and lay down and was immediately back in that peaceful meadow where nothing ever happened. The next time he woke Ali was still there, this time with a cup of tea and a plate of biscuits. 'One hour,' Ali said.

Then at last it was the turn of the police van. They moved down the red laterite slope on to the raft, and then edged foot by foot across the dark styx-like stream towards the woods on the other side. The two ferrymen pulling on the rope wore nothing but girdles, as though they had left their clothes behind on the bank where life ended, and a third man beat time to them, making do for instrument in this between-world with an empty sardine-tin.

The wailing tireless voice of the living singer shifted backwards.

This was only the first of three ferries that had to be crossed, with the same queue forming each time. Scobie never succeeded in sleeping properly again; his head began to ache from the heave of the van: he ate some aspirin and hoped for the best. He didn't want a dose of fever when he was away from home. It was not Pemberton that worried him now—let the dead bury their dead—it was the promise he had made to Louise. Two hundred pounds was so small a sum: the figures rang their changes in his aching head like a peal of bells: 200 002 020: it worried him that he could not find a fourth combination: 002 200 020.

They had come beyond the range of the tin-roofed shacks and the decayed wooden settlers' huts; the villages they passed through were bush villages of mud and thatch: no light showed anywhere: doors were closed and shutters were up, and only a few goats' eyes watched the headlamps of the convoy. 020 002 200 200 002 020. Ali squatting in the body of the van put an arm around his shoulder holding a mug of hot tea—somehow he had boiled another kettle in the lurching chassis. Louise was right—it was like the old days. If he had felt younger, if there had been no problem of 200 020 002, he would have been happy. Poor Pemberton's death would not have disturbed him—that was merely in the way of duty, and he had never liked Pemberton.

'My head humbug me, Ali.'

'Massa take plenty aspirin.'

'Do you remember, Ali, that two hundred 002 trek we did twelve years ago in ten days, along the border; two of the carriers went sick. . . .'

He could see in the driver's mirror Ali nodding and beaming. It seemed to him that this was all he needed of love and friendship. He could be happy with no more in the world than this—the grinding van, the hot tea against his lips, the heavy damp weight of the forest, even the aching head, the loneliness. If I could just arrange for her happiness first, he thought, and in the confusing night he forgot for the while what experience had taught him—that no human being can really understand another, and no one can arrange another's happiness.

'One hour more,' Ali said, and he noticed that the darkness was thinning. 'Another mug of tea, Ali, and put some whisky in it.' The convoy had separated from them a quarter of an hour ago, when the police van had turned away from the main road and bumped along a by-road farther into the bush. He shut his eyes and tried to draw his mind away from the broken peal of figures to the distasteful job. There was only a native police sergeant at Bamba, and he would like to be clear in his own mind as to what had happened before he received the sergeant's illiterate report. It would be better, he considered reluctantly, to go first to the Mission and see Father Clay.

Father Clay was up and waiting for him in the dismal little European house which had been built among the mud huts in laterite bricks to look like a Victorian presbytery. A hurricane-lamp shone on the priest's short red hair and his young freckled Liverpool face. He couldn't sit still for more than a few minutes at a time, and then he would be up, pacing his tiny room from hideous oleograph to plaster statue and back to oleograph again. 'I saw so little of him,' he wailed, motioning with his hands as though he were at the altar. 'He cared for nothing but cards and drinking. I don't drink and I've never played cards–except demon, you know, except demon, and that's a patience. It's terrible, terrible.'

'He hanged himself?'

'Yes. His boy came over to me yesterday. He hadn't seen him since the night before, but that was quite usual after a bout, you know, a bout. I told him to go to the police. That was right, wasn't it? There was nothing I could do. Nothing. He was quite dead.'

'Quite right. Would you mind giving me a glass of water and some aspirin?'

'Let me mix the aspirin for you. You know, Major Scobie, for weeks and months nothing happens here at all. I just walk up and down here, up and down, and then suddenly out of the blue . . . it's terrible.' His eyes were red and sleepless: he seemed to Scobie one of those who are quite unsuited to loneliness. There were no books to be seen except a little shelf with his breviary and a few religious tracts. He was a man without resources. He began to pace up and down again and suddenly, turning on Scobie, he shot out an excited question. 'Mightn't there be a hope that it's murder?'

'Hope?'

'Suicide,' Father Clay said. 'It's too terrible. It puts a man outside mercy. I've been thinking about it all night.'

'He wasn't a Catholic. Perhaps that makes a difference. Invincible ignorance, eh?'

'That's what I try to think.' Half-way between oleograph and statuette he suddenly started and stepped aside as though he had encountered another on his tiny parade. Then he looked quickly and slyly at Scobie to see whether his act had been noticed.

'How often do you get down to the port?' Scobie asked.

'I was there for a night nine months ago. Why?'

'Everybody needs a change. Have you many converts here?'

'Fifteen. I try to persuade myself that young Pemberton had time–time, you know, while he died, to realise . . .'

'Difficult to think clearly when you are strangling, Father.' He took a swig at the aspirin and the sour grains stuck in his throat. 'If it was murder you'd simply change your mortal sinner, Father,' he said with an attempt at humour which wilted between the holy picture and the holy statue.

'A murderer has time . . .' Father Clay said. He added wistfully, with nostalgia, 'I used to do duty sometimes at Liverpool Gaol.'

'Have you any idea why he did it?'

'I didn't know him well enough. We didn't get on together.'

'The only white men here. It seems a pity.'

'He offered to lend me some books, but they weren't at all the kind of books I care to read–love stories, novels. . . .'

'What do you read, Father?'

'Anything on the saints, Major Scobie. My great devotion is to the Little Flower.'

'He drank a lot, didn't he? Where did he get it from?'

'Yusef's store, I suppose.'

'Yes. He may have been in debt?'

'I don't know. It's terrible, terrible.'

Scobie finished his aspirin. 'I suppose I'd better go along.' It was day now outside, and there was a peculiar innocence about the light, gentle and clear and fresh before the sun climbed.

'I'll come with you, Major Scobie.'

The police sergeant sat in a deck-chair outside the D.C.'s bungalow. He rose and raggedly saluted, then immediately in his hollow unformed voice began to read his report. 'At 3.30 p.m. yesterday, sah, I was woken by D.C.'s boy, who reported that D.C. Pemberton, sah . . .'

'That's all right, sergeant, I'll go inside and have a look round.' The chief clerk waited for him just inside the door.

The living-room of the bungalow had obviously once been the D.C.'s pride—that must have been in Butterworth's day. There was an air of elegance and personal pride in the furniture; it hadn't been supplied by the Government. There were eighteenth-century engravings of the old colony on the wall and in one bookcase were the volumes that Butterworth had left behind him—Scobie noted some titles and authors, Maitland's *Constitutional History*, Sir Henry Maine, Bryce's *Holy Roman Empire*, Hardy's poems, and the *Doomsday Records of Little Withington*, privately printed. But imposed on all this were the traces of Pemberton—a gaudy leather pouf of so-called native work, the marks of cigarette-ends on the chairs, a stack of the books Father Clay had disliked—Somerset Maugham, an Edgar Wallace, two Horlers, and spread-eagled on the settee, *Death Laughs at Locksmiths*. The room was not properly dusted and Butterworth's books were stained with damp.

'The body is in the bedroom, sah,' the sergeant said.

Scobie opened the door and went in—Father Clay followed him. The body had been laid on the bed with a sheet over the face. When Scobie turned the sheet down to the shoulder he had the impression that he was looking at a child in a nightshirt quietly asleep: the pimples were the pimples of puberty and the dead face seemed to bear the trace of no experience beyond the classroom or the football field. 'Poor child,' he said aloud. The pious ejaculations of Father Clay irritated him. It seemed to him that unquestionably there must be mercy for someone so unformed. He asked abruptly, 'How did he do it?'

The police sergeant pointed to the picture rail that Butterworth had meticulously fitted—no Government contractor would have thought of it. A picture—an early native king receiving missionaries under a State umbrella—leant against the wall and a cord remained twisted over the brass picture hanger. Who would have expected the flimsy contrivance not to collapse? He can weigh very little, he thought, and he remembered a child's bones, light and brittle as a bird's. His feet when he hung must have been only fifteen inches from the ground.

'Did he leave any papers?' Scobie asked the clerk. 'They usually do.' Men who are going to die are apt to become garrulous with self-revelations.

'Yes, sah, in the office.'

It needed only a casual inspection to realise how badly the office had been kept. The filing cabinet was unlocked: the trays on the desk were filled by papers dusty with inattention. The native clerk had obviously followed the same ways as his chief. 'There, sah, on the pad.'

Scobie read, in a hand-writing unformed as the face, a script-writing which hundreds of his school contemporaries must have been turning out all over the world:

> Dear Dad,—Forgive all this trouble. There doesn't seem anything else to do. It's a pity I'm not in the army because then I might be killed. Don't go and pay the money I owe—the fellow doesn't deserve it. They may try and get it out of you. Otherwise I wouldn't mention it. It's a rotten business for you, but it can't be helped. Your loving son.

The signature was 'Dicky'. It was like a letter from school excusing a bad report.

He handed the letter to Father Clay. 'You are not going to tell me there's anything unforgivable there, Father. If you or I did it, it would be despair—I grant you anything with us. We'd be damned because we know, but *he* doesn't know a thing.'

'The Church's teaching . . .'

'Even the Church can't teach me that God doesn't pity the young. . . .' Scobie broke abruptly off. 'Sergeant, see that a grave's dug quickly before the sun gets too hot. And look out for any bills he owed. I want to have a word with someone about this.' When he turned towards the window the light dazzled him. He put his hand over his eyes and said, 'I wish to God my head . . .' and shivered. 'I'm in for a dose if I can't stop it. If you don't mind Ali putting up my bed at your place, Father, I'll try and sweat it out.'

He took a heavy dose of quinine and lay naked between the blankets. As the sun climbed it sometimes seemed to him that the stone walls of the small cell-like room sweated with cold and sometimes were baked with heat. The door was open and Ali squatted on the step just outside whittling a piece of wood. Occasionally he chased away villagers who raised their voices within the area of sick-room silence. The *peine forte et dure* weighed on Scobie's forehead: occasionally it pressed him into sleep.

But in this sleep there were no pleasant dreams. Pemberton and Louise were obscurely linked. Over and over again he was reading a letter which consisted only of variations on the figure 200 and the signature at the bottom was sometimes 'Dicky' and sometimes 'Ticki'; he had the sense of time passing and his own immobility between the blankets—there was something he had to do, someone he had to save, Louise or Dicky or Ticki, but he was tied to the bed and they laid weights on his forehead as you lay weights on loose papers. Once the sergeant came to the door and Ali chased him away, once Father Clay tiptoed in and took a tract off a shelf, and once, but that might have been a dream, Yusef came to the door.

Above five in the evening he woke feeling dry and cool and weak and called Ali in. 'I dreamed I saw Yusef.'

'Yusef come for to see you, sah.'

'Tell him I'll see him now.' He felt tired and beaten about the body: he turned to face the stone wall and was immediately asleep. In his sleep Louise wept silently beside him; he put out his hand and touched the stone wall again–'Everything shall be arranged. Everything. Ticki promises.' When he woke Yusef was beside him.

'A touch of fever, Major Scobie. I am very sorry to see you poorly.'

'I'm sorry to see you at all, Yusef.'

'Ah, you always make fun of me.'

'Sit down, Yusef. What did you have to do with Pemberton?'

Yusef eased his great haunches on the hard chair and noticing that his flies were open put down a large and hairy hand to deal with them. 'Nothing, Major Scobie.'

'It's an odd coincidence that you are here just at the moment when he commits suicide.'

'I think myself it is providence.'

'He owed you money, I suppose?'

'He owed my store-manager money.'

'What sort of pressure were you putting on him, Yusef?'

'Major, you give an evil name to a dog and the dog is finished. If the D.C. wants to buy at my store, how can my manager stop selling to him? If he does that, what will happen? Sooner or later there will be a first-class row. The Provincial Commissioner will find out. The D.C. will be sent home. If he does not stop selling, what happens then? The D.C. runs up more and more bills. My manager becomes afraid of me, he asks the D.C. to pay–there is a row that way. When you have a D.C. like poor young Pemberton, there will be a row one day whatever you do. And the Syrian is always wrong.'

'There's quite a lot in what you say, Yusef.' The pain was beginning again. 'Give me that whisky and quinine, Yusef.'

'You are not taking too much quinine, Major Scobie? Remember blackwater.'

'I don't want to be stuck up here for days. I want to kill this at birth. I've too many things to do.'

'Sit up a moment, Major, and let me beat your pillows.'

'You aren't a bad chap, Yusef.'

Yusef said, 'Your sergeant has been looking for bills, but he could not find any. Here are IOU's though. From my manager's safe.' He flapped his thigh with a little sheaf of papers.

'I see. What are you going to do with them?'

'Burn them,' Yusef said. He took out a cigarette-lighter and lit the corners. 'There,' Yusef said. 'He has paid, poor boy. There is no reason to trouble his father.'

'Why did you come up here?'

'My manager was worried. I was going to propose an arrangement.'

'One needs a long spoon to sup with you, Yusef.'

'My enemies do. Not my friends. I would do a lot for you, Major Scobie.'

'Why do you always call me a friend, Yusef?'

'Major Scobie,' Yusef said, leaning his great white head forward, reeking of hair oil, 'friendship is something in the soul. It is a thing one feels. It is not a return for something. You remember when you put me into court ten years ago?'

'Yes, yes.' Scobie turned his head away from the light of the door.

'You nearly caught me, Major Scobie, that time. It was a matter of import duties, you remember. You could have caught me if you had told your policeman to say something a little different. I was quite overcome with astonishment, Major Scobie, to sit in a police court and hear true facts from the mouths of policemen. You must have taken a lot of trouble to find out what was true, and to make them say it. I said to myself, Yusef, a Daniel has come to the Colonial Police.'

'I wish you wouldn't talk so much, Yusef. I'm not interested in your friendship.'

'Your words are harder than your heart, Major Scobie. I want to explain why in my soul I have always felt your friend. You have made me feel secure. You will not frame me. You need facts, and I am sure the facts will always be in my favour.' He dusted the ashes from his white trousers, leaving one more grey smear. 'These are facts. I have burned all the IOU's.'

'I may yet find traces, Yusef, of what kind of agreement you were intending to make with Pemberton. This station controls one of the main routes across the border from–damnation, I can't think of names with this head.'

'Cattle smugglers. I'm not interested in cattle.'

'Other things are apt to go back the other way.'

'You are still dreaming of diamonds, Major Scobie. Everybody has gone crazy about diamonds since the war.'

'Don't feel too certain, Yusef, that I won't find something when I go through Pemberton's office.'

'I feel quite certain, Major Scobie. You know I cannot read or write. Nothing is ever on paper. Everything is always in my head.' Even while Yusef talked, Scobie dropped asleep–into one of those shallow sleeps that last a few seconds and have only time to reflect a preoccupation. Louise was coming towards him with both hands held out and a smile that he hadn't seen upon her face for years. She said, 'I am so happy, so happy,' and he woke again to Yusef's voice going soothingly on. 'It is only your friends who do not trust you, Major Scobie. I trust you. Even that scoundrel Tallit trusts you.'

It took him a moment to get this other face into focus. His brain adjusted itself achingly from the phrase 'so happy' to the phrase 'do not trust'. He said, 'What are you talking about, Yusef?' He could feel the mechanism of his brain creaking, grinding, scraping, cogs failing to connect, all with pain.

'First, there is the Commissionership.'

'They need a young man,' he said mechanically, and thought, if I hadn't fever I would never discuss a matter like this with Yusef.

'Then the special man they have sent from London . . .'

'You must come back when I'm clearer, Yusef. I don't know what the hell you are talking about.'

'They have sent a special man from London to investigate the diamonds–they are crazy about diamonds–only the Commissioner must know about him–none of the other officers, not even you.'

'What rubbish you talk, Yusef. There's no such man.'

'Everybody guesses but you.'

'Too absurd. You shouldn't listen to rumour, Yusef.'

'And a third thing. Tallit says everywhere you visit me.'

'Tallit! Who believes what Tallit says?'

'Everybody everywhere believes what is bad.'

'Go away, Yusef. Why do you want to worry me now?'

'I just want you to understand, Major Scobie, that you can depend on me. I have friendship for you in my soul. That is true, Major Scobie, it is true.' The reek of hair oil came closer as he bent towards the bed: the deep brown eyes were damp with what seemed to be emotion. 'Let me pat your pillow, Major Scobie.'

'Oh, for goodness' sake, keep away,' Scobie said.

'I know how things are, Major Scobie, and if I can help . . . I am a well-off man.'

'I'm not looking for bribes, Yusef,' he said wearily and turned his head away to escape the scent.

'I am not offering you a bribe, Major Scobie. A loan at any time on a reasonable rate of interest – four per cent per annum. No conditions. You can arrest me next day if you have facts. I want to be your friend, Major Scobie. You need not be my friend. There is a Syrian poet who wrote, "Of two hearts one is always warm and one is always cold: the cold heart is more precious than diamonds: the warm heart has no value and is thrown away."'

'It sounds a very bad poem to me. But I'm no judge.'

'It is a happy chance for me that we should be here together. In the town there are so many people watching. But here, Major Scobie, I can be of real help to you. May I fetch you more blankets?'

'No, no, just leave me alone.'

'I hate to see a man of your characteristics, Major Scobie, treated badly.'

'I don't think the time's ever likely to come, Yusef, when I shall need *your* pity. If you want to do something for me, though, go away and let me sleep.'

But when he slept the unhappy dreams returned. Upstairs Louise was crying, and he sat at a table writing his last letter. 'It's a rotten business for you, but it can't be helped. Your loving husband, Dicky,' and then as he turned to look for a weapon or a rope, it suddenly occurred to him that this was an act he could never do. Suicide was for ever out of his power – he couldn't condemn himself for eternity – no cause was important enough. He tore up his letter and ran upstairs to tell Louise that after all everything was all right, but she had stopped crying and the silence welling out from inside the bedroom terrified him. He tried the door and the door was locked. He called out, 'Louise, everything's all right. I've booked your passage,' but there was no answer. He cried again, 'Louise,' and then a key turned and the door slowly opened with a sense of irrecoverable disaster, and he saw standing just inside Father Clay, who said to him, 'The teaching of the Church . . .' Then he woke again to the small stone room like a tomb.

I / ii

He was away for a week, for it took three days for the fever to run its course and another two days before he was fit to travel. He did not see Yusef again.

It was past midnight when he drove into town. The houses were white as bones in the moonlight; the quiet streets stretched out on either side like the arms of a skeleton, and the faint sweet smell of flowers lay on the air. If he had been returning to an empty house he knew that he would have been contented. He was tired and he didn't want to break the silence—it was too much to hope that Louise would be asleep, too much to hope that things would somehow have become easier in his absence and that he would see her free and happy as she had been in one of his dreams.

The small boy waved his torch from the door: the frogs croaked from the bushes, and the pye dogs wailed at the moon. He was home. Louise put her arms round him: the table was laid for a late supper, the boys ran to and fro with his boxes: he smiled and talked and kept the bustle going. He talked of Pemberton and Father Clay and mentioned Yusef, but he knew that sooner or later he would have to ask how things had been with her. He tried to eat, but he was too tired to taste the food.

'Yesterday I cleared up his office and wrote my report—and that was that.' He hesitated, 'That's all my news,' and went reluctantly on, 'How have things been here?' He looked quickly up at her face and away again. There had been one chance in a thousand that she would have smiled and said vaguely, 'Not so bad' and then passed on to other things, but he knew from her mouth that he wasn't so lucky as that. Something fresh had happened.

But the outbreak—whatever it was to be—was delayed. She said, 'Oh, Wilson's been attentive.'

'He's a nice boy.'

'He's too intelligent for his job. I can't think why he's out here as just a clerk.'

'He told me he drifted.'

'I don't think I've spoken to anybody else since you've been away, except the small boy and the cook. Oh, and Mrs Halifax.' Something in her voice told him that the danger point was reached. Always, hopelessly, he tried to evade it. He stretched and said, 'My God, I'm tired. The fever's left me limp as a rag. I think I'll go to bed. It's nearly half-past one, and I've got to be at the station at eight.'

She said, 'Ticki, have you done anything at all?'

'How do you mean, dear?'

'About the passage.'

'Don't worry. I'll find a way, dear.'

'You haven't found one yet?'

'No. I've got several ideas I'm working on. It's just a question of borrowing.' 200, 020, 002 rang in his brain.

'Poor dear,' she said, 'don't worry,' and put her hand against his cheek. 'You're tired. You've had fever. I'm not going to bait you now.' Her hand, her words broke through every defence: he had expected tears, but he found them now in his own eyes. 'Go up to bed, Henry,' she said.

'Aren't you coming up?'

'There are just one or two things I want to do.'

He lay on his back under the net and waited for her. It occurred to him, as it hadn't occurred to him for years, that she loved him. Poor dear, she loved him: she was someone of human stature with her own sense of responsibility, not simply the object of his care and kindness. The sense of failure deepened round him. All the way back from Bamba he had faced one fact—that there was only one man in the city capable of lending him, and willing to lend him, the two hundred pounds, and that was a man he must not borrow from. It would have been safer to accept the Portuguese captain's bribe. Slowly and drearily he had reached the decision to tell her that the money simply could not be found, and for the next six months at any rate, until his leave, she must stay. If he had not felt so tired he would have told her when she asked him and it would have been over now, but he had flinched away and she had been kind, and it would be harder now than it had ever been to disappoint her. There was silence all through the little house, but outside the half-starved pye dogs yapped and whined. He listened, leaning on his elbow; he felt oddly unmanned, lying in bed alone waiting for Louise to join him. She had always been the one to go first to bed. He felt uneasy, apprehensive, and suddenly his dream came to mind, how he had listened outside the door and knocked, and there was no reply. He struggled out from under the net and ran downstairs barefooted.

Louise was sitting at the table with a pad of notepaper in front of her, but she had written nothing but a name. The winged ants beat against the light and dropped their wings over the table. Where the light touched her head he saw the grey hairs.

'What is it, dear?'

'Everything was so quiet,' he said, 'I wondered whether something had happened. I had a bad dream about you the other night. Pemberton's suicide upset me.'

'How silly, dear. Nothing like that could ever happen with us.'

'Yes, of course. I just wanted to see you,' he said, putting his hand on her hair. Over her shoulder he read the only words she had written, 'Dear Mrs Halifax'. . . .

'You haven't got your shoes on,' she said. 'You'll be catching jiggers.'

'I just wanted to see you,' he repeated and wondered whether the stains on the paper were sweat or tears.

'Listen, dear,' she said. 'You are not to worry any more. I've baited you and baited you. It's like fever, you know. It comes and goes. Well, now it's gone—for a while. I know you can't raise the money. It's not your fault. If it hadn't been for that stupid operation . . . It's just the way things are, Henry.'

'What's it all got to do with Mrs Halifax?'

'She and another woman have a two-berth cabin in the next ship and the other woman's fallen out. She thought perhaps I could slip in—if her husband spoke to the agent.'

'That's in about a fortnight,' he said.

'Darling, give up trying. It's better just to give up. Anyway, I had to let Mrs Halifax know to-morrow. And I'm letting her know that I shan't be going.'

He spoke rapidly—he wanted the words out beyond recall. 'Write and tell her that you can go.'

'Ticki,' she said, 'what do you mean?' Her face hardened. 'Ticki, please don't promise something which can't happen. I know you're tired and afraid of a scene. But there isn't going to be a scene. I mustn't let Mrs Halifax down.'

'You won't. I know where I can borrow the money.'

'Why didn't you tell me when you came back?'

'I wanted to give you your ticket. A surprise.'

She was not so happy as he would have expected: she always saw a little farther than he hoped. 'And you are not worrying any more?' she asked.

'I'm not worrying any more. Are you happy?'

'Oh yes,' she said in a puzzled voice. 'I'm happy, dear.'

I / iii

The liner came in on a Saturday evening; from the bedroom window they could see its long grey form steal past the boom, beyond the palms. They watched it with a sinking of the heart—happiness is never really so welcome as changelessness—hand in hand they watched their separation anchor in the bay. 'Well,' Scobie said, 'that means to-morrow afternoon.'

'Darling,' she said, 'when this time is over, I'll be good to you again. I just couldn't stand this life any more.'

They could hear a clatter below stairs as Ali, who had also been watching the sea, brought out the trunks and boxes. It was as if the house were tumbling down around them, and the vultures took off from the roof, rattling the corrugated-iron as though they felt the tremor in the walls. Scobie said, 'While you are sorting your things upstairs, I'll pack your books.' It was as if they had been playing these last two weeks at infidelity, and now the process of divorce had them in its grasp: the division of one life into two: the sharing out of the sad spoils.

'Shall I leave you this photograph, Ticki?' He took a quick sideways glance at the first communion face and said, 'No. You have it.'

'I'll leave you this one of us with the Ted Bromleys.'

'Yes, leave that.' He watched her for a moment laying out her clothes and then he went downstairs. One by one he took out the books and wiped them with a cloth: the Oxford Verse, the Woolfs, the younger poets. Afterwards the shelves were almost empty: his own books took up so little room.

Next day they went to Mass together early. Kneeling together at the Communion rail they seemed to claim that this was not separation. He thought: I've prayed for peace and now I'm getting it. It's terrible the way that prayer is answered. It had better be good, I've paid a high enough price for it. As they walked back he said anxiously, 'You are happy?'

'Yes, Ticki, and you?'

'I'm happy as long as you are happy.'

'It will be all right when I've got on board and settled down. I expect I shall drink a bit to-night. Why don't you have someone in, Ticki?'

'Oh, I prefer being alone.'

'Write to me every week.'

'Of course.'

'And Ticki, you won't be lazy about Mass? You'll go when I'm not there?'

'Of course.'

Wilson came up the road. His face shone with sweat and anxiety. He said,

'Are you really off? Ali told me at the house that you are going on board this afternoon.'

'She's off,' Scobie said.

'You never told me it was close like this.'

'I forgot,' Louise said, 'there was so much to do.'

'I never thought you'd really go. I wouldn't have known if I hadn't run into Halifax at the agent's.'

'Oh well,' Louise said, 'you and Henry will have to keep an eye on each other.'

'It's incredible,' Wilson said, kicking the dusty road. He hung there, between them and the house, not stirring to let them by. He said, 'I don't know a soul but you–and Harris of course.'

'You'll have to start making acquaintances,' Louise said. 'You'll have to excuse us now. There's so much to do.'

They walked round him because he didn't move, and Scobie, looking back, gave him a kindly wave–he looked so lost and unprotected and out of place on the blistered road. 'Poor Wilson,' he said, 'I think he's in love with you.'

'He thinks he is.'

'It's a good thing for him you are going. People like that become a nuisance in this climate. I'll be kind to him while you are away.'

'Ticki,' she said, 'I shouldn't see too much of him. I wouldn't trust him. There's something phoney about him.'

'He's young and romantic.'

'He's too romantic. He tells lies. Why does he say he doesn't know a soul?'

'I don't think he does.'

'He knows the Commissioner. I saw him going up there the other night at dinner-time.'

'It's just a way of talking.'

Neither of them had any appetite for lunch, but the cook, who wanted to rise to the occasion, produced an enormous curry which filled a washing-basin in the middle of the table: round it were ranged the many small dishes that went with it–the fried bananas, red peppers, ground nuts, paw paw, orange-slices, chutney. They seemed to be sitting miles apart separated by a waste of dishes. The food chilled on their plates and there seemed nothing to talk about except, 'I'm not hungry,' 'Try and eat a little,' 'I can't touch a thing,' 'You ought to start off with a good meal,' an endless friendly bicker about food. Ali came in and out to watch them: he was like a figure on a clock that records the striking of the hours. It seemed horrible to both of them that now they would be glad when the separation was complete; they could settle down, when once this ragged leave-taking was over, to a different life which again would exclude change.

'Are you sure you've got everything?' This was another variant which enabled them to sit there not eating but occasionally picking at something easily swallowed, going through all the things that might have been forgotten.

'It's lucky there's only one bedroom. They'll have to let you keep the house to yourself.'

'They may turn me out for a married couple.'

'You'll write every week?'

'Of course.'

Sufficient time had elapsed: they could persuade themselves that they had lunched. 'If you can't eat any more I may as well drive you down. The sergeant's organised carriers at the wharf.' They could say nothing now which wasn't formal; unreality cloaked their movements. Although they could touch each other it was as if the whole coastline of a continent was already between them; their words were like the stilted sentences of a bad letter-writer.

It was a relief to be on board and no longer alone together. Halifax, of the Public Works Department, bubbled over with false bonhomie. He cracked risky jokes and told the two women to drink plenty of gin. 'It's good for the bow-wows,' he said. 'First thing to go wrong on board ship are the bow-wows. Plenty of gin at night and what will cover a sixpence in the morning.' The two women took stock of their cabin. They stood there in the shadow like cave-dwellers; they spoke in undertones that the men couldn't catch: they were no longer wives—they were sisters belonging to a different race. 'You and I are not wanted, old man,' Halifax said. 'They'll be all right now. Me for the shore.'

'I'll come with you.' Everything had been unreal, but this suddenly was real pain, the moment of death. Like a prisoner he had not believed in the trial: it had been a dream: the condemnation had been a dream and the truck ride, and then suddenly here he was with his back to the blank wall and everything was true. One steeled oneself to end courageously. They went to the end of the passage, leaving the Halifaxes the cabin.

'Good-bye, dear.'

'Good-bye. Ticki, you'll write every . . .'

'Yes, dear.'

'I'm an awful deserter.'

'No, no. This isn't the place for you.'

'It would have been different if they'd made you Commissioner.'

'I'll come down for my leave. Let me know if you run short of money before then. I can fix things.'

'You've always fixed things for me. Ticki, you'll be glad to have no more scenes.'

'Nonsense.'

'Do you love me, Ticki?'

'What do you think?'

'Say it. One likes to hear it—even if it isn't true.'

'I love you, Louise. Of course it's true.'

'If I can't bear it down there alone, Ticki, I'll come back.'

They kissed and went up on deck. From here the port was always beautiful; the thin layer of houses sparkled in the sun like quartz or lay in the shadow of the great green swollen hills. 'You are well escorted,' Scobie said. The destroyers and the corvettes sat around like dogs: signal flags rippled and a helio flashed. The fishing boats rested on the broad bay under their brown butterfly sails. 'Look after yourself, Ticki.'

Halifax came booming up behind them. 'Who's for shore? Got the police launch, Scobie? Mary's down in the cabin, Mrs Scobie, wiping off the tears and putting on the powder for the passengers.'

'Good-bye, dear.'

'Good-bye.' That was the real good-bye, the handshake with Halifax watching and the passengers from England looking curiously on. As the launch moved away she was almost at once indistinguishable; perhaps she had gone down to the cabin to join Mrs Halifax. The dream had finished: change was over: life had begun again.

'I hate these good-byes,' Halifax said. 'Glad when it's all over. Think I'll go up to the Bedford and have a glass of beer. Join me?'

'Sorry. I have to go on duty.'

'I wouldn't mind a nice little black girl to look after me now I'm alone,' Halifax said. 'However, faithful and true, old fidelity, that's me,' and as Scobie knew, it was.

In the shade of a tarpaulined dump Wilson stood, looking out across the bay. Scobie paused. He was touched by the plump sad boyish face. 'Sorry we didn't see you,' he said and lied harmlessly. 'Louise sent her love.'

I / iv

It was nearly one in the morning before he returned. The light was out in the kitchen quarters and Ali was dozing on the steps of the house until the headlamps woke him, passing across his sleeping face. He jumped up and lit the way from the garage with his torch.

'All right, Ali. Go to bed.'

He let himself into the empty house–he had forgotten the deep tones of silence. Many a time he had come in late, after Louise was asleep, but there had never then been quite this quality of security and impregnability in the silence: his ears had listened for, even though they could not catch, the faint rustle of another person's breath, the tiny movement. Now there was nothing to listen for. He went upstairs and looked into the bedroom. Everything had been tidied away; there was no sign of Louise's departure or presence: Ali had even removed the photograph and put it in a drawer. He was indeed alone. In the bathroom a rat moved, and once the iron roof crumpled as a late vulture settled for the night.

Scobie sat down in the living-room and put his feet upon another chair. He felt unwilling yet to go to bed, but he was sleepy–it had been a long day. Now that he was alone he could indulge in the most irrational act and sleep in a chair instead of a bed. The sadness was peeling off his mind, leaving contentment. He had done his duty: Louise was happy. He closed his eyes.

The sound of a car driving in off the road, headlamps moving across the window, woke him. He imagined it was a police car–that night he was the responsible officer and he thought that some urgent and probably unnecessary telegram had come in. He opened the door and found Yusef on the step. 'Forgive me, Major Scobie, I saw your light as I was passing, and I thought . . .'

'Come in,' he said, 'I have whisky or would you prefer a little beer. . .?'

Yusef said with surprise, 'This is very hospitable of you, Major Scobie.'

'If I know a man well enough to borrow money from him, surely I ought to be hospitable.'

'A little beer then, Major Scobie.'

'The Prophet doesn't forbid it?'

'The Prophet had no experience of bottled beer or whisky, Major Scobie. We have to interpret his words in a modern light.' He watched Scobie take the bottles from the ice chest. 'Have you no refrigerator, Major Scobie?'

'No. Mine's waiting for a spare part – it will go on waiting till the end of the war, I imagine.'

'I must not allow that. I have several spare refrigerators. Let me send one up to you.'

'Oh, I can manage all right, Yusef. I've managed for two years. So you were passing by.'

'Well, not exactly, Major Scobie. That was a way of speaking. As a matter of fact I waited until I knew your boys were asleep, and I borrowed a car from a garage. My own car is so well known. And I did not bring a chauffeur. I didn't want to embarrass you, Major Scobie.'

'I repeat, Yusef, that I shall never deny knowing a man from whom I have borrowed money.'

'You do keep harping on that so, Major Scobie. That was just a business transaction. Four per cent is a fair interest. I ask for more only when I have doubt of the security. I wish you would let me send you a refrigerator.'

'What did you want to see me about?'

'First, Major Scobie, I wanted to ask after Mrs Scobie. Has she got a comfortable cabin? Is there anything she requires? The ship calls at Lagos, and I could have anything she needs sent on board there. I would telegraph my agent.'

'I think she's quite comfortable.'

'Next, Major Scobie, I wanted to have a few words with you about diamonds.'

Scobie put two more bottles of beer on the ice. He said slowly and gently, 'Yusef, I don't want you to think I am the kind of man who borrows money one day and insults his creditor the next to reassure his ego.'

'Ego?'

'Never mind. Self-esteem. What you like. I'm not going to pretend that we haven't in a way become colleagues in a business, but my duties are strictly confined to paying you four per cent.'

'I agree, Major Scobie. You have said all this before and I agree. I say again that I am never dreaming to ask you to do one thing for me. I would rather do things for you.'

'What a queer chap you are, Yusef. I believe you do like me.'

'Yes, I do like you, Major Scobie.' Yusef sat on the edge of his chair which cut a sharp edge in his great expanding thighs: he was ill at ease in any house but his own. 'And now may I talk to you about diamonds, Major Scobie?'

'Fire away then.'

'You know I think the Government is crazy about diamonds. They waste your time, the time of the Security Police: they send special agents down the coast: we even have one here – you know who, though nobody is supposed to know but the Commissioner: he spends money on every black or poor Syrian who tells him stories. Then he telegraphs it to England and all down the coast. And after all this, do they catch a single diamond?'

'This has got nothing to do with us, Yusef.'

'I want to talk to you as a friend, Major Scobie. There are diamonds and diamonds and Syrians and Syrians. You people hunt the wrong men. You want to stop industrial diamonds going to Portugal and then to Germany, or across the border to the Vichy French. But all the time you are chasing people who are not interested in industrial diamonds, people who just want to get a few gem stones in a safe place for when peace comes again.'

'In other words you?'

'Six times this month police have been into my stores making everything untidy. They will never find any industrial diamonds that way. Only small men are interested in industrial diamonds. Why, for a whole matchbox full of them, you would only get two hundred pounds. I call them gravel collectors,' he said with contempt.

Scobie said slowly, 'Sooner or later, Yusef, I felt sure that you'd want something out of me. But you are going to get nothing but four per cent. To-morrow I am giving a full confidential report of our business arrangement to the Commissioner. Of course he may ask for my resignation, but I don't think so. He trusts me.' A memory pricked him. 'I think he trusts me.'

'Is that a wise thing to do, Major Scobie?'

'I think it's very wise. Any kind of secret between us two would go bad in time.'

'Just as you like, Major Scobie. But I don't want anything from you, I promise. I would like to give you things always. You will not take a refrigerator, but I thought you would perhaps take advice, information.'

'I'm listening, Yusef.'

'Tallit's a small man. He is a Christian. Father Rank and other people go to his house. They say, "If there's such a thing as an honest Syrian, then Tallit's the man." Tallit's not very successful, and that looks just the same as honesty.'

'Go on.'

'Tallit's cousin is sailing in the next Portuguese boat. His luggage will be searched, of course, and nothing will be found. He will have a parrot with him in a cage. My advice, Major Scobie, is to let Tallit's cousin go and keep his parrot.'

'Why let the cousin go?'

'You do not want to show your hand to Tallit. You can easily say the parrot is suffering from a disease and must stay. He will not dare to make a fuss.'

'You mean the diamonds are in its crop?'

'Yes.'

'Has that trick been used before on the Portuguese boats?'

'Yes.'

'It looks to me as if we'll have to buy an aviary.'

'Will you act on that information, Major Scobie?'

'You give me information, Yusef. I don't give you information.'

Yusef nodded and smiled. Raising his bulk with some care he touched Scobie's sleeve quickly and shyly. 'You are quite right, Major Scobie.

Believe me, I never want to do you any harm at all. I shall be careful and you be careful too, and everything will be all right.' It was as if they were in a conspiracy together to do no harm: even innocence in Yusef's hands took on a dubious colour. He said, 'If you were to say a good word to Tallit sometimes it would be safer. The agent visits him.'

'I don't know of any agent.'

'You are quite right, Major Scobie.' Yusef hovered like a fat moth on the edge of the light. He said, 'Perhaps if you were writing one day to Mrs Scobie you would give her my best wishes. Oh no, letters are censored. You cannot do that. You could say, perhaps–no, better not. As long as *you* know, Major Scobie, that you have my best wishes—' Stumbling on the narrow path, he made for his car. When he had turned on his lights he pressed his face against the glass: it showed up in the illumination of the dashboard, wide, pasty, untrustworthy, sincere. He made a tentative shy sketch of a wave towards Scobie, where he stood alone in the doorway of the quiet and empty house.

BOOK TWO

PART I

I / i

They stood on the verandah of the D.C.'s bungalow at Pende and watched the torches move on the other side of the wide passive river. 'So that's France,' Druce said, using the native term for it.

Mrs Perrot said, 'Before the war we used to picnic in France.'

Perrot joined them from the bungalow, a drink in either hand: bandy-legged, he wore his mosquito-boots outside his trousers like riding-boots, and gave the impression of having only just got off a horse. 'Here's yours, Scobie.' He said, 'Of course ye know I find it hard to think of the French as enemies. My family came over with the Huguenots. It makes a difference, ye know.' His lean long yellow face cut in two by a nose like a wound was all the time arrogantly on the defensive: the importance of Perrot was an article of faith with Perrot—doubters would be repelled, persecuted if he had the chance . . . the faith would never cease to be proclaimed.

Scobie said, 'If they ever joined the Germans, I suppose this is one of the points where they'd attack.'

'Don't I know it,' Perrot said, 'I was moved here in 1939. The Government had a shrewd idea of what was coming. Everything's prepared, ye know. Where's the doctor?'

'I think he's taking a last look at the beds,' Mrs Perrot said. 'You must be thankful your wife's arrived safely, Major Scobie. Those poor people over there. Forty days in the boats. It shakes one up to think of it.'

'It's the damned narrow channel between Dakar and Brazil that does it every time,' Perrot said.

The doctor came gloomily out on to the verandah.

Everything over the river was still and blank again: the torches were all out. The light burning on the small jetty below the bungalow showed a few feet of dark water sliding by. A piece of wood came out of the dark and floated so slowly through the patch of light that Scobie counted twenty before it went into darkness again.

'The Froggies haven't behaved too badly this time,' Druce said gloomily, picking a mosquito out of his glass.

'They've only brought the women, the old men and the dying,' the doctor said, pulling at his beard. 'They could hardly have done less.'

Suddenly like an invasion of insects the voices whined and burred upon the farther bank. Groups of torches moved like fireflies here and there: Scobie, lifting his binoculars, caught a black face momentarily illuminated: a hammock pole: a white arm: an officer's back. 'I think they've arrived,' he said. A long line of lights was dancing along the water's edge. 'Well,' Mrs Perrot said, 'we may as well go in now.' The mosquitoes whirred steadily around them like sewing machines. Druce exclaimed and struck his hand.

'Come in,' Mrs Perrot said. 'The mosquitoes here are all malarial.' The windows of the living-room were netted to keep them out; the stale air was heavy with the coming rains.

'The stretchers will be across at six a.m.,' the doctor said. 'I think we are all set, Perrot. There's one case of blackwater and a few cases of fever, but most are just exhaustion–the worst disease of all. It's what most of us die of in the end.'

'Scobie and I will see the walking cases,' Druce said. 'You'll have to tell us how much interrogation they can stand, doctor. Your police will look after the carriers, Perrot, I suppose–see that they all go back the way they came.'

'Of course,' Perrot said. 'We're stripped for action here. Have another drink?' Mrs Perrot turned the knob of the radio and the organ of the Orpheum Cinema, Clapham, sailed to them over three thousand miles. From across the river the excited voices of the carriers rose and fell. Somebody knocked on the verandah door. Scobie shifted uncomfortably in his chair: the music of the Würlitzer organ moaned and boomed. It seemed to him outrageously immodest. The verandah door opened and Wilson came in.

'Hello, Wilson,' Druce said. 'I didn't know you were here.'

'Mr Wilson's up to inspect the U.A.C. store,' Mrs Perrot explained. 'I hope the rest-house at the store is all right. It's not often used.'

'Oh yes, it's very comfortable,' Wilson said. 'Why Major Scobie, I didn't expect to see you.'

'I don't know why you didn't,' Perrot said. 'I told you he'd be here. Sit down and have a drink.' Scobie remembered what Louise had once said to him about Wilson–phoney, she had called him. He looked across at Wilson and saw the blush at Perrot's betrayal fading from the boyish face, and the little wrinkles that gathered round the eyes and gave the lie to his youth.

'Have you heard from Mrs Scobie, sir?'

'She arrived safely last week.'

'I'm glad. I'm so glad.'

'Well,' Perrot said, 'what are the scandals from the big city?' The words 'big city' came out with a sneer–Perrot couldn't bear the thought that there was a place where people considered themselves important and where he was not regarded. Like a Huguenot imagining Rome, he built up a picture of frivolity, viciousness and corruption. 'We bushfolk,' Perrot went heavily on, 'live very quietly.' Scobie felt sorry for Mrs Perrot; she had heard these phrases so often: she must have forgotten long ago the time of courtship when she had believed in them. Now she sat close up against the radio with the music turned low listening or pretending to listen to the old Viennese melodies, while her mouth stiffened in the effort to ignore her husband in the familiar part. 'Well, Scobie, what are our superiors doing in the city?'

'Oh,' said Scobie vaguely, watching Mrs Perrot, 'nothing very much has been happening. People are too busy with the war . . .'

'Oh, yes,' Perrot said, 'so many files to turn over in the Secretariat. I'd like to see them growing rice down here. They'd know what work was.'

'I suppose the greatest excitement recently,' Wilson said, 'would be the parrot, sir, wouldn't it?'

'Tallit's parrot?' Scobie asked.

'Or Yusef's according to Tallit,' Wilson said. 'Isn't that right, sir, or have I got the story wrong?'

'I don't think we'll ever know what's right,' Scobie said.

'But what *is* the story? We're out of touch with the great world of affairs here. We have only the French to think about.'

'Well, about three weeks ago Tallit's cousin was leaving for Lisbon on one of the Portuguese ships. We searched his baggage and found nothing, but I'd heard rumours that sometimes diamonds had been smuggled in a bird's crop, so I kept the parrot back, and sure enough there were about a hundred pounds' worth of industrial diamonds inside. The ship hadn't sailed, so we fetched Tallit's cousin back on shore. It seemed a perfect case.'

'But it wasn't?'

'You can't beat a Syrian,' the doctor said.

'Tallit's cousin's boy swore that it wasn't Tallit's cousin's parrot–and so of course did Tallit's cousin. Their story was that the small boy had substituted another bird to frame Tallit.'

'On behalf of Yusef, I suppose,' the doctor said.

'Of course. The trouble was the small boy disappeared. Of course there are two explanations of that–perhaps Yusef had given him his money and he'd cleared off, or just as possibly Tallit had given him money to throw the blame on Yusef.'

'Down here,' Perrot said, 'I'd have had 'em both in jail.'

'Up in town,' Scobie said, 'we have to think about the law.'

Mrs Perrot turned the knob of the radio and a voice shouted with unexpected vigour, 'Kick him in the pants.'

'I'm for bed,' the doctor said. 'To-morrow's going to be a hard day.'

Sitting up in bed under his mosquito-net Scobie opened his diary. Night after night for more years than he could remember he had kept a record–the barest possible record–of his days. If anyone argued a date with him he could check up; if he wanted to know which day the rains had begun in any particular year, when the last but one Director of Public Works had been transferred to East Africa, the facts were all there, in one of the volumes stored in the tin box under his bed at home. Otherwise he never opened a volume–particularly that volume where the barest fact of all was contained–*C. died.* He couldn't have told himself why he stored up this record–it was certainly not for posterity. Even if posterity were to be interested in the life of an obscure policeman in an unfashionable colony, it would have learned nothing from these cryptic entries. Perhaps the reason was that forty years ago at a preparatory school he had been given a prize–a copy of *Allan Quatermain*–for keeping a diary throughout one summer holiday, and the habit had simply stayed. Even the form the diary took had altered very little. *Had sausages for breakfast. Fine day. Walk in morning. Riding lesson in afternoon. Chicken for lunch. Treacle roll.* Almost imperceptibly this record had changed into *Louise left. Y. called in the evening. First typhoon 2 a.m.* His pen was powerless to convey the importance of any entry: only he himself, if he had cared to read back, could have seen in the last phrase but one the enormous breach pity had blasted through his integrity. *Y. not Yusef.*

Scobie wrote: *May 5. Arrived Pende to meet survivors of s.s. 43* (he used the code number for security). *Druce with me.* He hesitated for a moment and then added, *Wilson here.* He closed the diary, and lying flat on his back under the net he began to pray. This also was a habit. He said the Our Father, the Hail Mary, and then, as sleep began to clog his lids, he added an act of contrition. It was a formality, not because he felt himself free from serious sin but because it had never occurred to him that his life was important enough one way or another. He didn't drink, he didn't fornicate, he didn't even lie, but he never regarded this absence of sin as virtue. When he thought about it at all, he regarded himself as a man in the ranks, the member of an awkward squad, who had no opportunity to break the more serious military rules. 'I missed Mass yesterday for insufficient reason. I neglected my evening prayers.' This was no more than admitting what every soldier did—that he had avoided a fatigue when the occasion offered. 'O God, bless—' but before he could mention names he was asleep.

I /ii

They stood on the jetty next morning: the first light lay in cold strips along the eastern sky. The huts in the village were still shuttered with silver. At two that morning there had been a typhoon—a wheeling pillar of black cloud driving up from the coast, and the air was cold yet with the rain. They stood with coat-collars turned up watching the French shore, and the carriers squatted on the ground behind them. Mrs Perrot came down the path from the bungalow wiping the white sleep from her eyes, and from across the water very faintly came the bleating of a goat. 'Are they late?' Mrs Perrot asked.

'No, we are early.' Scobie kept his glasses focused on the opposite shore. He said, 'They are stirring.'

'Those poor souls,' Mrs Perrot said, and shivered with the morning chill.

'They are alive,' the doctor said.

'Yes.'

'In my profession we have to consider that important.'

'Does one ever get over a shock like that? Forty days in open boats.'

'If you survive at all,' the doctor said, 'you get over it. It's failure people don't get over, and this you see is a kind of success.'

'They are fetching them out of the huts,' Scobie said. 'I think I can count six stretchers. The boats are being brought in.'

'We were told to prepare for nine stretcher cases and four walking ones,' the doctor said. 'I suppose there've been some more deaths.'

'I may have counted wrong. They are carrying them down now. I think there are seven stretchers. I can't distinguish the walking cases.'

The flat cold light, too feeble to clear the morning haze, made the distance across the river longer than it would seem at noon. A native dugout canoe bearing, one supposed, the walking cases came blackly out of the haze: it was suddenly very close to them. On the other shore they were having trouble with the motor of a launch; they could hear the irregular putter, like an animal out of breath.

First of the walking cases to come on shore was an elderly man with an arm in a sling. He wore a dirty white topee and a native cloth was draped over his shoulders; his free hand tugged and scratched at the white stubble on his face. He said in an unmistakably Scottish accent, 'Ah'm Loder, chief engineer.'

'Welcome home, Mr Loder,' Scobie said. 'Will you step up to the bungalow and the doctor will be with you in a few minutes?'

'Ah have no need of doctors.'

'Sit down and rest. I'll be with you soon.'

'Ah want to make ma report to a proper official.'

'Would you take him up to the house, Perrot?'

'I'm the District Commissioner,' Perrot said. 'You can make your report to me.'

'What are we waitin' for then?' the engineer said. 'It's nearly two months since the sinkin'. There's an awful lot of responsibility on me, for the captain's dead.' As they moved up the hill to the bungalow, the persistent Scottish voice, as regular as the pulse of a dynamo, came back to them. 'Ah'm responsible to the owners.'

The other three had come on shore, and across the river the tinkering in the launch went on: the sharp crack of a chisel, the clank of metal, and then again the spasmodic putter. Two of the new arrivals were the cannon fodder of all such occasions: elderly men with the appearance of plumbers who might have been brothers if they had not been called Forbes and Newall, uncomplaining men without authority, to whom things simply happened. One had a crushed foot and walked with a crutch; the other had his hand bound up with shabby strips of tropical shirt. They stood on the jetty with as natural a lack of interest as they would have stood at a Liverpool street corner waiting for the local to open. A stalwart grey-headed woman in mosquito-boots followed them out of the canoe.

'Your name, madam?' Druce asked, consulting a list. 'Are you Mrs Rolt?'

'I am not Mrs Rolt. I am Miss Malcott.'

'Will you go up to the house? The doctor . . .'

'The doctor has far more serious cases than me to attend to.'

Mrs Perrot said, 'You'd like to lie down.'

'It's the last thing I want to do,' Miss Malcott said. 'I am not in the least tired.' She shut her mouth between every sentence. 'I am not hungry. I am not nervous. I want to get on.'

'Where to?'

'To Lagos. To the Educational Department.'

'I'm afraid there will be a good many delays.'

'I've been delayed two months. I can't stand delay. Work won't wait.' Suddenly she lifted her face towards the sky and howled like a dog.

The doctor took her gently by the arm and said, 'We'll do what we can to get you there right away. Come up to the house and do some telephoning.'

'Certainly,' Miss Malcott said, 'there's nothing that can't be straightened on a telephone.'

The doctor said to Scobie, 'Send those other two chaps up after us. They are all right. If you want to do some questioning, question them.'

Druce said, 'I'll take them along. You stay here, Scobie, in case the launch arrives. French isn't my language.'

Scobie sat down on the rail of the jetty and looked across the water. Now that the haze was lifting the other bank came closer; he could make out now with the naked eye the details of the scene: the white warehouse, the mud huts, the brasswork of the launch glittering in the sun: he could see the red fezzes of the native troops. He thought: Just such a scene as this and I might have been waiting for Louise to appear on a stretcher—or perhaps not waiting. Somebody settled himself on the rail beside him, but Scobie didn't turn his head.

'A penny for your thoughts, sir.'

'I was just thinking that Louise is safe, Wilson.'

'I was thinking that too, sir.'

'Why do you always call me sir, Wilson? You are not in the police force. It makes me feel very old.'

'I'm sorry, Major Scobie.'

'What did Louise call you?'

'Wilson. I don't think she liked my Christian name.'

'I believe they've got that launch to start at last, Wilson. Be a good chap and warn the doctor.'

A French officer in a stained white uniform stood in the bow: a soldier flung a rope and Scobie caught and fixed it. '*Bonjour*,' he said, and saluted.

The French officer returned his salute—a drained-out figure with a twitch in the left eyelid. He said in English, 'Good morning. I have seven stretcher cases for you here.'

'My signal says nine.'

'One died on the way and one last night. One from blackwater and one from—from, my English is bad, do you say fatigue?'

'Exhaustion.'

'That is it.'

'If you will let my labourers come on board they will get the stretchers off.' Scobie said to the carriers, 'Very softly. Go very softly.' It was an unnecessary command: no white hospital attendants could lift and carry more gently. 'Won't you stretch your legs on shore?' Scobie asked, 'or come up to the house and have some coffee?'

'No. No coffee, thank you. I will just see that all is right here.' He was courteous and unapproachable, but all the time his left eyelid flickered a message of doubt and distress.

'I have some English papers if you would like to see them.'

'No, no, thank you. I read English with difficulty.'

'You speak it very well.'

'That is a different thing.'

'Have a cigarette?'

'Thank you, no. I do not like American tobacco.'

The first stretcher came on shore—the sheets were drawn up to the man's chin and it was impossible to tell from the stiff vacant face what his age might be. The doctor came down the hill to meet the stretcher and led the carriers away to the Government rest-house where the beds had been prepared.

'I used to come over to your side,' Scobie said, 'to shoot with your police chief. A nice fellow called Durand—a Norman.'

'He is not here any longer,' the officer said.

'Gone home?'

'He's in prison at Dakar,' the French officer replied, standing like a figure-head in the bows, but the eye twitching and twitching. The stretchers slowly passed Scobie and turned up the hill: a boy who couldn't have been more than ten with a feverish face and a twig-like arm thrown out from his blanket: an old lady with grey hair falling every way who twisted and turned and whispered: a man with a bottle nose–a knob of scarlet and blue on a yellow face. One by one they turned up the hill–the carriers' feet moving with the certainty of mules. 'And Père Brûle?' Scobie asked. 'He was a good man.'

'He died last year of blackwater.'

'He was out here twenty years without leave, wasn't he? He'll be hard to replace.'

'He has not been replaced,' the officer said. He turned and gave a short savage order to one of his men. Scobie looked at the next stretcher load and looked away again. A small girl–she couldn't have been more than six–lay on it. She was deeply and unhealthily asleep; her fair hair was tangled and wet with sweat; her open mouth was dry and cracked, and she shuddered regularly and spasmodically. 'It's terrible,' Scobie said.

'What is terrible?'

'A child like that.'

'Yes. Both parents were lost. But it is all right. She will die.'

Scobie watched the bearers go slowly up the hill, their bare feet very gently flapping the ground. He thought: It would need all Father Brûle's ingenuity to explain that. Not that the child would die–that needed no explanation. Even the pagans realised that the love of God might mean an early death, though the reason they ascribed was different; but that the child should have been allowed to survive the forty days and nights in the open boat–that was the mystery, to reconcile that with the love of God.

And yet he could believe in no God who was not human enough to love what he had created. 'How on earth did she survive till now?' he wondered aloud.

The officer said gloomily, 'Of course they looked after her on the boat. They gave up their own share of the water often. It was foolish, of course, but one cannot always be logical. And it gave them something to think about.' It was like the hint of an explanation–too faint to be grasped. He said, 'Here is another who makes one angry.'

The face was ugly with exhaustion: the skin looked as though it were about to crack over the cheek-bones: only the absence of lines showed that it was a young face. The French officer said, 'She was just married–before she sailed. Her husband was lost. Her passport says she is nineteen. She may live. You see, she still has some strength.' Her arms as thin as a child's lay outside the blanket, and her fingers clasped a book firmly. Scobie could see the wedding-ring loose on her dried-up finger.

'What is it?'

'*Timbres*,' the French officer said. He added bitterly, 'When this damned war started, she must have been still at school.'

Scobie always remembered how she was carried into his life on a stretcher grasping a stamp-album with her eyes fast shut.

In the evening they gathered together again for drinks, but they were subdued. Even Perrot was no longer trying to impress them. Druce said, 'Well, to-morrow I'm off. You coming, Scobie?'

'I suppose so.'

Mrs Perrot said, 'You got all you wanted?'

'All I needed. That chief engineer was a good fellow. He had it ready in his head. I could hardly write fast enough. When he stopped he went flat out. That was what was keeping him together–"ma responsibility". You know they'd walked–the ones that could walk–five days to get here.'

Wilson said, 'Were they sailing without an escort?'

'They started out in convoy, but they had some engine trouble–and you know the rule of the road nowadays: no waiting for lame ducks. They were twelve hours behind the convoy and were trying to pick up when they were sniped. The submarine commander surfaced and gave them direction. He said he would have given them a tow, but there was a naval patrol out looking for him. You see, you can really blame nobody for this sort of thing,' and this sort of thing came at once to Scobie's mind's eye–the child with the open mouth, the thin hands holding the stamp-album. He said, 'I suppose the doctor will look in when he gets a chance?'

He went restlessly out on to the verandah, closing the netted door carefully behind him, and a mosquito immediately droned towards his ear. The skirring went on all the time, but when they drove to the attack they had the deeper tone of dive-bombers. The lights were showing in the temporary hospital, and the weight of that misery lay on his shoulders. It was as if he had shed one responsibility only to take on another. This was a responsibility he shared with all human beings, but that was no comfort, for it sometimes seemed to him that he was the only one who recognised his responsibility. In the Cities of the Plain a single soul might have changed the mind of God.

The doctor came up the steps on to the verandah. 'Hallo, Scobie,' he said in a voice as bowed as his shoulders, 'taking the night air? It's not healthy in this place.'

'How are they?' Scobie asked.

'There'll be only two more deaths, I think. Perhaps only one.'

'The child?'

'She'll be dead by morning,' the doctor said abruptly.

'Is she conscious?'

'Never completely. She asks for her father sometimes: she probably thinks she's in the boat still. They'd kept it from her there–said her parents were in one of the other boats. But of course they'd signalled to check up.'

'Won't she take you for her father?'

'No, she won't accept the beard.'

Scobie said, 'How's the school teacher?'

'Miss Malcott? She'll be all right. I've given her enough bromide to put her out of action till morning. That's all she needs—and the sense of getting somewhere. You haven't got room for her in your police van, have you? She'd be better out of here.'

'There's only just room for Druce and me with our boys and kit. We'll be sending proper transport as soon as we get back. The walking cases all right?'

'Yes, they'll manage.'

'The boy and the old lady?'

'They'll pull through.'

'Who is the boy?'

'He was at a prep. school in England. His parents in South Africa thought he'd be safer with them.'

Scobie said reluctantly, 'That young woman—with the stamp-album?' It was the stamp-album and not the face that haunted his memory for no reason that he could understand, and the wedding-ring loose on the finger, as though a child had dressed up.

'I don't know,' the doctor said. 'If she gets through to-night—perhaps—'

'You're dead tired, aren't you? Go in and have a drink.'

'Yes. I don't want to be eaten by mosquitoes.' The doctor opened the verandah door, and a mosquito struck at Scobie's neck. He didn't bother to guard himself. Slowly, hesitatingly, he retraced the route the doctor had taken, down the steps on to the tough rocky ground. The loose stones turned under his boots. He though of Pemberton. What an absurd thing it was to expect happiness in a world so full of misery. He had cut down his own needs to a minimum, photographs were put away in drawers, the dead were put out of mind: a razor-strop, a pair of rusty handcuffs for decoration. But one still has one's eyes, he thought, one's ears. Point me out the happy man and I will point you out either extreme egotism, evil—or else an absolute ignorance.

Outside the rest-house he stopped again. The lights inside would have given an extraordinary impression of peace if one hadn't known, just as the stars on this clear night gave also an impression of remoteness, security, freedom. If one knew, he wondered, the facts, would one have to feel pity even for the planets? if one reached what they called the heart of the matter?

'Well, Major Scobie?' It was the wife of the local missionary speaking to him. She was dressed in white like a nurse, and her flint-grey hair lay back from her forehead in ridges like wind erosion. 'Have you come to look on?' she asked forbiddingly.

'Yes,' he said. He had no other idea of what to say: he couldn't describe to Mrs Bowles the restlessness, the haunting images, the terrible impotent feeling of responsibility and pity.

'Come inside,' Mrs Bowles said, and he followed her obediently like a boy. There were three rooms in the rest-house. In the first the walking cases had been put: heavily dosed they slept peacefully, as though they had been taking healthy exercise. In the second room were the stretcher cases for whom there was reasonable hope. The third room was a small one and contained only two beds divided by a screen: the six-year-old girl with the dry mouth, the young woman lying unconscious on her back, still grasping the stamp-album. A night-light burned in a saucer and cast thin shadows between the beds. 'If you want to be useful,' Mrs Bowles said, 'stay here a moment. I want to go to the dispensary.'

'The dispensary?'

'The cook-house. One has to make the best of things.'

Scobie felt cold and strange. A shiver moved his shoulders. He said, 'Can't I go for you?'

Mrs Bowles said, 'Don't be absurd. Are you qualified to dispense? I'll only be away a few minutes. If the child shows signs of going call me.' If she had given him time, he would have thought of some excuse, but she was already out of the room and he sat heavily down in the only chair. When he looked at the child, he saw a white communion veil over her head: it was a trick of the light on the mosquito net and a trick of his own mind. He put his head in his hands and wouldn't look. He had been in Africa when his own child died. He had always thanked God that he had missed that. It seemed after all that one never really missed a thing. To be a human being one had to drink the cup. If one were lucky on one day, or cowardly on another, it was presented on a third occasion. He prayed silently into his hands, 'O God, don't let anything happen before Mrs Bowles comes back.' He could hear the heavy uneven breathing of the child. It was as if she were carrying a weight with great effort up a long hill: it was an inhuman situation not to be able to carry it for her. He thought: this is what parents feel year in and year out, and I am shrinking from a few minutes of it. They see their children dying slowly every hour they live. He prayed again, 'Father, look after her. Give her peace.' The breathing broke, choked, began again with terrible effort. Looking between his fingers he could see the six-year-old face convulsed like a navvy's with labour. 'Father,' he prayed, 'give her peace. Take away my peace for ever, but give her peace.' The sweat broke out on his hands. 'Father . . .'

He heard a small scraping voice repeat, 'Father,' and looking up he saw the blue and bloodshot eyes watching him. He thought with horror: this is what I thought I'd missed. He would have called Mrs Bowles, only he hadn't the voice to call with. He could see the breast of the child struggling for breath to repeat the heavy word; he came over to the bed and said, 'Yes, dear. Don't speak, I'm here.' The night-light cast the shadow of his clenched fist on the sheet and it caught the child's eye. An effort to laugh convulsed her, and he moved his hand away. 'Sleep, dear,' he said, 'you are sleepy. Sleep.' A memory that he had carefully buried returned and taking out his handkerchief he made the shadow of a rabbit's head fall on the pillow beside her. 'There's your rabbit,' he said, 'to go to sleep with. It will stay until you sleep. Sleep.' The sweat poured down his face and tasted in his mouth as salt as tears. 'Sleep.' He moved the rabbit's ears up and down, up and down. Then he heard Mrs Bowles's voice, speaking low just behind him. 'Stop that,' she said harshly, 'the child's dead.'

In the morning he told the doctor that he would stay till proper transport arrived: Miss Malcott could have his place in the police van. It was better to get her moving, for the child's death had upset her again, and it was by no means certain that there would not be other deaths. They buried the child next day, using the only coffin they could get: it had been designed for a tall man. In this climate delay was unwise. Scobie did not attend the funeral service which was read by Mr Bowles, but the Perrots were present, Wilson and some of the court messengers: the doctor was busy in the rest-house. Instead, Scobie walked rapidly through the rice-fields, talked to the agricultural officer about irrigation, kept away. Later, when he had exhausted the possibilities of irrigation, he went into the store and sat in the dark among all the tins, the tinned hams and the tinned soups, the tinned butter, the tinned biscuits, the tinned milk, the tinned potatoes, the tinned chocolates, and waited for Wilson. But Wilson didn't come: perhaps the funeral had been too much for all of them, and they had returned to the D.C.'s bungalow for drinks. Scobie went down to the jetty and watched the sailing boats move down towards the sea. Once he found himself saying aloud as though to a man at his elbow, 'Why didn't you let her drown?' A court messenger looked at him askance and he moved on, up the hill.

Mrs Bowles was taking the air outside the rest-house: taking it literally, in doses like medicine. She stood there with her mouth opening and closing, inhaling and expelling. She said, 'Good afternoon,' stiffly, and took another dose. 'You weren't at the funeral, major?'

'No.'

'Mr Bowles and I can seldom attend a funeral together. Except when we're on leave.'

'Are there going to be any more funerals?'

'One more, I think. The rest will be all right in time.'

'Which of them is dying?'

'The old lady. She took a turn for the worse last night. She had been getting on well.'

He felt a merciless relief. He said, 'The boy's all right?'

'Yes.'

'And Mrs Rolt?'

'She's not out of danger, but I think she'll do. She's conscious now.'

'Does she know her husband's dead?'

'Yes.' Mrs Bowles began to swing her arms, up and down, from the shoulder. Then she stood on tip-toe six times. He said, 'I wish there was something I could do to help.'

'Can you read aloud?' Mrs Bowles asked, rising on her toes.

'I suppose so. Yes.'

'You can read to the boy. He's getting bored and boredom's bad for him.'

'Where shall I find a book?'

'There are plenty at the Mission. Shelves of them.'

Anything was better than doing nothing. He walked up to the Mission and found, as Mrs Bowles said, plenty of books. He wasn't much used to books, but even to his eye these hardly seemed a bright collection for reading to a sick boy. Damp-stained and late Victorian, the bindings bore titles like *Twenty Years in the Mission Field*, *Lost and Found*, *The Narrow Way*, *The Missionary's Warning*. Obviously at some time there had been an appeal for books for the Mission library, and here were the scraping of many pious shelves at home. *The Poems of John Oxenham*, *Fishers of Men*. He took a book at random out of the shelf and returned to the rest-house. Mrs Bowles was in her dispensary mixing medicines.

'Found something?'

'Yes.'

'You are safe with any of those books,' Mrs Bowles said. 'They are censored by the committee before they come out. Sometimes people try to send the most unsuitable books. We are not teaching the children here to read in order that they shall read—well, novels.'

'No, I suppose not.'

'Let me see what you've chosen.'

He looked at the title himself for the first time: *A Bishop among the Bantus*.

'That should be interesting,' Mrs Bowles said. He agreed doubtfully.

'You know where to find him. You can read to him for a quarter of an hour—not more.'

The old lady had been moved into the innermost room where the child had died, the man with the bottle-nose had been shifted into what Mrs Bowles now called the convalescence ward, so that the middle room could be given up to the boy and Mrs Rolt. Mrs Rolt lay facing the wall with her eyes closed. They had apparently succeeded in removing the album from her clutch and it lay on a chair beside the bed. The boy watched Scobie with the bright intelligent gaze of fever.

'My name's Scobie. What's yours?'

'Fisher.'

Scobie said nervously, 'Mrs Bowles asked me to read to you.'

'What are you? A soldier?'

'No, a policeman.'

'Is it a murder story?'

'No. I don't think it is.' He opened the book at random and came on a photograph of the bishop sitting in his robes on a hard drawing-room chair outside a little tin-roofed church: he was surrounded by Bantus, who grinned at the camera.

'I'd like a murder story. Have you ever been in a murder?'

'Not what you'd call a real murder with clues and a chase.'

'What sort of a murder then?'

'Well, people get stabbed sometimes fighting.' He spoke in a low voice so as not to disturb Mrs Rolt. She lay with her fist clenched on the sheet—a fist not much bigger than a tennis ball.

'What's the name of the book you've brought? Perhaps I've read it. I read *Treasure Island* on the boat. I wouldn't mind a pirate story. What's it called?'

Scobie said dubiously, '*A Bishop among the Bantus.*'

'What does that mean?'

Scobie drew a long breath. 'Well, you see, Bishop is the name of the hero.'

'But you said *a* Bishop.'

'Yes. His name was Arthur.'

'It's a soppy name.'

'Yes, but he's a soppy hero.' Suddenly, avoiding the boy's eyes, he noticed that Mrs Rolt was not asleep: she was staring at the wall, listening. He went wildly on, 'The real heroes are the Bantus.'

'What are Bantus?'

'They were a peculiarly ferocious lot of pirates who haunted the West Indies and preyed on all the shipping in that part of the Atlantic.'

'Does Arthur Bishop pursue them?'

'Yes. It's a kind of detective story too because he's a secret agent of the British Government. He dresses up as an ordinary seaman and sails on a merchantman so that he can be captured by the Bantus. You know they always give the ordinary seamen a chance to join them. If he'd been an officer they would have made him walk the plank. Then he discovers all their secret passwords and hiding-places and their plans of raids, of course, so that he can betray them when the time is ripe.'

'He sounds a bit of a swine,' the boy said.

'Yes, and he falls in love with the daughter of the captain of the Bantus and that's when he turns soppy. But that comes near the end and we won't get as far as that. There are a lot of fights and murders before then.'

'It sounds all right. Let's begin.'

'Well, you see, Mrs Bowles told me I was only to stay a short time to-day, so I've just told you *about* the book, and we can start it to-morrow.'

'You may not be here to-morrow. There may be a murder or something.'

'But the book will be here. I'll leave it with Mrs Bowles. It's her book. Of course it may sound a bit different when *she* reads it.'

'Just begin it,' the boy pleaded.

'Yes, begin it,' said a low voice from the other bed, so low that he would have discounted it as an illusion if he hadn't looked up and seen her watching him, the eyes large as a child's in the starved face.

Scobie said, 'I'm a very bad reader.'

'Go on,' the boy said impatiently. 'Anyone can read aloud.'

Scobie found his eyes fixed on an opening paragraph which stated, *I shall never forget my first glimpse of the continent where I was to labour for thirty of the best years of my life.* He said slowly, 'From the moment that they left Bermuda the low lean rakehelly craft had followed in their wake. The captain was evidently worried, for he watched the strange ship continually through his spyglass. When night fell it was still on their trail, and at dawn it was the first sight that met their eyes. Can it be, Arthur Bishop wondered, that I am about to meet the object of my quest, Blackbeard, the leader of the Bantus himself, or his blood-thirsty lieutenant. . . .' He turned a page and was temporarily put out by a portrait of the bishop in whites with a clerical collar and a topee, standing before a wicket and blocking a ball a Bantu had just bowled him.

'Go on,' the boy said.

'. . . Batty Davis, so called because of his insane rages when he would send a whole ship's crew to the plank? It was evident that Captain Buller feared the worst, for he crowded on all canvas and it seemed for a time that he would show the strange ship a clean pair of heels. Suddenly over the water came the boom of a gun, and a cannon-ball struck the water twenty yards ahead of them. Captain Buller had his glass to his eye and called down from the bridge to Arthur Bishop, "The Jolly Roger, by God." He was the only one of the ship's company who knew the secret of Arthur's strange quest.'

Mrs Bowles came briskly in. 'There, that will do. Quite enough for the day. And what's he been reading you, Jimmy?'

'Bishop among the Bantus.'

'I hope you enjoyed it.'

'It's wizard.'

'You're a very sensible boy,' Mrs Bowles said approvingly.

'Thank you,' a voice said from the other bed and Scobie turned again reluctantly to take in the young devastated face. 'Will you read again to-morrow?'

'Don't worry Major Scobie, Helen,' Mrs Bowles rebuked her. 'He's got to get back to the port. They'll all be murdering each other without him.'

'You a policeman?'

'Yes.'

'I knew a policeman once—in our town—' the voice trailed off into sleep. He stood a minute looking down at her face. Like a fortune-teller's cards it showed unmistakably the past—a voyage, a loss, a sickness. In the next deal perhaps it would be possible to see the future. He took up the stamp-album and opened it at the fly-leaf: it was inscribed, 'Helen, from her loving father on her fourteenth birthday.' Then it fell open at Paraguay, full of the decorative images of parrakeets—the kind of picture stamps a child collects. 'We'll have to find her some new stamps,' he said sadly.

I / V

Wilson was waiting for him outside. He said, 'I've been looking for you, Major Scobie, ever since the funeral.'

'I've been doing good works,' Scobie said.

'How's Mrs Rolt?'

'They think she'll pull through—and the boy too.'

'Oh yes, the boy.' Wilson kicked a loose stone in the path and said, 'I want your advice, Major Scobie. I'm a bit worried.'

'Yes?'

'You know I've been down here checking up on our store. Well, I find that our manager has been buying military stuff. There's a lot of tinned food that never came from our exporters.'

'Isn't the answer fairly simple—sack him?'

'It seems a pity to sack the small thief if he could lead one to the big thief, but of course that's your job. That's why I wanted to talk to you.' Wilson paused and that extraordinary tell-tale blush spread over his face. He said,

'You see, he got the stuff from Yusef's man.'

'I could have guessed that.'

'You could?'

'Yes, but you see, Yusef's man is not the same as Yusef. It's easy for him to disown a country storekeeper. In fact, for all we know, Yusef may be innocent. It's unlikely, but not impossible. Your own evidence would point to it. After all you've only just learned yourself what your storekeeper was doing.'

'If there were clear evidence,' Wilson said, 'would the police prosecute?'

Scobie came to a standstill. 'What's that?'

Wilson blushed and mumbled. Then, with a venom that took Scobie completely by surprise, he said, 'There are rumours going about that Yusef is protected.'

'You've been here long enough to know what rumours are worth.'

'They are all round the town.'

'Spread by Tallit—or Yusef himself.'

'Don't misunderstand me,' Wilson said. 'You've been very kind to me—and Mrs Scobie has too. I thought you ought to know what's been said.'

'I've been here fifteen years, Wilson.'

'Oh, I know,' Wilson said, 'this is impertinent. But people are worried about Tallit's parrot. They say he was framed because Yusef wants him run out of town.'

'Yes, I've heard that.'

'They say that you and Yusef are on visiting terms. It's a lie, of course, but . . .'

'It's perfectly true. I'm also on visiting terms with the sanitary inspector, but it wouldn't prevent my prosecuting him. . . .' He stopped abruptly. He said, 'I have no intention of defending myself to you, Wilson.'

Wilson repeated, 'I just thought you ought to know.'

'You are too young for your job, Wilson.'

'My job?'

'Whatever it is.'

For the second time Wilson took him by surprise, breaking out with a crack in his voice, 'Oh, you are unbearable. You are too damned honest to live.' His face was aflame, even his knees seemed to blush with rage, shame, self-deprecation.

'You ought to wear a hat, Wilson,' was all Scobie said.

They stood facing each other on the stony path between the D.C.'s bungalow and the rest-house; the light lay flat across the rice-fields below them, and Scobie was conscious of how prominently they were silhouetted to the eyes of any watcher. 'You sent Louise away,' Wilson said, 'because you were afraid of me.'

Scobie laughed gently. 'This is sun, Wilson, just sun. We'll forget about it in the morning.'

'She couldn't stand your stupid, unintelligent . . . you don't know what a woman like Louise thinks.'

'I don't suppose I do. Nobody wants another person to know that, Wilson.'

Wilson said, 'I kissed her that evening. . . .'

'It's the colonial sport, Wilson.' He hadn't meant to madden the young man: he was only anxious to let the occasion pass lightly, so that in the morning they could behave naturally to each other. It was just a touch of sun, he told himself; he had seen this happen times out of mind during fifteen years.

Wilson said, 'She's too good for you.'

'For both of us.'

'How did you get the money to send her away? That's what I'd like to know. You don't earn all that. I know. It's printed in the Colonial Office List.' If the young man had been less absurd, Scobie might have been angered and they might have ended friends. It was his serenity that stoked the flames. He said now, 'Let's talk about it to-morrow. We've all been upset by that child's death. Come up to the bungalow and have a drink.' He made to pass Wilson, but Wilson barred the way: a Wilson scarlet in the face with tears in his eyes. It was as if he had gone so far that he realised the only thing to do was to go farther—there was no return the way he had come. He said, 'Don't think I haven't got my eye on you.'

The absurdity of the phrase took Scobie off his guard.

'You watch your step,' Wilson said, 'and Mrs Rolt . . .'

'What on earth has Mrs Rolt got to do with it?'

'Don't think I don't know why you've stayed behind, haunted the hospital. . . . While we were all at the funeral, you slunk down here. . . .'

'You really are crazy, Wilson,' Scobie said.

Suddenly Wilson sat down; it was as if he had been folded up by some large invisible hand. He put his head in his hands and wept.

'It's the sun,' Scobie said. 'Just the sun. Go and lie down,' and taking off his hat he put it on Wilson's head. Wilson looked up at him between his fingers—at the man who had seen his tears—with hatred.

2/i

The sirens were wailing for a total black-out, wailing through the rain which fell interminably; the boys scrambled into the kitchen quarters, and bolted the door as though to protect themselves from some devil of the bush. Without pause the hundred and forty-four inches of water continued their steady and ponderous descent upon the roofs of the port. It was incredible to imagine that any human beings, let alone the dispirited fever-soaked defeated of Vichy territory, would open an assault at this time of the year, and yet of course one remembered the Heights of Abraham. . . . A single feat of daring can alter the whole conception of what is possible.

Scobie went out into the dripping darkness holding his big striped umbrella: a mackintosh was too hot to wear. He walked all round his quarters; not a light showed, the shutters of the kitchen were closed, and the Creole houses were invisible behind the rain. A torch gleamed momentarily in the transport park across the road, but, when he shouted, it went out: a coincidence: no one there could have heard his voice above the hammering of the water on the roof. Up in Cape Station the officers' mess was shining wetly towards the sea, but that was not his responsibility. The headlamps of the military lorries ran like a chain of beads along the edge of the hills, but that too was someone else's affair.

Up the road behind the transport park a light went suddenly on in one of the Nissen huts where the minor officials lived; it was a hut that had been unoccupied the day before and presumably some visitor had just moved in. Scobie considered getting his car from the garage, but the hut was only a couple of hundred yards away, and he walked. Except for the sound of the rain, on the road, on the roofs, on the umbrella, there was absolute silence: only the dying moan of the sirens continued for a moment or two to vibrate within the ear. It seemed to Scobie later that this was the ultimate border he had reached in happiness: being in darkness, alone, with the rain falling, without love or pity.

He knocked on the door of the Nissen hut, loudly because of the blows of the rain on the black roof like a tunnel. He had to knock twice before the door opened. The light for a moment blinded him. He said, 'I'm sorry to bother you. One of your lights is showing.'

A woman's voice said, 'Oh, I'm sorry. It was careless . . .'

His eyes cleared, but for a moment he couldn't put a name to the intensely remembered features. He knew everyone in the colony. This was something that had come from outside . . . a river . . . early morning . . . a dying child. 'Why,' he said, 'it's Mrs Rolt, isn't it? I thought you were in hospital?'

'Yes. Who are you? Do I know you?'

'I'm Major Scobie of the police. I saw you at Pende.'

'I'm sorry,' she said. 'I don't remember a thing that happened there.'

'Can I fix your light?'

'Of course. Please.' He came in and drew the curtains close and shifted a table lamp. The hut was divided in two by a curtain: on one side a bed, a makeshift dressing-table: on the other a table, a couple of chairs—the few sticks of furniture of the pattern allowed to junior officials with salaries under £500 a year. He said, 'They haven't done you very proud, have they? I wish I'd known. I could have helped.' He took her in closely now: the young worn-out face, with the hair gone dead. . . . The pyjamas she was wearing were too large for her: the body was lost in them: they fell in ugly folds. He looked to see whether the ring was still loose upon her finger, but it had gone altogether.

'Everybody's been very kind,' she said. 'Mrs Carter gave me a lovely pouf.'

His eyes wandered: there was nothing personal anywhere: no photographs, no books, no trinkets of any kind, but then he remembered that she had brought nothing out of the sea except herself and a stamp-album.

'Is there any danger?' she asked anxiously.

'Danger?'

'The sirens.'

'Oh, none at all. These are just alarms. We get about one a month. Nothing ever happens.' He took another long look at her. 'They oughtn't to have let you out of hospital so soon. It's not six weeks . . .'

'I wanted to go. I wanted to be alone. People kept on coming to see me.'

'Well, I'll be going now myself. Remember if you ever want anything I'm just down the road. The two-storeyed white house beyond the transport park sitting in a swamp.'

'Won't you stay till the rain stops?' she asked.

'I don't think I'd better,' he said. 'You see, it goes on until September,' and won out of her a stiff unused smile.

'The noise is awful.'

'You get used to it in a few weeks. Like living beside a railway. But you won't have to. They'll be sending you home very soon. There's a boat in a fortnight.'

'Would you like a drink? Mrs Carter gave me a bottle of gin as well as the pouf.'

'I'd better help you to drink it then.' He noticed when she produced the bottle that nearly half had gone. 'Have you any limes?'

'No.'

'They've given you a boy, I suppose?'

'Yes, but I don't know what to ask him for. And he never seems to be around.'

'You've been drinking it neat?'

'Oh no, I haven't touched it. The boy upset it—that was his story.'

'I'll talk to your boy in the morning,' Scobie said. 'Got an ice-box?'

'Yes, but the boy can't get me any ice.' She sat weakly down in a chair. 'Don't think me a fool. I just don't know where I am. I've never been anywhere like this.'

'Where do you come from?'

'Bury St Edmunds. In Suffolk. I was there eight weeks ago.'

'Oh no, you weren't. You were in that boat.'

'Yes. I forgot the boat.'

'They oughtn't to have pushed you out of the hospital all alone like this.'

'I'm all right. They had to have my bed. Mrs Carter said she'd find room for me, but I wanted to be alone. The doctor told them to do what I wanted.'

Scobie said, 'I can understand you wouldn't want to be with Mrs Carter, and you've only got to say the word and I'll be off too.'

'I'd rather you waited till the All Clear. I'm a bit rattled, you know.' The stamina of women had always amazed Scobie. This one had survived forty days in an open boat and she talked about being rattled. He remembered the casualties in the report the chief engineer had made: the third officer and two seamen who had died, and the stoker who had gone off his head as a result of drinking sea water and drowned himself. When it came to strain it was always a man who broke. Now she lay back on her weakness as on a pillow.

He said, 'Have you thought out things? Shall you go back to Bury?'

'I don't know. Perhaps I'll get a job.'

'Have you had any experience?'

'No,' she confessed, looking away from him. 'You see, I only left school a year ago.'

'Did they teach you anything?' It seemed to him that what she needed more than anything else was just talk, silly aimless talk. She thought that she wanted to be alone, but what she was afraid of was the awful responsibility of receiving sympathy. How could a child like that act the part of a woman whose husband had been drowned more or less before her eyes? As well expect her to act Lady Macbeth. Mrs Carter would have had no sympathy with her inadequacy. Mrs Carter, of course, would have known how to behave, having buried one husband and three children.

She said, 'I was best at netball,' breaking in on his thoughts.

'Well,' he said, 'you haven't quite the figure for a gym instructor. Or have you, when you are well?'

Suddenly and without warning she began to talk. It was as if by the inadvertent use of a password he had induced a door to open: he couldn't tell now which word he had used. Perhaps it was 'gym instructor', for she began rapidly to tell him about the netball (Mrs Carter, he thought, had probably talked about forty days in an open boat and a three-weeks'-old husband). She said, 'I was in the school team for two years,' leaning forward excitedly with her chin on her hand and one bony elbow upon a bony knee. With her white skin—unyellowed yet by atabrine or sunlight—he was reminded of a bone the sea has washed and cast up. 'A year before that I was in the second team. I would have been captain if I'd stayed another year. In 1940 we beat Roedean and tied with Cheltenham.'

He listened with the intense interest one feels in a stranger's life, the interest the young mistake for love. He felt the security of his age sitting there listening with a glass of gin in his hand and the rain coming down. She told him her school was on the downs just behind Seaport: they had a French mistress called Mlle Dupont who had a vile temper. The headmistress could read Greek just like English—Virgil. . . .

'I always thought Virgil was Latin.'

'Oh yes. I meant Homer. I wasn't any good at Classics.'

'Were you good at anything besides netball?'

'I think I was next best at maths, but I was never any good at trigonometry.' In summer they went into Seaport and bathed, and every Saturday they had a picnic on the downs—sometimes a paper-chase on ponies, and once a disastrous affair on bicycles which spread out over the whole country, and two girls didn't return till one in the morning. He listened fascinated, revolving the heavy gin in his glass without drinking. The sirens squealed the All Clear through the rain, but neither of them paid any attention. He said, 'And then in the holidays you went back to Bury?'

Apparently her mother had died ten years ago, and her father was a clergyman attached in some way to the Cathedral. They had a very small house on Angel Hill. Perhaps she had not been as happy at Bury as at school, for she tacked back at the first opportunity to discuss the games mistress whose name was the same as her own—Helen, and for whom the whole of her year had an enormous *schwarmerei*. She laughed now at this passion in a superior way: it was the only indication she gave him that she was grown-up, that she was—or rather had been—a married woman.

She broke suddenly off and said, 'What nonsense it is telling you all this.'

'I like it.'

'You haven't once asked me about—you know—'

He did know, for he had read the report. He knew exactly the water ration for each person in the boat—a cupful twice a day, which had been reduced after twenty-one days to half a cupful. That had been maintained until within twenty-four hours of the rescue mainly because the deaths had left a small surplus. Behind the school buildings of Seaport, the totem-pole of the netball game, he was aware of the intolerable surge, lifting the boat and dropping it again, lifting it and dropping it. 'I was miserable when I left—it was the end of July. I cried in the taxi all the way to the station.' Scobie counted the months—July to April: nine months: the period of gestation, and what had been born was a husband's death and the Atlantic pushing them like wreckage towards the long flat African beach and the sailor throwing himself over the side. He said, 'This is more interesting. I can guess the other.'

'What a lot I've talked. Do you know, I think I shall sleep to-night.'

' Haven't you been sleeping?'

'It was the breathing all round me at the hospital. People turning and breathing and muttering. When the light was out, it was just like—you know.'

'You'll sleep quietly here. No need to be afraid of anything. There's a watchman always on duty. I'll have a word with him.'

'You've been so kind,' she said. 'Mrs Carter and the others—they've all been kind.' She lifted her worn, frank, childish face and said, 'I like you so much.'

'I like you too,' he said gravely. They both had an immense sense of security: they were friends who could never be anything else than friends—they were safely divided by a dead husband, a living wife, a father who was a clergyman, a games mistress called Helen, and years and years of experience. They hadn't got to worry about what they should say to each other.

He said, 'Good night. To-morrow I'm going to bring you some stamps for your album.'

'How did you know about my album?'

'That's my job. I'm a policeman.'

'Good night.'

He walked away, feeling an extraordinary happiness, but this he would not remember as happiness, as he would remember setting out in the darkness, in the rain, alone.

2/ii

From eight-thirty in the morning until eleven he dealt with a case of petty larceny; there were six witnesses to examine, and he didn't believe a word that any of them said. In European cases there are words one believes and words one distrusts: it is possible to draw a speculative line between the truth and the lies; at least the *cui bono* principle to some extent operates, and it is usually safe to assume, if the accusation is theft and there is no question of insurance, that something has at least been stolen. But here one could make no such assumption: one could draw no lines. He had known police officers whose nerves broke down in the effort to separate a single grain of incontestable truth; they ended, some of them, by striking a witness, they were pilloried in the local Creole papers and were invalided home or transferred. It woke in some men a virulent hatred of a black skin, but Scobie had long ago, during his fifteen years, passed through the dangerous stages; now lost in the tangle of lies he felt an extraordinary affection for these people who paralysed an alien form of justice by so simple a method.

At last the office was clear again. There was nothing further on the charge-sheet, and taking out a pad and placing some blotting-paper under his wrist to catch the sweat, he prepared to write to Louise. Letter-writing never came easily to him. Perhaps because of his police training, he could never put even a comforting lie upon paper over his signature. He had to be accurate: he could comfort only by omission. So now, writing the two words *My dear* upon the paper, he prepared to omit. He wouldn't write that he missed her, but he would leave out any phrase that told unmistakably that he was content. *My dear, you must forgive a short letter again. You know I'm not much of a hand at letter writing. I got your third letter yesterday, the one telling me that you were staying with Mrs Halifax's friend for a week outside Durban. Here everything is quiet. We had an alarm last night, but it turned out that an American pilot had mistaken a school of porpoises for submarines. The rains have started, of course. The Mrs Rolt I told you about in my last letter is out of hospital and they've put her to wait for a boat in one of the Nissen huts behind the transport park. I'll do what I can to make her comfortable. The boy is still in hospital, but all right. I really think that's about all the news. The Tallit affair drags on—I don't think anything will come of it in the end. Ali had to go and have a couple of teeth out the other day. What a fuss he made! I had to drive him to the hospital or he'd never have gone.* He paused: he hated the idea of the censors—who happened to be Mrs Carter and Calloway—reading these last phrases of affection. *Look after yourself, my dear, and don't worry about me. As long as you are happy, I'm happy. In another nine months I can take my leave and we'll be together.* He was going to write, 'You are in my mind always,' but that was not a statement he could sign. He wrote instead, *You are in my mind so often during the day*, and then pondered the signature. Reluctantly, because he believed it would please her, he wrote *Your Ticki*. For a moment he was reminded of that other letter signed 'Dicky' which had come back to him two or three times in dreams.

The sergeant entered, marched to the middle of the floor, turned smartly to face him, saluted. He had time to address the envelope while all this was going on. 'Yes, sergeant?'

'The Commissioner, sah, he ask you to see him.'

'Right.'

The Commissioner was not alone. The Colonial Secretary's face shone gently with sweat in the dusky room, and beside him sat a tall bony man Scobie had not seen before—he must have arrived by air, for there had been no ship in during the last ten days. He wore a colonel's badges as though they didn't belong to him on his loose untidy uniform.

'This is Major Scobie, Colonel Wright.' He could tell the Commissioner was worried and irritated. He said, 'Sit down, Scobie. It's about this Tallit business.' The rain darkened the room and kept out the air. 'Colonel Wright has come up from Cape Town to hear about it.'

'From Cape Town, sir?'

The Commissioner moved his legs, playing with a penknife. He said, 'Colonel Wright is the M.I.5 representative.'

The Colonial Secretary said softly, so that everybody had to bend their heads to hear him, 'The whole thing's been unfortunate.' The Commissioner began to whittle the corner of his desk, ostentatiously not listening. 'I don't think the police should have acted–quite in the way they did–not without consultation.'

Scobie said, 'I've always understood it was our duty to stop diamond smuggling.'

In his soft obscure voice the Colonial Secretary said, 'There weren't a hundred pounds' worth of diamonds found.'

'They are the only diamonds that have ever been found.'

'The evidence against Tallit, Scobie, was too slender for an arrest.'

'He wasn't arrested. He was interrogated.'

'His lawyers say he was brought forcibly to the police station.'

'His lawyers are lying. You surely realise that much.'

The Colonial Secretary said to Colonel Wright, 'You see the kind of difficulty we are up against. The Roman Catholic Syrians are claiming they are a persecuted minority and that the police are in the pay of the Moslem Syrians.'

Scobie said, 'The same thing would have happened the other way round–only it would have been worse. Parliament has more affection for Moslems than Catholics.' He had a sense that no one had mentioned the real purpose of this meeting. The Commissioner flaked chip after chip off his desk, disowning everything, and Colonel Wright sat back on his shoulder-blades saying nothing at all.

'Personally,' the Colonial Secretary said, 'I would always . . .' and the soft voice faded off into inscrutable murmurs which Wright, stuffing his fingers into one ear, leaning his head sideways as though he were trying to hear something through a defective telephone, might possibly have caught.

Scobie said, 'I couldn't hear what you said.'

'I said personally I'd always take Tallit's word against Yusef's.'

'That,' Scobie said, 'is because you have only been in this colony five years.'

Colonel Wright suddenly interjected, 'How many years have you been here, Major Scobie?'

'Fifteen.'

Colonel Wright grunted non-committally.

The Commissioner stopped whittling the corner of his desk and drove his knife viciously into the top. He said, 'Colonel Wright wants to know the source of your information, Scobie.'

'You know that, sir. Yusef.' Wright and the Colonial Secretary sat side by side watching him. He stood back with lowered head, waiting for the next move, but no move came. He knew they were waiting for him to amplify his bald reply, and he knew too that they would take it for a confession of weakness if he did. The silence became more and more intolerable: it was like an accusation. Weeks ago he had told Yusef that he intended to let the Commissioner know the details of his loan; perhaps he had really had that intention, perhaps he had been bluffing; he couldn't remember now. He only knew that now it was too late. That information should have been given before taking action against Tallit: it could not be an afterthought. In the corridor behind the office Fraser passed whistling his favourite tune; he opened the door of the office, said, 'Sorry, sir,' and retreated again, leaving a whiff of warm Zoo smell behind him. The murmur of the rain went on and on. The Commissioner took the knife out of the table and began to whittle again; it was as if, for a second time, he were deliberately disowning the whole business. The Colonial Secretary cleared his throat. 'Yusef,' he repeated.

Scobie nodded.

Colonel Wright said, 'Do you consider Yusef trustworthy?'

'Of course not, sir. But one has to act on what information is available—and this information proved correct up to a point.'

'Up to what point?'

'The diamonds were there.'

The Colonial Secretary said, 'Do you get much information from Yusef?'

'This is the first time I've had any at all.'

He couldn't catch what the Colonial Secretary said beyond the word 'Yusef'.

'I can't hear what you say, sir.'

'I said are you in touch with Yusef?'

'I don't know what you mean by that.'

'Do you see him often?'

'I think in the last three months I have seen him three—no, four times.'

'On business?'

'Not necessarily. Once I gave him a lift home when his car had broken down. Once he came to see me when I had fever at Bamba. Once . . .'

'We are not cross-examining you, Scobie,' the Commissioner said.

'I had an idea, sir, that these gentlemen were.'

Colonel Wright uncrossed his long legs and said, 'Let's boil it down to one question. Tallit, Major Scobie, has made counter-accusations—against the police, against you. He says in effect that Yusef has given you money. Has he?'

'No, sir. Yusef has given me nothing.' He felt an odd relief that he had not yet been called upon to lie.

The Colonial Secretary said, 'Naturally sending your wife to South Africa was well within your private means.' Scobie sat back in his chair, saying nothing. Again he was aware of the hungry silence waiting for his words.

'You don't answer?' the Colonial Secretary said impatiently.

'I didn't know you had asked a question. I repeat—Yusef has given me nothing.'

'He's a man to beware of, Scobie.'

'Perhaps when you have been here as long as I have you'll realise the police are meant to deal with people who are not received at the Secretariat.'

'We don't want our tempers to get warm, do we?'

Scobie stood up. 'Can I go, sir? If these gentlemen have finished with me. . . . I have an appointment.' The sweat stood on his forehead; his heart jumped with fury. This should be the moment of caution, when the blood runs down the flanks and the red cloth waves.

'That's all right, Scobie,' the Commissioner said.

Colonel Wright said, 'You must forgive me for bothering you. I received a report. I had to take the matter up officially. I'm quite satisfied.'

'Thank you, sir.' But the soothing words came too late: the damp face of the Colonial Secretary filled his field of vision. The Colonial Secretary said softly, 'It's just a matter of discretion, that's all.'

'If I'm wanted for the next half an hour, sir,' Scobie said to the Commissioner, 'I shall be at Yusef's.'

2/iii

After all they had forced him to tell a kind of lie: he had no appointment with Yusef. All the same he wanted a few words with Yusef; it was just possible that he might yet clear up, for his own satisfaction, if not legally, the Tallit affair. Driving slowly through the rain–his windscreen wiper had long ceased to function–he saw Harris struggling with his umbrella outside the Bedford Hotel.

'Can I give you a lift? I'm going your way.'

'The most exciting things have been happening,' Harris said. His hollow face shone with rain and enthusiasm. 'I've got a house at last.'

'Congratulations.'

'At least it's not a house: it's one of the huts up your way. But it's a home,' Harris said. 'I'll have to share it, but it's a home.'

'Who sharing it with you?'

'I'm asking Wilson, but he's gone away–to Lagos for a week or two. The damned elusive Pimpernel. Just when I wanted him. And that brings me to the second exciting thing. Do you know I've discovered we were both at Downham?'

'Downham?'

'The school, of course. I went into his room to borrow his ink while he was away, and there on his table I saw a copy of the old *Downhamian.*'

'What a coincidence,' Scobie said.

'And do you know–it's really been a day of extraordinary happenings–I was looking through the magazine and there at the end was a page which said, "The Secretary of the old Downhamian Association would like to get in touch with the following old boys with whom we have lost touch"–and there half-way down was my own name, in print, large as life. What do you think of that?'

'What did you do?'

'Directly I got to the office I sat down and wrote–before I touched a cable, except of course "the most immediates", but then I found I'd forgotten to put down the secretary's address, so back I had to go for the paper. You wouldn't care to come in, would you, and see what I've written?'

'I can't stay long.' Harris had been given an office in a small unwanted room in the Elder Dempster Company's premises. It was the size of an old-fashioned servant's bedroom and this appearance was enhanced by a primitive washbasin with one cold tap and a gas-ring. A table littered with cable forms was squashed between the washbasin and a window no larger than a port-hole which looked straight out on to the water-front and the grey creased bay. An abridged version of *Ivanhoe* for the use of schools, and half a loaf of bread stood in an out-tray. 'Excuse the muddle,' Harris said. 'Take a chair,' but there was no spare chair.

'Where've I put it?' Harris wondered aloud, turning over the cables on his desk, 'Ah, I remember.' He opened *Ivanhoe* and fished out a folded sheet. 'It's only a rough draft,' he said with anxiety. 'Of course I've got to pull it together. I think I'd better keep it back till Wilson comes. You see I've mentioned him.'

Scobie read,

> Dear Secretary,—It was just by chance I came on a copy of the 'Old Downhamian' which another old Downhamian, E. Wilson (1923–1928), had in his room. I'm afraid I've been out of touch with the old place for a great many years and I was very pleased and a bit guilty to see that you have been trying to get into touch with me. Perhaps you'd like to know a bit about what I'm doing in 'the white man's grave', but as I'm a cable censor you will understand that I can't tell you much about my work. That will have to wait till we've won the war. We are in the middle of the rains now—and how it does rain. There's a lot of fever about, but I've only had one dose and E. Wilson has so far escaped altogether. We are sharing a little house together, so that you can feel that old Downhamians even in this wild and distant part stick together. We've got an old Downhamian team of two and go out hunting together but only cockroaches (Ha! Ha!). Well, I must stop now and get on with winning the war. Cheerio to all old Downhamians from quite an old Coaster.

Scobie looking up met Harris's anxious and embarrassed gaze. 'Do you think it's on the right lines?' he asked. 'I was a bit doubtful about "Dear Secretary".'

'I think you've caught the tone admirably.'

'Of course you know it wasn't a very good school, and I wasn't very happy there. In fact I ran away once.'

'And now they've caught up with you.'

'It makes you think, doesn't it?' said Harris. He stared out over the grey water with tears in his bloodshot eyes. 'I've always envied people who were happy there,' he said.

Scobie said consolingly, 'I didn't much care for school myself.'

'To start off happy,' Harris said. 'It must make an awful difference afterwards. Why, it might become a habit, mightn't it?' He took the piece of bread out of the out-tray and dropped it into the wastepaper-basket. 'I always mean to get this place tidied up,' he said.

'Well, I must be going, Harris. I'm glad about the house—and the old Downhamian.'

'I wonder if Wilson was happy there,' Harris brooded. He took *Ivanhoe* out of the out-tray and looked around for somewhere to put it, but there wasn't any place. He put it back again. 'I don't suppose he was,' he said, 'or why should he have turned up here?'

Scobie left his car immediately outside Yusef's door: it was like a gesture of contempt in the face of the Colonial Secretary. He said to the steward, 'I want to see your master. I know the way.'

'Massa out.'

'Then I'll wait for him.' He pushed the steward to one side and walked in. The bungalow was divided into a succession of small rooms identically furnished with sofas and cushions and low tables for drinks like the rooms in a brothel. He passed from one to another, pulling the curtains aside, till he reached the little room where nearly two months ago now he had lost his integrity. On the sofa Yusef lay asleep.

He lay on his back in his white duck trousers with his mouth open, breathing heavily. A glass was on a table at his side, and Scobie noticed the small white grains at the bottom. Yusef had taken a bromide. Scobie sat down at his side and waited. The window was open, but the rain shut out the air as effectively as a curtain. Perhaps it was merely the want of air that caused the depression which now fell on his spirits, perhaps it was because he had returned to the scene of a crime. Useless to tell himself that he had committed no offence. Like a woman who has made a loveless marriage he recognised in the room as anonymous as an hotel bedroom the memory of an adultery.

Just over the window there was a defective gutter which emptied itself like a tap, so that all the time you could hear the two sounds of the rain–the murmur and the gush. Scobie lit a cigarette, watching Yusef. He couldn't feel any hatred of the man. He had trapped Yusef as consciously and as effectively as Yusef had trapped him. The marriage had been made by both of them. Perhaps the intensity of the watch he kept broke through the fog of bromide: the fat thighs shifted on the sofa. Yusef grunted, murmured, 'dear chap' in his deep sleep, and turned on his side, facing Scobie. Scobie stared again round the room, but he had examined it already thoroughly enough when he came here to arrange his loan: there was no change–the same hideous mauve silk cushions, the threads showing where the damp was rotting the covers, the tangerine curtains. Even the blue syphon of soda was in the same place: they had an eternal air like the furnishings of hell. There were no bookshelves, for Yusef couldn't read: no desk because he couldn't write. It would have been useless to search for papers–papers were useless to Yusef. Everything was inside that large Roman head.

'Why – Major Scobie. . . .' The eyes were open and sought his; blurred with bromide they found it difficult to focus.

'Good morning, Yusef.' For once Scobie had him at a disadvantage. For a moment Yusef seemed about to sink again into drugged sleep; then with an effort he got on an elbow.

'I wanted to have a word about Tallit, Yusef.'

'Tallit . . . forgive me, Major Scobie. . . .'

'And the diamonds.'

'Crazy about diamonds,' Yusef brought out with difficulty in a voice halfway to sleep. He shook his head, so that the white lick of hair flapped; then putting out a vague hand he stretched for the syphon.

'Did you frame Tallit, Yusef?'

Yusef dragged the syphon towards him across the table, knocking over the bromide glass; he turned the nozzle towards his face and pulled the trigger. The soda water broke on his face and splashed all round him on the mauve silk. He gave a sigh of relief and satisfaction, like a man under a shower on a hot day. 'What is it, Major Scobie, is anything wrong?'

'Tallit is not going to be prosecuted.'

He was like a tired man dragging himself out of the sea: the tide followed him. He said, 'You must forgive me, Major Scobie. I have not been sleeping well.' He shook his head up and down thoughtfully, as a man might shake a box to see whether anything rattles. 'You were saying something about Tallit, Major Scobie,' and he explained again, 'It is the stocktaking. All the figures. Three four stores. They try to cheat me because it's all in my head.'

'Tallit,' Scobie repeated, 'won't be prosecuted.'

'Never mind. One day he will go too far.'

'Were they your diamonds, Yusef?'

'My diamonds? They have made you suspicious of me, Major Scobie.'

'Was the small boy in your pay?'

Yusef mopped the soda water off his face with the back of his hand. 'Of course he was, Major Scobie. That was where I got my information.'

The moment of inferiority had passed; the great head had shaken itself free of the bromide, even though the limbs still lay sluggishly spread over the sofa. 'Yusef, I'm not your enemy. I have a liking for you.'

'When you say that, Major Scobie, how my heart beats.' He pulled his shirt wider, as though to show the actual movement of the heart and little streams of soda water irrigated the black bush on his chest. 'I am too fat,' he said.

'I would like to trust you, Yusef. Tell me the truth. Were the diamonds yours or Tallit's?'

'I always want to speak the truth to you, Major Scobie. I never told you the diamonds were Tallit's.'

'They were yours?'

'Yes, Major Scobie.'

'What a fool you have made of me, Yusef. If only I had a witness here, I'd run you in.'

'I didn't mean to make a fool of you, Major Scobie. I wanted Tallit sent away. It would be for the good of everybody if he was sent away. It is no good the Syrians being in two parties. If they were in one party you would be able to come to me and say, "Yusef, the Government wants the Syrians to do this or that," and I should be able to answer, "It shall be so."'

'And the diamond smuggling would be in one pair of hands.'

'Oh, the diamonds, diamonds, diamonds,' Yusef wearily complained. 'I tell you, Major Scobie, that I make more money in one year from my smallest store than I would make in three years from diamonds. You cannot understand how many bribes are necessary.'

'Well, Yusef, I'm taking no more information from you. This ends our relationship. Every month, of course, I shall send you the interest.' He felt a strange unreality in his own words: the tangerine curtains hung there immovably. There are certain places one never leaves behind; the curtains and cushions of this room joined an attic bedroom, an ink-stained desk, a lacy altar in Ealing–they would be there so long as consciousness lasted.

Yusef put his feet on the floor and sat bolt upright. He said, 'Major Scobie, you have taken my little joke too much to heart.'

'Good-bye, Yusef, you aren't a bad chap, but good-bye.'

'You are wrong, Major Scobie. I am a bad chap.' He said earnestly, 'My friendship for you is the only good thing in this black heart. I cannot give it up. We must stay friends always.'

'I'm afraid not, Yusef.'

'Listen, Major Scobie. I am not asking you to do anything for me except sometimes–after dark perhaps when nobody can see–to visit me and talk to me. Nothing else. Just that. I will tell you no more tales about Tallit. I will tell you nothing. We will sit here with the syphon and the whisky bottle. . . .'

'I'm not a fool, Yusef. I know it would be of great use to you if people believed we were friends. I'm not giving you that help.'

Yusef put a finger in his ear and cleared it of soda water. He looked bleakly and brazenly across at Scobie. This must be how he looks, Scobie thought, at the store manager who has tried to deceive him about the figures he carries in his head. 'Major Scobie, did you ever tell the Commissioner about our little business arrangement or was that all bluff?'

'Ask him yourself.'

'I think I will. My heart feels rejected and bitter. It urges me to go to the Commissioner and tell him everything.'

'Always obey your heart, Yusef.'

'I will tell him you took my money and together we planned the arrest of Tallit. But you did not fulfil your bargain, so I have come to him in revenge. In revenge,' Yusef repeated gloomily, his Roman head sunk on his fat chest.

'Go ahead. Do what you like, Yusef.' But he couldn't believe in any of this scene however hard he played it. It was like a lovers' quarrel. He couldn't believe in Yusef's threats and he had no belief in his own calmness: he did not even believe in this good-bye. What had happened in the mauve and orange room had been too important to become part of the enormous equal past. He was not surprised when Yusef, lifting his head, said, 'Of course I shall not go. One day you will come back and want my friendship. And I shall welcome you.'

Shall I really be so desperate? Scobie wondered, as though in the Syrian's voice he had heard the genuine accent of prophecy.

On his way home Scobie stopped his car outside the Catholic church and went in. It was the first Saturday of the month and he always went to confession on that day. Half a dozen old women, their hair bound like char-women's in dusters, waited their turn: a nursing sister: a private soldier with a Royal Ordnance insignia. Father Rank's voice whispered monotonously from the box.

Scobie, with his eyes fixed on the cross, prayed–the Our Father, the Hail Mary, the Act of Contrition. The awful languor of routine fell on his spirits. He felt like a spectator–one of those many people round the cross over whom the gaze of Christ must have passed, seeking the face of a friend or an enemy. It sometimes seemed to him that his profession and his uniform classed him inexorably with all those anonymous Romans keeping order in the streets a long way off. One by one the old Kru women passed into the box and out again, and Scobie prayed–vaguely and ramblingly–for Louise, that she might be happy now at this moment and so remain, that no evil should ever come to her through him. The soldier came out of the box and he rose.

'In the name of the Father, the Son and the Holy Ghost.' He said, 'Since my last confession a month ago I have missed one Sunday Mass and one holiday of obligation.'

'Were you prevented from going?'

'Yes, but with a little effort I could have arranged my duties better.'

'Yes?'

'All through this month I have done the minimum. I've been unnecessarily harsh to one of my men. . . .' He paused a long time.

'Is that everything?'

'I don't know how to put it, Father, but I feel–tired of my religion. It seems to mean nothing to me. I've tried to love God, but—' he made a gesture which the priest could not see, turned sideways through the grille. 'I'm not sure that I even believe.'

'It's easy,' the priest said, 'to worry too much about that. Especially here. The penance I would give to a lot of people if I could is six months' leave. The climate gets you down. It's easy to mistake tiredness for–well, disbelief.'

'I don't want to keep you, Father. There are other people waiting. I know these are just fancies. But I feel–empty. Empty.'

'That's sometimes the moment God chooses,' the priest said. 'Now go along with you and say a decade of your rosary.'

'I haven't a rosary. At least . . .'

'Well, five Our Fathers and five Hail Marys then.' He began to speak the words of absolution, but the trouble is, Scobie thought, there's nothing to absolve. The words brought no sense of relief because there was nothing to relieve. They were a formula: the Latin words hustled together–a hocus pocus. He went out of the box and knelt down again, and this too was part of a routine. It seemed to him for a moment that God was too accessible. There was no difficulty in approaching Him. Like a popular demagogue He was open to the least of His followers at any hour. Looking up at the cross he thought, He even suffers in public.

3/i

'I've brought you some stamps,' Scobie said. 'I've been collecting them for a week—from everybody. Even Mrs Carter has contributed a magnificent parrakeet—look at it—from somewhere in South America. And here's a complete set of Liberians surcharged for the American occupation. I got those from the Naval Observer.'

They were completely at ease: it seemed to both of them for that very reason they were safe.

'Why do you collect stamps?' he asked. 'It's an odd thing to do—after sixteen.'

'I don't know,' Helen Rolt said. 'I don't really collect. I carry them round. I suppose it's habit.' She opened the album and said, 'No, it's not just habit. I do love the things. Do you see this green George V halfpenny stamp? It's the first I ever collected. I was eight. I steamed it off an envelope and stuck it in a notebook. That's why my father gave me an album. My mother had died, so he gave me a stamp-album.'

She tried to explain more exactly. 'They are like snap-shots. They are so portable. People who collect china—they can't carry it around with them. Or books. But you don't have to tear the pages out like you do with snap-shots.'

'You've never told me about your husband,' Scobie said.

'No.'

'It's not really much good tearing out a page because you can see the place where it's been torn?'

'Yes.'

'It's easier to get over a thing,' Scobie said, 'If you talk about it.'

'That's not the trouble,' she said. 'The trouble is—it's so terribly easy to get over.' She took him by surprise; he hadn't believed she was old enough to have reached that stage in her lessons, that particular turn of the screw. She said, 'He's been dead—how long—is it eight weeks yet? and he's so dead, so completely dead. What a little bitch I must be.'

Scobie said, 'You needn't feel that. It's the same with everybody, I think. When we say to someone, "I can't live without you," what we really mean is, "I can't live feeling you may be in pain, unhappy, in want." That's all it is. When they are dead our responsibility ends. There's nothing more we can do about it. We can rest in peace.'

'I didn't know I was so tough,' Helen said. 'Horribly tough.'

'I had a child,' Scobie said, 'who died. I was out here. My wife sent me two cables from Bexhill, one at five in the evening and one at six, but they mixed up the order. You see she meant to break the thing gently. I got one cable just after breakfast. It was eight o'clock in the morning—a dead time of day for any news.' He had never mentioned this before to anyone, not even to Louise. Now he brought out the exact words of each cable, carefully. 'The cable said, *Catherine died this afternoon no pain God bless you*. The second cable came at lunch-time. It said, *Catherine seriously ill. Doctor has hope my diving*. That was the one sent off at five. "Diving" was a mutilation–I suppose for "darling". You see there was nothing more hopeless she could have put to break the news than "doctor has hope".'

'How terrible for you,' Helen said.

'No, the terrible thing was that when I got the second telegram, I was so muddled in my head, I thought, there's been a mistake. She must be still alive. For a moment until I realised what had happened, I was– disappointed. That was the terrible thing. I thought "now the anxiety begins, and the pain", but when I realised what had happened, then it was all right, she was dead, I could begin to forget her.'

'Have you forgotten her?'

'I don't remember her often. You see, I escaped seeing her die. My wife had that.'

It was astonishing to him how easily and quickly they had become friends. They came together over two deaths without reserve. She said, 'I don't know what I'd have done without you.'

'Everybody would have looked after you.'

'I think they are scared of me,' she said.

He laughed.

'They are. Flight-Lieutenant Bagster took me to the beach this afternoon, but he was scared. Because I'm not happy and because of my husband. Everybody on the beach was pretending to be happy about something, and I sat there grinning and it didn't work. Do you remember when you went to your first party and coming up the stairs you heard all the voices and you didn't know how to talk to people? That's how I felt, so I sat and grinned in Mrs Carter's bathing-dress, and Bagster stroked my leg, and I wanted to go home.'

'You'll be going home soon.'

'I don't mean *that* home. I mean here, where I can shut the door and not answer when they knock. I don't want to go away yet.'

'But surely you aren't happy here?'

'I'm so afraid of the sea,' she said.

'Do you dream about it?'

'No. I dream of John sometimes–that's worse. Because I've always had bad dreams of him, and I still have bad dreams of him. I mean we were always quarrelling in the dreams and we still go on quarrelling.'

'Did you quarrel?'

'No. He was sweet to me. We were only married a month, you know. It would be easy being sweet as long as that, wouldn't it? When this happened I hadn't really had time to know my way around.' It seemed to Scobie that she had never known her way around–at least not since she had left her netball team; was it a year ago? Sometimes he saw her lying back in the boat on that oily featureless sea, day after day, with the other child near death and the sailor going mad, and Miss Malcott, and the chief engineer who felt his responsibility to the owners, and sometimes he saw her carried past him on a stretcher grasping her stamp-album, and now he saw her in the borrowed un-becoming bathing-dress grinning at Bagster as he stroked her legs, listening to the laughter and the splashes, not knowing the adult etiquette. . . . Sadly like an evening tide he felt responsibility bearing him up the shore.

'You've written to your father?'

'Oh yes, of course. He cabled that he's pulling strings about the passage. I don't know what strings he can pull from Bury, poor dear. He doesn't know anybody at all. He cabled too about John, of course.' She lifted a cushion off the chair and pulled the cable out. 'Read it. He's very sweet, but of course he doesn't know a thing about me.'

Scobie read, *Terribly grieved for you, dear child, but remember his happiness, Your loving father.* The date stamp with the Bury mark made him aware of the enormous distance between father and child. He said, 'How do you mean, he doesn't know a thing?'

'You see, he believes in God and heaven, all that sort of thing.'

'You don't?'

'I gave up all that when I left school. John used to pull his leg about it, quite gently you know. Father didn't mind. But he never knew I felt the way John did. If you are a clergyman's daughter there are a lot of things you have to pretend about. He would have hated knowing that John and I went together, oh, a fortnight before we married.'

Again he had that vision of someone who didn't know her way around: no wonder Bagster was scared of her. Bagster was not a man to accept responsibility, and how could anyone lay the responsibility for any action, he thought, on this stupid bewildered child? He turned over the little pile of stamps he had accumulated for her and said, 'I wonder what you'll do when you get home?'

'I suppose,' she said, 'they'll conscript me.'

He thought: If my child had lived, she too would have been conscriptable, flung into some grim dormitory, to find her own way. After the Atlantic, the A.T.S. or the W.A.A.F., the blustering sergeant with the big bust, the cook-house and the potato peelings, the Lesbian officer with the thin lips and the tidy gold hair, and the men waiting on the Common outside the camp, among the gorse bushes . . . compared to that surely even the Atlantic was more a home. He said, 'Haven't you got any shorthand? any languages?' Only the clever and the astute and the influential escaped in war.

'No,' she said, 'I'm not really any good at anything.'

It was impossible to think of her being saved from the sea and then flung back like a fish that wasn't worth catching.

He said, 'Can you type?'

'I can get along quite fast with one finger.'

'You could get a job here, I think. We are very short of secretaries. All the wives, you know, are working in the secretariat, and we still haven't enough. But it's a bad climate for a woman.'

'I'd like to stay. Let's have a drink on it.' She called, 'Boy, boy.'

'You are learning,' Scobie said. 'A week ago you were so frightened of him . . .' The boy came in with a tray set out with glasses, limes, water, a new gin bottle.

'This isn't the boy I talked to,' Scobie said.

'No, that one went. You talked to him too fiercely.'

'And this one came?'

'Yes.'

'What's your name, boy?'

'Vande, sah.'

'I've seen you before, haven't I?'

'No, sah.'

'Who am I?'

'You big policeman, sah.'

'Don't frighten this one away,' Helen said.

'Who were you with?'

'I was with D.C. Pemberton up bush, sah. I was small boy.'

'Is that where I saw you?' Scobie said. 'I suppose I did. You look after this missus well now, and when she goes home, I get you big job. Remember that.'

'Yes, sah.'

'You haven't looked at the stamps,' Scobie said.

'No, I haven't, have I?' A spot of gin fell upon one of the stamps and stained it. He watched her pick it out of the pile, taking in the straight hair falling in rats' tails over the nape as though the Atlantic had taken the strength out of it for ever, the hollowed face. It seemed to him that he had not felt so much at ease with another human being for years–not since Louise was young. But this case was different, he told himself: they were safe with each other. He was more than thirty years the older; his body in this climate had lost the sense of lust; he watched her with sadness and affection and enormous pity because a time would come when he couldn't show her around in a world where she was at sea. When she turned and the light fell on her face she looked ugly, with the temporary ugliness of a child. The ugliness was like handcuffs on his wrists.

He said, 'That stamp's spoilt. I'll get you another.'

'Oh no,' she said, 'it goes in as it is. I'm not a real collector.'

He had no sense of responsibility towards the beautiful and the graceful and the intelligent. They could find their own way. It was the face for which nobody would go out of his way, the face that would never catch the covert look, the face which would soon be used to rebuffs and indifference that demanded his allegiance. The word 'pity' is used as loosely as the word 'love': the terrible promiscuous passion which so few experience.

She said, 'You see, whenever I see that stain I'll see this room. . . .'

'Then it's like a snapshot.'

'You can pull a stamp out,' she said with a terrible youthful clarity, 'and you don't know that it's ever been there.' She turned suddenly to him and said, 'It's so good to talk to you. I can say anything I like. I'm not afraid of hurting you. You don't want anything out of me. I'm safe.'

'We're both safe.' The rain surrounded them, falling regularly on the iron roof.

She said, 'I have a feeling that you'd never let me down.' The words came to him like a command he would have to obey however difficult. Her hands were full of the absurd scraps of paper he had brought her. She said, 'I'll keep these always. I'll never have to pull these out.'

Somebody knocked on the door and a voice said, 'Freddie Bagster. It's only me. Freddie Bagster,' cheerily.

'Don't answer,' she whispered, 'don't answer.' She put her arm in his and watched the door with her mouth a little open as though she were out of breath. He had the sense of an animal which had been chased to its hole.

'Let Freddie in,' the voice wheedled. 'Be a sport, Helen. Only Freddie Bagster.' The man was a little drunk.

She stood pressed against him with her hand on his side. When the sound of Bagster's feet receded, she raised her mouth and they kissed. What they had both thought was safety proved to have been the camouflage of an enemy who works in terms of friendship, trust and pity.

3/ii

The rain poured steadily down, turning the little patch of reclaimed ground on which his house stood back into swamp again. The window of his room blew to and fro. At some time during the night the catch had been broken by a squall of wind. Now the rain had blown in, his dressing-table was soaking wet, and there was a pool of water on the floor. His alarm clock pointed to 4.25. He felt as though he had returned to a house that had been abandoned years ago. It would not have surprised him to find cobwebs over the mirror, the mosquito-net hanging in shreds and the dirt of mice upon the floor.

He sat down on a chair and the water drained off his trousers and made a second pool around his mosquito-boots. He had left his umbrella behind, setting out on his walk home with an odd jubilation, as though he had rediscovered something he had lost, something which belonged to his youth. In the wet and noisy darkness he had even lifted his voice and tried out a line from Fraser's song, but his voice was tuneless. Now somewhere between the Nissen hut and home he had mislaid his joy.

At four in the morning he had woken. Her head lay in his side and he could feel her hair against his breast. Putting his hand outside the net he found the light. She lay in the odd cramped attitude of someone who has been shot in escaping. It seemed to him for a moment even then, before his tenderness and pleasure awoke, that he was looking at a bundle of cannon fodder. The first words she said when the light had roused her were, 'Bagster can go to hell.'

'Were you dreaming?'

She said, 'I dreamed I was lost in a marsh and Bagster found me.'

He said, 'I've got to go. If we sleep now, we shan't wake again till it's light.' He began to think for both of them, carefully. Like a criminal he began to fashion in his own mind the undetectable crime: he planned the moves ahead: he embarked for the first time in his life on the long legalistic arguments of deceit. If so-and-so . . . then that follows. He said, 'What time does your boy turn up?'

'About six I think. I don't know. He calls me at seven.'

'Ali starts boiling my water about a quarter to six. I'd better go.' He looked carefully everywhere for signs of his presence: he straightened a mat and hesitated over an ash-tray. Then at the end of it all he had left his umbrella standing against the wall. It seemed to him the typical action of a criminal. When the rain reminded him of it, it was too late to go back. He would have to hammer on her door, and already in one hut a light had gone on. Standing in his own room with a mosquito-boot in his hand, he thought wearily and drearily, In future I must do better than that.

In the future–that was where the sadness lay. Was it the butterfly that died in the act of love? But human beings were condemned to consequences. The responsibility as well as the guilt was his–he was not a Bagster: he knew what he was about. He had sworn to preserve Louise's happiness, and now he had accepted another and contradictory responsibility. He felt tired by all the lies he would some time have to tell; he felt the wounds of those victims who had not yet bled. Lying back on the pillow he started sleeplessly out towards the grey early morning tide. Somewhere on the face of those obscure waters moved the sense of yet another wrong and another victim, not Louise, nor Helen.

PART II

I / i

'There. What do you think of it?' Harris asked with ill-concealed pride. He stood in the doorway of the hut while Wilson moved cautiously forward between the brown sticks of Government furniture like a setter through stubble.

'Better than the hotel,' Wilson said cautiously, pointing his muzzle towards a Government easy-chair.

'I thought I'd give you a surprise when you got back from Lagos.' Harris had curtained the Nissen hut into three: a bedroom for each of them and a common sitting room. 'There's only one point that worries me. I'm not sure whether there are any cockroaches.'

'Well, we only played the game to get rid of them.'

'I know, but it seems almost a pity, doesn't it?'

'Who are our neighbours?'

'There's Mrs Rolt who was submarined, and there are two chaps in the Department of Works, and somebody called Clive from the Agricultural Department, Boling, who's in charge of Sewage–they all seem a nice friendly lot. And Scobie, of course, is just down the road.'

'Yes.'

Wilson moved restlessly around the hut and came to a stop in front of a photograph which Harris had propped against a Government inkstand. It showed three long rows of boys on a lawn: the first row sitting cross-legged on the grass: the second on chairs, wearing high stiff collars, with an elderly man and two women (one had a squint) in the centre: the third row standing. Wilson said, 'That woman with a squint–I could swear I'd seen her somewhere before.'

'Does the name Snakey convey anything to you?'

'Why, yes, of course.' He looked closer. 'So you were at that hole too?'

'I saw *The Downhamian* in your room and I fished this out to surprise you. I was in Jagger's house. Where were you?'

'I was a Prog,' Wilson said.

'Oh well,' Harris admitted in a tone of disappointment, 'there were some good chaps among the Progs.' He laid the photograph flat down again as though it were something that hadn't quite come off. 'I was thinking we might have an old Downhamian dinner.'

'Whatever for?' Wilson asked. 'There are only two of us.'

'We could invite a guest each.'

'I don't see the point.'

Harris said bitterly, 'Well, you are the real Downhamian, not me. I never joined the association. You get the magazine. I thought perhaps you had an interest in the place.'

'My father made me a life member and he always forwards the bloody paper,' Wilson said abruptly.

'It was lying beside your bed. I thought you'd been reading it.'

'I may have glanced at it.'

'There was a bit about me in it. They wanted my address.'

'Oh, but you know why that is?' Wilson said. 'They are sending out appeals to any old Downhamian they can rake up. The panelling in the Founders' Hall is in need of repair. I'd keep your address quiet if I were you.' He was one of those, it seemed to Harris, who always knew what was on, who gave advance information on extra halves, who knew why old So-and-So had not turned up to school, and what the row brewing at the Head's special meeting was about. A few weeks ago he had been a new boy whom Harris had been delighted to befriend, to show around. He remembered the evening when Wilson would have put on evening dress for a Syrian's dinner-party if he hadn't been warned. But Harris from his first year at school had been fated to see how quickly new boys grew up: one term he was their kindly mentor—the next he was discarded. He could never progress as quickly as the newest unlicked boy. He remembered how even in the cockroach game—that *he* had invented—his rules had been challenged on the first evening. He said sadly, 'I expect you are right. Perhaps I won't send a letter after all.' He added humbly, 'I took the bed on this side, but I don't mind a bit which I have. . . .'

'Oh, that's all right,' Wilson said.

'I've only engaged one steward. I thought we could save a bit by sharing.'

'The less boys we have knocking about here the better,' Wilson said.

That night was the first night of their new comradeship. They sat reading on their twin Government chairs behind the black-out curtains. On the table was a bottle of whisky for Wilson and a bottle of barley-water flavoured with lime for Harris. A sense of extraordinary peace came to Harris while the rain tingled steadily on the roof and Wilson read a Wallace. Occasionally a few drunks from the R.A.F. mess passed by, shouting or revving their cars, but this only enhanced the sense of peace inside the hut. Sometimes his eyes strayed to the walls seeking a cockroach, but you couldn't have everything.

'Have you got *The Downhamian* handy, old man? I wouldn't mind another glance at it. This book's so dull.'

'There's a new one unopened on the dressing-table.'

'You don't mind my opening it?'

'Why the hell should I?'

Harris turned first to the old Downhamian notes and read again how the whereabouts of H.R.Harris (1917–1921) was still wanted. He wondered whether it was possible that Wilson was wrong: there was no word here about the panelling in Hall. Perhaps after all he would send that letter and he pictured the reply he might receive from the Secretary. *My dear Harris*, it would go something like that, *we were all delighted to receive your letter from those romantic parts. Why not send us a full length contribution to the mag. and while I'm writing to you, what about membership of the Old Downhamian Association? I notice you've never joined. I'm speaking for all Old Downhamians when I say that we'll be glad to welcome you.* He tried out 'proud to welcome you' on his tongue, but rejected that. He was a realist.

The Downhamians had had a fairly successful Christmas term. They had beaten Harpenden by one goal, Merchant Taylors by two, and had drawn with Lancing. Ducker and Tierney were coming on well as forwards, but the scrum was still slow in getting the ball out. He turned a page and read how the Opera Society had given an excellent rendering of *Patience* in the Founders' Hall. F.J.K., who was obviously the English master, wrote:

> Lane as Bunthorne displayed a degree of æstheticism which surprised all his companions of Vb. We would not hitherto have described his hand as mediæval or associated him with lilies, but he persuaded us that we had misjudged him. A great performance, Lane.

Harris skimmed through the account of five matches, a fantasy called 'The Tick of the Clock' beginning *There was once a little old lady whose most beloved possession. . . .* The walls of Downham–the red brick laced with yellow, the extraordinary crockets, the mid-Victorian gargoyles–rose around him: boots beat on stone stairs and a cracked dinner-bell rang to rouse him to another miserable day. He felt the loyalty we feel to unhappiness–the sense that that is where we really belong. His eyes filled with tears, he took a sip of his barley-water and thought, 'I'll post that letter whatever Wilson says.' Somebody outside shouted, 'Bagster. Where are you, Bagster, you sod?' and stumbled in a ditch. He might have been back at Downham, except of course that they wouldn't have used *that* word.

Harris turned a page or two and the title of a poem caught his eye. It was called 'West Coast' and it was dedicated to 'L.S.'. He wasn't very keen on poetry, but it struck him as interesting that somewhere on this enormous coastline of sand and smells there existed a third old Downhamian.

> *Another Tristram on this distant coast*, he read
> *Raises the poisoned chalice to his lips,*
> *Another Mark upon the palm-fringed shore*
>   *Watches his love's eclipse.*

It seemed to Harris obscure: his eye passed rapidly over the intervening verses to the initials at the foot: E.W. He nearly exclaimed aloud, but he restrained himself in time. In such close quarters as they now shared it was necessary to be circumspect. There wasn't space to quarrel in. Who is L. S., he wondered, and thought, surely it can't be . . . the very idea crinkled his lips in a cruel smile. He said, 'There's not much in the mag. We beat Harpenden. There's a poem called West Coast. Another poor devil out here, I suppose.'

'Oh.'

'Lovelorn,' Harris said. 'But I don't read poetry.'

'Nor do I,' Wilson lied behind the barrier of the Wallace.

I /ii

It had been a very narrow squeak. Wilson lay on his back in bed and listened to the rain on the roof and the heavy breathing of the old Downhamian beyond the curtain. It was as if the hideous years had extended through the intervening mist to surround him again. What madness had induced him to send that poem to the Downhamian? But it wasn't madness: he had long since become incapable of anything so honest as madness: he was one of those condemned in childhood to complexity. He knew what he had intended to do: to cut the poem out with no indication of its source and to send it to Louise. It wasn't quite her sort of poem, he knew, but surely, he had argued, she would be impressed to some extent by the mere fact that the poem was in print. If she asked him where it had appeared, it would be easy to invent some convincing coterie name. The *Downhamian* luckily was well printed and on good paper. It was true, of course, that he would have to paste the cutting on opaque paper to disguise what was printed on the other side, but it would be easy to think up an explanation of that. It was as if his profession were slowly absorbing his whole life, just as school had done. His profession was to lie, to have the quick story ready, never to give himself away, and his private life was taking the same pattern. He lay on his back in a nausea of self-disgust.

The rain had momentarily stopped. It was one of those cool intervals that were the consolation of the sleepless. In Harris's heavy dreams the rain went on. Wilson got softly out and mixed himself a bromide; the grains fizzed in the bottom of the glass and Harris spoke hoarsely and turned over behind the curtain. Wilson flashed his torch on his watch and read 2.25. Tiptoeing to the door so as not to waken Harris, he felt the little sting of a jigger under his toe-nail. In the morning he must get his boy to scoop it out. He stood on the small cement pavement above the marshy ground and let the cool air play on him with his pyjama jacket flapping open. All the huts were in darkness, and the moon was patched with the rain-clouds coming up. He was going to turn away when he heard someone stumble a few yards away and he flashed his torch. It lit on a man's bowed back moving between the huts towards the road. 'Scobie,' Wilson exclaimed and the man turned.

'Hullo, Wilson,' Scobie said, 'I didn't know you lived up here.'

'I'm sharing with Harris,' Wilson said, watching the man who had watched his tears.

'I've been taking a walk,' Scobie said unconvincingly, 'I couldn't sleep.' It seemed to Wilson that Scobie was still a novice in the world of deceit: he hadn't lived in it since childhood, and he felt an odd elderly envy for Scobie, much as an old lag might envy the young crook serving his first sentence, to whom all this was new.

I /iii

Wilson sat in his little stuffy room in the U.A.C. office. Several of the firm's journals and day books bound in quarter pigskin formed a barrier between him and the door. Surreptitiously, like a schoolboy using a crib, Wilson behind the barrier worked at his code books, translating a cable. A commercial calendar showed a week old date—June 20, and a motto: *The best investments are honesty and enterprise. William P. Cornforth.* A clerk knocked and said, 'There's a nigger for you, Wilson, with a note.'

'Who from?'

'He says Brown.'

'Keep him a couple of minutes, there's a good chap, and then boot him in.' However diligently Wilson practised, the slang phrase sounded unnaturally on his lips. He folded up the cable and stuck it in the code book to keep his place: then he put the cable and the code book in the safe and pulled the door to. Pouring himself out a glass of water he looked out on the street; the mammies, their heads tied up in bright cotton cloths, passed under their coloured umbrellas. Their shapeless cotton gowns fell to the ankle: one with a design of match-boxes: another with kerosene lamps: the third—the latest from Manchester—covered with mauve cigarette-lighters on a yellow ground. Naked to the waist a young girl passed gleaming through the rain and Wilson watched her out of sight with melancholy lust. He swallowed and turned as the door opened.

'Shut the door.'

The boy obeyed. He had apparently put on his best clothes for this morning call: a white cotton shirt fell outside his white shorts. His gym shoes were immaculate in spite of the rain, except that his toes protruded.

'You small boy at Yusef's?'

'Yes, sah.'

'You got a message,' Wilson said, 'from my boy. He tell you what I want, eh? He's your young brother, isn't he?'

'Yes, sah.'

'Same father?'

'Yes, sah.'

'He says you good boy, honest. You want to be a steward, eh?'

'Yes, sah.'

'Can you read?'

'No, sah.'

'Write?'

'No, sah.'

'You got eyes in your head? Good ears? You see everything? You hear everything?' The boy grinned—a gash of white in the smooth grey elephant hide of his face: he had a look of sleek intelligence. Intelligence, to Wilson, was more valuable than honesty. Honesty was a double-edged weapon, but intelligence looked after number one. Intelligence realised that a Syrian might one day go home to his own land, but the English stayed. Intelligence knew that it was a good thing to work for Government, whatever the Government. 'How much you get as small boy?'

'Ten shillings.'

'I pay you five shillings more. If Yusef sack you I pay you ten shillings. If you stay with Yusef one year and give me good information–true information–no lies, I give you job as steward with white man. Understand?'

'Yes, sah.'

'If you give me lies, then you go to prison. Maybe they shoot you. I don't know. I don't care. Understand?'

'Yes, sah.'

'Every day you see your brother at meat market. You tell him who comes to Yusef's house. Tell him where Yusef goes. You tell him any strange boys who come to Yusef's house. You no tell lies, you tell truth. No humbug. If no one comes to Yusef's house you say no one. You no make big lie. If you tell lie, I know it and you go to prison straight away.' The wearisome recital went on. He was never quite sure how much was understood. The sweat ran off Wilson's forehead and the cool contained grey face of the boy aggravated him like an accusation he couldn't answer. 'You go to prison and you stay in prison plenty long time.' He could hear his own voice cracking with the desire to impress; he could hear himself, like the parody of a white man on the halls. He said, 'Scobie? Do you know Major Scobie?'

'Yes, sah. He very good man, sah.' They were the first words apart from yes and no the boy had uttered.

'You see him at your master's?'

'Yes, sah.'

'How often?'

'Once, twice, sah.'

'He and your master–they are friends?'

'My master he think Major Scobie very good man, sah.' The reiteration of the phrase angered Wilson. He broke furiously out, 'I don't want to hear whether he's good or not. I want to know where he meets Yusef, see? What do they talk about? You bring them in drinks some time when steward's busy? What do you hear?'

'Last time they have big palaver,' the boy brought ingratiatingly out, as if he were showing a corner of his wares.

'I bet they did. I want to know all about their palaver.'

'When Major Scobie go away one time, my master he put pillow right on his face.'

'What on earth do you mean by that?'

The boy folded his arms over his eyes in a gesture of great dignity and said, 'His eyes make pillow wet.'

'Good God,' Wilson said, 'what an extraordinary thing.'

'Then he drink plenty whisky and go to sleep–ten, twelve hours. Then he go to his store in Bond Street and make plenty hell.'

'Why?'

'He say they humbug him.'

'What's that got to do with Major Scobie?'

The boy shrugged. As so many times before Wilson had the sense of a door closed in his face; he was always on the outside of the door.

When the boy had gone he opened his safe again, moving the knob of the combination first left to 32–his age, secondly right to 10, the year of his birth, left again to 65, the number of his home in Western Avenue, Pinner, and took out the code books. 32946 78523 97042. Row after row of groups swam before his eyes. The telegram was headed Important, or he would have postponed the decoding till the evening. He knew how little important it really was–the usual ship had left Lobito carrying the usual suspects–diamonds, diamonds, diamonds. When he had decoded the telegram he would hand it to the long-suffering Commissioner, who had already probably received the same information or contradictory information from S.O.E. or one of the other secret organisations which took root on the coast like mangroves. *Leave alone but do not repeat not pinpoint P. Ferreira passenger 1st class repeat P. Ferreira passenger 1st class.* Ferreira was presumably an agent his organisation had recruited on board. It was quite possible that the Commissioner would receive simultaneously a message from Colonel Wright that P. Ferreira was suspected of carrying diamonds and should be rigorously searched. 72391 87052 63847 92034. How did one simultaneously leave alone, not repeat not pinpoint, and rigorously search Mr Ferreira? That luckily was not his worry. Perhaps it was Scobie who would suffer any headache there was.

Again he went to the window for a glass of water and again he saw the same girl pass. Or maybe it was not the same girl. He watched the water trickling down between the two thin wing-like shoulder-blades. He remembered there was a time when he had not noticed a black skin. He felt as though he had passed years and not months on this coast, all the years between puberty and manhood.

I /iv

'Going out?' Harris asked with surprise. 'Where to?'

'Just into town,' Wilson said, loosening the knot round his mosquito-boots.

'What on earth can you find to do in town at this hour?'

'Business,' Wilson said.

Well, he thought, it was business of a kind, the kind of joyless business one did alone, without friends. He had bought a second-hand car a few weeks ago, the first he had ever owned, and he was not yet a very reliable driver. No gadget survived the climate long and every few hundred yards he had to wipe the windscreen with his handkerchief. In Kru town the hut doors were open and families sat around the kerosene lamps waiting till it was cool enough to sleep. A dead pye-dog lay in the gutter with the rain running over its white swollen belly. He drove in second gear at little more than a walking pace, for civilian head-lamps had to be blacked out to the size of a visiting-card and he couldn't see more than fifteen paces ahead. It took him ten minutes to reach the great cotton tree near the police station. There were no lights on in any of the officer's rooms and he left his car outside the main entrance. If anyone saw it there they would assume he was inside. For a moment he sat with the door open hesitating. The image of the girl passing in the rain conflicted with the sight of Harris on his shoulder-blades reading a book with a glass of squash at his elbow. He thought sadly, as lust won the day, what a lot of trouble it was; the sadness of the after-taste fell upon his spirits beforehand.

He had forgotten to bring his umbrella and he was wet through before he had walked a dozen yards down the hill. It was the passion of curiosity more than of lust that impelled him now. Some time or another if one lived in a place one must try the local product. It was like having a box of chocolates shut in a bedroom drawer. Until the box was empty it occupied the mind too much. He thought: when this is over I shall be able to write another poem to Louise.

The brothel was a tin-roofed bungalow half-way down the hill on the right-hand side. In the dry season the girls sat outside in the gutter like sparrows; they chatted with the policeman on duty at the top of the hill. The road was never made up, so that nobody drove by the brothel on the way to the wharf or the Cathedral: it could be ignored. Now it turned a shuttered silent front to the muddy street, except where a door, propped open with a rock out of the roadway, opened on a passage. Wilson looked quickly this way and that and stepped inside.

Years ago the passage had been white-washed and plastered, but rats had torn holes in the plaster and human beings had mutilated the whitewash with scrawls and pencilled names. The walls were tattooed like a sailor's arm, with initials, dates, there were even a pair of hearts interlocked. At first it seemed to Wilson that the place was entirely deserted; on either side of the passage there were little cells nine feet by four with curtains instead of doorways and beds made out of old packing-cases spread with a native cloth. He walked rapidly to the end of the passage; then, he told himself, he would turn and go back to the quiet and somnolent security of the room where the old Downhamian dozed over his book.

He felt an awful disappointment, as though he had *not* found what he was looking for, when he reached the end and discovered that the left-hand cell was occupied; in the light of an oil lamp burning on the floor he saw a girl in a dirty shift spread out on the packing cases like a fish on a counter; her bare pink soles dangled over the words 'Tate's Sugar'. She lay there on duty, waiting for a customer. She grinned at Wilson, not bothering to sit up and said, 'Want jig jig, darling. Ten bob.' He had a vision of a girl with a rain-wet back moving forever out of his sight.

'No,' he said, 'no,' shaking his head and thinking, What a fool I was, what a fool, to drive all the way for only this. The girl giggled as if she understood his stupidity and he heard the slop slop of bare feet coming up the passage from the road; the way was blocked by an old mammy carrying a striped umbrella. She said something to the girl in her native tongue and received a grinning explanation. He had the sense that all this was only strange to *him*, that it was one of the stock situations the old woman was accustomed to meet in the dark regions which she ruled. He said weakly, 'I'll just go and get a drink first.'

'She get drink,' the mammy said. She commanded the girl sharply in the language he couldn't understand and the girl swung her legs off the sugar cases. 'You stay here,' the mammy said to Wilson, and mechanically like a hostess whose mind is elsewhere but who must make conversation with however uninteresting a guest, she said, 'Pretty girl, jig jig, one pound.' Market values here were reversed: the price rose steadily with his reluctance.

'I'm sorry. I can't wait,' Wilson said. 'Here's ten bob,' and he made the preliminary motions of departure, but the old woman paid him no attention at all, blocking the way, smiling steadily like a dentist who knows what's good for you. Here a man's colour had no value: he couldn't bluster as a white man could elsewhere; by entering this narrow plaster passage, he had shed every racial, social and individual trait, he had reduced himself to human nature. If he had wanted to hide, here was the perfect hiding-place; if he had wanted to be anonymous, here he was simply a man. Even his reluctance, disgust and fear were not personal characteristics; they were so common to those who came here for the first time that the old woman knew exactly what each move would be. First the suggestion of a drink, then the offer of money, after that . . .

Wilson said weakly, 'Let me by,' but he knew that she wouldn't move; she stood watching him, as though he were a tethered animal on whom she was keeping an eye for its owner. She wasn't interested in him, but occasionally she repeated calmly, 'Pretty girl jig jig by-an-by.' He held out a pound to her and she pocketed it and went on blocking the way. When he tried to push by, she thrust him backwards with a casual pink palm, saying, 'By-an-by. Jig jig.' It had all happened so many hundreds of times before.

Down the passage the girl came carrying a vinegar bottle filled with palm wine, and with a sigh of reluctance Wilson surrendered. The heat between the walls of rain, the musty smell of his companion, the dim and wayward light of the kerosene lamp reminded him of a vault newly opened for another body to be let down upon its floor. A grievance stirred in him, a hatred of those who had brought him here. In their presence he felt as though his dead veins would bleed again.

PART III

I / i

Helen said, 'I saw you on the beach this afternoon.' Scobie looked up from the glass of whisky he was measuring. Something in her voice reminded him oddly of Louise. He said, 'I had to find Rees—the Naval Intelligence man.'

'You didn't even speak to me.'

'I was in a hurry.'

'You are so careful, always,' she said, and now he realised what was happening and why he had thought of Louise. He wondered sadly whether love always inevitably took the same road. It was not only the act of love itself that was the same. . . . How often in the last two years he had tried to turn away at the critical moment from just such a scene–to save himself but also to save the other victim. He laughed with half a heart and said, 'For once I wasn't thinking of you. I had other things in mind.'

'What other things?'

'Oh, diamonds. . . .'

'Your work is much more important to you than I am.' Helen said, and the banality of the phrase, read in how many bad novels, wrung his heart.

'Yes,' he said gravely, 'but I'd sacrifice it for you.'

'Why?'

'I suppose because you are a human being. Somebody may love a dog more than any other possession, but he wouldn't run down even a strange child to save it.'

'Oh,' she said, 'why do you always tell me the truth? I don't want the truth all the time.'

He put the whisky glass in her hand and said, 'Dear, you are unlucky. You are tied up with a middle-aged man. We can't be bothered to lie all the time like the young.'

'If you knew,' she said, 'how tired I get of all your caution. You come here after dark and you go after dark. It's so–so ignoble.'

'Yes.'

'We always make love–here. Among the junior official's furniture. I don't believe we'd know how to do it anywhere else.'

'Poor you,' he said.

She said furiously, 'I don't want your pity.' But it was not a question of whether she wanted it–she had it. Pity smouldered like decay at his heart. He would never rid himself of it. He knew from experience how passion died away and how love went, but pity always stayed. Nothing ever diminished pity. The conditions of life nurtured it. There was only a single person in the world who was unpitiable, oneself.

'Can't you ever risk anything?' she asked. 'You never even write a line to me. You go away on trek for days, but you won't leave anything behind. I can't even have a photograph to make this place human.'

'But I haven't got a photograph.'

'I suppose you think I'd use your letters against you.' He thought, if I shut my eyes it might almost be Louise speaking–the voice was younger, that was all, and perhaps less capable of giving pain. Standing with the whisky glass in his hand he remembered another night–a hundred yards away–the glass had then contained gin. He said gently, 'You talk such nonsense.'

'You think I'm a child. You tiptoe in–bringing me stamps.'

'I'm trying to protect you.'

'I don't care a bloody damn if people talk.' He recognised the hard swearing of the netball team.

He said, 'If they talked enough, this would come to an end.'

'You are not protecting *me*. You are protecting your wife.'

'It comes to the same thing.'

'Oh,' she said, 'to couple me with–that woman.' He couldn't prevent the wince. He had underrated her power of giving pain. He could see how she had spotted her success: he had delivered himself into her hands. Now she would always know how to inflict the sharpest stab. She was like a child with a pair of dividers who knows her power to injure. You could never trust a child not to use her advantage.

'Dear,' he said, 'it's too soon to quarrel.'

'That woman,' she repeated, watching his eyes. 'You'd never leave her, would you?'

'We are married,' he said.

'If she knew of this, you'd go back like a whipped dog.' He thought with tenderness, she hasn't read the best books, like Louise.

'I don't know.'

'You'll never marry me.'

'I can't. You know that.'

'It's a wonderful excuse being a Catholic,' she said. 'It doesn't stop you sleeping with me—it only stops you marrying me.'

'Yes,' he said. He thought: how much older she is than she was a month ago. She hadn't been capable of a scene then, but she had been educated by love and secrecy: he was beginning to form her. He wondered whether if this went on long enough, she would be indistinguishable from Louise. In my school, he thought, they learn bitterness and frustration and how to grow old.

'Go on,' Helen said, 'justify yourself.'

'It would take too long,' he said. 'One would have to begin with the arguments for a God.'

'What a twister you are.'

He felt disappointed. He had looked forward to the evening. All day in the office dealing with a rent case and a case of juvenile delinquency he had looked forward to the Nissen hut, the bare room, the junior official's furniture like his own youth, everything that she had abused. He said, 'I meant well.'

'What do you mean?'

'I meant to be your friend. To look after you. To make you happier than you were.'

'Wasn't I happy?' she asked as though she were speaking of years ago.

He said, 'You were shocked, lonely . . .'

'I couldn't have been as lonely as I am now,' she said. 'I go out to the beach with Mrs Carter when the rain stops. Bagster makes a pass, they think I'm frigid. I come back here before the rain starts and wait for you . . . we drink a glass of whisky . . . you give me some stamps as though I were your small girl . . .'

'I'm sorry,' Scobie said. He put out his hand and covered hers: the knuckles lay under his palm like a small backbone that had been broken. He went slowly and cautiously on, choosing his words carefully, as though he were pursuing a path through an evacuated country sown with booby-traps: every step he took he expected the explosion. 'I'd do anything—almost anything—to make you happy. I'd stop coming here. I'd go right away—retire . . .'

'You'd be so glad to get rid of me,' she said.

'It would be like the end of life.'

'Go away if you want to.'

'I don't want to go. I want to do what you want.'

'You can go if you want to—or you can stay,' she said with contempt. 'I can't move, can I?'

'If you want it, I'll get you on the next boat somehow.'

'Oh, how pleased you'd be if this were over,' she said and began to weep. When he put out a hand to touch her she screamed at him, 'Go to hell. Go to hell. Clear out.'

'I'll go,' he said.

'Yes, go and don't come back.'

Outside the door, with the rain cooling his face, running down his hands, it occurred to him how much easier life might be if he took her at her word. He would go into his house and close the door and be alone again; he would write a letter to Louise without a sense of deceit and sleep as he hadn't slept for weeks, dreamlessly. Next day the office, the quiet going home, the evening meal, the locked door. . . . But down the hill, past the transport park, where the lorries crouched under the dripping tarpaulins, the rain fell like tears. He thought of her alone in the hut, wondering whether the irrevocable words had been spoken, if all the to-morrows would consist of Mrs Carter and Bagster until the boat came and she went home with nothing to remember but misery. Inexorably another's point of view rose on the path like a murdered innocent.

As he opened his door a rat that had been nosing at the food-safe retreated without haste up the stairs. This was what Louise had hated and feared; he had at least made her happy, and now ponderously, with planned and careful recklessness, he set about trying to make things right for Helen. He sat down at his table and taking a sheet of typewriting paper—official paper stamped with the Government watermark—he began to compose a letter.

He wrote: *My darling*—he wanted to put himself entirely in her hands, but to leave her anonymous. He looked at his watch and added in the right-hand corner, as though he were making a police report, *12.35 a.m. Burnside, September 5*. He went carefully on, *I love you more than myself, more than my wife. I am trying very hard to tell the truth. I want more than anything in the world to make you happy.* . . . The banality of the phrases saddened him; they seemed to have no truth personal to herself: they had been used too often. *If I were young*, he thought, *I would be able to find the right words, the new words, but all this has happened to me before.* He wrote again, *I love you. Forgive me*, signed and folded the paper.

He put on his mackintosh and went out again in the rain. Wounds festered in the damp, they never healed. Scratch your finger and in a few hours there would be a little coating of green skin. He carried a sense of corruption up the hill. A soldier shouted something in his sleep in the transport park—a single word like a hieroglyphic on a wall which Scobie could not interpret—the men were Nigerians. The rain hammered on the Nissen roofs, and he thought, Why did I write that? Why did I write 'more than God'? she would have been satisfied with 'more than Louise'. Even if it's true, why did I write it? The sky wept endlessly around him; he had the sense of wounds that never healed. He whispered, 'O God, I have deserted you. Do not you desert me.' When he came to her door he thrust the letter under it; he heard the rustle of the paper on the cement floor but nothing else. Remembering the childish figure carried past him on the stretcher, he was saddened to think how much had happened, how uselessly, to make him now say to himself with resentment: she will never again be able to accuse me of caution.

I /ii

'I was just passing by,' Father Rank said, 'so I thought I'd look in.' The evening rain fell in grey ecclesiastical folds, and a lorry howled its way towards the hills.

'Come in,' Scobie said. 'I'm out of whisky. But there's beer—or gin.'

'I saw you up at the Nissens, so I thought I'd follow you down. You are not busy?'

'I'm having dinner with the Commissioner, but not for another hour.'

Father Rank moved restlessly around the room, while Scobie took the beer out of the ice-box. 'Would you have heard from Louise lately?' he asked.

'Not for a fortnight,' Scobie said, 'but there've been more sinkings in the south.'

Father Rank let himself down in the Government armchair with his glass between his knees. There was no sound but the rain scraping on the roof. Scobie cleared his throat and then the silence came back. He had the odd sense that Father Rank, like one of his own junior officers, was waiting there for orders.

'The rains will soon be over,' Scobie said.

'It must be six months now since your wife went.'

'Seven.'

'Will you be taking your leave in South Africa?' Father Rank asked, looking away and taking a draught of his beer.

'I've postponed my leave. The young men need it more.'

'Everybody needs leave.'

'*You've* been here twelve years without it, Father.'

'Ah, but that's different,' Father Rank said. He got up again and moved restlessly down one wall and along another. He turned an expression of undefined appeal toward Scobie. 'Sometimes,' he said, 'I feel as though I weren't a working man at all.' He stopped and stared and half raised his hands, and Scobie remembered Father Clay dodging an unseen figure in his restless walk. He felt as though an appeal were being made to which he couldn't find an answer. He said weakly, 'There's no one works harder than you, Father.'

Father Rank returned draggingly to his chair. He said, 'It'll b′ ʀ,ood when the rains are over.'

'How's the mammy out by Congo Creek? I heard she was dying.'

'She'll be gone this week. She's a good woman.' He took another draught of beer and doubled up in the chair with his hand on his stomach. 'The wind,' he said. 'I get the wind badly.'

'You shouldn't drink bottled beer, Father.'

'The dying,' Father Rank said, 'that's what I'm here for. They send for me when they are dying.' He raised eyes bleary with too much quinine and said harshly and hopelessly, 'I've never been any good to the living, Scobie.'

'You are talking nonsense, Father.'

'When I was a novice, I thought that people talked to their priests, and I thought God somehow gave the right words. Don't mind me, Scobie, don't listen to me. It's the rains—they always get me down about this time. God doesn't give the right words, Scobie. I had a parish once in Northampton. They make boots there. They used to ask me out to tea, and I'd sit and watch their hands pouring out, and we'd talk of the Children of Mary and repairs to the church roof. They were very generous in Northampton. I only had to ask and they'd give. I wasn't of any use to a single living soul, Scobie. I thought, in Africa things will be different. You see I'm not a reading man, Scobie. I never had much talent for loving God as some people do. I wanted to be of use, that's all. Don't listen to me. It's the rains. I haven't talked like this for five years. Except to the mirror. If people are in trouble they'd go to you, Scobie, not to me. They ask me to dinner to hear the gossip. And if you were in trouble where would you go?' And Scobie was again aware of those bleary and appealing eyes, waiting through the dry seasons and the rains, for something that never happened. Could I shift my burden there, he wondered: could I tell him that I love two women: that I don't know what to do? What would be the use? I know the answers as well as he does. One should look after one's own soul at whatever cost to another, and that's what I can't do, what I shall never be able to do. It wasn't he who required the magic word, it was the priest, and he couldn't give it.

'I'm not the kind of man to get into trouble, Father. I'm dull and middle-aged,' and looking away, unwilling to see distress, he heard Father Rank's clapper miserably sounding, 'Ho! ho ho!'

I /iii

On his way to the Commissioner's bungalow, Scobie looked in at his office. A message was written in pencil on his pad. *I looked in to see you. Nothing important. Wilson.* It struck him as odd: he had not seen Wilson for some weeks, and if his visit had no importance why had he so carefully recorded it? He opened the drawer of his desk to find a packet of cigarettes and noticed at once that something was out of order: he considered the contents carefully: his indelible pencil was missing. Obviously Wilson had looked for a pencil with which to write his message and had forgotten to put it back. But why the message?

In the charge-room the sergeant said, 'Mr Wilson come to see you, sah.'

'Yes, he left a message.'

So that was it, he thought: I would have known anyway, so he considered it best to let me know himself. He returned to his office and looked again at his desk. It seemed to him that a file had been shifted, but he couldn't be sure. He opened his drawer, but there was nothing there which would

interest a soul. Only the broken rosary caught his eye–something which
should have been mended a long while ago. He took it out and put it in his
pocket.

'Whisky?' the Commissioner asked.

'Thank you,' Scobie said, holding the glass up between himself and the
Commissioner. 'Do *you* trust me?'

'Yes.'

'Am I the only one who doesn't know about Wilson?'

The Commissioner smiled, lying back at ease, unembarrassed. 'Nobody
knows officially–except myself and the manager of the U.A.C.–that was
essential of course. The Governor too and whoever deals with the cables
marked Most Secret. I'm glad you've tumbled to it.'

'I wanted you to know that–up to date of course–I've been trustworthy.'

'You don't need to tell me, Scobie.'

'In the case of Tallit's cousin we couldn't have done anything different.'

'Of course not.'

Scobie said, 'There is one thing you don't know though. I borrowed two
hundred pounds from Yusef so that I could send Louise to South Africa. I
pay him four per cent interest. The arrangement is purely commercial, but if
you want my head for it . . .'

'I'm glad you told me,' the Commissioner said. 'You see Wilson got the
idea that you were being blackmailed. He must have dug up those payments
somehow.'

'Yusef wouldn't blackmail for money.'

'I told him that.'

'Do you want my head?'

'I need your head, Scobie. You're the only officer I really trust.'

Scobie stretched out a hand with an empty glass in it: it was like a
handclasp.

'Say when.'

'When.'

Men can become twins with age. The past was their common womb; the
six months of rain and the six months of sun was the period of their common
gestation. They needed only a few words and a few gestures to convey their
meaning. They had graduated through the same fevers, they were moved by
the same love and contempt.

'Derry reports there've been some big thefts from the mines.'

'Commercial?'

'Gem stones. Is it Yusef–or Tallit?'

'It might be Yusef,' Scobie said. 'I don't think he deals in industrial
diamonds. He calls them gravel. But of course one can't be sure.'

'The *Esperança* will be in in a few days. We've got to be careful.'

'What does Wilson say?'

'He swears by Tallit. Yusef is the villain of his piece–and you, Scobie.'

'I haven't seen Yusef for a long while.'

'I know.'

'I begin to know what these Syrians feel–watched and reported on.'

'Wilson reports on all of us, Scobie. Fraser, Tod, Thimblerigg, myself.

He thinks I'm too easy-going. It doesn't matter though. Wright tears up his reports, and of course Wilson reports on him.'

'I suppose so.'

He walked up, at midnight, to the Nissen huts. In the black-out he felt momentarily safe, unwatched, unreported on; in the soggy ground his footsteps made the smallest sounds, but as he passed Wilson's hut he was aware again of the deep necessity for caution. An awful weariness touched him, and he thought: I will go home: I won't creep by to her to-night: her last words had been 'don't come back'. Couldn't one, for once, take somebody at their word? He stood twenty yards from Wilson's hut, watching the crack of light between the curtains. A drunken voice shouted somewhere up the hill and the first spatter of the returning rain licked his face. He thought: I'll go back and go to bed, in the morning I'll write to Louise and in the evening go to confession: the day after that God will return to me in a priest's hands: life will be simple again. Virtue, the good life, tempted him in the dark like a sin. The rain blurred his eyes, the ground sucked at his feet as they trod reluctantly towards the Nissen hut.

He knocked twice and the door immediately opened. He had prayed between the two knocks that anger might still be there behind the door, that he wouldn't be wanted. He couldn't shut his eyes or his ears to any human need of him; he was not the centurion, but a man in the ranks who had to do the bidding of a hundred centurions, and when the door opened, he could tell the command was going to be given again—the command to stay, to love, to accept responsibility, to lie.

'Oh darling,' she said, 'I thought you were never coming. I bitched you so.'

'I'll always come if you want me.'

'Will you?'

'Always. If I'm alive.' God can wait, he thought: how can one love God at the expense of one of his creatures? Would a woman accept the love for which a child had to be sacrificed?

Carefully they drew the curtains close before turning up the lamps.

She said, 'I've been afraid all day that you wouldn't come.'

'Of course I came.'

'I told you to go away. Never pay any attention to me when I tell you to go away. Promise.'

'I promise,' he said.

'If you hadn't come back . . .' she said, and became lost in thought between the lamps. He could see her searching for herself, frowning in the effort to see where she would have been . . . 'I don't know. Perhaps I'd have slutted with Bagster, or killed myself, or both. I think both.'

He said anxiously, 'You mustn't think like that. I'll always be here if you need me, as long as I'm alive.'

'Why do you keep on saying as long as I'm alive?'

'There are thirty years between us.'

For the first time that night they kissed. She said, 'I can't feel the years.'

'Why did you think I wouldn't come?' Scobie said. 'You got my letter.'

'Your letter?'

'The one I pushed under your door last night.'

She said with fear, 'I never saw a letter. What did you say?'

He touched her face and smiled. 'Everything. I didn't want to be cautious any longer. I put down everything.'

'Even your name?'

'I think so. Anyway it's signed with my handwriting.'

'There's a mat by the door. It must be under the mat.' But they both knew it wouldn't be there. It was as if all along they had foreseen how disaster would come in by that particular door.

'Who would have taken it?'

He tried to soothe her nerves. 'Probably your boy threw it away, thought it was waste paper. It wasn't in an envelope. Nobody could know whom I was writing to.'

'As if that mattered. Darling,' she said, 'I feel sick. Really sick. Somebody's getting something on you. I wish I'd died in that boat.'

'You're imagining things. Probably I didn't push the note far enough. When your boy opened the door in the morning it blew away or got trampled in the mud.' He spoke with all the conviction he could summon: it was just possible.

'Don't let me ever do you any harm,' she implored, and every phrase she used fastened the fetters more firmly round his wrists. He put out his hands to her and lied firmly, 'You'll never do me harm. Don't worry about a lost letter. I exaggerated. It said nothing really—nothing that a stranger would understand. Don't worry.'

'Listen, darling. Don't stay to-night. I'm nervous. I feel—watched. Say good night now and go away. But come back. Oh my dear, come back.'

The light was still on in Wilson's hut as he passed. Opening the door of his own dark house he saw a piece of paper on the floor. It gave him an odd shock as though the missing letter had returned, like a cat, to its old home. But when he picked it up, it wasn't his letter, though this too was a message of love. It was a telegram addressed to him at police headquarters and the signature written in full for the sake of censorship, Louise Scobie, was like a blow struck by a boxer with a longer reach than he possessed. *Have written am on my way home have been a fool stop love*—and then that name as formal as a seal.

He sat down. His head swam with nausea. He thought: if I had never written that other letter, if I had taken Helen at her word and gone away, how easily then life could have been arranged again. But he remembered his words in the last ten minutes, 'I'll always be here if you need me as long as I'm alive'—that constituted an oath as ineffaceable as the vow by the Ealing altar. The wind was coming up from the sea—the rains ended as they began with typhoons. The curtains blew in and he ran to the windows and pulled them shut. Upstairs the bedroom windows clattered to and fro, tearing at hinges. Turning from closing them he looked at the bare dressing-table where soon the photographs and the pots would be back again—one photograph in particular. The happy Scobie, he thought, my one success. A child in hospital said 'Father' as the shadow of a rabbit shifted on the pillow: a girl went by on a stretcher clutching a stamp-album—why me, he thought, why do they need me, a dull middle-aged police officer who had failed for promotion? I've got nothing to give them that they can't get elsewhere: why can't they leave me in peace? Elsewhere there was a younger and better love, more security. It sometimes seemed to him that all he could share with them was his despair.

Leaning back against the dressing-table, he tried to pray. The Lord's Prayer lay as dead on his tongue as a legal document: it wasn't his daily bread that he wanted but so much more. He wanted happiness for others and solitude and peace for himself. 'I don't want to plan any more,' he said suddenly aloud. 'They wouldn't need me if I were dead. No one needs the dead. The dead can be forgotten. O God, give me death before I give them unhappiness.' But the words sounded melodramatically in his own ears. He told himself that he mustn't get hysterical: there was far too much planning to do for an hysterical man, and going downstairs again he thought three aspirins or perhaps four were what he required in this situation—this banal situation. He took a bottle of filtered water out of the ice-box and dissolved the aspirin. He wondered how it would feel to drain death as simply as these aspirins which now stuck sourly in his throat. The priests told one it was the unforgivable sin, the final expression of an unrepentant despair, and of course one accepted the Church's teaching. But they taught also that God had sometimes broken his own laws, and was it less possible for him to put out a hand of forgiveness into the suicidal darkness than to have woken himself in the tomb, behind the stone? Christ had not been murdered—you couldn't murder God. Christ had killed himself: he had hung himself on the Cross as surely as Pemberton from the picture-rail.

He put his glass down and thought again, I must not get hysterical. Two people's happiness was in his hands and he must learn to juggle with strong nerves. Calmness was everything. He took out his diary and began to write against the date, Wednesday, September 6. *Dinner with the Commissioner. Satisfactory talk about W. Called on Helen for a few minutes. Telegram from Louise that she is on the way home.*

He hesitated for a moment and then wrote: *Father Rank called in for drink before dinner. A little overwrought. He needs leave.* He read this over and scored out the last two sentences. It was seldom in this record that he allowed himself an expression of opinion.

2/i

The telegram lay on his mind all day: ordinary life—the two hours in court on a perjury case—had the unreality of a country one is leaving for ever. One thinks, At this hour, in that village, these people I once knew are sitting down at table just as they did a year ago when I was there, but one is not convinced that any life goes on the same as ever outside the consciousness. All Scobie's consciousness was on the telegram, on that nameless boat edging its way now up the African coastline from the south. God forgive me, he thought, when his mind lit for a moment on the possibility that it might never arrive. In our hearts there is a ruthless dictator, ready to contemplate the misery of a thousand strangers if it will ensure the happiness of the few we love.

At the end of the perjury case Fellowes, the sanitary inspector, caught him at the door. 'Come to chop to-night, Scobie. We've got a bit of real Argentine beef.' It was too much of an effort in this dream world to refuse an invitation. 'Wilson's coming,' Fellowes said. 'To tell you the truth, he helped us with the beef. You like him, don't you?'

'Yes. I thought it was you who didn't.'

'Oh, the club's got to move with the times, and all sorts of people go into trade nowadays. I admit I was hasty. Bit boozed up, I wouldn't be surprised. He was at Downham: we used to play them when I was at Lancing.'

Driving out to the familiar house he had once occupied himself on the hills, Scobie thought listlessly, I must speak to Helen soon. She mustn't learn this from someone else. Life always repeated the same pattern; there was always, sooner or later, bad news that had to be broken, comforting lies to be uttered, pink gins to be consumed to keep misery away.

He came to the long bungalow living-room and there at the end of it was Helen. With a sense of shock he realised that never before had he seen her like a stranger in another man's house, never before dressed for an evening's party. 'You know Mrs Rolt, don't you?' Fellowes asked. There was no irony in his voice. Scobie thought with a tremor of self-disgust, how clever we've been: how successfully we've deceived the gossipers of a small colony. It oughtn't to be possible for lovers to deceive so well. Wasn't love supposed to be spontaneous, reckless. . . ?

'Yes,' he said, 'I'm an old friend of Mrs Rolt. I was at Pende when she was brought across.' He stood by the table a dozen feet away while Fellowes mixed the drinks and watched her while she talked to Mrs Fellowes, talked easily, naturally. Would I, he wondered, if I had come in to-night and seen her for the first time ever have felt any love at all?

'Now which was yours, Mrs Rolt?'

'A pink gin.'

'I wish I could get my wife to drink them. I can't bear her gin and orange.'

Scobie said, 'If I'd known you were going to be here, I'd have called for you.'

'I wish you had,' Helen said. 'You never come and see me.' She turned to Fellowes and said with an ease that horrified him, 'He was so kind to me in hospital at Pende, but I think he only likes the sick.'

Fellowes stroked his little ginger moustache, poured himself out some more gin and said, 'He's scared of you, Mrs Rolt. All we married men are.'

She said with false blandness, 'Do you think I could have one more without getting tight?'

'Ah, here's Wilson,' Fellowes said, and there he was with his pink, innocent, self-distrustful face and his badly tied cummerbund. 'You know everybody, don't you? You and Mrs Rolt are neighbours.'

'We haven't met though,' Wilson said, and began automatically to blush.

'I don't know what's come over the men in this place,' said Fellowes. 'You and Scobie both neighbours and neither of you see anything of Mrs Rolt,' and Scobie was immediately aware of Wilson's gaze speculatively turned upon him. '*I* wouldn't be so bashful,' Fellowes said, pouring out the pink gins.

'Dr Sykes late as usual,' Mrs Fellowes commented from the end of the room, but at that moment treading heavily up the outside stairs, sensible in a dark dress and mosquito-boots, came Dr Sykes. 'Just in time for a drink, Jessie,' Fellowes said. 'What's it to be?'

'Double Scotch,' Dr Sykes said. She glared around through her thick glasses and added, 'Evening all.'

As they went in to dinner, Scobie said, 'I've got to see you,' but catching Wilson's eye he added, 'about your furniture.'

'My furniture?'

'I think I could get you some extra chairs.' As conspirators they were much too young; they had not yet absorbed a whole code book into their memory and he was uncertain whether she had understood the mutilated phrase. All through dinner he sat silent, dreading the time when he would be alone with her, afraid to lose the least opportunity; when he put his hand in his pocket for a handkerchief the telegram crumpled in his fingers . . . *have been a fool stop love.*

'Of course you know more about it than we do, Major Scobie,' Dr Sykes said.

'I'm sorry. I missed . . .'

'We were talking about the Pemberton case.' So already in a few months it had become a case. When something became a case it no longer seemed to concern a human being: there was no shame or suffering in a case. The boy on the bed was cleaned and tidied, laid out for the text-book of psychology.

'I was saying,' Wilson said, 'that Pemberton chose an odd way to kill himself. I would have chosen a sleeping-draught.'

'It wouldn't be easy to get a sleeping-draught in Bamba,' Dr Sykes said. 'It was probably a sudden decision.'

'I wouldn't have caused all that fuss,' said Fellowes. 'A chap's got the right to take his own life, of course, but there's no need for fuss. An overdose of sleeping-draught—I agree with Wilson—that's the way.'

'You still have to get your prescription,' Dr Sykes said.

Scobie with his fingers on the telegram remembered the letter signed 'Dicky', the immature handwriting, the marks of cigarettes on the chairs, the novels of Wallace, the stigmata of loneliness. Through two thousand years, he thought, we have discussed Christ's agony in just this disinterested way.

'Pemberton was always a bit of a fool,' Fellowes said.

'A sleeping-draught is invariably tricky,' Dr Sykes said. Her big lenses reflected the electric globe as she turned them like a lighthouse in Scobie's direction. '*Your* experience will tell you how tricky. Insurance companies never like sleeping-draughts, and no coroner could lend himself to a deliberate fraud.'

'How can they tell?' Wilson asked.

'Take luminol, for instance. Nobody could really take enough luminol by accident. . . .' Scobie looked across the table at Helen. She ate slowly, without appetite, her eyes on her plate. Their silences seemed to isolate them: this was a subject the unhappy could never discuss impersonally. Again he was aware of Wilson looking from one to another of them, and Scobie drew desperately at his mind for any phrase that would end their dangerous solitude. They could not even be silent together with safety.

He said, 'What's the way out you'd recommend, Dr Sykes?'

'Well, there are bathing accidents—but even they need a good deal of explanation. If a man's brave enough to step in front of a car, but it's too uncertain . . .'

'And involves somebody else,' Scobie said.

'Personally,' Dr Sykes said, grinning under her glasses, 'I should have no difficulties. In my position, I should classify myself as an angina case and then get one of my colleagues to prescribe . . .'

Helen said with sudden violence, 'What a beastly talk this is. You've got no business to tell . . .'

'My dear,' Dr Sykes said, revolving her malevolent beams, 'when you've been a doctor as long as I have been you know your company. I don't think any of us are likely . . .'

Mrs Fellowes said, 'Have another helping of fruit salad, Mrs Rolt.'

'Are you a Catholic, Mrs Rolt?' Fellowes asked. 'Of course they take very strong views.'

'No, I'm not a Catholic.'

'But they do, don't they, Scobie?'

'We are taught,' Scobie said, 'that it's the unforgivable sin.'

'But do you really, seriously, Major Scobie,' Dr Sykes asked, 'believe in Hell?'

'Oh yes, I do.'

'In flames and torment?'

'Perhaps not quite that. They tell us it may be a permanent sense of loss.'

'That sort of Hell wouldn't worry *me*,' Fellowes said.

'Perhaps you've never lost anything of any importance,' Scobie said.

The real object of the dinner-party had been the Argentine beef. With that consumed there was nothing to keep them together (Mrs Fellowes didn't play cards). Fellowes busied himself about the beer, and Wilson was wedged between the sour silence of Mrs Fellowes and Dr Sykes' garrulity.

'Let's get a breath of air,' Scobie suggested.

'Wise?'

'It would look odd if we didn't,' Scobie said.

'Going to look at the stars?' Fellowes called, pouring out the beer. 'Making up for lost time, Scobie? Take your glasses with you.'

They balanced their glasses on the rail of the verandah. Helen said, 'I haven't found your letter.'

'Forget it.'

'Wasn't that what you wanted to see me about?'

'No.'

He could see the outline of her face against the sky doomed to go out as the rain clouds advanced. He said, 'I've got bad news.'

'Somebody knows?'

'Oh no, nobody knows.' He said, 'Last night I had a telegram from my wife. She's on the way home.' One of the glasses fell from the rail and smashed in the yard.

The lips repeated bitterly the word 'home' as if that were the only word she had grasped. He said quickly, moving his hand along the rail and failing to reach her, '*Her* home. It will never be my home again.'

'Oh yes, it will. Now it will be.'

He swore carefully, 'I shall never again want any home without you.' The rain clouds had reached the moon and her face went out like a candle in a sudden draught of wind. He had the sense that he was embarking now on a longer journey than he had ever intended. A light suddenly shone on both of them as a door opened. He said sharply, 'Mind the black-out,' and thought: at least we were not standing together, but how, how did our faces look? Wilson's voice said, 'We thought a fight was going on. We heard a glass break.'

'Mrs Rolt lost all her beer.'

'For God's sake call me Helen,' she said drearily, 'everybody else does, Major Scobie.'

'Am I interrupting something?'

'A scene of unbridled passion,' Helen said. 'It's left me shaken. I want to go home.'

'I'll drive you down,' Scobie said. 'It's getting late.'

'I wouldn't trust you, and anyway Dr Sykes is dying to talk to you about suicide. I won't break up the party. Haven't you got a car, Mr Wilson?'

'Of course. I'd be delighted.'

'You could always drive down and come straight back.'

'I'm an early bird myself,' Wilson said.

'I'll just go in then and say good night.'

When he saw her face again in the light, he thought: do I worry too much? Couldn't this for her be just the end of an episode? He heard her saying to Mrs Fellowes, 'The Argentine beef certainly was lovely.'

'We've got Mr Wilson to thank for it.'

The phrases went to and fro like shuttlecocks. Somebody laughed (it was Fellowes or Wilson) and said, 'You're right there,' and Dr Sykes' spectacles made a dot dash dot on the ceiling. He couldn't watch the car move off without disturbing the black-out; he listened to the starter retching and retching, the racing of the engine, and then the slow decline to silence.

Dr Sykes said, 'They should have kept Mrs Rolt in hospital a while longer.'

'Why?'

'Nerves. I could feel it when she shook hands.'

He waited another half an hour and then he drove home. As usual Ali was waiting for him, dozing uneasily on the kitchen step. He lit Scobie to the door with his torch. 'Missus leave letter,' he said, and took an envelope out of his shirt.

'Why didn't you leave it on my table?'

'Massa in there.'

'What massa?' but by that time the door was open, and he saw Yusef stretched in a chair, asleep, breathing so gently that the hair lay motionless on his chest.

'I tell him go away,' Ali said with contempt, 'but he stay.'

'That's all right. Go to bed.'

He had a sense that life was closing in on him. Yusef had never been here since the night he came to inquire after Louise and to lay his trap for Tallit. Quietly, so as not to disturb the sleeping man and bring *that* problem on his heels, he opened the note from Helen. She must have written it immediately she got home. He read, *My darling, this is serius. I can't say this to you, so I'm putting it on paper. Only I'll give it to Ali. You trust Ali. When I heard your wife was coming back* . . .

Yusef opened his eyes and said, 'Excuse me, Major Scobie, for intruding.'

'Do you want a drink? Beer. Gin. My whisky's finished.'

'May I send you a case?' Yusef began automatically and then laughed. 'I always forget. I must not send you things.'

Scobie sat down at the table and laid the note open in front of him. Nothing could be so important as those next sentences. He said, 'What do you want, Yusef?' and read on, *When I heard your wife was coming back, I was angry and bitter. It was stupid of me. Nothing is your fault.*

'Finish your reading, Major Scobie, I can wait.'

'It isn't really important,' Scobie said, dragging his eyes from the large immature letters, the mistake in spelling. 'Tell me what you want, Yusef,' and back his eyes went to the letter. *That's why I'm writing. Because last night you made promises about not leaving me and I don't want you ever to be bound to me with promises. My dear, all your promises* . . .

'Major Scobie, when I lent you money, I swear, it was for friendship, just friendship. I never wanted to ask anything of you, anything at all, not even the four per cent. I wouldn't even have asked for *your* friendship . . . I was *your* friend . . . this is very confusing, words are very complicated, Major Scobie.'

'You've kept the bargain, Yusef. I don't complain about Tallit's cousin.' He read on: *belong to your wife. Nothing you say to me is a promise. Please, please remember that. If you never want to see me again, don't write, don't speak. And, dear, if you just want to see me sometimes, see me sometimes. I'll tell any lies you like.*

'Do finish what you are reading, Major Scobie. Because what I have to speak about is very, very important.'

My dear, my dear, leave me if you want to or have me as your hore if you want to. He thought: she's only heard the word, never seen it spelt: they cut it out of the school Shakespeare. *Goodnight. Don't worry, my darling.* He said savagely, 'All right, Yusef. What is it that's so important?'

'Major Scobie, I have got after all to ask you a favour. It has nothing to do with the money I lent you. If you can do this for me it will be friendship, just friendship.'

'It's late, Yusef, tell me what it is.'

'The *Esperança* will be in the day after to-morrow. I want a small packet taken on board for me and left with the captain.'

'What's in the packet?'

'Major Scobie, don't ask. I am your friend. I would rather have this be a secret. It will harm no one at all.'

'Of course, Yusef, I can't do it. You know that.'

'I assure you, Major Scobie, on my word—' he leant forward in the chair and laid his hand on the black fur of his chest—'on my word as a friend the package contains nothing, nothing for the Germans. No industrial diamonds, Major Scobie.'

'Gem stones?'

'Nothing for the Germans. Nothing that will hurt your country.'

'Yusef, you can't really believe that I'd agree?'

The light drill trousers squeezed to the edge of the chair: for one moment Scobie thought that Yusef was going on his knees to him. He said, 'Major Scobie, I implore you. . . . It is important for you as well as for me.' His voice broke with genuine emotion, 'I want to be a friend.'

Scobie said, 'I'd better warn you before you say any more, Yusef, that the Commissioner *does* know about our arrangement.'

'I daresay, I daresay, but this is so much worse. Major Scobie, on my word of honour, this will do no harm to anyone. Just do this one act of friendship, and I'll never ask another. Do it of your own free will, Major Scobie. There is no bribe. I offer no bribe.'

His eye went back to the letter: *My dear, this is serius*. Serius—his eye this time read it as *servus*—a slave: a servant of the servants of God. It was like an unwise command which he had none the less to obey. He felt as though he were turning his back on peace for ever. With his eyes open, knowing the consequences, he entered the territory of lies without a passport for return.

'What were you saying, Yusef? I didn't catch . . .'

'Just once more I ask you . . .'

'No, Yusef.'

'Major Scobie,' Yusef said, sitting bolt upright in his chair, speaking with a sudden odd formality, as though a stranger had joined them and they were no longer alone, 'you remember Pemberton?'

'Of course.'

'His boy came into my employ.'

'Pemberton's boy?' *Nothing you say to me is a promise.*

'Pemberton's boy is Mrs Rolt's boy.'

Scobie's eyes remained on the letter, but he no longer read what he saw.

'Her boy brought me a letter. You see I asked him to keep his eyes—bare—is that the right word?'

'You have a very good knowledge of English, Yusef. Who read it to you?'

'That does not matter.'

The formal voice suddenly stopped and the old Yusef implored again, 'Oh, Major Scobie, what made you write such a letter? It was asking for trouble.'

'One can't be wise all the time, Yusef. One would die of disgust.'

'You see it has put you in my hands.'

'I wouldn't mind that so much. But to put three people in your hands . . .'

'If only you would have done an act of friendship . . .'

'Go on, Yusef. You must complete your blackmail. You can't get away with half a threat.'

'I wish I could dig a hole and put the package in it. But the war's going badly, Major Scobie. I am doing this not for myself, but for my father and mother, my half brother, my three sisters—and there are cousins too.'

'Quite a family.'

'You see if the English are beaten all my stores have no value at all.'

'What do you propose to do with the letter, Yusef?'

'I hear from a clerk in the cable company that your wife is on her way back. I will have the letter handed to her as soon as she lands.'

He remembered the telegram signed Louise Scobie: *have been a fool stop love*. It would be a cold welcome, he thought.

'And if I give your package to the captain of the *Esperança*?'

'My boy will be waiting on the wharf. In return for the captain's receipt he will give you an envelope with your letter inside.'

'You trust your boy?'

'Just as you trust Ali.'

'Suppose I demand the letter first and gave you my word . . .'

'It is the penalty of the blackmailer, Major Scobie, that he has no debts of honour. You would be quite right to cheat me.'

'Suppose you cheat me?'

'That wouldn't be right. And formerly I was your friend.'

'You very nearly were,' Scobie reluctantly admitted.

'I am the base Indian.'

'The base Indian?'

'Who threw away a pearl,' Yusef sadly said. 'That was in the play by Shakespeare the Ordnance Corps gave in the Memorial Hall. I have always remembered it.'

2/ii

'Well,' Druce said, 'I'm afraid we'll have to get to work now.'

'One more glass,' the captain of the *Esperança* said.

'Not if we are going to release you before the boom closes. See you later, Scobie.'

When the door of the cabin closed the captain said breathlessly, 'I am still here.'

'So I see. I told you there are often mistakes—minutes go to the wrong place, files are lost.'

'I believe none of that,' the captain said. 'I believe you helped me.' He dripped gently with sweat in the stuffy cabin. He added, 'I pray for you at Mass, and I have brought you this. It was all that I could find for you in Lobito. She is a very obscure saint,' and he slid across the table between them a holy medal the size of a nickel piece. 'Santa—I don't remember her name. She had something to do with Angola I think,' the captain explained.

'Thank you,' Scobie said. The package in his pocket seemed to him to weigh as heavily as a gun against his thigh. He let the last drops of port settle in the well of his glass and then drained them. He said, 'This time I have something for *you*.' A terrible reluctance cramped his fingers.

'For me?'

'Yes.'

How light the little package actually was now that it was on the table between them. What had weighed like a gun in the pocket might now have contained little more than fifty cigarettes. He said, 'Someone who comes on board with the pilot at Lisbon will ask you if you have any American cigarettes. You will give him this package.'

'Is this Government business?'

'No. The Government would never pay as well as this.' He laid a packet of notes upon the table.

'This surprises me,' the captain said with an odd note of disappointment. 'You have put yourself in my hands.'

'You were in mine,' Scobie said.

'I don't forget. Nor will my daughter. She is married outside the Church, but she has faith. She prays for you too.'

'The prayers we pray then don't count, surely?'

'No, but when the moment of Grace returns they rise,' the captain raised his fat arms in an absurd and touching gesture, 'all at once together like a flock of birds.'

'I shall be glad of them,' Scobie said.

'You can trust me, of course.'

'Of course. Now I must search your cabin.'

'You do not trust me very far.'

'That package,' Scobie said, 'has nothing to do with the war.'

'Are you sure?'

'I am nearly sure.'

He began his search. Once, pausing by a mirror, he saw poised over his own shoulder a stranger's face, a fat, sweating, unreliable face. Momentarily he wondered: who can that be? before he realised that it was only this new unfamiliar look of pity which made it strange to him. He thought: am I really one of those whom people pity?

BOOK THREE

PART I

I / i

The rains were over and the earth steamed. Flies everywhere settled in clouds, and the hospital was full of malaria patients. Farther up the coast they were dying of blackwater, and yet for a while there was a sense of relief. It was as if the world had become quiet again, now that the drumming on the iron roofs was over. In the town the deep scent of flowers modified the Zoo smell in the corridors of the police station. An hour after the boom was opened the liner moved in from the south unescorted.

Scobie went out in the police boat as soon as the liner anchored. His mouth felt stiff with welcome; he practised on his tongue phrases which would seem warm and unaffected, and he thought: what a long way I have travelled to make me rehearse a welcome. He hoped he would find Louise in one of the public rooms; it would be easier to greet her in front of strangers, but there was no sign of her anywhere. He had to ask at the purser's office for her cabin number.

Even then, of course, there was the hope that it would be shared. No cabin nowadays held less than six passengers.

But when he knocked and the door was opened, nobody was there but Louise. He felt like a caller at a strange house with something to sell. There was a question-mark at the end of his voice when he said, 'Louise?'

'Henry.' She added, 'Come inside.' When once he was within the cabin there was nothing to do but kiss. He avoided her mouth–the mouth reveals so much, but she wouldn't be content until she had pulled his face round and left the seal of her return on his lips. 'Oh my dear, here I am.'

'Here you are,' he said, seeking desperately for the phrases he had rehearsed.

'They've all been so sweet,' she explained. 'They are keeping away, so that I can see you alone.'

'You've had a good trip?'

'I think we were chased once.'

'I was very anxious,' he said and thought: that is the first lie. I may as well take the plunge now. He said, 'I've missed you so much.'

'I was a fool to go away, darling.' Through the porthole the houses sparkled like mica in the haze of heat. The cabin smelt closely of women, of powder, nail-varnish, and nightdresses. He said, 'Let's get ashore.'

But she detained him a little while yet. 'Darling,' she said, 'I've made a lot of resolutions while I've been away. Everything now is going to be different. I'm not going to rattle you any more.' She repeated, 'Everything will be different,' and he thought sadly that that at any rate was the truth, the bleak truth.

Standing at the window of his house while Ali and the small boy carried in the trunks he looked up the hill towards the Nissen huts. It was as if a landslide had suddenly put an immeasurable distance between him and them. They were so distant that at first there was no pain, any more than for an episode of youth remembered with the faintest melancholy. Did my lies really start, he wondered, when I wrote that letter? Can I really love her more than Louise? Do I, in my heart of hearts, love either of them, or is it only that this automatic pity goes out to any human need–and makes it worse? Any victim demands allegiance. Upstairs silence and solitude were being hammered away, tin-tacks were being driven in, weights fell on the floor and shook the ceiling. Louise's voice was raised in cheerful peremptory commands. There was a rattle of objects on the dressing-table. He went upstairs and from the doorway saw the face in the white communion veil staring back at him again: the dead too had returned. Life was not the same without the dead. The mosquito-net hung, a grey ectoplasm, over the double bed.

'Well, Ali,' he said, with the phantom of a smile which was all he could raise at this séance, 'Missus back. We're all together again.' Her rosary lay on the dressing-table, and he thought of the broken one in his pocket. He had always meant to get it mended: now it hardly seemed worth the trouble.

'Darling,' Louise said, 'I've finished up here. Ali can do the rest. There are so many things I want to speak to you about. . . .' She followed him downstairs and said at once, 'I must get the curtains washed.'

'They don't show the dirt.'

'Poor dear, you wouldn't notice, but I've been away.' She said, 'I really want a bigger bookcase now. I've brought a lot of books back with me.'

'You haven't told me yet what made you . . .'

'Darling, you'd laugh at me. It was so silly. But suddenly I saw what a fool I'd been to worry like that about the Commissionership. I'll tell you one day when I don't mind your laughing.' She put her hand out and tentatively touched his arm. 'You're really glad . . .?'

'So glad,' he said.

'Do you know one of the things that worried me? I was afraid you wouldn't be much of a Catholic without me around, keeping you up to things, poor dear.'

'I don't suppose I have been.'

'Have you missed Mass often?'

He said with forced jocularity, 'I've hardly been at all.'

'Oh, Ticki.' She pulled herself quickly up and said, 'Henry, darling, you'll think I'm very sentimental, but to-morrow's Sunday and I want us to go to communion together. A sign that we've started again–in the right way.' It was extraordinary the points in a situation one missed–this he had not considered. He said, 'Of course,' but his brain momentarily refused to work.

'You'll have to go to confession this afternoon.'

'I haven't done anything very terrible.'

'Missing Mass on Sunday's a mortal sin, just as much as adultery.'

'Adultery's more fun,' he said with attempted lightness.

'It's time I came back.'

'I'll go along this afternoon–after lunch. I can't confess on an empty stomach,' he said.

'Darling, you *have* changed, you know.'

'I was only joking.'

'I don't mind you joking. I like it. You didn't do it much though before.'

'You don't come back every day, darling.' The strained good humour, the jest with dry lips, went on and on: at lunch he laid down his fork for yet another 'crack'. 'Dear Henry,' she said, 'I've never known you so cheerful.' The ground had given way beneath his feet, and all through the meal he had the sensation of falling, the relaxed stomach, the breathlessness, the despair – because you couldn't fall so far as this and survive. His hilarity was like a scream from a crevasse.

When lunch was over (he couldn't have told what it was he'd eaten) he said, 'I must be off.'

'Father Rank?'

'First I've got to look in on Wilson. He's living in one of the Nissens now. A neighbour.'

'Won't he be in town?'

'I think he comes back for lunch.'

He thought as he went up the hill, what a lot of times in future I shall have to call on Wilson. But no – that wasn't a safe alibi. It would only do this once, because he knew that Wilson lunched in town. None the less, to make sure, he knocked and was taken aback momentarily when Harris opened to him. 'I didn't expect to see you.'

'I had a touch of fever,' Harris said.

'I wondered whether Wilson was in.'

'He always lunches in town,' Harris said.

'I just wanted to tell him he'd be welcome to look in. My wife's back, you know.'

'I thought I saw the activity through the window.'

'You must call on us too.'

'I'm not much of a calling man,' Harris said, drooping in the doorway. 'To tell you the truth women scare me.'

'You don't see enough of them, Harris.'

'I'm not a squire of dames,' Harris said with a poor attempt at pride, and Scobie was aware of how Harris watched him as he picked his way reluctantly towards a woman's hut, watched with the ugly asceticism of the unwanted man. He knocked and felt that disapproving gaze boring into his back. He thought: there goes my alibi: he will tell Wilson and Wilson . . . He thought: I will say that as I was up here, I called . . . and he felt his whole personality crumble with the slow disintegration of lies.

'Why did you knock?' Helen asked. She lay on her bed in the dusk of drawn curtains.

'Harris was watching me.'

'I didn't think you'd come to-day.'

'How did you know?'

'Everybody here knows everything – except one thing. How clever you are about that. I suppose it's because you are a police officer.'

'Yes.' He sat down on the bed and put his hand on her arm; immediately the sweat began to run between them. He said, 'What are you doing here? You are not ill?'

'Just a headache.'

He said mechanically, without even hearing his own words. 'Take care of yourself.'

'Something's worrying you,' she said. 'Have things gone- wrong?'

'Nothing of that kind.'

'Do you remember the first night you stayed here? We didn't worry about anything. You even left your umbrella behind. We were happy. Doesn't it seem odd?–we were happy.'

'Yes.'

'Why do we go on like this–being unhappy?'

'It's a mistake to mix up the ideas of happiness and love,' Scobie said with desperate pedantry, as though, if he could turn the whole situation into a textbook case, as they had turned Pemberton, peace might return to both of them, a kind of resignation.

'Sometimes you are so damnably old,' Helen said, but immediately she expressed with a motion of her hand towards him that she wasn't serious. To-day, he thought, she can't afford to quarrel–or so she believes. 'Darling,' she added, 'a penny for your thoughts.'

One ought not to lie to two people if it could be avoided–that way lay complete chaos, but he was tempted terribly to lie as he watched her face on the pillow. She seemed to him like one of those plants in nature films which you watch age under your eye. Already she had the look of the coast about her. She shared it with Louise. He said, 'It's just a worry I have to think out for myself. Something I hadn't considered.'

'Tell me, darling. Two brains . . .' She closed her eyes and he could see her mouth steady for a blow.

He said, 'Louise wants me to go to Mass with her, to communion. I'm supposed to be on the way to confession now.'

'Oh, is that all?' she asked with immense relief, and irritation at her ignorance moved like hatred unfairly in his brain.

'All?' he said. 'All?' Then justice reclaimed him. He said gently, 'If I don't go to communion, you see, she'll know there's something wrong–seriously wrong.'

'But can't you simply go?'

He said, 'To me that means–well, it's the worst thing I can do.'

'You don't really believe in hell?'

'That was what Fellowes asked me.'

'But I simply don't understand. If you believe in hell, why are you with me now?'

How often, he thought, lack of faith helps one to see more clearly than faith. He said, 'You are right, of course: it ought to prevent all this. But the villagers on the slopes of Vesuvius go on. . . . And then, against all the teaching of the Church, one has the conviction that love–any kind of love–does deserve a bit of mercy. One will pay, of course, pay terribly, but I don't believe one will pay for ever. Perhaps one will be given time before one dies. . . .

'A deathbed repentance,' she said with contempt.

'It wouldn't be easy,' he said, 'to repent of this.' He kissed the sweat off her hand. 'I can regret the lies, the mess, the unhappiness, but if I were dying now I wouldn't know how to repent the love.'

'Well,' she said with the same undertone of contempt that seemed to pull her apart from him, into the safety of the shore, 'can't you go and confess everything now? After all it doesn't mean you won't do it again.'

'It's not much good confessing if I don't intend to try. . . .'

'Well then,' she said triumphantly, 'be hung for a sheep. You are in–what do you call it?–mortal sin?–now. What difference does it make?'

He thought: pious people, I suppose, would call this the devil speaking, but he knew that evil never spoke in these crude answerable terms: this was innocence. He said, 'There *is* a difference–a big difference. It's not easy to explain. *Now* I'm just putting our love above–well, my safety. But the other–the other's really evil. It's like the Black Mass, the man who steals the sacrament to desecrate it. It's striking God when he's down–in my power.'

She turned her head wearily away and said, 'I don't understand a thing you are saying. It's all hooey to me.'

'I wish it were to me. But I believe it.'

She said sharply, 'I *suppose* you do. Or it is just a trick? I didn't hear so much about God when we began, did I? You aren't turning pious on me to give you an excuse. . . ?'

'My dear,' Scobie said, 'I'm not leaving you ever. I've got to think, that's all.'

I /ii

At a quarter-past six next morning Ali called them. Scobie woke at once, but Louise remained sleeping–she had had a long day. Scobie watched her–this was the face he had loved: this was the face he loved. She was terrified of death by sea and yet she had come back, to make him comfortable. She had borne a child by him in one agony, and in another agony had watched the child die. It seemed to him that he had escaped everything. If only, he thought, I could so manage that she never suffers again, but he knew that he had set himself an impossible task. He could delay the suffering, that was all, but he carried it about with him, an infection which sooner or later she must contract. Perhaps she was contracting it now, for she turned and whimpered in her sleep. He put his hand against her cheek to soothe her. He thought: if only she will go on sleeping, then I will sleep on too, I will oversleep, we shall miss Mass, another problem will be postponed. But as if his thoughts had been an alarm clock she awoke.

'What time is it, darling?'

'Nearly half-past six.'

'We'll have to hurry.' He felt as though he were being urged by a kindly and remorseless gaoler to dress for execution. Yet he still put off the saving lie: there was always the possibility of a miracle. Louise gave a final dab of powder (but the powder caked as it touched the skin) and said, 'We'll be off now.' Was there the faintest note of triumph in her voice? Years and years ago, in the other life of childhood, someone with his name Henry Scobie had acted in the school play, had acted Hotspur. He had been chosen for his seniority and his physique, but everyone said that it had been a good performance. Now he had to act again—surely it was as easy as the simpler verbal lie?

Scobie suddenly leant back against the wall and put his hand on his chest. He couldn't make his muscles imitate pain, so he simply closed his eyes. Louise looking in her mirror said, 'Remind me to tell you about Father Davis in Durban. He was a very good type of priest, much more intellectual than Father Rank.' It seemed to Scobie that she was never going to look round and notice him. She said, 'Well, we really must be off,' and dallied by the mirror. Some sweat-lank hairs were out of place. Through the curtain of his lashes at last he saw her turn and look at him. 'Come along, dear,' she said, 'you look sleepy.'

He kept his eyes shut and stayed where he was. She said sharply, 'Ticki, what's the matter?'

'A little brandy.'

'Are you ill?'

'A little brandy,' he repeated sharply, and when she had fetched it for him and he felt the taste on his tongue he had an immeasurable sense of reprieve. He sighed and relaxed. 'That's better.'

'What was it, Ticki?'

'Just a pain in my chest. It's gone now.'

'Have you had it before?'

'Once or twice while you've been away.'

'You must see a doctor.'

'Oh, it's not worth a fuss. They'll just say overwork.'

'I oughtn't to have dragged you up, but I wanted us to have communion together.'

'I'm afraid I've ruined that—with the brandy.'

'Never mind, Ticki.' Carelessly she sentenced him to eternal death. 'We can go any day.'

He knelt in his seat and watched Louise kneel with the other communicants at the altar rail: he had insisted on coming to the service with her Father Rank turning from the altar came to them with God in His hands. Scobie thought: God has just escaped me, but will He always escape? *Domine non sum dignus . . . domine non sum dignus . . . domine non sum dignus.* . . . His hand formally, as though he were at drill, beat on a particular button of his uniform. It seemed to him for a moment cruelly unfair of God to have exposed himself in this way, a man, a wafer of bread, first in the Palestinian villages and now here in the hot port, there, everywhere, allowing man to have his will of Him. Christ had told the rich young man to sell all and follow Him, but that was an easy rational step compared with this that God had taken, to put Himself at the mercy of men who hardly knew the meaning of the word. How desperately God must love, he thought with shame. The priest had reached Louise in his slow interrupted patrol, and suddenly Scobie was aware of the sense of exile. Over there, where all these people knelt, was a country to which he would never return. The sense of love stirred in him, the love one always feels for what one has lost, whether a child, a woman, or even pain.

Wilson tore the page carefully out of *The Downhamian* and pasted a thick sheet of Colonial Office notepaper on the back of the poem. He held it up to the light: it was impossible to read the sports results on the other side of his verses. Then he folded the page carefully and put it in his pocket; there it would probably stay, but one never knew.

He had seen Scobie drive away towards the town and with beating heart and a sense of breathlessness, much the same as he had felt when stepping into the brothel, even with the same reluctance—for who wanted at any given moment to change the routine of his life?—he made his way downhill towards Scobie's house.

He began to rehearse what he considered another man in his place would do: pick up the threads at once: kiss her quite naturally, upon the mouth if possible, say 'I've missed you', no uncertainty. But his beating heart sent out its message of fear which drowned thought.

'It's Wilson at last,' Louise said. 'I thought you'd forgotten me,' and held out her hand. He took it like a defeat.

'Have a drink.'

'I was wondering whether you'd like a walk.'

'It's too hot, Wilson.'

'I haven't been up there, you know, since. . . .'

'Up where?' He realised that for those who do not love time never stands still.

'Up at the old station.'

She said vaguely with a remorseless lack of interest, 'Oh yes . . . yes, I haven't been up there myself yet.'

'That night when I got back,' he could feel the awful immature flush expanding, 'I tried to write some verse.'

'What, you, Wilson?'

He said furiously, 'Yes, me, Wilson. Why not? And it's been published.'

'I wasn't laughing. I was just surprised. Who published it?'

'A new paper called *The Circle*. Of course they don't pay much.'

'Can I see it?'

Wilson said breathlessly, 'I've got it here.' He explained, 'There was something on the other side I couldn't stand. It was just too modern for me.' He watched her with hungry embarrassment.

'It's quite pretty,' she said weakly.

'You see the initials?'

'I've never had a poem dedicated to me before.'

Wilson felt sick; he wanted to sit down. Why, he wondered, does one ever begin this humiliating process: why does one imagine that one is in love? He had read somewhere that love had been invented in the eleventh century by the troubadours. Why had they not left us with lust? He said with hopeless venom, 'I love you.' He thought: it's a lie, the word means nothing off the printed page. He waited for her laughter.

'Oh, no, Wilson,' she said, 'no. You don't. It's just Coast fever.'

He plunged blindly, 'More than anything in the world.'

She said gently, 'No one loves like that, Wilson.'

He walked restlessly up and down, his shorts flapping, waving the bit of paper from *The Downhamian*. 'You ought to believe in love. You're a Catholic. Didn't God love the world?'

'Oh yes,' she said, 'He's capable of it. But not many of us are.'

'You love your husband. You told me so. And it's brought you back.'

Louise said sadly, 'I suppose I do. All I can. But it's not the kind of love *you* want to imagine you feel. No poisoned chalices, eternal doom, black sails. We don't *die* for love, Wilson—except, of course, in books. And sometimes a boy play-acting. Don't let's play-act, Wilson—it's no fun at our age.'

'I'm not play-acting,' he said with a fury in which he could hear too easily the histrionic accent. He confronted her bookcase as though it were a witness she had forgotten. 'Do *they* play-act?'

'Not much,' she said. 'That's why I like them better than *your* poets.'

'All the same you came back.' His face lit up with wicked inspiration. 'Or was that just jealousy?'

She said, 'Jealousy? What on earth have I got to be jealous about?'

'They've been careful,' Wilson said, 'but not as careful as all that.'

'I don't know what you are talking about.'

'Your Ticki and Helen Rolt.'

Louise struck at his cheek and missing got his nose, which began to bleed copiously. She said, 'That's for calling him Ticki. Nobody's going to do that except me. You know he hates it. Here, take my handkerchief if you haven't got one of your own.'

Wilson said, 'I bleed awfully easily. Do you mind if I lie on my back?' He stretched himself on the floor between the table and the meat safe, among the ants. First there had been Scobie watching his tears at Pende, and now—this.

'You wouldn't like me to put a key down your back?' Louise asked.

'No. No thank you.' The blood had stained the *Downhamian* page.

'I really *am* sorry. I've got a vile temper. This will cure you, Wilson.' But if romance is what one lives by, one must never be cured of it. The world has too many spoilt priests of this faith or that: better surely to pretend a belief than wander in that vicious vacuum of cruelty and despair. He said obstinately, 'Nothing will cure me, Louise. I love you. Nothing,' bleeding into her handkerchief.

'How strange,' she said, 'it would be if it were true.'

He grunted a query from the ground.

'I mean,' she explained, 'if you *were* one of those people who really love. I thought Henry was. It would be strange if really it was you all the time.' He felt an odd fear that after all he was going to be accepted at his own valuation, rather as a minor staff officer might feel during a rout when he finds that his claim to know the handling of the tanks will be accepted. It is too late to admit that he knows nothing but what he has read in the technical journals—'O lyric love, half angel and half bird.' Bleeding into the handkerchief, he formed his lips carefully round a generous phrase, 'I expect he loves—in his way.'

'Who?' Louise said. 'Me? This Helen Rolt you are talking about? Or just himself?'

'I shouldn't have said that.'

'Isn't it true? Let's have a bit of truth, Wilson. You don't know how tired I am of comforting lies. Is she beautiful?'

'Oh no, no. Nothing of that sort.'

'She's young, of course, and I'm middle-aged. But surely she's a bit worn after what she's been through.'

'She's very worn.'

'But she's not a Catholic. She's lucky. She's free, Wilson.'

Wilson sat up against the leg of the table. He said with genuine passion, 'I wish to God you wouldn't call me Wilson.'

'Edward. Eddie. Ted. Teddy.'

'I'm bleeding again,' he said dismally and lay back on the floor.

'What do you know about it all, Teddie?'

'I think I'd rather be Edward. Louise, I've seen him come away from her hut at two in the morning. He was up there yesterday afternoon.'

'He was at confession.'

'Harris saw him.'

'You're certainly watching him.'

'It's my belief Yusef is using him.'

'That's fantastic. You're going too far.'

She stood over him as though he were a corpse: the blood-stained handkerchief lay in his palm. They neither of them heard the car stop or the footsteps up to the threshold. It was strange to both of them, hearing a third voice from an outside world speaking into this room which had become as close and intimate and airless as a vault. 'Is anything wrong?' Scobie's voice asked.

'It's just . . .' Louise said and made a gesture of bewilderment—as though she were saying: where does one start explaining? Wilson scrambled to his feet and at once his nose began to bleed.

'Here,' Scobie said and taking out his bundle of keys dropped them inside Wilson's shirt collar. 'You'll see,' he said, 'the old-fashioned remedies are always best,' and sure enough the bleeding did stop within a few seconds. 'You should never lie on your back,' Scobie went reasonably on. 'Seconds use a sponge of cold water, and you certainly look as though you'd been in a fight, Wilson.'

'I always lie on my back,' Wilson said. 'Blood makes me ill.'

'Have a drink?'

'No,' Wilson said, 'no. I must be off.' He retrieved the keys with some difficulty and left the tail of his shirt dangling. He only discovered it when Harris pointed it out to him on his return to the Nissen, and he thought: that is how I looked while I walked away and they watched side by side.

'What did he want?' Scobie said.

'He wanted to make love to me.'

'Does he love you?'

'He thinks he does. You can't ask much more than that, can you?'

'You seem to have hit him rather hard,' Scobie said, 'on the nose?'

'He made me angry. He called you Ticki. Darling, he's spying on you.'

'I know that.'

'Is he dangerous?'

'He might be—under some circumstances. But then it would be my fault.'

'Henry, do you never get furious at anyone? Don't you mind him making love to me?'

He said, 'I'd be a hypocrite if I were angry at that. It's the kind of thing that happens to people. You know, quite pleasant normal people do fall in love.'

'Have you ever fallen in love?'

'Oh yes, yes.' He watched her closely while he excavated his smile. '*You* know I have.'

'Henry, did you really feel ill this morning?'

'Yes.'

'It wasn't just an excuse?'

'No.'

'Then, darling, let's go to communion together to-morrow morning.'

'If you want to,' he said. It was the moment he had known would come. With bravado, to show that his hand was not shaking, he took down a glass. 'Drink?'

'It's too early, dear,' Louise said; he knew she was watching him closely like all the others. He put the glass down and said, 'I've just got to run back to the station for some papers. When I get back it will be time for drinks.'

He drove unsteadily down the road, his eyes blurred with nausea. O God, he thought, the decisions you force on people, suddenly, with no time to consider. I am too tired to think: this ought to be worked out on paper like a problem in mathematics, and the answer arrived at without pain. But the pain made him physically sick, so that he retched over the wheel. The trouble is, he thought, we know the answers—we Catholics are damned by our knowledge. There's no need for me to work anything out—there is only one answer: to kneel down in the confessional and say, 'Since my last confession I have committed adultery so many times etcetera etcetera'; to hear Father Rank telling me to avoid the occasion: never see the woman alone (speaking in those terrible abstract terms: Helen—the woman, the occasion, no longer the bewildered child clutching the stamp-album, listening to Bagster howling outside the door: that moment of peace and darkness and tenderness and pity 'adultery'). And I to make my act of contrition, the promise 'never more to offend thee', and then to-morrow the communion: taking God in my mouth in what they call the state of grace. That's the right answer—there *is* no other answer: to save my own soul and abandon her to Bagster and despair. One must be reasonable, he told himself, and recognise that despair doesn't last (is that true?), that love doesn't last (but isn't that the very reason that despair does?), that in a few weeks or months she'll be all right again. She has survived forty days in an open boat and the death of her husband and can't she survive the mere death of love? As I can, as I know I can.

He drew up outside the church and sat hopelessly at the wheel. Death never comes when one desires it most. He thought: of course there's the ordinary honest *wrong* answer, to leave Louise, forget that private vow, resign my job. To abandon Helen to Bagster or Louise to what? I am trapped, he told himself, catching sight of an expressionless stranger's face in the driving mirror, trapped. Nevertheless he left the car and went into the church. While he was waiting for Father Rank to go into the confessional he knelt and prayed: the only prayer he could rake up. Even the words of the 'Our Father' and the 'Hail Mary' deserted him. He prayed for a miracle, 'O God convince me, help me, convince me. Make me feel that I am more important than that girl.' It was not Helen's face he saw as he prayed but the dying child who called him father: a face in a photograph staring from the dressing-table: the face of a black girl of twelve a sailor had raped and killed glaring blindly up at him in a yellow paraffin light. 'Make me put my own soul first. Give me trust in your mercy to the one I abandon.' He could hear Father Rank close the door of his box and nausea twisted him again on his knees. 'O God,' he said, 'if instead I should abandon you, punish me but let the others get some happiness.' He went into the box. He thought, a miracle may still happen. Even Father Rank may for once find the word, the right word. . . . Kneeling in the space of an upturned coffin he said, 'Since my last confession I have committed adultery.'

'How many times?'

'I don't know, Father, many times.'

'Are you married?'

'Yes.' He remembered that evening when Father Rank had nearly broken down before him, admitting his failure to help. . . . Was he, even while he was struggling to retain the complete anonymity of the confessional, remembering it too? He wanted to say, 'Help me, Father. Convince me that I would do right to abandon her to Bagster. Make me believe in the mercy of God,' but he knelt silently waiting: he was unaware of the slightest tremor of hope. Father Rank said, 'Is it one woman?'

'Yes.'

'You must avoid seeing her. Is that possible?'

He shook his head.

'If you must see her, you must never be alone with her. Do you promise to do that, promise God not me?' He thought: how foolish it was of me to expect the magic word. This is the formula used so many times on so many people. Presumably people promised and went away and came back and confessed again. Did they really believe they were going to try? He thought: I am cheating human beings every day I live, I am not going to try to cheat myself or God. He replied, 'It would be no good my promising that, Father.'

'You must promise. You can't desire the end without desiring the means.'

Ah, but one can, he thought, one can: one can desire the peace of victory without desiring the ravaged towns.

Father Rank said, 'I don't need to tell you surely that there's nothing automatic in the confessional or in absolution. It depends on your state of mind whether you are forgiven. It's no good coming and kneeling here unprepared. Before you come here you must know the wrong you've done.'

'I do know that.'

'And you must have a real purpose of amendment. We are told to forgive our brother seventy times seven and we needn't fear God will be any less forgiving than we are, but nobody can begin to forgive the uncontrite. It's better to sin seventy times and repent each time than sin once and never repent.' He could see Father Rank's hand go up to wipe the sweat out of his eyes: it was like a gesture of weariness. He thought: what is the good of keeping him in this discomfort? He's right, of course, he's right. I was a fool to imagine that somehow in this airless box I would find a conviction. . . . He said, 'I think I was wrong to come, Father.'

'I don't want to refuse you absolution, but I think if you would just go away and turn things over in your mind, you'd come back in a better frame of mind.'

'Yes, Father.'

'I will pray for you.'

When he came out of the box it seemed to Scobie that for the first time his footsteps had taken him out of sight of hope. There was no hope anywhere he turned his eyes: the dead figure of the God upon the cross, the plaster Virgin, the hideous stations representing a series of events that had happened a long time ago. It seemed to him that he had only left for his exploration the territory of despair.

He drove down to the station, collected a file and returned home. 'You've been a long time,' Louise said. He didn't even know the lie he was going to tell before it was on his lips. 'That pain came back,' he said, 'so I waited for a while.'

'Do you think you ought to have a drink?'

'Yes, until anybody tells me not to.'

'And you'll see a doctor?'

'Of course.'

That night he dreamed that he was in a boat drifting down just such an underground river as his boyhood hero Allan Quatermain had taken towards the lost city of Milosis. But Quatermain had companions while he was alone, for you couldn't count the dead body on the stretcher as a companion. He felt a sense of urgency, for he told himself that bodies in this climate kept for a very short time and the smell of decay was already in his nostrils. Then, sitting there guiding the boat down the mid-stream, he realised that it was not the dead body that smelt but his own living one. He felt as though his blood had ceased to run: when he tried to lift his arm it dangled uselessly from his shoulder. He woke and it was Louise who had lifted his arm. She said, 'Darling, it's time to be off.'

'Off?' he asked.

'We're going to Mass,' and again he was aware of how closely she was watching him. What was the good of yet another delaying lie? He wondered what Wilson had said to her. Could he go on lying week after week, finding some reason of work, of health, of forgetfulness for avoiding the issue at the altar rail? He thought hopelessly: I am damned already—I may as well go the whole length of my chain. 'Yes,' he said, 'of course. I'll get up,' and was suddenly surprised by her putting the excuse into his mouth, giving him his chance. 'Darling,' she said, 'if you aren't well, stay where you are. I don't want to drag you to Mass.'

But the excuse it seemed to him was also a trap. He could see where the turf had been replaced over the hidden stakes. If he took the excuse she offered he would have all but confessed his guilt. Once and for all now at whatever eternal cost, he was determined that he would clear himself in her eyes and give her the reassurance she needed. He said, 'No, no. I will come with you.' When he walked beside her into the church it was as if he had entered this building for the first time—a stranger. An immeasurable distance already separated him from these people who knelt and prayed and would presently receive God in peace. He knelt and pretended to pray.

The words of the Mass were like an indictment. 'I will go in unto the altar of God: to God who giveth joy to my youth.' But there was no joy anywhere. He looked up from between his hands and the plaster images of the Virgin and the saints seemed to be holding out hands to everyone, on either side, beyond him. He was the unknown guest at a party who is introduced to no one. The gentle painted smiles were unbearably directed elsewhere. When the Kyrie Eleison was reached he again tried to pray. 'Lord have mercy . . . Christ have mercy . . . Lord have mercy,' but the fear and the shame of the act he was going to commit chilled his brain. Those ruined priests who presided at a Black Mass, consecrating the Host over the naked body of a woman, consuming God in an absurd and horrifying ritual, were at least performing the act of damnation with an emotion larger than human love: they were doing it from hate of God or some odd perverse devotion to God's enemy. But he had no love of evil or hate of God. How was he to hate this God who of His own accord was surrendering Himself into his power? He was desecrating God because he loved a woman—was it even love, or was it just a feeling of pity and responsibility? He tried again to excuse himself: 'You can look after yourself. You survive the cross every day. You can only suffer. You can never be lost. Admit that you must come second to these others.' And myself, he thought, watching the priest pour the wine and water into the chalice, his own damnation being prepared like a meal at the altar, I must come last: I am the Deputy Commissioner of Police: a hundred men serve under me: I am the responsible man. It is my job to look after the others. I am conditioned to serve.

Sanctus. Sanctus. Sanctus. The Canon of the Mass had started: Father Rank's whisper at the altar hurried remorselessly towards the consecration. 'To order our days in thy peace . . . that we be preserved from eternal damnation. . . .' *Pax, pacis, pacem*: all the declinations of the word 'peace' drummed on his ears through the Mass. He thought: I have left even the hope of peace for ever. I am the responsible man. I shall soon have gone too far in my design of deception ever to go back. *Hoc est enim Corpus*: the bell rang, and Father Rank raised God in his fingers–this God as light now as a wafer whose coming lay on Scobie's heart as heavily as lead. *Hic est enim calix sanguinis* and the second bell.

Louise touched his hand. 'Dear, are you well?' He thought: here is the second chance. The return of my pain. I can go out. But if he went out of church now, he knew that there would be only one thing left to do–to follow Father Rank's advice, to settle his affairs, to desert, to come back in a few days' time and take God with a clear conscience and a knowledge that he had pushed innocence back where it properly belonged–under the Atlantic surge. Innocence must die young if it isn't to kill the souls of men.

'Peace I leave with you, my peace I give unto you.'

'I'm all right,' he said, the old longing pricking at the eyeballs, and looking up towards the cross on the altar he thought savagely: Take your sponge of gall. You made me what I am. Take the spear thrust. He didn't need to open his Missal to know how this prayer ended. 'May the receiving of Thy Body, O Lord Jesus Christ, which I unworthy presume to take, turn not to my judgment and condemnation.' He shut his eyes and let the darkness in. Mass rushed towards its end: *Domine, non sum dignus . . . Domine, non sum dignus . . . Domine, non sum dignus. . . .* At the foot of the scaffold he opened his eyes and saw the old black women shuffling up towards the altar rail, a few soldiers, an aircraft mechanic, one of his own policemen, a clerk from the bank: they moved sedately towards peace, and Scobie felt an envy of their simplicity, their goodness. Yes, now at this moment of time they were good.

'Aren't you coming, dear?' Louise asked, and again the hand touched him: the kindly firm detective hand. He rose and followed her and knelt by her side like a spy in a foreign land who has been taught the customs and to speak the language like a native. Only a miracle can save me now, Scobie told himself, watching Father Rank at the altar opening the tabernacle, but God would never work a miracle to save Himself. I am the cross, he thought, He will never speak the word to save Himself from the cross, but if only wood were made so that it didn't feel, if only the nails were senseless as people believed.

Father Rank came down the steps from the altar bearing the Host. The saliva had dried in Scobie's mouth: it was as though his veins had dried. He couldn't look up; he saw only the priest's skirt like the skirt of the mediæval war-horse bearing down upon him: the flapping of feet: the charge of God. If only the archers would let fly from ambush, and for a moment he dreamed that the priest's steps had indeed faltered: perhaps after all something may yet happen before he reaches me: some incredible interposition. . . . But with open mouth (the time had come) he made one last attempt at prayer, 'O God, I offer up my damnation to you. Take it. Use it for them,' and was aware of the pale papery taste of an eternal sentence on the tongue.

3/i

The bank manager took a sip of iced water and exlaimed with more than professional warmth, 'How glad you must be to have Mrs Scobie back well in time for Christmas.'

'Christmas is a long way off still,' Scobie said.

'Time flies when the rains are over,' the bank manager went on with his novel cheerfulness. Scobie had never before heard in his voice this note of optimism. He remembered the stork-like figure pacing to and fro, pausing at the medical books, so many hundred times a day.

'I came along . . .' Scobie began.

'About your life insurance–or an overdraft, would it be?'

'Well, it wasn't either this time.'

'You know I'll always be glad to help you, Scobie, whatever it is.' How quietly Robinson sat at his desk. Scobie said with wonder, 'Have you given up your daily exercise?'

'Ah, that was all stuff and nonsense,' the manager said. 'I had read too many books.'

'I wanted to look in your medical encyclopædia,' Scobie explained.

'You'd do much better to see a doctor,' Robinson surprisingly advised him. 'It's a doctor who's put me right, not the books. The time I would have wasted. . . . I tell you, Scobie, the new young fellow they've got at the Argyll Hospital's the best man they've sent to this colony since they discovered it.'

'And he's put you right?'

'Go and see him. His name's Travis. Tell him I sent you.'

'All the same, if I could just have a look . . .'

'You'll find it on the shelf. I keep 'em there still because they look important. A bank manager has to be a reading man. People expect him to have solid books around.'

'I'm glad your stomach's cured.'

The manager took another sip of water. He said, 'I'm not bothering about it any more. The truth of the matter is, Scobie, I'm . . .'

Scobie looked through the encyclopædia for the word Angina and now he read on: CHARACTER OF THE PAIN. *This is usually described as being 'gripping', 'as though the chest were in a vice'. The pain is situated in the middle of the chest and under the sternum. It may run down either arm, perhaps more commonly the left, or up into the neck or down into the abdomen. It lasts a few seconds, or at the most a minute or so.* THE BEHAVIOUR OF THE PATIENT. *This is characteristic. He holds himself absolutely still in whatever circumstances he may find himself. . . .* Scobie's eye passed rapidly down the cross-headings: CAUSE OF THE PAIN. TREATMENT. TERMINATION OF THE DISEASE. Then he put the book back on the shelf. 'Well,' he said, 'perhaps I'll drop in on your Doctor Travis. I'd rather see him than Doctor Sykes. I hope he cheers me up as he's done you.'

'Well, my case,' the manager said evasively, 'had peculiar features.'

'Mine looks straightforward enough.'

'You seem pretty well.'

'Oh, I'm all right—bar a bit of pain now and then and sleeping badly.'

'Your responsibilities do that for you.'

'Perhaps.'

It seemed to Scobie that he had sowed enough—against what harvest? He couldn't himself have told. He said good-bye and went out into the dazzling street. He carried his helmet and let the sun strike vertically down upon his thin greying hair. He offered himself for punishment all the way to the police station and was rejected. It had seemed to him these last three weeks that the damned must be in a special category; like the young men destined for some unhealthy foreign post in a trading company, they were reserved from their humdrum fellows, protected from the daily task, preserved carefully at special desks, so that the worst might happen later. Nothing now ever seemed to go wrong. The sun would not strike, the Colonial Secretary asked him to dinner . . . He felt rejected by misfortune.

The Commissioner said, 'Come in, Scobie. I've got good news for you,' and Scobie prepared himself for yet another rejection.

'Baker is not coming here. They need him in Palestine. They've decided after all to let the right man succeed me.' Scobie sat down on the window-ledge and watched his hand tremble on his knee. He thought: so all this need not have happened. If Louise had stayed I should never have loved Helen, I would never have been blackmailed by Yusef, never have committed that act of despair. I would have been myself still—the same self that lay stacked in fifteen years of diaries, not this broken cast. But, of course, he told himself, it's only because I have done these things that success comes. I am of the devil's party. He looks after his own in this world. I shall go now from damned success to damned success, he thought with disgust.

'I think Colonel Wright's word was the deciding factor. You impressed him, Scobie.'

'It's come too late, sir.'

'Why too late?'

'I'm too old for the job. It needs a younger man.'

'Nonsense. You're only just fifty.'

'My health's not good.'

'It's the first I've heard of it.'

'I was telling Robinson at the bank to-day. I've been getting pains, and I'm sleeping badly.' He talked rapidly, beating time on his knee. 'Robinson swears by Travis. He seems to have worked wonders with him.'

'Poor Robinson.'

'Why?'

'He's been given two years to live. That's in confidence, Scobie.'

Human beings never cease to surprise: so it was the death sentence that had cured Robinson of his imaginary ailments, his medical books, his daily walk from wall to wall. I suppose, Scobie thought, that is what comes of knowing the worst—one is left alone with the worst and it's like peace. He imagined Robinson talking across the desk to his solitary companion. 'I hope we all die as calmly,' he said. 'Is he going home?'

'I don't think so. I suppose presently he'll have to go to the Argyll.'

Scobie thought: I wish I had known what I had been looking at. Robinson was exhibiting the most enviable possession a man can own—a happy death. This tour would bear a high proportion of deaths—or perhaps not so high when you counted them and remembered Europe. First Pemberton, then the child at Pende, now Robinson . . . no, it wasn't many, but of course he hadn't counted the blackwater cases in the military hospital.

'So that's how matters stand,' the Commissioner said. 'Next tour you will be Commissioner. Your wife will be pleased.'

I must endure her pleasure, Scobie thought, without anger. I am the guilty man, and I have no right to criticise, to show vexation ever again. He said, 'I'll be getting home.'

Ali stood by his car, talking to another boy who slipped quietly away when he saw Scobie approach. 'Who was that, Ali?'

'My small brother, sah,' Ali said.

'I don't know him, do I? Same mother?'

'No, sah, same father.'

'What does he do?' Ali worked at the starting handle, his face dripping with sweat, saying nothing.

'Who does he work for, Ali?'

'Sah?'

'I said who does he work for?'

'For Mr Wilson, sah.'

The engine started and Ali climbed into the back seat. 'Has he ever made you a proposition, Ali? I mean has he asked you to report on me—for money?' He could see Ali's face in the driving mirror, set, obstinate, closed and rocky like a cave mouth. 'No, sah.'

'Lots of people are interested in me and pay good money for reports. They think me bad man, Ali.'

Ali said, 'I'm your boy,' staring back through the medium of the mirror. It seemed to Scobie one of the qualities of deceit that you lost the sense of trust. If I can lie and betray, so can others. Wouldn't many people gamble on my honesty and lose their stake? Why should I lose my stake on Ali? I have not been caught and he has not been caught, that's all. An awful depression weighed his head towards the wheel. He thought: I know that Ali is honest: I have known that for fifteen years; I am just trying to find a companion in this region of lies. Is the next stage the stage of corrupting others?

Louise was not in when they arrived. Presumably someone had called and taken her out—perhaps to the beach. She hadn't expected him back before sundown. He wrote a note for her, *Taking some furniture up to Helen. Will be back early with good news for you*, and then he drove up alone to the Nissen huts through the bleak empty middle day. Only the vultures were about—gathering round a dead chicken at the edge of the road, stooping their old men's necks over the carrion, their wings like broken umbrellas sticking out this way and that.

'I've brought you another table and a couple of chairs. Is your boy about?'

'No, he's at market.'

They kissed as formally now when they met as a brother and sister. When the damage was done adultery became as unimportant as friendship. The flame had licked them and gone on across the clearing: it had left nothing standing except a sense of responsibility and a sense of loneliness. Only if you trod barefooted did you notice the heat in the grass. Scobie said, 'I'm interrupting your lunch.'

'Oh no. I've about finished. Have some fruit salad.'

'It's time you had a new table. This one wobbles.' He said, 'They are making me Commissioner after all.'

'It will please your wife,' Helen said.

'It doesn't mean a thing to me.'

'Oh, of course it does,' she said briskly. This was another convention of hers—that only she suffered. He would for a long time resist, like Coriolanus, the exhibition of *his* wounds, but sooner or later he would give way: he would dramatise his pain in words until even to himself it seemed unreal. Perhaps, he would think, she is right after all: perhaps I don't suffer. She said, 'Of course the Commissioner must be above suspicion, mustn't he, like Cæsar.' (Her sayings, as well as her spelling, lacked accuracy.) 'This is the end of us, I suppose.'

'You know there is no end to us.'

'Oh, but the Commissioner can't have a mistress hidden away in a Nissen hut.' The sting, of course, was in the 'hidden away', but how could he allow himself to feel the least irritation, remembering the letter she had written to him, offering herself as a sacrifice any way he liked, to keep or to throw away? Human beings couldn't be heroic all the time: those who surrendered everything—for God or love—must be allowed sometimes in thought to take back their surrender. So many had never committed the heroic act, however rashly. It was the act that counted. He said, 'If the Commissioner can't keep you, then I shan't be the Commissioner.'

'Don't be silly. After all,' she said with fake reasonableness, and he recognised this as one of her bad days, 'what do we get out of it?'

'I get a lot,' he said, and wondered: is that a lie for the sake of comfort? There were so many lies nowadays he couldn't keep track of the small, the unimportant ones.

'An hour or two every other day perhaps when you can slip away. Never so much as a night.'

He said hopelessly, 'Oh, I have plans.'

'What plans?'

He said, 'They are too vague still.'

She said with all the acid she could squeeze out, 'Well, let me know in time. To fall in with your wishes, I mean.'

'My dear, I haven't come here to quarrel.'

'I sometimes wonder what you do come here for.'

'Well, to-day I brought some furniture.'

'Oh yes, the furniture.'

'I've got the car here. Let me take you to the beach.'

'Oh, we can't be seen there together.'

'That's nonsense. Louise is there now, I think.'

'For God's sake,' Helen said, 'keep that smug woman out of my sight.'

'All right then. I'll take you for a run in the car.'

'That would be safer, wouldn't it?'

Scobie took her by the shoulders and said, 'I'm not always thinking of safety.'

'I thought you were.'

Suddenly he felt his resistance give way and he shouted at her, 'The sacrifice isn't all on your side.' With despair he could see from a distance the scene coming up on both of them: like the tornado before the rains, that wheeling column of blackness which would soon cover the whole sky.

'Of course work must suffer,' she said with childish sarcasm. 'All these snatched half-hours.'

'I've given up hope,' he said.

'What do you mean?'

'I've given up the future. I've damned myself.'

'Don't be so melodramatic,' she said. 'I don't know what you are talking about. Anyway, you've just told me about the future—the Commissionership.'

'I mean the real future—the future that goes on.'

She said, 'If there's one thing I hate it's your Catholicism. I suppose it comes of having a pious wife. It's so bogus. If you really believed you wouldn't be here.'

'But I do believe and I am here.' He said with bewilderment, 'I can't explain it, but there it is. My eyes are open. I know what I'm doing. When Father Rank came down to the rail carrying the sacrament . . .'

Helen exclaimed with scorn and impatience, 'You've told me all that before. You are trying to impress me. You don't believe in hell any more than I do.'

He took her wrists and held them furiously. He said, 'You can't get out of it that way. I believe, I tell you. I believe that I'm damned for all eternity—unless a miracle happens. I'm a policeman. I know what I'm saying. What I've done is far worse than murder—that's an act, a blow, a stab, a shot: it's over and done, but I'm carrying my corruption around with me. It's the coating of my stomach.' He threw her wrists aside like seeds towards the stony floor. 'Never pretend I haven't shown my love.'

'Love for your wife, you mean. You were afraid she'd find out.'

Anger drained out of him. He said, 'Love for both of you. If it were just for her there'd be an easy straight way.' He put his hands over his eyes, feeling hysteria beginning to mount again. He said, 'I can't bear to see suffering, and I cause it all the time. I want to get out, get out.'

'Where to?'

Hysteria and honesty receded: cunning came back across the threshold like a mongrel dog. He said, 'Oh, I just mean take a holiday.' He added, 'I'm not sleeping well. And I've been getting an odd pain.'

'Darling, are you ill?' The pillar had wheeled on its course: the storm was involving others now: it had passed beyond them. Helen said, 'Darling, I'm a bitch. I get tired and fed up with things—but it doesn't mean anything. Have you seen a doctor?'

'I'll see Travis at the Argyll some time soon.'

'Everybody says Dr Sykes is better.'

'No, I don't want to see Dr Sykes.' Now that the anger and hysteria had passed he could see her exactly as she was that first evening when the sirens blew. He thought, O God, I can't leave her. Or Louise. You don't need me as they need me. You have your good people, your saints, all the company of the blessed. You can do without me. He said, 'I'll take you for a spin now in the car. It will do us both good.'

In the dusk of the garage he took her hands again and kissed her. He said, 'There are no eyes here ... Wilson can't see us. Harris isn't watching. Yusef's boys ...'

'Dear, I'd leave you to-morrow if it would help.'

'It wouldn't help.' He said, 'You remember when I wrote you a letter–which got lost. I tried to put down everything there, plainly, in black and white. So as not to be cautious any more. I wrote that I loved you more than my wife. ...' As he spoke he heard another's breath behind his shoulder, beside the car. He said, sharply, 'Who's that?'

'What, dear?'

'Somebody's here.' He came round to the other side of the car and said sharply, 'Who's there? Come out.'

'It's Ali,' Helen said.

'What are you doing here, Ali?'

'Missus sent me,' Ali said. 'I wait here for Massa tell him Missus back.' He was hardly visible in the shadow.

'Why were you waiting here?'

'My head humbug me,' Ali said. 'I go for sleep, small, small sleep.'

'Don't frighten him,' Helen said. 'He's telling the truth.'

'Go along home, Ali,' Scobie told him, 'and tell Missus I come straight down.' He watched him pad out into the hard sunlight between the Nissen huts. He never looked back.

'Don't worry about him,' Helen said. 'He didn't understand a thing.'

'I've had Ali for fifteen years,' Scobie said. It was the first time he had been ashamed before him in all those years. He remembered Ali the night after Pemberton's death, cup of tea in hand, holding him up against the shaking lorry, and then he remembered Wilson's boy slinking off along the wall by the police station.

'You can trust him anyway.'

'I don't know how,' Scobie said. 'I've lost the trick of trust.'

3/ii

Louise was asleep upstairs, and Scobie sat at the table with his diary open. He had written down against the date October 31: *Commissioner told me this morning I am to succeed him. Took some furniture to H.R. Told Louise news, which pleased her.* The other life–bare and undisturbed and built of facts–lay like Roman foundations under his hand. This was the life he was supposed to lead; no one reading this record would visualise the obscure shameful scene in the garage, the interview with the Portuguese captain, Louise striking out blindly with the painful truth, Helen accusing him of hypocrisy. ... He thought: this is how it ought to be. I am too old for emotion. I am too old to be a cheat. Lies are for the young. They have a lifetime of truth to recover in. He looked at his watch, 11.45, and wrote: *Temperature at 2 p.m. 92* . The lizard pounced upon the wall, the tiny jaws clamping on a moth. Something scratched outside the door–a pye-dog? He laid his pen down again and loneliness sat across the table opposite him. No man surely was less alone with his wife upstairs and his mistress little more than five hundred yards away up the hill, and yet it was loneliness that seated itself like a companion who doesn't need to speak. It seemed to him that he had never been so alone before.

There was nobody now to whom he could speak the truth. There were things the Commissioner must not know, Louise must not know, there were even limits to what he could tell Helen, for what was the use, when he had sacrificed so much in order to avoid pain, of inflicting it needlessly? As for God he could speak to Him only as one speaks to an enemy–there was bitterness between them. He moved his hand on the table, and it was as though his loneliness moved too and touched the tips of his fingers. 'You and I,' his loneliness said, 'you and I.' It occurred to him that the outside world if they knew the facts might envy him: Bagster would envy him Helen, and Wilson Louise. What a hell of a quiet dog, Fraser would exclaim with a lick of the lips. They would imagine, he thought with amazement, that I get something out of it, but it seemed to him that no man had ever got less. Even self-pity was denied him because he knew so exactly the extent of his guilt. He felt as though he had exiled himself so deeply in the desert that his skin had taken on the colour of the sand.

The door creaked gently open behind him. Scobie did not move. The spies, he thought, are creeping in. Is this Wilson, Harris, Pemberton's boy, Ali. . . ? 'Massa,' a voice whispered, and a bare foot slapped the concrete floor.

'Who are you?' Scobie asked, not turning round. A pink palm dropped a small ball of paper on the table and went out of sight again. The voice said, 'Yusef say come very quiet nobody see.'

'What does Yusef want now?'

'He send you dash–small small dash.' Then the door closed again and silence was back. Loneliness said, 'Let us open this together, you and I.'

Scobie picked up the ball of paper: it was light, but it had a small hard centre. At first he didn't realise what it was: he thought it was a pebble put in to keep the paper steady and he looked for writing which, of course, was not there, for whom would Yusef trust to write for him? Then he realised what it was–a diamond, a gem stone. He knew nothing about diamonds, but it seemed to him that it was probably worth at least as much as his debt to Yusef. Presumably Yusef had information that the stones he had sent by the *Esperança* had reached their destination safely. This was a mark of gratitude–not a bribe, Yusef would explain, the fat hand upon his sincere and shallow heart.

The door burst open and there was Ali. He had a boy by the arm who whimpered. Ali said, 'This stinking Mende boy he go all round the house. He try doors.'

'Who are you?' Scobie said.

The boy broke out in a mixture of fear and rage, 'I Yusef's boy. I bring

Massa letter,' and he pointed at the table where the pebble lay in the screw of paper. Ali's eyes followed the gesture. Scobie said to his loneliness, 'You and I have to think quickly.' He turned on the boy and said, 'Why you not come here properly and knock on the door? Why you come like a thief?'

He had the thin body and the melancholy soft eyes of all Mendes. He said, 'I not a thief,' with so slight an emphasis on the first word that it was just possible he was not impertinent. He went on, 'Massa tell me to come very quiet.'

Scobie said, 'Take this back to Yusef and tell him I want to know where he gets a stone like that. I think he steals stones and I find out by-and-by. Go on. Take it. Now, Ali, throw him out.' Ali pushed the boy ahead of him through the door, and Scobie could hear the rustle of their feet on the path. Were they whispering together? He went to the door and called out after them, 'Tell Yusef I call on him one night soon and make hell of a palaver.' He slammed the door again and thought, what a lot Ali knows, and he felt distrust of his boy moving again like fever with the bloodstream. He could ruin me, he thought: he could ruin *them*.

He poured himself out a glass of whisky and took a bottle of soda out of his ice-box. Louise called from upstairs, 'Henry.'

'Yes, dear?'

'Is it twelve yet?'

'Close on, I think.'

'You won't drink anything after twelve, will you? You remember to-morrow?' and of course he did remember, draining his glass: it was November the First—All Saints' Day, and this All Souls' Night. What ghost would pass over the whisky's surface? 'You are coming to communion, aren't you, dear?' and he thought wearily: there is no end to this: why should I draw the line now? One may as well go on damning oneself until the end. His loneliness was the only ghost his whisky could invoke, nodding across the table at him, taking a drink out of his glass. 'The next occasion,' loneliness told him, 'will be Christmas—the Midnight Mass—you won't be able to avoid that you know, and no excuse will serve you on that night, and after that'—the long chain of feast days, of early Masses in spring and summer, unrolled themselves like a perpetual calendar. He had a sudden picture before his eyes of a bleeding face, of eyes closed by the continuous shower of blows: the punch-drunk head of God reeling sideways.

'You *are* coming, Ticki?' Louise called with what seemed to him a sudden anxiety, as though perhaps suspicion had momentarily breathed on her again—and he thought again, can Ali really be trusted? and all the stale coast wisdom of the traders and the remittance men told him, 'Never trust a black. They'll let you down in the end. Had my boy fifteen years. . . .' The ghosts of distrust came out on All Souls' Night and gathered around his glass.

'Oh yes, my dear, I'm coming.'

'You have only to say the word,' he addressed God, 'and legions of angels . . .' and he struck with his ringed hand under the eye and saw the bruised skin break. He thought, 'And again at Christmas,' thrusting the child's face into the filth of the stable. He cried up the stairs, 'What's that you said, dear?'

'Oh, only that we've got so much to celebrate tomorrow. Being together and the Commissionership. Life is so happy, Ticki.' And that, he told his loneliness with defiance, is my reward, splashing the whisky across the table, defying the ghosts to do their worst, watching God bleed.

4/i

He could tell that Yusef was working late in his office on the quay. The little white two-storeyed building stood beside the wooden jetty on the edge of Africa, just beyond the army dumps of petrol, and a line of light showed under the curtains of the landward window. A policeman saluted Scobie as he picked his way between the crates. 'All quiet, corporal?'

'All quiet, sah.'

'Have you patrolled at the Kru Town end?'

'Oh yes, sah. All quiet, sah.' He could tell from the promptitude of the reply how untrue it was.

'The wharf rats out?'

'Oh no, sah. All very quiet like the grave.' The stale literary phrase showed that the man had been educated at a mission school.

'Well, good night.'

'Good night, sah.'

Scobie went on. It was many weeks now since he had seen Yusef—not since the night of the blackmail, and now he felt an odd yearning towards his tormentor. The little white building magnetised him, as though concealed there was his only companionship, the only man he could trust. At least his blackmailer knew him as no one else did: he could sit opposite that fat absurd figure and tell the whole truth. In this new world of lies his blackmailer was at home: he knew the paths: he could advise: even help. . . . Round the corner of a crate came Wilson. Scobie's torch lit his face like a map.

'Why, Wilson,' Scobie said, 'you are out late.'

'Yes,' Wilson said, and Scobie thought uneasily, how he hates me.

'You've got a pass for the quay?'

'Yes.'

'Keep away from the Kru Town end. It's not safe there alone. No more nose bleeding?'

'No,' Wilson said. He made no attempt to move; it seemed always his way—to stand blocking a path: a man one had to walk around.

'Well, I'll be saying good night, Wilson. Look in any time. Louise . . .'

Wilson said, 'I love her, Scobie.'

'I thought you did,' Scobie said. 'She likes you, Wilson.'

'I love her,' Wilson repeated. He plucked at the tarpaulin over the crate and said, 'You wouldn't know what that means.'

'What means?'

'Love. You don't love anybody except yourself, your dirty self.'

'You are overwrought, Wilson. It's the climate. Go and lie down.'

'You wouldn't act as you do if you loved her.' Over the black tide, from an invisible ship, came the sound of a gramophone playing some popular heart-rending tune. A sentry by the Field Security post challenged and somebody replied with a password. Scobie lowered his torch till it lit only Wilson's mosquito-boots. He said, 'Love isn't as simple as you think it is, Wilson. You read too much poetry.'

'What would you do if I told her everything–about Mrs Rolt?'

'But you have told her, Wilson. What you believe. But she prefers my story.'

'One day I'll ruin you, Scobie.'

'Would that help Louise?'

'I could make her happy,' Wilson claimed ingenuously, with a breaking voice that took Scobie back over fifteen years–to a much younger man than this soiled specimen who listened to Wilson at the sea's edge, hearing under the words the low sucking of water against wood. He said gently, 'You'd try. I know you'd try. Perhaps . . .' But he had no idea himself how that sentence was supposed to finish, what vague comfort for Wilson had brushed his mind and gone again. Instead an irritation took him against the gangling romantic figure by the crate who was so ignorant and yet knew so much. He said, 'I wish meanwhile you'd stop spying on me.'

'It's my job,' Wilson admitted, and his boots moved in the torchlight.

'The things you find out are so unimportant.' He left Wilson beside the petrol dump and walked on. As he climbed the steps to Yusef's office he could see, looking back, an obscure thickening of the darkness where Wilson stood and watched and hated. He would go home and draft a report. 'At 11.25 I observed Major Scobie going obviously by appointment. . . .'

Scobie knocked and walked right in where Yusef half lay behind his desk, his legs upon it, dictating to a black clerk. Without breaking his sentence–'five hundred rolls match-box design, seven hundred and fifty bucket and sand, six hundred poker dot artificial silk'–he looked up at Scobie with hope and apprehension. Then he said sharply to the clerk, 'Get out. But come back. Tell my boy that I see no one.' He took his legs from the desk, rose and held out a flabby hand, 'Welcome, Major Scobie,' then let it fall like an unwanted piece of material. 'This is the first time you have ever honoured my office, Major Scobie.'

'I don't know why I've come here now, Yusef.'

'It is a long time since we have seen each other.' Yusef sat down and rested his great head wearily on a palm like a dish. 'Time goes so differently for two people–fast or slow. According to their friendship.'

'There's probably a Syrian poem about that.'

'There is, Major Scobie,' he said eagerly.

'You should be friends with Wilson, not me, Yusef. He reads poetry. I have a prose mind.'

'A whisky, Major Scobie?'

'I wouldn't say no.' He sat down on the other side of the desk and the inevitable blue syphon stood between them.

'And how is Mrs Scobie?'

'Why did you send me that diamond, Yusef?'

'I was in your debt, Major Scobie.'

'Oh no, you weren't. You paid me off in full with a bit of paper.'

'I try so hard to forget that that was the way. I tell myself it was really friendship–at bottom it was friendship.'

'It's never any good lying to oneself, Yusef. One sees through the lie too easily.'

'Major Scobie, if I saw more of you, I should become a better man.' The soda hissed in the glasses and Yusef drank greedily. He said, 'I can feel in my heart, Major Scobie, that you are anxious, depressed. ... I have always wished that you would come to me in trouble.'

Scobie said, 'I used to laugh at the idea–that I should ever come to you.'

' In Syria we have a story of a lion and a mouse. ...'

'We have the same story, Yusef. But I've never thought of you as a mouse, and I'm no lion. No lion.'

'It is about Mrs Rolt you are troubled. And your wife, Major Scobie?'

'Yes.'

'You do not need to be ashamed with me, Major Scobie. I have had much woman trouble in my life. Now it is better because I have learned the way. The way is not to care a damn, Major Scobie. You say to each of them, "I do not care a damn. I sleep with whom I please. You take me or leave me. I do not care a damn." They always take you, Major Scobie.' He sighed into his whisky. 'Sometimes I have wished they would not take me.'

'I've gone to great lengths, Yusef, to keep things from my wife.'

'I know the lengths you have gone, Major Scobie.'

'Not the whole length. The business with the diamonds was very small compared . . .'

'Yes?'

'You wouldn't understand. Anyway somebody else knows now–Ali.'

'But you trust Ali?'

'I think I trust him. But he knows about you too. He came in last night and saw the diamond there. Your boy was very indiscreet.'

The big broad hand shifted on the table. 'I will deal with my boy presently.'

'Ali's half-brother is Wilson's boy. They see each other.'

'That is certainly bad,' Yusef said.

He had told all his worries now–all except the worst. He had the odd sense of having for the first time in his life shifted a burden elsewhere. And Yusef carried it–he obviously carried it. He raised himself from his chair and now moved his great haunches to the window, staring at the green black-out curtain as though it were a landscape. A hand went up to his mouth and he began to bite his nails–snip, snip, snip, his teeth closed on each nail in turn. Then he began on the other hand. 'I don't suppose it's anything to worry about really,' Scobie said. He was touched by uneasiness, as though he had accidentally set in motion a powerful machine he couldn't control.

'It is a bad thing not to trust,' Yusef said. 'One must always have boys one trusts. You must always know more about them than they do about you.' That, apparently, was his conception of trust. Scobie said, 'I used to trust him.'

Yusef looked at his trimmed nails and took another bite. He said, 'Do not worry. I will not have you worry. Leave everything to me, Major Scobie. I will find out for you whether you can trust him.' He made the startling claim, 'I will look after you.'

'How can you do that?' I feel no resentment, he thought with weary surprise. I am being looked after, and a kind of nursery peace descended.

'You mustn't ask me questions, Major Scobie. You must leave everything to me just this once. I understand the way.' Moving from the window Yusef turned on Scobie eyes like closed telescopes, blank and brassy. He said with a soothing nurse's gesture of the broad wet palm, 'You will just write a little note to your boy, Major Scobie, asking him to come here. I will talk to him. My boy will take it to him.'

'But Ali can't read.'

'Better still then. You will send some token with my boy to show that he comes from you. Your signet ring.'

'What are you going to do, Yusef?'

'I am going to help you, Major Scobie. That is all.' Slowly, reluctantly, Scobie drew at his ring. He said, 'He's been with me fifteen years. I always have trusted him until now.'

'You will see,' Yusef said. 'Everything will be all right.' He spread out his palm to receive the ring and their hands touched: it was like a pledge between conspirators. 'Just a few words.'

'The ring won't come off,' Scobie said. He felt an odd unwillingness. 'It's not necessary, anyway. He'll come if your boy tells him that I want him.'

'I do not think so. They do not like to come to the wharf at night.'

'He will be all right. He won't be alone. Your boy will be with him.'

'Oh yes, yes, of course. But I still think—if you would just send something to show—well, that it is not a trap. Yusef's boy is no more trusted, you see, than Yusef.'

'Let him come to-morrow, then.'

'To-night is better,' Yusef said.

Scobie felt in his pockets: the broken rosary grated on his nails. He said, 'Let him take this, but it's not necessary . . .' and fell silent, staring back at those blank eyes.

'Thank you,' Yusef said. 'This is most suitable.' At the door he said, 'Make yourself at home, Major Scobie. Pour yourself another drink. I must give my boy instructions. . . .'

He was away a very long time. Scobie poured himself a third whisky and then, because the little office was so airless, he drew the seaward curtains after turning out the light and let what wind there was trickle in from the bay. The moon was rising and the naval depot ship glittered like grey ice. Restlessly he made his way to the other window that looked up the quay towards the sheds and lumber of the native town. He saw Yusef's clerk coming back from there, and he thought how Yusef must have the wharf rats well under control if his clerk could pass alone through *their* quarters. I came for help, he told himself, and I am being looked after—how, and at whose cost? This was the day of All Saints and he remembered how mechanically, almost without fear or shame, he had knelt at the rail this second time and watched the priest come. Even that act of damnation could become as unimportant as a habit. He thought: my heart has hardened, and he pictured the fossilised shells one picks up on a beach: the stony convolutions like arteries. One can strike God once too often. After that does one care what happens? It seemed to him that he had rotted so far that it was useless to make any effort. God was lodged in his body and his body was corrupting outwards from that seed.

'It was too hot?' Yusef's voice said. 'Let us leave the room dark. With a friend the darkness is kind.'

'You have been a very long time.'

Yusef said with what must have been deliberate vagueness, 'There was much to see to.' It seemed to Scobie that now or never he must ask what was Yusef's plan, but the weariness of his corruption halted his tongue. 'Yes, it's hot,' he said, 'let's try and get a cross-draught,' and he opened the side window on to the quay. 'I wonder if Wilson has gone home.'

'Wilson?'

'He watched me come here.'

'You must not worry, Major Scobie. I think your boy can be made quite trustworthy.'

He said with relief and hope, 'You mean you have a hold on him?'

'Don't ask questions. You will see.' The hope and the relief both wilted. He said, 'Yusef, I *must* know . . .' but Yusef said, 'I have always dreamed of an evening just like this with two glasses by our side and darkness and time to talk about important things, Major Scobie. God. The family. Poetry. I have great appreciation of Shakespeare. The Royal Ordnance Corps have very fine actors and they have made me appreciate the gems of English literature. I am crazy about Shakespeare. Sometimes because of Shakespeare I would like to be able to read, but I am too old to learn. And I think perhaps I would lose my memory. That would be bad for business, and though I do not live for business I must do business to live. There are so many subjects I would like to talk to you about. I should like to hear the philosophy of your life.'

'I have none.'

'The piece of cotton you hold in your hand in the forest.'

'I've lost my way.'

'Not a man like you, Major Scobie. I have such an admiration for your character. You are a just man.'

'I never was, Yusef. I didn't know myself that's all. There's a proverb, you know, about in the end is the beginning. When I was born I was sitting here with you drinking whisky, knowing . . .'

'Knowing what, Major Scobie?'

Scobie emptied his glass. He said, 'Surely your boy must have got to my house now.'

'He has a bicycle.'

'Then they should be on their way back.'

'We must not be impatient. We may have to sit a long time, Major Scobie. You know what boys are.'

'I thought I did.' He found his left hand was trembling on the desk and he put it between his knees to hold it still. He remembered the long trek beside the border: innumerable lunches in the forest shade, with Ali cooking in an old sardine-tin, and again that last drive to Bamba came to mind—the long wait at the ferry, the fever coming down on him, and Ali always at hand. He wiped the sweat off his forehead and he thought for a moment: This is just a sickness, a fever, I shall wake soon. The record of the last six months—the first night in the Nissen hut, the letter which said too much, the smuggled diamonds, the lies, the sacrament taken to put a woman's mind at ease—seemed as insubstantial as shadows over a bed cast by a hurricane-lamp. He said to himself: I am waking up, and heard the sirens blowing the alert just as on that night, that night. . . . He shook his head and came awake to Yusef sitting in the dark on the other side of the desk, to the taste of the whisky, and the knowledge that everything was the same. He said wearily, 'They ought to be here by now.'

Yusef said, 'You know what boys are. They get scared by the siren and they take shelter. We must sit here and talk to each other, Major Scobie. It is a great opportunity for me. I do not want the morning ever to come.'

'The morning? I am not going to wait till morning for Ali.'

'Perhaps he will be frightened. He will know you have found him out and he will run away. Sometimes boys go back to bush. . . .'

'You are talking nonsense, Yusef.'

'Another whisky, Major Scobie?'

'All right. All right.' He thought: am I taking to drink too? It seemed to him that he had no shape left, nothing you could touch and say: this is Scobie.

'Major Scobie, there are rumours that after all justice is to be done and that you are to be Commissioner.'

He said with care, 'I don't think it will ever come to that.'

'I just wanted to say, Major Scobie, that you need not worry about me. I want your good, nothing so much as that. I will slip out of your life, Major Scobie. I will not be a millstone. It is enough for me to have had to-night—this long talk in the dark on all sorts of subjects. I will remember tonight always. You will not have to worry. I will see to that.' Through the window behind Yusef's head, from somewhere among the jumble of huts and warehouses, a cry came: pain and fear: it swam up like a drowning animal for air, and fell again into the darkness of the room, into the whisky, under the desk, into the basket of wastepaper, a discarded finished cry.

Yusef said too quickly, 'A drunk man.' He yelped apprehensively, 'Where are you going, Major Scobie? It's not safe—alone.' That was the last Scobie ever saw of Yusef, a silhouette stuck stiffly and crookedly on the wall, with the moonlight shining on the syphon and the two drained glasses. At the bottom of the stairs the clerk stood, staring down the wharf. The moonlight caught his eyes: like road studs they showed the way to turn.

There was no movement in the empty warehouses on either side or among the sacks and crates as he moved his torch: if the wharf rats had been out, that cry had driven them back to their holes. His footsteps echoed between the sheds, and somewhere a pye-dog wailed. It would have been quite possible to have searched in vain in this wilderness of litter until morning: what was it that brought him so quickly and unhesitatingly to the body, as though he had himself chosen the scene of the crime? Turning this way and that down the avenues of tarpaulin and wood, he was aware of a nerve in his forehead that beat out the whereabouts of Ali.

The body lay coiled and unimportant like a broken watchspring under a pile of empty petrol drums: it looked as though it had been shovelled there to wait for morning and the scavenger birds. Scobie had a moment of hope before he turned the shoulder over, for after all two boys had been together on the road. The seal grey neck had been slashed and slashed again. Yes, he thought, I can trust him now. The yellow eyeballs stared up at him like a stranger's, flecked with red. It was as if this body had cast him off, disowned him–'I know you not'. He swore aloud, hysterically. 'By God, I'll get the man who did this,' but under that anonymous stare insincerity withered. He thought: I am the man. Didn't I know all the time in Yusef's room that something was planned? Couldn't I have pressed for an answer? A voice said, 'Sah?'

'Who's that?'

'Corporal Laminah, sah.'

'Can you see a broken rosary anywhere around? Look carefully.'

'I can see nothing, sah.'

Scobie thought: if only I could weep, if only I could feel pain; have I really become so evil? Unwillingly he looked down at the body. The fumes of petrol lay all around in the heavy night and for a moment he saw the body as something very small and dark and a long way away–like a broken piece of the rosary he looked for: a couple of black beads and the image of God coiled at the end of it. Oh God, he thought, I've killed you: you've served me all these years and I've killed you at the end of them. God lay there under the petrol drums and Scobie felt the tears in his mouth, salt in the cracks of his lips. You served me and I did this to you. You were faithful to me, and I wouldn't trust you.

'What is it, sah?' the corporal whispered, kneeling by the body.

'I loved him,' Scobie said.

PART II

I / i

As soon as he had handed over his work to Fraser and closed his office for the day, Scobie started out for the Nissen. He drove with his eyes half-closed, looking straight ahead: he told himself, now, to-day, I am going to clean up, whatever the cost. Life is going to start again: this nightmare of love is finished. It seemed to him that it had died for ever the previous night under the petrol drums. The sun blazed down on his hands, which were stuck to the wheel by sweat.

His mind was so concentrated on what had to come–the opening of a door, a few words, and closing a door again for ever–that he nearly passed Helen on the road. She was walking down the hill towards him, hatless. She didn't even see the car. He had to run after her and catch her up. When she turned it was the face he had seen at Pende carried past him–defeated, broken, as ageless as a smashed glass.

'What are you doing here? In the sun, without a hat.'

She said vaguely, 'I was looking for you,' standing there, dithering on the laterite.

'Come back to the car. You'll get sunstroke.' A look of cunning came into her eyes. 'Is it as easy as all that?' she asked, but she obeyed him.

They sat side by side in the car. There seemed to be no object in driving farther: one could say good-bye here as easily as there. She said, 'I heard this morning about Ali. Did you do it?'

'I didn't cut his throat myself,' he said. 'But he died because I existed.'

'Do you know who did?'

'I don't know who held the knife. A wharf rat, I suppose. Yusef's boy who was with him has disappeared. Perhaps he did it or perhaps he's dead too. We will never prove anything. I doubt if Yusef intended it.'

'You know,' she said, 'this is the end for us. I can't go on ruining you any more. Don't speak. Let me speak. I never thought it would be like this. Other people seem to have love affairs which start and end and are happy, but with us it doesn't work. It seems to be all or nothing. So it's got to be nothing. Please don't speak. I've been thinking about this for weeks. I'm going to go away–right right away.'

'Where to?'

'I told you not to speak. Don't ask questions.' He could see in the windscreen a pale reflection of her desperation. It seemed to him as though he were being torn apart. 'Darling,' she said, 'don't think it's easy. I've never done anything so hard. It would be so much easier to die. You come into everything. I can never again see a Nissen hut–or a Morris car. Or taste a pink gin. See a black face. Even a bed . . . one has to sleep in a bed. I don't know where I'll get away from you. It's no use saying in a year it will be all right. It's a year I've got to get through. All the time knowing you are somewhere. I could send a telegram or a letter and you'd have to read it, even if you didn't reply.' He thought: how much easier it would be for her if I were dead. 'But I mustn't write,' she said. She wasn't crying: her eyes when he took a quick glance were dry and red, as he remembered them in hospital, exhausted. 'Waking up will be the worst. There's always a moment when one forgets that everything's different.'

He said, 'I came up here to say good-bye too. But there are things I can't do.'

'Don't talk, darling. I'm being good. Can't you see I'm being good? You don't have to go away from me–I'm going away from you. You won't ever know where to. I hope I won't be too much of a slut.'

'No,' he said, 'no.'

'Be quiet, darling. You are going to be all right. You'll see. You'll be able to clean up. You'll be a Catholic again–that's what you really want, isn't it, not a pack of women?'

'I want to stop giving pain,' he said.

'You want peace, dear. You'll have peace. You'll see. Everything will be all right.' She put her hand on his knee and began at last to weep in this effort to comfort him. He thought: where did she pick up this heart-breaking tenderness? Where do they learn to be so old so quickly?

'Look, dear. Don't come up to the hut. Open the car door for me. It's stiff. We'll say good-bye here, and you'll just drive home–or to the office if you'd rather. That's so much easier. Don't worry about me. I'll be all right.' He thought, I missed that one death and now I'm having them all. He leant over her and wrenched at the car door: her tears touched his cheek. He could feel the mark like a burn. 'There's no objection to a farewell kiss. We haven't quarrelled. There hasn't been a scene. There's no bitterness.' As they kissed he was aware of pain under his mouth like the beating of a bird's heart. They sat still, silent, and the door of the car lay open. A few black labourers passing down the hill looked curiously in.

She said, 'I can't believe that this is the last time: that I'll get out and you'll drive away, and we won't see each other again ever. I won't go outside more than I can help till I get right away. I'll be up here and you'll be down there. Oh, God, I wish I hadn't got the furniture you brought me.'

'It's just official furniture.'

'The cane is broken in one of the chairs where you sat down too quickly.'

'Dear, dear, this isn't the way.'

'Don't speak, darling. I'm really being quite good, but I can't say these things to another living soul. In books there's always a confidant. But I haven't got a confidant. I must say them all once.' He thought again: if I were dead, she would be free of me. One forgets the dead quite quickly; one doesn't wonder about the dead—what is he doing now, who is he with? This for her is the hard way.

'Now, darling, I'm going to do it. Shut your eyes. Count three hundred slowly, and I won't be in sight. Turn the car quickly and drive like hell. I don't want to see you go. And I'll stop my ears. I don't want to hear you change gear at the bottom of the hill. Cars do that a hundred times a day. I don't want to hear you change gear.'

O God, he prayed, his hands dripping over the wheel, kill me now, now. My God, you'll never have more complete contrition. What a mess I am. I carry suffering with me like a body smell. Kill me. Put an end to me. Vermin don't have to exterminate themselves. Kill me. Now. Now. Now.

'Shut your eyes, darling. This is the end. Really the end.' She said hopelessly, 'It seems so silly though.'

He said, 'I won't shut my eyes. I won't leave you. I promised that.'

'You aren't leaving me. I'm leaving you.'

'It won't work. We love each other. It won't work. I'd be up this evening to see how you were. I couldn't sleep . . .'

'You can always sleep. I've never known such a sleeper. Oh, my dear, look. I'm beginning to laugh at you again just as though we weren't saying good-bye.'

'We aren't. Not yet.'

'But I'm only ruining you. I can't give you any happiness.'

'Happiness isn't the point.'

'I'd made up my mind.'

'So had I.'

'But, darling, what do we *do*?' She surrendered completely. 'I don't mind going on as we are. I don't mind the lies. Anything.'

'Just leave it to me. I've got to think.' He leant over her and closed the door of the car. Before the lock had clicked he had made his decision.

Scobie watched the small boy as he cleared away the evening meal, watched him come in and go out, watched the bare feet flap the floor. Louise said, 'I know it's a terrible thing, dear, but you've got to put it behind you. You can't help Ali now.' A new parcel of books had come from England and he watched her cutting the leaves of a volume of verse. There was more grey in her hair than when she had left for South Africa, but she looked, it seemed to him, years younger because she was paying more attention to make-up: her dressing-table was littered with the pots and bottles and tubes she had brought back from the south. Ali's death meant little to her: why should it? It was the sense of guilt that made it so important. Otherwise one didn't grieve for a death. When he was young, he had thought love had something to do with understanding, but with age he knew that no human being understood another. Love was the wish to understand, and presently with constant failure the wish died, and love died too perhaps or changed into this painful affection, loyalty, pity. . . . She sat there, reading poetry, and she was a thousand miles away from the torment that shook his hand and dried his mouth. She would understand, he thought, if I were in a book, but would I understand her if she were just a character? I don't read that sort of book.

'Haven't you anything to read, dear?'

'I'm sorry. I don't feel much like reading.'

She closed her book, and it occurred to him that after all she had her own effort to make: she tried to help. Sometimes he wondered with horror whether perhaps she knew everything, whether that complacent face which she had worn since her return masked misery. She said, 'Let's talk about Christmas.'

'It's still a long way off,' he said quickly.

'Before you know it will be on us. I was wondering whether we could give a party. We've always been out to dinner: it would be fun to have people here. Perhaps on Christmas Eve.'

'Just what you like.'

'We could all go on then to Midnight Mass. Of course you and I would have to remember to drink nothing after ten – but the others could do as they pleased.'

He looked up at her with momentary hatred as she sat so cheerfully there, so smugly, it seemed to him, arranging his further damnation. He was going to be Commissioner. She had what she wanted – her sort of success, everything was all right with her now. He thought: it was the hysterical woman who felt the world laughing behind her back that I loved. I love failure: I can't love success. And how successful she looks, sitting there, one of the saved, and he saw laid across that wide face like a news-screen the body of Ali under the black drums, the exhausted eyes of Helen, and all the faces of the lost, his companions in exile, the unrepentant thief, the soldier with the sponge. Thinking of what he had done and was going to do, he thought, even God is a failure.

'What is it, Ticki? Are you still worrying . . .?'

But he couldn't tell her the entreaty that was on his lips: let me pity you again, be disappointed, unattractive, be a failure so that I can love you once more without this bitter gap between us. Time is short. I want to love you too at the end. He said slowly, 'It's the pain. It's over now. When it comes—' he remembered the phrase of the textbook–'it's like a vice.'

'You must see the doctor, Ticki.'

'I'll see him to-morrow. I was going to anyway because of my sleeplessness.'

'Your sleeplessness? But, Ticki, you sleep like a log.'

'Not the last week.'

'You're imagining it.'

'No. I wake up about two and can't sleep again–till just before we are called. Don't worry. I'll get some tablets.'

'I hate drugs.'

'I won't go on long enough to form a habit.'

'We must get you right for Christmas, Ticki.'

'I'll be all right by Christmas.' He came stiffly across the room to her, imitating the bearing of a man who fears that pain may return again, and put his hand against her breast. 'Don't worry.' Hatred went out of him at the touch–she wasn't as successful as all that: she would never be married to the Commissioner of Police.

After she had gone to bed he took out his diary. In this record at least he had never lied. At the worst he had omitted. He had checked his temperatures as carefully as a sea captain making up his log. He had never exaggerated or minimised, and he had never indulged in speculation. All he had written here was fact. *November 1. Early Mass with Louise. Spent morning on larceny case at Mrs Onoko's. Temperature 91° at 2. Saw Y. at his office. Ali found murdered.* The statement was as plain and simple as that other time when he had written: *C. died.*

'November 2.' He sat a long while with that date in front of him, so long that presently Louise called down to him. He replied carefully, 'Go to sleep, dear. If I sit up late, I may be able to sleep properly.' But already, exhausted by the day and by all the plans that had to be laid, he was near to nodding at the table. He went to his ice-box and wrapping a piece of ice in his handkerchief rested it against his forehead until sleep receded. *November 2.* Again he picked up his pen: this was his death-warrant he was signing. He wrote: *Saw Helen for a few minutes.* (It was always safer to leave no facts for anyone else to unearth.) *Temperature at 2, 92°. In the evening return of pain. Fear angina.* He looked up the pages of the entries for a week back and added an occasional note. *Slept very badly. Bad night. Sleeplessness continues.* He read the entries over carefully: they would be read later by the coroner, by the insurance inspectors. They seemed to him to be in his usual manner. Then he put the ice back on his forehead to drive sleep away. It was still only half after midnight: it would be better not to go to bed before two.

'It grips me,' Scobie said, 'like a vice.'

'And what do you do then?'

'Why nothing. I stay as still as I can until the pain goes.'

'How long does it last?'

'It's difficult to tell, but I don't think more than a minute.'

The stethoscope followed like a ritual. Indeed there was something clerical in all that Dr Travis did: an earnestness, almost a reverence. Perhaps because he was young he treated the body with great respect; when he rapped the chest he did it slowly, carefully, with his ear bowed close as though he really expected somebody or something to rap back. Latin words came softly on to his tongue as though in the Mass—*sternum* instead of *pacem*.

'And then,' Scobie said, 'there's the sleeplessness.'

The young man sat back behind his desk and tapped with an indelible pencil; there was a mauve smear at the corner of his mouth which seemed to indicate that sometimes—off guard—he sucked it. 'That's probably nerves,' Dr Travis said, 'apprehension of pain. Unimportant.'

'It's important to me. Can't you give me something to take? I'm all right when once I get to sleep, but I lie awake for hours, waiting. . . . Sometimes I'm hardly fit for work. And a policeman, you know, needs his wits.'

'Of course,' Dr Travis said. 'I'll soon settle you. Evipan's the stuff for you.' It was as easy as all that. 'Now for the pain—' he began his tap, tap, tap, with the pencil. He said, 'It's impossible to be certain, of course. . . . I want you to note carefully the circumstances of every attack . . . what seems to bring it on. Then it will be quite possible to regulate it, avoid it almost entirely.'

'But what's wrong?'

Dr Travis said, 'There are some words that always shock the layman. I wish we could call cancer by a symbol like H_2O. People wouldn't be nearly so disturbed. It's the same with the word angina.'

'You think it's angina?'

'It has all the characteristics. But men live for years with angina—even work in reason. We have to see exactly how much you can do.'

'Should I tell my wife?'

'There's no point in not telling her. I'm afraid this might mean—retirement.'

'Is that all?'

'You may die of a lot of things before angina gets you—given care.'

'On the other hand I suppose it could happen any day?'

'I can't guarantee anything, Major Scobie. I'm not even absolutely satisfied that this is angina.'

'I'll speak to the Commissioner then on the quiet. I don't want to alarm my wife until we are certain.'

'If I were you, I'd tell her what I've said. It will prepare her. But tell her you may live for years with care.'

'And the sleeplessness?'

'This will make you sleep.'

Sitting in the car with a little package on the seat beside him, he thought, I have only now to choose the date. He didn't start his car for quite a while; he was touched by a feeling of awe as if he had in fact been given his death sentence by the doctor. His eyes dwelt on the neat blob of sealing-wax like a dried wound. He thought, I have still got to be careful, so careful. If possible no one must even suspect. It was not only the question of his life insurance: the happiness of others had to be protected. It was not so easy to forget a suicide as a middle-aged man's death from angina.

He unsealed the package and studied the directions. He had no knowledge of what a fatal dose might be, but surely if he took ten times the correct amount he would be safe. That meant every night for nine nights removing a dose and keeping it secretly for use on the tenth night. More evidence must be invented in his diary which had to be written right up to the end–November 12. He must make engagements for the following week. In his behaviour there must be no hint of farewells. This was the worst crime a Catholic could commit–it must be a perfect one.

First the Commissioner. . . . He drove down towards the police station and stopped his car outside the church. The solemnity of the crime lay over his mind almost like happiness: it was action at last–he had fumbled and muddled too long. He put the package for safekeeping into his pocket and went in, carrying his death. An old mammy was lighting a candle before the Virgin's statue; another sat with her market basket beside her and her hands folded staring up at the altar. Otherwise the church was empty. Scobie sat down at the back: he had no inclination to pray–what was the good? If one was a Catholic, one had all the answers: no prayer was effective in a state of mortal sin, but he watched the other two with sad envy. They were still inhabitants of the country he had left. This was what human love had done to him–it had robbed him of love for eternity. It was no use pretending as a young man might that the price was worth while.

If he couldn't pray he could at least talk, sitting there at the back, as far as he could get from Golgotha. He said, O God, I am the only guilty one because I've known the answers all the time. I've preferred to give you pain rather than give pain to Helen or my wife because I can't observe your suffering. I can only imagine it. But there are limits to what I can do to you–or them. I can't desert either of them while I'm alive, but I can die and remove myself from their blood stream. They are ill with me and I can cure them. And you too, God–you are ill with me. I can't go on, month after month, insulting you. I can't face coming up to the altar at Christmas–your birthday feast–and taking your body and blood for the sake of a lie. I can't do that. You'll be better off if you lose me once and for all. I know what I'm doing. I'm not pleading for mercy. I am going to damn myself, whatever that means. I've longed for peace and I'm never going to know peace again. But you'll be at peace when I am out of your reach. It will be no use then sweeping the floor to find me or searching for me over the mountains. You'll be able to forget me, God, for eternity. One hand clasped the package in his pocket like a promise.

No one can speak a monologue for long alone–another voice will always make itself heard; every monologue sooner or later becomes a discussion. So now he couldn't keep the other voice silent; it spoke from the cave of his body: it was as if the sacrament which had lodged there for his damnation gave tongue. You say you love me, and yet you'll do this to me–rob me of you for ever. I made you with love. I've wept your tears. I've saved you from more than you will ever know; I planted in you this longing for peace only so that one day I could satisfy your longing and watch your happiness. And now you push me away, you put me out of your reach. There are no capital letters to separate us when we talk together. I am not Thou but simply you, when you speak to me; I am humble as any other beggar. Can't you trust me as you'd trust a faithful dog? I have been faithful to you for two thousand years. All you have to do now is ring a bell, go into a box, confess . . . the repentance is already there, straining at your heart. It's not repentance you lack, just a few simple actions: to go up to the Nissen hut and say good-bye. Or if you must, continue rejecting me but without lies any more. Go to your house and say good-bye to your wife and live with your mistress. If you live you will come back to me sooner or later. One of them will suffer, but can't you trust me to see that the suffering isn't too great?

The voice was silent in the cave and his own voice replied hopelessly: No. I don't trust you. I've never trusted you. If you made me, you made this feeling of responsibility that I've always carried about like a sack of bricks. I'm not a policeman for nothing–responsible for order, for seeing justice is done. There was no other profession for a man of my kind. I can't shift my responsibility to you. If I could, I would be someone else. I can't make one of them suffer so as to save myself. I'm responsible and I'll see it through the only way I can. A sick man's death means to them only a short suffering–everybody has to die. We are all of us resigned to death: it's life we aren't resigned to.

So long as you live, the voice said, I have hope. There's no human hopelessness like the hopelessness of God. Can't you just go on, as you are doing now? the voice pleaded, lowering the terms every time it spoke like a dealer in a market. It explained: there are worse acts. But no, he said, no. That's impossible. I won't go on insulting you at your own altar. You see it's an *impasse*, God, an *impasse*, he said, clutching the package in his pocket. He got up and turned his back on the altar and went out. Only when he saw his face in the driving mirror did he realise that his eyes were bruised with suppressed tears. He drove on towards the police station and the Commissioner.

3/i

November 3. Yesterday I told the Commissioner that angina had been diagnosed and that I should have to retire as soon as a successor could be found. Temperature at 2 p.m. 91°. Much better night as the result of Evipan.

November 4. Went with Louise to 7.30 Mass but as pain threatened to return did not wait for communion. In the evening told Louise that I should have to retire before end of tour. Did not mention angina but spoke of strained heart. Another good night as a result of Evipan. Temperature at 2 p.m. 89°.

November 5. Lamp thefts in Wellington Street. Spent long morning at Azikawe's store checking story of fire in storeroom. Temperature at 2 p.m. 90°. Drove Louise to Club for library night.

November 6–10. First time I've failed to keep up daily entries. Pain has become more frequent and unwilling to take on any extra exertion. Like a vice. Lasts about a minute. Liable to come on if I walk more than half a mile. Last night or two have slept badly in spite of Evipan, I think from the apprehension of pain.

November 11. Saw Travis again. There seems to be no doubt now that it is angina. Told Louise to-night, but also that with care I may live for years. Discussed with Commissioner an early passage home. In any case can't go for another month as too many cases I want to see through the courts in the next week or two. Agreed to dine with Fellowes on 13th. Commissioner on 14th. Temperature at 2 p.m. 88°.

3/ii

Scobie laid down his pen and wiped his wrist on the blotting-paper. It was just six o'clock on November 12 and Louise was out at the beach. His brain was clear, but the nerves tingled from his shoulder to his wrist. He thought: I have come to the end. What years had passed since he walked up through the rain to the Nissen hut, while the sirens wailed: the moment of happiness. It was time to die after so many years.

But there were still deceptions to be practised, just as though he were going to live through the night, good-byes to be said with only himself knowing that they were good-byes. He walked very slowly up the hill in case he was observed—wasn't he a sick man?—and turned off by the Nissens. He couldn't just die without some word—what word? O God, he prayed, let it be the right word, but when he knocked there was no reply, no words at all. Perhaps she was at the beach with Bagster.

The door was not locked and he went in. Years had passed in his brain, but here time had stood still. It might have been the same bottle of gin from which the boy had stolen—how long ago? The junior official's chairs stood stiffly around, as though on a film set: he couldn't believe they had ever moved, any more than the pouf presented by—was it Mrs Carter? On the bed the pillow had not been shaken after the siesta, and he laid his hand on the warm mould of a skull. O God, he prayed, I'm going away from all of you for ever: let her come back in time: let me see her once more, but the hot day cooled around him and nobody came. At 6.30 Louise would be back from the beach. He couldn't wait any longer.

I must leave some kind of a message, he thought, and perhaps before I have written it she will have come. He felt a constriction in his breast worse than any pain he had ever invented to Travis. I shall never touch her again. I shall leave her mouth to others for the next twenty years. Most lovers deceived themselves with the idea of an eternal union beyond the grave, but he knew all the answers: he went to an eternity of deprivation. He looked for paper and couldn't find so much as a torn envelope; he thought he saw a writing-case, but it was the stamp-album that he unearthed, and opening it at random for no reason, he felt fate throw another shaft, for he remembered that particular stamp and how it came to be stained with gin. She will have to tear it out, he thought, but that won't matter: she had told him that you can't see where a stamp has been torn out. There was no scrap of paper even in his pockets, and in a sudden rush of jealousy he lifted up the little green image of George VI and wrote in ink beneath it: *I love you*. She can't take that out, he thought with cruelty and disappointment, that's indelible. For a moment he felt as though he had laid a mine for an enemy, but this was no enemy. Wasn't he clearing himself out of her path like a piece of dangerous wreckage? He shut the door behind him and walked slowly down the hill—she might yet come. Everything he did now was for the last time—an odd sensation. He would never come this way again, and five minutes later taking a new bottle of gin from his cupboard, he thought: I shall never open another bottle. The actions which could be repeated became fewer and fewer. Presently there would be only one unrepeatable action left, the act of swallowing. He stood with the gin bottle poised and thought: then Hell will begin, and they'll be safe from me, Helen, Louise, and You.

At dinner he talked deliberately of the week to come; he blamed himself for accepting Fellowes's invitation and explained that dinner with the Commissioner the next day was unavoidable—there was much to discuss.

'Is there no hope, Ticki, that after a rest, a long rest . . .?'

'It wouldn't be fair to carry on—to them or you. I might break down at any moment.'

'It's really retirement?'

'Yes.'

She began to discuss where they were to live. He felt tired to death, and it needed all his will to show interest in this fictitious village or that, in the kind of house he knew they would never inhabit. 'I don't want a suburb,' Louise said. 'What I'd really like would be a weather-board house in Kent, so that one can get up to town quite easily.'

He said, 'Of course it will depend on what we can afford. My pension won't be very large.'

'I shall work,' Louise said. 'It will be easy in wartime.'

'I hope we shall be able to manage without that.'

'I wouldn't mind.'

Bed-time came, and he felt a terrible unwillingness to let her go. There was nothing to do when she had once gone but die. He didn't know how to keep her—they had talked about all the subjects they had in common. He said, 'I shall sit here a while. Perhaps I shall feel sleepy if I stay up half an hour longer. I don't want to take the Evipan if I can help it.'

'I'm very tired after the beach. I'll be off.'

When she's gone, he thought, I shall be alone for ever. His heart beat and he was held in the nausea of an awful unreality. I can't believe that I'm going to do this. Presently I shall get up and go to bed, and life will begin again.

Nothing, nobody, can force me to die. Though the voice was no longer speaking from the cave of his belly, it was as though fingers touched him, signalled their mute messages of distress, tried to hold him. . . .

'What is it, Ticki? You look ill. Come to bed too.'

'I wouldn't sleep,' he said obstinately.

'Is there nothing I can do?' Louise asked. 'Dear, I'd do anything. . . .' Her love was like a death sentence.

'There's nothing, dear,' he said. 'I mustn't keep you up.' But so soon as she turned towards the stairs he spoke again. 'Read me something,' he said, 'you got a new book to-day. Read me something.'

'You wouldn't like it, Ticki. It's poetry.'

'Never mind. It may send me to sleep.' He hardly listened while she read. People said you couldn't love two women, but what was this emotion if it were not love? This hungry absorption of what he was never going to see again? The greying hair, the line of nerves upon the face, the thickening body held him as her beauty never had. She hadn't put on her mosquito-boots, and her slippers were badly in need of mending. It isn't beauty that we love, he thought, it's failure—the failure to stay young for ever, the failure of nerves, the failure of the body. Beauty is like success: we can't love it for long. He felt a terrible desire to protect—but that's what I'm going to do, I am going to protect her from myself for ever. Some words she was reading momentarily caught his attention:

> We are all falling. This hand's falling too—
> all have this falling sickness none withstands.
>
> And yet there's always One whose gentle hands
> this universal falling can't fall through.

They sounded like truth, but he rejected them—comfort can come too easily. He thought, those hands will never hold my fall: I slip between the fingers, I'm greased with falsehood, treachery. Trust was a dead language of which he had forgotten the grammar.

'Dear, you are half asleep.'

'For a moment.'

'I'll go up now. Don't stay long. Perhaps you won't need your Evipan to-night.'

He watched her go. The lizard lay still upon the wall. Before she had reached the stairs he called her back. 'Say good night, Louise, before you go. You may be asleep.'

She kissed him perfunctorily on the forehead and he gave her hand a casual caress. There must be nothing strange of this last night, and nothing she would remember with regret. 'Good night, Louise. You know I love you,' he said with careful lightness.

'Of course and I love you.'

'Yes. Good night, Louise.'

'Good night, Ticki.' It was the best he could do with safety.

As soon as he heard the door close, he took out the cigarette carton in which he kept the ten doses of Evipan. He added two more doses for greater certainty–to have exceeded by two doses in ten days could not, surely, be regarded as suspicious. After that he took a long drink of whisky and sat still and waited for courage with the tablets in the palm of his hand. Now, he thought, I am absolutely alone: this was freezing-point.

But he was wrong. Solitude itself has a voice. It said to him, Throw away those tablets. You'll never be able to collect enough again. You'll be saved. Give up play-acting. Mount the stairs to bed and have a good night's sleep. In the morning you'll be woken by your boy, and you'll drive down to the police station for a day's ordinary work. The voice dwelt on the word 'ordinary' as it might have dwelt on the word 'happy' or 'peaceful'.

'No,' Scobie said aloud, 'no.' He pushed the tablets in his mouth six at a time, and drank them down in two draughts. Then he opened his diary and wrote against November 12, *Called on H.R., out; temperature at 2 p.m.* and broke abruptly off as though at that moment he had been gripped by the final pain. Afterwards he sat bolt upright and waited what seemed a long while for any indication at all of approaching death; he had no idea how it would come to him. He tried to pray, but the Hail Mary evaded his memory, and he was aware of his heart-beats like a clock striking the hour. He tried out an act of contrition, but when he reached, 'I am sorry and beg pardon', a cloud formed over the door and drifted down over the whole room and he couldn't remember what it was that he had to be sorry for. He had to hold himself upright with both hands, but he had forgotten the reason why he so held himself. Somewhere far away he thought he heard the sounds of pain. 'A storm,' he said aloud, 'there's going to be a storm,' as the clouds grew, and he tried to get up to close the windows. 'Ali,' he called, 'Ali.' It seemed to him as though someone outside the room were seeking him, calling him, and he made a last effort to indicate that he was here. He got to his feet and heard the hammer of his heart beating out a reply. He had a message to convey, but the darkness and the storm drove it back within the case of his breast, and all the time outside the house, outside the world that drummed like hammer blows within his ear, someone wandered, seeking to get in, someone appealing for help, someone in need of him. And automatically at the call of need, at the cry of a victim, Scobie strung himself to act. He dredged his consciousness up from an infinite distance in order to make some reply. He said aloud, 'Dear God, I love . . .' but the effort was too great and he did not feel his body when it struck the floor or hear the small tinkle of the medal as it span like a coin under the ice-box–the saint whose name nobody could remember.

PART III

I / i

Wilson said, 'I have kept away as long as I could, but I thought perhaps I could be of some help.'

'Everybody,' Louise said, 'has been very kind.'

'I had no idea that he was so ill.'

'Your spying didn't help you there, did it?'

'That was my job,' Wilson said, 'and I love you.'

'How glibly you use that word, Wilson.'

'You don't believe me?'

'I don't believe in anybody who says love, love, love. It means self, self, self.'

'You won't marry me then?'

'It doesn't seem likely, does it, but I might, in time. I don't know what loneliness may do. But don't let's talk about love any more. It was his favourite lie.'

'To both of you.'

'How has she taken it, Wilson?'

'I saw her on the beach this afternoon with Bagster. And I hear she was a bit pickled last night at the club.'

'She hasn't any dignity.'

'I never knew what he saw in her. I'd never betray you, Louise.'

'You know he even went up to see her the day he died.'

'How do you know?'

'It's all written there. In his diary. He never lied in his diary. He never said things he didn't mean–like love.'

Three days had passed since Scobie had been hastily buried. Dr Travis had signed the death certificate–*angina pectoris*. In that climate a post-mortem was difficult, and in any case unnecessary, though Dr Travis had taken the precaution of checking up on the Evipan.

'Do you know,' Wilson said, 'when my boy told me he had died suddenly in the night, I thought it was suicide?'

'It's odd how easily I can talk about him,' Louise said, 'now that he's gone. Yet I did love him, Wilson. I did love him, but he seems so very very gone.'

It was as if he had left nothing behind him in the house but a few suits of clothes and a Mende grammar: at the police station a drawer full of odds and ends and a pair of rusting handcuffs. And yet the house was no different: the shelves were as full of books; it seemed to Wilson that it must always have been *her* house, not his. Was it just imagination then that made their voices ring a little hollowly, as though the house were empty?

'Did you know all the time–about her?' Wilson asked.

'It's why I came home. Mrs Carter wrote to me. She said everybody was talking. Of course he never realised that. He thought he'd been so clever. And he nearly convinced me–that it was finished. Going to communion the way he did.'

'How did he square that with his conscience?'

'Some Catholics do, I suppose. Go to confession and start over again. I thought he was more honest though. When a man's dead one begins to find out.'

'He took money from Yusef.'

'I can believe it now.'

Wilson put his hand on Louise's shoulder and said, 'You can trust me, Louise. I love you.'

'I really believe you do.' They didn't kiss; it was too soon for that, but they sat in the hollow room, holding hands, listening to the vultures clambering on the iron roof.

'So that's his diary,' Wilson said.

'He was writing in it when he died—oh nothing interesting, just the temperatures. He always kept the temperatures. He wasn't romantic. God knows what she saw in him to make it worth while.'

'Would you mind if I looked at it?'

'If you want to,' she said, 'poor Ticki, he hasn't any secrets left.'

'His secrets were never very secret.' He turned a page and read and turned a page. He said, 'Had he suffered from sleeplessness very long?'

'I always thought that he slept like a log whatever happened.'

Wilson said, 'Have you noticed that he's written in pieces about sleeplessness—afterwards?'

'How do you know?'

'You've only to compare the colour of the ink. And all these records of taking his Evipan—it's very studied, very careful. But above all the colour of the ink.' He said, 'It makes one think.'

She interrupted him with horror, 'Oh no, he couldn't have done that. After all, in spite of everything, he *was* a Catholic.'

I /ii

'Just let me come in for one little drink,' Bagster pleaded.

'We had four at the beach.'

'Just one little one more.'

'All right,' Helen said. There seemed to be no reason so far as she could see to deny anyone anything any more for ever.

Bagster said, 'You know it's the first time you've let me come in. Charming little place you've made of it. Who'd have thought a Nissen hut could be so homey?' Flushed and smelling of pink gin, both of us, we are a pair, she thought. Bagster kissed her wetly on her upper lip and looked around again. 'Ha ha,' he said, 'the good old bottle.' When they had drunk one more gin he took off his uniform jacket and hung it carefully on a chair. He said, 'Let's take our back hair down and talk of love.'

'Need we?' Helen said. 'Yet?'

'Lighting up time,' Bagster said. 'The dusk. So we'll let George take over the controls. . . .'

'Who's George?'

'The automatic pilot, of course. You've got a lot to learn.'

'For God's sake teach me some other time.'

'There's no time like the present for a prang,' Bagster said, moving her firmly towards the bed. Why not? she thought, why not . . . if he wants it? Bagster is as good as anyone else. There's nobody in the world I love, and out of it doesn't count, so why not let them have their prangs (it was Bagster's phrase) if they want them enough. She lay back mutely on the bed and shut her eyes and was aware in the darkness of nothing at all. I'm alone, she thought without self-pity, stating it as a fact, as an explorer might after his companions have died from exposure.

'By God, you aren't enthusiastic,' Bagster said. 'Don't you love me a bit, Helen?' and his ginny breath fanned through her darkness.

'No,' she said, 'I don't love anyone.'

He said furiously, 'You loved Scobie,' and added quickly, 'Sorry. Rotten thing to say.'

'I don't love anyone,' she repeated. 'You can't love the dead, can you? They don't exist, do they? It would be like loving the dodo, wouldn't it?' questioning him as if she expected an answer, even from Bagster. She kept her eyes shut because in the dark she felt nearer to death, the death which had absorbed him. The bed trembled a little as Bagster shuffled his weight from off it, and the chair creaked as he took away his jacket. He said, 'I'm not all that of a bastard, Helen. You aren't in the mood. See you to-morrow?'

'I expect so.' There was no reason to deny anyone anything, but she felt an immense relief because nothing after all had been required.

'Good night, old girl,' Bagster said, 'I'll be seeing you.'

She opened her eyes and saw a stranger in dusty blue pottering round the door. One can say anything to a stranger—they pass on and forget like beings from another world. She asked, 'Do you believe in a God?'

'Oh well, I suppose so,' Bagster said, feeling at his moustache.

'I wish I did,' she said, 'I wish I did.'

'Oh well, you know,' Bagster said, 'a lot of people do. Must be off now. Good night.'

She was alone again in the darkness behind her lids, and the wish struggled in her body like a child: her lips moved, but all she could think of to say was, 'For ever and ever, Amen . . .' The rest she had forgotten. She put her hand out beside her and touched the other pillow, as though perhaps after all there was one chance in a thousand that she was not alone, and if she were not alone now she would never be alone again.

I /iii

'*I* should never have noticed it, Mrs Scobie,' Father Rank said.

'Wilson did.'

'Somehow I can't like a man who's quite so observant.'

'It's his job.'

Father Rank took a quick look at her. 'As an accountant?'

She said drearily, 'Father, haven't you any comfort to give me?' Oh, the conversations, he thought, that go on in a house after a death, the turnings over, the discussions, the questions, the demands—so much noise round the edge of silence.

'You've been given an awful lot of comfort in your life, Mrs Scobie. If what Wilson thinks is true, it's he who needs our comfort.'

'Do you know all that I know about him?'

'Of course I don't, Mrs Scobie. You've been his wife, haven't you, for fifteen years. A priest only knows the unimportant things.'

'Unimportant?'

'Oh, I mean the sins,' he said impatiently. 'A man doesn't come to us and confess his virtues.'

'I expect you know about Mrs Rolt. Most people did.'

'Poor woman.'

'I don't see why.'

'I'm sorry for anyone happy and ignorant who gets mixed up in that way with one of us.'

'He was a bad Catholic.'

'That's the silliest phrase in common use,' Father Rank said.

'And at the end this—horror. He must have known that he was damning himself.'

'Yes, he knew that all right. He never had any trust in mercy—except for other people.'

'It's no good even praying. . . .'

Father Rank clapped the cover of the diary to and said furiously, 'For goodness' sake, Mrs Scobie, don't imagine you—or I—know a thing about God's mercy.'

'The Church says . . .'

'I know the Church says. The Church knows all the rules. But it doesn't know what goes on in a single human heart.'

'You think there's some hope then?' she wearily asked.

'Are you so bitter against him?'

'I haven't any bitterness left.'

'And do you think God's likely to be more bitter than a woman?' he said with harsh insistence, but she winced away from the arguments of hope.

'Oh, why, why, did he have to make such a mess of things?'

Father Rank said, 'It may seem an odd thing to say—when a man's as wrong as he was—but I think, from what I saw of him, that he really loved God.'

She had denied just now that she felt any bitterness, but a little more of it drained out now like tears from exhausted ducts. 'He certainly loved no one else,' she said.

'And you may be in the right of it there too,' Father Rank replied.

STAMBOUL
TRAIN

ORIENT
EXPRESS

STAMBOUL TRAIN

For Vivien with love

Everything in nature is lyrical in its ideal essence:
tragic in its fate, and comic in its existence.
George Santayana

PART I

OSTEND

I

The purser took the last landing-card in his hand and watched the passengers cross the grey wet quay, over a wilderness of rails and points, round the corners of abandoned trucks. They went with coat-collars turned up and hunched shoulders; on the tables in the long coaches lamps were lit and glowed through the rain like a chain of blue beads. A giant crane swept and descended, and the clatter of the winch drowned for a moment the pervading sounds of water, water falling from the overcast sky, water washing against the sides of Channel steamer and quay. It was half-past four in the afternoon.

'A spring day, my God,' said the purser aloud, trying to dismiss the impressions of the last few hours, the drenched deck, the smell of steam and oil and stale Bass from the bar, the shuffle of black silk, as the stewardess moved here and there carrying tin basins. He glanced up the steel shafts of the crane, to the platform and the small figure in blue dungarees turning a great wheel, and felt an unaccustomed envy. The driver up there was parted by thirty feet of mist and rain from purser, passengers, the long lit express. I can't get away from their damned faces, the purser thought, recalling the young Jew in the heavy fur coat who had complained because he had been allotted a two-berth cabin; for two God-forsaken hours, that's all.

He said to the last passenger from the second class: 'Not that way, miss. The customs-shed's over there.' His mood relaxed a little at the unfamiliarity of the young face; this one had not complained. 'Don't you want a porter for your bag, miss?'

'I'd rather not,' she said. 'I can't understand what they say. It's not heavy.' She wrinkled her mouth at him over the top of her cheap white mackintosh. 'Unless you'd like to carry it–Captain.' Her impudence delighted him. 'Ah, if I were a young man now you wouldn't be wanting a porter. I don't know what they are coming to.' He shook his head as the Jew left the customs-shed, picking his way across the rails in grey suède shoes, followed by two laden porters. 'Going far?'

'All the way,' she said gazing unhappily past the rails, the piles of luggage, the lit lamps in the restaurant-car, to the dark waiting coaches.

'Got a sleeper?'

'No.'

'You ought to 'ave a sleeper,' he said, 'going all the way like that. Three nights in a train. It's no joke. What do you want to go to Constantinople for anyway? Getting married?'

'Not that I know of.' She laughed a little through the melancholy of departure and the fear of strangeness. 'One can't tell, can one?'

'Work?'

'Dancing. Variety.'

She said good-bye and turned from him. Her mackintosh showed the thinness of her body, which even while stumbling between the rails and sleepers retained its self-consciousness. A signal lamp turned from red to green, and a long whistle of steam blew through an exhaust. Her face, plain and piquant, her manner daring and depressed, lingered for a moment in his mind. 'Remember me,' he called after her. 'I'll see you again in a month or two.' But he knew that he would not remember her; too many faces would peer during the following weeks through the window of his office, wanting a cabin, wanting money changed, wanting a berth, for him to remember an individual, and there was nothing remarkable about her.

When he went on board, the decks were already being washed down for the return journey, and he felt happier to find the ship empty of strangers. This was how he would have liked it always to be: a few dagoes to boss in their own tongue, a stewardess with whom to drink a glass of ale. He grunted at the seamen in French and they grinned at him, singing an indecent song of a 'cocu' that made his plump family soul wither a little in envy. 'A bad crossing,' he said to the head steward in English. The man had been a waiter in London and the purser never spoke a word more French than was necessary. 'That Jew,' he said, 'did he give you a good tip?'

'What would you believe? Six francs.'

'Was he ill?'

'No. The old fellow with the moustaches—he was ill all the time. And I want ten francs. I win the bet. He was English.'

'Go on. You could cut his accent with a knife.'

'I see his passport. Richard John. Schoolteacher.'

'That's funny,' the purser said. And that's funny, he thought again, paying the ten francs reluctantly and seeing in his mind's eye the tired grey man in the mackintosh stride away from the ship's rail, as the gangway rose and the sirens blew out towards a rift in the clouds. He had asked for a newspaper, an evening newspaper. They wouldn't have been published in London as early as that, the purser told him, and when he heard the answer, he stood in a dream, fingering his long grey moustache. While the purser poured out a glass of Bass for the stewardess, before going through the accounts, he thought again of the schoolteacher, and wondered momentarily whether something dramatic had passed close by him, something weary and hunted and the stuff of stories. He too had made no complaint, and for that reason was more easily forgotten than the young Jew, the party of Cook's tourists, the sick woman in mauve who had lost a ring, the old man who had paid twice for his berth. The girl had been forgotten half an hour before. This was the first thing she shared with Richard John—below the tramp of feet, the smell of oil, the winking light of signals, worrying faces, clink of glasses, rows of numerals—a darkness in the purser's mind.

The wind dropped for ten seconds, and the smoke which had swept backwards and forwards across the quay and the metal acres in the quick gusts stayed for that time in the middle air. Like grey nomad tents the smoke seemed to Myatt, as he picked his way through the mud. He forgot that his suède shoes were ruined, that the customs officer had been impertinent over two pairs of silk pyjamas. From the man's rudeness and his contempt, the syllables 'Juif, Juif', he crept into the shade of those great tents. Here for a moment he was at home and required no longer the knowledge of his fur coat, of his suit from Savile Row, his money or his position in the firm to hearten him. But as he reached the train the wind rose, the tents of steam were struck, and he was again in the centre of a hostile world.

But he recognised with gratitude what money could buy. It could not always buy courtesy, but it had bought celerity. He was the first through the customs, and before the other passengers arrived, he could arrange with the guard for a sleeping compartment to himself. He had a hatred of undressing before another man, but the arrangement, he knew, would cost him more because he was a Jew; it would be no matter of a simple request and a tip. He passed the lit windows of the restaurant car, small mauve-shaded lamps shining on the linen laid ready for dinner. 'Ostend–Cologne–Vienne–Belgrade–Istanbul.' He passed the rows of names without a glance; the route was familiar to him; the names travelled back at the level of his eyes, like the spires of minarets, cupolas or domes of the cities themselves, offering no permanent settlement to one of his race.

The guard, as he had expected, was surly. The train was very full, he said, though Myatt knew he lied. April was too early in the year for crowded carriages, and he had seen few first-class passengers on the Channel steamer. While he argued, a bevy of tourists scrambled down the corridor, middle-aged ladies clutching shawls and rugs and sketch-books, an old clergyman complaining that he had mislaid his *Wide World Magazine*–'I always read a *Wide World* when I travel'–and in the rear, perspiring, genial under difficulties, their conductor wearing the button of an agency. 'Voilà,' the guard said and seemed to indicate with a gesture that his train was bearing an unaccustomed, a cruel burden. But Myatt knew the route too well to be deceived. The party, he guessed from its appearance of harassed culture, belonged to the slip-coach for Athens. When he doubled the tip, the guard gave way and pasted a reserved notice on the window of the compartment. With a sigh of relief Myatt found himself alone.

He watched the swim of faces separated by a safe wall of glass. Even through his fur coat the damp chill of the day struck him, and as he turned the heating-wheel, a mist from his breath obscured the pane, so that soon he could see of those who passed no more than unrelated features, a peering angry eye, a dress of mauve silk, a clerical collar. Only once was he tempted to break this growing solitude and wipe the glass with his fingers in time to catch sight of a thin girl in a white mackintosh disappearing along the corridor towards the second class. Once the door was opened and an elderly man glanced in. He had a grey moustache and wore glasses and a shabby soft hat. Myatt told him in French that the compartment was taken.

'One seat,' the man said.

'Do you want the second class?' Myatt asked, but the man shook his head and moved away.

Mr Opie sank with conscious luxury into his corner and regarded with curiosity and disappointment the small pale man opposite him. The man was extraordinarily commonplace in appearance; ill-health had ruined his complexion. Nerves, Mr Opie thought, watching the man's moving fingers, but they showed no other sign of acute sensibility. They were short, blunt and thick.

'I always think,' Mr Opie said, wondering whether he had been very unfortunate in his companion, 'that as long as one can get a sleeper, it is so unnecessary to travel first class. These second-class carriages are remarkably comfortable.'

'Yes–that's so–yes,' the other answered with alacrity. 'But 'ow did you know I was English?'

'I make a practice,' Mr Opie said with a smile, 'of always thinking the best of people.'

'Of course,' the pale man said, 'you as a clergyman—'

The newsboys were calling outside the window, and Mr Opie leant out. '*Le Temps de Londres.* Qu'est que c'est que ça? Rien du tout? *Le Matin* et un *Daily Mail.* C'est bon. Merci.' His French seemed to the other full of copybook phrases, used with gusto and inaccurately. 'Combien est cela? Trois francs. Oh la-la.'

To the white-faced man he said: 'Can I interpret for you? Is there any paper you want? Don't mind me if you want *La Vie*.'

'No, nothing, nothing, thank you. I've a book.'

Mr Opie looked at his watch. 'Three minutes and we shall be away.'

She had been afraid for several minutes that he would speak, or else the tall thin woman his wife. Silence for the time being she desired more than anything else. If I could have afforded a sleeper, she wondered, would I have been alone? In the dim carriage the lights flickered on, and the plump man remarked, 'Now we shan't be long.' The air was full of dust and damp, and the flicker of light outside reminded her for a moment of familiar things: the electric signs flashing and changing over the theatre in Nottingham High Street. The stir of life, the passage of porters and paper-boys, recalled for a moment the goose market, and to the memory of the market she clung, tried to externalise it in her mind, to build the bricks and lay the stalls, until they had as much reality as the cold rain-washed quay, the changing signal lamps. Then the man spoke to her, and she was compelled to emerge from her hidden world and wear a pose of cheerfulness and courage.

'Well, miss, we've got a long journey together. Suppose we exchange names. Mine's Peters, and this is my wife Amy.'

'Mine's Coral Musker.'

'Get me a sandwich,' the thin woman implored. 'I'm so empty I can hear my stomach.'

'Would you, miss? I don't know the lingo.'

And why, she would have liked to cry at him, do you suppose I do? I've never been out of England. But she had so schooled herself to accept responsibility wherever and in whatever form it came, that she made no protest, opened the door and would have run down the slippery dusky road between the rails in search of what he wanted if she had not seen a clock. 'There's no time,' she said, 'only one minute before we go.' Turning back she caught sight at the corridor's end of a face and figure that made her catch her breath with longing: a last dab of powder on the nose, a good-night to the door-keeper, and outside in the bright glittering betrayal of the dark, the young waiting Jew, the chocolates, the car round the corner, the rapid ride and the furtive dangerous embrace. But it was no one she knew; she was back in the unwanted, dreaded adventure of a foreign land, which could not be checked by a skilful word; no carefully-measured caress would satisfy the approaching dark.

The train's late, Myatt thought, as he stepped into the corridor. He felt in his waistcoat pocket for the small box of currants he always carried there. It was divided into four sections and his fingers chose one at random. As he put it into his mouth, he judged it by the feel. The quality's going off. That's Stein and Co. They are getting small and dry. At the end of the corridor a girl in a white mackintosh turned and gazed at him. Nice figure, he thought. Do I know her? He chose another currant and without a glance placed it. One of our own. Myatt, Myatt and Page. For a moment with the currant upon his tongue he might have been one of the lords of the world, carrying destiny with him. This is mine and this is good, he thought. Doors slammed along the line of coaches, and a horn was blown.

Richard John, with his mackintosh turned up above his ears, leant from the corridor window and saw the sheds begin to move backwards towards the slow wash of the sea. It was the end, he thought, and the beginning. Faces streamed away. A man with a pickaxe on his shoulder swung a red lamp; the smoke from the engine blew round him, and obscured his light. The brakes ground, the clouds parted, and the setting sun flashed on the line, the window and his eyes. If I could sleep, he thought with longing, I could remember more clearly all the things that have to be remembered.

The fire-hole door opened and the blaze and the heat of the furnace for a moment emerged. The driver turned the regulator full open, and the footplate shook with the weight of the coaches. Presently the engine settled smoothly to its work, the driver brought the cut-off back, and the last of the sun came out as the train passed through Bruges, the regulator closed, coasting with little steam. The sunset lit up tall dripping walls, alleys with stagnant water radiant for a moment with liquid light. Somewhere within the dingy casing lay the ancient city, like a notorious jewel, too stared at, talked of, trafficked over. Then a wilderness of allotments opened through the steam, sometimes the monotony broken by tall ugly villas, facing every way, decorated with coloured tiles, which now absorbed the evening. The sparks from the express became visible, like hordes of scarlet beetles tempted into the air by night; they fell and smouldered by the track, touched leaves and twigs and cabbage-stalks and turned to soot. A girl riding a cart-horse lifted her face and laughed; on the bank beside the line a man and woman lay embraced. Then darkness fell outside, and passengers through the glass could see only the transparent reflection of their own features.

2

'Premier Service, Premier Service.' The voice went echoing down the corridor, but Myatt was already seated in the restaurant-car. He did not wish to run the danger of sharing a table, of being forced into polite openings, of being, not improbably, snubbed. Constantinople, for many of the passengers the end of an almost interminable journey, approached him with the speed of the flying climbing telegraph-poles. When the journey was over, there would be no time to think; a waiting car, the rush of minarets, a dingy stair, and Mr Eckman rising from behind his desk. Subtleties, figures, contracts would encoil him. Here beforehand, in the restaurant-car, in the sleeping-berth, in the corridor, he must plan every word and rehearse every inflection. He wished that his dealings were with Englishmen or Turks, but Mr Eckman, and somewhere in the background the enigmatic Stein, were men of his own race, practised in reading a meaning into a tone of voice, the grip of fingers round a cigar.

Up the aisle the waiters came carrying the soup. Myatt felt in his breast-pocket and again he nibbled a currant, one of Stein's, small and dry, but, it had to be admitted, cheap. The eternal inevitable war between quality and quantity was fought out to no issue in his mind. Of one thing he had been as nearly certain as possible while tied to a desk in London, meeting only Stein's representatives and never Stein, hearing at best Stein's voice over the long-distance telephone, a ghost of a voice from whose inflections he could tell nothing: Stein was on the rocks. But what rocks? In mid-ocean or near shore? Was he desperate or only resigned to uncomfortable economies? The affair would have been simple if Myatt and Page's agent in Constantinople, the invaluable Mr Eckman, had not been suspected of intricate hidden relations with Stein skirting the outer fringe of the law.

He dipped his spoon into the tasteless Julienne; he preferred his food rich, highly seasoned, but full of a harsh nourishment. Out in the dark nothing was visible, except for the occasional flash of lights from a small station, the rush of flame in a tunnel, and always the transparent likeness of his own face, his hand floating like a fish through which water and weeds shine. He was a little irritated by its ubiquity and was about to pull down the blind when he noticed, behind his own reflection, the image of the shabby man in the mackintosh who had looked into his compartment. His clothes, robbed of colour and texture and opacity, the ghosts of ancient tailoring, had still a forced gentility; the mackintosh thrown open showed the high stiff collar, the over-buttoned jacket. The man waited patiently for his dinner—so Myatt at first thought, allowing his mind to rest a little from the subtleties of Stein and Mr Eckman—but before the waiter could reach him, the stranger was asleep. His face for a moment disappeared from view as the lights of a station turned the walls of the coach from mirrors to windows, through which became visible a throng of country passengers waiting with children and packages and string bags for some slow cross-country train. With the darkness the face returned, nodding into sleep.

Myatt forgot him, choosing a medium Burgundy, a Chambertin of 1923, to drink with the veal, though he knew it a waste of money to buy a good wine, for no bouquet could survive the continuous tremor. All down the coach the whimper and whine of shaken glass was audible as the express drove on at full steam towards Cologne. During the first glass Myatt thought again of Stein, waiting in Constantinople for his arrival with cunning or despair. He would sell out, Myatt felt sure, for a price, but another buyer was said to be in the field. That was where Mr Eckman was suspected of playing a double part, of trying to put up the price against his own firm with a fifteen per cent commission from Stein as the probable motive. Mr Eckman had written that Moult's were offering Stein a fancy price for his stock and goodwill; Myatt did not believe him. He had lunched one day with young Moult and casually introduced into their talk the name of Stein. Moult was not a Jew; he had no subtlety, no science of evasion; if he wished to lie, he would lie, but the lie would be confined to the words; he had no knowledge how the untrained hand gives the lie to the mouth. In dealing with an Englishman Myatt found one trick enough; as he introduced the important theme or asked the leading question, he would offer a cigar; if the man was lying, however prompt the answer, the hand would hesitate for the quarter of a second. Myatt knew what the Gentiles said of him: 'I don't like that Jew. He never looks you in the face.' You fools, he would triumph secretly, I know a trick worth two of that. He knew now for example that young Moult had not lied. It was Stein who was lying, or else Mr Eckman.

He poured himself out another glass. Curious, he thought, that it was he, travelling at the rate of sixty miles an hour, who was at rest, not Mr Eckman, locking up his desk, picking his hat from the rack, going downstairs, chewing, as it were, the firm's telegram between his sharp prominent teeth. 'Mr Carleton Myatt will arrive Istanbul 14th. Arrange meeting with Stein.' In the train, however fast it travelled, the passengers were compulsorily at rest; useless between the walls of glass to feel emotion, useless to try to follow any activity except of the mind; and that activity could be followed without fear of interruption. The world was beating now on Eckman and Stein, telegrams were arriving, men were interrupting the threads of their thought with speech, women were holding dinner-parties. But in the rushing reverberating express, noise was so regular that it was the equivalent of silence, movement was so continuous that after a while the mind accepted it as stillness. Only outside the train was violence of action possible, and the train would contain him safely with his plans for three days; by the end of that time he would know quite clearly how to deal with Stein and Mr Eckman.

The ice and the dessert over, the bill paid, he paused beside his table to light a cigar and thus faced the stranger and saw how again he had fallen into sleep between the courses; between the departure of the veal, *au Talleyrand*, and the arrival of the iced pudding he had fallen victim to what must have been a complete exhaustion.

Under Myatt's gaze he woke suddenly. 'Well?' he asked. Myatt apologised. 'I didn't mean to wake you.' The man watched him with suspicion, and something in the sudden change from sleep to a more accustomed anxiety, something in the well-meaning clothes betrayed by the shabby mackintosh, touched Myatt to pity. He presumed on their earlier encounter. 'You've found a compartment all right?'

'Yes.'

Myatt said impulsively: 'I thought perhaps you were finding it hard to rest. I have some aspirin in my bag. Can I lend you a few tablets?' The man snapped at him, 'I have everything I want. I am a doctor.' From habit Myatt watched his hands, thin with the bones showing. He apologised again with a little of the excessive humility of the bowed head in the desert. 'I'm sorry to have troubled you. You looked ill. If there is anything I can do for you—'

'No. Nothing. Nothing.' But as Myatt went, the other turned and called after him, 'The time. What is the right time?' Myatt said, 'Eight-forty. No, forty-two,' and saw the man's fingers adjust his watch with care for the exact minute.

As he reached the compartment the train was slowing down. The great blast furnaces of Liège rose along the line like ancient castles burning in a border raid. The train lurched and the points changed. Steel girders rose on either side, and very far below an empty street ran diagonally into the dark, and a lamp shone on a café door. The rails opened out, and unattached engines converged on the express, hooting and belching steam. The signals flashed green across the sleepers, and the arch of the station roof rose above the carriage. Newsboys shouted, and a line of stiff sedate men in black broadcloth and women in black veils waited along the platform; without interest, like a crowd of decorous strangers at a funeral, they watched the line of first-class coaches pass them, Ostend–Cologne–Vienne–Belgrade–Istanbul–the slip coach for Athens. Then with their string bags and their children they climbed into the rear coaches, bound perhaps for Pepinster or Verviers, fifteen miles down the line.

Myatt was tired. He had sat up till one o'clock the night before discussing with his father, Jacob Myatt, the affairs of Stein, and he had become aware as never before, watching the jerk of the white beard, of how affairs were slipping away from the old ringed fingers clasped round the glass of warm milk. 'They never pick off the skin,' Jacob Myatt complained, allowing his son to take the spoon and skim the surface clear. There were many things he now allowed his son to do, and Page counted for nothing; his directorship was a mere decoration awarded for twenty years' faithful service as head clerk. I am Myatt, Myatt and Page, he thought without a tremor at the idea of responsibility; he was the first born and it was the law of nature that the father should resign to the son.

They had disagreed last night over Eckman. Jacob Myatt believed that Stein had deceived the agent, and his son that the agent was in league with Stein. 'You'll see,' he promised, confident in his own cunning, but Jacob Myatt only said, 'Eckman's clever. We need a clever man there.'

It was no use, Myatt knew, settling down to sleep before the frontier at Herbesthal. He took out the figures that Eckman proposed as a basis for negotiation with Stein, the value of the stock in hand, the value of the goodwill, the amount which he believed Stein had been offered by another purchaser. It was true that Eckman had not named Moult in so many words; he had only hinted at the name and he could deny the hint. Moult's had never previously shown interest in currants; the nearest they had come to it was a brief flirtation with the date market. Myatt thought: I can't believe these figures. Stein's business is worth that to us, even if we dumped his stock into the Bosphorus, because we should gain a monopoly; but for any other firm it would be the purchase of a rocky business beaten by our competition.

The figures began to swim before his eyes in a mist of sleep. Ones, sevens, nines became Mr Eckman's small sharp teeth; sixes, fives, threes reformed themselves as in a trick film into Mr Eckman's dark polished eyes. Commissions in the form of coloured balloons floated across the carriage, growing in size, and he sought a pin to prick them one by one. He was brought back to full wakefulness by the sound of footsteps passing and re-passing along the corridor. Poor devil, he thought, seeing a brown mackintosh disappear past the window and two hands clasped.

But he felt no pity for Mr Eckman, following him back in fancy from his office to his very modern flat, into the shining lavatory, the silver-and-gilt bathroom, the bright cushioned drawing-room where his wife sat and sewed and sewed, making vests and pants and bonnets and socks for the Anglican Mission: Mr Eckman was a Christian. All along the line the blast furnaces flared.

The heat did not penetrate the wall of glass. It was bitterly cold, an April night like an old-fashioned Christmas card glittering with frost. Myatt took his fur coat from a peg and went into the corridor. At Cologne there was a wait of nearly forty-five minutes; time enough to get a cup of hot coffee or a glass of brandy. Until then he could walk, up and down, like the man in the mackintosh.

While there was nothing worth his notice in the outside air he knew who would be walking with him in spirit the length of the corridor, in and out of lavatories, Mr Eckman and Stein. Mr Eckman he thought, trying to coax some hot water into a gritty basin, kept a chained Bible by his lavatory seat. So at least he had been told. Large and shabby and very 'family' amongst the silver-and-gilt taps and plugs, it advertised to every man and woman who dined in his flat Mr Eckman's Christianity. There was no need of covert allusions to Church-goings, to the Embassy chaplain, merely a 'Would you like a wash, dear?' from his wife, his own hearty questions to the men after the coffee and the brandy. But of Stein, Myatt knew nothing.

'What a pity you are not getting out at Buda, as you are so interested in cricket. I'm trying—oh, so hard—to get up two elevens at the embassy.' A man with face as bleak and white and impersonal as his clerical collar was speaking to a little rat of a man who crouched opposite him, nodding and becking. The voice, robbed of its characteristic inflections by closed glass, floated out into the corridor as Myatt passed. It was the ghost of a voice and reminded Myatt again of Stein speaking over two thousand miles of cable, hoping that he would one day soon have the honour of entertaining Mr Carleton Myatt in Constantinople, agreeable, hospitable and anonymous.

He was passing the non-sleeping compartments in the second class; men with their waistcoats off sprawled along seats, blue about the chin; women with hair in dusty nets, like the string bags on the racks, tucked their skirts tightly round them and fell in odd shapes over the seats, large breasts and small thighs, small breasts and large thighs hopelessly confused. A tall thin woman woke for a moment to complain, 'That beer you got me. Shocking it was. I can't keep my stomach quiet.' On the seat opposite, the husband sat and smiled; he rubbed one hand over his rough chin, squinting sideways at the girl in the white mackintosh, who lay along the seat, her feet against his other hand. Myatt paused and lit a cigarette. He liked the girl's thin figure and her face, the lips tinted enough to lend her plainness an appeal. Nor was she altogether plain; the smallness of her features, of her skull, her nose and ears, gave her a spurious refinement, a kind of bright prettiness, like the window of a country shop at Christmas full of small lights and tinsel and coloured common gifts. Myatt remembered how she had gazed at him down the length of the corridor and wondered a little of whom he had reminded her. He was grateful that she had shown no distaste, no knowledge of his uneasiness in the best clothes that money could buy.

The man who shared her seat put his hand cautiously on her ankle and moved it very slowly up towards her knee. All the time he watched his wife. The girl woke and opened her eyes. 'How cold it is,' Myatt heard her say and knew from her elaborate and defensive friendliness that she was aware of the hand withdrawn. Then she looked up and saw him watching her. She was tactful, she was patient, but to Myatt she had little subtlety; he knew that his qualities, the possibilities of annoyance which he offered, were being weighed against her companion's. She wasn't looking for trouble: that was the expression she would use; and he found her courage, quickness and decision admirable. 'I think I'll have a cigarette outside,' she said, fumbling in her bag for a packet; then she was beside him.

'A match?'

'Thanks.' And moving out of view of her compartment they stared together into the murmuring darkness.

'I don't like your companion,' Myatt said.

'One can't pick and choose. He's not too bad. His name's Peters.'

Myatt for a moment hesitated. 'Mine's Myatt.'

'Mine's Coral—Coral Musker.'

'Dancing?'

'Sure.'

'American?'

'No. Why did you think so?'

'Something you said. You've got a bit of the accent. Ever been there?'

'Ever been there? Of course I have. Six nights a week and two afternoons. The Garden of the Country Club, Long Island; Palm Beach: A Bachelor's Apartment on Riverside Drive. Why, if you can't talk American you don't stand a chance in an English musical comedy.'

'You're clever,' said Myatt gravely, releasing Eckman and Stein from his consideration.

'Let's move,' the girl said, 'I'm cold.'

'Can't you sleep?'

'Not after that crossing. It's too cold, and that fellow's fingering my legs the whole time.'

'Why don't you smack his face?'

'Before we've reached Cologne? I'm not making trouble. We've got to live together to Buda-Pesth.'

'Is that where you are going?'

'Where he is. I'm going all the way.'

'So am I,' said Myatt, 'on business.'

'Well, we are neither of us going for pleasure, are we?' she said with a touch of gloom. 'I saw you when the train started. I thought you were someone I knew.'

'Who?'

'How do I know? I don't trouble to remember what a boy calls himself. It's not the name the post-office knows him by.' There seemed to Myatt something patient and courageous in her quiet acceptance of deceit. She flattened against the window a face a little blue with cold; she might have been a boy avidly examining the contents of a shop, the clasp-knives, the practical jokes, plate lifters, bombs that smell, buns that squeak, but all that was offered her was darkness and their own features. 'Do you think it will get any warmer,' she asked, 'as we go south?' as though she thought herself bound for a tropical climate. 'We don't go far enough for it to make much difference,' he said. 'I've known snow in Constantinople in April. You get the winds down the Bosphorus from the Black Sea. They cut round the corners. The city's all corners.'

'I hope the dressing-rooms are warm,' she said. 'You don't wear enough on the stage to keep the chill out. How I'd like something hot to drink.' She leant with blue face and bent knees against the window. 'Are we near Cologne? What's the German for coffee?' Her expression alarmed him. He ran down the corridor and closed the only open window. 'Are you feeling all right?'

She said slowly with half-closed eyes, 'That's better. You've made it quite stuffy. I'm warm enough now. Feel me.' She lifted her hand; he put it against his cheek and was startled by the heat. 'Look here,' he said. 'Go back to your carriage and I'll try and find some brandy for you. You are ill.' 'It's only that I can't keep warm,' she explained. 'I was hot and now it's cold again. I don't want to go back. I'll stay here.'

'You must have my coat,' he began reluctantly, but before he had time to limit his unwilling offer with 'for a while' or 'until you are warm', she slid to the floor. He took her hands and chafed them, watching her face with helpless anxiety. It seemed to him suddenly of vital necessity that he should aid her. Watching her dance upon the stage, or stand in a lit street outside a stage-door, he would have regarded her only as game for the senses, but helpless and sick under the dim unsteady lamp of the corridor, her body shaken by the speed of the train, she woke a painful pity. She had not complained of the cold; she had commented on it as a kind of necessary evil, and in a flash of insight he became aware of the innumerable necessary evils of which life for her was made up. He heard the monotonous tread of the man whom he had seen pass and re-pass his compartment and went to meet him. 'You are a doctor? There's a girl fainted.' The man stopped and asked reluctantly, 'Where is she?' Then he saw her past Myatt's shoulder. His hesitation angered the Jew. 'She looks really ill,' he urged him. The doctor sighed. 'All right, I'm coming.' He might have been nerving himself to an ordeal.

But the fear seemed to leave him as he knelt by the girl. He was tender towards her with the impersonal experienced tenderness of a doctor. He felt her heart and then lifted her lids. The girl came back to a confusing consciousness; she thought that it was she who was bending over a stranger with a long shabby moustache. She felt pity for the experience which had caused his great anxiety, and her solicitude went out to the friendliness she imagined in his eyes. She put her hands down to his face. He's ill, she thought, and for a moment shut out the puzzling shadows which fell the wrong way, the globe of light shining from the ground. 'Who are you?' she asked, trying to remember how it was that she had come to his help. Never, she thought, had she seen a man who needed help more.

'A doctor.'

She opened her eyes in astonishment and the world cleared. It was she who was lying in the corridor and the stranger who bent over her. 'Did I faint?' she asked. 'It was very cold.' She was aware of the heavy slow movement of the train. Lights streamed through the window across the doctor's face and on to the young Jew behind. Myatt, My'at. She laughed to herself in sudden contentment. It was as though, for the moment, she had passed to another all responsibility. The train lurched to a standstill, and the Jew was thrown against the wall. The doctor had not stirred. If he had swayed it was with the movement of the train and not against it. His eyes were on her face, his finger on her pulse; he watched her with a passion which was trembling on the edge of speech, but she knew that it was not passion for her or any attribute of her. She phrased it to herself: If I'd got Mistinguett's legs, he wouldn't notice. She asked him, 'What is it?' and lost all his answer in the voices crying down the platform and the entrance of blue uniformed men but 'my proper work'.

'Passports and luggage ready,' a foreign voice called to them, and Myatt spoke to her, asking for her bag: 'I'll see to your things.' She gave him her bag and helped by the doctor sat up against the wall.

'Passport?'

The doctor said slowly, and she became aware for the first time of his accent: 'My bags are in the first class. I can't leave this lady. I am a doctor.'

'English passport?'

'Yes.'

'All right.' Another man came up to them. 'Luggage?'

'Nothing to declare.' The man went on.

Coral Musker smiled. 'Is this really the frontier? Why, one could smuggle anything in. They don't look at the bags at all.'

'Anything,' the doctor said, 'with an English passport.' He watched the man out of sight and said nothing more until Myatt returned. 'I could go back to my carriage now,' she said.

'Have you a sleeper?'

'No.'

'Are you getting out at Cologne?'

'I'm going all the way.'

He gave her the same advice as the purser had done. 'You should have had a sleeper.' The uselessness of it irritated her and made her for a moment forget her pity for his age and anxiety. 'How could I have a sleeper? I'm in the chorus.' He flashed back at her with astonishing bitterness, 'No, you have not the money.'

'What shall I do?' she asked him. 'Am I ill?'

'How can I advise you?' he protested. 'If you were rich, I should say: Take six months' holiday. Go to North Africa. You fainted because of the crossing, because of the cold. Oh yes, I can tell you all that, but that's nothing. Your heart's bad. You've been overstraining it for years.'

She implored him, a little frightened, 'But what shall I do?' He opened his hands: 'Nothing. Carry on. Take what rest you can. Keep warm. You wear too little.'

A whistle blew, and the train trembled into movement. The station lamps sailed by them into darkness, and the doctor turned to leave her. 'If you want me again, I'm three coaches farther up. My name is John. Dr John.' She said with intimidated politeness, 'Mine's Coral Musker.' He gave her a little formal foreign bow and walked away. She saw in his eyes other thoughts falling like rain. Never before had she the sensation of being so instantly forgotten. 'A girl that men forget,' she hummed to keep up her courage.

But the doctor had not passed out of hearing before he was stopped. Treading softly and carefully along the shaking train, a hand clinging to the corridor rail, came a small pale man. She heard him speak to the doctor, 'Is anything the matter? Can I help?' He was a foot shorter and she laughed aloud at the sight of his avid face peering upwards. 'You mustn't think me inquisitive,' he said, one hand on the other's sleeve. 'A clergyman in my compartment thought someone was ill.' He added with eagerness, 'I said I'd find out.'

Up and down, up and down the corridor she had seen the doctor walking, clinging to its emptiness in preference to a compartment shared. Now, through no mistake on his part, he found himself in a crowd, questions and appeals sticking to his mind like burrs. She expected an outbreak, some damning critical remark which would send the fellow quivering down the corridor.

The softness of his reply surprised her. 'Did you say a priest?'

'Oh no,' the man apologised, 'I don't know yet what sect, what creed. Why? Is somebody dying?'

Dr John seemed to become aware of her fear and called down the corridor a reassurance before he brushed by the detaining hand. The little man remained for a moment in happy possession of a situation. When he had tasted it to the full, he approached. 'What's it all about?'

She took no notice, appealing to the only friendly presence she was left with. 'I'm not sick like that, am I?'

'What intrigues me,' the stranger said, 'is his accent. You'd say he was a foreigner, but he gave an English name. I think I'll follow him and talk.'

Her mind had worked clearly since she fainted; the sight of a world reversed, in which it had been the doctor who lay beneath her needing pity and care, had made the old images of the world sharp with unfamiliarity; but

words lagged behind intuition, and when she appealed, 'Don't bother him,'
the stranger was already out of hearing.

'What do you think?' Myatt asked. 'Is he right? Is there a mystery?'

'We've all got some secrets,' she said.

'He might be escaping from the police.'

She said with absolute conviction, 'He's good.' He accepted the phrase; it
dismissed the doctor from his thoughts. 'You must lie down,' he said, 'and
try to sleep,' but it did not need her evasive reply, 'How can I sleep with that
woman and her stomach?' to remind him of Mr Peters lurking in his corner
for her return and the renewal of his cheap easy harmless satisfactions. 'You
must have my sleeper.'

'What? In the first class?' Her disbelief and her longing decided him. He
determined to be princely on an Oriental scale, granting costly gifts and not
requiring, not wanting, any return. Parsimony was the traditional reproach
against his race, and he would show one Christian how undeserved it was.
Forty years in the wilderness, away from the flesh pots of Egypt, had
entailed harsh habits, the counted date and the hoarded water; nor had a
thousand years in the wilderness of a Christian world, where only the secret
treasure was safe, encouraged display; but the world was altering, the desert
was flowering; in stray corners here and there, in western Europe, the Jew
could show that other quality he shared with the Arab, the quality of the
princely host, who would wash the feet of beggars and feed them from his
own dish; sometimes he could cease to be the enemy of the rich to become
the friend of any poor man who sought a roof in the name of God. The roar of
the train faded from his consciousness, the light went out in his eyes, while
he built for his own pride the tent in the oasis, the well in the desert. He
spread his hands before her. 'Yes, you must sleep there. I'll arrange with the
guard. And my coat—you must take that. It will keep you warm. At Cologne
I'll find you coffee, but it will be better for you to sleep.'

'But I can't. Where will you sleep?'

'I shall find somewhere. The train's not full.' For the second time she
experienced an impersonal tenderness, but it was not frightening as the first
had been; it was a warm wave into which she let herself down, not too far, if
she felt afraid, for her feet to be aware of the sand, but only far enough to float
her without effort on her own part where she wanted to go—to a bed and a
pillow and a covering and sleep. She had an impression of how grace came
back to him with confidence, as he ceased to apologise or to assert and
became only a ministering shadow.

Myatt did not go to find the guard but wedged himself between the walls
of corridor and compartment, folded his arms and prepared to sleep. But
without his coat it was very cold. Although all the windows of the corridor
were shut, a draught blew past the swing door and over the footboard joining
coach to coach. Nor were the noises of the train regular enough now to be
indistinguishable from silence. There were many tunnels between
Herbesthal and Cologne, and in each the roar of the express was magnified.
Myatt slept uneasily, and the rush of the loosed steam and the draught on his
cheek contributed to his dream. The corridor became the long straight
Spaniards Road with the heath on either side. He was being driven slowly by
Isaacs in his Bentley, and they watched the girls' faces as they walked in pairs

along the lamp-lit eastern side, shopgirls offering themselves dangerously for a drink at the inn, a fast ride, and the fun of the thing; on the other side of the road, in the dark, on a few seats, the prostitutes sat, shapeless and shabby and old, with their backs to the sandy slopes and the thorn bushes, waiting for a man old and dumb and blind enough to offer them ten shillings. Isaacs drew up the Bentley under a lamp and they let the anonymous young beautiful animal faces stream by. Isaacs wanted someone fair and plump and Myatt someone thin and dark, but it was not easy to pick and choose, for all along the eastern side were lined the cars of their competitors, girls leaning across the open doors laughing and smoking; on the other side of the road a single two-seater kept patient watch. Myatt was irritated by Isaacs' uncompromising taste; it was cold in the Bentley with a draught on the cheek, and presently when he saw Coral Musker walking by, he jumped from the car and offered her a cigarette and after that a drink and after that a ride. That was one advantage with these girls, Myatt thought; they all knew what a ride meant, and if they didn't care for the look of you, they just said that they had to be going home now. But Coral Musker wanted a ride; she would take him for her companion in the dark of the car, with the lamps and the inns and the houses left behind and trees springing up like paper silhouettes in the green light of the head-lamps, and then the bushes with the scent of wet leaves holding the morning's rain and a short barbarous enjoyment in the stubble. As for Isaacs, he must just put up with his companion, although she was dark and broad and lightly clothed, with a great nose and prominent pointed teeth. But when she was seated next Isaacs in the front of the car she turned and gave him a long smile, saying, 'I've come out without a card, but my name's Stein.' And then in the teeth of the wind he was climbing a great stair with silver and gilt handrails, and she stood at the top wearing a small moustache, pointing to a woman who sat sewing, sewing, sewing, and called out to him, 'Meet Mrs Eckman.'

Coral Musker flung her hand away from the blankets in protest, as she danced and danced and danced in the glare of the spot-light, and the producer struck at her bare legs with a cane, telling her she was no good, that she was a month late, and she'd broken her contract. And all the time she danced and danced and danced, taking no notice of him while he beat at her legs with the cane.

Mrs Peters turned on her face and said to her husband, 'That beer. My stomach won't be quiet. It makes so much noise, I can't sleep.'

Mr Opie dreamed that in his surplice with cricket bat under his arm and batting-glove dangling from his wrist he mounted a great broad flight of marble steps towards the altar of God.

Dr John asleep at last with a bitter tablet dissolving on his tongue spoke once in German. He had no sleeper and sat bolt upright in the corner of his compartment, hearing outside the slow singing start, 'Köln, Köln. Köln.'

PART II

COLOGNE

I

'But of course, dear, I don't mind your being drunk,' said Janet Pardoe. The clock above Cologne station struck one, and a waiter began to turn out the lights on the terrace of the Excelsior. 'Look, dear, let me put your tie straight.' She leant across the table and adjusted Mabel Warren's tie.

'We've lived together for three years,' Miss Warren began to say in a deep melancholy voice, 'and I have never yet spoken to you harshly.'

Janet Pardoe put a little scent behind her ears. 'For heaven's sake, darling, look at the time. The train leaves in half an hour, and I've got to get my bags, and you've got to get your interview. Do drink up your gin and come along.'

Mabel Warren took her glass and drank. Then she rose and her square form swayed a little; she wore a tie and a stiff collar and a tweed 'sporting' suit. Her eyebrows were heavy, and her eyes were dark and determined and red with weeping.

'You know why I drink,' she protested.

'Nonsense, dear,' said Janet Pardoe, making certain in her compact mirror of the last niceties of appearance, 'you drank long before you ever met me. Have a little sense of proportion. I shall only be away a week.'

'These men,' said Miss Warren darkly, and then as Janet Pardoe rose to cross the square, she gripped her arm with extraordinary force. 'Promise me you'll be careful. If only I could come with you.' Almost on the threshold of the station she stumbled in a puddle. 'Oh, see what I've done now. What a great clumsy thing I am. To splash your beautiful new suit.' With a large rough hand, a signet ring on the small finger, she began to brush at Janet Pardoe's skirt.

'Oh, for God's sake, come on, Mabel,' Janet said.

Miss Warren's mood changed. She straightened herself and barred the way. 'You say I'm drunk. I am drunk. But I'm going to be drunker.'

'Oh, come on.'

'You are going to have one more drink with me or I shan't let you on the platform.'

Janet Pardoe gave way. 'One. Only one, mind.' She guided Mabel Warren across a vast black shining hall into a room where a few tired men and women were snatching cups of coffee. 'Another gin,' said Miss Warren, and Janet ordered it.

In a mirror on the opposite wall Miss Warren saw her own image, red, tousled, very shoddy, sitting beside another and far more familiar image, slim, dark, and beautiful. What do I matter? she thought, with the melancholy of drink. I've made her, I'm responsible for her, and with bitterness, I've paid for her. There's nothing she's wearing that I haven't paid for, sweated for, she thought (although the bitter cold defied the radiators in the restaurant), getting up at all hours, interviewing brothel-keepers in their cells, the mothers of murdered children, 'covering' this and 'covering' that. She knew with a certain pride what they said in the London office: 'When you want sob-stuff, send Dizzy Mabel.' All the way down the Rhine was her province; there wasn't a town of any size between Cologne and Mainz where she hadn't sought out human interest, forcing dramatic phrases onto the lips of sullen men, pathos into the mouths of women too overcome with grief to speak at all. There wasn't a suicide, a murdered woman, a raped child who had stirred her to the smallest emotion; she was an artist to examine critically, to watch, to listen; the tears were for paper. But now she sat and wept with ugly grunts because Janet Pardoe was leaving her for a week.

'Who is it you are interviewing?' Janet Pardoe asked. She was not at all interested, but she wanted to distract Mabel Warren from thoughts of separation; her tears were too conspicuous. 'You ought to comb your hair,' she added. Miss Warren wore no hat and her black hair, cut short like a man's, was hopelessly dishevelled.

'Savory,' said Miss Warren.

'Who's he?'

'Sold a hundred thousand copies. *The Great Gay Round*. Half a million words. Two hundred characters. The Cockney Genius. Drops his aitches when he can remember to.'

'What's he doing on the train?'

'Going East to collect material. It's not my job, but as I was seeing you off, I took it on. They've asked me for a quarter of a column, but they'll cut it down to a couple of sticks in London. He's chosen the wrong time. In the silly season he'd have got half a column among the mermaids and sea-horses.' The flare of professional interest guttered as she looked again at Janet Pardoe: no more of a morning would she see Janet in pyjamas pouring out coffee, no more of an evening come in to the flat and find Janet in pyjamas mixing a cocktail. She said huskily, 'Darling, which pair will you be wearing to-night?' The feminine question sounded oddly in Miss Warren's deep masculine voice.

'What do you mean?'

'Pyjamas, darling. I want to think of you tonight just as you are.'

'I don't suppose I shall even undress. Look, it's a quarter past one. We must go. You'll never get your interview.'

Miss Warren's professional pride was touched. 'You don't think I need to ask him questions?' she said. 'Just a look at him and I'll put the right words in his mouth. And he won't complain either. It's publicity.'

'But I must find the porter with my bags.' Everyone was leaving the restaurant. As the door opened and closed the cries of porters, the whistle of steam, came faintly down to where they sat. Janet Pardoe appealed again to

Miss Warren. 'We must go. If you want any more gin I shall leave you to it.'
But Miss Warren said nothing, Miss Warren ignored her; Janet Pardoe
found herself attending one of the regular rites of Mabel Warren's
journalistic career, the visible shedding of her drunkenness. First a hand put
the hair into order, then a powdered handkerchief, her compromise with
femininity, disguised the redness of her cheeks and lids. All the while she
was focusing her eyes, using whatever lay before her, cups, waiter, glasses
and so to the distant mirrors and her own image, as a kind of optician's
alphabetic scroll. On this occasion the first letter of the alphabet, the great
black A, was an elderly man in a mackintosh, who was standing beside a table
brushing away his crumbs before leaving to catch the train.

'My God,' said Miss Warren, covering her eyes with her hand, 'I'm
drunk. I can't see properly. Who's that there?'

'The man with the moustache?'

'Yes.'

'I've never seen him before.'

'I have,' said Miss Warren, 'I have. But where?' Something had diverted
her effectually from the thought of separation; her nose was on a scent and
leaving half a finger of gin in the bottom of her glass, she strode in the man's
wake to the door. He was out and walking quickly across the black shining
hall to a flight of stairs before Miss Warren could extricate herself from the
swing door. She crashed into a porter and fell on her knees, swaying her
head, trying to free it from the benevolence, the melancholy, the vagueness
of drink. He stopped to help her and she seized his arm and stayed him until
she could control her tongue. 'What train leaves platform five?' she asked.
'Vienna,' the man said.

'Belgrade?' 'Yes.'

It had been pure chance that she had said Belgrade and not
Constantinople, but the sound of her own voice brought her light. She called
out to Janet Pardoe: 'Take two seats. I'm coming with you as far as Vienna.'

'Your ticket?'

'I've got my reporter's pass.' It was she who was now impatient. 'Hurry.
Platform five. It's twenty-eight past. Only five minutes.' She still kept the
porter to her side with a muscular grip. 'Listen. I want you to take a message
for me. Kaiser Wilhelmstrasse 33.'

'I can't leave the station,' he told her.

'What time do you come off duty?'

'Six.'

'That's no good. You must slip out. You can do that, can't you? No one
will notice.'

'I'd get the sack.'

'Risk it,' said Miss Warren. 'Twenty marks.'

The man shook his head. 'The foreman would notice.'

'I'll give you another twenty for him.'

The foreman wouldn't do it, he said; there was too much to lose; the head
foreman might find out. Miss Warren opened her bag and began to count her
money. Above her head a clock struck the half-hour. The train left in three
minutes, but not for a moment did she allow her desperation to show; any
emotion would frighten the man. 'Eighty marks,' she said, 'and give the

foreman what you like. You'll only be away ten minutes.'

'It's a big risk,' the porter said, but he allowed her to press the notes into his hand. 'Listen carefully. Go to Kaiser Wilhelmstrasse 33. You'll find the offices of the London *Clarion*. Somebody's sure to be there. Tell him that Miss Warren has taken the Orient Express for Vienna. She won't be letting him have the interview tonight; she'll telephone it from Vienna tomorrow. Tell him she's on to a bill page lead. Now repeat that.' While he stumbled slowly through the message she kept an eye on the clock. One-thirty. One-thirty-one and a half. 'Right. Off with it. If you don't get it to them by one-fifty I'll report you for taking bribes.' She grinned at him with malicious playfulness, showing great square teeth, and then ran for the stairs. One-thirty-two. She thought that she heard a whistle blown and took the last three steps in one stride. The train was moving, a ticket-collector tried to block her way but she knocked him to one side and roared 'Pass' at him over her shoulder. The last third-class coaches were slipping by with increasing speed. My God, she thought, I'll give up drink. She got her hand on the bar of the last coach, while a porter shouted and ran at her. For a long ten seconds, with pain shooting up her arm, she thought that she would be dragged off the platform against the wheels of the guard's van. The high step daunted her. I can't make it. Another moment and her shoulder would give. Better drop on the platform and risk concussion than break both legs. But what a story to lose, she thought with bitterness, and jumped. She landed on her knees on the step just in time as the edge of the platform fell away. The last lamp vanished, the door under the pressure of her body opened inwards, and she fell on her back into the corridor. She propped herself up against the wall with care for her aching shoulder and thought with a wry triumph, Dizzy Mabel comes on board.

Morning light came through the slit in the blind and touched the opposite seat. When Coral Musker woke it was the seat and a leather suitcase that she first saw. She felt listless and apprehensive, thinking of the train which had to be caught at Victoria, the dry egg and the slices of the day before yesterday's loaf awaiting her downstairs. I wish I'd never taken the job, she thought, preferring now when the moment of departure was upon her the queue on the stairs of Shaftesbury Avenue, the forced cheerfulness of long waits outside the agent's door. She lifted the blind and was for a moment astonished by a telegraph-pole flashing past, a green river running by, touched with orange by the early sun, and wooded hills. Then she remembered.

It was still early, for the sun was low, only just emerging above the hills. A village on the opposite bank glittered with little lights; a few thin streams of smoke lay in the windless air above the small wooden houses, where early fires were being lit, breakfasts for labourers prepared. The village was so far from the line that it remained still, to be stared at, while the trees and cottages on the near bank, the tethered boats, fled backwards. She raised the other blind and in the corridor saw Myatt sleeping with his back against the wall. Her first instinct was to wake him; her second to let him sleep and lie back herself in the luxury of another's sacrifice. She felt tender towards him, as though he had given her new hope of a life which was not a continuous struggle for one's own hand; perhaps the world, she thought, was not so hard. She remembered how the purser had spoken to her kindly and called to her, 'Remember me'; it seemed not unlikely now, with the young man sleeping outside the door, ready to suffer some hours' discomfort for a stranger, that the purser might still remember her. She thought for the first time, with happiness: Perhaps I have a life in people's minds when I am not there to be seen or talked to. She looked out of the window again, but the village was gone, and the particular green hills she had stared at; only the river was the same. She fell asleep.

Miss Warren staggered down the train. She could not bear to hold the rail with her right hand, for her shoulder pained her still, although she had sat for nearly two hours in the third-class corridor. She felt battered, faint and drunk, and with difficulty arranged her thoughts, but her nose held yet the genuine aroma of the hunt. Never before in ten years of reporting, ten years of women's rights, rapes and murders, had she come so close to an exclusive bill page story, not a story which only the penny papers would trouble to print, but a story which *The Times* correspondent himself would give a year of life to know. It was not everyone, she thought with pride, who would have been capable of seizing the moment as she had done when drunk. As she lurched along the line of first-class compartments triumph sat oddly on her brow like a tip-tilted crown.

Luck favoured her. A man came out of a compartment and made his way towards the lavatory and, as she leant back against a window to let him by, she saw the man in the mackintosh dozing in a corner, for the moment alone. He looked up to see Miss Warren swaying a little forward and back in the doorway. 'Can I come in?' she asked. 'I got on the train at Cologne, and I can't find a seat.' Her voice was low, almost tender; she might have been urging a loved dog towards a lethal chamber.

'The seat's taken.'

'Only for a moment,' said Miss Warren. 'Just to rest my legs. I am so glad that you speak English. I am always so afraid of travelling on a train with nothing but a lot of foreigners. One might want anything almost in the night, mightn't one?' She grinned at him playfully. 'I believe that you are a doctor.'

'I was once a doctor,' the man admitted.

'And you are travelling out to Belgrade?' He looked at her sharply with a sense of uneasiness, and he caught her unawares, the square tweeded form leaning a little forward, the flash of the signet ring, the flushed hungry face. 'No,' he said, 'no. Not so far.'

'I am only going to Vienna,' said Miss Warren.

He said slowly, 'What made you think—?' wondering whether he did right to question her; he was unused to danger in the form of an English spinster a little drunk with gin; he could smell her all across the carriage. The risks he had faced before required only the ducked head, the quick finger, the plain lie. Miss Warren also hesitated, and her hesitation was like a breath of flame to an imprisoned man. She said, 'I thought I had seen you in Belgrade.'

'I have never been there.'

She came roughly into the open, tossing subterfuge aside. 'I was at

Belgrade,' she said, 'for my paper at the Kamnetz trial.' But she had given him all the warning he needed and he faced her with a complete lack of interest.

'The Kamnetz trial?'

'When General Kamnetz was charged with rape. Czinner was the chief evidence for the prosecution. But of course, the general was acquitted. The jury was packed. The Government would never have allowed a conviction. It was sheer stupidity on Czinner's part to give evidence.'

'Stupidity?' His polite interest angered her. 'Of course you've heard of Czinner. They had tried to shoot him a week before while he sat in a café. He was the head of the Social Democrats. He played into their hands by giving evidence against Kamnetz; they had a warrant out for his arrest for perjury twelve hours before the trial ended. They simply sat and waited for the acquittal.'

'How long ago was all this?'

'Five years.' He watched her narrowly, judging what reply would most irritate her. 'An old story now then. Is Czinner out of prison?'

'He got away from them. I'd give a lot to know how. It would make a wonderful story. He simply disappeared. Everyone assumed he'd been murdered.'

'And hadn't he?'

'No,' said Mabel Warren, 'he got away.'

'A clever man.'

'I don't believe it,' she said furiously. 'A clever man would never have given evidence. What did Kamnetz or the child matter to him? He was a quixotic fool.' A cold breath of air blew through the open door and set the doctor shivering. 'It's been a bitter night,' he said. She brushed the remark on one side with a square worn hand. 'To think,' she said with awe, 'that he never died. While the jury were away he walked out of the court before the eyes of the police. They sat there unable to do anything till the jury came back. Why, I swear that I saw the warrant sticking out of Hartep's breast pocket. He disappeared; he might never have existed; everything went on exactly as before. Even Kamnetz.'

He could not disguise a bitter interest. 'So? Even Kamnetz?' She seized her advantage, speaking huskily with unexpected imagination. 'Yes, if he went back now, he would find everything the same; the clock might have been put back. Hartep taking the same bribes; Kamnetz with his eye for a child; the same slums; the same cafés with the same concerts at six and eleven. Carl's gone from the Moscowa, that's all, the new waiter's a Frenchman. There's a new cinema, too, near the Park. Oh yes, there's one change. They've built over Kruger's beer garden. Flats for civil servants.' He remained silent, quite unable to meet this new move of his opponent. So Kruger's was gone with its fairy lights and brightly-coloured umbrellas and the gipsies playing softly from table to table in the dusk. And Carl had gone too. For a moment he would have bartered with the woman all his safety, and the safety of his friends, to know the news of Carl; had he gathered up his tips and retired to a new flat near the Park, folding up the napkins for his own table, drawing the cork for his own glass? He knew that he ought to interrupt the drunken dangerous woman opposite him, but he could not say a word, while she gave him news of Belgrade, the kind of news which his friends in their weekly coded letters never sent him.

There were other things, too, he would have liked to ask her. She had said the slums were the same, and he could feel under his feet the steep steps down into the narrow gorges; he bent under the bright rags stretched across the way, put his handkerchief across his mouth to shut out the smell of dogs, of children, of bad meat and human ordure. He wanted to know whether Dr Czinner was remembered there. He had known every inhabitant with an intimacy which they would have thought dangerous if they had not so implicitly trusted him, if he had not been by birth one of themselves. As it was, he had been robbed, confided in, welcomed, attacked and loved. Five years was a long time; he might already be forgotten.

Mabel Warren drew in her breath sharply. 'To come to facts. I want an exclusive interview for my paper. "How I escaped?" or "Why I am returning home?"'

'An interview?' His repetitions annoyed her; she had a splitting headache and felt 'wicked'. It was the term she used herself; it meant a hatred of men, of all the shifts and evasions they made necessary, of the way they spoiled beauty and stalked abroad in their own ugliness. They boasted of the women they had enjoyed; even the faded middle-aged face before her had in his time seen beauty naked, the hands which clasped his knee had felt and pried and enjoyed. And at Vienna she was losing Janet Pardoe, who was going alone into a world where men ruled. They would flatter her and give her bright cheap objects, as though she were a native to be cheated with Woolworth mirrors and glass beads. But it was not their enjoyment she most feared, it was Janet's. Not loving her at all, or only for the hour, the day, the year, they could make her weak with pleasure, cry aloud in her enjoyment. While she, Mabel Warren, who had saved her from a governess's buried life and fed her and clothed her, who could love her with the same passion until death, without satiety, had no means save her lips to express her love, was faced always by the fact that she gave no enjoyment and gained herself no more than an embittered sense of insufficiency. Now with her head aching, the smell of gin in her nostrils, the knowledge of her flushed ugliness, she hated men with a wicked intensity and their bright spurious graces.

'You are Doctor Czinner.' She noted with an increase of her anger that he did not trouble to deny his identity, proffering her carelessly the name he travelled under, 'My name is John.'

'Doctor Czinner,' she growled at him, closing her great teeth on her lower lip in an effort at self-control.

'Richard John, a schoolmaster, on holiday.'

'To Belgrade.'

'No.' He hesitated a moment. 'I am stopping at Vienna.' She did not believe him, but she won back her amiability with an effort. 'I'm getting out at Vienna, too. Perhaps you'll let me show you some of the sights.' A man stood in the doorway and she rose. 'I'm so sorry. This is your seat.' She grinned across the compartment, lurched sideways as the train clattered across a point, and failed to hold a belch which filled the compartment for a few seconds with the smell of gin and shaken motes of cheap powder. 'I'll see you again before Vienna,' she said, and moving down the corridor leant her red face against the cold smutty glass in a spasm of pain at her own drunkenness and squalor. 'I'll get him yet,' she thought, blushing at her belch as though she were a young girl at a dinner-party. 'I'll get him somehow. God damn his soul.'

A tender light flooded the compartments. It would have been possible for a moment to believe that the sun was the expression of something that loved and suffered for men. Human beings floated like fish in golden water, free from the urge of gravity, flying without wings, transparent, in a glass aquarium. Ugly faces and misshapen bodies were transmuted, if not into beauty, at least into grotesque forms fashioned by a mocking affection. On that golden tide they rose and fell, murmured and dreamed. They were not imprisoned, for they were not during the hour of dawn aware of their imprisonment.

Coral Musker woke for the second time. She stood up at once and went to the door; the man dozed wearily, his eyes jerking open to the rhythm of the train. Her mind was still curiously clear; it was as if the golden light had a quality of penetration, so that she could understand motives which were generally hidden, movements which as a rule had for her no importance or significance. Now as she watched him and he became aware of her, she saw his hands go out in a gesture which stayed half-way; she knew that it was a trick of his race which he was consciously repressing. She said softly, 'I'm a pig. You've been out there all night.' He shrugged his shoulders deprecatingly; he might have been a pawnbroker undervaluing a watch or vase. 'Why not? I didn't want you to be disturbed. I had to see the guard. Can I come in?'

'Of course. It's your compartment.'

He smiled and was unable to resist a spread of the hands, a slight bow from the hips. 'Pardon *me*. It's yours.' He took a handkerchief from his sleeve, rolled up his cuffs, made passes in the air. 'Look. See. A first-class ticket.' A ticket fell from his handkerchief and rolled on the floor between them.

'Yours.'

'No, yours.' He began to laugh with pleasure at her consternation.

'What do you mean? I couldn't take it. Why, it must have cost pounds.'

'Ten,' he said boastfully. 'Ten pounds.' He straightened his tie and said airily, 'That's nothing to me.'

But his confidence, his boastful eyes, alienated her. She said with a deep suspicion, 'What are you getting at? What do you think I am?' The ticket lay between them; nothing would induce her to pick it up. She stamped her foot as the gold faded and became no more than a yellow stain upon the glass and cushions. 'I'm going back to my seat.'

He said defiantly, 'I don't think about you. I've got other things to think about. If you don't want the ticket you can throw it away.' She saw him watching her, his shoulders raised again boastfully, carelessly, and she began to cry quietly to herself, turning to the window and the river and a bridge that fled by and a bare beech pricked with early buds. This is my gratitude for a calm long sleepy night; this is the way I take a present; and she thought with shame and disappointment of early dreams of great courtesans accepting gifts from princes. And I snap at him like a tired waitress.

She heard him move behind her and knew that he was stooping for the ticket; she wanted to turn to him and express her gratitude, say: 'It would be like heaven to sit on these deep cushions all the journey, sleep in the berth, forget that I'm on the way to a job, think myself rich. No one has ever been so good to me as you are,' but her earlier words, the vulgarity of her suspicion, lay like a barrier of class between them. 'Lend me your bag,' he said. She held it out behind her, and she felt his fingers open the clasp. 'There,' he said, 'I've put it inside. You needn't use it. Just sit here when you want to. And sleep here when you are tired.' I am tired, she thought. I could sleep here for hours. She said in a voice strained to disguise her tears, 'But how can I?'

'Oh,' he said, 'I'll find another compartment. I only slept outside last night because I was anxious about you. You might have needed something.' She began to cry again, leaning the top of her head against the window, half shutting her eyes, so that her lashes made a curtain between herself and the hard admonishments of old dry women of experience: 'There's only one thing a man wants.' 'Don't take presents from a stranger.' It was the size of the present she had been always told that made the danger. Chocolates and a ride, even in the dark, after a theatre, entailed no more than kisses on the mouth and neck, a little tearing of a dress. A girl was expected to repay, that was the point of all advice; one never got anything for nothing. Novelists like Ruby M. Ayres might say that chastity was worth more than rubies, but the truth was it was priced at a fur coat or thereabouts. One couldn't accept a fur coat without sleeping with a man. If you did, all the older women would tell you the man had a grievance. And the Jew had paid ten pounds.

He put his hand on her arm. 'What's the matter? Tell me. Do you feel ill?' She remembered the hand that shook the pillow, the whisper of his feet moving away. She said again, 'How can I?' but this time it was an appeal for him to speak and to deny the accumulated experience of poverty. 'Look,' he said, 'sit down and let me show you things. That's the Rhine.' She found herself laughing. 'I guessed that.' 'Did you see the rock we passed jutting out into the stream? That's the Lorelei rock. Heine.'

'What do you mean, Heine?' He said with pleasure, 'A Jew.' She began to forget the decision she was forced to make and watched him with interest, trying to find a stranger behind the too familiar features, the small eyes, the large nose, the black oiled hair. She had seen this man too often, like a waiter in a dinner-jacket sitting in the front row at provincial theatres, behind a desk at agents' offices, in the wings at rehearsal, outside the stage door at midnight; the world of the theatre vibrated with his soft humble imperative voice; he was mean with a commonplace habitual meanness, generous in fits and starts, never to be trusted. Soft praise at a rehearsal meant nothing, in the office afterwards he would be saying over a glass of whisky, 'That little girl in the front row, she's not worth her keep.' He was never angered or abusive, never spoke worse of anyone than as 'that little girl', and dismissal came in the shape of a typewritten note left in a pigeon-hole. She said gently, partly because none of these qualities prevented her liking Jews for their very quietness, partly because it was a girl's duty to be amiable, 'Jews are artistic, aren't they? Why, almost the whole orchestra at *Atta Girl* were Jewish boys.'

'Yes,' he said with a bitterness which she did not understand.

'Do you like music?'

'I can play the violin,' he said, 'not well.' For a moment it was as if behind the familiar eyes a strange life moved.

'I always wanted to cry at "Sonny Boy",' she said. She was aware of the space which divided her understanding from her expression; she was sensible of much and could say little, and what she said was too often the wrong thing. Now she saw the strange life die.

'Look,' he said sharply. 'No more river. We've left the Rhine. Not long before breakfast.'

She was a little pained by a sense of unfairness, but she was not given to argument. 'I'll have to fetch my bag,' she said, 'I've got sandwiches in it.'

He stared at her. 'Don't tell me you've brought provisions for three days.'

'Oh, no. Just supper last night and breakfast this morning. It saves about eight shillings.'

'Are you Scotch? Listen to me. You'll have breakfast with me.'

'What more do you expect me to have with you?'

He grinned. 'I'll tell you. Lunch, tea, dinner. And tomorrow—' She interrupted him with a sigh. 'I guess you're a bit rocky. You haven't escaped from anywhere, have you?' His face fell and he asked her with sudden humility, 'You couldn't put up with me? You'd be bored?'

'No,' she said, 'I shouldn't be bored. But why do you do all this for me? I'm not pretty. I guess I'm not clever.' She waited with longing for a denial. 'You are lovely, brilliant, witty,' the incredible words which would relieve her of any need to repay him or refuse his gifts; loveliness and wit were priced higher than any gift he offered, while if a girl were loved, even old women of hard experience would admit her right to take and never give. But he denied nothing. His explanation was almost insulting in its simplicity. 'I can talk so easily to you. I feel I know you.' She knew what that meant. 'Yes,' she said with the dry trivial grief of disappointment, 'I seem to know you too,' and what she meant were the long stairs, the agent's door, and the young friendly Jew, explaining gently and without interest that he had nothing to offer her, nothing to offer her at all.

Yes, she thought, they knew each other; they had both admitted the fact, and it had left them beggared of words. The world shifted and changed and passed them by. Trees and buildings rose and fell against a pale-blue clouded sky, beech changed to elm, and elm to fir, and fir to stone; a world, like lead upon a hot fire, bubbled into varying shapes now like a flame, now like a leaf of clover. Their thoughts remained the same and there was nothing to speak about, because there was nothing to discover.

'You don't really want me to have breakfast with you,' she said, trying to be sensible and break the embarrassment of their silence. But he would have nothing to do with her solution. 'I do,' he said, but there was a weakness in his voice which showed her that she had only to be masterful, to get up and leave him and go to her carriage, and he would make no resistance. But in her bag there were stale sandwiches and some of yesterday's milk in a wine bottle, while down the corridor came the smell of boiling coffee and fresh white loaves.

Mabel Warren poured out her coffee, black and strong with no sugar. 'It's the best story I've ever been after,' she said. 'I saw him five years ago walk out of court, while Hartep watched with the warrant in his pocket. Campbell, of the *News*, was after him at once, but he missed him in the street. He never went home, and no more was heard of him from that day to this. Everyone thought he had been murdered, but I never understood why, if they meant to murder him, they took out a warrant for his arrest.'

'Suppose,' said Janet Pardoe, without much interest, 'that he won't speak.'

Miss Warren broke a roll. 'I've never failed yet.'

'You'll invent something?'

'No, that's good enough for Savory, but not for him.' She said viciously, 'I'll make him speak. Somehow. Between here and Vienna. I've got nearly twelve hours. I'll think of a way.' She added thoughtfully, 'He says he's a schoolteacher. It may be true. That would be a good story. And where is he going? He says that he's getting out at Vienna. If he does I'll follow him. I'll follow him to Constantinople if necessary. But I don't believe it. He's going home.'

'To prison?'

'To trial. He's trusting the people perhaps. He was always popular in the slums. But he's a fool if he thinks they'll remember him. Five years. No one's ever remembered for so long.'

'Darling, how morbid you are.'

Mabel Warren came back with difficulty to her immediate surroundings, the coffee swaying in her cup, the gently-rocking table, and Janet Pardoe. Janet Pardoe had pouted and protested and grieved, but now she was squinting sideways at a Jew who shared a table with a girl, common to Miss Warren's eyes, but with a bright attraction. As for the man, his only merits were youth and money, but they were enough, Mabel Warren thought with bitter knowledge, to catch Janet's eye. 'You know it's true,' she said with useless anger. She tore at another roll with her square worn hand, while her emotion grew, how grotesquely she was aware. 'You'll have forgotten me in a week.'

'But of course I shan't, darling. Why, I owe you everything.' The words did not satisfy Mabel Warren. When I love, she thought, I do not think of what I owe. The world to her was divided into those who thought and those who felt. The first considered the dresses which had been bought them, the bills which had been paid, but presently the dresses went out of fashion and the wind caught the receipt from the desk and blew it away, and in any case the debt had been paid with a kiss or another kindness, and those who thought forgot; but those who felt remembered; they did not owe and they did not lend, they gave hatred or love. I am one of those, thought Miss Warren, her eyes filling with tears and the bread drying in her throat, I am one of those who love and remember always, who keep faith with the past in black dresses or black bands, I don't forget, and her eyes dwelt for a moment on the Jew's girl, as a tired motorist might eye with longing the common inn, the scarlet curtains and the watered ale, before continuing his drive towards the best hotel, with its music and its palms. She thought: 'I'll speak to her. She has a pretty figure.' For after all one could not live always with a low voice like music, with a tall figure like a palm. Faithfulness was not the same as remembrance; one could forget and be faithful and one could remember and be faithless.

She loved Janet Pardoe, she would always love Janet Pardoe, she protested inwardly; Janet had been a revelation to her of what love could mean ever since the first evening of their meeting in a cinema in Kaiser Wilhelmstrasse, and yet, and yet . . . They had come together in a mutual disgust of the chief actor; at least Mabel Warren had said aloud in English to relieve her feelings in the strained hush of the dark theatre, 'I can't bear these oiled men,' and had heard a low musical agreement. Yet even then Janet Pardoe had wished to stay till the end, till the last embrace, the final veiled lechery. Mabel Warren urged her to come and have a drink, but Janet Pardoe said that she wanted to see the news and they both stayed. That first evening seemed now to have revealed all of Janet's character that there was to reveal, the inevitable agreement which made no difference to what she did. Sharp words or disagreements had never ruffled her expressionless mood until the evening before, when she had thought herself rid of Mabel Warren. Miss Warren said viciously, not troubling to lower her voice at all, 'I don't like Jews,' and Janet Pardoe, turning her large luminous eyes back to Mabel Warren's, agreed, 'Nor do I, darling.'

Mabel Warren implored her with sudden desperation, 'Janet, when I've gone, you'll remember our love for each other? You won't let a man touch you?' She would have welcomed dissent, the opportunity to argue, to give reasons, to fix some kind of seal upon that fluid mind, but again all she got was an absent-minded agreement. 'But of course not, darling. How could I?' If she had faced a mirror she would have received more sense of an alien mind from the image there, but not, Miss Warren thought, the satisfaction of something beautiful. It was no good thinking of herself, her coarse hair, red lids, and obstinately masculine and discordant voice; there was no one, even the young Jew, who was not her physical rival. When she was gone, Janet Pardoe would remain for a little while a beautiful vacancy, hardly existing at all, save for the need of sleep, the need of food, the need of admiration. But soon she would be sitting back crumbling toast, saying, 'But of course I agree. I've always felt that.' The cup shook in Mabel Warren's hand, and the coffee trickled over the brim and drops fell to her skirt, already stained with grease and beer. What does it matter, she asked herself, what Janet does so long as I don't know? What does it matter to me if she lets a man take her to bed as long as she comes back? But the last qualification made her wince with mental pain, for would Janet, she wondered, ever return to an ageing plain infatuated woman? She'll tell him about me, Mabel Warren thought, of the two years she has lived with me, of the times when we have been happy, of the scenes I've made, even of the poems I've written her, and he'll laugh and she'll laugh and they'll go to bed laughing. I had better make up my mind that this is the end, that she will never come back from this holiday. I don't even know whether it's really her uncle she's visiting. There are as many fish in the sea as ever came out of it, Miss Warren thought, crumbling a roll, desperately aware of her uncared-for hands, the girl with the Jew, for instance. She was as poor as Janet was that evening in the cinema; she was not lovely as Janet was, so that it was happiness to sit for an hour and watch every motion of Janet's body, Janet doing her hair, Janet changing her dress, Janet pulling on her stockings, Janet mixing a drink, but she probably had twice the mind, common and shrewd though it might be.

'Darling,' Janet Pardoe asked with amusement, 'are you getting a pash for that little thing?' The train rocked and roared into a tunnel and out again, eliminating Mabel Warren's answer, taking it, as an angry hand might take a letter, tearing it across and scattering the pieces, only one phrase falling face upwards and in view: 'For ever,' so that no one but Mabel Warren could have said what her protest had been, whether she had sworn to remember always or had declared that one could not be faithful for ever to one person. When the train came out again into the sunlight, coffee-pots glimmering and white linen laid between an open pasture, where a few cows grazed, and a deep wood of firs, Miss Warren had forgotten what she had wished to say, for she recognised in a man who entered the restaurant-car Czinner's companion. At the same moment the girl rose. She and the young man had spoken so seldom Miss Warren could not decide whether they were acquainted; she hoped that they were strange to each other, for she was forming a plan which would not only give her speech with the girl but would help her to nail Czinner once and for all to the bill page of the paper, an exclusive crucifixion.

'Good-bye,' the girl said. Mabel Warren, watching them with the trained observer's eye, noted the Jew's raised shoulders, as of the ashamed habitual thief who leaning forward from the dock protests softly, more from habit than any real sense of injustice, that he has not had a fair trial. The casual observer might have read in their faces the result of a lover's quarrel; Mabel Warren knew better. 'I'll see you again?' the man asked, and she replied, 'If you want me, you'll know where to find me.'

Mabel Warren said to Janet, 'I'll see you later. There are things I must do,' and she followed the girl out of the car over the rocking bridge between the coaches, stumbling and grasping for support, but with the ache in her head quite gone in the warmth and illumination of her idea. For when she said there were things to do, 'things' meant nothing vague, but a throned triumphant concept for which her brain was the lit hall and a murmuring and approving multitude. Everything fitted, that she felt above all things, and she began to calculate what space they were likely to allow her in London; she had never led the paper before. There was the Disarmament Conference and the arrest of a peer for embezzlement and a baronet had married a Ziegfeld girl. None of these stories was exclusive; she had read them on the News Agency tape, before she went to the station. They will put the Disarmament Conference and the Ziegfeld girl on a back page, she thought. There's no doubt, short of a European war or the King's death, that my story will lead the paper, and with her eyes on the girl in front, she considered the image of Dr Czinner, tired and shabby and old-fashioned in the high collar and the little tight tie, sitting in the corner of his compartment with his hands gripped on his knee, while she told him a lot of lies about Belgrade. 'Dr Czinner Alive,' she thought, working at the headlines, but that would not do at the top, for five years had passed and not many people would remember his name. 'Mystery Man's Return. How Dr Czinner Escaped Death. Exclusive Story.'

'My dear,' she gasped, holding to the rail, apparently daunted by the second bridge, the shaking metal and the sound of the linked coaches straining. Her voice did not carry, and she had to repeat her exclamation in a shout, which fitted ill with the part she was assuming–an elderly woman struggling for breath. The girl turned and came back to her, her unschooled face white and miserable, with nothing hidden from any stranger. 'What's the matter? Are you ill?'

Miss Warren did not move, thinking intensely on the other side of the overlapping plates of steel. 'Oh, my dear, how glad I am that you are English. I feel so sick. I can't cross. I'm a silly old thing, I know.' Bitterly but of necessity she played upon her age. 'If you would give me your hand.' She thought: for this game I ought to have long hair, it would be more womanly. I wish my fingers weren't yellow. Thank God I don't still smell of drink. The girl came back. 'Of course. You needn't be afraid. Take my arm.' Miss Warren gripped it with strong fingers as she might have gripped the neck of a fighting dog.

When they reached the next corridor she spoke again. The noise of the train was softened, and she was able to subdue her voice to a husky whisper. 'If only there was a doctor on the train, my dear. I feel so ill.'

'But there is one. His name's Dr John. I came over faint last night and he helped me. Let me find him.'

'I'm so frightened of doctors, dear,' said Miss Warren with a glint of triumph; it was extraordinarily lucky that the girl knew Czinner. 'Talk to me a little first till I'm calmer. What's your name, my dear?'

'Coral Musker.'

'You must call me Mabel, Mabel Warren. I have a niece just like you. I work on a newspaper at Cologne. You must come and see me one day. The darlingest little flat. Are you on a holiday?'

'I dance. I'm off to Constantinople. A girl's ill in an English show there.' For a moment with the girl's hand in hers Mabel Warren felt flustered with a longing to be generous in an absurd obvious way. Why not give up the hope of keeping Janet Pardoe and invite the girl to break her contract and take Janet's place as her paid companion? 'You are so pretty,' she said aloud.

'Pretty,' said Coral Musker. No smile softened her incredulity. 'You're pulling my leg.'

'My dear, you are so kind and good.'

'You bet I am.' She spoke with a touch of vulgarity that spoiled for a moment Mabel Warren's vision. Coral Musker said with longing, 'Leave out the goodness. Say that again about my being pretty.' Mabel Warren acquiesced with complete conviction, 'My dear, you are lovely.' The astonished avidity with which the girl watched her was touching, the word 'virginity' passed through the urban darkness of Mabel Warren's mind. 'Has no one said that to you?' Eager and unbelieving Mabel Warren implored her: 'Not your young friend in the restaurant-car?'

'I hardly know him.'

'I think you are wise, my dear. Jews are not to be trusted.'

Coral Musker said slowly, 'Do you think he thought that? That I didn't like him because he was a Jew?'

'They are used to it, dear.'

'Then I shall go and tell him that I like him, that I've always liked Jews.'
Mabel Warren began to swear with a bitter obscene venom beneath her
breath.

'What did you say?'

'You won't leave me like this until you've found the doctor? Look. My
compartment's at the end of the corridor with my niece. I'll go there if you'll
fetch him.' She watched Coral Musker out of sight and slipped into the
lavatory. The train came to a sharp halt and then began to move backwards.
Miss Warren recognised through the window the spires of Würzburg, the
bridge over the Main; the train was shedding its third-class coaches,
shunting backwards and forwards between the signal boxes and the sidings.
Miss Warren left the door a little open, so that she could see the corridor.
When Coral Musker and Dr Czinner appeared she closed the door and
waited for the sound of their footsteps to pass. They had quite a long walk to
the end of the corridor; now, if she hurried, she would have time enough.
She slipped out. Before she could close the door the train started with a lurch
and the door slammed, but neither Coral Musker nor Dr Czinner looked
back.

She ran awkwardly, flung from one side to the other of the corridor by the
motion of the train, bruising a wrist and a knee. Passengers returning from
breakfast flattened themselves against the windows to let her by, and some of
them complained of her in German, knowing her to be English, and
imagining that she could not understand them. She grinned at them
maliciously, uncovering her great front teeth, and ran on. The right
compartment was easy to find, for she recognised the mackintosh hanging in
the corner, the soft stained hat. On the seat lay a morning paper that Czinner
must have bought a minute or two before Würzburg station. In the brief
pursuit of Coral Musker along the corridor she had thought out every move;
the stranger who shared the compartment was at breakfast, Dr Czinner,
seeking her at the other end of the train, would be away for at least three
minutes. In that time she must learn enough to make him speak.

First there was the mackintosh. There was nothing in the pockets but a
box of matches and a packet of Gold Flake. She picked up the hat and felt
along the band and inside the lining; she had sometimes found quite
valuable information concealed in hats, but the doctor's was empty. Now
she reached the dangerous moments of her search, for the examination of a
hat, even of the mackintosh pockets, could be disguised, but to drag the
suitcase from the rack, to lever the lock open with her pocket-knife and lift
the lid, laid her too obviously open to the charge of theft. And one blade of
her knife broke while she still laboured at the lock. Her purpose was patent
to anyone who passed the compartment, and she sweated a little on the
forehead, growing frenzied in her haste. If I am found it means the sack, she
thought: the cheapest rag in England could not stand for this; and if I'm
sacked, I lose Janet, I lose the chance of Coral. But if I succeed, she thought,
prying, pushing, scraping, there's nothing they won't do for me in return for
such a story; another four pounds a week wouldn't be too much to demand.
I'll be able to take a larger flat; when Janet knows of it, she'll return, she'll
never leave me. It is happiness, security, she thought, I'll be getting in
return for this, and the lock gave and the lid lifted and her fingers were on

the secrets of Dr Czinner. A woollen stomach-belt was the first of them.

She lifted it with care and found his passport. It gave his name as Richard John and his profession as teaching. His age was fifty-six. That proves nothing, she thought, these shady foreign politicians know where to buy a passport. She put it back where she had found it and began to slip her fingers between his suits, half-way down in the centre of the suitcase, the spot the customs officers always miss when they turn up the contents of a bag at the bottom and at the sides. She hoped to find a pamphlet or a letter, but there was only an old Baedeker published in 1914: *Konstantinopel und Kleinasien, Balkanstaaten, Archipel, Cypern*, slipped inside a pair of trousers. But Mabel Warren was thorough: she calculated that she had about one minute of safety left, and as there was nothing else to examine she opened the Baedeker, for it was curious to find it so carefully packed away. She looked at the fly-leaf and read with disappointment the name of Richard John written in a small fussy hand with a scratching nib, but under it was an address, The School House, Great Birchington-on-Sea, which was worth remembering; the *Clarion* could send a man down to interview the headmaster. A good story might be hidden there.

The guide-book seemed to have been bought second-hand, the cover was very worn and there was the label of a bookseller in Charing Cross Road on the fly-leaf. She turned to Belgrade. There was a one-page map, which had worked loose, but it was unmarked; she examined every page dealing with Belgrade and then every page dealing with Serbia, every page on any of the states which were now part of Yugo-Slavia. There was not so much as a smudge of ink. She would have given up the search if it were not for the position in which she had found the book. Obstinately and against the evidence of her eyes she believed that it had been hidden there and that therefore there must be something to hide. She skimmed the pages against her thumb, they ran unevenly because of the many folded maps, but on one of the early pages she found some lines and circles and triangles drawn in ink over the text. But the text dealt only with an obscure town in Asia Minor and the drawings might have been a child's scribble with ruler and compasses. Certainly, if the lines belonged to a code only an expert could decipher them. He's defeated me, she thought, with hatred, smoothing the surface of the suitcase, there's nothing here; but she felt unwilling to put back the Baedeker. He had hidden it, there must be something to find. She had risked so much already that it was easy to risk a little more. She closed the suitcase and put it back on the rack, but the Baedeker she slipped down her shirt and so under her armpit, where she could hold it with one arm pressed to her side.

But it was no use going back to her own seat, for she would meet Dr Czinner returning. It was then that she remembered Mr Quin Savory, whom she had come to the station to interview. His face was well known to her from photographs in the *Tatler*, cartoons in the *New Yorker*, pencil drawings in the *Mercury*. She looked cautiously down the corridor, her eyes blinking a little in a short-sighted manner, and then walked rapidly away. Mr Quin Savory was not to be found in the first-class carriages, but she ran him to earth in a second-class sleeper. With his chin buried in his overcoat, one hand round the bowl of a pipe, he watched with small glittering eyes the people who passed in the corridor. A clergyman dozed in the opposite corner.

Miss Warren opened the door and stepped inside. Her manner was masterful; she sat down without waiting for an invitation. She felt that she was offering this man something he wanted, publicity, and she was gaining nothing commensurate in return. There was no need to speak softly to him, to lure him into disclosures, as she had tried to lure Dr Czinner; she could insult him with impunity, for the Press had power to sell his books. 'You Mr Quin Savory?' she asked, and saw out of the corner of her eye how the clergyman's attitude changed to one of respectful attention; poor mutt, she thought, to be impressed by a 100,000 sale, we sell two million, twenty times as many people will have heard of Dr Czinner tomorrow. 'I represent the *Clarion*. Want an interview.'

'I'm a bit taken aback,' said Mr Savory, raising his chin, pulling at his overcoat.

'No need to be nervous,' said Miss Warren mechanically. She fetched her notebook from her bag and flipped it open. 'Just a few words for the English public. Travelling incognito?'

'Oh, no, no,' Mr Savory protested. 'I'm not royalty.'

Miss Warren began to write. 'Where are you going?'

'Why, first of all,' said Mr Savory brightly, as if pleased by Miss Warren's interest, which had already returned to the Baedeker and the scrawl of geometrical figures, 'to Constantinople. Then I may go to Ankara, the Far East. Baghdad. China.'

'Writing a travel book?'

'Oh, no, no, no. My public wants a novel. It'll be called *Going Abroad*. An adventure of the Cockney spirit. These countries, civilisations,' he made a circle in the air with his hand, 'Germany, Turkey, Arabia, they'll all take second pew to the chief character, a London tobacconist. D'you see?'

'Quite,' said Miss Warren, writing rapidly. '"Dr Richard Czinner, one of the greatest revolutionary figures of the immediate post-war period, is on his way home to Belgrade. For five years the world has thought him dead, but during that time he has been living as a schoolmaster in England, biding his time."' But for what? Miss Warren wondered. 'Your opinion of modern literature?' she asked. 'Joyce, Lawrence, all that?'

'It will pass,' Mr Savory said promptly with the effect of an epigram.

'You believe in Shakespeare, Chaucer, Charles Reade, that sort of thing?'

'They will live,' Mr Savory declared with a touch of solemnity.

'Bohemianism? You don't believe in that? Fitzroy Tavern?' ('A warrant for his arrest has been issued,' she wrote, 'but it could not be served till the trial was over. When the trial was over Dr Czinner had disappeared. Every station had been watched by the police, every car stopped. It was little wonder that the rumour of his murder by government agents spread rapidly.') 'You don't believe it's necessary to dress oddly, big black hat, velvet jacket and what not?'

'I think it's fatal,' Mr Savory said. He was now quite at his ease and watched the clergyman covertly while he talked. 'I'm not a poet. A poet's an individualist. He can dress as he likes; he depends only on himself. A novelist depends on other men; he's an average man with the power of expression. 'E's a spy,' Mr Savory added with confusing drama, dropping aitches right and left. "E 'as to see everything and pass unnoticed. If people recognised 'im they wouldn't talk, they'd pose before 'im; 'e wouldn't find things out.' Miss Warren's pencil raced. Now that she had got him started, she could think quickly: no need to press him with questions. Her pencil made meaningless symbols, which looked sufficiently like shorthand to convince Mr Savory that his remarks were being taken down in full, but behind the deceiving screen of squiggles and lines, circles and squares, Miss Warren thought. She thought of every possible aspect of the Baedeker. It had been published in 1914, but was in excellent condition; it had never been much used, except for the section dealing with Belgrade; the map of the city had been so often handled that it was loose.

'You do follow these views?' Mr Savory asked anxiously. 'They're important. They seem to me the touchstone of lit'ry integrity. One can 'ave that, you know, and yet sell one hundred thousand copies.' Miss Warren, annoyed at the interruption, only just prevented herself retorting, 'Do you think we should sell two million copies if we told the truth?' 'Very interesting,' she said. 'The public will be interested. Now what do you consider your contribution to English literature?' She grinned at him encouragingly and poised her pencil.

'Surely that's for somebody else to state,' said Mr Savory. 'But one 'opes, one 'opes, that it's something of this sort, to bring back cheerfulness and 'ealth to modern fiction. There's been too much of this introspection, too much gloom. After all, the world is a fine adventurous place.' The bony hand which held the pipe beat helplessly against his knee. 'To bring back the spirit of Chaucer,' he said. A woman passed along the corridor, and for a moment all Mr Savory's attention was visibly caught up to sail in her wake, bobbing, bobbing, bobbing, like his hand, 'Chaucer,' he said, 'Chaucer,' and suddenly, before Miss Warren's eyes he gave up the struggle, his pipe fell to the floor, and stooping to find it, he exclaimed irritably, 'Damn it all. Damn.' He was a man overworked, harassed by a personality which was not his own, by curiosities and lusts, a man on the edge of a nervous breakdown. Miss Warren gloated over him. It was not that she hated him, but that she hated any overpowering success, whether it meant the sale of a hundred thousand copies or the attainment of three hundred miles an hour, which made her an interviewer and a man the condescending interviewed. Failure of the same overwhelming kind was another matter, for then she was the avenging world, penetrating into prison cells, into hotel lounges, into mean back parlours. Then with a man at her mercy between the potted palms and the piano, when he was backed against the wedding photograph and the marble clock, she could almost love her victim, asking him little intimate questions, hardly listening to the answers. Well, not so great a gulf lay, she thought with satisfaction, between Mr Quin Savory, author of *The Great Gay Round*, and such a failure.

She harped on his phrase. 'Health,' she said. 'That's your mission? None of this "adults only" stuff. They give you as school prizes.'

Her irony had been a little too obvious. 'I'm proud of it,' he said. 'The younger generation's being brought up on 'ealthy traditions.' She noticed his dry lips, the squint towards the corridor. I'll put that in about healthy traditions, she thought, the public will like it, James Douglas will like it, and they will like it still better when he's a Hyde Park case, for that's what he'll be in a few years. I'll be alive to remind them. She was proud of her power of prophecy, though she had not yet lived to see any of her prophecies fulfilled. Take an expression in the present, a line of ill-health, a tone of voice, a gesture, no more illuminating to the average unobservant person than the lines and circles in the Baedeker, and fit them to what one knew of the man's surroundings, his friends and furniture, the house he lived in, and one saw the future, his shabby waiting fate. 'My God!' said Miss Warren, 'I've got it.'

Mr Savory jumped. 'What have you got?' he asked. 'Toothache?'

'No, no,' said Miss Warren. She felt grateful to him for the illumination which now flooded her mind with light, leaving no dark corners left in which Dr Czinner might hide from her. 'Such an excellent interview, I meant. I see the way to present you.'

'Do I see a proof?'

'Ah, we are not a weekly paper. Our public can't wait. Hungry, you know, for its lion's steak. No time for proofs. People in London will be reading the interview while they eat their breakfast tomorrow.' She left him with this assurance of the public interest, when she would far rather have sown in his overworked mind, grappling already with the problem of another half million popular words, the suggestion of how people forget, how they buy one day what they laugh at the next. But she could not afford the time; bigger game called, for she believed that she had guessed the secret of the Baedeker. It had been the consideration of her own prophecies which had given her the clue. The map was loose, the paper in a Baedeker she remembered was thin and insufficiently opaque; if one fitted the map against the pen drawings on the earlier page, the lines would show through.

My God, she thought, it's not everyone who would think of that. It deserves a drink. I'll find an empty compartment and call the steward. She did not even want Janet Pardoe to share this triumph; she would rather be alone with a glass of Courvoisier where she could think undisturbed and plan her next move. But when she had found the empty compartment she still acted with circumspection; she did not pull the Baedeker from under her shirt until the steward had fetched her the brandy. And not at once even then. She held the glass to her nostrils, allowing the fumes to reach that point at the back of her nose where brain and nose seemed one. The spirit she had drunk the night before was not all dissipated. It stirred like ground vapour on a wet hot day. Swimmy, she thought, I feel quite swimmy. Through the glass and the brandy she saw the outer world, so flat and regular that it never seemed to alter, neat fields and trees and small farms. Her eyes, short-sighted and flushed already with the mere fume of the brandy, could not catch the changing details, but she noticed the sky, grey and cloudless, and the pale sun. I shouldn't be surprised at snow, she thought, and looked to see whether the heating wheel was fully turned. Then she took the Baedeker from under her shirt. It would not be long before the train reached Nuremberg, and she wanted everything settled before fresh passengers came on board.

She had guessed right, that at least was certain. When she held the map and the marked page to the light the lines ran along the course of streets, the circles enclosed public buildings: the post office, the railway station, the courts of justice, the prison. But what did it all mean? She had assumed that Dr Czinner was returning to make some kind of personal demonstration, perhaps to stand his trial for perjury. The map in that context had no meaning. She examined it again. The streets were not marked haphazardly, there was a pattern, a nest of squares balanced on another square and the balancing square was the slum quarter. The next square was made on one side by the railway station, on another by the post office, on a third by the courts of justice. Inside this the squares became rapidly smaller, until they enclosed only the prison.

A bank mounted steeply on either side of the train and the sunlight was shut off; sparks, red in the overcast sky, struck the windows like hail, and darkness swept the carriages as the long train roared into a tunnel. Revolution, she thought, it means nothing less, with the map still raised to catch the first light returning.

The roar diminished and light came suddenly back. Dr Czinner was standing in the doorway, a newspaper under his arm. He was wearing the mackintosh again, and she regarded with contempt the glasses, the grey hair and shabby moustache, the small tight tie. She laid down the map and grinned at him. 'Well?'

Dr Czinner came in and shut the door. He sat down opposite her without a sign of hostility. He knows I've got him fixed, she thought; he's going to be reasonable? He asked her suddenly, 'Would your paper approve?'

'Of course not,' She said. 'I'd be sacked tomorrow. But when they get my story, that'll be a different matter.' She added with calculated insolence, 'I reckon that you are worth four pounds a week to me.'

Dr Czinner said thoughtfully, without anger, 'I don't intend to tell you anything.' She waved her hand at him. 'You've told me a lot already. There's this.' She tapped the Baedeker. 'You were a foreign master at Great Birchington-on-Sea. We'll get the story from your headmaster.' His head dropped. 'And then,' she said, 'there's this map. And these scrawls. I've put two and two together.' She had expected some protests of fear or indignation, but he was still brooding over her first guess. His attitude puzzled her and for an anguished moment she wondered, Am I missing the best story? Is the best story not here at all, but at a south-coast school among the red-brick buildings and the pitch-pine desks and ink-stands and cracked bells and the smell of boys' clothes? The doubt made her less certain of herself and she spoke gently, more gently than she had intended, for it was difficult to modulate her husky voice. 'We'll get together,' she growled in a winning way. 'I'm not here to let you down. I don't want to interfere with you. Why, if you succeed, my story's all the more valuable. I'll promise not to release anything at all until you give the word.' She said plaintively, as if she were an artist accused of deprecating paint, 'I wouldn't spoil your revolution. Why, it'll be a grand story.'

Age was advancing rapidly on Dr Czinner. It was as if he had warded off with temporary success five years of pitch-pine smells and the whine of chalk on blackboards, only to sit now in a railway carriage and allow the baulked years to come upon him, together and not one by one. For the moment he was an old man nodding into sleep, his face as grey as the snow sky over Nuremberg. 'Now first,' said Miss Warren, 'what are your plans? I can see you depend a good deal on the slums.'

He shook his head. 'I depend on no one.'

'You are keeping absolute control?'

'Least of all myself.'

Miss Warren struck her knee sharply. 'I want plain answers,' but she got the same reply, 'I shall tell you nothing.' He looks more like seventy than fifty-six, she thought; he's getting deaf, he doesn't understand what I've been saying. She was very forbearing; she felt certain that this was not success she faced, it resembled failure too closely, and failure she could love; she could be tender and soft-syllabled towards failure, wooing it with little whinnying words, as long as in the end it spoke. A weak man had sometimes gone away with the impression that Miss Warren was his best friend. She leant forward and tapped on Dr Czinner's knee, putting all the amiability of which she was capable into her grin. 'We are in this together, doctor. Don't you understand that? Why, we can even help you. Public opinion's just another name for the *Clarion*. I know you are afraid we'll be indiscreet, that we'll publish your story tomorrow and the government will be warned. But I tell you we won't breathe so much as a paragraph on the book page until you begin your show. Then I want to be able to put right across the middle page, "Dr Czinner's Own Story. Exclusive to the *Clarion*." Now, that's not unreasonable.'

'There's nothing I wish to say.'

Miss Warren withdrew her hand. Did the poor fool, she wondered, think that he would stand between her and another four pounds a week, between her and Janet Pardoe? He became, old and stupid and stubborn on the opposite seat, the image of all the men who threatened her happiness, who were closing round Janet with money and little toys and laughter at a woman's devotion to a woman. But the image was in her power; she could break the image. It was not a useless act of mischief on Cromwell's part to shatter statues. Some of the power of the Virgin lay in the Virgin's statue, and when the head was off and a limb gone and the seven swords broken, fewer candles were lit and the prayers said at her altar were not so many. One man like Dr Czinner ruined by a woman, and fewer stupid girls like Coral Musker would believe all strength and cunning to reside in a man. But she gave him, because of his age, and because he reeked to her nose of failure, one more chance. 'Nothing?'

'Nothing.'

She laughed at him angrily. 'You've said a mouthful already.' He was unimpressed and she explained slowly as if to a mental defective, 'We reach Vienna at eight-forty tonight. By nine I shall be telephoning to the Cologne office. They'll get my story through to London by ten o'clock. The paper doesn't go to press for the first London edition till eleven. Even if the message is delayed, it's possible to alter the bill page for the last edition up to three o'clock in the morning. My story will be read at breakfast tomorrow. Every paper in London will have a reporter round at the Yugo-Slavian Ministry by nine o'clock in the morning. Before lunch tomorrow the whole story will be known in Belgrade, and the train's not due there till six in the evening. And there won't be much left to the imagination either. Think what I shall be able to say. Dr Richard Czinner, the famous Socialist agitator, who disappeared from Belgrade five years ago at the time of the Kamnetz trial, is on his way home. He joined the Orient express at Ostend on Monday and his train is due at Belgrade this evening. It is believed that his arrival will coincide with a Socialist outbreak based on the slum quarters, where Doctor Czinner's name has never been forgotten, and an attempt will probably be made to seize the station, the post office and the prison.' Miss Warren paused. 'That's the story I shall telegraph. But if you'll say more I'll tell them to hold until you give the word. I'm offering you a straightforward bargain.'

'I tell you that I am leaving the train at Vienna.'

'I don't believe you.'

Dr Czinner sucked in his breath, staring through the window at the grey luminous sky, a group of factory chimneys, and a great black metal drum. The compartment filled with the smell of gas. Cabbages were growing in the allotments through the bad air, gross bouquets sprinkled with frost. He said so softly that she had to lean forward to catch the words, 'I have no reason to fear you.' He was subdued, he was certain, and his calmness touched her nerves. She protested uneasily and with anger, as if the criminal in the dock, the weeping man beside the potted fern, had been endowed suddenly with a mysterious reserve of strength, 'I can play hell with you.'

Dr Czinner said slowly, 'There's going to be snow.' The train was creeping into Nuremberg, and the great engines that ranged themselves on either side reflected the wet steel aspect of the sky. 'No,' he said, 'there's nothing you can do which will harm me.' She tapped the Baedeker and he remarked with a flash of humour: 'Keep it as a souvenir of our meeting.' She was certain then that her fear was justified; he was escaping her, and she stared at him with rage. If I could do him an injury, she thought, watching in the mirror behind him success, in the likeness of Janet Pardoe, wandering away, lovely and undeserving and vacant, down long streets and through the lounges of expensive hotels, if I could do him an injury.

It angered her the more to find herself speechless and Dr Czinner in control. He handed her the paper and asked her, 'Do you read German? Then read this.' All the while that the train stood in Nuremberg station, a long twenty minutes, she stared at it. The message it contained infuriated her. She had been prepared for news of some extraordinary success, of a king's abdication, a government's overthrow, a popular demand for Doctor Czinner's return, which would have raised him into the position of the condescending interviewed. What she read was more extraordinary, a failure which put him completely out of her power. She had been many times bullied by the successful, never before by one who had failed.

'Communist outbreak in Belgrade,' she read. 'An attempt was made late last night by a band of armed Communist agitators to seize the station and the prison at Belgrade. The police were taken by surprise and for nearly three hours the revolutionaries were in undisturbed possession of the general post office and the goods-yards. All telegraphic communication with Belgrade was interrupted until early this morning. At two o'clock, however, our representative at Vienna spoke to Colonel Hartep, the Chief of Police, by telephone and learned that order had been restored. The revolutionaries were few in number and lacked a proper leader; their attack on the prison was repulsed by the warders, and for some hours afterwards they stayed inactive in the post office, apparently in the hope that the inhabitants of the poorer quarters of the capital would come to their help. Meanwhile the government was able to muster police reinforcements, and with the help of a platoon of soldiers and a couple of field-guns, the police recaptured the post office after a siege lasting little more than three-quarters of an hour.' This summary was printed in large type; underneath in small type was a more detailed account of the outbreak. Miss Warren sat and stared at it; she frowned a little and was conscious of the dryness of her mouth. Her brain felt clear and empty. Dr Czinner explained, 'They were three days too early.'

Miss Warren snapped at him, 'What more could you have done?'

'The people would have followed me.'

'They've forgotten you. Five years is the hell of a time. The young men were children when you ran away.'

Five years, she thought, seeing them fall on her inevitably through future days, like the endless rain of a wet winter, watching in mind Janet Pardoe's face as it worried over the first wrinkle, the first greyness, or else the smooth tight lifted skin and dark dyed hair every three weeks whitening at the roots.

'What are you going to do now?' she asked, and the promptitude and plainness of his answer, 'I've told you. I'm getting out at Vienna,' filled her with suspicion. 'That's nice,' she said, 'we'll be together. We can talk. You'll have no objection to an interview now. If you are short of money, our Vienna office will advance you some.' She was aware that he was watching her more closely than ever before. 'Yes,' he said slowly, 'perhaps we can talk,' and she was certain this time that he was lying. He's going to double, she thought, but it was difficult to see his motive. He had no choice but to get out at Vienna or at Buda-Pesth; it would be unsafe to travel farther. Then she remembered him at the Kamnetz trial, fully aware that no jury would convict and yet giving his dangerous useless evidence while Hartep waited with the warrant. He's fool enough to do anything, she thought, and wondered for a moment whether, behind the quietness, he was already standing in the dock with his companions, uttering his defence with an eye to the packed gallery. If he goes on, she thought, I'll go, I'll stick to him, I'll have his story, but she felt curiously weak and undecided, for she had no threat left. He was beaten, leaning back in his corner old and hopeless, with the newspaper gathering dust on the floor between them, and he was triumphant, watching her leave the carriage, the Baedeker forgotten on the seat, with nothing but silence for her exclamation: 'I'll see you again at Vienna.'

When Miss Warren had gone, Dr Czinner stooped for the paper. His sleeve caught an empty glass and it fell and shattered on the floor. His hand rested on the paper and he stared at the glass, unable to concentrate his thought, unable to decide what it was he had to do, pick up the paper or gather the dangerous sharp scraps. Presently he laid the paper carefully folded across his knees and closed his eyes. He was haunted in his personal darkness by the details of the story that Miss Warren had read; he knew every turn in the stairs in the post office, he could see the exact spot where the barricade had been built. The muddling fools, he thought, and tried to feel hate for the men who had destroyed his hopes. They had ruined him with them. They had left him in an empty house which could not find a tenant because old ghosts were sometimes vocal in the rooms, and Dr Czinner himself now was not even the latest ghost.

If a face peered from a window or a voice was heard upstairs or a carpet whispered, it might have been Dr Czinner seeking to return to a sentient life after five years of burial, working his way round the corners of desks, exposing his transparency before the blackboard and the insubordinate children, crouched in chapel at a service in which the living man had never believed, asking God with the breathing discordant multitude to dismiss him with His blessing.

And sometimes it seemed as if a ghost might return to life, for he had learned that as a ghost he could suffer pain. The ghost had memories; it could remember the Doctor Czinner who had been so loved that it was worth while for a hired murderer to fire a revolver at his head. That was the proudest memory of all, of how Dr Czinner sat in the beer-house at the poor corner of the park and heard the shot shatter the mirror behind him and knew it for the final proof of how dearly the poor loved him. But the ghost of Czinner, huddled in a shelter while the east wind swept the front and the grey sea tossed the pebbles, had learned to weep at the memory before returning to the red-brick building and tea and to the children who fashioned subtle barbs of pain. But after the final service and the customary hymns and handshakes the ghost of Czinner found itself again touching the body of Czinner; a touch was all the satisfaction it could get. Now there was nothing left but to leave the train at Vienna and return. In ten days the voices would be singing: 'Lord receive us with Thy blessing, Once again assembled here.'

Dr Czinner turned a page of the paper and read a little. The nearest he could attain to hate of these muddled men was envy; he could not hate when he remembered details no newspaper correspondent thought it worth while to give, that the man who, after firing his last shot, was bayoneted outside the sorting-room had been left-handed and a lover of Delius's music, the melancholy idealistic music of a man without a faith in anything but death. And that another, who leapt from the third-floor window of the telephone exchange, had a wife scarred and blinded in a factory accident, whom he loved and to whom he was sadly and unwillingly faithless.

But what is left for me to do? Dr Czinner put down the paper and began to walk the compartment, three steps one way to the door, three steps the other way to the window, up and down. A few flakes of snow were falling, but the wind blew the smoke of the engine back across the window, and if the flakes touched the glass at all, they were already grey like scraps of paper. But six hundred feet up, on the hills which came down to the line at Neumarkt, the snow began to lie like beds of white flowers. If they had waited, if they had waited, thought Dr Czinner, and as his mind turned from the dead to the men who lived to be tried, the impossibility of his own easy escape presented itself with such force that he exclaimed in a whisper, 'I must go to them.' But what was the use? He sat down again and began to argue with himself that the gesture would have practical value. If I give myself up and stand my trial with them; the world will listen to my defence as it would never listen to me, safe in England. The strengthening of his resolution encouraged him; he grew more hopeful; the people he thought, will rise to save me, though they did not rise for the others. Again the ghost of Czinner felt close to life, and warmth touched its frozen transparency.

But there were many things to be considered. First he had to avoid the reporter. He must give her the slip at Vienna; it ought not to be difficult, for the train did not arrive till nearly nine, and by that hour of the evening, surely, he thought, she will be drunk. He shivered a little with the cold and the idea of any further contact with that hoarse dangerous woman. Well, he thought, picking up the Baedeker and letting the newspaper drop to the floor, her sting is drawn. She seemed to hate me; I wonder why; some strange pride of profession, I suppose. I may as well go back to my compartment. But when he reached it, he walked on, hands behind back and Baedeker under arm, absorbed by the idea that the ghostly years were over. I am alive again, he thought, because I am conscious of death as a future possibility, almost a certainty, for they will hardly let me escape again, even if I defend myself and others with the tongue of an angel. Faces which were familiar to him looked up as he passed, but they failed to break his absorption. I am afraid, he told himself with triumph, I am afraid.

2

'Not *the* Quin Savory?' asked Janet Pardoe.

'Well,' said Mr Savory, 'I don't know of another.'

'*The Great Gay Whirl?*'

'*Round*,' Mr Savory corrected her sharply. '*Great Gay Round*.' He put his hand on her elbow and began to propel her down the corridor. 'Time for a sherry. Fancy your being related to the woman who's been interviewing me. Daughter? Niece?'

'Well, not exactly related,' said Janet Pardoe. 'I'm her companion.'

'Better not.' Mr Savory's fingers closed more firmly on her arm. 'Get another job. You are too young. It's not 'ealthy.'

'How right you are,' said Janet Pardoe, stopping for a moment in the corridor and turning to him eyes luminous with admiration.

Miss Warren was writing a letter, but she saw them go by. She had laid her writing-pad upon her knee, and her fountain-pen spluttered across the paper, splashing ink and biting deep holes.

> Dear Cousin Con, *she wrote*, I'm writing to you because I've nothing better to do. This is the Orient Express, but I'm not going on to Constantinople. I'm getting out at Vienna. But that's another story. Could you get me five yards of ring velvet? Pink. I'm having my flat done up again, while Janet's away. She's on the same train, but I'm leaving her at Vienna. A job of work really, chasing a hateful old man half across Europe. *The Great Gay Round* is on board, but of course you don't read books. And a rather charming little dancer called Coral,

whom I think I shall take as my companion. I can't make up my mind whether to have my flat redecorated. Janet says she'll only be away a week. You mustn't on any account pay more than eight-and-eleven a yard. Blue, I think, would suit me, but of course, not navy. This man I was telling you about, *wrote Miss Warren following Janet Pardoe with her eyes, digging the pen into the paper*, thinks himself too clever for me, but you know as well as I do, don't you, Con, that I can play hell with anyone who thinks that. Janet is a bitch. I'm thinking of getting a new companion. There's a little actress on this train who would suit me. You should see her, the loveliest figure, Con. You'd admire her as much as I do. Not very pretty, but with lovely legs. I really think I must get my flat done up. Which reminds me. You can go up to ten-and-eleven with that ring velvet. I may be going to Belgrade, so wait till you hear from me again. Janet seems to be getting a pash for this Savory man. But I can play hell with him too if I want to. Good-bye. Look after yourself. Give my love to Elsie. I hope she looks after you better than Janet does me. You've always been luckier, but wait till you see Coral. For God's sake don't forget that ring velvet. Much love. Mabel. P.S. Did you hear that Uncle John died suddenly the other day almost on my doorstep?

Miss Warren's pen ended the letter in a large pool of ink. She enclosed it in a thick line and wrote *Sorry*. Then she wiped the pen on her skirt and rang the bell for a steward. Her mouth was terribly dry.

Coral Musker stood for a little while in the corridor, watching Myatt, wondering whether what Mabel Warren had suggested was true. He sat with head bent over a pile of papers, running a pencil up and down a row of figures, always returning it to the same numeral. Presently he laid down the pencil and put his head in his hands. Pity for a moment touched her, as well as gratitude. With the knowing eyes hidden he might have been a schoolboy, despairingly engaged on homework which would not come right. She could see that he had taken off his gloves the better to grip the pencil and his fingers were blue with cold; even the ostentation of his fur coat was pathetic to her, for it was hopelessly inadequate. It could not solve his sums or keep his fingers warm.

Coral opened the door and came in. He raised his face and smiled, but his work absorbed him. She wanted to take the work away from him and show him the solution and tell him not to let his master know that he had been helped. Who by? she wondered. Mother? Sister? Nothing so distant as a cousin, she thought, sitting down in the easy silence which was the measure of their familiarity.

Because she grew tired of watching through the window the gathering snow she spoke to him: 'You said that I could come in when I wanted to.'

'Of course.'

'I couldn't help feeling a beast,' she said, 'going away so suddenly and never thanking you properly. You were good to me last night.'

'I didn't like the idea of your staying in the compartment with that man when you were ill,' he said impatiently, tapping with his pencil. 'You needed proper sleep.'

'But why were you interested in me?' She received the fatal inevitable answer: 'I seemed to know you quite well.' He would have gone back to his calculations if it had not been for the unhappy quality of her silence. She could see how he was worried and surprised and a little harassed; he thinks I

want him to make love to me, she thought, and wondered, do I? Do I? It
would complete the resemblance to other men she had known if he rumpled
her hair a bit and pulled her dress open in getting his lips against her breast. I
owe him that, she thought, and the accumulated experience of other women
told her again that she owed him a good deal more. But how can I pay, she
asked herself, if he doesn't press for payment? And the mere thought of
performing that strange act when she was not drunk as she supposed some
women were, or passionate, but only grateful, chilled her more than the
falling snow. She was not even certain how one went about it, whether it
would be necessary to spend a whole night with him, to undress completely
in the cold carriage. But she began to comfort herself with the thought that
he was like other men she had known and was satisfied with very little; the
only difference was that he was more generous.

'Last night,' he said, watching her closely while he spoke, and his attitude
of attention and his misunderstanding of her silence told her that after all
they did not know everything of each other, 'last night I dreamed about you.'
He laughed nervously. 'I dreamed that I picked you up and took you for a
ride and presently you were going to . . .' He paused and evaded the issue. 'I
felt excited by you.'

She became frightened, as if a moneylender were leaning across his desk
and approaching very gently and inexorably to the subject of repayment. 'In
your dream,' she said. But he took no notice of her. 'Then the guard came
along and woke me up. The dream was very vivid. I was so excited that I
bought your ticket.'

'You mean that you thought–that you wanted—'

The moneylender raised his shoulders, the moneylender sat back behind
his desk, and the moneylender rang the bell for a servant to show her out to
the street and strangers and the freedom of being unknown. 'I just told you
this,' he said, 'so that you needn't feel you owe me anything. It was the effect
of a dream, and when I'd bought the ticket, I thought you might as well use
it,' and he picked up his pencil and turned back to his papers. He added
formally, without thought, 'It was brash of me to think that for ten
pounds—'

Those words did not at first reach her. She was too confused by her relief,
even by the shame of being desirable only in a dream, above all by her
gratitude. And then pursuing her out of the silence came the final words with
their hint of humility–this was unfamiliar. She faced her terror of the
bargain, putting out her hand and touching Myatt's face with a gratitude
which had borrowed its gesture from an unknown love. 'If you want me to,'
she said. 'I thought that you were bored with me. Shall I come tonight?' She
laid her fingers across the papers on his knee, small square hands with
powder lying thick in the hollow of the knuckles, nails reddened at the tip,
hiding the rows of numerals, Mr Eckman's calculations and subterfuges and
cunning concealments, offering herself with an engaging and pathetic
dubiety. He said slowly, half his mind still following Mr Eckman in and out
of hidden rooms, 'I thought that you disliked me'; he lifted her hands from
his papers and said absentmindedly: 'Perhaps because I was Jewish.'

'You're tired.'

'There's something here I can't get straight.'

'Leave it,' she said, 'until tomorrow.'

'I haven't the time. I've got to get this done. We are not sitting still.' But in fact all sense of motion had been rapt from them by the snow. It fell so heavily that the telegraph-poles were hidden. She took her hands away and asked him with resentment, 'Then you don't want me to come?' The calmness and familiarity with which he met her proposal chilled her gratitude.

'Yes,' he said, 'come. Come tonight.' He touched her hands. 'Don't think me cold. It's because we seem to know each other so well.' He appealed to her, 'Be a little strange.'

But before she could gather her wits for a pretence, she had admitted to him, 'Yes, I feel that too,' so that there was nothing else to say, and they sat on in silence like old friends, thinking without excitement of the night before them. Her brief passion of gratitude was over, for now it seemed as unnecessary as it was unwanted. You were not grateful to an acquaintance of so long standing; you took favours and gave favours and talked a little of the weather, not indignant at a caress or embittered by an indifference; and if you saw him in the stalls, you smiled once or twice as you danced, because something had to be done with your face which was a plain one, and a man liked to be recognised from the stage.

'The snow's getting worse.'

'Yes. It'll be cold tonight.' And you smiled in case a joke was intended and said as enticingly as possible to so old a friend, 'We'll be warm,' unable to forget that night was coming, remembering all that friends had said and advised and warned, puzzled and repelled that a man should feel indifference and lust at the same time. All that morning and all through lunch the snow continued to fall, lying deep at Passau on the roof of the customs-shed, melted on the line by the steam from the engine into grey icy streams, and the Austrian officials picked their way in gum-boots and swore a little, searching the luggage perfunctorily.

PART III

VIENNA

I

Josef Grünlich moved to the sheltered side of the chimney, while the snow piled itself all round him on the roof. Below the central station burned like a bonfire in the dark. A whistle screamed and a long line of lights came into view, moving slowly; he looked at his watch as a clock struck nine. That's the Istanbul Express, he thought, twenty minutes late; it may have been held up by snow. He adjusted his flat silver watch and replaced it in his waistcoast pocket, smoothing the creases over the curve of his belly. Well, he considered, it is lucky to be fat on a night like this. Before buttoning his overcoat he ran his hands between pants and trousers and adjusted the revolver which hung between his legs by a piece of string twisted around a button. Trust Josef for three things, he reminded himself comfortably, for a woman, a meal and a fat crib. He emerged from the shelter of the chimney.

It was very slippery on the roof and there was some danger. The snow beat against his eyes and caked into ice on the heels of his shoes. Once he slipped and saw for a moment rising like a fish through dark water to meet him the lit awning of á café. He whispered, 'Hail Mary, full of grace,' digging his heels into the snow, clutching with his fingers. Saved by the rim of a gutter, he rose to his feet and laughed softly; it was no good being angry with nature. A little later he found the iron arms of the fire-escape.

The climb that followed he considered the most dangerous part of the whole business, for although the escape ran down the back of the flats, out of sight of the street, it faced the goods-yard, and the yard was the limit of a policeman's beat. He appeared every three minutes, the dim lamp at the corner of a shed gleaming on his black polished gaiters, his leather belt, his pistol holster. The deep snow quietened the sound of feet, and Josef could expect no warning of his approach, but the ticking of his watch kept him in mind of danger. He waited at the head of the ladder, crouched low, uneasily conscious of his white background, until the policeman had come and gone again. Then he began his climb. He had only to pass one unoccupied storey, but as he reached the top window a light flashed on him and a whistle blew. I can't be caught, he thought incredulously, I've never been caught, it doesn't happen to me, and waited with his back to the yard for a word or a bullet, while his brain began to move like the little well-oiled wheels of a watch, one thought fitting into another and setting a third in motion. When nothing happened he turned his face from the ladder and the blank wall; the yard was empty, the light glowed from a lamp someone had carried into the loft of the goods-shed, and the whistle had been one of the many noises of the station. His mistake had wasted precious seconds, and he continued his descent with a reckless disregard of his icy shoes, two steps at a time.

When he came to the next window he tapped. There was no reply, and he murmured a mild imprecation, keeping his head turned to the corner of the yard where the policeman would very soon appear. He tapped again and this time heard the shuffle of loose slippers. The lock of the window was lifted, and a woman's voice said, 'Anton. Is that you?' 'Yes,' said Josef, 'this is Anton. Let me in quickly.' The curtain was drawn back and a thin hand pulled and pulled at the top pane. 'The bottom,' Josef whispered, 'not the top. You think me an acrobat.' When the window was raised he showed great agility for a man so fat in stepping from the escape to the sill, but he found it difficult to squeeze into the room. 'Can't you raise it another inch?' An engine hooted three times and his brain automatically noted the meaning of the signal: a heavy goods train on the down line. Then he was in the room, the woman had closed the window and the noise of the station faded.

Josef brushed the snow off his coat and his moustache and looked at his watch; nine-five; the train to Passau would not leave for another forty minutes, and he had his ticket ready. With his back to the window and the woman he took in the room casually, but every detail marched to its ordered place in his memory, the ewer and basin on the liver-coloured washstand, the chipped gilt mirror, the iron bedstead, the chamber-pot, the holy picture. He said, 'Better leave the window open. In case your master returns.'

A thin shocked voice said, 'I couldn't. Oh, I couldn't.' He turned to her with amiable mockery, 'Modest Anna,' and watched her with sharp knowledgeable eyes. She shared his age, but not his experience, standing lean and flustered and excited by the window; her black skirt lay across the bed, but she still wore her black blouse, her white domestic collar, and she held a towel before her legs to hide them.

He regarded her quizzically, 'Pretty Anna.' Her mouth fell open and she stared back at him, silent and fascinated. Josef noted with distaste her uneven and discoloured teeth: whatever else I have to do, he thought, I will not kiss her, but it was evident that she expected an embrace; her modesty was transformed into a horrible middle-aged coquetry, to which he was forced to respond. He began to talk to her in baby language, sitting down on the edge of her bed and keeping its width between them. 'What had the pretty Anna got now then? A great big man? Oh, how he will rumple you.' He wagged a finger at her playfully, 'You and I, Anna. We'll have a good time by and by. Eh?' He squinted sideways at the door and saw with relief that it was unlocked; it would have been just like the old bitch to have locked him in and hidden the key, but no reflection of his anxiety or his distaste ruffled the plump pink face. 'Eh?'

She smiled and let out a long whistling breath. 'Oh, Anton.' He jumped to his feet, and she dropped the towel and came towards him, with the thin tread of a bird, in her black cotton stockings. 'One moment,' he said, 'one moment,' raising his hand defensively, aghast at the antique lust he had aroused. Neither of us are beauties, he thought, and the presence of a pink-and-white Madonna gave the whole situation a kind of conscious blasphemy. He stopped her by his urgent whisper, 'Are you sure there's no one in the flat?' Her face reddened as if he had made a crude advance. 'No, Anton, we are quite alone.' His brain began to work again with precision; it was only personal relationships that confused him; when there was danger, or the need of action, his mind had the reliability of a tested machine. 'Have you the bag I gave you?'

'Yes, Anton, here under the bed.' She drew out a small black doctor's bag, and he chucked her under the chin and told her that she had pretty eyes. 'Get undressed,' he said, 'and into bed. I'll be with you again in a moment.' Before she could argue or ask him to explain, he had skipped gaily through the door on his toes and closed it behind him. Immediately he looked round for a chair and wedged it under the handle, so that the door could not be opened from inside.

He was familiar from a previous visit with the room he was in. It was a cross between an office and an old-fashioned drawing-room. There was a desk, a red velvet sofa, a swivel-chair, several occasional tables, a few large nineteenth-century engravings of children playing with dogs and ladies bending over garden walls. One wall was almost covered by a large roller map of the central station, with its platforms and goods-sheds, points and signal-boxes marked in primary colours. The shapes of furniture were dimly visible now in the half-dark, shadows falling like dust-sheets over the chairs from the street lights reflected on the ceiling and the glow of a reading-lamp on the desk. Josef struck his chin against an occasional table and nearly overturned a palm. He swore mildly, and Anna's voice called out from the bedroom, 'What is it, Anton? What are you doing?'

'Nothing,' he said, 'nothing. I'll be with you in a moment. Your master's left a light on. Are you sure he won't be back?'

She began to cough, but between the paroxysms she let him know, 'He's on duty till midnight. Anton, you won't be long?' He made a grimace. 'Just taking off a few things, Anna darling.' Through the open window the sounds of the road beat up into the room; there was a constant blowing of horns. Josef leant out and examined the street. Taxis sped up and down with luggage and passengers, but he ignored them and the flicker of sky signs, and the clinking café immediately below, questing down the pavements; few people were passing, for it was the hour of dinner, theatre, or cinema. There was no policeman to be seen.

'Anton.'

He snapped, 'Be quiet,' and drew the blinds lest he should be seen from one of the buildings opposite. He knew exactly where the safe was built into the wall; only a meal, a cinema, and a few drinks had been required to get the information from Anna. But he had feared to ask her for the combination; she might have realised that her charm was insufficient to bring him in the dark across an icy roof to her bedroom. From a small book-case behind the desk he drew six heavy volumes of *Railway Working and Railway Management*, which hid a small steel door. Josef Grünlich's mind was now clear and concentrated; he moved without hurry or hesitation. Before he set to work he noted the time, nine-ten, and calculated that he need not leave for half an hour. Ample time, he thought, and pressed a wet thumb on the safe door, the steel is not half an inch thick. He laid the black bag on the desk and unpacked his tools. His chisels were in beautiful condition, highly polished, with a sharp edge; he took a pride in the neatness of his tools as well as in the speed of his work. He might have broken the thin steel with a jemmy, but Anna would hear the blows and he could not trust her to keep silent. He therefore lit his smallest blow-pipe, first putting on smoked glasses to shield his eyes from the glare. The details of the room started out of the shadows at the first fierce jab of flame, the heat scorched his face, and the steel door began to sizzle like melting butter.

'Anton.' The woman shook the handle of the bedroom door. 'Anton. What are you doing? Why have you shut me in?' Through the low roar of the flame, he cried to her, 'Be quiet.' He heard her feeling at the lock and twisting the handle. Then she spoke again urgently, 'Anton, let me out.' Every time he removed his lips from the pipe to answer her, the flame shrank. Trusting to her timorous stupidity, he addressed her ferociously, 'Be quiet, or I'll twist your neck.' For a moment there was silence, the flame waxed, the steel door turned from a red to a white heat, then Anna called quite loudly, 'I know what you are doing, Anton.' Josef pressed his lips to the pipe and paid her no attention, but Anna's next cry startled him: 'You are at the safe, Anton.' She began to rattle the handle again, until he was forced to let the flame sink and shout at her, 'Be quiet. I meant what I said. I'll twist your ugly neck for you, you old bitch.' Her voice sank, but he could hear her quite distinctly; her lips must have been pressed to the key-hole. 'Don't, don't say that, Anton. Listen. Let me out. I've got something to tell you, to warn you.' He did not answer her, blowing the flame and the steel back to a white heat. 'I lied to you, Anton. Let me out. Herr Kolber is coming back.' He lowered the pipe and sprang round. 'What's that? What do you mean?'

'I thought you wouldn't come if you knew. There would have been time to love each other. Half an hour. And if he came in earlier, we could have lain quiet.' Josef's brain worked quickly, he wasted no time in cursing the woman, but blew out the pipe and packed it back in his bag with the chisels and the jemmy and the skeleton-key and the pot of pepper. He surendered without a second thought one of the easiest hauls of his career, but it was his pride that he took no avoidable risks. He had never been caught. Sometimes he had worked with partners and the partners had been caught, but they bore no malice. They recognised the extraordinary nature of Josef's record and went to prison with pride that he had escaped, and afterwards to their friends they would point him out: 'That's Josef. Five years now and never jugged.'

He closed his bag and jumped a little at a strange sound outside like the twanging of a bow. 'What's that?'

Anna whispered through the door, 'The lift. Someone has rung it down.' He picked up a volume of *Railway Management*, but the safe glowed red with heat and he put it back on the desk. From below came the clang of a gate closing, the high hum of the lift. Josef stepped towards the curtain and drew the string on which the revolver dangled a couple of inches higher. He wondered whether it would be possible to escape through the window, but he remembered that there was a straight drop of thirty feet to the awning of the café. Then the gates opened and closed. Anna whispered through the key-hole: 'The floor below.'

That's all right, then, Josef thought, I can take my time. Back into Anna's bedroom and then over the roof. I shall have to wait twenty minutes for the Passau train. The chair under the handle was tightly wedged. He had to put down his bag and use both hands. The chair slid along the hardwood floor and crashed over. At the same moment the light went on.

'Stay where you are,' said Herr Kolber, 'and put your hands up.'

Josef Grünlich obeyed at once. He turned round very slowly, and during those seconds formed his plan. 'I'm not armed,' he said gently, scanning Herr Kolber with mild reproachful eyes. Herr Kolber wore the blue uniform and the round peaked cap of an assistant station-master; he was small and thin with a brown crinkled face, and the hand holding the revolver shook a little with excitement and age and fury. For a moment Josef's mild eyes were narrowed and focused on the revolver, calculating the angle at which it would be fired, wondering whether the bullet would go astray. No, he thought, he will aim at my legs and hit my stomach. Herr Kolber had his back to the safe and could not yet have seen the disarranged books. 'You don't understand,' Josef said.

'What are you doing at that door?'

Josef's face was still red from the glow of the flame. 'Me and Anna,' he said.

Herr Kolber shouted at him, 'Speak up, you scoundrel.'

'Me and Anna are friends. I'm very sorry, Herr Superintendent, to be found like this. Anna invited me in.'

'Anna?' Herr Kolber said incredulously. 'Why?'

Josef's hips wriggled with embarrassment. 'Well, Herr Kolber, you see how it is. Me and Anna are friends.'

'Anna, come here.' The door opened slowly, and Anna came out. She had put on her skirt and tidied her hair. 'It's true, Herr Kolber.' She gazed with horror past him at the exposed safe. 'What's the matter with you? What are you staring at now? This is a fine kettle of fish. A woman of your age.'

'Yes, Herr Kolber, but—' She hesitated and Josef interrupted her before she could defend herself, or accuse him. 'I'm very fond of Anna.' She accepted his words with a pitiable gratitude. 'Yes, he told me that.'

Herr Kolber stamped his foot. 'You were a fool, Anna. Turn out his pockets. He's probably stolen your money.' It still did not occur to him to examine his safe, and Josef played up to the part assigned to him of an inferior thief. He knew the type to the last bluster and the last whine. He had worked with them, employed them, and seen them depart to gaol without regret. Pickpennies, he called them, and he meant by the term that they were men without ambition or resource. 'I haven't stolen her money,' he whined. 'I wouldn't do such a thing. I'm fond of Anna.'

'Turn out his pockets.' Anna obeyed, but her hands moved in his clothes like a caress. 'Now his hip pocket.'

'I don't carry a gun,' Josef said.

'His hip pocket,' Herr Kolber repeated, and Anna turned out the lining. When he saw that that pocket too was empty, Herr Kolber lowered his revolver, but he still quivered with elderly rage. 'Making my flat a brothel,' he said. 'What have you got to say for yourself, Anna? This is a fine kettle of fish.'

Anna, with her eyes on the floor, twisted her thin hands. 'I don't know what came over me, Herr Kolber', but even while she spoke she seemed to learn. She looked up and Josef Grünlich saw in her eyes affection turn to distaste and distaste to anger. 'He tempted me,' she said slowly. All the while Josef was conscious of his black bag on the desk behind Herr Kolber's back, of the pile of books and the exposed safe, but uneasiness did not hamper thought. Sooner or later Herr Kolber would discover what had brought him to the flat, and already he had noticed close to the station-master's hand a bell which probably rang in the porter's flat.

'Can I put my hands down, Herr Superintendent?'

'Yes, but don't move an inch.' Herr Kolber stamped his foot. 'I'm going to have the truth of this if I keep you here all night. I won't have men coming here seducing my maid.' The word 'men' took Josef for a second off his guard; the idea of the middle-aged Anna as an object of pursuit amused him, and he smiled. Anna saw the smile and guessed the reason. She said to Herr Kolber, 'Be careful. He didn't want me. He—' but Josef Grünlich took the accusation out of her mouth. 'I'll confess. It was not Anna I came for. Look, Herr Kolber,' and he waved his left hand towards the safe. Herr Kolber turned with his revolver pointing to the floor, and Josef shot him twice in the small of the back.

Anna put her hand to her throat and began to scream, looking away from the body. Herr Kolber had fallen on his knees with his forehead touching the floor; he wriggled once between the shots, and then the whole body would have fallen sideways if it had not been propped in its position by the wall. 'Shut your mouth,' said Josef, and when the woman continued to scream, he took her by the throat and shook her. 'If you don't keep quiet for ten minutes, I'll put you underground too–see?' He saw that she had fainted and threw her into a chair; then he shut and locked the window and the bedroom door, for he was afraid that if she returned to the bedroom, her screams might be heard by the policeman when his beat took him to the goods-yard. The key he pushed down the lavatory pan with the handle of a scrubbing-brush. He made a last survey of the study; but he had already decided to leave the black bag on the desk; he always wore gloves, and the bag would bear only Anna's finger-prints. It was a pity to lose such a fine set of tools, but he was prepared to sacrifice anything which might endanger him, even he thought, looking at his watch, the ticket to Passau. The train would not leave for another quarter of an hour, and he could not linger in Vienna so long. He remembered the express he had seen from the roof, the express to Istanbul, and wondered: Can I make it without buying a ticket? He was unwilling to leave the trail of his features behind him, and it even crossed his mind to blind Anna with one of the chisels so that she might not be able to identify him. It was a passing thought; unnecessary violence was abhorrent to him, not because he disliked violence, but because he liked to be precise in his methods, omitting nothing which was necessary and adding nothing which was superfluous. Now with great care to avoid the blood he searched Herr Kolber's pockets for the study key, and when he had found it, he paused for a moment before a mirror to tidy his hair and brush his hat. Then he left the room, locking the door behind him and dropping the key into an umbrella-stand in the hall: he intended to do no more roof-climbing that night.

His only hesitation was when he saw the lift waiting with open door, but he decided almost at once to use the staircase, for the noise of the lift would blaze his trail past other flats. All the way down the stairs he listened for Anna's screams, but only silence followed him. The snow was still falling outside, quietening the wheels of cars, the tread of feet; but the silence up the stairs seemed to fall faster and more thickly and to disguise the signs he had left behind, the pile of books, the black bag, the scorched safe. He had never before killed a man, but as long as silence lasted, he could forget that he had taken the final step which raised him to the dangerous peak of his profession.

A door on the first floor was open, and as he passed he heard a petulant woman's voice, 'Such drawers, I tell you. Well, I'm not the President's daughter, and I said to her, give me something respectable. Thin! You've never seen—'

Josef Grünlich twisted his thick grey moustache and stepped boldly out into the street, glancing this way, glancing that, as if he were expecting a friend. There was no policeman in sight, and as the pavements had been swept clear of snow, he left no prints. He turned smartly to the left towards the station, his ears pricked for the sound of screams, but he heard nothing but the hoot of taxi-cabs and the rustle of the snow. At the end of the street the great arch of the station enticed him like the lit façade of a variety theatre.

But it would be dangerous, he thought, to hang about the entrance like a seller of lottery tickets, and suddenly with the sense of dropping all the tenement's height, floor by floor, from Herr Kolber's flat, with the sense renewed of his own resource, the hand pointing to the safe, the quick pull on the string, and the revolver levelled and fired in one moment, pride filled him. I have killed a man. He let his overcoat flap open to the night breeze; he smoothed his waistcoat, fingered his silver chain; to an imaginary female friend he raised his soft grey hat, made by the best maker in Vienna, but a little too small for him, because it had been lifted from a lavatory peg. I, Josef Grünlich, have killed a man. I am clever, he thought, I'll be too much for them. Why should I hurry like a sneak thief to the station, slip inconspicuously through doorways, hide in the shadow of sheds? There's time for a cup of coffee, and he chose a table on the pavement, at the edge of the awning, which he had seen rise towards him when he slipped on the roof. He glanced upwards through the falling snow, one floor, two floors, three floors, and there was the lighted window of Herr Kolber's study; four floors, and the shadow of the building vanished in the grey loaded sky. It would have been an ugly fall.

'Der Kaffee mit Milch,' he said. He stirred the coffee thoughtfully, Josef Grünlich, the man of destiny. There was nothing else to be done, he didn't hesitate. A shadow of discontent passed across his features when he thought: But I can tell no one of this. It would be too dangerous. Even his best friend, Anton, whose Christian name he had used, must remain in ignorance, for there might be a reward offered for information. Nevertheless, sooner or later, he assured himself, they would guess, and they will point me out:

There's Josef. He killed Kolber at Vienna, but they never caught him. He's never been caught.'

He put down his glass and listened. Had it been a taxi or a noise from the station or a woman's scream? He looked round the tables; no one had heard anything odd, they were talking, drinking, laughing, and one man was spitting. But Josef Grünlich's thirst was a little dulled while he sat and listened. A policeman came down the street; he had probably been relieved from traffic duty and was on his way home, but Josef, lifting his glass, shielded his face and watched him covertly over the brim. Then quite certainly he heard a scream. The policeman stopped, and Josef, glancing anxiously round for the waiter, rose and laid some coins upon the table; the revolver between his legs had rubbed a small sore.

'Guten Abend.' The policeman bought an evening paper and went down the street. Josef put his gloved fingers to his forehead and brought them down damp with sweat. This won't do, he thought, I mustn't get nervous; I must have imagined that scream, and he was about to sit down and finish his coffee when he heard it again. It was extraordinary that it should have passed unnoticed in the café. How long, he wondered, before she unlocks the window? Then they'll hear her. He left his table and out in the street heard the screams more clearly, but the taxis went hooting by, a few hotel porters staggered down the slippery pavement carrying bags; no one stopped, no one heard.

Something struck the pavement with the clink of metal, and Josef looked down. It was a copper coin. That's curious, he thought, a lucky omen, but stooping to pick it up, he saw at intervals, all the way from the café, copper and silver coins lying in the centre of the pavement. He felt in his trouser pocket and found nothing but a hole. My goodness, he thought, have I been dropping them ever since I left the flat? And he saw himself standing at the end of a clear trail that led, paving stone by paving stone, and then stair by stair, to the door of Herr Kolber's study. He began to walk rapidly back along the pavement, picking up the coins and cramming them into his overcoat pocket, but he had not reached the café when the glass of a window broke high up above his head and a woman's voice screamed over and over again: 'Zu Hülfe! Zu Hülfe!' A waiter ran out of the café and stared upwards; a taxi-driver put on his brakes and ground his machine to a halt by the kerb; two men who had been playing chess left their pieces and ran into the road. Josef Grünlich had thought it very quiet under the falling snow, but only now was he confronted by real silence, as the taxi stopped and everyone in the café ceased speaking, and the woman continued to scream: 'Zu Hülfe! Zu Hülfe!' Somebody said, 'Die Polizei,' and two policemen came running down the street with clinking holsters. Then everything became again as usual, except that a small knot of idle people gathered at the entrance to the flats. The two chess players went back to their game; the taxi-driver pressed his self-starter, and then because the cold had already touched his engine, climbed out to wind the handle. Josef Grünlich walked, not too rapidly, towards the station, and a newspaper seller began to pick up the coins he had left on the pavement. Certainly, Josef thought, I cannot wait for the Passau train. But neither, he began to think, could he risk arrest for travelling without a ticket. But I haven't the money to get another; even my small change has gone. Josef, Josef, he abjured himself, don't make difficulties. You must get more. You are not going to give in now: Josef Grünlich, five years and never jugged. You've killed a man: surely for once you, the head of your profession, can do something which any pickpenny finds easy, steal a woman's handbag.

He kept his eyes alert as he went up the steps into the station. He must take no risks. If he was caught, he would have to face a life sentence, not a week in gaol. He must choose carefully. Several bags were almost thrust into his hands in the crowded hall, so carelessly were they guarded, but the owners looked too poor or too gad-about. The first would have only a few shillings; the others, as like as not, would keep in their bags not even small change, only a powder-puff, a lipstick, a mirror, perhaps some French letters.

At last he found what he wanted, something indeed better than he had hoped. A foreign woman, English probably, with short uncovered hair and red eyes, struggling with the door of a telephone-booth. Her bag had fallen at her feet while she put both hands to the handle. She was, he thought, a little drunk, and as she was foreign, she would have plenty of money in her bag. For Josef Grünlich the whole affair was child's play.

The door came open and Mabel Warren faced the black shining instrument which for ten years now had taken her best time and her best phrases. She stooped for her bag, but it was gone. Strange, she thought, I could have sworn—did I leave it in the train? She had eaten a farewell dinner on the train with Janet Pardoe. There had been a glass of sherry, the larger part of a bottle of hock, and two liqueur brandies. Afterwards she had been a little dazed. Janet had paid for the dinner and she had given Janet a cheque and taken the change; she had more than two pounds of small Austrian change in the pocket of her tweed jacket now, but in the bag were nearly eighty marks.

She had some difficulty in making the long distance exchange understand the number she wanted in Cologne, because her voice was a little muzzled. While she waited, balancing her top-heavy form on the small steel seat, she watched the barrier. Fewer and fewer passengers came from the platforms: there was no sign of Dr Czinner. And yet, when she looked into his compartment ten minutes from Vienna, he was wearing his hat and mackintosh and he had answered her, 'Yes, I am getting out.' She had not trusted him, and when the train drew up, she waited until he left his compartment, watched him fumbling on the platform for his ticket, and would not then have let him out of her sight if it had not been necessary to telephone the office. For if he was lying she was determined to follow him to Belgrade and she would have no further opportunity to telephone that night. Did I leave my bag in the train? she wondered again, and then the telephone rang.

She looked at her wrist-watch: I've got ten minutes. If he doesn't come out in five, I'll go back to the train. It won't pay him to lie to me. 'Hello. Is that the London *Clarion*? Edwards? Right. Get this down. No, my lad, this isn't the Savory story. I'll give you that in a moment. This is your bill-page lead, and you've got to hold it for half an hour. If I don't ring up again, shoot it off. The Communist outbreak at Belgrade, which was put down with some loss of life on Wednesday night, as reported in our later editions yesterday, was planned by the notorious agitator, Dr Richard Czinner, who disappeared during the Kamnetz trial (no Kamnetz, K for Kaiser, A for Arse, M for Mule, N for Navel, no not that kind. It doesn't matter; it's the same letter. E for Erotic, T for Tart, Z for Zebra. Got it?), Kamnetz trial. Note to sub-editor. See press cuttings, August, 1927. He was believed to have been murdered by Government agents, but although a warrant was out for his arrest, he escaped, and in an exclusive interview with our special correspondent described his life as a schoolmaster at Great Birchington-on-Sea. Note to news-editor: Can't get him to speak about this; get the dope from the headmaster. His name's John. The outbreak at Belgrade was untimely; it had been planned for Saturday night, by which time Dr Czinner, who left England on Wednesday evening, would have arrived in the capital and taken control. Dr Czinner learnt of the outbreak and its failure when the express by which he was travelling reached Würzburg and immediately decided to leave the train at Vienna. He was heartbroken and could only murmur over and over again to our special correspondent: "If only they had waited." He was confident that if he had been present in Belgrade, the whole working class of the city would have supported the rising. In broken accents he gave our correspondent the amazing tale of his escape from Belgrade in 1927 and described the plans now prematurely ruined. Got that? Now listen carefully. If you don't get the rest of the dope in half an hour cancel everything after "reaching Würzburg" and continue as follows: And after long and painful hesitation decided to continue his journey to Belgrade. He was heartbroken and could only murmur: "Those fine brave fellows. How can I desert them?" When he had a little recovered he explained to our special correspondent that he had decided to stand his trial with the survivors, thus living up to the quixotic reputation he gained for himself at the time of the Kamnetz trial. His popularity with the working classes is an open secret, and his action may prove a considerable embarrassment to the Government.'

Miss Warren took a long breath and looked at her watch. Only five minutes now before the train left. 'Hello. Don't run away. Here's the bromide about Savory. You've got to be quick in getting this down. They've asked for half a column, but I haven't the time. I'll give you a few sticks. Mr Quin Savory, author of *The Great Gay Round*, is on his way to the Far East in search of material for his new novel, *Going Abroad*. Although the book will have an eastern setting, the great novelist will not have quite deserted the London he loves so well, for he will view these distant lands through the eyes of a little London tobacconist. Mr Savory, a slim bronzed figure, welcomed our correspondent on the platform at Cologne. He has a curt (don't be funny. I said curt. C.U.R.T.) manner which does not hide a warm and sympathetic heart. Asked to estimate his place in literature he said: "I take my stand with sanity as opposed to the morbid introspection of such writers as Lawrence and Joyce. Life is a fine thing for the adventurous with a healthy mind in a healthy body." Mr Savory, who dresses quietly and without eccentricity, does not believe in the Bohemianism of some literary circles. "They give up to sex," he said, amusingly adapting Burke's famous phrase, "what is meant for mankind." Our correspondent pointed out the warm admiration which had been felt by countless readers for Emmy Tod, the little char in *The Great Gay Round* (which incidentally is now in its hundredth thousand). "You have a wonderful knowledge of the female heart, Mr Savory," he said. Mr Savory, who is unmarried, climbed back into his carriage with a debonair smile. "A novelist," he laughed, "is something of a spy," and he waved his hand gaily as the train carried him off. It is an open secret, by the way, that the Hon. Carol Delaine, the daughter of Lord Garthaway, will play the part of Emmy Tod, the chargirl, in the British film production of *The Great Gay Round*. Got that? Of course it's a bromide. What else can one do with the little swine?'

Miss Warren clapped down the receiver. Dr Czinner had not appeared. She was angry, but satisfied. He had thought to leave her behind in Vienna station, and she pictured with pleasure his disappointment when he looked up from his paper to find her again in the doorway of his compartment. Closer than mud, she whispered to herself, that's what I'll be.

The official at the barrier stopped her: 'Fahrkarte, bitte.' He was not looking at her, for he was busy collecting the tickets of passengers who had just arrived in some small local train, women with babies in arms and one man clasping a live hen. Miss Warren tried to brush her way through: 'Journalist's pass.' The ticket collector turned to her suspiciously. Where was it?

'I've left my bag behind,' said Miss Warren.

He collected the last ticket, shuffled the pasteboard into an even pile, round which with deliberation he twisted an india-rubber ring. The lady, he explained with stubborn courtesy, had told him when she came from the platform that she had a pass; she had waved a piece of card at him and brushed by before he could examine it. Now he would like to see that piece of card.

'Damn,' said Miss Warren. 'Then my bag has been stolen.'

But the lady had just said that it was in the train.

Miss Warren swore again. She knew that her appearance was against her; she wore no hat, her hair was rumpled, and her breath smelt of drink. 'I can't help it,' she said. 'I've got to get back on that train. Send a man with me and I'll give him the money.'

The ticket-collector shook his head. He could not leave the barrier himself, he explained, and it would be out of order to send any of the porters who were in the hall on to the platform to collect money for a ticket. Why should not the lady buy a ticket and then claim reimbursement from the company? 'Because,' said Miss Warren furiously, 'the lady hasn't enough money on her.'

'In that case,' the ticket-collector said gently, with a glance at the clock, 'the lady will have to go by a later train. The Orient Express will have gone. As for the bag, you need not worry. A telephone message can be sent to the next station.'

Somebody in the booking-hall was whistling a tune. Miss Warren had heard it before with Janet, the setting of a light voluptuous song, while hand in hand they listened in darkness, and the camera panned all the length of a studio street, picking a verse from this man's mouth as he leant from a window, from this woman who sold vegetables behind a barrow, from that youth who embraced a girl in the shadow of a wall. She put one hand to her hair. Into her thoughts and fears, into the company of Janet and Q.C. Savory, Coral and Richard Czinner, a young pink face was for a moment thrust, soft eyes beamed helpfully behind horn-rimmed glasses. 'I guess, ma'am, you're having some trouble with this man. I'd be vurra proud to interpret for you.'

Miss Warren spun round with fury. 'Go and eat corn,' she said and strode to the telephone box. The American had turned the scale between sentiment and anger, between regret and revenge. He thinks that he's safe, she thought, that he's shaken me off, that I can't do anything to him just because he's failed. But by the time the bell rang in the box she was quite calm. Janet might flirt with Savory, Coral with her Jew; Mabel Warren for the time being did not care. When there was a choice between love of a woman and hate of a man, her mind could cherish only one emotion, for her love might be a subject for laughter, but no one had ever mocked her hatred.

2

Coral Musker stared with bewilderment at the menu. 'Choose for me,' she said, and was glad that he ordered wine, for it will help, she thought, tonight. 'I like your ring.' The lights of Vienna fled by them into the dark, and the waiter leant across the table and pulled down the blind. Myatt said, 'It cost fifty pounds.' He was back in familiar territory, he was at home, no longer puzzled by the inconsistency of human behaviour. The wine list before him, the napkin folded on his plate, the shuffle of waiters passing his chair, all gave him confidence. He smiled and moved his hand, so that the stone glinted from different facets on the ceiling and on the wine glasses. 'It's worth nearly twice that.'

'Tell me about her,' said Mr Q.C. Savory; 'she's an odd type. Drinks?' 'So devoted to me.' 'But who wouldn't be?' He leant forward crumbling bread and asked with caution: 'I've never been able to understand. What can a woman like that *do?* . . .'

'No, I won't have any more of this foreign beer. My stomach won't stand it. Ask them, haven't they got a Guinness. I'd just fancy a Guinness.'

'Of course you are having a great sports revival in Germany,' said Mr Opie. 'Splendid types of young men, one sees. But still it's not the same as cricket. Take Hobbs and Sutcliffe . . .'

'Kisses. Always kisses.'

'But I don't speak the lingo, Amy.'

'Do you always say what a thing's worth? Do you know what I'm worth?' Her perplexity and fear broke into irritation. 'Of course you do. Ten pounds for a ticket.'

'I explained,' Myatt said, 'all about that.'

'If I was that girl there . . .' Myatt turned and saw the slender woman in her furs and was caught up and judged and set down again by her soft luminous eyes. 'You are prettier,' he said with open insincerity, trying again to catch the woman's gaze and learn the verdict. It's not a lie, he told himself, for Coral at her best is pretty, while with the stranger one could never use the insignificant measure of prettiness. But I should be dumb before her, he thought. I could not talk to her easily as I can to Coral; I should be conscious of my hands, of my race; and with a wave of gratitude he turned to Coral, 'You're good to me.'

He leant across the soup, the rolls and the cruet: 'You *will* be good to me.'

'Yes,' she said, 'tonight.'

'Why only tonight? When we get to Constantinople why shouldn't you, why shouldn't we . . .' He hesitated. There was something about her which puzzled him: one small unvisited grove in all the acres of their familiarity.

'Live with you there?'

'Why not?' But it was not the reasons against his proposal which thronged her mind, which so coloured her thoughts that she had to focus her eyes more clearly on reality, the swaying train, men and women as far as she could see eating and drinking between the drawn blinds, the scraps of other people's talk.

'Yes, that's all. Kisses. Just kisses.'

'Hobbs and Zudgliffe?'

It was all the reasons in favour: instead of the chill return at dawn to a grimy lodging and a foreign landlady, who would not understand her when she asked for a hot-water-bottle or a cup of tea, and would offer for a tired head some alien substitute for aspirin, to go back to a smart flat with shining taps and constant hot water and a soft bed with a flowered silk coverlet, that indeed would be worth any pain, any night's discomfort. But it's too good to be true, she thought, and tonight when he finds me cold and frightened and unused to things, he won't want me any longer. 'Wait,' she said. 'You may not want me.'

'But I do.'

'Wait till breakfast. Ask me at breakfast. Or just don't ask me.'

'No, not crickett. Not crickett,' said Josef Grünlich, wiping his moustache. 'In Germany we learn to run,' and the quaintness of his phrase made Mr Opie smile. 'Have you been a runner yourself?'

'In my day,' said Josef Grünlich, 'I was a great runner. Nobody runned as well as I. Nobody could catch me.'

'Heller.'

'Don't swear, Jim.'

'I wasn't swearing. It's the beer. Try some of this. It's not gassy. What you had before they call Dunkel.'

'I'm so glad you liked it.'

'That little char. I can't remember her name, she was lovely.'

'Come back and talk a little after dinner.'

'You won't be silly now, Mr Savory?'

'I shall ask you.'

'Don't promise. Don't promise anything. Talk about something else. Tell me what you are going to do in Constantinople.'

'That's only business. It's tricky. The next time you eat spotted dog, think of me. Currants. I am currants,' he added with a humorous pride.

'Then I'll call you spotted dog. I can't call you Carleton, can I? What a name.'

'Look, have a currant. I always carry a few with me. Have one of these in this division. Good, isn't it?'

'Juicy.'

'That's one of ours, Myatt, Myatt and Page. Now try one of these. What do you think of that?'

'Look through there in the first class, Amy. Can't you see her? Too good for us, that's what she is.'

'With that Jew? Well, one knows what to think.'

'I have the greatest respect of course, for the Roman Catholic Church,' said Mr Opie. 'I am not bigoted. As an example of organisation . . .'

'So?'

'I am silly now.'

'Juicy.'

'No, no, that one's not juicy.'

'Have I said the wrong thing?'

'That was one of Stein's. A cheap inferior currant. The vineyards are on the wrong side of the hills. It makes them dry. Have another. Can't you see the difference?'

'Yes, this is dry. It's quite different. But the other was juicy. You don't believe me, but it really was. You must have got them mixed.'

'No, I chose the sample myself. It's odd. It's very odd.'

All down the restaurant-cars fell the sudden concerted silence which is said to mean that an angel passes overhead. But through the human silence the tumblers tingled on the table, the wheels thudded along the iron track, the windows shook and sparks flickered like match heads through the darkness. Late for the last service Dr Czinner came down the restaurant-car in the middle of the silence, with knees a little bent as a sailor keeps firm foothold in a stormy sea. A waiter preceded him, but he was unaware of being led. Words glowed in his mind and became phrases. You say that I am a traitor to my country, but I do not recognise my country. The dark downward steps, the ordure against the unwindowed wall, the starving faces. These are not Slavs, he thought, who owe a duty to this frock-coated figure or to that: they are the poor of all the world. He faced the military tribunal sitting under the eagles and the crossed swords: It is you who are old-fashioned with your machine-guns and your gas and your talk of country. Unconsciously as he walked the aisle from table to table he touched and straightened the tightly-knotted tie and fingered the Victorian pin: I am of the present. But for a moment into his grandiloquent dream obtruded the memory of long rows of malicious adolescent faces, the hidden mockery, the nicknames, the caricatures, the notes passed in grammars, under desks, the ubiquitous whispers impossible to place and punish. He sat down and stared without comprehension at the bill of fare.

Yes, I wouldn't mind being that Jew, Mr Peters thought during the long angelic visitation, he's got a nice skirt all right, all right. Not pretty. I wouldn't say pretty, but a good figure, and that, said Mr Peters to himself, watching his wife's tall angularity, remembering her murmurous stomach, that's the most important thing.

It was odd. He had chosen the samples with particular care. It was natural of course that even Stein's currants should not all be inferior, but when so much was suspected, a further suspicion was easy. Suppose, for example, Mr Eckman had been doing a little trade on his own account, had allowed Stein some of the firm's consignment of currants, in order temporarily to raise the quality, had, on the grounds of that improved quality, indeed, induced Moults' to bid for the business. Mr Eckman must be having uneasy moments now, turning up the time-table, looking at his watch, thinking that half Myatt's journey was over. Tomorrow, he thought, I will send a telegram and put Joyce in charge; Mr Eckman shall have a month's holiday. Joyce will keep an eye on the books, and he pictured the scurryings to and fro, as in an ants' nest agitated by a man's foot, a telephone call from Eckman to Stein or from Stein to Eckman, a taxi ordered here and dismissed there, a lunch for once without wine, and then the steep office steps and at the top of them the faithful rather stupid Joyce keeping his eye upon the books. And all the time, at the modern flat, Mrs Eckman would sit on her steel sofa knitting baby clothes for the Anglican mission, and the great dingy Bible, Mr Eckman's first deception, would gather dust on its unturned leaf.

Q. C. Savory pushed the button of the spring blind and moonlight touched his face and his fish knife and turned the steel rails on the quiet up-line to silver. The snow had stopped falling and lay piled along the banks and between the sleepers, lightening the darkness. A few hundred yards away the Danube flickered like mercury. He could see tall trees fly backwards and telegraph-poles, which caught the moonlight on their metal arms as they passed. While silence held the carriage, he put the thought of Janet Pardoe away from him; he wondered what terms he could use to describe the night. It is all a question of choice and arrangement; I must show not all that I see but a few selected sharp points of vision. I must not mention the shadows across the snow, for their colour and shape are indefinite, but I may pick out the scarlet signal lamp shining against the white ground, the flame of the waiting-room fire in the country station, the bead of light on a barge beating back against the current.

Josef Grünlich stroked the sore on his leg where the revolver pressed and wondered: How many hours to the frontier? Would the frontier guards have received notice of the murder? But I am safe. My passport is in order. No one saw me take the bag. There's nothing to connect me with Kolber's flat. Ought I to have dropped the gun somewhere? he wondered, but he reassured himself: it might have been traced to me. They can tell miraculous things nowadays from a scratch on the bore. Crime grew more unsafe every year; he had heard rumours of a new finger-print stunt, some way by which they could detect the print even when the hand had been gloved. But they haven't caught me yet with all their science.

One thing the films had taught the eye, Savory thought, the beauty of landscape in motion, how a church tower moved behind and above the trees, how it dipped and soared with the uneven human stride, the loveliness of a chimney rising towards a cloud and sinking behind the further cowls. That sense of movement must be conveyed in prose, and the urgency of the need struck him, so that he longed for paper and pencil while the mood was on him and repented his invitation to Janet Pardoe to come back with him after dinner and talk. He wanted to work; he wanted for an hour or two to be free from any woman's intrusion. I don't want her, he thought, but as he snapped the blind down again, he felt again the prick of desire. She was well-dressed; she 'talked like a lady'; and she had read his books with admiration; these three facts conquered him, still aware of his birthplace in Balham, the fugitive Cockney intonation of his voice. After six years of accumulative success, success represented by the figures of sales, 2,000, 4,000, 10,000, 25,000, 100,000, he was still astonished to find himself in the company of well-dressed women, and not divided by a thick pane of restaurant glass or the width of a counter. One wrote, day by day, with labour and frequent unhappiness, but with some joy, a hundred thousand words; a clerk wrote as many in an office ledger, and yet the words which he, Q.C.Savory, the former shop assistant, wrote had a result that the hardest work on an office stool could not attain; and as he picked at his fish and watched Janet Pardoe covertly, he thought not of current accounts, royalties and shares, nor of readers who wept at his pathos or laughed at his Cockney humour, but the long stairs to London drawing-rooms, the opening of double doors, the announcement of his name, faces of women who turned towards him with interest and respect.

Soon in an hour or two he will be my lover; and at the thought and the touch of fear at a strange relationship the dark knowing face lost its familiarity. When she fainted in the corridor he had been kind, with hands that pulled a warm coat round her, a voice that offered her rest and luxury; gratitude pricked at her eyes, and but for the silence all down the car she would have said: 'I love you.' She kept the words on her lips, so that she might break their private silence with them when the public silence passed.

The Press will be there, Czinner thought, and saw the journalists' box as it had been at the Kamnetz trial full of men scribbling and one man who sketched the general's likeness. It will be my likeness. It will be the justification of the long cold hours on the esplanade, when I walked up and down and wondered whether I had done right to escape. I must have every word perfect, remember clearly the object of my fight, remember that it is not only the poor of Belgrade who matter, but the poor of every country. He had protested many times against the national outlook of the militant section of the Social-Democratic party. Even their great song was national, 'March, Slavs, march'; it had been adopted against his wishes. It pleased him that the passport in his pocket was English, the plan in his suitcase German. He had bought the passport at a little paper-shop near the British Museum, kept by a Pole. It was handed to him over the tea-table in the back parlour, and the thin spotty man, whose name he had already forgotten, had apologised for the price. 'The expense is very bad,' he complained, and while he helped his customer into his coat had asked mechanically and without interest: 'How is your business?' It was quite obvious that he thought Czinner a thief. Then he had to go into the shop to sell an *Almanach Gaulois* to a furtive schoolboy. 'March, Slavs, march.' The man who had written the music had been bayoneted outside the sorting-room.

'Braised chicken! Roast veal . . .' The waiters called their way along the carriage and broke the minute's silence. Everyone began talking at once.

'I find the Hungarians take to cricket quite naturally. We had six matches last season.'

'This beer's no better. I *would* just like a glass of Guinness.'

'I do believe these currants—' 'I love you.' 'Our agent—what did you say?' 'I said that I loved you.' The angel had gone, and noisily and cheerfully with the thud of wheels, the clatter of plates, voices talking and the tingle of mirrors, the express passed a long line of fir-trees and the flickering Danube. In the coach the pressure gauge rose, the driver turned the regulator open, and the speed of the train was increased by five miles an hour.

3

Coral Musker paused on the metal plates between the restaurant-car and the second-class coaches. She was jarred and shaken by the heave of the train, and for the moment she could not go on to fetch her bag from the compartment where Mr Peters sat with his wife Amy. Away from the rattling metal, the beating piston, she stepped in thought, wrapping a fur coat round her, up the stairs to her flat. On the drawing-room table was a basket of hot-house roses and a card 'with love from Carl', for she had decided to call him that. One could not say: 'I love you, Carleton,' but 'I adore you, Carl' was easy. She laughed aloud and clapped her hands with the sudden sense that love was a simple affair, made up of gratitude and gifts and familiar jokes, a flat, no work, and a maid.

She began to run down the corridor, buffeted from one side to the other, but caring not at all. I'll go into the theatre three days late, and I shall say: 'Is Mr Sidney Dunn to be found?' But of course the door-keeper will be a Turk and only mutter through his whiskers, so I'll have to find my own way along the passage to the dressing-rooms, over a litter of firehoses, and I shall say 'Good afternoon' or 'Bong jour', and put my head into the general dressing-room and say 'Where's Sid?' He'll be rehearsing in front, so I'll pop out of the wings at him, and he'll say, 'Who the hell are you?' beating time while Dunn's Babies dance and dance and dance. 'Coral Musker.' 'You're three days late. What the hell do you mean by it?' And I'll say, 'I just looked in to give notice.' She repeated the sentence aloud to hear how it would sound: 'I just looked in to give notice,' but the roar of the train beat her bravado into a sound more like a tremulous wail.

'Excuse me,' she said to Mr Peters, who was drowsing in his corner a little greasy after his meal. His legs were stretched across the compartment and barred her entry. 'Excuse me,' she repeated, and Mr Peters woke up and apologised. 'Coming back to us? That's right.'

'No,' she said, 'I'm fetching my bag.'

Amy Peters folded along a seat with a peppermint dissolving in her mouth said with sudden venom, 'Don't speak to her, Herbert. Let her get her bag. Thinks she's too good for us.'

'I only want my bag. What's getting your goat? I never said a word—'

'Don't get fussed, Amy,' said Mr Peters. 'It's none of our business what this young lady does. Have another peppermint. It's her stomach,' he said to Coral. 'She's got indigestion.'

'Young lady, indeed. She's a tart.'

Coral had pulled her bag from beneath the seat, but now she set it down again firmly on Mr Peters' toes. She put her hands on her hips and faced the woman, feeling very old and confident and settled, because the nature of the quarrel brought to mind her mother, arms akimbo, exchanging a few words with a neighbour, who had suggested that she was 'carrying on' with the lodger. For that moment she was her mother; she had sloughed her own experiences as easily as a dress, the feigned gentility of the theatre, the careful speech. 'Who do you think you are?' She knew the answer: shopkeepers on a spree, going out to Budapest on a Cook's tour, because it was a little farther than Ostend, because they could boast at home of being travellers, and show the bright labels of a cheap hotel on their suitcases. Once she would have been impressed herself, but she had learnt to take things casually, never to admit ignorance, to be knowing. 'Who do you think you are talking to? I'm not one of your shopgirls. Not that you have any in your back street.'

'Now, now,' said Mr Peters, touched on the raw by her discovery, 'there's no call to get angry.'

'Oh, isn't there. Did you hear what she called me? I suppose she saw you trying to get off with me.'

'We know he wasn't good enough for you. Easy money's what you want. Don't think we want you in this carriage. I know where you belong.'

'Take that stuff out of your mouth when you talk to me.'

'Arbuckle Avenue. Catch 'em straight off the train at Paddington.'

Coral laughed. It was her mother's histrionic laugh to call the neighbours to come and see the fight. Her fingers tingled upon her hips with excitement; she had been good so long, never dropped an aitch, or talked of a boy friend, or said 'pleased to meet you'. For years she had been hovering indecisively between the classes and belonged nowhere except to the theatre, with her native commonsense lost and natural refinement impossible. Now with pleasure she reverted to type. 'I wouldn't be a scarecrow like you, not if you paid me. No wonder you've got a belly-ache with a face like that. No wonder your old man wanted a change.'

'Now, now, ladies,' said Mr Peters.

'He wouldn't soil his hands with you. A dirty little Jew, that's all you're good for.'

Coral suddenly began to cry, although her hands still flaunted battle, and she had voice enough to reply, 'Keep off him,' but Mrs Peters' words remained smudged, like the dissolving smoke of an aerial advertisement, across the fair prospect.

'Oh, we know he's your boy.'

'My dear,' said a voice behind her, 'don't let them worry you.'

'Here's another of your friends.'

'So?' Dr Czinner put his hand under Coral's elbow and insinuated her out of the compartment.

'Jews and foreigners. You ought to be ashamed.'

Dr Czinner picked up the suitcase and laid it in the corridor. When he turned back to Mrs Peters, he showed her not the harassed miserable face of the foreign master, but the recklessness and the sarcasm which the journalists had noted when he took the witness-box against Kamnetz. 'So?' Mrs Peters took the peppermint out of her mouth; Dr Czinner, thrusting both hands into the pockets of his mackintosh, swayed backwards and forwards upon his toes. He appeared the master of the situation, but he was uncertain how to speak, for his mind was still full of grandiloquent phrases, of socialist rhetoric. He was made harsh by the signs of oppression, but he lacked for the moment words with which to contest it. They existed, he was aware, somewhere in the obscurity of his mind, glowing phrases, sentences as bitter as smoke. 'So?'

Mrs Peters began to find her courage. 'What are you barging your head in about? It's a bit too much. First one Nosey Parker, then another. Herbert, you do something.'

Dr Czinner began to speak. In his thick accent the words assumed a certain ponderous force that silenced, though they did not convince, Mrs Peters. 'I am a doctor.' He told them how useless it was to expect from them the sense of shame. The girl last night had fainted; he had ordered her for her health to have a sleeper. Suspicion only dishonoured the suspicious. Then he joined Coral Musker in the corridor. They were out of sight of the compartment, but Mrs Peters' voice was clearly audible, 'Yes, but who pays? That's what I'd like to know.' Dr Czinner pressed the back of his head against the glass and whispered with hatred, 'Bourgeois.'

'Thank you,' Coral said, and added, when she saw his expression of disappointment, 'Can I do anything? Are *you* ill?'

'No, no,' he said. 'But I was useless. I have not the gift of making speeches.' He leant back against the window and smiled at her. 'You were better. You talked very well.'

'Why were they such beasts?' she asked.

'They are always the same, the bourgeois,' he said. 'The proletariat have their virtues, and the gentleman is often good, just and brave. He is paid for something useful, for governing or teaching or healing, or his money is his father's. He does not deserve it perhaps, but he has done no one harm to get it. But the bourgeois—he buys cheap and sells dear. He buys from the worker and sells back to the worker. He is useless.'

Her question had not required an answer. She stared at him, bewildered by the flood of his explanation and the strength of his conviction, without understanding a word of what he said. 'I didn't do them any harm.'

'Ah, but you've done them great harm. So have I. We have come from the same class. But we earn our living honestly, doing no harm but some good. We are an example against them, and they do not like that.'

Out of this explanation she picked the only phrase she understood. 'Aren't you a gentleman?'

'No, and I am not a bourgeois.'

She could not understand the faint boastfulness of his reply, for ever since she left her home it had been her ambition to be mistaken for a lady. She had studied to that end with as much care as an ambitious subaltern studies for the staff college: every month her course included a new number of *Woman and Beauty*, every week a *Home Notes*; she examined in their pages the photographs of younger stars and of the daughters of the obscurer peers, learning what accessories were being worn and what powders in favour.

He began to advise her gently, 'If you cannot take a holiday, try to keep as quiet as possible. Do not get angry for no reason—'

'They called me a tart.' She could see that the word meant nothing to him. It did not for a moment ruffle the surface of his mind. He continued to talk gently about her health, not meeting her eyes. He's thinking of something else, she thought, and stooped impatiently for her bag, intending to leave him. He forestalled her by a spate of directions about sedatives and fruit juices and warm clothes. Obscurely she realised a change in his attitude. Yesterday he had wanted solitude, now he would seize any excuse to keep her company a minute longer. 'What did you mean,' she asked, 'when you said "My proper work"?'

'When did I say that?' he asked sharply.

'Yesterday when I was faint.'

'I was dreaming. I have only one work.' He said no more, and after a moment she picked up her bag and went.

Nothing in her experience would have enabled her to realise the extent of the loneliness to which she had abandoned him. 'I have only one work.' It was a confession which frightened him, for it had not been always true. He had not lived beside and grown accustomed to the idea of a unique employment. His life had once been lit by the multitude of his duties. If he had been born with a spirit like a vast bare room, covered with the signs of a house gone down in the world, scratches and peeling paper and dust, his duties, like the separate illuminations of a great candelabra too massive to pawn, had adequately lit it. There had been his duty to his parents who had gone hungry that he might be educated. He remembered the day when he took his degree, and how they had visited him in his bed-sitting-room and sat quiet in a corner watching him with respect, even with awe, and without love, for they could not love him now that he was an educated man; once he heard his father address him as 'Sir'. Those candles had blown out early, and he had hardly noticed the loss of two lights among so many, for he had his duty to his patients, his duty to the poor of Belgrade, and the slowly growing idea of his duty to his own class in every country. His parents had starved themselves that he might be a doctor, he himself had gone hungry and endangered his health that he might be a doctor, and it was only when he had practised for several years that he realised the uselessness of his skill. He could do nothing for his own people; he could not recommend rest to the worn-out or prescribe insulin to the diabetic, because they had not the money to pay for either.

He began to walk the corridor, muttering a little to himself. Small flakes of snow were again falling; they were blown against the windows like steam.

There had been his duty to God. He corrected himself: to a god. A god who had swayed down crowded aisles under a bright moth-worn canopy, a god the size of a crown-piece enclosed in a gold framework. It was a two-faced god, a deity who comforted the poor in their distress as they raised their eyes to his coming between the pillars, and a deity who had persuaded them, for the sake of a doubtful future, to endure their pain, as they bowed their heads, while the surge of the choristers and the priests and the singing passed by. He had blown that candle out with his own breath, telling himself that God was a fiction invented by the rich to keep the poor content; he had blown it out with a gesture, with a curious old-fashioned sense of daring, and he sometimes felt an unreasoning resentment against those who nowadays were born without religious sense and were able to laugh at the seriousness of the nineteenth-century iconoclast.

And now there was only one dim candle to light the vast room. I am not a son, he thought, nor a doctor, nor a believer, I am a Socialist; the word mouthed by politicians on innumerable platforms, printed in bad type on bad paper in endless newspapers rang cracked. I have failed even there. He was alone, and his single light was guttering, and he would have welcomed the company of anyone.

When he reached his compartment and found a stranger there he was glad. The man's back was turned, but he spun quickly round on short stout legs. The first thing which Dr Czinner noticed was a silver cross on his watch-chain, the next that his suitcase was not in the same spot where he had left it. He asked sadly, 'Are you, too, a reporter?'

'Ich spreche kein Englisch,' the man replied. Dr Czinner said in German, while he barred the way into the corridor, 'A police spy? You are too late.' His eyes were still on the silver cross, which swung backwards and forwards with the man's movement; it might have been lurching to the human stride, and for a moment Dr Czinner flattened himself against the wall of a steep street to let the armoured men, the spears and the horses pass, and the tired tortured man. He had not died to make the poor contented, to bind the chains tighter; his words had been twisted.

'I am not a police spy.'

Dr Czinner paid the stranger small attention as he faced the possibility that, if the words had been twisted, some of the words might have been true. He argued with himself that the doubt came only from the approach of death, because when the burden of failure was almost too heavy to bear, a man inevitably turned to the most baseless promise. 'I will give you rest.' Death did not give rest, for rest could not exist without the consciousness of rest.

'You misunderstand me, Herr—'

'Czinner.' He relinquished his name to the stranger without hesitation; the time was past for disguises, and in the new veracious air he had to doff not only the masks of identity. There were words which he had not inquired into closely, common slogans which he had accepted because they helped his cause: 'Religion is the rich man's friend.' He said to the stranger: 'If you are not a police spy, who are you? What have you been doing here?'

'My name,' and the fat man bobbed a little from the waist, while a finger twisted the bottom button of his waistcoat, 'is—' The name was tossed into the bright snow-lit darkness, drowned by the roar of the train, the clatter of steel piles, an echoing bridge; the Danube, like a silver eel, slipped from one side to the other of the line. The man had to repeat his name, 'Josef Grünlich.' He hesitated and then continued, 'I was looking for money, Herr Czinner.'

'You've stolen—'

'You came back too soon.' He began slowly to explain. 'I have escaped from the police. Nothing disgraceful, Herr Czinner, I can assure you.' He twisted and twisted his waistcoat button, an unconvincing alien talker in the newly-lit air of Dr Czinner's brain, populated only by incontestable truths, by a starving face, a bright rag, a child in pain, a man staggering up the road to Golgotha. 'It was a political offence, Herr Czinner. An affair of a newspaper. A great injustice has been done me, and so I had to fly. It was for the sake of the cause that I opened your suitcase.' He blew out the word 'cause' with a warm intense breath, cheapening it into a shibboleth, an easy emotion. 'You will call the guard?' He fixed his knees, and his finger tightened on the button.

'What do you mean by your cause?'

'I am a Socialist.' The realisation came sharply to Dr Czinner that a movement could not be judged by its officers; socialism was not condemned by the adherence of Grünlich, but he was anxious, none the less, to forget Grünlich. 'I will let you have some money.' He took out his pocket-book and handed the man five English pounds. 'Good night.'

It was easy to dismiss Grünlich and it had cost him little, for money would be of no value to him in Belgrade. He did not need a lawyer to defend him: his defence was his own tongue. But it was less easy to evade the thought which Grünlich had left behind, that a movement was not condemned by the dishonesty of its officers. He himself was not without dishonesty, and the truth of his belief was not altered because he was guilty of vanity, of several meannesses; once he had got a girl with child. Even his motives in travelling first class were not unmixed; it was easier to evade the frontier police, but it was also more comfortable, more fitted to his vanity as a leader. He found himself praying: 'God forgive me.' But he was shut off from any assurance of forgiveness, if there existed any power which forgave.

The guard came and looked at his ticket. 'Snowing again,' he said. 'It is worse up the line. It will be lucky if we get through without delay.' He showed an inclination to stay and talk. Three winters ago, he said, they had had a bad time. They had been snowed up for forty-eight hours on one of the worst patches of the line, one of the bare Balkan patches; no food to be got, and the fuel had to be saved.

'Shall we reach Belgrade to time?'

'One can't tell. My experience is—snow this side of Buda, twice as much snow before Belgrade. It's a different case before we reach the Danube. It can be snowing in Munich and like summer at Buda. Good night, Herr Doktor. You'll be having patients in this cold.' The guard went down the corridor beating his hands together.

Doctor Czinner did not stay long in his compartment; the man who had shared it had left the train at Vienna. Soon it would be impossible to see even passing lights through the window; the snow was caked in every crevice and ice was forming on the glass. When a signal-box or a station lamp went by its image was cut into wedges by the streaks of opaque ice, so that for a moment the window of the train became a kaleidoscope in which the jumbled pieces of coloured glass were shaken. Dr Czinner wrapped his hands for warmth in the loose folds of his mackintosh and began again to walk the corridor. He passed through the guard's van and came out into the third-class carriages which had been attached to the train at Vienna. Most of the compartments were in darkness except for a dim globe burning in the roof. On the wooden seats the passengers were settling themselves for the night with rolled coats under their heads; some of the compartments were so full that the men and women slept bolt upright in two rows, their faces green and impassive in the faint light. There was a smell of cheap red wine from the empty bottles under the seats, and a few scraps of sour bread lay on the floor. When he came near the lavatory he turned back, the smell was too much for him. Behind him the door blew open and shut with the shaking of the express.

I belong there, he thought without conviction; I should be travelling third class. I do not wish to be like a constitutional Labour member taking his first-class ticket to cast his vote in a packed parliament. But he comforted himself with the thought of how he would have been delayed by frequent changes and how he might have been held up at the frontier. He remained aware nevertheless of the mixture of his motives; they had only begun to worry him since his knowledge of failure; all his vanities, meannesses and small sins would have been swept to darkness in the thrill and unselfishness of victory. But he wished, now that all depended on his tongue, that he could make his speech from the dock with a conscience perfectly clear. Small things in his past, which his enemies would never know, might rise in his own mind to clog his tongue. I failed utterly with those two shopkeepers; shall I succeed any better in Belgrade?

Because his future had an almost certain limit, he began to dwell, as he was not accustomed to do, on the past. There had been a time when a clear conscience could be bought at the price of a moment's shame: 'since my last confession, I have done this or that.' If, he thought with longing and a little bitterness, I could get back my purity of motive so easily, I should be a fool not to take the chance. My regret for what I have done is not less now than then, but I have no conviction of forgiveness; I have no conviction that there is anyone to forgive. He came near to sneering at his last belief: Shall I go and confess my sins to the treasurer of the Social-Democratic party, to the third-class passengers? The priest's face turned away, the raised fingers, the whisper of a dead tongue, seemed to him suddenly as beautiful, as infinitely desirable and as hopelessly lost as youth and first love in the corner of the viaduct wall.

It was then that Dr Czinner caught sight of Mr Opie alone in a second-class compartment, writing in a notebook.

He watched him with a kind of ashamed greed, for he was about to surrender to a belief which it had been his pride to subdue. But if it gives me peace, he protested, and at the still darkling associations of the word he pulled the door back and entered the compartment. The long pale face and pale eyes, the impression of inherited culture, embarrassed him; by his request he would admit the priest's superiority; and he was again for a moment the boy with grubby hands blushing in the dark of the confessional at his commonplace sins. He said in his stiff betraying English, 'Will you excuse me? Perhaps I am disturbing you. You want to sleep?'

'Not at all. I get out at Buda. I don't suppose I shall sleep,' he laughed deprecatingly, 'until I am safe ashore.'

'My name is Czinner.'

'And mine is Opie.' To Mr Opie his name had conveyed nothing; perhaps it was kept in mind only by journalists. Dr Czinner drew the door to and sat down in the opposite seat. 'You are a priest?' He tried to add 'father', but the word stuck on his tongue; it meant too much, it meant a grey starved face, affection hardening into respect, sacrifice into suspicion of a son grown like an enemy. 'Not of the Roman persuasion,' said Mr Opie. Dr Czinner was silent for several minutes, uncertain how to word his request. His lips felt dry with a literal thirst for righteousness, which was like a glass of ice-cold water on a table in another man's room. Mr Opie seemed aware of his embarrassment and remarked cheerfully, 'I am making a little anthology.' Dr Czinner repeated mechanically, 'Anthology?'

'Yes,' said Mr Opie, 'a spiritual anthology for the lay mind, something to take the place in the English church of the Roman books of contemplation.' His thin white hand stroked the black wash-leather cover of his notebook. 'But I intend to strike deeper. The Roman books are, what shall I say? too exclusively religious. I want mine to meet all the circumstances of everyday life. Are you a cricketer?'

The question took Dr Czinner by surprise; he had again in memory been kneeling in darkness, making his act of contrition. 'No,' he said, 'no.'

'Never mind. You will understand what I mean. Suppose that you are the last man in; you have put on your pads; eight wickets have fallen; fifty runs must be made; you wonder whether the responsibility will fall upon you. You will get no strength for that crisis from any of the usual books of contemplation; you may indeed be a little suspicious of religion. I aim at supplying that man's need.'

Mr Opie had spoken rapidly and with enthusiasm, and Dr Czinner found his knowledge of English failing him. He did not understand the words 'pad', 'wickets', 'runs'; he knew that they were connected with the English game of cricket; he had become familiar with the words during the last five years and they were associated in his mind with salty wind-swept turf, the supervision of insubordinate children engaged on a game which he could not master; but the religious significance of the words escaped him. He supposed that the priest was using them metaphorically: 'responsibility', 'crisis', 'man's need', these phrases he understood, and they gave him the opportunity he required to make his request.

'I wished to speak to you,' he said, 'of confession.' At the sound of the word he was momentarily young again.

'It's a difficult subject,' said Mr Opie. He examined his hands for a moment and then began to speak rapidly. 'I am not dogmatic on the point. I think there is a great deal to be said for the attitude of the Roman church. Modern psychology is working on parallel lines. There is a similarity in the relationship between the confessor and the penitent and that between the psycho-analyst and the patient. There is, of course, this difference, that one claims to forgive the sins. But the difference,' Mr Opie continued hurriedly, as Dr Czinner tried to speak, 'is not after all very great. In the one case the sins are said to be forgiven and the penitent leaves the confessional with a clear mind and the intention of making a fresh start; in the other the mere expression of the patient's vices and the bringing to light of his unconscious motives in practising them are said to remove the force of the desire. The patient leaves the psycho-analyst with the power, as well as the intention, of making a fresh start.' The door into the corridor opened, and a man entered. 'From that point of view,' said Mr Opie, 'confession to the psycho-analyst seems to be more efficacious than confession to the priest.'

'You are discussing confession?' the newcomer asked. 'May I draw a red 'erring across your argument? There's a literary aspect to be considered.'

'Let me introduce you to each other,' said Mr Opie. 'Dr Czinner–Mr Q. C. Savory. We really have here the elements of a most interesting discussion; the doctor, the clergyman, and the writer.'

Dr Czinner said slowly: 'Have you not left out the penitent?'

'I was going to introduce him,' Mr Savory said. 'In a way surely *I* am the penitent. In so far as the novel is founded on the author's experience, the novelist is making a confession to the public. This puts the public in the position of the priest and the analyst.'

Mr Opie countered him with a smile. 'But your novel is a confession only in so far as a dream is a confession. The Freudian censor intervenes. The Freudian censor,' he had to repeat in a louder voice as the train passed under a bridge. 'What does the medical man say?' Their polite bright attentive gaze confused Dr Czinner. He sat with head a little bent, unable to bring the bitter phrases from his mind to his lips; speech was failing him for a second time that evening; how could he depend on it when he reached Belgrade?

'And then' said Mr Savory, 'there's Shakespeare.'

'Where is there not?' said Mr Opie. 'He strides this narrow world like a colossus. You mean—'

'What was his attitude to confession? He was born, of course, a Roman Catholic.'

'In *Hamlet*,' began Mr Opie, but Dr Czinner waited no longer. He rose and made two short bows. 'Good night,' he said. He wanted to express his anger and disappointment, but all he found to say was: 'So interesting.' The corridor, lit only by a chain of dim blue globes, sloped grey and vibrating towards the dark vans. Somebody turned in his sleep and said in German, 'Impossible. Impossible.'

When Coral left the doctor she began to run, as fast as was possible with a suitcase in a lurching train, so that she was out of breath and almost pretty when Myatt saw her pulling at the handle of his door. He had put away the correspondence from Mr Eckman and the list of market prices ten minutes ago, because he found that always, before the phrases or the figures could convey anything to his mind, he heard the girl's voice: 'I love you.'

What a joke, he thought, what a joke.

He looked at his watch. No stop now for seven hours and he had tipped the guard. He wondered whether they got used to this kind of affair on long-distance trains. When he was younger he used to read stories of king's messengers seduced by beautiful countesses travelling alone and wonder whether such good fortune would ever happen to him. He looked at himself in the glass and pressed back his oiled black hair. I am not bad-looking if my skin were not so sallow; but when he took off his fur coat, he could not help remembering that he was growing fat and that he was travelling in currants and not with a portfolio of sealed papers. Nor is she a beautiful Russian countess, but she likes me and she has a pretty figure.

He sat down, and then looked at his watch and got up again. He was excited. You fool, he thought, she's nothing new; pretty and kind and common, you can find her any night on the Spaniards road, and yet in spite of these persuasions he could not but feel that the adventure had in it a touch of freshness, of unfamiliarity. Perhaps it was only the situation: travelling at sixty miles an hour in a berth little more than two feet across. Perhaps it was her exclamation at dinner; the girls he had known were shy of using that phrase; they would say 'I love you' if they were asked, but their spontaneous tribute was more likely to be 'You're a nice boy'. He began to think of her as he had never thought before of any woman who was attainable: she is dear and sweet, I should like to do things for her. It did not occur to him for several moments that she had already reason for gratitude.

'Come in,' he said, 'come in.' He took the suitcase from her and pushed it under the seat and then took her hands.

'Well,' she said with a smile, 'I'm here, aren't I?' In spite of her smile he thought her frightened and wondered why. He loosed her hands in order to pull down the blinds of the corridor windows, so that they seemed suddenly to become alone in a small trembling box. He kissed her and found her mouth cool, soft, uncertainly responsive. She sat down on the seat which had become converted into a berth and asked him, 'Did you wonder whether I'd come?'

'You promised,' he reminded her.

'I might have changed my mind.'

'But why?' Myatt was becoming impatient. He did not want to sit about and talk; her legs, swinging freely without touching the floor, excited him. 'We'll have a nice time.' He took off her shoes and ran his hands up her stockings. 'You know a lot, don't you?' she said. He flushed. 'Do you mind that?'

'Oh, I'm glad,' she said, 'so glad. I couldn't bear it if you hadn't known a lot.' Her eyes large and scared, her face pale under the dim blue globe, first amused him, then attracted him. He wanted to shake her out of aloofness into passion. He kissed her again and tried to slip her frock over her shoulder. Her body trembled and moved under her dress like a cat tied in a bag; suddenly she put her lips to him and kissed his chin. 'I do love you,' she said, 'I do.'

The sense of unfamiliarity deepened round him. It was as if he had started out from home on a familiar walk, past the gas works, across the brick bridge over the Wimble, across two fields, and found himself not in the lane which ran uphill to the new road and the bungalows, but on the threshold of a strange wood, faced by a shaded path he had never taken, running God knows where. He took his hands from her shoulders and said without touching her: 'How sweet you are,' and then with astonishment: 'How dear.' He had never before felt the lust rising in him checked and increasing because of the check; he had always spilt himself into new adventures with an easy excitement.

'What shall I do? Shall I take off my clothes?' He nodded, finding it hard to speak, and saw her rise from the berth and go into a corner and begin to undress slowly and very methodically, folding each garment in turn and laying it neatly on the opposite seat. He was conscious as he watched her calm movements of the inadequacy of his body. He said, 'You are lovely,' and his words stumbled with an unfamiliar excitement. When she came across the carriage he saw that he had been deceived; her calm was like a skin tightly drawn; her face was flushed with excitement and her eyes were scared; she looked uncertain whether to laugh or cry. They came together quite simply in the narrow space between the seats. 'I wish the light would go right out,' she said. She stood close against him while he touched her with his hands, both swaying easily to the motion of the train. 'No,' he said.

'It would be more becoming,' she said and began to laugh quietly to herself. Her laughter lay, an almost imperceptible pool of sound, beneath the pounding and the clatter of the express, but when they spoke, instead of whispering, they had to utter the intimate words loudly and clearly.

The sense of strangeness survived even the customary gestures; lying in the berth she proved awkward in a mysterious innocent fashion which astonished him. Her laughter stopped, not coming gradually to an end, but vanishing so that he wondered whether he had imagined the sound or whether it had been a trick of the glancing wheels. She said suddenly and urgently, 'Be patient, I don't know much,' and then she cried out with pain. He could not have been more startled if a ghost had passed through the compartment dressed in an antique wear which antedated steam. He would have left her if she had not held him to her with her hands, while she said in a voice of which snatches only escaped the sound of the engine, 'Don't go. I'm sorry. I didn't mean . . .' Then the sudden stopping of the train lurched them apart. 'What is it?' she said. 'A station.' She protested with pain, 'Why must it now?'

Myatt opened the window a little way and leant out. The dim chain of lights lit the ground for only a few feet beside the line. Snow already lay inches thick; somewhere in the distance a red spark shone intermittently, like a revolving light between the white gusts. 'It isn't a station,' he said. 'Only a signal against us.' The stilling of the wheels made the night very quiet with one whistle of steam to break it; here and there men woke and put their heads out of windows and spoke to each other. From the third-class carriages at the rear of the train came the sound of a fiddle. The tune was bare, witty, mathematical, but in its passage through the dark and over the snow it became less determinate, until it picked from Myatt's mind a trace of perplexity and regret: 'I never knew. I never guessed.' There was such warmth in the carriage now between them that, without closing the window, he knelt beside the berth and put his hand to her face, touching her features with curious fingers. Again he was overwhelmed with the novel thought, 'How sweet, how dear.' She lay quiet, shaken a little by quick breaths of pain or excitement.

Somebody in the third-class carriages began to curse the fiddler in German, saying that he could not sleep for the noise. It seemed not to occur to him that he had slept through the racket of the train, and that it was the silence surrounding the precise slow notes which woke him. The fiddler swore back and went on fiddling, and a number of people began to talk at once, and someone laughed.

'Were you disappointed?' she asked. 'Was I awfully bad at it?'

'You were lovely,' he said. 'But I never knew. Why did you agree?'

She said in a tone as light as the fiddle's, 'A girl's got to learn some time.' He touched her face again. 'I hurt you.'

'It wasn't a picnic,' she said.

'Next time,' he began to promise, but she interrupted with a question which made him laugh by its gravity: 'There'll be another time? Did I pass all right?'

'You want another time?'

'Yes,' she said, but she was thinking not of his embrace, but of the flat in Constantinople and her own bedroom and going to bed at ten. 'How long will you stay out there?'

'Perhaps a month. Perhaps longer.' She whispered with so much regret, 'So soon,' that he began to promise many things he knew very well he would regret in daylight. 'You can come back with me. I'll give you a flat in town.' Her silence seemed to emphasise the wildness of his promises. 'Don't you believe me?'

'Oh,' she said in a voice of absolute trust, 'it's too good to be true.'

He was touched by the complete absence of coquetry, and remembered again with sudden force that he had been her first lover. 'Listen,' he said, 'will you come again tomorrow?' She protested with real apprehension that he would tire of her before they reached Constantinople.

He ignored her objection. 'I'd give a party to celebrate.'

'Where? In Constantinople?'

'No,' he said, 'I've no one to invite there,' and for a moment the thought of Mr Eckman cast a shadow over his pleasure.

'What, in the train?' She began to laugh again, but this time in a contented and unfrightened way.

'Why not?' he became a little boastful. 'I'll invite everyone. It'll be a kind of wedding dinner.'

She teased him, 'Without the wedding,' but he became the more pleased with his idea. 'I'll invite everyone: the doctor, that person in the second class, the inquisitive fellow (do you remember him?)' He hesitated for a second. 'That girl.' 'What girl?' 'The niece of your friend.' But his grandiloquence was a little dashed by the thought that she would never accept his invitation; she is not a chorus girl, he thought with shame at his own ingratitude, she is not pretty and easy and common, she is beautiful, she is the kind of woman I should like to marry; and for a moment he contemplated with a touch of bitterness her inaccessibility. Then he recovered his spirits. 'I'll get the fiddler,' he boasted, 'to play to us while we eat.'

'You wouldn't dare to invite them,' she said with shining eyes.

'I will. They'll never refuse the kind of dinner I'll pay for. We'll have the best wine they can give us,' he said, making rapid calculations of cost and choosing to forget that a train reduces all wine to a common mediocrity. 'It'll cost two pounds a head.'

She beat her hands together in approval. 'You'll never dare to tell them the reason.'

He smiled at her. 'I'll tell them it's to drink the health of my mistress.' For a long time then she lay quiet, dwelling on the word and its suggestion of comfort and permanence, almost of respectability. Then she shook her head, 'It's too good to be true,' but her expression of disbelief was lost in the whistle of steam and the grinding of the wheels into motion.

While the couplings between the carriages strained and the signal burning a green light lurched slowly by, Josef Grünlich was saying, 'I am the President of the Republic.' He woke as a gentleman in a tailcoat was about to present him with a golden key to open the new city safe deposits; he woke at once to a full knowledge of his surroundings and to a full memory of his dream. Leaning his hands upon his fat knees he began to laugh. President of the Republic, that's good, and why not? I can spin a yarn all right. Kolber and that doctor both deceived in one day. Five English pounds he gave me, because I was sharp and spotted what he was when he said, 'Police spy.' Quick, that's Josef Grünlich all over. 'Look over there, Herr Kolber.' Flick at the string, aim, fire, all in one second. And I've got away with it too. They can't catch Josef. What was it the priest said? Josef began to laugh deep down in his belly. 'Do you play cricket in Germany?' And I said, 'No, they teach us to run. I was a great runner in my time.' That was quick if you like, and he never saw the joke, said something about 'Sobs and Hudglich'.

But it was a bad moment all the same, thought Josef, staring out into the falling snow, when the doctor spotted that his bag had been moved. I'd got my finger on the string. If he'd tried to call the guard I'd have shot him in the stomach before he could shout a word. Josef laughed again happily, feeling his revolver rub gently against the sore on the inside of his knee: I'd have spilt his guts for him.

PART IV

SUBOTICA

I

The telegraph receiving set in the station-master's office at Subotica flickered; dots and dashes were spilt into the empty room. Through the open door Lukitch, the clerk, sat in a corner of the parcels office and cursed the importunate sounds. But he made no effort to rise. 'It can't be important at this hour,' he explained to the parcels clerk and to Ninitch, a young man in a grey uniform, one of the frontier guards. He shuffled a pack of cards and at the same time the clock struck seven. Outside an indeterminate sun was breaking over grey half-melted snow, the wet rails glinted. Ninitch sipped his glass of *rakia*; the heavy plum wine brought tears to his eyes; he was very young.

Lukitch went on shuffling. 'What do you think it's all about?' asked the parcels clerk. Lukitch shook his grimy tousled head. 'One can't tell of course. But I shouldn't be surprised all the same. It will serve her right.' The parcels clerk began to giggle. Ninitch raised his dark eyes, that could contain no expression save simplicity, and asked: 'Who is she?' To his imagination the telegraph began to speak in an imperious feminine way.

'Ah, you soldiers,' said the parcels clerk. 'You don't know half of what goes on.'

'That's true,' Ninitch said. 'We stand about for hours at a time with our bayonets fixed. There's not going to be another war, is there? Up to the barracks and down to the station. We don't have time to see things.' Dot, dot, dot, dash, went the telegraph. Lukitch dealt the pack into three equal piles; the cards sometimes stuck together and he licked his fingers to separate them. He ranged the three piles side by side in front of him. 'It's probably the station-master's wife,' he explained. 'When she goes away for a week she sends him telegrams at the oddest times, every day. Late in the evening or early in the morning. Full of tender expressions. In rhyme sometimes: "Your little dove sends all her love", or "I think of you faithfully and ever so tenderly".'

'Why does she do it?' asked Ninitch.

'She's afraid he may have one of the servants in bed with him. She thinks he'll repent if he gets a telegram from her just at the moment.'

The parcels clerk giggled. 'And of course the funny part is, he wouldn't look at his servants. His inclinations, if she only knew it, are all the other way.'

'Your bets, gentlemen,' said Lukitch and he watched them narrowly, while they put copper coins on two of the piles of cards. Then he dealt out each pack in turn. In the third pack, on which no money had been placed, was the knave of diamonds. He stopped dealing and pocketed the coins. 'Bank wins,' he said, and passed the cards to Ninitch. It was a very simple game.

The parcels clerk stubbed out his cigarette and lit another, while Ninitch shuffled. 'Was there any news on the train?'

'Everything quiet in Belgrade,' said Lukitch.

'Is the telephone working?'

'Worse luck.' The telegraph had stopped buzzing, and Lukitch sighed with relief. 'That's over, anyway.'

The soldier suddenly stopped shuffling and said in a puzzled voice, 'I'm glad I wasn't in Belgrade.'

'Fighting, my boy,' said the parcels clerk hilariously.

'Yes,' said Ninitch shyly, 'but they were, weren't they, our own people? It was not as if they were Bulgars.'

'Kill or be killed,' said the parcels clerk. 'Come, deal away, Ninitch, my boy.'

Ninitch began to deal; several times he lost count of the cards; it was obvious that something was on his mind. 'And then, what did they want? What did they want to get by it all?'

'They were Reds,' said Lukitch.

'Poor people? Make your bets, gentlemen,' he added mechanically. Lukitch piled all the coppers he had won on the same heap as the parcels clerk; he caught the clerk's eye and winked; and the other man increased his bet. Ninitch was too absorbed in his slow clumsy thoughts to realise that he had shown the position of the knave when he dealt. The parcels clerk could not restrain a giggle. 'After all,' said Ninitch, 'I am poor, too.'

'We've made our bets,' said Lukitch impatiently, and Ninitch dealt out the cards. His eyes opened a little wider when he saw that both bets had been successful; for a moment a faint suspicion affected his manner; then he counted out the coins and rose. 'Are you going to stop?' asked Lukitch.

'Must be getting back to the guard-room.'

The parcels clerk grinned. 'He's lost all his money. Give him some more *rakia* before he goes, Lukitch.' Lukitch poured out another glass and stood with bottle tipped. The telephone-bell was ringing. 'The devil,' he said. 'It's that woman.' He put the bottle down and went into the other room. A pale sun slanted through the window and touched the crates and trunks piled behind the counter. Ninitch raised his glass, and the parcels clerk sat with one finger on the pack of cards listening. 'Hello, hello!' bellowed Lukitch in a rude voice. 'Who do you want? The telegraph? I've heard nothing. I can't hang over it the whole time. I've got a lot to do in this station. Tell the woman to send her telegrams at a reasonable hour. What's that?' His voice suddenly changed. 'I'm very sorry, sir. I never dreamed . . .' The parcels clerk giggled. 'Of course. Immediately, sir, immediately. I'll send at once, sir. If you would not mind holding the line for two minutes, sir . . .'

Ninitch sighed and went out into the bitter air of the small platformless station. He had forgotten to put on his gloves, and before he could huddle them on, his fingers were nipped by the cold. He dragged his feet slowly through the first half-melted and then half-frozen mud and snow. No, I am glad I was not in Belgrade, he thought. It was all very puzzling; they were poor and he was poor; they had wives and children; he had a wife and a small daughter; they must have expected to gain something by it, those Reds. The sun getting up above the roof of the customs-shed touched his face with the ghost of warmth; a stationary engine stood like a stray dog panting steam on the up-line. No train would be passing through to Belgrade before the Orient express was due; for half an hour there would be clamour and movement, the customs-officers would arrive and the guards be posted conspicuously outside the guard-room, then the train would steam out, and there would be only one more train, a small cross-country one to Vinkovce, that day. Ninitch buried his hands in his empty pockets: then would be the time for more *rakia* and another game of cards: but he had no money. Again a slight suspicion that he had been cheated touched his stubborn mind.

'Ninitch. Ninitch.' He looked round and saw the station-master's clerk plunging after him through the slush without overcoat or gloves. Ninitch thought: He has robbed me, his heart has been touched by God, he is going to make restitution. He stopped and smiled at Lukitch, as much as to say: Have no fear, I am not angry with you. 'You fool, I thought I should never make you hear,' said the clerk, panting at his side, small and grimy and ill-natured. 'Go at once to Major Petkovitch. He's wanted on the telephone. I can't make the guard-room answer.'

'The telephone went out of order last night,' Ninitch explained, 'while the snow fell.'

'Incompetence,' fumed the clerk.

'A man was coming from the town to see to it today.' He hesitated. 'The major won't come out in the snow. He has a fire in his room so high.'

'Fool. Imbecile,' said the clerk. 'It's the Chief of Police speaking from Belgrade. They were trying to send through a telegram, but you were talking so hard, how could anyone hear? Be off.' Ninitch began to walk on towards the guard-room, but the clerk screamed after him, 'Run, you fool, run.' Ninitch broke into a trot, handicapped by his heavy boots. It's curious, he thought, one's treated like a dog, but a moment later he thought: After all, it's good of them to play cards with me; they must earn in a day what I earn in a week; and they get paid, too, he said to himself, considering the deductions from his own pay for mess, for quarters, for fires. 'Is the major in?' he asked in the guard-room and then knocked timidly on the door. He should have passed the message through the serjeant, but the serjeant was not in the room, and in any case one never knew when an opportunity for special service might arise, and that might lead to promotion, more pay, more food, a new dress for his wife.

'Come in.'

Major Petkovitch sat at his desk facing the door. He was short, thin, sharp-featured, and wore pince-nez. There was probably some foreign blood in his family, for he was fair-haired. He was reading an out-of-date German book on strategy and feeding his dog with pieces of sausage. Ninitch stared with envy at the roaring fire. 'Well, what is it?' the major asked irritably, like a schoolmaster disturbed while going through his pupils' exercises.

'The Chief of Police has rung up, sir, and wants you on the telephone in the station-master's office.'

'Isn't our own telephone working?' the major asked, trying, not very successfully, as he laid down the book, to hide his curiosity and excitement; he wanted to give the impression of being on intimate terms with the Chief of Police.

'No, sir, the man hasn't come from the town yet.'

'How very trying. Where is the serjeant?'

'He's gone out for a moment, sir.'

Major Petkovitch plucked at his gloves and smoothed them. 'You had better come with me. I may need a messenger. Can you write?'

'A very little, sir,' Ninitch was afraid that the major would choose another messenger, but all he said was, 'Tut.' Ninitch and the dog followed at the major's heels across the guard-room and over the rails. In the station-master's office Lukitch was making a great show of work in a corner, while the parcels clerk hung round the door totting up entries on a folio sheet. 'The line is quite clear, sir,' said Lukitch and scowled at Ninitch behind the major's back; he envied his proximity to the instrument.

'Hello, hello, hello,' called Major Petkovitch acidly. The private soldier leant his head a little towards the telephone. Over the long miles between the frontier and Belgrade came the ghost of a cultured insolent voice with an intonation so clear that even Ninitch, standing two feet away from the instrument, could catch the measured syllables. They fell, like a succession of pins, into a deep silence: Lukitch and the parcels clerk held their breath in vain; the stationary engine across the track had stopped panting. 'Colonel Hartep speaking.' It is the Chief of Police, Ninitch thought, I have heard him speak: how proud my wife will be this evening: the story will go all round the barracks, trust her for that. She has not much reason to be proud of me, he considered simply, without self-depreciation, she makes the very most of what she has.

'Yes, yes, this is Major Petkovitch.'

The insolent voice was a little lowered; Ninitch caught the words only in snatches. 'On no account . . . Belgrade . . . search the train.'

'Should I take him to the barracks?'

The voice rose a little in emphasis. 'No. As few people must see him as possible. . . . On the spot.'

'But really,' Major Petkovitch protested, 'we haven't the accommodation here. What can we do with him?'

'. . . a few hours only.'

'By court-martial? It's very irregular.' The voice began to laugh gently. 'Myself . . . with you by lunch . . .'

'But in the event of an acquittal?'

'. . . myself,' said the voice indistinctly, 'you, Major, Captain Alexitch.' It fell lower still. 'Discreet . . . among friends,' and then more clearly, 'He may not be alone . . . suspects . . . any excuse . . . the customs. No fuss, mind.'

Major Petkovitch said in a tone of the deepest disapproval, 'Is there anything else, Colonel Hartep?' The voice became a little animated. 'Yes,

yes. About lunch. I suppose you haven't got much choice up there. . . . At the station . . . a good fire . . . something hot . . . cold things in the car and wine.' There was a pause. 'Remember, you're responsible.'

'For something so irregular,' began Major Petkovitch. 'No, no, no,' said the voice, 'I was referring, of course, to lunch.'

'Is everything quiet in Belgrade?' Major Petkovitch asked stiffly. 'Fast asleep,' the voice said.

'May I ask one more question?'

Major Petkovitch called, 'Hello. Hello. Hello,' in an irritated voice and then slammed down the receiver. 'Where's that man? Come with me,' and again followed by Ninitch and his dog he plunged into the cold, crossed the rails and the guard-room, and slammed the door of his room behind him. Then he wrote a number of notes very briefly and handed them to Ninitch for delivery: he was so hurried and irritated that he forgot to seal two of them. These, of course, Ninitch read; his wife would be proud of him that evening. There was one to the chief customs officer, but that was sealed; there was one to the captain at the barracks telling him to double the station guard immediately and to serve out twenty rounds of ammunition per man. It made Ninitch uneasy; did it mean war, that the Bulgars were coming? Or the Reds? He remembered what had happened at Belgrade and was very much disturbed. After all, he thought, they are our own people, they are poor, they have wives and children. Last of all there was a note for the cook at the barracks, containing detailed instructions for a lunch for three, to be served hot in the major's room at one-thirty; 'Remember, you're responsible,' it ended.

When Ninitch left the room, Major Petkovitch was again reading the out-of-date German book on strategy, while he fed his dog with pieces of sausage.

2

Coral Musker had fallen asleep long before the train reached Budapest. When Myatt drew a cramped arm from under her head, she woke to a grey morning like the swell of a leaden sea. She scrambled quickly from the berth and dressed; she was hurried and excited and she mislaid things. She began to sing light-heartedly under her breath: *I'm so happy, Happy-go-lucky me.* The motion of the train flung her against the window, but she gave the grey morning only a hurried glance. Lights came out here and there, one after the other, but there was not yet day enough to see the houses by; a lamp-lit bridge across the Danube gleamed like the buckle of a garter. *I just go my way, Singing every day.* Somewhere down by the river a white house glowed; it might have been mistaken for a tree trunk in an orchard, but for two lights in ground-floor rooms; as she watched, they were turned out. They've been celebrating late; she wondered, what's been going on there? and laughed a little, feeling herself at one with all daring, scandalous and youthful things.

Things that worry you Never worry me. Summer follows Spring. I just smile and . . . Quite dressed now except for her shoes, she turned towards the berth and Myatt.

He was uneasily asleep and needed a shave; he lay in rumpled clothes, and she could connect him with the excitement and pain of the night only with difficulty. This man was a stranger; he would disclaim responsibility for words spoken by an intruder in the dark. So much had been promised her. But she told herself that that kind of good fortune did not come her way. The words of elderly experienced women were brought again to mind: 'They'll promise anything beforehand,' and the strange moral code of her class warned her: 'You mustn't remind them.' Nevertheless she approached him and with her hand tried gently to arrange his hair into some semblance of her lover's. As she touched his forehead he woke, and she faced with courage the glance which she feared to see momentarily blank with ignorance of who she was and what they had done together. She fortified herself with maxims: 'There's as good fish in the sea,' but to her glad amazement he said at once without any struggle to remember, 'Yes, we must have the fiddler.'

She clapped her hands together in relief: 'And don't forget the doctor.' She sat down on the edge of the berth and slipped on her shoes. *I'm so happy.* He remembers, he's going to keep his promise. She began to sing again: *Living in the sunlight, loving in the moonlight, Having a wonderful time.* The guard came down the corridor knocking on the door: 'Budapest.' The lights were clustering together; above the opposite bank of the river, apparently dropped half-way from the heavy sky, shone three stars. 'What's that? There. It's going. Quick.'

'The castle,' he said.

'Budapest.' Josef Grünlich, nodding in his corner, started awake and went to the window. He had a flashing glimpse of water between tall grey houses, of lights burning in upper rooms, cut off abruptly by the arch of the station, and then the train slid to rest in a great echoing hall. Mr Opie at once emerged, brisk and cheerful and laden, dumping two suitcases upon the ground, and then a golf bag, and a tennis racket in its case. Josef grinned and blew out his chest; the sight of Mr Opie reminded him of his crime. A man in Cook's uniform came by leading a tall crumpled woman and her husband; they stumbled at his heels, bewildered, and unhappy through the whistling steam and the calling of strange tongues. It seemed to Josef that he might leave the train. Immediately, because this was something which concerned his safety, he ceased to think either humorously or grandiloquently; the small precise wheels of his brain went round and like the auditing machine in a bank began to record with unfailing accuracy the debits and credits. In a train he was virtually imprisoned; the police could arrange his arrest at any point of his journey; therefore the sooner he was at liberty the better. As an Austrian he would pass unnoticed in Budapest. If he continued his journey to Constantinople, he would run the risk of three more customs examinations. The automatic machine ran again through the figures, added, checked and passed on to the debit side. The police in Budapest were efficient. In the Balkan countries they were corrupt and there was nothing to fear from the customs. He was farther from the scene of his crime. He had friends in

Istanbul. Josef Grünlich decided to go on. The decision made, he again leant back in a dream of triumph; images of revolvers quickly drawn flashed through his mind, voices spoke of him: 'There's Josef. Five years now and never jugged. He killed Kolber at Vienna.'

'Budapest.' Dr Czinner ceased writing for a little more than a minute. That small pause was the tribute he paid to the city in which his father had been born. His father had left Hungary when a young man and settled in Dalmatia; in Hungary he had been a peasant, toiling on another man's land; in Split and eventually in Belgrade he had been a shoemaker working for himself; and yet the previous more servile existence, the inheritance of a Hungarian peasant's blood, represented to Dr Czinner the breath of a larger culture blowing down the dark stinking Balkan alleys. It was as if an Athenian slave, become a freed man in barbarian lands, regretted a little the statuary, the poetry, the philosophy of a culture in which he had had no share. The station began to float away from him; names slipped by in a language which his father had never taught him: 'Restoracioj', 'Pôsto', 'Informoj'. A poster flapped close to the carriage window: 'Teatnoj Kaj Amuzejoj', and mechanically he noted the unfamiliar names, the entertainments which would be just opening as the train arrived at Belgrade, the Opera, the Royal Orfeum, the Tabarin, and the Jardin de Paris. He remembered how his father had often commented, in the dark basement parlour behind his shop: 'They enjoy themselves in Buda.' His father, too, had once enjoyed himself in the city, pressing his face against the glass of restaurants, watching, without envy, the food carried to the tables, the fiddlers moving from group to group, making merry himself in a simple vicarious way. He had been angered by his father's easy satisfaction.

He wrote for ten minutes more and then folded the paper and slipped it into the pocket of his mackintosh. He wished to be prepared for any eventuality; his enemies he knew had no scruples; they would rather see him quickly murdered in a back street than alive in the dock. The strength of his position lay in their ignorance of his coming; he had to proclaim his voluntary presence in Belgrade before they knew that he was there, for then there could be no quick assassination of an unidentified stranger; they would have no choice but to put him upon his trial. He opened his suitcases and took out the Baedeker. Then he lit a match and held it to the corner of the map; the shiny paper burned slowly. The railway shot up in a little lick of flame, and he watched the post office square turn into tough black ash. Then the green of the park, the Kalimagdan, turned brown. The streets of the slum quarter were the last to burn, and he blew the flame to hasten it.

When the map was quite burned he threw the ash under the seat, put a bitter tablet on his tongue, and tried to sleep. He found it difficult. He was a man without humour or he would have smiled at the sudden lightness of his heart, as he recognised, fifty miles beyond Buda, a sudden break in the gre Danube plain, a hill shaped like a thimble and shaggy with fir trees. A made a great circle to avoid it and then shot straight towards the cʲ and hill were both white now under the snow, which hung in

great lumps like the nests of rooks. He remembered the road and the hill and
the wood because they were the first things he had noted with a sense of full
security after escaping across the frontier five years before. His companion
who drove the car had broken silence for the first time since they left
Belgrade and called to him: 'We shall be in Buda in an hour and a quarter.'
Dr Czinner had not realised till then that he was safe. Now his lightness of
heart had opposite cause. He thought not that he was only fifty miles from
Budapest, but that he was only seventy miles from the frontier. He was
nearly home. Instinct for the moment was stronger in him than opinion. It
was no use telling himself that he had no home and that his destination was a
prison; for that one moment of light-hearted enjoyment it was to Kruger's
beer-garden, to the park at evening swimming in green light, to the steep
streets and the bright rags that he was journeying. After all, he told himself, I
shall see all this again; they'll drive me from the prison to the court. It was
then that he remembered with unreasoning melancholy that the beer-garden
had been turned into flats.

Across the breakfast table Coral and Myatt faced each other with
immeasurable relief as strangers. At dinner they had been old friends with
nothing to say to one another. All through breakfast they talked fast and
continuously as if the train was consuming time, not miles, and they had to
fill the hours with talk sufficient for a life together.

'And when I get to Constantinople, what shall I do? My room's been
booked.'

'Never mind that. I've taken a room at an hotel. You'll come with me and
we'll make it a double room.'

She accepted his solution with breathless pleasure, but there was no time
for silence, for sitting back. Rocks, houses, bare pastures were receding at
fifty miles an hour, and there was much to be said. 'We get in at breakfast
time, don't we? What shall we do all day?'

'We'll have lunch together. In the afternoon I'll have to go to the office
and see to things there. You can go shopping. I'll be back in the evening and
we'll have dinner and go to the theatre.'

'Yes, and what theatre?' It was extraordinary to her, the transformation
which the night had caused. His face no longer resembled that of all the
Jewish boys she had known with half intimacy; even the gesture with which
he gave and gave, the instinctive spreading of the hands, was different; his
emphasis on how much he would spend, on what a good time he would give
her, was unique because she believed him.

'We'll have the best seats at your theatre.'

'Dunn's Babies?'

'Yes, and we'll take them all out to dinner afterwards, if you like.'

'No.' She shook her head; she could not risk losing him now, and many
of Dunn's Babies would be prettier than she. 'Let's go back to bed after
the theatre.' They began to laugh over their coffee, spilling brown drops
upon the tablecloth. There was no apprehension in her laugh; she was
happy because pain was behind her. 'Do you know how long we've sat at
breakfast?' she asked. 'A whole hour. It's a scandal. I've never done it
~re. A cup of tea in bed at ten o'clock is my breakfast. And two pieces

of toast and some orange juice if I've got a nice landlady.'

'And when you haven't any work?'

She laughed. 'I leave out the orange juice. Are we near the frontier now?'

'Very near.' Myatt lit a cigarette. 'Smoke?'

'Not in the morning. I'll leave you to it.' She got up and at the same moment the train ground across a point and she was flung against him. She caught his arm to steady herself and over his shoulder saw a signal-box sway dizzily out of sight and a black shed against which the snow had drifted. She held his arm a moment till her giddiness passed. 'Darling, come soon. I'll be waiting for you.' Suddenly she wanted to say to him, 'Come now.' She felt afraid at being left alone when the train was in a station. Strangers might come in and take his seat, and she would be unable to make them understand. She would not know what the customs men said to her. But she told herself that he would soon tire if she made demands on him; it wasn't safe to trouble a man; her happiness was not so secure that she dared take the smallest risk with it. She looked back; he sat with head a little bent, caressing with his fingers a gold cigarette-case. She was glad later that she had taken that last glance, it was to serve as an emblem of fidelity, an image to carry with her, so that she might explain, 'I've never left you.'

The train stopped as she reached her seat, and she looked out of the window at a small muddy station. Subotica was printed in black letters on a couple of lamps; the station buildings were little more than a row of sheds, and there was a platform. A group of customs-officers in green uniforms came down between the lines with half a dozen soldiers; they seemed in no hurry to begin their search. They laughed and talked and went on towards the guard's van. A row of peasants stood watching the train, and one woman suckled a child. There were a good many soldiers about with nothing to do; one of them shooed the peasants off the rails, but they scrambled over them again twenty yards down the line. The passengers began to grow impatient; the train was half an hour late already, and no attempt had yet been made to search the luggage or examine the passports. Several people climbed on to the line and crossed the rails in hope of finding a refreshment-room; a tall thin German with a bullet head walked up and down, up and down. Coral Musker saw the doctor leave the train, wearing his soft hat and mackintosh and a pair of grey wool gloves. He and the German passed and repassed and passed again, but they might have been walking in different worlds for all the notice they took of each other. Once they stood side by side while an official looked at their passports, but they still belonged to different worlds, the German was fuming and impatient, and the doctor was smiling to himself.

When she came near him she could see the quality of his smile, vacuous and sentimental. It seemed out of place. 'Excuse me speaking to you,' she said humbly, a little frightened by his stiff respectful manner. He bowed and put his grey gloved hands behind him; she caught a glimpse of a hole in the thumb. 'I was wondering ... we were wondering ... if you would have dinner with us tonight.' The smile had been tidied away, and she saw him gathering together a forbidding weight of words. She explained, 'You have been so kind to me.' It was very cold in the open air and they both began to walk; the frozen mud crackled round the tops of her shoes and marked her stockings. 'It would have given me great pleasure,' he said, marshalling his words with terrible correctness, 'and it is my sorrow that I cannot accept. I am leaving the train tonight at Belgrade. I should have enjoyed . . .' He stopped in his stride with creased brows and seemed to forget what he was saying; he put the hand in the worn glove into his mackintosh pocket. 'I should have enjoyed . . .' Two men in uniform were walking up the line towards them.

The doctor put his hand on her arm and swung her gently round, and they began to walk back along the train. He was still frowning and he never finished his sentence. Instead, he began another, 'I wonder if you would mind–my glasses are frosted over–what do you see in front of us?'

'There are a few customs-officers coming down from the guard's van to meet us.'

'Is that all? In green uniform?'

'No, in grey.'

The doctor stopped. 'So?' He took her hand in his, and she felt an envelope folded into her palm. 'Go quickly back to your carriage. Hide this. When you get to Istanbul post it. Go now quickly. But don't seem in a hurry.' She obeyed without understanding him; twenty steps brought her up to the men in grey and she saw that they were soldiers; they carried no rifles, but she guessed it by their bayonet sheaths. They barred her way, and for a moment she thought they would stop her; they were talking rapidly among themselves, but when she came within a few feet of them, one man stepped aside to let her by. She was relieved but still a little frightened, feeling the letter folded in her hand. Was she being made to smuggle something? A drug? Then one of the soldiers came after her; she heard his boots cracking the mud; she reassured herself that she was imagining things, that if he wanted her he would call, and his silence encouraged her. Nevertheless, she walked more rapidly. Her compartment was only one carriage away, and her lover would be able to explain in German to the man who she was. But Myatt was not in the compartment; he was still smoking in the restaurant. For a second she hesitated. I will go to the restaurant and tap on the window, but her second's hesitation had been too long. A hand touched her elbow, and a voice said something to her gently in a foreign tongue.

She swung round to protest, to implore, ready, if need be, to break away and run to the restaurant-car, but her fears were a little quietened by the soldier's large gentle eyes. He smiled at her and nodded his head and pointed to the station buildings. She said, 'What do you want? Can't you speak English?' He shook his head and smiled again and pointed, and she saw the doctor meet the soldiers and walk with them towards the buildings. There could be nothing wrong, he was walking in front of them, they were not using force. The soldier nodded and smiled and then with a great effort brought out three words of English. 'All quite good,' he said and pointed again to the buildings.

'Can I just tell my friend?' she asked. He nodded and smiled and took her arm, leading her gently away from the train.

The waiting-room was empty except for the doctor. A stove burnt in the middle of the floor, and the view from the windows was broken by lines of frost. She was conscious all the while of the letter in her hand. The soldier ushered her in gently and politely and then closed the door without locking it. 'What do they want?' she asked. 'I mustn't miss the train.'

'Don't be frightened,' he said. 'I'll explain to them; they'll let you go in five minutes. You must let them search you if they want to. Have they taken the letter?'

'No.'

'Better give it to me. I don't want to get you into trouble.' She held out her hand and at the same moment the door opened. The soldier came in and smiled encouragingly and took the letter from her. Dr Czinner spoke to him, and the man talked rapidly; he had simple unhappy eyes. When he had gone again Dr Czinner said, 'He doesn't like it. He was told to look through the keyhole and see if anything passed between us.'

Coral Musker sat down on a wooden seat and stuck her feet out towards the stove. Dr Czinner noted with amazement, 'You are very calm.'

'It's no use getting shirty,' she said. 'They can't understand, anyway. My friend'll be looking for me soon.'

'That's true,' he said with relief. He hesitated for a moment. 'You must wonder why I do not apologise to you for this—discomfort. You see there's something I hold more important than any discomfort. I expect you don't understand.'

'Don't I, though,' she said, thinking with wry humour of the night. A long whistle shivered through the cold air and she sprang up apprehensively. 'That's not our train, is it? I can't miss it.' Dr Czinner was at the window. He freed the inner surface from steam with the palm of his hand and peered between the ridges of frost. 'No,' he said, 'it's an engine on the other line. I think they are changing engines. It will take them a long time. Don't be frightened.'

'Oh, I'm not scared,' she said, settling herself again on the hard seat. 'My friend'll be along soon. *They'll* be scared then. He's rich, you know.'

'So?' said Dr Czinner.

'Yes, and important too. He's the head of a firm. They do something with currants.' She began to laugh. 'He told me to think of him when I eat spotted dog.'

'So?'

'Yes. I like him. He's been sweet to me. He's quite different from other Jews. They're generally kind, but he—well, he's quiet.'

'I think that he must be a very lucky young man,' said Dr Czinner. The door was opened and two soldiers pushed a man in. Dr Czinner moved quickly forward and put his foot in the door. He spoke to them softly. One of them replied, the other thrust him back and closed and locked the door. 'I asked them,' he said, 'why they were keeping you here. I told you must catch the train. One of them said it was quite all right. An officer wants to ask you a question or two. The train doesn't go for half an hour.'

'Thank you,' Coral said.

'And me?' said the newcomer in a furious voice. 'And me?'

'I know nothing about you, Herr Grünlich.'

'The customs they came and they search me. They take my cannon. They say: "Why haven't you declared that you keep a cannon in possession?" I say: "No one would travel in your country without a cannon."' Coral Musker began to laugh: Josef Grünlich glared at her wickedly, then he smoothed his rumpled waistcoat, glanced at his watch, and sat down. With his hands on his fat knees he stared straight in front of him, considering.

He must have finished his cigarette by now, Coral thought. He'll have gone back to the compartment and found I'm not there. Perhaps he'll wait ten minutes before he asks one of the men at the station whether they've seen me. In twelve minutes he'll have found me. Her heart leapt when a key turned in the lock, wondering at the speed with which he had traced her, but it was not Myatt who entered, but a fair fussed officer. He snapped an order over his shoulder and two soldiers came in behind him and stood against the door.

'But what's it all about?' Coral asked Dr Czinner. 'Do they think we've smuggled something?' She could not understand what the foreigners said to each other, and suddenly she felt lost and afraid, knowing that however much these men might wish to help her, they could not understand what she said or what she wanted. She implored Dr Czinner, 'Tell them I must catch this train. Ask them to tell my friend.' He took no notice, but stood stiffly by the stove with his hands in his pockets answering questions. She turned to the German in the corner, staring at the toes of his shoes. 'Tell them that I've done nothing, please.' He raised his eyes for a moment and looked at her with hatred.

At last Dr Czinner said, 'I have tried to explain that you know nothing of the note I passed you. But he says he must keep you a little longer until the Chief of Police has questioned you.'

'But the train?' she implored, 'the train?'

'I think it will be all right. It will be here for another half an hour. I have asked him to let your friend know and he says that he will see what can be done.' She went to the officer and touched his arm. 'I must go by this train,' she said, 'I must. Do understand me, please.' He shook his arm free, and rebuked her in a sharp precise tone, his pince-nez nodding, but what the terms of the rebuke were she could not tell. Then he left the waiting-room.

Coral pressed her face to the window. Between two fronds of frost the German passed, walking up and down the track; she tried to see as far as the restaurant-car. 'Is he in sight?' Dr Czinner asked.

'It's going to snow again,' she said, and left the window. Suddenly she could bear her perplexity no longer. 'Why do they want me? What are they keeping me here for?'

He assured her, 'It's a mistake. They are frightened. There has been rioting in Belgrade. They want me, that's all.'

'But why? You're English, aren't you?'

'No, I'm one of them,' he said with some bitterness.

'What have you done?'

'I've tried to make things different.' He explained with an air of distaste for labels: 'I am a Communist.'

At once she exclaimed, 'Why? Why?' watching him fearfully, unable to hide that she felt her faith shaken in the only man, except Myatt, able and willing to help her. Even the kindness he had shown her on the train she now regarded with suspicion. She went to the bench and sat down as far as she could from the German.

'It would take a long time to tell you why,' he said. She took no notice, shutting her mind to the meaning of any words he uttered. She thought of him now as one of the untidy men who paraded on Saturday afternoons in Trafalgar Square bearing hideous banners: 'Workers of the World, Unite', 'Walthamstow Old Comrades', 'Balham Branch of the Juvenile Workers' League'. They were the kill-joys, who would hang the rich and close the theatres and drive her into dismal free love at a summer camp, and afterwards make her walk in procession down Oxford Street, carrying her baby behind a banner: 'British Women Workers'.

'Longer than I've got,' he said.

She took no notice. She was, for the moment in her thoughts, immeasurably above him. She was a rich man's mistress, and he was a workman. When she at last took notice of him it was with contempt: 'I suppose you'll go to gaol.'

'I think they'll shoot me,' he said.

She stared at him in amazement, forgetting their difference in class: 'Why?' He smiled with a touch of conceit: 'They're afraid.'

'In England,' she said, 'they let the Reds speak as much as they like. The police stand round.'

'Ah, but there's a difference. We do more than speak.'

'But there'll be a trial?'

'A sort of trial. They'll take me to Belgrade.'

Somewhere a horn was blowing, and the cold air was split by a whistle. 'They must be shunting,' Dr Czinner said to reassure her. A film of smoke was blown across the windows, darkening the waiting-room, and voices called and feet began to run along the track outside. Links between coaches groaned and pushed and strained, and then the thin walls shook to the grinding of pistons, the beat of heavy wheels. When the smoke cleared, Coral Musker sat quite still on the wooden bench. There was nothing to be said and her feet were stone cold. But after a while she began to read in Dr Czinner's silence an accusation, and she spoke with warmth, 'He'll come back for me,' she said. 'You wait and see.'

Ninitch let his rifle fall into the crook of his arm and beat his gloved hands together. 'That new engine's noisy,' he said, as he watched the train stretch like elastic round a bend and disappear. The points groaned back into place, and the signal on the passenger up-line rose. A man came down the steps from the box, crossed the line and disappeared in the direction of a cottage.

'Gone for lunch,' Ninitch's companion said enviously.

'I've never heard an engine as noisy as that,' Ninitch said, 'all the time I've been here.' Then his companion's remark reached him. 'The major's having a hot meal down from the barracks,' he said. But he did not tell his friend that the Chief of Police was coming from Belgrade; he kept the news for his wife.

'You are a lucky one,' his companion said. 'You'll be having a meal all right. I've often thought it must be good to be married when I see your wife come down of a morning.'

'It's not too bad,' said Ninitch modestly.

'Tell me, what does she bring you?'

'A loaf of bread and a piece of sausage. Sometimes a bit of butter. She's a good girl.' But his thoughts were not so temperate. *I am not good enough for her; I should like to be rich and give her a dress and a necklace and take her to Belgrade to the theatre.* He thought at first with envy of the foreign girl locked in the waiting-room, of her clothes which seemed to him very costly and of her green glass necklace, but in comparing her with his wife he soon forgot his envy and began to regard the foreigner, too, with affection. The beauty and fragility of women struck him with pathos, as he beat his great clumsy hands together.

'Wake up,' his friend whispered, and both men straightened and stood 'at ease' in a stiff attitude as a car plunged up the road to the station, breaking through the frozen surface and scattering water. 'Who the devil?' his friend whispered, hardly moving his lips, but Ninitch proudly knew; he knew that the tall ribboned officer was the Chief of Police, he even knew the name of the other officer who bounded out of the car like a rubber ball and held the door open for Colonel Hartep to alight.

'What a place,' said Colonel Hartep with amused distaste, looking first at the mud and then at his polished boots.

Captain Alexitch blew out his round red cheeks. 'They might have laid some boards.'

'No, no, we are the police. They don't like us. God knows what sort of a lunch they'll give us. Here, my man,' he beckoned to Ninitch, 'help the chauffeur out with these cases. Be careful to keep the wine steady and upright.'

'Major Petkovitch, sir . . .'

'Never mind Major Petkovitch.'

'Excuse me,' said a precise angry voice behind Ninitch.

'Certainly, Major,' Colonel Hartep smiled and bowed, 'but I am sure that there is no need to excuse you.'

'This man is on guard over the prisoners.'

'You have captured a number of them. I congratulate you.'

'Two men and a girl.'

'In that case I should imagine a good lock, a guard, a bayonet, a rifle, and twenty rounds of ammunition will meet the case.'

Major Petkovitch licked his lips. 'The police, of course, know best how to guard a prison. I bow to superior knowledge. Take the things out of the car,' he said to Ninitch, 'and bring them to my room.' He led the officers round the corner of the waiting-room and out of sight. Ninitch stared after them, until the chauffeur called out to him, 'I can't wait here in the car all day. Look lively. You soldiers aren't used to a spot of work.' He began to take the boxes out of the car, telling over their contents as he did so: 'A half case of champagne. A cold duck. Fruit. Two bottles of sherry. Sausage. Wine biscuits. Lettuce. Olives.'

'Well,' Ninitch's friend called out, 'is it a good meal?'

Ninitch stood and stared for a moment in silence. Then he said in a low voice, 'It's a feast.'

He had carried the sherry and champagne and the duck to the major's room when he saw his wife coming up the road bringing his own lunch wrapped in a white cloth. She was small and dark with her shawl twisted tightly round her shoulders; she had a malicious humorous face and big boots. He put down the case of fruit and went to meet her. 'I shall not be long,' he told her in a low voice, so that the chauffeur might not hear. 'Wait for me. I've something to tell you,' and very seriously he went back to his task. His wife sat down by the side of the road and watched him, but when he came back from the major's office, where the table was already spread and the officers were making headway with the wine, she was gone. She had left his lunch by the side of the road. 'Where is she?' he asked the other guard.

'She talked to the chauffeur and then she went back to the barracks. She seemed excited about something.'

Ninitch suffered a pang of disappointment. He had looked forward to telling his wife the story of Colonel Hartep's coming, and now the chauffeur had anticipated him. It was always the same. A soldier's life was a dog's life. It was the civilians who got high wages and robbed the soldiers at cards and abused them and even interfered between a soldier and his wife. But his resentment was brief. There were secrets he could yet discover for his wife, if he kept ears and eyes open. He waited for some time before he carried the last case to the major's room. The champagne was bubbling low; all three men spoke at once, and Major Petkovitch's glasses had fallen in his lap. 'Such bobbles,' Captain Alexitch was saying, 'such thighs. I said to His Excellency if I was in your place . . .' Major Petkovitch drew lines on the tablecloth with a finger dipped in wine. 'The first maxim is, never strike at the wings. Crumple the centre.' Colonel Hartep was quite sober. He leant back in his chair smoking. 'Take just a trifle of French mustard; two sprigs of parsley,' but neither of his juniors paid him any attention. He smiled gently and filled their glasses.

The snow was falling again, and through the wind-blown drifts Dr Czinner saw the peasants of Subotica straggling across the line, thrusting their inquisitive twisted bodies towards the waiting-room. One man got close enough to the window to stare in and examine the doctor's face. They were separated by a few feet and a sheet of glass and the lines of frost and the vapour of their breath. Dr Czinner could count his wrinkles, name the colour of his eyes and examine with brief professional interest a sore upon his cheek. But always the peasants were driven back by the two soldiers, who struck at them with the butts of their rifles. The peasants gave way and moved on to the line, but presently they swarmed back, obstinate, stupid and hopeless.

There had been silence in the waiting-room for a very long while. Dr Czinner went back to the stove. The girl sat with her thumbs joined and her head a little bent. He knew what she was doing; she was praying that her lover would come back for her soon, and from her secrecy he guessed that she was not accustomed to prayer. She was very frightened, and with a cold sympathy he was able to judge the measure of her fear. His experience told him two things, that prayers were not answered and that so casual a lover would not trouble to return.

He was sorry that he had involved her, but he regretted it only as he might have regretted a necessary lie. He had always recognised the need of sacrificing his own integrity; only a party in power could possess scruples;

scruples in himself would be a confession that he doubted the overwhelming value of his cause. But the reflection for some reason made him bitter; he found himself envying virtues which he was not rich or strong enough to cherish. He would have welcomed generosity, charity, meticulous codes of honour to his breast if he could have succeeded, if the world had been shaped again to the pattern he loved and longed for. He spoke to her angrily: 'You are lucky to believe that that will do good,' but he found to his amazement that she could instinctively outbid his bitterness, which was founded on theories laboriously worked out by a fallible reason. 'I don't,' she said, 'but one must do something.'

He was shocked by the ease of her disbelief, which did not come from the painful reading of rationalist writers and nineteenth-century scientists, she had been born to disbelief as securely as he had been born to belief. He had sacrificed security in order to reach the same position, and for a moment he longed to sow in her some dry plant of doubt, a half-belief which would make her mistrust her judgment. He allowed the inclination to pass and encouraged her. 'He'll come back for you from Belgrade.'

'Perhaps he can't afford the time.'

'He'll telegraph to the British Consul.'

She said, 'Of course,' without conviction. The events of the night, the experience of Myatt's tenderness, swam back from her, like a lit pier, into darkness. She strained her memory in the effort to recover sight of him, but he soon became an indistinguishable member of a crowd gathered to say good-bye. It was not long before she began to question his difference from all the other Jews she had known. Even her body, rested now and healed, but the deep peace gone with the pain, was aware of no difference. She repeated, 'Of course,' because she was ashamed at her lack of faith, because it was no use grumbling anyway, because at any rate she was no worse off except for being a day late for the show. There's as good fish in the sea, she told herself, but feeling none the less strangely tied to a memory which lacked all conviction.

The German sat bolt upright in his corner, sleeping; his eyelids twitched, ready to rise at the least unfamiliar sound. He was accustomed to rest in strange places and to take advantage of any respite. When the door opened, his eyes were at once attentive.

A guard entered and waved his hand at them and shouted. Dr Czinner repeated what he said in English. 'We are to come out.' The snow blew in at the open door, making a grey tidemark on the threshold. They could see the peasants huddled on the line. Josef Grünlich stood up and smoothed his waistcoat, and pressed his elbow in Dr Czinner's side. 'If we runned now, eh, through the snow, all together?' 'They would shoot,' Dr Czinner said. The guard shouted again and waved his hand. 'But they shoot anyway, eh? What do they want outside?'

Dr Czinner turned to Coral Musker. 'I don't think there's anything to fear. Are you coming?'

'Of course.' Then she implored him, 'Wait one moment for me. I've lost my handkerchief.' The tall thin form bent like a pair of grey compasses, went down on the knees and fetched it from beneath the seat. His awkwardness made her smile; she forgot her distrust and thanked him with disproportionate gratitude. Outside he walked with bent head to avoid the snow, smiling to himself. One guard led them and one walked behind with his rifle unslung and his bayonet fixed. They called to each other in a language she could not understand over the prisoner's heads, and she was being taken she did not know where. There was a scramble and splashing of feet over the rails and the mud as the peasants came nearer, hungry for a sight of them, and she was a little daunted by the olive faces and her own ignorance of what it was all about. She asked Dr Czinner, 'Why are you smiling?' and hoped to hear that he had seen a way to release them all, to catch the express, to put back the hands of the clock. He said, 'I don't know. Was I smiling? It is perhaps because I am home again.' For a moment his mouth was serious, then it fell again into a loose smile, and his eyes as they peered this way and that through his frosted glasses seemed moist and empty of anything but a kind of stupid happiness.

3

Myatt, with his eye on the lengthening ash of his cigar, thought. These were the moments he cherished, when he felt alone with himself and feared no rebuff, when his body was satisfied and his emotions stilled. The night before he had tried in vain to work; the girl's face had come between him and the figures; now she was relegated to her proper place. Presently, as evening came on, he might need her and she would be there, and at the thought he felt tenderness and even gratitude, not least because her physical presence gone, she had left no importunate ghost. He could remember now without looking at his papers the figures he had been unable to arrange. He multiplied, divided, subtracted, seeing the long columns arrange themselves down the window, across which the transparent bodies of customs-officials and porters passed unnoticed. Presently somebody asked to see his passport, and then the ash fell from his cigar and he went back to his compartment to open his luggage. Coral was not there, but he supposed that she was in the lavatory. The customs-officer tapped her bag. 'And this?'

'It's unlocked,' he said. 'The lady is not here. You will find nothing.' When he was alone again he lay back in his corner and closed his eyes, the better to consider the affairs of Mr Eckman, but by the time the train drew out of Subotica he was asleep. He dreamed that he was mounting the stairs to Mr Eckman's office. Narrow, uncarpeted and unlit, they might have led to a disreputable flat off Leicester Square, instead of to the headquarters of the biggest currant importers in Europe. He did not remember passing through the door; the next moment he was sitting face to face with Mr Eckman. A great pile of papers lay between them and Mr Eckman stroked his dark moustache and tapped the desk with his fountain-pen, while a spider drew the veins of its web across a dry ink-well. The electric light was dim and the window was sooty and in the corner Mrs Eckman sat on a steel sofa knitting baby clothes.

'I admit everything,' said Mr Eckman. Suddenly his chair rose, until he sat high overhead, tapping with an auctioneer's hammer. 'Answer me these questions,' said Mr Eckman. 'You are on oath. Don't prevaricate. Say yes or no. Did you seduce the girl?'

'In a way.'

Mr Eckman drew a sheet of paper from the middle of the pile, and another and another, till the pile tottered and fell to the floor with the noise of falling bricks. 'This affair of Jervis. Slim work I call it. You had contracted with the trustees and had only delayed to sign.'

'It was legal.'

'And this £10,000 to Stavrog when you'd already had an offer of £15,000.'

'It's business.'

'And the girl on the Spaniards Road.

'And the £1,000 to Moults' clerk for information.

'What have I done that you haven't done? Answer me quick. Don't prevaricate. Say yes or no. My lord and gentlemen of the jury, the prisoner at the bar . . .'

'I want to speak. I've got something to say. I'm not guilty.'

'Under what clause? What code? Law of Equity? Law of Tithes? Admiralty Court or the King's Bench? Answer me quick. Don't prevaricate. Say yes or no. Three strokes of the hammer. Going, going. This fine flourishing business, gentlemen.'

'Wait a moment. I'll tell you. George. Cap. III. Section 4. Vic. 2504. Honour among Thieves.'

Mr Eckman, suddenly very small in the dingy office, began to weep, stretching out his hands. And all the washerwomen who paddled in the stream knee-deep lifted up their heads and wept, while a dry wind tore up the sand from the sea-beaches and flung it rattling against the leaves of the forest, and a voice which might have been Mrs Eckman's implored him over and over again, 'Come back.' Then the desert shook under his feet and he opened his eyes. The train had stopped, and the snow was caking on the glass of the window. Coral had not returned.

Presently somebody at the back of the train began to laugh and jeer, and others joined in, whistling and catcalling. Myatt looked at his watch. He had slept for more than two hours, and perhaps because he remembered the voice in his dream, he felt uneasy at Coral's absence. Smoke poured from the engine and a man in dungarees with a blackened face stood apart from it, gazing hopelessly. Several people called to him from the third class and he turned and shook his head and shrugged in a graceful bewildered way. The *chef de train* walked rapidly down the track away from the engine. Myatt stopped him. 'What has happened?'

'Nothing. Nothing at all. A little defect.'

'Are we stuck here for long?'

'Oh, a mere trifle. An hour, an hour and a half perhaps. We are telephoning for a new engine.'

Myatt closed the window and went into the corridor; there was no sign of Coral. He passed down the whole length of the train, looking into compartments, trying the doors of lavatories until he reached the third class. There he remembered the man with the violin and sought him through the hard wooden odorous compartments, until he ran him to earth, a small pinched fellow with a swollen eye.

'I am giving a dinner tonight,' Myatt said to him in German, 'and I want you to play for me. I'll give you fifty paras.'

'Seventy-five, your excellency.'

Myatt was hurried; he wanted to find Coral. 'Seventy-five, then.'

'Something dreamy, melancholy, to bring tears, your excellency?'

'Of course not. I want something light and cheerful.'

'Ah, well, of course? That is more expensive.'

'What do you mean? Why more expensive?'

His excellency, of course, was a foreigner. He did not understand. It was the custom of the country to charge more for light songs than for melancholy. Oh, an age-old custom. One and a half dinas?—Suddenly, dispelling his impatience and his anxiety, the joy of bargaining gripped Myatt. The money was nothing; there was less than half a crown at stake, but this was business; he would not give in. 'Seventy-five paras. Not a para more.'

The man grinned at him with pleasure: this was a stranger after his own heart. 'One dina thirty paras. It is my last word, your excellency. I should disgrace my profession if I accepted less.' The odour of stale bread and sour wine no longer disturbed Myatt; it was the smell of the ancestral market-place. This was the pure poetry of business: gain and loss hardly entered into a transaction fought out in paras, each of which was worth less than a farthing. He came a little way into the carriage, but he did not sit down. 'Eighty paras.'

'Your excellency, one must live. One dina twenty-five. It would shame me to take less.'

Myatt offered the man a cigarette. 'A glass of *rakia*, your excellency?' Myatt nodded and took without distaste the thick chipped tumbler. 'Eighty-five paras. Take it or leave it.' Smoking and drinking together in a close understanding they grew fierce with each other. 'You insult me, your excellency. I am a musician.'

'Eight-seven paras, that is my last word.'

The three officers sat round the table, which had been cleared of the glasses. Two soldiers stood before the door with fixed bayonets. Dr Czinner watched Colonel Hartep with curiosity; he had last seen him at the Kamnetz trial marshalling his lying witnesses with a graceful disregard of justice. That was five years ago, but the years had done little to alter his appearance. His hair was a fine silver above his ears and there were a few kindly wrinkles at the corners of his eyes. 'Major Petkovitch,' he said, 'will you read the charge against the prisoners? Let the lady have a chair.'

Dr Czinner took his hands from the pockets of his mackintosh and wiped his glasses. He could keep emotion from his voice, but not from his hands, which trembled a little. 'A charge?' he said. 'What do you mean? Is this a court?'

Major Petkovitch, paper in hand, snapped at him, 'Be quiet.'

'It's a reasonable question, Major,' said Colonel Hartep. 'The doctor has been abroad. You see,' he said, speaking gently and with great kindness, 'measures have had to be taken for your safety. Your life would not be safe in Belgrade. People are angry about the rising.'

'I still don't understand your right,' Dr Czinner said, 'to make more than a preliminary inquiry.'

Colonel Hartep explained. 'This is a court martial. Martial Law was proclaimed early yesterday morning. Now, Major Petkovitch.'

Major Petkovitch began to read a long document in a manuscript which he found often illegible. 'The prisoner, Richard Czinner . . . conspiracy against the Government . . . unserved sentence for perjury . . . false passport. The prisoner, Josef Grünlich, found in possession of arms. The prisoner, Coral Musker, conspiracy with Richard Czinner, against the Government.' He laid the paper down and said to Colonel Hartep, 'I am uncertain of the legality of this court as it stands. The prisoners should be represented by counsel.'

'Dear, dear, that is certainly an oversight. Perhaps you, Major . . . ?'

'No. The court must consist of not less than three officers.'

Dr Czinner interrupted. 'Don't trouble yourselves. I will do without counsel. These others cannot understand a word of what you say. They won't object.'

'It's irregular,' said Major Petkovitch. The Chief of Police looked at his watch. 'I have noted your protest, Major. Now we can begin.' The fat officer hiccuped, put his hand to his mouth, and winked.

'Ninety paras.'

'One dina.'

Myatt stubbed out his cigarette. He had played the game long enough. 'One dina, then. Tonight at nine.' He walked rapidly back to his compartment, but Coral was not there. Passengers were scrambling from the train, talking and laughing and stretching their arms. The engine-driver was the centre of a small crowd to whom he was explaining the breakdown with humour. Although there was no house in sight two or three villagers had already appeared and were offering for sale bottled mineral waters and sweets on the end of sticks. The road ran parallel to the line, separated only by a ridge of snow; the driver of a motor-car honked his horn and shouted again and again. 'Quick car to Belgrade. A hundred and twenty dinas. Quick car to Belgrade.' It was an exorbitant rate and only one stout merchant paid him attention. A long wrangle began beside the road. 'Mineral waters. Mineral waters.' A German with cropped head paced up and down muttering angrily to himself. Myatt heard a voice saying behind him in English, 'There's going to be more snow.' He turned in the hope that it might be Coral, but it was the woman whom he had seen in the restaurant-car.

'It will be no fun to be stuck here,' he said. 'They may be hours bringing another engine. What about sharing a car to Belgrade?'

'Is that an invitation?'

'A Dutch one,' Myatt said hastily.

'But I haven't a sou.' She turned and waved her hand. 'Mr Savory, come and share a car. You'll pay my share won't you?' Mr Savory elbowed his way out of the group of people round the driver. 'I can't make out what the fellow's saying. Something about a boiler,' he said. 'Share a car?' he went on more slowly. 'That'll be rather expensive, won't it?' He eyed the woman carefully and waited, as if he expected her to answer his question; he is wondering, of course, Myatt thought, what he will get out of it. Mr Savory's hesitation, the woman's waiting silence, aroused his competitive instincts. He wanted to unfurl the glory of wealth like a peacock's tail before her and dazzle her with the beauty of his possessions. 'Sixty dinas,' he said, 'for the two of you.'

'I'll just go along,' said Mr Savory, 'and see the *chef de train*. He may know how long . . .' The first snow began to fall. 'If you would be my guest,' said Myatt, 'Miss—'

'My name's Janet Pardoe,' she said, and drew her fur coat up above her ears. Her cheeks glowed where the snow touched them, and Myatt could follow through the fur the curve of her concealed body and compare it with Coral's thin nakedness. I shall have to take Coral too, he thought. 'Have you seen,' he said, 'a girl in a mackintosh, thin, shorter than you?'

'Oh yes,' Janet Pardoe said, 'she got out of the train at Subotica. I know whom you mean. You had supper with her last night.' She smiled at him. 'She's your mistress, isn't she?'

'Do you mean she got out with her bag?'

'Oh no. She had nothing with her. I saw her going across to the station with a customs man. She's a funny little thing, isn't she? A chorus girl?' she asked with polite interest, but her tone conveyed to Myatt a criticism not of the girl but of himself for spending his money to so little advantage. It angered him as much as if she had criticised the quality of his currants; it was a reflection on his discernment and his discretion. After all, he thought, I have spent on her no more than I should spend on you by taking you into Belgrade, and would you pay me back so readily in kind? But the unlikelihood woke desire and bitterness, for this girl was silver polished goods, while Coral was at the best a piece of pretty coloured glass, valued for sentimental reasons; the other had intrinsic worth. She is the kind, he thought, who needs more than money: a handsome body to meet her own lust, and wit and education. I am a Jew, and I have learned nothing except how to make money. But none the less her criticism angered him and made it easier to relinquish the unattainable.

'She must have missed the train. I'll have to go back for her.' He did not apologise for his broken promise, but went quickly while it was still easy to go.

The merchant was haggling with the driver. He had brought the price down to a hundred dinas, and his own offer had risen to ninety. Myatt was ashamed of his interruption, and of the contempt both men must feel for his hasty unbusinesslike manner. 'I'll give you a hundred and twenty dinas to take me to Subotica and back.' When he saw that the driver was ready to begin another argument he raised his offer. 'A hundred and fifty dinas if you take me there and back before this train leaves.'

The car was old, battered and very powerful. They drove into the face of the storm at sixty miles an hour along a road which had not been mended in a lifetime. The springs were broken and Myatt was flung from side to side, as the car fell into holes and climbed and heeled. It groaned and panted like a human being, driven to the edge of endurance by a merciless master. The snow fell faster; the telegraph-poles along the line seemed glimpses of dark space in the gaps of a white wall. Myatt leant over to the driver and shouted in German above the roar of the ancient engine, 'Can you see?' The car twisted and swerved across the road and the man yelled back at him that there was nothing to fear, they would meet nothing on the road; he did not say that he could see.

Presently the wind rose. The road which had before been hidden from them by a straight wall of snow now rose and fell back on them, like a wave of which the snow was the white stinging spume. Myatt shouted to the driver to go slower; if a tyre bursts now, he thought, we are dead. He saw the driver look at his watch and put his foot upon the accelerator and the ancient engine responded with a few more miles an hour, like one of those strong obstinate old men of whom others say, 'They are the last. We don't breed that kind now.' Myatt shouted again, 'Slower,' but the driver pointed to his watch and drove his car to its creaking, unsafe, and gigantic limit of strength. He was a man to whom thirty dinas, the difference between catching and losing the train, meant months of comfort; he would have risked his life and the life of his passenger for far less money. Suddenly, as the wind took the snow and blew it aside, a cart appeared in the gap ten yards away and right in front of them. Myatt had just time to see the bemused eyes of the oxen, to calculate where their horns would smash the glass of the windscreen; an elderly man screamed and dropped his goad and jumped. The driver wrenched his wheel round, the car leapt a bank, rode crazily on two wheels, while the others hummed and revolved between the wind and earth, leant farther and farther over till Myatt could see the ground rise like boiling milk, left the bank, touched two wheels to the ground, touched four, and roared down the road at sixty-five miles an hour, while the snow closed behind them, and hid the oxen and cart and the astonished terrified old man.

'Drive slower,' Myatt gasped, but the driver turned and grinned at him and waved an untrembling hand.

The officers sitting in a row at the table, the guards at the door, the doctor answering question after question after question receded. Coral Musker fell asleep. The night had tired her; she could not understand a word that was said; she did not know why she was there; she was frightened and beginning to despair. She dreamed first that she was a child and everything was very simple and very certain and everything had an explanation and a moral. And then she dreamed that she was very old and was looking back over her life and she knew everything and she knew what was right and what was wrong, and why this and that had happened and everything was very simple and had a moral. But this second dream was not like the first one, for she was nearly awake and she ruled the dream to suit herself, and always in the background the talking went on. In this dream she began to remember from the safety of age the events of the night and the day and how everything had turned out for the best and how Myatt had come back for her from Belgrade.

Dr Czinner too had been given a chair. He could tell from the fat officer's expression that the lie was nearly done with, for he had ceased to pay any attention to the questions, nodding and hiccuping and nodding again. Colonel Hartep kept up the appearance of justice from a genuine kindliness.

He had no scruples, but he did not wish to give unnecessary pain. If it had been possible he would have left Dr Czinner until the end some scraps of hope. Major Petkovitch continually raised objections; he knew as well as anyone what the outcome of the trial would be, but he was determined that it should have a superficial legality, that everything should be done in the proper order according to the regulations in the 1929 handbook.

With his hands folded quietly in front of him, and his shabby soft hat on the floor at his feet, Dr Czinner fought them without hope. The only satisfaction he could expect to gain would be the admission of the hollowness of his trial; he was going to be quietly tucked away in earth at the frontier station after dark, without publicity. 'On the ground of perjury,' he said, 'I have not yet been tried. It's outside the jurisdiction of a court martial.'

'You were tried in your absence,' Colonel Hartep said, 'and sentenced to five years' imprisonment.'

'I think you will find that I must still be brought up before a civil judge for sentence.'

'He's quite right,' said Major Petkovitch. 'We have no jurisdiction there. If you look up Section 15—'

'I believe you, Major. We'll waive then the sentence for perjury. There remains the false passport.'

Dr Czinner said quickly, 'You must prove that I have not become a naturalised British subject. Where are your witnesses? Will you telegraph to the British Ambassador?'

Colonel Hartep smiled. 'It would take so long. We'll waive the false passport. You agree, Major?'

'No,' said Major Petkovitch, 'I think it would be more correct to postpone trial on the smaller charge until sentence—that is to say, a verdict—has been declared on the greater.'

'It is all the same to me,' said Colonel Hartep. 'And you, Captain?' The captain nodded and grinned and closed his eyes.

'And now,' Colonel Hartep said, 'the charge of conspiring.' Major Petkovitch interrupted, 'I have been thinking it over. I think "treason" should have been the word used in the indictment.'

'Treason, then.'

'No, no, Colonel. It is impossible to alter the indictment now. "Conspiracy" will have to stand.'

'The maximum penalty—?'

'Is the same.'

'Well then, Dr Czinner, do you wish to plead guilty or not guilty?'

Dr Czinner sat for a moment considering. Then he said, 'It makes little difference?' Colonel Hartep looked at his watch, and then touched a letter which lay on the table. 'In the opinion of the court this is sufficient to convict.' He had the air of a man who wishes politely but firmly to put an end to an interview.

'I have the right, I suppose, to demand that it should be read, to cross-examine the soldier who took it?'

'Without doubt,' said Major Petkovitch eagerly.

Dr Czinner smiled. 'I won't trouble you. I plead guilty.' But if this had been a court in Belgrade, he told himself, with the pressmen scribbling in their box, I would have fought every step. Now that he had nobody to address, his mind was flooded with eloquence, words which could stab and words which would have brought tears. He was no longer the angry tongue-tied man who had failed to impress Mrs Peters. 'The court adjourns,' Colonel Hartep said. In the short silence the wind could be heard wandering like an angry watch-dog round the station buildings. It was a very brief interval, just long enough for Colonel Hartep to write a few sentences on a sheet of paper and push it across the table to his companions to sign. The two guards a little eased their position.

'The court finds all the prisoners guilty,' Colonel Hartep read. 'The prisoner, Josef Grünlich, is sentenced to a month's imprisonment, after which he will be repatriated. The prisoner, Coral Musker, is sentenced to twenty-four hours' imprisonment and will then be repatriated. The prisoner . . .'

Dr Czinner interrupted: 'Can I speak to the court before sentence is passed?'

Colonel Hartep glanced quickly at the window: it was shut; at the guards: their disciplined faces were uncomprehending and empty. 'Yes,' he said.

Major Petkovitch's face flushed. 'Impossible,' he said. 'Quite impossible. Regulation 27a. The prisoner should have spoken before the court adjourned.' The Chief of Police looked past the major's sharp profile to where Dr Czinner sat, bunched up on the chair, his hands folded together in grey woollen gloves. An engine hooted outside and ground slowly down the line. The snow whispered at the window. He was aware of the long ribbons on his coat and of the hole in Dr Czinner's glove. 'It would be most irregular,' Major Petkovitch railed on, while with one hand he absent-mindedly felt for his dog under the table and pulled the beast's ears. 'I note your protest,' Colonel Hartep said, and then he spoke to Dr Czinner. 'You know as well as I do,' he said kindly, 'that nothing you can say will alter the verdict. But if it pleases you, if it will make you any happier to speak, you may.'

Dr Czinner had expected opposition or contempt and his words would have flown to meet them. Kindness and consideration for a moment made him dumb. He envied again the qualities which only confidence and power could give the possessor. Before Colonel Hartep's kindly waiting silence he was tongue-tied. Captain Alexitch opened his eyes and closed them again. The doctor said slowly, 'Those medals you won in the service of your country during the war. I have no medals, because I love my country too much. I won't kill men because they also love their country. What I am fighting for is not new territory but a new world.' His words halted; there was no audience to bear him up; and he became conscious of the artificiality of his words which did not bear witness to the great love and the great hate driving him on. Sad and beautiful faces, thin from bad food, old before their time, resigned to despair, passed through his mind; they were people he had known, whom he had attended and failed to save. The world was in chaos to leave so much nobility unused, while the great financiers and the soldiers prospered. He said, 'You are employed to bolster up an old world which is full of injustice and muddle. For people like Vuskovitch, who steal the small savings of the poor, and live for ten years fast, full, stupid lives, and then shoot themselves. And yet you are paid to defend the only system which would protect men like him. You put the small thief in prison, but the big thief lives in a palace.'

Major Petkovitch said, 'What the prisoner is saying has no bearing on the case. It is a political speech.'

'Let him go on.' Colonel Hartep shaded his face with his hands and closed his eyes. Dr Czinner thought that he was feigning sleep to mask his indifference, but he opened them again when Dr Czinner called out to him angrily, 'How old-fashioned you are with your frontiers and your patriotism. The aeroplane doesn't know a frontier; even your financiers don't recognise frontiers.' Then Dr Czinner saw that something saddened him and the thought that perhaps Colonel Hartep had no desire for his death made him again at a loss for words. He moved his eyes restlessly from point to point, from the map on the wall to the little shelf below the clock full of books on strategy and military history in worn jackets. At last his eyes reached the two guards; one stared past him, paying him no attention, careful to keep his eyes on one spot and his rifle at the correct angle. The other watched him with wide stupid unhappy eyes. That face joined the sad procession through his brain, and he was aware for a moment that he had a better audience than pressmen, that here was a poor man to be converted from the wrong service to the right, and words came to him, the vague and sentimental words which had once appealed to him and would appeal to the other. But he was cunning now with the guile of his class, staring away from the man at the floor and only letting his gaze flicker back once like a lizard's tail. He addressed him in the plural as 'Brothers'. He urged that there was no shame in poverty that they should seek to be rich, and that there was no crime in poverty that they should be oppressed. When all were poor, no one would be poor. The wealth of the world belonged to everyone. If it was divided, there would be no rich men, but every man would have enough to eat, and would have no reason to feel ashamed beside his neighbour.

Colonel Hartep lost interest. Dr Czinner was losing the individuality of the grey wool gloves and the hole in the thumb; he was becoming a tub orator, no more. He looked at his watch and said, 'I think I have allowed you enough time.' Major Petkovitch muttered something under his breath and becoming suddenly irritable kicked his dog in the ribs and said, 'Be off with you. Always wanting attention.' Captain Alexitch woke up and said in a tone of great relief, 'Well, that's over.' Dr Czinner, staring at the floor five yards to the left of the guard, said slowly, 'This wasn't a trial. They had sentenced me to death before they began. Remember, I'm dying to show you the way. I don't mind dying. Life has not been so good as that. I think I shall be of more use dead.' But while he spoke his clearer mind told him that the chances were few that his death would have any effect.

'The prisoner Richard Czinner is sentenced to death,' Colonel Hartep read, 'the sentence to be carried out by the officer commanding the garrison at Subotica in three hours' time.' It will be dark by then, the doctor thought. No one will know of this.

For a moment everyone sat still as though they were at a concert and a movement had ended and they were uncertain whether to applaud. Coral

Musker woke. She could not understand what was happening. The officers were speaking together, shuffling papers. Then one of them gave a command and the guards opened the door and motioned towards the wind and the snow and the white veiled buildings.

The prisoners passed out. They kept close to each other in the storm of snow which struck them. They had not gone far when Josef Grünlich seized Dr Czinner's sleeve. 'You tell me nothing. What shall happen to me? You walk along and say nothing.' He grumbled and panted.

'A month's imprisonment,' Dr Czinner said, 'and then you are to be sent home.'

'They think that, do they? They think they are damned clever.' He became silent, studying with close attention the position of the buildings. He stumbled on the edge of the line and muttered angrily to himself.

'And me?' Coral asked. 'What's to happen to me?'

'You'll be sent home tomorrow.'

'But I can't. There's my job. I shall lose it. And my friend.' She had been afraid of this journey, because she could not understand what porters said to her, because of the strange food, and the uncertainty at the end of it: there had been a moment as the purser called after her across the wet quay at Ostend when she would gladly have turned back. But 'things' had happened since then: she would be returning to the same lodgings, to the toast and orange juice for breakfast, the long wait on the agent's stairs with Ivy and Flo and Phil and Dick, all the affectionate people one kissed and called by their front names and didn't know from Adam. Intimacy with one person could do this—empty the world of friendships, give a distaste for women's kisses and their bright chatter, make the ordinary world a little unreal and very uninteresting. Even the doctor did not matter to her as he stalked along in a different world, but she remembered as they reached the door of the waiting-room to ask him, 'And you? What's happening to you?'

He said vaguely, forgetting to stand aside for her to enter, 'I'm being kept here.'

'Where will they take me?' Josef Grünlich asked as the door closed.

'And me?'

'To the barracks, I expect, for tonight. There's no train to Belgrade. They've let the stove out.' Through the window he tried to catch a view of the peasants, but apparently they had grown tired of waiting and had gone home. He said with relief, 'There's nothing to be done,' and with obscure humour, 'It's something to be at home.' He saw himself for a moment facing a desert of pitch-pine desks, row on row of malicious faces, and he remembered the times when he had felt round his heart the little cold draughts of disobedience, the secret signals and spurts of disguised laughter threatening his livelihood, for a master who could not keep order must eventually be dismissed. His enemies were offering him the one thing he had never known, security. There was no need to decide anything. He was at peace.

Dr Czinner began to hum a tune. He said to Coral Musker, 'It's an old song. The lover says: 'I cannot come in daylight, for I am poor and your father will set the dogs on me. But at night I will come to your window and ask you to let me in." And the girl says: "If the dogs bark, stay very still in the shadow of the wall and I will come down to you, and we will go together to the orchard at the bottom of the garden.'" He sang the first verse in a voice a little harsh from lack of use; Josef Grünlich, sitting in the corner, scowled at the singer, and Coral stood by the cold stove and listened with surprise and pleasure because he seemed to be younger and full of hope. 'At night I will come to your window and ask you to let me in.' He was not addressing a lover: the words had no power to bring a girl's face from his dry purposeful political years, but his parents bobbed at him their humorous wrinkled faces, no longer with awe for the educated man, for the doctor, for the almost gentleman. Then in a lower voice he sang the girl's part. His voice was less harsh and might once have been beautiful; one of the guards came to the window and looked in and Josef Grünlich began to weep in a meaningless Teutonic way, thinking of orphans in the snow and princesses with hearts of ice and not for a moment of Herr Kolber, whose body was borne now through the grey city snow followed by two officials in a car and one mourner in a taxi, an elderly bachelor, a great draughts player. 'Stay very still in the shadow of the wall and I will come down to you.' The world was chaotic; when the poor were starved and the rich were not happier for it; when the thief might be punished or rewarded with titles; when wheat was burned in Canada and coffee in Brazil, and the poor in his own country had no money for bread and froze to death in unheated rooms; the world was out of joint and he had done his best to set it right, but that was over. He was powerless now and happy. 'We will go to the orchard at the bottom of the garden.' Again it was no memory of a girl which comforted him, but the sad and beautiful faces of the poor who promised him rest. He had done all that he could do; nothing more was expected of him; they surrendered him their hopelessness, the secret of their beauty and their happiness as well as of their grief, and led him towards the leafy rustling darkness. The guard pressed his face to the window, and Dr Czinner stopped singing. 'It's your turn,' he said to Coral.

'Oh, I don't know any songs that you'd like,' she told him seriously, searching her memory at the same time for something a little old-fashioned and melancholy, something which would share the quality of a sad idyll with the song he had sung.

'We must pass the time somehow,' he said, and suddenly she began to sing in a small clear voice like the tinkle of a musical box:

> *'I was sitting in a car*
> *With Michael;*
> *I looked at a star*
> *With John;*
> *I had a glass of bitter*
> *With Peter*
> *In a bar;*
> *But the pips went wrong; they never go right.*
> *This year, next year*
> *(You may have counted wrong, count again, dear),*
> *Some day, never.*
> *I'll be a good girl for ever and ever.'*

'Is this Subotica?' Myatt shouted, as a few mud cottages plunged at them through the storm, and the driver nodded and waved his hand forward. A small child ran out into the middle of the road and the car swerved to avoid it; a chicken squawked and handfuls of grey feathers were flung up into the snow. An old woman ran out of a cottage and shouted after them. 'What's she saying?' The driver grinned over his shoulder: 'Dirty Jew.'

The arrow on the speedometer wavered and retreated: fifty miles, forty miles, thirty miles, twenty. 'Soldiers about,' the man said.

'You mean there's a speed limit?'

'No, no. These damned soldiers if they see a good car, they commandeer it. Same with the horses.' He pointed at the fields through the driving snow. 'The peasants, they are all starving. I worked here once, but I thought: no, the city for me. The country's dead, anyway.' He nodded towards the line which disappeared into the storm. 'One or two trains a day, that's all. You can't blame the Reds for making trouble.'

'Has there been trouble?'

'Trouble? You should have seen it. The goods yard all in flames; the post-office smashed to bits. The police were scared. There's martial law in Belgrade.'

'I wanted to send a telegram from there. Will it get through?' The car panted its way on second gear up a small hill and came into a street of dingy brick houses plastered with advertisements. 'If you want to send a telegram,' the driver said, 'I should send it from here. There are queues of newspaper men at Belgrade, and the post-office is smashed and they've had to commandeer old Nikola's restaurant. You know what that means; but you don't because you are a foreigner. It's not the bugs, nobody minds a few bugs, it's healthy, but the smells—'

'Have I got time to send a telegram here and catch the train?'

'That train,' the driver said, 'won't go for hours and hours. They've sent for a new engine, but nobody's going to pay any attention to them in the city. You should see the station, the mess—You had better let me drive you into Belgrade. I'll show you the sights too. I know all the best houses.'

Myatt interrupted him, 'I'll go to the post-office first. And then we'll try the hotels for the lady.'

'There's only one.'

'And then the station.'

The sending of the telegram took some time; first he had to write the message to Joyce in such a way that no action for libel could be brought by Mr Eckman. He decided at last on: 'Eckman granted a month's holiday to start immediately. Please take charge at once. Arriving tomorrow.' That ought to convey what he wanted, but it then had to be put into the office code, and when the coded telegram was handed across the counter, the clerk refused to accept it. All telegrams were liable to censorship, and no coded messages could be transmitted. At last he got away, only to find that nothing was known of Coral at the hotel, which smelt of dried plants and insect powder. She must be still at the station, he thought. He left the car a hundred yards down the road in order to get rid of the driver who was proving too talkative and too helpful and pushed forward alone through the wind and snow.

He passed two sentries outside a building and asked them the way to the waiting-room. One of them said that there was no waiting-room now.

'Where can I make inquiries?'

The tallest of the guards suggested the station-master. 'And where is his office?' The man pointed to a second building, but added gently that the station-master was away; he was in Belgrade. Myatt checked his impatience, the man was so obviously good-natured. His companion spat to show his contempt and muttered remarks about Jews under his breath. 'Where can I go then to make inquiries?'

'There's the major,' the man said doubtfully, 'or there's the station-master's clerk.'

'You can't see the major. He's gone to the barracks,' the other guard said. Myatt absent-mindedly drew a little nearer to the door; he could hear low voices inside. The surly guard became suddenly angry and brutal; he struck at Myatt's legs with the butt of his rifle. 'Go away. We don't want spies round here. Go away, you Jew.' With the calm of his race Myatt drew away; it was a superficial calm carried unconsciously like an inherited feature; beneath it he felt the resentment of a young man aware of his own importance. He leant towards the soldier with the intention of lodging in the flushed animal face some barb of speech, but he stopped in time, aware with amazement and horror of the presence of danger; in the small hungry eyes shone hatred and a desire to kill; it was as if all the oppressions, the pogroms, the chains, and the envy and superstition which caused them, had been herded into a dark cup of the earth and now he stared down at them from the rim. He moved back with his eyes on the soldier while the man's fingers felt round the trigger. 'I'll see the station-master's clerk,' he said, but his instinct told him to walk quickly back to his car and rejoin the train.

'That's not the way,' the friendly guard called after him. 'Over there. Across the line.' Myatt was thankful for the storm that roared along the line and blew gustily between him and the soldiers. Where he stood there was no prevailing wind, for it was trapped in the alleys between the buildings and sent swirling round the corners in contrary directions. He wondered at his own persistence in staying in the empty dangerous station; he told himself that he owed the girl nothing, and he knew that she would agree with him. 'We're quits,' she would say. 'You've given me the ticket, and I've given you a nice time.' But he was tied by her agreement, by her refusal to make any claim. Before so complete a humility one could be nothing else but generous. He picked his way across the line and pushed open a door. A tousled man sat at a desk drinking wine. His back was turned, and Myatt said in what he hoped was an intimidating authoritative tone, 'I want to make an inquiry.' He had no reason to be afraid of a civilian, but when the man turned and he saw the eyes grow cunning and insolent at the sight of him, he despaired. A mirror hung above the desk, and in it Myatt saw the reflection of himself quite clearly for a moment, short and stout and nasal in his heavy fur coat, and it occurred to him that perhaps these people hated him not only because he was a Jew but because he carried the traces of money into their resigned surroundings. 'Well?' said the clerk.

'I want to make an inquiry,' Myatt said, 'about a girl who was left behind here from the Orient express this morning.'

'What do you mean?' the clerk asked insolently. 'If anybody leaves the train, they leave it. They aren't left behind. Why, the train was waiting here this morning for more than half an hour.'

'Well, then, did a girl get out?'

'No.'

'Will you just examine your tickets and check that?'

'No. I said no one got out, didn't I? What are you waiting here for? I'm a busy man.'

Myatt knew suddenly that he would not be sorry to accept the clerk's word and end his search; he would have done all that lay in his power, and he would be free. He thought of Coral for a moment as a small alley, enticing a man's footsteps, but blind at the end with a windowless wall; there were others, and he thought for a moment of Janet Pardoe, who were like streets lined with shops full of glitter and warmth, streets which led somewhere. He was reaching an age when he wanted to marry and have children, set up his tent and increase his tribe. But his thoughts had been too precise; they roused his conscience on behalf of someone who had not shown the slightest hope of marriage but had been intent only on honest payment and her own affection. It came to him again as a strange and unexpected cry, her exclamation, 'I love you.' He returned from the doorway to the clerk's desk determined to do all that he could do, to scamp no effort; she might now be somewhere in discomfort, stranded without money, possibly afraid. 'She was seen to leave the train.'

The clerk groaned at him: 'What do you want me to do? Come out in the snow looking for her? I tell you I don't know a thing about her. I haven't seen any girl.' His voice trailed off as he watched Myatt take out his note-case. Myatt removed a five-dina note and smoothed it between his fingers. 'If you can tell me where she is, you can have two of these.' The clerk stammered a little, tears came to his eyes, and he said with poignant regret, 'If I could, if I only could. I am sure I should be glad to help.' His face lit up and he suggested hopefully, 'You ought to try the hotel.' Myatt put the case back in his pocket; he had done all that he could do; and he went out to find his car.

For the last few hours the sun had been obscured, but its presence had been shown in the glitter of the falling snow, in the whiteness of the drifts; now it was sinking and the snow was absorbing the greyness of the sky; he would not get back to the train before dark. But even the hope of catching the train became faint, for he found when he reached his car that the engine had frozen, in spite of the rugs spread across the radiator.

4

Josef Grünlich said: 'It is all very well to sing.' Although he complained of their inanition his eyes were red with weeping, and it was with an effort that he put away from him the little match girls and the princesses with hearts of ice. 'They will not catch me so easily.' He began to walk round the walls of the waiting-room pressing a wet thumb to the woodwork. 'Never have I been imprisoned. It may surprise you, but it is true. At my time of life one cannot start something like that. And they are sending me back to Austria.'

'Are you wanted there?'

Josef Grünlich pulled down his waistcoat and set the little silver cross shaking. 'I do not mind telling you. We are all together, eh?' He twisted his neck a little in a sudden access of modesty. 'I have slaughtered a man at Vienna.'

Coral said with horror, 'Do you mean that you are a murderer?' Josef Grünlich thought: I should like to tell them. It's too good to be a secret. Quickness? Why–'Look over there, Herr Kolber,' flick of the string, aim, fire twice, wriggle, man dead, all in two seconds; but better not. He encouraged himself with the cautious motto of his profession, the poker-work injunction to keep pride in bounds–'One never knows.' He ran his finger inside his collar and said airily, 'I had to. It was an affair of honour.' His hesitation was infinitesimal. 'He had–how do you say it?–made my daughter big.' With difficulty he prevented himself laughing as he thought of Herr Kolber, small and dry, and of his petulant exclamation, 'This is a pretty kettle of fish.'

'You mean you killed him,' Coral asked with amazement, 'just because he'd played around with your daughter?'

Josef Grünlich raised his hands and asked absent-mindedly, his eyes straying to the window and measuring its height from the ground, 'What could I do? Her honour, my honour . . .'

'Gosh,' said Coral, 'I'm glad I haven't a father.'

Josef Grünlich said suddenly, 'A hairpin perhaps.'

'What do you mean, a hairpin?'

'Or a pocket knife?'

'I haven't got any hairpins. What would I want hairpins for?'

'I have a paper-cutter,' Dr Czinner said. As he handed it over, he said, 'My watch has stopped. Could you tell me how long we have been back here?'

'An hour,' said Josef.

'Two hours more then,' Dr Czinner remarked thoughtfully. Neither of the others heard him. Josef tiptoed to the door, paper-cutter in hand, and Coral watched him. 'Come here, Fraülein,' Josef said, and when she was beside him he whispered to her, 'Have you some grease?' She gave him a pot of cold cream from her bag and he spread the cream thickly over the lock of the door, leaving a little space clear. He began to laugh gently to himself, bent almost double, with his eye to the lock. 'Such a lock,' he whispered jubilantly, 'such a lock.'

'What do you want the cream for?'

'Quiet,' he said. 'It will make what I do quieter.'

He came back to the cold stove and waved them together. 'That lock,' he told them in an undertone, 'is nothing. If we could send one guard away we could run.'

'You'll be shot,' Dr Czinner said.

'They cannot shoot all three at once,' Grünlich said. He dropped two suggestions into their silence: 'The dark. The snow,' and then stood back, waiting for their decision. His own mind worked smoothly. He would be the first out of the door, the first away; he could run faster than an old man and a girl; the guard would fire at the nearest fugitive.

'I should advise you to stay,' Dr Czinner said to Coral. 'You aren't in any danger here.'

Grünlich opened his mouth to protest, but he said nothing. They all three watched the window and the passing of one of the guards, rifle slung across his shoulder. 'How long will it take you to open the door?' Dr Czinner asked.

'Five minutes.'

'Get to work then.' Dr Czinner tapped on the window and the other guard came. His large friendly eyes were pressed close to the glass and he stared into the waiting-room. The room was darker than the open air and he could see nothing but dim shapes moving restlessly here and there for warmth. Dr Czinner put his mouth close to the glass and spoke to him in his own tongue. 'What is your name?' Scratch, scratch, scratch went the paper knife, but when it slipped the whine was hushed by the layer of cream.

'Ninitch,' said the ghost of a voice through the glass.

'Ninitch,' Dr Czinner repeated slowly. 'Ninitch. I used to know your father, I think, in Belgrade.' Ninitch showed no doubt of the easy lie, flattening his nose against the window, but all his view of the waiting-room was cut off by the doctor's features. 'He died six years ago,' he said.

Dr Czinner took what was only a small risk to one acquainted with the poor in Belgrade and of the food they eat. 'Yes. He was ill when I knew him. Cancer of the stomach.'

'Cancer?'

'Pains.'

'Yes, yes, in the belly. That was him. They came on at night, and he would get very hot in the face. My mother used to lie beside him with a cloth to dry his skin. Fancy you knowing him, your honour. Shall I open the window so that we can talk better?' Grünlich's knife scratched and scratched and scratched; a screw came out and tinkled like a needle on the floor.

'No,' Dr Czinner said. 'Your companion might not like it.'

'He's gone up to the town to the barracks to see the major. There's a foreigner been here making inquiries. He thinks there's something wrong.'

'A foreigner?' Dr Czinner asked. His mouth had gone dry with hope. 'Has he gone?'

'He's just gone back to his car, down the road.' The waiting-room was full of shadows. Dr Czinner turned for a moment from the window and asked softly, 'How is it going? Can you be quick?'

'Two minutes more,' Grünlich said.

'There's a foreigner with a car down the road. He's been making inquiries.'

Coral put her hands together and said softly, 'He's come back for me. You see. You said he wouldn't.' She began to laugh gently, and when Dr Czinner whispered to her to keep calm, she said, 'I'm not hysterical. I'm just happy,' for it had occurred to her that this frightening adventure had been, after all, for the best; it had shown that he was fond of her, otherwise he would never have troubled to come back. He must have missed the train, she thought, and we shall have to spend the night together in Belgrade, perhaps two nights, and she began to dream of smart hotels, and dinners and his hand on her arm.

Dr Czinner turned back to the window. 'We are very thirsty,' he said. 'Have you any wine?'

Ninitch shook his head. 'No.' He added doubtfully, 'Lukitch has a bottle of *rakia* across the way.' Dusk had already made the way longer; there was no moon to light the steel of the rails and the lamp in the station-master's office might have been a hundred yards away and not a hundred feet.

'Be a good fellow and get us a drink.'

He shook his head. 'I mustn't leave the door.'

Dr Czinner did not offer him money; instead he called through the glass that he had attended Ninitch's father. 'I gave him tablets to take when the pain was too bad.'

'Little round tablets?' Ninitch asked.

'Yes. Morphia tablets.'

Ninitch with his face pressed against the glass considered. It was possible to see the thoughts moving like fish in the translucent eyes. He said, 'Fancy your giving him those tablets. He used to take one whenever the pain came, and one at night too. It made him sleep.'

'Yes.'

'What a lot I shall have to tell my wife.'

'The drink,' Dr Czinner prompted him.

Ninitch said slowly, 'If you tried to escape while I was gone, I should get into trouble.' Dr Czinner said, 'How could we escape? The door's locked and the window is too small.'

'Very well, then.'

Dr Czinner saw him go and turned with a sigh of unhappiness to the others. 'Now,' he said. His sigh was for the loss of his security. The struggle was renewed. It was his distasteful duty to escape if he could.

'One moment,' Grünlich said, scratching at the door.

'There's no one outside. The guard's the other side of the line. When you come out of the door turn to the left and turn to the left again between the buildings. The car's down the road.'

'I know all that,' said Grünlich, and another screw tinkled to the floor. 'Ready.'

'I should stay here.' Dr Czinner said to Coral.

'But I couldn't. My friend's just down the road.'

'Ready,' Grünlich said again, scowling at them. They gathered at the door. 'If they fire,' Dr Czinner said, 'run crookedly.' Grünlich pulled the door open and the snow blew in. It was not so dark outside as it had been in the room; the station-master's lamp across the rails lit up the figure of the guard in the window. Grünlich dived first into the storm; with head bent almost to his knees he bounced forward like a ball. The others followed. It was not easy to run. The wind and snow were enemies allied to drive them back: the wind broke their speed and the snow blinded them. Coral gasped with pain as she ran into a tall iron pillar with a trunk like an elephant's used for watering engines. Grünlich was far ahead of her; Dr Czinner was a little behind; she could hear the painful effort of his lungs. Their footsteps made no sound in the snow, and they dared not shout to the driver of the car.

Before Grünlich had reached the gap between the buildings, a door slammed, someone called, and a rifle was fired. Grünlich's first effort had exhausted him. The distance between him and Coral lessened. The guard fired twice, and Coral could hear the buzz of the bullets far overhead. She wondered whether he was deliberately aiming high. Ten seconds more and they would pass the corner out of his sight and be visible from the car. She heard a door open again, a bullet whipped up the snow beside her and she ran the faster. She was almost side by side with Grünlich when they reached the corner. Dr Czinner exclaimed behind her and she thought he was urging her to run faster, but before she turned the corner she looked back and saw that he was hugging the wall with both hands. She stopped and called out, 'Herr Grünlich,' but he paid her no attention, bundling round the building and out of sight.

'Go on,' Dr Czinner said.

The light shining from the horizon behind the thinner clouds faded. 'Take my arm,' she said. He obeyed, but his weight was too much for her, though he tried to ease it with one hand against the wall. They reached the corner. The rear lamp of the car blinked through the dusk and snow a hundred yards away, and she stopped. 'I can't do it,' she said. He made no answer, and when she took her hand away he slid down to the snow.

For a few seconds she wondered whether to leave him. She told herself with conviction that he would never have waited for her. But then she was in no great danger and he was. She stood hesitating, bent down to watch his pale old face; she noticed that there was blood on his moustache. Voices sounded round the corner, and she found she had no time to decide. Dr Czinner was sitting with his back to a wooden door which was on the latch, and she pulled him inside and closed it again, but she was afraid to shoot the bolt. Someone ran by, an engine spluttered. Then the car roared into activity and distance took the sound and subdued it to a murmur. The shed had no windows: it was quite dark, and it was too late now for her to leave him.

She felt in Dr Czinner's pockets and found a box of matches. When she struck one the roof shot above her like a bean-stalk. Something blocked the shed at one end, stacked half-way to the roof. Another match showed her fat sacks piled more than twice the height of a man. In Dr Czinner's right-hand pocket was a folded newspaper. She tore off a page and made a spill, so that she might have enough light to drag him across the shed, for she was afraid that at any moment the guard would open the door. But his weight was too much for her. She held the spill close to his eyes to see whether he was conscious, and the stinging smoke woke him. He opened his eyes and watched her with perplexity. She whispered to him, 'I want to hide you in the sacks.' He did not seem to understand and she repeated the sentence very slowly and distinctly.

He said, 'Ich spreche kein Englisch.'

Oh, she thought, I wish I'd left him; I wish I was in the car now. He must be dying; he can't understand a word I say, and she was terrified at the idea of being left all alone in the shed with a dead man. Then the flame went out, choked in its own ash. She searched for the newspaper again on hands and knees and tore a page and folded it and made another spill. Then she found that she had mislaid the matches, and on hands and knees she felt the floor all round her. Dr Czinner began to cough, and something moved on the floor close to her hands. She nearly screamed for fear of rats, but when at last she had found the matches and lit a spill, she saw it was the doctor who had moved. He was crawling crookedly towards the end of the shed. She tried to guide him, but he seemed unaware of her. All the slow way across she wondered why no one came to look in the shed.

Dr Czinner was completely exhausted when he reached the sacks and he lay down with his face buried against them; he had been bleeding from the mouth. Again all the responsibility was hers. She wondered whether he was dying and she put her mouth close to his ear. 'Shall I get help?' She was afraid that he would answer her in German, but this time he said quite clearly, 'No, no.' After all, she thought, he's a doctor; he must know. She asked him, 'What can I do for you?' He shook his head and closed his eyes; he was no longer bleeding and she thought him better. She pulled sacks down from the pile and made a kind of cave large enough to shelter them, piling the sacks at the entrance, so that no one could see them from the door. The sacks were heavy with grain, and the work was unfinished when she heard voices. She crouched low in the hole with her fingers crossed for luck, and the door opened, a torch flashed over the sacks above her head. Then the door was shut and quiet returned. It was a long time before she had the courage to finish her work.

'We'll miss the train,' Myatt said as he watched the driver turn and turn the starting handle; the self-starter was useless.

'I will take you back quicker,' the man said. At last the engine began to wake, grumble, fall asleep and wake again. 'Now we're off,' he said. He climbed into his seat and turned on the front lamps, but while he was coaxing the engine into a steady roar, there was an explosion in the dusk behind. 'What's that?' Myatt asked thinking the car had back-fired. Then it happened again, and a little afterwards there was another sound like the popping of a cork. 'They are firing in the station,' the driver said, pushing at the self-starter. Myatt knocked his hand away. 'We'll wait.'

The man repeated, 'Wait?' He explained hurriedly, 'It's the soldiers. We had better be off.' He could not know how closely Myatt echoed his advice. Myatt was frightened; he had seen in the soldiers' attitude the spirit which made pogroms possible; but he remained obstinate; he was not quite satisfied that he had done everything he could to find the girl in Subotica.

'They are coming,' the man said. Along the road from the station someone was running. At first he eluded them in the falling snow. Then they could make out a man dodging a little this way and a little that. He was upon them with surprising speed, short and fat, clawing at the door to climb in. 'What's up?' Myatt asked him. He spluttered a little at the mouth. 'Drive off quick.' The door stuck and he bundled himself over the top and collapsed out of breath in the back seat.

'Is there anybody else?' Myatt asked. 'Are you alone?'

'Yes, yes, alone,' the man assured him. 'Drive away quick.'

Myatt leant back and tried to see his face. 'No girl?'

'No. No girl.'

There was a flash of light somewhere by the station buildings and a bullet scraped the mudguard. The driver, without waiting for an order, thrust down his foot and sent the car ricocheting from hole to hole along the road. Myatt again studied the stranger's face. 'Weren't you on the Istanbul express?' The man nodded. 'And you haven't seen a girl at the station?' The man became voluble. 'I will tell you all about it.' His speech was indistinct; many phrases were taken from his mouth by the plunging car; he said he had been detained for not declaring a little piece of lace, a very small little piece of lace, and had been badly treated by the soldiers and fired on when he escaped. 'And you saw no girl?'

'No. No girl.' He met Myatt's gaze with a complete honesty. It would have needed a long inquisition to spy at the back of the blank eyes the spark of malice, the little glint of cunning.

Although the wooden walls trembled with the wind, it was warm among the sacks, in the dark, in the unwindowed shed. Dr Czinner turned to escape the pain in his chest and turned again, but it pursued him; only in the moment of turning did he gain a few strides; when he was still, the pain was on him. So all through the night he turned and turned. There were times when he became conscious of the wind outside and mistook the rustle of the snow for the movement of the pebbles at the sea's edge. During those moments a memory of his years of exile took shape in the barn, so that he began to recite declensions and French irregular verbs. But his resistance was weakened, and instead of showing an obstinate sarcastic front to his tormentors, he wept.

Coral Musker laid his head in an easier position, but he moved it again, turning it and turning it, muttering rhythmically, tears falling down his cheeks and on to his moustache. She gave up the attempt to help him and tried to escape into the past from her own fear, so that if their thoughts had been given a form visible to each other, a strange medley would have filled the barn. Under coloured lights which spilt out 'It's a Baby' a clergyman rumpled his gown across his arm and dived at a black-board with a piece of chalk; several children pursued another with taunts in and out of stage doors, up and down agents' stairs. In a glass shelter on a grey sea-front a woman gave a neighbour a piece of her mind, while a bell tolled for tea or chapel.

'Wasser,' Dr Czinner whispered. 'What do you want?' She bent down to him and tried to see his face. 'Wasser.'

'Shall I fetch someone?' He did not hear her.

'Do you want something to drink?' He paid her no attention, repeating 'Wasser' again and again. She knew that he was not conscious, but her nerves were worn and she was irritated by his failure to answer her. 'All right then, lie there. I've done all I can, I'm sure.' She scrambled as far away from him as she could and tried to sleep, but the trembling of the walls kept her awake, the moaning of the wind made her aware of desolation, and she crept back to Dr Czinner's side for company and comfort. 'Wasser,' he whispered again. Her hand touched his face and she was astonished at the heat and dryness of the skin. Perhaps he wants water, she thought, and was at a loss for a minute where to find it until she realised that it was falling all round her and piling itself against the walls of the shed. She was warned by a faint doubt: should somebody in a fever be given water? But remembering the dryness of his skin, she gave way to pity.

Although water was all round her, it was not easily or quickly reached. She had to light two spills and climb from the hole among the sacks without extinguishing them. She opened the door of the shed boldly, for she would half have welcomed discovery now, but the night was dark and there was no one to be seen. She gathered a handful of snow and went back into the shed and closed the door; the draught of the closing door blew out her light.

She called to Dr Czinner, but he made no reply, and she was frightened at the thought that he might be dead. With one hand held in front of her face she walked forward and was brought up short by the wall. She waited a moment before trying again and was glad to hear a movement. She went to it and was again stopped by the wall. She thought with rising fear: it must have been a rat that moved. The snow in her hand was beginning to melt. She called out again, and this time a whisper answered. She jumped, it was so close to her, and feeling sideways her hand immediately touched the barricade of sacks. She began to laugh, but rebuked herself: Now don't be hysterical. Everything depends on you; and she tried to comfort herself with the assurance that this was her first star part. But it was difficult to play with confidence in the dark without applause.

When she had found the hole among the sacks most of the snow was melted or spilt, but she pressed what was left against the doctor's mouth. It seemed to ease him. He lay still, while the snow upon his lips melted and trickled between his teeth. He was so quiet that she lit a spill to see his face and was astonished at his shrewd conscious gaze. She spoke to him, but he was too full of thought to answer.

He was taking in his position, the force of his second failure. He knew that he was dying; he had been brought to consciousness by the touch of cold upon the tongue; and after a moment of bewilderment, remembered everything. He could tell where he had been shot from the pain; he was aware of his own fever and of the secret fatal bleeding within. For a moment he thought it his duty to brush the snow from his lips, but then he realised that he had no more duties to anyone but himself.

When the girl lit the spill he was thinking: Grünlich has escaped. It amused him to consider how hard it would be for a Christian to reconcile the escape with his own death. He smiled a little, maliciously. But then, his Christian training took an ironical revenge, for he too began to try to reconcile the events of the last few days and to wonder in what he had erred and how it was that others had succeeded. He saw the express in which they had travelled breaking the dark sky like a rocket. They clung to it with every stratagem in their power, leaning this way and leaning that, altering the balance now in this direction, now in that. One had to be very alive, very flexible, very opportunist. The snow on the lips had all melted and its effect was passing. Before the spill had flickered to its end, his sight had dimmed, and the great shed with its cargo of sacks floated away from him into darkness. He had no sense that he was within it; he thought that he was left behind, watching it disappear. His mind became confused; and soon he was falling through endless space, breathless, with a windy vacancy in head and chest, because he had been unable to retain his foothold on what was sometimes a ship and at other times a comet, the world itself, or only a fast train from Ostend to Istanbul. His mother and father bobbed at him their seamed thin faces, followed him through the ether, past the rush of stars, telling him that they were glad and grateful, that he had done what he could, that he had been faithful. He was breathless and could not answer them, tugged downward in great pain by gravity. He wanted to say to them that he had been damned by his faithfulness, that one must lean this way and that, but he had to listen all the way to their false comfort, falling and falling in great pain.

It was impossible to tell in the barn the progress of the dark; when Coral struck a match to see her watch, she was disappointed to find how slowly time went by. After a while the store of matches became low and she did not dare to strike another. She wondered whether to leave the shed and surrender herself, for she began to despair now of seeing Myatt again. He had done more than could have been expected of him by returning; it was unlikely that he would come back again. But she was frightened of the world outside, not of the soldiers, but of the agents, the long stairs, the landladies, the old life. As long as she lay by Dr Czinner's side, she retained something of Myatt, a memory they both possessed.

Of course, she told herself, I can write to him, but months might pass before he was again in London, and she couldn't expect either his affection or desire to last when she was away. She knew too, that she could make him see her when he returned. He would feel that it was his duty at least to give her lunch, but 'I'm not after his money', she whispered aloud in the dark barn beside the dying man. Her sense of desolation, the knowledge that for some reason, God alone knew why, she loved him, made her for a moment protestant. Why not? Why shouldn't I write to him? He might like it; he might want me still, and if he doesn't, why shouldn't I put up a fight? I'm tired of being decent, of doing the right thing. Her thoughts were very close to Dr Czinner's when she exclaimed to herself that it didn't pay.

But she knew too well that it was her nature, she was born so and she must make the best of it. She would be a fumbler at the other game; relentless when she ought to be weak, forgiving when she ought to be hard. Even now she could not dwell long with envy and admiration at the thought of Grünlich driving away into the dark beside Myatt; her thoughts returned with a stupid fidelity to Myatt himself, to her last sight of him in the restaurant-car with his fingers caressing his gold cigarette case. But she was aware all the time that there was no quality in Myatt to justify her fidelity; it was just that she was like that and he had been kind. She wondered for a moment whether Dr Czinner's case was not the same; he had been too faithful to people who could have been served better by cunning. She heard his difficult breathing through the dark and thought again without bitterness or criticism, it just doesn't pay.

The fork of roads sprang towards the headlights. The driver hesitated for a fraction too long, then twisted his wheel and sent the car spinning round on two wheels. Josef Grünlich fell from one end of the seat to the other, gasping with fear. He did not dare to open his eyes again until the four wheels were on the ground. They had left the main road, and the car was bounding down the ruts of a country lane, splashing a fierce light on the budding trees and turning them to cardboard. Myatt leaned back from his seat beside the driver and explained, 'He's avoiding Subotica and is going over the line by a cattle crossing. You had better hold tight.' The trees vanished and suddenly they were roaring downhill between bare snow-draped fields. The lane had been churned by cattle into mud which had frozen. Two red lights sprang up towards them from below, and a short stretch of rail glinted with emerald drops. The lights swung backward and forward and a voice could be heard above the engine, calling.

'Shall I drive through them?' the man asked calmly, his foot ready to fall on the accelerator. 'No, no!' Myatt exclaimed. He saw no reason why he should get into trouble for a stranger's sake. He could see the men holding the lanterns. They wore grey uniforms and carried revolvers. The car stopped between them, jumping the first rail and coming to rest tilted like a stranded boat. One of the soldiers said something which the driver translated into German. 'He wants to see our papers.'

Josef Grünlich leant back quietly against the cushions with his legs crossed. One hand played idly with his silver chain. When one of the soldiers caught his eye he smiled gently and nodded; anyone would have taken him for a rich and amiable business man, travelling with his secretary. It was Myatt who was flurried, sunk in his fur coat, remembering the woman's cry of 'Dirty Jew', the sentry's eyes, the clerk's insolence. It was in some such barren quarter of the world, among frozen fields and thin cattle, that one might expect to find old hatreds the world was outgrowing still alive. A soldier flashed his lamp in his face and repeated his demand with impatience and contempt. Myatt took out his passport, the man held it upside down and examined closely the lion and the unicorn; then he brought out his one word of German:

'Englander?'

Myatt nodded and the man threw the passport back on the seat and became absorbed in the driver's papers, which opened out into a long streamer like a child's book. Josef Grünlich leant cautiously forward and took Myatt's passport from the seat in front. He grinned when the red light was flashed on his face and flourished the passport. The guard called his friend, they stood and examined him under the light, speaking together in low voices, paying no attention to his gesture. 'What do they want?' he complained without altering his fixed fat smile. One of the men gave an order, which the driver translated. 'Stand up.'

With Myatt's passport in one hand, the other on his silver chain, he obeyed, and they moved the lights from his feet to his head. He had no overcoat and shivered with the cold. One of the men laughed and prodded him in the stomach with a finger. 'They want to see if it's real,' the driver explained.

'What's real?'

'Your roundness.'

Josef Grünlich had to feign amusement at the insult and smile and smile. His self-esteem had been pricked by two anonymous fools whom he would never see again. Someone else would have to bear the pain of his indignity, for it had been his pride, as it was now his grief, that he never forgot an injury. He did his best by pleading with the driver in German, 'Can't you run them down?' and he grinned at the men and waggled the passport, while they discussed him point by point. Then they stood back and nodded, and the driver pressed the starter. The car lifted over the rails, then slowly climbed a long rutted lane, and Josef Grünlich looking back saw the two red lamps bobbing like paper lanterns in the darkness.

'What did they want?'

'They were looking for someone,' the driver said. But that Josef knew well. Hadn't he killed Kolber in Vienna? Hadn't he escaped only an hour ago from Subotica under the eyes of a sentry? Wasn't he the cute one, the cunning fellow, who was quick and never hesitated? They had closed every road to cars and yet he slipped through. But like a small concealed draught the thought came to him that if they had been seeking him they would have found him. They were looking for someone else. They thought someone else of more importance. They had circulated the description of the old slow doctor and not of Josef Grünlich, who had killed Kolber and whose boast it was—'five years now and never jugged.' The fear of speed left him. As they hurtled through the dark in the creaking antique car, he sat still, brooding on the injustice of it all.

Coral Musker woke with the sense of strangeness, of difference. She sat up and the sack of grain creaked under her. It was the only sound; the whisper of falling snow had stopped. She listened, and realised with fear that she was alone. Dr Czinner had gone; she could no longer hear his breathing. Somewhere from far away the sound of a car changing gear reached her through the dusk. It came to her side like a friendly dog, fawning and nuzzling.

If Dr Czinner is gone, she thought, there's nothing to keep me here. I'll go and find that car. If it's the soldiers they won't do anything to me; it may be ... Longing kept the sentence open like the beak of a hungry bird. She put out a hand to steady herself, while she got upon her knees, and touched the doctor's face. He did not move, and though the face was warm, she could feel the blood as crisp and dry round his mouth as old skin. She screamed once and then was quiet and purposeful, feeling for the matches, lighting a spill. But her hand shook. Her nerves were bending, even though they had not given way, beneath the weight of her responsibilities. It seemed to her that every day for the past week had loaded her with something to decide, some fear which she must disguise. 'Here's this job at Constantinople. Take it or leave it. There are a dozen girls on the stairs'; Myatt pressing the ticket into her bag; her landlady advising this and that; the sudden terror of strangeness on the quay at Ostend with the purser calling after her to remember him.

In the light of the spill she was again surprised by the doctor's knowledgeable stare, but it was a frozen knowledge which never changed. She looked away and looked back and it was the same. I never knew he was as bad as that, she thought. I can't stay here. She even wondered whether they would accuse her of his death. These foreigners, whose language she could not understand, were capable of anything. But she delayed too long, while the spill burned down, because of an odd curiosity. Had he too once had a girl? The thought robbed him of impressiveness, he was no longer terrifying dead, and she examined his face more closely than she had ever dared before. Manners went out with life. She noticed for the first time that his face was curiously coarse-featured; if it had not been so thin it might have been repulsive; perhaps it was only anxiety and scant food which had lent it intelligence and a certain sensibility. Even in death, under the shaking blue light of a slip of newspaper, the face was remarkable for its lack of humour. Perhaps, unlike most men, he had never had a girl. If he had lived with somebody who laughed at him a bit, she thought, he would not now be here like this; he wouldn't have taken things so seriously; he'd have learnt not to fuss, to let things slide; it's the only way. She touched the long moustaches. They were comic; they were pathetic; they could never let him seem tragic. Then the spill went out and he might have been buried already for all she could see of him and soon for all she thought of him, her mind swept away by faint sounds of a cruising car and of footsteps. Her scream had not gone unheard.

A narrow wash of light flowed under the ill-fitting door; voices spoke; and the car came humming gently down the road outside. The footsteps moved away, a door opened, and through the thin walls of the barn she heard somebody routing among the sacks next door; a dog snuffled. It brought back the level dull Nottingham fields, on a Sunday, the little knot of miners with whom she once went ratting, a dog called Spot. In and out of barns the dog went while they all stood in a circle armed with sticks. There was an argument going on outside, but she could not recognise any of the voices. The car stopped, but the engine was left softly running.

Then the door of the shed opened and the light leaped upwards to the sacks. She raised herself on an elbow and saw, through a crack of her barricade, the pale officer in pince-nez and the soldier who had been on guard outside the waiting-room. They crossed the floor towards her and her nerves gave way; she could not bear to wait all the slow time till she was discovered. They were half turned from her and when she got to her feet and called out, 'Here I am,' the officer jumped round, pulling out his revolver. Then he saw who it was, and asked her a question, standing still in the middle of the floor with his revolver levelled. She thought she understood him and said, 'He's dead.'

The officer gave an order and the soldier advanced and began to pull away the sacks slowly. It was the same man who had stopped her on the way to the restaurant-car, and she hated him for a moment until he raised his face and smiled at her miserably and apologetically, while the officer bombarded him from behind with little barbed impatiences. Suddenly, as he pulled away the last sack at the cave mouth, their faces almost touched, and in that instant she got as much from him as from conversation with a quiet man.

Major Petkovitch, when he saw that the doctor made no movement, crossed the shed and shone the light full on the dead face. The long moustaches paled in the glow and the open eyes cast back the light like plates. The major held out his revolver to the soldier. The good humour, the remnants of simple happiness, which had remained somewhere behind the façade of misery, collapsed. It was as if all the floors of a house fell and left the walls standing. He was horrified and inarticulate and motionless; and the revolver remained lying in the major's palm. Major Petkovitch did not lose his temper; he watched the other with curiosity and determination through his gold pince-nez. He had all the feeling of a barracks at his finger's end; beside the worn books on German strategy there stood on his shelves a little row of volumes on psychology; he knew every one of his privates with the intimacy of a confessor, how far they were brutal, how far kind, how far cunning and how far simple; he knew what their pleasures were—*rakia* and gaming and women; their ambitions, though these might be no more than an exciting or a happy story to tell a wife. He knew best of all how to adjust punishment to character, and how to break the will. He had been impatient with the soldier as he pulled so slowly at the sacks, but he was not impatient now; he let the revolver lie in his palm and repeated his command quite calmly, gazing through the gold rims.

The soldier lowered his head and wiped his nose with his hand and squinted painfully along the floor. Then he took the revolver and put it to Dr Czinner's mouth. Again he hesitated. He laid his hand on Coral's arm, and with a push sent her face downwards to the floor, and as she lay there, she heard the shot. The soldier had saved her from the sight, but he could not save her from her imagination. She got up and fled to the door, retching as she ran. She had expected the relief of darkness, and the glare of the headlamps outside came like a blow on the head. She leant against the door and tried to steady herself, feeling infinitely more alone than when she woke and found Dr Czinner dead; she wanted Myatt desperately, with pain. People were still arguing beside the car, and there was a faint smell of liquor in the air.

'What the hell?' a voice said. The knot of people was torn in two, and Miss Warren appeared between them. Her face was red and sore and triumphant. She gripped Coral's arm. 'What's happening? No, don't tell me now. You're sick. You're coming with me straight out of this.' The soldiers stood between her and the car, and the officer came from the shed and joined them. Miss Warren said rapidly in a low voice, 'Promise anything. Don't mind what you say.' She put a large square hand on the officer's sleeve and began to talk ingratiatingly. He tried to interrupt her, but his words were swept away. He took off his glasses and wiped them and was lost. Threats would have been idle, she might have protested all night, but she offered him the one bait it would have been against his nature to refuse, reason. And behind the reason she offered she allowed him to catch a glimpse of a different, a more valuable reason, a high diplomatic motive. He wiped his glasses again, nodded, and gave in. Miss Warren seized his hand and squeezed it, imprinting deep on the wincing finger the mark of her signet ring.

Coral slid to the ground. Miss Warren touched her and she tried to shake herself free. After the great noise the earth was swimming up to her in silence. Very far away a voice said, 'Your heart's bad,' and she opened her eyes again, expecting to see an old face beneath her. But she was stretched along the back seat of a car and Miss Warren was covering her with a rug. She poured out a glass of brandy and held it to Coral's mouth; the car starting shook them together and spilled the brandy over her chin; Coral smiled back at the flushed, tender, rather drunken face.

'Listen, darling,' Miss Warren said, 'I'm taking you back with me to Vienna first. I can wire the story from there. If any dirty skunk tries to get at you say nothing. Don't even open your mouth to say no.'

The words conveyed nothing to Coral. She had a pain in her breast. She saw the station lights go out as the car turned away towards Vienna and she wondered with an obstinate fidelity where Myatt was. The pain made breathing difficult, but she was determined not to speak. To speak, to describe her pain, to ask for help would be to empty her mind for a moment of his face; her ears would lose the sound of his voice whispering to her of what they would do together in Constantinople. I won't be the first to forget, she thought with obstinacy, fighting with all the other images which strove for supremacy, the scarlet blink of the car down the dusky road, Dr Czinner's stare in the light of the spill; fighting desperately at last against pain, against breathlessness, against a desire to cry out, against a darkness of the brain which was robbing her even of the images she fought.

I remember. I haven't forgotten. But she could not restrain one cry. It was so low that the humming motor drowned it. It never reached Miss Warren's ears any more than the renewed whisper which followed it: I haven't forgotten.

'Exclusive,' Miss Warren said, drumming with her fingers on the rugs. 'I want it exclusive. It's my story,' she claimed with pride, allowing somewhere at the back of her mind, behind the headlines and the leaded type, a dream to form of Coral in pyjamas pouring out coffee, Coral in pyjamas mixing a cocktail, Coral asleep in the redecorated and rejuvenated flat.

PART V

CONSTANTINOPLE

I

'Hello, hello. Has Mr Carleton Myatt arrived yet?'

The small lively Armenian, with a flower in his buttonhole, answered, in an English as trim and well cut as his morning coat, 'No. I am afraid not. Is there any message?'

'Surely the train is in?'

'No. It is three hours late. I believe the engine broke down near Belgrade.'

'Tell him Mr Joyce . . .'

'And now,' said the reception clerk, leaning confidentially over the counter towards two rapt American girls, who watched him with parted lips, under beautiful plucked brows, 'what can I advise for you two ladies this afternoon? You should have a guide for the bazaars.'

'Perhaps you, Mr Kalebdjian,' they said almost in the same breath; their wide avaricious virginal eyes followed him as he swung round at the buzz of the telephone: 'Hello. Hello. Long-distance personal call? Right. Hello. No, Mr Carleton Myatt has not arrived yet. We expect him any moment. Shall I take a message? You will ring up again at six. Thank you.'

'Ah,' he said to the two Americans, 'if I could, it would be such a pleasure. But duty keeps me here. I have a second cousin though, and I will arrange that he shall meet you here tomorrow morning and take you to the bazaar. Now this afternoon I would suggest that you take a taxi to the Blue Mosque by way of the Hippodrome, and afterwards visit the Roman cisterns. Then if you took tea at the Russian restaurant in Pera, and came back here for dinner, I would recommend you to a theatre for the evening. Now if that suits you, I'll order you a taxi for the afternoon from a reliable garage.'

They both opened their mouths at once and said, 'That'll be swell, Mr Kalebdjian,' and while he was ringing up his third cousin's garage in Pera, they moved across the hall to the dusty confectionery stall and wondered whether to buy him a box of candies. The great garish hotel with its tiled floors and international staff and its restaurant in imitation of the Blue Mosque had been built before the war; now that the Government had shifted to Ankara and Constantinople was feeling the competition of the Piraeus, the hotel had sunk a little in the world. The staff had been cut, and it was possible to wander through the great empty lounge without meeting a page and the bells notoriously did not ring. But at the reception counter Mr

Kalebdjian opposed the general inertia in his well-cut coat.

'Is Mr Carleton Myatt in, Kalebdjian?'

'No, sir, the train's late. Would you care to wait?'

'He's got a sitting-room?'

'Oh, naturally. Here, boy, show this gentleman to Mr Myatt's room.'

'Give him my card when he comes in.'

The two Americans decided not to give Mr Kalebdjian a box of Turkish delight, but he was so sweet and pretty they wanted to do something for him and they stood lost in thought, until he appeared suddenly at their elbow: 'Your taxi is here, ladies. I will give the driver full directions. You will find him most reliable.' He led them out and saw them safely away. The little stir and bustle subsided like dust, and Mr Kalebdjian went back into the silent hall. For a moment it had been almost as in the old days at the height of the season.

No one came in for a quarter of an hour; an early fly nipped by the cold died noisily against a window-pane. Mr Kalebdjian rang up the housekeeper's room to make sure that the heating was turned on in the rooms, and then he sat with his hands between his knees with nothing to think about and nothing to do.

The swing doors turned and turned, and a knot of people entered. Myatt was the first of them. Janet Pardoe and Mr Savory followed him and three porters with their luggage. Myatt was happy. This was his chosen ground; an international hotel was his familiar oasis, however bare. The nightmare of Subotica faded and lost all reality before Mr Kalebdjian advancing to meet him. He was glad that Janet Pardoe should see how he was recognised in the best hotels far away from home.

'How are you, Mr Carleton Myatt? This is a great joy.' Mr Kalebdjian shook hands, bowing from the hips, his incredibly white teeth flashing with genuine pleasure.

'Glad to see you, Kalebdjian. Manager away as usual? These are my friends, Miss Pardoe and Mr Savory. The whole of this hotel is on Kalebdjian's shoulders,' he explained to them. 'You are making us comfortable? That's right. See that there's a box of sweets in Miss Pardoe's room.'

Janet Pardoe began softly, 'My uncle's meeting me,' but Myatt swept aside her objection. 'He can wait one day. You must be my guest here tonight.' He was beginning to unfurl again his peacock tail with a confidence which he borrowed from the palms and pillars and Mr Kalebdjian's deference.

'There've been two telephone calls for you, Mr Carleton Myatt, and a gentleman is waiting to see you in your room.'

'Good. Give me his card. See to my friends. My room the usual one?' He walked rapidly to the lift, his lips pursed with exhilaration, for there had been in the last few days too much that had been uncertain and difficult to understand, and now he was back at work. It will be Mr Eckman, he thought, not troubling to look at the card, and suddenly quite certain of what he would say to him. The lift rose uneasily to the first floor and the boy led him down a dusty passage and opened a door. The sunlight poured into the room and he could hear the yapping of cars through the open window. A fair

stocky man in a tweed suit got up from the sofa. 'Mr Carleton Myatt?' he
asked.

Myatt was surprised. He had never seen this man before. He looked at the
card in his hand and read Mr Leo Stein. 'Ah, Mr Stein.'

'Surprised to see me?' said Mr Stein. 'Hope you don't think me
precipitate.' He was very bluff and cordial. Very English, Myatt thought,
but the nose betrayed him, the nose which had been straightened by an
operation and bore the scar. The hostility between the open Jew and the
disguised Jew showed itself at once in the conjurer's smiles, the hearty
handclasp, the avoidance of the eyes. 'I had expected our agent,' Myatt said.

'Ah, poor Eckman, poor Eckman,' Stein sighed, shaking his blond head.

'What do you mean?'

'My business here really. To ask you to come and see Mrs Eckman. Very
worrying for her.'

'You mean he's gone?'

'Disappeared. Never went home last night. Very mysterious.'

It was cold. Myatt shut the window and with his hands in the pockets of
his fur coat walked up and down the room, three paces this way and three
paces that. He said slowly, 'I'm not surprised. He couldn't face me, I
suppose.'

'He told me a few days ago that he felt you didn't trust him. He was hurt,
very hurt.'

Myatt said slowly and carefully, 'I never trust a Jew who has turned
Christian.'

'Oh come, Mr Myatt, isn't that a little dogmatic?' Stein said with a trace of
discomfort.

'Perhaps. I suppose,' Myatt said, stopping in the middle of the room,
with his back to Stein, but with Stein's body reflected to the knees in a gilt
mirror, 'he had gone further in his negotiations than he had ever let me
know.'

'Oh, the negotiations,' Stein's image in the mirror was less comfortable
than his voice, 'they, of course, were finished.'

'He had told you we wouldn't buy?'

'He'd bought.'

Myatt nodded. He was not surprised. There must have been a good deal
behind Eckman's disappearance. Stein said slowly, 'I'm really worried
about poor Eckman. I can't bear to think he may have killed himself.'

'I don't think you need worry. He's just retired from business, I expect. A
little hurriedly.'

'You see,' Stein said, 'he had worries.'

'Worries?'

'Well, there was the feeling that you didn't trust him. And then he didn't
have any children. He wanted children. He had a lot to worry him, Mr
Myatt. One must be charitable.'

'But I am not a Christian, Mr Stein. I don't believe that charity is the chief
virtue. Can I see the paper he signed?'

'Of course.' Mr Stein drew a long envelope folded in two from the pocket
of the tweed coat. Myatt sat down, spread the pages out on a table, and read
them carefully. He made no comment and his expression conveyed nothing.

No one could have told how great was his happiness at being back with figures, with something that he could understand and that had no feelings. When he had finished reading, he leant back and stared at his nails; they had been manicured before he left London, but they needed attention already.

Mr Stein asked gently, 'Had a good journey? Trouble in Belgrade didn't affect you, I suppose?'

'No,' Myatt said, with an absent mind. It was true. It seemed to him that the whole unexplained incident at Subotica was unreal. Very soon he would have forgotten it because it was isolated from ordinary life and because it had no explanation. He said, 'Of course you know we could drive a coach through this agreement.'

'I don't think so,' Mr Stein said. 'Poor Eckman was your accredited agent. You left him in charge of the negotiations.'

'He never had the authority to sign this. No, Mr Stein, this is no good to you, I'm afraid.'

Mr Stein sat down on the sofa and crossed his legs. He smelt of pipe smoke and tweeds. 'Of course, Mr Myatt,' he said, 'I don't want to force anything down your throat. My motto is: Never let down a fellow business man. I'd tear that agreement up now, Mr Myatt, if it was the fair thing to do. But you see, since poor Eckman signed this, Moult's have given up. They won't reopen their offer now.'

'I know just how far Moult's were interested in currants,' Myatt said.

'Well, you see, under the circumstances, and in all friendliness, Mr Myatt, if you tear that agreement up, I shall have to fight it. Mind if I smoke?'

'Have a cigar.'

'Mind if I have a pipe?' He began to stuff a pale sweet tobacco into the bowl.

'I suppose Eckman got a commission on this?'

'Ah, poor Eckman,' Mr Stein said enigmatically. 'I'd really like you to come along and see Mrs Eckman. She's very worried.'

'She has no need to worry if his commission was big enough.' Mr Stein smiled and lit his pipe. Myatt began to read the agreement over again. It was true that it could be upset, but courts of law were chancy things. A good barrister might give a lot of trouble. There were figures one would rather not see published. After all Stein's business was of value to the firm. What he disliked was the price and the directorship granted to Stein. Even the price was not out of the question, but he could not bear the intrusion of a stranger into the family business. He said, 'I'll tell you what I'll do. We'll tear this up and make you a new offer.'

Mr Stein shook his head. 'Come now, that wouldn't be quite fair to me, would it, Mr Myatt?' Myatt decided what he would do. He did not want to worry his father with a lawsuit. He would accept the agreement on condition that Stein resigned the directorship. But he was not going to show his hand yet; Stein might crumple. 'Sleep on it, Mr Stein,' he advised.

'Well, that,' Mr Stein said cheerfully, 'I doubt if I shall be allowed to do. Not if I know the girls of today. I'm meeting a niece here his afternoon. She travelled out on your train from Cologne. Poor Pardoe's child.'

Myatt took out his cigar-case, and while he chose and cut a cigar, decided what he would do. He began to despise Stein. He talked too much and gave away unnecessary information. No wonder his business had not prospered. At the same time Myatt's vague attraction to Stein's niece crystallised. The knowledge that her mother had been a Jewess made him feel suddenly at home with her. She became approachable, and he was ashamed of the stiffness of his company the night before. They had dined together in the train on his return from Subotica, but all the time he had been on his best behaviour. He said slowly, 'Oh yes, I met Miss Pardoe on the train. In fact she's down below now. We came from the station together.'

It was Mr Stein's turn to weigh his words. When he spoke it was at a slight significant tangent. 'Poor girl, she's got no parents. My wife thought we ought to have her to stay. I'm her guardian, you see.' They sat side by side with the table between them. On it lay the agreement signed by Mr Eckman. They did not mention it; business seemed laid aside, but Stein and Myatt knew that the whole discussion had been reopened. Each was aware of the thought in the other's mind, but they spoke in evasions.

'Your sister,' Myatt said, 'must have been a lovely woman.'

'She got her looks from my father,' Mr Stein said. Neither would admit that they were interested in Janet Pardoe's beauty. Even her grandparents were mentioned before her. 'Did your family come from Leipzig?' Myatt asked.

'That's right. It was my father who brought the business here.'

'You found it a mistake?'

'Oh, come now, Mr Myatt, you've seen the figures. It wasn't as bad as that. But I want to sell out and retire while I can still enjoy life.'

'How do you mean?' Myatt asked with curiosity. 'How enjoy life?'

'Well, I'm not very much interested in business,' Mr Stein said.

Myatt repeated with amazement, 'Not interested in business?'

'Golf,' said Mr Stein, 'and a little place in the country. That's what I look forward to.'

The shock passed, and Myatt again noted that Stein gave away too much information. Stein's expansive manner was his opportunity; he flashed the conversation back to the agreement: 'Why do you want this directorship then? I think perhaps I could come near to meeting you on the money question if you resigned the directorship.'

'I don't want it for myself necessarily,' said Mr Stein, puffing at his pipe between his phrases, squinting sideways at Myatt's lengthening ash, 'but I'd like—for the sake of tradition, you know—to have one of the family on the board.' He gave a long candid chuckle. 'But I have no son. Not even a nephew.'

Myatt said thoughtfully, 'You'll have to encourage your niece,' and they both laughed and walked downstairs together. Janet Pardoe was nowhere to be seen.

'Miss Pardoe gone out?' he asked Mr Kalebdjian.

'No, Mr Myatt, Miss Pardoe has just gone to the restaurant with Mr Savory.'

'Ask them to wait lunch twenty minutes, and Mr Stein and I will join them.'

There was a slight tussle to be last through the swing door; the friendship between Myatt and Mr Stein grew rapidly.

When they were in a taxi on the way to Mr Eckman's flat, Stein spoke. 'This Savory,' he said, 'who's he?'

'Just a writer,' said Myatt.

'Is he hanging round Janet?'

'Friendly,' Myatt said. 'They met on the train.' He clasped his hands over his knees and sat silent, contemplating seriously the subject of marriage. She is very lovely, he thought, she is refined, she would make a good hostess, she is half Jewish.

'I'm her guardian,' said Mr Stein. 'Ought I perhaps to speak to him?'

'He's well off.'

'Yes, but a writer,' said Mr Stein. 'I don't like it. They are chancy. I'd like to see her married to a steady fellow in business.'

'She was introduced to him, I think, by this woman she's been living with in Cologne.'

'Oh yes,' said Mr Stein, uncomfortably, 'she's been earning her own living since her poor parents died. I didn't interfere. It's good for a girl, but my wife thought we ought to see something of her, so I invited her here. Thought perhaps we could find her a better job near us.'

They swerved round a miniature policeman standing on a box to direct traffic and climbed a hill. Below them, between a tall bare tenement and a telegraph-pole, the domes of the Blue Mosque floated up like a cluster of azure soap bubbles.

Mr Stein was still uneasy. 'It's good for a girl,' he repeated. 'And the firm's been taking up all my time lately. But when this sale is through,' he added brightly, 'I'll settle something on her.'

The taxi drew into a small dark courtyard, containing a solitary dustbin, but the long stair they climbed was lighted by great windows and the whole of Stamboul seemed to flow out beneath them. They could see St Sophia and the Fire Tower and a long stretch of water up the western side of the Golden Horn towards Eyub. 'A fine situation,' said Mr Stein. 'There's not a better flat in Constantinople,' and he rang the bell, but Myatt was thinking of the cost and wondering how much the firm had contributed to Mr Eckman's view.

The door opened. Mr Stein did not trouble to give his name to the maid, but led the way down a white panelled passage which trapped the sun like a tawny beast between its windows. 'A friend of the family?' Myatt suggested. 'Oh, poor Eckman and I have been quite intimate for some time now,' said Mr Stein, flinging open a door on to a great glassy drawing-room, in which a piano and a bowl of flowers and a few steel chairs floated in primrose air. 'Well, Emma,' said Mr Stein, 'I've brought along Mr Carleton Myatt to see you.'

There were no dark corners in the room, no shelter from the flow of soft benevolent light, but Mrs Eckman had done her best to hide behind the piano which stretched like a polished floor between them. She was small and grey and fashionably dressed, but her clothes did not suit her. She reminded Myatt of an old family maid who wears her mistress's discarded frocks. She had a pile of sewing under her arm and she whispered her welcome from where she stood, not venturing any farther on to the sun-splashed floor.

'Well, Emma,' said Mr Stein, 'have you heard anything from your husband?'

'No. Not yet. No,' she said. She added with bright misery, 'He's such a bad correspondent,' and asked them to sit down. She began to hide away needles and cotton and balls of wool and pieces of flannel in a large work-bag. Mr Stein stared uncomfortably from steel chair to steel chair. 'Can't think why poor Eckman bought all this stuff,' he breathed to Myatt.

Myatt said: 'You mustn't worry, Mrs Eckman. I've no doubt you'll hear from your husband today.'

She stopped in the middle of her tidying and watched Myatt's lips.

'Yes, Emma,' said Mr Stein, 'directly poor Eckman knows how well Mr Myatt and I agree, he'll come hurrying home.'

'Oh,' Mrs Eckman whispered from her corner, away across the shining floor, 'I don't mind if he doesn't come back here. I'd go to him anywhere. This isn't *home*,' she said with a small emphatic gesture and dropped a needle and two pearl buttons.

'Well, I agree,' Mr Stein remarked and blew out his cheeks. 'I don't understand what your husband sees in all this steel stuff. Give me some good mahogany pieces and a couple of arm-chairs a man can go to sleep in.'

'Oh, but my husband has very good taste,' Mrs Eckman whispered hopelessly, her frightened eyes peering out from under her fashionable hat like a mouse lost in a wardrobe.

'Well,' Myatt said impatiently, 'I'm sure you needn't worry at all about your husband. He's been upset about business, that's all. There's no reason to think that he's—that anything has happened to him.'

Mrs Eckman emerged from behind the piano and came across the floor, twisting her hands nervously. 'I'm not afraid of that,' she said. She stopped between them and then turned round and went back quickly to her corner. Myatt was startled. 'Then what are you afraid of?' he asked.

She nodded her head at the bright steely room. 'My husband's so modern,' she said with fear and pride. Then her pride went out, and with her hands plunged in her work-basket, among the buttons and the balls of wool, she said, 'He may not want to come back for me.'

'Well, what do you think of that?' Mr Stein said as he went downstairs.

'Poor woman,' Myatt said.

'Yes, yes, poor woman,' Mr Stein repeated, blowing his nose in an honest emotional way. He felt hungry, but Myatt had more to do before lunch, and Mr Stein stuck close. He felt that with every taxi they shared, their intimacy grew, and apart altogether from their plans for Janet Pardoe, intimacy with Myatt was worth several thousand pounds a year to him. The taxi rattled down a steep cobbled street out into the cramped square by the general post office, and then down-hill again to Galata and the docks. At the top of a dingy stair they reached the small office, crammed with card indexes and dispatch-boxes, with only one window that looked out on to a high wall and the top of a steamer's funnel. Dust lay thick on the sill. It was the room which had given birth to the great glassy drawing-room, as an elderly mother may bear an artist as her last child. A grandfather clock, which with the desk filled most of the remaining space, struck two, but early as it was Joyce was there. A typist disappeared into a kind of boot cupboard at the back of the room.

'Any news of Eckman?'

'No, sir,' said Joyce. Myatt glanced at a few letters and then left him, crouched like a faithful dog over Eckman's desk and Eckman's transgressions. 'And now lunch,' he said. Mr Stein moistened his lips. 'Hungry?' Myatt asked.

'I had an early breakfast,' said Mr Stein without reproach.

But Janet Pardoe and Mr Savory had not waited for them. They were drinking coffee and liqueurs in the blue tiled restaurant when Myatt and Mr Stein exclaimed how lucky it was that his niece and Myatt had met already and were friends. Janet Pardoe said nothing, but watched him with peaceful eyes, and smiled once at Myatt. She seemed to Myatt to be saying, 'How little does he know of us,' and he smiled back before he remembered that there was nothing to know.

'So I suppose you two,' said Mr Stein, 'kept each other company all the way from Cologne.'

Mr Savory asserted himself, 'Well, I think your niece saw more of me,' but Mr Stein swept on, eliminating him. 'Got to know each other well, eh?'

Janet Pardoe opened her soft pronounced lips a little way and said softly, 'Oh, Mr Myatt had another friend he knew better than me.' Myatt turned his head to order lunch, and when he gave his attention again to them, Janet Pardoe was saying with a sweet gentle malice, 'Oh, she was his mistress, you know.'

Mr Stein laughed heartily. 'Look at the wicked fellow. He's blushing.'

'And you know she ran away from him,' said Janet Pardoe.

'Ran away from him? Did he beat her?'

'Well, if you ask him he'll try and make a mystery about it. When the train broke down he motored all the way back to the last station and looked for her. He was away ages. And the mystery he tries to make of it. He helped someone to escape from the customs.'

'But the girl?' Mr Stein asked, eyeing Myatt roguishly.

'She ran away with a doctor,' Mr Savory said.

'He'll never admit it,' Janet Pardoe said, nodding at Myatt.

'Well, really, I'm a little uneasy about it,' Myatt said. 'I shall telephone to the consul at Belgrade.'

'Telephone to your grandmother,' Mr Savory exclaimed and looked with a bright nervousness from one to the other. It was his habit when he was quite certain of his company to bring out some disarming colloquialism which drew attention to the shop counter, the apprentices' dormitory, in his past. He was still at times swept by an intoxicating happiness at being accepted, at finding himself at the best hotel, talking on equal terms to people whom he had once thought he would never know except across the bales of silk, the piles of tissue-paper. The great ladies who invited him to their literary At Homes were delighted by his expressions. What was the good of displaying a novelist who had risen from the bargain counter if he did not carry with him some faint trace of his ancestry, some remnant from the sales?

Mr Stein glared at him. 'I think you would be quite right,' he said to Myatt. Mr Savory was abashed. These people were among the minority who had never read his books, who did not know his claim to attention. They thought him merely vulgar. He sank a little in his seat and said to Janet Pardoe, 'The doctor. Wasn't *your* friend interested in the doctor?' but she was aware of the others' disapproval, and did not trouble to search her mind for the long dull story Miss Warren had told her. She cut him short, 'I can't keep count of all the people Mabel's interested in. I don't remember anything about the doctor.'

It was only the vulgarity of Mr Savory's expression to which Mr Stein objected. He was very much in favour of a little honest chaff about the girl. It would seal his valuable intimacy with Myatt. When the first course was on the table, he brought the conversation round again. 'Now tell us some more of what Mr Myatt's been up to.'

'She's very pretty,' said Janet Pardoe, with audible charity. Mr Savory glanced at Myatt to see whether he was taking offence, but Myatt was too hungry; he was enjoying his late lunch. 'On the stage, isn't she?' he asked.

'Yes. Variety.'

'I said she was a chorus girl,' Janet Pardoe remarked. 'There was something just the faintest bit common. Had you met her before?'

'No, no,' Myatt said hurriedly. 'Just a chance meeting.'

'The things that go on in these long-distance trains,' Mr Stein exclaimed with relish. 'Did she cost you much?' He caught his niece's eye and winked. When she smiled back, he was pleased. It would have been tiresome if she had been one of those old-fashioned girls in front of whom one could not talk openly; there was nothing he liked better than a little bit of smut in female company; so long, of course, he thought, with his eye turning with disapproval to Mr Savory, as it was quite refined.

'Ten pounds,' Myatt said, nodding to the waiter.

'My dear, how expensive,' said Janet Pardoe, and she watched him with respect.

'I'm joking,' Myatt said. 'I didn't give her any money. I got her a ticket. Besides, it was just a friendship. She's a good creature.'

'Ah, ha,' said Mr Stein. Myatt drained his glass. Across the blue tiles a waiter came, pushing a trolley. 'The food's very good here,' said Mr Savory. Myatt expanded in the air of home, faintly aromatic with cooking; in one of the public rooms a Rachmaninoff Concerto was being played. One might have been in London. At the sound of the music a memory swam up into his mind and broke in scarlet light; people stuck their heads out of windows, laughing, talking, jeering at the fiddler. He said slowly to himself, 'She was in love with me.' He had never meant the words to drop audibly into the bare blue restaurant; he was embarrassed and a little shocked to hear them; they sounded boastful, and he had not meant to boast; there was nothing to boast about in being loved by a chorus girl. He blushed when they all laughed at him.

'Ah, these girls,' Mr Stein said, shaking his head, 'they know how to get round a man. It's the glamour of the stage. I remember when I was a young fellow how I'd wait outside the stage door for hours just to see some little hussy from the front row. Chocolates. Suppers.' He was stopped for a moment by the sight of a duck's grey breast on his plate. 'The lights of London,' he said.

'Talking of theatres, Janet,' Myatt said, 'will you do a show with me tonight?' He used her Christian name, feeling quite at ease now that he knew that her mother was Jewish and that her uncle was in his pocket.

'I should love to, but I've promised Mr Savory to have dinner with him.'

'We could go along to a late cabaret.' But he had no intention of allowing her to dine with Mr Savory. All the afternoon he was too busy to see her; there were hours he had to spend at the office, straightening out all the affairs which Mr Eckman had so ingeniously tangled; he had visits to pay. At half-past three driving through the Hippodrome he saw Mr Savory taking photographs in the middle of a group of children; he worked rapidly; three times he squeezed his bulb while the taxi went by, and each time the children laughed at him. It was half-past six when Myatt returned to the hotel.

'Is Miss Pardoe about, Kalebdjian?' Mr Kalebdjian knew everything that went on in the hotel. Only his restlessness explained the minuteness of his information; he would make sudden dives from the deserted hall, rattle upstairs and down again, penetrate into distant lounges, and then be back at his desk with his hands between his knees, doing nothing. 'Miss Pardoe is changing for dinner, Mr Carleton Myatt.' Once when a member of the Government was staying in the hotel, Mr Kalebdjian had startled a meticulous caller from the British Embassy: 'His Excellency is in the lavatory. But he will not be more than another three minutes.' Trotting down corridors, listening at bathroom doors, back again with nothing to do but turn over in his mind a little sheaf of information, that was Mr Kalebdjian's life.

Myatt tapped on Janet Pardoe's door. 'Who's that?'

'May I come in?'

'The door's not locked.'

Janet Pardoe had nearly finished dressing. Her frock lay across the bed and she sat before her dressing-table powdering her arms. 'Are you really going to have dinner with Savory?' Myatt asked.

'Well, I promised to,' Janet said.

'We could have had dinner at the Pera Palace, and then gone on to the Petits Champs.'

'It would have been lovely, wouldn't it,' Janet Pardoe said. She began to brush her eyelashes.

'Who's that?' Myatt pointed at a large photograph in a folding frame of a woman's square face. The hair was bobbed and the photographer had tried to dissolve in mist the rocky outline of the jaw.

'That's Mabel. She came with me on the train as far as Vienna.'

'I don't remember seeing her.'

'Her hair's cut short now. That's an old photograph. She doesn't like being taken.'

'She looks grim.'

'I put it up there in case I began to feel naughty. She writes poetry. There's some on the back. It's very bad, I think. I don't know anything about poetry.'

'Can I read it?'

'Of course. I expect you think it very funny that anyone should write me poetry.' Janet Pardoe stared into the mirror.

Myatt turned the photograph round and read.

> 'Naiad, slim, water-cool,
> Borne for a river,

> *Running to the sea:*
> *Endure a year longer*
> *Salt, rocky, narrow pool'*

'It doesn't rhyme. Or does it?' Myatt asked. 'What does it mean, anyway?'

'I think it's meant as a compliment,' Janet Pardoe said, polishing her nails.

Myatt sat down on the edge of the bed and watched her. What would she do, he wondered, if I tried to seduce her? He knew the answer: she would laugh. Laughter was the perfect defence of chastity. He said, 'You aren't going to have dinner with Savory. I wouldn't be seen dead with a man like that. A counter-jumper.'

'My dear,' Janet Pardoe said, 'I promised. Besides he's a genius.'

'You are going to come downstairs with me, jump into a taxi, and have dinner at the Pera Palace.'

'Poor man, he'll never forgive me. It would be fun.'

And that's that. Myatt thought, pulling at his black tie, everything is easy now that I know her mother was Jewish. It was easy to talk hard all through dinner and to put his arm round her as they walked from the Pera Palace to the Petits Champs near the British Embassy. The night was warm, for the wind had dropped, and the tables in the garden were crowded. Subotica became the more unreal when he remembered the snow driven against his face. On the stage, a Frenchwoman in a dinner-jacket pranced up and down with a cane under her arm, singing a song about 'Ma Tante', which Spinelli had made popular in Paris more than five years before. The Turkish gentlemen, drinking coffee, laughed and chattered and shook their small dark feathery heads like noisy domestic birds, but their wives, so lately freed from the veil, sat silent and stared at the singer, their faces pasty and expressionless. Myatt and Janet Pardoe walked along the garden's edge, looking for a table, while the Frenchwoman screeched and laughed and pranced, flinging her desperate indecencies towards the inattentive and the unamused. Pera fell steeply away below them, the lights of fishing boats in the Golden Horn flashed like pocket torches, and the waiters went round serving coffee. 'I don't believe there's a table. We shall have to go into the theatre.' A fat man waved his hand and grinned. 'Do you know him?' Myatt thought for a moment, walking on. 'Yes, I think. . . . A man called Grünlich.' He had seen him clearly only twice, once when he had climbed into the car and once when he had climbed out into the light of the waiting train. His memory therefore was dim, as of someone he had known better a long while ago in another country. When they had passed the table, he forgot him.

'There's an empty one.' Under the table their legs touched. The Frenchwoman disappeared, swinging her hips, and a man flung cartwheels on to the stage from the wings. He got to his feet, took off his hat, and said something in Turkish which made everyone laugh.

'What did he say?'

'I couldn't hear,' Myatt said. The man threw his hat into the air, caught it, leant forward until he was bent double, and called out a single word. All the Turkish gentlemen laughed again, and even the pasty faces smiled. 'What did he say?'

'It must have been dialect. I couldn't understand it.'

'I'd like something sentimental,' Janet Pardoe said. 'I drank too much at dinner. I'm feeling sentimental.'

'They give you a good dinner, don't they?' Myatt said with pride.

'Why don't you stay there? People say that it's the best hotel.'

'Oh well, you know, ours is pretty good, and I like Kalebdjian. He always makes me comfortable.'

'Still the best people—'

A troupe of girls in shorts danced on the stage. They wore guards' caps and they had hung whistles round their necks, but the significance was lost on the Turkish audience, which was not used to guards dressed in shorts. 'I believe they are English girls,' Myatt said, and he suddenly leant forward.

'Do you know one of them?'

'I thought–I hoped,' but he was not sure that it had not been fear he felt at the appearance of Dunn's Babies. Coral had not told him she was going to dance at the Petits Champs, but very likely she had not known. He remembered her staring with brave bewilderment into the noisy dark.

'I like the Pera Palace.'

'Well, I did stay there once,' Myatt said, 'but something embarrassing happened. That's why I never went again.'

'Tell me. But don't be silly, you must. Do tell me.'

'Well, I had a friend with me. She seemed quite a nice young thing.'

'A chorus girl?'

Dunn's Babies began to sing:

> *'If you want to express*
> *That feeling you've got,*
> *When you're sometimes cold,*
> *   sometimes hot.'*

'No, no. She was the secretary of a friend of mine. Shipping.'

'Come up here,' Dunn's Babies sang. *'Come up here,'* and some English sailors sitting at the back of the garden clapped and shouted: 'Wait for us. We're coming.' One sailor began to push his way between the tables towards the stage.

> *'If you want to express*
> *That kind of gloom*
> *You feel alone in a double*
> *   room . . .'*

The man fell on his back and everyone laughed. He was very drunk.

Myatt said, 'It was terrible. She suddenly went mad at about two o'clock in the morning. Shouting and breaking things. The night porter came upstairs, and everybody stood about in the passage. They thought I was doing something to her.'

'And were you?'

'No. I'd been fast asleep. It was terrible. I've never spent a night there since.'

'Come up here. Come up here.'

'What was she like?'

'I can't remember a thing about her.'

Janet Pardoe said softly, 'You can't think how tired I am of living with a woman.' Accidentally their hands touched on the table and then stayed side by side. The fairy lights hanging in the bushes gleamed back at him from her necklace, and at the very end of the garden, over her shoulder Myatt saw Mr Stein pressing his way between the tables, pipe in hand. It was a mass attack. He knew that he only had to lean forward now to ask her to marry him and he would have arranged far more than his domestic future; he would have bought Mr Stein's business at Mr Stein's figure, and Mr Stein would have a nephew on the board and be satisfied. Mr Stein came nearer and waved his pipe; he had to make a detour to avoid the drunk man on the ground, and during that moment's grace Myatt summoned to his assistance any thoughts likely to combat the smooth and settled future. He remembered Coral and the sudden strangeness of their meeting, when he had thought that all was as familiar as cigarette smoke, but her face eluded him, perhaps because the train at that moment had been almost in darkness. She was fair, she was thin, but he could not remember her features. I have done all I can for her, he told himself; we should have said good-bye in any case in a few weeks. It's about time I settled down.

Mr Stein waved his pipe again, and Dunn's Babies stamped their feet and blew their whistles.

> '*Waiting at the station*
> *For a near relation,*
> *Puff, puff, puff, puff—*'

Myatt said, 'Don't go back to her. Stay with me.'

> '*Puff, puff, puff, puff,*
> *The Istanbul train.*'

She nodded and their hands moved together. He wondered whether Mr Stein had the contract in his pocket.

A BURNT-OUT
CASE

To Docteur Michel Lechat

Dear Michel,

I hope you will accept the dedication of this novel which owes any merit it may have to your kindness and patience; the faults, failures and inaccuracies are the author's alone. Dr. Colin has borrowed from you his experience of leprosy and nothing else. Dr. Colin's leproserie is not your leproserie–which now, I fear, has probably ceased to exist. Even geographically it is placed in a region far from Yonda. Every leproserie, of course, has features in common, and from Yonda and other leproseries which I visited in the Congo and the Cameroons I may have taken superficial characteristics. From the fathers of your Mission I have stolen the Superior's cheroots–that is all, and from your Bishop the boat that he was so generous as to lend me for a journey up the Ruki. It would be a waste of time for anyone to try to identify Querry, the Ryckers, Parkinson, Father Thomas–they are formed from the flotsam of thirty years as a novelist. This is not a *roman à clef*, but an attempt to give dramatic expression to various types of belief, half-belief and non-belief, in the kind of setting, removed from world-politics and household-preoccupations, where such differences are felt acutely and find expression. This Congo is a region of the mind, and the reader will find no place called Luc on any map, nor did its Governor and Bishop exist in any regional capital.

You, if anyone, will know how far I have failed in what I attempted. A doctor is not immune from 'the long despair of doing nothing well,' the *cafard* that hangs around a writer's life. I only wish I had dedicated to you a better book in return for the limitless generosity I was shown at Yonda by you and the fathers of the mission.

Affectionately yours,
Graham Greene

A BURNT-OUT CASE

'Io non mori', e non rimasi vivo.'
(I did not die, yet nothing of life remained.)

Dante

'Within limits of normality, every individual loves
himself. In cases where he has a deformity or
abnormality or develops it later, his own aesthetic
sense revolts and he develops a sort of disgust towards
himself. Though with time, he becomes reconciled to
his deformities, it is only at the conscious level. His
sub-conscious mind, which continues to bear the mark
of injury, brings about certain changes in his whole
personality, making him suspicious of society.'

R. V. Wardekar
(in a pamphlet on leprosy)

PART I

CHAPTER I

I

The cabin-passenger wrote in his diary a parody of Descartes: 'I feel discomfort, therefore I am alive,' then sat pen in hand with no more to record. The captain in a white soutane stood by the open windows of the saloon reading his breviary. There was not enough air to stir the fringes of his beard. The two of them had been alone together on the river for ten days—alone, that is to say, except for the six members of the African crew and the dozen or so deck-passengers who changed, almost indistinguishably, at each village where they stopped. The boat, which was the property of the Bishop, resembled a small battered Mississippi paddle-steamer with a high nineteenth-century fore-structure, the white paint badly in need of renewal. From the saloon windows they could see the river before them unwind, and below them on the pontoons the passengers sat and dressed their hair among the logs of wood for the engine.

If no change means peace, this certainly was peace, to be found like a nut at the centre of the hard shell of discomfort—the heat that engulfed them where the river narrowed to a mere hundred metres: the shower that was always hot from the ship's engine: in the evening the mosquitoes, and in the day the tsetse flies with wings raked back like tiny jet-fighters (a board above the bank at the last village had warned them in three languages: 'Zone of sleeping sickness. Be careful of the tsetse flies.'). The captain read his breviary with a fly-whisk in his hand, and whenever he made a kill he held up the tiny corpse for the passenger's inspection, saying 'tsetse'—it was nearly the limit of their communication, for neither spoke the other's language with ease or accuracy.

This was somewhat the way in which the days passed. The passenger would be woken at four in the morning by the tinkling sound of the sanctus-bell in the saloon, and presently from the window of the Bishop's cabin, which he shared with a crucifix, a chair, a table, a cupboard where cockroaches lurked, and one picture—the nostalgic photograph of some church in Europe covered in a soutane of heavy snow—he would see the congregation going home across the gang-plank. He would watch them as they climbed the steep bank and disappeared into the bush, swinging lanterns like the carol-singers he had once seen during his stay in a New England village. By five the boat was on the move again, and at six as the sun rose he would eat his breakfast with the captain. The next three hours, before the great heat had begun, were for both men the best of the day, and the passenger found that he could watch, with a kind of inert content, the thick, rapid, khaki-coloured stream against which the small boat fought its way at about three knots, the engine, somewhere below the altar and the Holy Family, groaning like an exhausted animal and the big wheel churning away at the stern. A lot of effort it seemed for so slow a progress. Every few hours a fishing-village came into sight, the houses standing high on stilts to guard them against the big rains and the rats. At times a member of the crew called up to the captain, and the captain would take his gun and shoot at some small sign of life that only he and the sailor had eyes to detect among the green and blue shadows of the forest: a baby crocodile sunning on a fallen log, or a fishing eagle which waited motionless among the leaves. At nine the heat had really begun, and the captain, having finished reading his breviary, would oil his gun or kill a few more tsetse flies, and sometimes, sitting down at the dining-table with a box of beads, he would set himself the task of manufacturing cheap rosaries.

After the midday meal both men retired to their cabins as the forests sauntered by under the exhausting sun. Even when the passenger was naked it was difficult for him to sleep, and he was never finally able to decide between letting a little draught pass through his cabin or keeping the hot air out. The boat possessed no fan, and so he woke always with a soiled mouth, and while the warm water in the shower cleaned his body it could not refresh it.

There yet remained another hour or two of peace towards the end of the day, when he sat below on a pontoon while the Africans prepared their chop in the early dark. The vampire-bats creaked over the forest and candles flickered, reminding him of the Benedictions of his youth. The laughter of the cooks went back and forth from one pontoon to the other, and it was never long before someone sang, but he couldn't understand the words.

At dinner they had to close the windows of the saloon and draw the curtains to, so that the steersman might see his way between the banks and snags, and then the pressure-lamp gave out too great a heat for so small a room. To delay the hour of bed they played *quatre cent vingt et un* wordlessly like a ritual mime, and the captain invariably won as though the god he believed in, who was said to control the winds and waves, controlled the dice too in favour of his priest.

This was the moment for talk in garbled French or garbled Flemish if they were going to talk, but they never talked much. Once the passenger asked, 'What are they singing, father? What kind of song? A love song?'

'No,' the captain said, 'not a love song. They sing only about what has happened during the day, how at the last village they bought some fine cooking-pots which they will sell for a good profit further up the river, and of course they sing of you and me. They call me the great fetishist,' he added with a smile and nodded at the Holy Family and the pull-out altar over the cupboard where he kept the cartridges for his gun and his fishing-tackle. He killed a mosquito with a slap on his naked arm and said, 'There is a motto in the Mongo language, "The mosquito has no pity for the thin man".'

'What do they sing about me?'

'They are singing now, I think.' He put the dice and counters away and listened. 'Shall I translate for you? It is not altogether complimentary.'

'Yes, if you please.'

'Here is a white man who is neither a father nor a doctor. He has no beard. He comes from a long way away—we do not know from where—and he tells no one to what place he is going nor why. He is a rich man, for he drinks whisky every evening and he smokes all the time. Yet he offers no man a cigarette.'

'That had never occurred to me.'

'Of course,' the captain said, 'I know where you are going, but you have never told me why.'

'The road was closed by floods. This was the only route.'

'That wasn't what I meant.'

About nine in the evening they usually, if the river had not widened and thus made navigation easy, pulled into the bank. Sometimes they would find there a rotting upturned boat which served as shelter when it rained for unlikely passengers. Twice the captain disembarked his ancient bicycle and bounced off into the dark interior to try to obtain some cargo from a *colon* living miles away and save it from the hands of the O.T.R.A.C.O. company, the great monopolist of the river and the tributaries, and there were times, if they were not too late in tying up, when they received unexpected visitors. On one occasion a man, a woman and a child, with sickly albino skins that came from years of heat and humidity, emerged from the thick rain-forest in an old station-wagon; the man drank a glass or two of whisky, while he and the priest complained of the price that Otraco charged for fuelling wood and spoke of the riots hundreds of miles away in the capital, while the woman sat silent holding the child's hand and stared at the Holy Family. When there were no European visitors there were always the old women, their heads tied up in dusters, their bodies wrapped in mammy-cloths, the once bright colours so faded that you could scarcely detect the printed designs of match-boxes, soda-water siphons, telephones, or other gimmicks of the white man. They shuffled into the saloon on their knees and patiently waited under the roaring pressure-lamp until they were noticed. Then, with an apology to his passenger, the captain would send him to his cabin, for these were confessions that he had to hear in secret. It was the end of one more day.

2

For several mornings they were pursued by yellow butterflies which were a welcome change from the tsetses. The butterflies came tacking into the saloon as soon as it was light, while the river still lay under a layer of mist like steam on a vat. When the mist cleared they could see one bank lined with white nenuphars which from a hundred yards away resembled a regiment of swans. The colour of the water in this wider reach was pewter, except where the wheel churned the wake to chocolate, and the green reflection of the woods was not mirrored on the surface but seemed to shine up from underneath the paper-thin transparent pewter. Two men who stood in a pirogue had their legs extended by their shadows so that they appeared to be wading knee-deep in the water. The passenger said, 'Look, father, over there. Doesn't that suggest to you an explanation of how Christ was thought to be walking on the water?' but the captain, who was taking aim at a heron standing behind the rank of nenuphars, did not bother to answer. He had a passion for slaughtering any living thing, as though only man had the right to a natural death.

After six days they came to an African seminary standing like an ugly red-brick university at the top of the clay bank. At this seminary the captain had once taught Greek, and so they stopped here for the night, partly for old times' sake and partly to enable them to buy wood at a cheaper price than Otraco charged. The loading began immediately–the young black seminarists were standing ready, before the ship's bell rang twice, to carry the wood on to the pontoons so that the boat might be cast off again at the first hint of light. After their dinner the priests gathered in the common-room. The captain was the only one to wear a soutane. One father, with a trim pointed beard, dressed in an open khaki shirt, reminded the passenger of a young officer of the Foreign Legion he had once known in the East whose recklessness and ill-discipline had led to an heroic and wasteful death; another of the fathers might have been taken for a professor of economics, a third for a lawyer, a fourth for a doctor, but the too easy laughter, the exaggerated excitement over some simple game of cards with matches for stakes had the innocence and immaturity of isolation–the innocence of explorers marooned on an ice-cap or of men imprisoned by a war which has long passed out of hearing. They turned the radio on for the evening news, but this was just habit, the imitation of an act performed years ago for a motive they no longer remembered clearly; they were not interested in the tensions and changing cabinets of Europe, they were barely interested in the riots a few hundred miles away on the other side of the river, and the passenger became aware of his own safety among them–they would ask no intrusive questions. He was again reminded of the Foreign Legion. If he had been a murderer escaping from justice, not one would have had the curiosity to probe his secret wound.

And yet–he could not tell why–their laughter irritated him, like a noisy child or a disc of jazz. He was vexed by the pleasure which they took in small things–even in the bottle of whisky he had brought for them from the boat. Those who marry God, he thought, can become domesticated too–it's just as hum-drum a marriage as all the others. The word 'Love' means a formal touch of the lips as in the ceremony of the Mass, and 'Ave Maria' like 'dearest' is a phrase to open a letter. This marriage like the world's marriages was held together by habits and tastes shared in common between God and themselves–it was God's taste to be worshipped and their taste to worship, but only at stated hours like a suburban embrace on a Saturday night.

The laughter rose higher. The captain had been caught cheating, and now each priest in turn tried to outdo his neighbour by stealing matches, making surreptitious discards, calling the wrong suit–the game, like so many children's games, was about to reach an end in chaos, and would there be tears before bed? The passenger got impatiently up and walked away from them around the dreary common-room. The face of the new Pope, looking like an eccentric headmaster, stared at him from the wall. On top of a chocolate-coloured dresser lay a few *romans policiers* and a stock of missionary journals. He opened one: it reminded him of a school magazine. There was an account of a football match at a place called Oboko and an old boy was writing the first instalment of an essay called 'A Holiday in Europe'. A wall-calendar bore the photograph of another mission: there was the same kind of hideous church built of unsuitable brick beside a verandahed priest's house. Perhaps it was a rival school. Grouped in front of the buildings were the fathers: they were laughing too. The passenger wondered when it was that he had first begun to detest laughter like a bad smell.

He walked out into the moonlit dark. Even at night the air was so humid that it broke upon the cheek like tiny beads of rain. Some candles still burned on the pontoons and a torch moved along the upper deck, showing him where the boat was moored. He left the river and found a rough track which started behind the classrooms and led towards what geographers might have called the centre of Africa. He followed it a short way, for no reason that he knew, guided by the light of moon and stars; ahead of him he could hear a kind of music. The track brought him into a village and out the other side. The inhabitants were awake, perhaps because the moon was full: if so they had marked its exact state better than his diary. Men were beating on old tins they had salvaged from the mission, tins of sardines and Heinz beans and plum jam, and someone was playing a kind of home-made harp. Faces peered at him from behind small fires. An old woman danced awkwardly, cracking her hips under a piece of sacking, and again he felt taunted by the innocence of the laughter. They were not laughing at him, they were laughing with each other, and he was abandoned, as he had been in the living-room of the seminary, to his own region where laughter was like the unknown syllables of an enemy tongue. It was a very poor village: the thatch of the clay huts had been gnawed away a long time since by rats and rain, and the women wore only old clouts, which had once seen service for sugar or grain, around their waists. He recognised them as pygmoids—bastard descendants of the true pygmies. They were not a powerful enemy. He turned and went back to the seminary.

The room was empty, the card-game had broken up, and he passed to his bedroom. He had become so accustomed to the small cabin that he felt defenceless in this vast space which held only a washstand with a jug, basin and glass, a chair, a narrow bed under a mosquito-net, and a bottle of boiled water on the floor. One of the fathers, who was presumably the Superior, knocked and came in. He said, 'Is there anything you want?'

'Nothing. I want nothing.' He nearly added, 'That is my trouble.'

The Superior looked in the jug to see whether it was full. 'You will find the water very brown,' he said, 'but it is quite clean.' He lifted the lid of a soap-dish to assure himself that the soap had not been forgotten. A brand new orange tablet lay there.

'Lifebuoy,' the Superior said proudly.

'I haven't used Lifebuoy,' the passenger said, 'since I was a child.'

'Many people say it is good for prickly heat. But I never suffer from that.'

Suddenly the passenger found himself unable any longer not to speak. He said, 'Nor I. I suffer from nothing. I no longer know what suffering is. I have come to the end of all that too.'

'Too?'

'Like all the rest. To the end of everything.'

The Superior turned away from him without curiosity. He said, 'Oh well, you know, suffering is something which will aways be provided when it is required. Sleep well. I will call you at five.'

CHAPTER 2

I

Doctor Colin examined the record of the man's tests—for six months now the search for the leprosy bacilli in smears taken from the skin had shown a negative result. The African who stood before him with a staff under his shoulder had lost all his toes and fingers. Doctor Colin said, 'Excellent. You are cured.'

The man took a step or two nearer to the doctor's desk. His toeless feet looked like rods and when he walked it was as though he were engaged in pounding the path flat. He said with apprehension, 'Must I go away from here?'

Doctor Colin looked at the stump the man held out like a piece of wood which had been roughly carved into the beginnings of a human hand. There was a rule that the leproserie should take contagious cases only: the cured had to return to their villages, or, if it were possible, continue what treatment was necessary as outpatients in the hospital at Luc, the provincial capital. But Luc was many days away whether by road or river. Colin said, 'It would be hard for you to find work outside. I will see what can be done for you. Go and speak to the sisters.' The stump seemed useless, but it was extraordinary what a mutilated hand could be taught to do; there was one man in the leproserie without fingers who had been taught to knit as well as any sister. But even success could be saddening, for it showed the value of the material they had so often to discard. For fifteen years the doctor had dreamt of a day when he would have funds available for constructing special tools to fit each mutilation, but now he hadn't money enough even to provide decent mattresses in the hospital.

'What's your name?' he asked.

'Deo Gratias.'

Impatiently the doctor called out the next number.

It was a young woman with palsied fingers—a claw-hand. The doctor tried to flex her fingers, but she winced with the stab of the nerves, though she continued to smile with a kind of brave coquetry as though she thought in that way she might induce him to spare her further pain. She had made up her mouth with a mauve lipstick which went badly with the black skin, and her right breast was exposed, for she had been feeding her baby on the dispensary step. Her arm was scarred for half its length where the doctor had made an incision to release the ulnar nerve which had been strangled by its sheath. Now the girl was able with an effort to move her fingers a further degree. The doctor wrote on her card, for the sisters' attention, 'Paraffin wax' and turned to the next patient.

In fifteen years Doctor Colin had only known two days hotter than this one. Even the Africans were feeling the heat, and half the usual number of patients had come to the dispensary. There was no fan, and Doctor Colin worked below a make-shift awning on the verandah: a table, a hard wooden chair, and behind him the little office that he dreaded to enter because of the insufficient ventilation. His filing cabinets were there, and the steel was hot to the touch.

Patient after patient exposed his body to him; in all the years he had never become quite accustomed to the sweet gangrenous smell of certain leprous skins, and it had become to him the smell of Africa. He ran his fingers over the diseased surface and made his notes almost mechanically. The notes had small value, but his fingers, he knew, gave the patients comfort: they realised that they were not untouchable. Now that a cure had been found for the physical disease, he had always to remember that leprosy remained a psychological problem.

From the river Doctor Colin heard the sound of a ship's bell. The Superior passed by the dispensary on his bicycle, riding towards the beach. He waved, and the doctor raised his hand in answer. It was probably the day for the Otraco boat which was long overdue. It was supposed to call once a fortnight with mail, but they could never depend on it, for it was delayed more often than not by unexpected cargo or by a faulty pipe.

A baby began to cry and immediately like dogs all the babies around the dispensary started to howl together. 'Henri,' Doctor Colin called; his young African dispenser rapped out a phrase in his native tongue—'Babies to the breast' and instantaneously peace returned. At twelve-thirty the doctor broke off for the day. In the little hot office he wiped his hands with spirit.

He walked down towards the beach. He had been expecting a book to be sent him from Europe: a Japanese Atlas of Leprosy, and perhaps it had come with the mail. The long street of the leper village led towards the river: small two-roomed houses built of brick with mud huts in the yards behind. When he had arrived fifteen years ago there had been only the mud huts—now they served as kitchens, and yet still when anyone was about to die, he would retire into the yard. He couldn't die peacefully in a room furnished with a radio-set and a picture of the latest Pope; he was prepared to die only where his ancestors had died, in the darkness surrounded by the smell of dry mud and leaves. In the third yard on the left an old man was dying now, sitting in a battered deckchair, inside the shadow of the kitchen-door.

Beyond the village, just before the river came into sight, the ground was being cleared for what would one day be the new hospital block. A gang of lepers was pounding the last square yards supervised by Father Joseph, who worked beside them, beating away himself at the ground in his old khaki pants and a soft hat which looked as though it had been washed up on the beach many years ago.

'Otraco?' Doctor Colin called out to him.

'No, the Bishop's boat,' Father Joseph replied, and he paced away, feeling the ground with his feet. He had long ago caught the African habit of speaking as he moved, with his back turned, and his voice had the high

African inflection. 'They say there's a passenger on board.'

'A passenger?'

Doctor Colin came into sight of the funnel where it stuck up between the long avenue of logs that had been cut ready for fuel. A man was walking up the avenue towards him. He raised his hat, a man of his own age, in the late fifties with a grizzled morning stubble, wearing a crumpled tropical suit. 'My name is Querry,' he introduced himself, speaking in an accent which Colin could not quite place as French or Flemish any more than he could immediately identify the nationality of the name.

'Doctor Colin,' he said. 'Are you stopping here?'

'The boat goes no further,' the man answered, as if that were indeed the only explanation.

2

Once a month Doctor Colin and the Superior went into a confidential huddle over figures. The support of the leproserie was the responsibility of the Order; the doctor's salary and the cost of medicine were paid by the State. The State was the richer and the more unwilling partner, and the doctor made every effort to shift what burden he could from the Order. In the struggle with the common enemy the two of them had become close friends–Doctor Colin was even known occasionally to attend Mass, though he had long ago, before he had come to this continent of misery and heat, lost faith in any god that a priest would have recognised. The only trouble the Superior ever caused him was with the cheroot which the priest was never without, except when saying Mass and in sleep; the cheroots were strong and Doctor Colin's quarters cramped, and the ash always found a way between his pamphlets and reports. Now he had to shake the ash off the accounts he had prepared for the chief medical officer in Luc; in them he had deftly and unobtrusively transferred to the State the price of a new clock and three mosquito-nets for the mission.

'I am sorry,' the Superior apologised, dropping yet more ash on to an open page of the Atlas of Leprosy. The thick bright colours and the swirling designs resembled the reproduction of a Van Gogh landscape, and the doctor had been turning the pages with a purely aesthetic pleasure before the Superior joined him. 'Really I am impossible,' the Superior said, brushing at the page. 'Worse than usual, but then I've had a visit from M. Rycker. The man upsets me.'

'What did he want?'

'Oh, he wanted to find out about our visitor. And of course he was very ready to drink our visitor's whisky.'

'Was it worth three days' journey?'

'Well, at least he got the whisky. He said the road had been impossible for four weeks and he had been starved of intellectual conversation.'

'How is his wife–and the plantation?'

'Rycker seeks information. He never gives it. And he was anxious to discuss his spiritual problems.'

'I would never have guessed he had any.'

'When a man has nothing else to be proud of,' the Superior said, 'he is proud of his spiritual problems. After two whiskies he began to talk to me about Grace.'

'What did you do?'

'I lent him a book. He won't read it, of course. He knows all the answers—six years wasted in a seminary can do a lot of harm. What he really wanted was to discover who Querry might be, where he came from and how long he was going to stay. I would have been tempted to tell him if I had known the answer myself. Luckily Rycker is afraid of lepers, and Querry's boy happened to come in. Why did you give Querry Deo Gratias?'

'He's cured, but he's a burnt-out case, and I don't want to send him away. He can sweep a floor and make a bed without fingers or toes.'

'Our visitors are sometimes fastidious.'

'I assure you Querry doesn't mind. In fact he asked for him. Deo Gratias was the first leper whom he saw when he came off the boat. Of course I told him the man was cured.'

'Deo Gratias brought me a note. I don't think Rycker liked me touching it. I noticed that he didn't shake hands with me when he said goodbye. What strange ideas people have about leprosy, doctor.'

'They learn it from the Bible. Like sex.'

'It's a pity people pick and choose what they learn from the Bible,' the Superior said, trying to knock the end of his cheroot into the ashtray. But he was always doomed to miss.

'What do you think of Querry, father? Why do you think he's here?'

'I'm too busy to pry into a man's motives. I've given him a room and a bed. One more mouth to feed is not an embarrassment. And to do him justice he seemed very ready to help—if there were any help that he was capable of giving. Perhaps he is only looking for somewhere quiet to rest in.'

'Few people would choose a leproserie as a holiday resort. When he asked me for Deo Gratias I was afraid for a moment that we might have a leprophil on our hands.'

'A leprophil? Am I a leprophil?'

'No, father. You are here under obedience. But you know very well that leprophils exist, though I daresay they are more often women than men. Schweitzer seems to attract them. They would rather wash the feet with their hair like the woman in the gospel than clean them with something more antiseptic. Sometimes I wonder whether Damien was a leprophil. There was no need for him to become a leper in order to serve them well. A few elementary precautions—I wouldn't be a better doctor without my fingers, would I?'

'I don't find it very rewarding looking for motives. Querry does no harm.'

'The second day he was here, I took him to the hospital. I wanted to test his reactions. They were quite normal ones—nausea not attraction. I had to give him a whiff of ether.'

'I'm not as suspicious of leprophils as you are, doctor. There are people who love and embrace poverty. Is that so bad? Do we have to invent a word ending in phil for them?'

'The leprophil makes a bad nurse and ends by joining the patients.'

'But all the same, doctor, you've said it yourself, leprosy is a psychological problem. It may be very valuable for the leper to feel loved.'

'A patient can always detect whether he is loved or whether it is only his leprosy which is loved. I don't want leprosy loved. I want it eliminated. There are fifteen million cases in the world. We don't want to waste time with neurotics, father.'

'I wish you had a little time to waste. You work too hard.'

But Doctor Colin was not listening. He said, 'You remember that little leproserie in the bush that the nuns ran. When D.D.S. was discovered to be a cure, they were soon reduced to half a dozen patients. Do you know what one of the nuns said to me? "It's terrible, doctor. Soon we'll have no lepers at all." There surely was a leprophil.'

'Poor woman,' the Superior said. 'You don't see the other side.'

'What other side?'

'An old maid, without imagination, anxious to do good, to be of use. There aren't so many places in the world for people like that. And the practice of her vocation is being taken away from her by the weekly doses of D.D.S. tablets.'

'I thought you didn't look for motives.'

'Oh, mine's a very superficial reading like your own diagnosis, doctor. But it would be a good thing for all of us if we were even more superficial. There's no real harm in a superficial judgment, but if I begin to probe into what lies behind that desire to be of use, oh well, I might find some terrible things, and we are all tempted to stop when we reach that point. Yet if we dug further, who knows?–the terrible too might be only a few skins deep. Anyway it's safer to make superficial judgments. They can always be shrugged off. Even by the victims.'

'And Querry? What of him? Superficially speaking, of course.'

PART II

CHAPTER I

I

In an unfamiliar region it is always necessary for the stranger to begin at once to construct the familiar, with a photograph perhaps or a row of books if they are all that he has brought with him from the past. Querry had no photographs and no books except his diary. The first morning when he was woken at six by the sound of prayers from the chapel next door, he felt the panic of complete abandonment. He lay on his back listening to the pious chant, and if there had been some magic power in his signet ring, he would have twisted it and asked whatever djinn answered him to be transferred again to that place which for want of a better name he called his home. But magic, if such a thing existed at all, was more likely to lie in the rhythmical and incomprehensible chant next door. It reminded him, like the smell of a medicine, of an illness from which he had long recovered. He blamed himself for not realising that the area of leprosy was also the area of this other sickness. He had expected doctors and nurses: he had forgotten that he would find priests and nuns.

Deo Gratias was knocking on the door. Querry heard the scrape of his stump as it attempted to raise the latch. A pail of water hung on his wrist like a coat on a cloakroom-knob. Querry had asked Doctor Colin before engaging him whether he suffered pain, and the doctor had reassured him, answering that mutilation was the alternative to pain. It was the palsied with their stiffened fingers and strangled nerves who suffered—suffered almost beyond bearing (you heard them sometimes crying in the night), but the suffering was in some sort a protection against mutilation. Querry did not suffer, lying on his back in bed, flexing his fingers.

And so from the first morning he set himself to build a routine, the familiar within the unfamiliar. It was the condition of survival. Every morning at seven he breakfasted with the fathers. They drifted into their common-room from whatever task they had been engaged on for the last hour, since the chanting had ceased. Father Paul with Brother Philippe was in charge of the dynamo which supplied electricity to the Mission and the leper village; Father Jean had been saying Mass at the nuns' house; Father Joseph had already started the labourers to work on clearing the ground for the new hospital; Father Thomas, with eyes sunk like stones in the pale clay of his face, swallowed his coffee in a hurry, like a nauseating medicine, and was off to superintend the two schools. Brother Philippe sat silent, taking no part in any conversation: he was older than the fathers, he could speak nothing but Flemish and he had the kind of face which seems worn away by weather and patience. As the faces began to develop features as negatives do in a hypo-bath, Querry separated himself all the more from their company. He was afraid of the questions they might ask, until he began to realise that, like the priests in the seminary on the river, they were going to ask none of any importance. Even the questions they found necessary were phrased like statements–'On Sundays a bus calls here at six-thirty if you wish to go to Mass,'–and Querry was not required to answer that he had given up attending Mass more than twenty years before. His absence was never remarked.

After breakfast he would take a book he had borrowed from the doctor's small library and go down to the bank of the river. It had widened out in this reach and was nearly a mile across. An old tin barge, rusty with long disuse, enabled him to avoid the ants; and he sat there until the sun, soon after nine, became too high for comfort. Sometimes he read, sometimes he simply watched the steady khaki flow of the stream, which carried little islands of grass and water jacinth endlessly down at the pace of crawling taxis, out of the heart of Africa, towards the far-off sea.

On the other shore the great trees, with roots above the ground like the ribs of a half-built ship, stood out over the green jungle wall, brown at the top like stale cauliflowers. The cold grey trunks, unbroken by branches, curved a little this way and a little that, giving them a kind of reptilian life. Porcelain-white birds stood on the backs of coffee-coloured cows, and once for a whole hour he watched a family who sat in a pirogue by the bank doing nothing; the mother wore a bright yellow dress, the man, wrinkled like bark, sat bent over a paddle he never used, and a girl with a baby on her lap smiled and smiled like an open piano. When it was too hot to sit any longer in the sunlight he joined the doctor at the hospital or the dispensary, and when that was over half the day had safely gone. He no longer felt nausea from anything he saw, and the bottle of ether was not required. After a month he spoke to the doctor.

'You are very short-handed, aren't you, for dealing with eight hundred people?'

'Yes.'

'If I could be of any use to you–I know I am not trained . . .'

'You will be leaving soon, won't you?'

'I have no plans.'

'Have you any knowledge of electro-therapy?'

'No.'

'You could be trained, if you were interested. Six months in Europe.'

'I don't want to return to Europe,' Querry said.

'Never?'

'Never. I am afraid to return.' The phrase sounded in his own ears melodramatic and he tried to withdraw it. 'I don't mean afraid. Just for this reason and that.'

The doctor ran his fingers over the patches on a child's back. To the unpractised eye the child looked perfectly healthy. 'This is going to be a bad case,' Doctor Colin said. 'Feel this.'

Querry's hesitation was no more perceptible than the leprosy. At first his fingers detected nothing, but then they stumbled on places where the child's skin seemed to have grown an extra layer. 'Have you no kind of electrical knowledge?'

'I'm sorry.'

'Because I'm expecting some apparatus from Europe. It's long overdue. With it I will be able to take the temperature of the skin simultaneously in twenty places. You can't detect it with your fingers, but this nodule here is warmer than the skin around it. I hope one day to be able to forestall a patch. They are trying that in India now.'

'You are suggesting things too complicated for me,' Querry said. 'I'm a man of one trade, one talent.'

'What trade is that?' the doctor asked. 'We are a city in miniature here, and there are few trades for which we could not find a place.' He looked at Querry with sudden suspicion. 'You are not a writer, are you? There's no room for a writer here. We want to work in peace. We don't want the press of the world discovering us as they discovered Schweitzer.'

'I'm not a writer.'

'Or a photographer? The lepers here are not going to be exhibits in any horror museum.'

'I'm not a photographer. Believe me I want peace as much as you do. If the boat had gone any further, I would not have landed here.'

'Then tell me what your trade is, and we will fit you in.'

'I have abandoned it,' Querry said. A sister passed on a bicycle busy about something. 'Is there nothing simple I can do to earn my keep?' he asked. 'Bandaging? I've had no training there either, but it can't be difficult to learn. Surely there has to be someone who washes the bandages. I could release a more valuable worker.'

'That is the sisters' province. My life here would not be worth living if I interfered with their arrangements. Are you feeling restless? Perhaps next time the boat calls you could go back to the capital. There are plenty of opportunities in Luc.'

'I am never going to return,' Querry said.

'In that case you had better warn the fathers,' the doctor said with irony. He called to the dispenser, 'That's enough. No more this morning.' While he washed his hands in spirits he took a look at Querry over his shoulder. The dispenser was shepherding the lepers out and they were alone. He said, 'Are you wanted by the police? You needn't be afraid of telling me—or any of us. You'll find a leproserie just as safe as the Foreign Legion.'

'No. I've committed no crime. I assure you there's nothing of interest in my case. I have retired, that's all. If the fathers don't want me here, I can always go on.'

'You've said it yourself—the boat goes no further.'

'There's the road.'

'Yes. In one direction. The way you came. It's not often open though. This is the season of rains.'

'There are always my feet,' Querry said.

Colin looked for a smile, but there was none on Querry's face. He said, 'If you really want to help me and you don't mind a rough journey you might take the second truck to Luc. The boat may not be back for weeks. My new apparatus should have arrived by now in the town. It will take you about eight days there and back–if you are lucky. Will you go? It will mean sleeping in the bush, and if the ferries are not working you'll have to return. You can hardly call it a road,' he went on; he was determined that the Superior should not accuse him of persuading Querry to go. 'It's only if you want to help . . . you can see how impossible it is for any of us. We can't be spared.'

'Of course. I'll start right away.'

It occurred to the doctor that perhaps here too was a man under obedience, but not to any divine or civil authority, only to whatever wind might blow. He said, 'You could pick up some frozen vegetables too and some steak. The fathers and I could do with a change of diet. There's a cold storage at Luc. Tell Deo Gratias to fetch a camp-bed from my place. If you put a bicycle in the back you could spend the first night at the Perrins', but you can't reach them by truck. They are down by the river. Then there are the Chantins about eight hours further on–unless they've gone home, I can't remember. And last of all there's always Rycker at the second ferry, about six hours from Luc. You'd get a warm welcome from him, I'm sure of that.'

'I'd rather sleep in the lorry,' Querry said. 'I'm not a sociable man.'

'I warn you, it's not an easy journey. And we could always wait for the boat.'

He paused for a while for Querry to answer, but all that Querry found to say was 'I shall be glad to be of use.' The distrust between them deadened intercourse; it seemed to the doctor that the only sentences he could find to speak with any safety had been preserved for a long time in a jar in the dispensary and smelt of formaldehyde.

2

The river drew a great bow through the bush, and generations of administrators, who had tried to cut across the arc with a road from the regional capital of Luc, had been defeated by the forest and the rain. The rain formed quagmires and swelled the tributary streams until the ferries were unusable, while at long intervals, spaced like a layer of geological time, the forest dropped trees across the way. In the deep bush trees grew unnoticeably old through centuries and here and there one presently died, lying half collapsed for a while in the ropy arms of the lianas until sooner or later they gently lowered the corpse into the only space large enough to receive it, and that was the road, narrow like a coffin or a grave. There were no hearses to drag the corpse away; if it was to be removed at all it could only be by fire.

During the rains no one ever tried to use the road; a few *colons* in the forest would then be completely isolated unless, by bicycle, they could reach the river and camp there in a fisherman's village until a boat came. Then, when the rains were over, weeks had still to pass before the local government could spare the men to build the necessary fires and clear the road. After a few years of complete neglect the road would have disappeared completely and forever. The forest would soon convert it to a surface scrawl, like the first scratches on a wall of early man, and there would remain then reptiles, insects, a few birds and primates, and perhaps the pygmoids—the only human beings in the forest who had the capacity to survive without a road.

The first night Querry stopped the truck at a turn in the road where a track led off towards the Perrins' plantation. He opened a tin of soup and a tin of Frankfurters, while Deo Gratias put up a bed for him in the back of the truck and lit the paraffin-cooker. He offered to share his food with Deo Gratias, but the man had some mess of his own ready prepared in a pot wrapped in an old rag, and the two of them sat in silence with the truck between them as though they were in separate rooms. When the meal was over Querry moved round the bonnet with the intention of saying something to Deo Gratias, but the 'boy' by rising to his feet made the occasion as formal as though Querry had entered his hut in the village, and the words, whatever they were, died before they had been spoken. If the boy had possessed an ordinary name, Pierre, Jean, Marc, it might have been possible to begin some simple sentence in French, but Deo Gratias—the absurd name stuck on Querry's tongue.

He walked a little way from the truck, because he knew how far he was from sleep, up the path which led eventually to the river or to the Perrins, and he heard the thud of Deo Gratias's feet behind him. Perhaps he had followed with the idea of protecting him or perhaps because he feared to be left alone in the dark beside the truck. Querry turned with impatience because he had no wish for company, and there the man stood on his two rounded toeless feet, supported on his staff, like something which had grown on that spot ages ago and to which people on one special day made offerings.

'Is this the path to the Perrins?'

The man said yes, but Querry guessed it was what Africans always replied to a question couched like that. He went back to the truck and lay down on the camp-bed. He could hear Deo Gratias settling himself for the night under the belly of the truck, and he lay on his back, staring up at where the stars ought to have been visible, but the gauze of the mosquito-net obscured them. As usual there was no silence. Silence belonged to cities. He dreamt of a girl whom he had once known and thought he loved. She came to him in tears because she had broken a vase which she valued, and she became angry with him because he didn't share her suffering. She struck him in the face, but he felt the blow no more than a dab of butter against his cheek. He said, 'I am sorry, I am too far gone, I can't feel at all, I am a leper.' As he explained his sickness to her he awoke.

This was a specimen of his days and nights. He had no trouble beyond the boredom of the bush. The ferries worked; the rivers were not in flood, in spite of the rain which came torrentially down on their last night. Deo Gratias made a tent over the back of the truck with a ground-sheet and lay down himself as he had done every night in the shelter of the chassis. Then the sun was out again and the track became a road a few miles out of Luc.

3

They searched a long time for the doctor's apparatus before they found a clue. The cargo-department of Otraco knew nothing of it and suggested the customs, which was no more than a wooden hut by a jetty in the tiny river port, where bat-eared dogs yapped and ran. The customs were uninterested and uncooperative, so that Querry had to dig out the European controller who was having an after-lunch siesta in a block of blue and pink modern flats by a little public garden where no one sat on the hot cement benches. The door of the apartment was opened by an African woman, tousled and sleepy, who looked as though she had been sharing the controller's siesta. The controller was an elderly Fleming who spoke very little French. The pouches under his eyes were like purses that contained the smuggled memories of a disappointing life. Querry had already become so accustomed to the bush-life that this man seemed to belong to another age and race than his own. The commercial calendar on the wall with a coloured reproduction of a painting by Vermeer, the triptych of wife and children on the locked piano, and a portrait of the man himself in a uniform of antique cut belonging to an antique war were like the deposits of a dead culture. They could be dated accurately, but no research would disclose the emotions that had once been attached to them.

The controller was very cordial and confused, as though he were anxious to hide with hospitality some secret of his siesta; he had forgotten to do up his flies. He invited Querry to sit down and take a glass, but when he heard that Querry had come from the leproserie he became restless and anxious, eyeing the chair on which Querry sat. Perhaps he expected to see the bacilli of leprosy burrowing into the upholstery. He knew nothing, he said, of any apparatus and suggested that it might be at the cathedral. When Querry stopped on the landing outside he could hear the tap running in the bathroom. The controller was obviously disinfecting his hands.

True enough the apparatus some time ago had been lodged at the cathedral, although the priest in charge, who had assumed the crates contained a holy statue or books for the fathers' library, at first denied all knowledge. They had gone off by the last Otraco boat and were somewhere stuck on the river. Querry drove to the cold storage. The hour of siesta was over, and he had to queue for string-beans.

The high vexed colonial voices, each angry about something different, rose around him, competing for attention. It seemed to him for a moment that he was back in Europe, and his shoulders instinctively hunched through fear of recognition. In the crowded store he realised how on the river and in the streets of the leproserie there had been a measure of peace. 'But you simply must have potatoes,' a woman's voice was saying. 'How dare you deny it? They came in on yesterday's plane. The pilot told me.' She was obviously playing her last card, when she appealed to the European manager. 'I am expecting the Governor to dinner.' Surreptitiously the potatoes emerged, ready wrapped in cellophane.

A voice said, 'You are Querry, aren't you?'

He turned. The man who spoke to him was tall, stooping and overgrown. He was like the kind of plant people put in bathrooms, reared on humidity, shooting too high. He had a small black moustache like a smear of city soot and his face was narrow and flat and endless, like an illustration of the law that two parallel lines never meet. He put a hot restless hand on Querry's arm. 'My name is Rycker. I missed you the other day when I called at the leproserie. How did you get over here? Is a boat in?'

'I came by truck.'

'You were fortunate to get through. You must stay a night at my place on your way home.'

'I have got to get back to the leproserie.'

'They can do without you. They'll have to do without you. After last night's rain there'll be too much water for the ferry. Why are you waiting here?'

'I only wanted some *haricots verts* and some . . .'

'Boy! Some *haricots verts* for this master. You know you have to shout at them a little. They understand nothing else. The only alternative to staying with us is to remain here till the water goes down, and I can assure you, you won't like the hotel. This is a very provincial town. Nothing here to interest a man like you. You are *the* Querry, aren't you?' and Rycker's mouth shut trapwise, while his eyes gleamed roguishly like a detective's.

'I don't know what you mean.'

'We don't all live quite out of the world like the fathers and our dubious friend the doctor. Of course this is a bit of a desert, but all the same one manages—somehow—to keep in touch. Two dozen lagers, boy, and make it quick. Of course I shall respect your incognito. I will say nothing. You can trust me not to betray a guest. You'll be far safer at my place than at the hotel. Only myself and my wife. As a matter of fact it was my wife who said to me, "Do you suppose he can possibly be *the* Querry?"'

'You've made a mistake.'

'Oh no, I haven't. I can show you a photograph when you come to my house—in one of the papers that lie around in case they may prove useful. Useful! This one certainly has, hasn't it, because otherwise we would have thought you were only a relation of Querry's or that the name was pure coincidence, for who would expect to find *the* Querry holed up in a leproserie in the bush? I have to admit I am somewhat curious. But you can trust me, trust me all the way. I have serious enough problems of my own, so I can sympathise with those of another man. I've buried myself too. We'd better go outside, for in a little town like this even the walls have ears.'

'I'm afraid . . . they are expecting me to return. . . .'

'God rules the weather. I assure you, M. Querry, you have no choice.'

CHAPTER 2

House and factory overlooked the ferry; no situation could have been better chosen for a man with Rycker's devouring curiosity. It was impossible for anyone to use the road that led from the town to the interior without passing the two wide windows which were like the lenses of a pair of binoculars trained on the river. They drove under the deep blue shadows of the palm trees towards the river; Rycker's chauffeur and Deo Gratias followed in Querry's lorry.

'You see, M. Querry, how it is. The river's far too high. Not a chance to pass tonight. Who knows whether even tomorrow . . . ? So we have time for some interesting talks, you and I.'

As they drove through the yard of the factory, among the huge boilers abandoned to rust, a smell like stale margarine lay heavily around them. A blast of hot air struck from an open doorway, and the reflection of a furnace billowed into the waning light. 'To you, of course,' Rycker said, 'accustomed to the factories of the West, this must appear a bit ramshackle. Though I can't remember whether you ever were closely concerned with any factories.'

'No.'

'There were so many spheres in which *the* Querry led the way.'

He recurred again and again to the word 'the' as though it were a title of nobility.

'The place functions,' he said as the car bumped among the boilers, 'it functions in its ugly way. We waste nothing. When we finish with the nut there's nothing left. Nothing. We've crushed out the oil,' he said with relish rolling the r, 'and as for the husk–into the furnace with it. We don't need any other fuel to keep the furnaces alive.'

They left the two cars in the yard and walked over to the house. 'Marie, Marie,' Rycker called, scraping the mud off his shoes, stamping across the verandah. 'Marie.'

A girl in blue jeans with a pretty unformed face came quickly round the corner in answer to his call. Querry was on the point of asking 'Your daughter?' when Rycker forestalled him. 'My wife,' he said. 'And here, *chérie*, is *the* Querry. He tried to deny it, but I told him we had a photograph.'

'I am very glad to meet you,' she said. 'We will try to make you comfortable.' Querry had the impression that she had learnt such occasional speeches by heart from her governess or from a book of etiquette. Now she had said her piece she disappeared as suddenly as she had come; perhaps the school-bell had rung for class.

'Sit down,' Rycker said. 'Marie is fixing the drinks. You can see I've trained her to know what a man needs.'

'Have you been married long?'

'Two years. I brought her out after my last leave. In a post like this it's necessary to have a companion. You married?'

'Yes–that is to say I have been married.'

'Of course I know you are thinking that she is very young for me. But I look ahead. If you believe in marriage you have to look to the future. I've still got twenty years of–let's call it active life ahead of me, and what would a woman of thirty be like in twenty years? A man keeps better in the tropics. Don't you agree?'

'I've never thought about it. And I don't yet know the tropics.'

'There are enough problems without sex I can assure you. St Paul wrote, didn't he, that it was better to marry than burn. Marie will stay young long enough to save me from the furnace.' He added quickly, 'Of course I'm only joking. We have to joke, don't we, about serious things. At the bottom of my heart I believe very profoundly in love.' He made the claim as some men might claim to believe in fairies.

The steward came along the verandah carrying a tray and Mme. Rycker followed him. Querry took a glass and Mme. Rycker stood at his elbow while the steward poised the syphon–a division of duties. 'Will you tell me how much soda?' Mme. Rycker asked.

'And now, my dear, you'll change into a proper dress,' Rycker said.

Over the whisky he turned again to what he called 'Your case.' He had now less the manner of a detective than of a counsel who by the nature of his profession is an accomplice after the fact. 'Why are you here, Querry?'

'One must be somewhere.'

'All the same, as I said this morning, no one would expect to find you working in a leproserie.'

'I am not working.'

'When I drove over some weeks ago, the fathers said that you were at the hospital.'

'I was watching the doctor work. I stand around, that's all. There's nothing I can do.'

'It seems a waste of talent.'

'I have no talent.'

Rycker said, 'You mustn't despise us poor provincials.'

When they had gone into dinner, and after Rycker had said a short grace, Querry's hostess spoke again. She said, 'I hope you will be comfortable,' and 'Do you care for salad?' Her fair hair was streaked and darkened with sweat and he saw her eyes widen with apprehension when a black-and-white moth, with the wing-spread of a bat, swooped across the table. 'You must make yourself at home here,' she said, her gaze following the moth as it settled like a piece of lichen on the wall. He wondered whether she had ever felt at home herself. She said, 'We don't have many visitors,' and he was reminded of a child forced to entertain a caller until her mother returns. She had changed, between the whisky and the dinner, into a cotton frock covered with a pattern of autumnal leaves which was like a memory of Europe.

'Not visitors like *the* Querry anyway,' Rycker interrupted her. It was as though he had turned off a knob on a radio-set which had been tuned in to a lesson in deportment after he had listened enough. The sound of the voice was shut off the air, but still, behind the shy and wary eyes, the phrases were going on for no one to hear. 'The weather has been a little hot lately, hasn't it? I hope you had a good flight from Europe.'

Querry said, 'Do you like the life here?' The question startled her; perhaps the answer wasn't in her phrase-book. 'Oh yes,' she said, 'yes. It's very interesting,' staring over his shoulder through the window to where the boilers stood like modern statues in the floodlit yard; then she shifted her eyes back to the moth on the wall and the gecko pointing at his prey.

'Fetch that photograph, dear,' Rycker said.

'What photograph?'

'The photograph of our guest.'

She trailed reluctantly out, making a detour to avoid the wall where the moth rested and the lizard pointed, and returned soon with an ancient copy of *Time*. Querry remembered the ten years younger face upon the cover (the issue had coincided with his first visit to New York). The artist, drawing from a photograph, had romanticised his features. It wasn't the face he saw when he shaved, but a kind of distant cousin. It reflected emotions, thoughts, hopes, profundities that he had certainly expressed to no reporter. The background of the portrait was a building of glass and steel which might have been taken for a concert-hall, or perhaps even for an *orangerie*, if a great cross planted like a belfry outside the door had not indicated it was a church.

'So you see,' Rycker said, 'we know all.'

'I don't remember that the article was very accurate.'

'I suppose the Government—or the Church—have commissioned you to do something out here?'

'No. I've retired.'

'I thought a man of your kind never retired.'

'Oh, one comes to an end, just as soldiers do and bank-managers.'

When the dinner was over the girl left, like a child after the dessert. 'I expect she's gone to write up her journal,' Rycker said. 'This is a red-letter day for her, meeting *the* Querry. She'll have plenty to put down in it.'

'Does she find much to write?'

'I wouldn't know. At the beginning I used to take a quiet look, but she discovered that, and now she locks it up. I expect I teased her a little too much. I remember one entry: "Letter from mother. Poor Maxime has had five puppies." It was the day I was decorated by the Governor, but she forgot to put anything about the ceremony.'

'It must be a lonely life at her age.'

'Oh, I don't know. There are a lot of household duties even in the bush. To be quite frank, I think it's a good deal more lonely for me. She's hardly—you can see it for yourself—an intellectual companion. That's one of the disadvantages of marrying a young wife. If I want to talk about things which really interest me, I have to drive over to the fathers. A long way to go for a conversation. Living in the way I do, one has a lot of time to think things over. I'm a good Catholic, I hope, but that doesn't prevent me from having spiritual problems. A lot of people take their religion lightly, but I had six years when I was a young man with the Jesuits. If a novice master had been less unfair you wouldn't have found me here. I gathered from that article in *Time* that you are a Catholic too.'

'I've retired,' Querry said for the second time.

'Oh come now, one hardly retires from *that*.'

The gecko on the wall leapt at the moth, missed and lay motionless again, the tiny paws spread on the wall like ferns.

'To tell you the truth,' Rycker said, 'I find those fathers at the leproserie an unsatisfactory lot. They are more interested in electricity and building than in questions of faith. Ever since I heard you were here I've looked forward to a conversation with an intellectual Catholic.'

'I wouldn't call myself that.'

'In the long years I've been out here I've been thrown back on my own thoughts. Some men can manage, I suppose, with clock-golf. I can't. I've read a great deal on the subject of love.'

'Love?'

'The love of God. Agape not Eros.'

'I'm not qualified to talk about that.'

'You underrate yourself,' Rycker replied. He went to the sideboard and fetched a tray of liqueurs, disturbing the gecko who disappeared behind a reproduction of some primitive Flight into Egypt. 'A glass of Cointreau,' Rycker said, 'or would you prefer a Van Der Hum?' Beyond the verandah Querry saw a thin figure in a gold-leafed dress move towards the river. Perhaps out of doors the moths had lost their terror.

'In the seminary I formed the habit of thinking more than most men,' Rycker said. 'A faith like ours, when profoundly understood, sets us many problems. For instance—no, it's not a mere instance, I'm jumping to the heart of what really troubles me, I don't believe my wife understands the true nature of Christian marriage.'

Out in the darkness there was a plop-plop-plop. She must be throwing small pieces of wood into the river.

'It sometimes seems to me,' Rycker said, 'that she's ignorant of almost everything. I find myself wondering whether the nuns taught her at all. You saw for yourself—she doesn't even cross herself at meals when I say grace. Ignorance, you know, beyond a certain point might even invalidate a marriage in canon law. That's one of the matters I have tried in vain to discuss with the fathers. They would much prefer to talk about turbines. Now you are here . . .'

'I'm not competent to discuss it,' Querry said. In the moments of silence he could hear the river flooding down.

'At least you listen. The fathers would already have started talking about the new well they propose to dig. A well, Querry, a well against a human soul.' He drank down his Van Der Hum and poured himself another. 'They don't realise . . . just suppose that we weren't properly married, she could leave me at any time, Querry.'

'It's easy to leave what you call a proper marriage, too.'

'No, no. It's much more difficult. There are social pressures—particularly here.'

'If she loves you . . .'

'That's no protection. We are men of the world, Querry, you and I. A love like that doesn't last. I tried to teach her the importance of loving God. Because if she loved Him, she wouldn't want to offend Him, would she? And that would be some security. I have tried to get her to pray, but I don't think she knows any prayers except the Pater Noster and the Ave Maria. What prayers do you use, Querry?'

'None—except occasionally, from habit, in a moment of danger.' He added sadly, 'Then I pray for a brown teddy bear.'

'You are joking, I know that, but this is very serious. Have another Cointreau?'

'What's really worrying you, Rycker? A man?'

The girl came back into the light of the lamp which hung at the corner of the verandah. She was carrying a *roman policier* in the *Série Noire*. She gave a whistle that was scarcely audible, but Rycker heard it. 'That damn puppy,' he said. 'She loves her puppy more than she loves me—or God.' Perhaps the Van Der Hum affected the logic of his transitions. He said, 'I'm not jealous. It's not a man I worry about. She hasn't enough feeling for that. Sometimes she even refuses her duties.'

'What duties?'

'Her duties to me. Her married duties.'

'I've never thought of those as duties.'

'You know very well the Church does. No one has any right to abstain except by mutual consent.'

'I suppose there may be times when she doesn't want you.'

'Then what am I supposed to do? Have I given up the priesthood for nothing at all?'

'I wouldn't talk to her too much, if I were you, about loving God,' Querry said with reluctance. 'She mightn't see a parallel between that and your bed.'

'There's a close parallel for a Catholic,' Rycker said rapidly. He put up his hand as though he were answering a question before his fellow novices. The bristles of hair between the knuckles were like a row of little moustaches.

'You seem to be very well up in the subject,' Querry said.

'At the seminary I always came out well in moral theology.'

'I don't fancy you need me then—or the fathers either. You have obviously thought everything out satisfactorily yourself.'

'That goes without saying. But sometimes one needs confirmation and encouragement. You can't imagine, Querry, what a relief it is to go over these problems with an educated Catholic.'

'I don't know that I would call myself a Catholic.'

Rycker laughed. 'What? *The* Querry? You can't fool me. You are being too modest. I wonder they haven't made you a count of the Holy Roman Empire—like that Irish singer, what was his name?'

'I don't know. I am not musical.'

'You should read what they say about you in *Time*.'

'On matters like that *Time* isn't necessarily well informed. Would you mind if I went to bed? I'll have to be up early in the morning if I'm to reach the next ferry before dark.'

'Of course. Though I doubt if you'll be able to cross the river tomorrow.'

Rycker followed him along the verandah to his room. The darkness was noisy with frogs, and for a long while after his host had said goodnight and gone, they seemed to croak with Rycker's hollow phrases: grace: sacrament: duty: love, love, love.

CHAPTER 3

I

'You want to be of use, don't you?' the doctor asked sharply. 'You don't want menial jobs just for the sake of menial jobs? You aren't either a masochist or a saint.'

'Rycker promised me that he would tell no one.'

'He kept his word for nearly a month. That's quite an achievement for Rycker. When he came here the other day he only told the Superior in confidence.'

'What did the Superior say?'

'That he would listen to nothing in confidence outside the confessional.'

The doctor continued to unpack the crate of heavy electrical apparatus which had arrived at last by the Otraco boat. The lock on the dispensary door was too insecure for him to trust the apparatus there, so he unpacked it on the floor of his living-room. One could never be certain of the African's reaction to anything unfamiliar. In Leopoldville six months before, when the first riots broke out, the attack had been directed at the new glass-and-steel hospital intended for African patients. The most monstrous rumours were easily planted and often believed. It was a land where Messiahs died in prison and rose again from the dead: where walls were said to fall at the touch of fingernails sanctified by a little holy dust. A man whom the doctor had cured of leprosy wrote him a threatening letter once a month; he really believed that he had been turned out of the leproserie, not because he was cured, but because the doctor had personal designs on the half acre of ground on which he used to grow bananas. It only needed someone, in malice or ignorance, to suggest that the new machines were intended to torture the patients and some fools would break into the dispensary and destroy them. Yet in our century you could hardly call them fools. Hola Camp, Sharpeville and Algiers had justified all possible belief in European cruelty.

So it was better, the doctor explained, to keep the machines out of sight at home until the new hospital was finished. The floor of his sitting-room was covered with straw from the crates.

'The position of the power-plugs will have to be decided now.' The doctor asked, 'Do you know what this is?'

'No.'

'I've wanted it for so long,' the doctor said, touching the metal shape tenderly as a man might stroke the female flank of one of Rodin's bronzes. 'Sometimes I despaired. The papers I have had to fill in, the lies I've told. And here at last it *is*.'

'What does it do?'

'It measures to one twenty-thousandth of a second the reaction of the
nerves. One day we are going to be proud of this leproserie. Of you too and
the part you will have played.'

'I told you I've retired.'

'One never retires from a vocation.'

'Oh yes, make no mistake, one does. One comes to an end.'

'What are you here for then? To make love to a black woman?'

'No. One comes to an end of that too. Possibly sex and a vocation are born
and die together. Let me roll bandages or carry buckets. All I want is to pass
the time.'

'I thought you wanted to be of use.'

'Listen,' Querry said and then fell silent.

'I *am* listening.'

'I don't deny my profession once meant a lot to me. So have women. But
the use of what I made was never important to me. I wasn't a builder of
council-houses or factories. When I made something I made it for my own
pleasure.'

'Is that the way you loved women?' the doctor asked, but Querry hardly
heard him. He was talking as a hungry man eats.

'Your vocation is quite a different one, doctor. You are concerned with
people. I wasn't concerned with the people who occupied my space—only
with the space.'

'I wouldn't have trusted your plumbing then.'

'A writer doesn't write for his readers, does he? Yet he has to take
elementary precautions all the same to make them comfortable. My interest
was in space, light, proportion. New materials interested me only in the
effect they might have on those three. Wood, brick, steel, concrete,
glass—space seems to alter with what you use to enclose it. Materials are the
architect's plot. They are not his motive for work. Only the space and the
light and the proportion. The subject of a novel is not the plot. Who
remembers what happened to Lucien de Rubempré in the end?'

'Two of your churches are famous. Didn't you care what happened inside
them—to people?'

'The acoustics had to be good of course. The high altar had to be visible to
all. But people hated them. They said they weren't designed for prayer.
They meant that they were not Roman or Gothic or Byzantine. And in a year
they had cluttered them up with their cheap plaster saints; they took out my
plain windows and put in stained glass dedicated to dead pork-packers who
had contributed to diocesan funds, and when they had destroyed my space
and my light, they were able to pray again, and they even became proud of
what they had spoilt. I became what they called a great Catholic architect,
but I built no more churches, doctor.'

'I am not a religious man, I don't know much about these things, but I
suppose they had a right to believe their prayers were more important than a
work of art.'

'Men have prayed in prison, men have prayed in slums and concentration
camps. It's only the middle-classes who demand to pray in suitable
surroundings. Sometimes I feel sickened by the word prayer. Rycker used it
a great deal. Do you pray, doctor?'

'I think the last time I prayed was before my final medical exam. And you?'

'I gave it up a long time ago. Even in the days when I believed, I seldom prayed. It would have got in the way of work. Before I went to sleep, even if I was with a woman, the last thing I had always to think about was work. Problems which seemed insoluble would often solve themselves in sleep. I had my bedroom next to my office, so that I could spend two minutes in front of the drawing-board the last thing of all. The bed, the bidet, the drawing-board, and then sleep.'

'It sounds a little hard on the woman.'

'Self-expression is a hard and selfish thing. It eats everything, even the self. At the end you find you haven't even got a self to express. I have no interest in anything any more, doctor. I don't want to sleep with a woman nor design a building.'

'Have you no children?'

'I once had, but they disappeared into the world a long time ago. We haven't kept in touch. Self-expression eats the father in you too.'

'So you thought you could just come and die here?'

'Yes. That *was* in my mind. But chiefly I wanted to be in an empty place, where no new building or woman would remind me that there was a time when I was alive, with a vocation and a capacity to love—if it was love. The palsied suffer, their nerves feel, but I am one of the mutilated, doctor.'

'Twenty years ago we might have been able to offer you your death, but now we deal only in cures. D.D.S. costs three shillings a year. It's much cheaper than a coffin.'

'Can you cure me?'

'Perhaps your mutilations haven't gone far enough yet. When a man comes here too late the disease has to burn itself out.' The doctor laid a cloth tenderly over his machine. 'The other patients are waiting. Do you want to come or would you like to sit here thinking of your own case? It's often the way with the mutilated—they want to retire too, out of sight.'

The air in the hospital lay heavily and sweetly upon them: it was never moved by a fan or a breeze. Querry was conscious of the squalor of the bedding—cleanliness was not important to the leper, only to the healthy. The patients brought their own mattresses which they had probably possessed for a lifetime—rough sacking from which the straw had escaped. The bandaged feet lay in the straw like ill-wrapped packages of meat. On the verandah the walking cases sat out of the sun—if you could call a walking case a man who, when he moved, had to support his huge swollen testicles with both hands. A woman with palsied eyelids who could not close her eyes or even blink sat in a patch of shade out of the merciless light. A man without fingers nursed a baby on his knee, and another man lay flat on the verandah with one breast long and drooping and teated like a woman's. There was little the doctor could do for any of these; the man with elephantiasis had too weak a heart for an operation, and though he could have sewn up the woman's eyelids, she had refused to have it done from fear, and as for the baby it would be a leper too in time. Nor could he help those in the first ward who were dying of tuberculosis, or the woman who dragged herself between the beds, her legs withered with polio. It had always seemed to the doctor unfair that leprosy did not preclude all other diseases (leprosy was enough for one human being to bear), and yet it was from the other diseases that most of his patients died. He passed on and Querry tagged at his heels, saying nothing.

In the mud kitchen at the back of one of the lepers' houses an old man sat in the dark on an ancient deck-chair. He made an effort to rise when the doctor crossed the yard, but his legs wouldn't support him and he made a gesture of courteous apology. 'High blood pressure,' the doctor said softly. 'No hope. He has come to his kitchen to die.' His legs were as thin as a child's and he wore a clout like a baby's napkin round the waist for decency. Querry had seen where his clothes had been left neatly folded in the new brick cottage under the Pope's portrait. A holy medal lay in the hollow of his breast among the scarce grey hairs. He had a face of great kindness and dignity, a face that must have always accepted life without complaint, the face of a saint. Now he enquired after the doctor's health as though it were the doctor who was sick, not he.

'Is there anything that I can fetch you?' the doctor asked, and no, the old man replied, he had everything he needed. He wanted to know whether the doctor had heard recently from his family and he made enquiries after the health of the doctor's mother.

'She has been in Switzerland, in the mountains. A holiday in the snow.'

'Snow?'

'I forgot. You have never seen snow. It is frozen vapour, frozen mist. The air is so cold that it never melts and it lies on the ground white and soft like the feathers of a *pique-bœuf*, and the lakes are covered with ice.'

'I know what ice is,' the old man said proudly, 'I have seen ice in a refrigerator. Is your mother old like me?'

'Older.'

'Then she ought not to travel far away from her home. One should die in one's own village if it is possible.' He looked sadly at his own thin legs. 'They will not carry me or I should walk to mine.'

'I would arrange for a lorry to take you,' the doctor said, 'but I don't think you would stand the journey.'

'It would be too much trouble for you,' the old man said, 'and in any case there is no time because I am going to die tomorrow.'

'I will tell the Superior to come and see you as soon as he can.'

'I do not wish to be any trouble to him. He has many duties. I will not be dead till the evening.'

By the old deck-chair stood a bottle with a Johnny Walker label. It contained a brown liquid and some withered plants tied together with a loop of beads. 'What has he got there,' Querry asked after they left him, 'in the bottle?'

'Medicine. Magic. An appeal to his God Nzambi.'

'I thought he was a Catholic.'

'If I sign a form I call myself a Catholic too. So does he. I believe in nothing most of the time. He half believes in Christ and half believes in Nzambi. There's not much difference between us as far as Catholicism is concerned. I only wish I were as good a man.'

'Will he really die tomorrow?'

'I think so. They have a wonderful knack of knowing.'

In the dispensary a leper with bandaged feet stood waiting with a small boy in her arms. Every rib in the child's body showed. It was like a cage over which a dark cloth has been flung at night to keep a bird asleep, and like a bird his breath moved under the cloth. It was not leprosy that would kill him, the doctor said, but sicklaemia, an incurable disease of the blood. There was no hope. The child would not live long enough even to become a leper, but there was no point in telling the mother that. He touched the little hollow chest with his finger, and the child winced away. The doctor began to abuse the woman in her own language, and she argued unconvincingly back, clutching the boy against her hip. The boy stared passively over the doctor's shoulder with sad frog-like eyes as though nothing that anyone said would ever concern him seriously again. When the woman had gone, Doctor Colin said, 'She promises it won't happen any more. But how can I tell?'

'What won't happen?'

'Didn't you see the little scar on his breast? They have been cutting a pocket in his skin to put their native medicines in. She says it was the grandmother who did it. Poor child. They won't let him die in peace without pain. I told her that if it happened again, I would cease treating her for leprosy, but I daresay they won't let me see the boy a second time. In that state he's as easy to hide as a needle.'

'Can't you put him in the hospital?'

'You've seen what sort of a hospital I've got. Would you want a boy of yours to die there? Next,' he called angrily, 'next,' and the next was a child too, a boy of six. His father accompanied him, and his fingerless fist rested on the boy's shoulder to give him comfort. The doctor turned the child round and ran his hand over the young skin.

'Well,' he said, 'you should be noticing things by this time. What do you think of this case?'

'One of his toes has gone already.'

'That's not important. He's had jiggers and they've neglected them. It happens often in the bush. No—here's the first patch. The leprosy has just begun.'

'Is there no way to protect the children?'

'In Brazil they take them away at birth, and thirty per cent of the babies die. I prefer a leper to a dead child. We'll cure him in a couple of years.' He looked up quickly at Querry and away again. 'One day—in the new hospital—I'll have a special children's ward and dispensary. I'll anticipate the patch. I'll live to see leprosy in retreat. Do you know there are some areas, a few hundred miles from here, where one in five of the people are lepers? I dream of movable prefabricated hospitals. War has changed. In 1914 generals organised battles from country houses, but in 1944 Rommel and Montgomery fought from moving caravans. How can I convey what I want to Father Joseph? I can't draw. I can't even design one room to the best advantage. I'll only be able to tell him what's wrong after the hospital is built. He's not even a builder. He's a good bricklayer. He's putting one brick on another for the love of God as they used to build monasteries. So you see I need you,' Doctor Colin said. The boy's four toes wriggled impatiently on the cement floor, waiting for the meaningless conversation between the white men to reach a conclusion.

2

Querry wrote in his journal: 'I haven't enough feeling left for human beings to do anything for them out of pity.' He carefully recalled the scar on the immature breast and the four toes, but he was unmoved; an accumulation of pinpricks cannot amount to the sensation of pain. A storm was on the way, and the flying ants swarmed into the room, striking against the light until he shut the window. Then they fell on the cement floor and lost their wings and ran this way and that as though they were confused at finding themselves so suddenly creatures of earth not air. With the window closed the wet heat increased and he had to put blotting paper under his wrist to catch the sweat.

He wrote, in an attempt to make clear his motives to Doctor Colin: 'A vocation is an act of love: it is not a professional career. When desire is dead one cannot continue to make love. I've come to the end of desire and to the end of a vocation. Don't try to bind me in the loveless marriage and to make me imitate what I used to perform with passion. And don't talk to me like a priest about my duty. A talent—we used to learn that lesson as children in scripture-lessons—should not be buried when it still has purchasing power, but when the currency has changed and the image has been superseded and no value is left in the coin but the weight of a wafer of silver, a man has every right to hide it. Obsolete coins, like corn, have always been found in graves.'

The notes were rough and disjointed: he had no talent to organise his thought in words. He ended: 'What I have built, I have always built for myself, not for the glory of God or the pleasure of a purchaser. Don't talk to me of human beings. Human beings are not my country. And haven't I offered anyway to wash their filthy bandages?'

He tore the pages out and sent them by Deo Gratias to Doctor Colin. At the end a half-sentence had been thrust out into the void—'I will do anything for you in reason, but don't ask me to try to revive . . .' like a plank from a ship's deck off which a victim has been thrust.

Doctor Colin came to his room later and tossed the letter, crumpled into a paper ball, on to his table. 'Scruples,' the doctor said impatiently. 'Just scruples.'

'I tried to explain. . . .'

'Who cares?' the doctor said, and that question 'Who cares?' went echoing obsessively on in Querry's brain like a line of verse learnt in adolescence.

He had a dream that night from which he woke in terror. He was walking down a long railway-track, in the dark, in a cold country. He was hurrying because he had to reach a priest and explain to him that, in spite of the clothes he was wearing, he was a priest also and he must make his confession and obtain wine with which to celebrate Mass. He was under orders of some kind from a superior. He had to say his Mass now that night. Tomorrow would be too late. He would lose his chance forever. He came to a village and left the railway-track (the small station was shuttered and deserted:

perhaps the whole branch line had been closed long since by the authorities) and presently found himself outside the priest's door, heavy and mediaeval, studded with great nails the size of Roman coins. He rang and was admitted. A lot of chattering pious women surrounded the priest, but he was friendly and accessible in spite of them. Querry said, 'I must see you at once, alone. There is something I have to tell you,' and already he began to feel the enormous relief and security of his confession. He was nearly home again. The priest took him aside into a little room where a decanter of wine stood on a table, but before he had time to speak the holy women came billowing in through the curtain after them, full of little pious jests and whimsicalities. 'But we must be alone,' Querry cried, 'I have to speak to you,' and the priest pushed the women back through the curtain, and they swayed for a moment to and fro like clothes on hangers in a cupboard. All the same the two of them were sufficiently alone now for him to speak, and with his eyes on the wine he was able at last really to begin. 'Father . . .' but at that moment, when he was about to lose the burden of his fear and responsibility, a second priest entered the room and taking the father on one side began to explain to him how he had run short of wine and had come to borrow his, and still talking he picked up the decanter from the table. Then Querry broke down. It was as though he had had an appointment with hope at this turn of the road and had arrived just too late. He let out a cry like that of an animal in pain and woke. It was raining hard on all the tin roofs, and when the lightning flashed he could see the small white cell that his mosquito-net made, the size of a coffin, and in one of the leper-houses nearby a quarrel had begun between a man and a woman. He thought, 'I was too late,' and an obsessional phrase bobbed up again, like a cork attached to some invisible fishing-net below the water, 'Who cares?' 'Who cares?'

When the morning came at last he went to the carpenter in the leproserie and showed him how to make the kind of desk and drawing-board that he required, and only when that was done did he seek out Doctor Colin to tell him of his decision.

'I am glad,' Doctor Colin said, 'for you.'

'Why for me?'

'I know nothing about you,' Doctor Colin said, 'but we are all made much the same way. You have been trying an impossible experiment. A man can't live with nothing but himself.'

'Oh yes, he can.'

'Sooner or later he would kill himself.'

'If he had enough interest,' Querry replied.

CHAPTER 4

I

After two months a measure of natural confidence had grown between Querry and Deo Gratias. At first it was based only on the man's disabilities. Querry was not angry with him when he spilt water; he kept his temper when one of his drawings was smeared by ink from a broken bottle. It takes a long time to learn even the simplest tasks without fingers and toes, and in any case a man who cares for nothing finds it difficult—or absurd—to be angry. There was one occasion when the crucifix which the fathers had left hanging on Querry's wall was broken by some maladroitness on the part of the mutilated man and he expected Querry to react as he might have reacted himself if a fetish of his own had been carelessly or heartlessly destroyed. It was easy for him to mistake indifference for sympathy.

One night when the moon was full Querry became aware of the man's absence as one might become aware of some hitherto unnoticed object missing from a mantelpiece in a temporary home. His ewer had not been filled and the mosquito-net had not been drawn down, and later, as he was on his way to the doctor's house, where he had to discuss a possible cut in the cost of building, he met Deo Gratias stumbling with his staff down the central road of the leproserie as quickly as he was able on toeless feet. The man's face was wet with sweat and when Querry spoke to him he swerved away into someone's backyard. When Querry returned half-an-hour later he stood there still, like a tree-stump that the owner had not bothered to move. The sweat looked like traces of the night's rain on the bark and he appeared to be listening to something a long way off. Querry listened too, but he could hear nothing except the rattle of the crickets and the swelling diapason of the frogs. In the morning Deo Gratias had not returned, and Querry felt an unimportant disappointment that the servant had not spoken a word to him before he left. He told the doctor that the boy had gone. 'If he doesn't come back tomorrow will you find me another?'

'I don't understand,' Doctor Colin said. 'I only gave him the job so that he might stay in the leproserie. He had no wish to go.' Later that day a leper picked up the man's staff from a path that led into the thickest bush, and brought it to Querry's room where he was at work, taking advantage of the last light.

'But how do you know that the staff is his? All the mutilated lepers have them,' Querry asked and the man simply repeated that it belonged to Deo Gratias—no argument, no reason, just one more of the things they knew that he knew nothing about.

'You think some accident has happened to him?'

Something, the man said in his poor French, had happened, and Querry got the impression that an accident was what the man feared least of all.

'Why don't you go and look for him then?' Querry asked.

There was not enough light left, the man said, under the trees. They would have to wait till morning.

'But he's been gone already nearly twenty-four hours. If there has been an accident we have waited long enough. You can take my torch.'

The morning would be better, the man repeated, and Querry saw that he was scared.

'If I go with you, will you come?'

The man shook his head, so Querry went alone.

He could not blame these people for their fears: a man had to believe in nothing if he was not to be afraid of the big bush at night. There was little in the forest to appeal to the romantic. It was completely empty. It had never been humanised, like the woods of Europe, with witches and charcoal-burners and cottages of marzipan; no one had ever walked under these trees lamenting lost love, nor had anyone listened to the silence and communed like a lake-poet with his heart. For there was no silence; if a man here wished to be heard at night he had to raise his voice to counter the continuous chatter of the insects as in some monstrous factory where thousands of sewing-machines were being driven against time by myriads of needy seamstresses. Only for an hour or so, in the midday heat, silence fell, the siesta of the insect.

But if, like these Africans, one believed in some kind of divine being, wasn't it just as possible for a god to exist in this empty region as in the empty spaces of the sky where men had once located him? These woody spaces would remain unexplored, it seemed likely now, for longer than the planets. The craters of the moon were already better known than the forest at the door that one could enter any day on foot. The sharp sour smell of chlorophyl from rotting vegetation and swampwater fell like a dentist's mask over Querry's face.

It was a stupid errand. He was no hunter. He had been bred in a city. He couldn't possibly hope to discover a human track even in daylight, and he had accepted too easily the evidence of the staff. Shining his torch on this side and that he elicited only stray gleams and flashes among the foliage which might have been the reflection of eyes, but were more probably little pools of rainwater caught in the curls of the leaves. He must have been walking now for half an hour, and he had probably covered a mile along the narrow path. Once his finger slipped on the trigger of the torch and in the moment of darkness he walked off the twisting path slap into the forest-wall. He thought: I have no reason to believe that my battery will see me home. He continued to digest the thought as he walked further in. He had said to Doctor Colin to explain the reason for his stay, 'the boat goes no further', but it is always possible to go a little deeper on one's own feet. He called 'Deo Gratias! Deo Gratias!' above the noise of the insects, but the absurd name which sounded like an invocation in a church received no response.

His own presence here was hardly more explicable than that of Deo Gratias. The thought of his servant lying injured in the forest waiting for the call or footstep of any human being would perhaps at an earlier time have vexed him all night until he was forced into making a token gesture. But now that he cared for nothing, perhaps he was being driven only by a vestige of intellectual curiosity. What had brought Deo Gratias here out of the safety and familiarity of the leproserie? The path, of course, might be leading somewhere—to a village perhaps where Deo Gratias had relations—but he had already learned enough of Africa to know that it was more likely to peter out—to be the relic of a track made by men who had come searching for caterpillars to fry; it might well mark the furthest limit of human penetration. What was the meaning of the sweat he had seen pouring down the man's face? It might have been caused by fear or anxiety or even, in the heavy river-heat, by the pressure of thought. Interest began to move painfully in him like a nerve that has been frozen. He had lived with inertia so long that he examined his 'interest' with clinical detachment.

He must have been walking now, he told himself, over an hour. How had Deo Gratias come so far without his staff on mutilated feet? He felt more than ever doubtful whether the battery would last him home. Nonetheless, he went on. He realised how foolish he had been not to tell the doctor or one of the fathers where he was going in case of accident, but wasn't an accident perhaps exactly what he was seeking? In any case he went on, while the mosquitoes droned to the attack. There was no point in waving them away. He trained himself to submit.

Fifty yards further he was startled by a harsh animal sound—the kind of grunt he could imagine a wild boar giving. He stopped and moved his waning light in a circle round him. He saw that many years ago this path must have been intended to lead somewhere, for in front of him were the remains of a bridge made from the trunks of trees that had long ago rotted. Two more steps and he would have fallen down the gap, not a great fall, a matter of feet only, into a shallow overgrown marsh, but for a man mutilated in hands and feet far enough: the light shone on the body of Deo Gratias, half in the water, half out. He could see the tracks made in the wet and slippery ground by hands like boxing gloves which had tried to catch hold. Then the body grunted again, and Querry climbed down beside it.

Querry couldn't tell whether Deo Gratias was conscious or not. His body was too heavy to lift, and he made no effort to co-operate. He was warm and wet like a hummock of soil; he felt like part of the bridge that had fallen in many years ago. After ten minutes of struggle Querry managed to drag his limbs out of the water—it was all he could do. The obvious thing now, if his torch would last long enough, was to fetch help. Even if the Africans refused to return with him two of the fathers would certainly aid him. He made to climb up on to the bridge and Deo Gratias howled, as a dog or a baby might howl. He raised a stump and howled, and Querry realised that he was crippled with fear. The fingerless hand fell on Querry's arm like a hammer and held him there.

There was nothing to be done but wait for the morning. The man might die of fear, but neither of them would die from damp or mosquito-bites. He settled himself down as comfortably as he could by the boy and by the last light of the torch examined the rocky feet. As far as he could tell an ankle was broken—that seemed to be all. Soon the light was so dim that Querry could see the shape of the filament in the dark, like a phosphorescent worm; then it went out altogether. He took Deo Gratias's hand to reassure him, or rather laid his own hand down beside it; you cannot 'take' a fingerless hand. Deo

Gratias grunted twice, and then uttered a word. It sounded like 'Pendélé'. In the darkness the knuckles felt as a rock might that has been eroded for years by the weather.

2

'We both had a lot of time to think,' Querry said to Doctor Colin. 'It wasn't light enough to leave him till about six. I suppose it was about six—I had forgotten to wind my watch.'

'It must have been a long bad night.'

'One has had worse alone.' He seemed to be searching his memory for an example. 'Nights when things end. Those are the interminable nights. In a way you know this seemed a night when things begin. I've never much minded physical discomfort. And after about an hour when I tried to move my hand, he wouldn't let it go. His fist lay on it like a paper-weight. I had an odd feeling that he needed me.'

'Why odd?' Doctor Colin asked.

'Odd to me. I've needed people often enough in my life. You might accuse me of having used people more than I have ever loved them. But to be needed is a different sensation, a tranquilliser, not an excitement. Do you know what the word "Pendélé" means? Because after I moved my hand he began to talk. I had never properly listened to an African talking before. You know how one listens with half an ear, as one does to children. It wasn't easy to follow the mixture of French and whatever language it is that Deo Gratias speaks. And this word "Pendélé" continually cropped up. What does it mean, doctor?'

'I've an idea that it means something the same as *Bunkasi*—and that means pride, arrogance, perhaps a kind of dignity and independence if you look at the good side of the word.'

'It's not what he meant. I am certain he meant a place—somewhere in the forest, near water, where something of great importance to him was happening. He had felt strangled his last day in the leproserie; of course he didn't use the word "strangled", he told me there wasn't enough air, he wanted to dance and shout and run and sing. But, poor fellow, he couldn't run or dance, and the fathers would have taken a poor view of the kind of songs he wanted to sing. So he set out to find this place beside the water. He had been taken there once by his mother when he was a child, and he could remember how there had been singing and dancing and games and prayers.'

'But Deo Gratias comes from hundreds of miles away.'

'Perhaps there is more than one Pendélé in the world.'

'A lot of people left the leproserie three nights ago. They've most of them come back. I expect they had some kind of witchcraft going on. He started too late and he couldn't catch up with them.'

'I asked him what prayers. He said they prayed to Yezu Klisto and someone called Simon. Is that the same as Simon Peter?'

'No, not quite the same. The fathers could tell you about Simon. He died in gaol nearly twenty years ago. They think he'll rise again. It's a strange

Christianity we have here, but I wonder whether the Apostles would find it as difficult to understand as the collected works of Thomas Aquinas. If Peter could have understood those, it would have been a greater miracle than Pentecost, don't you think? Even the Nicaean Creed—it has the flavour of higher mathematics to me.'

'That word Pendélé runs in my head.'

'We always connect hope with youth,' Doctor Colin said, 'but sometimes it can be one of the diseases of age. The cancerous growth you find unexpectedly in the dying after a deep operation. These people here are all dying—oh, I don't mean of leprosy, I mean of us. And their last disease is hope.'

'Then you'll know where to look for me,' Querry said, 'if I should be missing.' An unexpected sound made the doctor look up; Querry's face was twisted into the rictus of a laugh. The doctor realised with astonishment that Querry had perpetrated a joke.

PART III

CHAPTER I

I

Rycker and his wife drove into town for cocktails with the Governor. In a village by the road stood a great wooden cage on stilts where once a year at a festival a man danced above the flames lit below; in the bush thirty kilometres before they had passed something sitting in a chair constructed out of a palm-nut and woven fibres into the rough and monstrous appearance of a human being. Inexplicable objects were the fingerprints of Africa. Naked women smeared white with grave-clay fled up the banks as the car passed, hiding their faces.

Rycker said, 'When Mme. Guelle asks you what you will drink, say a glass of Perrier.'

'Not an *orange pressée*?'

'Not unless you can see a jug of it on the sideboard. We mustn't inconvenience her.'

Marie Rycker took in the advice seriously and then turned her eyes from her husband and stared away at the dull forest wall. The only path that led inside was closed with fibre-mats for a ceremony no white man must see.

'You heard what I said, darling?'

'Yes. I will remember.'

'And the *canapés*. Don't eat too many of them like you did last time. We haven't come to the Residence to take a meal. It creates a bad impression.'

'I won't touch a thing.'

'That would be just as bad. It would look as though you had noticed they were stale. They usually are.'

The little medal of Saint Christopher jingle-jangled like a fetish below the windscreen.

'I am frightened,' the girl said. 'It is all so complicated and Mme. Guelle does not like me.'

'It isn't that she doesn't like you,' Rycker explained kindly. 'It is only that last time, you remember, you began to leave before the wife of the Commissioner. Of course, we are not bound by these absurd colonial rules, but we don't want to seem pushing and it is generally understood that as leading *commerçants* we come after the Public Works. Watch for Mme. Cassin to leave.'

'I never remember any of their names.'

'The very fat one. You can't possibly miss her. By the way if Querry should be there don't be shy of inviting him for the night. In a place like this one longs for intelligent conversation. For the sake of Querry I would even put up with that atheist Doctor Colin. We could make up another bed on the verandah.'

But neither Querry nor Colin was there.

'A Perrier if you are sure it's no trouble,' Marie Rycker said. Everybody had been driven in from the garden, for it was the hour when the D.D.T. truck cannoned a stinging hygienic fog over the town.

Mme. Guelle graciously brought the Perrier with her own hands. 'You are the only people,' she said, 'who seem to have met M. Querry. The mayor would have liked him to sign the Golden Book, but he seems to spend all his time in that sad place out there. Now you perhaps could pry him out for all our sakes.'

'We don't really know him,' Marie Rycker said. 'He spent the night with us when the river was in flood, that's all. He wouldn't have stayed otherwise. I don't think he wants to see people. My husband promised not to tell . . .'

'Your husband was quite right to tell *us*. We should have looked such fools, having *the* Querry in our own territory without being aware of it. How did he strike you, dear?'

'I hardly spoke to him.'

'His reputation in certain ways is very bad they tell me. Have you read the article in *Time*? Oh yes, of course, your husband showed it to us. Not of course that they write of *that*. It's only what they say in Europe. One has to remember though that some of the great saints of the Church passed through a certain period of—how shall I put it?'

'Do I hear you talking of saints, Mme. Guelle?' Rycker asked. 'What excellent whisky you always have.'

'Not exactly saints. We were discussing M. Querry.'

'In my opinion,' Rycker said, raising his voice a little like a monitor in a noisy classroom, 'he may well be the greatest thing to happen in Africa since Schweitzer, and Schweitzer after all is a Protestant. I found him a most interesting companion when he stayed with us. And have you heard the latest story?' Rycker asked the room at large, shaking the ice in his glass like a hand-bell. 'He went out into the bush two weeks ago, they say, to find a leper who had run away. He spent the whole night with him in the forest, arguing and praying, and he persuaded the man to return and complete his treatment. It rained in the night and the man was sick with fever, so he covered him with his body.'

'What an unconventional thing to do,' Mme. Guelle said. 'He's not, is he . . .?'

The Governor was a very small man with a short sight which gave him an appearance of moral intensity; physically he had the air of looking to his wife for protection, but like a small nation, proud of its culture, he was an unwilling satellite. He said, 'There are more saints in the world than the Church recognises.' This remark stamped with official approval what might otherwise have been regarded as an eccentric or even an ambiguous action.

'Who is this man Querry?' the Director of Public Works asked the Manager of Otraco.

'They say he's a world-famous architect. You should know. He comes into your province.'

'He's not here officially, is he?'

'He's helping with the new hospital at the leproserie.'

'But I passed those plans months ago. They don't need an architect. It's a simple building job.'

'The hospital,' Rycker said, interrupting them and drawing them within his circle, 'you can take it from me, is only a first step. He is designing a modern African church. He hinted at that to me himself. He's a man of great vision. What be builds lasts. A prayer in stone. There's Monseigneur coming in. Now we shall learn what the Church thinks of Querry.'

The Bishop was a tall rakish figure with a neatly trimmed beard and the roving eye of an old-fashioned cavalier of the boulevards. He generously avoided putting out his hand to the men so that they might escape a genuflection. Women however liked to kiss his ring (it was a form of innocent flirtation), and he readily allowed it.

'So we have a saint among us, Monseigneur,' Mme. Guelle said.

'You honour me too much. And how is the Governor? I don't see him here.'

'He's gone to unlock some more whisky. To tell the truth, Monseigneur, I was not referring to you. I'd be sorry to see you become a saint—for the time being, that is.'

'An Augustinian thought,' the Bishop said obscurely.

'We were talking about Querry, *the* Querry,' Rycker explained. 'A man in that position burying himself in a leproserie, spending a night praying with a leper in the bush—you must admit, Monseigneur, that self-sacrifices like that are rare. What do you think?'

'I am wondering, does he play bridge?' Just as the Governor's comment had given administrative approval to Querry's conduct, so the Bishop's question was taken to mean that the Church in her wise and traditional fashion reserved her opinion.

The Bishop accepted a glass of orange juice. Marie Rycker looked at it sadly. She had parked her Perrier and didn't know what to do with her hands. The Bishop said to her kindly, 'You should learn bridge, Mme. Rycker. We have too few players round here now.'

'I am frightened of cards, Monseigneur.'

'I will bless the pack and teach you myself.' Marie Rycker was uncertain whether the Bishop was joking; she tried out an unnoticeable kind of smile.

Rycker said, 'I can't imagine how a man of Querry's calibre can work with that atheist Colin. That's a man, you can take it from me, who doesn't know the meaning of the word charity. Do you remember last year when I tried to organise a Lepers' Day? He would have nothing to do with it. He said he couldn't afford to accept charity. Four hundred dresses and suits had been accumulated and he refused to distribute them, just because there weren't enough to go round. He said he would have had to buy the rest out of his own pocket to avoid jealousy—why should a leper be jealous? You should talk to him one day, Monseigneur, on the nature of charity.'

But Monseigneur had moved on, his hand under Marie Rycker's elbow. 'Your husband seems very taken up with this man Querry,' he said.

'He thinks he may be somebody he can talk to.'

'Are you so silent?' the Bishop asked, teasing her gently as though he had indeed picked her up outside a café on the boulevards.

'I can't talk about his subjects.'

'What subjects?'

'Free Will and Grace and—Love.'

'Come now—love . . . you know about that, don't you?'

'Not that kind of love,' Marie Rycker said.

2

By the time the Ryckers came to go—they had to wait a long time for Mme. Cassin–Rycker had drunk to the margin of what was dangerous; he had passed from excessive amiability to dissatisfaction, the kind of cosmic dissatisfaction which, after probing faults in others' characters, went on to the examination of his own. Marie Rycker knew that if he could be induced at this stage to take a sleeping-pill all might yet be well; he would probably reach unconsciousness before he reached religion which, like the open doorway in a red-lamp district, led inevitably to sex.

'There are times,' Rycker said, 'when I wish we had a more spiritual bishop.'

'He was kind to me,' Marie Rycker said.

'I suppose he talked to you of cards.'

'He offered to teach me bridge.'

'I suppose he knew that I had forbidden you to play.'

'He couldn't. I've told no one.'

'I will not have my wife turned into a typical *colon*.'

'I think I am one already.' She added in a low voice, 'I don't want to be different.'

He said sharply, 'Spending all their time in small talk . . .'

'I wish I could. How I wish I could. If anyone could only teach me that . . .'

It was always the same. She drank nothing but Perrier, and yet the alcohol on his breath would make her talk as though the whisky had entered her own blood, and what she said then was always too close to the truth. Truth, which someone had once written made us free, irritated Rycker as much as one of his own hang-nails. He said, 'What nonsense. Don't talk like that for effect. There are times when you remind me of Mme. Guelle.' The night sang discordantly at them from either side of the road, and the noises from the forest were louder than the engine. She had a longing for all the shops which climbed uphill along the rue de Namur: she tried to look through the lighted dashboard into a window full of shoes. She stretched out her foot beside the brake and said in a whisper, 'I take size six.'

'What did you say?'

'Nothing.'

In the light of the headlamp she saw the cage strutting by the road like a Martian.

'You are getting into a bad habit of talking to yourself.'

She said nothing. She couldn't tell him, 'There is no one else to speak to,' about the pâtisserie at the corner, the day when Sister Thérèse broke her ankle, the *plage* in August with her parents.

'A lot of it is my own fault,' Rycker said, reaching his second stage. 'I realise that. I have failed to teach you the real values as I see them. What can you expect from the manager of a palm-oil factory? I was not meant for this life. I should have thought even you could have seen that.' His vain yellow face hung like a mask between her and Africa. He said, 'When I was young I wanted to be a priest.' He must have told her this, after drinks, at least once a month since they married, and every time he spoke she remembered their first night in the hotel at Antwerp, when he had lifted his body off her like a half-filled sack and dumped it at her side, and she, feeling some tenderness because she thought that in some way she had failed him, touched his shoulder (which was hard and round like a swede in the sack), and he asked her roughly, 'Aren't you satisfied? A man can't go on and on.' Then he had turned on his side away from her: the holy medal that he always wore had got twisted by their embrace and now lay in the small of his back, facing her like a reproach. She wanted to defend herself, 'It was you who married me. I know about chastity too–the nuns taught me.' But the chastity she had been taught was something which she connected with clean white garments and light and gentleness, while his was like old sackcloth in a desert.

'What did you say?'

'Nothing.'

'You are not even interested when I tell you my deepest feelings.'

She said miserably, 'Perhaps it was a mistake.'

'Mistake?'

'Marrying me. I was too young.'

'You mean I am too old to give you satisfaction.'

'No–no. I didn't mean . . .'

'You know only one kind of love, don't you? Do you suppose that's the kind of love the saints feel?'

'I don't know any saints,' she said desperately.

'You don't believe I am capable in my small way of going through the Dark Night of the Soul? I am o ly your husband who shares your bed. . . .'

She whispered, 'I don't understand. Please, I don't understand.'

'What don't you understand?'

'I thought that love was supposed to make you happy.'

'Is that what they taught you in the convent?'

'Yes.'

He made a grimace at her, breathing heavily, and the coupé was filled momentarily with the scent of Vat 69. They passed beside the grim constructed figure in the chair; they were nearly home.

'What are you thinking?' he asked.

She had been back in the shop in the rue de Namur watching an elderly man who was gently, so gently, easing her foot into a stiletto-heeled shoe. So she said, 'Nothing.'

Rycker said in a voice suddenly kind, 'That is the opportunity for prayer.'

'Prayer?' She knew, but without relief, that the quarrel was over, for from experience she knew too that, after the rain had swept by, the lightning always came nearer.

'When I have nothing else to think of, I mean that I *have* to think of, I always say a Pater Noster, an Ave Maria or even an Act of Contrition.'

'Contrition?'

'That I have been unjustly angry with a dear child whom I love.' His hand fell on her thigh and his fingers kneaded gently the silk of her skirt, as though they were seeking some muscle to fasten on. Outside the rusting abandoned cylinders showed they were approaching the house; they would see the lights of the bedrooms when they turned.

She wanted to go straight to her room, the small hot uninviting room where he sometimes allowed her to be alone during her monthly or unsafe periods, but he stopped her with a touch; she hadn't really expected to get away with it. He said, 'You aren't angry with me, Mawie?' He always lisped her name childishly at the moments when he felt least childish.

'No. It's only—it wouldn't be safe.' Her hope of escape was that he feared a child.

'Oh come. I looked up the calendar before I came out.'

'I've been so irregular the last two months.' Once she had bought a douche, but he had found it and thrown it away and afterwards he had lectured her on the enormity and unnaturalness of her act, speaking so long and emotionally on the subject of Christian marriage that the lecture had ended on the bed.

He put his hand below her waist and propelled her gently in the direction he required. 'Tonight,' he said, 'we'll take a risk.'

'But it's the worst time. I promise . . .'

'The Church doesn't intend us to avoid all risk. The safe period mustn't be abused, Mawie.'

She implored him, 'Let me go to my room for a moment. I've left my things there,' for she hated undressing in front of his scrutinising gaze. 'I won't be long. I promise I won't be long.'

'I'll be waiting for you,' Rycker promised.

She undressed as slowly as she dared and took a pyjama jacket from under her pillow. There was no room here for anything but a small iron bed, a chair, a wardrobe, a chest-of-drawers. On the chest was a photograph of her parents—two happy elderly people who had married late and had one child. There was a picture postcard of Bruges sent by a cousin, and an old copy of *Time*. Underneath the chest she had hidden a key and now she unlocked the bottom drawer. Inside the drawer was her secret museum: a too-clean Missal which she had been given at the time of her first communion, a seashell, the programme of a concert in Brussels, André Lejeune's History of Europe in one volume for the use of schools, and an exercise book containing an essay which she had written during her last term (she had received the maximum marks) on the Wars of Religion. Now she added to her collection the old copy of *Time*. Querry's face covered Lejeune's History: it lay, a discord, among the relics of childhood. She remembered Mme. Guelle's words exactly, 'His reputation in certain ways is very bad.' She locked the drawer and hid the key—it was unsafe to delay any further. Then she walked along the verandah to *their* room, where Rycker was stretched naked inside the mosquito tent of the double-bed under the wooden body on the cross. He looked like a drowned man fished up in a net—hair lay like seaweed on his belly and legs; but at her entrance he came immediately to life, lifting the side of the tent. 'Come, Mawie,' he said. A Christian marriage, how often she had been told it by her religious instructors, symbolised the marriage of Christ and his Church.

2

The Superior with old-fashioned politeness ground out his cheroot, but Mme. Rycker was no sooner seated than absent-mindedly he lit another. His desk was littered with hardware catalogues and scraps of paper on which he had made elaborate calculations that always came out differently, for he was a bad mathematician—multiplication with him was an elaborate form of addition and a series of subtractions would take the place of long division. One page of a catalogue was open at the picture of a bidet which the Superior had mistaken for a new kind of foot-bath. When Mme. Rycker entered he was trying to calculate whether he could afford to buy three dozen of these for the leproserie: they were just the thing for washing leprous feet.

'Why, Mme. Rycker, you are an unexpected visitor. Is your husband . . . ?'

'No.'

'It's a long way to come alone.'

'I had company as far as the Perrins'. I spent the night there. My husband asked me to bring you two drums of oil.'

'How very kind of him.'

'I am afraid we do too little for the leproserie.'

It occurred to the Superior that he might ask the Ryckers to supply a few of the novel foot-baths, but he was uncertain how many they could afford. To a man without possessions any man with money appears rich—should he ask for one foot-bath or the whole three dozen? He began to turn the photographs towards Marie Rycker, cautiously, so that it might look as though he were only fiddling with his papers. It would be so much easier for him to speak if she were to exclaim, 'What an interesting new foot-bath,' so that he could follow up by saying—

Instead of that she confused him by changing the subject. 'How are the plans for the new church, father?'

'New church?'

'My husband told me you were building a wonderful new church as big as a cathedral, in an African style.'

'What an extraordinary idea. If I had the money for that'—not with all his scraps of paper could he calculate the cost of a 'church like a cathedral'—'why, we could build a hundred houses, each with a foot-bath.' He turned the catalogue a little more towards her. 'Doctor Colin would never forgive me for wasting money on a church.'

'I wonder why my husband . . . ?'

Was it possibly a hint, the Superior wondered, that the Ryckers were prepared to finance . . . He could hardly believe that the manager of a palm-oil factory had made himself sufficiently rich, but Mme. Rycker of course might have been left a fortune. Her inheritance would certainly be the talk of Luc, but he only made the journey to the town once a year. He said, 'The old church, you know, will serve us a long time yet. Only half our people are Catholics. Anyway it's no use having a great church if the people still live in mud huts. Now our friend Querry sees a way of cutting the cost of a cottage by a quarter. We were such amateurs here until he came.'

'My husband has told everyone that M. Querry is building a church.'

'Oh no, we have better uses for him than that. The new hospital too is a long way from being finished. Any money we can beg or steal must go to equipping it. I've just been looking at these catalogues. . . .'

'Where is M. Querry now?'

'Oh, I expect he's working in his room unless he's with the doctor.'

'Everybody was talking about him at the Governor's two weeks ago.'

'Poor M. Querry.'

A small black child hardly more than two feet high walked into the room without knocking, coming in like a scrap of shadow from the noonday glare outside. He was quite naked and his little tassel hung like a bean-pod below the pot-belly. He opened a drawer in the Superior's desk and pulled out a sweet. Then he walked out again.

'They were being quite complimentary,' Mme. Rycker said. 'Is it true—about his boy getting lost . . . ?'

'Something of the sort happened. I don't know what *they* are saying.'

'That he stayed all night and prayed . . .'

'M. Querry is hardly a praying man.'

'My husband thinks a lot of him. There are so few people my husband can talk to. He asked me to come here and invite . . .'

'We are very grateful for the two drums of oil. What you have saved us with those, we can spend . . .' He turned the photograph of the bidet a little further towards Mme. Rycker.

'Do you think I could speak to him?'

'The trouble is, Mme. Rycker, this is his hour for work.'

She said imploringly, 'I only want to be able to tell my husband that I've asked him,' but her small toneless voice contained no obvious appeal and the Superior was looking elsewhere, at a feature of the foot-bath which he did not fully understand. 'What do you think of that?' he asked.

'What?'

'This foot-bath. I want to get three dozen for the hospital.'

He looked up because of her silence and was surprised to see her blushing. It occurred to him that she was a very pretty child. He said, 'Do you think . . . ?'

She was confused, remembering the ambiguous jokes of her more dashing companions at the convent. 'It's not really a foot-bath, father.'

'What else could it be for then?'

She said with the beginnings of humour, 'You'd better ask the doctor—or M. Querry.' She moved a little in her chair, and the Superior took it for a sign of departure.

'It's a long ride back to the Perrins', my dear. Can I offer you a cup of coffee, or a glass of beer?'

'No. No thank you.'

'Or a little whisky?' In all the long years of his abstinence the Superior had never learnt that whisky was too strong for the midday sun.

'No thank you. Please, father, I know you are busy. I don't want to be a nuisance, but if I could just see M. Querry and ask him . . .'

'I will give him your message, my dear. I promise I won't forget. See, I am writing it down.' He hesitated which sum to disfigure with the memo–'Querry-Rycker.' It was impossible for him to tell her that he had given his promise to Querry to leave him undisturbed, 'particularly by that pious imbecile, Rycker'.

'It won't do, father. It won't do. I promised I'd see him myself. He won't believe I've tried.' She broke off and the Superior thought later, 'I really believe she was going to ask me for a note, the kind of note children take to school, saying that they have been genuinely ill.'

'I'm not even sure where he is,' the Superior said, emphasising the word 'sure' to avoid a lie.

'If I could just look for him.'

'We can't have you wandering around in this sun. What would your husband say?'

'That's what I am afraid of. He'll never believe that I did my best.' She was obviously close to tears and this made her look younger, so that it was easy to discount the tears as the facile meaningless grief of childhood.

'I tell you what,' the Superior said, 'I will get him to telephone–when the line is in order.'

'I know that he doesn't like my husband,' she said with sad frankness.

'My dear child, it's all in your imagination.' He was at his wit's end. He said, 'Querry's a strange fellow. None of us really know him. Perhaps he likes none of us.'

'He stays with you. He doesn't avoid you.'

The Superior felt a stab of anger against Querry. These people had sent him two drums of oil. Surely they deserved in return a little civility. He said, 'Stay here. I'll see if Querry's in his room We can't have you looking all over the leproserie. . . .'

He left his study and turning the corner of the verandah made for Querry's room. He passed the rooms of Father Thomas and Father Paul which were distinguished from each other by nothing more personal than an individual choice of crucifix and a differing degree of untidiness: then the chapel: then Querry's room. It was the only one in the place completely bare of symbols, bare indeed of almost everything. No photographs of a community or a parent. The room struck the Superior even in the heat of the day as cold and hard, like a grave without a cross. Querry was sitting at his table, a letter before him, when the Superior entered. He didn't look up.

'I'm sorry to disturb you,' the Superior said.

'Sit down, father. Just a moment while I finish this.' He turned the page and said, 'How do you end your letters, father?'

'It depends. Your brother in Christ perhaps?'

'*Toute à toi.* I remember I used to put that phrase too. How false it sounds now.'

'You have a visitor. I've kept my word and defended you to the last ditch. I can do no more. I wouldn't have disturbed you otherwise.'

'I'm glad you came. I don't relish being alone with this. You see–the mail has caught up with me. How did anyone know I was here? Does that damned local *Journal* in Luc circulate even in Europe?'

'Mme. Rycker is here, asking for you.'

'Oh well, at least it's not her husband.'

He picked up the envelope. 'Do you see, she's even got the post box number right. What patience. She must have written to the Order.'

'Who is she?'

'She was once my mistress. I left her three months ago, poor woman–and that's hypocrisy. I feel no pity. I'm sorry, father. I didn't mean to embarrass you.'

'You haven't. It's Mme. Rycker who has done that. She brought us two drums of oil and she wants to speak to you.'

'Am I worth that much?'

'Her husband sent her.'

'Is that the custom here? Tell him I'm not interested.'

'She's only brought you an invitation, poor young woman. Can't you see her and thank her and say no? She seems half afraid to go back unless she can say that she had talked to you. You aren't afraid of her, are you?'

'Perhaps. In a way.'

'Forgive me for saying it, M. Querry, but you don't strike me as a man who is afraid of women.'

'Have you never come across a leper, father, who is afraid of striking his fingers because he knows they won't hurt any more?'

'I've known men rejoice when the feeling returns–even pain. But you have to give pain a chance.'

'One can have a mirage of pain. Ask the amputated. All right, father, bring her in. It's a great deal better than seeing her wretched husband anyway.'

The Superior opened the door, and there the girl was on the threshold, in the glare of sun, caught with her mouth open, like someone surprised by a camera in a night-club, looking up in the flash, with an ungainly grimace of pain. She turned sharply round and walked away to where her car was parked and they heard her inefficient attempts at starting. The Superior followed her. A line of women returning from the market delayed him. He scampered a little way after the car, the cheroot still in his mouth and his white sun-helmet tip-tilted, but she drove away under the big arch which bore the name of the leproserie, her boy watching his antics curiously through the side-window. He came limping back because he had stubbed a toe.

'Silly child,' he said, 'why didn't she stay in my room? She could have spent the night with the nuns. She'll never get to the Perrins' by dark. I only hope her boy's reliable.'

'Do you suppose she heard?'

'Of course she heard. You didn't exactly lower your voice when you spoke of Rycker. If you love a man it can't be very pleasant to hear how unwelcome . . .'

'And it's far worse, father, when you don't love him at all.'

'Of course she loves him. He's her husband.'

'Love isn't one of the commonest characteristics of marriage, father.'

'They're both Catholics.'

'Nor is it of Catholics.'

'She's a very good young woman,' the Superior said obstinately.

'Yes, father. And what a desert she must live in out there alone with that man.' He looked at the letter which lay on his desk and that phrase of immolation which everyone used and some people meant–'*toute à toi*'. It occurred to him that one could still feel the reflection of another's pain when one had ceased to feel one's own. He put the letter in his pocket: it was fair at least that he should feel the friction of the paper. 'She's been taken a long way from Pendélé,' he said.

'What's Pendélé?'

'I don't know–a dance at a friend's house, a young man with a shiny simple face, going to Mass on Sunday with the family, falling asleep in a single bed perhaps.'

'People have to grow up. We are called to more complicated things than that.'

'Are we?'

'"When we are a child we think as a child".'

'I can't match quotations from the Bible with you, father, but surely there's also something about having to be as little children if we are to inherit . . . We've grown up rather badly. The complications have become too complex–we should have stopped with the amoeba–no, long before that with the silicates. If your god wanted an adult world he should have given us an adult brain.'

'We most of us make our own complications, M. Querry.'

'Why did he give us genitals then if he wanted us to think clearly? A doctor doesn't prescribe marijuana for clear thought.'

'I thought you said you had no interest in anything.'

'I haven't. I've come through to the other side, to nothing. All the same I don't like looking back,' he said and the letter crackled softly as he shifted.

'Remorse is a kind of belief.'

'Oh no, it isn't. You try to draw everything into the net of your faith, father, but you can't steal all the virtues. Gentleness isn't Christian, self-sacrifice isn't Christian, charity isn't, remorse isn't. I expect the caveman wept to see another's tears. Haven't you even seen a dog weep? In the last cooling of the world, when the emptiness of your belief is finally exposed, there'll always be some bemused fool who'll cover another's body with his own to give it warmth for an hour more of life.'

'You believe that? But once I remember you saying you were incapable of love.'

'I am. The awful thing is I know it would be my body someone would cover. Almost certainly a woman. They have a passion for the dead. Their missals are stuffed with memorial cards.'

The Superior stubbed out his cheroot and then lit another as he moved towards the door. Querry called after him, 'I've come far enough, haven't I? Keep that girl away and her bloody tears.' He struck his hand furiously on the table because it seemed to him that he had used a phrase applicable only to the stigmata.

When the Superior had gone Querry called to Deo Gratias. The man came in propped on his three toeless feet. He looked to see if the wash-basin needed emptying.

'It's not that,' Querry said. 'Sit down. I want to ask you something.'

The man put down his staff and squatted on the ground. Even the act of sitting was awkward without toes or fingers. Querry lit a cigarette and put it in the man's mouth. He said, 'Next time you try to leave here, will you take me with you?'

The man made no answer. Querry said, 'No, you needn't answer. Of course you won't. Tell me, Deo Gratias, what was the water like? Like the big river out there?'

The man shook his head.

'Like the lake at Bikoro?'

'No.'

'What was it like, Deo Gratias?'

'It fell from the sky.'

'A waterfall?' But the word had no meaning to Deo Gratias in this flat region of river and deep bush.

'You were a child in those days on your mother's back. Were there many other children?'

He shook his head.

'Tell me what happened?'

'*Nous étions heureux*,' Deo Gratias said.

PART IV

CHAPTER I

I

Querry and Doctor Colin sat on the steps of the hospital in the cool of the early day. Every pillar had its shadow and every shadow its crouching patient. Across the road the Superior stood at the altar saying Mass, for it was a Sunday morning. The church had open sides, except for a lattice of bricks to break the sun, so that Querry and Colin were able to watch the congregation cut into shapes like a jig-saw pattern, the nuns on chairs in the front row and behind them the lepers sitting on long benches raised a foot from the ground, built of stone because stone could be disinfected more thoroughly and quickly than wood. At this distance it was a gay scene with the broken sun spangled on the white nuns' robes and the bright mammy cloths of the women. The rings which the women wore round their thighs jingled like rosaries when they knelt to pray, and all the mutilations were healed by distance and by the brickwork which hid their feet. Beyond the doctor on the top step sat the old man with elephantiasis, his scrotum supported on the step below. They talked in a whisper, so that their voices would not disturb the Mass which went on across the way—a whisper, a tinkle, a jingle, a shuffle, private movements of which they had both almost forgotten the meaning, it was so long since they had taken any part.

'Is it really impossible to operate?' Querry asked.

'Too risky. His heart mightn't stand the anaesthetic.'

'Has he got to carry that thing around then till death?'

'Yes. It doesn't weigh as much as you would think. But it seems unfair, doesn't it, to suffer all that and leprosy too.'

In the church there was a sigh and a shuffle as the congregation sat. The doctor said, 'One day I'll screw some money out of someone and have a few wheelchairs made for the worst cases. He would need a special one, of course. Could a famous ecclesiastical architect design a chair for swollen balls?'

'I'll get you out a blue print,' Querry said.

The voice of the Superior reached them from across the road. He was preaching in a mixture of French and Creole; even a Flemish phrase crept in here and there, and a word or two that Querry assumed to be Mongo or some other tongue of the river tribes.

'And I tell you truth I was ashamed when this man he said to me, "You

Klistians are all big thieves—you steal this, you steal that, you steal all the time. Oh, I know you don't steal money. You don't creep into Thomas Olo's hut and take his new radio-set, but you are thieves all the same. Worse thieves than that. You see a man who lives with one wife and doesn't beat her and looks after her when she gets a bad pain from medicines at the hospital, and you say that's Klistian love. You go to the courthouse and you hear a good judge, who say to the piccin that stole sugar from the white man's cupboard, 'You're a very sorry piccin. I not punish you, and you, you will not come here again. No more sugar palaver,' and you say that's Klistian mercy. But you are a mighty big thief when you say that—for you steal this man's love and that man's mercy. Why do you not say when you see man with knife in his back bleeding and dying, 'There's Klistian anger'?''

'I really believe he's answering something I said to him,' Querry said with a twitch of the mouth that Colin was beginning to recognise as a rudimentary smile, 'but I didn't put it quite like that.'

'Why not say when Henry Okapa got a new bicycle and someone came and tore his brake, "There's Klistian envy"? You are like a man who steals only the good fruit and leaves the bad fruit rotting on the tree.

'All right. You tell me I'm number one thief, but I say you make big mistake. Any man may defend himself before his judge. All of you in this church, you are my judges now, and this is my defence.'

'It's a long time since I listened to a sermon,' Doctor Colin said. 'It brings back the long tedious hours of childhood, doesn't it?'

'You pray to Yezu,' the Superior was saying. He twisted his mouth from habit as though he were despatching a cheroot from one side to the other. 'But Yezu is not just a holy man. Yezu is God and Yezu made the world. When you make a song you are in the song, when you bake bread you are in the bread, when you make a baby you are in the baby, and because Yezu made you, he is in you. When you love it is Yezu who loves, when you are merciful it is Yezu who is merciful. But when you hate or envy it is not Yezu, for everything that Yezu made is good. Bad things are not there—they are nothing. Hate means no love. Envy means no justice. They are just empty spaces, where Yezu ought to be.'

'He begs a lot of questions,' Doctor Colin said.

'Now I tell you that when a man loves, he must be Klistian. When a man is merciful he must be Klistian. In this village do you think you are the only Klistians—you who come to church? There is a doctor who lives near the well beyond Marie Akimbu's house and he prays to Nzambe and he makes bad medicine. He worships a false God, but once when a piccin was ill and his father and mother were in the hospital he took no money; he gave bad medicine but he took no money: he made a big God palaver with Nzambe for the piccin but took no money. I tell you then he was a Klistian, a better Klistian than the man who broke Henry Okapa's bicycle. He not believe in Yezu, but he a Klistian. I am not a thief, who steal away his charity to give to Yezu. I give back to Yezu only what Yezu made. Yezu made love, he made mercy. Everybody in the world has something that Yezu made. Everybody in the world is that much a Klistian. So how can I be a thief? There is no man so wicked he never once in his life show in his heart something that God made.'

'That would make us both Christians,' Querry said. 'Do you feel a Christian, Colin?'

'I'm not interested,' Colin said. 'I wish Christianity could reduce the price of cortisone, that's all. Let's go.'

'I hate simplifications,' Querry said, and sat on.

The Superior said, 'I do not tell you to do good things for the love of God. That is very hard. Too hard for most of us. It is much easier to show mercy because a child weeps or to love because a girl or a young man pleases your eye. That's not wrong, that's good. Only remember that the love you feel and the mercy you show were made in you by God. You must go on using them and perhaps if you pray Klistian prayers it makes it easier for you to show mercy a second time and a third time. . . .'

'And to love a second and a third girl,' Querry said.

'Why not?' the doctor asked.

'Mercy . . . love . . .' Querry said. 'Hasn't he ever known people to kill with love and kill with mercy? When a priest speaks those words they sound as though they had no meaning outside the vestry and the guild-meetings.'

'I think that is the opposite of what he's trying to say.'

'Does he want us to blame God for love? I'd rather blame man. If there is a God, let him be innocent at least. Come away, Colin, before you are converted and believe yourself an unconscious Christian.'

They rose and walked past the mutter of the Credo towards the dispensary.

'Poor man,' Colin said. 'It's a hard life, and he doesn't get many thanks. He does his best for everybody. If he believes I'm a crypto-Christian it's convenient for me, isn't it? There are many priests who wouldn't be happy to work with an atheist for a colleague.'

'He should have learnt from you that it's possible for an intelligent man to make his life without a god.'

'My life is easier than his—I have a routine that fills my day. I know when a man is cured by the negative skin-tests. There are no skin-tests for a good action. What were your motives, Querry, when you followed your boy into the forest?'

'Curiosity. Pride. Not Klistian love, I assure you.'

Colin said, 'All the same you talk as if you'd lost something you'd loved. I haven't. I think I have always liked my fellow men. Liking is a great deal safer than love. It doesn't demand victims. Who is your victim, Querry?'

'I have none now. I'm safe. I'm cured, Colin,' he added without conviction.

2

Father Paul took a helping of what was meant to be a cheese soufflé, then poured himself out a glass of water to ease it down. He said, 'Querry is wise today to lunch with the doctor. Can't you persuade the sisters to vary the *plat du jour*? Sunday after all is a feast-day.'

'This is meant to be a treat for us,' the Superior said. 'They believe we look forward to it all through the week. I wouldn't like to disillusion the poor things. They use a lot of eggs.'

All the cooking for the priests' house was done by the nuns and the food had to be carried a quarter of a mile in the sun. It had never occurred to the nuns that this might be disastrous for soufflés and omelettes and even for after-dinner coffee.

Father Thomas said, 'I do not think Querry minds much about his food.' He was the only priest in the leproserie with whom the Superior felt ill at ease; he still seemed to carry with him the strains and anxieties of the seminary. He had left it longer ago than any of the others, but he seemed doomed to a perpetual and unhappy youth; he was ill at ease with men who had grown up and were more concerned over the problems of the electric-light plant or the quality of the brick-making than over the pursuit of souls. Souls could wait. Souls had eternity.

'Yes, he's a good enough guest,' the Superior said, steering a little away from the course that he suspected Father Thomas wished to pursue.

'He's a remarkable man,' Father Thomas said, struggling to regain direction.

'We have enough funds now,' the Superior said at large, 'for an electric fan in the delivery-ward.'

'We'll have air-conditioning in our rooms yet,' Father Jean said, 'and a drug-store and all the latest movie magazines including pictures of Brigitte Bardot.' Father Jean was tall, pale and concave with a beard which struggled like an unpruned hedge. He had once been a brilliant moral theologian before he joined the Order and now he carefully nurtured the character of a film-fan, as though it would help him to wipe out an ugly past.

'I'd rather have a boiled egg for Sunday lunch,' Father Paul said.

'You wouldn't like stale eggs boiled,' Father Jean said, helping himself to more soufflé; in spite of his cadaverous appearance he had a Flemish appetite.

'They wouldn't be stale,' Father Joseph said, 'if they only learnt to manage the chickens properly. I'd be quite ready to put some of my men on to building them proper houses for intensive production. It would be easy enough to carry the electric power down from their houses. . . .'

Brother Philippe spoke for the first time. He was always reluctant to intrude on the conversation of men who he considered belonged to another less mundane world. 'Electric fans, chicken houses: be careful, father, or you will be overloading the dynamos before you've done.'

The Superior was aware that Father Thomas was smouldering at his elbow. He said tactfully, 'And the new classroom, father? Have you everything that's needed?'

'Everything but a catechist who knows the first thing about his faith.'

'Oh well, so long as he can teach the alphabet. First things first.'

'I should have thought the Catechism was rather more important than the alphabet.'

'Rycker was on the telephone this morning,' Father Jean said, coming to the Superior's rescue.

'What did he want?'

'Querry of course. He said he had a message—something about an Englishman, but he refused to give it. He threatened to be over one day soon, when the ferries are working again. I asked him if he could bring me some film magazines, but he said he didn't read them. He also wants to borrow Father Garrigou-Lagrange on Predestination.'

'There are moments,' the Superior said with moderation, 'when I almost regret M. Querry's arrival.'

'Surely we should be very glad,' Father Thomas said, 'of any small inconvenience he may bring us. We don't live a very troubled life.' The helping of soufflé he had taken remained untasted on his plate. He kneaded a piece of bread into a hard pellet and washed it down like a pill. 'You can't expect people to leave us alone while he is here. It's not only that he's a famous man. He's a man of profound faith.'

'I hadn't noticed it,' Father Paul said. 'He wasn't at Mass this morning.' The Superior lit another cheroot.

'Oh yes he was. I can tell you his eyes never left the altar. He was sitting across the way with the sick. That's as good a way of attending Mass as sitting up in front with his back to the lepers, isn't it?'

Father Paul opened his mouth to reply, but the Superior stopped him with a covert wink. 'At any rate it is a charitable way of putting it,' the Superior said. He balanced his cheroot on the edge of his plate and rose to give thanks. Then he crossed himself and picked up his cheroot again. 'Father Thomas,' he said, 'can you spare me a minute?'

He led the way to his room and installed Father Thomas in the one easy chair that he kept for visitors by the filing-cabinet. Father Thomas watched him tensely, sitting bolt upright, like a cobra watching a mongoose. 'Have a cheroot, father?'

'You know I don't smoke.'

'Of course. I'm sorry. I was thinking of someone else. Is that chair uncomfortable? I'm afraid the springs may have gone. It's foolish having springs in the tropics, but it was given us with a lot of junk. . . .'

'It's quite comfortable, thank you.'

'I'm sorry you don't find your catechist satisfactory. It's not so easy to find a good one now that we have three classes for boys. The nuns seem to manage better than we do.'

'Only if you consider Marie Akimbu a suitable teacher.'

'She works very hard I'm told by Mother Agnes.'

'Certainly, if you call having a baby every year by a different man hard work. I can't see that it's right allowing her to teach with her cradle in the class. She's pregnant again. What kind of an example is that?'

'Oh well, you know, *autres pays autres mœurs*. We are here to help, father, not condemn, and I don't think we can teach the sisters their business. They know the young woman better than we do. Here, you must remember, there are few people who know their own fathers. The children belong to the mother. Perhaps that's why they prefer us, and the Mother of God, to the Protestants.' The Superior searched for words. 'Let me see, father, you've been with us now—it must be over two years?'

'Two years next month.'

'You know you don't eat enough. That soufflé wasn't exactly inviting . . .'

'I have no objection to the soufflé. I happen to be fasting for a private intention.'

'Of course you have your confessor's consent?'

'It wasn't necessary for just one day, father.'

'The soufflé day was a good day to choose then, but you know this climate is very difficult for Europeans, especially at the beginning. By the time our leave comes at the end of six years we have become accustomed to it. Sometimes I almost dread going home. The first years . . . one mustn't drive oneself.'

'I am not aware of driving myself unduly, father.'

'Our first duty, you know, is to survive, even if that means taking things a little more easily. You have a great spirit of self-sacrifice, father. It's a wonderful quality, but it's not always what's required on the battlefield. The good soldier doesn't court death.'

'I am quite unaware . . .'

'We all of us have a feeling of frustration sometimes. Poor Marie Akimbu, we have to take the material we have to hand. I'm not sure that you'd find better material in some of the parishes of Liège, though sometimes I've wondered whether perhaps you might be happier there. The African mission is not for everyone. If a man feels himself ill-adapted here, there's no defeat in asking for a transfer. Do you sleep properly, father?'

'I have enough sleep.'

'Perhaps you ought to have a check-up with Doctor Colin. It's wonderful what a pill will do at the right time.'

'Father, why are you so against M. Querry?'

'I hope I'm not. I'm unaware of it.'

'What other man in his position—he's world-famous, father, even though Father Paul may never have heard of him—would bury himself here, helping with the hospital?'

'I don't look for motives, Father Thomas. I hope I accept what he does with gratitude.'

'Well, I do look for motives. I've been talking to Deo Gratias. I hope I would have done what he did, going out at night into the bush looking for a servant, but I doubt . . .'

'Are you afraid of the dark?'

'I'm not ashamed to say that I am.'

'Then it would have needed more courage in your case. I have still to find what does frighten M. Querry.'

'Well, isn't that heroic?'

'Oh no. I am disturbed by a man without fear as I would be by a man without a heart. Fear saves us from so many things. Not that I'm saying, of course, that M. Querry . . .'

'Does it show a lack of heart staying beside his boy all night, praying with him?'

'They are telling that story in the city, I know, but did he pray? It's not what Querry told the doctor.'

'I asked Deo Gratias. He said yes. I asked him what prayers—the Ave Maria, I asked him? He said yes.'

'Father Thomas, when you have been in Africa a little longer, you will learn not to ask an African a question which may be answered by yes. It is their form of courtesy to agree. It means nothing at all.'

'I think after two years I can tell when an African is lying.'

'Those are not lies. Father Thomas, I can well understand why you are attracted to Querry. You are both men of extremes. But in our way of life, it is better for us not to have heroes—not live heroes, that is. The saints should be enough for us.'

'You are not suggesting there are not live saints?'

'Of course not. But don't let's recognise them before the Church does. We shall be saved a lot of disappointment that way.'

3

Father Thomas stood by his netted door staring through the wire-mesh at the ill-lighted avenue of the leproserie. Behind him on his table he had prepared a candle and the flame shone palely below the bare electric globe; in five minutes all the lights would go out. This was the moment he feared; prayers were of no avail to heal the darkness. The Superior's words had reawakened his longing for Europe. Liège might be an ugly and brutal city, but there was no hour of the night when a man, lifting his curtain, could not see a light shining on the opposite wall of the street or perhaps a late passer-by going home. Here at ten o'clock, when the dynamos ceased working, it needed an act of faith to know that the forest had not come up to the threshold of the room. Sometimes it seemed to him that he could hear the leaves brushing on the mosquito-wire. He looked at his watch—four minutes to go.

He had admitted to the Superior that he was afraid of the dark. But the Superior had brushed away his fear as of no account. He felt an enormous longing to confide, but it was almost impossible to confide in men of his own Order, any more than a soldier could admit his cowardice to another soldier. He couldn't say to the Superior, 'Every night I pray that I won't be summoned to attend someone dying in the hospital or in his kitchen, that I won't have to light the lamp of my bicycle and pedal through the dark.' A few weeks ago an old man had so died, but it was Father Joseph who went out to find the corpse where it sat in a rickety deck-chair with some fetish or other for Nzambe placed in its lap and a holy medal round its neck; he had given conditional absolution by the light of the bicycle-lamp because there were no candles to be found.

He believed that the Superior grudged the admiration he felt for Querry. His companions, it seemed to him, spent their lives with small concerns which they could easily discuss together—the cost of foot-baths, a fault in the dynamo, a holdup at the brick-kiln, but the things which worried him he could discuss with no one. He envied the happily married man who had a ready confidante at bed and board. Father Thomas was married to the Church and the Church responded to his confidence only in the clichés of the confessional. He remembered how even in the seminary his confessor had checked him whenever he had gone further than the platitudes of his problem. The word 'scruple' was posted like a traffic sign in whichever direction the mind drove. 'I want to talk, I want to talk,' Father Thomas cried silently to himself as all the lights went out and the beat of the dynamos stopped. Somebody came down the verandah in the dark; the steps passed the room of Father Paul and would have passed his own if he had not called out, 'Is it you, M. Querry?'

'Yes.'

'Won't you come in for a moment?'

Querry opened the door and came into the small radiance of the candle. He said, 'I've been explaining to the Superior the difference between a bidet and a foot-bath.'

'Please won't you sit down? I can never sleep so early as this and my eyes are not good enough to read by candle-light.' Already in one sentence he had admitted more to Querry than he had ever done to his Superior, for he knew that the Superior would only too readily have given him a torch and permission to read for as long as he liked after the lights went out, but that permission would have drawn attention to his weakness. Querry looked for a chair. There was only one and Father Thomas began to pull back the mosquito-net from the bed.

'Why not come to my room?' Querry asked. 'I have some whisky there.'

'Today I am fasting,' Father Thomas said. 'Please take the chair. I will sit here.' The candle burnt straight upwards to a smoky tip like a crayon. 'I hope you are happy here,' Father Thomas said.

'Everyone has been very kind to me.'

'You are the first visitor to stay here since I came.'

'Is that so?'

Father Thomas's long narrow nose was oddly twisted at the end; it gave him the effect of smelling sideways at some elusive odour. 'Time is needed to settle in a place like this.' He laughed nervously. 'I'm not sure that I'm settled myself yet.'

'I can understand that,' Querry said mechanically for want of anything better to say, but the bromide was swallowed like wine by Father Thomas.

'Yes, you have great understanding. I sometimes think a layman has more capacity for understanding than a priest. Sometimes,' he added, 'more faith.'

'That's certainly not true in my case,' Querry said.

'I have told this to no one else,' Father Thomas said, as though he were handing over some precious object which would leave Querry forever in his debt. 'When I finished at the seminary I sometimes thought that only by martyrdom could I save myself—if I could die before I lost everything.'

'One doesn't die,' Querry said.

'I wanted to be sent to China, but they wouldn't accept me.'

'Your work here must be just as valuable,' Querry said, dealing out his replies quickly and mechanically like cards.

'Teaching the alphabet?' Father Thomas shifted on the bed and the drape of mosquito-net fell over his face like a bride's veil or a beekeeper's. He turned it back and it fell again, as though even an inanimate object had enough consciousness to know the best moment to torment.

'Well, it's time for bed,' Querry said.

'I'm sorry. I know I'm keeping you up. I'm tiring you.'

'Not at all,' Querry said. 'Besides I sleep badly.'

'You do? It's the heat. I can't sleep for more than a few hours.'

'I could let you have some pills.'

'Oh no, no, thank you. I must learn somehow–this is the place God has sent me to.'

'Surely you volunteered?'

'Of course, but if it hadn't been His will . . .'

'Perhaps it's his will that you should take a nembutal. Let me fetch you one.'

'It does me so much more good just to talk to you for a little. You know in a community one doesn't talk–about anything important. I'm not keeping you from your work, am I?'

'I can't work by candle-light.'

'I'll release you very soon,' Father Thomas said, smiling weakly, and then fell silent again. The forest might be approaching, but for once he had a companion. Querry sat with his hands between his knees waiting. A mosquito hummed near the candle-flame. The dangerous desire to confide grew in Father Thomas's mind like the pressure of an orgasm. He said, 'You won't understand how much one needs, sometimes, to have one's faith fortified by talking to a man who believes.'

Querry said, 'You have the fathers.'

'We talk only about the dynamo and the schools.' He said, 'Sometimes I think if I stay here I'll lose my faith altogether. Can you understand that?'

'Oh yes, I can understand that. But I think it's your confessor you should talk to, not me.'

'Deo Gratias talked to you, didn't he?'

'Yes. A little.'

'You make people talk. Rycker . . .'

'God forbid.' Querry moved restlessly on the hard chair. 'What I would say to you wouldn't help you at all. You must believe that. I'm not a man of–faith.'

'You are a man of humility,' Father Thomas said. 'We've all noticed that.'

'If you knew the extent of my pride . . .'

'Pride which builds churches and hospitals is not so bad a pride.'

'You mustn't use me to buttress your faith, father. I'd be the weak spot. I don't want to say anything that could disturb you more–but I've nothing for you–nothing. I wouldn't even call myself a Catholic unless I were in the army or in a prison. I am a legal Catholic, that's all.'

'We both of us have our doubts,' Father Thomas said. 'Perhaps I have more than you. They even come to me at the altar with the Host in my hands.'

'I've long ceased to have doubts. Father, if I must speak plainly, I don't believe at all. Not at all. I've worked it out of my system–like women. I've no desire to convert others to disbelief, or even to worry them. I want to keep my mouth shut, if only you'd let me.'

'You can't think what a lot of good our conversation has done me,' Father Thomas said with excitement. 'There's not a priest here to whom I can talk as we're talking. One sometimes desperately needs a man who has experienced the same weaknesses as oneself.'

'But you've misunderstood me, father.'

'Don't you see that perhaps you've been given the grace of aridity? Perhaps even now you are walking in the footsteps of St John of the Cross, the *noche oscura*.'

'You are so very far from the truth,' Querry said, making a movement with his hands of bewilderment or rejection.

'I've watched you here,' Father Thomas said, 'I am capable of judging a man's actions.' He leant forward until his face was not very far from Querry's and Querry could smell the lotion Father Thomas used against mosquito-bites. 'For the first time since I came to this place, I feel I can be of use. If you ever have the need to confess, always remember I am here.'

'The only confession I am ever likely to make,' Querry said, 'would be to an examining magistrate.'

'Ha, ha.' Father Thomas caught the joke in mid-air and confiscated it, like a schoolboy's ball, under his soutane. He said, 'Those doubts you have. I can assure you I know them too. But couldn't we perhaps go over together the philosophical arguments . . . to help us both?'

'They wouldn't help me, father. Any sixteen-year-old student could demolish them, and anyway I need no help. I don't want to be harsh, father, but I don't wish to believe. I'm cured.'

'Then why do I get more sense of faith from you than from anyone here?'

'It's in your own mind, father. You are looking for faith and so I suppose you find it. But I'm not looking. I don't want any of the things I've known and lost. If faith were a tree growing at the end of the avenue, I promise you I'd never go that way. I don't mean to say anything to hurt you, father. I would help you if I could. If you feel in pain because you doubt, it is obvious that you are feeling the pain of faith, and I wish you luck.'

'You really do understand, don't you?' Father Thomas said, and Querry could not restrain an expression of tired despair. 'Don't be irritated. Perhaps I know you better than you do yourself. I haven't found so much understanding, "not in all Israel" if you can call the community that. You have done so much good. Perhaps—another night—we could have a talk again. On our problems—yours and mine.'

'Perhaps, but—'

'And pray for me, M. Querry. I would value your prayers.'

'I don't pray.'

'I have heard differently from Deo Gratias,' Father Thomas said, fetching up a smile like a liquorice-stick, dark and sweet and prehensile. He said, 'There are interior prayers, the prayers of silence. There are even unconscious prayers when men have goodwill. A thought from you may be a prayer in the eyes of God. Think of me occasionally, M. Querry.'

'Of course.'

'I would like to be of help to you as you have been to me.' He paused as though he were waiting for some appeal, but Querry only put a hand to his face and brushed away the sticky tendrils which a spider had left dangling between him and the door. 'I shall sleep tonight,' Father Thomas said, threateningly.

CHAPTER 2

I

About twice a month the Bishop's boat was due to come in with the heavier provisions for the leproserie, but sometimes many weeks went by without a visit. They waited for it with forced patience; perhaps the captain of the Otraco boat which brought the mail would also bring news of her small rival–a snag in the river might have pierced its bottom: it might be stranded on a mud-bank; perhaps the rudder had been twisted in collision with a fallen tree-trunk; or the captain might be down with fever or have been appointed a professor of Greek by the Bishop who had not yet found a priest to take his place. It was not a very popular job among members of the Order. No knowledge of navigation was required, not even of machinery, for the African mate was in virtual charge of the engine and the bridge. Four weeks of loneliness on the river every trip, the attempt at each halt to discover some cargo which had not been pledged to Otraco, such a life compared unfavourably with employment at the cathedral in Luc or even at a seminary in the bush.

It was dusk when the inhabitants of the leproserie heard the bell of the long-overdue boat; the sound came to Colin and Querry where they sat over the first drink of the evening on the doctor's verandah. 'At last,' Colin said, finishing his whisky, 'if only they have brought the new X-ray . . .'

White flowers had opened with twilight on the long avenue; fires were being lit for the evening meal, and the mercy of darkness was falling at last over the ugly and the deformed. The wrangles of the night had not yet begun, and peace was there, something you could touch like a petal or smell like wood-smoke. Querry said to Colin, 'You know I am happy here.' He closed his mouth on the phrase too late; it had escaped him on the sweet evening air like an admission.

2

'I remember the day you came,' Colin said. 'You were walking up this road and I asked you how long you were going to stay. You said–do you remember?—'

But Querry was silent and Colin saw that he already regretted having spoken at all.

The white boat came slowly round the bend of the river; a lantern was alight at the bow, and the pressure-lamp was burning in the saloon. A black figure, naked except for a loin-cloth, was poised with a rope on the pontoon, preparing to throw it. The fathers in their white soutanes gathered on the verandah like moths round a treacle-jar, and when Colin looked behind him he could see the glow of the Superior's cheroot following them down the road.

Colin and Querry halted at the top of the steep bank above the river. An African dived in from the pontoon and swam ashore as the engines petered out. He caught the rope and made it fast around a rock and the top-heavy boat eased in. A sailor pushed a plank across for a woman who came ashore carrying two live turkeys on her head; she fussed with her mammy-cloths, draping and redraping them about her waist.

'The great world comes to us,' Colin said.

'What do you mean?'

The captain waved from the window of the saloon. Along the narrow deck the door of the Bishop's cabin was closed, but a faint light shone through the mosquito-netting.

'Oh, you never know what the boat may bring. After all, it brought you.'

'They seem to have a passenger,' Querry said.

The captain gesticulated to them from the window; his arm invited them to come aboard. 'Has he lost his voice?' the Superior said, joining them at the top of the bank, and cupping his hands he yelled as loudly as he could, 'Well, captain, you are late.' The sleeve of a white soutane moved in the dusk; the captain had put a finger to his lips. 'In God's name,' the Superior said, 'has he got the Bishop on board?' He led the way down the slope and across the gang-plank.

Colin said, 'After you.' He was aware of Querry's hesitation. He said, 'We'll have a glass of beer. It's the custom,' but Querry made no move. 'The captain will be glad to see you again,' he went on, his hand under Querry's elbow to help him down the bank. The Superior was picking his way among the women, the goats and the cooking-pots, which littered the pontoon, towards the iron ladder by the engine.

'What you said about the world?' Querry said. 'You don't really suppose, do you . . . ?' and he broke off with his eyes on the cabin that he had once occupied, where the candle-flame was wavering in the river-draught.

'It was a joke,' Colin said. 'I ask you–does it look like the great world?' Night which came in Africa so quickly had wiped the whole boat out, except the candle in the Bishop's cabin, the pressure-lamp in the saloon where two white figures silently greeted each other, and the hurricane-lamp at the foot of the ladder where a woman sat preparing her husband's chop.

'Let's go,' Querry said.

At the top of the ladder the captain greeted them. He said, 'So you are still here, Querry. It is a pleasure to see you again.' He spoke in a low voice; he might have been exchanging a confidence. In the saloon the beer was already uncapped and awaiting them. The captain shut the door and for the first time raised his voice. He said, 'Drink up quickly, Doctor Colin. I have a patient for you.'

'One of the crew?'

'Not one of the crew,' the captain said, raising his glass. 'A real passenger. I've only had two real passengers in two years, first there was M. Querry and now this man. A passenger who pays, not a father.'

'Who is he?'

'He comes from the great world,' the captain said, echoing Colin's phrase. 'It has been difficult for me. He speaks no Flemish and very little French, and that made it yet more complicated when he went down with fever. I am very glad to be here,' he said and seemed about to lapse into his more usual silence.

'Why has he come?' the Superior asked.

'How do I know? I tell you—he speaks no French.'

'Is he a doctor?'

'He is certainly not a doctor or he wouldn't be so frightened of a little fever.'

'Perhaps I should see him right away,' Colin said. 'What language does he speak?'

'English. I tried him in Latin,' the captain said. 'I even tried him in Greek, but it was no good.'

'I can speak English,' Querry said with reluctance.

'How is his fever?' Colin asked.

'This is the worst day. Tomorrow it will be better. I said to him, "Finitum est," but I think he believed that I meant he was dying.'

'Where did you pick him up?'

'At Luc. He had some kind of introduction to the Bishop—from Rycker, I think. He had missed the Otraco boat.'

Colin and Querry went down the narrow deck to the Bishop's cabin. Hanging at the end of the deck was the misshapen lifebelt looking like a dried eel, the steaming shower, the lavatory with the broken door, and beside it the kitchen-table and the hutch where two rabbits munched in the dark; nothing, except presumably the rabbits, had changed. Colin opened the cabin-door, and there was the photograph of the church under snow, but in the rumpled bed which Querry had somehow imagined would still bear, like a hare's form, his own impression, lay the naked body of a very fat man. His neck as he lay on his back was forced into three ridges like gutters and the sweat filled them and drained round the curve of his head on to the pillow.

'I suppose we'll have to take him ashore,' Colin said. 'If there's a spare room at the fathers'.' On the table stood a Rolleiflex camera and a portable Remington, and inserted in the typewriter was a sheet of paper on which the man had begun to type. When Querry brought the candle closer he could read one sentence in English: 'The eternal forest broods along the banks unchanged since Stanley and his little band—' It petered out without punctuation. Colin lifted the man's wrist and felt his pulse. He said, 'The captain's right. He'll be up in a few days. This sleep marks the end.'

'Then why not leave him here?' Querry said.

'Do you know him?'

'I've never seen him before.'

'I thought you sounded afraid,' Colin said. 'We can hardly ship him back if he's paid his passage here.'

The man woke as Colin dropped his wrist. 'Are you the doctor?' he asked in English.

'Yes. My name is Doctor Colin.'

'I'm Parkinson,' the man said firmly as though he were the sole survivor of a whole tribe of Parkinsons. 'Am I dying?'

'He wants to know if he is dying,' Querry translated.

Colin said, 'You will be all right in a few days.'

'It's bloody hot,' Parkinson said. He looked at Querry. 'Thank God there's someone here at last who speaks English.' He turned his head towards the Remington and said, 'The white man's grave.'

'Your geography's wrong. This is not West Africa,' Querry corrected him with dry dislike.

'They won't know the bloody difference,' Parkinson said.

'And Stanley never came this way,' Querry went on, without attempting to disguise his antagonism.

'Oh yes he did. This river's the Congo, isn't it?'

'No. You left the Congo a week ago after Luc.'

The man said again ambiguously, 'They won't know the bloody difference. My head's splitting.'

'He's complaining about his head,' Querry told Colin.

'Tell him I'll give him something when we've taken him ashore. Ask him if he can walk as far as the fathers'. He would be a terrible weight to carry.'

'Walk!' Parkinson exclaimed. He twisted his head and the sweat-gutters drained on to the pillow. 'Do you want to kill me? It would be a bloody good story, wouldn't it, for everyone but me. Parkinson buried where Stanley once . . .'

'Stanley was never here,' Querry said.

'I don't care whether he was or not. Why keep bringing it up? I'm bloody hot. There ought to be a fan. If the chap here is a doctor, why can't he take me to a proper hospital?'

'I doubt if you'd like the hospital we have,' Querry said. 'It's for lepers.'

'Then I'll stay where I am.'

'The boat returns to Luc tomorrow.'

Parkinson said, 'I can't understand what the doctor says. Is he a good doctor? Can I trust him?'

'Yes, he's a good doctor.'

'But they never tell the patient, do they?' Parkinson said. 'My old man died thinking he only had a duodenal ulcer.'

'You are not dying. You have got a touch of malaria, that's all. You are over the worst. It would be much easier for all of us if you'd walk ashore. Unless you want to return to Luc.'

'When I start a job,' Parkinson said obscurely, 'I finish a job.' He wiped his neck dry with his fingers. 'My legs are like butter,' he said. 'I must have lost a couple of stone. It's the strain on the heart I'm afraid of.'

'It's no use,' Querry told Colin. 'We'll have to have him carried.'

'I will see what can be done,' Colin said and left them. When they were alone, Parkinson said, 'Can you use a camera?'

'Of course.'

'With a flash bulb?'

'Yes.'

He said, 'Would you do me a favour and take some pictures of me carried ashore? Get as much atmosphere in as you can—you know the kind of thing, black faces gathered round looking worried and sympathetic.'

'Why should they be worried?'

'You can easily fix that,' Parkinson said. 'They'll be worried enough anyway in case they drop me–and *they* won't know the difference.'

'What do you want the picture for?'

'It's the kind of thing they like to have. You can't distrust a photograph, or so people think. Do you know, since you came into the cabin and I could talk again, I've been feeling better? I'm not sweating so much, am I? And my head . . .' He twisted it tentatively and gave a groan again. 'Oh well, if I hadn't had this malaria, I daresay I'd have had to invent it. It gives the right touch.'

'I wouldn't talk so much if I were you.'

'I'm bloody glad the boat-trip's over, I can tell you that.'

'Why have you come here?'

'Do you know a man called Querry?' Parkinson said.

The man had struggled round on to his side. The reflection from the candle shone back from the dribbles and pools of sweat so that the face appeared like a too-travelled road after rain. Querry knew for certain he had never seen the man before, and yet he remembered how Doctor Colin had said to him, 'The great world comes to us.'

'Why do you want Querry?' he asked.

'It's my job to want him,' Parkinson said. He groaned again. 'It's no bloody picnic this. You wouldn't lie to me, would you, about the doctor? And what he said?'

'No.'

'It's my heart, as I told you. Two stone in a week. This too solid flesh is surely melting. Shall I tell you a secret? The daredevil Parkinson is sometimes damned afraid of death.'

'Who are you?' Querry asked. The man turned his face away with irritable indifference and closed his eyes. Soon he was asleep again.

He was still asleep when they carried him off the boat wrapped in a piece of tarpaulin like a dead body about to be committed to the deep. It needed six men to lift him and they got in each other's way, so that once as they struggled up the bank, a man slipped and fell. Querry was in time to prevent the body falling. The head rammed his chest and the smell of hair-oil poisoned the night. He wasn't used to supporting such a weight and he was breathless and sweating as they got the body over the rise and came on Father Thomas standing there holding a hurricane-lamp. Another African took Querry's place and Querry walked behind at Father Thomas's side. Father Thomas said, 'You shouldn't have done that–a weight like that, in this heat–it's rash at your age. Who is he?'

'I don't know. A stranger.'

Father Thomas said, 'Perhaps a man can be judged by his rashness.' The glow of the Superior's cheroot approached them through the dark. 'You won't find much rashness here,' Father Thomas went angrily on. 'Bricks and mortar and the monthly bills–that's what we think about. Not the Samaritan on the road to Jericho.'

'Nor do I. I just took a hand for a few minutes, that's all.'

'We could all learn from you,' Father Thomas said, taking Querry's arm above the elbow as though he were an old man who needed the support of a disciple.

The Superior overtook them. He said, 'I don't know where we are going to put him. We haven't a room free.'

'Let him share mine. There's room for the two of us,' Father Thomas said, and he squeezed Querry's arm as if he wished to convey to him 'I at least have learnt your lesson. I am not as my brothers are.'

CHAPTER 3

I

Doctor Colin had before him a card which carried the outline-drawing of a man. He had made the drawing himself; the cards he had ordered in Luc because he despaired of obtaining any like them from home. The trouble was they cost too little; the invoices had fallen like fine dust through the official tray that sifted his requests for aid. There was nobody on the lower levels of the Ministry at home with authority to allow an expenditure of six hundred francs, and nobody with courage enough to worry a senior officer with such a paltry demand. Now whenever he used the charts he felt irritated by his own bad drawings. He ran his fingers over a patient's back and detected a new thickening of the skin below the left shoulder-blade. He drew the shading on his chart and called 'Next.' Perhaps he might have forestalled that patch if the new hospital had been finished and the new apparatus installed for taking the temperature of the skin. 'It is not a case of what I have done,' he thought, 'but of what I am going to do.' This optimistic phrase had an ironic meaning for Doctor Colin.

When he first came to this country, there was an old Greek shopkeeper living in Luc–a man in his late seventies who was famous for his reticence. A few years before he had married a young African woman who could neither read nor write. People wondered what kind of contact they could have, at his age, with his reticence and her ignorance. One day he saw his African clerk bedding her down at the back of the warehouse behind some sacks of coffee. He said nothing at all, but next day he went to the bank and took out his savings. Most of the savings he put in an envelope and posted in at the door of the local orphanage which was always chock-a-block with unwanted half-castes. The rest he took with him up the hill behind the courthouse to a garage which sold ancient cars, and there he bought the cheapest car they could sell him. It was so old and so cheap that even the manager, perhaps because he too was a Greek, had scruples. The car could only be trusted to start on top of a hill, but the old man said that didn't matter. It was his ambition to drive a car once before he died–his whim if you liked to call it that. So they showed him how to put it into gear and how to accelerate, and shoving behind they gave him a good running start. He rode down to the square in Luc where his store was situated and began hooting as soon as he got there. People stopped to look at the strange sight of the old man driving his first car, and as he passed the store his clerk came out to see the fun. The old man drove all round the square a second time–he couldn't have stopped the car anyway because it would not start on the flat. Round he came with his clerk waving in the doorway to encourage him, then he twisted the wheel, trod down on the accelerator and drove straight over his clerk into the store, where the car came to the final halt of all time up against the cash register. Then he got out of the car, and leaving it just as it was, he went into his parlour and waited for the police to arrive. The clerk was not dead, but both his legs were crushed and the pelvis was broken and he wouldn't be any good for a woman ever again. Presently the Commissioner of Police walked in. He was a young man and this was his first case and the Greek was highly respected in Luc. 'What have you done?' he demanded when he came into the parlour. 'It is not a case of what have I done,' the old man said, 'but of what I am going to do,' and he took a gun from under the cushion and shot himself through the head. Doctor Colin since those days had often found comfort in the careful sentence of the old Greek storekeeper.

He called again, 'Next.' It was a day of extreme heat and humidity and the patients were languid and few. It had never ceased to surprise the doctor how human beings never became acclimatised to their own country; an African suffered from the heat like any European, just as a Swede he once knew suffered from the long winter night as though she had been born in a southern land. The man who now came to stand before the doctor would not meet his eyes. On the chart he was given the name of Attention, but now any attention he had was certainly elsewhere.

'Trouble again like the other night?' the doctor asked.

The man looked over the doctor's shoulder as if someone he feared were approaching and said, 'Yes.' His eyes were heavy and bloodshot; he pushed his shoulders forward on either side of his sunken chest as though they were the corners of a book he was trying to close.

'It will be over soon,' the doctor said. 'You must be patient.'

'I am afraid,' the man said in his own tongue. 'Please when night comes let them bind my hands.'

'Is it as bad as that?'

'Yes. I am afraid for my boy. He sleeps beside me.'

The D.D.S. tablets were not a simple cure. Reactions from the drug were sometimes terrible. When it was only a question of pain in the nerves you could treat a patient with cortisone, but in a few cases a kind of madness came over the mind in the hours of darkness. The man said, 'I am afraid of killing my boy.'

The doctor said, 'This will pass. One more night, that's all. Remember you have just to hold on. Can you read the time?'

'Yes.'

'I will give you a clock that shines so that you can read it in the dark. The trouble will start at eight o'clock. At eleven o'clock you will feel worse. Don't struggle. If we tie your hands you will struggle. Just look at the clock. At one you will feel very bad, but then it will begin to pass. At three you will feel no worse than you do now, and after that less and less—the madness will go. Just look at the clock and remember what I say. Will you do that?'

'Yes.'

'Before dark I will bring you the clock.'

'My child . . .'

'Don't worry about your child. I will tell the sisters to look after him till the madness has gone. You must just watch the clock. As the hands move the madness will move too. And at five the clock will ring a bell. You can sleep then. Your madness will have gone. It won't come back.'

He tried to speak with conviction, but he felt the heat blurring his intonation. When the man had gone he felt that something had been dragged out of him and thrown away. He said to the dispenser, 'I can't see anyone today.'

'There are only six more.'

'Am I the only one who must not feel the heat?' But he felt some of the shame of a deserter as he walked away from his tiny segment of the world's battlefield.

Perhaps it was shame that led his steps towards another patient. As he passed Querry's room he saw him busied at his drawing-board; he went on and came to Father Thomas's room. Father Thomas too had taken the morning off—his schools like the dispensary would have been all but emptied by the heat. Parkinson sat on the only chair, wearing the bottom of his pyjamas: the cord looked as if it were tied insecurely round an egg. Father Thomas was talking excitedly as Colin entered, in what even the doctor recognised to be very odd English. He heard the name 'Querry'. There was hardly space to stand between the two beds.

'Well,' Colin said, 'you see, M. Parkinson, you are not dead. One doesn't die of a small fever.'

'What's he saying?' Parkinson asked Father Thomas. 'I'm tired of not understanding. What was the good of the Norman Conquest if we don't speak the same language now?'

'Why has he come here, Father Thomas? Have you found that out?'

'He is asking me a great many questions about Querry.'

'Why? What business is it of his?'

'He told me that he had come here specially to talk to him.'

'Then he would have done better to have gone back with the boat because Querry won't talk.'

'Querry, that's right, Querry,' Parkinson said. 'It's stupid of him to pretend to hide away. No one really wants to hide from Montagu Parkinson. Aren't I the end of every man's desire? Quote. Swinburne.'

'What have you told him, father?'

Father Thomas said defensively, 'I've done no more than confirm what Rycker told him.'

'Rycker! Then he's been listening to a pack of lies.'

'Is the story of Deo Gratias a lie? Is the new hospital a lie? I hope that I have been able to put the story in the right context, that's all.'

'What is the right context?'

'The Catholic context,' Father Thomas replied.

The Remington portable had been set up on Father Thomas's table beside the crucifix. On the other side of the crucifix, like the second thief, the Rolleiflex hung by its strap from a nail. Doctor Colin looked at the typewritten sheet upon the table. He could read English more easily than he could speak it. He read the heading: 'The Recluse of the Great River', then looked accusingly at Father Thomas. 'Do you know what this is about?'

'It is the story of Querry,' Father Thomas said.

'This nonsense!'

Colin looked again at the typewritten sheet. 'That is the name which the natives have given to a strange newcomer in the heart of darkest Africa.' Colin said, '*Qui êtes-vous?*'

'Parkinson,' the man said. 'I've told you already. Montagu Parkinson.' He added with disappointment, 'Doesn't the name mean anything at all to you?'

Lower down the page Colin read, 'three weeks by boat to reach this wild territory. Struck down after seven days by the bites of tsetse flies and mosquitoes I was carried ashore unconscious. Where once Stanley battled his way with Maxim guns, another fight is being waged—this time in the cause of the African—against the deadly infection of leprosy . . . woke from my fever to find myself a patient in a leper hospital. . . .'

'But these are lies,' Colin said to Father Thomas.

'What's he grousing about?' Parkinson asked.

'He says that what you have written there is—not altogether true.'

'Tell him it's more than the truth,' Parkinson said. 'It's a page of modern history. Do you really believe Caesar said "*Et tu, Brute*"? It's what he ought to have said and someone on the spot—old Herodotus, no he was the Greek, wasn't he, it must have been someone else, Suetonius perhaps, spotted what was needed. The truth is always forgotten. Pitt on his deathbed asked for Bellamy's Pork Pies, but history altered that.' Even Father Thomas could not follow the convolutions of Parkinson's thoughts. 'My articles have to be remembered like history. At least from one Sunday to another. Next Sunday's instalment, "The Saint with a Past".'

'Do you understand a word of all this, father?' Colin asked.

'Not very much,' Father Thomas admitted.

'Has he come here to make trouble?'

'No, no. Nothing like that. Apparently his paper sent him to Africa to write about some disturbances in British territory. He arrived too late, but by that time we had our own trouble in the capital, so he came on.'

'Not even knowing French?'

'He had a first-class return ticket to Nairobi. He told me that his paper could not afford two star writers in Africa, so they cabled him to move on into our territory. He was too late again, but then he heard some rumours of Querry. He said that he had to bring *something* back. When he got to Luc he happened at the Governor's to meet Rycker.'

'What does he know of Querry's past? Even we . . .'

Parkinson was watching the discussion closely; his eyes travelled from one face to another. Here and there a word must have meant something to him and he drew his rapid, agile, erroneous conclusions.

'It appears,' Father Thomas said, 'that the British newspapers have what they call a *morgue*. He has only to cable them and they will send him a précis of all that has ever been published about Querry.'

'It's like a police persecution.'

'Oh, I'm convinced they'll find nothing to his discredit.'

'Have neither of you,' Parkinson asked sorrowfully, 'heard my name Montagu Parkinson? Surely it's memorable enough.' It was impossible to tell whether he was laughing at himself.

Father Thomas began to answer him. 'To be quite truthful until you came . . .'

'My name is writ in water. Quote. Shelley,' Parkinson said.

'Does Querry know what it's all about?' Colin asked Father Thomas.

'Not yet.'

'He was beginning to be happy here.'

'You mustn't be hasty,' Father Thomas said. 'There is another side to all of this. Our leproserie may become famous—as famous as Schweitzer's hospital, and the British, one has heard, are a generous people.'

Perhaps the name Schweitzer enabled Parkinson to catch at Father Thomas's meaning. He brought quickly out, 'My articles are syndicated in the United States, France, Germany, Japan and South America. No other living journalist . . .'

'We have managed without publicity until now, father,' Colin said.

'Publicity is only another name for propaganda. And we have a college for that in Rome.'

'Perhaps it is more fitted for Rome, father, than Central Africa.'

'Publicity can be an acid test for virtue. Personally I am convinced that Querry . . .'

'I have never enjoyed blood-sports, father. And a man-hunt least of all.'

'You exaggerate, doctor. A great deal of good can come from all of this. You know how you have always lacked money. The mission can't provide it. The State will not. Your patients deserve to be considered.'

'Perhaps Querry is also a patient,' Colin said.

'That's nonsense. I was thinking of the lepers—you have always dreamt of a school for rehabilitation, haven't you, if you could get the funds. For those poor burnt-out cases of yours.'

'Querry may be also a burnt-out case,' the doctor said. He looked at the fat man in the chair. 'Where now will he be able to find *his* therapy? Limelight is not very good for the mutilated.'

The heat of the day and the anger they momentarily felt for each other made them careless, and it was only Parkinson who saw that the man they were discussing was already over the threshold of Father Thomas's room.

'How are you, Querry?' Parkinson said. 'I didn't recognise you when I met you on the boat.'

Querry said, 'Nor I you.'

'Thank God,' Parkinson said, 'you aren't finished like the riots were. I've caught up with one story anyway. We've got to have a talk, you and I.'

2

'So that's the new hospital,' Parkinson said. 'Of course I don't know about these things, but there seems to me nothing very original . . .' He bent over the plans and said with the obvious intention of provoking, 'It reminds me of something in one of our new satellite towns. Hemel Hempstead perhaps. Or Stevenage.'

'This is not architecture,' Querry said. 'It's a cheap building job. Nothing more. The cheaper the better, so long as it stands up to heat, rain and humidity.'

'Do they require a man like you for that?'

'Yes. They have no builder here.'

'Are you going to stay till it's finished?'

'Longer than that.'

'Then what Rycker told me must be partly true.'

'I doubt if anything that man says could ever be true.'

'You'd need to be a kind of a saint, wouldn't you, to bury yourself here.'

'No. Not a saint.'

'Then what are you? What are your motives? I know a lot about you already. I've briefed myself,' Parkinson said. He sat his great weight down on the bed and said confidingly, 'You aren't exactly a man who loves his fellows, are you? Leaving out women, of course.' There is a strong allurement in corruption and there was no doubt of Parkinson's; he carried it on the surface of his skin like phosphorus, impossible to mistake. Virtue had died long ago within that mountain of flesh for lack of air. A priest might not be shocked by human failings, but he could be hurt or disappointed; Parkinson would welcome any kind of failing. Nothing would hurt Parkinson or disappoint him but the size of a cheque.

'You heard what the doctor called me just now—one of the burnt-out cases. They are the lepers who lose everything that can be eaten away before they are cured.'

'You are a whole man as far as one can see,' said Parkinson, looking at the fingers resting on the drawing-board.

'I've come to an end. This place, you might say, is the end. Neither the road nor the river go any further. You have been washed up here too, haven't you?'

'Oh, no, I came with a purpose.'

'I was afraid of you on the boat, but I am afraid of you no longer.'

'I can't understand what you had to fear. I'm a man like other men.'

'No,' Querry said, 'you are a man like me. Men with vocations are different from the others. They have more to lose. Behind all of us in various ways lies a spoilt priest. You once had a vocation, admit it, if it was only a vocation to write.'

'That's not important. Most journalists begin that way.' The bed bent below Parkinson's weight as he shifted his buttocks like sacks.

'And end your way?'

'What are you driving at? Are you trying to insult me? I'm beyond insult, Mr Querry.'

'Why should I insult you? We are two of a kind. I began as an architect and I am ending as a builder. There's little pleasure in that kind of progress. Is there pleasure in *your* final stage, Parkinson?' He looked at the typewritten sheet that he had picked up in Father Thomas's room and carried in with him.

'It's a job.'

'Of course.'

'It keeps me alive,' Parkinson said.

'Yes.'

'It's no use saying I'm like you. At least I enjoy life.'

'Oh yes. The pleasures of the senses. Food, Parkinson?'

'I have to be careful.' He took the dangling corner of the mosquito-net to mop his forehead with. 'I weigh eighteen stone.'

'Women, Parkinson?'

'I don't know why you are asking me these questions. I came to interview *you*. Of course I screw a bit now and then, but there comes a time in every man's life . . .'

'You're younger than I am.'

'My heart's not all that strong.'

'You really have come to an end like me, haven't you, Parkinson, so here we find ourselves together. Two burnt-out cases. There must be many more of us in the world. We should have a masonic sign to recognise each other.'

'I'm not burnt-out. I have my work. The biggest syndication . . .' He seemed determined to prove that he was dissimilar to Querry. Like a man presenting his skin to a doctor he wanted to prove that there was no thickening, no trace of a nodule, nothing that might class him with the other lepers.

'There was a time,' Querry said, 'when you would not have written that sentence about Stanley.'

'It's a small mistake in geography, that's all. One has to dramatise. It's the first thing they teach a reporter on the *Post*—he has to make every story stand up. Anyway no one will notice.'

'Would you write the real truth about me?'

'There are laws of libel.'

'I would never bring an action. I promise you that.' He read the advance announcement aloud. 'The Past of a Saint. What a saint!'

'How do you know that Rycker's not right about you? We none of us really know ourselves.'

'We have to if we are to be cured. When we reach the furthest point, there's no mistaking it. When the fingers are gone and the toes too and the smear-reactions are all negative, we can do no more harm. Would you write the truth, Parkinson, even if I told it to you? I know you wouldn't. You aren't burnt-out after all. You are still infectious.'

Parkinson looked at Querry with bruised eyes. He was like a man who has reached the limit of the third degree, when there is nothing else to do but admit everything. 'They would sack me if I tried,' he said. 'It's easy enough to take risks when you are young. To think I am further off from heaven etc. etc. Quote. Edgar Allan Poe.'

'It wasn't Poe.'

'Nobody notices things like that.'

'What is the past you have given me?'

'Well, there was the case of Anne Morel, wasn't there? It even reached the English papers. After all you had an English mother. And you had just completed that modern cathedral in Bruges.'

'It wasn't Bruges. What story did they tell about that?'

'That she killed herself for love of you. At eighteen. For a man of forty.'

'It was more than fifteen years ago. Do papers have so long a memory?'

'No. But the *morgue* serves us instead. I shall describe in my best Sunday-paper style how you came here in expiation. . . .'

'Papers like yours invariably make small mistakes. The woman's name was Marie and not Anne. She was twenty-five and not eighteen. Nor did she kill herself for love of me. She wanted to escape me. That was all. So you see I am expiating nothing.'

'She wanted to escape the man she loved?'

'Exactly that. It must be a terrible thing for a woman to make love nightly with an efficient instrument. I never failed her. She tried to leave me several times, and each time I got her to come back. You see it hurt my vanity to be left by a woman. I always wanted to do the leaving.'

'How did you bring her back?'

'Those of us who practise one art are usually adept at another. A painter writes. A poet makes a tune. I happened in those days to be a good actor for an amateur. Once I used tears. Another time an overdose of nembutal, but not, of course, a dangerous dose. Then I made love to a second woman to show her what she was going to miss if she left me. I even persuaded her that I couldn't do my work without her. I made her think that I would leave the Church if I hadn't her support to my faith–she was a good Catholic, even in bed. In my heart of course I had left the Church years before, but she never realised that. I believed a little of course, like so many do, at the major feasts, Christmas and Easter, when memories of childhood stir us to a kind of devotion. She always mistook it for the love of God.'

'All the same there must be some reason that you came out here, among the lepers. . . .'

'Not in expiation, Mr Parkinson. There were plenty of women after Marie Morel as there had been women before her. Perhaps for ten more years I managed to believe in my own emotion–"my dearest love", "*toute à toi*" and all the rest. One always tries not to repeat the same phrases, just as one tries to preserve some special position in the act of sex, but there are only thirty-two positions according to Aretine and there are less than that number of endearing words, and in the end most women reach their climax most easily in the commonest position of all and with the commonest phrase upon the tongue. It was only a question of time before I realised that I didn't love at all. I've never really loved. I'd only accepted love. And then the worst boredom settled in. Because if I had deceived myself with women I had deceived myself with work too.'

'No one has ever questioned your reputation.'

'The future will. Somewhere in a back street of Brussels now there's a boy at a drawing-board who will show me up. I wish I could see the cathedral he will build. . . . No, I don't. Or I wouldn't be here. He'll be no spoilt priest. He'll pass the novice-master.'

'I don't know what you are talking about, Querry. Sometimes you talk like Rycker.'

'Do I? Perhaps he has the Masonic sign too. . . .'

'If you are so bored, why not be bored in comfort? A little apartment in Brussels or a villa in Capri. After all, you are a rich man, Querry.'

'Boredom is worse in comfort. I thought perhaps out here there would be enough pain and enough fear to distract. . . .' He looked at Parkinson. 'Surely *you* can understand me if anyone can.'

'I can't understand a word.'

'Am I such a monster that even you . . . ?'

'What about your work, Querry? Whatever you say, you can't be bored with that. You've been a raging success.'

'You mean money? Haven't I told you that the work wasn't good enough? What were any of my churches compared with the cathedral at Chartres? They were all signed with my name of course—nobody could mistake a Querry for a Corbusier, but which one of us knows the architect of Chartres? He didn't care. He worked with love not vanity—and with belief too, I suppose. To build a church when you don't believe in a god seems a little indecent, doesn't it? When I discovered I was doing that, I accepted a commission for a city hall, but I didn't believe in politics either. You never saw such an absurd box of concrete and glass as I landed on the poor city square. You see I discovered what seemed only to be a loose thread in my jacket—I pulled it and all the jacket began to unwind. Perhaps it's true that you can't believe in a god without loving a human being or love a human being without believing in a god. They use the phrase "make love," don't they? But which of us are creative enough to "make" love? We can only be loved—if we are lucky.'

'Why are you telling me this, Mr Querry—even if it's true?'

'Because at least you are someone who won't mind the truth, though I doubt whether you'll ever write it. Perhaps—who knows?—I might persuade you to drop altogether this absurd pious nonsense that Rycker talks about me. I am no Schweitzer. My God, he almost tempts me to seduce his wife. That at least might change his tune.'

'Could you?'

'It's an awful thing when experience and not vanity makes one say yes.'

Parkinson made an oddly humble gesture. He said, 'Let me have men about me that are fat. Quote. Shakespeare. I got that one right anyway. As for me I wouldn't even know how to begin.'

'Begin with readers of the *Post*. You are famous among your readers and fame is a potent aphrodisiac. Married women are the easiest, Parkinson. The young girl too often has her weather-eye open on security, but a married woman has already found it. The husband at the office, the children in the nursery, a condom in the bag. Say that she's been married at twenty, she's ready for a limited excursion before she's reached thirty. If her husband is young too, don't be afraid; she may have had enough of youth. With a man of my age and yours she needn't expect jealous scenes.'

'What you are talking about doesn't have much to do with love, does it? You said you'd been loved. You complained of it if I remember right, but I probably don't. As you realise well enough, I'm only a bloody journalist.'

'Love comes quickly enough with gratitude, only too quickly. The loveliest of women feels gratitude, even to an ageing man like me, if she learns to feel pleasure again. Ten years in the same bed withers the little bud, but now it blooms once more. Her husband notices the way she looks. Her children cease to be a burden. She takes an interest again in housekeeping as she used to in the old days. She confides a little in her intimate friends, because to be the mistress of a famous man increases her self-respect. The adventure is over. Romance has begun.'

'What a cold-blooded bastard you are,' Parkinson said with deep respect, as though he were talking of the *Post*'s proprietor.

'Why not write that instead of this pious nonsense you are planning?'

'I couldn't. My newspaper is for family reading. Although of course that word the Past has a certain meaning. But it means abandoned follies, doesn't it? not abandoned virtues. We'll touch on Mlle. Morel–delicately. And there was somebody else, wasn't there, called Grison?'

Querry didn't answer.

'It's no use denying things now,' Parkinson said. 'Grison is mummified in the *morgue* too.'

'Yes, I do remember him. I don't care to because I don't like farce. He was a senior employee in the Post Office. He challenged me to a duel after I had left his wife. One of those bogus modern duels where nobody fires straight. I was tempted to break the conventions and to wing him, but his wife would have mistaken it for passion. Poor man, he was quite content so long as we were together, but when I left her he had to suffer such scenes with her in public. . . . She had much less mercy on him than I had.'

'It's odd that you admit all this to me,' Parkinson said. 'People are more cautious with me as a rule. Except that I remember once there was a murderer–he talked as much as you.'

'Perhaps it's the mark of a murderer, loquacity.'

'They didn't hang this chap and I pretended to be his brother and visited him twice a month. All the same I'm puzzled by your attitude. You didn't strike me when I saw you first as exactly a talking man.'

'I have been waiting for you, Parkinson, or someone like you. Not that I didn't fear you too.'

'Yes, but why?'

'You are my looking-glass. I can talk to a looking-glass, but one can be a little afraid of one too. It returns such a straight image. If I talked to Father Thomas as I've talked to you, he'd twist my words.'

'I'm grateful for your good opinion.'

'A good opinion? I dislike you as much as I dislike myself. I was nearly happy when you arrived, Parkinson, and I've only talked to you now so that you'll have no excuse to stay. The interview is over, and you've never had a better one. You don't want my opinion, do you, on Gropius? Your public hasn't heard of Gropius.'

'All the same I jotted down some questions,' Parkinson said. 'We might get on to those now that we've cleared the way.'

'I said the interview was over.'

Parkinson leaned forward on the bed and then swayed back like a Chinese wobbling toy made in the likeness of the fat God of Prosperity. He said, 'Do you consider that the love of God or the love of humanity is your principal driving force, Querry? What in your opinion is the future of Christianity? Has the Sermon on the Mount influenced your decision to give your life to the lepers? Who is your favourite saint? Do you believe in the efficacy of prayer?' He began to laugh, the great belly rolling like a dolphin. 'Do miracles still occur? Have you yet visited Fatima?'

He got off the bed. 'We can forget the rest of the crap. "In his bare cell in the heart of the dark continent one of the greatest of modern architects and one of the most famous Catholics of his day bared his conscience to the correspondent of the *Post*. Montagu Parkinson, who was on the spot last month in South Korea, is on the spot again. He will reveal to our readers in his next instalment how remorse for the past is Querry's driving force. Querry is atoning for a reckless youth by serving others. Saint Francis was the gayest spark in all the gay old city of Firenze–Florence to you and me."'

Parkinson went out into the hard glare of the Congo day, but he hadn't said enough. He returned and put his face close up against the net and blew his words through it in a fine spray. '"Next Sunday's instalment: A girl dies for love." I don't like you any more than you like me, Querry, but I'm going to build you up. I'll build you up so high they'll raise a statue to you by the river. In the worst possible taste, you know the sort of thing, you won't be able to avoid it because you'll be dead and buried–you on your knees surrounded by your bloody lepers teaching them to pray to the god you don't believe in and the birds shitting on your hair. I don't mind you being a religious fake, Querry, but I'll show you that you can't use me to ease your bleeding conscience. I wouldn't be surprised if there weren't pilgrims at your shrine in twenty years, and that's how history's written, believe you me. *Exegi monumentum*. Quote. Virgil.'

Querry took from his pocket the meaningless letter with the all-inclusive phrase which might, of course, be genuine. The letter had not come to him from one of the women Parkinson had mentioned: the *morgue* of the *Post* was not big enough to hold all possible bodies. He read it through again in the mood that Parkinson had elicited. 'Do you remember?' She was one of those who would never admit that when an emotion was dead, the memory of the occasion was dead as well. He had to take her memories on trust, because she had always been a truthful woman. She reminded him of a guest who claims one particular matchbox as her own out of the debris of a broken party.

He went to his bed and lay down. The pillow gathered heat under his neck, but this noonday he couldn't face the sociabilities of lunch with the fathers. He thought: there was only one thing I could do and that is reason enough for being here. I can promise you, Marie, *toute à toi*, all of you, never again from boredom or vanity to involve another human being in my lack of love. I shall do no more harm, he thought, with the kind of happiness a leper must feel when he is freed at last by his seclusion from the fear of passing on contagion to another. For years he had not thought of Marie Morel; now he remembered the first time he had heard her name spoken. It was spoken by a young architectural student whom he had been helping with his studies. They had come back together from a day at Bruges into the neon-lighted Brussels evening and they had passed the girl accidentally outside the northern station. He had envied a little his dull undistinguished companion when he saw her face brighten under the lamps. Has anyone ever seen a man smile at a woman as a woman smiles at the man she loves, fortuitously, at a bus-stop, in a railway carriage, at some chain-store in the middle of buying groceries, a smile so naturally joyful, without premeditation and without caution? The converse, of course, is probably true also. A man can never smile quite so falsely as the girl in a brothel-parlour. But the girl in the brothel, Querry thought, is imitating something true. The man has nothing to imitate.

He soon had no cause to feel envy for his companion of that night. Even in those early days he had known how to alter the direction of a woman's need to love. Woman? She was not even as old as the architectural student whose name he couldn't now remember—an ugly name like Hoghe. Unlike Marie Morel the former student was probably still alive, building in some suburb his bourgeois villas—machines for living in. Querry addressed him from the bed. 'I am sorry. I really believed that I meant you no harm. I really thought in those days that I acted from love.' There is a time in life when a man with a little acting ability is able to deceive even himself.

PART V

CHAPTER I

It is characteristic of Africa the way that people come and go, as though the space and emptiness of an undeveloped continent encourage drift; the high tide deposits the flotsam on the edge of the shore and sweeps it away again in its withdrawal, to leave elsewhere. No one had expected Parkinson, he had come unannounced, and a few days later he went again, carrying his Rolleiflex and Remington down to the Otraco boat bound for some spot elsewhere. Two weeks later a motor-boat came up the river in the late evening carrying a young administrator who played a game of liar-dice with the fathers, drank one glass of whisky before bed, and left behind him, as if it had been the sole intention of his voyage, a copy of an English journal, the *Architectural Review*, before departing without so much as breakfast into the grey and green immensity. (The review contained–apart from the criticism of a new arterial road–some illustrations of a hideous cathedral newly completed in a British colony. Perhaps the young man thought that it would serve as a warning to Querry.) Again a few weeks went unnoticed by–a few deaths from tuberculosis, the hospital climbing a few feet higher from its foundations–and then two policemen got off the Otraco boat to make enquiries about a Salvation Army leader who was wanted in the capital. He was said to have persuaded the people of a neighbouring tribe to sell their blankets to him because they would be too heavy to wear at the Resurrection of the Dead and then to give him the money back so that he might keep it for them in a secure place where no thieves would break in and steal. As a recompense he had given certificates insuring them against the danger of being kidnapped by the Catholic and Protestant missionaries who, he said, were exporting bodies with the help of witchcraft wholesale to Europe in sealed railway trucks where they were turned into canned food labelled Best African Tunny. The policemen could learn nothing of the fugitive at the leproserie, and they departed again on the same boat two hours later, floating away with the small islands of water-jacinth at the same speed and in the same direction, as though they were all a part of nature too.

Querry in time began to forget Parkinson. The great world had done its worst and gone, and a kind of peace descended. Rycker stayed aloof, and no echo from any newspaper article out of distant Europe came to disturb Querry. Even Father Thomas moved away for a while from the leproserie to a seminary in the bush from which he hoped to obtain a teacher for yet another new class. Querry's feet were becoming familiar with the long laterite road that stretched between his room and the hospital; in the evening, when the worst heat was over, the laterite glowed, like a night-blooming flower, in shades of rose and red.

The fathers were unconcerned with private lives. A husband, after he had been cured, left the leproserie and his wife moved into the hut of another man, but the fathers asked no questions. One of the catechists, a man who had reached the limit of mutilation, having lost nose, fingers, toes (he looked as though he had been lopped, scraped and tidied by a knife), fathered a baby with the woman, crippled by polio, who could only crawl upon the ground dragging her dwarfed legs behind her. The man brought the baby to the Church for baptism and there it was baptised Emanuel—there were no questions and no admonitions. The fathers were too busy to bother themselves with what the Church considered sin (moral theology was the subject they were least concerned with). In Father Thomas some thwarted instinct might be seen deviously at work, but Father Thomas was no longer there to trouble the leproserie with his scruples and anxieties.

The doctor was a less easy character to understand. Unlike the fathers he had no belief in a god to support him in his hard vocation. Once when Querry made a comment on his life—a question brought to his mind by the sight of some pitiable and squalid case—the doctor looked up at him with much the same clinical eye with which he had just examined the patient. He said, 'Perhaps if I tested your skin now I would get a second negative reaction.'

'What do you mean?'

'You are showing curiosity again about another human being.'

'Who was the first?' Querry asked.

'Deo Gratias. You know I have been luckier in my vocation than you.'

Querry looked down the long row of worn-out mattresses where bandaged people lay in the awkward postures of the bedridden. The sweet smell of sloughed skin was in the air. 'Lucky?' he said.

'It needs a very strong man to survive an introspective and solitary vocation. I don't think you were strong enough. I know I couldn't have stood your life.'

'Why does a man choose a vocation like this?' Querry asked.

'He's chosen. Oh, I don't mean by god. By accident. There is an old Danish doctor still going the rounds who became a leprologist late in life. By accident. He was excavating an ancient cemetery and found skeletons there without finger-bones—it was an old leper-cemetery of the fourteenth century. He X-rayed the skeletons and he made discoveries in the bones, especially in the nasal area, which were quite unknown to any of us—you see most of us haven't the chance to work with skeletons. He became a leprologist after that. You will meet him at any international conference on leprosy carrying his skull with him in an airline's overnight bag. It has passed through a lot of douaniers' hands. It must be rather a shock, that skull, to them, but I believe they don't charge duty on it.'

'And you, Doctor Colin? What was your accident?'

'Only the accident of temperament, perhaps,' the doctor replied evasively. They came out together into the unfresh and humid air. 'Oh, don't mistake me. I had no death-wish as Damien had. Now that we can cure leprosy, we shall have fewer of those vocations of doom, but they weren't uncommon once.' They began to cross the road to the shade of the dispensary where the lepers waited on the steps; the doctor halted in the hot centre of the laterite. 'There used to be a high suicide-rate among leprologists—I suppose they couldn't wait for that positive test they all expected some time. Bizarre suicides for a bizarre vocation. There was one man I knew quite well who injected himself with a dose of snake-venom, and another who poured petrol over his furniture and his clothes and then set himself alight. There is a common feature, you will have noticed, in both cases—unnecessary suffering. That can be a vocation too.'

'I don't understand you.'

'Wouldn't you rather suffer than feel discomfort? Discomfort irritates our ego like a mosquito-bite. We become aware of ourselves, the more uncomfortable we are, but suffering is quite a different matter. Sometimes I think that the search for suffering and the remembrance of suffering are the only means we have to put ourselves in touch with the whole human condition. With suffering we become part of the Christian myth.'

'Then I wish you'd teach me how to suffer,' Querry said. 'I only know the mosquito-bites.'

'You'll suffer enough if we stand here any longer,' Doctor Colin said and he drew Querry off the laterite into the shade. 'Today I am going to show you a few interesting eye-cases.' He sat at his surgery table and Querry took the chair beside him. Only on the linen masks that children wear at Christmas had he seen such scarlet eyes, representing avarice or senility, as now confronted them. 'You only need a little patience,' Doctor Colin said. 'Suffering is not so hard to find,' and Querry tried to remember who it was that had said much the same to him months ago. He was irritated by his own failure of memory.

'Aren't you being glib about suffering?' he asked. 'That woman who died last week . . .'

'Don't be too sorry for those who die after some pain. It makes them ready to go. Think of how a death sentence must sound when you are full of health and vigour.' Doctor Colin turned away from him to speak in her native tongue to an old woman whose palsied eyelids never once moved to shade the eyes.

That night, after taking dinner with the fathers, Querry strolled over to the doctor's house. The lepers were sitting outside their huts to make the most of the cool air which came with darkness. At a little stall, lit by a hurricane-lamp, a man was offering for five francs a handful of caterpillars he had gathered in the forest. Somebody was singing a street or two away, and by a fire Querry came upon a group of dancers gathered round his boy Deo Gratias, who squatted on the ground and used his fists like drum-sticks to beat the rhythm on an old petrol-tin. Even the bat-eared dogs lay quiet as though carved on tombs. A young woman with bare breasts kept a rendezvous where a path led away into the forest. In the moonlight the nodules on her face ceased for a while to exist, and there were no patches on her skin. She was any young girl waiting for a man. It seemed to Querry that some persistent poison had been drained from his system after his outbreak to the Englishman. He could remember no evening peace to equal this since the night when he had given the last touches to his first architectural plans, perhaps the only ones which had completely satisfied him. The owners, of course, had spoilt the building afterwards as they spoiled everything. No building was safe from the furniture, the pictures, the human beings that it would presently contain. But first there had been this peace. *Consummatum est:* pain over and peace falling round him like a little death.

When he had drunk his second whisky he said to the doctor, 'When a smear-test is negative, does it always stay so?'

'Not always. It's too early to loose the patient on the world until the tests have been negative–oh, for six months. There are relapses even with our present drugs.'

'Do they sometimes find it hard to be loosed?'

'Very often. You see they become attached to their hut and their patch of land, and of course for the burnt-out cases life outside isn't easy. They carry the stigma of leprosy. People are apt to think once a leper, always a leper.'

'I begin to find your vocation a little easier to understand. All the same–the fathers believe they have the Christian truth behind them, and it helps them in a place like this. You and I have no such truth. Is the Christian myth that you talked about enough for you?'

'I want to be on the side of change,' the doctor said. 'If I had been born an amoeba who could think, I would have dreamed of the day of the primates. I would have wanted anything I did to contribute to that day. Evolution, as far as we can tell, has lodged itself finally in the brains of man. The ant, the fish, even the ape has gone as far as it can go, but in our brain evolution is moving–my God–at what a speed! I forget how many hundreds of millions of years passed between the dinosaurs and the primates, but in our own lifetime we have seen the change from diesel to jet, the splitting of the atom, the cure of leprosy.'

'Is change so good?'

'We can't avoid it. We are riding a great ninth evolutionary wave. Even the Christian myth is part of the wave, and perhaps, who knows, it may be the most valuable part. Suppose love were to evolve as rapidly in our brains as technical skill has done. In isolated cases it may have done, in the saints . . . in Christ, if the man really existed.'

'You can really comfort yourself with all that?' Querry asked. 'It sounds like the old song of progress.'

'The nineteenth century wasn't as far wrong as we like to believe. We have become cynical about progress because of the terrible things we have seen men do during the last forty years. All the same through trial and error the amoeba did become the ape. There were blind starts and wrong turnings even then, I suppose. Evolution today can produce Hitlers as well as St John of the Cross. I have a small hope, that's all, a very small hope, that someone they call Christ was the fertile element, looking for a crack in the wall to plant its seed. I think of Christ as an amoeba who took the right turning. I want to be on the side of the progress which survives. I'm no friend of pterodactyls.'

'But if we are incapable of love?'

'I'm not sure such a man exists. Love is planted in man now, even uselessly in some cases, like an appendix. Sometimes of course people call it hate.'

'I haven't found any trace of it in myself.'

'Perhaps you are looking for something too big and too important. Or too active.'

'What you are saying seems to me every bit as superstitious as what the fathers believe.'

'Who cares? It's the superstition I live by. There was another superstition–quite unproven–Copernicus had it–that the earth went round the sun. Without that superstition we shouldn't be in a position now to shoot rockets at the moon. One has to gamble on one's superstitions. Like Pascal gambled on his.' He drank his whisky down.

'Are you a happy man?' Querry asked.

'I suppose I am. It's not a question that I've ever asked myself. Does a happy man ever ask it? I go on from day to day.'

'Swimming on your wave,' Querry said with envy. 'Do you never need a woman?'

'The only one I ever needed,' the doctor said, 'is dead.'

'So that's why you came out here.'

'You are wrong,' Colin said. 'She's buried a hundred yards away. She was my wife.'

CHAPTER 2

In the last three months the hospital had made great progress. It was no longer a mere ground-plan looking like the excavation of a Roman villa; the walls had risen; the window-spaces were there waiting for wire nets. It was even possible to estimate the time when the roof would be fixed. The lepers worked more rapidly as the end came in sight. Querry was walking through the building with Father Joseph; they passed through non-existent doors like revenants, into rooms that did not yet exist, into the future operating-theatre, the X-ray room, the fire-proof room with the vats of paraffin wax for the palsied hands, into the dispensary, into the two main wards.

'What will you do,' Father Joseph said, 'when this is finished?'

'What will you, father?'

'Of course it's for the Superior and the doctor to decide, but I would like to build a place where the mutilated can learn to work–occupational therapy, I suppose they call it at home. The sisters do what they can with individuals, especially the mutilated. No one wants to be a special case. They would learn much quicker in a class where they could joke a bit.'

'And after that?'

'There's always more building to be done for the next twenty years, if only lavatories.'

'Then there'll always be something for me to do, father.'

'An architect like you is wasted on the work we have here. These are only builders' jobs.'

'I have become a builder.'

'Don't you ever want to see Europe again?'

'Do you, father?'

'There's a big difference between us. Europe is much the same as this for those of our Order–a group of buildings, very like the ones we have here, our rooms aren't any different, nor the chapel (even the Stations are the same), the same classrooms, the same food, the same clothes, the same kind of faces. But surely to you Europe means more than that–theatres, friends, restaurants, bars, books, shops, the company of your equals–the fruits of fame whatever that means.'

Querry said, 'I am content here.'

It was nearly time for the midday meal, and they walked back together towards the mission, passing the nuns' house and the doctor's and the small shabby cemetery. It was not kept well–the service of the living took up too much of the fathers' time. Only on All Souls night was the graveyard properly remembered when a lamp or a candle shone on every grave, pagan and Christian. About half the graves had crosses, and they were as simple and uniform as those of the mass dead in a war-cemetery. Querry knew now which grave belonged to Mme. Colin. It stood crossless and a little apart, but the only reason for the separation was to leave space for Doctor Colin to join her.

'I hope you'll find room for me there too,' Querry said. 'I won't rate a cross.'

'We shall have trouble with Father Thomas over that. He'll argue that once baptized you are always a Christian.'

'I would do well to die then before he returns.'

'Better be quick about it. He will be back sooner than we think.' Even his brother priests were happier without Father Thomas; it was impossible not to feel a grudging pity for so unattractive a man.

Father Joseph's warning proved wise too quickly. Absorbed in examining the new hospital they had failed to hear the bell of the Otraco boat. Father Thomas was already ashore with the cardboard box in which he carried all his personal belongings. He stood in the doorway of his room and greeted them as they passed. He had the curious and disquieting air of receiving them like guests.

'Well, Father Joseph, you see that I am back before my time.'

'We do see,' Father Joseph said.

'Ah, M. Querry, I have something very important to discuss with you.'

'Yes?'

'All in good time. Patience. Much has happened while I have been away.'

'Don't keep us on tenterhooks,' Father Joseph said.

'At lunch, at lunch,' Father Thomas replied, carrying his cardboard box elevated like a monstrance into his room.

As they passed the next window they could see the Superior standing by his bed. He was pushing a hair-brush, a sponge-bag and a box of cheroots into his khaki knapsack, a relic of the last war which he carried with him across the world like a memory. He took the cross from his desk and packed it away wrapped in a couple of handkerchiefs. Father Joseph said, 'I begin to fear the worst.'

The Superior at lunch sat silent and preoccupied. Father Thomas was on his right. He crumbled his bread with the closed face of importance. Only when the meal was over did the Superior speak. He said, 'Father Thomas has brought me a letter. The Bishop wants me in Luc. I may be away some weeks or even months and I am asking Father Thomas to act for me during my absence. You are the only one, father,' he added, 'with the time to look after the accounts.' It was an apology to the other fathers and a hidden rebuke to the pride which Father Thomas was already beginning to show—he had very little in common with the doubting pitiful figure of a month ago. Perhaps even a temporary promotion could cure a failing vocation.

'You know you can trust me,' Father Thomas said.

'I can trust everyone here. My work is the least important in the place. I can't build like Father Joseph or look after the dynamos like Brother Philippe.'

'I will try not to let the school suffer,' Father Thomas said.

'I am sure you will succeed, father. You will find that my work will take up very little of your time. A superior is always replaceable.'

The more bare a life is, the more we fear change. The Superior said grace and looked around for his cheroots, but he had already packed them. He accepted a cigarette from Querry, but he wore it as awkwardly as he would have worn a suit of lay clothes. The fathers stood unhappily around unused to departures. Querry felt like a stranger present at some domestic grief.

'The hospital will be finished, perhaps, before I return,' the Superior said with a certain sadness.

'We will not put up the roof-tree till you are back,' Father Joseph replied.

'No, no, you must promise me to delay nothing. Father Thomas, those are my last instructions. The roof-tree at the earliest moment and plenty of champagne—if you can find a donor—to celebrate.'

For years in their quiet unchanging routine they had been apt to forget that they were men under obedience, but now, suddenly, they were reminded of it. Who knew what was intended for the Superior, what letters might not have passed between the Bishop and the General in Europe? He spoke of returning in a few weeks (the Bishop, he had explained, had summoned him for a consultation), but all of them were aware that he might never return. Decisions might already have been taken elsewhere. They watched him now unobtrusively, with affection, as one might watch a dying man (only Father Thomas was absent: he had already gone to move his papers into the other's room), and the Superior in turn looked at them and the bleak refectory in which he had spent his best years. It was true what Father Joseph had said. The buildings, wherever he went, would always be very much the same; the refectories would vary as little as colonial airports, but for that very reason a man became more accustomed to the minute differences. There would always be the same coloured reproduction of the Pope's portrait, but this one had a stain in the corner where the leper who made the frame had spilt the walnut colouring. The chairs too had been fashioned by lepers, who had taken as a model the regulation kind supplied to the junior grade of government officials, a kind you would find in every mission, but one of the chairs had become unique by its unreliability; they had always kept it against the wall since a visiting priest, Father Henri, had tried to imitate a circus trick by balancing on the back. Even the bookcase had an individual weakness: one shelf slanted at an angle, and there were stains upon the wall that reminded each man of something. The stains on a different wall would evoke different pictures. Wherever one went one's companions would have much the same names (there are not so many saints in common use to choose from), but the new Father Joseph would not be quite the same as the old.

From the river came the summons of the ship's bell. The Superior took the cigarette out of his mouth and looked at it as though he wondered how it had come there. Father Joseph said, 'I think we should have a glass of wine. . . .' He rummaged in the cupboard for a bottle and found one which had been two-thirds finished some weeks ago on the last major feast-day. However there was a thimbleful left for all. '*Bon voyage*, father.' The ship's bell rang again. Father Thomas came to the door and said, 'I think you should be off now, father.'

'Yes. I must fetch my knapsack.'

'I have it here,' Father Thomas said.

'Well then . . .' The Superior gave one more furtive look at the room: the stained picture, the broken chair, the slanting shelf.

'A safe return,' Father Paul said. 'I will fetch Doctor Colin.'

'No, no, this is his time for a siesta. M. Querry will explain to him how it is.'

They walked down to the river bank to see the last of him and Father Thomas carried his knapsack. By the gang-plank the Superior took it and slung it over his shoulder with something of a military gesture. He touched Father Thomas on the arm. 'I think you'll find the accounts in good order. Leave next month's as late as you can . . . in case I'm back.' He hesitated and said with a deprecating smile, 'Be careful of yourself, Father Thomas. Not too much enthusiasm.' Then the ship and the river took him away from them.

Father Joseph and Querry returned to the house together. Querry said, 'Why has he chosen Father Thomas? He has been here a shorter time than any of you.'

'It is as the Superior said. We all have our proper jobs, and to tell you the truth Father Thomas is the only one who has the least notion of book-keeping.'

Querry lay down on his bed. At this hour of the day the heat made it impossible to work and almost as impossible to sleep except for brief superficial spells. He thought he was with the Superior on the boat going away, but in his dream the boat took the contrary direction to that of Luc. It went on down the narrowing river into the denser forest, and it was now the Bishop's boat. A corpse lay in the Bishop's cabin and the two of them were taking it to Pendélé for burial. It surprised him to think that he had been so misled as to believe that the boat had reached the furthest point of its journey into the interior when it reached the leproserie. Now he was in motion again, going deeper.

The scrape of a chair woke him. He thought it was the ship's bottom grinding across a snag in the river. He opened his eyes and saw Father Thomas sitting by his bedside.

'I had not meant to wake you,' Father Thomas said.

'I was only half asleep.'

'I have brought you messages from a friend of yours,' Father Thomas said.

'I have no friends in Africa except those I have made here.'

'You have more friends than you know. My message is from M. Rycker.'

'Rycker is no friend of mine.'

'I know he is a little impetuous, but he is a man with a great admiration for you. He feels, from something his wife has said, that he was perhaps wrong to speak of you to the English journalist.'

'His wife has more sense than he has then.'

'Luckily it has all turned out for the best,' Father Thomas said, 'and we owe it to M. Rycker.'

'The best?'

'He has written about you and all of us here in the most splendid fashion.'

'Already?'

'He telegraphed his first article from Luc. M. Rycker helped him at the post-office. He made it a condition that he should read the article first – M. Rycker, of course, would never have allowed anything damaging to us to pass. He has written a real appreciation of your work. It has already been translated in *Paris Dimanche*.'

'That rag?'

'It reaches a very wide public,' Father Thomas said.

'A scandal-sheet.'

'All the more creditable then that your message should appear there.'

'I don't know what you are talking about – I have no message.' He turned impatiently away from Father Thomas's searching and insinuating gaze and lay facing the wall. He heard the rustle of paper – Father Thomas was drawing something from the pocket of his soutane. He said, 'Let me read a little bit of it to you. I assure you that it will give you great pleasure. The article is called: "An Architect of Souls. The Hermit of the Congo."'

'What nauseating rubbish. I tell you, father, nothing that man could write would interest me.'

'You are really much too harsh. I am only sorry I had no time to show it to the Superior. He makes a slight mistake about the name of the Order, but you can hardly expect anything different from an Englishman. Listen to the way he ends. "When a famous French statesman once retired into the depths of the country, to avoid the burden of office, it was said that the world made a path to his door."'

'He can get nothing right,' Querry said. 'Nothing. It was an author, not a statesman. And the author was American, not French.'

'These are trifles,' Father Thomas said rebukingly. 'Listen to this. "The whole Catholic world has been discussing the mysterious disappearance of the great architect Querry. Querry whose range of achievement extended from the latest cathedral in the United States, a palace of glass and steel, to a little white Dominican chapel on the Côte d'Azur . . ."'

'Now he's confusing me with that amateur, Matisse,' Querry said.

'Never mind small details.'

'I hope for your sake that the gospels are more accurate in small details than Parkinson.'

'"Querry has not been seen for a long while in his usual haunts. I have tracked him all the way from his favourite restaurant, l'Epaule de Mouton . . ."'

'This is absurd. Does he think I'm a gourmandising tourist?'

'"To the heart of Africa. Near the spot where Stanley once pitched his camp among the savage tribes, I at last came on Querry. . . ."' Father Thomas looked up. He said, 'It is here that he writes a great many gracious things about our work. "Selfless . . . devoted . . . in the white robes of their blameless lives." Really, you know, he does have a certain sense of style.'

'"What is it that has induced the great Querry to abandon a career that brought him honour and riches to give up his life to serving the world's untouchables? I was in no position to ask him that when suddenly I found that my quest had ended. Unconscious and burning with fever, I was carried on shore from my pirogue, the frail bark in which I had penetrated what Joseph Conrad called the Heart of Darkness, by a few faithful natives who had followed me down the great river with the same fidelity their grandfathers had shown to Stanley."'

'He can't keep Stanley out of it,' Querry said. 'There have been many others in Central Africa, but I suppose the English would never have heard of them.'

'"I woke to find Querry's hand upon my pulse and Querry's eyes gazing into mine. Then I sensed the great mystery."'

'Do you really enjoy this stuff?' Querry asked. He sat up impatiently on his bed.

'I have read many lives of saints that were far worse written,' Father Thomas said. 'Style is not everything. The man's intentions are sound. Perhaps you are not the best judge. He goes on, "It was from Querry's lips that I learned the meaning of the mystery. Though Querry spoke to me as perhaps he had never spoken to another human soul, with a burning remorse for a past as colourful and cavalier as that St Francis once led in the dark alleys of the city by the Arno . . ." I wish I had been there.' Father Thomas said wistfully, 'when you spoke of that. I'm leaving out the next bit which deals mainly with the lepers. He seems to have noticed only the mutilated—a pity since it gives a rather too sombre impression of our home here.' Father Thomas, as the acting Superior, was already taking a more favourable view of the mission than he had a month before.

'Here is where he reaches what he calls the heart of the matter. "It was from Querry's most intimate friend, André Rycker, the manager of a palm-oil plantation, that I learned the secret. It is perhaps typical of Querry that what he keeps humbly hidden from the priests for whom he works he is ready to disclose to this planter—the last person you would expect to find on terms of close friendship with the great architect. 'You want to know what makes him tick?' M. Rycker said to me. 'I am sure that it is love, a completely selfless love without the barrier of colour or class. I have never known a man more deeply instructed in faith. I have sat at this very table late into the night discussing the nature of divine love with the great Querry.' So the two strange halves of Querry meet—to me Querry had spoken of the women he had loved in the world of Europe, and to his obscure friend, in his factory in the bush, he had spoken of his love of God. The world in this atomic day has need of saints. When a famous French statesman once retired into the depths of the country, to avoid the burden of office, it was said that the world made a path to his door. It is unlikely that the world which discovered the way to Schweitzer at Lambarene will fail to seek out the hermit of the Congo." I think he might have left out the reference to St Francis,' Father Thomas said, 'it might be misunderstood.'

'What lies the man does tell,' Querry exclaimed. He got up from his bed and stood near his drawing-board and the stretched sheet of blueprint. He said, 'I won't allow that man . . .'

'He is a journalist, of course,' Father Thomas said. 'These are just professional exaggerations.'

'I don't mean Parkinson. It's his job. I mean Rycker. I have never spoken to Rycker about Love or God.'

'He told me that he once had an interesting discussion with you.'

'Never. There was no discussion. All the talking, I assure you, was done by him.'

Father Thomas looked down at the newspaper cutting. He said, 'There's to be a second article, it appears, in a week's time. It says here, "Next Sunday. A Saint's Past. Redemption by Suffering. The Leper Lost in the Jungle." That will be Deo Gratias I imagine,' Father Thomas said. 'There's also a photograph of the Englishman talking to Rycker.'

'Give it to me.' Querry tore the paper into pieces and dropped them on the floor. He said, 'Is the road open?'

'It was when I left Luc. Why?'

'I'm going to take a truck then.'

'Where to?'

'To have a word with Rycker. Can't you see, father, that I must silence him? This mustn't go on. I'm fighting for my life.'

'Your life?'

'My life here. It's all I have.' He sat wearily down on the bed. He said, 'I've come a long way. There's nowhere else for me to go if I leave here.'

Father Thomas said, 'For a good man fame is always a problem.'

'But, father, I'm not a good man. Can't you believe me? Must you too twist everything like Rycker and that man? I had no good motive in coming here. I am looking after myself as I have always done, but surely even a selfish man has the right to a little happiness?'

'You have a truly wonderful quality of humility,' Father Thomas said.

PART VI

CHAPTER I

I

Marie Rycker stopped her reading of *The Imitation of Christ* as soon as she saw that her husband was asleep, but she was afraid to move in case she might wake him, and of course there was always the possibility of a trap. She could imagine how he would reproach her, 'Could you not watch by me one hour?' for her husband was not afraid to carry imitation to great lengths. The hollow face was turned away from her so that she could not see his eyes. She thought that so long as he was ill she need not tell him her news, for one had no duty to give such unwelcome news as hers to a sick man. Through the net of the window there blew in the smell of stale margarine which she would always associate with marriage, and from where she sat she could see the corner of the engine-house, where they were feeding the ovens with the husks.

She felt ashamed of her fear and boredom and nausea. She had been bred a *colon* and she knew very well that this was not how a *colon* ought to behave. Her father had represented the same company as her husband, in a different, a roving capacity, but because his wife was delicate he had sent her home to Europe before his child's birth. Her mother had fought to stay with him, for she was a true *colon*, and in her turn the daughter of a *colon*. The word spoken in Europe so disparagingly was a badge of honour to them. Even in Europe on leave they lived in groups, went to the same restaurants and café-bars kept by former *colons* and took villas for the season at the same watering-places. Wives waited among the potted palms for their husbands to return from the land of palms; they played bridge and read aloud to each other their husbands' letters, which contained the gossip of the colony. The letters bore bright postage stamps of beasts and birds and flowers and the postmarks of exotic places. Marie began to collect them at six, but she always preserved the envelopes and the postmarks as well, so that she had to keep them in a box instead of an album. One of the postmarks was Luc. She did not foresee that one day she would begin to know Luc better than she knew the rue de Namur.

With the tenderness that came from a sense of guilt she wiped Rycker's face with a handkerchief soaked in eau-de-cologne, even at the risk of waking him. She knew that she was a false *colon*. It was like betraying one's country–all the worse because one's country was so remote and so maligned.

One of the labourers came out of the shed to make water against the wall. When he turned back he saw her watching him and they stared across the few yards at each other, but they were like people watching with telescopes over an immense distance. She remembered a breakfast, with the pale European sun on the water outside and the bathers going in for an early dip, and her father teaching her the Mongo for 'bread' and 'coffee' and 'jam'. They were still the only three words in Mongo that she knew. But it was not enough to say coffee and bread and jam to the man outside. They had no means of communication: she couldn't even curse him, as her father or her husband could have done, in words that he understood. He turned and went into the shed and again she felt the loneliness of her treachery to this country of *colons*. She wanted to apologise to her old father at home; she couldn't blame him for the postmarks and the stamps. Her mother had yearned to remain with him. She had not realised how fortunate her weakness was. Rycker opened his eyes and said, 'What time is it?'

'I think it's about three o'clock.'

He was asleep again before he could have heard her reply, and she sat on. In the yard a lorry backed towards the shed. It was piled high with nuts for the presses and the ovens; they were like dried and withered heads, the product of a savage massacre. She tried to read, but the *Imitation of Christ* could not hold her attention. Once a month she received a copy of *Marie-Chantal*, but she had to read the serial in secret when Rycker was occupied, for he despised what he called women's fiction and spoke critically of day-dreams. What other resources had she than dreams? They were a form of hope, but she hid them from him as a member of the Resistance used to hide his pill of cyanide. She refused to believe that this was the end, growing old in solitude with her husband and the smell of margarine and the black faces and the scrap-metal, in the heat and the humidity. She awaited day by day some radio-signal which would announce the hour of liberation. Sometimes she thought that there were no lengths to which she would not go for the sake of liberation.

Marie-Chantal came by surface-mail; it was always two months out-of-date, but that hardly mattered, since the serial story, as much as any piece of literature, had eternal values. In the story she was reading now a girl in the Salle Privée at Monte Carlo had placed 12,000 francs, the last money she had in the world, upon the figure 17, but a hand had reached over her shoulder while the ball ran and shifted her tokens to 19. Then the 19 socket caught the ball and she turned to see who her benefactor could be . . . but she would have to wait another three weeks before she discovered his identity. He was approaching her now down the West African coast, by mail-boat, but even when he arrived at Matadi, there was still the long river-journey ahead of him. The dogs began barking in the yard and Rycker woke.

'See who it is,' he said, 'but keep him away.' She heard a car draw up. It was probably the representative of one of the two rival breweries. Each man made the tour of the out-stations three times a year and gave a party to the local chief and the villagers with his brand of beer gratis for everyone. In some mysterious way it was supposed to aid consumption.

They were shovelling the dried heads out of the *camion* when she came into the yard. Two men sat in a small Peugeot truck. One of them was

African, but she couldn't see who the other was because the sun on the windshield dazzled her, but she heard him say, 'What I have to do here should take no time at all. We will reach Luc by ten.' She came to the door of the car and saw that it was Querry. She recalled the shameful scene weeks before when she had run to her car in tears. Afterwards she had spent the night by the roadside bitten by mosquitoes rather than face another human being who might despise her husband too.

She thought gratefully, 'He has come of his own accord. What he said was just a passing mood. It was his *cafard* which spoke, not he.' She wanted to go in and see her husband and tell him, but then she remembered that he had told her, 'Keep him away.'

Querry climbed out of the truck and she saw that the boy with him was one of the *mutilés* from the leproserie. She said to Querry, 'You've come to call on us? My husband will be so glad . . .'

'I am on my way to Luc,' Querry said, 'but I want to have a word with M. Rycker first.' There was something in his expression which recalled her husband at certain moments. If *cafard* had dictated that insulting phrase the *cafard* still possessed him.

She said, 'He is ill. I'm afraid you can't see him.'

'I must. I have been three days on the road from the leproserie. . . .'

'You will have to tell me.' He stood by the door of the truck. She said, 'Can't you give me your message?'

'I can hardly strike a woman,' Querry said. A sudden rictus round the mouth startled her. Perhaps he was trying to soften the phrase with a smile, but it made his face all the uglier.

'Is that your message?'

'More or less,' Querry said.

'Then you'd better come inside.' She walked slowly away without looking back. He seemed to her like an armed savage from whom she must disguise her fear. When she reached the house she would be safe. Violence in their class always happened in the open air; it was restrained by sofas and bric-à-brac. When she passed through the door she was tempted to escape to her room, leaving the sick man at Querry's mercy, but she steeled herself by the thought of what Rycker might say to her when he had gone, and with no more than a glance down the passage where safety lay she went to the verandah and heard Querry's steps following behind.

When she reached the verandah she put on the voice of a hostess as she might have done a clean frock. She said, 'Can I get you something to drink?'

'It's a little early. Is your husband really sick?'

'Of course he is. I told you. The mosquitoes are bad here. We are too close to water. He hadn't been taking his paludrin. I don't know why. You know he has moods.'

'I suppose it was here that Parkinson got his fever?'

'Parkinson?'

'The English journalist.'

'That man,' she said with distaste. 'Is he still around?'

'I don't know. You were the last people to see him. After your husband had put him on my track.'

'I am sorry if he troubled you. I wouldn't answer any of his questions.'

Querry said, 'I had made it quite clear to your husband that I had come here to be private. He forced himself on me in Luc. He sent you out to the leproserie after me. He sent Parkinson. He has been spreading grotesque stories about me in the town. Now there's this newspaper article and another one is threatened. I have come to tell your husband that this persecution has got to stop.'

'Persecution?'

'Have you another name for it?'

'You don't understand. My husband was excited by your coming here. At finding you. There are not so many people he can talk to about what interests him. He's very alone.' She was looking across the river and the winding-gear of the ferry and the forest on the other side. 'When he's excited by something he wants to possess it. Like a child.'

'I have never cared for children.'

'It's the only young thing about him,' she said, the words coming quickly and unintentionally out, like the spurt from a wound.

He said, 'Can't you persuade him to stop talking about me?'

'I have no influence. He doesn't listen to me. After all why should he?'

'If he loves you . . .'

'I don't know whether he does. He says sometimes that he only loves God.'

'Then I must speak to him myself. A touch of fever is not going to stop him hearing what I have to say.' He added, 'I'm not sure of his room, but there aren't many in this house. I can find it.'

'No. Please no. He'll think it's my fault. He'll be angry. I don't want him angry. I've got something to tell him. I can't if he's angry. It's ghastly enough as it is.'

'What's ghastly?'

She looked at him with an expression of despair. Tears formed in her eyes and began to drip gracelessly like sweat. She said, 'I think I have a baby on the way.'

'But I thought women usually liked . . .'

'He doesn't want one. But he wouldn't allow me to be safe.'

'Have you seen a doctor?'

'No. There's been no excuse for me to go to Luc, and we've only the one car. I didn't want him to be suspicious. He usually wants to know after a time if everything's all right.'

'Hasn't he asked you?'

'I think he's forgotten that we did anything since the time before.'

He was moved unwillingly by her humility. She was very young and surely she was pretty enough, yet it seemed never to occur to her that a man ought not to forget such an act. She said, as if that explained everything, 'It was after the Governor's cocktail party.'

'Are you sure about it?'

'I've missed twice.'

'My dear, in this climate that often happens.' He said, 'I advise you—what's your name?'

'Marie.' It was the commonest woman's name of all, but it sounded to him like a warning.

'Yes,' she said eagerly, 'you advise me . . .?'

'Not to tell your husband yet. We must find some excuse for you to go to Luc and see the doctor. But don't worry too much. Don't you want the child?'

'What would be the use of wanting it if *he* doesn't?'

'I would take you in with me now—if we could find you an excuse.'

'If anybody can persuade him, you can. He admires you so much.'

'I have some medicines to pick up for Doctor Colin at the hospital, and I was going to buy some surprise provisions for the fathers too, champagne for when the roof-tree goes up. But I wouldn't be able to deliver you back before tomorrow evening.'

'Oh,' she said, 'his boy can look after him far better than I can. He's been with him longer.'

'I meant that perhaps he mightn't trust me. . . .'

'There hasn't been rain for days. The roads are quite good.'

'Shall I talk to him then?'

'It isn't really what you came to say, is it?'

'I'll treat him as gently as I can. You've drawn my sting.'

She said, 'It will be fun—to go to Luc alone. I mean with you.' She wiped her eyes dry with the back of her hand; she was no more ashamed of her tears than a child would have been.

'Perhaps the doctor will say you have nothing to fear. Which is his room?'

'Through the door at the end of the passage. You really won't be harsh to him?'

'No.'

Rycker was sitting up in bed when he entered. He was wearing a look of grievance like a mask, but he took it off quickly and substituted another representing welcome when he saw his visitor. 'Why, Querry? Was it you?'

'I came to see you on the way to Luc.'

'It's good of you to visit me on a bed of sickness.'

Querry said, 'I wanted to see you about that stupid article by the Englishman.'

'I gave it to Father Thomas to take to you.' Rycker's eyes were bright with fever or pleasure. 'There has never been such a sale in Luc for *Paris-Dimanche*, I can tell you that. The bookshop has sent for extra copies. They say they have ordered a hundred of the next issue.'

'Did it never occur to you how detestable it would be to me?'

'I know the paper is not a very high-class one, but the article was highly laudatory. Do you realise that it's even been reprinted in Italy? The bishop, so I'm told, has had an enquiry from Rome.'

'Will you listen to me, Rycker? I'm trying to speak gently because you are sick. But all this has to stop. I am not a Catholic, I am not even a Christian. I won't be adopted by you and your Church.'

Rycker sat under the crucifix, wearing a smile of understanding.

'I have no belief whatever in a god, Rycker. No belief in the soul, in eternity. I'm not even interested.'

'Yes. Father Thomas has told me how terribly you have been suffering from aridity.'

'Father Thomas is a pious fool, and I came out here to escape fools,

Rycker. Will you promise to leave me in peace or must I go again the way I came? I was happy before this started. I found I could work. I was feeling interested, involved in something. . . .'

'It's a penalty of genius to belong to the world.'

If he had to have a tormentor how gladly he would have chosen the cynical Parkinson. There were interstices in that cracked character where the truth might occasionally seed. But Rycker was like a wall so plastered over with church-announcements that you couldn't even see the brickwork behind. He said, 'I'm no genius, Rycker. I am a man who had a certain talent, not a very great talent, and I have come to the end of it. There was nothing new I could do. I could only repeat myself. So I gave up. It's as simple and commonplace as that. Just as I have given up women. After all there are only thirty-two ways of driving a nail into a hole.'

'Parkinson told me of the remorse you felt. . . .'

'I have never felt remorse. Never. You all dramatise too much. We can retire from feeling just as naturally as we retire from a job. Are you sure that you still feel anything, Rycker, that you aren't pretending to feel? Would you greatly care if your factory were burnt down tomorrow in a riot?'

'My heart is not in that.'

'And your heart isn't in your wife either. You made that clear to me the first time we met. You wanted someone to save you from St Paul's threat of burning.'

'There is nothing wrong in a Christian marriage,' Rycker said. 'It's far better than a marriage of passion. But if you want to know the truth, my heart has always been in my faith.'

'I begin to think we are not so different, you and I. We don't know what love is. You pretend to love a god because you love no one else. But I won't pretend. All I have left me is a certain regard for the truth. It was the best side of the small talent I had. You are inventing all the time, Rycker, aren't you? There are men who talk about love to prostitutes—they daren't even sleep with a woman without inventing some sentiment to excuse them. You've even invented this idea of me to justify yourself. But I won't play your game, Rycker.'

'When I look at you,' Rycker said, 'I can see a man tormented.'

'Oh no you can't. I haven't felt any pain at all in twenty years. It needs something far bigger than you to cause me pain.'

'Whether you like it or not, you have set an example to all of us.'

'An example of what?'

'Unselfishness and humility,' Rycker said.

'I warn you, Rycker, that unless you stop spreading this rubbish about me . . .'

But he felt his powerlessness. He had been trapped into words. A blow would have been simpler and better, but it was too late now for blows.

Rycker said, 'Saints used to be made by popular acclaim. I'm not sure that it wasn't a better method than a trial in Rome. We have taken you up, Querry. You don't belong to yourself any more. You lost yourself when you prayed with that leper in the forest.'

'I didn't pray. I only . . .' He stopped. What was the use? Rycker had stolen the last word. Only after he had slammed the door shut did he remember that he had said nothing of Marie Rycker and of her journey to Luc.

And of course there she was waiting for him eagerly and patiently, at the other end of the passage. He wished that he had brought a bag of sweets with which to comfort her. She said excitedly, 'Did he agree?'

'I never asked him.'

'You promised.'

'I got angry, and I forgot. I'm very sorry.'

She said, 'I'll come with you to Luc all the same.'

'You'd better not.'

'Were you very angry with him?'

'Not very. I kept most of the anger to myself.'

'Then I'm coming.' She left him before he had time to protest, and a few moments later she was back with no more than a Sabena night-bag for the journey.

He said, 'You travel light.'

When they reached the truck he asked, 'Wouldn't it be better if I went back and spoke to him?'

'He might say no. Then what could I do?'

They left behind them the smell of the margarine and the cemetery of old boilers, and the shadow of the forest fell on either side. She said politely in her hostess voice, 'Is the hospital going well?'

'Yes.'

'How is the Superior?'

'He is away.'

'Did you have a heavy storm last Saturday? We did.'

He said. 'You don't have to make conversation with me.'

'My husband says that I am too silent.'

'Silence is not a bad thing.'

'It is when you are unhappy.'

'I'm sorry. I had forgotten . . .'

They drove a few more kilometres without words. Then she asked, 'Why did you come here and not some other place?'

'Because it is a long way off.'

'Other places are a long way off. The South Pole.'

'When I was at the airport there was no plane leaving for the South Pole.' She giggled. It was easy to amuse the young, even the unhappy young. 'There was one going to Tokyo,' he added, 'but somehow this place seemed a lot further off. And I was not interested in geishas or cherry-blossom.'

'You don't mean you really didn't know where . . . ?'

'One of the advantages of having a credit card is that you don't need to make up your mind where you are going till the last moment.'

'Haven't you any family to leave?'

'Not a family. There was someone, but she was better off without me.'

'Poor her.'

'Oh no. She's lost nothing of value. It's hard for a woman to live with a man who doesn't love her.'

'Yes.'

'There are always the times of day when one ceases to pretend.'

'Yes.' They were silent again until darkness began to fall and he switched the headlights on. They shone on a human effigy with a coconut-head, sitting on a rickety chair. She gave a gasp of fright and pressed against his shoulder. She said, 'I'm scared of things I don't understand.'

'Then you must be frightened of a great deal.'

'I am.'

He put his arm round her shoulders to reassure her. She said, 'Did you say goodbye to her?'

'No.'

'But she must have seen you packing.'

'No. I travel light too.'

'You came away without anything?'

'I had a razor and a toothbrush and a letter of credit from a bank in America.'

'Do you really mean you didn't know where you were going?'

'I had no idea. So it wasn't any good taking clothes.'

The track was rough and he needed both hands on the wheel. He had never before scrutinised his own behaviour. It had seemed to him at the time the only logical thing to do. He had eaten a larger breakfast than usual because he could not be certain of the hour of his next meal, and then he had taken a taxi. His journey began in the great all-but-empty airport built for a world-exhibition which had closed a long time ago. One could walk a mile through the corridors without seeing more than a scattering of human beings. In an immense hall people sat apart waiting for the plane to Tokyo. They looked like statues in an art-gallery. He had asked for a seat to Tokyo before he noticed an indicator with African names.

He had said, 'Is there a seat on that plane too?'

'Yes, but there's no connection to Tokyo after Rome.'

'I shall go the whole way.' He gave the man his credit card.

'Where is your luggage?'

'I have no luggage.'

He supposed now that his conduct must have seemed a little odd. He said to the clerk, 'Mark my ticket with my surname only, please. On the passenger list too. I don't want to be bothered by the Press.' It was one of the few advantages which fame brought a man that he was not automatically regarded with suspicion because of unusual behaviour. Thus simply he had thought to cover his tracks, but he had not entirely succeeded or the letter signed *toute à toi* could never have reached him. Perhaps she had been to the airport herself to make enquiries. The man there must have had quite a story to tell her. Even so, at his destination, no one had known him, and at the small hotel he went to—without air-conditioning and with a shower which didn't work, no one knew his name. So it could have been no one but Rycker who had betrayed his whereabouts; the ripple of Rycker's interest had gone out across half the world like radio-waves, reaching the international Press. He said abruptly, 'How I wish I'd never met your husband.'

'So do I.'

'It's done you no harm, surely?'

'I mean—I wish I hadn't met him either.' The headlamps caught the wooden poles of a cage high in the air. She said, 'I hate this place. I want to go home.'

'We've come too far to turn back now.'

'That's not home,' she said. 'That's the factory.'

He knew very well what she expected him to say, but he refused to speak. You uttered a few words of sympathy—however false and conventional—and experience taught him what nearly always followed. Unhappiness was like a hungry animal waiting beside the track for any victim. He said, 'Have you friends in Luc to put you up?'

'We have no friends there. I'll go with you to the hotel.'

'Did you leave a note for your husband?'

'No.'

'It would have been better.'

'Did you leave a note behind before you caught the plane?'

'That was different. I was not returning.'

She said, 'Would you lend me money for a ticket home—I mean, to Europe?'

'No.'

'I was afraid you wouldn't.' As if that settled everything and there was nothing more to do about it, she fell asleep. He thought rashly: poor frightened beast—this one was too young to be a great danger. It was only when they were fully grown you couldn't trust them with your pity.

2

It was nearly eleven at night before they drove into Luc past the little river-port. The Bishop's boat was lying at her moorings. A cat stopped halfway up the gang-plank and regarded them, and Querry swerved to avoid a dead piedog stretched in their track waiting for the morning vulture. The hotel across the square from the Governor's house was decked out with the relics of gaiety. Perhaps the directors of the local brewery had been giving their annual party or some official, who thought himself lucky, had been celebrating his recall home. In the bar there were mauve and pink paper-chains hanging over the tubular steel chairs that gave the whole place the cheerless and functional look of an engine-room; shades which represented the man in the moon beamed down from the light-brackets.

There was no air-conditioning in the rooms upstairs, and the walls stopped short of the ceiling so that any privacy was impossible. Every movement was audible from the neighbouring room, and Querry could follow every stage of the girl's retirement—the zipping of the all-night bag, the clatter of a coat-hanger, the tinkle of a glass bottle on a porcelain basin. Shoes were dropped on bare boards, and water ran. He sat and wondered what he ought to do to comfort her if the doctor told her in the morning she was pregnant. He was reminded of his long night's vigil with Deo Gratias. It had been fear then too that he had contended with. He heard the bed creak.

He took a bottle of whisky from his sack and poured himself a glass. Now it was his turn to tinkle, run water, clatter; he was like a prisoner in a cell answering by code the signals of a fellow-convict. An odd sound reached him through the wall—it sounded to him as though she were crying. He felt no pity, only irritation. She had forced herself on him and she was threatening now to spoil his night's sleep. He had not yet undressed. He took the bottle of whisky with him and knocked on her door.

He saw at once that he had been wrong. She was sitting up in bed reading a paper-back—she must have had time to stow that away too in the Sabena bag. He said, 'I'm sorry—I thought I heard you crying.'

'Oh no,' she said. 'I was laughing.' He saw that it was a popular novel dealing with the life in Paris of an English major. 'It's terribly funny.'

'I brought this along in case you needed comfort.'

'Whisky? I've never drunk it.'

'You can begin. But you probably won't like it.' He washed her toothmug out and poured her a weak drink.

'You don't like it?'

She said, 'I like the idea. Drinking whisky at midnight in a room of my own.'

'It's not midnight yet.'

'You know what I mean. And reading in bed. My husband doesn't like me reading in bed. Especially a book like this.'

'What's wrong with the book?'

'It's not serious. It's not about God. Of course,' she said, 'he has good reason. I'm not properly educated. The nuns did their best, but it simply didn't stick.'

'I'm glad you're not worrying about tomorrow.'

'There may be good news. I've got a bit of a stomach-ache at this moment. It can't be the whisky yet, can it? and it might be the curse.' The hostess-phrases had gone to limbo where the nuns' learning lay, and she had reverted to the school-dormitory. It was absurd to consider that anyone so immature could be in any way a danger.

He asked, 'Were you happy when you were at school?'

'It was bliss.' She bunched her knees higher and said, 'Why don't you sit down?'

'It's quite time you were asleep.' He found it impossible not to treat her as a child. Rycker, instead of rupturing her virginity, had sealed it safely down once and for all.

She said, 'What are you going to do? When the hospital's finished, I mean?' That was the question they were all asking him, but this time he did not evade it: there was a theory that one should always tell the direct truth to the young.

He said, 'I am going to stay. I am never going back.'

'You'll have to—sometime—on leave.'

'The others perhaps, but not me.'

'You'll get sick in the end if you stay.'

'I'm very tough. Anyway what do I care? We all sooner or later get the same sickness, age. Do you see those brown marks on the backs of my hands—my mother used to call them grave-marks.'

'They are only freckles,' she said.

'Oh no, freckles come from the sunlight. These come from the darkness.'

'You are very morbid,' she said, speaking like the head of the school. 'I don't really understand you. I have to stay here, but my God if I were free like you . . .'

'I will tell you a story,' he said and poured himself out a second treble Scotch.

'That's a very large whisky. You aren't a heavy drinker, are you? My husband is.'

'I'm only a steady one. This one is to help me with the story. I'm not used to telling stories. How does one begin?' He drank slowly. 'Once upon a time.'

'Really,' she said, 'you and I are much too old for fairy stories.'

'Yes. That in a way *is* the story as you'll see. Once upon a time there was a boy who lived in the deep country.'

'Were you the boy?'

'No, you mustn't draw close parallels. They always say a novelist chooses from his general experience of life, not from special facts. I have never lived out of cities until now.'

'Go on.'

'This boy lived with his parents on a farm—not a very large farm, but it was big enough for them and two servants and six labourers, a dog, a cat, a cow . . . I suppose there was a pig. I don't know much about farms.'

'There seems to be an awful lot of characters. I shall fall asleep if I try to remember them all.'

'That's exactly what I'm trying to make you do. His parents used to tell the boy stories about the King who lived in a city a hundred miles away—about the distance of the furthest star.'

'That's nonsense. A star is billions and billions . . .'

'Yes, but the boy *thought* the star was a hundred miles away. He knew nothing about light-years. He had no idea that the star he was watching had probably been dead and dark before the world was made. They told him that, even though the King was far away, he was watching everything that went on everywhere. When a pig littered, the King knew of it, or when a moth died against a lamp. When a man and woman married, he knew that too. He was pleased by their marriage because when *they* came to litter it would increase the number of his subjects; so he rewarded them—you couldn't see the reward, for the woman frequently died in childbirth and the child was sometimes born deaf or blind, but, after all, you cannot see the air—and yet it exists according to those who know. When a servant slept with another servant in a haystack the King punished them. You couldn't always see the punishment—the man found a better job and the girl was more beautiful with her virginity gone and afterwards married the foreman, but that was only because the punishment was postponed. Sometimes it was postponed until the end of life, but that made no difference because the King was the King of the dead too and you couldn't tell what terrible things he might do to them in the grave.

'The boy grew up. He married properly and was rewarded by the King, although his only child died and he made no progress in his profession—he had always wanted to carve statues, as large and important as the Sphinx. After his child's death he quarrelled with his wife and was punished by the King for it. Of course you couldn't have seen the punishment any more than you could see the reward: you had to take both on trust. He became in time a famous jeweller, for one of the women whom he had satisfied gave him money for his training, and he made many beautiful things in honour of his mistress and of course the King. Lots of rewards began to come his way. Money too. From the King. Everyone agreed that it all came from the King. He left his wife and his mistress, he left a lot of women, but he always had a great deal of fun with them first. They called it love and so did he, he broke all the rules he could think of, and he must surely have been punished for breaking them, but you couldn't see the punishment nor could he. He grew richer and he made better and better jewellery, and women were kinder and kinder to him. He had, everyone agreed, a wonderful time. The only trouble was that he became bored, more and more bored. Nobody ever seemed to say no to him. Nobody ever made him suffer—it was always other people who suffered. Sometimes just for a change he would have welcomed feeling the pain of the punishment that the King must all the time have been inflicting on him. He could travel wherever he chose and after a while it seemed to him that he had gone much further than the hundred miles that separated him from the King, further than the furthest star, but wherever he went he always came to the same place where the same things happened: articles in the papers praised his jewellery, women cheated their husbands and went to bed with him, and servants of the King acclaimed him as a loyal and faithful subject.

'Because people could only see the reward, and the punishment was invisible, he got the reputation of being a very good man. Sometimes people were a little perplexed that such a good man should have enjoyed quite so many women—it was, on the surface anyway, disloyal to the King who had made quite other rules. But they learnt in time to explain it; they said he had a great capacity for love and love had always been regarded by them as the highest of virtues. Love indeed was the greatest reward even the King could give, all the greater because it was more invisible than such little material rewards as money and success and membership of the Academy. Even the man himself began to believe that he loved a great deal better than all the so-called good people who obviously could not be so good if you knew all (you had only to look at the punishments they received—poverty, children dying, losing both legs in a railway accident and the like). It was quite a shock to him when he discovered one day that he didn't love at all.'

'How did he discover that?'

'It was the first of several important discoveries which he made about that time. Did I tell you that he was a very clever man, much cleverer than the people around him? Even as a boy he had discovered all by himself about the King. Of course there were his parents' stories, but they proved nothing. They might have been old wives' tales. They loved the King, they said, but he went one better. He proved that the King existed by historical, logical, philosophical and etymological methods. His parents told him that was a waste of time: they knew: they had seen the King. "Where?" "In our hearts of course." He laughed at them for their simplicity and their superstition. How could the King possibly be in their hearts when he was able to prove that he had never stirred from the city a hundred miles away? His King existed objectively and there was no other King but his.'

'I don't like parables much, and I don't like your hero.'

'He doesn't like himself much, and that's why he's never spoken before—except in this way.'

'What you said about "no other king but his" reminds me a little of my husband.'

'You mustn't accuse a story-teller of introducing real characters.'

'When are you going to reach a climax? Has it a happy ending? I don't want to stay awake otherwise. Why don't you describe some of the women?'

'You are like so many critics. You want me to write your own sort of story.'

'Have you read *Manon Lescaut*?'

'Years ago.'

'We all loved it at the convent. Of course it was strictly forbidden. It was passed from hand to hand, and I pasted the cover of Lejeune's History of the Wars of Religion on it. I have it still.'

'You must let me finish my story.'

'Oh well,' she said with resignation, leaning back against the pillows, 'if you must.'

'I have told you about my hero's first discovery. His second came much later when he realised that he was not born to be an artist at all: only a very clever jeweller. He made one gold jewel in the shape of an ostrich egg: it was all enamel and gold and when you opened it you found inside a little gold figure sitting at a table and a little gold and enamel egg on the table, and when you opened that there was a little figure sitting at a table and a little gold and enamel egg and when you opened that . . . I needn't go on. Everyone said he was a master-technician, but he was highly praised too for the seriousness of his subject-matter because on the top of each egg there was a gold cross set with chips of precious stones in honour of the King. The trouble was that he wore himself out with the ingenuity of his design, and suddenly when he was making the contents of the final egg with an optic glass—that was what they called magnifying glasses in the old days in which this story is set, for of course it contains no reference to our time and no likeness to any living character. . . .' He took another long drink of whisky; he couldn't remember how long it was since he had experienced the odd elation he was feeling now. He said, 'What am I saying? I think I am a little drunk. The whisky doesn't usually affect me in this way.'

'Something about an egg,' her sleepy voice replied from under the sheet.

'Oh yes, the second discovery.' It was, he began to think, a sad story, so that it was hard to understand this sense of freedom and release, like that of a prisoner who at last 'comes clean,' admitting everything to his inquisitor. Was this the reward perhaps which came sometimes to a writer? 'I have told all: you can hang me now.' 'What did you say?'

'The last egg.'

'Oh yes, that was it. Suddenly our hero realised how bored he was—he never wanted to turn his hand any more to mounting any jewel at all. He was finished with his profession—he had come to an end of it. Nothing could ever be so ingenious as what he had done already, or more useless, and he could never hear any praise higher than what he had received. He knew what the damned fools could do with their praise.'

'So what?'

'He went to a house number 49 in a street called the Rue des Remparts where his mistress had kept an apartment ever since she left her husband. Her name was Marie like yours. There was a crowd outside. He found the doctor and the police there because an hour before she had killed herself.'

'How ghastly.'

'Not for him. A long time ago he had got to the end of pleasure just as now he had got to the end of work, although it is true he went on practising pleasure as a retired dancer continues to rehearse daily at the bar, because he has spent all his mornings that way and it never occurs to him to stop. So our hero felt only relief: the bar had been broken, he wouldn't bother, he thought, to obtain another. Although, of course, after a month or two he did. However it was too late then—the morning-habit had been broken and he never took it up again with quite the same zeal.'

'It's a very unpleasant fairy story,' the voice said. He couldn't see her face because the sheet was pulled over it. He paid no attention to her criticism.

'I tell you it isn't easy leaving a profession any more than you would find it easy leaving a husband. In both cases people talk a lot to you about duty. People came to him to demand eggs with crosses (it was his duty to the King and the King's followers). It almost seemed from the fuss they made that no one else was capable of making eggs or crosses. To try and discourage them and show them how his mind had changed, he did cut a few more stones as frivolously as he knew how, exquisite little toads for women to wear in their navels—navel-jewels became quite a fashion for a time. He even fashioned little soft golden coats of mail, with one hollow stone like a knowing eye at the top, with which men might clothe their special parts—they came to be known for some reason as Letters of Marque and for a while they too were quite fashionable as gifts. (You know how difficult it is for a woman to find anything to give a man at Christmas.) So our hero received yet more money and praise, but what vexed him most was that even these trifles were now regarded as seriously as his eggs and crosses had been. He was the King's jeweller and nothing could alter that. People declared that he was a moralist and that these were serious satires on the age—in the end the idea rather spoilt the sale of the letters, as you can imagine. A man hardly wants to wear a moral satire in that place, and women were chary of touching a moral satire in the way they had liked touching a soft jewelled responsive coat.

'However the fact that his jewels ceased to be popular with people in general only made him more popular with the connoisseurs who distrust popular success. They began to write books about his art; especially those who claimed to know and love the King wrote about him. The books all said much the same thing, and when our hero had read one he had read them all. There was nearly always a chapter called The Toad in the Hole: the Art of Fallen Man, or else there was one called From Easter Egg to Letters of Marque, the Jeweller of Original Sin.'

'Why do you keep on calling him a jeweller?' the voice said from under the sheet. 'You know very well he was an architect.'

'I warned you not to attach real characters to my story. You'll be identifying yourself with the other Marie next. Although, thank God, you're not the kind to kill yourself.'

'You'd be surprised what I could do,' she said. 'Your story isn't a bit like *Manon Lescaut*, but it's pretty miserable all the same.'

'What none of these people knew was that one day our hero had made a startling discovery—he no longer believed all those arguments historical, philosophical, logical and etymological that he had worked out for the existence of the King. There was left only a memory of the King who had lived in his parents' heart and not in any particular place. Unfortunately his heart was not the same as the one his parents shared: it was calloused with pride and success, and it had learned to beat only with pride when a building . . .'

'You said building.'

'When a jewel was completed or when a woman cried under him, "*donne, donne, donne*".' He looked at the whisky in the bottle: it wasn't worth preserving the little that remained; he emptied it into his glass and he didn't bother to add water.

'You know,' he said, 'he had deceived himself, just as much as he had deceived the others. He had believed quite sincerely that when he loved his work he was loving the King and that when he made love to a woman he was at least imitating in a faulty way the King's love for his people. The King after all had so loved the world that he had sent a bull and a shower of gold and a son . . .'

'You are getting it all confused,' the girl said.

'But when he discovered there was no such King as the one he had believed in, he realised too that anything that he had ever done must have been done for love of himself. How could there be any point any longer in making jewels or making love for his own solitary pleasure? Perhaps he had reached the end of his sex and the end of his vocation before he made his discovery about the King or perhaps that discovery brought about the end of everything? I wouldn't know, but I'm told that there were moments when he wondered if his unbelief were not after all a final and conclusive proof of the King's existence. This total vacancy might be his punishment for the rules he had wilfully broken. It was even possible that this was what people meant by pain. The problem was complicated to the point of absurdity, and he began to envy his parents' simple and uncomplex heart, in which they had always believed that the King lived—and not in the cold palace as big as St Peter's a hundred miles away.'

'So then?'

'I told you, didn't I, that it's just as difficult to leave a profession as to leave a husband. If you left your husband there would be acres and acres of daylight you wouldn't know how to cross, and acres of darkness as well, and of course there would always be telephone calls and the kind enquiries of friends and the chance paragraphs in the newspapers. But that part of the story has no real interest.'

'So he took a credit card . . .' she said.

The whisky was finished. He said, 'I've kept you awake.'

'I wish you'd told me a romantic story. All the same it took my mind off things.' She giggled under the sheet. 'I could almost say to him, couldn't I, that we'd spent the night together. Do you think that he'd divorce me? I suppose not. The Church won't allow divorce. The Church says, the Church orders . . .'

'Are you really so unhappy?' He got no reply. To the young sleep comes as quickly as day to the tropical town. He opened the door very quietly and went out into the passage that was still dark with one all-night globe palely burning. Some late-sleeper or early-riser closed a door five rooms away: a flush choked and swallowed in the silence. He sat on his bed. It was the hour of coolness. He thought: the King is dead, long live the King. Perhaps he had found here a country and a life.

CHAPTER 2

I

Querry was out early to do as many as he could of the doctor's errands before the day became too hot. There was no sign of Marie Rycker at breakfast, and no sound over the partition of their rooms. At the Cathedral he collected the letters which had been waiting for the next boat—he was glad to find that not one of them was addressed to him. *Toute à toi* had made her one gesture towards his unknown region, and he hoped for her sake that it had been a gesture of duty and convention and not of love, for in that case his silence would do her no further hurt.

By midday he was feeling parched and finding himself not far from the wharf he went down to the river and up the gang-plank of the Bishop's boat to see whether the captain were on board. He hesitated a moment at the foot of the ladder surprised by his own action. It was the first time for a long while that he had voluntarily made a move towards companionship. He remembered how fearful he had been when he last set foot on board and the light was burning in the cabin. The crew had piled logs on the pontoons ready for another voyage, and a woman was hanging her washing between the companion-way and the boiler; he called 'Captain,' as he climbed the ladder, but the priest who sat at the saloon-table going through the bills of lading was a stranger to him.

'May I come in?'

'I think I know who you are. You must be M. Querry. Shall we open a bottle of beer?'

Querry asked after the former captain. 'He has been sent to teach moral theology,' his successor said, 'at Wakanga.'

'Was he sorry to go?'

'He was delighted. The river-life did not appeal to him.'

'To you it does?'

'I don't know yet. This is my first voyage. It is a change from canon law. We start tomorrow.'

'To the leproserie?'

'We shall end there. A week. Ten days. I'm not sure yet about the cargo.'

Querry when he left the boat felt that he had aroused no curiosity. The captain had not even asked him about the new hospital. Perhaps *Paris-*

Dimanche had done its worst; there was nothing more that Rycker or Parkinson could inflict on him. It was as though he were on the verge of acceptance into a new country; like a refugee he watched the consul lift his pen to fill in the final details of his visa. But the refugee remains apprehensive to the last; he has had too many experiences of the sudden afterthought, the fresh question or requirement, the strange official who comes into the room carrying another file. A man was in the hotel-bar, drinking below the man in the moon and the chains of mauve paper; it was Parkinson.

Parkinson raised a glass of pink gin and said, 'Have one on me.'

'I thought you had gone away.'

'Only as far as Stanleyville for the riots. Now I've filed my story and I'm a free man again until something turns up. What's yours?'

'How long are you staying here?'

'Until I get a cable from home. Your story has gone over well. They may want a third instalment.'

'You didn't use what I gave you.'

'It wasn't family reading.'

'You can get no more from me.'

'You'd be surprised,' Parkinson said, 'what sometimes comes one's way by pure good luck.' He chinked the ice against the side of his glass. 'Quite a success that first article had. Full syndication, even the Antipodes—except of course behind the curtain. The Americans are lapping it up. Religion and an anti-colonialist angle—you couldn't have a better mixture for them. There's just one thing I do rather regret—you never took that photograph of me carried ashore with fever. I had to make do with a photograph which Mme. Rycker took. But now I've got a fine one of myself in Stanleyville, beside a burnt-out car. Wasn't it you who contradicted me about Stanley? He must have been there or they wouldn't have called the place after him. Where are you going?'

'To my room.'

'Oh yes, you are number six, aren't you, in my corridor?'

'Number seven.'

Parkinson stirred the ice round with his finger. 'Oh I see. Number seven. You aren't vexed with me, are you? I assure you those angry words the other day, they didn't mean a thing. It was just a way to get you talking. A man like me can't afford to be angry. The darts the picador sticks into the bull are not the real thing.'

'What is?'

'The next instalment. Wait till you read it.'

'I hardly expect to find the moment of truth.'

'*Touché*,' Parkinson said. 'It's a funny thing about metaphors—they never really follow through. Perhaps you won't believe me, but there was a time when I was interested in style.' He looked into his glass of gin as though into a well. 'What the hell of a long life it is, isn't it?'

'The other day you seemed afraid to lose it.'

'It's all I've got,' Parkinson said.

The door opened from the blinding street and Marie Rycker walked in. Parkinson said in a jovial voice, 'Well, fancy, look who's here.'

'I gave Mme. Rycker a lift from the plantation.'

'Another gin,' Parkinson said to the barman.

'I do not drink gin,' Marie Rycker told him in her stilted phrase-book English.

'What *do* you drink? Now that I come to think of it, I don't remember ever seeing you with a glass in your hand all the time I stayed with you. Have an *orange pressée*, my child?'

'I am very fond of whisky,' Marie Rycker said with pride.

'Good for you. You are growing up fast.' He went down the length of the bar to give the order and on his way he made a little jump, agile in so fat a man, and set the paper-chains rocking with the palm of his hand.

'Any news?' Querry asked.

'He can't tell me—not until the day after tomorrow. He thinks . . .'

'Yes.'

'He thinks I'm caught,' she said gloomily and then Parkinson was back beside them holding the glass. He said, 'I heard your old man had the fever.'

'Yes.'

'Don't I know what it feels like!' Parkinson said. 'He's lucky to have a young wife to look after him.'

'He does not need me for a nurse.'

'Are you staying here long?'

'I do not know. Two days perhaps.'

'Time for a meal with me then?'

'Oh no. No time for that,' she said without hesitation.

He grinned without mirth. '*Touché* again.'

When she had drained her whisky she said to Querry, 'We're lunching together, aren't we, you and I? Give me just a minute for a wash. I'll fetch my key.'

'Allow *me*,' Parkinson said, and before she had time to protest, he was already back at the bar, swinging her key on his little finger. 'Number six,' he said, 'so we are all three on the same floor.'

Querry said, 'I'll come up with you.'

She looked into her room and came quickly back to his. She asked, 'Can I come in? You can't think how squalid it is in mine. I got up too late and they haven't made the bed.' She wiped her face with his towel, then looked ruefully at the marks which her powder had left. 'I'm sorry. What a mess I've made. I didn't mean to.'

'It doesn't matter.'

'Women are disgusting, aren't they?'

'In a long life I haven't found them so.'

'See what I've landed you with now. Twenty-four more hours in a hole like this.'

'Can't the doctor write to you about the result?'

'I can't go back until I know. Don't you see how impossible that would be? If the answer's yes, I've got to tell him right away. It was my only excuse for coming anyway.'

'And if the answer's no?'

'I'll be so happy then I won't care about anything. Perhaps I won't even go back.' She asked him, 'What *is* a rabbit test?'

'I don't know exactly. I believe they take your urine, and cut the rabbit open . . .'

'Do they do *that*?' she asked with horror.

'They sew the rabbit up again. I think it survives for another test.'

'I wonder why we all have to know the worst so quickly. At a poor beast's expense.'

'Haven't you any wish at all for a child?'

'For a young Rycker? No.' She took the comb out of his brush and without examining it pushed it through her hair. 'I didn't trap you into lunch, did I? You weren't eating with anyone else?'

'No.'

'It's just that I can't stand that man out there.'

But it was impossible to get far away from him in Luc. There were only two restaurants in the town and they chose the same one. The three of them were the only people there; he watched them between bites from his table by the door. He had slung his Rolleiflex on the chair-back beside him much as civilians slung their revolvers in those uncertain days. At least you could say of him that he went hunting with a camera only.

Marie Rycker gave herself a second helping of potatoes. 'Don't tell me,' she said, 'that I'm eating enough for two.'

'I won't.'

'It's the stock *colon* joke, you know, for someone with worms.'

'How is your stomach-ache?'

'Alas, it's gone. The doctor seemed to think that it had no connection.'

'Hadn't you better telephone to your husband? Surely he'll be anxious if you don't come back today.'

'The lines are probably down. They usually are.'

'There hasn't been a storm.'

'The Africans are always stealing the wire.'

She finished off a horrible mauve dessert before she spoke again. 'I expect you are right. I'll telephone,' and she left him alone with his coffee. His cup and Parkinson's clinked in unison over the empty tables.

Parkinson called across, 'The mail's not in. I've been expecting a copy of my second article. I'll drop it in your room if it comes. Let me see. Is it six or seven? It wouldn't do to get the wrong room, would it?'

'You needn't bother.'

'You owe me a photograph. Perhaps you and Mme. Rycker would oblige.'

'You'll get no photograph from me, Parkinson.'

Querry paid the bill and went to find the telephone. It stood on a desk where a woman with blue hair and blue spectacles was writing her accounts with an orange pen. 'It's ringing,' Marie Rycker said, 'but he doesn't answer.'

'I hope his fever's not worse.'

'He's probably gone across to the factory.' She put the telephone down and said, 'I've done my best, haven't I?'

'You could try again this evening before we have dinner.'

'You *are* stuck with me, aren't you?'

'No more than you with me.'

'Have you any more stories to tell?'

'No. I only know the one.'

She said, 'It's an awful time till tomorrow. I don't know what to do until I know.'

'Lie down awhile.'

'I can't. Would it be very stupid if I went to the cathedral and prayed?'

'Nothing is stupid that makes the time pass.'

'But if the thing is here,' she said, 'inside me, it couldn't suddenly disappear, could it, if I prayed?'

'I wouldn't think so.' He said reluctantly, 'Even the priests don't ask you to believe that. They would tell you, I suppose, to pray that God's will be done. But don't expect me to talk to you about prayer.'

'I'd want to know what his will was before I prayed anything like that,' she said. 'All the same, I think I'll go and pray. I could pray to be happy, couldn't I?'

'I suppose so.'

'That would cover almost everything.'

2

Querry too found the hours hanging heavily. Again he walked down to the river. Work had stopped upon the Bishop's boat, and there was no one on board. In the little square the shops were shuttered. It seemed as though all the world were asleep except himself and the girl who, he supposed, was still praying. But when he returned to the hotel he found that Parkinson at least was awake. He stood under the mauve-and-pink paper streamers, with his eyes upon the door. After Querry had crossed the threshold, he came tiptoeing forward and said with sly urgent importance, 'I must have a word with you quietly before you go to your room.'

'What about?'

'The general situation,' Parkinson said. 'Storm over Luc. Do you know who's up there?'

'Up where?'

'On the first floor.'

'You seem very anxious to tell me. Go ahead.'

'The husband,' Parkinson said heavily.

'What husband?'

'Rycker. He's looking for his wife.'

'I think he'll find her in the cathedral.'

'It's not as simple as all that. He knows you're with her.'

'Of course he does. I was at his house yesterday.'

'All the same I don't think he expected to find you here in adjoining rooms.'

'You think like a gossip-writer,' Querry said. 'What difference does it make whether rooms adjoin? You can sleep together from opposite ends of a passage just as easily.'

'Don't underrate the gossip-writers. They write history. From Fair Rosamund to Eva Braun.'

'I don't think history will be much concerned with the Ryckers.' He went to the desk and said, 'My bill, please. I'm leaving now.'

'Running away?' Parkinson asked.

'Why running away? I was only staying here to give her a lift back. Now I can leave her with her husband. She's his responsibility.'

'You *are* a cold-blooded devil,' Parkinson said. 'I begin to believe some of the things you told me.'

'Print them instead of your pious rubbish. It might be interesting to tell the truth for once.'

'But which truth? You aren't as simple-minded as you make out, Querry, and there weren't any lies of fact in what I wrote. Leaving out Stanley, of course.'

'And your *pirogue* and your faithful servants.'

'Anyway, what I wrote about *you* was true.'

'No.'

'You have buried yourself here, haven't you? You are working for the lepers. You did pursue that man into the forest. . . . It all adds up, you know, to what people like to call goodness.'

'I know my own motives.'

'Do you? And did the saints? What about "most miserable sinner" and all that crap?'

'You talk—almost—as Father Thomas does. Not quite, of course.'

'History's just as likely to take my interpretation as your own. I told you I was going to build you up, Querry. Unless, of course, as now seems likely, I find it makes a better story if I pull you down.'

'Do you really believe you have all that power?'

'Montagu Parkinson has a very wide syndication.'

The woman with blue hair said, 'Your bill, M. Querry,' and he turned to pay. 'Isn't it worth your while,' Parkinson said, 'to ask me a favour?'

'I don't understand.'

'I've been threatened often in my time. I've had my camera smashed twice. I've spent a night in a police-cell. Three times in a restaurant somebody hit me.' For a moment he sounded like St Paul: 'Three times I was beaten with rods, once I was stoned; I have been shipwrecked three times. . . .' He said, 'The strange thing is that no one has ever appealed to my better nature. It might work. It's probably there, you know, some-where. . . .' It was like a genuine grief.

Querry said gently, 'Perhaps I would, if I cared at all.'

Parkinson said, 'I can't bear that damned indifference of yours. Do you know what he found up there? But you wouldn't ask a journalist for information, would you? There's a towel in your room. I showed it him myself. And a comb with long hair in it.' The misery of being Parkinson for a moment looked out of his wounded eyes. He said, 'I'm disappointed in you, Querry. I'd begun to believe my own story about you.'

'I'm sorry,' Querry said.

'A man's got to believe a bit or contract out altogether.'

Somebody stumbled at the turn of the stairs. It was Rycker coming down. He had a book of some kind in his hand in a pulpy scarlet cover. The fingers on the rail shook as he came, from the remains of fever or from nerves. He stopped and the fat-boy mask of the man in the moon grinned at him from a neighbouring light-bracket. He said, 'Querry.'

'Hello, Rycker, are you feeling better?'

'I can't understand it,' Rycker said. 'You of all men in the world. . . .' He seemed to be searching desperately for clichés, the clichés from the *Marie-Chantal* serials rather than the clichés he was accustomed to from his reading in theology. 'I thought you were my friend, Querry.'

The orange pen was suspiciously busy behind the desk and the blue head was unconvincingly bent. 'I don't know what you are talking about, Rycker,' Querry said. 'You'd better come into the bar. We'll be more alone there.' Parkinson prepared to follow them, but Querry blocked the door. He said, 'No, this isn't a story for the *Post*.'

'I have nothing to hide from Mr Parkinson,' Rycker said in English.

'As you wish.' The heat of the afternoon had driven away even the barman. The paper streamers hung down like old man's beard. Querry said, 'Your wife tried to telephone you at lunch-time, but there was no reply.'

'What do you suppose? I was on the road by six this morning.'

'I'm glad you've come. I shall be able to leave now.'

Rycker said, 'It's no good denying anything, Querry, anything at all. I've been to my wife's room, number six, and you've got the key of number seven in your pocket.'

'You needn't jump to stupid conclusions, Rycker. Even about towels and combs. What if she did wash in my room this morning? As for rooms they were the only ones prepared when we arrived.'

'Why did you take her away without so much as a word . . .?'

'I meant to tell you, but you and I talked about other things.' He looked at Parkinson leaning on the bar. He was watching their mouths closely as though in that way he might come to understand the language they were using.

'She went and left me ill with a high fever. . . .'

'You had your boy. There were things she had to do in town.'

'What things?'

'I think that's for her to tell you, Rycker. A woman can have her secrets.'

'You seem to share them all right. Hasn't a husband got the right . . . ?'

'You are too fond of talking about rights, Rycker. She has her rights too. But I'm not going to stand and argue. . . .'

'Where are you going?'

'To find my boy. I want to start for home. We can do nearly four hours before dark.'

'I've got a lot more to talk to you about.'

'What? The love of God?'

'No,' Rycker said, 'about this.' He held the book open at a page headed with a date. Querry saw that it was a diary with ruled lines and between them the kind of careful script girls learn to write at school. 'Go on,' Rycker said, 'read it.'

'I don't read other people's diaries.'

'Then I'll read it to you. "Spent night with Q".'

Querry smiled. He said, 'It's true—in a way. We sat drinking whisky and I told her a long story.'

'I don't believe a word you're saying.'

'You deserve to be a cuckold, Rycker, but I have never gone in for seducing children.'

'I can imagine what the Courts would say to this.'

'Be careful, Rycker. Don't threaten me. I might change my mind.'

'I could make you pay,' Rycker said, 'pay heavily.'

'I doubt whether any court in the world would take your word against hers and mine. Goodbye, Rycker.'

'You can't walk out of here as though nothing has happened.'

'I would have liked to leave you in suspense, but it wouldn't be fair to her. Nothing has happened, Rycker. I haven't even kissed your wife. She doesn't attract me in that way.'

'What right have you to despise us as you do?'

'Be a sensible man. Put that diary back where you found it and say nothing.'

'"Spent the night with Q" and say nothing?'

Querry turned to Parkinson. 'Give your friend a drink and talk some sense into him. You owe him an article.'

'A duel would make a good story,' Parkinson said wistfully.

'It's lucky for her I'm not a violent man,' Rycker said. 'A good thrashing . . .'

'Is that a part of Christian marriage, too?'

He felt an extraordinary weariness; he had lived a lifetime in the middle of some such scene as this, he had been born to such voices, and if he were not careful, he would die with them in his ears. He walked out on the two of them, paying no attention at all to the near-scream of Rycker, 'I've got a right to demand . . .' In the cabin of the truck sitting beside Deo Gratias he was at peace again. He said, 'You've never been back, have you, into the forest, and I know you'll never take me there. . . . All the same, I wish . . . Is Pendélé very far away?'

Deo Gratias sat with his head down, saying nothing.

'Never mind.'

Outside the cathedral Querry stopped the truck and got out. It would be wiser to warn her. The doors were open for ventilation, and the hideous windows through which the hard light glared in red and blue made the sun more clamorous than outside. The boots of a priest going to the sacristy squealed on the tiled floor, and a mammy chinked her beads. It was not a church for meditation; it was as hot and public as a market-place, and in the side-chapels stood plaster stallholders, offering a baby or a bleeding heart. Marie Rycker was sitting under a statue of Sainte Thérèse of Lisieux. It seemed a less than suitable choice. The two had nothing in common but youth.

He asked her, 'Still praying?'

'Not really. I didn't hear you come.'

'Your husband's at the hotel.'

'Oh,' she said flatly, looking up at the saint who had disappointed her.

'He's been reading a diary you left in your room. You oughtn't to have written what you did—"Spent the night with Q."'

'It was true, wasn't it? Besides I put in an exclamation mark to show.'

'Show what?'

'That is wasn't serious. The nuns never minded if you put an exclamation mark. "Mother Superior in a tearing rage!" They always called it the "exaggeration mark".'

'I don't think your husband knows the convent code.'

'So he really believes . . . ?' she asked and giggled.

'I've tried to persuade him otherwise.'

'It seems such a waste, doesn't it, if he believes that. We might just as well have really done it. Where are you going now?'

'I'm driving home.'

'I'd come with you if you liked. Only I know you don't like.'

He looked up at the plaster face with its simpering and holy smile. 'What would she say?'

'I don't consult her about everything. Only *in extremis*. Though this is pretty *extremis* now, I suppose, isn't it? What with this and that. Have I got to tell him about the baby?'

'It would be better to tell him before he finds out.'

'And I prayed to her so hard for happiness,' she said disdainfully. 'What a hope. Do you believe in prayer at all?'

'No.'

'Did you never?'

'I suppose I believed once. When I believed in giants.'

He looked around the church, at the altar, the tabernacle, the brass candles and the European saints, pale like albinos in the dark continent. He could detect in himself a dim nostalgia for the past, but everyone always felt that, he supposed, in middle age, even for a past of pain, when pain was associated with youth. If there were a place called Pendélé, he thought, I would never bother to find my way back.

'You think I've been wasting my time, don't you, praying?'

'It was better than lying on your bed brooding.'

'You don't believe in prayer at all—or in God?'

'No.' He said gently, 'Of course, I may be wrong.'

'And Rycker does,' she said, calling him by his surname as though he were no longer her husband. 'I wish it wasn't always the wrong people who believed.'

'Surely the nuns . . .'

'Oh, they are professionals. They believe in anything. Even the Holy House of Loretto. They ask us to believe too much and then we believe less and less.' Perhaps she was talking in order to postpone the moment of return. She said, 'Once I got into trouble drawing a picture of the Holy House in full flight with jet-engines. How much did you believe—when you believed?'

'I suppose, like the boy in the story I told you, I persuaded myself to believe almost everything with arguments. You can brainwash yourself into anything you want—even into marriage or a vocation. Then the years pass and the marriage or the vocation fails and it's better to get out. It's the same with belief. People hang on to a marriage for fear of a lonely old age or to a vocation for fear of poverty. It's not a good reason. And it's not a good reason to hang on to the Church for the sake of some mumbo-jumbo when you come to die.'

'And what about the mumbo-jumbo of birth?' she asked. 'If there's a baby inside me now, I'll have to have it christened, won't I? I'm not sure that I'd be happy if it wasn't. Is that dishonest? If only it hadn't *him* for a father.'

'Of course it isn't dishonest. You mustn't think your marriage has failed yet.'

'Oh but it has.'

'I didn't mean with Rycker, I meant . . .' He said sharply, 'For God's sake, don't you start taking me for an example, too.'

CHAPTER 3

I

The rather sweet champagne was the best that Querry had been able to find in Luc, and it had not been improved by the three-day drive in the truck and a breakdown at the first ferry. The nuns provided tinned pea-soup, four lean roast chickens and an ambiguous sweet omelette which they had made with guava jelly: the omelette had sat down half way between their house and the fathers'. But on this day, when the ceremony of raising the roof-tree was over at last, no one felt in a mood to criticise. An awning had been set up outside the dispensary, and at long trestle tables the priests and nuns had provided a feast for the lepers who had worked on the hospital and their families, official and unofficial; beer was there for the men and fizzy fruit drinks and buns for the women and children. The nuns' own celebration had been prepared in strict privacy, but it was rumoured to consist mainly of extra strong coffee and some boxes of *petits fours* that had been kept in reserve since the previous Christmas and had probably turned musty in the interval.

Before the feast there was a service. Father Thomas traipsed round the new hospital, supported by Father Joseph and Father Paul, sprinkling the walls with holy water, and several hymns were sung in the Mongo language. There had been prayers and a sermon from Father Thomas which went on far too long—he had not yet learned enough of the native tongue to make himself properly understood. Some of the younger lepers grew impatient and wandered away, and a child was found by Brother Philippe arrosing the new walls with his own form of water.

Nobody cared that a small dissident group who had nothing to do with the local tribe sang their own hymns apart. Only the doctor, who had once worked in the Lower Congo, recognised them for what they were, trouble-makers from the coast more than a thousand kilometres away. It was unlikely that any of the lepers could understand them, so he let them be. The only sign of their long journey by path and water and road was an unfamiliar stack of bicycles up a side-path into the bush which he had happened to take that morning.

'*E ku Kinshasa ka bazeyi ko:*
E ku Luozi ka bazeyi ko. . . .'
'In Kinshasa they know nothing:
In Luozi they know nothing.'

The proud song of superiority went on: superiority to their own people, to the white man, to the Christian god, to everyone beyond their own circle of six, all of them wearing the peaked caps that advertised Polo beer.

'In the Upper Congo they know nothing:
In heaven they know nothing:
Those who revile the Spirit know nothing:
The Chiefs know nothing:
The whites know nothing.'

Nzambe had never been humiliated as a criminal: he was an exclusive god. Only Deo Gratias moved some way towards them; he squatted on the ground between them and the hospital, and the doctor remembered that as a child he had come west from the Lower Congo too.

'Is that the future?' Querry said. He couldn't understand the words, only the aggressive slant of the Polo-beer caps.

'Yes.'

'Do you fear it?'

'Of course. But I don't want my own liberty at the expense of anyone else's.'

'They do.'

'We taught them.'

What with one delay and another it was nearly sunset before the tree was raised on to the roof and the feast began. By that time the awning outside the dispensary was no longer needed to shelter the workmen from the heat, but judging from the black clouds massing beyond the river, Father Joseph decided that it might yet serve to protect them from the rain.

Father Thomas's decision to raise the roof-tree had not been made without argument. Father Joseph wished to wait a month in the hope that the Superior would return, and Father Paul had at first supported him, but when Doctor Colin agreed with Father Thomas they had withdrawn their opposition. 'Let Father Thomas have his feast and his hymns,' the doctor said to them. 'I want the hospital.'

Doctor Colin and Querry left the group from the east and turned back to the last of the ceremony. 'We were right, but all the same,' the doctor said, 'I wish the Superior were here. He would have enjoyed the show and at least he would have talked to these people in a language they can understand.'

'More briefly too,' Querry said. The hollow African voices rose around them in another hymn.

'And yet you stay and watch,' the doctor said.

'Oh yes, I stay.'

'I wonder why.'

'Ancestral voices. Memories. Did you ever lie awake when you were a child listening to them talking down below? You couldn't understand what they were saying, but it was a noise that somehow comforted. So it is now with me. I am happy listening, saying nothing. The house is not on fire, there's no burglar lurking in the next room: I don't want to understand or believe. I would have to think if I believed. I don't want to think any more. I can build you all the rabbit-hutches you need without thought.'

Afterwards at the mission there was a great deal of raillery over the champagne. Father Paul was caught pouring himself a glass out of turn; somebody–Brother Philippe seemed an unlikely culprit–filled an empty bottle with soda-water, and the bottle had circulated half around the table before anyone noticed. Querry remembered an occasion months ago: a night at a seminary on the river when the priests cheated over their cards. He had walked out into the bush unable to bear their laughter and their infantility. How was it that he could sit here now and smile with them? He even found himself resenting the strict face of Father Thomas who sat at the end of the table unamused.

The doctor proposed the toast of Father Joseph and Father Joseph proposed the toast of the doctor. Father Paul proposed the toast of Brother Philippe, and Brother Philippe lapsed into confusion and silence. Father Jean proposed the toast of Father Thomas who did not respond. The champagne had almost reached an end, but someone disinterred from the back of the cupboard a half-finished bottle of Sandeman's port and they drank it out of liqueur glasses to make it go further. 'After all the English drink port at the end of a meal,' Father Jean said. 'An extraordinary custom, Protestant perhaps, but nevertheless . . .'

'Are you sure there's nothing against it in moral theology?' Father Paul asked.

'Only in canon law. *Lex contra Sandemanium*, but even that, of course, was interpreted by that eminent Benedictine, Dom. . . .'

'Father Thomas, won't you have a glass of port?'

'No thank you, father. I have drunk enough.'

The darkness outside the open door suddenly drew back and for a moment they could see the palm trees bending in a strange yellow light the colour of old photographs. Then everything went dark again, and the wind blew in, rustling the pages of Father Jean's film magazines. Querry got up to close it against the coming storm, but on a second thought he stepped outside and shut it behind him. The northern sky lightened again, in a long band above the river. From where the lepers were celebrating came the sound of drums and the thunder answered like the reply of a relieving force. Somebody moved on the verandah. When the lightning flashed he saw that it was Deo Gratias.

'Why aren't you at the feast, Deo Gratias?' Then he remembered that the feast was only for the non-mutilated, for the masons and carpenters and bricklayers. He said, 'Well, they've done a good job on the hospital.' The man made no reply. Querry said, 'You aren't planning to run away again, are you?' and he lit a cigarette and put it between the man's lips.

'No,' Deo Gratias said.

In the darkness Querry felt himself prodded by the man's stump. He said, 'What's troubling you, Deo Gratias?'

'You will go,' Deo Gratias said, 'now that the hospital house is built.'

'Oh no, I won't. This is where I'm going to end my days. I can't go back where I came from, Deo Gratias. I don't belong there any more.'

'Have you killed a man?'

'I have killed everything.' The thunder came nearer, and then the rain: first it was like skirmishers rustling furtively among the palm-tree fans, creeping through the grass; then it was the confident tread of a great watery host beating a way from across the river to sweep up the verandah steps. The drums of the lepers were extinguished; even the thunder could be heard only faintly behind the great charge of rain.

Deo Gratias hobbled closer. 'I want to go with you,' he said.

'I tell you I'm staying here. Why won't you believe me? For the rest of my life. I shall be buried here.'

Perhaps he had not made himself heard through the rain, for Deo Gratias repeated, 'I will go with you.' Somewhere a telephone began to ring—a trivial human sound persisting like an infant's cry through the rain.

2

After Querry had left the room Father Thomas said, 'We seem to have toasted everyone except the man to whom we owe most.'

Father Joseph said, 'He knows well enough how grateful we are. Those toasts were not very seriously meant, Father Thomas.'

'I think I ought to express the gratitude of the community, formally, when he comes back.'

'You'll only embarrass him,' Doctor Colin said. 'All he wants of any of us is to be left alone.' The rain pounded on the roof; Brother Philippe began to light candles on the dresser in case the electric current failed.

'It was a happy day for all of us when he arrived here,' Father Thomas said. 'Who could have foreseen it? The great Querry.'

'An even happier day for him,' the doctor replied. 'It's much more difficult to cure the mind than the body, and yet I think the cure is nearly complete.'

'The better the man the worse the aridity,' Father Thomas said.

Father Joseph looked guiltily at his champagne and then at his companions; Father Thomas made them all feel as though they were drinking in church. 'A man with little faith doesn't feel the temporary loss of it.' His sentiments were impeccable. Father Paul winked at Father Jean.

'Surely,' the doctor said, 'you assume too much. His case may be much simpler than that. A man can believe for half his life on insufficient reason, and then he discovers his mistake.'

'You talk, doctor, like all atheists, as though there were no such thing as grace. Belief without grace is unthinkable, and God will never rob a man of grace. Only a man himself can do that—by his own actions. We have seen Querry's actions here, and they speak for themselves.'

'I hope you won't be disappointed,' the doctor said. 'In our treatment we get burnt-out cases, too. But we don't say they are suffering from aridity. We only say the disease has run its course.'

'You are a very good doctor, but all the same I think we are better judges of a man's spiritual condition.'

'I dare say you are–if such a thing exists.'

'You can detect a patch on the skin where we see nothing at all. You must allow us to have a nose for–well . . .' Father Thomas hesitated and then said '. . . heroic virtue.' Their voices were raised a little against the storm. The telephone began to ring.

Doctor Colin said, 'That's probably the hospital. I'm expecting a death tonight.' He went to the sideboard where the telephone stood and lifted the receiver. He said, 'Who is it? Is that Sister Clare?' He said to Father Thomas, 'It must be one of your sisters. Will you take it? I can't hear what she is saying.'

'Perhaps they have got at our champagne,' Father Joseph said.

Doctor Colin surrendered the receiver to Father Thomas and came back to the table. 'She sounded agitated, whoever she was,' he said.

'Please speak more slowly,' Father Thomas said. 'Who is it? Sister Hélène? I can't hear you–the storm is too loud. Say that again. I don't understand.'

'It's lucky for us all,' Father Joseph said, 'that the sisters don't have a feast every day of the week.'

Father Thomas turned furiously from the telephone. He said, 'Be quiet, father. I can't hear if you talk. This is no joke. A terrible thing seems to have happened.'

'Is somebody ill?' the doctor asked.

'Tell Mother Agnes,' Father Thomas said, 'that I'll be over as soon as I can. I had better find him and bring him with me.' He put the receiver down and stood bent like a question-mark over the telephone.

'What is it, father?' the doctor said. 'Can I be of use?'

'Does anyone know where Querry's gone?'

'He went outside a few minutes ago.'

'How I wish the Superior were here.' They looked at Father Thomas with astonishment. He could not have given a more extreme signal of distress.

'You had better tell us what it's all about,' Father Paul said.

Father Thomas said, 'I envy you your skin-test, doctor. You were right to warn me against disappointment. The Superior too. He said much the same thing as you. I have trusted too much to appearances.'

'Has Querry done something?'

'God forbid one should condemn any man without hearing all the facts. . . .'

The door opened and Querry entered. The rain splashed in behind him and he had to struggle with the door. He said, 'The gauge outside shows nearly half a centimetre already.'

Nobody spoke. Father Thomas came a little way towards him.

'M. Querry, is it true that when you went into Luc you went with Mme. Rycker?'

'I drove her in. Yes.'

'Using *our* truck?'

'Of course.'

'While her husband was sick?'

'Yes.'

'What is this all about?' Father Joseph asked.

'Ask M. Querry,' Father Thomas replied.

'Ask me what?'

Father Thomas drew on his rubber-boots and fetched his umbrella from the coat-rack.

'What am I supposed to have done?' Querry said and he looked first to Father Joseph and then to Father Paul. Father Paul made a gesture with his hand of noncomprehension.

'You had better tell us what is going on, father,' Doctor Colin said.

'I must ask you to come with me, M. Querry. We will discuss what has to be done next with the sisters. I had hoped against hope that there was some mistake. I even wish you had tried to lie. It would have been less brazen. I don't want you found here by Rycker if he should arrive.'

'What would Rycker want here?' Father Jean said.

'He might be expected to want his wife, mightn't he? She's with the sisters now. She arrived half an hour ago. After three days by herself on the road. She is with child,' Father Thomas said. The telephone began to ring again. 'Your child.'

Querry said, 'That's nonsense. She can't have told anyone that.'

'Poor girl. I suppose she hadn't the nerve to tell him to his face. She came from Luc to find you.'

The telephone rang again.

'It seems to be my turn to answer it,' Father Joseph said, approaching the telephone with trepidation.

'We gave you a warm welcome here, didn't we? We asked you no questions. We didn't pry into your past. And in return you present us with this—scandal. Weren't there enough women for you in Europe?' Father Thomas said. 'Did you have to make our little community here a base for your operations?' Suddenly he was again the nervy and despairing priest who couldn't sleep and was afraid of the dark. He began to weep, clinging to his umbrella as an African might cling to a totem-pole. He looked as though he had been left out all night like a scarecrow.

'Hullo, hullo,' Father Joseph called into the telephone. 'In the name of all the known saints, can't you speak up, whoever you are?'

'I'll go and see her with you right away,' Querry said.

'It's your right,' Father Thomas said. 'She's in no condition to argue, though. She's had nothing but a packet of chocolate to eat the last three days. She hadn't even a boy with her when she arrived. If only the Superior . . . Mme. Rycker of all people. Such kindness to the mission. For God's sake, what is it now, Father Joseph?'

'It's only the hospital,' Father Joseph said with relief. He gave the receiver to Doctor Colin. 'It is the death I was expecting,' the doctor said. 'Thank goodness something tonight seems to be following a normal course.'

3

Father Thomas walked silently ahead below his great umbrella. The rain had stopped for a while, but the aftermath dripped from the ribs. Father Thomas was only visible at intervals when the lightning flared. He had no torch, but he knew the path by heart in the dark. Many omelettes and soufflés had come to grief along this track. The nuns' white house was suddenly close to them in a simultaneous flash and roar—the lightning had struck a tree somewhere close by and all the lights of the mission fused at once.

One of the sisters met them at the door carrying a candle. She looked at Querry over Father Thomas's shoulder as though he were the devil himself—with fear, distaste and curiosity. She said, 'Mother's sitting with Mme. Rycker.'

'We'll go in,' Father Thomas said gloomily.

She led them to a white painted room, where Marie Rycker lay in a white painted bed under a crucifix, with a night-light burning beside her. Mother Agnes sat by the bed with a hand touching Marie Rycker's cheek. Querry had the impression of a daughter who had come safely home, after a long visit to a foreign land.

Father Thomas said in an altar-whisper, 'How is she?'

'She's taken no harm,' Mother Agnes said, 'not in the body, that is.'

Marie Rycker turned in the bed and looked up at them. Her eyes had the transparent honesty of a child who has prepared a cast-iron lie. She smiled at Querry and said, 'I am sorry. I had to come. I was scared.'

Mother Agnes withdrew her hand and watched Querry closely as though she feared a violent act against her charge.

Querry said gently, 'You mustn't be frightened. It was the long journey which scared you—that's all. Now you are safe among friends you will explain, won't you. . . .' He hesitated.

'Oh yes,' she whispered, 'everything.'

'They haven't understood what you told them. About our visit to Luc together. And the baby. There's going to be a baby?'

'Yes.'

'Just tell them whose baby it is.'

'I have told them,' she said. 'It's yours. Mine, too, of course,' she added, as though by adding that qualification she were making everything quite clear and beyond blame.

Father Thomas said, 'You see.'

'Why are you telling them that? You know it's not true. We have never been in each other's company except in Luc.'

'That first time,' she said, 'when my husband brought you to the house.'

It would have been easier if he had felt anger, but he felt none: to lie is as natural at a certain age as to play with fire. He said, 'You know what you are saying is all nonsense. I'm certain you don't want to do me any harm.'

'Oh no,' she said, 'never. *Je t'aime, chéri. Je suis toute à toi.*'

Mother Agnes wrinkled her nose with distaste.

'That's why I've come to you,' Marie Rycker said.

'She ought to rest now,' Mother Agnes said. 'All this can be discusssed in the morning.'

'You must let me talk to her alone.'

'Certainly not,' Mother Agnes said. 'That would not be right. Father Thomas, you won't permit him. . . .'

'My good woman, do you think I'm going to beat her? You can come to her rescue at her first scream.'

Father Thomas said, 'We can hardly say no if Mme. Rycker wishes it.'

'Of course I wish it,' she said. 'I came here only for that.' She put her hand on Querry's sleeve. Her smile of sad and fallen trust was worthy of Bernhardt's Marguerite Gauthier on her death bed.

When they were alone she gave a happy sigh. 'That's that.'

'Why have you told them these lies?'

'They aren't all lies,' she said. 'I do love you.'

'Since when?'

'Since I spent a night with you.'

'You know very well that was nothing at all. We drank some whisky. I told you a story to send you to sleep.'

'Yes. That was when I fell in love. No, it wasn't. I'm afraid I'm lying again' she said with unconvincing humility. 'It was when you came to the house the first time. *Un coup de foudre.*'

'The night you told them we slept together?'

'That was really a lie too. The night I slept with you properly was after the Governor's party.'

'What on earth are you talking about now?'

'I didn't want him. The only way I could manage was to shut my eyes and think it was you.'

'I suppose I ought to thank you,' Querry said, 'for the compliment.'

'It was then that the baby must have started. So you see it wasn't a lie that I told.'

'Not a lie?'

'Only half a lie. If I hadn't thought all the time of you, I'd have been all dried up and babies don't come so easily then, do they? So in a way it is your child.'

He looked at her with a kind of respect. It would have needed a theologian to appreciate properly the tortuous logic of her argument, to separate good from bad faith, and only recently he had thought of her as someone too simple and young to be a danger. She smiled up at him winningly, as though she hoped to entice him into yet another of his stories to postpone the hour of bed. He said, 'You'd better tell me exactly what happened when you saw your husband in Luc.'

She said, 'It was ghastly. Really ghastly. I thought once he was going to kill me. He wouldn't believe about the diary. He went on and on all that night until I was tired out and I said, "All right. Have it your own way then. I did sleep with him. Here and there and everywhere." Then he hit me. He would have hit me again, I think, if M. Parkinson hadn't interfered.'

'Was Parkinson there too, then?'

'He heard me cry and came along.'

'To take some photographs, I suppose.'

'I don't think he took any photographs.'

'And then what happened?'

'Well, of course, he found out about things in general. You see, he wanted to go home right away, and I said no, I had to stay in Luc until I knew. "Know?" he said. And then it all came out. I went and saw the doctor in the morning and when I knew the worst I just took off without going back to the hotel.'

'Rycker thinks the baby is mine?'

'I tried very hard to convince him it was his—because of course, you could say in a way that it was.' She stretched herself down in the bed with a sigh of comfort and said, 'Goodness, I'm glad to be here. It was really scary driving all the way alone. I didn't wait in the house to get any food and I forgot a bed and I just slept in the car.'

'In his car?'

'Yes. But I expect M. Parkinson will have given him a lift home.'

'Is it any use asking you to tell Father Thomas the truth?'

'Well, I've rather burned my boats, haven't I?'

'You've burned the only home I have,' Querry said.

'I just had to escape,' she explained apologetically. For the first time he was confronted by an egoism as absolute as his own. The other Marie had been properly avenged: as for *toute à toi* the laugh was on her side now.

'What do you expect me to do?' Querry said. 'Love you in return?'

'It would be nice if you could, but you can't, they'll have to send me home, won't they?'

He went to the door and opened it. Mother Agnes was lurking at the end of the passage. He said, 'I've done all I can.'

'I suppose you've tried to persuade the poor girl to protect you.'

'Oh, she admits the lie to me, of course, but I have no tape-recorder. What a pity the Church doesn't approve of hidden microphones.'

'May I ask you, M. Querry, from now on to stay away from our house?'

'You don't need to ask me that. Be very careful yourselves of that little packet of dynamite in there.'

'She's a poor innocent young . . .'

'Oh, innocent . . . I daresay you are right. God preserve us from all innocence. At least the guilty know what they are about.'

The electric fuses had not yet been repaired, and only the feel of the path under his feet guided him towards the mission buildings. The rain had passed to the south, but the lightning flapped occasionally above the forest and the river. Before he reached the mission he had to pass the doctor's house. An oil lamp burned behind the window and the doctor stood beside it, peering out. Querry knocked on the door.

Colin asked, 'What has happened?'

'She'll stick to her lies. They are her only way of escape.'

'Escape?'

'From Rycker and Africa.'

'Father Thomas is talking to the others now. It was no concern of mine, so I came home.'

'They want me to go away, I suppose?'

'I wish to God the Superior were here. Father Thomas is not exactly a well-balanced man.'

Querry sat down at the table. The Atlas of Leprosy was open at a gaudy page of swirling colour. He said, 'What's this?'

'We call these "the fish swimming upstream". The bacilli—those coloured spots there—are swarming along the nerves.'

'I thought I had come far enough,' Querry said, 'when I reached this place.'

'It may blow over. Let them talk. You and I have more important things to do. Now that the hospital's finished we can get down to the mobile units and the new lavatories I talked to you about.'

'We are not dealing with your sick people, doctor, and your coloured fish. They are predictable. These are normal people, healthy people with unforeseeable reactions. It looks as though I shall get no nearer to Pendélé than Deo Gratias did.'

'Father Thomas has no authority over me. You can stay in my house from now on if you don't mind sleeping in the workroom.'

'Oh no. You can't risk quarrelling with them. You are too important to this place. I shall have to go away.'

'Where will you go to?'

'I don't know. It's strange, isn't it, how worried I was when I came here, because I thought I had become incapable of feeling pain. I suppose a priest I met on the river was right. He said one only had to wait. You said the same to me too.'

'I'm sorry.'

'I don't know that I am. You said once that when one suffers, one begins to feel part of the human condition, on the side of the Christian myth, do you remember? "I suffer, therefore I am." I wrote something like that once in my diary, but I can't remember what or when, and the word wasn't "suffer".'

'When a man is cured,' the doctor said, 'we can't afford to waste him.'

'Cured?'

'No further skin-tests are required in your case.'

4

Father Joseph absent-mindedly wiped a knife with the skirt of his soutane; he said, 'We mustn't forget that it's only her word against his.'

'Why should she invent such a shocking story like that?' Father Thomas asked. 'In any case the baby is presumably real enough.'

'Querry has been of great use to us here,' Father Paul said. 'We've reason to be grateful . . .'

'Grateful? Can you really think that, father, after he's made us a laughing stock? The Hermit of the Congo. The Saint with a Past. All those stories the papers printed. What will they print now?'

'You were more pleased with the stories than he was,' Father Jean said.

'Of course I was pleased. I believed in him. I thought his motives for coming here were good. I even defended him to the Superior when he warned me. . . . But I hadn't realised then what his true motives were.'

'If you know them tell us what they were,' Father Jean said. He spoke in the dry precise tones that he was accustomed to use in discussions on moral theology so as to rob of emotion any question dealing with sexual sin.

'I can only suppose he was flying from some woman-trouble in Europe.'

'Woman-trouble is not a very exact description, and aren't we all supposed to run away from it? St Augustine's wish to wait awhile is not universally recommended.'

'Querry is a very good builder,' Father Joseph said obstinately.

'What do you propose then, that he should stay here in the mission, living in sin with Mme. Rycker?'

'Of course not,' Father Jean said. 'Mme. Rycker must leave tomorrow. From what you have told us he has no wish to go with her.'

'The matter will not end there,' Father Thomas said. 'Rycker will want a separation. He may even sue Querry for divorce, and the newspapers will print the whole edifying story. They are interested enough as it is in Querry. Do you suppose the General will be pleased when he reads at his breakfast-table the scandal at our leproserie?'

'The roof-tree is safely up,' Father Joseph said, rubbing away at his knife, 'but a great deal still remains to be done.'

'There is no possible harm in simply waiting,' Father Paul said. 'The girl may be lying. Rycker may take no action. The newspapers may print nothing (it's not the picture of Querry they wanted to give the world). The story may not even reach the General's ears—or eyes.'

'Do you suppose the Bishop won't hear of it? It will be all over Luc by this time. In the absence of the Superior I am responsible . . .'

Brother Philippe spoke for the first time. 'There's a man outside,' he said. 'Had I better unlock the door?'

It was Parkinson, sodden and speechless. He had been walking very fast. He ran his hand back and forth over his heart as though he were trying to soothe an animal that he carried like a Spartan under his shirt.

'Give him a chair,' Father Thomas said.

'Where's Querry?' Parkinson asked.

'I don't know. In his room perhaps.'

'Rycker's looking for him. He went to the sisters' house, but Querry had gone.'

'How did he know where to look?'

'She had left a note for Rycker at home. We would have caught her up, but we had car-trouble at the last ferry.'

'Where's Rycker now?'

'God knows. It's so pitch-dark out there. He may have walked into the river for all I know.'

'Did he see his wife?'

'No—an old nun pushed us both out and locked the door. That made him madder than ever, I can tell you. We haven't had six hours sleep since Luc, and that was more than three days ago.'

He rocked backwards and forwards in the chair. 'Oh that this too too solid flesh. Quote. Shakespeare. I've got a weak heart,' he explained to Father Thomas who was finding it difficult with his inadequate English to follow the drift of Parkinson's thoughts. The others watched closely and understood little. The situation seemed to all of them to have got hopelessly out of control.

'Please give me a drink,' Parkinson said. Father Thomas found that there was a little champagne left at the bottom of one of the many bottles which still littered the table among the carcasses of the chickens and the remains of the mutilated uneaten soufflé.

'Champagne?' Parkinson exclaimed. 'I'd rather have had a spot of gin.' He looked at the glasses and the bottles: one glass still held an inch of port. He said, 'You do yourselves pretty well here.'

'It was a very special day,' Father Thomas said with some embarrassment, seeing the table for a moment with the eyes of a stranger.

'A special day—I should think it has been. I never thought we'd make the ferry, and now with this storm I suppose we may be stuck here. How I wish I'd never come to this damned dark continent. Quoth the raven never more. Quote. Somebody.'

Outside a voice shouted unintelligibly.

'That's him,' Parkinson said, 'roaming around. He's fighting mad. I said to him I thought Christians were supposed to forgive, but it's no use talking to him now.'

The voice came nearer. 'Querry,' they heard it cry, 'Querry. Where are you, Querry?'

'What a damned fuss about nothing. And I wouldn't be surprised if there had been no hanky-panky after all. I told him that. "They talked most of the night," I said, "I heard them. Lovers don't talk like that. There are intervals of silence."'

'Querry. Where are you, Querry?'

'I think he *wants* to believe the worst. It makes him Querry's equal, don't you see, when they fight over the same girl.' He added with a somewhat surprising insight, 'He can't bear not being important.'

The door opened yet again and a tousled, rain-soaked Rycker stood in the doorway; he looked from one father to another as though among them he expected to find Querry, perhaps in the disguise of a priest.

'M. Rycker,' Father Thomas began.

'Where's Querry?'

'Please come in and sit down and talk things . . .'

'How can I sit?' Rycker said. 'I am a man in agony.' He sat down, nonetheless, on the wrong chair—the weak back splintered. 'I'm suffering from a terrible shock, father. I opened my soul to that man, I told him my inmost thoughts, and this is my reward.'

'Let us talk quietly and sensibly. . . .'

'He laughed at me and despised me,' Rycker said. 'What right had he to despise me? We are all equal in the sight of God. Even a poor plantation manager and *the* Querry. Breaking up a Christian marriage.' He smelt very strongly of whisky. He said, 'I'll be retiring in a couple of years. Does he think I'm going to keep his bastard on my pension?'

'You've been on the road for three days, Rycker. You need a night's sleep. Afterwards . . .'

'She never wanted to sleep with me. She always made her excuses, but then the first time he comes along, just because he's famous . . .'

Father Thomas said, 'We all want to avoid scandal.'

'Where's the doctor?' Rycker asked sharply. 'They were as thick as thieves.'

'He's at home. He has nothing to do with this.'

Rycker made for the door. He stood there for a moment as though he were on a stage and had forgotten his exit line. 'There isn't a jury that would convict me,' he said and went out again into the dark and rain. For a moment nobody spoke and then Father Joseph asked them all, 'What did he mean by that?'

'We shall laugh at this in the morning,' Father Jean said.

'I don't see the humour of the situation,' Father Thomas replied.

'What I mean is it's a little like one of those Palais Royal farces that one has read. . . . The injured husband pops in and out.'

'I don't read Palais Royal farces, father.'

'Sometimes I think God was not entirely serious when he gave man the sexual instinct.'

'If that is one of the doctrines you teach in moral theology . . .'

'Nor when he invented moral theology. After all, it was St Thomas Aquinas who said that he made the world in play.'

Brother Philippe said, 'Excuse me . . .'

'You are lucky not to have my responsibility, Father Jean. I can't treat the affair as a Palais Royal farce whatever St Thomas may have written. Where are you going, Brother Philippe?'

'He said something about a jury, father, and it occurred to me that, well, perhaps he's carrying a gun. I think I ought to warn . . .'

'This is too much,' Father Thomas said. He turned to Parkinson and asked him in English, 'Has he a gun with him?'

'I'm sure I don't know. A lot of people are carrying them nowadays, aren't they? But he wouldn't have the nerve to use it. I told you, he only wants to seem important.'

'I think, if you will excuse me, father, I had better go over to Doctor Colin's,' Brother Philippe said.

'Be careful, brother,' Father Paul said.

'Oh, I know a great deal about firearms,' Brother Philippe replied.

5

'Was that someone shouting?' Doctor Colin asked.

'I heard nothing.' Querry went to the window and looked into the dark. He said, 'I wish Brother Philippe would get the lights back. It's time I went home, and I haven't a torch.'

'They won't start the current now. It's gone ten o'clock.'

'They'll want me to go as soon as I can, won't they? But the boat's unlikely to be here for at least a week. Perhaps someone can drive me out. . . .'

'I doubt if the road will be passable now after the rain, and there's more to come.'

'Then we have a few days, haven't we, for talking about those mobile units you dream of. But I'm no engineer, doctor. Brother Philippe will be able to help you more than I could ever do.'

'This is a make-shift life we lead here,' Doctor Colin said. 'All I want is a kind of pre-fab on wheels. Something we can fit on to the chassis of a half-ton truck. What did I do with that sheet of paper? There's an idea I wanted to show you. . . .' The doctor opened the drawer in his desk. Inside was the photograph of a woman. She lay there in wait, unseen by strangers, gathering no dust, always present when the drawer opened.

'I shall miss this room–wherever I am. You've never told me about your wife, doctor. How she came to die.'

'It was sleeping-sickness. She used to spend a lot of time out in the bush in the early days trying to persuade the lepers to come in for treatment. We didn't have such effective drugs for sleeping-sickness as we have now. People die too soon.'

'It was my hope to end up in the same patch of ground as you and she. We would have made an atheist corner between us.'

'I wonder if you would have qualified for that.'

'Why not?'

'You're too troubled by your lack of faith, Querry. You keep on fingering it like a sore you want to get rid of. I am content with the myth; you are not–you have to believe or disbelieve.'

Querry said, 'Somebody is calling out there. I thought for a moment it was my name. . . . But one always seems to hear one's own name, whatever anyone really calls. It only needs a syllable to be the same. We are such egoists.'

'You must have had a lot of belief once to miss it the way you do.'

'I swallowed their myth whole, if you call that a belief. This is my body and this is my blood. Now when I read that passage it seems so obviously symbolic, but how can you expect a lot of poor fishermen to recognise symbols? Only in moments of superstition I remember that I gave up the sacrament before I gave up the belief and the priests would say there was a connection. Rejecting grace Rycker would say. Oh well, I suppose belief is a kind of vocation and most men haven't room in their brains or hearts for two vocations. If we really believe in something we have no choice, have we, but to go further. Otherwise life slowly whittles the belief away. My architecture stood still. One can't be a half-believer or a half-architect.'

'Are you saying that you've ceased to be even a half?'

'Perhaps I hadn't a strong enough vocation in either, and the kind of life I lived killed them both. It needs a very strong vocation to withstand success. The popular priest and the popular architect–their talents can be killed easily by disgust.'

'Disgust?'

'Disgust of praise. How it nauseates, doctor, by its stupidity. The very people who ruined my churches were loudest afterwards in their praise of what I'd built. The books they have written about my work, the pious motives they've attributed to me–they were enough to sicken me of the drawing-board. It needed more faith than I possessed to withstand all that. The praise of priests and pious people–the Ryckers of the world.'

'Most men seem to put up with success comfortably enough. But you came here.'

'I think I'm cured of pretty well everything, even disgust. I've been happy here.'

'Yes, you were learning to use your fingers pretty well, in spite of the mutilation. Only one sore seems to remain, and you rub it all the time.'

'You are wrong, doctor. Sometimes you talk like Father Thomas.'

'Querry,' a voice unmistakably called. 'Querry.'

'Rycker,' Querry said. 'He must have followed his wife here. I hope to God the sisters didn't let him in to see her. I'd better go and talk . . .'

'Let him cool off first.'

'I've got to make him see reason.'

'Then wait till morning. You can't see reason at night.'

'Querry. Querry. Where are you, Querry?'

'What a grotesque situation it is,' Querry said. 'That this should happen to me. The innocent adulterer. That's not a bad title for a comedy.' His mouth moved in the effort of a smile. 'Lend me the lamp.'

'You'd do much better to keep out of it, Querry.'

'I must do something. He's making so much noise. . . . It will only add to what Father Thomas calls the scandal.'

The doctor reluctantly followed him out. The storm had come full circle and was beating up towards them again, from across the river. 'Rycker,' Querry called, holding the lamp up, 'I'm here.' Somebody came running towards them, but when he reached the area of light, they saw that it was Brother Philippe. 'Please go back into the house,' Brother Philippe said, 'and shut the door. We think that Rycker may be carrying a gun.'

'He wouldn't be mad enough to use it,' Querry said.

'All the same . . . to avoid unpleasantness . . .'

'Unpleasantness . . . you have a wonderful capacity, Brother Philippe, for understatement.'

'I don't know what you mean.'

'Never mind. I'll take your advice and hide under Doctor Colin's bed.'

He had walked a few steps back when Rycker's voice said, 'Stop. Stop where you are.' The man came unsteadily out of the dark. He said in a tone of trivial complaint, 'I've been looking everywhere for you.'

'Well, here I am.'

All three looked where Rycker's right hand was hidden in his pocket.

'I've got to talk to you, Querry.'

'Then talk, and when you've finished, I'd like a word too with you.' Silence followed. A dog barked somewhere in the leproserie. Lightning lit them all like a flash-bulb.

'I'm waiting, Rycker.'

'You–you renegade.'

'Are we here for a religious argument? I'll admit you know much more than I do about the love of God.'

Rycker's reply was partly buried under the heavy fall of the thunder. The last sentence stuck out like a pair of legs from beneath the rubble.

'. . . persuade me what she wrote meant nothing, and all the time you must have known there was a child coming.'

'Your child. Not mine.'

'Prove it. You'd better prove it.'

'It's difficult to prove a negative, Rycker. Of course, the doctor can make a test of my blood, but you'll have to wait six months for the . . .'

'How dare you laugh at me?'

'I'm not laughing at you, Rycker. Your wife has done us both an injury. I'd call her a liar if I thought she even knew what a lie was. She thinks the truth is anything that will protect her or send her home to her nursery.'

'You sleep with her and then you insult her. You're a coward, Querry.'

'Perhaps I am.'

'Perhaps. Perhaps. Nothing that I can say would ever anger *the* Querry, would it? He's so infernally important, how could he care what the mere manager of a palm-oil factory – I've got an immortal soul as much as you, Querry.'

'I don't make any claims to one. You can be God's important man, Rycker, for all I care. I'm not *the* Querry to anyone but you. Certainly not to myself.'

'Please come to the mission, M. Rycker,' Brother Philippe pleaded. 'We'll put up a bed for you there. We shall all of us feel better after a night's sleep. And a cold shower in the morning,' he added, and as though to illustrate his words, a waterfall of rain suddenly descended on them. Querry made an odd awkward sound which the doctor by now had learned to interpret as a laugh, and Rycker fired twice. The lamp fell with Querry and smashed; the burning wick flared up once under the deluge of rain, lighting an open mouth and a pair of surprised eyes, and then went out.

The doctor plumped down on his knees in the mud and felt for Querry's body. Rycker's voice said, 'He laughed at me. How dare he laugh at me?' The doctor said to Brother Philippe, 'I have his head. Can you find his legs? We've got to get him inside.' He called to Rycker, 'Put down that gun, you fool, and help!'

'Not at Rycker,' Querry said. The doctor leant down closer: he could hardly hear him. He said, 'Don't speak. We are going to lift you now. You'll be all right.'

Querry said, 'Laughing at myself.'

They carried him on to the verandah and laid him down out of the rain. Rycker fetched a cushion for his head. He said, 'He shouldn't have laughed.'

'He doesn't laugh easily,' the doctor said, and again there was a noise that resembled a distorted laugh.

'Absurd,' Querry said, 'this is absurd or else . . .' but what alternative, philosophical or psychological, he had in mind they never knew.

6

The Superior had returned a few days after the funeral, and he visited the cemetery with Doctor Colin. They had buried Querry not far from Mme. Colin's grave, but with enough space left for the doctor in due course. Under the special circumstances Father Thomas had given way in the matter of the cross—only a piece of hard wood from the forest was stuck up there, carved with Querry's name and dates. Nor had there been a Catholic ceremony, though Father Joseph had said unofficially a prayer at the grave. Someone—it was probably Deo Gratias—had put an old jam-pot beside the mound filled with twigs and plants curiously twined. It looked more like an offering to Nzambe than a funeral wreath. Father Thomas would have thrown it away, but Father Joseph dissuaded him.

'It's a very ambiguous offering,' Father Thomas protested, 'for a Christian cemetery.'

'He was an ambiguous man,' Father Joseph replied.

Parkinson had procured in Luc a formal wreath which was labelled 'From three million readers of the *Post*. Nature I loved and next to Nature Art. Robert Browning.' He had photographed it for future use, but with unexpected modesty he refused to be taken beside it.

The Superior said to Colin, 'I can't help regretting that I wasn't here. I might have been able to control Rycker.'

'Something was bound to happen sooner or later,' Colin said. 'They would never have let him alone.'

'Who do you mean by "they"?'

'The fools, the interfering fools, they exist everywhere, don't they? He had been cured of all his success; but you can't cure success, any more than I can give my *mutilés* back their fingers and toes. I return them to the town, and people look at them in the stores and watch them in the street and draw the attention of others to them as they pass. Succcess is like that too—a mutilation of the natural man. Are you coming my way?'

'Where are you going?'

'To the dispensary. Surely we've wasted enough time on the dead.'

'I'll come a little way with you,' The Superior felt in the pocket of his soutane for a cheroot, but there wasn't one there.

'Did you see Rycker before you left Luc?' Colin asked.

'Of course. They've made him quite comfortable at the prison. He has been to confession and he intends to go to communion every morning. He's working very hard at Garrigou-Lagrange. And of course he's quite a hero in Luc. M. Parkinson has already telegraphed an interview with him and the metropolitan journalists will soon begin to pour in. I believe M. Parkinson's article was headed "Death of a Hermit. The Saint who Failed." Of course, the result of the trial is a foregone conclusion.'

'Acquittal?'

'Naturally. *Le crime passionnel*. Everybody will have got what they wanted—it's really quite a happy ending, isn't it? Rycker feels he has become important both to God and man. He even spoke to me about the possibility of the Belgian College at Rome and an annulment. I didn't encourage him. Mme. Rycker will soon be free to go home and she will keep the child. M. Parkinson has a much better story than he had ever hoped to find. I'm glad, by the way, that Querry never read his second article.'

'You can hardly say it was a happy ending for Querry.'

'Wasn't it? Surely he always wanted to go a bit further.' The Superior added shyly, 'Do you think there was anything between him and Mme. Rycker?'

'No.'

'I wondered. Judging from Parkinson's second article he would seem to have been a man with a great capacity—well—for what they call love.'

'I'm not so sure of that. Nor was he. He told me once that all his life he had only made use of women, but I think he saw himself always in the hardest possible light. I even wondered sometimes whether he suffered from a kind of frigidity. Like a woman who changes partners constantly in the hope that one day she will experience the true orgasm. He said that he always went through the motions of love efficiently, even towards God in the days when he believed, but then he found that the love wasn't really there for anything except his work, so in the end he gave up the motions. And afterwards, when he couldn't even pretend that what he felt was love, the motives for work failed him. That was like the crisis of a sickness—when the patient has no more interest in life at all. It is then that people sometimes kill themselves, but he was tough, very tough.'

'You spoke just now as though he had been cured.'

'I really think he was. He'd learned to serve other people, you see, and to laugh. An odd laugh, but it was a laugh all the same. I'm frightened of people who don't laugh.'

The Superior said shyly, 'I thought perhaps you meant that he was beginning to find his faith again.'

'Oh no, not that. Only a reason for living. You try too hard to make a pattern, father.'

'But if the pattern's there . . . you haven't a cheroot have you?'

'No.'

The Superior said, 'We all analyse motives too much. I said that once to Father Thomas. You remember what Pascal said, that a man who starts looking for God has already found him. The same may be true of love—when we look for it, perhaps we've already found it.'

'He was inclined—I only know what he told me himself—to confine his search to a woman's bed.'

'It's not so bad a place to look for it. There are a lot of people who only find hate there.'

'Like Rycker?'

'We don't know enough about Rycker to condemn him.'

'How persistent you are, father. You never let anyone go, do you? You'd like to claim even Querry for your own.'

'I haven't noticed that you relax much before a patient dies.'

They had reached the dispensary. The lepers sat on the hot cement steps waiting for something to happen. At the new hospital the ladders leant against the roof, and the last work was in progress. The roof-tree had been battered and bent by the storm, but it was held in place still by its strong palm-fibre thongs.

'I see from the accounts,' the Superior said, 'that you've given up using vitamin tablets. Is that a wise economy?'

'I don't believe the anaemia comes from the D.D.S. treatment. It comes from the hookworm. It's cheaper to build lavatories than to buy vitamin tablets. That's our next project. I mean it was to have been. How many patients have turned up today?' he asked the dispenser.

'About sixty.'

'Your god must feel a bit disappointed,' Doctor Colin said, 'when he looks at this world of his.'

'When you were a boy they can't have taught you theology very well. God cannot feel disappointment or pain.'

'Perhaps that's why I don't care to believe in him.'

The doctor sat down at the table and drew forward a blank chart. 'Number one,' he called.

It was a child of three, quite naked, with a little pot-belly and a dangling tassel and a finger stuck in the corner of his mouth. The doctor ran his fingers over the skin of the back while the child's mother waited.

'I know that little fellow,' the Superior said. 'He always came to me for sweets.'

'He's infected all right,' Doctor Colin said. 'Feel the patches here and here. But you needn't worry,' he added in a tone of suppressed rage, 'we shall be able to cure him in a year or two, and I can promise you that there will be no mutilations.'

THE
THIRD MAN

THE THIRD MAN

to Carol Reed

in admiration and affection and in memory of so many
early morning Vienna hours at Maxim's, the
Casanova, the Oriental.

I

One never knows when the blow may fall. When I saw Rollo Martins first I made this note on him for my security police files: 'In normal circumstances a cheerful fool. Drinks too much and may cause a little trouble. Whenever a woman passes raises his eyes and makes some comment, but I get the impression that really he'd rather not be bothered. Has never really grown up and perhaps that accounts for the way he worshipped Lime.' I wrote there that phrase 'in normal circumstances' because I met him first at Harry Lime's funeral. It was February, and the gravediggers had been forced to use electric drills to open the frozen ground in Vienna's Central Cemetery. It was as if even nature were doing its best to reject Lime, but we got him in at last and laid the earth back on him like bricks. He was vaulted in, and Rollo Martins walked quickly away as though his long gangly legs wanted to break into a run, and the tears of a boy ran down his thirty-five-year-old face. Rollo Martins believed in friendship, and that was why what happened later was a worse shock to him than it would have been to you or me (you because you would have put it down to an illusion and me because at once a rational explanation–however wrongly–would have come to my mind). If only he had come to tell me then, what a lot of trouble would have been saved.

If you are to understand this strange, rather sad story you must have an impression at least of the background–the smashed dreary city of Vienna divided up in zones among the Four Powers–the Russian, the British, the American, the French zones, regions marked only by notice boards, and in the centre of the city, surrounded by the Ring with its heavy public buildings and its prancing statuary, the Innere Stadt under the control of all Four Powers. In this once fashionable Inner City each power in turn, for a month at a time, takes, as we call it, 'the chair', and becomes responsible for security; at night, if you were fool enough to waste your Austrian schillings on a night club, you would be fairly certain to see the International Power at work–four military police, one from each power, communicating with each other, if they communicated at all, in the common language of their enemy. I never knew Vienna between the wars, and I am too young to remember the old Vienna with its Strauss music and its bogus easy charm; to me it is simply a city of undignified ruins which turned that February into great glaciers of snow and ice. The Danube was a grey flat muddy river a long way off across the Second Bezirk, the Russian zone where the Prater lay smashed and desolate and full of weeds, only the Great Wheel revolving slowly over the foundations of merry-go-rounds like abandoned millstones, the rusting iron of smashed tanks which nobody had cleared away, the frost-nipped weeds where the snow was thin. I haven't enough imagination to picture it as it had once been, any more than I can picture Sacher's Hotel as other than a transit hotel for English officers or see the Kärntnerstrasse as a fashionable shopping street instead of a street which exists, most of it, only at eye level, repaired up to the first storey. A Russian soldier in a fur cap goes by with a rifle over his shoulder, a few tarts cluster round the American Information Office, and men in overcoats sip erstaz coffee in the windows of the Old Vienna. At night it is just as well to stick to the Inner City or the zones of three of the Powers, though even there the kidnappings occur – such senseless kidnappings they sometimes seemed to us – a Ukrainian girl without a passport, an old man beyond the age of usefulness, sometimes, of course, the technician or the traitor. This was roughly the Vienna to which Rollo Martins came on February seventh last year. I have reconstructed the affair as best I can from my own files and from what Martins told me. It is as accurate as I can make it – I have tried not to invent a line of dialogue, though I can't vouch for Martins' memory; an ugly story if you leave out the girl: grim and sad and unrelieved, if it were not for that absurd episode of the British Council lecturer.

2

A British subject can still travel if he is content to take with him only five English pounds which he is forbidden to spend abroad, but if Rollo Martins had not received an invitation from Lime of the International Refugee Office he would not have been allowed to enter Austria, which counts still as occupied territory. Lime had suggested that Martins might write up the business of looking after the international refugees, and although it wasn't Martins' usual line, he had consented. It would give him a holiday, and he badly needed a holiday after the incident in Dublin and the other incident in Amsterdam; he always tried to dismiss women as 'incidents', things that simply happened to him without any will of his own, acts of God in the eyes of insurance agents. He had a haggard look when he arrived in Vienna and a habit of looking over his shoulder that for a time made me suspicious of him until I realized that he went in fear that one of, say, six people might turn up unexpectedly. He told me vaguely that he had been mixing his drinks – that was another way of putting it.

Rollo Martins' usual line was the writing of cheap paper-covered Westerns under the name of Buck Dexter. His public was large but unremunerative. He couldn't have afforded Vienna if Lime had not offered to pay his expenses when he got there out of some vaguely described propaganda fund. Lime could also, he said, keep him supplied with paper bafs – the only currency in use from a penny upwards in British hotels and clubs. So it was with exactly five unusable pound notes that Martins arrived in Vienna.

An odd incident had occurred at Frankfurt, where the plane from London grounded for an hour. Martins was eating a hamburger in the American canteen (a kindly airline supplied the passengers with a voucher for sixty-five cents' worth of food) when a man he could recognize from twenty feet away as a journalist approached his table.

'You Mr Dexter?' he asked.

'Yes,' Martins said, taken off his guard.

'You look younger than your photographs,' the man said. 'Like to make a statement? I represent the local forces paper here. We'd like to know what you think of Frankfurt.'

'I only touched down ten minutes ago.'

'Fair enough,' the man said. 'What about views on the American novel?'

'I don't read them,' Martins said.

'The well-known acid humour,' the journalist said. He pointed at a small grey-haired man with protruding teeth, nibbling a bit of bread. 'Happen to know if that's Carey?'

'No. What Carey?'

'J. G. Carey of course.'

'I've never heard of him.'

'You novelists live out of the world. He's my real assignment,' and Martins watched him make across the room for the great Carey, who greeted him with a false headline smile, laying down his crust. Dexter wasn't the man's assignment, but Martins couldn't help feeling a certain pride—nobody had ever before referred to him as a novelist; and that sense of pride and importance carried him over the disappointment when Lime was not there to meet him at the airport. We never get accustomed to being less important to other people than they are to us—Martins felt the little jab of dispensability, standing by the bus door, watching the snow come sifting down, so thinly and softly that the great drifts among the ruined buildings had an air of permanence, as though they were not the result of this meagre fall, but lay, for ever, above the line of perpetual snow.

There was no Lime to meet him at the Hotel Astoria, the terminus where the bus landed him, and no message—only a cryptic one for Mr Dexter from someone he had never heard of called Crabbin. 'We expected you on tomorrow's plane. Please stay where you are. On the way round. Hotel room booked.' But Rollo Martins wasn't the kind of man who stayed around. If you stayed around in a hotel lounge, sooner or later incidents occurred; one mixed one's drinks. I can hear Rollo Martins saying to me, 'I've done with incidents. No more incidents,' before he plunged head first into the most serious incident of all. There was always a conflict in Rollo Martins—between the absurd Christian name and the sturdy Dutch (four generations back) surname. Rollo looked at every woman that passed, and Martins renounced them for ever. I don't know which one of them wrote the Westerns.

Martins had been given Lime's address and he felt no curiosity about the man called Crabbin; it was too obvious that a mistake had been made, though he didn't yet connect it with the conversation at Frankfurt. Lime had written that he could put Martins up in his own flat, a large apartment on the edge of Vienna that had been requisitioned from a Nazi owner. Lime could pay for the taxi when he arrived, so Martins drove straight away to the building lying in the third (British) zone. He kept the taxi waiting while he mounted to the third floor.

How quickly one becomes aware of silence even in so silent a city as
Vienna with the snow steadily settling. Martins hadn't reached the second
floor before he was convinced that he would not find Lime there, but the
silence was deeper than just absence—it was as if he would not find Lime
anywhere in Vienna, and, as he reached the third floor and saw the big black
bow over the door handle, anywhere in the world at all. Of course it might
have been a cook who had died, a housekeeper, anybody but Harry Lime,
but he knew—he felt he had known twenty stairs down—that Lime, the Lime
he had hero-worshipped now for twenty years, since the first meeting in a
grim school corridor with a cracked bell ringing for prayers, was gone.
Martins wasn't wrong, not entirely wrong. After he had rung the bell half a
dozen times a small man with a sullen expression put his head out from
another flat and told him in a tone of vexation, 'It's no use. There's nobody
there. He's dead.'

'Herr Lime?'

'Herr Lime, of course.'

Martins said to me later, 'At first it didn't mean a thing. It was just a bit of
information, like those paragraphs in *The Times* they call "News in Brief". I
said to him, "When did it happen? How?"'

'He was run over by a car,' the man said. 'Last Thursday.' He added
sullenly, as if really this were none of his business, 'They're burying him this
afternoon. You've only just missed them.'

'Them?'

'Oh, a couple of friends and the coffin.'

'Wasn't he in hospital?'

'There was no sense in taking him to hospital. He was killed here on his
own doorstep—instantaneously. The right-hand mudguard struck him on
his shoulder and bowled him over like a rabbit.'

It was only then, Martins told me, when the man used the word 'rabbit',
that the dead Harry Lime came alive, became the boy with a gun which he
had shown Martins the means of 'borrowing'; a boy starting up among the
long sandy burrows of Brickworth Common saying, 'Shoot, you fool, shoot!
There,' and the rabbit limped to cover, wounded by Martins' shot.

'Where are they burying him?' he asked the stranger on the landing.

'In the Central Cemetery. They'll have a hard time of it in this frost.'

He had no idea how to pay for his taxi, or indeed where in Vienna he could
find a room in which he could live for five English pounds, but that problem
had to be postponed until he had seen the last of Harry Lime. He drove
straight out of town into the suburb (British zone) where the Central
Cemetery lay. One passed through the Russian zone to reach it, and took a
short cut through the American zone, which you couldn't mistake because of
the ice-cream parlours in every street. The trams ran along the high wall of
the Central Cemetery, and for a mile on the other side of the rails stretched
the monumental masons and the market gardeners—an apparently endless
chain of gravestones waiting for owners and wreaths waiting for mourners.

Martins had not realized the size of this huge snowbound park where he
was making his last rendezvous with Lime. It was as if Harry had left a
message for him, 'Meet me in Hyde Park', without specifying a spot between
the Achilles statue and Lancaster Gate; the avenues of graves, each avenue

numbered and lettered, stretched out like the spokes of an enormous wheel; they drove for a half-mile towards the west, and then turned and drove a half-mile north, turned south. . . . The snow gave the great pompous family headstones an air of grotesque comedy; a toupée of snow slipped sideways over an angelic face, a saint wore a heavy white moustache, and a shako of snow tipped at a drunken angle over the bust of a superior civil servant called Wolfgang Gottmann. Even this cemetery was zoned between the Powers: the Russian zone was marked by huge tasteless statues of armed men, the French by rows of anonymous wooden crosses and a torn tired tricolour flag. Then Martins remembered that Lime was a Catholic and was unlikely to be buried in the British zone for which they had been vainly searching. So back they drove through the heart of a forest where the graves lay like wolves under the trees, winking white eyes under the gloom of the evergreens. Once from under the trees emerged a group of three men in strange eighteenth-century black and silver uniforms with three-cornered hats pushing a kind of barrow: they crossed a ride in the forest of graves and disappeared again.

It was just chance that they found the funeral in time—one patch in the enormous park where the snow had been shovelled aside and a tiny group was gathered, apparently bent on some very private business. A priest had finished speaking, his words coming secretively through the thin patient snow, and a coffin was on the point of being lowered into the ground. Two men in lounge suits stood at the graveside; one carried a wreath that he obviously had forgotten to drop on to the coffin, for his companion nudged his elbow so that he came to with a start and dropped the flowers. A girl stood a little way away with her hands over her face, and I stood twenty yards away by another grave, watching with relief the last of Lime and noticing carefully who was there—just a man in a mackintosh I was to Martins. He came up to me and said, 'Could you tell me who they are burying?'

'A fellow called Lime,' I said, and was astonished to see the tears start to this stranger's eyes: he didn't look like a man who wept, nor was Lime the kind of man whom I thought likely to have mourners—genuine mourners with genuine tears. There was the girl of course, but one excepts women from all such generalizations.

Martins stood there, till the end, close beside me. He said to me later that as an old friend he didn't want to intrude on these newer ones—Lime's death belonged to them, let them have it. He was under the sentimental illusion that Lime's life—twenty years of it anyway—belonged to him. As soon as the affair was over—I am not a religious man and always feel a little impatient with the fuss that surrounds death—Martins strode away on his long legs, which always seemed likely to get entangled together, back to his taxi. He made no attempt to speak to anyone, and the tears now were really running, at any rate the few meagre drops that any of us can squeeze out at our age.

One's file, you know, is never quite complete; a case is never really closed, even after a century, when all the participants are dead. So I followed Martins: I knew the other three: I wanted to know the stranger. I caught him up by his taxi and said, 'I haven't any transport. Would you give me a lift into town?'

'Of course,' he said. I knew the driver of my jeep would spot me as we came out and follow us unobtrusively. As we drove away I noticed Martins never looked behind–it's nearly always the fake mourners and the fake lovers who take that last look, who wait waving on platforms, instead of clearing quickly out, not looking back. Is it perhaps that they love themselves so much and want to keep themselves in the sight of others, even of the dead?

I said, 'My name's Calloway.'

'Martins,' he said.

'You were a friend of Lime?'

'Yes.' Most people in the last week would have hesitated before they admitted quite so much.

'Been here long?'

'I only came this afternoon from England. Harry had asked me to stay with him. I hadn't heard.'

'Bit of a shock?'

'Look here,' he said. 'I badly want a drink, but I haven't any cash–except five pounds sterling. I'd be awfully grateful if you'd stand me one.'

It was my turn to say 'Of course'. I thought for a moment and told the driver the name of a small bar in the Kärntnerstrasse. I didn't think he'd want to be seen for a while in a busy British bar full of transit officers and their wives. This bar–perhaps because it was exorbitant in its prices–seldom had more than one self-occupied couple in at a time. The trouble was too that it really only had one drink–a sweet chocolate liqueur that the waiter improved at a price with cognac–but I got the impression that Martins had no objection to any drink so long as it cast a veil over the present and the past. On the door was the usual notice saying the bar opened from six till ten, but one just pushed the door and walked through the front rooms. We had a whole small room to ourselves; the only couple were next door, and the waiter, who knew me, left us alone with some caviare sandwiches. It was lucky that we both knew I had an expense account.

Martins said over his second quick drink, 'I'm sorry, but he was the best friend I ever had.'

I couldn't resist saying, knowing what I knew, and because I was anxious to vex him–one learns a lot that way–'That sounds like a cheap novelette.'

He said quickly, 'I write cheap novelettes.'

I had learned something anyway. Until he had had a third drink I was under the impression that he wasn't an easy talker, but I felt fairly certain he was one of those who turn unpleasant after their fourth glass.

I said, 'Tell me about yourself–and Lime.'

'Look here,' he said, 'I badly need another drink, but I can't keep on scrounging on a stranger. Could you change me a pound or two into Austrian money?'

'Don't bother about that,' I said and called the waiter. 'You can treat me when I come to London on leave. You were going to tell me how you met Lime?'

The glass of chocolate liqueur might have been a crystal, the way he looked at it and turned it this way and that. He said, 'It was a long time ago. I don't suppose anyone knows Harry the way I do,' and I thought of the thick file of agents' reports in my office, each claiming the same thing. I believe in my agents; I've sifted them all very thoroughly.'

'How long?'

'Twenty years—or a bit more. I met him my first term at school. I can see the place. I can see the notice board and what was on it. I can hear the bell ringing. He was a year older and knew the ropes. He put me wise to a lot of things.' He took a quick dab at his drink and then turned the crystal again as if to see more clearly what there was to see. He said, 'It's funny. I can't remember meeting any woman quite as well.'

'Was he clever at school?'

'Not the way they wanted him to be. But what things he did think up! He was a wonderful planner. I was far better at subjects like History and English than Harry, but I was a hopeless mug when it came to carrying out his plans.' He laughed: he was already beginning, with the help of drink and talk, to throw off the shock of the death. He said, 'I was always the one who got caught.'

'That was convenient for Lime.'

'What the hell do you mean?' he asked. Alcoholic irritation was setting in.

'Well, wasn't it?'

'That was my fault, not his. He could have found someone cleverer if he'd chosen, but he liked me.' Certainly, I thought, the child is father to the man, for I too had found Lime patient.

'When did you see him last?'

'Oh, he was over in London six months ago for a medical congress. You know, he qualified as a doctor, though he never practised. That was typical of Harry. He just wanted to see if he could do a thing and then he lost interest. But he used to say that it often came in handy.' And that too was true. It was odd how like the Lime he knew was to the Lime I knew: it was only that he looked at Lime's image from a different angle or in a different light. He said, 'One of the things I liked about Harry was his humour.' He gave a grin which took five years off his age. 'I'm a buffoon. I like playing the silly fool, but Harry had real wit. You know, he could have been a first-class light composer if he had worked at it.'

He whistled a tune—it was oddly familiar to me. 'I always remember that. I saw Harry write it. Just in a couple of minutes on the back of an envelope. That was what he always whistled when he had something on his mind. It was his signature tune.' He whistled the tune a second time, and I knew then who had written it—of course it wasn't Harry. I nearly told him so, but what was the point? The tune wavered and went out. He stared down into his glass, drained what was left, and said, 'It's a damned shame to think of him dying the way he did.'

'It was the best thing that ever happened to him,' I said.

He didn't take in my meaning at once: he was a little hazy with his drinks. 'The best thing?'

'Yes.'

'You mean there wasn't any pain?'

'He was lucky in that way, too.'

It was my tone of voice and not my words that caught Martins' attention. He asked gently and dangerously—I could see his right hand tighten—'Are you hinting at something?'

There is no point at all in showing physical courage in all situations: I eased my chair far enough back to be out of reach of his fist. I said, 'I mean that I had his case completed at police headquarters. He would have served a long spell—a very long spell—if it hadn't been for the accident.'

'What for?'

'He was about the worst racketeer who ever made a dirty living in this city.'

I could see him measuring the distance between us and deciding that he couldn't reach me from where he sat. Rollo wanted to hit out, but Martins was steady, careful. Martins, I began to realize, was dangerous. I wondered whether after all I had made a complete mistake: I couldn't see Martins being quite the mug that Rollo had made out. 'You're a policeman?' he asked.

'Yes.'

'I've always hated policemen. They are always either crooked or stupid.'

'Is that the kind of book you write?'

I could see him edging his chair round to block my way out. I caught the waiter's eye and he knew what I meant—there's an advantage in always using the same bar for interviews.

Martins brought out a surface smile and said gently, 'I have to call them sheriffs.'

'Been in America?' It was a silly conversation.

'No. Is this an interrogation?'

'Just interest.'

'Because if Harry was that kind of racketeer, I must be one too. We always worked together.'

'I daresay he meant to cut you in—somewhere in the organization. I wouldn't be surprised if he had meant to give you the baby to hold. That was his method at school—you told me, didn't you? And, you see, the headmaster was getting to know a thing or two.'

'You are running true to form, aren't you? I suppose there was some petty racket going on with petrol and you couldn't pin it on anyone, so you've picked a dead man. That's just like a policeman. You're a real policeman, I suppose?'

'Yes, Scotland Yard, but they've put me into a colonel's uniform when I'm on duty.'

He was between me and the door now. I couldn't get away from the table without coming into range. I'm no fighter, and he had six inches of advantage anyway. I said, 'It wasn't petrol.'

'Tyres, saccharin—why don't you policemen catch a few murderers for a change?'

'Well, you could say that murder was part of his racket.'

He pushed the table over with one hand and made a dive at me with the other; the drink confused his calculations. Before he could try again my driver had his arms round him. I said, 'Don't treat him rough. He's only a writer with too much drink in him.'

'Be quiet, can't you, sir,' my driver said. He had an exaggerated sense of officer-class. He would probably have called Lime 'sir'.

'Listen, Callaghan, or whatever your bloody name is . . .'

'Calloway. I'm English, not Irish.'

'I'm going to make you look the biggest bloody fool in Vienna. There's one dead man you aren't going to pin your unsolved crimes on.'

'I see. You're going to find me the real criminal? It sounds like one of your stories.'

'You can let me go, Callaghan. I'd rather make you look the fool you are than black your bloody eye. You'd only have to go to bed for a few days with a black eye. But when I've finished with you, you'll leave Vienna.'

I took out a couple of pounds' worth of bafs and stuck them in his breast pocket. 'These will see you through tonight,' I said, 'and I'll make sure they keep a seat for you on tomorrow's London plane.'

'You can't turn me out. My papers are in order.'

'Yes, but this is like other cities: you need money here. If you change your sterling on the black market I'll catch up on you inside twenty-four hours. Let him go.'

Rollo Martins dusted himself down. He said, 'Thank for the drinks.'

'That's all right.'

'I'm glad I don't have to feel grateful. I suppose they were on expenses?'

'Yes.'

'I'll be seeing you again in a week or two when I've got the dope.' I knew he was angry. I didn't believe then that he was serious. I thought he was putting over an act to cheer up his self-esteem.

'I might come and see you off tomorrow.'

'I shouldn't waste your time. I won't be there.'

'Paine here will show you the way to Sacher's. You can get a bed and dinner there. I'll see to that.'

He stepped to one side as though to make way for the waiter and slashed out at me. I just avoided him, but stumbled against the table. Before he could try again Paine had landed him one on the mouth. He went bang over in the alleyway between the tables and came up bleeding from a cut lip. I said, 'I thought you promised not to fight.'

He wiped some of the blood away with his sleeve and said, 'Oh, no, I said I'd rather make you a bloody fool. I didn't say I wouldn't give you a black eye as well.'

I had had a long day and I was tired of Rollo Martins. I said to Paine, 'See him safely into Sacher's. Don't hit him again if he behaves,' and turning away from both of them towards the inner bar (I deserved one more drink), I heard Paine say respectfully to the man he had just knocked down, 'This way, sir. It's only just around the corner.'

3

What happened next I didn't hear from Paine but from Martins a long time afterwards, as I reconstructed the chain of events which did indeed–though not quite in the way he had expected–prove me to be a fool. Paine simply saw him to the head porter's desk and explained there, 'This gentleman came in on the plane from London. Colonel Calloway says he's to have a room.' Having made that clear, he said, 'Good evening, sir,' and left. He was probably a bit embarrassed by Martins' bleeding lip.

'Had you already got a reservation, sir?' the porter asked.

'No. No, I don't think so,' Martins said in a muffled voice, holding his handkerchief to his mouth.

'I thought perhaps you might be Mr Dexter. We had a room reserved for a week for Mr Dexter.'

Martins said, 'Oh, I am Mr Dexter.' He told me later that it occurred to him that Lime might have engaged a room for him in that name because perhaps it was Buck Dexter and not Rollo Martins who was to be used for propaganda purposes. A voice said at his elbow, 'I'm so sorry you were not met at the plane, Mr Dexter. My name's Crabbin.'

The speaker was a stout middle-aged young man with a natural tonsure and one of the thickest pairs of horn-rimmed glasses that Martins had ever seen. He went apologetically on, 'One of our chaps happened to ring up Frankfurt and heard you were on the plane. H.Q. made one of their usual foolish mistakes and wired you were not coming. Something about Sweden, but the cable was badly mutilated. Directly I heard from Frankfurt I tried to meet the plane, but I just missed you. You got my note?'

Martins held his handkerchief to his mouth and said obscurely, 'Yes. Yes?'

'May I say at once, Mr Dexter, how excited I am to meet you?'

'Good of you.'

'Ever since I was a boy, I've thought you the greatest novelist of our century.'

Martins winced. It was painful opening his mouth to protest. He took an angry look instead at Mr Crabbin, but it was impossible to suspect that young man of a practical joke.

'You have a big Austrian public, Mr Dexter, both for your originals and your translations. Especially for *The Curved Prow*, that's my own favourite.'

Martins was thinking hard. 'Did you say—room for a week?'

'Yes.'

'Very kind of you.'

'Mr Schmidt here will give you tickets every day, to cover all meals. but I expect you'll need a little pocket money. We'll fix that. Tomorrow we thought you'd like a quiet day—to look about.'

'Yes.'

'Of course any of us are at your service if you need a guide. Then the day after tomorrow in the evening there's a little quiet discussion at the Institute—on the contemporary novel. We thought perhaps you'd say a few words just to set the ball rolling, and then answer questions.'

Martins at that moment was prepared to agree to anything to get rid of Mr Crabbin and also to secure a week's free board and lodging; and Rollo, of course, as I was to discover later, had always been prepared to accept any suggestion—for a drink, for a girl, for a joke, for a new excitement. He said now, 'Of course, of course,' into his handkerchief.

'Excuse me, Mr Dexter, have you got toothache? I know a very good dentist.'

'No. Somebody hit me, that's all.'

'Good God! Were they trying to rob you?'

'No, it was a soldier. I was trying to punch his bloody colonel in the eye.' He removed the handkerchief and gave Crabbin a view of his cut mouth. He told me that Crabbin was at a complete loss for words. Martins couldn't understand why because he had never read the work of his great contemporary, Benjamin Dexter: he hadn't even heard of him. I am a great admirer of Dexter, so that I could understand Crabbin's bewilderment. Dexter has been ranked as a stylist with Henry James, but he has a wider feminine streak than his master—indeed his enemies have sometimes described his subtle, complex, wavering style as old-maidish. For a man still just on the right side of fifty his passionate interest in embroidery and his habit of calming a not very tumultuous mind with tatting—a trait beloved by his disciples—certainly to others seems a little affected.

'Have you ever read a book called *The Lone Rider of Santa Fé*?'

'No, I don't think so.'

Martins said, 'This lone rider had his best friend shot by the sheriff of a town called Lost Claim Gulch. The story is how he hunted that sheriff down—quite legally—until his revenge was completed.'

'I never imagined you reading Westerns, Mr Dexter,' Crabbin said, and it needed all Martins' resolution to stop Rollo saying, 'But I write them.'

'Well, I'm gunning just the same way for Colonel Callaghan.'

'Never heard of him.'

'Heard of Harry Lime?'

'Yes,' Crabbin said cautiously, 'but I didn't really know him.'

'I did. He was my best friend.'

'I shouldn't have thought he was a very—literary character.'

'None of my friends are.'

Crabbin blinked nervously behind the horn-rims. He said with an air of appeasement, 'He was interested in the theatre though. A friend of his—an actress, you know—is learning English at the Institute. He called once or twice to fetch her.'

'Young or old?'

'Oh, young, very young. Not a good actress in my opinion.'

Martins remembered the girl by the grave with her hands over her face. He said, 'I'd like to meet any friend of Harry's.'

'She'll probably be at your lecture.'

'Austrian?'

'She claims to be Austrian, but I suspect she's Hungarian. She works at the Josefstadt.'

'Why claims to be Austrian?'

'The Russians sometimes get interested in the Hungarians. I wouldn't be surprised if Lime had helped her with her papers. She calls herself Schmidt. Anna Schmidt. You can't imagine a young English actress calling herself Smith, can you? And a pretty one, too. It always struck me as a bit too anonymous to be true.'

Martins felt he had got all he could from Crabbin, so he pleaded tiredness, a long day, promised to ring up in the morning, accepted ten pounds' worth of bafs for immediate expenses, and went to his room. It seemed to him that he was earning money rapidly—twelve pounds in less than an hour.

He *was* tired: he realized that when he stretched himself out on the bed in his boots. Within a minute he had left Vienna far behind him and was walking through a dense wood, ankle-deep in snow. An owl hooted, and he felt suddenly lonely and scared. He had an appointment to meet Harry under a particular tree, but in a wood so dense how could he recognize any one tree from the rest? Then he saw a figure and ran towards it: it whistled a familiar tune and his heart lifted with relief and joy at not after all being alone. The figure turned and it was not Harry at all—just a stranger who grinned at him in a little circle of wet slushy melted snow, while the owl hooted again and again. He woke suddenly to hear the telephone ringing by his bed.

A voice with a trace of foreign accent—only a trace—said, 'Is that Mr Rollo Martins?'

'Yes.' It was a change to be himself and not Dexter.

'You wouldn't know me,' the voice said unnecessarily, 'but I was a friend of Harry Lime.'

It was a change too to hear anyone claim to be a friend of Harry's. Martins' heart warmed towards the stranger. He said, 'I'd be glad to meet you.'

'I'm just round the corner at the Old Vienna.'

'Couldn't you make it tomorrow? I've had a pretty awful day with one thing and another.'

'Harry asked me to see that you were all right. I was with him when he died.'

'I thought—' Rollo Martins said and stopped. He had been going to say, 'I thought he died instantaneously,' but something suggested caution. He said instead, 'You haven't told me your name.'

'Kurtz,' the voice said. 'I'd offer to come round to you, only, you know, Austrians aren't allowed in Sacher's.'

'Perhaps we could meet at the Old Vienna in the morning.'

'Certainly,' the voice said, 'if you are *quite* sure that you are all right till then?'

'How do you mean?'

'Harry had it on his mind that you'd be penniless.' Rollo Martins lay back on his bed with the receiver to his ear and thought: Come to Vienna to make money. This was the third stranger to stake him in less than five hours. He said cautiously, 'Oh, I can carry on till I see you.' There seemed no point in turning down a good offer till he knew what the offer was.

'Shall we say eleven, then, at the Old Vienna in the Kärntnerstrasse? I'll be in a brown suit and I'll carry one of your books.'

'That's fine. How did you get hold of one?'

'Harry gave it to me.' The voice had enormous charm and reasonableness, but when Martins had said good night and rung off, he couldn't help wondering how it was that if Harry had been so conscious before he died he had not had a cable sent to stop him. Hadn't Callaghan too said that Lime died instantaneously—or without pain, was it?—or had he put the words into Callaghan's mouth? It was then the idea first lodged firmly in Martins' mind that there was something wrong about Lime's death, something the police had been too stupid to discover. He tried to discover it himself with the help to two cigarettes, but he fell asleep without his dinner and with the mystery still unsolved. It had been a long day, but not quite long enough for that.

4

'What I disliked about him at first sight,' Martins told me, 'was his toupée. It was one of those obvious toupées—flat and yellow, with the hair cut straight at the back and not fitting close. There *must* be something phoney about a man who won't accept baldness gracefully. He had one of those faces too where the lines have been put in carefully, like a make-up, in the right places—to express charm, whimsicality, lines at the corner so the eyes. He was made up to appeal to romantic schoolgirls.'

This conversation took place some days later—he brought out his whole story when the trail was nearly cold. We were sitting in the Old Vienna at the table he had occupied that first morning with Kurtz, and when he made that remark about the romantic schoolgirls I saw his rather hunted eyes focus suddenly. It was a girl—just like any other girl, I thought, hurrying by outside in the driving snow.

'Something pretty?'

He brought his gaze back and said, 'I'm off that for ever. You know, Calloway, a time comes in a man's life when he gives up all that sort of thing . . .'

'I see. I thought you were looking at a girl.'

'I was. But only because she reminded me for a moment of Anna—Anna Schmidt.'

'Who's she? Isn't she a girl?'

'Oh, yes, in a way.'

'What do you mean, in a way?'

'She was Harry's girl.'

'Are you taking her over?'

'She's not that kind, Calloway. Didn't you see her at his funeral? I'm not mixing my drinks any more. I've got a hangover to last me a lifetime.'

'You were telling me about Kurtz,' I said.

It appeared that Kurtz was sitting there, making a great show of reading *The Lone Rider of Santa Fé*. When Martins sat down at his table he said with indescribably false enthusiasm, 'It's wonderful how you keep the tension.'

'Tension?'

'Suspense. You're a master at it. At the end of every chapter one's left guessing . . .'

'So you were a friend of Harry's,' Martins said.

'I think his best,' But Kurtz added with the smallest pause, in which his brain must have registered the error, 'except you, of course.'

'Tell me how he died.'

'I was with him. We came out together from the door of his flat and Harry saw a friend he knew across the road–an American called Cooler. He waved to Cooler and started across the road to him when a jeep came tearing round the corner and bowled him over. It was Harry's fault really–not the driver's.'

'Somebody told me he died instantaneously.'

'I wish he had. He died before the ambulance could reach us though.'

'He could speak, then?'

'Yes. Even in his pain he worried about you.'

'What did he say?'

'I can't remember the exact words, Rollo–I may call you Rollo, mayn't I? He always called you that to us. He was anxious that I should look after you when you arrived. See that you were looked after. Get your return ticket for you.' In telling me, Martins said, 'You see I was collecting return tickets as well as cash.'

'But why didn't you cable to stop me?'

'We did, but the cable must have missed you. What with censorship and the zones, cables can take anything up to five days.'

'There was an inquest?'

'Of course.'

'Did you know that the police have a crazy notion that Harry was mixed up in some racket?'

'No. But everyone in Vienna is. We all sell cigarettes and exchange schillings for bafs and that kind of thing. You won't find a single member of the Control Commission who hasn't broken the rules.'

'The police meant something worse than that.'

'They get rather absurd ideas sometimes,' the man with the toupée said cautiously.

'I'm going to stay here till I prove them wrong.'

Kurtz turned his head sharply and the toupée shifted very very slightly. He said, 'What's the good? Nothing can bring Harry back.'

'I'm going to have that police officer run out of Vienna.'

'I don't see what you can do.'

'I'm going to start working back from his death. You were there and this man Cooler and the chauffeur. You can give me their addresses.'

'I don't know the chauffeur's.'

'I can get it from the coroner's records. And then there's Harry's girl . . .'

Kurtz said, 'It will be painful for her.'

'I'm not concerned about her. I'm concerned about Harry.'

'Do you know what it is that the police suspect?'

'No. I lost my temper too soon.'

'Has it occurred to you,' Kurtz said gently, 'that you might dig up something–well, discreditable to Harry?'

'I'll risk that.'

'It will take a bit of time–and money.'

'I've got time and you were going to lend me some money, weren't you?'

'I'm not a rich man,' Kurtz said. 'I promised Harry to see you were all right and that you got your plane back . . .'

'You needn't worry about the money–or the plane,' Martins said. 'But I'll make a bet with you—in pounds sterling—five pounds against two hundred schillings—that there's something queer about Harry's death.'

It was a shot in the dark, but already he had this firm instinctive sense that there was something wrong, though he hadn't yet attached the word 'murder' to the instinct. Kurtz had a cup of coffee half-way to his lips and Martins watched him. The shot apparently went wide; an unaffected hand held the cup to the mouth and Kurtz drank, a little noisily, in long sips. Then he put down the cup and said, 'How do you mean—queer?'

'It was convenient for the police to have a corpse, but wouldn't it have been equally convenient, perhaps, for the real racketeers?' When he had spoken he realized that after all Kurtz might not have been unaffected by his wild statement: hadn't he perhaps been frozen into caution and calm? The hands of the guilty don't necessarily tremble; only in stories does a dropped glass betray agitation. Tension is more often shown in the studied action. Kurtz had drunk his coffee as though nothing had been said.

'Well'— he took another sip—'of course I wish you luck, though I don't believe there's anything to find. Just ask me for any help you want.'

'I want Cooler's address.'

'Certainly. I'll write it down for you. Here it is. In the American zone.'

'And yours?'

'I've already put it—underneath. I'm unlucky enough to be in the Russian zone—so don't visit me very late. Things sometimes happen round our way.' He was giving one of his studied Viennese smiles, the charm carefully painted in with a fine brush in the little lines about the mouth and eyes. 'Keep in touch,' he said, 'and if you need any help . . . but I still think you are very unwise.' He touched *The Lone Rider*. 'I'm so proud to have met you. A master of suspense,' and one hand smoothed the toupée, while another, passing softly over the mouth, brushed out the smile as though it had never been.

5

Martins sat on a hard chair just inside the stage door of the Josefstadt Theatre. He had sent up his card to Anna Schmidt after the matinée, marking it 'a friend of Harry's'. An arcade of little windows, with lace curtains and the lights going out one after another, showed where the artists were packing up for home, for the cup of coffee without sugar, the roll without butter to sustain them for the evening performance. It was like a little street built indoors for a film set, but even indoors it was cold, even cold to a man in a heavy overcoat, so that Martins rose and walked up and down underneath the little windows. He felt, he said, rather like a Romeo who wasn't sure of Juliet's balcony.

He had had time to think: he was calm now, Martins not Rollo was in the ascendant. When a light went out in one of the windows and an actress descended into the passage where he walked, he didn't even turn to take a look. He was done with all that. He thought, Kurtz is right. They are all right. I'm behaving like a romantic fool. I'll just have a word with Anna Schmidt, a word of commiseration, and then I'll pack and go. He had quite forgotten, he told me, the complication of Mr Crabbin.

A voice over his head called 'Mr Martins,' and he looked up at the face that watched him from between the curtains a few feet above his head. It wasn't a beautiful face, he firmly explained to me, when I accused him of once again mixing his drinks. Just an honest face; dark hair and eyes which in that light looked brown; a wide forehead, a large mouth which didn't try to charm. No danger anywhere, it seemed to Rollo Martins, of that sudden reckless moment when the scent of hair or a hand against the side alters life. She said, 'Will you come up, please? The second door on the right.'

There are some people, he explained to me carefully, whom one recognizes instantaneously as friends. You can be at ease with them because you know that never, never will you be in danger. 'That was Anna,' he said, and I wasn't sure whether the past tense was deliberate or not.

Unlike most actresses' rooms this one was almost bare; no wardrobe packed with clothes, no clutter of cosmetics and grease-paints; a dressing-gown on the door, one sweater he recognized from Act II on the only easy chair, a tin of half-used paints and grease. A kettle hummed softly on a gas ring. She said, 'Would you like a cup of tea? Someone sent me a packet last week—sometimes the Americans do, instead of flowers, you know, on the first night.'

'I'd like a cup,' he said, but if there was one thing he hated it was tea. He watched her while she made it, made it, of course, all wrong: the water not on the boil, the teapot unheated, too few leaves. She said, 'I never quite understand why English people like tea.'

He drank his cupful quickly like a medicine and watched her gingerly and delicately sip at hers. He said, 'I wanted very much to see you. About Harry.'

It was the dreadful moment; he could see her mouth stiffen to meet it.

'Yes?'

'I had known him twenty years. I was his friend. We were at school together, you know, and after that—there weren't many months running when we didn't meet . . .'

She said, 'When I got your card, I couldn't say no. But there's nothing really for us to talk about, is there?—nothing.'

'I wanted to hear—'

'He's dead. That's the end. Everything's over, finished. What's the good of talking?'

'We both loved him.'

'I don't know. You can't know a thing like that—afterwards. I don't know anything any more except—'

'Except?'

'That I want to be dead too.'

Martins told me, 'Then I nearly went away. What was the good of tormenting her because of this wild idea of mine? But instead I asked her one question. "Do you know a man called Cooler?"'

'An American?' she asked. 'I think that was the man who brought me some money when Harry died. I didn't want to take it, but he said Harry had been anxious—at the last moment.'

'So he didn't die instantaneously?'

'Oh, no.'

Martins said to me, 'I began to wonder why I had got that idea so firmly into my head, and then I thought it was only the man in the flat who told me so—no one else. I said to her, "He must have been very clear in his head at the end—because he remembered about me too. That seems to show that there wasn't really any pain."'

'That's what I tell myself all the time.'

'Did you see the doctor?'

'Once. Harry sent me to him. He was Harry's own doctor. He lived near by, you see.'

Martins suddenly saw in that odd chamber of the mind that constructs such pictures, instantaneously, irrationally, a desert place, a body on the ground, a group of birds gathered. Perhaps it was a scene from one of his own books, not yet written, forming at the gate of consciousness. It faded, and he thought how odd that they were all there, just at that moment, all Harry's friends—Kurtz, the doctor, this man Cooler; only the two people who loved him seemed to have been missing. He said, 'And the driver? Did you hear his evidence?'

'He was upset, scared. But Cooler's evidence exonerated him. No, it wasn't his fault, poor man. I've often heard Harry say what a careful driver he was.'

'He knew Harry too?' Another bird flapped down and joined the others round the silent figure on the sand who lay face down. Now he could tell that it was Harry, by the clothes, by the attitude like that of a boy asleep in the grass at a playing-field's edge, on a hot summer afternoon.

Somebody called outside the window, 'Fräulein Schmidt.'

She said, 'They don't like one to stay too long. It uses up *their* electricity.'

He had given up the idea of sparing her anything. He told her, 'The police say they were going to arrest Harry. They'd pinned some racket on him.'

She took the news in much the same way as Kurtz. 'Everybody's in a racket.'

'I don't believe he was in anything serious.'

'No.'

'But he may have been framed. Do you know a man named Kurtz?'

'I don't think so.'

'He wears a toupée.'

'Oh.' He could tell that that struck home. He said, 'Don't you think that it was very odd they were all there—at the death? Everybody knew Harry. Even the driver, the doctor . . .'

She said with hopeless calm, 'I've wondered that too, though I didn't know about Kurtz. I wondered whether they'd murdered him, but what's the use of wondering?'

'I'm going to get those bastards,' Rollo Martins said.

'It won't do any good. Perhaps the police are right. Perhaps poor Harry got mixed up—'

'Fräulein Schmidt,' the voice called again.

'I must go.'

'I'll walk with you a bit of the way.'

The dark was almost down; the snow had ceased for a while to fall, and the great statues of the Ring, the prancing horses, the chariots and eagles, were gun-shot grey with the end of evening. 'It's better to give up and forget,' Anna said. The moon-lit snow lay ankle-deep on the unswept pavements.

'Will you give me the doctor's address?'

They stood in the shelter of a wall while she wrote it down for him.

'And yours too?'

'Why do you want that?'

'I might have news for you.'

'There isn't any news that would do any good now.' He watched her from a distance board her tram, bowing her head against the wind, a dark question mark on the snow.

6

An amateur detective has this advantage over the professional, that he doesn't work set hours. Rollo Martins was not confined to the eight-hour day: his investigations didn't have to pause for meals. In his one day he covered as much ground as one of my men would have covered in two, and he had this initial advantage over us, that he was Harry's friend. He was, as it were, working from inside, while we pecked at the perimeter.

Dr Winkler was at home. Perhaps he would not have been at home to a police officer. Again Martins had marked his card with the open-sesame phrase: 'A friend of Harry Lime's.'

Dr Winkler's waiting-room reminded Martins of an antique shop—an antique shop that specializes in religious *objets d'art*. There were more crucifixes than he could count, none of later date probably than the seventeenth century. There were statues in wood and ivory. There were a number of reliquaries: little bits of bone marked with saints' names and set in oval frames on a background of tinfoil. If they were genuine, what an odd fate it was, Martins thought, for a portion of Saint Susanna's knuckle to come to rest in Dr Winkler's waiting-room. Even the high-backed hideous chairs looked as if they had once been sat in by cardinals. The room was stuffy, and one expected the smell of incense. In a small gold casket was a splinter of the True Cross. A sneeze disturbed him.

Dr Winkler was the cleanest doctor Martins had ever seen. He was very small and neat, in a black tail-coat and a high stiff collar; his little black moustache was like an evening tie. He sneezed again: perhaps he was cold because he was so clean. He said, 'Mr Martins?'

An irresistible desire to sully Dr Winkler assailed Rollo Martins. He said, 'Dr Winkle?'

'Dr Winkler.'

'You've got an interesting collection here.'

'Yes.'

'These saints' bones . . .'

'The bones of chickens and rabbits.' Dr Winkler took a large white handkerchief out of his sleeve rather as though he were a conjurer producing his country's flag, and blew his nose neatly and thoroughly twice, closing each nostril in turn. You expected him to throw away the handkerchief after one use. 'Would you mind, Mr Martins, telling me the purpose of your visit? I have a patient waiting.'

'We were both friends of Harry Lime.'

'I was his medical adviser,' Dr Winkler corrected him and waited obstinately between the crucifixes.

'I arrived too late for the inquest. Harry had invited me out here to help him in something. I don't quite know what. I didn't hear of his death till I arrived.'

'Very sad,' Dr Winkler said.

'Naturally, under the circumstances, I want to hear all I can.'

'There is nothing I can tell you that you don't know. He was knocked over by a car. He was dead when I arrived.'

'Would he have been conscious at all?'

'I understand he was for a short time, while they carried him into the house.'

'In great pain?'

'Not necessarily.'

'You are quite certain that it was an accident?'

Dr Winkler put out a hand and straightened a crucifix. 'I was not there. My opinion is limited to the cause of death. Have you any reason to be dissatisfied?'

The amateur has another advantage over the professional: he can be reckless. He can tell unnecessary truths and propound wild theories. Martins said, 'The police have implicated Harry in a very serious racket. It seemed to me that he might have been murdered–or even killed himself.'

'I am not competent to pass an opinion,' Dr Winkler said.

'Do you know a man called Cooler?'

'I don't think so.'

'He was there when Harry was killed.'

'Then of course I have met him. He wears a toupée.'

'That was Kurtz.'

Dr Winkler was not only the cleanest, he was also the most cautious doctor that Martins had ever met. His statements were so limited that you could not for a moment doubt their veracity. He said, 'There was a second man there.' If he had to diagnose a case of scarlet fever he would, you felt, have confined himself to a statement that a rash was visible, that the temperature was so and so. He would never find himself in error at an inquest.

'Had you been Harry's doctor for long?' He seemed an odd man for Harry to choose–Harry who liked men with a certain recklessness, men capable of making mistakes.

'For about a year.'

'Well, it's good of you to have seen me.' Dr Winkler bowed. When he bowed there was a very slight creak as though his shirt were made of celluloid. 'I mustn't keep you from your patients any longer.' Turning away from Dr Winkler, he confronted yet another crucifix, the figure hanging with arms above the head: a face of elongated El Greco agony. 'That's a strange crucifix,' he said.

'Jansenist,' Dr Winkler commented and closed his mouth sharply as though he had been guilty of giving away too much information.

'Never heard the word. Why are the arms above the head?'

Dr Winkler said reluctantly, 'Because He died, in their view, only for the elect.'

7

As I see it, turning over my files, the notes of conversations, the statements of various characters, it would have been still possible, at this moment, for Rollo Martins to have left Vienna safely. He had shown an unhealthy curiosity, but the disease had been checked at every point. Nobody had given anything away. The smooth wall of deception had as yet shown no real crack to his roaming fingers. When Rollo Martins left Dr Winkler's he was in no danger. He could have gone home to bed at Sacher's and slept with a quiet mind. He could even have visited Cooler at this stage without trouble. No one was seriously disturbed. Unfortunately for him—and there would always be periods of his life when he bitterly regretted it—he chose to go back to Harry's flat. He wanted to talk to the little vexed man who said he had seen the accident—or had he really not said so much? There was a moment in the dark frozen street when he was inclined to go straight to Cooler, to complete his picture of those sinister birds who sat around Harry's body, but Rollo, being Rollo, decided to toss a coin and the coin fell for the other action, and the deaths of two men.

Perhaps the little man—who bore the name of Koch—had drunk a glass too much of wine, perhaps he had simply spent a good day at the office, but this time, when Rollo Martins rang his bell, he was friendly and quite ready to talk. He had just finished dinner and had crumbs on his moustache. 'Ah, I remember you. You are Herr Lime's friend.'

He welcomed Martins in with great cordiality and introduced him to a mountainous wife whom he obviously kept under very strict control. 'Ah, in the old days, I would have offered you a cup of coffee, but now—'

Martins passed round his cigarette case and the atmosphere of cordiality deepened. 'When you came yesterday I was a little abrupt,' Herr Koch said, 'but I had a touch of migraine and my wife was out, so I had to answer the door myself.'

'Did you tell me that you had actually seen the accident?'

Herr Koch exchanged glances with his wife. 'The inquest is over, Ilse. There is no harm. You can trust my judgement. The gentleman is a friend. Yes, I saw the accident, but you are the only one who knows. When I say that I saw it, perhaps I should say that I heard it. I heard the brakes put on and the sound of the skid, and I got to the window in time to see them carry the body to the house.'

'But didn't you give evidence?'

'It is better not to be mixed up in such things. My office cannot spare me. We are short of staff, and of course I did not actually *see*—'

'But you told me yesterday how it happened.'

'That was how they described it in the papers.'

'Was he in great pain?'

'He was dead. I looked right down from my window here and I saw his face. I know when a man is dead. You see, it is, in a way, my business. I am the head clerk at the mortuary.'

'But the others say that he did not die at once.'

'Perhaps they don't know death as well as I do.'

'He was dead, of course, when the doctor arrived. He told me that.'

'He was dead at once. You can take the word of a man who knows.'

'I think, Herr Koch, that you should have given evidence.'

'One must look after oneself, Herr Martins. I was not the only one who should have been there.'

'How do you mean?'

'There were three people who helped to carry your friend to the house.'

'I know–two men and the driver.'

'The driver stayed where he was. He was very much shaken, poor man.'

'Three men . . .' It was as though suddenly, fingering that bare wall, his fingers had encountered, not so much a crack perhaps, but at least a roughness that had not been smoothed away by the careful builders.

'Can you describe the men?'

But Herr Koch was not trained to observe the living: only the man with the toupée had attracted his eyes–the other two were just men, neither tall nor short, thick nor thin. He had seen them from far above, foreshortened, bent over their burden; they had not looked up, and he had quickly looked away and closed the window, realizing at once the wisdom of not being seen himself.

'There was no evidence I could really give, Herr Martins.'

No evidence, Martins thought, no evidence! He no longer doubted that murder had been done. Why else had they lied about the moment of death? They wanted to quieten with their gifts of money and their plane ticket the only two friends Harry had in Vienna. And the third man? Who was he?

He said, 'Did you see Herr Lime go out?'

'No.'

'Did you hear a scream?'

'Only the brakes, Herr Martins.'

It occurred to Martins that there was nothing–except the word of Kurtz and Cooler and the driver–to prove that in fact Harry had been killed at that precise moment. There was the medical evidence, but that could not prove more than that he had died, say, within a half-hour, and in any case the medical evidence was only as strong as Dr Winkler's word: that clean controlled man creaking among his crucifixes.

'Herr Martins, it just occurs to me–you are staying in Vienna?'

'Yes.'

'If you need accommodation and spoke to the authorities quickly, you might secure Herr Lime's flat. It is a requisitioned property.'

'Who has the keys?'

'I have them.'

'Could I see the flat?'

'Ilse, the keys.'

Herr Koch led the way into the flat that had been Harry's. In the little dark hall there was still the smell of cigarette smoke—the Turkish cigarettes that Harry always smoked. It seemed odd that a man's smell should cling in the folds of a curtain so long after the man himself had become dead matter, a gas, a decay. One light, in a heavily beaded shade, left them in semi-darkness, fumbling for door handles.

The living-room was completely bare—it seemed to Martins too bare. The chairs had been pushed up against the walls; the desk at which Harry must have written was free from dust or any papers. The parquet reflected the light like a mirror. Herr Koch opened a door and showed the bedroom: the bed neatly made with clean sheets. In the bathroom not even a used razor blade indicated that a few days ago a living man had occupied it. Only the dark hall and the cigarette smell gave a sense of occupation.

'You see,' Herr Koch said, 'it is quite ready for a newcomer. Ilse has cleaned up.'

That she certainly had done. After a death there should have been more litter left than this. A man can't go suddenly and unexpectedly on his longest journey without forgetting this or that, without leaving a bill unpaid, an official form unanswered, the photograph of a girl. 'Were there no papers, Herr Koch?'

'Herr Lime was always a very tidy man. His wastepaper basket was full and his brief-case, but his friend fetched that away.'

'His friend?'

'The gentleman with the toupée.'

It was possible, of course, that Lime had not taken the journey so unexpectedly, and it occurred to Martins that Lime had perhaps hoped he would arrive in time to help. He said to Herr Koch, 'I believe my friend was murdered.'

'Murdered?' Herr Koch's cordiality was snuffed out by the word. He said, 'I would not have asked you in here if I had thought you would talk such nonsense.'

'Why should it be nonsense?'

'We do not have murders in this zone.'

'All the same, your evidence may be very valuable.'

'I have no evidence. I saw nothing. I am not concerned. You must leave here at once, please. You have been very inconsiderate.' He hustled Martins back through the hall; already the smell of the smoke was fading a little more. Herr Koch's last words before he slammed his own door was, 'It's no concern of mine.' Poor Herr Koch! We do not choose our concerns. Later, when I was questioning Martins closely, I said to him, 'Did you see anybody at all on the stairs, or in the street outside?'

'Nobody.' He had everything to gain by remembering some chance passer-by, and I believed him. He said, 'I noticed myself how quiet and dead the whole street looked. Part of it had been bombed, you know, and the moon was shining on the snow slopes. It was so very silent. I could hear my own feet creaking in the snow.'

'Of course, it proves nothing. There is a basement where anybody who had followed you could have hidden.'

'Yes.'

'Or your whole story may be phoney.'

'Yes.'

'The trouble is I can see no motive for you to have done it. It's true you are already guilty of getting money on false pretences. You came out here to join Lime, perhaps to help him . . .'

Martins said to me, 'What was this precious racket you keep on hinting at?'

'I'd have told you all the facts when I first saw you if you hadn't lost your temper so damned quickly. Now I don't think I shall be acting wisely to tell you. It would be disclosing official information, and your contacts, you know, don't inspire confidence. A girl with phoney papers supplied by Lime, this man Kurtz . . .'

'Dr Winkler . . .'

'I've got nothing against Dr Winkler. No, if you are phoney, you don't need the information, but it might help you to learn exactly what we know. You see, our facts are not complete.'

'I bet they aren't. I could invent a better detective than you in my bath.'

'Your literary style does not do your namesake justice.' Whenever he was reminded of Mr Crabbin, that poor harassed representative of the British Council, Rollo Martins turned pink, with annoyance, embarrassment, shame. That too inclined me to trust him.

He had certainly given Crabbin some uncomfortable hours. On returning to Sacher's Hotel after his interview with Herr Koch he had found a desperate note waiting for him from the representative.

'I have been trying to locate you all day,' Crabbin wrote. 'It is essential that we should get together and work out a proper programme for you. This morning by telephone I have arranged lectures at Innsbruck and Salzburg for next week, but I must have your consent to the subjects, so that proper programmes can be printed. I would suggest two lectures: "The Crisis of Faith in the Western World" (you are very respected here as a Christian writer, but this lecture should be quite unpolitical and no references should be made to Russia or Communism) and "The Technique of the Contemporary Novel". The same lectures would be given in Vienna. Apart from this, there are a great many people here who would like to meet you, and I want to arrange a cocktail party for early next week. But for all this I must have a few words with you.' The letter ended on a note of acute anxiety. 'You will be at the discussion tomorrow night, won't you? We all expect you at 8.30 and, needless to say, look forward to your coming. I will send transport to the hotel at 8.15 sharp.'

Rollo Martins read the letter and, without bothering any further about Mr Crabbin, went to bed.

8

After two drinks Rollo Martins' mind would always turn towards women—in a vague, sentimental, romantic way, as a sex, in general. After three drinks, like a pilot who dives to find direction, he would begin to focus on one available girl. If he had not been offered a third drink by Cooler, he would probably not have gone quite so soon to Anna Schmidt's house, and if—but there are too many 'ifs' in my style of writing, for it is my profession to balance possibilities, human possibilities, and the drive of destiny can never find a place in my files.

Martins had spent his lunch-time reading up the reports of the inquest, thus again demonstrating the superiority of the amateur to the professional, and making him more vulnerable to Cooler's liquor (which the professional in duty bound would have refused). It was nearly five o'clock when he reached Cooler's flat, which was over an ice-cream parlour in the American zone: the bar below was full of G.I.s with their girls, and the clatter of the long spoons and the curious free unformed laughter followed him up the stairs.

The Englishman who objects to Americans in general usually carries in his mind's eye just such an exception as Cooler: a man with tousled grey hair and a worried kindly face and long-sighted eyes, the kind of humanitarian who turns up in a typhus epidemic or a world war or a Chinese famine long before his countrymen have discovered the place in an atlas. Again the card marked 'Harry's friend' was like an entrance ticket. Cooler was in officer's uniform, with mysterious letters on his flash, and no badges of rank, although his maid referred to him as Colonel Cooler. His warm frank handclasp was the most friendly act that Martins had encountered in Vienna.

'Any friend of Harry is all right with me,' Cooler said. 'I've heard of you, of course.'

'From Harry?'

'I'm a great reader of Westerns,' Cooler said, and Martins believed him as he did not believe Kurtz.

'I wondered—you were there, weren't you?—if you'd tell me about Harry's death.'

'It was a terrible thing,' Cooler said. 'I was just crossing the road to go to Harry. He and Mr Kurtz were on the sidewalk. Maybe if I hadn't started across the road, he'd have stayed where he was. But he saw me and stepped straight off to meet me and this jeep—it was terrible, terrible. The driver braked, but he didn't stand a chance. Have a Scotch, Mr Martins. It's silly of me, but I get shaken up when I think of it.' He said as he splashed in the soda, 'In spite of this uniform, I'd never seen a man killed before.'

'Was the other man in the car?'

Cooler took a long pull and then measured what was left with his tired kindly eyes. 'What man would you be referring to, Mr Martins?'

'I was told there was another man there.'

'I don't know how you got that idea. You'll find all about it in the inquest reports.' He poured out two more generous drinks. 'There were just the three of us—me and Mr Kurtz and the driver. The doctor, of course. I expect you were thinking of the doctor.'

'This man I was talking to happened to look out of a window—he has the next flat to Harry's—and he said he saw three men and the driver. That's before the doctor arrived.'

'He didn't say that in court.'

'He didn't want to get involved.'

'You'll never teach these Europeans to be good citizens. It was his duty.' Cooler brooded sadly over his glass. 'It's an odd thing, Mr Martins, with accidents. You'll never get two reports that coincide. Why, even Mr Kurtz and I disagreed about details. The thing happens so suddenly, you aren't concerned to notice things, until bang crash, and then you have to reconstruct, remember. I expect he got too tangled up trying to sort out what happened before and what after, to distinguish the four of us.'

'The four?'

'I was counting Harry. What else did he see, Mr Martins?'

'Nothing of interest—except he says Harry was dead when he was carried to the house.'

'Well, he was dying—not much difference there. Have another drink, Mr Martins?'

'No, I don't think I will.'

'Well, I'd like another spot. I was very fond of your friend, Mr Martins, and I don't like talking about it.'

'Perhaps one more—to keep you company. Do you know Anna Schmidt?' Martins asked, while the whisky tingled on his tongue.

'Harry's girl? I met her once, that's all. As a matter of fact, I helped Harry fix her papers. Not the sort of thing I should confess to a stranger, I suppose, but you have to break the rules sometimes. Humanity's a duty too.'

'What was wrong?'

'She was Hungarian and her father had been a Nazi, so they said. She was scared the Russians would pick her up.'

'Why should they want to?'

'We can't always figure out why they do these things. Perhaps just to show that it's not healthy being friends with an Englishman.'

'But she lives in the British zone.'

'That wouldn't stop them. It's only five minutes' ride in a jeep from the Commandatura. The streets aren't well lighted, and you haven't many police around.'

'You took her some money from Harry, didn't you?'

'Yes, but I wouldn't have mentioned that. Did she tell you?'

The telephone rang, and Cooler drained his glass. 'Hullo,' he said. 'Why, yes. This is Colonel Cooler.' Then he sat with the receiver at his ear and an expression of sad patience, while some voice a long way off drained into the room. 'Yes,' he said once. 'Yes.' His eyes dwelt on Martins' face, but they seemed to be looking a long way beyond him: flat and tired and kind, they might have been gazing out across the sea. He said, 'You did quite right,' in a tone of commendation, and then, with a touch of asperity, 'Of course they will be delivered. I gave my word. Good-bye.'

He put the receiver down and passed a hand across his forehead wearily. It was as though he were trying to remember something he had to do. Martins said, 'Had you heard anything of this racket the police talk about?'

'I'm sorry. What's that?'

'They say Harry was mixed up in some racket.'

'Oh, no,' Cooler said. 'No. That's quite impossible. He had a great sense of duty.'

'Kurtz seemed to think it was possible.'

'Kurtz doesn't understand how an Anglo-Saxon feels,' Cooler replied.

9

It was nearly dark when Martins made his way along the banks of the canal: across the water lay the half-destroyed Diana baths and in the distance the great black circle of the Prater Wheel, stationary above the ruined houses. Over there across the grey water was the Second Bezirk, in Russian ownership. St Stephanskirche shot its enormous wounded spire into the sky above the Inner City, and, coming up the Kärntnerstrasse, Martins passed the lit door of the Military Police station. The four men of the International Patrol were climbing into their jeep; the Russian M.P. sat beside the driver (for the Russians had that day taken over the chair for the next four weeks) and the Englishman, the Frenchman, and the American mounted behind. The third stiff whisky fumed into Martins' brain, and he remembered the girl in Amsterdam, the girl in Paris; loneliness moved along the crowded pavement at his side. He passed the corner of the street where Sacher's lay and went on. Rollo was in control and moved towards the only girl he knew in Vienna.

I asked him how he knew where she lived. Oh, he said, he'd looked up the address she had given him the night before, in bed, studying a map. He wanted to know his way about, and he was good with maps. He could memorize turnings and street names easily because he always went one way on foot.

'One way?'

'I mean when I'm calling on a girl—or someone.'

He hadn't, of course, known that she would be in, that her play was not on that night in the Josefstadt, or perhaps he had memorized that too from the posters. In at any rate she was, if you could really call it being in, sitting alone in an unheated room, with the bed disguised as a divan, and a typewritten script lying open at the first page on the inadequate too-fancy topply table—because her thoughts were so far from being 'in'. He said awkwardly (and nobody could have said, not even Rollo, how much his awkwardness was part of his technique), 'I thought I'd just look in and look you up. You see, I was passing . . .'

'Passing? Where to?' It had been a good half an hour's walk from the Inner City to the rim of the English zone, but he always had a reply. 'I had too much whisky with Colonel Cooler. I needed a walk and I just happened to find myself this way.'

'I can't give you a drink here. Except tea. There's some of that packet left.'

'No, no thank you.' He said, 'You are busy,' looking at the script.

'I didn't get beyond the first line.'

He picked it up and read: '*Enter Louise.* LOUISE: I heard a child crying.'

'Can I stay a little?' he asked with a gentleness that was more Martins than Rollo.

'I wish you would.' He slumped down on the divan, and he told me a long time later (for lovers reconstruct the smallest details if they can find a listener) that then it was he took his second real look at her. She stood there as awkward as himself in a pair of old flannel trousers which had been patched badly in the seat; she stood with her legs firmly straddled as though she were opposing someone and was determined to hold her ground–a small rather stocky figure with any grace she had folded and put away for use professionally.

'One of those bad days?' he asked.

'It's always bad about this time.' She explained, 'He used to look in, and when I heard you ring, just for a moment, I thought . . .' She sat down on a hard chair opposite him and said, 'Please talk. You knew him. Just tell me anything.'

And so he talked. The sky blackened outside the window while he talked. He noticed after a while that their hands had met. He said to me, 'I never meant to fall in love, not with Harry's girl.'

'When did it happen?' I asked him.

'It was very cold and I got up to close the window curtains. I only noticed my hand was on hers when I took it away. As I stood up I looked down at her face and she was looking up. It wasn't a beautiful face–that was the trouble. It was a face to live with, day in, day out. A face for wear. I felt as though I'd come into a new country where I couldn't speak the language. I had always thought it was beauty one loved in a woman. I stood there at the curtains, waiting to pull them, looking out. I couldn't see anything but my own face, looking back into the room, looking for her. She said, "And what did Harry do that time?" and I wanted to say, "Damn Harry. He's dead. We both loved him, but he's dead. The dead are made to be forgotten." Instead, of course, all I said was, "What do you think? He just whistled his old tune as if nothing was the matter," and I whistled it to her as well as I could. I heard her catch her breath, and I looked round and before I could think: Is this the right way, the right card, the right gambit?–I'd already said, "He's dead. You can't go on remembering him for ever."'

She said, 'I know, but perhaps something will happen first.'

'What do you mean–something happen?'

'Oh, I mean perhaps there'll be another war, or I'll die, or the Russians will take me.'

'You'll forget him in time. You'll fall in love again.'

'I know, but I don't want to. Don't you see I don't want to?'

So Rollo Martins came back from the window and sat down on the divan again. When he had risen half a minute before he had been the friend of Harry, comforting Harry's girl; now he was a man in love with Anna Schmidt who had been in love with a man they had both once known called Harry Lime. He didn't speak again that evening about the past. Instead he began to tell her of the people he had seen. 'I can believe anything of Winkler,' he told her, 'but Cooler—I liked Cooler. He was the only one of his friends who stood up for Harry. The trouble is, if Cooler's right, then Koch is wrong, and I really thought I had something there.'

'Who's Koch?'

He explained how he had returned to Harry's flat and he described his interview with Koch, the story of the third man.

'If it's true,' she said, 'it's very important.'

'It doesn't prove anything. After all, Koch backed out of the inquest; so might this stranger.'

'That's not the point,' she said. 'It means that *they* lied: Kurtz and Cooler.'

'They might have lied so as not to inconvenience this fellow—if he was a friend.'

'Yet another friend—on the spot. And where's your Cooler's honesty then?'

'What do we do? Koch clamped down like an oyster and turned me out of his flat.'

'He won't turn me out,' she said, 'or his Ilse won't.'

They walked up the long road to the flat together; the snow clogged on their shoes and made them move slowly like convicts weighed down by irons. Anna Schmidt said, 'Is it far?'

'Not very far now. Do you see that knot of people up the road? It's somewhere about there.' The group was like a splash of ink on the whiteness, a splash that flowed, changed shape, spread out. When they came a little nearer Martins said, 'I think that's his block. What do you suppose this is, a political demonstration?'

Anna Schmidt stopped. She said, 'Who else have you told about Koch?'

'Only you and Colonel Cooler. Why?'

'I'm frightened. It reminds me . . .' She had her eyes fixed on the crowd and he never knew what memory out of her confused past had risen to warn her. 'Let's go away,' she implored him.

'You're crazy. We're on to something here, something big . . .'

'I'll wait for you.'

'But you're going to talk to him.'

'Find out first what all those people . . .' She said, strangely for one who worked behind the footlights, 'I hate crowds.'

He walked slowly on alone, the snow caking on his heels. It wasn't a political meeting, for no one was making a speech. He had the impression of heads turning to watch him come, as though he were somebody who was expected. When he reached the fringe of the little crowd, he knew for certain that it was the house. A man looked hard at him and said, 'Are you another of them?'

'What do you mean?'

'The police.'

'No. What are they doing?'

'They've been in and out all day.'

'What's everybody waiting for?'

'They want to see him brought out.'

'Who?'

'Herr Koch.' It occurred to Martins that somebody besides himself had discovered Herr Koch's failure to give evidence, though that was hardly a police matter. He said, 'What's he done?'

'Nobody knows that yet. They can't make their minds up in there–it might be suicide, you see, and it might be murder.'

'Herr Koch?'

'Of course.'

A small child came up to his informant and pulled at his hand. 'Papa, Papa.' He wore a wool cap on his head, like a gnome; his face was pinched and blue with cold.

'Yes, my dear, what is it?'

'I heard them talking through the grating, Papa.'

'Oh, you cunning little one. Tell us what you heard, Hansel.'

'I heard Frau Koch crying, Papa.'

'Was that all, Hansel?'

'No. I heard the big man talking, Papa.'

'Ah, you cunning little Hansel. Tell Papa what he said.'

'He said, "Can you tell me, Frau Koch, what the foreigner looked like?"'

'Ha, ha, you see, they think it's murder. And who's to say they are wrong? Why should Herr Koch cut his own throat in the basement?'

'Papa, Papa.'

'Yes, little Hansel?'

'When I looked through the grating, I could see some blood on the coke.'

'What a child you are. How could you tell it was blood? The snow leaks everywhere.' The man turned to Martins and said, 'The child has such an imagination. Maybe he will be a writer when he grows up.'

The pinched face stared solemnly up at Martins. The child said, 'Papa.'

'Yes, Hansel?'

'He's a foreigner too.'

The man gave a big laugh that caused a dozen heads to turn. 'Listen to him, sir, listen,' he said proudly. 'He thinks you did it just because you are a foreigner. As though there weren't more foreigners here these days than Viennese.'

'Papa, Papa.'

'Yes, Hansel?'

'They are coming out.'

A knot of police surrounded the covered stretcher which they lowered carefully down the steps for fear of sliding on the trodden snow. The man said, 'They can't get an ambulance into this street because of the ruins. They have to carry it round the corner.' Frau Koch came out at the tail of the procession; she had a shawl over her head and an old sackcloth coat. Her thick shape looked like a snowman as she sank in a drift at the pavement's

edge. Someone gave her a hand and she looked round with a lost hopeless
gaze at this crowd of strangers. If there were friends there she did not
recognize them, looking from face to face. Martins bent as she passed,
fumbling at his shoelace, but looking up from the ground he saw at his own
eyes' level the scrutinizing cold-blooded gnome-gaze of little Hansel.

Walking back down the street towards Anna, he looked back once. The
child was pulling at his father's hand and he could see the lips forming round
those syllables like the refrain of a grim ballad, 'Papa, Papa.'

He said to Anna, 'Koch has been murdered. Come away from here.' He
walked as rapidly as the snow would let him, turning this corner and that.
The child's suspicion and alertness seemed to spread like a cloud over the
city—they could not walk fast enough to evade its shadow. He paid no
attention when Anna said to him, 'Then what Koch said was true. There *was*
a third man,' nor a little later when she said, 'It must have been murder. You
don't kill a man to hide anything less.'

The tramcars flashed like icicles at the end of the street: they were back at
the Ring. Martins said, 'You had better go home alone. I'll keep away from
you awhile till things have sorted out.'

'But nobody can suspect you.'

'They are asking about the foreigner who called on Koch yesterday.
There may be some unpleasantness for a while.'

'Why don't you go to the police?'

'They are so stupid. I don't trust them. See what they've pinned on Harry.
And then I tried to hit this man Callaghan. They'll have it in for me. The
least they'll do is send me away from Vienna. But if I stay quiet—there's only
one person who can give me away. Cooler.'

'And he won't want to.'

'Not if he's guilty. But then I can't believe he's guilty.'

Before she left him, she said, 'Be careful. Koch knew so very little and they
murdered him. You know as much as Koch.'

The warning stayed in his brain all the way to Sacher's: after nine o'clock
the streets are very empty, and he would turn his head at every padding step
coming up the street behind him, as though that third man whom they had
protected so ruthlessly were following him like an executioner. The Russian
sentry outside the Grand Hotel looked rigid with the cold, but he was
human, he had a face, an honest peasant face with Mongol eyes. The third
man had no face: only the top of a head seen from a window. At Sacher's Mr
Schmidt said, 'Colonel Calloway has been in, asking for you, sir. I think
you'll find him in the bar.'

'Back in a moment,' Martins said and walked straight out of the hotel
again: he wanted time to think. But immediately he stepped outside a man
came forward, touched his cap, and said firmly, 'Please, sir.' He flung open
the door of a khaki-painted truck with a Union Jack on the windscreen and
firmly urged Martins within. He surrendered without protest; sooner or
later, he felt sure, inquiries would be made; he had only pretended optimism
to Anna Schmidt.

The driver drove too fast for safety on the frozen road, and Martins
protested. All he got in reply was a sullen grunt and a muttered sentence
containing the word 'orders'. 'Have you orders to kill me?' Martins asked

facetiously and got no reply at all. He caught sight of the Titans on the Hofburg balancing great globes of snow above their heads, and then they plunged into ill-lit streets beyond, where he lost all sense of direction.

'Is it far?' But the driver paid no attention at all. At least, Martins thought, I am not under arrest: they have not sent a guard; I am being invited–wasn't that the word they used?–to visit the station to make a statement.

The car drew up and the driver led the way up two flights of stairs; he rang the bell of a great double door, and Martins was aware of many voices beyond it. He turned sharply to the driver and said, 'Where the hell . . . ?' but the driver was already half-way down the stairs, and already the door was opening. His eyes were dazzled from the darkness by the lights inside; he heard, but he could hardly see, the advance of Crabbin. 'Oh, Mr Dexter, we have been so anxious, but better late than never. Let me introduce you to Miss Wilbraham and the Gräfin von Meyersdorf.'

A buffet laden with coffee cups; an urn steaming; a woman's face shiny with exertion; two young men with the happy intelligent faces of sixth-formers; and, huddled in the background, like faces in a family album, a multitude of the old-fashioned, the dingy, the earnest and cheery features of constant readers. Martins looked behind him, but the door had closed.

He said desperately to Mr Crabbin, 'I'm sorry, but—'

'Don't think any more about it,' Mr Crabbin said. 'One cup of coffee and then let's go on to the discussion. We have a very good gathering tonight. They'll put you on your mettle, Mr Dexter.' One of the young men placed a cup in his hand, the other shovelled in sugar before he could say he preferred his coffee unsweetened. The younger man breathed into his ear, 'Afterwards would you mind signing one of your books, Mr Dexter?' A large woman in black silk bore down upon him and said, 'I don't mind if the Gräfin does hear me, Mr Dexter, but I don't like your books, I don't approve of them. I think a novel should tell a good story.'

'So do I,' Martins said hopelessly.

'Now, Mrs Bannock, wait for question time.'

'I know I'm downright, but I'm sure Mr Dexter values *honest* criticism.'

An old lady, who he supposed was the Gräfin, said, 'I do not read many English books, Mr Dexter, but I am told that yours . . .'

'Do you mind drinking up?' Crabbin said and hustled him through into an inner room where a number of elderly people were sitting on a semi-circle of chairs with an air of sad patience.

Martins was not able to tell me very much about the meeting; his mind was still dazed with the death; when he looked up he expected to see at any moment the child Hansel and hear that persistent pedantic refrain, 'Papa, Papa.' Apparently Crabbin opened the proceedings, and, knowing Crabbin, I am sure that it was a very lucid, very fair and unbiased picture of the contemporary English novel. I have heard him give that talk so often, varied only by the emphasis given to the work of the particular English visitor. He would have touched lightly on various problems of technique–the point of view, the passage of time–and then he would have declared the meeting open for questions and discussion.

Martins missed the first question altogether, but luckily Crabbin filled the gap and answered it satisfactorily. A woman wearing a brown hat and a piece of fur round her throat said with passionate interest, 'May I ask Mr Dexter if he is engaged on a new work?'

'Oh, yes—yes.'

'May I ask the title?'

'"The Third Man",' Martins said and gained a spurious confidence as the result of taking that hurdle.

'Mr Dexter, could you tell us what author has chiefly influenced you?'

Martins, without thinking, said, 'Grey.' He meant of course the author of *Riders of the Purple Sage*, and he was pleased to find his reply gave general satisfaction—to all save an elderly Austrian who asked, 'Grey. What Grey? I do not know the name.'

Martins felt he was safe now and said, 'Zane Grey—I don't know any other,' and was mystified at the low subservient laughter from the English colony.

Crabbin interposed quickly for the sake of the Austrians, 'That is a little joke of Mr Dexter's. He meant the poet Gray—a gentle, mild, subtle genius—one can see the affinity.'

'And he is called Zane Grey?'

'That was Mr Dexter's joke. Zane Grey wrote what we call Westerns—cheap popular novelettes about bandits and cowboys.'

'He is not a great writer?'

'No, no. Far from it,' Mr Crabbin said. 'In the strict sense I would not call him a writer at all.' Martins told me that he felt the first stirrings of revolt at that statement. He had never regarded himself before as a writer, but Crabbin's self-confidence irritated him—even the way the light flashed back from Crabbin's spectaclewwmed an added cause of vexation. Crabbin said, 'He was just a popular entertainer.'

'Why the hell not?' Martins said fiercely.

'Oh, well, I merely meant—'

'What was Shakespeare?'

Somebody with great daring said, 'A poet.'

'Have you ever read Zane Grey?'

'No, I can't say—'

'Then you don't know what you are talking about.'

One of the young men tried to come to Crabbin's rescue.

'And James Joyce, where would you put James Joyce, Mr Dexter?'

'What do you mean put? I don't want to put anybody anywhere,' Martins said. It had been a very full day: he had drunk too much with Colonel Cooler; he had fallen in love; a man had been murdered—and now he had the quite unjust feeling that he was being got at. Zane Grey was one of his heroes: he was damned if he was going to stand any nonsense.

'I mean would you put him among the really great?'

'If you want to know, I've never heard of him. What did he write?'

He didn't realize it, but he was making an enormous impression. Only a great writer could have taken so arrogant, so original a line. Several people wrote Zane Grey's name on the backs of envelopes and the Gräfin whispered hoarsely to Crabbin, 'How do you spell Zane?'

'To tell you the truth, I'm not quite sure.'

A number of names were simultaneously flung at Martins—little sharp pointed names like Stein, round pebbles like Woolf. A young Austrian with an intellectual black forelock called out, 'Daphne du Maurier,' and Mr Crabbin winced and looked sideways at Martins. He said in an undertone, 'Be gentle with them.'

A kind-faced woman in a hand-knitted jumper said wistfully, 'Don't you agree, Mr Dexter, that no one, no one has written about *feelings* so poetically as Virginia Woolf? In prose, I mean.'

Crabbin whispered, 'You might say something about the stream of consciousness.'

'Stream of what?'

A note of despair came into Crabbin's voice. 'Please, Mr Dexter, these people are you genuine admirers. They want to hear your views. If you knew how they have *besieged* the Institute.'

An elderly Austrian said, 'Is there any writer in England today of the stature of the late John Galsworthy?'

There was an outburst of angry twittering in which the names of Du Maurier, Priestley, and somebody called Layman were flung to and fro. Martins sat gloomily back and saw again the snow, the stretcher, the desperate face of Frau Koch. He thought: if I had never returned, if I had never asked questions, would that little man still be alive? How had he benefited Harry by supplying another victim to assuage the fear of whom?—Herr Kurtz, Colonel Cooler (he could not believe that), Dr Winkler? Not one of them seemed adequate to the drab gruesome crime in the basement; he could hear the child saying, 'I saw blood on the coke,' and somebody turned towards him a blank face without features, a grey plasticine egg, the third man.

Martins could not have said how he got through the rest of the discussion. Perhaps Crabbin took the brunt; perhaps he was helped by some of the audience who got into an animated discussion about the film version of a popular American novel. He remembered very little more before Crabbin was making a final speech in his honour. Then one of the young men led him to a table stacked with books and asked him to sign them. 'We have only allowed each member one book.'

'What have I got to do?'

'Just a signature. That's all they expect. This is my copy of *The Curved Prow*. I would be so grateful if you'd just write a little something . . .'

Martins took his pen and wrote: 'From B. Dexter, author of *The Lone Rider of Santa Fé*,' and the young man read the sentence and blotted it with a puzzled expression. As Martins sat down and started signing Benjamin Dexter's title pages, he could see in a mirror the young man showing the inscription to Crabbin. Crabbin smiled weakly and stroked his chin, up and down, up and down. 'B. Dexter, B. Dexter, B. Dexter,' Martins wrote rapidly—it was not, after all, a lie. One by one the books were collected by their owners; little half-sentences of delight and compliment were dropped like curtsies—was this what it was to be a writer? Martins began to feel distinct irritation towards Benjamin Dexter. The complacent, tiring, pompous ass, he thought, signing the twenty-seventh copy of *The Curved Prow*. Every time he looked up and took another book he saw Crabbin's worried speculative gaze. The members of the Institute were beginning to go home with their spoils: the room was emptying. Suddenly in the mirror Martins saw a military policeman. He seemed to be having an argument with one of Crabbin's young henchmen. Martins thought he caught the sound of his own name. It was then he lost his nerve and with it any relic of common sense. There was only one book left to sign; he dashed off a last 'B. Dexter' and made for the door. The young man, Crabbin, and the policeman stood together at the entrance.

'And this gentleman?' the policeman asked.

'It's Mr. Benjamin Dexter,' the young man said.

'Lavatory. Is there a lavatory?' Martins said.

'I understand a Mr Rollo Martins came here in one of your cars.'

'A mistake. An obvious mistake.'

'Second door on the left,' the young man said.

Martins grabbed his coat from the cloakroom as he went and made down the stairs. On the first-floor landing he heard someone mounting the stairs and, looking over, saw Paine, whom I had sent to identify him. He opened a door at random and shut it behind him. He could hear Paine going by. The room where he stood was in darkness; a curious moaning sound made him turn and face whatever room it was.

He could see nothing and the sound had stopped. He made a tiny movement and once more it started, like an impeded breath. He remained still and the sound died away. Outside somebody called, 'Mr Dexter, Mr Dexter.' Then a new sound started. It was like somebody whispering—a long continuous monologue in the darkness. Martins said, 'Is anybody there?' and the sound stopped again. He could stand no more of it. He took out his lighter. Footsteps went by and down the stairs. He scraped and scraped at the little wheel and no light came. Somebody shifted in the dark, and something rattled in mid-air like a chain. He asked once more with the anger of fear, 'Is anybody there?' and only the click-click of metal answered him.

Martins felt desperately for a light switch, first to his right hand and then to his left. He did not dare go farther because he could no longer locate his fellow occupant; the whisper, the moaning, the click had all stopped. Then he was afraid that he had lost the door and felt wildly for the knob. He was far less afraid of the police than he was of the darkness, and he had no idea of the noise he was making.

Paine heard it from the bottom of the stairs and came back. He switched on the landing light, and the glow under the door gave Martins his direction. He opened the door and, smiling weakly at Paine, turned back to take a second look at the room. The eyes of a parrot chained to a perch stared beadily back at him. Paine said respectfully, 'We were looking for you, sir. Colonel Calloway wants a word with you.'

'I lost my way,' Martins said.

'Yes, sir. We thought that was what had happened.'

10

I had kept a very careful record of Martins' movements from the moment I knew that he had not caught the plane home. He had been seen with Kurtz, and at the Josefstadt Theatre; I knew about his visit to Dr Winkler and to Colonel Cooler, his first return to the block where Harry had lived. For some reason my man lost him between Cooler's and Anna Schmidt's flats; he reported that Martins had wandered widely, and the impression we both got was that he had deliberately thrown off his shadower. I tried to pick him up at the hotel and just missed him.

Events had taken a disquieting turn, and it seemed to me that the time had come for another interview. He had a lot to explain.

I put a good wide desk between us and gave him a cigarette. I found him sullen but ready to talk, within strict limits. I asked him about Kurtz and he seemed to me to answer satisfactorily. I then asked him about Anna Schmidt and I gathered from his reply that he must have been with her after visiting Colonel Cooler; that filled in one of the missing points. I tried him with Dr Winkler, and he answered readily enough. 'You've been getting around,' I said, 'quite a bit. And have you found out anything about your friend?'

'Oh, yes,' he said. 'It was under your nose but you didn't see it.'

'What?'

'That he was murdered.' That took me by surprise: I had at one time played with the idea of suicide, but I had ruled even that out.

'Go on,' I said. He tried to eliminate from his story all mention of Koch, talking about an informant who had seen the accident. This made his story rather confusing, and I couldn't grasp at first why he attached so much importance to the third man.

'He didn't turn up at the inquest, and the others lied to keep him out.'

'Nor did your man turn up – I don't see much importance in that. If it was a genuine accident, all the evidence needed was there. Why get the other chap in trouble? Perhaps his wife thought he was out of town; perhaps he was an official absent without leave – people sometimes take unauthorized trips to Vienna from places like Klagenfurt. The delights of the great city, for what they are worth.'

'There was more to it than that. The little chap who told me about it – they've murdered him. You see, they obviously didn't know what else he had seen.'

'Now we have it,' I said. 'You mean Koch.'

'Yes.'

'As far as we know, you were the last person to see him alive.' I questioned him then, as I've written, to find out if he had been followed to Koch's by somebody who was sharper than my man and had kept out of sight. I said, 'The Austrian police are anxious to pin this on you. Frau Koch told them how disturbed her husband was by your visit. Who else knew about it?'

'I told Cooler.' He said excitedly, 'Suppose immediately I left he telephoned the story to someone–to the third man. They had to stop Koch's mouth.'

'When you told Colonel Cooler about Koch, the man was already dead. That night he got out of bed, hearing someone, and went downstairs—'

'Well, that rules me out. I was in Sacher's.'

'But he went to bed very early. Your visit brought back the migraine. It was soon after nine when he got up. You returned to Sacher's at nine-thirty. Where were you before that?'

He said gloomily, 'Wandering round and trying to sort things out.'

'Any evidence of your movements?'

'No.'

I wanted to frighten him, so there was no point in telling him that he had been followed all the time. I knew that he hadn't cut Koch's throat, but I wasn't sure that he was quite so innocent as he made out. The man who owns the knife is not always the real murderer.

'Can I have another cigarette?'

'Yes.'

He said, 'How did you know that I went to Koch's? That was why you pulled me in here, wasn't it?'

'The Austrian police—'

'They hadn't identified me.'

'Immediately you left Colonel Cooler's, he telephoned to me.'

'Then that lets him out. If he had been concerned, he wouldn't have wanted me to tell you my story–to tell Koch's story, I mean.'

'He might assume that you were a sensible man and would come to me with your story as soon as you learned of Koch's death. By the way, how did you learn of it?'

He told me promptly and I believed him. It was then I began to believe him altogether. He said, 'I still can't believe Cooler's concerned. I'd stake anything on his honesty. He's one of those Americans with a real sense of duty.'

'Yes,' I said, 'he told me about that when he phoned. He apologized for it. He said it was the worst of having been brought up to believe in citizenship. He said it made him feel a prig. To tell you the truth, Cooler irritates me. Of course, he doesn't know that I know about his tyre deals.'

'Is he in a racket, too, then?'

'Not a very serious one. I daresay he's salted away twenty-five thousand dollars. But I'm not a good citizen. Let the Americans look after their own people.'

'I'm damned.' He said thoughtfully, 'Is that the kind of thing Harry was up to?'

'No. It was not so harmless.'

He said, 'You know, this business–Koch's death–has shaken me. Perhaps Harry did get mixed up in something bad. Perhaps he was trying to clear out again, and that's why they murdered him.'

'Or perhaps,' I said, 'they wanted a bigger cut of the spoils. Thieves fall out.'

He took it this time without any anger at all. He said, 'We won't agree about motives, but I think you check your facts pretty well. I'm sorry about the other day.'

'That's all right.' There are times when one has to make a flash decision—this was one of them. I owed him something in return for the information he had given me. I said, 'I'll show you enough of the facts in Lime's case for you to understand. But don't fly off the handle. It's going to be a shock.'

It couldn't help being a shock. The war and the peace (if you can call it peace) let loose a great number of rackets, but none more vile than this one. The black marketeers in food did at least supply food, and the same applied to all the other racketeers who provided articles in short supply at extravagant prices. But the penicillin racket was a different affair altogether. Penicillin in Austria was supplied only to the military hospitals; no civilian doctor, not even a civilian hospital, could obtain it by legal means. As the racket started, it was relatively harmless. Penicillin would be stolen by military orderlies and sold to Austrian doctors for very high sums—a phial would fetch anything up to seventy pounds. You might say that this was a form of distribution—unfair distribution because it benefited only the rich patient, but the original distribution could hardly have a claim to greater fairness.

This racket went on quite happily for a while. Occasionally an orderly was caught and punished, but the danger simply raised the price of penicillin. Then the racket began to get organized: the big men saw big money in it, and while the original thief got less for his spoils, he received instead a certain security. If anything happened to him he would be looked after. Human nature too was curious twisted reasons that the heart certainly knows nothing of. It eased the conscience of many small men to feel that they were working for an employer: they were almost as respectable soon in their own eyes as wage-earners; they were one of a group, and if there was guilt, the leaders bore the guilt. A racket works like a totalitarian party.

This I have sometimes called stage two. Stage three was when the organizers decided that the profits were not large enough. Penicillin would not always be impossible to obtain legitimately; they wanted more money and quicker money while the going was good. They began to dilute the penicillin with coloured water, and, in the case of penicillin dust, with sand. I keep a small museum in one drawer in my desk, and I showed Martins examples. He wasn't enjoying the talk, but he hadn't yet grasped the point. He said, 'I suppose that makes the stuff useless.'

I said, 'We wouldn't worry so much if that was all, but just consider. You can be immunized from the effects of penicillin. At the best you can say that the use of this stuff makes a penicillin treatment for the particular patient ineffective in the future. That isn't so funny, of course, if you are suffering from V.D. Then the use of sand on a wound that requires penicillin—well, it's not healthy. Men have lost their legs and arms that way—and their lives. But perhaps what horrified me most was visiting the children's hospital here. They had bought some of this penicillin for use against meningitis. A

number of children simply died, and a number went off their heads. You can
see them now in the mental ward.'

He sat on the other side of the desk, scowling into his hands. I said, 'It
doesn't bear thinking about very closely, does it?'

'You haven't showed me any evidence yet that Harry—'

'We are coming to that now,' I said. 'Just sit still and listen.' I opened
Lime's file and began to read. At the beginning the evidence was purely
circumstantial, and Martins fidgeted. So much consisted of
coincidence—reports from agents that Lime had been at a certain place at a
certain time; the accumulation of opportunities; his acquaintance with
certain people. He protested once, 'But the same evidence would apply
against me—now.'

'Just wait,' I said. For some reason Harry Lime had grown careless: he
may have realized that we suspected him and got rattled. He held a quite
distinguished position in the Relief Organization, and a man like that is the
more easily rattled. We put one of our agents as an orderly in the British
Military Hospital: we knew by this time the name of our go-between, but we
have never succeeded in getting the line right back to the source. Anyway, I
am not going to bother the reader now, as I bothered Martins then, with all
the stages—the long tussle to win the confidence of the go-between, a man
called Harbin. At last we had the screws on Harbin, and we twisted them
until he squealed. This kind of police work is very similar to secret service
work: you look for a double agent whom you can really control, and Harbin
was the man for us. But even he only led us as far as Kurtz.

'Kurtz!' Martins exclaimed. 'But why haven't you pulled him in?'

'Zero hour is almost here,' I said.

Kurtz was a great step forward, for Kurtz was in direct communication
with Lime—he had a small outside job in connection with international
relief. With Kurtz, Lime sometimes put things on paper—if he was pressed.
I showed Martins the photostat of a note. 'Can you identify that?'

'It's Harry's hand.' He read it through. 'I don't see anything wrong.'

'No, but now read this note from Harbin to Kurtz—which we dictated.
Look at the date. This is the result.'

He read them both through twice.

'You see what I mean?' If one watched a world come to an end, a plane
dive from its course, I don't suppose one would chatter, and a world for
Martins had certainly come to an end, a world of easy friendship, hero-
worship, confidence that had begun twenty years before in a school corridor.
Every memory—afternoons in the long grass, the illegitimate shoots on
Brickworth Common, the dreams, the walks, every shared experience—was
simultaneously tainted, like the soil of an atomized town. One could not walk
there with safety for a long while. While he sat there, looking at his hands
and saying nothing, I fetched a precious bottle of whisky out of a cupboard
and poured out two large doubles. 'Go on,' I said, 'drink that,' and he
obeyed me as though I were his doctor. I poured him out another.

He said slowly, 'Are you certain that he was the real boss?'

'It's as far back as we have got so far.'

'You see, he was always apt to jump before he looked.'

I didn't contradict him, though that wasn't the impression he had before given of Lime. He was searching round for some comfort.

'Suppose,' he said, 'someone had got a line on him, forced him into this racket, as you forced Harbin to double-cross . . .'

'It's possible.'

'And they murdered him in case he talked when he was arrested.'

'It's not impossible.'

'I'm glad they did,' he said. 'I wouldn't have liked to hear Harry squeal.' He made a curious little dusting movement with his hand on his knee as much as to say, 'That's that.' He said, 'I'll be getting back to England.'

'I'd rather you didn't just yet. The Austrian police would make an issue if you tried to leave Vienna at the moment. You see, Cooler's sense of duty made him call them up too.'

'I see,' he said hopelessly.

'When we've found the third man . . .' I said.

'I'd like to hear *him* squeal,' he said. 'The bastard. The bloody bastard.'

I I

After he left me, Martins went straight off to drink himself silly. He chose the Oriental to do it in, the dreary smoky little night club that stands behind a sham Eastern façade. The same semi-nude photographs on the stairs, the same half-drunk Americans at the bar, the same bad wine and extraordinary gins—he might have been in any third-rate night haunt in any other shabby capital of a shabby Europe. At one point of the hopeless early hours the International Patrol took a look at the scene, and a Russian soldier made a bolt for the stairs at the sight of them, moving with bent averted head like a small harvest animal. The Americans never stirred and nobody interfered with them. Martins had drink after drink; he would probably have had a woman too, but the cabaret performers had all gone home, and there were practically no women left in the place, except for one beautiful shrewd-looking French journalist who made one remark to her companion and fell contemptuously asleep.

Martins moved on: at Maxim's a few couples were dancing rather gloomily, and at a place called Chez Victor the heating had failed and people sat in overcoats drinking cocktails. By this time the spots were swimming in front of Martins' eyes, and he was oppressed by a sense of loneliness. His mind reverted to the girl in Dublin, and the one in Amsterdam. That was one thing that didn't fool you—the straight drink, the simple physical act: one didn't expect fidelity from a woman. His mind revolved in circles—from sentiment to lust and back again from belief to cynicism.

The trams had stopped, and he set out obstinately on foot to find Harry's girl. He wanted to make love to her—just like that: no nonsense, no sentiment. He was in the mood for violence, and the snowy road heaved like a lake and set his mind on a new course towards sorrow, eternal love, renunciation. In the corner of a sheltering wall he was sick in the snow.

It must have been about three in the morning when he climbed the stairs to Anna's room. He was nearly sober by that time and had only one idea in his head, that she must know about Harry too. He felt that somehow this knowledge would pay the mortmain that memory levies on human beings, and he would stand a chance with Harry's girl. If you are in love yourself, it never occurs to you that the girl doesn't know: you believe you have told it plainly in a tone of voice, the touch of a hand. When Anna opened the door to him, with astonishment at the sight of him tousled on the threshold, he never imagined that she was opening the door to a stranger.

He said, 'Anna, I've found out everything.'

'Come in,' she said, 'you don't want to wake the house.' She was in a dressing-gown; the divan had become a bed, the kind of tumbled bed that showed how sleepless the occupant had been.

'Now,' she said, while he stood there, fumbling for words, 'what is it? I thought you were going to keep away. Are the police after you?'

'No.'

'You didn't really kill that man, did you?'

'Of course not.'

'You're drunk, aren't you?'

'I am a bit,' he said sulkily. The meeting seemed to be going on the wrong lines. He said angrily, 'I'm sorry.'

'Why? I would like a drink myself.'

He said, 'I've been with the British police. They are satisfied I didn't do it. But I've learned everything from them. Harry was in a racket—a bad racket.' He said hopelessly, 'He was no good at all. We were both wrong.'

'You'd better tell me,' Anna said. She sat down on the bed and he told her, swaying slightly beside the table where her typescript part still lay open at the first page. I imagine he told it to her pretty confusedly, dwelling chiefly on what had stuck most in his mind, the children dead with meningitis, and the children in the mental ward. He stopped and they were silent. She said, 'Is that all?'

'Yes.'

'You were sober when they told you? They really proved it?'

'Yes.' He added drearily, 'So that, you see, was Harry.'

'I'm glad he's dead now,' she said. 'I wouldn't have wanted him to rot for years in prison.'

'But can you understand how Harry—your Harry, my Harry—could have got mixed up . . . ?' He said hopelessly, 'I feel as though he had never really existed, that we'd dreamed him. Was he laughing at fools like us all the time?'

'He may have been. What does it matter?' she said. 'Sit down. Don't worry.' He had pictured himself comforting *her*—not this other way about. She said, 'If he was alive now, he might be able to explain, but we've got to remember him as he was to us. There are always so many things that one doesn't know about a person, even a person one loves—good things, bad things. We have to leave plenty of room for them.'

'Those children—'

She said angrily, 'For God's sake stop making people in *your* image. Harry was real. He wasn't just your hero and my lover. He was Harry. He was in a racket. He did bad things. What about it? He was the man we knew.'

He said, 'Don't talk such bloody wisdom. Don't you see that I love you?'

She looked at him in astonishment. 'You?'

'Yes, me. I don't kill people with fake drugs. I'm not a hypocrite who persuades people that I'm the greatest—I'm just a bad writer who drinks too much and falls in love with girls . . .'

She said, 'But I don't even know what colour your eyes are. If you'd rung me up just now and asked me whether you were dark or fair or wore a moustache, I wouldn't have known.'

'Can't you get him out of your mind?'

'No.'

He said, 'As soon as they've cleared up this Koch murder, I'm leaving Vienna. I can't feel interested any longer in whether Kurtz killed Harry—or the third man. Whoever killed him it was a kind of justice. Maybe I'd kill him myself under these circumstances. But you still love him. You love a cheat, a murderer.'

'I loved a man,' she said. 'I told you—a man doesn't alter because you find out more about him. He's still the same man.'

'I hate the way you talk. I've got a splitting headache, and you talk and talk . . .'

'I didn't ask you to come.'

'You make me cross.'

Suddenly she laughed. She said, 'You are so comic. You come here at three in the morning—a stranger—and say you love me. Then you get angry and pick a quarrel. What do you expect me to do—or say?'

'I haven't seen you laugh before. Do it again. I like it.'

'There isn't enough for two laughs,' she said.

He took her by the shoulders and shook her gently. He said, 'I'd make comic faces all day long. I'd stand on my head and grin at you between my legs. I'd learn a lot of jokes from the books on after-dinner speaking.'

'Come away from the window. There are no curtains.'

'There's nobody to see.' But automatically checking his statement, he wasn't quite so sure: a long shadow that had moved, perhaps with the movement of clouds over the moon, was motionless again. He said, 'You still love Harry, don't you?'

'Yes.'

'Perhaps I do. I don't know.' He dropped his hands and said, 'I'll be pushing off.'

He walked rapidly away. He didn't bother to see whether he was being followed, to check up on the shadow. But, passing by the end of a street, he happened to turn, and there just around the corner, pressed against a wall to escape notice, was a thick stocky figure. Martins stopped and stared. There was something familiar about that figure. Perhaps, he thought, I have grown unconsciously used to him during these last twenty-four hours; perhaps he is one of those who have so assiduously checked my movements. Martins stood there, twenty yards away, staring at the silent motionless figure in the dark side street who stared back at him. A police spy, perhaps, or an agent of those other men, those men who had corrupted Harry first and then killed him—even possibly, the third man?

It was not the face that was familiar, for he could not make out so much as the angle of the jaw; nor a movement, for the body was so still that he began to believe that the whole thing was an illusion caused by shadow. He called sharply, 'Do you want anything?' and there was no reply. He called again with the irascibility of drink, 'Answer, can't you,' and an answer came, for a window curtain was drawn petulantly back by some sleeper he had awakened, and the light fell straight across the narrow street and lit up the features of Harry Lime.

12

'Do you believe in ghosts?' Martins said to me.

'Do you?'

'I do now.'

'I also believe that drunk men see things—sometimes rats, sometimes worse.'

He hadn't come to me at once with his story—only the danger to Anna Schmidt tossed him back into my office, like something the sea had washed up, tousled, unshaven, haunted by an experience he couldn't understand. He said, 'If it had been just the face, I wouldn't have worried. I'd been thinking about Harry, and I might easily have mistaken a stranger. The light was turned off again at once, you see. I only got one glimpse, and the man made off down the street—if he was a man. There was no turning for a long way, but I was so startled I gave him another thirty yards' start. He came to one of those advertisement kiosks and for a moment moved out of sight. I ran after him. It only took me ten seconds to reach the kiosk, and he must have heard me running, but the strange thing was he never appeared again. I reached the kiosk. There wasn't anybody there. The street was empty. He couldn't have reached a doorway without my seeing him. He simply vanished.'

'A natural thing for ghosts—or illusions.'

'But I can't believe I was as drunk as all that!'

'What did you do then?'

'I had to have another drink. My nerves were all in pieces.'

'Didn't that bring him back?'

'No, but it sent me back to Anna's.'

I think he would have been ashamed to come to me with his absurd story if it had not been for the attempt on Anna Schmidt. My theory, when he did tell me his story, was that there had been a watcher—though it was drink and hysteria that had pasted on the man's face the features of Harry Lime. The watcher had noted his visit to Anna, and the member of the ring—the penicillin ring—had been warned by telephone. Events that night moved fast. You remember that Kurtz lived in the Russian zone—in the Second Bezirk to be exact, in a wide, empty, desolate street that runs down to the Prater Platz. A man like that had probably obtained his influential contacts.

It was ruin for a Russian to be observed on very friendly terms with an American or an Englishman, but the Austrian was a potential ally—and in any case one doesn't fear the influence of the ruined and defeated.

You must understand that at this period cooperation between the Western Allies and the Russians had practically, though not yet completely, broken down.

The original police agreement in Vienna between the Allies confined the military police (who had to deal with crimes involving allied personnel) to their particular zones, unless permission was given to them to enter the zone of another Power. This agreement worked well enough between the three Western Powers. I only had to get on the phone to my opposite number in the American or French zones before I sent in my men to make an arrest or pursue an investigation. During the first six months of the occupation it had worked reasonably well with the Russians: perhaps forty-eight hours would pass before I received permission, and in practice there are few occasions when it is necessary to work quicker than that. Even at home it is not always possible to obtain a search warrant or permission from one's superiors to detain a suspect with any greater speed. Then the forty-eight hours turned into a week or a fortnight, and I remember my American colleague suddenly taking a look at his records and discovering that there were forty cases dating back more than three months where not even an acknowledgement of his requests had been received. Then the trouble started. We began to turn down, or not to answer, the Russian requests, and sometimes without permission they would send in police, and there were clashes. . . . At the date of this story the Western Powers had more or less ceased to put in applications or reply to the Russian ones. This meant that if I wanted to pick up Kurtz it would be as well to catch him outside the Russian zone, though of course it was always possible his activities might offend the Russians and his punishment be more sudden and severe than any we should inflict. Well, the Anna Schmidt case was one of the clashes: when Rollo Martins went drunkenly back at four o'clock in the morning to tell Anna that he had seen the ghost of Harry, he was told by a frightened porter who had not yet gone back to sleep that she had been taken away by the International Patrol.

What happened was this. Russia, you remember, was in the chair as far as the Innere Stadt was concerned, and when Russia was in the chair, you expected certain irregularities. On this occasion, half-way through the patrol, the Russian policeman pulled a fast one on his colleagues and directed the car to the street where Anna Schmidt lived. The British military policeman that night was new to his job: he didn't realize, till his colleagues told him, that they had entered a British zone. He spoke a little German and no French, and the Frenchman, a cynical hard-bitten Parisian, gave up the attempt to explain to him. The American took on the job. 'It's all right by me,' he said, 'but is it all right by you?' The British M.P. tapped the Russian's shoulder, who turned his Mongol face and launched a flood of incomprehensible Slav at him. The car drove on.

Outside Anna Schmidt's block the American took a hand in the game and demanded in German what it was all about. The Frenchman leaned against the bonnet and lit a stinking Caporal. France wasn't concerned, and anything that didn't concern France had no genuine importance to him. The

Russian dug out a few words of German and flourished some papers. As far as they could tell, a Russian national wanted by the Russian police was living there without proper papers. They went upstairs and the Russian tried Anna's door. It was firmly bolted, but he put his shoulder to it and tore out the bolt without giving the occupant an opportunity of letting him in. Anna was in bed, though I don't suppose, after Martins' visit, she was asleep.

There is a lot of comedy in these situations if you are not directly concerned. You need a background of Central European terror, of a father who belonged to a losing side, of house-searches and disappearances, before the fear outweighs the comedy. The Russian, you see, refused to leave the room while Anna dressed: the Englishman refused to remain in the room: the American wouldn't leave a girl unprotected with a Russian soldier, and the Frenchman—well, I think the Frenchman must have thought it was fun. Can't you imagine the scene? The Russian was just doing his duty and watched the girl all the time, without a flicker of sexual interest; the American stood with his back chivalrously turned, but aware, I am sure, of every movement; the Frenchman smoked his cigarette and watched with detached amusement the reflection of the girl dressing in the mirror of the wardrobe; and the Englishman stood in the passage wondering what to do next.

I don't want you to think the English policeman came too badly out of the affair. In the passage, undistracted by chivalry, he had time to think, and his thoughts led him to the telephone in the next flat. He got straight through to me at my flat and woke me out of that deepest middle sleep. That was why when Martins rang up an hour later I already knew what was exciting him; it gave him an undeserved but very useful belief in my efficiency. I never heard another crack from him about policemen or sheriffs after that night.

I must explain another point of police procedure. If the International Patrol made an arrest, they had to lodge their prisoner for twenty-four hours at the International Headquarters. During that period it would be determined which Power could justifiably claim the prisoner. It was this rule that the Russians were most ready to break. Because so few of us can speak Russian and the Russian is almost debarred from explaining his point of view (try and explain your own point of view on any subject in a language you don't know well—it's not as easy as ordering a meal), we are apt to regard any breach of an agreement by the Russians as deliberate and malign. I think it quite possible that they understood this agreement as referring only to prisoners about whom there was a dispute. It's true that there was a dispute about nearly every prisoner they took, but there was no dispute in their own minds, and no one has a greater sense of self-righteousness than a Russian. Even in his confessions a Russian is self-righteous—he pours out his revelations, but he doesn't excuse himself, he needs no excuse. All this had to form the background of one's decision. I gave my instructions to Corporal Starling.

When he went back to Anna's room a dispute was raging. Anna had told the American that she had Austrian papers (which was true) and that they were quite in order (which was rather stretching the truth). The American told the Russian in bad German that they had no right to arrest an Austrian citizen. He asked Anna for her papers and when she produced them, the Russian snatched them from her hand.

'Hungarian,' he said, pointing at Anna. 'Hungarian,' and then, flourishing the papers, 'bad, bad.'

The American, whose name was O'Brien, said, 'Give the goil back her papers,' which the Russian naturally didn't understand. The American put his hand on his gun, and Corporal Starling said gently, 'Let it go, Pat.'

'If these papers ain't in order we got a right to look.'

'Just let it go. We'll see the papers at H.Q.'

'If you get to H.Q. You can't trust these Russian drivers. As like as not he'll drive straight through to his zone.

'We'll see,' Starling said.

'The trouble about you British is you never know when to make a stand.'

'Oh, well,' Starling said; he had been at Dunkirk, but he knew when to be quiet.

They got back into the car with Anna, who sat in the front between the two Russians dumb with fear. After they had gone a little way the American touched the Russian on the shoulder, 'Wrong way,' he said. 'H.Q. that way.' The Russian chattered back in his own tongue making a conciliatory gesture, while they drove on. 'It's what I said,' O'Brien told Starling. 'They are taking her to the Russian zone.' Anna stared out with terror through the windscreen. 'Don't worry, little goil,' O'Brien said, 'I'll fix them all right.' His hand was fidgeting round his gun again. Starling said, 'Look here, Pat, this is a British case. You don't have to get involved.'

'You are new to this game. You don't know these bastards.'

'It's not worth making an incident about.'

'For Christ's sake,' O'Brien said, 'not worth . . . that little goil's got to have protection.' American chivalry is always, it seems to me, carefully canalized—one still awaits the American saint who will kiss a leper's sores.

The driver put on his brakes suddenly: there was a road block. You see, I knew they would have to pass this military post if they did not make their way to the International H.Q. in the Inner City. I put my head in at the window and said to the Russian haltingly, in his own tongue, 'What are you doing in the British zone?'

He grumbled that it was 'orders'.

'Whose orders? Let me see them.' I noted the signature—it was useful information. I said, 'This tells you to pick up a certain Hungarian national and war criminal who is living with faulty papers in the British zone. Let me see the papers.'

He started on a long explanation, but I saw the papers sticking in his pocket and I pulled them out. He made a grab at his gun, and I punched his face—I felt really mean at doing so, but it's the conduct they expect from an angry officer and it brought him to reason—that and seeing three British soldiers approaching his headlights. I said, 'These papers look to me quite in order, but I'll investigate them and send a report of the result to your colonel. He can, of course, ask for the extradition of this lady at any time. All we want is proof of her criminal activities. I'm afraid we don't regard Hungarian as Russian nationality.' He goggled at me (my Russian was probably half incomprehensible) and I said to Anna, 'Get out of the car.' She couldn't get by the Russian, so I had to pull him out first. Then I put a packet of cigarettes in his hand, said, 'Have a good smoke,' waved my hand to the others, gave a sigh of relief, and that incident was closed.

13

While Martins told me how he went back to Anna's and found her gone, I did some hard thinking. I wasn't satisfied with the ghost story or the idea that the man with Harry Lime's features had been a drunken illusion. I took out two maps of Vienna and compared them. I rang up my assistant and, keeping Martins silent with a glass of whisky, asked him if he had located Harbin yet. He said no; he understood he'd left Klagenfurt a week ago to visit his family in the adjoining zone. One always wants to do everything oneself; one has to guard against blaming one's juniors. I am convinced that I would never have let Harbin out of our clutches, but then I would probably have made all kinds of mistakes that my junior would have avoided. 'All right,' I said. 'Go on trying to get hold of him.'

'I'm sorry, sir.'

'Forget it. It's just one of those things.'

His young enthusiastic voice—if only one could still feel that enthusiasm for a routine job; how many opportunities, flashes of insight one misses simply because a job has become just a job—tingled up the wire. 'You know, sir, I can't help feeling that we ruled out the possibility of murder too easily. There are one or two points—'

'Put them on paper, Carter.'

'Yes, sir. I think, sir, if you don't mind my saying so,' (Carter is a very young man) 'we ought to have him dug up. There's no real evidence that he died just when the others said.'

'I agree, Carter. Get on to the authorities.'

Martins was right. I had made a complete fool of myself, but remember that police work in an occupied city is not like police work at home. Everything is unfamiliar: the methods of one's foreign colleagues, the rules of evidence, even the procedure at inquests. I suppose I had got into the state of mind when one trusts too much to one's personal judgement. I had been immensely relieved by Lime's death. I was satisfied with the accident.

I said to Martins, 'Did you look inside the kiosk or was it locked?'

'Oh, it wasn't a newspaper kiosk,' he said. 'It was one of those solid iron kiosks you see everywhere plastered with posters.'

'You'd better show me the place.'

'But is Anna all right?'

'The police are watching the flat. They won't try anything else yet.'

I didn't want to make a fuss in the neighbourhood with a police car, so we took trams—several trams—changing here and there, and came into the district on foot. I didn't wear my uniform, and I doubted anyway, after the failure of the attempt on Anna, whether they would risk a watcher. 'This is the turning,' Martins said and led me down a side street. We stopped at the kiosk. 'You see, he passed behind here and simply vanished—into the ground.'

'That was exactly where he did vanish to,' I said.

'How do you mean?'

An ordinary passer-by would never have noticed that the kiosk had a door, and of course it had been dark when the man disappeared. I pulled the door open and showed Martins the little curling iron staircase that disappeared into the ground. He said, 'Good God, then I didn't imagine him!'

'It's one of the entrances to the main sewer.'

'And anyone can go down?'

'Anyone. For some reason the Russians object to these being locked.'

'How far can one go?'

'Right across Vienna. People used them in air raids; some of our prisoners hid for two years down there. Deserters have used them—and burglars. If you know your way about you can emerge again almost anywhere in the city through a manhole or a kiosk like this one. The Austrians have to have special police for patrolling these sewers.' I closed the door of the kiosk again. I said, 'So that's how your friend Harry disappeared.'

'You really believe it was Harry?'

'The evidence points that way.'

'Then whom did they bury?'

'I don't know yet, but we soon shall, because we are digging him up again. I've got a shrewd idea, though, that Koch wasn't the only inconvenient man they murdered.'

Martins said, 'It's a bit of a shock.'

'Yes.'

'What are you going to do about it?'

'I don't know. It's no good applying to the Russians, and you can bet he's hiding out now in the Russian zone. We have no line now on Kurtz, for Harbin's blown—he must have been blown or they wouldn't have staged that mock death and funeral.'

'But it's odd, isn't it, that Koch didn't recognize the dead man's face from the window?'

'The window was a long way up and I expect the face had been damaged before they took the body out of the car.'

He said thoughtfully, 'I wish I could speak to him. You see, there's so much I simply can't believe.'

'Perhaps you are the only one who could speak to him. It's risky though, because you know too much.'

'I still can't believe—I only saw the face for a moment.' He said, 'What shall I do?'

'He won't leave the Russian zone now. Perhaps that's why he tried to have the girl taken over—because he loves her? Because he doesn't feel secure? I don't know. I do know that the only person who could persuade him to come over would be you—or her, if he still believes you are his friend. But first you've got to speak to him. I can't see the line.'

'I could go and see Kurtz. I have the address.'

I said, 'Remember. Lime may not want you to leave the Russian zone when once you are there, and I can't protect you there.'

'I want to clear the whole damned thing up,' Martins said, 'but I'm not going to act as a decoy. I'll talk to him. That's all.'

14

Sunday had laid its false peace over Vienna; the wind had dropped and no snow had fallen for twenty-four hours. All the morning trams had been full, going out to Grinzing where the young wine is drunk and to the slopes of snow on the hills outside. Walking over the canal by the makeshift military bridge, Martins was aware of the emptiness of the afternoon: the young were out with their toboggans and their skis, and all around him was the after-dinner sleep of age. A notice board told him that he was entering the Russian zone, but there were no signs of occupation. You saw more Russian soldiers in the Inner City than here.

Deliberately he had given Kurtz no warning of his visit. Better to find him out than a reception prepared for him. He was careful to carry with him all his papers, including the *laissez-passer* of the Four Powers that on the face of it allowed him to move freely through all the zones of Vienna. It was extraordinarily quiet over here on the other side of the canal, and a melodramatic journalist had painted a picture of silent terror, but the truth was simply the wider streets, the greater shell damage, the fewer people–and Sunday afternoon. There was nothing to fear, but all the same, in this huge empty street where all the time you heard your own feet moving, it was difficult not to look behind.

He had no difficulty in finding Kurtz's block, and when he rang the bell the door was opened quickly, as though Kurtz expected a visitor, by Kurtz himself.

'Oh,' Kurtz said, 'it's you, Mr Martins,' and made a perplexed motion with his hand to the back of his head. Martins had been wondering why he looked so different, and now he knew. Kurtz was not wearing the toupée, and yet his head was not bald. He had a perfectly normal head of hair cut close. He said, 'It would have been better to have telephoned to me. You nearly missed me; I was going out.'

'May I come in a moment?'

'Of course.'

In the hall a cupboard door stood open, and Martins saw Kurtz's overcoat, his raincoat, a couple of soft hats, and, hanging sedately on a peg like a wrap, Kurtz's toupée. He said, 'I'm glad to see your hair has grown,' and saw, in the mirror on the cupboard door, the hatred flame and blush on Kurtz's face. When he turned Kurtz smiled at him like a conspirator and said vaguely, 'It keeps the head warm.'

'Whose head?' Martins asked, for it had suddenly occurred to him how useful that toupée might have been on the day of the accident. 'Never mind,' he went quickly on, for his errand was not with Kurtz. 'I'm here to see Harry.'

'Harry?'

'I want to talk to him.'

'Are you mad?'

'I'm in a hurry, so let's assume that I am. Just make a note of my madness. If you should see Harry—or his ghost—let him know that I want to talk to him. A ghost isn't afraid of a man, is it? Surely it's the other way round. I'll be waiting in the Prater by the Big Wheel for the next two hours—if you can get in touch with the dead, hurry.' He added, 'Remember, I was Harry's friend.'

Kurtz said nothing, but somewhere, in a room off the hall, somebody cleared his throat. Martins threw open a door; he had half expected to see the dead rise yet again, but it was only Dr Winkler who rose from a kitchen chair, in front of the kitchen stove, and bowed very stiffly and correctly with the same celluloid squeak.

'Dr Winkle,' Martins said. Dr Winkler looked extraordinarily out of place in a kitchen. The debris of a snack lunch littered the kitchen table, and the unwashed dishes consorted very ill with Dr Winkler's cleanness.

'Winkler,' the doctor corrected him with stony patience.

Martins said to Kurtz, 'Tell the doctor about my madness. He might be able to make a diagnosis. And remember the place—by the Great Wheel. Or do ghosts only rise by night?' He left the flat.

For an hour he waited, walking up and down to keep warm, inside the enclosure of the Great Wheel; the smashed Prater with its bones sticking crudely through the snow was nearly empty. One stall sold thin flat cakes like cartwheels, and the children queued with their coupons. A few courting couples would be packed together in a single car of the Wheel and revolve slowly above the city, surrounded by empty cars. As the car reached the highest point of the Wheel, the revolutions would stop for a couple of minutes and far overhead the tiny faces would press against the glass. Martins wondered who would come for him. Was there enough friendship left in Harry for him to come alone, or would a squad of police arrive? It was obvious from the raid on Anna Schmidt's flat that he had a certain pull. And then as his watch-hand passed the hour, he wondered: Was it all an invention of my mind? Are they digging up Harry's body now in the Central Cemetery?

Somewhere behind the cakestall a man was whistling, and Martins knew the tune. He turned and waited. Was it fear or excitement that made his heart beat—or just the memories that tune ushered in, for life had always quickened when Harry came, came just as he came now, as though nothing much had happened, nobody had been lowered into a grave or found with cut throat in a basement, came with his amused, deprecating, take-it-or-leave-it manner—and of course one always took it.

'Harry.'

'Hullo, Rollo.'

Don't picture Harry Lime as a smooth scoundrel. He wasn't that. The picture I have of him in my files is an excellent one: he is caught by a street photographer with his stocky legs apart, big shoulders a little hunched, a

belly that has known too much good food for too long, on his face a look of
cheerful rascality, a geniality, a recognition that *his* happiness will make the
world's day. Now he didn't make the mistake of putting out a hand that
might have been rejected, but instead just patted Martins on the elbow and
said, 'How are things?'

'We've got to talk, Harry.'

'Of course.'

'Alone.'

'We couldn't be more alone than here.'

He had always known the ropes, and even in the smashed pleasure park he
knew them, tipping the woman in charge of the Wheel, so that they might
have a car to themselves. He said, 'Lovers used to do this in the old days, but
they haven't the money to spare, poor devils, now,' and he looked out of the
window of the swaying, rising car at the figures diminishing below with what
looked like genuine commiseration.

Very slowly on one side of them the city sank; very slowly on the other the
great cross-girders of the Wheel rose into sight. As the horizon slid away the
Danube became visible, and the piers of the Reichsbrücke lifted above
the houses. 'Well,' Harry said, 'it's good to see you, Rollo.'

'I was at your funeral.'

'That was pretty smart of me, wasn't it?'

'Not so smart for your girl. She was there too–in tears.'

'She's a good little thing,' Harry said. 'I'm very fond of her.'

'I didn't believe the police when they told me about you.'

Harry said, 'I wouldn't have asked you to come if I'd known what was
going to happen, but I didn't think the police were on to me.'

'Were you going to cut me in on the spoils?'

'I've never kept you out of anything, old man, yet.' He stood with his back
to the door as the car swung upwards, and smiled back at Rollo Martins, who
could remember him in just such an attitude in a secluded corner of the
school-quad, saying, 'I've learned a way to get out at night. It's absolutely
safe. You are the only one I'm letting in on it.' For the first time Rollo
Martins looked back through the years without admiration, as he thought:
He's never grown up. Marlowe's devils wore squibs attached to their tails:
evil was like Peter Pan–it carried with it the horrifying and horrible gift of
eternal youth.

Martins said, 'Have you ever visited the children's hospital? Have you
seen any of your victims?'

Harry took a look at the toy landscape below and came away from the
door. 'I never feel quite safe in these things,' he said. He felt the back of the
door with his hand, as though he were afraid that it might fly open and
launch him into that iron-ribbed space. 'Victims?' he asked. 'Don't be
melodramatic, Rollo. Look down there,' he went on, pointing through the
window at the people moving like black flies at the base of the Wheel.
'Would you really feel any pity if one of those dots stopped moving–for
ever? If I said you can have twenty thousand pounds for every dot that stops,
would you really, old man, tell me to keep my money–without hesitation?
Or would you calculate how many dots you could afford to spare? Free of
income tax, old man. Free of income tax.' He gave his boyish conspiratorial

smile. 'It's the only way to save nowadays.'

'Couldn't you have stuck to tyres?'

'Like Cooler? No. I've always been ambitious.'

'You are finished now. The police know everything.'

'But they can't catch me, Rollo, you'll see. I'll pop up again. You can't keep a good man down.'

The car swung to a standstill at the highest point of the curve and Harry turned his back and gazed out of the window. Martins thought: One good shove and I could break the glass, and he pictured the body falling, falling, through the iron struts, a piece of carrion dropping among the flies. He said, 'You know the police are planning to dig up your body. What will they find?'

'Harbin,' Harry replied with simplicity. He turned away from the window and said, 'Look at the sky.'

The car had reached the top of the Wheel and hung there motionless, while the stain of the sunset ran in streaks over the wrinkled papery sky beyond the black girders.

'Why did the Russians try to take Anna Schmidt?'

'She had false papers, old man.'

'Who told them?'

'The price of living in this zone, Rollo, is service. I have to give them a little information now and then.'

'I thought perhaps you were just trying to get her here—because she was your girl? Because you wanted her?'

Harry smiled. 'I haven't all that influence.'

'What would have happened to her?'

'Nothing very serious. She'd have been sent back to Hungary. There's nothing against her really. A year in a labour camp perhaps. She'd be infinitely better off in her own country than being pushed around by the British police.'

'She hasn't told them anything about you.'

'She's a good little thing,' Harry repeated with satisfaction and pride.

'She loves you.'

'Well, I gave her a good time while it lasted.'

'And I love her.'

'That's fine, old man. Be kind to her. She's worth it. I'm glad.' He gave the impression of having arranged everything to everybody's satisfaction. 'And you can help to keep her mouth shut. Not that she knows anything that matters.'

'I'd like to knock you through the window.'

'But you won't, old man. Our quarrels never last long. You remember that fearful one in the Monaco, when we swore we were through. I'd trust you anywhere, Rollo. Kurtz tried to persuade me not to come, but I know you. Then he tried to persuade me to, well, arrange an accident. He told me it would be quite easy in this car.'

'Except that I'm the stronger man.'

'But I've got the gun. You don't think a bullet wound would show when you hit *that* ground?' Again the car began to move, sailing slowly down, until the flies were midgets, were recognizable human beings. 'What fools we are, Rollo, talking like this, as if I'd do that to you—or you to me.' He turned his back and leaned his face against the glass. One thrust. . . . 'How much do you earn a year with your Westerns, old man?'

'A thousand.'

'Taxed. I earn thirty thousand free. It's the fashion. In these days, old man, nobody thinks in terms of human beings. Governments don't, so why should we? They talk of the people and the proletariat, and I talk of the mugs. It's the same thing. They have their five-year plans and so have I.'

'You used to be a Catholic.'

'Oh, I still *believe*, old man. In God and mercy and all that. I'm not hurting anybody's soul by what I do. The dead are happier dead. They don't miss much here, poor devils,' he added with that odd touch of genuine pity, as the car reached the platform and the faces of the doomed-to-be-victims, the tired pleasure-hoping Sunday faces, peered in at them. 'I could cut you in, you know. It would be useful. I have no one left in the Inner City.'

'Except Cooler? and Winkler?'

'You really mustn't turn policeman, old man.' They passed out of the car and he put his hand again on Martins' elbow. 'That was a joke. I know you won't. Have you heard anything of old Bracer recently?'

'I had a card at Christmas.'

'Those were the days, old man. Those were the days. I've got to leave you here. We'll see each other sometime. If you are in a jam, you can always get me at Kurtz's.' He moved away and, turning, waved the hand he had had the tact not to offer: it was like the whole past moving off under a cloud. Martins suddenly called after him, 'Don't trust me, Harry,' but there was too great a distance now between them for the words to carry.

15

'Anna was at the theatre,' Martins told me, 'for the Sunday matinée. I had to see the whole dreary comedy through a second time. About a middle-aged composer and an infatuated girl and an understanding–a terribly understanding–wife. Anna acted very badly–she wasn't much of an actress at the best of times. I saw her afterwards in her dressing-room, but she was badly fussed. I think she thought I was going to make a serious pass at her all the time, and she didn't want a pass. I told her Harry was alive–I thought she'd be glad and that I would hate to see how glad she was, but she sat in front of her make-up mirror and let the tears streak the grease-paint and I wished afterwards that she had been glad. She looked awful and I loved her. Then I told her about my interview with Harry, but she wasn't really paying much attention because when I'd finished she said, "I wish he was dead."

'"He deserves to be," I said.

'"I mean he would be safe then–from everybody."'

I asked Martins, 'Did you show her the photographs I gave you–of the children?'

'Yes. I thought, it's got to be kill or cure this time. She's got to get Harry out of her system. I propped the pictures up among the pots of grease. She couldn't avoid seeing them. I said, "The police can't arrest Harry unless they get him into this zone, and we've got to help."'

'She said, "I thought he was your friend." I said, "He *was* my friend." She said, "I'll never help you to get Harry. I don't want to see him again, I don't want to hear his voice. I don't want to be touched by him, but I won't do a thing to harm him."

'I felt bitter—I don't know why, because after all I had done nothing for her. Even Harry had done more for her than I had. I said, "You want him still," as though I were accusing her of a crime. She said, "I don't want him, but he's in me. That's a fact—not like friendship. Why, when I have a sex dream, he's always the man."'

I prodded Martins on when he hesitated. 'Yes?'

'Oh, I just got up and left her then. Now it's your turn to work on me. What do you want me to do?'

'I want to act quickly. You see, it was Harbin's body in the coffin, so we can pick up Winkler and Cooler right away. Kurtz is out of our reach for the time being, and so is the driver. We'll put in a formal request to the Russians for permission to arrest Kurtz and Lime: it makes our files tidy. If we are going to use you as our decoy, your message must go to Lime straight away—not after you've hung around in this zone for twenty-four hours. As I see it, you were brought here for a grilling almost as soon as you got back into the Inner City; you heard then from me about Harbin; you put two and two together and you go and warn Cooler. We'll let Cooler slip for the sake of the bigger game—we have no evidence that he was in on the penicillin racket. He'll escape into the Second Bezirk to Kurtz, and Lime will know you've played the game. Three hours later you send a message that the police are after you: you are in hiding and must see him.'

'He won't come.'

'I'm not so sure. We'll choose our hiding place carefully—where he'll think there's a minimum of risk. It's worth trying. It would appeal to his pride and sense of humour if he could scoop you out. And it would stop your mouth.'

Martins said, 'He never used to scoop me out—at school.' It was obvious that he had been reviewing the past with care and coming to conclusions.

'That wasn't such serious trouble and there was no danger of your squealing.'

He said, 'I told Harry not to trust me, but he didn't hear.'

'Do you agree?'

He had given me back the photographs of the children and they lay on my desk. I could see him take a long look at them. 'Yes,' he said, 'I agree.'

16

All the arrangements went according to plan. We delayed arresting Winkler, who had returned from the Second Bezirk, until after Cooler had been warned. Martins enjoyed his short interview with Cooler. Cooler greeted him without embarrassment and with considerable patronage. 'Why, Mr Martins, it's good to see you. Sit down. I'm glad everything went off all right between you and Colonel Calloway. A very straight chap, Calloway.'

'It didn't,' Martins said.

'You don't bear any ill-will, I'm sure, about my letting him know about you seeing Koch. The way I figured it was this—if you were innocent you'd clear yourself right away, and if you were guilty, well, the fact that I liked you oughtn't to stand in the way. A citizen has his duties.'

'Like giving false evidence at an inquest.'

Cooler said, 'Oh, that old story. I'm afraid you are riled at me, Mr Martins. Look at it this way—you as a citizen, owing allegiance—'

'The police have dug up the body. They'll be after you and Winkler. I want you to warn Harry . . .'

'I don't understand.'

'Oh, yes, you do.' And it was obvious that he did. Martins left him abruptly. He wanted no more of that kindly humanitarian face.

It only remained then to bait the trap. After studying the map of the sewer system I came to the conclusion that a café anywhere near the main entrance of the great sewer, which was placed like all the others in an advertisement kiosk, would be the most likely spot to tempt Lime. He had only to rise once again through the ground, walk fifty yards, bring Martins back with him, and sink again into the obscurity of the sewers. He had no idea that this method of evasion was known to us: he probably knew that one patrol of the sewer police ended before midnight, and the next did not start till two, and so at midnight Martins sat in the little cold café in sight of the kiosk, drinking coffee after coffee. I had lent him a revolver; I had men posted as close to the kiosk as I could, and the sewer police were ready when zero hour struck to close the manholes and start sweeping the sewers inwards from the edge of the city. But I intended, if I could, to catch him before he went underground again. It would save trouble—and risk to Martins. So there, as I say, in the café Martins sat.

The wind had risen again, but it had brought no snow; it came icily off the Danube and in the little grassy square by the café it whipped up the snow like the surf on top of a wave. There was no heating in the café, and Martins sat warming each hand in turn on a cup of ersatz coffee—innumerable cups. There was usually one of my men in the café with him, but I changed them every twenty minutes or so irregularly. More than an hour passed. Martins had long given up hope and so had I, where I waited at the end of a phone several streets away, with a party of the sewer police ready to go down if it became necessary. We were luckier than Martins because we were warm in our great boots up to the thighs and our reefer jackets. One man had a small searchlight about half as big again as a car headlight strapped to his breast, and another man carried a brace of Roman candles. The telephone rang. It was Martins. He said, 'I'm perishing with cold. It's a quarter past one. Is there any point in going on with this?'

'You shouldn't telephone. You must stay in sight.'

'I've drunk seven cups of this filthy coffee. My stomach won't stand much more.'

'He can't delay much longer if he's coming. He won't want to run into the two o'clock patrol. Stick it another quarter of an hour, but keep away from the telephone.'

Martins' voice said suddenly, 'Christ, he's here! He's—' and then the telephone went dead. I said to my assistant, 'Give the signal to guard all manholes,' and to my sewer police, 'We are going down.'

What had happened was this. Martins was still on the telephone to me when Harry Lime came into the café. I don't know what he heard, if he heard anything. The mere sight of a man wanted by the police and without friends in Vienna speaking on the telephone would have been enough to warn him. He was out of the café again before Martins had put down the receiver. It was one of those rare moments when none of my men was in the café. One had just left and another was on the pavement about to come in. Harry Lime brushed by him and made for the kiosk. Martins came out of the café and saw my man. If he had called out then it would have been an easy shot, but I suppose it was not Lime, the penicillin racketeer, who was escaping down the street; it was Harry. Martins hesitated just long enough for Lime to put the kiosk between them; then he called out 'That's him,' but Lime had already gone to ground.

What a strange world unknown to most of us lies under our feet: we live above a cavernous land of waterfalls and rushing rivers, where tides ebb and flow as in the world above. If you have ever read the adventures of Allan Quatermain and the account of his voyage along the underground river to the city of Milosis, you will be able to picture the scene of Lime's last stand. The main sewer, half as wide as the Thames, rushes by under a huge arch, fed by tributary streams: these streams have fallen in waterfalls from higher levels and have been purified in their fall, so that only in these side channels is the air foul. The main stream smells sweet and fresh with a faint tang of ozone, and everywhere in the darkness is the sound of falling and rushing water. It was just past high tide when Martins and the policeman reached the river: first the curving iron staircase, then a short passage so low they had to stoop, and then the shallow edge of the water lapped at their feet. My man shone his torch along the edge of the current and said, 'He's gone that way,' for just as a deep stream when it shallows at the rim leaves an accumulation of debris, so the sewer left in the quiet water against the wall a scum of orange peel, old cigarette cartons, and the like, and in this scum Lime had left his trail as unmistakably as if he had walked in mud. My policeman shone his torch ahead with his left hand, and carried his gun in his right. He said to Martins, 'Keep behind me, sir, the bastard may shoot.'

'Then why the hell should you be in front?'

'It's my job, sir.' The water came half-way up their legs as they walked; the policeman kept his torch pointing down and ahead at the disturbed trail at the sewer's edge. He said, 'The silly thing is the bastard doesn't stand a chance. The manholes are all guarded and we've cordoned off the way into the Russian zone. All our chaps have to do now is to sweep inwards down the side passages from the manholes.' He took a whistle out of his pocket and blew, and very far away, here and again there, came the notes of a reply. He said, 'They are all down here now. The sewer police, I mean. They know this place just as I know the Tottenham Court Road. I wish my old woman could see me now,' he said, lifting his torch for a moment to shine it ahead, and at that moment the shot came. The torch flew out of his hand and fell into the stream. He said, 'God blast the bastard!'

'Are you hurt?'

'Scraped my hand, that's all. A week off work. Here, take this other torch, sir, while I tie my hand up. Don't shine it. He's in one of the side passages.' For a long time the sound of the shot went on reverberating: when the last echo died a whistle blew ahead of them, and Martins' companion blew an answer.

Martins said, 'It's an odd thing—I don't even know your name.'

'Bates, sir.' He gave a low laugh in the darkness. 'This isn't my usual beat. Do you know the Horseshoe, sir?'

'Yes.'

'And the Duke of Grafton?'

'Yes.'

'Well, it takes a lot to make a world.'

Martins said, 'Let me come in front. I don't think he'll shoot at me, and I want to talk to him.'

'I had orders to look after you, sir. Careful.'

'That's all right.' He edged round Bates, plunging a foot deeper in the stream as he went. When he was in front he called out, 'Harry,' and the name sent up an echo, 'Harry, Harry, Harry!' that travelled down the stream and woke a whole chorus of whistles in the darkness. He called again, 'Harry. Come out. It's no use.'

A voice startlingly close made them hug the wall. 'Is that you, old man?' it called. 'What do you want me to do?'

'Come out. And put your hands above your head.'

'I haven't a torch, old man. I can't see a thing.'

'Be careful, sir,' Bates said.

'Get flat against the wall. He won't shoot at me,' Martins said. He called, 'Harry, I'm going to shine the torch. Play fair and come out. You haven't got a chance.' He flashed the torch on, and twenty feet away, at the edge of the light and the water, Harry stepped into view. 'Hands above the head, Harry.' Harry raised his hand and fired. The shot ricocheted against the wall a foot from Martins' head, and he heard Bates cry out. At the same moment a searchlight from fifty yards away lit the whole channel, caught Harry in its beams, then Martins, then the staring eyes of Bates slumped at the water's edge with the sewage washing to his waist. An empty cigarette carton wedged into his armpit and stayed. My party had reached the scene.

Martins stood dithering there above Bates's body, with Harry Lime half-way between us. We couldn't shoot for fear of hitting Martins, and the light of the searchlight dazzled Lime. We moved slowly on, our revolvers trained for a chance, and Lime turned this way and that like a rabbit dazzled by headlights; then suddenly he took a flying jump into the deep central rushing stream. When we turned the searchlight after him he was submerged, and the current of the sewer carried him rapidly on, past the body of Bates, out of the range of the searchlight into the dark. What makes a man, without hope, cling to a few more minutes of existence? Is it a good quality or a bad one? I have no idea.

Martins stood at the outer edge of the searchlight beam, staring downstream. He had his gun in his hand now, and he was the only one of us who could fire with safety. I thought I saw a movement and called out to him, 'There. There. Shoot.' He lifted his gun and fired, just as he had fired at the same command all those years ago on Brickworth Common, fired, as he did then, inaccurately. A cry of pain came tearing back like calico down the cavern: a reproach, an entreaty. 'Well done,' I called and halted by Bates's body. He was dead. His eyes remained blankly open as we turned the searchlight on him; somebody stooped and dislodged the carton and threw it in the river, which whirled it on—a scrap of yellow Gold Flake: he was certainly a long way from the Tottenham Court Road.

I looked up and Martins was out of sight in the darkness. I called his name and it was lost in a confusion of echoes, in the rush and the roar of the underground river. Then I heard a third shot.

Martins told me later, 'I walked downstream to find Harry, but I must have missed him in the dark. I was afraid to lift the torch: I didn't want to tempt him to shoot again. He must have been struck by my bullet just at the entrance of a side passage. Then I suppose he crawled up the passage to the foot of the iron stairs. Thirty feet above his head was the manhole, but he wouldn't have had the strength to lift it, and even if he had succeeded the police were waiting above. He must have known all that, but he was in great pain, and just as an animal creeps into the dark to die, so I suppose a man makes for the light. He wants to die at home, and the darkness is never home to *us*. He began to pull himself up the stairs, but then the pain took him and he couldn't go on. What made him whistle that absurd scrap of a tune I'd been fool enough to believe he had written himself? Was he trying to attract attention, did he want a friend with him, even the friend who had trapped him, or was he delirious and had he no purpose at all? Anyway I heard his whistle and came back along the edge of the stream, and felt where the wall ended and found my way up the passage where he lay. I said, "Harry," and the whistling stopped, just above my head. I put my hand on an iron hand-rail, and climbed. I was still afraid he might shoot. Then, only three steps up, my foot stamped down on his hand, and he was there. I shone my torch on him: he hadn't got a gun; he must have dropped it when my bullet hit him. For a moment I thought he was dead, but then he whimpered with pain. I said, "Harry," and he swivelled his eyes with a great effort to my face. He was trying to speak, and I bent down to listen. "Bloody fool," he said—that was all. I don't know whether he meant that for himself—some sort of act of contrition, however inadequate (he was a Catholic)–or was it for me–with my thousand a year taxed and my imaginary cattle-rustlers who couldn't even shoot a rabbit clean? Then he began to whimper again. I couldn't bear it any more and I put a bullet through him.'

'We'll forget that bit,' I said.

Martins said, 'I never shall.'

17

A thaw set in that night, and all over Vienna the snow melted, and the ugly ruins came to light again; steel rods hanging like stalactites, and rusty girders thrusting like bones through the grey slush. Burials were much simpler than they had been a week before when electric drills had been needed to break the frozen ground. It was almost as warm as a spring day when Harry Lime had his second funeral. I was glad to get him under earth again, but it had taken two men's deaths. The group by the grave was smaller now: Kurtz wasn't there, nor Winkler–only the girl and Rollo Martins and myself. And there weren't any tears.

After it was over the girl walked away without a word to either of us down the long avenue of trees that led to the main entrance and the tram stop, splashing through the melted snow. I said to Martins, 'I've got transport. Can I give you a lift?'

'No,' he said, 'I'll take a tram back.'

'You win. You've proved me a bloody fool.'

'I haven't won,' he said. 'I've lost.' I watched him striding off on his overgrown legs after the girl. He caught her up and they walked side by side. I don't think he said a word to her: it was like the end of a story except that before they turned out of my sight her hand was through his arm–which is how a story usually begins. He was a very bad shot and a very bad judge of character, but he had a way with Westerns (a trick of tension) and with girls (I wouldn't know what). And Crabbin? Oh, Crabbin is still arguing with the British Council about Dexter's expenses. They say they can't pass simultaneous payments in Stockholm and Vienna. Poor Crabbin. Poor all of us, when you come to think of it.

THE QUIET AMERICAN

THE QUIET AMERICAN

Dear Réné and Phuong,

I have asked permission to dedicate this book to you not only in memory of the happy evenings I have spent with you in Saigon over the last five years, but also because I have quite shamelessly borrowed the location of your flat to house one of my characters, and your name, Phuong, for the convenience of readers because it is simple, beautiful and easy to pronounce, which is not true of all your country-women's names. You will both realise I have borrowed little else, certainly not the characters of anyone in Viet Nam. Pyle, Granger, Fowler, Vigot, Joe–these have had no originals in the life of Saigon or Hanoi, and General Thé is dead: shot in the back, so they say. Even the historical events have been in at least one case rearranged. For example, the big bomb near the Continental preceded and did not follow the bicycle bombs. I have no scruples about such small changes. This is a story and not a piece of history, and I hope that as a story about a few imaginary characters it will pass for both of you one hot Saigon evening.

Yours affectionately,
Graham Greene

'I do not like being moved: for the will is
    excited; and action
Is a most dangerous thing; I tremble for
    something factitious,
Some malpractice of heart and
    illegitimate process;
We're so prone to these things, with our
    terrible notions of duty.'

A.H.CLOUGH

'This is the patent age of new inventions
    For killing bodies, and for saving souls,
All propagated with the best intentions.'

BYRON

PART I

CHAPTER I

After dinner I sat and waited for Pyle in my room over the rue Catinat; he had said, 'I'll be with you at latest by ten,' and when midnight struck I couldn't stay quiet any longer and went down into the street. A lot of old women in black trousers squatted on the landing: it was February and I suppose too hot for them in bed. One trishaw driver pedalled slowly by towards the river-front and I could see lamps burning where they had disembarked the new American planes. There was no sign of Pyle anywhere in the long street.

Of course, I told myself, he might have been detained for some reason at the American Legation, but surely in that case he would have telephoned to the restaurant—he was very meticulous about small courtesies. I turned to go indoors when I saw a girl waiting in the next doorway. I couldn't see her face, only the white silk trousers and the long flowered robe, but I knew her for all that. She had so often waited for me to come home at just this place and hour.

'Phuong,' I said—which means Phœnix, but nothing nowadays is fabulous and nothing rises from its ashes. I knew before she had time to tell me that she was waiting for Pyle too. 'He isn't here.'

'*Je sais. Je t'ai vu seul à la fenêtre.*'

'You may as well wait upstairs.' I said. 'He will be coming soon.'

'I can wait here.'

'Better not. The police might pick you up.'

She followed me upstairs. I thought of several ironic and unpleasant jests I might make, but neither her English nor her French would have been good enough for her to understand the irony, and, strange to say, I had no desire to hurt her or even to hurt myself. When we reached the landing all the old women turned their heads, and as soon as we had passed their voices rose and fell as though they were singing together.

'What are they talking about?'

'They think I have come home.'

Inside my room the tree I had set up weeks ago for the Chinese New Year had shed most of its yellow blossoms. They had fallen between the keys of my typewriter. I picked them out. '*Tu es troublé,*' Phuong said.

'It's unlike him. He's such a punctual man.'

I took off my tie and my shoes and lay down on the bed. Phuong lit the gas stove and began to boil the water for tea. It might have been six months ago. 'He says you are going away soon now,' she said.

'Perhaps.'

'He is very fond of you.'

'Thank him for nothing,' I said.

I saw that she was doing her hair differently, allowing it to fall black and straight over her shoulders. I remembered that Pyle had once criticised the elaborate hairdressing which she thought became the daughter of a mandarin. I shut my eyes and she was again the same as she used to be: she was the hiss of steam, the clink of a cup, she was a certain hour of the night and the promise of rest.

'He will not be long,' she said as though I needed comfort for his absence.

I wondered what they talked about together. Pyle was very earnest and I had suffered from his lectures on the Far East, which he had known for as many months as I had years. Democracy was another subject of his—he had pronounced and aggravating views on what the United States was doing for the world. Phuong on the other hand was wonderfully ignorant; if Hitler had come into the conversation she would have interrupted to ask who he was. The explanation would be all the more difficult because she had never met a German or a Pole and had only the vaguest knowledge of European geography, though about Princess Margaret of course she knew more than I. I heard her put a tray down on the end of the bed.

'Is he still in love with you, Phuong?'

To take an Annamite to bed with you is like taking a bird: they twitter and sing on your pillow. There had been a time when I thought none of their voices sang like Phuong's. I put out my hand and touched her arm—their bones too were as fragile as a bird's.

'Is he, Phuong?'

She laughed and I heard her strike a match, 'In love?'—perhaps it was one of the phrases she didn't understand.

'May I make your pipe?' she asked.

When I opened my eyes she had lit the lamp and the tray was already prepared. The lamplight made her skin the colour of dark amber as she bent over the flame with a frown of concentration, heating the small paste of opium, twirling her needle.

'Does Pyle still not smoke?' I asked her.

'No.'

'You ought to make him or he won't come back.' It was a superstition among them that a lover who smoked would always return, even from France. A man's sexual capacity might be injured by smoking, but they would always prefer a faithful to a potent lover. Now she was kneading the little ball of hot paste on the convex margin of the bowl and I could smell the opium. There is no smell like it. Beside the bed my alarm-clock showed twelve-twenty, but already my tension was over. Pyle had diminished. The lamp lit her face as she tended the long pipe, bent over it with the serious attention she might have given to a child. I was fond of my pipe: more than two feet of straight bamboo, ivory at either end. Two-thirds of the way down was the bowl, like a convolvulus reversed, the convex margin polished and darkened by the frequent kneading of the opium. Now with a flick of the wrist she plunged the needle into the tiny cavity, released the opium and reversed the bowl over the flame, holding the pipe steady for me. The bead of opium bubbled gently and smoothly as I inhaled.

The practised inhaler can draw a whole pipe down in one breath, but I always had to take several pulls. Then I lay back, with my neck on the leather pillow, while she prepared the second pipe.

I said, 'You know, really, it's as clear as daylight. Pyle knows I smoke a few pipes before bed, and he doesn't want to disturb me. He'll be round in the morning.'

In went the needle and I took my second pipe. As I laid it down, I said, 'Nothing to worry about. Nothing to worry about at all.' I took a sip of tea and held my hand in the pit of her arm. 'When you left me,' I said, 'it was lucky I had this to fall back on. There's a good house in the rue d'Ormay. What a fuss we Europeans make about nothing. You shouldn't live with a man who doesn't smoke, Phuong.'

'But he's going to marry me,' she said. 'Soon now.'

'Of course, that's another matter.'

'Shall I make your pipe again?'

'Yes.'

I wondered whether she would consent to sleep with me that night if Pyle never came, but I knew that when I had smoked four pipes I would no longer want her. Of course it would be agreeable to feel her thigh beside me in the bed–she always slept on her back, and when I woke in the morning I could start the day with a pipe, instead of with my own company. 'Pyle won't come now,' I said. 'Stay here, Phuong.' She held the pipe out to me and shook her head. By the time I had drawn the opium in, her presence or absence mattered very little.

'Why is Pyle not here?' she asked.

'How do I know?' I said.

'Did he go to see General Thé?'

'I wouldn't know.'

'He told me if he could not have dinner with you, he wouldn't come here.'

'Don't worry. He'll come. Make me another pipe.' When she bent over the flame the poem of Baudelaire's came into my mind: '*Mon enfant, ma sœur. . . .*' How did it go on?

> *Aimer à loisir,*
> *Aimer et mourir*
> *Au pays qui te ressemble.*

Out on the waterfront slept the ships, '*dont l'humeur est vagabonde*'. I thought that if I smelt her skin it would have the faintest fragrance of opium, and her colour was that of the small flame. I had seen the flowers on her dress beside the canals in the north, she was indigenous like a herb, and I never wanted to go home.

'I wish I were Pyle,' I said aloud, but the pain was limited and bearable–the opium saw to that. Somebody knocked on the door.

'Pyle,' she said.

'No. It's not his knock.'

Somebody knocked again impatiently. She got quickly up, shaking the yellow tree so that it showered its petals again over my typewriter. The door opened. 'Monsieur Fowlair,' a voice commanded.

'I'm Fowler,' I said. I was not going to get up for a policeman–I could see his khaki shorts without lifting my head.

He explained in almost unintelligible Vietnamese French that I was needed immediately–at once–rapidly–at the Sureté.

'At the French Sureté or the Vietnamese?'

'The French.' In his mouth the word sounded like '*Françung*'.

'What about?'

He didn't know: it was his orders to fetch me.

'*Toi aussi*,' he said to Phuong.

'Say *vous* when you speak to a lady,' I told him. 'How did you know she was here?'

He only repeated that they were his orders.

'I'll come in the morning.'

'*Sur le chung*,' he said, a little, neat, obstinate figure. There wasn't any point in arguing, so I got up and put on my tie and shoes. Here the police had the last word: they could withdraw my order of circulation: they could have me barred from Press Conferences: they could even, if they chose, refuse me an exit permit. These were the open legal methods, but legality was not essential in a country at war. I knew a man who had suddenly and inexplicably lost his cook–he had traced him to the Vietnamese Sureté, but the officers there assured him that he had been released after questioning. His family never saw him again. Perhaps he had joined the Communists; perhaps he had been enlisted in one of the private armies which flourished round Saigon–the Hoa-Haos or the Caodaists or General Thé. Perhaps he was in a French prison. Perhaps he was happily making money out of girls in Cholon, the Chinese suburb. Perhaps his heart had given way when they questioned him. I said, 'I'm not going to walk. You'll have to pay for a trishaw.' One had to keep one's dignity.

That was why I refused a cigarette from the French officer at the Sureté. After three pipes I felt my mind clear and alert: it could take such decisions easily without losing sight of the main question–what do they want from me? I had met Vigot before several times at parties–I had noticed him because he appeared incongruously in love with his wife, who ignored him, a flashy and false blonde. Now it was two in the morning and he sat tired and depressed in the cigarette smoke and the heavy heat, wearing a green eye-shade, and he had a volume of Pascal open on his desk to while away the time. When I refused to allow him to question Phuong without me he gave way at once, with a single sigh that might have represented his weariness with Saigon, with the heat, or with the whole human condition.

He said in English, 'I'm so sorry I had to ask you to come.'

'I wasn't asked. I was ordered.'

'Oh, these native police–they don't understand.' His eyes were on a page of *Les Pensées* as though he were still absorbed in those sad arguments. 'I wanted to ask you a few questions–about Pyle.'

'You had better ask him the questions.'

He turned to Phuong and interrogated her sharply in French. 'How long have you lived with Monsieur Pyle?'

'A month–I don't know,' she said.

'How much has he paid you?'

'You've no right to ask her that,' I said. 'She's not for sale.'

'She used to live with you, didn't she?' he asked abruptly. 'For two years.'

'I'm a correspondent who's supposed to report your war–when you let him. Don't ask me to contribute to your scandal sheet as well.'

'What do you know about Pyle? Please answer my questions, Monsieur Fowler. I don't want to ask them. But this is serious. Please believe me it is very serious.'

'I'm not an informer. You know all I can tell you about Pyle. Age thirty-two, employed in the Economic Aid Mission, nationality American.'

'You sound like a friend of his,' Vigot said, looking past me at Phuong. A native policeman came in with three cups of black coffee.

'Or would you rather have tea?' Vigot asked.

'I *am* a friend,' I said. 'Why not? I shall be going home one day, won't I? I can't take her with me. She'll be all right with him. It's a reasonable arrangement. And he's going to marry her, he says. He might, you know. He's a good chap in his way. Serious. Not one of those noisy bastards at the Continental. A quiet American,' I summed him precisely up as I might have said, 'a blue lizard', 'a white elephant'.

Vigot said, 'Yes.' He seemed to be looking for words on his desk with which to convey his meaning as precisely as I had done. 'A very quiet American.' He sat there in the little hot office waiting for one of us to speak. A mosquito droned to the attack and I watched Phuong. Opium makes you quick-witted–perhaps only because it calms the nerves and stills the emotions. Nothing, not even death, seems so important. Phuong, I thought, had not caught his tone, melancholy and final, and her English was very bad. While she sat there on the hard office-chair, she was still waiting patiently for Pyle. I had at that moment given up waiting, and I could see Vigot taking those two facts in.

'How did you meet him first?' Vigot asked me.

Why should I explain to him that it was Pyle who had met me? I had seen him last September coming across the square towards the bar of the Continental: an unmistakably young and unused face flung at us like a dart. With his gangly legs and his crew-cut and his wide campus gaze he seemed incapable of harm. The tables on the street were most of them full. 'Do you mind?' he had asked with serious courtesy. 'My name's Pyle. I'm new here,' and he had folded himself around a chair and ordered a beer. Then he looked quickly up into the hard noon glare.

'Was that a grenade?' he asked with excitement and hope.

'Most likely the exhaust of a car,' I said, and was suddenly sorry for his disappointment. One forgets so quickly one's own youth: once I was interested myself in what for want of a better term they call news. But grenades had staled on me; they were something listed on the back page of the local paper–so many last night in Saigon, so many in Cholon: they never made the European Press. Up the street came the lovely flat figures–the white silk trousers, the long tight jackets in pink and mauve patterns slit up the thigh. I watched them with the nostalgia I knew I would feel when I had left these regions for ever. 'They are lovely, aren't they?' I said over my beer, and Pyle cast them a cursory glance as they went up the rue Catinat.

'Oh, sure,' he said indifferently: he was a serious type. 'The Minister's very concerned about these grenades. It would be very awkward, he says, if there was an incident—with one of us, I mean.'

'With one of you? Yes, I suppose that would be serious. Congress wouldn't like it.' Why does one want to tease the innocent? Perhaps only ten days ago he had been walking back across the Common in Boston, his arms full of the books he had been reading in advance on the Far East and the problems of China. He didn't even hear what I said; he was absorbed already in the dilemmas of Democracy and the responsibilities of the West; he was determined—I learnt that very soon—to do good, not to any individual person but to a country, a continent, a world. Well, he was in his element now with the whole universe to improve.

'Is he in the mortuary?' I asked Vigot.

'How did you know he was dead?' It was a foolish policeman's question, unworthy of the man who read Pascal, unworthy also of the man who so strangely loved his wife. You cannot love without intuition.

'Not guilty,' I said. I told myself that it was true. Didn't Pyle always go his own way? I looked for any feeling in myself, even resentment at a policeman's suspicion, but I could find none. No one but Pyle was responsible. Aren't we all better dead? the opium reasoned within me. But I looked cautiously at Phuong, for it was hard on her. She must have loved him in her way: hadn't she been fond of me and hadn't she left me for Pyle? She had attached herself to youth and hope and seriousness and now they had failed her more than age and despair. She sat there looking at the two of us and I thought she had not yet understood. Perhaps it would be a good thing if I could get her away before the fact got home. I was ready to answer any questions if I could bring the interview quickly and ambiguously to an end, so that I might tell her later, in private, away from a policeman's eye and the hard office-chairs and the bare globe where the moths circled.

I said to Vigot, 'What hours are you interested in?'

'Between six and ten.'

'I had a drink at the Continental at six. The waiters will remember. At six forty-five I walked down to the quay to watch the American planes unloaded. I saw Wilkins of the Associated News by the door of the Majestic. Then I went into the cinema next door. They'll probably remember—they had to get me change. From there I took a trishaw to the Vieux Moulin—I suppose I arrived about eight thirty—and had dinner by myself. Granger was there—you can ask him. Then I took a trishaw back about a quarter to ten. You could probably find the driver. I was expecting Pyle at ten, but he didn't turn up.'

'Why were you expecting him?'

'He telephoned me. He said he had to see me about something important.'

'Have you any idea what?'

'No. Everything was important to Pyle.'

'And this girl of his?—do you know where she was?'

'She was waiting for him outside at midnight. She was anxious. She knows nothing. Why, can't you see she's waiting for him still?'

'Yes,' he said.

'And you can't really believe I killed him for jealousy—or she for what? He was going to marry her.'

'Yes.'

'Where did you find him?'

'He was in the water under the bridge to Dakow.'

The Vieux Moulin stood beside the bridge. There were armed police on the bridge and the restaurant had an iron grille to keep out grenades. It wasn't safe to cross the bridge at night, for all the far side of the river was in the hands of the Vietminh after dark. I must have dined within fifty yards of his body.

'The trouble was,' I said, 'he got mixed up.'

'To speak plainly,' Vigot said, 'I am not altogether sorry. He was doing a lot of harm.'

'God save us always,' I said, 'from the innocent and the good.'

'The good?'

'Yes, good. In his way. You're a Roman Catholic. You wouldn't recognise his way. And anyway, he was a damned Yankee.'

'Would you mind identifying him? I'm sorry. It's a routine, not a very nice routine.'

I didn't bother to ask him why he didn't wait for someone from the American Legation, for I knew the reason. French methods are a little old-fashioned by our cold standards: they believe in the conscience, the sense of guilt, a criminal should be confronted with his crime, for he may break down and betray himself. I told myself again I was innocent, while he went down the stone stairs to where the refrigerating plant hummed in the basement.

They pulled him out like a tray of ice-cubes, and I looked at him. The wounds were frozen into placidity. I said, 'You see, they don't re-open in my presence.'

'*Comment?*'

'Isn't that one of the objects? Ordeal by something or other? But you've frozen him stiff. They didn't have deep freezes in the Middle Ages.'

'You recognise him?'

'Oh yes.'

He looked more than ever out of place: he should have stayed at home. I saw him in a family snapshot album, riding on a dude ranch, bathing on Long Island, photographed with his colleagues in some apartment on the twenty-third floor. He belonged to the skyscraper and the express elevator, the ice-cream and the dry Martinis, milk at lunch, and chicken sandwiches on the Merchant Limited.

'He wasn't dead from this,' Vigot said, pointing at a wound in the chest. 'He was drowned in the mud. We found the mud in his lungs.'

'You work quickly.'

'One has to in this climate.'

They pushed the tray back and closed the door. The rubber padded.

'You can't help us at all?' Vigot asked.

'Not at all.'

I walked back with Phuong towards my flat. I was no longer on my dignity. Death takes away vanity—even the vanity of the cuckold who mustn't show his pain. She was still unaware of what it was about, and I had no technique for telling her slowly and gently. I was a correspondent: I thought in headlines. 'American official murdered in Saigon.' Working on a newspaper one does not learn the way to break bad news, and even now I had to think of my paper and to ask her, 'Do you mind stopping at the cable office?' I left her in the street and sent my wire and came back to her. It was only a gesture: I knew too well that the French correspondents would already be informed, or if Vigot had played fair (which was possible), then the censors would hold my telegram till the French had filed theirs. My paper would get the news first under a Paris date-line. Not that Pyle was very important. It wouldn't have done to cable the details of his true career, that before he died he had been responsible for at least fifty deaths, for it would have damaged Anglo-American relations, the Minister would have been upset. The Minister had a great respect for Pyle—Pyle had taken a good degree in—well, one of those subjects Americans can take degrees in: perhaps public relations or theatrecraft, perhaps even Far Eastern studies (he had read a lot of books).

'Where is Pyle?' Phuong asked. 'What did they want?'

'Come home,' I said.

'Will Pyle come?'

'He's as likely to come there as anywhere else.'

The old women were still gossiping on the landing, in the relative cool. When I opened my door I could tell my room had been searched: everything was tidier than I ever left it.

'Another pipe?' Phuong asked.

'Yes.'

I took off my tie and my shoes; the interlude was over; the night was nearly the same as it had been. Phuong crouched at the end of the bed and lit the lamp. *Mon enfant, ma sœur*—skin the colour of amber. *Sa douce langue natale.*

'Phuong,' I said. She was kneading the opium on the bowl. '*Il est mort*, Phuong.' She held the needle in her hand and looked up at me like a child trying to concentrate, frowning. '*Tu dis?*'

'Pyle *est mort. Assassiné.*'

She put the needle down and sat back on her heels, looking at me. There was no scene, no tears, just thought—the long private thought of somebody who has to alter a whole course of life.

'You had better stay here tonight,' I said.

She nodded and taking up the needle again began to heat the opium. That night I woke from one of those short deep opium sleeps, ten minutes long, that seem a whole night's rest, and found my hand where it had always lain at night, between her legs. She was asleep and I could hardly hear her breathing. Once again after so many months I was not alone, and yet I thought suddenly with anger, remembering Vigot and his eye-shade in the police station and the quiet corridors of the Legation with no one about and the soft hairless skin under my hand, 'Am I the only one who really cared for Pyle?'

CHAPTER 2

I

The morning Pyle arrived in the square by the Continental I had seen enough of my American colleagues of the Press, big, noisy, boyish and middle-aged, full of sour cracks against the French, who were, when all was said, fighting this war. Periodically, after an engagement had been tidily finished and the casualties removed from the scene, they would be summoned to Hanoi, nearly four hours' flight away, addressed by the Commander-in-Chief, lodged for one night in a Press Camp where they boasted that the barman was the best in Indo-China, flown over the late battlefield at a height of 3,000 feet (the limit of a heavy machine-gun's range) and then delivered safely and noisily back, like a school-treat, to the Continental Hotel in Saigon.

Pyle was quiet, he seemed modest, sometimes that first day I had to lean forward to catch what he was saying. And he was very, very serious. Several times he seemed to shrink up within himself at the noise of the American Press on the terrace above—the terrace which was popularly believed to be safer from hand-grenades. But he criticised nobody.

'Have you read York Harding?' he asked.

'No. No, I don't think so. What did he write?'

He gazed at a milk-bar across the street and said dreamily, 'That looks like a soda-fountain.' I wondered what depth of homesickness lay behind his odd choice of what to observe in a scene so unfamiliar. But hadn't I on my first walk up the rue Catinat noticed first the shop with the Guerlain perfume and comforted myself with the thought that, after all, Europe was only distant thirty hours? He looked reluctantly away from the milk-bar and said, 'York wrote a book called *The Advance of Red China*. It's a very profound book.'

'I haven't read it. Do you know him?'

He nodded solemnly and lapsed into silence. But he broke it again a moment later to modify the impression he had given. 'I don't know him well,' he said. 'I guess I only met him twice.' I liked him for that—to consider it was boasting to claim acquaintance with—what was his name? York Harding. I was to learn later that he had an enormous respect for what he called serious writers. That term excluded novelists, poets and dramatists unless they had what he called a contemporary theme, and even then it was better to read the straight stuff as you got it from York.

I said, 'You know, if you live in a place for long you cease to read about it.'

'Of course I always like to know what the man on the spot has to say,' he replied guardedly.

'And then check it with York?'

'Yes.' Perhaps he had noticed the irony, because he added with his habitual politeness, 'I'd take it as a very great privilege if you could find time

to brief me on the main points. You see, York was here more than two years
ago.'

I liked his loyalty to Harding—whoever Harding was. It was a change from
the denigrations of the Pressmen and their immature cynicism. I said, 'Have
another bottle of beer and I'll try to give you an idea of things.'

I began, while he watched me intently like a prize pupil, by explaining the
situation in the North, in Tonkin, where the French in those days were
hanging on to the delta of the Red River, which contained Hanoi and the
only northern port, Haiphong. Here most of the rice was grown, and when
the harvest was ready the annual battle for the rice always began.

'That's the North,' I said. 'The French may hold, poor devils, if the
Chinese don't come to help the Vietminh. A war of jungle and mountain and
marsh, paddy fields where you wade shoulder-high and the enemy simply
disappear, bury their arms, put on peasant dress. But you can rot
comfortably in the damp in Hanoi. They don't throw bombs there. God
knows why. You could call it a regular war.'

'And here in the South?'

'The French control the main roads until seven in the evening: they
control the watch towers after that, and the towns—part of them. That
doesn't mean you are safe, or there wouldn't be iron grilles in front of the
restaurants.'

How often I had explained all this before. I was a record always turned on
for the benefit of newcomers—the visiting Member of Parliament, the new
British Minister. Sometimes I would wake up in the night saying, 'Take the
case of the Caodaists.' Or the Hoa-Haos or the Binh Xuyen, all the private
armies who sold their services for money or revenge. Strangers found them
picturesque, but there is nothing picturesque in treachery and distrust.

'And now,' I said. 'there's General Thé. He was Caodaist Chief of
Staff, but he's taken to the hills to fight both sides, the French, the
Communists. . . .'

'York,' Pyle said, 'wrote that what the East needed was a Third Force.'
Perhaps I should have seen that fanatic gleam, the quick response to a
phrase, the magic sound of figures: Fifth Column, Third Force, Seventh
Day. I might have saved all of us a lot of trouble, even Pyle, if I had realised
the direction of that indefatigable young brain. But I left him with the arid
bones of background and took my daily walk up and down the rue Catinat.
He would have to learn for himself the real background that held you as a
smell does: the gold of the rice-fields under a flat late sun: the fishers' fragile
cranes hovering over the fields like mosquitoes: the cups of tea on an old
abbot's platform, with his bed and his commercial calendars, his buckets
and broken cups and the junk of a lifetime washed up around his chair: the
mollusc hats of the girls repairing the road where a mine had burst: the gold
and the young green and the bright dresses of the south, and in the north the
deep browns and the black clothes and the circle of enemy mountains and
the drone of planes. When I first came I counted the days of my assignment,
like a schoolboy marking off the days of term; I thought I was tied to what
was left of a Bloomsbury square and the 73 bus passing the portico of Euston
and springtime in the local in Torrington Place. Now the bulbs would be out
in the square garden, and I didn't care a damn. I wanted a day punctuated by

those quick reports that might be car-exhausts or might be grenades, I wanted to keep the sight of those silk-trousered figures moving with grace through the humid noon, I wanted Phuong, and my home had shifted its ground eight thousand miles.

I turned at the High Commissioner's house, where the Foreign Legion stood on guard in their white képis and their scarlet epaulettes, crossed by the Cathedral and came back by the dreary wall of the Vietnamese Sureté that seemed to smell of urine and injustice. And yet that too was a part of home, like the dark passages on upper floors one avoided in childhood. The new dirty magazines were out on the bookstalls near the quay–*Tabu* and *Illusion*, and the sailors were drinking beer on the pavement, an easy mark for a home-made bomb. I thought of Phuong, who would be haggling over the price of fish in the third street down on the left before going for her elevenses to the milk-bar (I always knew where she was in those days), and Pyle ran easily and naturally out of my mind. I didn't even mention him to Phuong, when we sat down to lunch together in our room over the rue Catinat and she wore her best flowered silk robe because it was two years to a day since we had met in the Grand Monde in Cholon.

2

Neither of us mentioned him when we woke on the morning after his death. Phuong had risen before I was properly awake and had our tea ready. One is not jealous of the dead, and it seemed easy to me that morning to take up our old life together.

'Will you stay tonight?' I asked Phuong over the *croissants* as casually as I could.

'I will have to fetch my box.'

'The police may be there,' I said. 'I had better come with you.' It was the nearest we came that day to speaking of Pyle.

Pyle had a flat in a new villa near the rue Duranton, off one of those main streets which the French continually subdivided in honour of their generals–so that the rue de Gaulle became after the third intersection the rue Leclerc, and that again sooner or later would probably turn abruptly into the rue de Lattre. Somebody important must have been arriving from Europe by air, for there was a policeman facing the pavement every twenty yards along the route to the High Commissioner's Residence.

On the gravel drive to Pyle's apartment were several motor-cycles and a Vietnamese policeman examined my press-card. He wouldn't allow Phuong into the house, so I went in search of a French officer. In Pyle's bathroom Vigot was washing his hands with Pyle's soap and drying them on Pyle's towel. His tropical suit had a stain of oil on the sleeve–Pyle's oil, I supposed.

'Any news?' I asked.

'We found his car in the garage. It's empty of petrol. He must have gone off last night in a trishaw–or in somebody else's car. Perhaps the petrol was drained away.'

'He might even have walked,' I said. 'You know what Americans are.'

'Your car was burnt, wasn't it?' he went thoughtfully on. 'You haven't a new one yet?'

'No.'

'It's not an important point.'

'No.'

'Have you any views?' he asked.

'Too many,' I said.

'Tell me.'

'Well, he might have been murdered by the Vietminh. They have murdered plenty of people in Saigon. His body was found in the river by the bridge to Dakow–Vietminh territory when your police withdraw at night. Or he might have been killed by the Vietnamese Sureté–it's been known. Perhaps they didn't like his friends. Perhaps he was killed by Caodaists because he knew General Thé.'

'Did he?'

'They say so. Perhaps he was killed by General Thé because he knew the Caodaists. Perhaps he was killed by the Hoa-Haos for making passes at the General's concubines. Perhaps he was just killed by someone who wanted his money.'

'Or a simple case of jealousy,' Vigot said.

'Or perhaps by the French Sureté,' I continued, 'because they didn't like his contacts. Are you really looking for the people who killed him?'

'No,' Vigot said. 'I'm just making a report, that's all. So long as it's an act of war–well, there are thousands killed every year.'

'You can rule me out,' I said. 'I'm not involved. Not involved,' I repeated. It had been an article of my creed. The human condition being what it was, let them fight, let them love, let them murder, I would not be involved. My fellow journalists called themselves correspondents; I preferred the title of reporter. I wrote what I saw. I took no action–even an opinion is a kind of action.

'What are you doing here?'

'I've come for Phuong's belongings. Your police wouldn't let her in.'

'Well, let us go and find them.'

'It's nice of you, Vigot.'

Pyle had two rooms, a kitchen and bathroom. We went to the bedroom. I knew where Phuong would keep her box–under the bed. We pulled it out together; it contained her picture books. I took her few spare clothes out of the wardrobe, her two good robes and her spare trousers. One had a sense that they had been hanging there for a few hours only and didn't belong, they were in passage like a butterfly in a room. In a drawer I found her small triangular *culottes* and her collection of scarves. There was really very little to put in the box, less than a week-end visitor's at home.

In the sitting-room there was a photograph of herself and Pyle. They had been photographed in the botanical gardens beside a large stone dragon. She held Pyle's dog on a leash–a black chow with a black tongue. A too black dog. I put the photograph in her box. 'What's happened to the dog?' I said.

'It isn't here. He may have taken it with him.'

'Perhaps it will return and you can analyse the earth on its paws.'

'I'm not Lecoq, or even Maigret, and there's a war on.'

I went across to the bookcase and examined the two rows of books—Pyle's library. *The Advance of Red China, The Challenge to Democracy, The Rôle of the West*—these, I suppose, were the complete works of York Harding. There were a lot of Congressional Reports, a Vietnamese phrase book, a history of the War in the Philippines, a Modern Library Shakespeare. On what did he relax? I found his light reading on another shelf: a portable Thomas Wolfe and a mysterious anthology called *The Triumph of Life* and a selection of American poetry. There was also a book of chess problems. It didn't seem much for the end of the working day, but, after all, he had had Phuong. Tucked away behind the anthology there was a paper-backed book called *The Physiology of Marriage*. Perhaps he was studying sex, as he had studied the East, on paper. And the keyword was marriage. Pyle believed in being involved.

His desk was quite bare. 'You've made a clean sweep.' I said.

'Oh,' Vigot said, 'I had to take charge of these on behalf of the American Legation. You know how quickly rumour spreads. There might have been looting. I had all his papers sealed up.' He said it seriously without even smiling.

'Anything damaging?'

'We can't afford to find anything damaging against an ally,' Vigot said.

'Would you mind if I took one of these books—as a keepsake?'

'I'll look the other way.'

I chose York Harding's *The Rôle of the West* and packed it in the box with Phuong's clothes.

'As a friend,' Vigot said, 'is there nothing you could tell me in confidence? My report's all tied up. He was murdered by the Communists. Perhaps the beginning of a campaign against American aid. But between you and me—listen, it's dry talking, what about a vermouth cassis round the corner?'

'Too early.'

'He didn't confide anything to you the last time he saw you?'

'No.'

'When was that?'

'Yesterday morning. After the big bang.'

He paused to let my reply sink in—to my mind, not to his: he interrogated fairly. 'You were out when he called on you last night?'

'Last night? I must have been. I didn't think . . .'

'You may be wanting an exit visa. You know we could delay it indefinitely.'

'Do you really believe,' I said, 'that I want to go home?'

Vigot looked through the window at the bright cloudless day. He said sadly, 'Most people do.'

'I like it here. At home there are—problems.'

'*Merde*,' Vigot said, 'here's the American Economic Attaché.' He repeated with sarcasm, 'Economic Attaché.'

'I'd better be off. He'll want to seal me up too.'

Vigot said wearily, 'I wish you luck. He'll have a terrible lot to say to me.'

The Economic Attaché was standing by his Packard when I came out, trying to explain something to his driver. He was a stout middle-aged man with an exaggerated bottom and a face that looked as if it never needed a razor. He called out, 'Fowler. Could you explain to this darned driver . . .?'

I explained.

He said, 'But that's just what I told him, but he always pretends not to understand French.'

'It may be a matter of accent.'

'I was three years in Paris. My accent's good enough for one of these darned Vietnamese.'

'The voice of Democracy,' I said.

'What's that?'

'I expect it's a book by York Harding.'

'I don't get you.' He took a suspicious look at the box I carried. 'What've you got there?' he said.

'Two pairs of white silk trousers, two silk robes, some girl's underpants—three pairs, I think. All home products. No American aid.'

'Have you been up there?' he asked.

'Yes.'

'You heard the news?'

'Yes.'

'It's a terrible thing,' he said, 'terrible.'

'I expect the Minister's very disturbed.'

'I should say. He's with the High Commissioner now, and he's asked for an interview with the President.' He put his hand on my arm and walked me away from the cars. 'You knew young Pyle well, didn't you? I can't get over a thing like that happening to him. I knew his father. Professor Harold C. Pyle—you'll have heard of him?'

'No.'

'He's the world authority on underwater erosion. Didn't you see his picture on the cover of *Time* the other month?'

'Oh, I think I remember. A crumbling cliff in the background and gold-rimmed glasses in the foreground.'

'That's him. I had to draft the cable home. It was terrible. I loved that boy like he was my son.'

'That makes you closely related to his father.'

He turned his wet brown eyes on me. He said, 'What's getting you? That's not the way to talk when a fine young fellow . . .'

'I'm sorry,' I said. 'Death takes people in different ways.' Perhaps he had really loved Pyle. 'What did you say in your cable?' I asked.

He replied seriously and literally, '"Grieved to report your son died a soldier's death in cause of Democracy." The Minister signed it.'

'A soldier's death,' I said. 'Mightn't that prove a bit confusing? I mean to the folks at home. The Economic Aid Mission doesn't sound like the Army. Do you get Purple Hearts?'

He said in a low voice, tense with ambiguity, 'He had special duties.'

'Oh yes, we all guessed that.'

'He didn't talk, did he?'

'Oh no,' I said, and Vigot's phrase came back to me, 'He was a very quiet American.'

'Have you any hunch,' he asked, 'why they killed him? and who?'

Suddenly I was angry; I was tired of the whole pack of them with their private stores of Coca-Cola and their portable hospitals and their too wide cars and their not quite latest guns. I said, 'Yes. They killed him because he was too innocent to live. He was young and ignorant and silly and he got involved. He had no more of a notion than any of you what the whole affair's about, and you gave him money and York Harding's books on the East and said, "Go ahead. Win the East for Democracy." He never saw anything he hadn't heard in a lecture-hall, and his writers and his lecturers made a fool of him. When he saw a dead body he couldn't even see the wounds. A red menace, a soldier of democracy.'

'I thought you were his friend,' he said in a tone of reproach.

'I *was* his friend. I'd have liked to see him reading the Sunday supplements at home and following the baseball. I'd have liked to see him safe with a standardised American girl who subscribed to the Book Club.'

He cleared his throat with embarrassment. 'Of course,' he said, 'I'd forgotten that unfortunate business. I was quite on your side, Fowler. He behaved very badly. I don't mind telling you I had a long talk with him about the girl. You see, I had the advantage of knowing Professor and Mrs Pyle.'

I said, 'Vigot's waiting,' and walked away. For the first time he spotted Phuong and when I looked back at him he was watching me with pained perplexity: an eternal brother who didn't understand.

CHAPTER 3

I

The first time Pyle met Phuong was again at the Continental, perhaps two months after his arrival. It was the early evening, in the momentary cool which came when the sun had just gone down, and the candles were lit on the stalls in the side streets. The dice rattled on the tables where the French were playing *Quatre Cent Vingt-et-un* and the girls in the white silk trousers bicycled home down the rue Catinat. Phuong was drinking a glass of orange juice and I was having a beer and we sat in silence, content to be together. Then Pyle came tentatively across, and I introduced them. He had a way of staring hard at a girl as though he hadn't seen one before and then blushing. 'I was wondering whether you and your lady,' Pyle said, 'would step across and join my table. One of our attachés . . .'

It was the Economic Attaché. He beamed down at us from the terrace above, a great warm welcoming smile, full of confidence, like the man who keeps his friends because he uses the right deodorants. I had heard him called Joe a number of times, but I had never learnt his surname. He made a noisy show of pulling out chairs and calling for the waiter, though all that activity could possibly produce at the Continental was a choice of beer, brandy-and-soda or vermouth cassis. 'Didn't expect to see you here, Fowler,' he said. 'We are waiting for the boys back from Hanoi. There seems to have been quite a battle. Weren't you with them?'

'I'm tired of flying four hours for a Press Conference,' I said.

He looked at me with disapproval. He said, 'These guys are real keen.

Why, I expect they could earn twice as much in business or on the radio without any risk.'

'They might have to work,' I said.

'They seem to sniff the battle like war-horses,' he went on exultantly, paying no attention to words he didn't like. 'Bill Granger—you can't keep him out of a scrap.'

'I expect you're right. I saw him in one the other evening at the bar of the Sporting.'

'You know very well I didn't mean that.'

Two trishaw drivers came pedalling furiously down the rue Catinat and drew up in a photo-finish outside the Continental. In the first was Granger. The other contained a small, grey, silent heap which Granger now began to pull out on to the pavement. 'Oh, come on, Mick,' he said, 'come on.' Then he began to argue with his driver about the fare. 'Here,' he said, 'take it or leave it,' and flung five times the correct amount into the street for the man to stoop for.

The Economic Attaché said nervously, 'I guess these boys deserve a little relaxation.'

Granger flung his burden on to a chair. Then he noticed Phuong. 'Why,' he said, 'you old so-and-so, Joe. Where did you find her? Didn't know you had a whistle in you. Sorry, got to find the can. Look after Mick.'

'Rough soldierly manners,' I said.

Pyle said earnestly, blushing again, 'I wouldn't have invited you two over if I'd thought . . .'

The grey heap stirred in the chair and the head fell on the table as though it wasn't attached. It sighed, a long whistling sigh of infinite tedium, and lay still.

'Do you know him?' I asked Pyle.

'No. Isn't he one of the Press?'

'I heard Bill call him Mick,' the Economic Attaché said.

'Isn't there a new U.P. correspondent?'

'It's not him. I know him. What about your Economic Mission? You can't know all your people—there are hundreds of them.'

'I don't think he belongs,' the Economic Attaché said. 'I can't recollect him.'

'We might find his identity card,' Pyle suggested.

'For God's sake don't wake him. One drunk's enough. Anyway Granger will know.'

But he didn't. He came gloomily back from the lavatory. 'Who's the dame?' he asked morosely.

'Miss Phuong is a friend of Fowler's,' Pyle said stiffly. 'We want to know who . . .'

'Where'd he find her? You got to be careful in this town.' He added gloomily, 'Thank God for penicillin.'

'Bill,' the Economic Attaché said, 'we want to know who Mick is.'

'Search me.'

'But you brought him here.'

'The Frogs can't take Scotch. He passed out.'

'Is he French? I thought you called him Mick.'

'Had to call him something,' Granger said. He leant over to Phuong and said, 'Here. You. Have another glass of orange? Got a date tonight?'

I said, 'She's got a date every night.'

The Economic Attaché said hurriedly, 'How's the war, Bill?'

'Great victory north-west of Hanoi. French recaptured two villages they never told us they'd lost. Heavy Vietminh casualties. Haven't been able to count their own yet but will let us know in a week or two.'

The Economic Attaché said, 'There's a rumour that the Vietminh have broken into Phat Diem, burned the Cathedral, chased out the Bishop.'

'They wouldn't tell us about that in Hanoi. That's not a victory.'

'One of our medical teams couldn't get beyond Nam Dinh,' Pyle said.

'You didn't get down as far as that, Bill?' the Economic Attaché asked.

'Who do you think I am? I'm a correspondent with an *Ordre de Circulation* which shows when I'm out of bounds. I fly to Hanoi airport. They give us a car to the Press Camp. They lay on a flight over the two towns they've recaptured and show us the tricolour flying. It might be any darned flag at that height. Then we have a Press Conference and a colonel explains to us what we've been looking at. Then we file our cables with the censor. Then we have drinks. Best barman in Indo-China. Then we catch the plane back.'

Pyle frowned at his beer.

'You underrate yourself, Bill,' the Economic Attaché said. 'Why, that account of Road 66—what did you call it? Highway to Hell—that was worthy of the Pulitzer. You know the story I mean—the man with his head blown off kneeling in the ditch, and that other you saw walking in a dream . . .'

'Do you think I'd really go near their stinking highway? Stephen Crane could describe a war without seeing one. Why shouldn't I? It's only a damned colonial war anyway. Get me another drink. And then let's go and find a girl. You've got a piece of tail. I want a piece of tail too.'

I said to Pyle, 'Do you think there's anything in the rumour about Phat Diem?'

'I don't know. Is it important? I'd like to go and have a look,' he said, 'if it's important.'

'Important to the Economic Mission?'

'Oh, well,' he said, 'you can't draw hard lines. Medicine's a kind of weapon, isn't it? These Catholics, they'd be pretty strong against the Communists, wouldn't they?'

'They trade with the Communists. The Bishop gets his cows and the bamboo for his building from the Communists. I wouldn't say they were exactly York Harding's Third Force,' I teased him.

'Break it up,' Granger was shouting. 'Can't waste the whole night here. I'm off to the House of Five Hundred Girls.'

'If you and Miss Phuong would have dinner with me . . .' Pyle said.

'You can eat at the Chalet,' Granger interrupted him, 'while I'm knocking the girls next door. Come on, Joe. Anyway you're a man.'

I think it was then, wondering what a man is, that I felt my first affection for Pyle. He sat a little turned away from Granger, twisting his beer mug, with an expression of determined remoteness. He said to Phuong, 'I guess you get tired of all this shop—about your country, I mean?'

'*Comment?*'

'What are you going to do with Mick?' the Economic Attaché asked.

'Leave him here,' Granger said.

'You can't do that. You don't even know his name.'

'We could bring him along and let the girls look after him.'

The Economic Attaché gave a loud communal laugh. He looked like a face on television. He said, 'You young people can do what you want, but I'm too old for games. I'll take him home with me. Did you say he was French?'

'He spoke French.'

'If you can get him into my car . . .'

After he had driven away, Pyle took a trishaw with Granger, and Phuong and I followed along the road to Cholon. Granger had made an attempt to get into the trishaw with Phuong, but Pyle diverted him. As they pedalled us down the long suburban road to the Chinese town a line of French armoured cars went by, each with its jutting gun and silent officer motionless like a figurehead under the stars and the black, smooth, concave sky–trouble again probably with a private army, the Binh Xuyen, who ran the Grand Monde and the gambling halls of Cholon. This was a land of rebellious barons. It was like Europe in the Middle Ages. But what were the Americans doing here? Columbus had not yet discovered their country. I said to Phuong, 'I like that fellow, Pyle.'

'He's quiet,' she said, and the adjective which she was the first to use stuck like a schoolboy name, till I heard even Vigot use it, sitting there with his green eye-shade, telling me of Pyle's death.

I stopped our trishaw outside the Chalet and said to Phuong, 'Go in and find a table. I had better look after Pyle.' That was my first instinct–to protect him. It never occurred to me that there was greater need to protect myself. Innocence always calls mutely for protection when we would be so much wiser to guard ourselves against it: innocence is like a dumb leper who has lost his bell, wandering the world, meaning no harm.

When I reached the House of the Five Hundred Girls, Pyle and Granger had gone inside. I asked at the military police post just inside the doorway, '*Deux Américains?*'

He was a young Foreign Legion corporal. He stopped cleaning his revolver and jutted his thumb towards the doorway beyond, making a joke in German. I couldn't understand it.

It was the hour of rest in the immense courtyard which lay open to the sky. Hundreds of girls lay on the grass or sat on their heels talking to their companions. The curtains were undrawn in the little cubicles around the square–one tired girl lay alone on a bed with her ankles crossed. There was trouble in Cholon and the troops were confined to quarters and there was no work to be done: the Sunday of the body. Only a knot of fighting, scrabbling, shouting girls showed me where custom was still alive. I remembered the old Saigon story of the distinguished visitor who had lost his trousers fighting his way back to the safety of the police post. There was no protection here for the civilian. If he chose to poach on military territory, he must look after himself and find his own way out.

I had learnt a technique–to divide and conquer. I chose one in the crowd that gathered round me and edged her slowly towards the spot where Pyle and Granger struggled.

'*Je suis un vieux,*' I said. '*Trop fatigué.*' She giggled and pressed. '*Mon ami,*' I said, '*il est très riche, très vigoureux.*'

'*Tu es sale,*' she said.

I caught sight of Granger flushed and triumphant; it was as though he took this demonstration as a tribute to his manhood. One girl had her arm through Pyle's and was trying to tug him gently out of the ring. I pushed my girl in among them and called to him, 'Pyle, over here.'

He looked at me over their heads and said, 'It's terrible. Terrible.' It may have been a trick of the lamplight, but his face looked haggard. It occurred to me that he was quite possibly a virgin.

'Come along, Pyle,' I said. 'Leave them to Granger.' I saw his hand move towards his hip pocket. I really believe he intended to empty his pockets of piastres and greenbacks. 'Don't be a fool, Pyle,' I called sharply. 'You'll have them fighting.' My girl was turning back to me and I gave her another push into the inner ring round Granger. '*Non, non,*' I said, '*je suis un Anglais, pauvre, très pauvre.*' Then I got hold of Pyle's sleeve and dragged him out, with the girl hanging on to his other arm like a hooked fish. Two or three girls tried to intercept us before we got to the gateway where the corporal stood watching, but they were half-hearted.

'What'll I do with this one?' Pyle said.

'She won't be any trouble,' and at that moment she let go his arm and dived back into the scrimmage round Granger.

'Will he be all right?' Pyle asked anxiously.

'He's got what he wanted—a bit of tail.'

The night outside seemed very quiet with only another squadron of armoured cars driving by like people with a purpose. He said, 'It's terrible. I wouldn't have believed . . .' He said with sad awe, 'They were so pretty.' He was not envying Granger, he was complaining that anything good—should be marred or ill-treated. Pyle could see pain when it was in front of his eyes. (I don't write that as a sneer; after all there are many of us who can't.)

I said, 'Come back to the Chalet. Phuong's waiting.'

'I'm sorry,' he said. 'I quite forgot. You shouldn't have left her.'

'*She* wasn't in danger.'

'I just thought I'd see Granger safely . . .' He dropped again into his thoughts, but as we entered the Chalet he said with obscure distress, 'I'd forgotten how many men there are . . .'

2

Phuong had kept us a table at the edge of the dance-floor and the orchestra was playing some tune which had been popular in Paris five years ago. Two Vietnamese couples were dancing, small, neat, aloof, with an air of civilisation we couldn't match. (I recognised one, an accountant from the Banque de l'Indo-Chine and his wife.) They never, one felt, dressed carelessly, said the wrong word, were a prey to untidy passion. If the war seemed medieval, they were like the eighteenth-century future. One would have expected Mr Pham-Van-Tu to write Augustans in his spare time, but I happened to know he was a student of Wordsworth and wrote nature poems. His holidays he spent at Dalat, the nearest he could get to the atmosphere of the English lakes. He bowed slightly as he came round. I wondered how Granger had fared fifty yards up the road.

Pyle was apologising to Phuong in bad French for having kept her waiting. '*C'est impardonable,*' he said.

'Where have you been?' she asked him.

He said, 'I was seeing Granger home.'

'Home?' I said and laughed, and Pyle looked at me as though I were another Granger. Suddenly I saw myself as he saw me, a man of middle age, with eyes a little bloodshot, beginning to put on weight, ungraceful in love, less noisy than Granger perhaps but more cynical, less innocent, and I saw Phuong for a moment as I had seen her first, dancing past my table at the Grand Monde in a white ball-dress, eighteen years old, watched by an elder sister who had been determined on a good European marriage. An American had bought a ticket and asked her for a dance: he was a little drunk—not harmfully, and I suppose he was new to the country and thought the hostesses of the Grand Monde were whores. He held her much too close as they went round the floor the first time, and then suddenly there she was, going back to sit with her sister, and he was left, stranded and lost among the dancers, not knowing what had happened or why. And the girl whose name I didn't know sat quietly there, occasionally sipping her orange juice, owning herself completely.

'*Peut-on avoir l'honneur?*' Pyle was saying in his terrible accent, and a moment later I saw them dancing in silence at the other end of the room, Pyle holding her so far away from him that you expected him at any moment to sever contact. He was a very bad dancer, and she had been the best dancer I had ever known in her days at the Grand Monde.

It had been a long and frustrating courtship. If I could have offered marriage and a settlement everything would have been easy, and the elder sister would have slipped quietly and tactfully away whenever we were together. But three months passed before I saw her so much as momentarily alone, on a balcony at the Majestic, while her sister in the next room kept on asking when we proposed to come in. A cargo boat from France was being unloaded in Saigon River by the light of flares, the trishaw bells rang like telephones, and I might have been a young and inexperienced fool for all I found to say. I went back hopelessly to my bed in the rue Catinat and never dreamed that four months later she would be lying beside me, a little out of breath, laughing as though with surprise because nothing had been quite what she expected.

'Monsieur Fowlair.' I had been watching them dance and hadn't seen her sister signalling to me from another table. Now she came over and I reluctantly asked her to sit down. We had never been friends since the night she was taken ill in the Grand Monde and I had seen Phuong home.

'I haven't seen you for a whole year,' she said.

'I am away so often at Hanoi.'

'Who is your friend?' she asked.

'A man called Pyle.'

'What does he do?'

'He belongs to the American Economic Mission. You know the kind of thing–electrical sewing machines for starving seamstresses.'

'Are there any?'

'I don't know.'

'But they don't use sewing machines. There wouldn't be any electricity where they live.' She was a very literal woman.

'You'll have to ask Pyle,' I said.

'Is he married?'

I looked at the dance floor. 'I should say that's as near as he ever got to a woman.'

'He dances very badly,' she said.

'Yes.'

'But he looks a nice reliable man.'

'Yes.'

'Can I sit with you for a little? My friends are very dull.'

The music stopped and Pyle bowed stiffly to Phuong, then led her back and drew out her chair. I could tell that his formality pleased her. I thought how much she missed in her relation to me.

'This is Phuong's sister,' I said to Pyle. 'Miss Hei.'

'I'm very glad to meet you,' he said and blushed.

'You come from New York?' she asked.

'No. From Boston.'

'That is in the United States too?'

'Oh yes. Yes.'

'Is your father a business man?'

'Not really. He's a professor.'

'A teacher?' she asked with a faint note of disappointment.

'Well, he's a kind of authority, you know. People consult him.'

'About health? Is he a doctor?'

'Not that sort of doctor. He's a doctor of engineering though. He understands all about underwater erosion. You know what that is?'

'No.'

Pyle said with a dim attempt at humour, 'Well, I'll leave it to Dad to tell you about that.'

'He is here?'

'Oh no.'

'But he is coming?'

'No. That was just a joke,' Pyle said apologetically.

'Have you got another sister?' I asked Miss Hei.

'No. Why?'

'It sounds as though you were examining Mr Pyle's marriageability.'

'I have only one sister,' Miss Hei said, and she clamped her hand heavily down on Phuong's knee, like a chairman with his gavel marking a point of order.

'She's a very pretty sister,' Pyle said.

'She is the most beautiful girl in Saigon,' Miss Hei said, as though she were correcting him.

'I can believe it.'

I said, 'It's time we ordered dinner. Even the most beautiful girl in Saigon must eat.'

'I am not hungry,' Phuong said.

'She is delicate,' Miss Hei went firmly on. There was a note of menace in her voice. 'She needs care. She deserves care. She is very, very loyal.'

'My friend is a lucky man,' Pyle said gravely.

'She loves children,' Miss Hei said.

I laughed and then caught Pyle's eye; he was looking at me with shocked surprise, and suddenly it occurred to me that he was genuinely interested in what Miss Hei had to say. While I was ordering dinner (though Phuong had told me she was not hungry, I knew she could manage a good steak tartare with two raw eggs and etceteras), I listened to him seriously discussing the question of children. 'I've always thought I'd like a lot of children,' he said. 'A big family's a wonderful interest. It makes for the stability of marriage. And it's good for the children too. I was an only child. It's a great disadvantage being an only child.' I had never heard him talk so much before.

'How old is your father?' Miss Hei asked with gluttony.

'Sixty-nine.'

'Old people love grandchildren. It is very sad that my sister has no parents to rejoice in her children. When the day comes,' she added with a baleful look at me.

'Nor you either,' Pyle said, rather unnecessarily I thought.

'Our father was of a very good family. He was a mandarin in Hué.'

I said, 'I've ordered dinner for all of you.'

'Not for me,' Miss Hei said. 'I must be going to my friends. I would like to meet Mr Pyle again. Perhaps you could manage that.'

'When I get back from the north,' I said.

'Are you going to the north?'

'I think it's time I had a look at the war.'

'But the Press are all back,' Pyle said.

'That's the best time for me. I don't have to meet Granger.'

'Then you must come and have dinner with me and my sister when Monsieur Fowlair is gone.' She added with morose courtesy, 'To cheer her up.'

After she had gone Pyle said, 'What a very nice cultivated woman. And she spoke English so well.'

'Tell him my sister was in business once in Singapore,' Phuong said proudly.

'Really? What kind of business?'

I translated for her. 'Import, export. She can do shorthand.'

'I wish we had more like her in the Economic Mission.'

'I will speak to her,' Phuong said. 'She would like to work for the Americans.'

After dinner they danced again. I am a bad dancer too and I hadn't the unselfconsciousness of Pyle—or had I possessed it, I wondered, in the days when I was first in love with Phuong? There must have been many occasions at the Grand Monde before the memorable night of Miss Hei's illness when I had danced with Phuong just for an opportunity to speak to her. Pyle was taking no such opportunity as they came round the floor again; he had relaxed a little, that was all, and was holding her less at arm's length, but they were both silent. Suddenly watching her feet, so light and precise and mistress of his shuffle, I was in love again. I could hardly believe that in an hour, two hours, she would be coming back to me to that dingy room with the communal closet and the old women squatting on the landing.

I wished I had never heard the rumour about Phat Diem, or that the rumour had dealt with any other town than the one place in the north where my friendship with a French naval officer would allow me to slip in, uncensored, uncontrolled. A newspaper scoop? Not in those days when all the world wanted to read about was Korea. A chance of death? Why should I want to die when Phuong slept beside me every night? But I knew the answer to that question. From childhood I had never believed in permanence, and yet I had longed for it. Always I was afraid of losing happiness. This month, next year, Phuong would leave me. If not next year, in three years. Death was the only absolute value in my world. Lose life and one would lose nothing again for ever. I envied those who could believe in a God and I distrusted them. I felt they were keeping their courage up with a fable of the changeless and the permanent. Death was far more certain than God, and with death there would be no longer the daily possibility of love dying. The nightmare of a future of boredom and indifference would lift. I could never have been a pacifist. To kill a man was surely to grant him an immeasurable benefit. Oh yes, people always, everywhere, loved their enemies. It was their friends they preserved for pain and vacuity.

'Forgive me for taking Miss Phuong from you,' Pyle's voice said.

'Oh, I'm no dancer, but I like watching her dance.' One always spoke of her like that in the third person as though she were not there. Sometimes she seemed invisible like peace.

The first cabaret of the evening began: a singer, a juggler, a comedian—he was very obscene, but when I looked at Pyle he obviously couldn't follow the argot. He smiled when Phuong smiled and laughed uneasily when I laughed. 'I wonder where Granger is now,' I said, and Pyle looked at me reproachfully.

Then came the turn of the evening: a troupe of female impersonators. I had seen many of them during the day in the rue Catinat walking up and down, in old slacks and sweaters, a bit blue about the chin, swaying their hips. Now in low-cut evening dresses, with false jewellery and false breasts and husky voices, they appeared at least as desirable as most of the European women in Saigon. A group of young Air Force officers whistled to them and they smiled glamorously back. I was astonished by the sudden violence of Pyle's protest. 'Fowler,' he said, 'let's go. We've had enough, haven't we? This isn't a bit suitable for *her*.'

CHAPTER 4

I

From the bell tower of the Cathedral the battle was only picturesque, fixed like a panorama of the Boer War in an old *Illustrated London News*. An aeroplane was parachuting supplies to an isolated post in the *calcaire*, those strange weather-eroded mountains on the Annam border that look like piles of pumice, and because it always returned to the same place for its glide, it might never have moved, and the parachute was always there in the same spot, half-way to earth. From the plain the mortar-bursts rose unchangingly, the smoke as solid as stone, and in the market the flames burnt palely in the sunlight. The tiny figures of the parachutists moved in single file along the canals, but at this height they appeared stationary. Even the priest who sat in a corner of the tower never changed his position as he read in his breviary. The war was very tidy and clean at that distance.

I had come in before dawn in a landing-craft from Nam Dinh. We couldn't land at the naval station because it was cut off by the enemy who completely surrounded the town at a range of six hundred yards, so the boat ran in beside the flaming market. We were an easy target in the light of the flames, but for some reason no one fired. Everything was quiet, except for the flop and crackle of the burning stalls. I could hear a Senegalese sentry on the river's edge shift his stance.

I had known Phat Diem well in the days before the attack—the one long narrow street of wooden stalls, cut up every hundred yards by a canal, a church and a bridge. At night it had been lit only by candles or small oil lamps (there was no electricity in Phat Diem except in the French officers' quarters), and day or night the street was packed and noisy. In its strange medieval way, under the shadow and protection of the Prince Bishop, it had been the most living town in all the country, and now when I landed and walked up to the officers' quarters it was the most dead. Rubble and broken glass and the smell of burnt paint and plaster, the long street empty as far as the sight could reach, it reminded me of a London thoroughfare in the early morning after an all-clear: one expected to see a placard, 'Unexploded Bomb'.

The front wall of the officers' house had been blown out, and the houses across the street were in ruins. Coming down the river from Nam Dinh I had learnt from Lieutenant Peraud what had happened. He was a serious young man, a Freemason, and to him it was like a judgement on the superstitions of his fellows. The Bishop of Phat Diem had once visited Europe and acquired there a devotion to Our Lady of Fatima—that vision of the Virgin which appeared, so Roman Catholics believe, to a group of children in Portugal. When he came home, he built a grotto in her honour in the Cathedral precincts, and he celebrated her feast-day every year with a procession.

Relations with the colonel in charge of the French and Vietnamese troops had always been strained since the day when the authorities had disbanded the Bishop's private army. This year the colonel—who had some sympathy with the Bishop, for to each of them his country was more important than Catholicism—made a gesture of amity and walked with his senior officers in the front of the procession. Never had a greater crowd gathered in Phat Diem to do honour to Our Lady of Fatima. Even many of the Buddhists—who formed about half the population—could not bear to miss the fun, and those who had belief in neither God nor Buddha believed that somehow all these banners and incense-burners and the golden monstrance would keep war from their homes. All that was left of the Bishop's army—his brass band—led the procession, and the French officers, pious by order of the colonel, followed like choirboys through the gateway into the Cathedral precincts, past the white statue of the Sacred Heart that stood on an island in the little lake before the Cathedral, under the bell tower with spreading oriental wings and into the carved wooden Cathedral with its gigantic pillars formed out of single trees and the scarlet lacquer work of the altar, more Buddhist than Christian. From all the villages between the canals, from that Low Country landscape where young green rice-shoots and golden harvests take the place of tulips and churches of windmills, the people poured in.

Nobody noticed the Vietminh agents who had joined the procession too, and that night as the main Communist battalion moved through the passes in the *calcaire*, into the Tonkin plain, watched helplessly by the French outpost in the mountains above, the advance agents struck in Phat Diem.

Now after four days, with the help of parachutists, the enemy had been pushed back half a mile around the town. This was a defeat: no journalists were allowed, no cables could be sent, for the papers must carry only victories. The authorities would have stopped me in Hanoi if they had known of my purpose, but the further you get from headquarters, the looser becomes the control until, when you come within range of the enemy's fire, you are a welcome guest—what has been a menace for the *Etat Major* in Hanoi, a worry for the full colonel in Nam Dinh, to the lieutenant in the field is a joke, a distraction, a mark of interest from the outer world, so that for a few blessed hours he can dramatise himself a little and see in a false heroic light even his own wounded and dead.

The priest shut his breviary and said, 'Well, that's finished.' He was a European, but not a Frenchman, for the Bishop would not have tolerated a French priest in his diocese. He said apologetically, 'I have to come up here, you understand, for a bit of quiet from all those poor people.' The sound of the mortar-fire seemed to be closing in, or perhaps it was the enemy at last replying. The strange difficulty was to find them: there were a dozen narrow fronts, and between the canals, among the farm buildings and the paddy fields, innumerable opportunities for ambush.

Immediately below us stood, sat and lay the whole population of Phat Diem. Catholics, Buddhists, pagans, they had all packed their most valued possessions—a cooking-stove, a lamp, a mirror, a wardrobe, some mats, a holy picture—and moved into the Cathedral precincts. Here in the north it would be bitterly cold when darkness came, and already the Cathedral was full: there was no more shelter; even on the stairs to the bell tower every step was occupied, and all the time more people crowded through the gates, carrying their babies and household goods. They believed, whatever their religion, that here they would be safe. While we watched, a young man with a rifle in Vietnamese uniform pushed his way through: he was stopped by a priest, who took his rifle from him. The father at my side said in explanation, 'We are neutral here. This is God's territory.' I thought, "It's a strange poor population God has in his kingdom, frightened, cold, starving–'I don't know how we are going to feed these people,' the priest told me–you'd think a great King would do better than that." But then I thought, "It's always the same wherever one goes–it's not the most powerful rulers who have the happiest populations."

Little shops had already been set up below. I said, 'It's like an enormous fair, isn't it, but without one smiling face.'

The priest said, 'They were terribly cold last night. We have to keep the monastery gates shut or they would swamp us.'

'You all keep warm in here?' I asked.

'Not very warm. And we would not have room for a tenth of them.' He went on, 'I know what you are thinking. But it is essential for some of us to keep well. We have the only hospital in Phat Diem, and our only nurses are these nuns.'

'And your surgeon?'

'I do what I can.' I saw then that his soutane was speckled with blood. He said, 'Did you come up here to find me?'

'No. I wanted to get my bearings.'

'I asked you because I had a man up here last night. He wanted to go to confession. He had got a little frightened, you see, with what he had seen along the canal. One couldn't blame him.'

'It's bad along there?'

'The parachutists caught them in a cross-fire. Poor souls. I thought perhaps you were feeling the same.'

'I'm not a Roman Catholic. I don't think you could even call me a Christian.'

'It's strange what fear does to a man.'

'It would never do that to me. If I believed in any God at all, I should still hate the idea of confession. Kneeling in one of your boxes. Exposing myself to another man. You must excuse me, Father, but to me it seems morbid–unmanly even.'

'Oh,' he said lightly, 'I expect you are a good man. I don't suppose you've ever had much to regret.'

I looked along the churches, where they ran down evenly spaced between the canals, towards the sea. A light flashed from the second tower. I said, 'You haven't kept all your churches neutral.'

'It isn't possible,' he said. 'The French have agreed to leave the Cathedral precincts alone. We can't expect more. That's a Foreign Legion post you are looking at.'

'I'll be going along. Goodbye, Father.'

'Goodbye and good luck. Be careful of snipers.'

I had to push my way through the crowd to get out, past the lake and the white statue with its sugary outspread arms, into the long street. I could see for nearly three quarters of a mile each way, and there were only two living beings in all that length besides myself—two soldiers with camouflaged helmets going slowly away up the edge of the street, their sten guns at the ready. I say the living because one body lay in a doorway with its head in the road. The buzz of flies collecting there and the squelch of the soldiers' boots growing fainter and fainter were the only sounds. I walked quickly past the body, turning my head the other way. A few minutes later when I looked back I was quite alone with my shadow and there were no sounds except the sounds I made. I felt as though I were a mark on a firing range. It occurred to me that if something happened to me in this street it might be many hours before I was picked up: time for the flies to collect.

When I had crossed two canals, I took a turning that led to a church. A dozen men sat on the ground in the camouflage of parachutists, while two officers examined a map. Nobody paid me any attention when I joined them. One man, who wore the long antennae of a walkie-talkie, said, 'We can move now,' and everybody stood up.

I asked them in my bad French whether I could accompany them. An advantage of this war was that a European face proved in itself a passport on the field: a European could not be suspected of being an enemy agent. 'Who are you?' the lieutenant asked.

'I am writing about the war,' I said.

'American?'

'No, English.'

He said, 'It is a very small affair, but if you wish to come with us . . .' He began to take off his steel helmet. 'No, no,' I said, 'that is for combatants.'

'As you wish.'

We went out behind the church in single file, the lieutenant leading, and halted for a moment on a canal-bank for the soldier with the walkie-talkie to get contact with the patrols on either flank. The mortar shells tore over us and burst out of sight. We had picked up more men behind the church and were now about thirty strong. The lieutenant explained to me in a low voice, stabbing a finger at his map, 'Three hundred have been reported in this village here. Perhaps massing for tonight. We don't know. No one has found them yet.'

'How far?'

'Three hundred yards.'

Words came over the wireless and we went on in silence, to the right the straight canal, to the left low scrub and fields and scrub again. 'All clear,' the lieutenant whispered with a reassuring wave as we started. Forty yards on, another canal, with what was left of a bridge, a single plank without rails, ran across our front. The lieutenant motioned to us to deploy and we squatted down facing the unknown territory ahead, thirty feet off, across the plank. The men looked at the water and then, as though by a word of command, all together, they looked away. For a moment I didn't see what they had seen, but when I saw, my mind went back, I don't know why, to the Chalet and the female impersonators and the young soldiers whistling and Pyle saying, 'This isn't a bit suitable.'

The canal was full of bodies: I am reminded now of an Irish stew containing too much meat. The bodies overlapped: one head, seal-grey, and anonymous as a convict with a shaven scalp, stuck up out of the water like a buoy. There was no blood: I suppose it had flowed away a long time ago. I have no idea how many there were: they must have been caught in a cross-fire, trying to get back, and I suppose every man of us along the bank was thinking, "Two can play at that game." I too took my eyes away; we didn't want to be reminded of how little we counted, how quickly, simply and anonymously death came. Even though my reason wanted the state of death, I was afraid like a virgin of the act. I would have liked death to come with due warning, so that I could prepare myself. For what? I didn't know, nor how, except by taking a look around at the little I would be leaving.

The lieutenant sat beside the man with the walkie-talkie and stared at the ground between his feet. The instrument began to crackle instructions and with a sigh as though he had been roused from sleep he got up. There was an odd comradeliness about all their movements, as though they were equals engaged on a task they had performed together times out of mind. Nobody waited to be told what to do. Two men made for the plank and tried to cross it, but they were unbalanced by the weight of their arms and had to sit astride and work their way across a few inches at a time. Another man had found a punt hidden in some bushes down the canal and he worked it to where the lieutenant stood. Six of us got in and be began to pole it towards the other bank, but we ran on a shoal of bodies and stuck. He pushed away with his pole, sinking it into this human clay, and one body was released and floated up all its length beside the boat like a bather lying in the sun. Then we were free again, and once on the other side we scrambled out, with no backward look. No shots had been fired: we were alive: death had withdrawn perhaps as far as the next canal. I heard somebody just behind me say with great seriousness, '*Gott sei dank.*' Except for the lieutenant they were most of them Germans.

Beyond was a group of farm-buildings; the lieutenant went in first, hugging the wall, and we followed at six-foot intervals in single file. Then the men, again without an order, scattered through the farm. Life had deserted it—not so much as a hen had been left behind, though hanging on the walls of what had been the living room were two hideous oleographs of the Sacred Heart and the Mother and Child which gave the whole ramshackle group of buildings a European air. One knew what these people believed even if one didn't share their belief: they were human beings, not just grey drained cadavers.

So much of the war is sitting around and doing nothing, waiting for somebody else. With no guarantee of the amount of time you have left it doesn't seem worth starting even a train of thought. Doing what they had done so often before, the sentries moved out. Anything that stirred ahead of us now was enemy. The lieutenant marked his map and reported our position over the radio. A noonday hush fell: even the mortars were quiet and the air was empty of planes. One man doodled with a twig in the dirt of the farmyard. After a while it was as if we had been forgotten by war. I hoped that Phuong had sent my suits to the cleaners. A cold wind ruffled the straw of the yard, and a man went modestly behind a barn to relieve himself. I tried to remember whether I had paid the British Consul in Hanoi for the bottle of whisky he had allowed me.

Two shots were fired to our front, and I thought, "This is it. Now it comes." It was all the warning I wanted. I awaited, with a sense of exhilaration, the permanent thing.

But nothing happened. Once again I had 'over-prepared the event'. Only long minutes afterwards one of the sentries entered and reported something to the lieutenant. I caught the phrase, '*Deux civils.*'

The lieutenant said to me, 'We will go and see,' and following the sentry we picked our way along a muddy overgrown path between two fields. Twenty yards beyond the farm buildings, in a narrow ditch, we came on what we sought: a woman and a small boy. They were very clearly dead: a small neat clot of blood on the woman's forehead, and the child might have been sleeping. He was about six years old and he lay like an embryo in the womb with his little bony knees drawn up. '*Mal chance*,' the lieutenant said. He bent down and turned the child over. He was wearing a holy medal round his neck, and I said to myself, 'The juju doesn't work.' There was a gnawed piece of loaf under his body. I thought, "I hate war."

The lieutenant said, 'Have you seen enough?' speaking savagely, almost as though I had been responsible for these deaths. Perhaps to the soldier the civilian is the man who employs him to kill, who includes the guilt of murder in the pay-envelope and escapes responsibility. We walked back to the farm and sat down again in silence on the straw, out of the wind, which like an animal seemed to know that dark was coming. The man who had doodled was relieving himself, and the man who had relieved himself was doodling. I thought how in those moments of quiet, after the sentries had been posted, they must have believed it safe to move from the ditch. I wondered whether they had lain there long–the bread had been very dry. This farm was probably their home.

The radio was working again. The lieutenant said wearily, 'They are going to bomb the village. Patrols are called in for the night.' We rose and began our journey back, punting again around the shoal of bodies, filing past the church. We hadn't gone very far, and yet it seemed a long enough journey to have made with the killing of those two as the only result. The planes had gone up, and behind us the bombing began.

Dark had fallen by the time I reached the officers' quarters, where I was spending the night. The temperature was only a degree above zero, and the sole warmth anywhere was in the blazing market. With one wall destroyed by a bazooka and the doors buckled, canvas curtains couldn't shut out the draughts. The electric dynamo was not working, and we had to build barricades of boxes and books to keep the candles burning. I played *Quatre Cent Vingt-et-un* for Communist currency with a Captain Sorel: it wasn't possible to play for drinks as I was a guest of the mess. The luck went wearisomely back and forth. I opened my bottle of whisky to try to warm us a little, and the others gathered round. The colonel said, 'This is the first glass of whisky I have had since I left Paris.'

A lieutenant came in from his round of the sentries. 'Perhaps we shall have a quiet night,' he said.

'They will not attack before four,' the colonel said. 'Have you a gun?' he asked me.

'No.'

'I'll find you one. Better keep it on your pillow.' He added courteously, 'I am afraid you will find you mattress rather hard. And at three-thirty the mortar-fire will begin. We try to break up any concentrations.'

'How long do you suppose this will go on?'

'Who knows? We can't spare any more troops from Nam Dinh. This is just a diversion. If we can hold out with no more help than we got two days ago, it is, one may say, a victory.'

The wind was up again, prowling for an entry. The canvas curtain sagged (I was reminded of Polonius stabbed behind the arras) and the candle wavered. The shadows were theatrical. We might have been a company of barnstormers.

'Have your posts held?'

'As far as we know.' He said with an effect of great tiredness, 'This is nothing, you understand, an affair of no importance compared with what is happening a hundred kilometres away at Hoa Binh. That is a battle.'

'Another glass, Colonel?'

'Thank you, no. It is wonderful, your English whisky, but it is better to keep a little for the night in case of need. I think, if you will excuse me, I will get some sleep. One cannot sleep after the mortars start. Captain Sorel, you will see that Monsieur Fowlair has everything he needs, a candle, matches, a revolver.' He went into his room.

It was the signal for all of us. They had put a mattress on the floor for me in a small store-room and I was surrounded by wooden cases. I stayed awake only a very short time—the hardness of the floors was like rest. I wondered, but oddly without jealousy, whether Phuong was at the flat. The possession of a body tonight seemed a very small thing—perhaps that day I had seen too many bodies which belonged to no one, not even to themselves. We were all expendable. When I fell asleep I dreamed of Pyle. He was dancing all by himself on a stage, stiffly, with his arms held out to an invisible partner, and I sat and watched him from a seat like a music-stool with a gun in my hand in case anyone should interfere with his dance. A programme set up by the stage, like the numbers in an English music-hall, read, 'The Dance of Love. "A" certificate.' Somebody moved at the back of the theatre and I held my gun tighter. Then I woke.

My hand was on the gun they had lent me, and a man stood in the doorway with a candle in his hand. He wore a steel helmet which threw a shadow over his eyes, and it was only when he spoke that I knew he was Pyle. He said shyly, 'I'm awfully sorry to wake you up. They told me I could sleep in here.'

I was still not fully awake. 'Where did you get that helmet?' I asked.

'Oh, somebody lent it to me,' he said vaguely. He dragged in after him a military kitbag and began to pull out a wool-lined sleeping-bag.

'You are very well equipped,' I said, trying to recollect why either of us should be here.

'This is the standard travelling kit,' he said, 'of our medical aid teams. They lent me one in Hanoi.' He took out a thermos and a small spirit stove, a hair-brush, a shaving-set and a tin of rations. I looked at my watch. It was nearly three in the morning.

2

Pyle continued to unpack. He made a little ledge of cases, on which he put his shaving-mirror and tackle. I said, 'I doubt if you'll get any water.'

'Oh,' he said, 'I've enough in the thermos for the morning.' He sat down on his sleeping-bag and began to pull off his boots.

'How on earth did you get here?' I asked.

'They let me through as far as Nam Dinh to see our trachoma team, and then I hired a boat.'

'A boat?'

'Oh, some kind of a punt—I don't know the name for it. As a matter of fact I had to buy it. It didn't cost much.'

'And you came down the river by yourself?'

'It wasn't really difficult, you know. The current was with me.'

'You are crazy.'

'Oh no. The only real danger was running aground.'

'Or being shot up by a naval patrol, or a French plane. Or having your throat cut by the Vietminh.'

He laughed shyly. 'Well, I'm here anyway,' he said.

'Why?'

'Oh, there are two reasons. But I don't want to keep you awake.'

'I'm not sleepy. The guns will be starting soon.'

'Do you mind if I move the candle? It's a little too bright here.' He seemed nervous.

'What's the first reason?'

'Well, the other day you made me think this place was rather interesting. You remember when we were with Granger . . . and Phuong.'

'Yes?'

'I thought I ought to take a look at it. To tell you the truth, I was a little ashamed of Granger.'

'I see. As simple as all that.'

'Well, there wasn't any real difficulty, was there?' He began to play with his bootlaces, and there was a long silence. 'I'm not being quite honest,' he said at last.

'No?'

'I really came to see you.'

'You came here to see me?'

'Yes.'

'Why?'

He looked up from his bootlaces in an agony of embarrassment. 'I had to tell you—I've fallen in love with Phuong.'

I laughed. I couldn't help it. He was so unexpected and serious. I said, 'Couldn't you have waited till I got back? I shall be in Saigon next week.'

'You might have been killed,' he said. 'It wouldn't have been honourable.

And then I don't know if I could have stayed away from Phuong all that time.'

'You mean, you *have* stayed away?'

'Of course. You don't think I'll tell *her*—without you knowing?'

'People do,' I said. 'When did it happen?'

'I guess it was that night at the Chalet, dancing with her.'

'I didn't think you ever got close enough.'

He looked at me in a puzzled way. If his conduct seemed crazy to me, mine was obviously inexplicable to him. He said, 'You know, I think it was seeing all those girls in that house. They were so pretty. Why, she might have been one of them. I wanted to protect her.'

'I don't think she's in need of protection. Has Miss Hei invited you out?'

'Yes, but I haven't gone. I've kept away.' He said gloomily, 'It's been terrible. I feel such a heel, but you do believe me, don't you, that if you'd been married—why, I wouldn't ever come between a man and his wife.'

'You seem pretty sure you *can* come between,' I said. For the first time he had irritated me.

'Fowler,' he said, 'I don't know your Christian name . . . ?'

'Thomas. Why?'

'I can call you Tom, can't I? I feel in a way this has brought us together. Loving the same woman, I mean.'

'What's your next move?'

He sat up enthusiastically against the packing-cases. 'Everything seems different now that you know,' he said. 'I shall ask her to marry me, Tom.'

'I'd rather you called me Thomas.'

'She'll just have to choose between us, Thomas. That's fair enough.' But was it fair? I felt for the first time the premonitory chill of loneliness. It was all fantastic, and yet . . . He might be a poor lover, but I was the poor man. He had in his hand the infinite riches of respectability.

He began to undress and I thought, "He has youth too." How sad it was to envy Pyle.

I said, 'I can't marry her. I have a wife at home. She would never divorce me. She's High Church—if you know what that means.'

'I'm sorry, Thomas. By the way, my name's Alden, if you'd care . . .'

'I'd rather stick to Pyle,' I said. 'I think of you as Pyle.'

He got into his sleeping-bag and stretched his hand out for the candle. 'Whew,' he said, 'I'm glad that's over, Thomas. I've been feeling awfully bad about it.' It was only too evident that he no longer did.

When the candle was out, I could just see the outline of his crew-cut against the light of the flames outside. 'Good-night, Thomas. Sleep well,' and immediately at those words like a bad comedy cue the mortars opened up, whirring, shrieking, exploding.

'Good God,' Pyle said, 'is it an attack?'

'They are trying to stop an attack.'

'Well, I suppose, there'll be no sleep for us now?'

'No sleep.'

'Thomas, I want you to know what I think of the way you've taken all this—I think you've been swell, swell, there's no other word for it.'

'Thank you.'

'You've seen so much more of the world than I have. You know, in some ways Boston is a bit–cramping. Even if you aren't a Lowell or a Cabot. I wish you'd advise me, Thomas.'

'What about?'

'Phuong.'

'I wouldn't trust my advice if I were you. I'm biased. I want to keep her.'

'Oh, but I know you're straight, absolutely straight, and we both have her interests at heart.'

Suddenly I couldn't bear his boyishness any more. I said, 'I don't care that for her interests. You can have her interests. I only want her body. I want her in bed with me. I'd rather ruin her and sleep with her than, than . . . look after her damned interests.'

He said, 'Oh,' in a weak voice, in the dark.

I went on, 'If it's only her interests you care about, for God's sake leave Phuong alone. Like any other woman she'd rather have a good . . .' The crash of a mortar saved Boston ears from the Anglo-Saxon word.

But there was a quality of the implacable in Pyle. He had determined I was behaving well and I had to behave well. He said, 'I know what you are suffering, Thomas.'

'I'm not suffering.'

'Oh yes, you are. I know what I'd suffer if I had to give up Phuong.'

'But I haven't given her up.'

'I'm pretty physical too, Thomas, but I'd give up all hope of that if I could see Phuong happy.'

'She is happy.'

'She can't be–not in her situation. She needs children.'

'Do you really believe all that nonsense her sister . . .'

'A sister sometimes knows better . . .'

'She was just trying to sell the notion to you, Pyle, because she thinks you have more money. And, my God, she has sold it all right.'

'I've only got my salary.'

'Well, you've got a favourable rate of exchange anyway.'

'Don't be bitter, Thomas. These things happen. I wish it had happened to anybody else but you. Are those our mortars?'

'Yes, "our" mortars. You talk as though she was leaving me, Pyle.'

'Of course,' he said without conviction, 'she may choose to stay with you.'

'What would you do then?'

'I'd apply for a transfer.'

'Why don't you just go away, Pyle, without causing trouble?'

'It wouldn't be fair to her, Thomas,' he said quite seriously. I never knew a man who had better motives for all the trouble he caused. He added, 'I don't think you quite understand Phuong.'

And waking that morning months later with Phuong beside me, I thought, "And did you understand her either? Could you have anticipated this situation? Phuong so happily asleep beside me and you dead?" Time has its revenges, but revenges seem so often sour. Wouldn't we all do better not trying to understand, accepting the fact that no human being will ever understand another, not a wife a husband, a lover a mistress, nor a parent a child? Perhaps that's why men have invented God–a being capable of understanding. Perhaps if I wanted to be understood or to understand I would bamboozle myself into belief, but I am a reporter; God exists only for leader-writers.

'Are you sure there's anything much to understand?' I asked Pyle. 'Oh, for God's sake, let's have a whisky. It's too noisy to argue.'

'It's a little early,' Pyle said.

'It's damned late.'

I poured out two glasses and Pyle raised his and stared through the whisky at the light of the candle. His hand shook whenever a shell burst, and yet he had made that senseless trip from Nam Dinh.

Pyle said, 'It's a strange thing that neither of us can say "Good luck".' So we drank saying nothing.

CHAPTER 5

I had thought I would be only one week away from Saigon, but it was nearly three weeks before I returned. In the first place it proved more difficult to get out of the Phat Diem area than it had been to get in. The road was cut between Nam Dinh and Hanoi and aerial transport could not be spared for one reporter who shouldn't have been there anyway. Then when I reached Hanoi the correspondents had been flown up for briefing on the latest victory and the plane that took them back had no seat left for me. Pyle got away from Phat Diem the morning he arrived: he had fulfilled his mission—to speak to me about Phuong, and there was nothing to keep him. I left him asleep when the mortar-fire stopped at five-thirty and when I returned from a cup of coffee and some biscuits in the mess he wasn't there. I assumed that he had gone for a stroll—after punting all the way down the river from Nam Dinh a few snipers would not have worried him; he was as incapable of imagining pain or danger to himself as he was incapable of conceiving the pain he might cause others. On one occasion—but that was months later—I lost control and thrust his foot into it, into the pain I mean, and I remember how he turned away and looked at his stained shoe in perplexity and said, 'I must get a shine before I see the Minister.' I knew then he was already forming his phrases in the style he had learnt from York Harding. Yet he was sincere in his way: it was coincidence that the sacrifices were all paid by others, until that final night under the bridge to Dakow.

It was only when I returned to Saigon that I learnt how Pyle, while I drank my coffee, had persuaded a young naval officer to take him on a landing-craft which after a routine patrol dropped him surreptitiously at Nam Dinh. Luck was with him and he got back to Hanoi with his trachoma team twenty-four hours before the road was officially regarded as cut. When I reached Hanoi he had already left for the south, leaving me a note with the barman at the Press Camp.

'Dear Thomas,' he wrote, 'I can't begin to tell you how swell you were the other night. I can tell you my heart was in my mouth when I walked into that room to find you.' (Where had it been on the long boat-ride down the river?) 'There are not many men who would have taken the whole thing so calmly. You were great, and I don't feel half as mean as I did, now that I've told you.' (Was he the only one that mattered? I wondered angrily, and yet I knew that he didn't intend it that way. To him the whole affair would be happier as soon as he didn't feel mean–I would be happier, Phuong would be happier, the whole world would be happier, even the Economic Attaché and the Minister. Spring had come to Indo-China now that Pyle was mean no longer.) 'I waited for you here for twenty-four hours, but I shan't get back to Saigon for a week if I don't leave today, and my real work is in the south. I've told the boys who are running the trachoma teams to look you up–you'll like them. They are great boys and doing a man-size job. Don't worry in any way that I'm returning to Saigon ahead of you. I promise you I won't see Phuong until you return. I don't want you to feel later that I've been unfair in any way. Cordially yours, Alden.'

Again this calm assumption that 'later' it would be I who would lose Phuong. Is confidence based on a rate of exchange? We used to speak of sterling qualities. Have we got to talk now about a dollar love? A dollar love, of course, would include marriage and Junior and Mother's Day, even though later it might include Reno or the Virgin Islands or wherever they go nowadays for their divorces. A dollar love had good intentions, a clear conscience, and to Hell with everybody. But my love had no intentions: it knew the future. All one could do was try to make the future less hard, to break the future gently when it came, and even opium had its value there. But I never foresaw that the first future I would have to break to Phuong would be the death of Pyle.

I went–for I had nothing better to do–to the Press Conference. Granger, of course, was there. A young and too beautiful French colonel presided. He spoke in French and a junior officer translated. The French correspondents sat together like a rival football-team. I found it hard to keep my mind on what the colonel was saying: all the time it wandered back to Phuong and the one thought–suppose Pyle is right and I lose her: where does one go from here?

The interpreter said, 'The colonel tells you that the enemy has suffered a sharp defeat and severe losses–the equivalent of one complete battalion. The last detachments are now making their way back across the Red River on improvised rafts. They are shelled all the time by the Air Force.' The colonel ran his hand through his elegant yellow hair and, flourishing his pointer, danced his way down the long maps on the wall. An American correspondent asked, 'What are the French losses?'

The colonel knew perfectly well the meaning of the question–it was usually put at this stage of the conference, but he paused, pointer raised with a kind smile like a popular schoolmaster, until it was interpreted. Then he answered with patient ambiguity.

'The colonel says our losses have not been heavy. The exact number is not yet known.'

This was always the signal for trouble. You would have thought that sooner or later the colonel would have found a formula for dealing with his refractory class, or that the headmaster would have appointed a member of his staff more efficient at keeping order.

'Is the colonel seriously telling us,' Granger said, 'that he's had time to count the enemy dead and not his own?'

Patiently the colonel wove his web of evasion, which he knew perfectly well would be destroyed again by another question. The French correspondents sat gloomily silent. If the American correspondents stung the colonel into an admission they would be quick to seize it, but they would not join in baiting their countryman.

'The colonel says the enemy forces are being over-run. It is possible to count the dead behind the firing-line, but while the battle is still in progress you cannot expect figures from the advancing French units.'

'It's not what *we* expect,' Granger said, 'it's what the *Etat Major* knows or not. Are you seriously telling us that platoons do not report their casualties as they happen by walkie-talkie?'

The colonel's temper was beginning to fray. If only, I thought, he had called our bluff from the start and told us firmly that he knew the figures but wouldn't say. After all it was their war, not ours. We had no God-given right to information. We didn't have to fight Left-Wing deputies in Paris as well as the troops of Ho Chi Minh between the Red and the Black Rivers. We were not dying.

The colonel suddenly snapped out the information that French casualties had been in a proportion of one to three, then turned his back on us, to stare furiously at his map. These were his men who were dead, his fellow officers, belonging to the same class at St Cyr—not numerals as they were to Granger. Granger said, 'Now we are getting somewhere,' and stared round with oafish triumph at his fellows; the French with heads bent made their sombre notes.

'That's more than can be said in Korea,' I said with deliberate misunderstanding, but I had only given Granger a new line.

'Ask the colonel,' he said, 'what the French are going to do next? He says the enemy's on the run across the Black River . . .'

'Red River,' the interpreter corrected him.

'I don't care what the colour of the river is. What we want to know is what the French are going to do now.'

'The enemy are in flight.'

'What happens when they get to the other side? What are you going to do then? Are you just going to sit down on the other bank and say that's over?' The French officers listened with gloomy patience to Granger's bullying voice. Even humility is required today of the soldier. 'Are you going to drop them Christmas cards?'

The captain interpreted with care, even to the phrase, '*cartes de Noël*'. The colonel gave us a wintry smile. 'Not Christmas cards,' he said.

I think the colonel's youth and beauty particularly irritated Granger. The colonel wasn't—at least not by Granger's interpretation—a man's man. He said, 'You aren't dropping much else.'

The colonel spoke suddenly in English, good English. He said, 'If the supplies promised by the Americans had arrived, we should have more to drop.' He was really in spite of his elegance a simple man. He believed that a newspaper correspondent cared for his country's honour more than for news. Granger said sharply (he was efficient: he kept dates well in his head),

'You mean that none of the supplies promised for the beginning of September have arrived?'

'No.'

Granger had got his news: he began to write.

'I am sorry,' the colonel said, 'that is not for printing: that is for background.'

'But, colonel,' Granger protested, 'that's news. We can help you there.'

'No, it is a matter for the diplomats.'

'What harm can it do?'

The French correspondents were at a loss: they could speak very little English. The colonel had broken the rules. They muttered angrily together.

'I am no judge,' the colonel said. 'Perhaps the American newspapers would say, "Oh, the French are always complaining, always begging." And in Paris the Communists would accuse, "The French are spilling their blood for America and America will not even send a second-hand helicopter." It does no good. At the end of it we should still have no helicopters, and the enemy would still be there, fifty miles from Hanoi.'

'At least I can print that, can't I, that you need helicopters bad?'

'You can say,' the colonel said, 'that six months ago we had three helicopters and now we have one. One,' he repeated with a kind of amazed bitterness. 'You can say that if a man is wounded in this fighting, not seriously wounded, just wounded, he knows that he is probably a dead man. Twelve hours, twenty-four hours perhaps, on a stretcher to the ambulance, then bad tracks, a breakdown, perhaps an ambush, gangrene. It is better to be killed outright.' The French correspondents leant forward, trying to understand. 'You can write that,' he said, looking all the more venomous for his physical beauty. '*Interprètez*,' he ordered, and walked out of the room, leaving the captain the unfamiliar task of translating from English into French.

'Got him on the raw,' said Granger with satisfaction, and he went into a corner by the bar to write his telegram. Mine didn't take long: there was nothing I could write from Phat Diem that the censors would pass. If the story had seemed good enough I could have flown to Hong Kong and sent it from there, but was any news good enough to risk expulsion? I doubted it. Expulsion meant the end of a whole life, it meant the victory of Pyle, and there, when I returned to my hotel, waiting in my pigeon-hole, was in fact his victory, the end of the affair—a congratulatory telegram of promotion. Dante never thought up that turn of the screw for his condemned lovers. Paolo was never promoted to Purgatory.

I went upstairs to my bare room and the dripping cold-water tap (there was no hot water in Hanoi) and sat on the edge of my bed with the bundle of the mosquito-net like a swollen cloud overhead. I was to be the new foreign editor, arriving every afternoon at half past three, at that grim Victorian building near Blackfriars station with a plaque of Lord Salisbury by the lift. They had sent the good news on from Saigon, and I wondered whether it had already reached Phuong's ears. I was to be a reporter no longer: I was to have opinions, and in return for that empty privilege I was deprived of my last hope in the contest with Pyle. I had experience to match his virginity, age was as good a card to play in the sexual game as youth, but now I hadn't even the limited future of twelve more months to offer, and a future was trumps. I envied the most homesick officer condemned to the chance of death. I would have liked to weep, but the ducts were as dry as the hot-water pipes. Oh, they could have home – I only wanted my room in the rue Catinat.

It was cold after dark in Hanoi and the lights were lower than those of Saigon, more suited to the darker clothes of the women and the fact of war. I walked up the rue Gambetta to the Pax Bar – I didn't want to drink in the Metropole with the senior French officers, their wives and their girls, and as I reached the bar I was aware of the distant drumming of the guns out towards Hoa Binh. In the day they were drowned in traffic-noises, but everything was quiet now except for the tring of bicycle-bells where the trishaw drivers plied for hire. Pietri sat in his usual place. He had an odd elongated skull which sat on his shoulders like a pear on a dish; he was a Sureté officer and was married to a pretty Tonkinese who owned the Pax Bar. He was another man who had no particular desire to go home. He was a Corsican, but he preferred Marseilles, and to Marseilles he preferred any day his seat on the pavement in the rue Gambetta. I wondered whether he already knew the contents of my telegram.

'*Quatre Cent Vingt-et-un?*' he asked.

'Why not?'

We began to throw and it seemed impossible to me that I could ever have a life again, away from the rue Gambetta and the rue Catinat, the flat taste of vermouth cassis, the homely click of dice, and the gunfire travelling like a clock-hand around the horizon.

I said, 'I'm going back.'

'Home?' Pietri asked, throwing a four-two-one.

'No. England.'

PART II

CHAPTER I

Pyle had invited himself for what he called a drink, but I knew very well he didn't really drink. After the passage of weeks that fantastic meeting in Phat Diem seemed hardly believable: even the details of the conversation were less clear. They were like the missing letters on a Roman tomb and I the archaeologist filling in the gaps according to the bias of my scholarship. It even occurred to me that he had been pulling my leg, and that the conversation had been an elaborate and humorous disguise for his real purpose, for it was already the gossip of Saigon that he was engaged in one of those services so ineptly called secret. Perhaps he was arranging American arms for a Third Force—the Bishop's brass band, all that was left of his young scared unpaid levies. The telegram that awaited me in Hanoi I kept in my pocket. There was no point in telling Phuong, for that would be to poison the few months we had left with tears and quarrels. I wouldn't even go for my exit-permit till the last moment in case she had a relation in the immigration-office.

I told her, 'Pyle's coming at six.'

'I will go and see my sister,' she said.

'I expect he'd like to see you.'

'He does not like me or my family. When you were away he did not come once to my sister, although she had invited him. She was very hurt.'

'You needn't go out.'

'If he wanted to see me, he would have asked us to the Majestic. He wants to talk to you privately—about business.'

'What is his business?'

'People say he imports a great many things.'

'What things?'

'Drugs, medicines . . .'

'Those are for the trachoma teams in the north.'

'Perhaps. The Customs must not open them. They are diplomatic parcels. But once there was a mistake—the man was discharged. The First Secretary threatened to stop all imports.'

'What was in the case?'

'Plastic.'

'You don't mean bombs?'

'No. Just plastic.'

When Phuong had gone, I wrote home. A man from Reuter's was leaving for Hong Kong in a few days and he could mail my letter from there. I knew my appeal was hopeless, but I was not going to reproach myself later for not taking every possible measure. I wrote to the Managing Editor that this was the wrong moment to change their correspondent. General de Lattre was dying in Paris: the French were about to withdraw altogether from Hoa Binh: the north had never been in greater danger. I wasn't suitable, I told him, for a foreign editor–I was a reporter, I had no real opinions about anything. On the last page I even appealed to him on personal grounds, although it was unlikely that any human sympathy could survive under the strip-light, among the green eye-shades and the stereotyped phrases–'the good of the paper', 'the situation demands . . .'

I wrote: 'For private reasons I am very unhappy at being moved from Vietnam. I don't think I can do my best work in England, where there will be not only financial but family strains. Indeed, if I could afford it I would resign rather than return to the U.K. I only mention this as showing the strength of my objection. I don't think you have found me a bad correspondent, and this is the first favour I have ever asked of you.' Then I looked over my article on the battle of Phat Diem, so that I could send it out to be posted under a Hong Kong dateline. The French would not seriously object now–the siege had been raised: a defeat could be played as a victory. Then I tore up the last page of my letter to the editor. It was no use–the 'private reasons' would become only the subject of sly jokes. Every correspondent, it was assumed, had his local girl. The editor would joke to the night-editor, who would take the envious thought back to his semi-detached villa at Streatham and climb into bed with it beside the faithful wife he had carried with him years back from Glasgow. I could see so well the kind of house that has no mercy–a broken tricycle stood in the hall and somebody had broken his favourite pipe; and there was a child's shirt in the living-room waiting for a button to be sewn on. 'Private reasons': drinking in the Press Club I wouldn't want to be reminded by their jokes of Phuong.

There was a knock on the door. I opened it to Pyle and his black dog walked in ahead of him. Pyle looked over my shoulder and found the room empty. 'I'm alone,' I said, 'Phuong is with her sister.' He blushed. I noticed that he was wearing a Hawaii shirt, even though it was comparatively restrained in colour and design. I was surprised: had he been accused of un-American activities? He said, 'I hope I haven't interrupted . . .'

'Of course not. Have a drink?'

'Thanks. Beer?'

'Sorry. We haven't a frig–we send out for ice. What about a Scotch?'

'A small one, if you don't mind. I'm not very keen on hard liquor.'

'On the rocks?'

'Plenty of soda–if you aren't short.'

I said, 'I haven't seen you since Phat Diem.'

'You got my note, Thomas?'

When he used my Christian name, it was like a declaration that he hadn't been humorous, that he hadn't been covering up, that he was here to get Phuong. I noticed that his crew-cut had recently been trimmed; was even the Hawaii shirt serving the function of male plumage?

'I got your note,' I said. 'I suppose I ought to knock you down.'

'Of course,' he said, 'you've every right, Thomas. But I boxed at college—and I'm so much younger.'

'No, it wouldn't be a good move for me, would it?'

'You know, Thomas (I'm sure you feel the same), I don't like discussing Phuong behind her back. I thought she would be here.'

'Well, what shall we discuss—plastic?' I hadn't meant to surprise him.

He said, 'You know about that?'

'Phuong told me.'

'How could she . . . ?'

'You can be sure it's all over the town. What's so important about it? Are you going into the toy business?'

'We don't like the details of our aid to get around. You know what Congress is like—and then one has visiting Senators. We had a lot of trouble about our trachoma teams because they were using one drug instead of another.'

'I still don't understand the plastic.'

His black dog sat on the floor taking up too much room, panting; its tongue looked like a burnt pancake. Pyle said vaguely, 'Oh, you know, we want to get some of these local industries on their feet, and we have to be careful of the French. They want everything bought in France.'

'I don't blame them. A war needs money.'

'Do you like dogs?'

'No.'

'I thought the British were great dog lovers.'

'We think Americans love dollars, but there must be exceptions.'

'I don't know how I'd get along without Duke. You know sometimes I feel so darned lonely . . .'

'You've got a great many companions in your branch.'

'The first dog I ever had was called Prince. I called him after the Black Prince. You know, the fellow who . . .'

'Massacred all the women and children in Limoges.'

'I don't remember that.'

'The history books gloss it over.'

I was to see many times that look of pain and disappointment touch his eyes and mouth when reality didn't match the romantic ideas he cherished, or when someone he loved or admired dropped below the impossible standard he had set. Once, I remember, I caught York Harding out in a gross error of fact, and I had to comfort him: 'It's human to make mistakes.' He had laughed nervously and said, 'You must think me a fool, but—well, I almost thought him infallible.' He added, 'My father took to him a lot the only time they met, and my father's darned difficult to please.'

The big black dog called Duke, having panted long enough to establish a kind of right to the air, began to poke about the room. 'Could you ask your dog to be still?' I said.

'Oh, I'm so sorry. Duke. Duke. Sit down, Duke.' Duke sat down and began noisily to lick his private parts. I filled our glasses and managed in passing to disturb Duke's toilet. The quiet lasted a very short time; he began to scratch himself.

'Duke's awfully intelligent,' said Pyle.

'What happened to Prince?'

'We were down on the farm in Connecticut and he got run over.'

'Were you upset?'

'Oh, I minded a lot. He meant a great deal to me, but one has to be sensible. Nothing could bring him back.'

'And if you lose Phuong, will you be sensible?'

'Oh yes, I hope so. And you?'

'I doubt it. I might even run amok. Have you thought about that, Pyle?'

'I wish you'd call me Alden, Thomas.'

'I'd rather not. Pyle has got—associations. Have you thought about it?'

'Of course I haven't. You're the straightest guy I've ever known. When I remember how you behaved when I barged in . . .'

'I remember thinking before I went to sleep how convenient it would be if there were an attack and you were killed. A hero's death. For Democracy.'

'Don't laugh at me, Thomas.' He shifted his long limbs uneasily. 'I must seem a bit dumb to you, but I know when you're kidding.'

'I'm not.'

'I know if you come clean you want what's best for her.'

It was then I heard Phuong's step. I had hoped against hope that he would have gone before she returned. He heard it too and recognised it. He said, 'There she is,' although he had had only one evening to learn her footfall. Even the dog got up and stood by the door, which I had left open for coolness, almost as though he accepted her as one of Pyle's family. I was an intruder.

Phuong said, 'My sister was not in,' and looked guardedly at Pyle.

I wondered whether she were telling the truth or whether her sister had ordered her to hurry back.

'You remember Monsieur Pyle?' I said.

'*Enchantée.*' She was on her best behaviour.

'I'm so pleased to see you again,' he said, blushing.

'*Comment?*'

'Her English is not very good,' I said.

'I'm afraid my French is awful. I'm taking lessons though. And I can understand—if Phuong will speak slowly.'

'I'll act as interpreter,' I said. 'The local accent takes some getting used to. Now what do you want to say? Sit down, Phuong. Monsieur Pyle has come specially to see you. Are you sure,' I added to Pyle, 'that you wouldn't like me to leave you two alone?'

'I want you to hear everything I have to say. It wouldn't be fair otherwise.'

'Well, fire away.'

He said solemnly, as though this part he had learned by heart, that he had a great love and respect for Phuong. He had felt it ever since the night he had danced with her. I was reminded a little of a butler showing a party of tourists over a 'great house'. The great house was his heart, and of the private apartments where the family lived we were given only a rapid and surreptitious glimpse. I translated for him with meticulous care—it sounded worse that way, and Phuong sat quiet with her hands in her lap as though she were listening to a movie.

'Has she understood that?' he asked.

'As far as I can tell. You don't want me to add a little fire to it, do you?'

'Oh no,' he said, 'just translate. I don't want to sway her emotionally.'

'I see.'

'Tell her I want to marry her.'

I told her.

'What was that she said?'

'She asked me if you were serious. I told her you were the serious type.'

'I suppose this is an odd situation,' he said. 'Me asking you to translate.'

'Rather odd.'

'And yet it seems so natural. After all you are my best friend.'

'It's kind of you to say so.'

'There's nobody I'd go to in trouble sooner than you,' he said.

'And I suppose being in love with my girl is a kind of trouble?'

'Of course. I wish it was anybody but you, Thomas.'

'Well, what do I say to her next. That you can't live without her?'

'No, that's too emotional. It's not quite true either. I'd have to go away, of course, but one gets over everything.'

'While you are thinking what to say, do you mind if I put in a word for myself?'

'No, of course not, it's only fair, Thomas.'

'Well, Phuong,' I said, 'are you going to leave me for him? He'll marry you. I can't. You know why.'

'Are you going away?' she asked and I thought of the editor's letter in my pocket.

'No.'

'Never?'

'How can one promise that? He can't either. Marriages break. Often they break quicker than an affair like ours.'

'I do not want to go,' she said, but the sentence was not comforting; it contained an unexpressed 'but'.

Pyle said, 'I think I ought to put all my cards on the table. I'm not rich. But when my father dies I'll have about fifty thousand dollars. I'm in good health—I've got a medical certificate only two months old, and I can let her know my blood-group.'

'I don't know how to translate that. What's it for?'

'Well, to make certain we can have children together.'

'Is that how you make love in America—figures of income and blood-group?'

'I don't know, I've never done it before. Maybe at home my mother would talk to her mother.'

'About your blood-group?'

'Don't laugh at me, Thomas. I expect I'm old-fashioned. You know I'm a little lost in this situation.'

'So am I. Don't you think we might call it off and dice for her?'

'Now you are pretending to be tough, Thomas. I know you love her in your way as much as I do.'

'Well, go on Pyle.'

'Tell her I don't expect her to love me right away. That will come in time, but tell her what I offer is security and respect. That doesn't sound very exciting, but perhaps it's better than passion.'

'She can always get passion,' I said, 'with your chauffeur when you are away at the office.'

Pyle blushed. He got awkwardly to his feet and said, 'That's a dirty crack. I won't have her insulted. You've no right . . .'

'She's not your wife yet.'

'What can you offer her?' he asked with anger. 'A couple of hundred dollars when you leave for England, or will you pass her on with the furniture?'

'The furniture isn't mine.'

'She's not either. Phuong, will you marry me?'

'What about the blood-group?' I said. 'And a health certificate. You'll need hers, surely? Maybe you ought to have mine too. And her horoscope—no, that's an Indian custom.'

'Will you marry me?'

'Say it in French,' I said, 'I'm damned if I'll interpret for you any more.'

I got to my feet and the dog growled. It made me furious. 'Tell your damned Duke to be quiet. This is my home, not his.'

'Will you marry me?' he repeated. I took a step towards Phuong and the dog growled again.

I said to Phuong, 'Tell him to go away and take his dog with him.'

'Come away with me now,' Pyle said. '*Avec moi.*'

'No,' Phuong said, 'no.' Suddenly all the anger in both of us vanished; it was a problem as simple as that: it could be solved with a word of two letters. I felt an enormous relief; Pyle stood there with his mouth a little open and an expression of bewilderment on his face. He said, 'She said no.'

'She knows that much English.' I wanted to laugh now: what fools we had both made of each other. I said, 'Sit down and have another Scotch, Pyle.'

'I think I ought to go.'

'One for the road.'

'Mustn't drink all your whisky,' he muttered.

'I get all I want through the Legation.' I moved towards the table and the dog bared its teeth.

Pyle said furiously, 'Down, Duke. Behave yourself.' He wiped the sweat off his forehead. 'I'm awfully sorry, Thomas, if I said anything I shouldn't. I don't know what came over me.' He took the glass and said wistfully, 'The best man wins. Only please don't leave her, Thomas.'

'Of course I shan't leave her,' I said.

Phuong said to me, 'Would he like to smoke a pipe?'

'Would you like to smoke a pipe?'

'No, thank you. I don't touch opium and we have strict rules in the service. I'll just drink this up and be off. I'm sorry about Duke. He's very quiet as a rule.'

'Stay to supper.'

'I think, if you don't mind, I'd rather be alone.' He gave an uncertain grin. 'I suppose people would say we'd both behaved rather strangely. I wish you could marry her, Thomas.'

'Do you really?'

'Yes. Ever since I saw that place—you know, that house near the Chalet—I've been so afraid.'

He drank his unaccustomed whisky quickly, not looking at Phuong, and when he said goodbye he didn't touch her hand, but gave an awkward little bobbing bow. I noticed how her eyes followed him to the door and as I passed the mirror I saw myself: the top button of my trousers undone, the beginning of a paunch. Outside he said, 'I promise not to see her, Thomas. You won't let this come between us, will you? I'll get a transfer when I finish my tour.'

'When's that?'

'About two years.'

I went back to the room and I thought, "What's the good? I might as well have told them both that I was going." He had only to carry his bleeding heart for a few weeks as a decoration. . . . My lie would even ease his conscience.

'Shall I make you a pipe?' Phuong asked.

'Yes, in a moment. I just want to write a letter.'

It was the second letter of the day, but I tore none of this up, though I had as little hope of a response. I wrote: 'Dear Helen, I am coming back to England next April to take the job of foreign editor. You can imagine I am not very happy about it. England is to me the scene of my failure. I had intended our marriage to last quite as much as if I had shared your Christian beliefs. To this day I'm not certain what went wrong (I know we both tried), but I think it was my temper. I know how cruel and bad my temper can be. Now I think it's a little better—the East has done that for me—not sweeter, but quieter. Perhaps it's simply that I'm five years older—at the end of life when five years becomes a high proportion of what's left. You have been very generous to me, and you have never reproached me once since our separation. Would you be even more generous? I know that before we married you warned me there could never be a divorce. I accepted the risk and I've nothing to complain of. At the same time I'm asking for one now.'

Phuong called out to me from the bed that she had the tray ready.

'A moment,' I said.

'I could wrap this up,' I wrote, 'and make it sound more honourable and more dignified by pretending it was for someone else's sake. But it isn't, and we always used to tell each other the truth. It's for my sake and only mine. I love someone very much, we have lived together for more than two years, she has been very loyal to me, but I know I'm not essential to her. If I leave her, she'll be a little unhappy I think, but there won't be any tragedy. She'll marry someone else and have a family. It's stupid of me to tell you this. I'm putting a reply into your mouth. But because I've been truthful so far, perhaps you'll believe me when I tell you that to lose her will be, for me, the beginning of death. I'm not asking you to be "reasonable" (reason is all on your side) or to be merciful. It's too big a word for my situation and anyway I don't particularly deserve mercy. I suppose what I'm really asking you is to behave, all of a sudden, irrationally, out of character. I want you to feel' (I hesitated over the word and then I didn't get it right) 'affection and to act before you have time to think. I know that's easier done over a telephone than over eight thousand miles. If only you'd just cable me "I agree"!'

When I had finished I felt as though I had run a long way and strained unconditioned muscles. I lay down on the bed while Phuong made my pipe. I said, 'He's young.'

'Who?'

'Pyle.'

'That's not so important.'

'I would marry you if I could, Phuong.'

'I think so, but my sister does not believe it.'

'I have just written to my wife and I have asked her to divorce me. I have never tried before. There is always a chance.'

'A big chance?'

'No, but a small one.'

'Don't worry. Smoke.'

I drew in the smoke and she began to prepare my second pipe. I asked her again, 'Was your sister really not at home, Phuong?'

'I told you—she was out.' It was absurd to subject her to this passion for truth, an Occidental passion, like the passion for alcohol. Because of the whisky I had drunk with Pyle, the effect of the opium was lessened. I said, 'I lied to you, Phuong. I have been ordered home.'

She put the pipe down. 'But you won't go?'

'If I refused, what would we live on?'

'I could come with you. I would like to see London.'

'It would be very uncomfortable for you if we were not married.'

'But perhaps your wife will divorce you.'

'Perhaps.'

'I will come with you anyway,' she said. She meant it, but I could see in her eyes the long train of thought begin, as she lifted the pipe again and began to warm the pellet of opium. She said, 'Are there skyscrapers in London?' and I loved her for the innocence of her question. She might lie from politeness, from fear, even for profit, but she would never have the cunning to keep her lie concealed.

'No,' I said, 'you have to go to America for them.'

She gave me a quick look over the needle and registered her mistake. Then as she kneaded the opium she began to talk at random of what clothes she would wear in London, where we should live, of the Tube-trains she had read about in a novel, and the double-decker buses: would we fly or go by sea? 'And the Statue of Liberty . . .' she said.

'No, Phuong, that's American too.'

CHAPTER 2

I

At least once a year the Caodaists hold a festival at the Holy See in Tanyin, which lies eighty kilometres to the north-west of Saigon, to celebrate such and such a year of Liberation, or of Conquest, or even a Buddhist,

Confucian or Christian festival. Caodaism was always the favourite chapter of my briefing to visitors. Caodaism, the invention of a Cochin civil servant, was a synthesis of the three religions. The Holy See was at Tanyin. A Pope and female cardinals. Prophecy by planchette. Saint Victor Hugo. Christ and Buddha looking down from the roof of the Cathedral on a Walt Disney fantasia of the East, dragons and snakes in technicolour. Newcomers were always delighted with the description. How could one explain the dreariness of the whole business: the private army of twenty-five thousand men, armed with mortars made out of the exhaust-pipes of old cars, allies of the French who turned neutral at the moment of danger? To these celebrations, which helped to keep the peasants quiet, the Pope invited members of the Government (who would turn up if the Caodaists at the moment held office), the Diplomatic Corps (who would send a few second secretaries with their wives or girls) and the French Commander-in-Chief, who would detail a two-star general from an office job to represent him.

Along the route to Tanyin flowed a fast stream of staff and C.D. cars, and on the more exposed sections of the road Foreign Legionaries threw out cover across the rice-fields. It was always a day of some anxiety for the French High Command and perhaps a certain hope for the Caodaists, for what could more painlessly emphasise their own loyalty than to have a few important guests shot outside their territory?

Every kilometre a small mud watch tower stood up above the flat fields like an exclamation-mark, and every ten kilometres there was a larger fort manned by a platoon of Legionaries, Moroccans or Senegalese. Like the traffic into New York the cars kept one pace – and as with the traffic into New York you had a sense of controlled impatience, watching the next car ahead and in the mirror the car behind. Everybody wanted to reach Tanyin, see the show and get back as quickly as possible: curfew was at seven.

One passed out of the French-controlled rice-fields into the rice-fields of the Hoa-Haos and thence into the rice-fields of the Caodaists, who were usually at war with the Hoa-Haos: only the flags changed on the watch towers. Small naked boys sat on the buffaloes which waited genital-deep among the irrigated fields; where the gold harvest was ready the peasants in their hats like limpets winnowed the rice against little curved shelters of plaited bamboo. The cars drove rapidly by, belonging to another world.

Now the churches of the Caodaists would catch the attention of strangers in every village; pale blue and pink plasterwork and a big eye of God over the door. Flags increased: troops of peasants made their way along the road: we were approaching the Holy See. In the distance the sacred mountain stood like a green bowler hat above Tanyin – that was where General Thé held out, the dissident Chief of Staff who had recently declared his intention of fighting both the French and the Vietminh. The Caodaists made no attempt to capture him, although he had kidnapped a cardinal, but it was rumoured that he had done it with the Pope's connivance.

It always seemed hotter in Tanyin than anywhere else in the Southern Delta; perhaps it was the absence of water, perhaps it was the sense of interminable ceremonies which made one sweat vicariously, sweat for the troops standing to attention through the long speeches in a language they didn't understand, sweat for the Pope in his heavy chinoiserie robes. Only the female cardinals in their white silk trousers chatting to the priests in sun-helmets gave an impression of coolness under the glare; you couldn't believe it would ever be seven o'clock and cocktail-time on the roof of the Majestic, with a wind from Saigon river.

After the parade I interviewed the Pope's deputy. I didn't expect to get anything out of him and I was right: it was a convention on both sides. I asked him about General Thé.

'A rash man,' he said and dismissed the subject. He began his set speech, forgetting that I had heard it two years before–it reminded me of my own gramophone records for newcomers. Caodaism was a religious synthesis . . . the best of all religions . . . missionaries had been despatched to Los Angeles . . . the secrets of the Great Pyramid. . . . He wore a long white soutane and he chain-smoked. There was something cunning and corrupt about him: the word 'love' occurred often. I was certain he knew that all of us were there to laugh at his movement; our air of respect was as corrupt as his phoney hierarchy, but we were less cunning. Our hypocrisy gained us nothing–not even a reliable ally, while theirs had procured arms, supplies, even cash down.

'Thank you, your Eminence.' I got up to go. He came with me to the door, scattering cigarette-ash.

'God's blessing on your work,' he said unctuously. 'Remember God loves the truth.'

'Which truth?' I asked.

'In the Caodaist faith all truths are reconciled and truth is love.'

He had a large ring on his finger and, when he held out his hand I really think he expected me to kiss it, but I am not a diplomat.

Under the bleak vertical sunlight I saw Pyle; he was trying in vain to make his Buick start. Somehow, during the last two weeks, at the bar of the Continental, in the only good bookshop in the rue Catinat, I had continually run into Pyle. The friendship which he had imposed from the beginning he now emphasised more than ever. His sad eyes would inquire mutely after Phuong, while his lips expressed with even more fervour the strength of his affection and of his admiration–God save the mark–for me.

A Caodaist commandant stood beside the car talking rapidly. He stopped when I came up. I recognised him–he had been one of Thé's assistants before Thé took to the hills.

'Hullo, commandant,' I said, 'how's the General?'

'Which general?' he asked with a shy grin.

'Surely in the Caodaist faith,' I said, 'all generals are reconciled.'

'I can't make this car move, Thomas,' Pyle said.

'I will get a mechanic,' the commandant said, and left us.

'I interrupted you.'

'Oh, it was nothing,' Pyle said. 'He wanted to know how much a Buick cost. These people are so friendly when you treat them right. The French don't seem to know how to handle them.'

'The French don't trust them.'

Pyle said solemnly, 'A man becomes trustworthy when you trust him.' It sounded like a Caodaist maxim. I began to feel the air of Tanyin was too ethical for me to breathe.

'Have a drink,' Pyle said.

'There's nothing I'd like better.'

'I brought a thermos of lime-juice with me.' He leant over and busied himself with a basket in the back.

'Any gin?'

'No, I'm awfully sorry. You know,' he said encouragingly, 'lime juice is very good for you in this climate. It contains–I'm not sure which vitamins.' He held out a cup to me and I drank.

'Anyway, it's wet,' I said.

'Like a sandwich? They're really awfully good. A new sandwich-spread called Vit-Health. My mother sent it from the States.'

'No, thanks, I'm not hungry.'

'It tastes rather like Russian salad–only sort of drier.'

'I don't think I will.'

'You don't mind if I do?'

'No, no, of course not.'

He took a large mouthful and it crunched and crackled. In the distance Buddha in white and pink stone rode away from his ancestral home and his valet–another statue–pursued him running. The female cardinals were drifting back to their house and the Eye of God watched us from above the Cathedral door.

'You know they are serving lunch here?' I said.

'I thought I wouldn't risk it. The meat–you have to be careful in this heat.'

'You are quite safe. They are vegetarian.'

'I suppose it's all right–but I like to know what I'm eating.' He took another munch at his Vit-Health. 'Do you think they have any reliable mechanics?'

'They know enough to turn your exhaust pipe into a mortar. I believe Buicks make the best mortars.'

The commandant returned and, saluting us smartly, said he had sent to the barracks for a mechanic. Pyle offered him a Vit-Health sandwich, which he refused politely. He said with a man-of-the-world air, 'We have so many rules here about food.' (He spoke excellent English.) 'So foolish. But you know what it is in a religious capital. I expect it is the same thing in Rome–or Canterbury,' he added with a neat natty little bow to me. Then he was silent. They were both silent. I had a strong impression that my company was not wanted. I couldn't resist the temptation to tease Pyle–it is, after all, the weapon of weakness and I was weak. I hadn't youth, seriousness, integrity, a future. I said, 'Perhaps after all I'll have a sandwich.'

'Oh, of course,' Pyle said, 'of course.' He paused before turning to the basket in the back.

'No, no,' I said. 'I was only joking. You two want to be alone.'

'Nothing of the kind,' Pyle said. He was one of the most inefficient liars I have ever known–it was an art he had obviously never practised. He explained to the commandant, 'Thomas here's the best friend I have.'

'I know Mr Fowler,' the commandant said.

'I'll see you before I go, Pyle.' And I walked away to the Cathedral. I could get some coolness there.

Saint Victor Hugo in the uniform of the French Academy with a halo round his tricorn hat pointed at some noble sentiment Sun Yat Sen was inscribing on a tablet, and then I was in the nave. There was nowhere to sit except in the Papal chair, round which a plaster cobra coiled, the marble floor glittered like water and there was no glass in the windows. We make a cage for air with holes, I thought, and man makes a cage for his religion in much the same way—with doubts left open to the weather and creeds opening on innumerable interpretations. My wife had found her cage with holes and sometimes I envied her. There is a conflict between sun and air: I lived too much in the sun.

I walked the long empty nave—this was not the Indo-China I loved. The dragons with lion-like heads climbed the pulpit: on the roof Christ exposed his bleeding heart. Buddha sat, as Buddha always sits, with his lap empty. Confucius's beard hung meagrely down like a waterfall in the dry season. This was play-acting: the great globe above the altar was ambition: the basket with the movable lid in which the Pope worked his prophecies was trickery. If this Cathedral had existed for five centuries instead of two decades, would it have gathered a kind of convincingness with the scratches of feet and the erosion of weather? Would somebody who was convincible like my wife find here a faith she couldn't find in human beings? And if I had really wanted faith would I have found it in her Norman church? But I had never desired faith. The job of a reporter is to expose and record. I had never in my career discovered the inexplicable. The Pope worked his prophecies with a pencil in a movable lid and the people believed. In any vision somewhere you could find the planchette. I had no visions or miracles in my repertoire of memory.

I turned my memories over at random like pictures in an album: a fox I had seen by the light of an enemy flare over Orpington stealing along beside a fowl run, out of his russet place in the marginal country: the body of a bayoneted Malay which a Gurkha patrol had brought at the back of a lorry into a mining camp in Pahang, and the Chinese coolies stood by and giggled with nerves, while a brother Malay put a cushion under the dead head: a pigeon on a mantelpiece, poised for flight in a hotel bedroom: my wife's face at a window when I came home to say goodbye for the last time. My thoughts had begun and ended with her. She must have received my letter more than a week ago, and the cable I did not expect had not come. But they say if a jury remains out for long enough there is hope for the prisoner. In another week, if no letter arrived, could I begin to hope? All round me I could hear the cars of the soldiers and the diplomats revving up: the party was over for another year. The stampede back to Saigon was beginning, and curfew called. I went out to look for Pyle.

He was standing in a patch of shade with the commandant, and no one was doing anything to his car. The conversation seemed to be over, whatever it had been about, and they stood silently there, constrained by mutual politeness. I joined them.

'Well,' I said, 'I think I'll be off. You'd better be leaving too if you want to be in before curfew.'

'The mechanic hasn't turned up.'

'He will come soon,' the commandant said. 'He was in the parade.'

'You could spend the night,' I said. 'There's a special Mass—you'll find it quite an experience. It lasts three hours.'

'I ought to get back.'

'You won't get back unless you start now.' I added unwillingly, 'I'll give you a lift if you like and the commandant can have your car sent in to Saigon tomorrow.'

'You need not bother about curfew in Caodaist territory,' the commandant said smugly. 'But beyond . . . Certainly I will have your car sent tomorrow.'

'Exhaust intact,' I said, and he smiled brightly, neatly, efficiently, a military abbreviation of a smile.

2

The procession of cars was well ahead of us by the time we started. I put on speed to try to overtake it, but we had passed out of the Caodaist zone into the zone of the Hoa-Haos with not even a dust cloud ahead of us. The world was flat and empty in the evening.

It was not the kind of country one associates with ambush, but men could conceal themselves neck-deep in the drowned fields within a few yards of the road.

Pyle cleared his throat and it was the signal for an approaching intimacy. 'I hope Phuong's well,' he said.

'I've never known her ill.' One watch tower sank behind, another appeared, like weights on a balance.

'I saw her sister out shopping yesterday.'

'And I suppose she asked you to look in,' I said.

'As a matter of fact she did.'

'She doesn't give up hope easily.'

'Hope?'

'Of marrying you to Phuong.'

'She told me you are going away.'

'These rumours get about.'

Pyle said, 'You'd play straight with me, Thomas, wouldn't you?'

'Straight?'

'I've applied for a transfer,' he said. 'I wouldn't want her to be left without either of us.'

'I thought you were going to see your time out.'

He said without self-pity, 'I found I couldn't stand it.'

'When are you leaving?'

'I don't know. They thought something could be arranged in six months.'

'You can stand six months?'

'I've got to.'

'What reason did you give?'

'I told the Economic Attaché—you met him—Joe—more or less the facts.'

'I suppose he thinks I'm a bastard not to let you walk off with my girl.'

'Oh no, he rather sided with you.'

The car was spluttering and heaving—it had been spluttering for a minute, I think, before I noticed it, for I had been examining Pyle's innocent question: 'Are you playing straight?' It belonged to a psychological world of great simplicity, where you talked of Democracy and Honor without the *u* as it's spelt on old tombstones, and you meant what your father meant by the same words. I said, 'We've run out.'

'Gas?'

'There was plenty. I crammed it full before I started. Those bastards in Tanyin have syphoned it out. I ought to have noticed. It's like them to leave us enough to get out of their zone.'

'What shall we do?'

'We can just make the next watch tower. Let's hope they have a little.'

But we were out of luck. The car reached within thirty yards of the tower and gave up. We walked to the foot of the tower and I called up in French to the guards that we were friends, that we were coming up. I had no wish to be shot by a Vietnamese sentry. There was no reply: nobody looked out. I said to Pyle, 'Have you a gun?'

'I never carry one.'

'Nor do I.'

The last colours of sunset, green and gold like the rice, were dripping over the edge of the flat world: against the grey neutral sky the watch tower looked as black as print. It must be nearly the hour of curfew. I shouted again and nobody answered.

'Do you know how many towers we passed since the last fort?'

'I wasn't noticing.'

'Nor was I.' It was probably at least six kilometres to the next fort—an hour's walk. I called a third time, and silence repeated itself like an answer.

I said, 'It seems to be empty: I'd better climb up and see.' The yellow flag with red stripes faded to orange showed that we were out of the territory of the Hoa-Haos and in the territory of the Vietnamese army.

Pyle said, 'Don't you think if we waited here a car might come?'

'It might, but *they* might come first.'

'Shall I go back and turn on the lights? For a signal.'

'Good God, no. Let it be.' It was dark enough now to stumble, looking for the ladder. Something cracked under foot; I could imagine the sound travelling across the fields of paddy, listened to by whom? Pyle had lost his outline and was a blur at the side of the road. Darkness, when once it fell, fell like a stone. I said, 'Stay there until I call.' I wondered whether the guard would have drawn up his ladder, but there it stood—though an enemy might climb it, it was their only way of escape. I began to mount.

I have read so often of people's thoughts in the moment of fear: of God, or family, or a woman. I admire their control. I thought of nothing, not even of the trap-door above me: I ceased, for those seconds, to exist: I was fear taken neat. At the top of the ladder I banged my head because fear couldn't count steps, hear, or see. Then my head came over the earth floor and nobody shot at me and fear seeped away.

3

A small oil lamp burned on the floor and two men crouched against the wall, watching me. One had a sten gun and one a rifle, but they were as scared as I'd been. They looked like schoolboys, but with the Vietnamese age drops suddenly like the sun—they are boys and then they are old men. I was glad that the colour of my skin and the shape of my eyes were a passport—they wouldn't shoot now even from fear.

I came up out of the floor, talking to reassure them, telling them that my car was outside, that I had run out of petrol. Perhaps they had a little I could buy. It didn't seem likely as I stared around. There was nothing in the little round room except a box of ammunition for the sten gun, a small wooden bed, and two packs hanging on a nail. A couple of pans with the remains of rice and some wooden chopsticks showed they had been eating without much appetite.

'Just enough to get us to the next fort?' I asked.

One of the men sitting against the wall—the one with the rifle—shook his head.

'If you can't we'll have to stay the night here.'

'*C'est défendu.*'

'Who by?'

'You are a civilian.'

'Nobody's going to make me sit out there on the road and have my throat cut.'

'Are you French?'

Only one man had spoken. The other sat with his head turned sideways, watching the slit in the wall. He could have seen nothing but a postcard of sky: he seemed to be listening and I began to listen too. The silence became full of sound: noises you couldn't put a name to—a crack, a creak, a rustle, something like a cough, and a whisper. Then I heard Pyle: he must have come to the foot of the ladder. 'You all right, Thomas?'

'Come up,' I called back. He began to climb the ladder and the silent soldier shifted his sten gun—I don't believe he'd heard a word of what we'd said: it was an awkward, jumpy movement. I realised that fear had paralysed him. I rapped out at him like a sergeant-major, 'Put that gun down!' and I used the kind of French obscenity I thought he would recognise. He obeyed me automatically. Pyle came up into the room. I said, 'We've been offered the safety of the tower till morning.'

'Fine,' Pyle said. His voice was a little puzzled. He said, 'Oughtn't one of those mugs to be on sentry?'

'They prefer not to be shot at. I wish you'd brought something stronger than lime-juice.'

'I guess I will next time,' Pyle said.

'We've got a long night ahead.' Now that Pyle was with me, I didn't hear the noises. Even the two soldiers seemed to have relaxed a little.

'What happens if the Viets attack them?' Pyle asked.

'They'll fire a shot and run. You read it every morning in the *Extrême Orient*. "A post south-west of Saigon was temporarily occupied last night by the Vietminh."'

'It's a bad prospect.'

'There are forty towers like this between us and Saigon. The chances always are that it's the other chap who's hurt.'

'We could have done with those sandwiches,' Pyle said. 'I do think one of them should keep a look-out.'

'He's afraid a bullet might look in.' Now that we too had settled on the floor, the Vietnamese relaxed a little. I felt some sympathy for them: it wasn't an easy job for a couple of ill-trained men to sit up here night after night, never sure of when the Viets might creep up on the road through the fields of paddy. I said to Pyle, 'Do you think they know they are fighting for Democracy? We ought to have York Harding here to explain it to them.'

'You always laugh at York,' said Pyle.

'I laugh at anyone who spends so much time writing about what doesn't exist—mental concepts.'

'They exist for him. Haven't you got any mental concepts? God, for instance?'

'I've no reason to believe in a God. Do you?'

'Yes. I'm a Unitarian.'

'How many hundred million Gods do people believe in? Why, even a Roman Catholic believes in quite a different God when he's scared or happy or hungry.'

'Maybe, if there is a God, he'd be so vast he'd look different to everyone.'

'Like the great Buddha in Bangkok,' I said. 'You can't see all of him at once. Anyway *he* keeps still.'

'I guess you're just trying to be tough,' Pyle said. 'There's something you must believe in. Nobody can go on living without some belief.'

'Oh, I'm not a Berkeleian. I believe my back's against this wall. I believe there's a sten gun over there.'

'I didn't mean that.'

'I believe what I report, which is more than most of your correspondents do.'

'Cigarette?'

'I don't smoke—except opium. Give one to the guards. We'd better stay friends with them.' Pyle got up and lit their cigarettes and came back. I said, 'I wish cigarettes had a symbolic significance like salt.'

'Don't you trust them?'

'No French officer,' I said, 'would care to spend the night alone with two scared guards in one of these towers. Why, even a platoon have been known to hand over their officers. Sometimes the Viets have a better success with a megaphone than a bazooka. I don't blame them. They don't believe in anything either. You and your like are trying to make a war with the help of people who just aren't interested.'

'They don't want Communism.'

'They want enough rice,' I said. 'They don't want to be shot at. They want one day to be much the same as another. They don't want our white skins around telling them what they want.'

'If Indo-China goes . . .'

'I know that record. Siam goes. Malaya goes. Indonesia goes. What does "go" mean? If I believed in your God and another life, I'd bet my future harp against your golden crown that in five hundred years there may be no New York or London, but they'll be growing paddy in these fields, they'll be carrying their produce to market on long poles wearing their pointed hats. The small boys will be sitting on the buffaloes. I like the buffaloes, they don't like our smell, the smell of Europeans. And remember–from a buffalo's point of view you are a European too.'

'They'll be forced to believe what they are told, they won't be allowed to think for themselves.'

'Thought's a luxury. Do you think the peasant sits and thinks of God and Democracy when he gets inside his mud hut at night?'

'You talk as if the whole country were peasant. What about the educated? Are they going to be happy?'

'Oh no,' I said, 'we've brought them up in *our* ideas. We've taught them dangerous games, and that's why we are waiting here, hoping we don't get our throats cut. We deserve to have them cut. I wish your friend York was here too. I wonder how he'd relish it.'

'York Harding's a very courageous man. Why, in Korea . . .'

'He wasn't an enlisted man, was he? He had a return ticket. With a return ticket courage becomes an intellectual exercise, like a monk's flagellation. How much can I stick? Those poor devils can't catch a plane home, Hi,' I called to them, 'what are your names?' I thought that knowledge somehow would bring them into the circle of our conversation. They didn't answer: just lowered back at us behind the stumps of their cigarettes. 'They think we are French,' I said.

'That's just it,' Pyle said. 'You shouldn't be against York, you should be against the French. Their colonialism.'

'Isms and ocracies. Give me facts. A rubber planter beats his labourer–all right, I'm against him. He hasn't been instructed to do it by the Minister of the Colonies. In France I expect he'd beat his wife. I've seen a priest, so poor he hasn't a change of trousers, working fifteen hours a day from hut to hut in a cholera epidemic, eating nothing but rice and salt fish, saying his Mass with an old cup–a wooden platter. I don't believe in God and yet I'm for that priest. Why don't you call that colonialism?'

'It *is* colonialism. York says it's often the good administrators who make it hard to change a bad system.'

'Anyway the French are dying every day–that's not a mental concept. They aren't leading these people on with half-lies like your politicians–and ours. I've been in India, Pyle, and I know the harm liberals do. We haven't a liberal party any more–liberalism's infected all the other parties. We are all either liberal conservatives or liberal socialists: we all have a good conscience. I'd rather be an exploiter who fights for what he exploits, and dies with it. Look at the history of Burma. We go and invade the country: the local tribes support us: we are victorious: but like you Americans we weren't colonialists in those days. Oh no, we made peace with the king and we handed him back his province and left our allies to be crucified and sawn in two. They were innocent. They thought we'd stay. But we were liberals and we didn't want a bad conscience.'

'That was a long time ago.'

'We shall do the same thing here. Encourage them and leave them with a little equipment and a toy industry.'

'Toy industry?'

'Your plastic.'

'Oh yes, I see.'

'I don't know what I'm talking politics for. They don't interest me and I'm a reporter. I'm not *engagé*.'

'Aren't you?' Pyle said.

'For the sake of an argument–to pass this bloody night, that's all. I don't take sides. I'll be still reporting, whoever wins.'

'If they win, you'll be reporting lies.'

'There's usually a way round, and I haven't noticed much regard for truth in our papers either.'

I think the fact of our sitting there talking encouraged the two soldiers: perhaps they thought the sound of our white voices–for voices have a colour too, yellow voices sing and black voices gargle, while ours just speak–would give an impression of numbers and keep the Viets away. They picked up their pans and began to eat again, scraping with their chopsticks, eyes watching Pyle and me over the rim of the pan.

'So you think we've lost?'

'That's not the point,' I said. 'I've no particular desire to see you win. I'd like those two poor buggers there to be happy–that's all. I wish they didn't have to sit in the dark at night scared.'

'You have to fight for liberty.'

'I haven't seen any Americans fighting around here. And as for liberty, I don't know what it means. Ask them.' I called across the floor in French to them. '*La liberté–qu'est ce que c'est la liberté?*' They sucked in the rice and stared back and said nothing.

Pyle said, 'Do you want everybody to be made in the same mould? You're arguing for the sake of arguing. You're an intellectual. You stand for the importance of the individual as much as I do–or York.'

'Why have we only just discovered it?' I said. 'Forty years ago no one talked that way.'

'It wasn't threatened then.'

'Ours wasn't threatened, oh no, but who cared about the individuality of the man in the paddy field–and who does now? The only man to treat him as a man is the political commissar. He'll sit in his hut and ask his name and listen to his complaints; he'll give up an hour a day to teaching him–it doesn't matter what, he's being treated like a man, like someone of value. Don't go on in the East with that parrot cry about a threat to the individual soul. Here you'd find yourself on the wrong side–it's they who stand for the individual and we just stand for Private 23987, unit in the global strategy.'

'You don't mean half what you are saying,' Pyle said uneasily.

'Probably three quarters. I've been here a long time. You know, it's lucky I'm not *engagé*, there are things I might be tempted to do–because here in the East—well, I don't like Ike. I like—well, these two. This is their country. What's the time? My watch has stopped.'

'It's turned eight-thirty.'

'Ten hours and we can move.'

'It's going to be quite chilly,' Pyle said and shivered. 'I never expected that.'

'There's water all round. I've got a blanket in the car. That will be enough.'

'Is it safe?'

'It's early for the Viets.'

'Let me go.'

'I'm more used to the dark.'

When I stood up the soldiers stopped eating. I told them, '*Je reviens, tout de suite.*' I dangled my legs over the trap door, found the ladder and went down. It is odd how reassuring conversation is, especially on abstract subjects: it seems to normalise the strangest surroundings. I was no longer scared: it was as though I had left a room and would be returning there to pick up the argument—the watch tower was the rue Catinat, the bar of the Majestic, or even a room off Gordon Square.

I stood below the tower for a minute to get my vision back. There was starlight, but no moonlight. Moonlight reminds me of a mortuary and the cold wash of an unshaded globe over a marble slab, but starlight is alive and never still, it is almost as though someone in those vast spaces is trying to communicate a message of good will, for even the names of the stars are friendly. Venus is any woman we love, the Bears are the bears of childhood, and I suppose the Southern Cross, to those, like my wife, who believe, may be a favourite hymn or a prayer beside the bed. Once I shivered as Pyle had done. But the night was hot enough, only the shallow stretch of water on either side gave a kind of icing to the warmth. I started out towards the car, and for a moment when I stood on the road I thought it was no longer there. That shook my confidence, even after I remembered that it had petered out thirty yards away. I couldn't help walking with my shoulders bent: I felt more unobtrusive that way.

I had to unlock the boot to get the blanket and the click and squeak startled me in the silence. I didn't relish being the only noise in what must have been a night full of people. With the blanket over my shoulder I lowered the boot more carefully than I had raised it, and then, just as the catch caught, the sky towards Saigon flared with light and the sound of an explosion came rumbling down the road. A bren spat and spat and was quiet again before the rumbling stopped. I thought, "Somebody's had it," and very far away heard voices crying with pain or fear or perhaps even triumph. I don't know why, but I had thought all the time of an attack coming from behind, along the road we had passed, and I had a moment's sense of unfairness that the Viets should be there ahead, between us and Saigon. It was as though we had been unconsciously driving towards danger instead of away from it, just as I was now walking in its direction, back towards the tower. I walked because it was less noisy than to run, but my body wanted to run.

At the foot of the ladder I called up to Pyle, 'It's me—Fowler.' (Even then I couldn't bring myself to use my Christian name to him.) The scene inside the hut had changed. The pans of rice were back on the floor; one man held his rifle on his hip and sat against the wall staring at Pyle and Pyle knelt a little way out from the opposite wall with his eyes on the sten gun which lay between him and the second guard. It was as though he had begun to crawl towards it but had been halted. The second guard's arm was extended towards the gun: no one had fought or even threatened, it was like that child's game when you mustn't be seen to move or you are sent back to base to start again.

'What's going on?' I said.

The two guards looked at me and Pyle pounced, pulling the sten to his side of the room.

'Is it a game?' I asked.

'I don't trust him with the gun,' Pyle said, 'if they are coming.'

'Ever used a sten?'

'No.'

'That's fine. Nor have I. I'm glad it's loaded—we wouldn't know how to reload it.'

The guards had quietly accepted the loss of the gun. The one lowered his rifle and laid it across his thighs; the other slumped against the wall and shut his eyes as though like a child he believed himself invisible in the dark. Perhaps he was glad to have no more responsibility. Somewhere far away the bren started again—three bursts and then silence. The second guard screwed his eyes closer shut.

'They don't know we can't use it,' Pyle said.

'They are supposed to be on our side.'

'I thought you didn't have a side.'

'*Touché*,' I said. 'I wish the Viets knew it.'

'What's happening out there?'

I quoted again tomorrow's *Extrême Orient*: 'A post fifty kilometres outside Saigon was attacked and temporarily captured last night by Vietminh irregulars.'

'Do you think it would be safer in the fields?'

'It would be terribly wet.'

'You don't seem worried,' Pyle said.

'I'm scared stiff—but things are better than they might be. They don't usually attack more than three posts in a night. Our chances have improved.'

'What's that?'

It was the sound of a heavy car coming up the road, driving towards Saigon. I went to the rifle slit and looked down, just as a tank went by.

'The patrol,' I said. The gun in the turret shifted now to this side, now to that. I wanted to call out to them, but what was the good? They hadn't room on board for two useless civilians. The earth floor shook a little as they passed, and they had gone. I looked at my watch—eight fifty-one, and waited, straining to read when the light flapped. It was like judging the distance of lightning by the delay before the thunder. It was nearly four minutes before the gun opened up. Once I thought I detected a bazooka replying, then all was quiet again.

'When they come back,' Pyle said, 'we could signal them for a lift to the camp.'

An explosion set the floor shaking. 'If they come back,' I said. 'That sounded like a mine.' When I looked at my watch again it had passed nine fifteen and the tank had not returned. There had been no more firing.

I sat down beside Pyle and stretched out my legs. 'We'd better try to sleep,' I said. 'There's nothing else we can do.'

'I'm not happy about the guards,' Pyle said.

'They are all right so long as the Viets don't turn up. Put the sten under your leg for safety.' I closed my eyes and tried to imagine myself somewhere else—sitting up in one of the fourth-class compartments the German railways ran before Hitler came to power, in the days when one was young and sat up all night without melancholy, when waking dreams were full of hope and not of fear. This was the hour when Phuong always set about preparing my evening pipes. I wondered whether a letter was waiting for me—I hoped not, for I knew what a letter would contain, and so long as none arrived I could day-dream of the impossible.

'Are you asleep?' Pyle asked.

'No.'

'Don't you think we ought to pull up the ladder?'

'I begin to understand why they don't. It's the only way out.'

'I wish that tank would come back.'

'It won't now.'

I tried not to look at my watch except at long intervals, and the intervals were never as long as they had seemed. Nine forty, ten five, ten twelve, ten thirty-two, ten forty-one.

'You awake?' I said to Pyle.

'Yes.'

'What are you thinking about?'

He hesitated. 'Phuong,' he said.

'Yes?'

'I was just wondering what she was doing.'

'I can tell you that. She'll have decided that I'm spending the night at Tanyin—it won't be the first time. She'll be lying on the bed with a joss stick burning to keep away the mosquitoes and she'll be looking at the pictures in an old *Paris-Match*. Like the French she has a passion for the Royal Family.'

He said wistfully, 'It must be wonderful to know exactly,' and I could imagine his soft dog's eyes in the dark. They ought to have called him Fido, not Alden.

'I don't really know—but it's probably true. There's no good in being jealous when you can't do anything about it. "No barricado for a belly."'

'Sometimes I hate the way you talk, Thomas. Do you know how she seems to me? She seems fresh, like a flower.'

'Poor flower,' I said. 'There are a lot of weeds around.'

'Where did you meet her?'

'She was dancing at the Grand Monde.'

'Dancing,' he exclaimed, as though the idea were painful.

'It's a perfectly respectable profession,' I said. 'Don't worry.'

'You have such an awful lot of experience, Thomas.'

'I have an awful lot of years. When you reach my age . . .'

'I've never had a girl,' he said, 'not properly. Not what you'd call a real experience.'

'A lot of energy with your people seems to go into whistling.'

'I've never told anybody else.'

'You're young. It's nothing to be ashamed of.'

'Have you had a lot of women, Fowler?'

'I don't know what a lot means. Not more than four women have had any importance to me—or me to them. The other forty-odd—one wonders why one does it. A notion of hygiene, of one's social obligations, both mistaken.'

'You think they *are* mistaken?'

'I wish I could have those nights back. I'm still in love, Pyle, and I'm a wasting asset. Oh, and there was pride, of course. It takes a long time before we cease to feel proud of being wanted. Though God knows why we should feel it, when we look around and see who is wanted too.'

'You don't think there's anything wrong with me, do you, Thomas?'

'No, Pyle.'

'It doesn't mean I don't *need* it, Thomas, like everybody else. I'm not—odd.'

'Not one of us needs it as much as we say. There's an awful lot of self-hypnosis around. Now I know I need nobody—except Phuong. But that's a thing one learns with time. I could go a year without one restless night if she wasn't there.'

'But she *is* there,' he said in a voice I could hardly catch.

'One starts promiscuous and ends like one's grandfather, faithful to one woman.'

'I suppose it seems pretty naïve to start that way . . .'

'No.'

'It's not in the Kinsey Report.'

'That's why it's not naïve.'

'You know, Thomas, it's pretty good being here, talking to you like this. Somehow it doesn't seem dangerous any more.'

'We used to feel that in the blitz,' I said, 'when a lull came. But they always returned.'

'If somebody asked you what your deepest sexual experience had been, what would you say?'

I knew the answer to that. 'Lying in bed early one morning and watching a woman in a red dressing-gown brush her hair.'

'Joe said it was being in bed with a Chink and a negress at the same time.'

'I'd have thought that one up too when I was twenty.'

'Joe's fifty.'

'I wonder what mental age they gave him in the war.'

'Was Phuong the girl in the red dressing-gown?'

I wished that he hadn't asked that question.

'No,' I said, 'that woman came earlier. When I left my wife.'

'What happened?'

'I left her, too.'

'Why?'

Why indeed? 'We are fools,' I said, 'when we love. I was terrified of losing her. I thought I saw her changing—I don't know if she really was, but I couldn't bear the uncertainty any longer. I ran towards the finish just like a coward runs towards the enemy and wins a medal. I wanted to get death over.'

'Death?'

'It was a kind of death. Then I came east.'

'And found Phuong?'

'Yes.'

'But don't you find the same thing with Phuong?'

'Not the same. You see, the other one loved me. I was afraid of losing love. Now I'm only afraid of losing Phuong.' Why had I said that, I wondered? He didn't need encouragement from me.

'But she loves you, doesn't she?'

'Not like that. It isn't in their nature. You'll find that out. It's a cliché to call them children–but there's one thing which is childish. They love you in return for kindness, security, the presents you give them–they hate you for a blow or an injustice. They don't know what it's like–just walking into a room and loving a stranger. For an ageing man, Pyle, it's very secure–she won't run away from home so long as the home is happy.'

I hadn't meant to hurt him. I only realised I had done it when he said with muffled anger, 'She might prefer greater security or more kindness.'

'Perhaps.'

'Aren't you afraid of that?'

'Not so much as I was of the other.'

'Do you love her at all?'

'Oh yes, Pyle, yes. But that other way I've only loved once.'

'In spite of the forty-odd women,' he snapped at me.

'I'm sure it's below the Kinsey average. You know, Pyle, women don't want virgins. I'm not sure *we* do, unless we are a pathological type.'

'I didn't mean I was a virgin,' he said. All my conversations with Pyle seemed to take grotesque directions. Was it because of his sincerity that they so ran off the customary rails? His conversation never took the corners.

'You can have a hundred women and still be a virgin, Pyle. Most of your G.I.s who were hanged for rape in the war were virgins. We don't have so many in Europe. I'm glad. They do a lot of harm.'

'I just don't understand you, Thomas.'

'It's not worth explaining. I'm bored with the subject anyway. I've reached the age when sex isn't the problem so much as old age and death. I wake up with these in mind and not a woman's body. I just don't want to be alone in my last decade, that's all. I wouldn't know what to think about all day long. I'd sooner have a woman in the same room–even one I didn't love. But if Phuong left me, would I have the energy to find another? . . .'

'If that's all she means to you . . .'

'All, Pyle? Wait until you're afraid of living ten years alone with no companion and a nursing home at the end of it. Then you'll start running in any direction, even away from that girl in the red dressing-gown, to find someone, anyone, who will last until you are through.'

'Why don't you go back to your wife, then?'

'It's not easy to live with someone you've injured.'

A sten gun fired a long burst–it couldn't have been more than a mile away.

Perhaps a nervous sentry was shooting at shadows: perhaps another attack had begun. I hoped it was an attack–it increased our chances.

'Are you scared, Thomas?'

'Of course I am. With all my instincts. But with my reason I know it's better to die like this. That's why I came east. Death stays with you.' I looked at my watch. It had gone eleven. An eight-hour night and then we could relax. I said, 'We seem to have talked about pretty nearly everything except God. We'd better leave him to the small hours.'

'You don't believe in Him, do you?'

'No.'

'Things to me wouldn't make sense without Him.'

'They don't make sense to me with him.'

'I read a book once . . .'

I never knew what book Pyle had read. (Presumably it wasn't York Harding or Shakespeare or the anthology of contemporary verse or *The Physiology of Marriage*–perhaps it was *The Triumph of Life*.) A voice came right into the tower with us, it seemed to speak from the shadows by the trap–a hollow megaphone voice saying something in Vietnamese. 'We're for it,' I said. The two guards listened, their faces turned to the rifle slit, their mouths hanging open.

'What is it?' Pyle asked.

Walking to the embrasure was like walking through the voice. I looked quickly out: there was nothing to be seen–I couldn't even distinguish the road and when I looked back into the room the rifle was pointed, I wasn't sure whether at me or at the slit. But when I moved round the wall the rifle wavered, hesitated, kept me covered: the voice went on saying the same thing over again. I sat down and the rifle was lowered.

'What's he saying?' Pyle asked.

'I don't know. I expect they've found the car and are telling these chaps to hand us over or else. Better pick up that sten before they make up their minds.'

'He'll shoot.'

'He's not sure yet. When he is he'll shoot anyway.'

Pyle shifted his leg and the rifle came up.

'I'll move along the wall,' I said. 'When his eyes waver get him covered.'

Just as I rose the voice stopped: the silence made me jump. Pyle said sharply, 'Drop your rifle.' I had just time to wonder whether the sten was unloaded–I hadn't bothered to look–when the man threw his rifle down.

I crossed the room and picked it up. Then the voice began again–I had the impression that no syllable had changed. Perhaps they used a record. I wondered when the ultimatum would expire.

'What happens next?' Pyle asked, like a schoolboy watching a demonstration in the laboratory: he didn't seem personally concerned.

'Perhaps a bazooka, perhaps a Viet.'

Pyle examined his sten. 'There doesn't seem any mystery about this,' he said. 'Shall I fire a burst?'

'No, let them hesitate. They'd rather take the post without firing and it gives us time. We'd better clear out fast.'

'They may be waiting at the bottom.'

'Yes.'

The two men watched us—I write men, but I doubt whether they had accumulated forty years between them. 'And these?' Pyle asked, and he added with a shocking directness, 'Shall I shoot them?' Perhaps he wanted to try the sten.

'They've done nothing.'

'They were going to hand us over.'

'Why not?' I said. 'We've no business here. It's their country.'

I unloaded the rifle and laid it on the floor. 'Surely you're not leaving that,' he said.

'I'm too old to run with a rifle. And this isn't my war. Come on.'

It wasn't my war, but I wished those others in the dark knew that as well. I blew the oil-lamp out and dangled my legs over the trap, feeling for the ladder. I could hear the guards whispering to each other like crooners, in their language like a song. 'Make straight ahead,' I told Pyle, 'aim for the rice. Remember there's water—I don't know how deep. Ready?'

'Yes.'

'Thanks for the company.'

'Always a pleasure,' Pyle said.

I heard the guards moving behind us: I wondered if they had knives. The megaphone voice spoke peremptorily as though offering a last chance. Something shifted softly in the dark below us, but it might have been a rat. I hesitated. 'I wish to God I had a drink,' I whispered.

'Let's go.'

Something was coming up the ladder: I heard nothing, but the ladder shook under my feet.

'What's keeping you?' Pyle said.

I don't know why I thought of it as something, that silent stealthy approach. Only a man could climb a ladder, and yet I couldn't think of it as a man like myself—it was as though an animal were moving in to kill, very quietly and certainly with the remorselessness of another kind of creation. The ladder shook and shook and I imagined I saw its eyes glaring upwards. Suddenly I could bear it no longer and I jumped, and there was nothing there at all but the spongy ground, which took my ankle and twisted it as a hand might have done. I could hear Pyle coming down the ladder; I realised I had been a frightened fool who could not recognise his own trembling, and I had believed I was tough and unimaginative, all that a truthful observer and reporter should be. I got on my feet and nearly fell again with the pain. I started out for the field dragging one foot after me and heard Pyle coming behind me. Then the bazooka shell burst on the tower and I was on my face again.

4

'Are you hurt?' Pyle said.

'Something hit my leg. Nothing serious.'

'Let's get on,' Pyle urged me. I could just see him because he seemed to be covered with a fine white dust. Then he simply went out like a picture on the screen when the lamps of the projector fail: only the soundtrack continued. I got gingerly up on to my good knee and tried to rise without putting any weight on my bad left ankle, and then I was down again breathless with pain. It wasn't my ankle: something had happened to my left leg. I couldn't worry—pain took away care. I lay very still on the ground hoping that pain wouldn't find me again. I even held my breath, as one does with toothache. I didn't think about the Viets who would soon be searching the ruins of the tower: another shell exploded on it—they were making quite sure before they came in. What a lot of money it costs, I thought as the pain receded, to kill a few human beings—you can kill horses so much cheaper. I can't have been fully conscious, for I began to think I had strayed into a knacker's yard which was the terror of my childhood in the small town where I was born. We used to think we heard the horses whinnying with fear and the explosion of the painless killer.

It was some while since the pain had returned, now that I was lying still and holding my breath—that seemed to me just as important. I wondered quite lucidly whether perhaps I ought to crawl towards the fields. The Viets might not have time to search far. Another patrol would be out by now trying to contact the crew of the first tank. But I was more afraid of the pain than of the partisans, and I lay still. There was no sound anywhere of Pyle: he must have reached the fields. Then I heard someone weeping. It came from the direction of the tower, or what had been the tower. It wasn't like a man weeping: it was like a child who is frightened of the dark and yet afraid to scream. I supposed it was one of the two boys—perhaps his companion had been killed. I hoped that the Viets wouldn't cut his throat. One shouldn't fight a war with children and a little curled body in a ditch came back to mind. I shut my eyes—that helped to keep the pain away, too, and waited. A voice called something I didn't understand. I almost felt I could sleep in this darkness and loneliness and absence of pain.

Then I heard Pyle whispering, 'Thomas. Thomas.' He had learnt footcraft quickly; I had not heard him return.

'Go away,' I whispered back.

He found me then and lay down flat beside me. 'Why didn't you come? Are you hurt?'

'My leg. I think it's broken.'

'A bullet?'

'No, no. Log of wood. Stone. Something from the tower. It's not bleeding.'

'You've got to make an effort.'

'Go away, Pyle. I don't want to, it hurts too much.'

'Which leg?'

'Left.'

He crept round to my side and hoisted my arm over his shoulder. I wanted to whimper like the boy in the tower and then I was angry, but it was hard to express anger in a whisper. 'God damn you, Pyle, leave me alone. I want to stay.'

'You can't.'

He was pulling me half on to his shoulder and the pain was intolerable.

'Don't be a bloody hero. I don't want to go.'

'You've got to help,' he said, 'or we are both caught.'

'You . . .'

'Be quiet or they'll hear you.' I was crying with vexation–you couldn't use a stronger word. I hoisted myself against him and let my left leg dangle–we were like awkward contestants in a three-legged race and we wouldn't have stood a chance if, at the moment we set off, a bren had not begun to fire in quick short bursts somewhere down the road towards the next tower. Perhaps a patrol was pushing up or perhaps they were completing their score of three towers destroyed. It covered the noise of our slow and clumsy flight.

'I'm not sure whether I was conscious all the time: I think for the last twenty yards Pyle must have almost carried my weight. He said, 'Careful here. We are going in.' The dry rice rustled around us and the mud squelched and rose. The water was up to our waists when Pyle stopped. He was panting and a catch in his breath made him sound like a bull-frog.

'I'm sorry,' I said.

'Couldn't leave you,' Pyle said.

The first sensation was relief; the water and mud held my leg tenderly and firmly like a bandage, but soon the cold set us chattering. I wondered whether it had passed midnight yet; we might have six hours of this if the Viets didn't find us.

'Can you shift your weight a little,' Pyle said, 'just for a moment?' And my unreasoning irritation came back–I had no excuse for it but the pain. I hadn't asked to be saved, or to have death so painfully postponed. I thought with nostalgia of my couch on the hard dry ground. I stood like a crane on one leg trying to relieve Pyle of my weight, and when I moved, the stalks of rice tickled and cut and crackled.

'You saved my life there,' I said, and Pyle cleared his throat for the conventional response, 'so that I could die here. I prefer dry land.'

'Better not talk,' Pyle said as though to an invalid.

'Who the hell asked you to save my life? I came east to be killed. It's like your damned impertinence . . .' I staggered in the mud and Pyle hoisted my arm around his shoulder. 'Ease it off,' he said.

'You've been seeing war-films. We aren't a couple of marines and you can't win a war-medal.'

'Sh-sh.' Footsteps could be heard, coming down to the edge of the field. The bren up the road stopped firing and there was no sound except the footsteps and the slight rustle of the rice when we breathed. Then the footsteps halted: they only seemed the length of a room away. I felt Pyle's hand on my good side pressing me slowly down; we sank together into the mud very slowly so as to make the least disturbance of the rice. On one knee, by straining my head backwards, I could just keep my mouth out of the water. The pain came back to my leg and I thought, "If I faint here I drown"–I had always hated and feared the thought of drowning. Why can't one choose one's death? There was no sound now: perhaps twenty feet away they were waiting for a rustle, a cough, a sneeze–"Oh God," I thought, "I'm going to sneeze." If only he had left me alone, I would have been responsible only for my own life–not his–and he wanted to live. I pressed my free fingers against my upper lip in that trick we learn when we are children playing at Hide and Seek, but the sneeze lingered, waiting to burst, and silent in the darkness the others waited for the sneeze. It was coming, coming, came . . .

But in the very second that my sneeze broke, the Viets opened with stens, drawing a line of fire through the rice—it swallowed my sneeze with its sharp drilling like a machine punching holes through steel. I took a breath and went under—so instinctively one avoids the loved thing, coquetting with death, like a woman who demands to be raped by her lover. The rice was lashed down over our heads and the storm passed. We came up for air at the same moment and heard the footsteps going away back towards the tower.

'We've made it,' Pyle said, and even in my pain I wondered what we'd made: for me, old age, an editor's chair, loneliness; and as for him, I know now that he spoke prematurely. Then in the cold we settled down to wait. Along the road to Tanyin a bonfire burst into life: it burnt merrily like a celebration.

'That's my car,' I said.

Pyle said, 'It's a shame, Thomas. I hate to see waste.'

'There must have been just enough petrol in the tank to set it going. Are you as cold as I am, Pyle?'

'I couldn't be colder.'

'Suppose we get out and lie flat on the road?'

'Let's give them another half hour.'

'The weight's on you.'

'I can stick it, I'm young.' He had meant the claim humorously, but it struck as cold as the mud. I had intended to apologise for the way my pain had spoken, but now it spoke again. 'You're young all right. You can afford to wait, can't you.'

'I don't get you, Thomas.'

We had spent what seemed to have been a week of nights together, but he could no more understand me than he could understand French. I said, 'You'd have done better to let me be.'

'I couldn't have faced Phuong,' he said, and the name lay there like a banker's bid. I took it up.

'So it was for her,' I said. What made my jealousy more absurd and humiliating was that it had to be expressed in the lowest of whispers—it had no tone, and jealousy likes histrionics. 'You think these heroics will get her. How wrong you are. If I were dead you could have had her.'

'I didn't mean that,' Pyle said. 'When you are in love you want to play the game, that's all.' That's true, I thought, but not as he innocently means it. To be in love is to see yourself as someone else sees you, it is to be in love with the falsified and exalted image of yourself. In love we are incapable of honour—the courageous act is no more than playing a part to an audience of two. Perhaps I was no longer in love but I remembered.

'If it had been you, I'd have left you,' I said.

'Oh no, you wouldn't, Thomas.' He added with unbearable complacency, 'I know you better than you do yourself.' Angrily I tried to move away from him and take my own weight, but the pain came roaring back like a train in a tunnel and I leant more heavily against him, before I began to sink into the water. He got both arms round me and held me up, and then inch by inch he began to edge me to the bank and the roadside. When he got me there he lowered me flat in the shallow mud below the bank at the edge of the field, and when the pain retreated and I opened my eyes and ceased to hold my breath, I could see only the elaborate cypher of the constellations—a foreign cypher which I couldn't read: they were not the stars of home. His face wheeled over me, blotting them out. 'I'm going down the road, Thomas, to find a patrol.'

'Don't be a fool,' I said. 'They'll shoot you before they know who you are. If the Viets don't get you.'

'It's the only chance. You can't lie in the water for six hours.'

'Then lay me in the road.'

'It's no good leaving you the sten?' he asked doubtfully.

'Of course it's not. If you are determined to be a hero, at least go slowly through the rice.'

'The patrol would pass before I could signal it.'

'You don't speak French.'

'I shall call out "*Je suis Frongçais*". Don't worry, Thomas. I'll be very careful.' Before I could reply he was out of a whisper's range—he was moving as quietly as he knew how, with frequent pauses. I could see him in the light of the burning car, but no shot came; soon he passed beyond the flames and very soon the silence filled the footprints. Oh yes, he was being careful as he had been careful boating down the river into Phat Diem, with the caution of a hero in a boy's adventure-story, proud of his caution like a Scout's badge and quite unaware of the absurdity and the improbability of his adventure.

I lay and listened for the shots from the Viets or a Legion patrol, but none came—it would probably take him an hour or even more before he reached a tower, if he ever reached it. I turned my head enough to see what remained of our tower, a heap of mud and bamboo and struts which seemed to sink lower as the flames of the car sank. There was peace when the pain went—a kind of Armistice Day of the nerves: I wanted to sing. I thought how strange it was that men of my profession would make only two news-lines out of all this night—it was just a common-or-garden night and I was the only strange thing about it. Then I heard a low crying begin again from what was left of the tower. One of the guards must still be alive.

I thought, "Poor devil, if we hadn't broken down outside *his* post, he could have surrendered as they nearly all surrendered, or fled, at the first call from the megaphone. But we were there—two white men, and we had the sten and they didn't dare to move. When we left it was too late." I was responsible for that voice crying in the dark: I had prided myself on detachment, on not belonging to this war, but those wounds had been inflicted by me just as though I had used the sten, as Pyle had wanted to do.

I made an effort to get over the bank into the road. I wanted to join him. It was the only thing I could do, to share his pain. But my own personal pain pushed me back. I couldn't hear him any more. I lay still and heard nothing but my own pain beating like a monstrous heart and held my breath and prayed to the God I didn't believe in, 'Let me die or faint. Let me die or faint'; and then I suppose I fainted and was aware of nothing until I dreamed that my eyelids had frozen together and someone was inserting a chisel to prise them apart, and I wanted to warn them not to damage the eyeballs beneath but couldn't speak and the chisel bit through and a torch' was shining on my face.

'We made it, Thomas,' Pyle said. I remember that, but I don't remember what Pyle later described to others: that I waved my hand in the wrong direction and told them there was a man in the tower and they had to see to him. Anyway I couldn't have made the sentimental assumption that Pyle made. I know myself, and I know the depth of my selfishness. I cannot be at ease (and to be at ease is my chief wish) if someone else is in pain, visibly or audibly or tactually. Sometimes this is mistaken by the innocent for unselfishness, when all I am doing is sacrificing a small good—in this case postponement in attending to my hurt—for the sake of a far greater good, a peace of mind when I need think only of myself.

They came back to tell me the boy was dead, and I was happy—I didn't even have to suffer much pain after the hypodermic of morphia had bitten my leg.

CHAPTER 3

I

I came slowly up the stairs to the flat in the rue Catinat, pausing and resting on the first landing. The old women gossiped as they always had done, squatting on the floor outside the urinoir, carrying Fate in the lines of their faces as others on the palm. They were silent as I passed and I wondered what they might have told me, if I had known their language, of what had passed while I had been away in the Legion Hospital back on the road towards Tanyin. Somewhere in the tower and the fields I had lost my keys, but I had sent a message to Phuong which she must have received, if she was still there. That 'if' was the measure of my uncertainty. I had had no news of her in hospital, but she wrote French with difficulty, and I couldn't read Vietnamese. I knocked on the door and it opened immediately and everything seemed to be the same. I watched her closely while she asked how I was and touched my splinted leg and gave me her shoulder to lean on, as though one could lean with safety on so young a plant. I said, 'I'm glad to be home.'

She told me that she had missed me, which of course was what I wanted to hear: she always told me what I wanted to hear, like a coolie answering questions, unless by accident. Now I awaited the accident.

'How have you amused yourself?' I asked.

'Oh, I have seen my sister often. She has found a post with the Americans.'

'She has, has she? Did Pyle help?'

'Not Pyle, Joe.'

'Who's Joe?'

'You know him. The Economic Attaché.'

'Oh, of course, Joe.'

He was a man one always forgot. To this day I cannot describe him, except his fatness and his powdered clean-shaven cheeks and his big laugh; all his identity escapes me—except that he was called Joe. There are some men whose names are always shortened.

With Phuong's help I stretched myself on the bed. 'Seen any movies?' I asked.

'There is a very funny one at the Catinat,' and immediately she began to tell me the plot in great detail, while I looked around the room for the white envelope that might be a telegram. So long as I didn't ask, I could believe that she had forgotten to tell me, and it might be there on the table by the typewriter, or on the wardrobe, perhaps put for safety in the cupboard-drawer where she kept her collection of scarves.

'The postmaster—I think he was the postmaster, but he may have been the mayor—followed them home, and he borrowed a ladder from the baker and he climbed through Corinne's window, but, you see, she had gone into the next room with François, but he did not hear Mme Bompierre coming and she came in and saw him at the top of the ladder and thought . . .'

'Who was Mme Bompierre?' I asked, turning my head to see the wash-basin, where sometimes she propped reminders among the lotions.

'I told you. She was Corinne's mother and she was looking for a husband because she was a widow . . .'

She sat on the bed and put her hand inside my shirt. 'It was very funny,' she said.

'Kiss me, Phuong.' She had no coquetry. She did at once what I asked and she went on with the story of the film. Just so she would have made love if I had asked her to, straight away, peeling off her trousers without question, and afterwards have taken up the thread of Mme Bompierre's story and the postmaster's predicament.

'Has a call come for me?'

'Yes.'

'Why didn't you give it me?'

'It is too soon for you to work. You must lie down and rest.'

'This may not be work.'

She gave it me and I saw that it had been opened. It read: 'Four hundred words background wanted effect de Lattre's departure on military and political situation.'

'Yes,' I said. 'It *is* work. How did you know? Why did you open it?'

'I thought it was from your wife. I hoped that it was good news.'

'Who translated it for you?'

'I took it to my sister.'

'If it had been bad news would you have left me, Phuong?'

She rubbed her hand across my chest to reassure me, not realising that it was words this time I required, however untrue. 'Would you like a pipe? There *is* a letter for you. I think perhaps it is from her.'

'Did you open that too?'

'I don't open your letters. Telegrams are public. The clerks read them.'

This envelope was among the scarves. She took it gingerly out and laid it on the bed. I recognised the handwriting. 'If this is bad news what will you . . .?' I knew well that it could be nothing else but bad. A telegram might have meant a sudden act of generosity: a letter could only mean explanation, justification . . . so I broke off my question, for there was no honesty in asking for the kind of promise no one can keep.

'What are you afraid of?' Phuong asked, and I thought, "I'm afraid of the loneliness, of the Press Club and the bed-sitting-room, I'm afraid of Pyle."

'Make me a brandy-and-soda,' I said. I looked at the beginning of the letter, 'Dear Thomas,' and the end, 'Affectionately, Helen,' and waited for the brandy.

'It is from *her*?'

'Yes.' Before I read it I began to wonder whether at the end I should lie or tell the truth to Phuong.

'Dear Thomas,
'I was not surprised to get your letter and to know that you were not alone. You are not a man, are you? to remain alone for very long. You pick up women like your coat picks up dust. Perhaps I would feel more sympathy with your case if I didn't feel that you would find consolation very easily when you return to London. I don't suppose you'll believe me, but what gives me pause and prevents me cabling you a simple No is the thought of the poor girl. We are apt to be more involved than you are.'

I had a drink of brandy. I hadn't realised how open the sexual wounds remain over the years. I had carelessly–not choosing my words with skill–set hers bleeding again. Who could blame her for seeking my own scars in return? When we are unhappy we hurt.

'Is it bad?' Phuong asked.

'A bit hard,' I said. 'But she has the right . . .' I read on.

'I always believed you loved Anne more than the rest of us until you packed up and went. Now you seem to be planning to leave another woman because I can tell from your letter that you don't really expect a "favourable" reply. "I'll have done my best"–aren't you thinking that? What would you do if I cabled "Yes"? Would you actually marry her? (I have to write "her"–you don't tell me her name.) Perhaps you would. I suppose like the rest of us you are getting old and don't like living alone. I feel very lonely myself sometimes. I gather Anne has found another companion. But you left her in time.'

She had found the dried scab accurately. I drank again. An issue of blood–the phrase came into my mind.

'Let me make you a pipe,' Phuong said.

'Anything,' I said, 'anything.'

'That is one reason why I ought to say No. (We don't need to talk about the religious reason, because you've never understood or believed in that.) Marriage doesn't prevent you leaving a woman, does it? It only delays the process, and it would be all the more unfair to the girl in this case if you lived with her as long as you lived with me. You would bring her back to England where she would be lost and a stranger, and when you left her, how terribly abandoned she would feel. I don't suppose she even uses a knife and fork, does she? I'm being harsh because I'm thinking of her good more than I am of yours. But, Thomas dear, I do think of yours too.

I felt physically sick. It was a long time since I had received a letter from my wife. I had forced her to write it and I could feel her pain in every line.

Her pain struck at my pain: we were back at the old routine of hurting each other. If only it were possible to love without injury—fidelity isn't enough: I had been faithful to Anne and yet I had injured her. The hurt is in the act of possession: we are too small in mind and body to possess another person without pride or to be possessed without humiliation. In a way I was glad that my wife had struck out at me again—I had forgotten her pain for too long, and this was the only kind of recompense I could give her. Unfortunately the innocent are always involved in any conflict. Always, everywhere, there is some voice crying from a tower.

Phuong lit the opium lamp. 'Will she let you marry me?'

'I don't know yet.'

'Doesn't she say?'

'If she does, she says it very slowly.'

I thought, "How much you pride yourself on being *dégagé*, the reporter, not the leader-writer, and what a mess you make behind the scenes. The other kind of war is more innocent than this. One does less damage with a mortar."

'If I go against my deepest conviction and say "Yes", would it even be good for *you*? You say you are being recalled to England and I can realise how you will hate that and do anything to make it easier. I can see you marrying after a drink too many. The first time we really tried—you as well as me—and we failed. One doesn't try so hard the second time. You say it will be the end of life to lose this girl. Once you used exactly that phrase to me—I could show you the letter, I have it still—and I suppose you wrote in the same way to Anne. You say that we've always tried to tell the truth to each other, but, Thomas, your truth is always so temporary. What's the good of arguing with you, or trying to make you see reason? It's easier to act as my faith tells me to act—as you think unreasonably—and simply to write: I don't believe in divorce: my religion forbids it, and so the answer, Thomas, is no—no.'

There was another half-page, which I didn't read, before 'Affectionately, Helen'. I think it contained news of the weather and an old aunt of mine I loved.

I had no cause for complaint, and I had expected this reply. There was a lot of truth in it. I only wished that she had not thought aloud at quite such length, when the thoughts hurt her as well as me.

'She says "No"?'

I said with hardly any hesitation, 'She hasn't made up her mind. There's still hope.'

Phuong laughed. 'You say "hope" with such a long face.' She lay at my feet like a dog on a crusader's tomb, preparing the opium, and I wondered what I should say to Pyle. When I had smoked four pipes I felt more ready for the future and I told her the hope was a good one—my wife was consulting a lawyer. Any day now I would get the telegram of release.

'It would not matter so much. You could make a settlement,' she said, and I could hear her sister's voice speaking through her mouth.

'I have no savings,' I said. 'I can't outbid Pyle.'

'Don't worry. Something may happen. There are always ways,' she said. 'My sister says you could take out a life-insurance,' and I thought how realistic it was of her not to minimise the importance of money and not to make any great and binding declarations of love. I wondered how Pyle over the years would stand that hard core, for Pyle was a romantic; but then of course in his case there would be a good settlement, the hardness might soften like an unused muscle when the need for it vanished. The rich had it both ways.

That evening, before the shops had closed in the rue Catinat, Phuong bought three more silk scarves. She sat on the bed and displayed them to me, exclaiming at the bright colours, filling a void with her singing voice, and then folding them carefully she laid them with a dozen others in her drawer: it was as though she were laying the foundation of a modest settlement. And I laid the crazy foundation of mine, writing a letter that very night to Pyle with the unreliable clarity and foresight of opium. This was what I wrote—I found it again the other day tucked into York Harding's *Rôle of the West*. He must have been reading the book when my letter arrived. Perhaps he had used it as a bookmark and then not gone on reading.

'Dear Pyle,' I wrote, and was tempted for the only time to write, 'Dear Alden,' for, after all, this was a bread-and-butter letter of some importance and it differed from other bread-and-butter letters in containing a falsehood:

'Dear Pyle, I have been meaning to write from the hospital to say thank you for the other night. You certainly saved me from an uncomfortable end. I'm moving about again now with the help of a stick—I broke apparently in just the right place and age hasn't yet reached my bones and made them brittle. We must have a party together some time to celebrate.' (My pen stuck on that word, and then, like an ant meeting an obstacle, went round it by another route.) 'I've got something else to celebrate and I know you will be glad of this, too, for you've always said that Phuong's interests were what we both wanted. I found a letter from my wife waiting when I got back, and she's more or less agreed to divorce me. So you don't need to worry any more about Phuong'—it was a cruel phrase, but I didn't realise the cruelty until I read the letter over and then it was too late to alter. If I were going to scratch that out, I had better tear the whole letter up.

'Which scarf do you like best?' Phuong asked. 'I love the yellow.'

'Yes. The yellow. Go down to the hotel and post this letter for me.'

She looked at the address. 'I could take it to the Legation. It would save a stamp.'

'I would rather you posted it.'

Then I lay back and in the relaxation of the opium I thought, "At least she won't leave me now before I go, and perhaps, somehow, tomorrow, after a few more pipes, I shall think of a way to remain."

2

Ordinary life goes on—that has saved many a man's reason. Just as in an air-raid it proved impossible to be frightened all the time, so under the bombardment of routine jobs, of chance encounters, of impersonal anxieties, one lost for hours together the personal fear. The thoughts of the coming April, of leaving Indo-China, of the hazy future without Phuong, were affected by the day's telegrams, the bulletins of the Vietnam Press, and by the illness of my assistant, an Indian called Dominguez (his family had come from Goa by way of Bombay) who had attended in my place the less important Press Conferences, kept a sensitive ear open to the tones of gossip and rumour, and took my messages to the cable-offices and the censorship. With the help of Indian traders, particularly in the north, in Haiphong, Nam Dinh and Hanoi, he ran his own personal intelligence service for my benefit, and I think he knew more accurately than the French High Command the location of Vietminh battalions within the Tonkin delta.

And because we never used our information except when it became news, and never passed any reports to the French intelligence, he had the trust and the friendship of several Vietminh agents hidden in Saigon-Cholon. The fact that he was an Asiatic, in spite of his name, unquestionably helped.

I was fond of Dominguez. Where other men carry their pride like a skin-disease on the surface, sensitive to the least touch, his pride was deeply hidden, and reduced to the smallest proportion possible, I think, for any human being. All that you encountered in daily contact with him was gentleness and humility and an absolute love of truth: you would have had to be married to him to discover the pride. Perhaps truth and humility go together; so many lies come from our pride–in my profession a reporter's pride, the desire to file a better story than the other man's, and it was Dominguez who helped me not to care–to withstand all those telegrams from home asking why I had not covered so and so's story or the report of someone else which I knew to be untrue.

Now that he was ill I realised how much I owed him–why, he would even see that my car was full of petrol, and yet never once, with a phrase or a look, had he encroached on my private life. I believe he was a Roman Catholic, but I had no evidence for it beyond his name and the place of his origin–for all I knew from his conversation, he might have worshipped Krishna or gone on annual pilgrimages, pricked by a wire frame, to the Batu Caves. Now his illness came like a mercy, reprieving me from the treadmill of private anxiety. It was I now who had to attend the wearisome Press Conferences and hobble to my table at the Continental for a gossip with my colleagues; but I was less capable than Dominguez of telling truth from falsehood, and so I formed the habit of calling in on him in the evenings to discuss what I had heard. Sometimes one of his Indian friends was there, sitting beside the narrow iron bed in the lodgings Dominguez shared in one of the meaner streets off the Boulevard Galliéni. He would sit up straight in his bed with his feet tucked under him so that you had less the impression of visiting a sick man than of being received by a rajah or a priest. Sometimes when his fever was bad his face ran with sweat, but he never lost the clarity of his thought. It was as though his illness were happening to another person's body. His landlady kept a jug of fresh lime by his side, but I never saw him take a drink–perhaps that would have been to admit that it was his own thirst, and his own body which suffered.

Of all the days that I visited him I remember one in particular. I had given up asking him how he was for fear that the question sounded like a reproach, and it was always he who inquired with great anxiety about my health and apologised for the stairs I had to climb. Then he said, 'I would like you to meet a friend of mine. He has a story you should listen to.'

'Yes.'

'I have his name written down because I know you find it difficult to remember Chinese names. We must not use it, of course. He has a warehouse on the Quai Mytho for junk metal.'

'Important?'

'It might be.'

'Can you give me an idea?'

'I would rather you heard from him. There is something strange, but I don't understand it.' The sweat was pouring down his face, but he just let it run as though the drops were alive and sacred—there was that much of the Hindu in him, he would never have endangered the life of a fly. He said, 'How much do you know of your friend Pyle?'

'Not very much. Our tracks cross, that's all. I haven't seen him since Tanyin.'

'What job does he do?'

'Economic Mission, but that covers a multitude of sins. I think he's interested in home-industries—I suppose with an American business tie-up. I don't like the way they keep the French fighting and cut out their business at the same time.'

'I heard him talking the other day at a party the Legation was giving to visiting Congressmen. They had put him on to brief them.'

'God help Congress,' I said, 'he hasn't been in the country six months.'

'He was talking about the old colonial powers—England and France, and how you two couldn't expect to win the confidence of the Asiatics. That was where America came in now with clean hands.'

'Hawaii, Puerto Rico,' I said, 'New Mexico.'

'Then someone asked him some stock question about the chances of the Government here ever beating the Vietminh and he said a Third Force could do it. There was always a Third Force to be found free from Communism and the taint of colonialism—national democracy he called it; you only had to find a leader and keep him safe from the old colonial powers.'

'It's all in York Harding,' I said. 'He had read it before he came out here. He talked about it his first week and he's learned nothing.'

'He may have found his leader,' Dominguez said.

'Would it matter?'

'I don't know. I don't know what he does. But go and talk to my friend on the Quai Mytho.'

I went home to leave a note for Phuong in the rue Catinat and then drove down past the port as the sun set. The tables and chairs were out on the *quai* beside the steamers and the grey naval boats, and the little portable kitchens burned and bubbled. In the Boulevard de la Somme the hairdressers were busy under the trees and the fortune-tellers squatted against the walls with their soiled packs of cards. In Cholon you were in a different city where work seemed to be just beginning rather than petering out with the daylight. It was like driving into a pantomime set: the long vertical Chinese signs and the bright lights and the crowd of extras led you into the wings, where everything was suddenly so much darker and quieter. One such wing took me down again to the *quai* and a huddle of sampans, where the warehouses yawned in the shadow and no one was about.

I found the place with difficulty and almost by accident, the godown gates were open, and I could see the strange Picasso shapes of the junk-pile by the light of an old lamp: bedsteads, bathtubs, ashcans, the bonnets of cars, stripes of old colour where the light hit. I walked down a narrow track carved in the iron quarry and called out for Mr Chou, but there was no reply. At the end of the godown a stair led up to what I supposed might be Mr Chou's house – I had apparently been directed to the back door, and I supposed that Dominguez had his reasons. Even the staircase was lined with junk, pieces of scrap-iron which might come in useful one day in this jackdaw's nest of a house. There was one big room on the landing and a whole family sat and lay about in it with the effect of a camp which might be struck at any moment. Small tea-cups stood about everywhere and there were lots of cardboard boxes full of unidentifiable objects and fibre suitcases ready strapped; there was an old lady sitting on a big bed, two boys and two girls, a baby crawling on the floor, three middle-aged women in old brown peasant-trousers and jackets, and two old men in a corner in blue silk mandarin coats playing mah jongg. They paid no attention to my coming; they played rapidly, identifying each piece by touch, and the noise was like shingle turning on a beach after a wave withdraws. No one paid any more attention than they did; only a cat leapt on to a cardboard box and a lean dog sniffed at me and withdrew.

'Monsieur Chou?' I asked, and two of the women shook their heads, and still no one regarded me, except that one of the women rinsed out a cup and poured tea from a pot which had been resting warm in its silk-lined box. I sat down on the end of the bed next the old lady and a girl brought me the cup: it was as though I had been absorbed into the community with the cat and the dog – perhaps they had turned up the first time as fortuitously as I had. The baby crawled across the floor and pulled at my laces and no one reproved it: one didn't in the East reprove children. Three commercial calendars were hanging on the walls, each with a girl in gay Chinese costume with bright pink cheeks. There was a big mirror mysteriously lettered Café de la Paix – perhaps it had got caught up accidentally in the junk: I felt caught up in it myself.

I drank slowly the green bitter tea, shifting the handleless cup from palm to palm as the heat scorched my fingers, and I wondered how long I ought to stay. I tried the family once in French, asking when they expected Monsieur Chou to return, but no one replied: they had probably not understood. When my cup was empty they refilled it and continued their own occupations: a woman ironing, a girl sewing, the two boys at their lessons, the old lady looking at her feet, the tiny crippled feet of old China – and the dog watching the cat, which stayed on the cardboard boxes.

I began to realise how hard Dominguez worked for his lean living.

A Chinese of extreme emaciation came into the room. He seemed to take up no room at all: he was like the piece of greaseproof paper that divides the biscuits in a tin. The only thickness he had was in his striped flannel pyjamas. 'Monsieur Chou?' I asked.

He looked at me with the indifferent gaze of a smoker: the sunken cheeks, the baby wrists, the arms of a small girl—many years and many pipes had been needed to whittle him down to these dimensions. I said, 'My friend, M. Dominguez, said that you had something to show me. You *are* Monsieur Chou?'

Oh yes, he said, he was Monsieur Chou and waved me courteously back to my seat. I could tell that the object of my coming had been lost somewhere within the smoky corridors of his skull. I would have a cup of tea? he was much honoured by my visit. Another cup was rinsed on to the floor and put like a live coal into my hands—the ordeal by tea. I commented on the size of his family.

He looked round with faint surprise as though he had never seen it in that light before. 'My mother,' he said, 'my wife, my sister, my uncle, my brother, my children, my aunt's children.' The baby had rolled away from my feet and lay on its back kicking and crowing. I wondered to whom it belonged. No one seemed young enough—or old enough—to have produced that.

I said, 'Monsieur Dominguez told me it was important.'

'Ah, Monsieur Dominguez. I hope Monsieur Dominguez is well?'

'He has had a fever.'

'It is an unhealthy time of year.' I wasn't convinced that he even remembered who Dominguez was. He began to cough, and under his pyjama jacket, which had lost two buttons, the tight skin twanged like a native drum.

'You should see a doctor yourself,' I said. A newcomer joined us—I hadn't heard him enter. He was a young man neatly dressed in European clothes. He said in English, 'Mr Chou has only one lung.'

'I am very sorry . . .'

'He smokes one hundred and fifty pipes every day.'

'That sounds a lot.'

'The doctor says it will do him no good, but Mr Chou feels much happier when he smokes.'

I made an understanding grunt.

'If I may introduce myself, I am Mr Chou's manager.'

'My name is Fowler. Mr Dominguez sent me. He said that Mr Chou had something to tell me.'

'Mr Chou's memory is very much impaired. Will you have a cup of tea?'

'Thank you, I have had three cups already.' It sounded like a question and an answer in a phrase-book.

Mr Chou's manager took the cup out of my hand and held it out to one of the girls, who after spilling the dregs on the floor again refilled it.

'That is not strong enough,' he said, and took it and tasted it himself, carefully rinsed it and refilled it from a second teapot. 'That is better?' he asked.

'Much better.'

Mr Chou cleared his throat, but it was only for an immense expectoration into a tin spittoon decorated with pink blooms. The baby rolled up and down among the tea-dregs and the cat leapt from a cardboard box on to a suitcase.

'Perhaps it would be better if you talked to me,' the young man said.

'My name is Mr Heng.'

'If you would tell me . . .'

'We will go down to the warehouse,' Mr Heng said. 'It is quieter there.'

I put out my hand to Mr Chou, who allowed it to rest between his palms with a look of bewilderment, then gazed around the crowded room as though he were trying to fit me in. The sound of the turning shingle receded as we went down the stairs. Mr Heng said, 'Be careful. The last step is missing,' and he flashed a torch to guide me.

We were back among the bedsteads and the bathtubs and Mr Heng led the way down a side aisle. When he had gone about twenty paces he stopped and shone his light on to a small iron drum. He said, 'Do you see that?'

'What about it?'

He turned it over and showed the trade mark: 'Diolacton.'

'It still means nothing to me.'

He said, 'I had two of those drums here. They were picked up with other junk at the garage of Mr Phan-Van-Muoi. You know him?'

'No; I don't think so.'

'His wife is a relation of General Thé.'

'I still don't quite see . . . ?'

'Do you know what this is?' Mr Heng asked, stooping and lifting a long concave object like a stick of celery which glistened chromium in the light of his torch.

'It might be a bath-fixture.'

'It is a mould,' Mr Heng said. He was obviously a man who took a tiresome pleasure in giving instruction. He paused for me to show my ignorance again. 'You understand what I mean by a mould?'

'Oh yes, of course, but I still don't follow . . .'

'This mould was made in U.S.A. Diolacton is an American trade name. You begin to understand?'

'Frankly, no.'

'There is a flaw in the mould. That was why it was thrown away. But it should not have been thrown away with the junk—nor the drum either. That was a mistake. Mr Muoi's manager came here personally. I could not find the mould, but I let him have back the other drum. I said it was all I had, and he told me he needed them for storing chemicals. Of course, he did not ask for the mould—that would have given too much away—but he had a good search. Mr Muoi himself called later at the American Legation and asked for Mr Pyle.'

'You seem to have quite an Intelligence Service,' I said. I still couldn't imagine what it was all about.

'I asked Mr Chou to get in touch with Mr Dominguez.'

'You mean you've established a kind of connection between Pyle and the General,' I said. 'A very slender one. It's not news anyway. Everybody here goes in for Intelligence.'

Mr Heng beat his heel against the black iron drum and the sound reverberated among the bedsteads. He said, 'Mr Fowler, you are English. You are neutral. You have been fair to all of us. You can sympathise if some of us feel strongly on whatever side.'

I said, 'If you are hinting that you are a Communist, or a Vietminh, don't worry. I'm not shocked. I have no politics.'

'If anything unpleasant happens here in Saigon, it will be blamed on us. My Committee would like you to take a fair view. That is why I have shown you this and this.'

'What is Diolacton?' I said. 'It sounds like condensed milk.'

'It has something in common with milk.' Mr Heng shone his torch inside the drum. A little white powder lay like dust on the bottom. 'It is one of the American plastics,' he said.

'I heard a rumour that Pyle was importing plastics for toys.' I picked up the mould and looked at it. I tried in my mind to divine its shape. This was not how the object itself would look: this was the image in a mirror, reversed.

'Not for toys,' Mr Heng said.

'It is like parts of a rod.'

'The shape is unusual.'

'I can't see what it could be for.'

Mr Heng turned away. 'I only want you to remember what you have seen,' he said, walking back in the shadows of the junk-pile. 'Perhaps one day you will have a reason for writing about it. But you must not say you saw the drum here.'

'Nor the mould?' I asked.

'Particularly not the mould.'

3

It is not easy the first time to meet again one who has saved—as they put it—one's life. I had not seen Pyle while I was in the Legion Hospital, and his absence and silence, easily accountable (for he was more sensitive to embarrassment than I), sometimes worried me unreasonably, so that at night before my sleeping drug had soothed me I would imagine him going up my stairs, knocking at my door, sleeping in my bed. I had been unjust to him in that, and so I had added a sense of guilt to my other more formal obligation. And then I suppose there was also the guilt of my letter. (What distant ancestors had given me this stupid conscience? Surely they were free of it when they raped and killed in their palaeolithic world.)

Should I invite my saviour to dinner, I sometimes wondered, or should I suggest a meeting for a drink in the bar of the Continental? It was an unusual social problem, perhaps depending on the value one attributed to one's life. A meal and a bottle of wine or a double whisky?—it had worried me for some days until the problem was solved by Pyle himself, who came and shouted at me through my closed door. I was sleeping through the hot afternoon, exhausted by the morning's effort to use my leg, and I hadn't heard his knock.

'Thomas, Thomas.' The call dropped into a dream I was having of walking down a long empty road looking for a turning which never came. The road unwound like a tape-machine with a uniformity that would never have altered if the voice hadn't broken in—first of all like a voice crying in pain from a tower and then suddenly a voice speaking to me personally,

'Thomas, Thomas.'

Under my breath I said, 'Go away, Pyle. Don't come near me. I don't want to be saved.'

'Thomas.' He was hitting at my door, but I lay possum as though I were back in the rice-field and he was an enemy. Suddenly I realised that the knocking had stopped, someone was speaking in a low voice outside and someone was replying. Whispers are dangerous. I couldn't tell who the speakers were. I got carefully off the bed and with the help of my stick reached the door of the other room. Perhaps I had moved too hurriedly and they had heard me, because a silence grew outside. Silence like a plant put out tendrils: it seemed to grow under the door and spread its leaves in the room where I stood. It was a silence I didn't like, and I tore it apart by flinging the door open. Phuong stood in the passage and Pyle had his hands on her shoulders: from their attitude they might have parted from a kiss.

'Why, come in,' I said, 'come in.'

'I couldn't make you hear,' Pyle said.

'I was asleep at first, and then I didn't want to be disturbed. But I *am* disturbed, so come in.' I said in French to Phuong, 'Where did you pick him up?'

'Here. In the passage,' she said. 'I heard him knocking, so I ran upstairs to let him in.'

'Sit down,' I said to Pyle. 'Will you have some coffee?'

'No, and I don't want to sit down, Thomas.'

'I must. This leg gets tired. You got my letter?'

'Yes. I wish you hadn't written it.'

'Why?'

'Because it was a pack of lies. I trusted you, Thomas.'

'You shouldn't trust anyone when there's a woman in the case.'

'Then you needn't trust me after this. I'll come sneaking up here when you go out, I'll write letters in typewritten envelopes. Maybe I'm growing up, Thomas.' But there were tears in his voice, and he looked younger than he had ever done. 'Couldn't you have won without lying?'

'No. This is European duplicity, Pyle. We have to make up for our lack of supplies. I must have been clumsy though. How did you spot the lies?'

'It was her sister,' he said. 'She's working for Joe now. I saw her just now. She knows you've been called home.'

'Oh, that,' I said with relief. 'Phuong knows it too.'

'And the letter from your wife? Does Phuong know about that? Her sister's seen it.'

'How?'

'She came here to meet Phuong when you were out yesterday and Phuong showed it to her. You can't deceive her. She reads English.'

'I see.' There wasn't any point in being angry with anyone—the offender was too obviously myself, and Phuong had probably only shown the letter as a kind of boast—it wasn't a sign of mistrust.

'You knew all this last night?' I asked Phuong.

'Yes.'

'I noticed you were quiet.' I touched her arm. 'What a fury you might have been, but you're Phuong—you are no fury.'

'I had to think,' she said, and I remembered how waking in the night I had told from the irregularity of her breathing that she was not asleep. I'd put my arm out to her and asked her '*Le cauchemar?*' She used to suffer from nightmares when she first came to the rue Catinat, but last night she had shaken her head at the suggestion: her back was turned to me and I had moved my leg against her–the first move in the formula of intercourse. I had noticed nothing wrong even then.

'Can't you explain, Thomas, why . . .'

'Surely it's obvious enough. I wanted to keep her.'

'At any cost to her?'

'Of course.'

'That's not love.'

'Perhaps it's not your way of love, Pyle.'

'I want to protect her.'

'I don't. She doesn't need protection. I want her around, I want her in my bed.'

'Against her will?'

'She wouldn't stay against her will, Pyle.'

'She can't love you after this.' His ideas were as simple as that. I turned to look for her. She had gone through to the bedroom and was pulling the counterpane straight where I had lain; then she took one of her picture books from a shelf and sat on the bed as though she were quite unconcerned with our talk. I could tell what book it was–a pictorial record of the Queen's life. I could see upside-down the state coach on the way to Westminster.

'Love's a Western word,' I said. 'We use it for sentimental reasons or to cover up an obsession with one woman. These people don't suffer from obsessions. You're going to be hurt, Pyle, if you aren't careful.'

'I'd have beaten you up if it wasn't for that leg.'

'You should be grateful to me–and Phuong's sister, of course. You can go ahead without scruples now–and you are very scrupulous in some ways, aren't you, when it doesn't come to plastics.'

'Plastics?'

'I hope to God you know what you are doing there. Oh, I know your motives are good, they always are.' He looked puzzled and suspicious. 'I wish sometimes you had a few bad motives, you might understand a little more about human beings. And that applies to your country too, Pyle.'

'I want to give her a decent life. This place–smells.'

'We keep the smell down with joss sticks. I suppose you'll offer her a deep freeze and a car for herself and the newest television set and . . .'

'And children,' he said.

'Bright young American citizens ready to testify.'

'And what will you give her? You weren't going to take her home.'

'No, I'm not that cruel. Unless I can afford her a return ticket.'

'You'll just keep her as a comfortable lay until you leave.'

'She's a human being, Pyle. She's capable of deciding.'

'On faked evidence. And a child at that.'

'She's no child. She's tougher than you'll ever be. Do you know the kind of polish that doesn't take scratches? That's Phuong. She can survive a dozen of us. She'll get old, that's all. She'll suffer from childbirth and hunger and cold and rheumatism, but she'll never suffer like we do from thoughts, obsessions—she won't scratch, she'll only decay.' But even while I made my speech and watched her turn the page (a family group with Princess Anne), I knew I was inventing a character just as much as Pyle was. One never knows another human being; for all I could tell, she was as scared as the rest of us: she didn't have the gift of expression, that was all. And I remembered that first tormenting year when I had tried so passionately to understand her, when I had begged her to tell me what she thought and had scared her with my unreasoning anger at her silences. Even my desire had been a weapon, as though when one plunged one's sword towards the victim's womb, she would lose control and speak.

'You've said enough,' I told Pyle. 'You know all there is to know. Please go.'

'Phuong,' he called.

'Monsieur Pyle?' she inquired, looking up from the scrutiny of Windsor Castle, and her formality was comic and reassuring at that moment.

'He's cheated you.'

'*Je ne comprends pas.*'

'Oh, go away,' I said. 'Go to your Third Force and York Harding and the *Rôle of Democracy*. Go away and play with plastics.'

Later I had to admit that he had carried out my instructions to the letter.

PART III

CHAPTER I

I

It was nearly a fortnight after Pyle's death before I saw Vigot again. I was going up the Boulevard Charner when his voice called to me from Le Club. It was the restaurant most favoured in those days by members of the Sureté, who, as a kind of defiant gesture to those who hated them, would lunch and drink on the ground-floor while the general public fed upstairs out of the reach of a partisan with a hand-grenade. I joined him and he ordered me a vermouth cassis. 'Play for it?'

'If you like,' and I took out my dice for the ritual game of *Quatre Cent Vingt-et-un*. How those figures and the sight of dice bring back to mind the war-years in Indo-China. Anywhere in the world when I see two men dicing I am back in the streets of Hanoi or Saigon or among the blasted buildings of Phat Diem, I see the parachutists, protected like caterpillars by their strange markings, patrolling by the canals, I hear the sound of the mortars closing in, and perhaps I see a dead child.

'*Sans vaseline*,' Vigot said, throwing a four-two-one. He pushed the last match towards me. The sexual jargon of the game was common to all the Sureté; perhaps it had been invented by Vigot and taken up by his junior officers, who hadn't however taken up Pascal. '*Sous-lieutenant*.' Every game you lost raised you a rank—you played till one or other became a captain or a commandant. He won the second game as well and while he counted out the matches, he said, 'We've found Pyle's dog.'

'Yes?'

'I suppose it had refused to leave the body. Anyway they cut its throat. It was in the mud fifty yards away. Perhaps it dragged itself that far.'

'Are you still interested?'

'The American Minister keeps bothering us. We don't have the same trouble, thank God, when a Frenchman is killed. But then those cases don't have rarity value.'

We played for the division of matches and then the real game started. It was uncanny how quickly Vigot threw a four-two-one. He reduced his matches to three and I threw the lowest score possible. '*Nanette*,' Vigot said, pushing me over two matches. When he had got rid of his last match he said, '*Capitaine*,' and I called the waiter for drinks. 'Does anybody ever beat you?' I asked.

'Not often. Do you want your revenge?'

'Another time. What a gambler you could be, Vigot. Do you play any other game of chance?'

He smiled miserably, and for some reason I thought of that blonde wife of his who was said to betray him with his junior officers.

'Oh well,' he said, 'there's always the biggest of all.'

'The biggest?'

'"Let us weigh the gain and loss," he quoted, "in wagering that God is, let us estimate these two chances. If you gain, you gain all; if you lose you lose nothing."'

I quoted Pascal back at him—it was the only passage I remembered. '"Both he who chooses heads and he who chooses tails are equally at fault. They are both in the wrong. The true course is not to wager at all."'

'"Yes; but you must wager. It is not optional. You are embarked." You don't follow your own principles, Fowler. You're *engagé*, like the rest of us.'

'Not in religion.'

'I wasn't talking about religion. As a matter of fact,' he said, 'I was thinking about Pyle's dog.'

'Oh.'

'Do you remember what you said to me—about finding clues on its paws, analysing the dirt and so on?'

'And you said you weren't Maigret or Lecoq.'

'I've not done so badly after all,' he said. 'Pyle usually took the dog with him when he went out, didn't he?'

'I suppose so.'

'It was too valuable to let it stray by itself?'

'It wouldn't be very safe. They eat chows, don't they, in this country?' He began to put the dice in his pocket. 'My dice, Vigot.'

'Oh, I'm sorry. I was thinking . . .'

'Why did you say I was *engagé*?'

'When did you last see Pyle's dog, Fowler?'

'God knows. I don't keep an engagement-book for dogs.'

'When are you due to go home?'

'I don't know exactly.' I never like giving information to the police. It saves them trouble.

'I'd like—tonight—to drop in and see you. At ten? If you will be alone.'

'I'll send Phuong to the cinema.'

'Things all right with you again—with her?'

'Yes.'

'Strange. I got the impression that you are—well—unhappy.'

'Surely there are plenty of possible reasons for that, Vigot.' I added bluntly, 'You should know.'

'Me?'

'You're not a very happy man yourself.'

'Oh, I've nothing to complain about. "A ruined house is not miserable."'

'What's that?'

'Pascal again. It's an argument for being proud of misery. "A tree is not miserable."'

'What made you into a policeman, Vigot?'

'There were a number of factors. The need to earn a living, a curiosity about people, and—yes, even that, a love of Gaboriau.'

'Perhaps you ought to have been a priest.'

'I didn't read the right authors for that—in those days.'

'You still suspect me, don't you, of being concerned?'

He rose and drank what was left of his vermouth cassis.

'I'd like to talk to you, that's all.'

I thought after he had turned and gone that he had looked at me with compassion, as he might have looked at some prisoner, for whose capture he was responsible, undergoing his sentence for life.

2

I *had* been punished. It was as though Pyle, when he left my flat, had sentenced me to so many weeks of uncertainty. Every time that I returned home it was with the expectation of disaster. Sometimes Phuong would not be there, and I found it impossible to settle to any work till she returned, for I always wondered whether she would ever return. I would ask her where she had been (trying to keep anxiety or suspicion out of my voice) and sometimes she would reply the market or the shops and produce her piece of evidence (even her readiness to confirm her story seemed at that period unnatural), and sometimes it was the cinema, and the stub of her ticket was there to prove it, and sometimes it was her sister's—that was where I believed she met Pyle. I made love to her in those days savagely as though I hated her, but what I hated was the future. Loneliness lay in my bed and I took loneliness into my arms at night. She didn't change; she cooked for me, she made my pipes, she gently and sweetly laid out her body for my pleasure (but it was no longer a pleasure), and just as in those early days I wanted her mind, now I wanted to read her thoughts, but they were hidden away in a language I couldn't speak. I didn't want to question her. I didn't want to make her lie (as long as no lie was spoken openly I could pretend that we were the same to each other as we had always been), but suddenly my anxiety would speak for me, and I said, 'When did you last see Pyle?'

She hesitated—or was it that she was really thinking back? 'When he came here,' she said.

I began—almost unconsciously—to run down everything that was American. My conversation was full of the poverty of American literature, the scandals of American politics, the beastliness of American children. It was as though she were being taken away from me by a nation rather than by a man. Nothing that America could do was right. I became a bore on the subject of America, even with my French friends who were ready enough to share my antipathies. It was as if I had been betrayed, but one is not betrayed by an enemy.

It was just at that time that the incident occurred of the bicycle bombs. Coming back from the Imperial Bar to an empty flat (was she at the cinema or with her sister?) I found that a note had been pushed under the door. It was from Dominguez. He apologised for being still sick and asked me to be outside the big store at the corner of the Boulevard Charner around ten-thirty the next morning. He was writing at the request of Mr Chou, but I suspected that Mr Heng was the more likely to require my presence.

The whole affair, as it turned out, was not worth more than a paragraph, and a humorous paragraph at that. It bore no relation to the sad and heavy war in the north, those canals in Phat Diem choked with the grey days-old bodies, the pounding of the mortars, the white glare of napalm. I had been waiting for about a quarter of an hour by a stall of flowers when a truck-load of police drove up with a grinding of brakes and a squeal of rubber from the direction of the Sureté Headquarters in the rue Catinat; the men disembarked and ran for the store, as though they were charging a mob, but there was no mob—only a zareba of bicycles. Every large building in Saigon is fenced in by them—no university city in the West contains so many bicycle-owners. Before I had time to adjust my camera the comic and inexplicable action had been accomplished. The police had forced their way among the bicycles and emerged with three which they carried over their heads into the boulevard and dropped into the decorative fountain. Before I could intercept a single policeman they were back in their truck and driving hard down the Boulevard Bonnard.

'*Operation Bicyclette*,' a voice said. It was Mr Heng.

'What is it?' I asked. 'A practise? For what?'

'Wait a while longer,' Mr Heng said.

A few idlers began to approach the fountain, where one wheel stuck up like a buoy as though to warn shipping away from the wrecks below: a policeman crossed the road shouting and waving his hands.

'Let's have a look,' I said.

'Better not,' Mr Heng said, and examined his watch. The hands stood at four minutes past eleven.

'You're fast,' I said.

'It always gains.' And at that moment the fountain exploded over the pavement. A bit of decorative coping struck a window and the glass fell like the water in a bright shower. Nobody was hurt. We shook the water and glass from our clothes. A bicycle wheel hummed like a top in the road, staggered and collapsed. 'It must be just eleven,' Mr Heng said.

'What on earth . . . ?'

'I thought you would be interested,' Mr Heng said, 'I *hope* you were interested.'

'Come and have a drink?'

'No, I am sorry. I must go back to Mr Chou's, but first let me show you something.' He led me to the bicycle park and unlocked his own machine. 'Look carefully.'

'A Raleigh,' I said.

'No, look at the pump. Does it remind you of anything?' He smiled patronisingly at my mystification and pushed off. Once he turned and waved his hand, pedalling towards Cholon and the warehouse of junk. At the Sureté, where I went for information, I realised what he meant. The mould I had seen in his warehouse had been shaped like a half-section of a bicycle-pump. That day all over Saigon innocent bicycle-pumps had proved to contain bombs which had gone off at the stroke of eleven, except where the police, acting on information that I suspect emanated from Mr Heng, had been able to anticipate the explosions. It was all quite trivial–ten explosions, six people slightly injured, and God knows how many bicycles. My colleagues–except for the correspondent of the *Extrême Orient*, who called it an 'outrage'–knew they could only get space by making fun of the affair. 'Bicycle Bombs' made a good headline. All of them blamed the Communists. I was the only one to write that the bombs were a demonstration on the part of General Thé, and my account was altered in the office. The General wasn't news. You couldn't waste space by identifying him. I sent a message of regret through Dominguez to Mr Heng–I had done my best. Mr Heng sent a polite verbal reply. It seemed to me then that he–or his Vietminh committee–had been unduly sensitive; no one held the affair seriously against the Communists. Indeed, if anything could have done so, it would have given them the reputation for a sense of humour. 'What'll they think of next?' people said at parties, and the whole absurd affair was symbolised for me too in the bicycle-wheel gaily spinning like a top in the middle of the boulevard. I never even mentioned to Pyle what I had heard of his connection with the General. Let him play harmlessly with plastic moulds: it might keep his mind off Phuong. All the same, because I happened to be in the neighbourhood one evening, because I had nothing better to do, I called in at Mr Muoi's garage.

It was a small, untidy place, not unlike a junk warehouse itself, in the Boulevard de la Somme. A car was jacked up in the middle of the floor with its bonnet open, gaping like the cast of some pre-historic animal in a provincial museum which nobody ever visits. I don't believe anyone remembered it was there. The floor was littered with scraps of iron and old boxes–the Vietnamese don't like throwing anything away, any more than a Chinese cook partitioning a duck into seven courses will dispense with so much as a claw. I wondered why anybody had so wastefully disposed of the empty drums and the damaged mould–perhaps it was a theft by an employee making a few piastres, perhaps somebody had been bribed by the ingenious Mr Heng.

Nobody seemed about, so I went in. Perhaps, I thought, they are keeping away for a while in case the police call. It was possible that Mr Heng had some contact in the Sureté, but even then it was unlikely that the police would act. It was better from their point of view to let people assume that the bombs were Communist.

Apart from the car and the junk strewn over the concrete floor there was nothing to be seen. It was difficult to picture how the bombs could have been manufactured at Mr Muoi's. I was very vague about how one turned the white dust I had seen in the drum into plastic, but surely the process was too complex to be carried out here, where even the two petrol pumps in the street seemed to be suffering from neglect. I stood in the entrance and looked out into the street. Under the trees in the centre of the boulevard the barbers were at work: a scrap of mirror nailed to a tree-trunk caught the flash of the sun. A girl went by at a trot under her mollusc hat carrying two baskets slung on a pole. The fortune-teller squatting against the wall of Simon Frères had found a customer, an old man with a whisp of beard like Ho Chi Minh's who watched impassively the shuffling and turning of the ancient cards. What possible future had he got that was worth a piastre? In the Boulevard de la Somme you lived in the open; everybody here knew all about Mr Muoi, but the police had no key which would unlock their confidence. This was the level of life where everything was known, but you couldn't step down to that level as you could step into the street. I remembered the old women gossiping on our landing beside the communal lavatory: they heard everything too, but I didn't know what they knew.

I went back into the garage and entered a small office at the back. There was the usual Chinese commercial calendar, a littered desk—price-lists and a bottle of gum and an adding-machine, some paper-clips, a teapot and three cups and a lot of unsharpened pencils, and for some reason an unwritten picture-postcard of the Eiffel Tower. York Harding might write in graphic abstractions about the Third Force, but this was what it came down to—this was It. There was a door in the back wall; it was locked, but the key was on the desk among the pencils. I opened the door and went through.

I was in a small shed about the size of the garage. It contained one piece of machinery that at first sight seemed like a cage of rods and wires furnished with innumerable perches to hold some wingless adult bird—it gave the impression of being tied up with old rags, but the rags had probably been used for cleaning when Mr Muoi and his assistants had been called away. I found the name of a manufacturer—somebody in Lyons and a patent number—patenting what? I switched on the current and the old machine came alive: the rods had a purpose—the contraption was like an old man gathering his last vital force, pounding down his fist, pounding down . . . This thing was still a press, though in its own sphere it must have belonged to the same era as the nickelodeon, but I suppose that in this country where nothing was ever wasted, and where everything might be expected to come one day to finish its career (I remembered seeing that ancient movie *The Great Train Robbery* jerking its way across a screen, giving entertainment, in a back-street in Nam Dinh), the press was still employable.

I examined the press more closely; there were traces of a white powder. Diolacton, I thought, something in common with milk. There was no sign of a drum or a mould. I went back into the office and into the garage. I felt like giving the old car a pat on the mudguard; it had a long wait ahead of it, perhaps, but it too one day . . . Mr Muoi and his assistants were probably by this time somewhere among the rice-fields on the way to the sacred mountain where General Thé had his headquarters. When now at last I raised my voice and called 'Monsieur Muoi!' I could imagine I was far away from the garage and the boulevard and the barbers, back among those fields where I had taken refuge on the road to Tanyin. 'Monsieur Muoi!' I could see a man turn his head among the stalks of rice.

I walked home and up on my landing the old women burst into their twitter of the hedges which I could understand no more than the gossip of the birds. Phuong was not in—only a note to say that she was with her sister. I lay down on the bed—I still tired easily—and fell asleep. When I woke I saw the illuminated dial of my alarm pointing to one twenty-five and I turned my head expecting to find Phuong asleep beside me. But the pillow was undented. She must have changed the sheet that day—it carried the coldness of the laundry. I got up and opened the drawer where she kept her scarves, and they were not there. I went to the bookshelf–the pictorial Life of the Royal Family had gone too. She had taken her dowry with her.

In the moment of shock there is little pain; pain began about three a.m. when I began to plan the life I had still somehow to live and to remember memories in order somehow to eliminate them. Happy memories are the worst, and I tried to remember the unhappy. I was practised. I had lived all this before. I knew I could do what was necessary, but I was so much older–I felt I had little energy left to reconstruct.

3

I went to the American Legation and asked for Pyle. It was necessary to fill in a form at the door and give it to a military policeman. He said, 'You haven't put the purpose of the visit.'

'He'll know,' I said.

'You're by appointment, then?'

'You can put it that way if you like.'

'Seems silly to you, I guess, but we have to be very careful. Some strange types come around here.'

'So I've heard.' He shifted his chewing-gum to another side and entered the lift. I waited. I had no idea what to say to Pyle. This was a scene I had never played before. The policeman returned. He said grudgingly, 'I guess you can go up. Room 12A. First floor.'

When I entered the room I saw that Pyle wasn't there. Joe sat behind the desk: the Economic Attaché: I still couldn't remember his surname. Phuong's sister watched me from behind a typing desk. Was it triumph that I read in those brown acquisitive eyes?

'Come in, come in, Tom,' Joe called boisterously. 'Glad to see you. How's your leg? We don't often get a visit from you to our little outfit. Pull up a chair. Tell me how you think the new offensive's going. Saw Granger last night at the Continental. He's for the north again. That boy's *keen*. Where there's news there's Granger. Have a cigarette. Help yourself. You know Miss Hei? Can't remember all these names–too hard for an old fellow like me. I call her "Hi, there!"–she likes it. None of this stuffy colonialism. What's the gossip of the market, Tom? You fellows certainly do keep your ears to the ground. Sorry to hear about your leg. Alden told me . . .'

'Where's Pyle?'

'Oh, Alden's not in the office this morning. Guess he's at home. Does a lot of his work at home.'

'I know what he does at home.'

'That boy's keen. Eh, what's that you said?'

'Anyway, I know one of the things he does at home.'

'I don't catch on, Tom. Slow Joe–that's me. Always was. Always will be.'

'He sleeps with my girl–your typist's sister.'

'I don't know what you mean.'

'Ask her. She fixed it. Pyle's taken my girl.'

'Look here, Fowler, I thought you'd come here on business. We can't have scenes in the office, you know.'

'I came here to see Pyle, but I suppose he's hiding.'

'Now, you're the very last man who ought to make a remark like that. After what Alden did for you.'

'Oh yes, yes, of course. He saved my life, didn't he? But I never asked him to.'

'At great danger to himself. That boy's got guts.'

'I don't care a damn about his guts. There are other parts of his body that are more àpropos.'

'Now we can't have any innuendoes like that, Fowler, with a lady in the room.'

'The lady and I know each other well. She failed to get her rake-off from me, but she's getting it from Pyle. All right. I know I'm behaving badly, and I'm going to go on behaving badly. This is a situation where people do behave badly.'

'We've got a lot of work to do. There's a report on the rubber output . . .'

'Don't worry, I'm going. But just tell Pyle if he phones that I called. He might think it polite to return the visit.' I said to Phuong's sister, 'I hope you've had the settlement witnessed by the notary public and the American Consul and the Church of Christ Scientist.'

I went into the passage. There was a door opposite me marked Men. I went in and locked the door and sitting with my head against the cold wall I cried. I hadn't cried until now. Even their lavatories were air-conditioned, and presently the temperate tempered air dried my tears as it dries the spit in your mouth and the seed in your body.

4

I left affairs in the hands of Dominguez and went north. At Haiphong I had friends in the Squadron Gascogne, and I would spend hours in the bar up at the airport, or playing bowls on the gravel-path outside. Officially I was at the front: I could qualify for keenness with Granger, but it was of no more value to my paper than had been my excursion to Phat Diem. But if one writes about war, self-respect demands that occasionally one shares the risks.

It wasn't easy to share them for even the most limited period, since orders had gone out from Hanoi that I was to be allowed only on horizontal raids—raids in this war as safe as a journey by bus, for we flew above the range of the heavy machine-gun; we were safe from anything but a pilot's error or a fault in the engine. We went out by time-table and came home by time-table: the cargoes of bombs sailed diagonally down and the spiral of smoke blew up from the road-junction or the bridge, and then we cruised back for the hour of the aperitif and drove our iron bowls across the gravel.

One morning in the mess in the town, as I drank brandies-and-sodas with a young officer who had a passionate desire to visit Southend Pier, orders for a mission came in. 'Like to come?' I said yes. Even a horizontal raid would be a way of killing time and killing thought. Driving out to the airport he remarked, 'This is a vertical raid.'

'I thought I was forbidden . . .'

'So long as you write nothing about it. It will show you a piece of country up near the Chinese border you will not have seen before. Near Lai Chau.'

'I thought all was quiet there–and in French hands?'

'It was. They captured this place two days ago. Our parachutists are only a few hours away. We want to keep the Viets head down in their holes until we have recaptured the post. It means low diving and machine-gunning. We can only spare two planes–one's on the job now. Ever dive-bombed before?'

'No.'

'It is a little uncomfortable when you are not used to it.'

The Gascogne Squadron possessed only small B.26 bombers–the French called them prostitutes because with their short wing-span they had no visible means of support. I was crammed on to a little metal pad the size of a bicycle seat with my knees against the navigator's back. We came up the Red River, slowly climbing, and the Red River at this hour was really red. It was as though one had gone far back in time and saw it with the old geographer's eyes who had named it first, at just such an hour when the late sun filled it from bank to bank; then we turned away at 9,000 feet towards the Black River, really black, full of shadows, missing the angle of the light, and the huge majestic scenery of gorge and cliff and jungle wheeled around and stood upright below us. You could have dropped a squadron into those fields of green and grey and left no more trace than a few coins in a harvest-field. Far ahead of us a small plane moved like a midge. We were taking over.

We circled twice above the tower and the green-encircled village, then corkscrewed up into the dazzling air. The pilot–who was called Trouin–turned to me and winked. On his wheel were the studs that controlled the gun and the bomb-chamber. I had that loosening of the bowels, as we came into position for the dive, that accompanies any new experience–the first dance, the first dinner-party, the first love. I was reminded of the Great Racer at the Wembley Exhibition when it came to the top of the rise–there was no way to get out: you were trapped with your experience. On the dial I had just time to read 3,000 metres when we drove down. All was feeling now, nothing was sight. I was forced up against the navigator's back: it was as though something of enormous weight were pressing on my chest. I wasn't aware of the moment when the bombs were released; then the gun chattered and the cockpit was full of the smell of cordite, and the weight was off my chest as we rose, and it was the stomach that fell away, spiralling down like a suicide to the ground we had left. For forty seconds Pyle had not existed: even loneliness hadn't existed. As we climbed in a great arc I could see the smoke through the side window pointing at me. Before the second dive I felt fear–fear of humiliation, fear of vomiting over the navigator's back, fear that my ageing lungs would not stand the pressure. After the tenth dive I was aware only of irritation–the affair had gone on too long, it was time to go home. And again we shot steeply up out of machine-gun range and swerved away and the smoke pointed. The village was surrounded on all sides by mountains. Every time we had to make the same approach, through the same gap. There was no way to vary our attack. As we dived for the fourteenth time I thought, now that I was free from the fear of humiliation, "They have only to fix one machine-gun into position." We lifted our nose again into the safe air—perhaps they didn't even have a gun. The forty minutes of the patrol had seemed interminable, but it had been free from the discomfort of personal thought. The sun was sinking as we turned for home: the geographer's moment had passed: the Black River was no longer black, and the Red River was only gold.

Down we went again, away from the gnarled and fissured forest towards the river, flattening out over the neglected rice-fields, aimed like a bullet at one small sampan on the yellow stream. The cannon gave a single burst of tracer, and the sampan blew apart in a shower of sparks: we didn't even wait to see our victims struggling to survive, but climbed and made for home. I thought again as I had thought when I saw the dead child at Phat Diem, "I hate war," There had been something so shocking in our sudden fortuitous choice of a prey—we had just happened to be passing, one burst only was required, there was no one to return our fire, we were gone again, adding our little quota to the world's dead.

I put on my earphones for Captain Trouin to speak to me. He said, 'We will make a little detour. The sunset is wonderful on the *calcaire*. You must not miss it,' he added kindly, like a host who is showing the beauty of his estate, and for a hundred miles we trailed the sunset over the Baie d'Along. The helmeted Martian face looked wistfully out, down the golden groves among the great humps and arches of porous stone, and the wounds of murder ceased to bleed.

5

Captain Trouin insisted that night on being my host in the opium house, though he would not smoke himself. He liked the smell, he said, he liked the sense of quiet at the end of the day, but in his profession relaxation could go no further. There were officers who smoked, but they were Army men—he had to have his sleep. We lay in a small cubicle in a row of cubicles like a dormitory at school, and the Chinese proprietor prepared my pipes. I hadn't smoked since Phuong left me. Across the way a *métisse* with long and lovely legs lay coiled after her smoke reading a glossy woman's paper, and in the cubicle next to her two middle-aged Chinese transacted business, sipping tea, their pipes laid aside.

I said, 'That sampan—this evening—was it doing any harm?'

Trouin said, 'Who knows? In those reaches of the river we have orders to shoot up anything in sight.'

I smoked my first pipe. I tried not to think of all the pipes I had smoked at home. Trouin said, 'Today's affair—that is not the worst for someone like myself. Over the village they could have shot us down. Our risk was as great as theirs. What I detest is napalm bombing. From 3,000 feet, in safety.' He made a hopeless gesture. 'You see the forest catching fire. God knows what you would see from the ground. The poor devils are burnt alive, the flames go over them like water. They are wet through with fire.' He said with anger against a whole world that didn't understand, 'I'm not fighting a colonial war. Do you think I'd do these things for the planters of Terre Rouge? I'd rather be court-martialled. We are fighting all of your wars, but you leave us the guilt.'

'That sampan,' I said.

'Yes, that sampan too.' He watched me as I stretched out for my second pipe. 'I envy you your means of escape.'

'You don't know what I'm escaping from. It's not from the war. That's no concern of mine. I'm not involved.'

'You will all be. One day.'

'Not me.'

'You are still limping.'

'They had the right to shoot at me, but they weren't even doing that. They were knocking down a tower. One should always avoid demolition squads. Even in Piccadilly.'

'One day something will happen. You will take a side.'

'No, I'm going back to England.'

'That photograph you showed me once . . .'

'Oh, I've torn that one up. She left me.'

'I'm sorry.'

'It's the way things happen. One leaves people oneself and then the tide turns. It almost makes me believe in justice.'

'I do. The first time I dropped napalm I thought, this is the village where I was born. That is where M. Dubois, my father's old friend, lives. The baker—I was very fond of the baker when I was a child—is running away down there in the flames I've thrown. The men of Vichy did not bomb their own country. I felt worse than them.'

'But you still go on.'

'Those are moods. They come only with the napalm. The rest of the time I think that I am defending Europe. And you know, those others—they do some monstrous things also. When they were driven out of Hanoi in 1946 they left terrible relics among their own people—people they thought had helped us. There was one girl in the mortuary—they had not only cut off her breasts, they had mutilated her lover and stuffed his . . .'

'That's why I won't be involved.'

'It's not a matter of reason or justice. We all get involved in a moment of emotion and then we cannot get out. War and Love—they have always been compared.' He looked sadly across the dormitory to where the *métisse* sprawled in her great temporary peace. He said, 'I would not have it otherwise. *There* is a girl who was involved by her parents—what is her future when this port falls? France is only half her home . . .'

'Will it fall?'

'You are a journalist. You know better than I do that we can't win. You know the road to Hanoi is cut and mined every night. You know we lose one class of St Cyr every year. We were nearly beaten in '50. De Lattre has given us two years of grace—that's all. But we are professionals: we have to go on fighting till the politicians tell us to stop. Probably they will get together and agree to the same peace that we could have had at the beginning, making nonsense of all these years.' His ugly face which had winked at me before the dive wore a kind of professional brutality like a Christmas mask from which a child's eyes peer through the holes in the paper. 'You would not understand the nonsense, Fowler. You are not one of us.'

'There are other things in one's life which make nonsense of the years.'

He put his hand on my knee with an odd protective gesture as though he were the older man. 'Take her home,' he said. 'That is better than a pipe.'

'How do you know she would come?'

'I have slept with her myself, and Lieutenant Perrin. Five hundred piastres.'

'Expensive.'

'I expect she would go for three hundred, but under the circumstances one does not care to bargain.'

But his advice did not prove sound. A man's body is limited in the acts which it can perform and mine was frozen by memory. What my hands touched that night might be more beautiful than I was used to, but we are not trapped only by beauty. She used the same perfume, and suddenly at the moment of entry the ghost of what I'd lost proved more powerful than the body stretched at my disposal. I moved away and lay on my back and desire drained out of me.

'I am sorry,' I said, and lied, 'I don't know what is the matter with me.'

She said with great sweetness and misunderstanding, 'Don't worry. It often happens that way. It is the opium.'

'Yes,' I said, 'the opium.' And I wished to heaven that it had been.

CHAPTER 2

I

It was strange, this first return to Saigon with nobody to welcome me. At the airport I wished there were somewhere else to which I could direct my taxi than the rue Catinat. I thought to myself: "Is the pain a little less than when I went away?" and tried to persuade myself that it was so. When I reached the landing I saw that the door was open, and I became breathless with an unreasonable hope. I walked very slowly towards the door. Until I reached the door hope would remain alive. I heard a chair creak, and when I came to the door I could see a pair of shoes, but they were not a woman's shoes. I went quickly in, and it was Pyle who lifted his awkward weight from the chair Phuong used to use.

He said, 'Hullo, Thomas.'

'Hullo, Pyle. How did you get in?'

'I met Dominguez. He was bringing your mail. I asked him to let me stay.'

'Has Phuong forgotten something?'

'Oh no, but Joe told me you'd been to the Legation. I thought it would be easier to talk here.'

'What about?'

He gave a lost gesture, like a boy put up to speak at some school function who cannot find the grown-up words. 'You've been away?'

'Yes. And you?'

'Oh, I've been travelling around.'

'Still playing with plastics?'

He grinned unhappily. He said, 'Your letters are over there.'

I could see at a glance there was nothing which could interest me now: there was one from my office in London and several that looked like bills, and one from my bank. I said, 'How's Phuong?'

His face lit up automatically like one of those electric toys which respond to a particular sound. 'Oh, she's fine,' he said, and then clamped his lips together as though he'd gone too far.

'Sit down, Pyle,' I said. 'Excuse me while I look at this. It's from my office.'

I opened it. How inopportunely the unexpected can occur. The editor wrote that he had considered my last letter and that in view of the confused situation in Indo-China, following the death of General de Lattre and the retreat from Hoa Binh, he was in agreement with my suggestion. He had appointed a temporary foreign editor and would like me to stay on in Indo-China for at least another year. 'We shall keep the chair warm for you,' he reassured me with complete incomprehension. He believed I cared about the job, and the paper.

I sat down opposite Pyle and re-read the letter which had come too late. For a moment I had felt elation as on the instant of waking before one remembers.

'Bad news?' Pyle asked.

'No.' I told myself that it wouldn't have made any difference anyway: a reprieve for one year couldn't stand up against a marriage settlement.

'Are you married yet?' I asked.

'No.' He blushed—he had a great facility in blushing. 'As a matter of fact I'm hoping to get special leave. Then we could get married at home—properly.'

'Is it more proper when it happens at home?'

'Well, I thought—it's difficult to say these things to you, you are so darned cynical, Thomas, but it's a mark of respect. My father and mother would be there—she'd kind of enter the family. It's important in view of the past.'

'The past?'

'You know what I mean. I wouldn't want to leave her behind there with any stigma . . .'

'Would you leave her behind?'

'I guess so. My mother's a wonderful woman—she'd take her around, introduce her, you know, kind of fit her in. She'd help her to get a home ready for me.'

I didn't know whether to feel sorry for Phuong or not—she had looked forward so to the skyscrapers and the Statue of Liberty, but she had so little idea of all they would involve, Professor and Mrs Pyle, the women's lunch clubs; would they teach her Canasta? I thought of her that first night in the Grand Monde, in her white dress, moving so exquisitely on her eighteen-year-old feet, and I thought of her a month ago, bargaining over meat at the butcher's stores in the Boulevard de la Somme. Would she like those bright clean little New England grocery stores where even the celery was wrapped in cellophane? Perhaps she would. I couldn't tell. Strangely I found myself saying as Pyle might have done a month ago, 'Go easy with her, Pyle. Don't force things. She can be hurt like you or me.'

'Of course, of course, Thomas.'

'She looks so small and breakable and unlike our women, but don't think of her as—as an ornament.'

'It's funny, Thomas, how differently things work out. I'd been dreading this talk. I thought you'd be tough.'

'I've had time to think, up in the north. There was a woman there. . . . Perhaps I saw what you saw at that whorehouse. It's a good thing she went away with you. I might one day have left her behind with someone like Granger. A piece of tail.'

'And we can remain friends, Thomas?'

'Yes, of course. Only I'd rather not see Phuong. There's quite enough of her around here as it is. I must find another flat—when I've got time.'

He unwound his legs and stood up. I'm so glad, Thomas. I can't tell you how glad I am. I've said it before, I know, but I do really wish it hadn't been you.'

'I'm glad it's you, Pyle.' The interview had not been the way I had foreseen: under the superficial angry schemes, at some deeper level, the genuine plan of action must have been formed. All the time that his innocence had angered me, some judge within myself had summed up in his favour, had compared his idealism, his half-baked ideas founded on the works of York Harding, with my cynicism. Oh, I was right about the facts, but wasn't he right too to be young and mistaken, and wasn't he perhaps a better man for a girl to spend her life with?

We shook hands perfunctorily, but some half-formulated fear made me follow him out to the head of the stairs and call after him. Perhaps there is a prophet as well as a judge in those interior courts where our true decisions are made. 'Pyle, don't trust too much in York Harding.'

'York!' He stared up at me from the first landing.

'We are the old colonial peoples, Pyle, but we've learnt a bit of reality, we've learned not to play with matches. This Third Force—it comes out of a book, that's all. General Thé's only a bandit with a few thousand men: he's not a national democracy.'

It was as if he had been staring at me through a letterbox to see who was there and now, letting the flap fall, had shut out the unwelcome intruder. His eyes were out of sight. 'I don't know what you mean, Thomas.'

'Those bicycle bombs. They were a good joke, even though one man did lose a foot. But, Pyle, you can't trust men like Thé. They aren't going to save the East from Communism. We know their kind.'

'We?'

'The old colonialists.'

'I thought you took no sides.'

'I don't, Pyle, but if someone has got to make a mess of things in your outfit, leave it to Joe. Go home with Phuong. Forget the Third Force.'

'Of course I always value your advice, Thomas,' he said formally. 'Well, I'll be seeing you.'

'I suppose so.'

The weeks moved on, but somehow I hadn't yet found myself a new flat. It wasn't that I hadn't time. The annual crisis of the war had passed again: the hot wet *crachin* had settled on the north: the French were out of Hoa Binh, the rice-campaign was over in Tonkin and the opium-campaign in Laos. Dominguez could cover easily all that was needed in the south. At last I did drag myself to see one apartment in a so-called modern building (Paris Exhibition 1934?) up at the other end of the rue Catinat beyond the Continental Hotel. It was the Saigon pied-à-terre of a rubber planter who was going home. He wanted to sell it lock, stock and barrel. I have always wondered what the barrels contain: as for the stock, there were a large number of engravings from the Paris Salon between 1880 and 1900. Their highest common factor was a big-bosomed woman with an extraordinary hair-do and gauzy draperies which somehow always exposed the great cleft buttocks and hid the field of battle. In the bathroom the planter had been rather more daring with his reproductions of Rops.

'You like art?' I asked and he smirked back at me like a fellow conspirator. He was fat with a little black moustache and insufficient hair.

'My best pictures are in Paris,' he said.

There was an extraordinary tall ash-tray in the living-room made like a naked woman with a bowl in her hair, and there were china ornaments of naked girls embracing tigers, and one very odd one of a girl stripped to the waist riding a bicycle. In the bedroom facing his enormous bed was a great glazed oil painting of two girls sleeping together. I asked him the price of his apartment without his collection, but he would not agree to separate the two.

'You are not a collector?' he asked.

'Well, no.'

'I have some books also,' he said, 'which I would throw in, though I intended to take these back to France.' He unlocked a glass-fronted bookcase and showed me his library—there were expensive illustrated editions of *Aphrodite* and *Nana*, there was *La Garçonne*, and even several Paul de Kocks. I was tempted to ask him whether he would sell himself with his collection: he went with them: he was period too. He said, 'If you live alone in the tropics a collection is company.'

I thought of Phuong just because of her complete absence. So it always is: when you escape to a desert the silence shouts in your ear.

'I don't think my paper would allow me to buy an art-collection.'

He said, 'It would not, of course, appear on the receipt.'

I was glad Pyle had not seen him: the man might have lent his features to Pyle's imaginary 'old colonialist', who was repulsive enough without him. When I came out it was nearly half past eleven and I went down as far as the Pavillon for a glass of iced beer. The Pavillon was a coffee centre for European and American women and I was confident that I would not see

Phuong there. Indeed I knew exactly where she would be at this time of day—she was not a girl to break her habits, and so, coming from the planter's apartment, I had crossed the road to avoid the milk-bar where at this time of day she had her chocolate malt. Two young American girls sat at the next table, neat and clean in the heat, scooping up ice-cream. They each had a bag slung on the left shoulder and the bags were identical, with brass eagle badges. Their legs were identical too, long and slender, and their noses, just a shade tilted, and they were eating their ice-cream with concentration as though they were making an experiment in the college laboratory. I wondered whether they were Pyle's colleagues: they were charming, and I wanted to send them home, too. They finished their ices and one looked at her watch. 'We'd better be going,' she said, 'to be on the safe side.' I wondered idly what appointment they had.

'Warren said we musn't stay later than eleven-twenty-five.'

'It's past that now.'

'It would be exciting to stay. I don't know what it's all about, do you?'

'Not exactly, but Warren said better not.'

'Do you think it's a demonstration?'

'I've seen so many demonstrations,' the other said wearily, like a tourist glutted with churches. She rose and laid on their table the money for the ices. Before going she looked around the café, and the mirrors caught her profile at every freckled angle. There was only myself left and a dowdy middle-aged Frenchwoman who was carefully and uselessly making up her face. Those two hardly needed make-up, the quick dash of lipstick, a comb through the hair. For a moment her glance had rested on me—it was not like a woman's glance, but a man's, very straightforward, speculating on some course of action. Then she turned quickly to her companion. 'We'd better be off.' I watched them idly as they went out side by side into the sun-splintered street. It was impossible to conceive either of them a prey to untidy passion: they did not belong to rumpled sheets and the sweat of sex. Did they take deodorants to bed with them? I found myself for a moment envying them their sterilised world, so different from this world that I inhabited—which suddenly inexplicably broke in pieces. Two of the mirrors on the wall flew at me and collapsed halfway. The dowdy Frenchwoman was on her knees in a wreckage of chairs and tables. Her compact lay open and unhurt in my lap and oddly enough I sat exactly where I had sat before, although my table had joined the wreckage around the Frenchwoman. A curious garden-sound filled the café: the regular drip of a fountain, and looking at the bar I saw rows of smashed bottles, which let out their contents in a multi-coloured stream—the red of porto, the orange of cointreau, the green of chartreuse, the cloudy yellow of pastis, across the floor of the café. The Frenchwoman sat up and calmly looked around for her compact. I gave it her and she thanked me formally, sitting on the floor. I realised that I didn't hear her very well. The explosion had been so close that my ear-drums had still to recover from the pressure.

I thought rather petulantly, "Another joke with plastics: what does Mr Heng expect me to write now?" but when I got into the Place Garnier, I realised by the heavy clouds of smoke that this was no joke. The smoke came from the cars burning in the car-park in front of the national theatre, bits of cars were scattered over the square, and a man without his legs lay twitching at the edge of the ornamental gardens. People were crowding in from the rue Catinat, from the Boulevard Bonnard. The sirens of police-cars, the bells of the ambulances and fire-engines came at one remove to my shocked ear-drums. For one moment I had forgotten that Phuong must have been in the milk-bar on the other side of the square. The smoke lay between. I couldn't see through.

I stepped out into the square and a policeman stopped me. They had formed a cordon round the edge to prevent the crowd increasing, and already the stretchers were beginning to emerge. I implored the policeman in front of me, 'Let me across. I have a friend . . .'

'Stand back,' he said. 'Everybody here has friends.'

He stood on one side to let a priest through, and I tried to follow the priest, but he pulled me back. I said, 'I am the Press,' and searched in vain for the wallet in which I had my card, but I couldn't find it: had I come out that day without it? I said, 'At least tell me what happened to the milk-bar': the smoke was clearing and I tried to see, but the crowd between was too great. He said something I didn't catch.

'What did you say?'

He repeated, 'I don't know. Stand back. You are blocking the stretchers.'

Could I have dropped my wallet in the Pavillon? I turned to go back and there was Pyle. He exclaimed, 'Thomas.'

'Pyle,' I said, 'for Christ's sake, where's your Legation pass? We've got to get across. Phuong's in the milk-bar.'

'No, no,' he said.

'Pyle, she is. She always goes there. At eleven thirty. We've got to find her.'

'She isn't there, Thomas.'

'How do you know? Where's your card?'

'I warned her not to go.'

I turned back to the policeman, meaning to throw him to one side and make a run for it across the square: he might shoot: I didn't care—and then the word 'warn' reached my consciousness. I took Pyle by the arm. 'Warn?' I said. 'What do you mean "warn"?'

'I told her to keep away this morning.'

The pieces fell together in my mind. 'And Warren?' I said, 'Who's Warren? He warned those girls too.'

'I don't understand.'

'There mustn't be any American casualties, must there?' An ambulance forced its way up the rue Catinat into the square and the policeman who had stopped me moved to one side to let it through. The policeman beside him was engaged in an argument. I pushed Pyle forward and ahead of me into the square before we could be stopped.

We were among a congregation of mourners. The police could prevent others entering the square; they were powerless to clear the square of the survivors and the first-comers. The doctors were too busy to attend to the dead, and so the dead were left to their owners, for one can own the dead as one owns a chair. A woman sat on the ground with what was left of her baby in her lap; with a kind of modesty she had covered it with her straw peasant hat. She was still and silent, and what struck me most in the square was the silence. It was like a church I had once visited during Mass—the only sounds came from those who served, except where here and there the Europeans wept and implored and fell silent again as though shamed by the modesty, patience and propriety of the East. The legless torso at the edge of the garden still twitched, like a chicken which has lost its head. From the man's shirt, he had probably been a trishaw driver.

Pyle said, 'It's awful.' He looked at the wet on his shoes and said in a sick voice, 'What's that?'

'Blood,' I said. 'Haven't you ever seen it before?'

He said, 'I must get them cleaned before I see the Minister.' I don't think he knew what he was saying. He was seeing a real war for the first time: he had punted down into Phat Diem in a kind of schoolboy dream, and anyway in his eyes soldiers didn't count.

I forced him, with my hand on his shoulder, to look around. I said, 'This is the hour when the place is always full of women and children—it's the shopping hour. Why choose that of all hours?'

He said weakly, 'There was to have been a parade.'

'And you hoped to catch a few colonels. But the parade was cancelled yesterday, Pyle.'

'I didn't know.'

'Didn't know!' I pushed him into a patch of blood where a stretcher had lain. 'You ought to be better informed.'

'I was out of town,' he said, looking down at his shoes. 'They should have called it off.'

'And missed the fun?' I asked him. 'Do you expect General Thé to lose his demonstration? This is better than a parade. Women and children are news, and soldiers aren't, in a war. This will hit the world's Press. You've put General Thé on the map all right, Pyle. You've got the Third Force and National Democracy all over your right shoe. Go home to Phuong and tell her about your heroic dead—there are a few dozen less of her people to worry about.'

A small fat priest scampered by, carrying something on a dish under a napkin. Pyle had been silent a long while, and I had nothing more to say. Indeed I had said too much already. He looked white and beaten and ready to faint, and I thought, "What's the good? he'll always be innocent, you can't blame the innocent, they are always guiltless. All you can do is control them or eliminate them. Innocence is a kind of insanity."

He said, 'Thé wouldn't have done this. I'm sure he wouldn't. Somebody deceived him. The Communists . . .'

He was impregnably armoured by his good intentions and his ignorance. I left him standing in the square and went on up the rue Catinat to where the hideous pink Cathedral blocked the way. Already people were flocking in: it must have been a comfort to them to be able to pray for the dead to the dead.

Unlike them, I had reason for thankfulness, for wasn't Phuong alive? Hadn't Phuong been 'warned'? But what I remembered was the torso in the square, the baby on its mother's lap. They had not been warned: they had not been sufficiently important. And if the parade had taken place would they not have been there just the same, out of curiosity, to see the soldiers, and hear the speakers, and throw the flowers? A two-hundred-pound bomb does not discriminate. How many dead colonels justify a child's or a trishaw driver's death when you are building a national democratic front? I stopped a motor-trishaw and told the driver to take me to the Quai Mytho.

PART IV

CHAPTER I

I had given Phuong money to take her sister to the cinema so that she would be safely out of the way. I went out to dinner myself with Dominguez and was back in my room waiting when Vigot called sharp on ten. He apologised for not taking a drink–he said he was too tired and a drink might send him to sleep. It had been a very long day.

'Murder and sudden death?'

'No. Petty thefts. And a few suicides. These people love to gamble and when they have lost everything they kill themselves. Perhaps I would not have become a policeman if I had known how much time I would have to spend in mortuaries. I do not like the smell of ammonia. Perhaps after all I will have a beer.'

'I haven't a refrigerator, I'm afraid.'

'Unlike the mortuary. A little English whisky, then?'

I remembered the night I had gone down to the mortuary with him and they had slid out Pyle's body like a tray of ice-cubes.

'So you are not going home?' he asked.

'You've been checking up?'

'Yes.'

I held the whisky out to him, so that he could see how calm my nerves were. 'Vigot, I wish you'd tell me why you think I was concerned in Pyle's death. Is it a question of motive? That I wanted Phuong back? Or do you imagine it was revenge for losing her?'

'No. I'm not so stupid. One doesn't take one's enemy's book as a souvenir. There it is on your shelf. *The Rôle of the West*. Who is this York Harding?'

'He's the man you are looking for, Vigot. He killed Pyle–at long range.'

'I don't understand.'

'He's a superior sort of journalist–they call them diplomatic correspondents. He gets hold of an idea and then alters every situation to fit the idea. Pyle came out here full of York Harding's idea. Harding had been here once for a week on his way from Bangkok to Tokyo. Pyle made the mistake of putting his idea into practice. Harding wrote about a Third Force. Pyle formed one–a shoddy little bandit with two thousand men and a couple of tame tigers. He got mixed up.'

'You never do, do you?'

'I've tried not to be.'

'But you failed, Fowler.' For some reason I thought of Captain Trouin and that night which seemed to have happened years ago in the Haiphong opium house. What was it he had said? something about all of us getting involved sooner or later in a moment of emotion. I said, 'You would have made a good priest, Vigot. What is it about you that would make it so easy to confess—if there were anything to confess?'

'I have never wanted any confessions.'

'But you've received them?'

'From time to time.'

'Is it because like a priest it's your job not to be shocked, but to be sympathetic? "M. Flic, I must tell you exactly why I battered in the old lady's skull." "Yes, Gustave, take your time and tell me why it was."'

'You have a whimsical imagination. Aren't you drinking, Fowler?'

'Surely it's unwise for a criminal to drink with a police officer?'

'I have never said you were a criminal.'

'But suppose the drink unlocked even in me the desire to confess? There are no secrets of the confessional in your profession.'

'Secrecy is seldom important to a man who confesses: even when it's to a priest. He has other motives.'

'To cleanse himself?'

'Not always. Sometimes he only wants to see himself clearly as he is. Sometimes he is just weary of deception. You are not a criminal, Fowler, but I would like to know why you lied to me. You saw Pyle the night he died.'

'What gives you that idea?'

'I don't for a moment think you killed him. You would hardly have used a rusty bayonet.'

'Rusty?'

'Those are the kind of details we get from an autopsy. I told you, though, that was not the cause of death. Dakow mud.' He held out his glass for another whisky. 'Let me see now. You had a drink at the Continental at six ten?'

'Yes.'

'And at six forty-five you were talking to another journalist at the door of the Majestic?'

'Yes, Wilkins. I told you all this, Vigot, before. That night.'

'Yes. I've checked up since then. It's wonderful how you carry such petty details in your head.'

'I'm a reporter, Vigot.'

'Perhaps the times are not quite accurate, but nobody could blame you, could they, if you were a quarter of an hour out here and ten minutes out there. You had no reason to think the times important. Indeed how suspicious it would be if you had been completely accurate.'

'Haven't I been?'

'Not quite. It was at five to seven that you talked to Wilkins.'

'Another ten minutes.'

'Of course. As I said. And it had only just struck six when you arrived at the Continental.'

'My watch is always a little fast,' I said. 'What time do you make it now?'

'Ten eight.'

'Ten eighteen by mine. You see.'

He didn't bother to look. He said. 'Then the time you said you talked to Wilkins was twenty-five minutes out–by your watch. That's quite a mistake, isn't it?'

'Perhaps I readjusted the time in my mind. Perhaps I'd corrected my watch that day. I sometimes do.'

'What interests me,' Vigot said, '(could I have a little more soda?–you have made this rather strong) is that you are not at all angry with me. It is not very nice to be questioned as I am questioning you.'

'I find it interesting, like a detective-story. And, after all, you know I didn't kill Pyle–you've said so.'

Vigot said, 'I know you were not present at his murder.'

'I don't know what you hope to prove by showing that I was ten minutes out here and five there.'

'It gives a little space,' Vigot said, 'a little gap in time.'

'Space for what?'

'For Pyle to come and see you.'

'Why do you want so much to prove that?'

'Because of the dog,' Vigot said.

'And the mud between its toes?'

'It wasn't mud. It was cement. You see, somewhere that night, when it was following Pyle, it stepped into wet cement. I remembered that on the ground-floor of the apartment there are builders at work–they are still at work. I passed them tonight as I came in. They work long hours in this country.'

'I wonder how many houses have builders in them–and wet cement. Did any of them remember the dog?'

'Of course I asked them that. But if they had they would not have told me. I am the police.' He stopped talking and leant back in his chair, staring at his glass. I had a sense that some analogy had struck him and he was miles away in thought. A fly crawled over the back of his hand and he did not brush it away–any more than Dominguez would have done. I had the feeling of some force immobile and profound. For all I knew, he might have been praying.

I rose and went through the curtains into the bedroom. There was nothing I wanted there, except to get away for a moment from that silence sitting in a chair. Phuong's picture-books were back on the shelf. She had stuck a telegram for me up among the cosmetics–some message or other from the London office. I wasn't in the mood to open it. Everything was as it had been before Pyle came. Rooms don't change, ornaments stand where you place them: only the heart decays.

I returned to the sitting-room and Vigot put the glass to his lips. I said, 'I've got nothing to tell you. Nothing at all.'

'Then I'll be going,' he said. 'I don't suppose I'll trouble you again.'

At the door he turned as though he were unwilling to abandon hope–his hope or mine. 'That was a strange picture for you to go and see that night. I wouldn't have thought you cared for costume drama. What was it? *Robin Hood*?'

'*Scaramouche*, I think. I had to kill time. And I needed distraction.'

'Distraction?'

'We all have our private worries, Vigot,' I carefully explained.

When Vigot was gone there was still an hour to wait for Phuong and living company. It was strange how disturbed I had been by Vigot's visit. It was as though a poet had brought me his work to criticise and through some careless action I had destroyed it. I was a man without a vocation—one cannot seriously consider journalism as a vocation, but I could recognise a vocation in another. Now that Vigot was gone to close his uncompleted file, I wished I had the courage to call him back and say, 'You are right. I did see Pyle the night he died.'

CHAPTER 2

I

On the way to the Quai Mytho I passed several ambulances driving out of Cholon heading for the Place Garnier. One could almost reckon the pace of rumour from the expression of the faces in the street, which at first turned on someone like myself coming from the direction of the Place with looks of expectancy and speculation. By the time I entered Cholon I had outstripped the news: life was busy, normal, uninterrupted: nobody knew.

I found Mr Chou's godown and mounted to Mr Chou's house. Nothing had changed since my last visit. The cat and the dog moved from floor to cardboard box to suitcase, like a couple of chess knights who cannot get to grips. The baby crawled on the floor, and the two old men were still playing mah jongg. Only the young people were absent. As soon as I appeared in the doorway one of the women began to pour out tea. The old lady sat on the bed and looked at her feet.

'Monsieur Heng,' I asked. I shook my head at the tea: I wasn't in the mood to begin another long course of that trivial bitter brew. 'Il faut absolument que je voie Monsieur Heng.' It seemed impossible to convey to them the urgency of my request, but perhaps the very abruptness of my refusal of tea caused some disquiet. Or perhaps like Pyle I had blood on my shoes. Anyway after a short delay one of the women led me out and down the stairs, along two bustling bannered streets and left me before what they would have called I suppose in Pyle's country a 'funeral parlour', full of stone jars in which the resurrected bones of the Chinese dead are eventually placed. 'Monsieur Heng,' I said to an old Chinese in the doorway, 'Monsieur Heng.' It seemed a suitable halting place on a day which had begun with the planter's erotic collection and continued with the murdered bodies in the square. Somebody called from an inner room and the Chinese stepped aside and let me in.

Mr Heng himself came cordially forward and ushered me into a little inner room lined with the black carved uncomfortable chairs you find in every Chinese anteroom, unused, unwelcoming. But I had the sense that on this occasion the chairs had been employed, for there were five little tea-cups on the table, and two were not empty. 'I have interrupted a meeting,' I said.

'A matter of business,' Mr Heng said evasively, 'of no importance. I am always glad to see you, Mr Fowler.'

'I've come from the Place Garnier,' I said.

'I thought that was it.'

'You've heard . . .'

'Someone telephoned to me. It was thought best that I keep away from Mr Chou's for a while. The police will be very active today.'

'But you had nothing to do with it.'

'It is the business of the police to find a culprit.'

'It was Pyle again,' I said.

'Yes.'

'It was a terrible thing to do.'

'General Thé is not a very controlled character.'

'And bombs aren't for boys from Boston. Who is Pyle's chief, Heng?'

'I have the impression that Mr Pyle is very much his own master.'

'What is he? O.S.S.?'

'The initial letters are not very important. I think now they are different.'

'What can I do, Heng? He's got to be stopped.'

'You can publish the truth. Or perhaps you cannot?'

'My paper's not interested in General Thé. They are only interested in your people, Heng.'

'You really want Mr Pyle stopped, Mr Fowler?'

'If you'd seen him, Heng. He stood there and said it was all a sad mistake, there should have been a parade. He said he'd have to get his shoes cleaned before he saw the Minister.'

'Of course, you could tell what you know to the police.'

'They aren't interested in Thé either. And do you think they would dare to touch an American? He has diplomatic privileges. He's a graduate of Harvard. The Minister's very fond of Pyle. Heng, there was a woman there whose baby—she kept it covered under her straw hat. I can't get it out of my head. And there was another in Phat Diem.'

'You must try to be calm, Mr Fowler.'

'What'll he do next, Heng?'

'Would you be prepared to help us, Mr Fowler?'

'He comes blundering in and people have to die for his mistakes. I wish your people had got him on the river from Nam Dinh. It would have made a lot of difference to a lot of lives.'

'I agree with you, Mr Fowler. He has to be restrained. I have a suggestion to make.' Somebody coughed delicately behind the door, then noisily spat. He said, 'If you would invite him to dinner tonight at the Vieux Moulin. Between eight-thirty and nine-thirty.'

'What good . . . ?'

'We would talk to him on the way,' Heng said.

'He may be engaged.'

'Perhaps it would be better if you asked him to call on you—at six-thirty. He will be free then: he will certainly come. If he is able to have dinner with you, take a book to your window as though you want to catch the light.'

'Why the Vieux Moulin?'

'It is by the bridge to Dakow—I think we shall be able to find a spot and talk undisturbed.'

'What will you do?'

'You do not want to know that, Mr Fowler. But I promise you we will act as gently as the situation allows.'

The unseen friends of Heng shifted like rats behind the wall. 'Will you do this for us, Mr Fowler?'

'I don't know,' I said, 'I don't know.'

'Sooner or later,' Heng said, and I was reminded of Captain Trouin speaking in the opium house, 'one has to take sides. If one is to remain human.'

2

I left a note at the Legation asking Pyle to come and then I went up the street to the Continental for a drink. The wreckage was all cleared away; the fire-brigade had hosed the square. I had no idea then how the time and the place would become important. I even thought of sitting there throughout the evening and breaking my appointment. Then I thought that perhaps I could frighten Pyle into inactivity by warning him of his danger–whatever his danger was, and so I finished my beer and went home, and when I reached home I began to hope that Pyle would not come. I tried to read, but there was nothing on my shelves to hold the attention. Perhaps I should have smoked, but there was no one to prepare my pipe. I listened unwillingly for footsteps and at last they came. Somebody knocked. I opened the door, but it was only Dominguez.

I said, 'What do you want, Dominguez?'

He looked at me with an air of surprise. 'Want?' He looked at his watch. 'This is the time I always come. Have you any cables?'

'I'm sorry–I'd forgotten. No.'

'But a follow-up on the bomb? Don't you want something filed?'

'Oh, work one out for me, Dominguez. I don't know how it is–being there on the spot, perhaps I got a bit shocked. I can't think of the thing in terms of a cable.' I hit out at a mosquito which came droning at my ear and saw Dominguez wince instinctively at my blow. 'It's all right, Dominguez, I missed it.' He grinned miserably. He could not justify this reluctance to take life: after all he was a Christian–one of those who had learnt from Nero how to make human bodies into candles.

'Is there anything I can do for you?' he asked. He didn't drink, he didn't eat meat, he didn't kill–I envied him the gentleness of his mind.

'No, Dominguez. Just leave me alone tonight.' I watched him from the window, going away across the rue Catinat. A trishaw driver had parked beside the pavement opposite my window; Dominguez tried to engage him, but the man shook his head. Presumably he was waiting for a client in one of the shops, for this was not a parking place for trishaws. When I looked at my watch it was strange to see that I had been waiting for little more than ten minutes, and, when Pyle knocked, I hadn't even heard his step.

'Come in.' But as usual it was the dog that came in first.

'I was glad to get your note, Thomas. This morning I thought you were mad at me.'

'Perhaps I was. It wasn't a pretty sight.'

'You know so much now, it won't hurt to tell you a bit more. I saw Thé this afternoon.'

'Saw him? Is he in Saigon? I suppose he came to see how his bomb worked.'

'That's in confidence, Thomas. I dealt with him very severely.' He spoke like the captain of a school-team who has found one of his boys breaking his training. All the same I asked him with a certain hope, 'Have you thrown him over?'

'I told him that if he made another uncontrolled demonstration we would have no more to do with him.'

'But haven't you finished with him already, Pyle?' I pushed impatiently at his dog which was nosing around my ankles.

'I can't. (Sit down, Duke.) In the long run he's the only hope we have. If he came to power with our help, we could rely on him . . .'

'How many people have to die before you realise . . . ?' But I could tell that it was a hopeless argument.

'Realise what, Thomas?'

'That there's no such thing as gratitude in politics.'

'At least they won't hate us like they hate the French.'

'Are you sure? Sometimes we have a kind of love for our enemies and sometimes we feel hate for our friends.'

'You talk like a European, Thomas. These people aren't complicated.'

'Is that what you've learned in a few months? You'll be calling them childlike next.'

'Well—in a way.'

'Find me an uncomplicated child, Pyle. When we are young we are a jungle of complications. We simplify as we get older.' But what good was it to talk to him? There was an unreality in both our arguments. I was becoming a leader-writer before my time. I got up and went to the bookshelf.

'What are you looking for, Thomas?'

'Oh, just a passage I used to be fond of. Can you have dinner with me, Pyle?'

'I'd love to, Thomas. I'm so glad you aren't mad any longer. I know you disagree with me, but we can disagree, can't we, and be friends?'

'I don't know. I don't think so.'

'After all, Phuong was much more important than this.'

'Do you really believe that, Pyle?'

'Why, she's the most important thing there is. To me. And to you, Thomas.'

'Not to me any longer.'

'It was a terrible shock today, Thomas, but in a week, you'll see, we'll have forgotten it. We are looking after the relatives too.'

'We?'

'We've wired to Washington. We'll get permission to use some of our funds.'

I interrupted him. 'The Vieux Moulin? Between nine and nine-thirty?'

'Where you like, Thomas.' I went to the window. The sun had sunk below the roofs. The trishaw driver still waited for his fare. I looked down at him and he raised his face to me.

'Are you waiting for someone, Thomas?'

'No. There was just a piece I was looking for.' To cover my action I read, holding the book up to the last light:

> *'I drive through the streets and I care not a damn,*
> *The people they stare, and they ask who I am;*
> *And if I should chance to run over a cad,*
> *I can pay for the damage if ever so bad.*
> *So pleasant it is to have money, heigh ho!*
> *So pleasant it is to have money.'*

'That's a funny kind of poem,' Pyle said with a note of disapproval.

'He was an adult poet in the nineteenth century. There weren't so many of them.' I looked down into the street again. The trishaw driver had moved away.

'Have you run out of drink?' Pyle asked.

'No, but I thought you didn't . . .'

'Perhaps I'm beginning to loosen up,' Pyle said. 'Your influence. I guess you're good for me, Thomas.'

I got the bottle and glasses — I forgot one of them the first journey and then I had to go back for water. Everything that I did that evening took a long time. He said, 'You know, I've got a wonderful family, but maybe they were a little on the strict side. We have one of those old houses in Chestnut Street, as you go up the hill on the right-hand side. My mother collects glass, and my father — when he's not eroding his old cliffs — picks up all the Darwin manuscripts and association-copies he can. You see, they live in the past. Maybe that's why York made such an impression on me. He seemed kind of open to modern conditions. My father's an isolationist.'

'Perhaps I would like your father,' I said. 'I'm an isolationist too.'

For a quiet man Pyle that night was in a talking mood. I didn't hear all that he said, for my mind was elsewhere. I tried to persuade myself that Mr Heng had other means at his disposal but the crude and obvious one. But in a war like this, I knew, there is no time to hesitate: one uses the weapon to hand — the French the napalm bomb, Mr Heng the bullet or the knife. I told myself too late that I wasn't made to be a judge — I would let Pyle talk awhile and then I would warn him. He could spend the night at my house. They would hardly break in there. I think he was speaking of the old nurse he had had — 'She really meant more to me than my mother, and the blueberry pies she used to make!' when I interrupted him. 'Do you carry a gun now — since that night?'

'No. We have orders in the Legation . . .'

'But you're on special duties?'

'It wouldn't do any good — if they wanted to get me, they always could. Anyway I'm as blind as a coot. At college they called me Bat — because I could see in the dark as well as they could. Once when we were fooling around . . .' He was off again. I returned to the window.

A trishaw driver waited opposite. I wasn't sure–they looked so much alike, but I thought he was a different one. Perhaps he really had a client. It occurred to me that Pyle would be safest at the Legation. They must have laid their plans, since my signal, for later in the evening: something that involved the Dakow bridge. I couldn't understand why or how: surely he would not be so foolish as to drive through Dakow after sunset and our side of the bridge was always guarded by armed police.

'I'm doing all the talking,' Pyle said. 'I don't know how it is, but somehow this evening . . .'

'Go on,' I said, 'I'm in a quiet mood, that's all. Perhaps we'd better cancel that dinner.'

'No, don't do that. I've felt cut off from you, since . . . well . . .'

'Since you saved my life,' I said and couldn't disguise the bitterness of my self-inflicted wound.

'No, I didn't mean that. All the same how we talked, didn't we, that night? As if it was going to be our last. I learned a lot about you, Thomas. I don't agree with you, mind, but for you maybe it's right–not being involved. You kept it up all right, even after your leg was smashed you stayed neutral.'

'There's always a point of change,' I said. 'Some moment of emotion . . .'

'You haven't reached it yet. I doubt if you ever will. And I'm not likely to change either–except with death,' he added merrily.

'Not even with this morning? Mightn't that change a man's views?'

'They were only war casualties,' he said. 'It was a pity, but you can't always hit your target. Anyway they died in the right cause.'

'Would you have said the same if it had been your old nurse with her blueberry pie?'

He ignored my facile point. 'In a way you could say they died for democracy,' he said.

'I wouldn't know how to translate that into Vietnamese.' I was suddenly very tired. I wanted him to go away quickly and die. Then I could start life again–at the point before he came in.

'You'll never take me seriously, will you, Thomas?' he complained, with that schoolboy gaiety which he seemed to have kept up his sleeve for this night of all nights. 'I tell you what–Phuong's at the cinema–what about you and me spending the whole evening together? I've nothing to do now.' It was as though someone from outside were directing him how to choose his words in order to rob me of any possible excuse. He went on, 'Why don't we go to the Chalet? I haven't been there since that night. The food is just as good as the Vieux Moulin, and there's music.'

I said, 'I'd rather not remember that night.'

'I'm sorry. I'm a dumb fool sometimes, Thomas. What about a Chinese dinner in Cholon?'

'To get a good one you have to order in advance. Are you scared of the Vieux Moulin, Pyle? It's well wired and there are always police on the bridge. And you wouldn't be such a fool, would you, as to drive through Dakow?'

'It wasn't that. I just thought it would be fun tonight to make a long evening of it.'

He made a movement and upset his glass, which smashed upon the floor. 'Good luck,' he said mechanically. 'I'm sorry, Thomas.' I began to pick up the pieces and pack them into the ash-tray. 'What about it, Thomas?' The smashed glass reminded me of the bottles in the Pavillon bar dripping their contents. 'I warned Phuong I might be out with you.' How badly chosen was the word 'warn'. I picked up the last piece of glass. 'I have got an engagement at the Majestic,' I said, 'and I can't manage before nine.'

'Well, I guess I'll have to go back to the office. Only I'm always afraid of getting caught.'

There was no harm in giving him that one chance. 'Don't mind being late,' I said. 'If you do get caught, look in here later. I'll come back at ten, if you can't make dinner, and wait for you.'

'I'll let you know . . .'

'Don't bother. Just come to the Vieux Moulin—or meet me here.' I handed back the decision to that Somebody in whom I didn't believe: You can intervene if You want to: a telegram on his desk: a message from the Minister. You cannot exist unless you have the power to alter the future. 'Go away now, Pyle. There are things I have to do.' I felt a strange exhaustion, hearing him go away and the pad of his dog's paws.

3

There were no trishaw drivers nearer than the rue d'Ormay when I went out. I walked down to the Majestic and stood awhile watching the unloading of the American bombers. The sun had gone and they worked by the light of arc-lamps. I had no idea of creating an alibi, but I told Pyle I was going to the Majestic and I felt an unreasoning dislike of telling more lies than were needed.

'Evening, Fowler.' It was Wilkins.

'Evening.'

'How's the leg?'

'No trouble now.'

'Got a good story filed?'

'I left it to Dominguez.'

'Oh, they told me you were there.'

'Yes, I was. But space is tight these days. They won't want much.'

'The spice has gone out of the dish, hasn't it?' Wilkins said. 'We ought to have lived in the days of Russell and the old *Times*. Dispatches by balloon. One had time to do some fancy writing then. Why, he'd even have made a column out of *this*. The luxury hotel, the bombers, night falling. Night never falls nowadays, does it, at so many piastres a word.' From far up in the sky you could faintly hear the noise of laughter: somebody broke a glass as Pyle had done. The sound fell on us like icicles. "The lamps shone o'er fair women and brave men," Wilkins malevolently quoted. 'Doing anything tonight, Fowler? Care for a spot of dinner?'

'I'm dining as it is. At the Vieux Moulin.'

'I wish you joy. Granger will be there. They ought to advertise special

Granger nights. For those who like background noise.'

I said good-night to him and went into the cinema next door–Errol Flynn, or it may have been Tyrone Power (I don't know how to distinguish them in tights), swung on ropes and leapt from balconies and rode bareback into technicolour dawns. He rescued a girl and killed his enemy and led a charmed life. It was what they call a film for boys, but the sight of Œdipus emerging with his bleeding eyeballs from the palace at Thebes would surely give a better training for life today. No life is charmed. Luck had been with Pyle at Phat Diem and on the road from Tanyin, but luck doesn't last, and they had two hours to see that no charm worked. A French soldier sat beside me with his hand in a girl's lap, and I envied the simplicity of his happiness or his misery, whichever it might be. I left before the film was over and took a trishaw to the Vieux Moulin.

The restaurant was wired in against grenades and two armed policemen were on duty at the end of the bridge. The *patron*, who had grown fat on his own rich Burgundian cooking, let me through the wire himself. The place smelt of capons and melting butter in the heavy evening heat.

'Are you joining the party of M. Granjair?' he asked me.

'No.'

'A table for one?' It was then for the first time that I thought of the future and the questions I might have to answer. 'For one,' I said, and it was almost as though I had said aloud that Pyle was dead.

There was only one room and Granger's party occupied a large table at the back; the *patron* gave me a small one closest to the wire. There were no window-panes, for fear of splintered glass. I recognised a few of the people Granger was entertaining, and I bowed to them before I sat down: Granger himself looked away. I hadn't seen him for months–only once since the night Pyle fell in love. Perhaps some offensive remark I had made that evening had penetrated the alcoholic fog, for he sat scowling at the head of the table while Madame Desprez, the wife of a public-relations officer, and Captain Duparc of the Press Liaison Service nodded and becked. There was a big man whom I think was an *hôtelier* from Pnom Penh and a French girl I'd never seen before and two or three other faces that I had only observed in bars. It seemed for once to be a quiet party.

I ordered a pastis because I wanted to give Pyle time to come–plans go awry and so long as I did not begin to eat my dinner it was as though I still had time to hope. And then I wondered what I hoped for. Good luck to the O.S.S. or whatever his gang were called? Long life to plastic bombs and General Thé? Or did I–I of all people–hope for some kind of miracle: a method of discussion arranged by Mr Héng which wasn't simply death? How much easier it would have been if we had both been killed on the road from Tanyin. I sat for twenty minutes over my pastis and then I ordered dinner. It would soon be half past nine: he wouldn't come now.

Against my will I listened: for what? a scream? a shot? some movement by the police outside? but in any case I would probably hear nothing, for Granger's party was warming up. The *hôtelier*, who had a pleasant untrained voice, began to sing and as a new champagne cork popped others joined in, but not Granger. He sat there with raw eyes glaring across the room at me. I wondered if there would be a fight: I was no match for Granger.

They were singing a sentimental song, and as I sat hungerless over my apology for a *Chapon duc Charles* I thought, for almost the first time since I had known that she was safe, of Phuong. I remembered how Pyle, sitting on the floor waiting for the Viets, had said, 'She seems fresh like a flower,' and I had flippantly replied, 'Poor flower.' She would never see New England now or learn the secrets of Canasta. Perhaps she would never know security: what right had I to value her less than the dead bodies in the square? Suffering is not increased by numbers: one body can contain all the suffering the world can feel. I had judged like a journalist in terms of quantity and I had betrayed my own principles; I had become as *engagé* as Pyle, and it seemed to me that no decision would ever be simple again. I looked at my watch and it was nearly a quarter to ten. Perhaps, after all, he had been caught; perhaps that 'someone' in whom he believed had acted on his behalf and he sat now in his Legation room fretting at a telegram to decode, and soon he would come stamping up the stairs to my room in the rue Catinat. I thought, "If he does I shall tell him everything."

Granger suddenly got up from his table and came at me. He didn't even see the chair in his way and he stumbled and laid his hand on the edge of my table. 'Fowler,' he said, 'come outside.' I laid enough notes down and followed him. I was in no mood to fight with him, but at that moment I would not have minded if he had beaten me unconscious. We have so few ways in which to assuage the sense of guilt.

He leant on the parapet of the bridge and the two policemen watched him from a distance. He said, 'I've got to talk to you, Fowler.'

I came within striking distance and waited. He didn't move. He was like an emblematic statue of all I thought I hated in America—as ill-designed as the Statue of Liberty and as meaningless. He said without moving, 'You think I'm pissed. You're wrong.'

'What's up, Granger?'

'I got to talk to you, Fowler. I don't want to sit there with those Frogs tonight. I don't like you, Fowler, but you talk English. A kind of English.' He leant there, bulky and shapeless in the half-light, an unexplored continent.

'What do you want, Granger?'

'I don't like Limies,' Granger said. 'I don't know why Pyle stomachs you. Maybe it's because he's Boston. I'm Pittsburgh and proud of it.'

'Why not?'

'There you are again.' He made a feeble attempt to mock my accent. 'You all talk like poufs. You're so damned superior. You think you know everything.'

'Good-night, Granger. I've got an appointment.'

'Don't go, Fowler. Haven't you got a heart? I can't talk to those Froggies.'

'You're drunk.'

'I've had two glasses of champagne, that's all, and wouldn't you be drunk in my place? I've got to go north.'

'What's wrong in that?'

'Oh, I didn't tell you, did I? I keep on thinking everyone knows. I got a cable this morning from my wife.'

'Yes?'

'My son's got polio. He's bad.'

'I'm sorry.'

'You needn't be. It's not your kid.'

'Can't you fly home?'

'I can't. They want a story about some damned mopping-up operations near Hanoi and Connolly's sick.' (Connolly was his assistant.)

'I'm sorry, Granger. I wish I could help.'

'It's his birthday tonight. He's eight at half past ten our time. That's why I laid on a party with champagne before I knew. I had to tell someone, Fowler, and I can't tell these Froggies.'

'They can do a lot for polio nowadays.'

'I don't mind if he's crippled, Fowler. Not if he lives. Me, I'd be no good crippled, but he's got brains. Do you know what I've been doing in there while that bastard was singing? I was praying. I thought maybe if God wanted a life he could take mine.'

'Do you believe in a God, then?'

'I wish I did,' Granger said. He passed his whole hand across his face as though his head ached, but the motion was meant to disguise the fact that he was wiping tears away.

'I'd get drunk if I were you,' I said.

'Oh, no, I've got to stay sober. I don't want to think afterwards I was stinking drunk the night my boy died. My wife can't drink, can she?'

'Can't you tell your paper . . . ?'

'Connolly's not really sick. He's off after a bit of tail in Singapore. I've got to cover for him. He'd be sacked if they knew.' He gathered his shapeless body together. 'Sorry I kept you, Fowler. I just had to tell someone. Got to go in now and start the toasts. Funny it happened to be you, and you hate my guts.'

'I'd do your story for you. I could pretend it was Connolly.'

'You wouldn't get the accent right.'

'I don't dislike you, Granger. I've been blind to a lot of things . . .'

'Oh, you and me, we're cat and dog. But thanks for the sympathy.'

Was I so different from Pyle, I wondered? Must I too have my foot thrust in the mess of life before I saw the pain? Granger went inside and I could hear the voices rising to greet him. I found a trishaw and was pedalled home. There was nobody there, and I sat and waited till midnight. Then I went down into the street without hope and found Phuong there.

CHAPTER 3

'Has Monsieur Vigot been to see you?' Phuong asked.

'Yes. He left a quarter of an hour ago. Was the film good?' She had already laid out the tray in the bedroom and now she was lighting the lamp.

'It was very sad,' she said, 'but the colours were lovely. What did Monsieur Vigot want?'

'He wanted to ask me some questions.'

'What about?'

'This and that. I don't think he will bother me again.'

'I like films with happy endings best,' Phuong said. 'Are you ready to smoke?'

'Yes.' I lay down on the bed and Phuong set to work with her needle. She said, 'They cut off the girl's head.'

'What a strange thing to do.'

'It was in the French Revolution.'

'Oh. Historical. I see.'

'It was very sad all the same.'

'I can't worry much about people in history.'

'And her lover—he went back to his garret—and he was miserable and he wrote a song—you see, he was a poet, and soon all the people who had cut off the head of his girl were singing his song. It was the Marseillaise.'

'It doesn't sound very historical,' I said.

'He stood there at the edge of the crowd while they were singing, and he looked very bitter and when he smiled you knew he was even more bitter and that he was thinking of her. I cried a lot and so did my sister.'

'Your sister? I can't believe it.'

'She is very sensitive. That horrid man Granger was there. He was drunk and he kept on laughing. But it was not funny at all. It was sad.'

'I don't blame him,' I said. 'He has something to celebrate. His son's out of danger. I heard today at the Continental. I like happy endings too.'

After I had smoked two pipes I lay back with my neck on the leather pillow and rested my hand in Phuong's lap. 'Are you happy?'

'Of course,' she said carelessly. I hadn't deserved a more considered answer.

'It's like it used to be,' I lied, 'a year ago.'

'Yes.'

'You haven't bought a scarf for a long time. Why don't you go shopping tomorrow?'

'It is a feast day.'

'Oh yes, of course. I forgot.'

'You have not opened your telegram,' Phuong said.

'No, I'd forgotten that too. I don't want to think about work tonight. And it's too late to file anything now. Tell me more about the film.'

'Well, her lover tried to rescue her from prison. He smuggled in boy's clothes and a man's cap like the one the gaoler wore, but just as she was passing the gate all her hair fell down and they called out "*Une aristocrate, une aristocrate*". I think that was a mistake in the story. They ought to have let her escape. Then they would both have made a lot of money with his song and they would have gone abroad to America—or England,' she added with what she thought was cunning.

'I'd better read the telegram,' I said. 'I hope to God I don't have to go north tomorrow. I want to be quiet with you.'

She loosed the envelope from among the pots of cream and gave it to me. I opened it and read: 'Have thought over your letter again stop am acting irrationally as you hoped stop have told my lawyer start divorce proceedings grounds desertion stop God bless you affectionately Helen.'

'Do you have to go?'

'No,' I said, 'I don't have to go. I'll read it to you. Here's your happy ending.'

She jumped from the bed. 'But it is wonderful. I must go and tell my sister. She will be so pleased. I will say to her, "Do you know who I am? I am the second Mrs Fowlair."'

Opposite me in the bookcase *The Rôle of the West* stood out like a cabinet portait—of a young man with a crew-cut and a black dog at his heels. He could harm no one any more. I said to Phuong, 'Do you miss him much?'

'Who?'

'Pyle.' Strange how even now, even to her, it was impossible to use his first name.

'Can I go please? My sister will be so excited.'

'You spoke his name once in your sleep.'

'I never remember my dreams.'

'There was so much you could have done together. He was young.'

'You are not old.'

'The skyscrapers. The Empire State Building.'

She said with a small hesitation, 'I want to see the Cheddar Gorge.'

'It isn't the Grand Canyon.' I pulled her down on to the bed. 'I'm sorry, Phuong.'

'What are you sorry for? It is a wonderful telegram. My sister . . .'

'Yes, go and tell your sister. Kiss me first.' Her excited mouth skated over my face, and she was gone.

I thought of the first day and Pyle sitting beside me at the Continental, with his eye on the soda-fountain across the way. Everything had gone right with me since he had died, but how I wished there existed someone to whom I could say that I was sorry.

March 1952–June 1955

LOSER
TAKES ALL

LOSER TAKES ALL

Dear Frere,

As we have been associated in business and
friendship for a quarter of a century I am dedicating
this frivolity without permission to you. Unlike some
of my Catholic critics, you, I know, when reading this
little story, will not mistake me for 'I', nor do I need to
explain to you that this tale has not been written for
the purposes of encouraging adultery, the use of
pyjama tops, or registry office marriages. Nor is it
meant to discourage gambling.

Affectionately and gratefully,

Graham Greene

PART I

I

I suppose the small greenish statue of a man in a wig on a horse is one of the famous statues of the world. I said to Cary, 'Do you see how shiny the right knee is? It's been touched so often for luck, like St Peter's foot in Rome.'

She rubbed the knee carefully and tenderly as though she were polishing it. 'Are you superstitious?' I said.

'Yes.'

'I'm not.'

'I'm so superstitious I never walk under ladders. I throw salt over my right shoulder. I try not to tread on the cracks in pavements. Darling, you're marrying the most superstitious woman in the world. Lots of people aren't happy. We are. I'm not going to risk a thing.'

'You've rubbed that knee so much, we ought to have plenty of luck at the tables.'

'I wasn't asking for luck at the tables,' she said.

2

That night I thought that our luck had begun in London two weeks before. We were to be married at St Luke's Church, Maida Hill, and we were going to Bournemouth for the honeymoon. Not, on the face of it, an exhilarating programme, but I thought I didn't care a damn where we went so long as Cary was there. Le Touquet was within our means, but we thought we could be more alone in Bournemouth–the Ramages and the Truefitts were going to Le Touquet. 'Besides, you'd lose all our money at the Casino,' Cary said, 'and we'd have to come home.'

'I know too much about figures. I live with them all day.'

'You won't be bored at Bournemouth?'

'No. I won't be bored.'

'I wish it wasn't your second honeymoon. Was the first very exciting–in Paris?'

'We could only afford a week-end,' I said guardedly.

'Did you love her a terrible lot?'

'Listen,' I said, 'it was more than fifteen years ago. You hadn't started school. I couldn't have waited all that time for you.'

'But did you?'

'The night after she left me I took Ramage out to dinner and stood him the best champagne I could get. Then I went home and slept for nine hours right across the bed. She was one of those people who kick at night and then say you are taking up too much room.'

'Perhaps I'll kick.'

'That would feel quite different. I hope you'll kick. Then I'll know you are there. Do you realize the terrible amount of time we'll waste asleep, not knowing a thing? A quarter of our life.'

It took her a long time to calculate that. She wasn't good at figures as I was. 'More,' she said, 'much more. I like ten hours.'

'That's even worse,' I said. 'And eight hours at the office without you. And food—this awful business of having meals.'

'I'll try to kick,' she said.

That was at lunch-time the day when our so-called luck started. We used to meet as often as we could for a snack at the Volunteer which was just round the corner from my office—Cary drank cider and had an unquenchable appetite for cold sausages. I've seen her eat five and then finish off with a hard-boiled egg.

'If we were rich,' I said, 'you wouldn't have to waste time cooking.'

'But think how much more time we'd waste eating. These sausages—look, I'm through already. We shouldn't even have finished the caviare.'

'And then the *sole meunière*,' I said.

'A little fried spring chicken with new peas.'

'A *soufflé Rothschild*.'

'Oh, don't be rich, please,' she said. 'We mightn't like each other if we were rich. Like me growing fat and my hair falling out . . .'

'That wouldn't make any difference.'

'Oh yes, it would,' she said. 'You know it would,' and the talk suddenly faded out. She was not too young to be wise, but she was too young to know that wisdom shouldn't be spoken aloud when you are happy.

I went back to the huge office block with its glass, glass, glass, and its dazzling marble floor and its pieces of modern carving in alcoves and niches like statues in a Catholic church. I was the assistant accountant (an ageing assistant accountant) and the very vastness of the place made promotion seem next to impossible. To be raised from the ground floor I would have to be a piece of sculpture myself.

In little uncomfortable offices in the city people die and people move on: old gentlemen look up from steel boxes and take a Dickensian interest in younger men. Here, in the great operational room with the computers ticking and the tape machines clicking and the soundless typewriters padding, you felt there was no chance for a man who hadn't passed staff college. I hadn't time to sit down before a loudspeaker said, 'Mr Bertram wanted in Room 10.' (That was me.)

'Who lives in Room 10?' I asked.

Nobody knew. Somebody said, 'It must be on the eighth floor.' (He spoke with awe as though he were referring to the peak of Everest–the eighth floor was as far as the London County Council regulations in those days allowed us to build towards Heaven.)

'Who lives in Room 10?' I asked the liftman again.

'Don't you know?' he said sourly: 'How long have you been here?'

'Five years.'

We began to mount. He said, 'You ought to know who lives in Room 10.'

'But I don't.'

'Five years and you don't know that.'

'Be a good chap and tell me.'

'Here you are. Eighth floor, turn left.' As I got out, he said gloomily, 'Not know Room 10!' He relented as he shut the gates. 'Who do you think? The Gom, of course.'

Then I began to walk very slowly indeed.

I have no belief in luck. I am not superstitious, but it is impossible, when you have reached forty and are conspicuously unsuccessful, not sometimes to half-believe in a malign providence. I had never met the Gom: I had only seen him twice; there was no reason so far as I could tell why I should ever see him again. He was elderly; he would die first, I would contribute grudgingly to a memorial. But to be summoned from the ground floor to the eighth shook me. I wondered what terrible mistake could justify a reprimand in Room 10; it seemed to be quite possible that our wedding now would never take place at St Luke's, nor our fortnight at Bournemouth. In a way I was right.

3

The Gom was called the Gom by those who disliked him and by all those too far removed from him for any feeling at all. He was like the weather–unpredictable. When a new tape machine was installed, or new computers replaced the old reliable familiar ones, you said, 'The Gom, I suppose,' before settling down to learn the latest toy. At Christmas little typewritten notes came round, addressed personally to each member of the staff (it must have given the typing pool a day's work, but the signature below the seasonal greeting, Herbert Dreuther, was rubber stamped). I was always a little surprised that the letter was not signed Gom. At that season of bonuses and cigars, unpredictable in amount, you sometimes heard him called by his full name, the Grand Old Man.

And there was something grand about him with his mane of white hair, his musician's head. Where other men collected pictures to escape death duties, he collected for pleasure. For a month at a time he would disappear in his yacht with a cargo of writers and actresses and oddments–a hypnotist, a man who had invented a new rose or discovered something about the endocrine glands. We on the ground floor, of course, would never have missed him: we should have known nothing about it if we had not read an account in the papers–the cheaper Sunday papers followed the progress of the yacht from port to port: they associated yachts with scandal, but there would never be any scandal on Dreuther's boat. He hated unpleasantness outside office hours.

I knew a little more than most from my position: diesel oil was included with wine under the general heading of Entertainment. At one time that caused trouble with Sir Walter Blixon. My chief told me about it. Blixon was the other power at No. 45. He held about as many shares as Dreuther, but he was not proportionally consulted. He was small, spotty, undistinguished, and consumed with jealousy. He could have had a yacht himself, but nobody would have sailed with him. When he objected to the diesel oil, Dreuther magnanimously gave way and then proceeded to knock all private petrol from the firm's account. As he lived in London he employed the firm's car, but Blixon had a house in Hampshire. What Dreuther courteously called a compromise was reached – things were to remain as they were. When Blixon managed somehow to procure himself a knighthood, he gained a momentary advantage until the rumour was said to have reached him that Dreuther had refused one in the same Honours List. One thing was certainly true – at a dinner party to which Blixon and my chief had been invited, Dreuther was heard to oppose a knighthood for a certain artist. 'Impossible. He couldn't accept it. An O.M. (or possibly a C.H.) are the only honours that remain respectable.' It made matters worse that Blixon had never heard of the C.H.

But Blixon bided his time. One more packet of shares would give him control and we used to believe that his chief prayer at night (he was a churchwarden in Hampshire) was that these shares would reach the market while Dreuther was at sea.

4

With despair in my heart I knocked in the door of No.10 and entered, but even in my despair I memorized details – they would want to know them on the ground floor. The room was not like an office at all – there was a bookcase containing sets of English classics and it showed Dreuther's astuteness that Trollope was there and not Dickens, Stevenson and not Scott, thus giving an appearance of personal taste. There was an unimportant Renoir and a lovely little Boudin on the far wall, and one noticed at once that there was a sofa but not a desk. The few visible files were stacked on a Regency table, and Blixon and my chief and a stranger sat uncomfortably on the edge of easy chairs. Dreuther was almost out of sight – he lay practically on his spine in the largest and deepest chair, holding some papers above his head and scowling at them through the thickest glasses I have ever seen on a human face.

'It is fantastic and it cannot be true,' he was saying in his deep guttural voice.

'I don't see the importance . . .' Blixon said.

Dreuther took off his glasses and gazed across the room at me. 'Who are you?' he asked.

'This is Mr Bertram, my assistant,' the chief accountant said.

'What is he doing here?'

'You told me to send for him.'

'I remember,' Dreuther said. 'But that was half an hour ago.'

'I was out at lunch, sir.'

'Lunch?' Dreuther asked as though it were a new word.

'It was during the lunch hour, Mr Dreuther,' the chief accountant said.

'And they go out for lunch?'

'Yes, Mr Dreuther.'

'All of them?'

'Most of them, I think.'

'How very interesting. I did not know. Do you go out to lunch, Sir Walter?'

'Of course I do, Dreuther. Now, for goodness sake, can't we leave this in the hands of Mr Arnold and Mr Bertram? The whole discrepancy only amounts to seven pounds fifteen and fourpence. I'm hungry, Dreuther.'

'It's not the amount that matters, Sir Walter. You and I are in charge of a great business. We cannot leave our responsibilities to others. The shareholders . . .'

'You are talking highfalutin rubbish, Dreuther. The shareholders are you and I . . .'

'And the Other, Sir Walter. Surely you never forget the Other. Mr Bertrand, please sit down and look at these accounts. Did they pass through your hands?'

With relief I saw that they belonged to a small subsidiary company with which I did not deal. 'I have nothing to do with General Enterprises, sir.'

'Never mind. You may know something about figures—it is obvious that no one else does. Please see if you notice anything wrong.'

The worst was obviously over. Dreuther had exposed an error and he did not really worry about a solution. 'Have a cigar, Sir Walter. You see, you cannot do without me yet.' He lit his own cigar. 'You have found the error, Mr Bertrand?'

'Yes. In the General Purposes account.'

'Exactly. Take your time, Mr Bertrand.'

'If you don't mind, Dreuther, I have a table at the Berkeley . . .'

'Of course, Sir Walter, if you are so hungry . . . I can deal with this matter.'

'Coming, Naismith?' The stranger rose, made a kind of bob at Dreuther and sidled after Blixon.

'And you, Arnold, you have had no lunch?'

'It really doesn't matter, Mr Dreuther.'

'You must pardon me. It had never crossed my mind . . . this—lunch hour—you call it?'

'Really it doesn't . . .'

'Mr Bertrand has had lunch. He and I will worry out this problem between us. Will you tell Miss Bullen that I am ready for my glass of milk? Would you like a glass of milk, Mr Bertrand?'

'No thank you, sir.'

I found myself alone with the Gom. I felt exposed as he watched me fumble with the papers—on the eighth floor, on a mountain top, like one of those Old Testament characters to whom a King commanded, 'Prophesy.'

'Where do you lunch, Mr Bertrand?'

'At the Volunteer.'

'Is that a good restaurant?'

'It's a public house, sir.'

'They serve meals?'

'Snacks.'

'How very interesting.' He fell silent and I began all over again to add, carry, subtract. I was for a time puzzled. Human beings are capable of the most simple errors, the failing to carry a figure on, but we had all the best machines and a machine should be incapable . . .

'I feel at sea, Mr Bertrand,' Dreuther said.

'I confess, sir, I *am* a little too.'

'Oh, I didn't mean in that way, not in that way at all. There is no hurry. We will put all that right. In our good time. I mean that when Sir Walter leaves my room I have a sense of calm, peace. I think of my yacht.' The cigar smoke blew between us. '*Luxe, calme et volupté*,' he said.

'I can't find any *ordre* or *beauté* in these figures, sir.'

'You read Baudelaire, Mr Bertrand?'

'Yes.'

'He is my favourite poet.'

'I prefer Racine, sir. But I expect that is the mathematician in me.'

'Don't depend too much on his classicism. There are moments in Racine, Mr Bertrand, when–the abyss opens.' I was aware of being watched while I started checking all over again. Then came the verdict. 'How very interesting.'

But now at last I was really absorbed. I have never been able to understand the layman's indifference to figures. The veriest fool vaguely appreciates the poetry of the solar system–'the army of unalterable law'–and yet he cannot see glamour in the stately march of the columns, certain figures moving upwards, crossing over, one digit running the whole length of every column, emerging, like some elaborate drill at Trooping the Colour. I was following one small figure now, dodging in pursuit.

'What computers do General Enterprises use, sir?'

'You must ask Miss Bullen.'

'I'm certain it's the Revolg. We gave them up five years ago. In old age they have a tendency to slip, but only when the 2 and the 7 are in relationship, and then not always, and then only in subtraction not addition. Now, here, sir, if you'll look, the combination happens four times, but only once has the slip occurred . . .'

'Please don't explain to me, Mr Bertrand. It would be useless.'

'There's nothing wrong except mechanically. Put these figures through one of our new machines. And scrap the Revolg (they've served long enough).'

I sat back on the sofa with a gasp of triumph. I felt the equal of any man. It had really been a very neat piece of detection. So simple when you knew, but everyone before me had accepted the perfection of the machine and no machine is perfect; in every join, rivet, screw lies original sin. I tried to explain that to Dreuther, but I was out of breath.

'How very interesting, Mr Bertrand. I'm glad we have solved the problem while Sir Walter is satisfying his carnal desires. Are you sure you won't have a glass of milk?'

'No thank you, sir. I must be getting back to the ground floor.'

'No hurry. You look tired, Mr Bertrand. When did you last have a holiday?'

'My annual leave's just coming round, sir. As a matter of fact I'm taking the opportunity to get married.'

'Really. How interesting. Have you received your clock?'

'Clock?'

'I believe they always give a clock here. The first time, Mr Bertrand?'

'Well . . . the second.'

'Ah, the second stands much more chance.'

The Gom had certainly a way with him. He made you talk, confide, he gave an effect of being really interested—and I think he always was, for a moment. He was a prisoner in his room, and small facts of the outer world came to him with the shock of novelty; he entertained them as an imprisoned man entertains a mouse or treasures a leaf blown through the bars. I said, 'We are going to Bournemouth for our honeymoon.'

'Ah, that I do not think is a good idea. That is *too* classical. You should take the young woman to the south—the bay of Rio de Janeiro . . .'

'I'm afraid I couldn't afford it, sir.'

'The sun would do you good, Mr Bertrand. You are pale. Some would suggest South Africa, but that is no better than Bournemouth.'

'I'm afraid that anyway . . .'

'I have it, Mr Bertrand. You and your beautiful young wife will come on my yacht. All my guests leave me at Nice and Monte Carlo. I will pick you up then on the 30th. We will sail down the coast of Italy, the Bay of Naples, Capri, Ischia.'

'I'm afraid, sir, it's a bit difficult. I'm very, very grateful, but you see we are getting married on the 30th.'

'Where?'

'St Luke's, Maida Hill.'

'St Luke's! You are being too classical again, my friend. We must not be too classical with a beautiful young wife. I assume she is young, Mr Bertrand?'

'Yes.'

'And beautiful?'

'I think so, sir.'

'Then you must be married at Monte Carlo. Before the mayor. With myself as witness. On the 30th. At night we sail for Portofino. That is better than St Luke's or Bournemouth.'

'But surely, sir, there would be legal difficulties . . .'

But he had already rung for Miss Bullen. I think he would have made a great actor; he already saw himself in the part of a Haroun who could raise a man from obscurity and make him the ruler over provinces. I have an idea too that he thought it would make Blixon jealous. It was the same attitude which he had taken to the knighthood. Blixon was probably planning to procure the Prime Minister to dinner. This would show how little Dreuther valued rank. It would take the salt out of any social success Blixon might have.

Miss Bullen appeared with a second glass of milk. 'Miss Bullen, please arrange with our Nice office to have Mr Bertrand married in Monte Carlo on the 30th at 4 p.m.'

'On the 30th, sir?'

'There may be residence qualifications – they must settle those. They can include him on their staff for the last six months. They will have to see the British Consul too. You had better speak on the telephone to M. Tissand, but don't bother me about it. I want to hear no more of it. Oh, and tell Sir Walter Blixon that we have found an error in the Revolg machines. They have got to be changed at once. He had better consult Mr Bertrand who will advise him. I want to hear no more of that either. The muddle has given us a most exhausting morning. Well, Mr Bertrand, until the 30th then. Bring a set of Racine with you. Leave the rest to Miss Bullen. Everything is settled.' So he believed, of course, but there was still Cary.

5

The next day was a Saturday. I met Cary at the Volunteer and walked all the way home with her: it was one of those spring afternoons when you can smell the country in a London street, tree smells and flower smells blew up into Oxford Street from Hyde Park, the Green Park, St James's, Kensington Gardens.

'Oh,' she said, 'I wish we could go a long, long way to somewhere very hot and very gay and very—' I had to pull her back or she would have been under a bus. I was always saving her from buses and taxis – sometimes I wondered how she kept alive when I wasn't there.

'Well,' I said, 'we can,' and while we waited for the traffic lights to change I told her.

I don't know why I expected such serious opposition: perhaps it was partly because she had been so set on a church wedding, the choir and the cake and all the nonsense. 'Think,' I said, 'to be married in Monte Carlo instead of Maida Hill. The sea down below and the yacht waiting . . .' As I had never been there, the details rather petered out.

She said, 'There's sea at Bournemouth too. Or so I've heard.'

'The Italian coast.'

'In company with your Mr Dreuther.'

'We won't share a cabin with him,' I said, 'and I don't suppose the hotel in Bournemouth will be quite empty.'

'Darling, I did want to be married at St Luke's.'

'Think of the Town Hall at Monte Carlo – the mayor in all his robes – the, the . . .'

'Does it count?'

'Of course it counts.'

'It would be rather fun if it didn't count, and then we could marry at St Luke's when we came back.'

'That would be living in sin.'

'I'd love to live in sin.'

'You could,' I said, 'any time. This afternoon.'

'Oh, I don't count London,' she said. 'That would be just making love. Living in sin is—oh, striped umbrellas and 80 in the shade and grapes—and a fearfully gay bathing suit. I'll have to have a new bathing suit.'

I thought all was well then, but she caught sight of one of those pointed spires sticking up over the plane trees a square ahead. 'We've sent out all the invitations. What will Aunt Marion say?' (She had lived with Aunt Marion ever since her parents were killed in the blitz.)

'Just tell her the truth. She'd much rather get picture-postcards from Italy than from Bournemouth.'

'It will hurt the Vicar's feelings.'

'Only to the extent of a fiver.'

'Nobody will really believe we are married.' She added a moment later (she was nothing if not honest), 'That will be fun.'

Then the pendulum swung again and she went thoughtfully on, 'You are only hiring your clothes. But my dress is being made.'

'There's time to turn it into an evening dress. After all, that's what it would have become anyway.'

The church loomed in sight: it was a hideous church, but no more hideous than St Luke's. It was grey and flinty and soot-stained, with reddish steps to the street the colour of clay and a text on a board that said, 'Come to Me all ye who are heavy laden,' as much as to say, 'Abandon Hope.' A wedding had just taken place, and there was a dingy high-tide line of girls with perambulators and squealing children and dogs and grim middle-aged matrons who looked as though they had come to curse.

I said, 'Let's watch. This might be happening to us.'

A lot of girls in long mauve dresses with lacy Dutch caps came out and lined the steps: they looked with fear at the nursemaids and the matrons and one or two giggled nervously—you could hardly blame them. Two photographers set up cameras to cover the entrance, an arch which seemed to be decorated with stone clover leaves, and then the victims emerged followed by a rabble of relatives.

'It's terrible,' Cary said, 'terrible. To think that might be you and me.'

'Well, you haven't an incipient goitre and I'm—well, damn it, I don't blush and I know where to put my hands.'

A car was waiting decorated with white ribbons and all the bridesmaids produced bags of paper rose petals and flung them at the young couple.

'They are lucky,' I said. 'Rice is still short, but I'm certain Aunt Marion can pull strings with the grocer.'

'She'd never do such a thing.'

'You can trust no one at a wedding. It brings out a strange atavistic cruelty. Now that they are not allowed to bed the bride, they try to damage the bridegroom. Look,' I said, clutching Cary's arm. A small boy, encouraged by one of the sombre matrons, had stolen up to the door of the car and, just as the bridegroom stooped to climb in, he launched at close range a handful of rice full in the unfortunate young man's face.

'When you can only spare a cupful,' I said, 'you are told to wait until you can see the white of your enemy's eyes.'

'But it's terrible,' Cary said.

'That, my dear child, is what is called a church marriage.'

'But ours wouldn't be like that. It's going to be very quiet—only near relatives.'

'You forget the highways and the hedges. It's a Christian tradition. That boy wasn't a relation. Trust me. I know. I've been married in church myself.'

'You were married in church? You never told me,' she said. 'In that case I'd *much* rather be married in a town hall. You haven't been married in a town hall too, have you?'

'No, it will be the first time—and the last time.'

'Oh, for God's sake,' Cary said, 'touch wood.'

So there she was two weeks later rubbing away at the horse's knee, asking for luck, and the great lounge of the Monte Carlo hotel spread emptily around us, and I said, 'That's that. We're alone, Cary.' (One didn't count the receptionist and the cashier and the concierge and the two men with our luggage and the old couple sitting on a sofa, for Mr Dreuther, they told me, had not yet arrived and we had the night to ourselves.)

6

We had dinner on the terrace of the hotel and watched people going into the Casino. Cary said, 'We ought to look in for the fun. After all, we aren't gamblers.'

'We couldn't be,' I said, 'not with fifty pounds basic.' We had decided not to use her allowance in case we found ourselves able to go to Le Touquet for a week in the winter.

'You are an accountant,' Cary said. 'You ought to know all the systems.'

'Systems are damned expensive,' I said. I had discovered that we had a suite already booked for us by Miss Bullen and I had no idea what it would cost. Our passports were still under different names, so I suppose it was reasonable that we should have two rooms, but the sitting-room seemed unnecessary. Perhaps we were supposed to entertain in it after the wedding. I said, 'You need a million francs★ to play a system, and then you are up against the limit. The bank can't lose.'

'I thought someone broke the bank once.'

'Only in a comic song,' I said.

'It would be awful if we were really gamblers,' she said. 'You've got to care so much about money. You don't, do you?'

'No,' I said and meant it. All I had in my mind that night was the wonder whether we would sleep together. We never had. It was that kind of marriage. I had tried the other kind, and now I would have waited months if I could gain in that way all the rest of the years. But tonight I didn't want to wait any longer. I was as fussed as a young man—I found I could no longer

---

★ At the period of this story the franc stood at about 1200 francs to the pound.

see into Cary's mind. She was twenty years younger, she had never been married before, and the game was all in her hands. I couldn't even interpret what she said to me. For instance as we crossed to the Casino she said, 'We'll only stay ten minutes. I'm terribly tired.' Was that hint in my favour or against me? Or was it just a plain statement of fact? Had the problem in my mind never occurred to her, or had she already made up her mind so certainly that the problem didn't exist? Was she assuming I knew the reason?

I had thought when they showed us our rooms I would discover, but all she had said with enormous glee was, 'Darling. What extravagance.'

I took the credit for Miss Bullen. 'It's only for one night. Then we'll be on the boat.' There was one huge double room and one very small single room and a medium-sized sitting-room in between: all three had balconies. I felt as though we had taken the whole front of the hotel. First she depressed me by saying, 'We could have two single rooms,' and then she contradicted that by saying, 'All the beds are double ones,' and then down I went again when she looked at the sofa in the sitting-room and said, 'I wouldn't have minded sleeping on that.' I was no wiser, and so we talked about systems. I didn't care a damn for systems.

After we had shown our passports and got our tickets we entered what they call the *cuisine*, where the small stakes are laid. 'This is where I belong,' Cary said, and nothing was less true. The old veterans sat around the tables with their charts and their pads and their pencils, making notes of every number. They looked, some of them, like opium smokers, dehydrated. There was a very tiny brown old lady with a straw hat of forty years ago covered in daisies: her left claw rested on the edge of the table like the handle of an umbrella and her right held a chip worth one hundred francs. After the ball had rolled four times she played her piece and lost it. Then she began waiting again. A young man leant over her shoulder, staked 100 on the last twelve numbers, won and departed. 'There goes a wise man,' I said, but when we came opposite the bar, he was there with a glass of beer and a sandwich. 'Celebrating three hundred francs,' I said.

'Don't be mean. Watch him, I believe that's the first food he's had today.'

I was on edge with wanting her, and I flared suddenly up; foolishly, for she would never have looked twice at him otherwise. So it is we prepare our own dooms. I said, 'You wouldn't call me mean if he weren't young and good-looking.'

'Darling,' she said with astonishment, 'I was only—' and then her mouth hardened. 'You *are* mean now,' she said. 'I'm damned if I'll apologise.' She stood and stared at the young man until he raised his absurd romantic hungry face and looked back at her. 'Yes,' she said, 'he is young, he is good-looking,' and walked straight out of the Casino. I followed saying, 'Damn, damn, damn,' under my breath. I knew now how we'd spend the night.

We went up in the lift in a dead silence and marched down the corridor and into the sitting-room.

'You can have the large room,' she said.

'No, you can.'

'The small one's quite big enough for me. I don't like huge rooms.'

'Then I'll have to change the luggage. They've put yours in the large room.'

'Oh, all right,' she said and went into it and shut the door without saying good night. I began to get angry with her as well as myself–'a fine first night of marriage,' I said aloud, kicking my suitcase, and then I remembered we weren't married yet, and everything seemed silly and wasteful.

I put on my dressing-gown and went out on to my balcony. The front of the Casino was floodlit: it looked a cross between a Balkan palace and a super-cinema with the absurd statuary sitting on the edge of the green roof looking down at the big portico and the commissionaires; everything stuck out in the white light as though projected in 3D. In the harbour the yachts were all lit up, and a rocket burst in the air over the hill of Monaco. It was so stupidly romantic I could have wept.

'Fireworks, darling,' a voice said, and there was Cary on her balcony with all the stretch of the sitting-room between us. 'Fireworks,' she said, 'isn't that just our luck?' so I knew all was right again.

'Cary,' I said–we had to raise our voices to carry. 'I'm so sorry . . .'

'Do you think there'll be a Catherine-wheel?'

'I wouldn't be surprised.'

'Do you see the lights in the harbour?'

'Yes.'

'Do you think Mr Dreuther's arrived?'

'I expect he'll sail in at the last moment tomorrow.'

'Could we get married without him? I mean he's a witness, isn't he, and his engine might have broken down or he might have been wrecked at sea or there might be a storm or something.'

'I think we could manage without him.'

'You do think it's arranged all right, don't you?'

'Oh yes, Miss Bullen's done it all. Four o'clock tomorrow.'

'I'm getting hoarse, are you, from shouting? Come on to the next balcony, darling.'

I went into the sitting-room and out on to the balcony there. She said, 'I suppose we'll all have to have lunch together–you and me and your Gom?'

'If he gets in for lunch.'

'It would be rather fun, wouldn't it, if he were a bit late. I like this hotel.'

'We'd have just enough money for two days, I suppose.'

'We could always run up terrible bills,' she said, and then added, 'not so much fun really as living in sin, I suppose. I wonder if that young man's in debt.'

'I wish you'd forget him.'

'Oh, I'm not a bit interested in him, darling. I don't like young men. I expect I've got a father fixation.'

'Damn it, Cary,' I said, 'I'm not as old as that.'

'Oh yes, you are,' she said, 'puberty begins at fourteen.'

'Then in fifteen years from tonight you may be a grandmother.'

'Tonight?' she said nervously, and then fell silent. The fireworks exploded in the sky. I said, 'There's your Catherine-wheel.'

She turned and looked palely at it.

'What are you thinking, Cary?'

'It's so strange,' she said. 'We are going to be together now for years and years and years. Darling, do you think we'll have enough to talk about?'

'We needn't only talk.'

'Darling, I'm serious. Have we got *anything* in common? I'm terribly bad at mathematics. And I don't understand poetry. You do.'

'You don't need to—you are the poetry.'

'No, but really—I'm serious.'

'We haven't dried up yet, and we've been doing nothing else but talk.'

'It would be so terrible,' she said, 'if we became a couple. You know what I mean. You with your paper. Me with my knitting.'

'You don't know how to knit.'

'Well, playing patience then. Or listening to the radio. Or watching television. We'll never have a television, will we?'

'Never.'

The rockets were dying down: there was a long pause: I looked away from the lights in the harbour. She was squatted on the floor of the balcony, her head against the side, and she was fast asleep. When I leant over I could touch her hair. She woke at once.

'Oh, how silly. I was dozing.'

'It's bed-time.'

'Oh. I'm not a bit tired really.'

'You said you were.'

'It's the fresh air. It's so nice in the fresh air.'

'Then come on my balcony.'

'Yes, I could, couldn't I?' she said dubiously.

'We don't need both balconies.'

'No.'

'Come round.'

'I'll climb over.'

'No. Don't. You might . . .'

'Don't argue,' she said, 'I'm here.'

They must have thought us crazy when they came to do the rooms—three beds for two people and not one of them had been slept in.

7

After breakfast we took a taxi to the Mairie—I wanted to be quite certain Miss Bullen had not slipped up, but everything was fixed; the marriage was to be at four sharp. They asked us not to be late as there was another wedding at 4.30.

'Like to go to the Casino?' I asked Cary. 'We could spend, say, 1000 francs now that everything's arranged.'

'Let's take a look at the port first and see if he's come.' We walked down the steps which reminded me of Montmartre except that everything was so creamy and clean and glittering and new, instead of grey and old and historic. Everywhere you were reminded of the Casino—the bookshops sold systems in envelopes, '2500 francs a week guaranteed', the toyshops sold small roulette boards, the tobacconists sold ashtrays in the form of a wheel, and even in the women's shops there were scarves patterned with figures and *manqué* and *pair* and *impair* and *rouge* and *noir*.

There were a dozen yachts in the harbour, and three carried British flags, but none of them was Dreuther's *Seagull*. 'Wouldn't it be terrible if he's forgotten?' Cary said.

'Miss Bullen would never let him forget. I expect he's unloading passengers at Nice. Anyway last night you wanted him to be late.'

'Yes, but this morning it feels scary. Perhaps we oughtn't to play in the Casino–just in case.'

'We'll compromise,' I said. 'Three hundred francs. We can't leave Monaco without playing once.'

We hung around the *cuisine* for quite a while before we played. This was the serious time of day–there were no tourists and the *Salle Privée* was closed and only the veterans sat there. You had a feeling with all of them that their lunch depended on victory. It was a long, hard, dull employment for them–a cup of coffee and then to work till lunch-time–if their system was successful and they could afford the lunch. Once Cary laughed–I forget what at, and an old man and an old woman raised their heads from opposite sides of the table and stonily stared. They were offended by our frivolity: this was no game to them. Even if the system worked, what a toil went into earning the 2500 francs a week. With their pads and their charts they left nothing to chance, and yet over and over again chance nipped in and shovelled away their tokens.

'Darling, let's bet.' She put all her three hundred francs on the number of her age, and crossed her fingers for luck. I was more cautious: I put one *carré* on the same figure, and backed *noir* and *impair* with my other two. We both lost on her age, but I won on my others.

'Have you won a fortune, darling? How terribly clever.'

'I've won two hundred and lost one hundred.'

'Well, buy a cup of coffee. They always say you ought to leave when you win.'

'We haven't really won. We are down four bob.'

'*You've* won.'

Over the coffee I said, 'Do you know, I think I'll buy a system just for fun? I'd like to see just how they persuade themselves . . .'

'If anybody could think up a system, it should be you.'

'I can see the possibility if there were no limit to the stakes, but then you'd have to be a millionaire.'

'Darling, you won't really think one up, will you? It's fun pretending to be rich for two days, but it wouldn't be fun if it were true. Look at the guests in the hotel, they are rich. Those women with lifted faces and dyed hair and awful little dogs.' She said again with one of her flashes of disquieting wisdom, 'You seem to get afraid of being old when you're rich.'

'There may be worse fears when you are poor.'

'They are ones we are used to. Darling, let's go and look at the harbour again. It's nearly lunch-time. Perhaps Mr Dreuther's in sight. This place–I don't like it terribly.'

We leant over a belvedere and looked down at the harbour–there wasn't any change there. The sea was very blue and very still and we could hear the voice of a cox out with an eight–it came clearly over the water and up to us. Very far away, beyond the next headland, there was a white boat, smaller than a celluloid toy in a child's bath.

'Do you think that's Mr Dreuther?' Cary asked.

'It might be. I expect it is.'

But it wasn't. When we came back after lunch there was no *Seagull* in the harbour and the boat we had seen was no longer in sight: it was somewhere on the way to Italy. Of course there was no need for anxiety: even if he failed to turn up before night, we could still get married. I said, 'If he's been held up, he'd have telegraphed.'

'Perhaps he's simply forgotten,' Cary said.

'That's impossible,' I said, but my mind told me that nothing was impossible with the Gom.

I said, 'I think I'll tell the hotel we'll keep on one room–just in case.'

'The small room,' Cary said.

The receptionist was a little crass. '*One* room, sir?'

'Yes, one room. The small one.'

'The small one? For you and madame, sir?'

'Yes.' I had to explain. 'We are being married this afternoon.'

'Congratulations, sir.'

'Mr Dreuther was to have been here.'

'We've had no word from Mr Dreuther, sir. He usually lets us know . . . We were not expecting him.'

Nor was I now, but I did not tell Cary that. This, after all, Gom or no Gom, was our wedding day. I tried to make her return to the Casino and lose a few hundred, but she said she wanted to walk on the terrace and look at the sea. It was an excuse to keep a watch for the *Seagull*. And of course the *Seagull* never came. That interview had meant nothing, Dreuther's kindness had meant nothing, a whim had flown like a wild bird over the snowy waste of his mind, leaving no track at all. We were forgotten. I said, 'It's time to go to the Mairie.'

'We haven't even a witness,' Cary said.

'They'll find a couple,' I said with a confidence I did not feel.

I thought it would be gay to arrive in a horse-cab and we climbed romantically into a ramshackle vehicle outside the Casino and sat down under the off-white awning. But we'd chosen badly. The horse was all skin and bone and I had forgotten that the road was uphill. An old gentleman with an ear-appliance was being pushed down to the Casino by a middle-aged woman, and she made far better progress down than we made up. As they passed us I could hear her precise English voice. She must have been finishing a story. She said, 'and so they lived unhappily ever after'; the old man chuckled and said, 'Tell me that one again.' I looked at Cary and hoped she hadn't heard but she had. 'Darling,' I said, 'don't be superstitious, not today.'

'There's a lot of sense in superstition. How do you know fate doesn't send us messages–so that we can be prepared. Like a kind of code. I'm always inventing new ones. For instance'–she thought a moment–'it will be lucky if a confectioner's comes before a flower shop. Watch your side.'

I did, and of course a flower shop came first. I hoped she hadn't noticed, but 'You can't cheat fate,' she said mournfully.

The cab went slower and slower: it would have been quicker to walk. I looked at my watch: we had only ten minutes to go. I said, 'You ought to have sacrificed a chicken this morning and found what omens there were in the entrails.'

'It's all very well to laugh,' she said. 'Perhaps our horoscopes don't match.'

'You wouldn't like to call the whole thing off, would you? Who knows? We'll be seeing a squinting man next.'

'Is that bad?'

'It's awful.' I said to the cabby, 'Please. A little faster. *Plus vite.*'

Cary clutched my arm. 'Oh,' she said.

'What's the matter?'

'Didn't you see him when he looked round. He's got a squint.'

'But, Cary, I was only joking.'

'That doesn't make any difference. Don't you see? It's what I said, you invent a code and fate uses it.'

I said angrily, 'Well, it doesn't make any difference. We are going to be too late anyway.'

'Too late?' She grabbed my wrist and looked at my watch. She said, 'Darling, we can't be late. Stop. *Arrêtez.* Pay him off.'

'We can't run uphill,' I said, but she was already out of the cab and signalling wildly to every car that passed. No one took any notice. Fathers of families drove smugly by. Children pressed their noses on the glass and made faces at her. She said, 'It's no use. We've got to run.'

'Why bother? Our marriage was going to be unlucky–you've read the omens, haven't you?'

'I don't care,' she said, 'I'd rather be unlucky with you than lucky with anyone else.' That was the sudden way she had–of dissolving a quarrel, an evil mood, with one clear statement. I took her hand and we began to run. But we would never have made it in time if a furniture-van had not stopped and given us a lift all the way. Has anyone else arrived at their wedding sitting on an old-fashioned brass bedstead? I said, 'From now on brass bedsteads will always be lucky.'

She said, 'There's a brass bedstead in the small room at the hotel.'

We had two minutes to spare when the furniture man helped us out on to the little square at the top of the world. To the south there was nothing higher, I suppose, before the Atlas mountains. The tall houses stuck up like cacti towards the heavy blue sky, and a narrow terracotta street came abruptly to an end at the edge of the great rock of Monaco. A Virgin in pale blue with angels blowing round her like a scarf looked across from the church opposite, and it was warm and windy and very quiet and all the roads of our life had led us to this square.

I think for a moment we were both afraid to go in. Nothing inside could be as good as this, and nothing was. We sat on a wooden bench, and another couple soon sat down beside us, the girl in white, the man in black: I became painfully conscious that I wasn't dressed up. Then a man in a high stiff collar made a great deal of fuss about papers and for a while we thought the marriage wouldn't take place at all: then there was a to-do, because we had turned up without witnesses, before they consented to produce a couple of sad clerks. We were led into a large empty room with a chandelier, and a desk—a notice on the door said *Salle des Mariages*, and the mayor, a very old man who looked like Clemenceau, wearing a blue and red ribbon of office, stood impatiently by while the man in the collar read out our names and our birth-dates. Then the mayor repeated what sounded like a whole code of laws in rapid French and we had to agree to them—apparently they were the clauses from the *Code Napoléon*. After that the mayor made a little speech in very bad English about our duty to society and our responsibility to the State, and at last he shook hands with me and kissed Cary on the cheek, and we went out again past the waiting couple on to the little windy square.

It wasn't an impressive ceremony, there was no organ like at St Luke's and no wedding guests. 'I don't feel I've been married,' Cary said, but then she added, 'It's fun not feeling married.'

8

There are so many faces in streets and bars and buses and stores that remind one of Original Sin, so few that carry permanently the sign of Original Innocence. Cary's face was like that—she would always until old age look at the world with the eyes of a child. She was never bored: every day was a new day: even grief was eternal and every joy would last for ever. 'Terrible' was her favourite adjective—it wasn't in her mouth a *cliché*—there *was* terror in her pleasures, her fears, her anxieties, her laughter—the terror of surprise, of seeing something for the first time. Most of us only see resemblances, every situation has been met before, but Cary saw only differences, like a wine-taster who can detect the most elusive flavour.

We went back to the hotel and the *Seagull* hadn't come and Cary met this anxiety quite unprepared as though it were the first time we had felt it. Then we went to the bar and had a drink, and it might have been the first drink we had ever had together. She had an insatiable liking for gin and Dubonnet which I didn't share. I said, 'He won't be in now till tomorrow.'

'Darling, shall we have enough for the bill?'

'Oh, we can manage tonight.'

'We might win enough at the Casino.'

'We'll stick to the cheap room. We can't afford to risk much.'

I think we lost about two thousand francs that night and in the morning and in the afternoon we looked down at the harbour and the *Seagull* wasn't there. 'He *has* forgotten,' Cary said. 'He'd have telegraphed otherwise.' I knew she was right, and I didn't know what to do, and when the next day came I knew even less.

'Darling,' Cary said, 'we'd better go while we can still pay,' but I had secretly asked for the bill (on the excuse that we didn't want to play beyond our resources), and I knew that already we had insufficient. There was nothing to do but wait. I telegraphed to Miss Bullen and she replied that Mr

Dreuther was at sea and out of touch. I was reading the telegram out to Cary as the old man with the ear-appliance sat on a chair at the top of the steps, watching the people go by in the late afternoon sun.

He asked suddenly, 'Do you know Dreuther?'

I said, 'Well, Mr Dreuther is my employer.'

'You think he is,' he said sharply. 'You are in Sitra, are you?'

'Yes.'

'Then I'm your employer, young man. Don't you put your faith in Dreuther.'

'You are Mr Bowles?'

'Of course I'm Mr Bowles. Go and find my nurse. It's time we went to the tables.'

When we were alone again, Cary asked, 'Who was that horrible old man? Is he really your employer?'

'In a way. In the firm we call him A.N.Other. He owns a few shares in Sitra—only a few, but they hold the balance between Dreuther and Blixon. As long as he supports Dreuther, Blixon can do nothing, but if Blixon ever managed to buy the shares, I'd be sorry for the Gom. A way of speaking,' I added. 'Nothing could make me sorry for him now.'

'He's only forgetful, darling.'

'Forgetfulness like that only comes when you don't care a damn about other people. None of us has a right to forget anyone. Except ourselves. The Gom never forgets himself. Oh hell, let's go to the Casino.'

'We can't afford to.'

'We are so in debt we may as well.'

That night we didn't bet much: we stood there and watched the veterans. The young man was back in the *cuisine*. I saw him change a thousand francs into tokens of a hundred, and presently when he'd lost those, he went out—no coffee or rolls for him that evening. Cary said, 'Do you think he'll go hungry to bed?'

'We all will,' I said, 'if the *Seagull* doesn't come.'

I watched them playing their systems, losing a little, gaining a little, and I thought it was strange how the belief persisted—that somehow you could beat the bank. They were like theologians, patiently trying to rationalize a mystery. I suppose in all lives a moment comes when we wonder—suppose after all there is a God, suppose the theologians are right. Pascal was a gambler, who staked his money on a divine system. I thought, I am a far better mathematician than any of these—is that why I don't believe in their mystery, and yet if this mystery exists, isn't it possible that I might solve it where they have failed? It was almost like a prayer when I thought: it's not for the sake of money—I don't want a fortune—just a few days with Cary free from anxiety.

Of all the systems round the table there was only one that really worked, and that did not depend on the so-called law of chance. A middle-aged woman with a big bird's nest of false blonde hair and two gold teeth lingered around the most crowded table. If anybody made a *coup* she went up to him and touching his elbow appealed quite brazenly—so long as the croupier was looking elsewhere—for one of his 200-franc chips. Perhaps charity, like a hunched back, is considered lucky. When she received a chip she would change it for two one-hundred-franc tokens, put one in her pocket and stake the other *en plein*. She couldn't lose her hundreds, and one day she stood to gain 3,500 francs. Most nights she must have left the table a thousand francs to the good from what she had in her pocket.

'Did you see her?' Cary asked as we walked to the bar for a cup of coffee–we had given up the gins and Dubonnets. 'Why should't I do that too?'

'We haven't come to that.'

'I've made a decision,' Cary said. 'No more meals at the hotel.'

'Do we starve?'

'We have coffee and rolls at a café instead–or perhaps milk–it's more nourishing.'

I said sadly, 'It's not the honeymoon I'd intended. Bournemouth would have been better.'

'Don't fret, darling. Everything will be all right when the *Seagull* comes.'

'I don't believe in the *Seagull* any more.'

'Then what do we do when the fortnight's over?'

'Go to gaol, I should think. Perhaps the prison is run by the Casino and we shall have recreation hours round a roulette wheel.'

'Couldn't you borrow from the Other?'

'Bowles? He's never lent without security in his life. He's sharper than Dreuther and Blixon put together–otherwise they'd have had his shares years ago.'

'But there must be something we can do, darling?'

'Madam, there is.' I looked up from my cooling coffee and saw a small man in frayed and dapper clothes with co-respondent shoes. His nose seemed bigger than the rest of his face: the experience of a lifetime had swollen the veins and bleared the eyes. He carried jauntily under his arm a walking stick that had lost its ferrule, with a duck's head for a handle. He said with blurred courtesy, 'I think I am unpardonably intruding, but you have had ill-success at the tables and I carry with me good tidings, sir and madam.'

'Well,' Cary said, 'we were just going . . .' She told me later that his use of a biblical phrase gave her a touch of shivers, of *diablerie*–the devil at his old game of quoting scripture.

'It is better for you to stay, for I have shut in my mind here a perfect system. That system I am prepared to let you have for a mere ten thousand francs.'

'You are asking the earth,' I said. 'We haven't got that much.'

'But you are staying at the Hôtel de Paris. I have seen you.'

'It's a matter of currency,' Cary said quickly. 'You know how it is with the English.'

'One thousand francs.'

'No,' Cary said, 'I'm sorry.'

'I tell you what I'll do,' I said, 'I'll stand you a drink for it.'

'Whisky,' the little man replied sharply. I realized too late that whisky cost 500 francs. He sat down at the table with his stick between his knees so that the duck seemed to be sharing his drink. I said, 'Go on.'

'It is a very small whisky.'

'You won't get another.'

'It is very simple,' the little man said, 'like all great mathematical discoveries. You bet first on one number and when your number wins you stake your gains on the correct transversal of six numbers. The correct transversal on one is 31 to 36; on two 13 to 18; òn three . . .'

'Why?'

'You can take it that I am right. I have studied very carefully here for many years. For five hundred francs I will sell you a list of all the winning numbers which came up last June.'

'But suppose the number doesn't come up?'

'You wait to start the system until it does.'

'It might take years.'

The little man got up, bowed and said, 'That is why one must have capital. I had too little capital. If instead of five million I had possessed ten million I would not be selling you my system for a glass of whisky.'

He retired with dignity, the ferruleless stick padding on the polished floor, the duck staring back at us as though it wanted to stay.

'I think my system's better,' Cary said. 'If that woman can get away with it, I can . . .'

'It's begging. I don't like my wife to beg.'

'I'm only a new wife. And I don't count it begging–it's not money, only tokens.'

'You know there was something that man said which made me think. It's a pure matter of reducing what one loses and increasing what one gains.'

'Yes, darling. But in my system I don't lose anything.'

She was away for nearly half an hour and then she came back almost at a run. 'Darling, put away your doodles. I want to go home.'

'They aren't doodles. I'm working out an idea.'

'Darling, please come at once or I'm going to cry.'

When we were outside she dragged me up through the gardens, between the floodlit palm trees and the flowerbeds like sugar sweets. She said, 'Darling, it was a terrible failure.'

'What happened?'

'I did exactly what that woman did. I waited till someone won a lot of money and then I sort of nudged his elbow and said, "Give." But he didn't give, he said quite sharply, "Go home to your mother," and the croupier looked up. So I went to another table. And the man there just said, "Later. Later. On the terrace." Darling, he thought I was a tart. And when I tried a third time–oh, it was terrible. One of those attendants who light people's cigarettes touched me on my arm and said, "I think Mademoiselle has played enough for tonight." Calling me Mademoiselle made it worse. I wanted to fling my marriage lines in his face, but I'd left them in the bathroom at the hotel.'

'In the bathroom?'

'Yes, in my sponge bag, darling, because for some reason I never lose my sponge bag–I've had it for years and years. But that's not why I want to cry. Darling, please let's sit down on this seat. I can't cry walking about–it's like eating chocolate in the open air. You get so out of breath you can't taste the chocolate.'

'For goodness' sake,' I said. 'If that's not the worst let me know the worst.

Do you realize we shall never be able to go into the Casino again–just when I've started on a system, a real system.'

'Oh, it's not as bad as that, darling. The attendant gave me such a nice wink at the door. I know *he* won't mind my going back–but I never want to go back, never.'

'I wish you'd tell me.'

'That nice young man saw it all.'

'What young man?'

'The hungry young man. And when I went out into the hall he followed me and said very sweetly, "Madame, I can only spare a token of one hundred francs, but it is yours."'

'You didn't take it?'

'Yes–I couldn't refuse it. He was so polite, and he was gone before I had time to thank him for it. And I changed it and used the francs in the slot machines at the entrance and I'm sorry I'm howling like this, but I simply can't help it, he was so terribly courteous, and he must be so terribly hungry and he's got a mind above money or he wouldn't have lent me a hundred francs, and when I'd won five hundred I looked for him to give him half and he'd gone.'

'You won five hundred? It'll pay for our coffee and rolls tomorrow.'

'Darling, you are so sordid. Don't you see that for ever after he'll think I was one of those old harpies like Bird's Nest in there?'

'I expect he was only making a pass.'

'You are so sexual. He was doing nothing of the kind. He's much too hungry to make a pass.'

'They say starvation sharpens the passions.'

9

We still had breakfast at the hotel in order to keep up appearances, but we found ourselves wilting even before the liftman. I have never liked uniforms–they remind me that there are those who command and those who are commanded–and now I was convinced that everybody in uniform knew that we couldn't pay the bill. We always kept our key with us, so that we might never have to go to the desk, and as we had changed all our travellers' cheques on our arrival, we didn't even have to approach the accountant. Cary had found a small bar called the Taxi Bar at the foot of one of the great staircases, and there we invariably ate our invariable lunch and our dinner. It was years before I wanted to eat rolls again and even now I always drink tea instead of coffee. Then, on our third lunch-time, coming out of the bar we ran into the assistant receptionist from the hotel who was passing along the street. He bowed and went by, but I knew that our hour had struck.

We sat in the gardens afterwards in the early evening sun and I worked hard on my system, for I felt as though I were working against time. I said to Cary, 'Give me a thousand francs. I've got to check up.'

'But, darling,' she said, 'do you realize we've only got five thousand left. Soon we shan't have anything even for rolls.'

'Thank God for that. I can't bear the sight of a roll.'

'Then let's change to ices instead. They don't cost any more. And, think, we can change our diet, darling. Coffee ices for lunch, strawberry ices for dinner. Darling, I'm longing for dinner.'

'If my system is finished in time, we'll have steaks . . .'

I took the thousand and went into the *cuisine*. Paper in hand I watched the table carefully for a quarter of an hour before betting and then quite quietly and steadily I lost, but when I had no more tokens to play my numbers came up in just the right order. I went out again to Cary. I said, 'The devil was right. It's a question of capital.'

She said sadly, 'You are getting like all the others.'

'What do you mean?'

'You think numbers, you dream numbers. You wake up in the night and say "*Zéro deux*". You write on bits of paper at meals.'

'Do you call them meals?'

'There are four thousand francs in my bag and they've got to last us till the *Seagull* comes. We aren't going to gamble any more. I don't believe in your system. A week ago you said you couldn't beat the bank.'

'I hadn't studied . . .'

'That's what the devil said—he'd studied. You'll be selling your system soon for a glass of whisky.'

She got up and walked back to the hotel and I didn't follow. I thought, a wife ought to believe in her husband to the bitter end and we hadn't been married a week; and then after a while I began to see her point of view. For the last few days I hadn't been much company, and what a life it had been—afraid to meet the porter's eye, and that was exactly what I met as I came into the hotel.

He blocked my way and said, 'The manager's compliments, sir, and could you spare him a few moments. In his room.' I thought: they can't send her to prison too, only me, and I thought: the Gom, that egotistical bastard on the eighth floor who has let us in for all this because he's too great to remember his promises. He makes the world and then goes and rests on the seventh day and his creation can go to pot that day for all he cares. If only for one moment I could have had him in my power—if he could have depended on my remembering *him*, but it was as if I was doomed to be an idea of his, he would never be an idea of mine.

'Sit down, Mr Bertram,' the manager said. He pushed a cigarette box across to me. 'Smoke?' He had the politeness of a man who has executed many people in his time.

'Thanks,' I said.

'The weather has not been quite so warm as one would expect at this time of year.'

'Oh, better than England, you know.'

'I do hope you are enjoying your stay.' This, I supposed, was the routine—just to show there was no ill-feeling—one has one's duty. I wished he would come to an end.

'Very much, thank you.'

'And your wife too?'

'Oh yes. Yes.'

He paused, and I thought: now it comes. He said, 'By the way, Mr Bertram, I think this is your first visit?'

'Yes.'

'We rather pride ourselves here on our cooking. I don't think you will find better food in Europe.'

'I'm sure you're right.'

'I don't want to be intrusive, Mr Bertram, please forgive me if I am, but we have noticed that you don't seem to care for our restaurant, and we are very anxious that you and your wife should be happy here in Monte Carlo. Any complaint you might have–the service, the wine . . .?'

'Oh, I've no complaint. No complaint at all.'

'I didn't think you would have, Mr Bertram. I have great confidence in our service here. I came to the conclusion–you will forgive me if I'm intrusive–'

'Yes. Oh yes.'

'I know that our English clients often have trouble over currency. A little bad luck at the tables can so easily upset their arrangements in these days.'

'Yes. I suppose so.'

'So it occurred to me, Mr Bertram, that perhaps–how shall I put it–you might be, as it were, a little–you will forgive me, won't you–well, short of funds?'

My mouth felt very dry now that the moment had come. I couldn't find the bold frank words I wanted to use. I said, 'Well,' and goggled across the desk. There was a portrait of the Prince of Monaco on the wall and a huge ornate inkstand on the desk and I could hear the train going by to Italy. It was like a last look at freedom.

The manager said, 'You realize that the Administration of the Casino and of this hotel are most anxious–really most anxious–you realize we are in a very special position here, Mr Bertram, we are not perhaps'–he smiled at his fingernails–'quite ordinary *hôteliers*. We have had clients here whom we have looked after for–well, thirty years'–he was incredibly slow at delivering his sentence. 'We like to think of them as friends rather than clients. You know here in the Principality we have a great tradition–well, of discretion, Mr Bertram. We don't publish names of our guests. We are the repository of many confidences.'

I couldn't bear the man's rigmarole any more. It had become less like an execution than like the Chinese water-torture. I said, 'We are quite broke–there's a confidence for you.'

He smiled again at his nails. 'That was what I suspected, Mr Bertram, and so I hope you will accept a small loan. For a friend of Mr Dreuther. Mr Dreuther is a very old client of ours and we should be most distressed if any friend of his failed to enjoy his stay with us.' He stood up, bowed and presented me with an envelope–I felt like a child receiving a good-conduct prize from a bishop. Then he led me to the door and said in a low confidential voice, 'Try our *Château Gruaud Larose* 1934: you will not be disappointed.'

I opened the envelope on the bed and counted the notes. I said, 'He's lent us 250,000 francs.'

'I don't believe it.'

'What it is to be a friend of the Gom. I wish I liked the bastard.'

'How will we ever repay it?'

'The Gom will have to help. He kept us here.'

'We'll spend as little as we can, won't we, darling?'

'But no more coffee and rolls. Tonight we'll have a party–the wedding party.' I didn't care a damn about the *Gruaud Larose* 1934: I hired a car and we drove to a little village in the mountains called Peille. Everything was rocky grey and gorse-yellow in the late sun which flowed out between the cold shoulders of the hills where the shadows waited. Mules stood in the street and the car was too large to reach the inn, and in the inn there was only one long table to seat fifty people. We sat at it and watched the darkness come, and they gave us their own red wine which wasn't very good and fat pigeons roasted and fruit and cheese. The villagers laughed in the next room over their drinks, and soon we could hardly see the enormous hump of hills.

'Happy?'

'Yes.'

She said after a while, 'I wish we weren't going back to Monte Carlo. Couldn't we send the car home and stay? We wouldn't mind about toothbrushes tonight, and tomorrow we could go–shopping.' She said the last word with an upward inflexion as though we were at the Ritz and the Rue de la Paix round the corner.

'A toothbrush at Cartier's,' I said.

'Lanvin for two pyjama tops.'

'Soap at Guerlain.'

'A few cheap handkerchiefs in the Rue de Rivoli.' She said, 'I can't think of anything else we'd want, can you? Did you ever come to a place like this with Dirty?' Dirty was the name she always used for my first wife who had been dark and plump and sexy with pekingese eyes.

'Never.'

'I like being somewhere without footprints.'

I looked at my watch. It was nearly ten and there was half an hour's drive back. I said, 'I suppose we'd better go.'

'It's not late.'

'Well, tonight I want to give my system a real chance. If I use 200-franc tokens I've got just enough capital.'

'You aren't going to the Casino?'

'Of course I am.'

'But that's stealing.'

'No it isn't. He gave us the money to enjoy ourselves with.'

'Then half of it's mine. You shan't gamble with my half.'

'Dear, be reasonable. I need the capital. The system needs the capital. When I've won you shall have the whole lot back with interest. We'll pay our bills, we'll come back here if you like for all the rest of our stay.'

'You'll never win. Look at the others.'

'They aren't mathematicians. I am.'

An old man with a beard guided us to our car through the dark arched streets: she wouldn't speak, she wouldn't even take my arm. I said, 'This is our celebration night, darling. Don't be mean.'

'What have I said that's mean?' How they defeat us with their silences: one can't repeat a silence or throw it back as one can a word. In the same silence we drove home. As we came out over Monaco the city was floodlit, the Museum, the Casino, the Cathedral, the Palace–the fireworks went up from the rock. It was the last day of a week of illuminations: I remembered the first day and our quarrel and the three balconies.

I said, 'We've never seen the *Salle Privée*. We must go there tonight.'

'What's special about tonight?' she said.

'*Le mari doit protection à sa femme, la femme obéissance à son mari.*'

'What on earth are you talking about?'

'You told the mayor you agreed to that. There's another article you agreed to–"The wife is obliged to live with her husband and to follow him wherever he judges it right to reside." Well, tonight we are damned well going to reside in the *Salle Privée*.'

'I didn't understand what he was saying.' The worst was always over when she consented to argue.

'Please, dear, come and see my system win.'

'I shall only see it lose,' she said and she spoke with strict accuracy.

At 10.30 exactly I began to play and to lose and I lost steadily. I couldn't change tables because this was the only table in the *Salle Privée* at which one could play with a 200-franc minimum. Cary wanted me to stop when I had lost half of the manager's loan, but I still believed that the moment would come, the tide turn, my figures prove correct.

How much is left?' she asked.

'This.' I indicated the five two-hundred-franc tokens. She got up and left me: I think she was crying, but I couldn't follow her without losing my place at the table.

And when I came back to our rooms in the hotel I was crying too–there are occasions when a man can cry without shame. She was awake: I could tell by the way she had dressed herself for bed how coldly she was awaiting me. She never wore the bottoms of her pyjamas except to show anger or indifference, but when she saw me sitting there on the end of the bed, shaking with the effort to control my tears, her anger went. She said, 'Darling, don't take on so. We'll manage somehow.' She scrambled out of bed and put her arms round me. 'Darling,' she said, 'I've been mean to you. It might happen to anybody. Look, we'll try the ices, not the coffee and rolls, and the *Seagull*'s sure to come. Sooner or later.'

'I don't mind now if it never comes,' I said.

'Don't be bitter, darling. It happens to everybody, losing.'

'But I haven't lost,' I said, 'I've won.'

She took her arms away. 'Won?'

'I've won five million francs.'

'Then why are you crying?'

'I'm laughing. We are rich.'

'Oh, you beast,' she said, 'and I was sorry for you,' and she scrambled back under the bedclothes.

PART II

I

One adapts oneself to money much more easily than to poverty: Rousseau might have written that man was born rich and is everywhere impoverished. It gave me great satisfaction to pay back the manager and leave my key at the desk. I frequently rang the bell for the pleasure of confronting a uniform without shame. I made Cary have an Elizabeth Arden treatment, and I ordered the *Gruaud Larose* 1934 (I even sent it back because it was not the right temperature). I had our things moved to a suite and I hired a car to take us to the beach. At the beach I hired one of the private bungalows where we could sunbathe, cut off by bushes and shrubs from the eyes of common people. There all day I worked in the sun (for I was not yet quite certain of my system) while Cary read (I had even bought her a new book).

I discovered that, as on the stock exchange, money bred money. I would now use ten-thousand-franc squares instead of two-hundred-franc tokens, and inevitably at the end of the day I found myself richer by several million. My good fortune became known: casual players would bet on the squares where I had laid my biggest stake, but they had not protected themselves, as I had with my other stakes, and it was seldom that they won. I noted a strange aspect of human nature, that though my system worked and theirs did not, the veterans never lost faith in their own calculations—not one abandoned his elaborate schemes, which led to nothing but loss, to follow my victorious method. The second day, when I had already increased my five million to nine, I heard an old lady say bitterly, 'What deplorable luck,' as though it were my good fortune alone that prevented the wheel revolving to her system.

On the third day I began to attend the Casino for longer hours—I would put in three hours in the morning in the kitchen and the same in the afternoon, and then of course in the evening I settled down to my serious labour in the *Salle Privée*. Cary had accompanied me on the second day and I had given her a few thousand francs to play with (she invariably lost them), but on the third day I thought it best to ask her to stay away. I found her anxious presence at my elbow distracting, and twice I made a miscalculation because she spoke to me. 'I love you very much, darling,' I said to her, 'but work is work. You go and sunbathe, and we'll see each other for meals.'

'Why do they call it a game of chance?' she said.

'How do you mean?'

'It's not a game. You said it yourself–it's work. You've begun to commute. Breakfast at nine thirty sharp, so as to catch the first table. What a lot of beautiful money you're earning. At what age will you retire?'

'Retire?'

'You mustn't be afraid of retirement, darling. We shall see so much more of each other, and we could fit up a little roulette wheel in your study. It will be so nice when you don't have to cross the road in all weathers.'

That night I brought my winnings up to fifteen million francs before dinner, and I felt it called for a celebration. I *had* been neglecting Cary a little–I realized that, so I thought we would have a good dinner and go to the ballet instead of my returning to the tables. I told her that and she seemed pleased. 'Tired businessman relaxes,' she said.

'As a matter of fact I am a little tired.' Those who have not played roulette seriously little know how fatiguing it can be. If I had worked less hard during the afternoon I wouldn't have lost my temper with the waiter in the bar. I had ordered two very dry Martinis and he brought them to us quite drowned in Vermouth–I could tell at once from the colour without tasting. To make matters worse he tried to explain away the colour by saying he had used Booth's gin. 'But you know perfectly well that I only take Gordon's,' I said, and sent them back. He brought me two more and he had put lemon peel in them. I said, 'For God's sake how long does one have to be a customer in this bar before you begin to learn one's taste?'

'I'm sorry, sir. I only came yesterday.'

I could see Cary's mouth tighten. I was in the wrong, of course, but I had spent a very long day at the Casino, and she might have realized that I am not the kind of man who is usually crotchety with servants. She said, 'Who would think that a week ago we didn't even dare to speak to a waiter in case he gave us a bill?'

When we went in to dinner there was a little trouble about our table on the terrace: we were earlier than usual, but as I said to Cary we had been good customers and they could have taken some small trouble to please. However, this time I was careful not to let my irritation show more than very slightly–I was determined that this dinner should be one to remember.

Cary as a rule likes to have her mind made up for her, so I took the menu and began to order. 'Caviare,' I said.

'For one,' Cary said.

'What will you have? Smoked salmon?'

'You order yours,' Cary said.

I ordered '*bresse à l'estragon à la broche*', a little Roquefort, and some wild strawberries. This, I thought, was a moment too for the *Gruaud Larose* '34 (they would have learnt their lesson about the temperature). I leant back feeling pleased and contented: my dispute with the waiter was quite forgotten, and I knew that I had behaved politely and with moderation when I found that our table was occupied.

'And Madame?' the waiter asked.

'A roll and butter and a cup of coffee,' Cary said.

'But Madame perhaps would like . . .' She gave him her sweetest smile as though to show me what I had missed. She said, 'Just a roll and butter please. I'm not hungry. To keep Monsieur company.'

I said angrily, 'In *that* case I'll cancel . . .' but the waiter had already gone. I said, 'How dare you?'

'What's the matter, darling?'

'You know very well what's the matter. You let me order . . .'

'But truly I'm not hungry, darling. I just wanted to be sentimental, that's all. A roll and butter reminds me of the days when we weren't rich. Don't you remember that little café at the foot of the steps?'

'You are laughing at me.'

'But *no*, darling. Don't you like thinking of those days at all?'

'Those days, those days—why don't you talk about last week and how you were afraid to send anything to the laundry and we couldn't afford the English papers and you couldn't read the French ones and . . .'

'Do you remember how reckless you were when you gave five francs to a beggar? Oh, that reminds me . . .'

'What of?'

'I never meet the hungry young man now.'

'I don't suppose he goes sunbathing.'

My caviare came and my vodka. The waiter said, 'Would Madame like her coffee now?'

'No. No, I think I'll toy with it while Monsieur has his—his . . .'

'*Bresse à l'estragon*, Madame.'

I've never enjoyed caviare less. She watched every helping I took, her chin in her hand, leaning forward in what I suppose she meant to be a devoted and wifely way. The toast crackled in the silence, but I was determined not to be beaten. I ate the next course grimly to an end and pretended not to notice how she spaced out her roll—she couldn't have been enjoying her meal much either. She said to the waiter, 'I'll have another cup of coffee to keep my husband company with his strawberries. Wouldn't you like a half bottle of champagne, darling?'

'No. If I drink any more I might lose my self-control . . .'

'Darling, what have I said? Don't you like me to remember the days when we were poor and happy? After all, if I had married you now it might have been for your money. You know you were terribly nice when you gave me five hundred francs to gamble with. You watched the wheel so seriously.'

'Aren't I serious now?'

'You don't watch the wheel any longer. You watch your paper and your figures. Darling, we are on *holiday*.'

'We would have been if Dreuther had come.'

'We can afford to go by ourselves now. Let's take a plane tomorrow—anywhere.'

'Not tomorrow. You see, according to my calculations the cycle of loss comes up tomorrow. Of course I'll only use 1,000-franc tokens, so as to reduce the incident.'

'Then the day after . . .'

'That's when I have to win back on double stakes. If you've finished your coffee it's time for the ballet.'

'I've got a headache. I don't want to go.'

'Of course you've got a headache eating nothing but rolls.'

'I ate nothing but rolls for three days and I never had a headache.' She got up from the table and said slowly, 'But in those days I was in love.' I refused to quarrel and I went to the ballet alone.

I can't remember which ballet it was–I don't know that I could have remembered even the same night. My mind was occupied. I had to lose next day if I were to win the day after, otherwise my system was at fault. My whole stupendous run would prove to have been luck only–the kind of luck that presumably by the laws of chance turns up in so many centuries, just as those long-lived laborious monkeys who are set at typewriters eventually in the course of centuries produce the works of Shakespeare. The ballerina to me was hardly a woman so much as a ball spinning on the wheel: when she finished her final movement and came before the curtain alone it was as though she had come to rest triumphantly at zero and all the counters around her were shovelled away into the back–the two thousand francs from the cheap seats with the square tokens from the stalls, all jumbled together. I took a turn on the terrace to clear my head: this was where we had stood the first night watching together for the *Seagull*. I wished Cary had been with me and I nearly returned straight away to the hotel to give her all she asked. She was right: system or chance, who cared? We could catch a plane, extend our holiday: I had enough now to buy a partnership in some safe modest business without walls of glass and modern sculpture and a Gom on the eighth floor, and yet–it was like leaving a woman one loved untouched, untasted, to go away and never know the truth of how the ball had come to rest in that particular order–the poetry of absolute chance or the determination of a closed system? I would be grateful for the poetry, but what pride I should feel if I proved the determinism.

The regiment was all assembled: strolling by the tables I felt like a commanding officer inspecting his unit. I would have liked to reprove the old lady for wearing the artificial daisies askew on her hat and to speak sharply to Mr Bowles for a lack of polish on his ear-appliance. A touch on my elbow and I handed out my 200 token to the lady who cadged. 'Move more smartly to it,' I wanted to say to her, 'the arm should be extended at full length and not bent at the elbow, and it's time you did something about your hair.' They watched me pass with expressions of nervous regret, waiting for me to choose my table, and when I halted somebody rose and offered me a seat. But I had not come to win–I had come symbolically to make my first loss and go. So courteously I declined the seat, laid out a pattern of tokens and with a sense of triumph saw them shovelled away. Then I went back to the hotel.

Cary wasn't there, and I was disappointed. I wanted to explain to her the importance of that symbolic loss, and instead I could only undress and climb between the humdrum sheets. I slept fitfully. I had grown used to Cary's company, and I put on the light at one to see the time, and I was still alone. At half past two Cary woke me as she felt her way to bed in the dark.

'Where've you been?' I asked.

'Walking,' she said.

'All by yourself?'

'No.' The space between the beds filled with her hostility, but I knew better than to strike the first blow–she was waiting for that advantage. I pretended to roll over and settle for sleep. After a long time she said, 'We walked down to the Sea Club.'

'It's closed.'

'We found a way in–it was very big and eerie in the dark with all the chairs stacked.'

'Quite an adventure. What did you do for light?'

'Oh, there was bright moonlight. Philippe told me all about his life.'

'I hope you unstacked a chair.'

'We sat on the floor.'

'If it was a madly interesting life tell it me. Otherwise it's late and I have to be . . .'

'"Up early for the Casino." I don't suppose you'd find it an interesting life. It was so simple, idyllic. And he told it with such intensity. He went to school at a *lycée*.'

'Most people do in France.'

'His parents died and he lived with his grandmother.'

'What about his grandfather?'

'He was dead too.'

'Senile mortality is very high in France.'

'He did military service for two years.'

I said, 'It certainly seems a life of striking originality.'

'You can sneer and sneer,' she said.

'But, dear, I've said nothing.'

'Of course you wouldn't be interested. You are never interested in anybody different from yourself, and he's young and very poor. He feeds on coffee and rolls.'

'Poor fellow,' I said with genuine sympathy.

'You are so uninterested you don't even ask his name.'

'You said it was Philippe.'

'Philippe who?' she asked triumphantly.

'Dupont,' I said.

'It isn't. It's Chantier.'

'Ah well, I mixed him up with Dupont.'

'Who's Dupont?'

'Perhaps they look alike.'

'I said who's Dupont.'

'I've no idea,' I said. 'But it's awfully late.'

'You're unbearable.' She slapped her pillow as though it were my face. There was a pause of several minutes and then she said bitterly, 'You haven't even asked whether I slept with him.'

'I'm sorry. Did you?'

'No. But he asked me to spend the night with him.'

'On the stacked chairs?'

'I'm having dinner with him tomorrow night.'

She was beginning to get me in the mood she wanted. I could stop myself no longer. I said, 'Who the hell is this Philippe Chantier?'

'The hungry young man, of course.'

'Are you going to dine on coffee and rolls?'

'I'm paying for the dinner. He's very proud, but I insisted. He's taking me somewhere very cheap and quiet and simple—a sort of students' place.'

'That's lucky,' I said, 'because I'm dining out too. Someone I met tonight at the Casino.'

'Who?'

'A Madame Dupont.'

'There's no such name.'

'I couldn't tell you the right one. I'm careful of a woman's honour.'

'Who is she?'

'She was winning a lot tonight at baccarat and we got into conversation. Her husband died recently, she was very fond of him, and she's sort of drowning her sorrows. I expect she'll soon find comfort, because she's young and beautiful and intelligent and rich.'

'Where are you having dinner?'

'Well, I don't want to bring her here—there might be talk. And she's too well known at the *Salle Privée*. She suggested driving to Cannes where nobody would know us.'

'Well, don't bother to come back early. I shall be late.'

'Exactly what I was going to say to you, dear.'

It was that sort of night. As I lay awake—and was aware of her wakefulness a few feet away—I thought it's the Gom's doing, he's even ruining our marriage now. I said, 'Dear, if you'll give up your dinner, I'll give up mine.'

She said, 'I don't even believe in yours. You invented it.'

'I swear to you—word of honour—that I'm giving a woman dinner tomorrow night.'

She said, 'I can't let Philippe down.' I thought gloomily: now I've got to do it, and where the hell can I find a woman?

2

We were very polite to each other at breakfast and at lunch. Cary even came into the Casino with me in the early evening, but I think her sole motive was to spot my woman. As it happened a young woman of great beauty was sitting at one of the tables, and Cary obviously drew the incorrect conclusion. She tried to see whether we exchanged glances and at last she could restrain her curiosity no longer. She said to me, 'Aren't you going to speak to her?'

'Who?'

'That girl.'

'I don't know what you mean,' I said, and tried to convey in my tone of voice that I was still guarding the honour of another. Cary said furiously, 'I must be off. I can't keep Philippe waiting. He's so sensitive.'

My system was working: I was losing exactly what I had anticipated losing, but all the exhilaration had gone out of my calculations. I thought: suppose this isn't what they call a lovers' quarrel; suppose she's really interested in this man; suppose this is the end. What do I do? What's left for me? Fifteen thousand pounds was an inadequate answer.

I was not the only one who was losing regularly. Mr Bowles sat in his wheeled chair, directing his nurse who put the tokens on the cloth for him, leaning over his shoulder, pushing with her private rake. He too had a system, but I suspected that his system was not working out. He sent her back twice to the desk for more money, and the second time I saw that his pocket-book was empty except for a few thousand-franc notes. He rapped out his directions and she laid out his remaining tokens—a hundred and fifty thousand francs' worth of them—the ball rolled and he lost the lot. Wheeling from the table he caught sight of me. 'You,' he said, 'what's your name?'

'Bertram.'

'I've cashed too little. Don't want to go back to the hotel. Lend me five million.'

'I'm sorry,' I said.

'You know who I am. You know what I'm worth.'

'The hotel . . .' I began.

'They can't let me have that amount till the banks open. I want it tonight. You've been winning plenty. I've watched you. I'll pay you back before the evening's out.'

'People have been known to lose.'

'I can't hear what you say,' he said shifting his earpiece.

'I'm sorry, Mr Other,' I said.

'My name's not Other. You know me. I'm A. N. Bowles.'

'We call you A. N. Other in the office. Why don't you go to the bank here and cash a cheque? There's someone always on duty.'

'I haven't got a French account, young man. Haven't you heard of currency regulations?'

'They don't seem to be troubling either of us much,' I said.

'You'd better come and have a cup of coffee and discuss the matter.'

'I'm busy just now.'

'Young man,' the Other said, 'I'm your employer.'

'I don't recognize anybody but the Gom.'

'Who on earth is the Gom?'

'Mr Dreuther.'

'The Gom. A. N. Other. There seems to be a curious lack of respect for the heads of your firm. Sir Walter Blixon—has he a name?'

'I believe the junior staff know him as the Blister.'

A thin smile momentarily touched the grey powdery features. 'At least that name is expressive,' A. N. Other remarked. 'Nurse, you can take a walk for half an hour. You can go as far as the harbour and back. You've always told me you like boats.'

When I turned the chair and began to push Bowles into the bar, a slight sweat had formed on my forehead and hands. An idea had come to me so fantastic that it drove away the thought of Cary and her hungry squire. I couldn't even wait till I got to the bar. I said, 'I've got fifteen million francs in my safe deposit box at the hotel. You can have them tonight in return for your shares.'

'Don't be a fool. They are worth twenty million at par, and Dreuther or Blixon would give me fifty million for them. A glass of Perrier water, please.'

I got him his water. He said, 'Now fetch me that five million.'

'No.'

'Young man,' he said, 'I have an infallible system. I have promised myself for twenty years to break the bank. I will not be foiled by a mere five million. Go and fetch them. Unless you do I shall order your dismissal.'

'Do you think that threat means anything to a man with fifteen million in the safe? And tomorrow I shall have twenty million.'

'You've been losing all tonight. I've watched you.'

'I had expected to lose. It proves my system's right.'

'There can't be two infallible systems.'

'Yours, I'm afraid, will prove only too fallible.'

'Tell me how yours works.'

'No. But I'll advise you on what is wrong with yours.'

'My system is my own.'

'How much have you won by it?'

'I have not yet begun to win. I am only at the first stage. Tonight I begin to win. Damn you, young man, fetch me that five million.'

'My system has won over fifteen million.'

I had got a false impression that the Other was a calm man. It is easy to appear calm when your movements are so confined. But when his fingers moved an inch on his knee he was exhibiting an uncontrollable emotion: his head swayed a minute degree and set the cord of his ear-appliance flapping. It was like the tiny stir of air clinking a shutter that is yet the sign of a tornado's approach.

He said, 'Suppose we have hit on the same system.'

'We haven't. I've been watching yours. I know it well. You can buy it in a paper packet at the stationer's for a thousand francs.'

'That's false. I thought it out myself, over the years, young man, in this chair. Twenty years of years.'

'It's not only *great* minds that think alike. But the bank will never be broken by a thousand-franc system marked on the envelope Infallible.'

'I'll prove you wrong. I'll make you eat that packet. Fetch me the five million.'

'I've told you my terms.'

Backward and forward and sideways moved the hands in that space to which illness confined him. They ran like mice in a cage—I could imagine them nibbling at the intolerable bars. 'You don't know what you are asking. Don't you realize you'd control the company if you chose to side with Blixon?'

'At least I would know something about the company I controlled.'

'Listen. If you let me have the five million tonight, I will repay it in the morning and give you half my winnings.'

'There won't be any winnings with your system.'

'You seem very sure of yours.'

'Yes.'

'I might consider selling the shares for twenty million plus your system.'

'I haven't got twenty million.'

'Listen, if you are so sure of yourself you can take an option on the shares for fifteen million now. You pay the balance in twenty-four hours—9 p.m. tomorrow—or you forfeit your fifteen million. In addition you give me your system.'

'It's a crazy proposal.'

'This is a crazy place.'

'If I don't win five million tomorrow, I don't have a single share?'

'Not a single share.' The fingers had stopped moving.

I laughed. 'Doesn't it occur to you that I've only got to phone the office tomorrow, and Blixon would advance me the money on the option? He wants the shares.'

'Tomorrow is Sunday and the agreement is for cash.'

'I don't give you the system till the final payment,' I said.

'I shan't want it if you've lost.'

'But I need money to play with.'

He took that carefully in. I said, 'You can't run a system on a few thousand francs.'

'You can pay ten million now,' he said, 'on account of fifteen. If you lose, you'll owe me five million.'

'How would you get it?'

He gave me a malign grin. 'I'll have your wages docked five hundred a year for ten years.'

I believe he meant it. In the world of Dreuther and Blixon he and his small packet of shares had survived only by the hardness, the meanness and the implacability of his character.

'I shall have to win ten million with five million.'

'You said you had the perfect system.'

'I thought I had.'

The old man was bitten by his own gamble: he jeered at me. 'Better just lend me the five million and forget the option.'

I thought of the Gom at sea in his yacht with his headline guests and the two of us forgotten—what did he care about his assistant accountant? I remembered the way he had turned to Miss Bullen and said, 'Arrange for Mr Bertrand (he couldn't bother to get my name right) to be married.' Would he arrange through Miss Bullen for our children to be born and our parents to be buried? I thought, with these shares at Blixon's call I shall have him fixed—he'll be powerless, I'll be employing him for just as long as I want him to feel the sting: then no more room on the eighth floor, no more yacht, no more of his '*luxe, calme et volupté*'. He had taken me in with his culture and his courtesy and his phoney kindness until I had nearly accepted him for the great man he believed himself to be. Now, I thought with a sadness for which I couldn't account, he will be small enough to be in my hands, and I looked at my ink-stained fingers with disrelish.

'You see,' the Other said, 'you don't believe any longer.'

'Oh, yes, I do,' I said, 'I'll take your bet. I was just thinking of something else—that's all.'

3

I went and fetched the money and we drew up the option right away on a sheet of notepaper and the nurse—who had returned by then—and the barman witnessed it. The option was to be taken up at 9 p.m. prompt in the same spot next day: the Other didn't want his gambling to be interrupted before his dinner-hour whether by good or bad news. Then I made him buy me a glass of whisky, though Moses had less trouble in extracting his drink from a rock in Sinai, and I watched him being pushed back to the *Salle Privée*. To all intents and purposes, for the next twenty-four hours, I was the owner of Sitra. Neither Dreuther nor Blixon in their endless war could make a move without the consent of their assistant accountant. It was strange to think that neither was aware of how the control of the business had changed—from a friend of Dreuther to an enemy of Dreuther. Blixon would be down in Hampshire reading up tomorrow's lessons, polishing up his pronunciation of the names in Judges—he would feel no exhilaration. And Dreuther—Dreuther was at sea, out of reach, playing bridge probably with his social lions—he would not be touched by the sense of insecurity. I ordered another whisky: I no longer doubted my system and I had no sense of regret. Blixon would be the first to hear: I would telephone to the office on Monday morning. It would be tactful to inform him of the new position through my chief, Arnold. There must be no temporary *rapprochement* between Dreuther and Blixon against the intruder: I would have Arnold explain to Blixon that for the time being he could count on me. Dreuther would not even hear of the matter unless he rang up his office from some port of call. Even that I could prevent: I could tell Arnold that the secret must be kept till Dreuther's return, for then I would have the pleasure of giving him the information in person.

I went out to tell Cary the news, forgetting about our engagements: I wanted to see her face when I told her she was the wife of the man who controlled the company. You've hated my system, I wanted to say to her, and the hours I have spent at the Casino, but there was no vulgar cause—it wasn't money I was after, and I quite forgot that until that evening I had no other motive than money. I began to believe that I had planned this from the first two-hundred-franc bet in the *cuisine*.

But of course there was no Cary to be found—'Madame went out with a gentleman,' the porter needlessly told me, and I remembered the date at the simple students' café. Well, there had been a time in my life when I had found little difficulty in picking up a woman and I went back to the Casino to fulfil my word. But the beautiful woman had got a man with her now: their fingers nuzzled over their communal tokens, and I soon realized that single women who came to the Casino to gamble were seldom either beautiful or interested in men. The ball and not the bed was the focal point. I thought of Cary's questions and my own lies—and there wasn't a lie she wouldn't see through.

I watched Bird's Nest circling among the tables, making a quick pounce here and there, out of the croupier's eye. She had a masterly technique: when a pile was large enough she would lay her fingers on a single piece and give a tender ogle at the owner as much as to say, 'You are so generous and I am all yours for the taking.' She was so certain of her own appeal that no one had the heart to expose her error. Tonight she was wearing long amber ear-rings and a purple evening dress that exposed her best feature–her shoulders. Her shoulders were magnificent, wide and animal, but then, like a revolving light, her face inevitably came round, the untidy false blonde hair tangled up with the ear-rings (I am sure she thought of her wisps and strands as 'wanton locks'), and that smile fixed like a fossil. Watching her revolve I began to revolve too: I was caught into her orbit, and I became aware that here alone was the answer. I had to dine with a woman and in the whole Casino this was the only woman who would dine with me. As she swerved away from an attendant with a sweep of drapery and a slight clank, clank from her evening bag where I supposed she had stowed her hundred-franc tokens, I touched her hand. 'Dear lady,' I said–the phrase astonished me: it was as though it had been placed on my tongue, and certainly it seemed to belong to the same period as the mauve evening dress, the magnificent shoulders. 'Dear lady,' I repeated with increasing astonishment (I almost expected a small white moustache to burgeon on my upper lip), 'you will I trust excuse a stranger . . .'

I think she must have gone in constant fear of the attendants because her instinctive ogle expanded with her relief at seeing me into a positive blaze of light: it flapped across the waste of her face like sheet lightning. 'Oh, not a stranger,' she said, and I was relieved to find that she was English and that at least I would not have to talk bad French throughout the evening. 'I have been watching with such admiration your great good fortune.' (She had indeed profited from it on several occasions.)

'I was wondering, dear lady,' (the extraordinary phrase slipped out again) 'if you would do me the honour of dining. I have no one with whom to celebrate my luck.'

'But, of course, colonel, it would be a great pleasure.' At that I really put my hand up to my mouth to see if the moustache were there. We both seemed to have learnt parts in a play–I began to fear what the third act might hold. I noticed she was edging towards the restaurant of the *Salle Privée*, but all my snobbery revolted at dining there with so notorious a figure of fun. I said, 'I thought perhaps–if we could take a little air–it's such a beautiful evening, the heat of these rooms, some small exclusive place . . .' I would have suggested a private room if I had not feared that my intentions might have been misunderstood and welcomed.

'Nothing would give me greater pleasure, colonel.'

We swept out (there was no other word for it) and I prayed that Cary and her young man were safely at dinner in their cheap café; it would have been intolerable if she had seen me at that moment. The woman imposed unreality. I was persuaded that to the white moustache had now been added a collapsible opera hat and a scarlet lined cloak.

I said, 'A horse-cab, don't you think, on a night so balmy . . .'

'Barmy, colonel?'

'Spelt with an L,' I explained, but I don't think she understood.

When we were seated in the cab I appealed for her help. 'I am really quite a stranger here. I have dined out so seldom. Where can we go that is quiet . . . and exclusive?' I was determined that the place should be exclusive: if it excluded all the world but the two of us, I would be the less embarrassed.

'There is a small new restaurant—a club really, very *comme il faut*. It is called *Orphée*. Rather expensive, I fear, colonel.'

'Expense is no object.' I gave the name to the driver and leant back. As she was sitting bolt upright I was able to shelter behind her bulk. I said, 'When were you last in Cheltenham . . . ?'

The devil was about us that night. Whatever I said had been written into my part. She replied promptly, 'Dear Cheltenham . . . how did you discover . . . ?'

'Well, you know, a handsome woman catches one's eye.'

'You live there too?'

'One of those little houses off Queen's Parade.'

'We must be near neighbours,' and to emphasize our nearness I could feel her massive flank move ever so slightly against me. I was glad that the cab drew up: we hadn't gone more than two hundred yards from the Casino.

'A bit highbrow, what?' I said, glaring up as I felt a colonel should do at the lit mask above the door made out of an enormous hollowed potato. We had to brush our way through shreds of cotton which were meant, I suppose, to represent cobwebs. The little room inside was hung with photographs of authors, actors and film stars, and we had to sign our name in a book, thus apparently becoming life members of the club. I wrote Robert Devereux. I could feel her leaning against my shoulder, squinnying at the signature.

The restaurant was crowded and rather garishly lit by bare globes. There were a lot of mirrors that must have been bought at the sale of some old restaurant, for they advertised ancient specialities like 'Mutton Chopps'.

She said, 'Cocteau was at the opening.'

'Who's he?'

'Oh, colonel,' she said, 'you are laughing at me.'

I said, 'Oh well, you know, in my kind of life one hasn't much time for books,' and suddenly, just under the word Chopps, I saw Cary gazing back at me.

'How I envy a life of action,' my companion said, and laid down her bag—chinkingly—on the table. The whole bird's nest shook and the amber ear-rings swung as she turned to me and said confidingly, 'Tell me, colonel. I love—passionately—to hear men talk of their lives.' (Cary's eyes in the mirror became enormous: her mouth was a little open as though she had been caught in mid-sentence.)

I said, 'Oh well, there's not much to tell.'

'Men are so much more modest than women. If I had deeds of derring-do to my credit I would never tire of telling them. Cheltenham must seem very quiet to you.' I heard a spoon drop at a neighbouring table. I said weakly, 'Oh well, I don't mind quiet. What will you eat?'

'I have such a teeny-weeny appetite, colonel. A *langouste thermidor* . . .'

'And a bottle of the Widow?' I could have bitten my tongue—the hideous words were out before I could stop them. I wanted to turn to Cary and say, 'This isn't me. I didn't write this. It's my part. Blame the author.'

A voice I didn't know said, 'But I adore you. I adore everything you do, the way you talk, the way you are so silent. I wish I could speak English much much better so that I could tell you . . .' I turned slowly sideways and looked at Cary. I had never, since I kissed her first, seen so complete a blush. Bird's Nest said, 'So young and so romantic, aren't they? I always think the English are too reticent. That's what makes our encounter so strange. Half an hour ago we didn't even know each other, and now here we are with–what did you call it?–a bottle of the Widow. How I love these masculine phrases. Are you married, colonel?'

'Well, in a way . . .'

'How do you mean?'

'We're sort of separated.'

'How sad. I'm separated too–by death. Perhaps that's less sad.'

A voice I had begun to detest said, 'Your husband does not deserve you to be faithful. To leave you all night while he gambles . . .'

'He's not gambling tonight,' Cary said. She added in a strangled voice, 'He's in Cannes having dinner with a young, beautiful, intelligent widow.'

'Don't cry, *chérie*.'

'I'm not crying, Philippe. I'm, I'm, I'm laughing. If he could see me now . . .'

'He would be wild with jealousy, I hope. Are you jealous?'

'So touching,' Bird's Nest said. 'One can't help listening. One seems to glimpse an entire life . . .'

The whole affair seemed to me abominably one-sided. 'Women are so gullible,' I said, raising my voice a little. 'My wife started going around with a young man because he looked hungry. Perhaps he was hungry. He would take her to expensive restaurants like this and make her pay. Do you know what they charge for a *langouste thermidor* here? It's so expensive, they don't even put the price on the bill. A simple inexpensive café for students.'

'I don't understand, colonel. Has something upset you?'

'And the wine. Don't you think I had to draw the line at his drinking wine at my expense?'

'You must have been treated shamefully.'

Somebody put down a glass so hard that it broke. The detestable voice said, '*Chérie*, that is good fortune for us. Look–I put some wine behind your ears, on the top of your head . . . Do you think your husband will sleep with the beautiful lady in Cannes?'

'Sleep is about all he's capable of doing.'

I got to my feet and shouted at her–I could stand no more. 'How dare you say such things?'

'Philippe,' Cary said, 'let's go.' She put some notes on the table and led him out. He was too surprised to object.

Bird's Nest said, 'They are really going too far, weren't they? Talking like that in public. I love your old-fashioned chivalry, colonel. The young must learn.'

She took nearly an hour before she got through her *langouste thermidor* and her strawberry ice. She began to tell me the whole story of her life, beginning over the *langouste* with a childhood in an old rectory in Kent and ending over the ice-cream with her small widow's portion at Cheltenham. She was staying in a little *pension* in Monte Carlo because it was 'select', and I suppose her methods at the Casino very nearly paid for her keep.

I got rid of her at last and went home. I was afraid that Cary wouldn't be there, but she was sitting up in bed reading one of those smart phrase books that are got up like a novel and are terribly bright and gay. When I opened the door she looked up over the book and said, '*Entrez, mon colonel.*'

'What are you reading that for?' I said.

'*J'essaye de faire mon français un peu meilleur.*'

'Why?'

'I might live in France one day.'

'Oh? Who with? The hungry student?'

'Philippe has asked me to marry him.'

'After what his dinner must have cost you tonight, I suppose he had to take an honourable line.'

'I told him there was a temporary impediment.'

'You mean your bad French?'

'I meant you, of course.'

Suddenly she began to cry, burying her head under the phrase book so that I shouldn't see. I sat down on the bed and put my hand on her side: I felt tired: I felt we were very far from the public house at the corner: I felt we had been married a long time and it hadn't worked. I had no idea how to pick up the pieces–I have never been good with my hands.

I said, 'Let's go home.'

'Not wait any more for Mr Dreuther?'

'Why should we? I practically own Mr Dreuther now.'

I hadn't meant to tell her, but out it came, all of it. She emerged from under the phrase book and she stopped crying. I told her that when I had extracted the last fun out of being Dreuther's boss, I would sell my shares at a good profit to Blixon–and that would be the final end of Dreuther. 'We'll be comfortably off,' I said.

'*We* won't.'

'What do you mean?'

'Darling, I'm not hysterical now and I'm not angry. I'm talking really seriously. I didn't marry a well-off man. I married a man I met in the bar of the Volunteer–someone who liked cold sausages and travelled by bus because taxis were too expensive. He hadn't had a very good life. He married a bitch who ran away from him. I wanted–oh, enormously–to give him fun. Now suddenly I've woken up in bed with a man who can buy all the fun he wants and his idea of fun is to ruin an old man who was kind to him. What if Dreuther did forget he'd invited you? He meant it at the time. He looked at you and you seemed tired and he liked you–just like that, for no reason, just as I liked you the first time in the Volunteer. That's how human beings work. They don't work on a damned system like your roulette.'

'The system hasn't done so badly for you.'

'Oh yes, it has. It's destroyed me. I've lived for you and now I've lost you.'

'You haven't. I'm here.'

'When I return home and go into the bar of the Volunteer, you won't be there. When I'm waiting at the 19 bus stop you won't be there either. You won't be anywhere where *I* can find you. You'll be driving down to your place in Hampshire like Sir Walter Blixon. Darling, you've been very lucky and you've won a lot of money, but I don't like you any more.'

I sneered back at her, but there wasn't any heart in my sneer. 'You only love the poor, I suppose?'

'Isn't that better than only loving the rich? Darling, I'm going to sleep on the sofa in the sitting-room.' We had a sitting-room again now, and a dressing-room for me, just as at the beginning. I said, 'Don't bother. I've got my own bed.'

I went out on to the balcony. It was like the first night when we had quarrelled, but this time she didn't come out on to her balcony, and we hadn't quarrelled. I wanted to knock on her door and say something, but I didn't know what words to use. All my words seemed to chink like the tokens in Bird's Nest's bag.

4

I didn't see her for breakfast, nor for lunch. I went into the Casino after lunch and for the first time I didn't want to win. But the devil was certainly in my system and win I did. I had the money to pay Bowles, I owned the shares, and I wished I had lost my last two hundred francs in the kitchen. After that I walked along the terrace—sometimes one gets ideas walking, but I didn't. And then looking down into the harbour I saw a white boat which hadn't been there before. She was flying the British flag and I recognized her from newspaper photographs. She was the *Seagull*. The Gom had come after all—he wasn't much more than a week late. I thought, you bastard, if only you'd troubled to keep your promise, I wouldn't have lost Cary. I wasn't important enough for you to remember and now I'm too important for her to love. Well, if I've lost her, you are going to lose everything too—Blixon will probably buy your boat.

I walked into the bar and the Gom was there. He had just ordered himself a Pernod and he was talking with easy familiarity to the barman, speaking perfect French. Whatever the man's language he would have spoken it perfectly—he was of the Pentecostal type. Yet he wasn't the Dreuther of the eighth floor now—he had put an old yachting cap on the bar, he had several days' growth of white beard and he wore an old and baggy pair of blue trousers and a sweat shirt. When I came in he didn't stop talking, but I could see him examining me in the mirror behind the bar. He kept on glancing at me as though I pricked a memory. I realized that he had not only forgotten his invitation, he had even forgotten me.

'Mr Dreuther,' I said.

He turned as slowly as he could; he was obviously trying to remember. 'You don't remember me,' I said.

'Oh, my dear chap, I remember you perfectly. Let me see, the last time we met . . .'

'My name's Bertram.' I could see it didn't mean a thing to him. He said, 'Of course. Of course. Been here long?'

'We arrived about nine days ago. We hoped you'd be in time for our wedding.'

'Wedding?' I could see it all coming back to him and for a moment he was foxed for an explanation.

'My dear chap, I hope everything was all right. We were caught with engine trouble. Out of touch. You know how it can be at sea. Now you are coming on board tonight, I hope. Get your bags packed. I want to sail at midnight. Monte Carlo is too much of a temptation for me. How about you? Been losing money?' He was sweeping his mistake into limbo on a tide of words.

'No, I've gained a little.'

'Hang on to it. It's the only way.' He was rapidly paying for his Pernod—he wanted to get away from his mistake as quickly as possible. 'Follow me down. We'll eat on board tonight. The three of us. No one else joins the boat until Portofino. Tell them I'll settle the bill.'

'It's not necessary. I can manage.'

'I can't have you out of pocket because I'm late.' He snatched his yachting cap and was gone. I could almost imagine he had a seaman's lurch. He had given me no time to develop my hatred or even to tell him that I didn't know where my wife was. I put the money for Bowles in an envelope and asked the porter to have it waiting for him in the bar of the Casino at nine. Then I went upstairs and began to pack my bags. I had a wild hope that if I could get Cary to sea our whole trouble might be left on shore in the luxury hotel, in the great ornate *Salle Privée*. I would have liked to stake all our troubles *en plein* and to lose them. It was only when I had finished my packing and went into her room that I knew I hadn't a hope. The room was more than empty—it was vacant. It was where somebody had been and wouldn't be again. The dressing-table was waiting for another user—the only thing left was the conventional letter. Women read so many magazines—they know the formula for parting. I think they have even learned the words by heart from the glossy pages—they are impersonal. 'Darling, I'm off. I couldn't bear to tell you that and what's the use? We don't fit any more.' I thought of nine days ago and how we'd urged the old horse-cab on. Yes, they said at the desk, Madame had checked out an hour ago.

I told them to keep my bags. Dreuther wouldn't want me to stay on board after what I was going to tell him.

5

Dreuther had shaved and changed his shirt and was reading a book in his little lounge. He again had the grand air of the eighth floor. The bar stood hospitably open and the flowers looked as though they had been newly arranged. I wasn't impressed. I knew about his kindness, but kindness at the skin-deep level can ruin people. Kindness has got to care. I carried a knife in my mind and waited to use it.

'But your wife has not come with you?'

'She'll be following,' I said.

'And your bags?'

'The bags too. Could I have a drink?'

I had no compunction in gaining the Dutch courage for assassination at his own expense. I had two whiskies very quickly. He poured them out himself, got the ice, served me like an equal. And he had no idea that in fact I was his superior.

'You look tired,' he said. 'The holiday had not done you good.'

'I have worries.'

'Did you remember to bring the Racine?'

'Yes.' I was momentarily touched that he had remembered that detail.

'Perhaps after dinner you would read a little. I was once fond of him like you. There is so much that I have forgotten. Age is a great period of forgetting.' I remembered what Cary had said—after all, at his age, hadn't he a right to forget? But when I thought of Cary I could have cried into my glass.

'We forget a lot of things near at hand, but we remember the past. I am often troubled by the past. Unnecessary misunderstanding. Unnecessary pain.'

'Could I have another whisky?'

'Of course.' He got up promptly to serve me. Leaning over his little bar, with his wide patriarchal back turned to me, he said, 'Do not mind talking. We are not on the eighth floor now. Two men on holiday. Friends I hope. Drink. There is no harm, if one is unhappy, in being a little drunk.'

I was a little drunk—more than a little. I couldn't keep my voice steady when I said, 'My wife isn't coming. She's left me.'

'A quarrel?'

'Not a real quarrel. Not words you can deny or forget.'

'Is she in love with someone else?'

'I don't know. Perhaps.'

'Tell me. I can't help. But one needs a listener.' Using the pronoun 'one' he made mine a general condition from which all men were destined to suffer. 'One' is born, 'one' dies, 'one' loses love. I told him everything—except what I had come to the boat to tell him. I told him of our coffee-and-roll lunches, of my winnings, of the hungry student and the Bird's Nest. I told him of our words over the waiter, I told him of her simple statement, 'I don't like you any more.' I even (it seems incredible to me now) showed him her letter.

He said, 'I am very sorry. If I had not been—delayed, this would not have happened. On the other hand you would not have won all this money.'

I said, 'Damn the money.'

'That is very easy to say. I have said it so often myself. But here I am—' he waved his hand round the little modest saloon that it took a very rich man to afford. 'If I had meant what I said, I wouldn't be here.'

'I do mean it.'

'Then you have hope.'

'She may be sleeping with him at this moment.'

'That does not destroy hope. So often one has discovered how much one loves by sleeping with another.'

'What shall I do?'

'Have a cigar.'

'I don't like them.'

'You will not mind–' He lit one himself. 'These too cost money. Certainly I do not like money–who could? The coins are badly designed and the paper is unclean. Like newspapers picked up in a public park, but I like cigars, this yacht, hospitality, and I suppose, I am afraid, yes,' he added lowering his cigar-point like a flag, 'power.' I had even forgotten that he no longer had it. 'One had to put up with this money.'

'Do you know where they will be?' he asked me.

'Celebrating, I imagine–on coffee and rolls.'

'I have had four wives. Are you sure you want her back?'

'Yes.'

'It can be very peaceful without them.'

'I'm not looking for peace–yet.'

'My second wife–I was still young then–she left me, and I made the mistake of winning her back. It took me years to lose her again after that. She was a good woman. It is not easy to lose a good woman. If one must marry it is better to marry a bad woman.'

'I did the first time and it wasn't much fun.'

'How interesting.' He took a long pull and watched the smoke drift and dissolve. 'Still, it didn't last. A good woman lasts. Blixon is married to a good woman. She sits next to him in the pew on Sundays, thinking about the menu for dinner. She is an excellent housekeeper and has great taste in interior decoration. Her hands are plump–she says proudly that they are good pastry hands–but that is not what a woman's hands should be for. She is a moral woman and when he leaves her during the week, he feels quite secure. But he has to go back, that is the terrible thing, he has to go back.'

'Cary isn't that good.' I looked at the last of my whisky. 'I wish to hell you could tell me what to do.'

'I am too old and the young would call me cynical. People don't like reality. They don't like common sense. Until age forces it on them. I would say–bring your bags, forget the whole matter–my whisky supply is large, for a few days anaesthetize yourself. I have some most agreeable guests coming on board tomorrow at Portofino–you will like Celia Charteris very much. At Naples there are several bordels if you find celibacy difficult. I will telephone to the office extending your leave. Be content with adventure. And don't try to domesticate adventure.'

I said, 'I want Cary. That's all. Not adventure.'

'My second wife left me because she said I was too ambitious. She didn't realize that it is only the dying who are free from ambition. And they probably have the ambition to live. Some men disguise their ambition–that's all. I was in a position to help this young man my wife loved. He soon showed his ambition then. There are different types of ambition–that is all, and my wife found she preferred mine. Because it was limitless. They do not feel the infinite as an unworthy rival, but for a man to prefer the desk of an assistant manager–that is an insult.' He looked mournfully at his long cigar-ash. 'All the same one should not meddle.'

'I would do anything . . .'

'Your wife is romantic. This young man's poverty appeals to her. I think I see a plan. Help yourself to another drink while I tell it to you . . .'

PART III

I

I went down the gang-plank, swaying slightly from the effect of the whisky, and walked up the hill from the port. It was a quarter past eight, and the sight of a clock reminded me for the first time of what I had not told Dreuther. Dreuther had said, 'Don't use money. Money is so obviously sordid. But those little round scarlet disks . . . You will see, no gambler can resist them.' I went to the Casino and looked for the pair: they were not there. Then I changed all the spare money I had, and when I came out my pocket clinked like Bird's Nest's bag.

It took me only a quarter of an hour to find them: they were in the café where we used to go for our meals. I watched them for a little, unseen from the door. Cary didn't look happy. She had gone there, she told me later, to prove to herself that she no longer loved me, that no sentiment attached to the places where we had been together, and she found that the proof didn't work out. She was miserable to see a stranger sitting in my chair, and the stranger had a habit she detested–he stuffed the roll into his mouth and bit off the buttered end. When he had finished he counted his resources and then asked her if she would mind not talking for a minute while he checked his system. 'We can go up to five hundred francs tonight in the kitchen,' he said, 'that is five one-hundred-franc stakes.' He was sitting there with a pencil and paper when I arrived.

I said 'Hullo,' from the doorway and Cary turned. She nearly smiled at me from habit–I could see the smile sailing up in her eyes and then she plucked it down like a boy might pluck his kite back to earth, out of the wind.

'What are you doing here?' she said.

'I wanted to make sure you were all right.'

'I am all right.'

'Sometimes one does something and wishes one hadn't.'

'Not me.'

'I wish you'd be quiet,' the young man said. 'What I am working out is very complicated.'

'Philippe, it's–my husband.'

He looked up, 'Oh, good evening,' and began to tap nervously on the table with the end of his pencil.

'I hope you are looking after my wife properly.'

'That's nothing to do with you,' he said.

'There are certain things you ought to know in order to make her happy. She hates skin on hot milk. Look, her saucer's full of scraps. You should attend to that before you pour out. She hates small sharp noises—for instance, the crackle of toast—or that roll you are eating. You must never chew nuts either. I hope you are listening. That noise with the pencil will not please her.'

'I wish you would go away,' the young man said.

'I would rather like to talk to my wife alone.'

'I don't want to be alone with you,' Cary said.

'You heard her. Please go.' It was strange how cleverly Dreuther had forecast our dialogue. I began to have hope.

'I'm sorry. I must insist.'

'You've no right . . .'

Cary said, 'Unless you leave us, we'll both walk out of here. Philippe, pay the bill.'

'*Chérie*, I do want to get my system straight.'

'I tell you what I'll do,' I said. 'I'm a much older man than you are, but I'll offer to fight you. If I win, I talk to Cary alone. If you win, I go away and never trouble you again.'

'I won't have you fighting,' Cary said.

'You heard her.'

'Alternatively, I'll pay for half an hour with her.'

'How dare you?' Cary said.

I put my hand in my pocket and pulled out fistfuls of yellow and red tokens—five-hundred-franc tokens, thousand-franc tokens, shooting them out on to the table between the coffee cups. He couldn't keep his eyes off them. They covered his system. I said, 'I'd rather fight. This is all the money I've got left.'

He stared at them. He said, 'I don't want to brawl.'

Cary said, 'Philippe, you wouldn't . . .'

I said, 'It's the only way you can get out of here without fighting.'

'*Chérie*, he only wants half an hour. After all, it's his right. There are things for you to settle together, and with this money I can really prove my system.'

She said to him in a voice to which in the past week I had become accustomed, 'All right. Take his money. Get along into that damned Casino. You've been thinking of nothing else all the evening.'

He had just enough grace to hesitate. 'I'll see you in half an hour, *chérie*.'

I said, 'I promise I'll bring her to the Casino myself. I have something to do there.' Then I called him back from the door, 'You've dropped a piece,' and he came back and felt for it under the table. Watching Cary's face I almost wished I hadn't won.

She was trying hard not to cry. She said, 'I suppose you think you've been very clever.'

'No.'

'You exposed him all right. You've demonstrated your point. What do I do now?'

'Come on board for one night. You've got a separate cabin. We can put you off in Genoa tomorrow.'

'I suppose you hope I'll change my mind?'

'Yes. I hope. It's not a very big hope, but it's better than despair. You see, I love you.'

'Would you promise never to gamble again?'

'Yes.'

'Would you throw away that damned system?'

'Yes.'

There was a song when I was young—'and then my heart stood still'. That was what I felt when she began to make conditions. 'Have you told him,' she asked, 'about the shares?'

'No.'

'I can't go on that boat with him not knowing. It would be too mean.'

'I promise I'll clear it up—before sleep.'

She had her head lowered, so that I couldn't see her face, and she sat very silent. I had used all my arguments: there was nothing more for me to say either. The night was full of nothing but clinking cups and running water. At last she said, 'What are we waiting for?'

We picked up all the bags and then we walked across to the Casino. She hadn't wanted to come, but I said, 'I promised to bring you.' I left her in the hall and went through to the kitchen—he wasn't there. Then I went to the bar, and then on to the *Salle Privée*. There he was, playing for the first time with a 500-franc minimum. A.N. Other was at the same table—the five-thousand squares littered the table around him. He sat in his chair with his fingers moving like mice. I leant over his shoulder and gave him *his* news, but he made no sign of interest, for the ball was bouncing now around the wheel. It came to rest in zero as I reached Philippe and the bank raked in their winnings.

I said to Philippe, 'Cary's here. I kept my promise.'

'Tell her not to come in. I am winning—except the last round. I do not want to be disturbed.'

'She won't disturb you ever again.'

'I have won 10,000.'

'But it's loser takes all,' I said. 'Lose these for me. It's all I've got left.'

I didn't wait for him to protest—and I don't think he would have protested.

2

The Gom that night was a perfect host. He showed himself so ignorant of our trouble that we began to forget it ourselves. There were cocktails before dinner and champagne at dinner and I could see that Cary was getting a little uncertain in her choice of words. She went to bed early because she wanted to leave me alone with the Gom. We both came out on to the deck to say good night to her. A small breeze went by, tasting of the sea, and the clouds hid moon and stars and made the riding lights on the yachts shine the brighter.

The Gom said, 'Tomorrow night you shall persuade me that Racine is the greatest poet, but tonight let me think of Baudelaire.' He leant on the rail and recited in a low voice, and I wondered to whom it was in the past that the old wise man with limitless ambitions was speaking.

> '*Vois sur ces canaux*
> *Dormir ces vaisseaux*
> *Dont l'humeur est vagabonde;*
> *C'est pour asssouvir*
> *Ton moindre désir*
> *Qu'ils viennent du bout du monde.*'

He turned and said, 'I am speaking that to you, my dear, from him,' and he put his arm around her shoulder, and then gave her a push towards the companion-way. She gave a sound like a small animal in pain and was gone.

'What was the matter?' the Gom asked.

'She was remembering something.' I knew what it was she was remembering, but I didn't tell him.

We went back into the saloon and the Gom poured out our drinks. He said, 'I'm glad the trick worked.'

'She may still decide to get off at Genoa.'

'She won't. In any case we'll leave out Genoa.' He added thoughtfully, 'It's not the first time I've kidnapped a woman.'

He gave me my glass. 'I shan't keep you up drinking tonight, but I wanted to tell you something. I'm getting a new assistant accountant.'

'You mean—you are giving me notice?'

'Yes.'

Unpredictable, the old bastard, I thought—to tell me this now, as his guest. Could it be that in my absence he had met and spoken with the Other? He said, 'You'll need a bigger income now you are married. I'm putting Arnold in charge of General Enterprises. You are to be chief accountant in his place. Drink your whisky and go to bed. They are getting up the anchor now.'

When I went down I wondered whether Cary's cabin would be locked, but it wasn't. She sat on one bunk with her knees drawn up to her chin staring through the porthole. The engines had started and we were moving out. The lights of the port wheeled around the wall. She said, 'Have you told him?'

'No.'

'You promised,' she said. 'I can't go sailing down Italy in this boat with him not knowing. He's been so terribly kind . . .'

'I owe him everything,' I said. 'It was he who told me how to act to get you back. The trick was his. I could think of nothing. I was in despair.'

'Then you must tell him. Now. At once.'

'There's nothing to tell. You don't think after he'd done that for me, I'd cheat him with Blixon?'

'But the shares?'

'When I went to find Philippe, I took back the money I'd left for the Other. The option's forfeited. The Other's fifteen million richer—and Philippe has our last five million if he hasn't lost it. We are back where we were.' The words were the wrong ones. I said, 'If only we could be.'

'We never can be.'

'Never?'

'I love you so much more. Because I've been terribly mean to you and nearly lost you.'

We said very little for a long time: there was no room for anything but our bodies in the cramped berth, but some time towards morning, when the circle of the porthole was grey, I woke her and told her what the Gom had said to me. 'We shan't be rich,' I added quickly for fear of losing her again, 'but we can afford Bournemouth next year . . .'

'No,' she said sleepily. 'Let's go to Le Touquet. They have a Casino there. But don't let's have a system.'

There was a promise I'd forgotten. I got up and took the great system out of my jacket-pocket and tore it in little pieces and threw them through the porthole–the white scraps blew back in our wake.

The sleepy voice said, 'Darling, it's terribly cold. It's snowing.'

'I'll close the porthole.'

'No. Just come back.'

THE POWER
AND THE GLORY

THE POWER AND THE GLORY

For Gervase

Th'inclosure narrow'd; the sagacious power
Of hounds and death drew nearer every hour.

Dryden

PART I

I

THE PORT

Mr Tench went out to look for his ether cylinder, into the blazing Mexican sun and the bleaching dust. A few vultures looked down from the roof with shabby indifference: he wasn't carrion yet. A faint feeling of rebellion stirred in Mr Tench's heart, and he wrenched up a piece of the road with splintering finger-nails and tossed it feebly towards them. One rose and flapped across the town: over the tiny plaza, over the bust of an ex-president, ex-general, ex-human being, over the two stalls which sold mineral water, towards the river and the sea. It wouldn't find anything there: the sharks looked after the carrion on that side. Mr Tench went on across the plaza.

He said 'Buenos días' to a man with a gun who sat in a small patch of shade against a wall. But it wasn't like England: the man said nothing at all, just stared malevolently up at Mr Tench, as if he had never had any dealings with the foreigner, as if Mr Tench were not responsible for his two gold bicuspid teeth. Mr Tench went sweating by, past the Treasury which had once been a church, towards the quay. Half-way across he suddenly forgot what he had come out for—a glass of mineral water? That was all there was to drink in this prohibition state—except beer, but that was a government monopoly and too expensive except on special occasions. An awful feeling of nausea gripped Mr Tench in the stomach—it couldn't have been mineral water he wanted. Of course his ether cylinder . . . the boat was in. He had heard its exultant piping while he lay on his bed after lunch. He passed the barbers' and two dentists' and came out between a warehouse and the customs on to the river bank.

The river went heavily by towards the sea between the banana plantations; the *General Obregon* was tied up to the bank, and beer was being unloaded—a hundred cases were already stacked upon the quay. Mr Tench stood in the shade of the customs house and thought: what am I here for? Memory drained out of him in the heat. He gathered his bile together and spat forlornly into the sun. Then he sat down on a case and waited. Nothing to do. Nobody would come to see him before five.

The *General Obregon* was about thirty yards long. A few feet of damaged rail, one lifeboat, a bell hanging on a rotten cord, an oil-lamp in the bow, she looked as if she might weather two or three more Atlantic years, if she didn't strike a Norther in the gulf. That, of course, would be the end of her. It didn't really matter: everybody was insured when he bought a ticket, automatically. Half a dozen passengers leant on the rail, among the hobbled turkeys, and stared at the port, the warehouse, the empty baked street with the dentists and the barbers.

Mr Tench heard a revolver holster creak just behind him and turned his head. A customs officer was watching him angrily. He said something which Mr Tench did not catch. 'Pardon me,' Mr Tench said.

'My teeth,' the customs man said indistinctly.

'Oh,' Mr Tench said, 'yes, your teeth.' The man had none: that was why he couldn't talk clearly. Mr Tench had removed them all. He was shaken with nausea—something was wrong—worms, dysentery. . . . He said, 'The set is nearly finished. To-night,' he promised wildly. It was, of course, quite impossible; but that was how one lived, putting off everything. The man was satisfied: he might forget, and in any case what could he *do*? He had paid in advance. That was the whole world to Mr Tench: the heat and the forgetting, the putting off till to-morrow, if possible cash down—for what? He stared out over the slow river: the fin of a shark moved like a periscope at the river's mouth. In the course of years several ships had stranded and they now helped to prop up the bank, the smoke-stacks leaning over like guns pointing at some distant objective across the banana trees and the swamps.

Mr Tench thought: ether cylinder: I nearly forgot. His mouth fell open and he began moodily to count the bottles of Cerveza Moctezuma. A hundred and forty cases. Twelve times a hundred and forty: the heavy phlegm gathered in his mouth: twelve fours are forty-eight. He said aloud in English, 'My God, a pretty one': twelve hundred, sixteen hundred and eighty: he spat, staring with vague interest at a girl in the bows of the *General Obregon*—a fine thin figure, they were generally so thick, brown eyes, of course, and the inevitable gleam of the gold tooth, but something fresh and young. . . . Sixteen hundred and eighty bottles at a peso a bottle.

Somebody whispered in English, 'What did you say?'

Mr Tench swivelled round. 'You English?' he asked in astonishment, but at the sight of the round and hollow face charred with a three-days' beard, he altered his question: 'You speak English?'

Yes, the man said, he spoke a little English. He stood stiffly in the shade, a small man dressed in a shabby dark city suit, carrying a small attaché case. He had a novel under his arm: bits of an amorous scene stuck out, crudely coloured. He said, 'Excuse me. I thought just now you were talking to me.' He had protuberant eyes; he gave an impression of unstable hilarity, as if perhaps he had been celebrating a birthday, alone.

Mr Tench cleared his mouth of phlegm. 'What did I say?' He couldn't remember a thing.

'You said my God a pretty one.'

'Now what could I have meant by that?' He stared up at the merciless sky. A vulture hung there, an observer. 'What? Oh just the girl I suppose. You don't often see a pretty piece round here. Just one or two a year worth looking at.'

'She is very young.'

'Oh, I don't have intentions,' Mr Tench said wearily. 'A man may look. I've lived alone for fifteen years.'

'Here?'

'Hereabouts.'

They fell silent and time passed, the shadow of the customs house shifted a few inches further towards the river: the vulture moved a little, like the black hand of a clock.

'You came in *her?*' Mr Tench asked.

'No.'

'Going in her?'

The little man seemed to evade the question, but then as if some explanation were required: 'I was just looking,' he said. 'I suppose she'll be sailing quite soon?'

'To Vera Cruz,' Mr Tench said. 'In a few hours.'

'Without calling anywhere?'

'Where could she call?' He asked, 'How did you get here?'

The stranger said vaguely, 'A canoe.'

'Got a plantation, eh?'

'No.'

'It's good hearing English spoken,' Mr Tench said. 'Now you learnt yours in the States?'

The man agreed. He wasn't very garrulous.

'Ah, what wouldn't I give,' Mr Tench said, 'to be there now.' He said in a low anxious voice, 'You don't happen, do you, to have a drink in that case of yours? Some of you people back there—I've known one or two—a little for medical purposes.'

'Only medicine,' the man said.

'You a doctor?'

The bloodshot eyes looked slyly out of their corners at Mr Tench. 'You would call me perhaps a—quack?'

'Patent medicines? Live and let live,' Mr Tench said.

'Are *you* sailing?'

'No, I came down here for—for . . . oh well, it doesn't matter anyway.' He put his hand on his stomach and said, 'You haven't got any medicine, have you, for—oh hell. I don't know what. It's just this bloody land. You can't cure me of that. No one can.'

'You want to go home?'

'Home,' Mr Tench said, 'my home's here. Did you see what the peso stands at in Mexico City? Four to the dollar. Four. O God. Ora pro nobis.'

'Are you a Catholic?'

'No, no. Just an expression. I don't believe in anything like that.' He said irrelevantly, 'It's too hot anyway.'

'I think I must find somewhere to sit.'

'Come up to my place,' Mr Tench said. 'I've got a spare hammock. The boat won't leave for hours—if you want to watch it go.'

The stranger said, 'I was expecting to see someone. The name was Lopez.'

'Oh, they shot him weeks ago,' Mr Tench said.

'Dead?'

'You know how it is round here. Friend of yours?'

'No, no,' the man protested hurriedly. 'Just a friend of a friend.'

'Well, that's how it is,' Mr Tench said. He brought up his bile again and spat it out into the hard sunlight. 'They say he used to help ... oh, undesirables ... well, to get out. His girl's living with the Chief of Police now.'

'His girl? Do you mean his daughter?'

'He wasn't married. I mean the girl he lived with.' Mr Tench was momentarily surprised by an expression on the stranger's face. He said again, 'You know how it is.' He looked across at the *General Obregon*. 'She's a pretty bit. Of course, in two years she'll be like all the rest. Fat and stupid. O God, I'd like a drink. Ora pro nobis.'

'I have a little brandy,' the stranger said.

Mr Tench regarded him sharply. 'Where?'

The hollow man put his hand to his hip–he might have been indicating the source of his odd nervous hilarity. Mr Tench seized his wrist. 'Careful,' he said. 'Not here.' He looked down the carpet of shadow: a sentry sat on an empty crate asleep beside his rifle. 'Come to my place,' Mr Tench said.

'I meant,' the little man said reluctantly, 'just to see her go.'

'Oh, it will be hours yet,' Mr Tench assured him again.

'Hours? Are you certain? It's very hot in the sun.'

'You'd better come home.'

Home: it was a phrase one used to mean four walls behind which one slept. There had never been a home. They moved across the little burnt plaza where the dead general grew green in the damp and the gaseosa stalls stood under the palms. Home lay like a picture postcard on a pile of other postcards: shuffle the pack and you had Nottingham, a Metroland birthplace, an interlude in Southend. Mr Tench's father had been a dentist too–his first memory was finding a discarded cast in a wastepaper basket–the rough toothless gaping mouth of clay, like something dug up in Dorset–Neanderthal or Pithecanthropus. It had been his favourite toy: they tried to tempt him with Meccano, but fate had struck. There is always one moment in childhood when the door opens and lets the future in. The hot wet river-port and the vultures lay in the wastepaper basket, and he picked them out. We should be thankful we cannot see the horrors and degradations lying around our childhood, in cupboards and bookshelves, everywhere.

There was no paving; during the rains the village (it was really no more) slipped into the mud. Now the ground was hard under the feet like stone. The two men walked in silence past barbers' shops and dentists'; the vultures on the roofs looked contented, like domestic fowls: they searched under wide dusty wings for parasites. Mr Tench said, 'Excuse me,' stopping at a little wooden hut, one storey high, with a veranda where a hammock swung. The hut was a little larger than the others in the narrow street which petered out two hundred yards away in swamp. He said, nervously, 'Would you like to take a look around? I don't want to boast, but I'm the best dentist here. It's not a bad place. As places go.' Pride wavered in his voice like a plant with shallow roots.

He led the way inside, locking the door behind him, through a dining-room where two rocking-chairs stood on either side of a bare table: an oil lamp, some copies of old American papers, a cupboard. He said, 'I'll get the glasses out, but first I'd like to show you–you're an educated man ...' The dentist's operating-room looked out on a yard where a few turkeys moved with shabby nervous pomp: a drill which worked with a pedal, a dentist's chair gaudy in bright red plush, a glass cupboard in which instruments were dustily jumbled. A forceps stood in a cup, a broken spirit-lamp was pushed into a corner, and gags of cotton-wool lay on all the shelves.

'Very fine,' the stranger commented.

'It's not so bad, is it,' Mr Tench said, 'for this town. You can't imagine the difficulties. That drill,' he continued bitterly, 'is made in Japan. I've only had it a month and it's wearing out already. But I can't afford American drills.'

'The window,' the stranger said, 'is very beautiful.'

One pane of stained glass had been let in: a Madonna gazed out through the mosquito wire at the turkeys in the yard. 'I got it,' Mr Tench said, 'when they sacked the church. It didn't feel right—a dentist's room without some stained glass. Not civilised. At home—I mean in England—it was generally the Laughing Cavalier—I don't know why—or else a Tudor rose. But one can't pick and choose.'

He opened another door and said, 'My workroom.' The first thing one saw was a bed under a mosquito tent. Mr Tench said, 'You understand—I'm pressed for room.' A ewer and basin stood at one end of a carpenter's bench, and a soap-dish: at the other a blow-pipe, a tray of sand, pliers, a little furnace. 'I cast in sand,' Mr Tench said. 'What else can I do in this place?' He picked up the cast of a lower jaw. 'You can't always get them accurate,' he said. 'Of course, they complain.' He laid it down, and nodded at another object on the bench—something stringy and intestinal in appearance, with two little bladders of rubber. 'Congenital fissure,' he said. 'It's the first time I've tried. The Kingsley cast. I doubt if I can do it. But a man must try to keep abreast of things.' His mouth fell open: the look of vacancy returned: the heat in the small room was overpowering. He stood there like a man lost in a cavern among the fossils and instruments of an age of which he knows very little. The stranger said, 'If we could sit down . . .'

Mr Tench stared at him blankly.

'We could open the brandy.'

'Oh yes, the brandy.'

Mr Tench got two glasses out of a cupboard under the bench, and wiped off traces of sand. Then they went and sat in rocking-chairs in the front room. Mr Tench poured out.

'Water?' the stranger asked.

'You can't trust the water,' Mr Tench said. 'It's got me here.' He put his hand on his stomach and took a long draught. 'You don't look too well yourself,' he said. He took a longer look. 'Your teeth.' One canine had gone, and the front teeth were yellow with tartar and carious. He said, 'You want to pay attention to them.'

'What is the good?' the stranger said. He held a small spot of brandy in his glass warily—as if it was an animal to which he gave shelter, but not trust. He had the air, in his hollowness and neglect, of somebody of no account who had been beaten up incidentally, by ill-health or restlessness. He sat on the very edge of the rocking-chair, with his small attaché case balanced on his knee and the brandy staved off with guilty affection.

'Drink up,' Mr Tench encouraged him (it wasn't his brandy). 'It will do you good.' The man's dark suit and sloping shoulders reminded him uncomfortably of a coffin, and death was in his carious mouth already. Mr Tench poured himself out another glass. He said, 'It gets lonely here. It's good to talk English, even to a foreigner. I wonder if you'd like to see a picture of my kids.' He drew a yellow snapshot out of his note-case and handed it over. Two small children struggled over the handle of a watering-can in a back garden. 'Of course,' he said, 'that was sixteen years ago.'

'They are young men now.'

'One died.'

'Oh, well,' the other replied gently, 'in a Christian country.' He took a gulp of his brandy and smiled at Mr Tench rather foolishly.

'Yes, I suppose so,' Mr Tench said with surprise. He got rid of his phlegm and said, 'It doesn't seem to me, of course, to matter much.' He fell silent, his thoughts ambling away; his mouth fell open, he looked grey and vacant, until he was recalled by a pain in the stomach and helped himself to some more brandy. 'Let me see. What was it we were talking about? The kids . . . oh yes, the kids. It's funny what a man remembers. You know, I can remember that watering-can better than I can remember the kids. It cost three and elevenpence three farthings, green; I could lead you to the shop where I bought it. But as for the kids,' he brooded over his glass into the past, 'I can't remember much else but them crying.'

'Do you get news?'

'Oh, I gave up writing before I came here. What was the use? I couldn't send any money. It wouldn't surprise me if the wife had married again. Her mother would like it—the old sour bitch: she never cared for me.'

The stranger said in a low voice, 'It is awful.'

Mr Tench examined his companion again with surprise. He sat there like a black question mark, ready to go, ready to stay, poised on his chair. He looked disreputable in his grey three-days' beard, and weak: somebody you could command to do anything. He said, 'I mean the world. The way things happen.'

'Drink up your brandy.'

He sipped at it. It was like an indulgence. He said, 'You remember this place before—before the Red Shirts came?'

'I suppose I do.'

'How happy it was then.'

'Was it? I didn't notice.'

'They had at any rate—God.'

'There's no difference in the teeth,' Mr Tench said. He gave himself some more of the stranger's brandy. 'It was always an awful place. Lonely. My God. People at home would have said romance. I thought: five years here, and then I'll go. There was plenty of work. Gold teeth. But then the peso dropped. And now I can't get out. One day I will.' He said, 'I'll retire. Go home. Live as a gentleman ought to live. This'—he gestured at the bare base room—'I'll forget all this. Oh, it won't be long now. I'm an optimist,' Mr Tench said.

The stranger asked suddenly, 'How long will she take to Vera Cruz?'

'Who?'

'The boat.'

Mr Tench said gloomily, 'Forty hours from now and we'd be there. The Diligencia. A good hotel. Dance places too. A gay town.'

'It makes it seem close,' the stranger said. 'And a ticket, how much would that be?'

'You'd have to ask Lopez,' Mr Tench said. 'He's the agent.'

'But Lopez . . .'

'Oh yes, I forgot. They shot him.'

Somebody knocked on the door. The stranger slipped the attaché case under his chair, and Mr Tench went cautiously up towards the window. 'Can't be too careful,' he said. 'Any dentist who's worth the name has enemies.'

A faint voice implored them, 'A friend,' and Mr Tench opened up. Immediately the sun came in like a white-hot bar.

A child stood in the doorway asking for a doctor. He wore a big hat and had stupid brown eyes. Beyond him two mules stamped and whistled on the hot beaten road. Mr Tench said he was not a doctor: he was a dentist. Looking round he saw the stranger crouched in the rocking-chair, gazing with an effect of prayer, entreaty. . . . The child said there was a new doctor in town: the old one had fever and wouldn't stir. His mother was sick.

A vague memory stirred in Mr Tench's brain. He said with an air of discovery, 'Why, you're a doctor, aren't you?'

'No, no. I've got to catch that boat.'

'I thought you said . . .'

'I've changed my mind.'

'Oh well, it won't leave for hours yet,' Mr Tench said. 'They're never on time.' He asked the child how far. The child said it was six leagues away.

'Too far,' Mr Tench said. 'Go away. Find someone else.' He said to the stranger, 'How things get around. Everyone must know you are in town.'

'I could do no good,' the stranger said anxiously: he seemed to be asking for Mr Tench's opinion, humbly.

'Go away,' Mr Tench commanded. The child did not stir. He stood in the hard sunlight looking in with infinite patience. He said his mother was dying. The brown eyes expressed no emotion: it was a fact. You were born, your parents died, you grew old, you died yourself.

'If she's dying,' Mr Tench said, 'there's no point in a doctor seeing her.'

But the stranger got up as though unwillingly he had been summoned to an occasion he couldn't pass by. He said sadly, 'It always seems to happen. Like this.'

'You'll have a job not to miss the boat.'

'I shall miss it,' he said. 'I am meant to miss it.' He was shaken by a tiny rage. 'Give me my brandy.' He took a long pull at it, with his eyes on the impassive child, the baked street, the vultures moving in the sky like indigestion spots.

'But if she's dying . . .' Mr Tench said.

'I know these people. She will be no more dying than I am.'

'You can do no good.'

The child watched them as if he didn't care. The argument in a foreign language going on in there was something abstract: he wasn't concerned. He would just wait here till the doctor came.

'You know nothing,' the stranger said fiercely. 'That is what everyone all the time says—you do no good.' The brandy had affected him. He said with monstrous bitterness, 'I can hear them saying it all over the world.'

'Anyway,' Mr Tench said, 'there'll be another boat. In a fortnight. Or three weeks. You are lucky. You can get out. You haven't got your capital here.' He thought of his capital: the Japanese drill, the dentist's chair, the spirit-lamp and the pliers and the little oven for the gold fillings: a stake in the country.

'Vamos,' the man said to the child. He turned back to Mr Tench and told him that he was grateful for the rest out of the sun. He had the kind of dwarfed dignity Mr Tench was accustomed to—the dignity of people afraid of a little pain and yet sitting down with some firmness in his chair. Perhaps he didn't care for mule travel. He said with an effect of old-fashioned ways, 'I will pray for you.'

'You were welcome,' Mr Tench said. The man got up on to the mule, and the child led the way, very slowly under the bright glare, towards the swamp, the interior. It was from there the man had emerged this morning to take a look at the *General Obregon*: now he was going back. He swayed very slightly in his saddle from the effect of the brandy. He became a minute disappointed figure at the end of the street.

It had been good to talk to a stranger, Mr Tench thought, going back into his room, locking the door behind him (one never knew). Loneliness faced him there, vacancy. But he was as accustomed to both as to his own face in the glass. He sat down in the rocking-chair and moved up and down, creating a faint breeze in the heavy air. A narrow column of ants moved across the room to the little patch on the floor where the stranger had spilt some brandy: they milled in it, then moved on in an orderly line to the opposite wall and disappeared. Down in the river the *General Obregon* whistled twice, he didn't know why.

The stranger had left his book behind. It lay under his rocking-chair: a woman in Edwardian dress crouched sobbing upon a rug embracing a man's brown polished pointed shoes. He stood above her disdainfully with a little waxed moustache. The book was called *La Eterna Martyr*. After a time Mr Tench picked it up. When he opened it he was taken aback—what was printed inside didn't seem to belong; it was Latin. Mr Tench grew thoughtful: he shut the book up and carried it into his workroom. You couldn't burn a book, but it might be as well to hide it if you were not sure—sure, that is, of what it was all about. He put it inside the little oven for gold alloy. Then he stood by the carpenter's bench, his mouth hanging open: he had remembered what had taken him to the quay—the ether cylinder which should have come down-river in the *General Obregon*. Again the whistle blew from the river, and Mr Tench ran without his hat into the sun. He had said the boat would not go before morning, but you could never trust these people *not* to keep to time-table, and sure enough, when he came out on to the bank between the customs and the warehouse, the *General Obregon* was already ten feet off in the sluggish river, making for the sea. He bellowed after it, but it wasn't any good: there was no sign of a cylinder anywhere on the quay. He shouted once again, and then didn't trouble any more. It didn't matter so much after all: a little additional pain was hardly noticeable in the huge abandonment.

On the *General Obregon* a faint breeze became evident: banana plantations on either side, a few wireless aerials on a point, the port slipped behind. When you looked back you could not have told that it had ever existed at all. The wide Atlantic opened up; the great grey cylindrical waves lifted the bows, and the hobbled turkeys shifted on the deck. The captain stood in the tiny deck-house with a toothpick in his hair. The land went backward at a slow even roll, and the dark came quite suddenly, with a sky of low and brilliant stars. One oil-lamp was lit in the bows, and the girl whom Mr Tench had spotted from the bank began to sing gently—a melancholy, sentimental and contented song about a rose which had been stained with true love's blood. There was an enormous sense of freedom and air upon the gulf with the low tropical shore-line buried in darkness as deeply as any mummy in a tomb. I am happy, the young girl said to herself without considering why, I am happy.

Far back inside the darkness the mules plodded on. The effect of the brandy had long ago worn off, and the man bore in his brain along the marshy tract, which, when the rains came, would be quite impassable, the sound of the *General Obregon*'s siren. He knew what it meant: the ship had kept to time-table: he was abandoned. He felt an unwilling hatred of the child ahead of him and the sick woman—he was unworthy of what he carried. A smell of damp came up all round him; it was as if this part of the world had never been dried in the flame when the world spun off into space: it had absorbed only the mist and cloud of those awful regions. He began to pray, bouncing up and down to the lurching slithering mule's stride, with his brandied tongue: 'Let me be caught soon. . . . Let me be caught.' He had tried to escape, but he was like the King of a West African tribe, the slave of his people, who may not even lie down in case the winds should fail.

2

THE CAPITAL

The squad of police made their way back to the station. They walked raggedly with rifles slung anyhow: ends of cotton where buttons should have been: a puttee slipping down over the ankle: small men with black secret Indian eyes. The little plaza on the hill-top was lighted with globes strung together in threes and joined by trailing overhead wires. The Treasury, the Presidencia, a dentist's, the prison—a low white colonnaded building which dated back three hundred years—and then the steep street down past the back wall of a ruined church: whichever way you went you came ultimately to water and to river. Pink classical façades peeled off and showed the mud beneath, and the mud slowly reverted to mud. Round the plaza the evening parade went on—women in one direction, men in the other; young men in red shirts milled boisterously round the gaseosa stalls.

The lieutenant walked in front of his men with an air of bitter distaste. He might have been chained to them unwillingly—perhaps the scar on his jaw was the relic of an escape. His gaiters were polished, and his pistol-holster: his buttons were all sewn on. He had a sharp crooked nose jutting out of a lean dancer's face; his neatness gave an effect of inordinate ambition in the shabby city. A sour smell came up to the plaza from the river and the vultures were bedded on the roofs, under the tent of their rough black wings. Sometimes a little moron head peered out and down and a claw shifted. At nine-thirty exactly all the lights in the plaza went out.

A policeman clumsily presented arms and the squad marched into barracks; they waited for no order, hanging up their rifles by the officer's room, lurching on into the court-yard, to their hammocks or the excusados. Some of them kicked off their boots and lay down. Plaster was peeling off the mud walls; a generation of policemen had scrawled messages on the whitewash. A few peasants waited on a bench, hands between their knees. Nobody paid them any attention. Two men were fighting in the lavatory.

'Where is the jefe?' the lieutenant asked. No one knew for certain: they thought he was playing billiards somewhere in the town. The lieutenant sat down with dapper irritation at the chief's table; behind his head two hearts were entwined in pencil on the whitewash. 'All right,' he said, 'what are you waiting for? Bring in the prisoners.' They came in bowing, hat in hand, one behind the other. 'So-and-so drunk and disorderly.' 'Fined five pesos.' 'But I can't pay, your excellency.' 'Let him clean out the lavatory and the cells then.' 'So-and-so. Defaced an election poster.' 'Fined five pesos.' 'So-and-so found wearing a holy medal under his shirt.' 'Fined five pesos.' The duty drew to a close: there was nothing of importance. Through the open door the mosquitoes came whirring in.

Outside the sentry could be heard presenting arms. The Chief of Police came breezily in, a stout man with a pink fat face, dressed in white flannels with a wide-awake hat and a cartridge-belt and a big pistol clapping his thigh. He held a handkerchief to his mouth: he was in distress. 'Toothache again,' he said, 'toothache.'

'Nothing to report,' the lieutenant said with contempt.

'The Governor was at me again to-day,' the chief complained.

'Liquor?'

'No, a priest.'

'The last was shot weeks ago.'

'He doesn't think so.'

'The devil of it is,' the lieutenant said, 'we haven't photographs.' He glanced along the wall to the picture of James Calver, wanted in the United States for bank robbery and homicide: a tough uneven face taken at two angles: description circulated to every station in Central America: the low forehead and the fanatic bent-on-one-thing eyes. He looked at it with regret: there was so little chance that he would ever get south; he would be picked up in some dive at the border—in Juarez or Piedras Negras or Nogales.

'He says we have,' the chief complained. 'My tooth, oh, my tooth.' He tried to find something in his hip-pocket, but the holster got in the way. The lieutenant tapped his polished boot impatiently, 'There,' the chief said. A large number of people sat round a table: young girls in white muslin: older women with untidy hair and harassed expressions: a few men peered shyly and solicitously out of the background. All the faces were made up of small dots. It was a newspaper photograph of a first communion party taken years ago; a youngish man in a Roman collar sat among the women. You could imagine him petted with small delicacies, preserved for their use in the stifling atmosphere of intimacy and respect. He sat there, plump, with protuberant eyes, bubbling with harmless feminine jokes. 'It was taken years ago.'

'He looks like all the rest,' the lieutenant said. It was obscure, but you could read into the smudgy photograph a well-shaved, well-powdered jowl much too developed for his age. The good things of life had come to him too early–the respect of his contemporaries, a safe livelihood. The trite religious word upon the tongue, the joke to ease the way, the ready acceptance of other people's homage . . . a happy man. A natural hatred as between dog and dog stirred in the lieutenant's bowels. 'We've shot him half a dozen times,' he said.

'The Governor has had a report . . . he tried to get away last week to Vera Cruz.'

'What are the Red Shirts doing that he comes to *us*?'

'Oh, they missed him, of course. It was just luck that he didn't catch the boat.'

'What happened to him?'

'They found his mule. The Governor says he must have him this month. Before the rains come.'

'Where was his parish?'

'Concepción and the villages around. But he left there years ago.'

'Is anything known?'

'He can pass as a gringo. He spent six years at some American seminary. I don't know what else. He was born in Carmen–the son of a storekeeper. Not that that helps.'

'They all look alike to me,' the lieutenant said. Something you could almost have called horror moved him when he looked at the white muslin dresses–he remembered the smell of incense in the churches of his boyhood, the candles and the laciness and the self-esteem, the immense demands made from the altar steps by men who didn't know the meaning of sacrifice. The old peasants knelt there before the holy images with their arms held out in the attitude of the cross: tired by the long day's labour in the plantations they squeezed out a further mortification. And the priest came round with the collecting-bag taking their centavos, abusing them for their small comforting sins, and sacrificing nothing at all in return–except a little sexual indulgence. And that was easy, the lieutenant thought, easy. Himself he felt no need of women. He said, 'We will catch him. It is only a question of time.'

'My tooth,' the chief wailed again. He said, 'It poisons the whole of life. To-day my biggest break was twenty-five.'

'You will have to change your dentist.'

'They are all the same.'

The lieutenant took the photograph and pinned it on the wall. James Calver, bank robber and homicide, stared in harsh profile towards the first communion party. 'He is a man at any rate,' the lieutenant said with approval.

'Who?'

'The gringo.'

The chief said, 'You heard what he did in Houston. Got away with ten thousand dollars. Two G men were shot.'

'G men?'

'It's a honour—in a way—to deal with such people.' He slapped furiously out at a mosquito.

'A man like that,' the lieutenant said, 'does no real harm. A few men dead. We all have to die. The money—somebody has to spend it. We do more good when we catch one of these.' He had the dignity of an idea, standing in the little whitewashed room with his polished boots and his venom. There was something disinterested in his ambition: a kind of virtue in his desire to catch the sleek respected guest of the first communion party.

The chief said mournfully, 'He must be devilishly cunning if he's been going on for years.'

'Anybody could do it,' the lieutenant said. 'We haven't really troubled about them—unless they put themselves in our hands. Why, I could guarantee to fetch this man in, inside a month if . . .'

'If what?'

'If I had the power.'

'It's easy to talk,' the chief said. 'What would you do?'

'This is a small state. Mountains on the north, the sea on the south. I'd beat it as you beat a street, house by house.'

'Oh, it sounds easy,' the chief moaned indistinctly with his handkerchief against his mouth.

The lieutenant said suddenly, 'I will tell you what I'd do. I would take a man from every village in the state as a hostage. If the villagers didn't report the man when he came, the hostage would be shot—and then we'd take another.'

'A lot of them would die, of course.'

'Wouldn't it be worth it?' the lieutenant demanded. 'To be rid of those people for ever.'

'You know,' the chief said, 'you've got something there.'

⋆　　⋆　　⋆

The lieutenant walked home through the shuttered town. All his life had lain here: the Syndicate of Workers and Peasants had once been a school. He had helped to wipe out that unhappy memory. The whole town was changed: the cement playground up the hill near the cemetery where iron swings stood like gallows in the moony darkness was the site of the cathedral. The new children would have new memories: nothing would ever be as it was. There was something of a priest in his intent observant walk—a theologian going back over the errors of the past to destroy them again.

He reached his own lodging. The houses were all one-storeyed, whitewashed, built round small patios, with a well and a few flowers. The windows on the street were barred. Inside the lieutenant's room there was a bed made of old packing-cases with a straw mat laid on top, a cushion and a sheet. There was a picture of the President on the wall, a calendar, and on the tiled floor a table and a rocking-chair. In the light of a candle it looked as comfortless as a prison or a monastic cell.

The lieutenant sat down upon his bed and began to take off his boots. It was the hour of prayer. Blackbeetles exploded against the walls like crackers. More than a dozen crawled over the tiles with injured wings. It infuriated him to think that there were still people in the state who believed in a loving and merciful God. There are mystics who are said to have experienced God directly. He was a mystic, too, and what he had experienced was vacancy—a complete certainty in the existence of a dying, cooling world, of human beings who had evolved from animals for no purpose at all. He knew.

He lay down in his shirt and breeches on the bed and blew out the candle. Heat stood in the room like an enemy. But he believed against the evidence of his senses in the cold empty ether spaces. A radio was playing somewhere: music from Mexico City, or perhaps even from London or New York, filtered into this obscure neglected state. It seemed to him like a weakness: this was his own land, and he would have walled it in if he could with steel until he had eradicated from it everything which reminded him of how it had once appeared to a miserable child. He wanted to destroy everything: to be alone without any memories at all. Life began five years ago.

The lieutenant lay on his back with his eyes open while the beetles detonated on the ceiling. He remembered the priest the Red Shirts had shot against the wall of the cemetery up the hill, another little fat man with popping eyes. He was a monsignor, and he thought that would protect him. He had a sort of contempt for the lower clergy, and right up to the last he was explaining his rank. Only at the very end had he remembered his prayers. He knelt down and they had given him time for a short act of contrition. The lieutenant had watched: he wasn't directly concerned. Altogether they had shot about five priests—two or three had escaped, the bishop was safely in Mexico City, and one man had conformed to the Governor's law that all priests must marry. He lived now near the river with his housekeeper. That, of course, was the best solution of all, to leave the living witness to the weakness of their faith. It showed the deception they had practised all these years. For if they really believed in heaven or hell, they wouldn't mind a little pain now, in return for what immensities . . . The lieutenant, lying on his hard bed, in the damp hot dark, felt no sympathy at all with the weakness of the flesh.

*   *   *

In the back room of the Academia Commercial a woman was reading to her family. Two small girls of six and ten sat on the edge of their bed, and a boy of fourteen leant against the wall with an expression of intense weariness.

'Young Juan,' the mother read, 'from his earliest years was noted for his humility and piety. Other boys might be rough and revengeful; young Juan followed the precept of Our Lord and turned the other cheek. One day his father thought that he had told a lie and beat him. Later he learnt that his son had told the truth, and he apologised to Juan. But Juan said to him, "Dear father, just as our Father in heaven has the right to chastise when he pleases . . ."'

The boy rubbed his face impatiently against the whitewash and the mild voice droned on. The two little girls sat with beady intense eyes, drinking in the sweet piety.

'We must not think that young Juan did not laugh and play like other children, though there were times when he would creep away with a holy picture-book to his father's cow-house from the circle of his merry play-mates.'

The boy squashed a beetle with his bare foot and thought gloomily that after all everything had an end—some day they would reach the last chapter and young Juan would die against a wall shouting, 'Viva el Christo Rey.' But then, he supposed, there would be another book; they were smuggled in every month from Mexico City: if only the customs men had known where to look.

'No, young Juan was a true young Mexican boy, and if he was more thoughtful than his fellows, he was also always the first when any play-acting was afoot. One year his class acted a little play before the bishop, based on the persecution of the early Christians, and no one was more amused than Juan when he was chosen to play the part of Nero. And what comic spirit he put into his acting—this child, whose young manhood was to be cut short by a ruler far worse than Nero. His class-mate, who later became Father Miguel Cerra, S.J., writes: "None of us who were there will ever forget that day . . ."'

One of the little girls licked her lips secretively. This was life.

'The curtain rose on Juan wearing his mother's best bath-robe, a charcoal moustache and a crown made from a tin biscuit-box. Even the good old bishop smiled when Juan strode to the front of the little home-made stage and began to declaim . . .'

The boy strangled a yawn against the whitewashed wall. He said wearily, 'Is he really a saint?'

'He will be, one day soon, when the Holy Father pleases.'

'And are they all like that?'

'Who?'

'The martyrs.'

'Yes. All.'

'Even Padre José?'

'Don't mention him,' the mother said. 'How dare you? That despicable man. A traitor to God.'

'He told me he was more of a martyr than the rest.'

'I've told you many times not to speak to him. My dear child, oh, my dear child . . .'

'And the other one—the one who came to see us?'

'No, he is not—exactly—like Juan.'

'Is he despicable?'

'No, no. Not despicable.'

The smallest girl said suddenly, 'He smelt funny.'

The mother went on reading: 'Did any premonition touch young Juan that night that he, too, in a few short years, would be numbered among the martyrs? We cannot say, but Father Miguel Cerra tells how that evening Juan spent longer than usual upon his knees, and when his class-mates teased him a little, as boys will . . .'

The voice went on and on, mild and deliberate, inflexibly gentle; the small girls listened intently, framing in their minds little pious sentences with which to surprise their parents, and the boy yawned against the whitewash. Everything has an end.

Presently the mother went in to her husband. She said, 'I am so worried about the boy.'

'Why not about the girls? There is worry everywhere.'

'They are two little saints already. But the boy–he asks such questions–about that whisky priest. I wish we had never had him in the house.'

'They would have caught him if we hadn't, and then he would have been one of your martyrs. They would write a book about him and you would read it to the children.'

'That man–never.'

'Well, after all,' her husband said, 'he carries on. I don't believe all that they write in these books. We are all human.'

'You know what I heard to-day? About a poor woman who took to him her son to be baptised. She wanted him called Pedro–but he was so drunk that he took no notice at all and baptised the boy Brigitta. Brigitta!'

'Well, it's a good saint's name.'

'There are times,' the mother said, 'when I lose all patience with you. And now the boy has been talking to Padre José.'

'This is a small town,' her husband said. 'And there is no use pretending. We have been abandoned here. We must get along as best we can. As for the Church–the Church is Padre José and the whisky priest–I don't know of any other. If we don't like the Church, well, we must leave it.'

He watched her with patience. He had more education than his wife; he could use a typewriter and knew the elements of book-keeping: once he had been to Mexico City: he could read a map. He knew the extent of their abandonment–the ten hours down-river to the port, the forty-two hours on the Gulf to Vera Cruz–that was one way out. To the north the swamps and rivers petering out against the mountains which divided them from the next state. And on the other side no roads–only mule-tracks and an occasional unreliable plane: Indian villages and the huts of herds: two hundred miles away, the Pacific.

She said, 'I would rather die.'

'Oh,' he said, 'of course. That goes without saying. But we have to go on living.'

* * *

The old man sat on a packing-case in the little dry patio. He was very fat and short of breath; he panted a little as if after great exertion in the heat. Once he had been something of an astronomer and now he tried to pick out the constellations, staring up into the night sky. He wore only a shirt and trousers; his feet were bare, but there remained something unmistakably clerical in his manner. Forty years of the priesthood had branded him. There was complete silence over the town: everybody was asleep.

The glittering worlds lay there in space like a promise–the world was not the universe. Somewhere Christ might not have died. He could not believe that to a watcher there *this* world could shine with such brilliance: it would roll heavily in space under its fog like a burning and abandoned ship. The whole globe was blanketed with his own sin.

A woman called from the only room he possessed, 'José, José.' He crouched like a galley-slave at the sound; his eyes left the sky, and the constellations fled upwards: the beetles crawled over the patio. 'José, José.' He thought with envy of the men who had died: it was over so soon. They were taken up there to the cemetery and shot against the wall: in two minutes life was extinct. And they called that martyrdom. Here life went on and on; he was only sixty-two. He might live to ninety. Twenty-eight years–that immeasurable period between his birth and his first parish: all childhood and youth and the seminary lay there.

'José. Come to bed.' He shivered: he knew that he was a buffoon. An old man who married was grotesque enough, but an old priest. . . . He stood outside himself and wondered whether he was even fit for hell. He was just a fat old impotent man mocked and taunted between the sheets. But then he remembered the gift he had been given which nobody could take away. That was what made him worthy of damnation–the power he still had of turning the wafer into the flesh and blood of God. He was a sacrilege. Wherever he went, whatever he did, he defiled God. Some mad renegade Catholic, puffed up with the Governor's politics, had once broken into a church (in the days when there were still churches) and seized the Host. He had spat on it, trampled it, and then the people had got him and hung him as they did the stuffed Judas on Holy Thursday from the belfry. He wasn't so bad a man, Padre José thought–he would be forgiven, he was just a politician; but he himself, he was worse than that–he was like an obscene picture hung here every day to corrupt children with.

He belched on his packing-case shaken by wind. 'José. What are you doing? You come to bed.' There was never anything to do at all–no daily Office, no Masses, no Confessions, and it was no good praying any longer at all: a prayer demanded an act and he had no intention of acting. He had lived for two years now in a continuous state of mortal sin with no one to hear his Confession: nothing to do at all but to sit and eat–eat far too much; she fed him and fattened him and preserved him like a prize boar. 'José.' He began to hiccup with nerves at the thought of facing for the seven hundred and thirty-eighth time his harsh housekeeper–his wife. There she would be lying in the big shameless bed that filled half the room, a bony shadow within the mosquito-tent, a lanky jaw and a short grey pigtail and an absurd bonnet. She thought she had a position to keep up: a Government pensioner: the wife of the only married priest. She was proud of it. 'José.' 'I'm–hic–coming, my love,' he said and lifted himself from the crate. Somebody somewhere laughed.

He lifted little pink eyes like those of a pig conscious of the slaughter-room. A high child's voice said, 'José.' He stared in a bewildered way around the patio. At a barred window opposite three children watched him with deep gravity. He turned his back and took a step or two towards his door, moving very slowly because of his bulk. 'José,' somebody squeaked again. 'José.' He looked back over his shoulder and caught the faces out in expressions of wild glee; his little pink eyes showed no anger–he had no right to be angry: he moved his mouth into a ragged, baffled, disintegrated smile, and as if that sign of weakness gave them all the licence they needed, they squealed back at him without disguise, 'José, José. Come to bed, José.' Their little shameless voices filled the patio, and he smiled humbly and sketched small gestures for silence, and there was no respect anywhere left for him in his home, in the town, in the whole abandoned star.

3

THE RIVER

Captain Fellows sang loudly to himself, while the little motor chugged in the bows of the canoe. His big sunburned face was like the map of a mountain region—patches of varying brown with two small blue lakes that were his eyes. He composed his songs as he went, and his voice was quite tuneless. 'Going home, going home, the food will be good for me-e-e. I don't like the food in the bloody citee.' He turned out of the main stream into a tributary: a few alligators lay on the sandy margin. 'I don't like your snouts, O trouts. I don't like your snouts, O trouts.' He was a happy man.

The banana plantations came down on either bank: his voice boomed under the hard sun: that and the churr of the motor were the only sounds anywhere—he was completely alone. He was borne up on a big tide of boyish joy—doing a man's job, the heart of the wild: he felt no responsibility for anyone. In only one other country had he felt more happy, and that was in war-time France, in the ravaged landscape of trenches. The tributary cork-screwed farther into the marshy overgrown state, and a vulture lay spread out in the sky; Captain Fellows opened a tin box and ate a sandwich—food never tasted so good as out of doors. A monkey made a sudden chatter at him as he went by, and Captain Fellows felt happily at one with nature—a wide shallow kinship with all the world moved with the bloodstream through the veins: he was at home anywhere. The artful little devil, he thought, the artful little devil. He began to sing again—somebody else's words a little jumbled in his friendly unretentive memory. 'Give to me the life I love, bread I dip in the river, under the wide and starry sky, the hunter's home from the sea.' The plantations petered out, and far behind the mountains came into view, heavy black lines drawn low-down across the sky. A few bungalows rose out of the mud. He was home. A very slight cloud marred his happiness.

He thought: after all, a man likes to be welcomed.

He walked up to his bungalow; it was distinguished from the others which lay along the bank by a tiled roof, a flagpost without a flag, a plate on the door with the title, 'Central American Banana Company'. Two hammocks were strung up on the veranda, but there was nobody about. Captain Fellows knew where to find his wife. He burst boisterously through a door and shouted, 'Daddy's home.' A scared thin face peeked at him through a mosquito-net; his boots ground peace into the floor; Mrs Fellows flinched away into the white muslin tent. He said, 'Pleased to see me, Trix?' and she drew rapidly on her face the outline of her frightened welcome. It was like a trick you do with a blackboard. Draw a dog in one line without lifting the chalk–and the answer, of course, is a sausage.

'I'm glad to be home,' Captain Fellows said, and he believed it. It was his one firm conviction–that he really felt the correct emotions of love and joy and grief and hate. He had always been a good man at zero hour.

'All well at the office?'

'Fine,' Fellows said, 'fine.'

'I had a bit of fever yesterday.'

'Ah, you need looking after. You'll be all right now,' he said vaguely, 'that I'm home.' He shied merrily away from the subject of fever–clapping his hands, a big laugh, while she trembled in her tent. 'Where's Coral?'

'She's with the policeman,' Mrs Fellows said.

'I hoped she'd meet me,' he said, roaming aimlessly about the little interior room, full of boot-trees, while his brain caught up with her. 'Policeman? What policeman?'

'He came last night and Coral let him sleep on the veranda. He's looking for somebody, she says.'

'What an extraordinary thing. *Here*?'

'He's not an ordinary policeman. He's an officer. He left his men in the village–Coral says.'

'I do think you ought to be up,' he said. 'I mean–these fellows, you can't trust them.' He felt no conviction when he added, 'She's just a kid.'

'I tell you I had fever,' Mrs Fellows wailed, 'I felt so terribly ill.'

'You'll be all right. Just a touch of the sun. You'll see–now *I'm* home.'

'I had such a headache. I couldn't read or sew. And then this man . . .'

Terror was always just behind her shoulder: she was wasted by the effort of not turning round. She dressed up her fear, so that she could look at it–in the form of fever, rats, unemployment. The real thing was taboo–death coming nearer every year in the strange place: everybody packing up and leaving, while she stayed in a cemetery no one visited, in a big above-ground tomb.

He said, 'I suppose I ought to go and see the man.' He sat down on the bed and put his hand upon her arm. They had something in common–a kind of diffidence. He said absent-mindedly, 'That dago secretary of the boss has gone.'

'Where?'

'West.' He could feel her arm go stiff: she strained away from him towards the wall. He had touched the taboo–the bond was broken, he couldn't tell why. 'Headache, darling?'

'Hadn't you better see the man?'

'Oh yes, yes. I'll be off.' But he didn't stir: it was the child who came to him.

She stood in the doorway watching them with a look of immense responsibility. Before her serious gaze they became a boy you couldn't trust and a ghost you could almost puff away, a piece of frightened air. She was very young–about thirteen–and at that age you are not afraid of many things, age and death, all the things which may turn up, snake-bite and fever and rats and a bad smell. Life hadn't got at her yet; she had a false air of impregnability. But she had been reduced already, as it were, to the smallest terms–everything was there but on the thinnest lines. That was what the sun did to a child, reduced it to a framework. The gold bangle on the bony wrist was like a padlock on a canvas door which a fist could break. She said, 'I told the policeman you were home.'

'Oh yes, yes,' Captain Fellows said. 'Got a kiss for your old dad?'

She came solemnly across the room and kissed him formally upon the forehead—he could feel the lack of meaning. She had other things to think about. She said, 'I told cook that Mother would not be getting up for dinner.'

'I think you ought to make the effort, dear,' Captain Fellows said.

'Why?' Coral asked.

'Oh, well . . .'

Coral said, 'I want to talk to you alone.' Mrs Fellows shifted inside her tent. Common sense was a horrifying quality she had never possessed: it was common sense which said, 'The dead can't hear' or 'She can't know now' or 'Tin flowers are more practical'.

'I don't understand,' Captain Fellows said uneasily, 'why your mother shouldn't hear.'

'She wouldn't want to. It would only scare her.'

Coral—he was accustomed to it by now—had an answer to everything. She never spoke without deliberation; she was prepared—but sometimes the answers she had prepared seemed to him of a wildness. . . . They were based on the only life she could remember, the swamp and vultures and no children anywhere, except a few in the village with bellies swollen by worms who ate dirt from the bank, inhumanly. A child is said to draw parents together, and certainly he felt an immense unwillingness to entrust himself to this child. Her answers might carry him anywhere. He felt through the net for his wife's hand, secretively: they were adults together. This was the stranger in their house. He said boisterously, 'You're frightening us.'

'I don't think,' the child said, with care, 'that *you'll* be frightened.'

He said weakly, pressing his wife's hand, 'Well, my dear, our daughter seems to have decided . . .'

'First you must see the policeman. I want him to go. I don't like him.'

'Then he must go, of course,' Captain Fellows said, with a hollow unconfident laugh.

'I told him that. I said we couldn't refuse him a hammock for the night when he arrived so late. But now he must go.'

'And he disobeyed you?'

'He said he wanted to speak to you.'

'He little knew,' Captain Fellows said, 'he little knew.' Irony was his only defence, but it was not understood; nothing was understood which was not clear—like an alphabet or a simple sum or a date in history. He relinquished his wife's hand and allowed himself to be led unwillingly into the afternoon sun. The police officer stood in front of the veranda, a motionless olive figure; he wouldn't stir a foot to meet Captain Fellows.

'Well, lieutenant?' Captain Fellows said breezily. It occurred to him that Coral had more in common with the policeman than with himself.

'I am looking for a man,' the lieutenant said. 'He has been reported in this district.'

'He can't be here.'

'Your daughter tells me the same.'

'She knows.'

'He is wanted on a very serious charge.'

'Murder?'

'No. Treason.'

'Oh, treason,' Captain Fellows said, all his interest dropping; there was so much treason everywhere—it was like petty larceny in a barracks.

'He is a priest. I trust you will report at once if he is seen.' The lieutenant paused. 'You are a foreigner living under the protection of our laws. We expect you to make a proper return for our hospitality. You are not a Catholic?'

'No.'

'Then I can trust you to report?' the lieutenant said.

'I suppose so.'

The lieutenant stood there like a little dark menacing question-mark in the sun: his attitude seemed to indicate that he wouldn't even accept the benefit of shade from a foreigner. But he had used a hammock; that, Captain Fellows supposed, he must have regarded as a requisition. 'Have a glass of gaseosa?'

'No. No, thank you.'

'Well,' Captain Fellows said, 'I can't offer you anything else, can I? It's treason to drink spirits.'

The lieutenant suddenly turned on his heel as if he could no longer bear the sight of them and strode away along the path which led to the village: his gaiters and his pistol holster winked in the sunlight. When he had gone some way they could see him pause and spit; he had not been discourteous, he had waited till he supposed that they no longer watched him before he got rid of his hatred and contempt for a different way of life, for ease, safety, toleration and complacency.

'I wouldn't want to be up against him,' Captain Fellows said.

'Of course he doesn't trust us.'

'They don't trust anyone.'

'I think,' Coral said, 'he smelt a rat.'

'They smell them everywhere.'

'You see, I wouldn't let him search the place.'

'Why ever not?' Captain Fellows asked, and then his vague mind went off at a tangent. 'How did you stop him?'

'I said I'd loose the dogs on him—and complain to the Minister. He hadn't any right . . .'

'Oh, right,' Captain Fellows said. 'They carry their right on their hips. It wouldn't have done any harm to let him look.'

'I gave him my word.' She was as inflexible as the lieutenant: small and black and out of place among the banana groves. Her candour made allowances for nobody: the future, full of compromises, anxieties, and shame, lay outside. But at any moment now a word, a gesture, the most trivial act might be her sesame—to what? Captain Fellows was touched with fear; he was aware of an inordinate love which robbed him of authority. You cannot control what you love—you watch it driving recklessly towards the broken bridge, the torn-up track, the horror of seventy years ahead. He closed his eyes—he was a happy man—and hummed a tune.

Coral said, 'I shouldn't have liked a man like that to catch me out–lying, I mean.'

'Lying? Good God,' Captain Fellows said, 'you don't mean he's here.'

'Of course he's here,' Coral said.

'Where?'

'In the big barn,' she explained gently. 'We couldn't let them catch him.'

'Does your mother know about this?'

She said with devastating honesty, 'Oh no. I couldn't trust *her*.' She was independent of both of them: they belonged together in the past. In forty years' time they would be dead as last year's dog. He said, 'You'd better show me.'

He walked slowly; happiness drained out of him more quickly and completely than out of an unhappy man: an unhappy man is always prepared. As she walked in front of him, her two meagre tails of hair bleaching in the sunlight, it occurred to him for the first time that she was of an age when Mexican girls were ready for their first man. What was to happen? He flinched away from problems which he had never dared to confront. As they passed the window of his bedroom he caught sight of a thin shape lying bunched and bony and alone in a mosquito-net. He remembered with self-pity and nostalgia his happiness on the river, doing a man's job without thinking of other people. If I had never married. . . . He wailed like a child at the merciless immature back, 'We've no business interfering with politics.'

'This isn't politics,' she said gently. 'I know about politics. Mother and I are doing the Reform Bill.' She took a key out of her pocket and unlocked the big barn in which they stored bananas before sending them down the river to the port. It was very dark inside after the glare. There was a scuffle in a corner. Captain Fellows picked up an electric torch and shone it on somebody in a torn dark suit–a small man who blinked and needed a shave.

'Que es usted?' Captain Fellows said.

'I speak English.' He clutched a small attaché case to his side, as if he were waiting to catch a train he must on no account miss.

'You've no business here.'

'No,' the man said, 'no.'

'It's nothing to do with us,' Captain Fellows said. 'We are foreigners.'

The man said, 'Of course. I will go.' He stood with his head a little bent like a man in an orderly-room listening to an officer's decision. Captain Fellows relented a little. He said, 'You'd better wait till dark. You don't want to be caught.'

'No.'

'Hungry?'

'A little. It does not matter.' He said with a rather repulsive humility, 'If you would do me a favour . . .'

'What?'

'A little brandy.'

'I'm breaking the law enough for you as it is,' Captain Fellows said. He strode out of the barn, feeling twice the size, leaving the small bowed figure in the darkness among the bananas. Coral locked the door and followed him. 'What a religion,' Captain Fellows said. 'Begging for brandy. Shameless.'

'But you drink it sometimes.'

'My dear,' Captain Fellows said, 'when you are older you'll understand the difference between drinking a little brandy after dinner and—well, needing it.'

'Can I take him some beer?'

'*You* won't take him anything.'

'The servants wouldn't be safe.'

He was powerless and furious. He said, 'You see what a hole you've put us in.' He stumped back into the house and into his bedroom, roaming aimlessly among the boot-trees. Mrs Fellows slept uneasily, dreaming of weddings. Once she said aloud, 'My train. Be careful of my train.'

'What's that?' he asked petulantly. 'What's that?'

Dark fell like a curtain: one moment the sun was there, the next it had gone. Mrs Fellows woke to another night. 'Did you speak, dear?'

'It was you who spoke,' he said. 'Something about trains.'

'I must have been dreaming.'

'It will be a long time before they have trains here,' he said, with gloomy satisfaction. He came and sat on the bed, keeping away from the window; out of sight, out of mind. The crickets were beginning to chatter and beyond the mosquito wire fireflies moved like globes. He put his heavy, cheery, needing-to-be-reassured hand on the shape under the sheet and said, 'It's not such a bad life, Trixy. Is it now? Not a bad life?' But he could feel her stiffen: the word 'life' was taboo: it reminded you of death. She turned her face away from him towards the wall and then hopelessly back again—the phrase 'turn to the wall' was taboo too. She lay panic-stricken, while the boundaries of her fear widened to include every relationship and the whole world of inanimate things: it was like an infection. You could look at nothing for long without becoming aware that it, too, carried the germ . . . the word 'sheet' even. She threw the sheet off her and said, 'It's so hot, it's so hot.' The usually happy and the always unhappy one watched the night thicken from the bed with distrust. They were companions cut off from all the world: there was no meaning anywhere outside their own hearts: they were carried like children in a coach through the huge spaces without any knowledge of their destination. He began to hum with desperate cheerfulness a song of the war years; he wouldn't listen to the footfall in the yard outside, going in the direction of the barn.

★   ★   ★

Coral put down the chicken legs and tortillas on the ground and unlocked the door. She carried a bottle of Cerveza Moctezuma under her arm. There was the same scuffle in the dark: the noise of a frightened man. She said, 'It's me,' to quieten him, but she didn't turn on the torch. She said, 'There's a bottle of beer here, and some food.'

'Thank you. Thank you.'

'The police have gone from the village—south. You had better go north.'

He said nothing.

She asked, with the cold curiosity of a child, 'What would they do to you if they found you?'

'Shoot me.'

'You must be very frightened,' she said with interest.

He felt his way across the barn towards the door and the pale starlight. He said, 'I *am* frightened,' and stumbled on a bunch of bananas.

'Can't you escape from here?'

'I tried. A month ago. The boat was leaving and then I was summoned.'

'Somebody needed you?'

'She didn't need me,' he said bitterly. She could just see his face now, as the world swung among the stars: what her father would call an untrustworthy face. He said, 'You see how unworthy I am. Talking like this.'

'Unworthy of what?'

He clasped his little attaché case closely and said, 'Could you tell me what month it is. Is it still February?'

'No. It's the seventh of March.'

'I don't often meet people who know. That means another month—six weeks—before the rains. He went on, 'When the rains come I am nearly safe. You see, the police can't get about.'

'The rains are best for you?' she asked: she had a keen desire to learn. The Reform Bill and Senlac and a little French lay like treasure trove in her brain. She expected answers to every question, and she absorbed them hungrily.

'Oh no, no. They mean another six months living like this.' He tore at a chicken leg. She could smell his breath: it was disagreeable, like something which has lain about too long in the heat. He said, 'I'd rather be caught.'

'But can't you,' she said logically, 'just give yourself up?'

He had answers as plain and understandable as her questions. He said, 'There's the pain. To choose pain like that—it's not possible. And it's my duty not to be caught. You see, my bishop is no longer here.' Curious pedantries moved him. 'This is my parish.' He found a tortilla and began to eat ravenously.

She said solemnly, 'It's a problem.' She could hear a gurgle as he drank out of the bottle. He said, 'I try to remember how happy I was once.' A firefly lit his face like a torch and then went out—a tramp's face: what could ever have made it happy? He said, 'In Mexico City now they are saying Benediction. The Bishop's there. . . . Do you imagine he ever thinks . . . ? They don't even know I'm alive.'

She said, 'Of course you could—renounce.'

'I don't understand.'

'Renounce your faith,' she explained, using the words of her European History.

He said, 'It's impossible. There's no way. I'm a priest. It's out of my power.'

The child listened intently. She said, 'Like a birthmark.' She could hear him sucking desperately at the bottle. She said, 'I think I could find my father's brandy.'

'Oh no, you mustn't steal.' He drained the beer: a long glassy whistle in the darkness: the last drop must have gone. He said, 'I must leave. At once.'

'You can always come back here.'

'Your father would not like it.'

'He needn't know,' she said. 'I could look after you. My room is just opposite this door. You would just tap at my window. Perhaps,' she went seriously on, 'it would be better to have a code. You see, somebody else might tap.'

He said in a horrified voice, 'Not a man?'

'Yes. You never know. Another fugitive from justice.'

'Surely,' he asked in bewilderment, 'that is not likely?'

She said airily, 'These things do happen.'

'Before to-day?'

'No, but I expect they will again. I want to be prepared. You must tap three times. Two long taps and a short one.'

He giggled suddenly like a child. 'How do you tap a long tap?'

'Like this.'

'Oh, you mean a loud one?'

'I call them long taps–because of Morse.' He was hopelessly out of his depth. He said, 'You are very good. Will you pray for me?'

'Oh,' she said, 'I don't believe in that.'

'Not in praying?'

'You see, I don't believe in God. I lost my faith when I was ten.'

'Well, well,' he said. 'Then I will pray for you.'

'You can,' she said patronisingly, 'if you like. If you come again I shall teach you the Morse code. It would be useful to you.'

'How?'

'If you were hiding in the plantation I could flash to you with my mirror news of the enemy's movements.'

He listened seriously. 'But wouldn't they see you?'

'Oh,' she said, 'I would invent an explanation.' She moved logically forward a step at a time, eliminating all objections.

'Good-bye, my child,' he said.

He lingered by the door. 'Perhaps–you do not care for prayers. Perhaps you would like . . . I know a good conjuring trick.'

'I like tricks.'

'You do it with cards. Have you any cards?'

'No.'

He sighed, 'Then that's no good,' and giggled–she could smell the beer on his breath–'I shall just have to pray for you.'

She said, 'You don't sound afraid.'

'A little drink,' he said, 'will work wonders in a cowardly man. With a little brandy, why, I'd defy–the devil.' He stumbled in the doorway.

'Good-bye,' she said. 'I hope you'll escape.' A faint sigh came out of the darkness. She said gently, 'If they kill you I shan't forgive them–ever.' She was ready to accept any responsibility, even that of vengeance, without a second thought. It was her life.

*   *   *

Half a dozen huts of mud and wattle stood in a clearing; two were in ruins. A few pigs routed round, and an old woman carried a burning ember from hut to hut, lighting a little fire on the centre of each floor to fill the hut with smoke and keep mosquitoes away. Women lived in two of the huts, the pigs in another; in the last unruined hut where maize was stored, an old man and a boy and a tribe of rats. The old man stood in the clearing watching the fire being carried round; it flickered through the darkness like a ritual repeated at the same hour for a lifetime. White hair, a white stubbly beard, and hands brown and fragile as last year's leaves, he gave an effect of immense permanence. Living on the edge of subsistence nothing much could ever change him. He had been old for years.

The stranger came into the clearing. He wore what used to be town shoes, black and pointed; only the uppers were left, so that he walked to all intents barefoot. The shoes were symbolic, like the cobwebbed flags in churches. He wore a shirt and a pair of black torn trousers and he carried his attaché case, as if he were a season-ticket holder. He had nearly reached the state of permanency too, but he carried about with him the scars of time—the damaged shoes implied a different past, the lines of his face suggested hopes and fears of the future. The old woman with the ember stopped between two huts and watched him. He came on into the clearing with his eyes on the ground and his shoulders hunched, as if he felt exposed. The old man advanced to meet him; he took the stranger's hand and kissed it.

'Can you let me have a hammock for the night?'

'Ah, father, for a hammock you must go to a town. Here you must take only the luck of the road.'

'Never mind. Anywhere to lie down. Can you give me—a little spirit?'

'Coffee, father. We have nothing else.'

'Some food.'

'We have no food.'

'Never mind.'

The boy came out of the hut and watched them: everybody watched. It was like a bull-fight. The animal was tired and they waited for the next move. They were not hard-hearted; they were watching the rare spectacle of something worse off than themselves. He limped on towards the hut. Inside it was dark from the knees upwards; there was no flame on the floor, just a slow burning away. The place was half filled by a stack of maize, and rats rustled among the dry outer leaves. There was a bed made of earth with a straw mat on it, and two packing-cases made a table. The stranger lay down, and the old man closed the door on them both.

'Is it safe?'

'The boy will watch. He knows.'

'Were you expecting me?'

'No, father. But it is five years since we have seen a priest . . . it was bound to happen one day.'

He fell uneasily asleep, and the old man crouched on the floor, fanning the fire with his breath. Somebody tapped on the door and the priest jerked upright. 'It is all right,' the old man said. 'Just your coffee, father.' He brought it to him—grey maize coffee smoking in a tin mug, but the priest was too tired to drink. He lay on his side perfectly still: a rat watched him from the maize.

'The soldiers were here yesterday,' the old man said. He blew on the fire. The smoke poured up and filled the hut. The priest began to cough, and the rat moved quickly like the shadow of a hand into the stack.

'The boy, father, has not been baptised. The last priest who was here wanted two pesos. I had only one peso. Now I have only fifty centavos.'

'To-morrow,' the priest said wearily.

'Will you say Mass, father, in the morning?'

'Yes, yes.'

'And confession, father, will you hear our confessions?'

'Yes, but let me sleep first.' He turned on his back and closed his eyes to keep out the smoke.

'We have no money, father, to give you. The other priest, Padre José . . .'

'Give me some clothes instead,' he said impatiently.

'But we have only what we wear.'

'Take mine in exchange.'

The old man hummed dubiously to himself, glancing sideways at what the fire showed of the black torn cloth. 'If I must, father,' he said. He blew quietly at the fire for a few minutes. The priest's eyes closed again.

'After five years there is so much to confess.'

The priest sat up quickly. 'What was that?' he said.

'You were dreaming, father. The boy will warn us if the soldiers come. I was only saying—'

'Can't you let me sleep for five minutes?' He lay down again. Somewhere, in one of the women's huts, someone was singing–'I went down to my field and there I found a rose.'

The old man said softly, 'It would be a pity if the soldiers came before we had time . . . such a burden on poor souls, father . . .' The priest shouldered himself upright against the wall and said furiously, 'Very well. Begin. I will hear your confession.' The rats scuffled in the maize. 'Go on then,' he said. 'Don't waste time. Hurry. When did you last . . . ?' The old man knelt beside the fire, and across the clearing the woman sang: 'I went down to my field and the rose was withered.'

'Five years ago.' He paused and blew at the fire. 'It's hard to remember, father.'

'Have you sinned against purity?'

The priest leant against the wall with his legs drawn up beneath him, and the rats accustomed to the voices moved again in the maize. The old man picked out his sins with difficulty, blowing at the fire. 'Make a good act of contrition,' the priest said, 'and say–say–have you a rosary?–then say the Joyful Mysteries.' His eyes closed, his lips and tongue stumbled over the absolution, failed to finish . . . he sprang awake again.

'Can I bring the women?' the old man was saying. 'It is five years . . .'

'Oh, let them come. Let them all come,' the priest cried angrily. 'I am your servant.' He put his hand over his eyes and began to weep. The old man opened the door: it was not completely dark outside under the enormous arc of starry ill-lit sky. He went across to the women's huts and knocked. 'Come,' he said. 'You must say your confessions. It is only polite to the father.' They wailed at him that they were tired . . . the morning would do. 'Would you insult him?' he said. 'What do you think he has come here for? He is a very holy father. There he is in my hut now weeping for our sins.' He hustled them out; one by one they picked their way across the clearing towards the hut, and the old man set off down the path towards the river to take the place of the boy who watched the ford for soldiers.

4

THE BYSTANDERS

It was years since Mr Tench had written a letter. He sat before the work-table sucking at a steel nib; an odd impulse had come to him to project this stray letter towards the last address he had—in Southend. Who knew who was alive still? He tried to begin. It was like breaking the ice at a party where you knew nobody. He started to write the envelope—Mrs Henry Tench, care of Mrs Marsdyke, 3, The Avenue, Westcliff. It was her mother's house: the dominating interfering creature who had induced him to set up his plate in Southend for a fatal while. 'Please forward,' he wrote. She wouldn't do it if she knew, but she had probably forgotten his handwriting by this time.

He sucked the inky nib—how to go on? It would have been easier if there had been some purpose behind it other than the vague desire to put on record to somebody that he was still alive. It might prove awkward if she had married again, but in that case she wouldn't hesitate to tear the letter up. He wrote: *Dear Sylvia*, in a big clear immature script, listening to the furnace purring on the bench. He was making a gold alloy—there were no depots here where he could buy his material ready-made. Besides, the depots didn't favour 14-carat gold for dental work, and he couldn't afford finer material.

The trouble was—nothing ever happened here. His life was as sober, respectable, regular as even Mrs Marsdyke could require.

He took a look at the crucible. The gold was on the point of fusion with the alloy, so he flung in a spoonful of vegetable charcoal to protect the mixture from the air, took up his pen again and sat mooning over the paper. He couldn't remember his wife clearly—only the hats she wore. How surprised she would be at hearing from him after this long while; there had been one letter written by each of them since the little boy died. The years really meant nothing to him—they drifted fairly rapidly by without changing a habit. He had meant to leave six years ago, but the peso dropped with a revolution, and so he had come south. Now he had more money saved, but a month ago the peso dropped again—another revolution somewhere. There was nothing to do but wait . . . the nib went back between his teeth and memory melted in the little hot room. Why write at all? He couldn't remember now what had given him the odd idea. Somebody knocked at the outer door and he left the letter on the bench—*Dear Sylvia*, staring up, big and bold and hopeless. A boat's bell rang by the riverside: it was the *General Obregon* back from Vera Cruz. A memory stirred. It was as if something alive and in pain moved in the little front room among the rocking-chairs—'an interesting afternoon: what happened to him, I wonder, when'—then died, or got away. Mr Tench was used to pain: it was his profession. He waited cautiously till a hand beat on the door again and a voice said, 'Con amistad'—there was no trust anywhere—before he drew the bolts and opened up, to admit a patient.

★   ★   ★

Padre José went in, under the big classical gateway marked in black letters 'Silencio' to what people used to call the Garden of God. It was like a building estate where nobody had paid attention to the architecture of the next house. The big stone tombs of above-ground burial were any height and any shape; sometimes an angel stood on the roof with lichenous wings: sometimes through a glass window you could see some rusting metal flowers upon a shelf—it was like looking into the kitchen of a house whose owners have moved on, forgetting to clean the vases out. There was a sense of intimacy—you could go anywhere and see anything. Life here had withdrawn altogether.

He walked very slowly because of his bulk among the tombs; he could be alone here, there were no children about, and he could waken a faint sense of homesickness which was better than no feeling at all. He had buried some of these people. His small inflamed eyes turned here and there. Coming round the huge grey bulk of the Lopez tomb—a merchant family which fifty years ago had owned the only hotel in the capital—he found he was not alone. A grave was being dug at the edge of the cemetery next the wall: two men were rapidly at work: a woman stood by and an old man. A child's coffin lay at their feet—it took no time at all in the spongy soil to get down far enough. A little water collected. That was why those who could afford it lay above ground.

They all paused a moment and looked at Padre José, and he sidled back towards the Lopez tomb as if he were an intruder. There was no sign of grief anywhere in the bright hot day: a vulture sat on a roof outside the cemetery. Somebody said, 'Father.'

Padre José put up his hand deprecatingly as if he were trying to indicate that he was not there, that he was gone, away, out of sight.

The old man said, 'Padre José.' They all watched him hungrily; they had been quite resigned until he had appeared, but now they were anxious, eager. . . . He ducked and dodged away from them. 'Padre José,' the old man repeated. 'A prayer?' They smiled at him, waiting. They were quite accustomed to people dying, but an unforeseen hope of happiness had bobbed up among the tombs: they could boast after this that one at least of their family had gone into the ground with an official prayer.

'It's impossible,' Padre José said.

'Yesterday was her saint's day,' the woman said, as if that made a difference. 'She was five.' She was one of those garrulous women who show to strangers the photographs of their children, but all she had to show was a coffin.

'I am sorry.'

The old man pushed the coffin aside with his foot the better to approach Padre José; it was small and light and might have contained nothing but bones. 'Not a whole service, you understand—just a prayer. She was—innocent,' he said. The word in the little stony town sounded odd and archaic and local, outdated like the Lopez tomb, belonging only here.

'It is against the law.'

'Her name,' the woman went on, 'was Anita. I was sick when I had her,' she explained, as if to excuse the child's delicacy which had led to all this inconvenience.

'The law . . .'

The old man put his finger to his nose. 'You can trust us. It is just the case of a short prayer. I am her grandfather. This is her mother, her father, her uncle. You can trust us.'

But that was the trouble—he could trust no one. As soon as they got back home one or other of them would certainly begin to boast. He walked backwards all the time, weaving his plump fingers, shaking his head, nearly bumping into the Lopez tomb. He was scared, and yet a curious pride bubbled in his throat because he was being treated as a priest again, with respect. 'If I could,' he said, 'my children . . .'

Suddenly and unexpectedly there was agony in the cemetery. They had been used to losing children, but they hadn't been used to what the rest of the world knows best of all—the hope which peters out. The woman began to cry, dryly, without tears, the trapped noise of something wanting to be released; the old man fell on his knees with his hands held out. 'Padre José,' he said, 'there is no one else . . .' He looked as if he were asking for a miracle. An enormous temptation came to Padre José to take the risk and say a prayer over the grave. He felt the wild attraction of doing one's duty and stretched a sign of the cross in the air; then fear came back, like a drug. Contempt and safety waited for him down by the quay: he wanted to get away. He sank hopelessly down on his knees and entreated them: 'Leave me alone.' He said, 'I am unworthy. Can't you see?—I am a coward.' The two old men faced each other on their knees among the tombs, the small coffin shoved aside like a pretext—an absurd spectacle. He knew it was absurd: a lifetime of self-analysis enabled him to see himself as he was, fat and ugly and old and humiliated. It was as if a whole seducing choir of angels had silently withdrawn and left the voices of the children in the patio—'Come to bed, José, come to bed,' sharp and shrill and worse then they had ever been. He knew he was in the grip of the unforgivable sin, despair.

*   *   *

'At last the blessed day arrived,' the mother read aloud, 'when the days of Juan's novitiate were over. Oh, what a joyful day was that for his mother and sisters. And a little sad too, for the flesh cannot always be strong, and how could they help mourning a while in their hearts for the loss of a small son and an elder brother? Ah, if they had known that they were gaining that day a saint in heaven to pray for them.'

The younger girl on the bed said, 'Have *we* got a saint?'

'Of course.'

'Why did they want another saint?'

The mother went on reading: 'Next day the whole family received communion from the hands of a son and brother. Then they said a fond good-bye—they little knew that it was the last—to the new soldier of Christ and returned to their homes in Morelos. Already clouds were darkening the heavens, and President Calles was discussing the anti-Catholic laws in the Palace at Chapultepec. The devil was ready to assail poor Mexico.'

'Is the shooting going to begin soon?' the boy asked, moving restlessly against the wall. His mother went relentlessly on: 'Juan unknown to all but his confessor was preparing himself for the evil days ahead with the most rigorous mortifications. His companions suspected nothing, for he was always the heart and soul of every merry conversation, and on the feast-day of the founder of the Order it was he . . .'

'I know, I know,' the boy said. 'He acted a play.'

The little girls opened astounded eyes.

'And why not, Luis?' the mother said, pausing with her finger on the prohibited book. He stared sullenly back at her. 'And why not, Luis?' she repeated. She waited a while, and then read on; the little girls watched their brother with horror and admiration. 'It was he,' she said, 'who obtained permission to perform a little one-act play founded on . . .'

'I know, I know,' the boy said, 'the catacombs.'

The mother, compressing her lips, continued: '. . . the persecution of the early Christians. Perhaps he remembered that occasion in his boyhood when he acted Nero before the good old bishop, but this time he insisted on taking the comic part of a Roman fishmonger . . .'

'I don't believe a word of it,' the boy said, with sullen fury, 'not a word of it.'

'How dare you!'

'Nobody could be such a fool.'

The little girls sat motionless, their eyes large and brown and pious.

'Go to your father.'

'Anything to get away from this–this—' the boy said.

'Tell him what you've told me.'

'This . . .'

'Leave the room.'

He slammed the door behind him. His father stood at the barred window of the *sala*, looking out; the beetles detonated against the oil-lamp and crawled with broken wings across the stone floor. The boy said, 'My mother told me to tell you that I told her that I didn't believe that the book she's reading . . .'

'What book?'

'The holy book.'

He said sadly, 'Oh that.' Nobody passed in the street, nothing happened; it was after nine-thirty and all the lights were out. He said, 'You must make allowances. For us, you know, everything seems over. That book–it is like our own childhood.'

'It sounds so silly.'

'You don't remember the time when the Church was here. I was a bad Catholic, but it meant–well, music, lights, a place where you could sit out of this heat–and for your mother, well, there was always something for her to do. If we had a theatre, anything at all instead, we shouldn't feel so–left.'

'But this Juan,' the boy said. 'He sounds so silly.'

'He was killed, wasn't he?'

'Oh, so were Villa, Obregon, Madero . . .'

'Who tells you about them?'

'We all of us play them. Yesterday I was Madero. They shot me in the plaza–the law of flight.' Somewhere in the heavy night a drum beat. The sour river smell filled the room: it was familiar like the taste of soot in cities. 'We tossed up. I was Madero: Pedro had to be Huerta. He fled to Vera Cruz down by the river. Manuel chased him–he was Carranza.' His father struck a beetle off his shirt, staring into the street: the sound of marching feet came nearer. He said, 'I suppose your mother's angry.'

'You aren't,' the boy said.

'What's the good? It's not your fault. We have been deserted.'

The soldiers went by, returning to barracks, up the hill near what had once been the cathedral; they marched out of step in spite of the drum-beat, they looked under-nourished; they hadn't yet made much of war. They passed lethargically by in the dark street and the boy watched them out of sight with excited and hopeful eyes.

★   ★   ★

Mrs Fellows rocked backwards and forwards, backwards and forwards. 'And so Lord Palmerston said if the Greek Government didn't do right to Don Pacífico . . .' She said, 'My darling, I've got such a headache I think we must stop to-day.'

'Of course. I have a little one too.'

'I expect yours will be better soon. Would you mind putting the books away?' The little shabby books had come by post from a firm in Paternoster Row called Private Tutorials, Ltd–a whole education which began with 'Reading Without Tears' and went methodically on to the Reform Bill and Lord Palmerston and the poems of Victor Hugo. Once every six months an examination paper was delivered, and Mrs Fellows laboriously worked through the answers and awarded marks. These she sent back to Paternoster Row, and there, weeks later, they were filed: once she had forgotten her duty when there was shooting in Zapata, and had received a printed slip beginning: 'Dear Parent, I regret to see . . .' The trouble was, they were years ahead of schedule by now–there were so few other books to read–and so the examination papers were years behind. Sometimes the firm sent embossed certificates for framing, announcing that Miss Coral Fellows had passed third with honours into the second grade, signed with a rubber stamp Henry Beckley, B.A., Director of Private Tutorials, Ltd, and sometimes there would be little personal letters type-written, with the same blue smudgy signature, saying: *Dear Pupil, I think you should pay more attention this week to. . . .* The letters were always six weeks out of date.

'My darling,' Mrs Fellows said, 'will you see the cook and order lunch? Just yourself. I can't eat a thing, and your father's out on the plantation.'

'Mother,' the child said, 'do you believe there's a God?'

The question scared Mrs Fellows. She rocked furiously up and down and said, 'Of course.'

'I mean the Virgin Birth–and everything.'

'My dear, what a thing to ask. Who have you been talking to?'

'Oh,' she said. 'I've been thinking, that's all.' She didn't wait for any further answer; she knew quite well there would be none–it was always her job to make decisions. Henry Beckley, B.A., had put it all into an early lesson–it hadn't been any more difficult to accept then than the giant at the top of the beanstalk, and at the age of ten she had discarded both relentlessly. By that time she was starting algebra.

'Surely your father hasn't . . .'

'Oh no.'

She put on her sun-helmet and went out into the blazing ten o'clock heat to find the cook—she looked more fragile than ever and more indomitable. When she had given her orders she went to the warehouse to inspect the alligator skins tacked out on a wall, then to the stables to see that the mules were in good shape. She carried her responsibilities carefully like crockery across the hot yard: there was no question she wasn't prepared to answer; the vultures rose languidly at her approach.

She returned to the house and her mother. She said, 'It's Thursday.'

'Is it, dear?'

'Hasn't father got the bananas down to the quay?'

'I'm sure I don't know, dear.'

She went briskly back into the yard and rang a bell. An Indian came. No, the bananas were still in the store; no orders had been given. 'Get them down,' she said, 'at once, quickly. The boat will be here soon.' She fetched her father's ledger and counted the bunches as they were carried out—a hundred bananas or more to a bunch which was worth a few pence. It took more than two hours to empty the store; somebody had got to do the work, and once before her father had forgotten the day. After half an hour she began to feel tired—she wasn't used to weariness so early in the day. She leant against the wall and it scorched her shoulder-blades. She felt no resentment at all at being there, looking after things: the word 'play' had no meaning to her at all—the whole of life was adult. In one of Henry Beckley's early reading-books there had been a picture of a doll's tea-party: it was incomprehensible like a ceremony she hadn't learned: she couldn't see the point of pretending. Four hundred and fifty-six. Four hundred and fifty-seven. The sweat poured down the peons' bodies steadily like a shower-bath. An awful pain took her suddenly in the stomach—she missed a load and tried to catch up in her calculations: she felt the sense of responsibility for the first time like a load borne for too many years. Five hundred and twenty-five. It was a new pain (not worms this time), but it didn't scare her; it was as if her body had expected it, had grown up to it, as the mind grows up to the loss of tenderness. You couldn't call it childhood draining out of her: of childhood she had never really been conscious.

'Is that the last?' she said.

'Yes, señorita.'

'Are you sure?'

'Yes, señorita.'

But she had to see for herself. Never before had it occurred to her to do a job unwillingly—if she didn't do a thing nobody would—but to-day she wanted to lie down, to sleep: if all the bananas didn't get away it was her father's fault. She wondered whether she had fever, her feet felt so cold on the hot ground. Oh well, she thought, and went patiently into the barn, found the torch, and switched it on. Yes, the place seemed empty enough, but she never left a job half done. She advanced towards the back wall, holding the torch in front of her. An empty bottle rolled away—she dropped the light on it: Cerveza Moctezuma. Then the torch lit the back wall: low down near the ground somebody had scrawled in chalk–she came closer: a lot of little crosses leant in the circle of light. He must have lain down among the bananas and tried to relieve his fear by writing something, and this was all he could think of. The child stood in her woman's pain and looked at them: a horrible novelty enclosed her whole morning: it was as if to-day everything were memorable.

★   ★   ★

The Chief of Police was in the cantina playing billiards when the lieutenant found him. He had a handkerchief tied all round his face with some idea that it relieved the tooth-ache. He was chalking his cue for a difficult shot as the lieutenant pushed through the swing door. On the shelves behind were nothing but gaseosa bottles and a yellow liquid called Sidral–warranted non-alcoholic. The lieutenant stood protestingly in the doorway. The situation was ignoble; he wanted to eliminate anything in the state at which a foreigner might have cause to sneer. He said, 'Can I speak to you?' The jefe winced at a sudden jab of pain and came with unusual alacrity towards the door; the lieutenant glanced at the score, marked in rings strung on a cord across the room–the jefe was losing. 'Back–moment,' the jefe said, and explained to the lieutenant, 'Don't want open mouth.' As they pushed the door somebody raised a cue and surreptitiously pushed back one of the jefe's rings.

They walked up the street side by side, the fat one and the lean. It was a Sunday and all the shops closed at noon–that was the only relic of the old time. No bells rang anywhere. The lieutenant said, 'Have you seen the Governor?'

'You can do anything,' the jefe said, 'anything.'

'He leaves it to us?'

'On conditions,' he winced.

'What are they?'

'He'll hold you–responsible–if–not caught before–rains.'

'As long as I'm not responsible for anything else . . .' the lieutenant said moodily.

'You asked for it. You got it.'

'I'm glad.' It seemed to the lieutenant that all the world he cared about now lay at his feet. They passed the new hall built for the Syndicate of Workers and Peasants: through the window they could see the big bold clever murals–of one priest caressing a woman in the confessional, another tippling on the sacramental wine. The lieutenant said, 'We will soon make these unnecessary.' He looked at the pictures with the eye of a foreigner: they seemed to him barbarous.

'Why? They are–fun.'

'One day they'll forget there ever was a Church here.'

The jefe said nothing. The lieutenant knew he was thinking, what a fuss about nothing. He said sharply, 'Well, what are my orders?'

'Orders?'

'You are my chief.'

The jefe was silent. He studied the lieutenant unobtrusively with little astute eyes. Then he said, 'You know I trust you. Do what you think best.'

'Will you put that in writing?'

'Oh—not necessary. We know each other.'

All the way up the road they fenced warily for positions.

'Didn't the Governor give you anything in writing?' the lieutenant asked.

'No. He said we knew each other.'

It was the lieutenant who gave way because it was he who really cared. He was indifferent to his personal future. He said, 'I shall take hostages from every village.'

'Then he won't stay in the villages.'

'Do you imagine,' the lieutenant asked bitterly, 'that they don't know where he is? He has to keep some touch—or what good is he?'

'Just as you like,' the jefe said.

'And I shall shoot as often as it's necessary.'

The jefe said with facetious brightness, 'A little blood never hurt anyone. Where will you start?'

'His parish, I think, Concepcion, and then—perhaps—his home.'

'Why there?'

'He may think he's safe there.' He brooded past the shuttered shops. 'It's worth a few deaths, but will *he*, do you think, support me if they make a fuss in Mexico City?'

'It isn't likely, is it?' the jefe said. 'But it's what—' he was stopped by a stab of pain.

'It's what I wanted,' the lieutenant said for him.

He made his way on alone towards the police station, and the chief went back to billiards. There were few people about; it was too hot. If only, he thought, we had a proper photograph—he wanted to know the features of his enemy. A swarm of children had the plaza to themselves. They were playing some obscure and intricate game from bench to bench. An empty gaseosa bottle sailed through the air and smashed at the lieutenant's feet. His hand went to his holster and he turned; he caught a look of consternation on a boy's face.

'Did you throw that bottle?'

The heavy brown eyes stared sullenly back at him.

'What were you doing?'

'It was a bomb.'

'Were you throwing it at me?'

'No.'

'What then?'

'A gringo.'

The lieutenant smiled—an awkward movement of the lips. 'That's right, but you must aim better.' He kicked the broken bottle into the road and tried to think of words which would show these children that they were on the same side. He said, 'I suppose the gringo was one of those rich Yankees . . .' and surprised an expression of devotion in the boy's face; it called for something in return, and the lieutenant became aware in his own heart of a sad and unsatisfiable love. He said, 'Come here.' The child approached, while his companions stood in a scared semi-circle and watched from a safe distance. 'What is your name?'

'Luis.'

'Well,' the lieutenant said, at a loss for words, 'you must learn to aim properly.'

The boy said passionately, 'I wish I could.' He had his eye on the holster.

'Would you like to see my gun?' the lieutenant asked. He pulled his heavy automatic from the holster and held it out: the children drew cautiously in. He said, 'This is the safety-catch. Lift it. So. Now it's ready to fire.'

'Is it loaded?' Luis asked.

'It's always loaded.'

The tip of the boy's tongue appeared: he swallowed. Saliva came from the glands as if he smelt food. They all stood close in now. A daring child put out his hand and touched the holster. They ringed the lieutenant round: he was surrounded by an insecure happiness as he fitted the gun back on his hip.

'What is it called?' Luis asked.

'A Colt .38.'

'How many bullets?'

'Six.'

'Have you killed somebody with it?'

'Not yet,' the lieutenant said.

They were breathless with interest. He stood with his hand on his holster and watched the brown intent patient eyes: it was for these he was fighting. He would eliminate from their childhood everything which had made him miserable, all that was poor, superstitious and corrupt. They deserved nothing less than the truth—a vacant universe and a cooling world, the right to be happy in any way they chose. He was quite prepared to make a massacre for their sakes—first the Church and then the foreigner and then the politician—even his own chief would one day have to go. He wanted to begin the world again with them, in a desert.

'Oh,' Luis said, 'I wish . . . I wish . . .' as if his ambition were too vast for definition. The lieutenant put out his hand in a gesture of affection—a touch, he didn't know what to do with it. He pinched the boy's ear and saw him flinch away with the pain; they scattered from him like birds and he went on alone across the plaza to the police station, a little dapper figure of hate carrying his secret of love. On the wall of the office the gangster still stared stubbornly in profile towards the first communion party. Somebody had inked round the priest's head to detach him from the girls' and the women's faces: the unbearable grin peeked out of a halo. The lieutenant called furiously out into the patio, 'Is there nobody here?' Then he sat down at the desk while the gun-butts scraped the floor.

PART II

I

The mule suddenly sat down under the priest. It was not an unnatural thing to do, for they had been travelling through the forest for nearly twelve hours. They had been going west, but news of soldiers met them there and they had turned east; the Red Shirts were active in that direction, so they had tacked north, wading through the swamps, diving into the mahogany darkness. Now they were both tired out and the mule simply sat down. The priest scrambled off and began to laugh. He was feeling happy. It is one of the strange discoveries a man can make that life, however you lead it, contains moments of exhilaration; there are always comparisons which can be made with worse times: even in danger and misery the pendulum swings.

He came cautiously out of the belt of trees into a marshy clearing. The whole state was like that, river and swamp and forest. He knelt down in the late sunlight and bathed his face in a brown pool which reflected back at him like a piece of glazed pottery the round, stubbly and hollow features. They were so unexpected that he grinned at them—with the shy evasive untrustworthy smile of a man caught out. In the old days he often practised a gesture a long while in front of a glass so that he had come to know his own face as well as an actor does. It was a form of humility—his own natural face hadn't seemed the right one. It was a buffoon's face, good enough for mild jokes to women, but unsuitable at the altar-rail. He had tried to change it—and indeed, he thought, indeed I have succeeded, they'll never recognise me now, and the cause of his happiness came back to him like the taste of brandy, promising temporary relief from fear, loneliness, a lot of things. He was being driven by the presence of soldiers to the very place where he most wanted to be. He had avoided it for six years, but now it wasn't his fault—it was his duty to go there—it couldn't count as sin. He went back to his mule and kicked it gently, 'Up, mule, up,' a small gaunt man in torn peasant's clothes going for the first time in many years, like any ordinary man, to his home.

In any case, even if he could have gone south and avoided the village, it was only one more surrender. The years behind him were littered with similar surrenders—feast days and fast days and days of abstinence had been the first to go: then he had ceased to trouble more than occasionally about his breviary—and finally he had left it behind altogether at the port in one of his periodic attempts at escape. Then the altar stone went–too dangerous to carry with him. He had no business to say Mass without it; he was probably liable to suspension, but penalties of the ecclesiastical kind began to seem unreal in a state where the only penalty was the civil one of death. The routine of his life like a dam was cracked and forgetfulness came dribbling through, wiping out this and that. Five years ago he had given way to despair–the unforgivable sin–and he was going back now to the scene of his despair with a curious lightening of the heart. For he had got over despair too. He was a bad priest, he knew it. They had a word for his kind–a whisky priest, but every failure dropped out of sight and mind: somewhere they accumulated in secret–the rubble of his failures. One day they would choke up, he supposed, altogether the source of grace. Until then he carried on, with spells of fear, weariness, with a shamefaced lightness of heart.

The mule splashed across the clearing and they entered the forest again. Now that he no longer despaired it didn't mean, of course, that he wasn't damned–it was simply that after a time the mystery became too great, a damned man putting God into the mouths of men: an odd sort of servant, that, for the devil. His mind was full of a simplified mythology: Michael dressed in armour slew a dragon, and the angels fell through space like comets with beautiful streaming hair because they were jealous, so one of the Fathers had said, of what God intended for men–the enormous privilege of life–this life.

There were signs of cultivation; stumps of trees and the ashes of fires where the ground was being cleared for a crop. He stopped beating the mule on; he felt a curious shyness . . . A woman came out of a hut and watched him lagging up the path on the tired mule. The tiny village, not more than two dozen huts round a dusty plaza, was made to pattern, but it was a pattern which lay close to his heart. He felt secure–he was confident of a welcome, confident that in this place there would be at least one person he could trust not to betray him to the police. When he was quite close the mule sat down again–this time he had to roll on the ground to escape. He picked himself up and the woman watched him as if he were an enemy. 'Ah, Maria,' he said, 'and how are you?'

'Well,' she exclaimed, 'it is you, father?'

He didn't look directly at her: his eyes were sly and cautious. He said, 'You didn't recognise me?'

'You've changed.' She looked him up and down with a kind of contempt. She said, 'When did you get those clothes, father?'

'A week ago.'

'What did you do with yours?'

'I gave them in exchange.'

'Why? They were good clothes.'

'They were very ragged–and conspicuous.'

'I'd have mended them and hidden them away. It's a waste. You look like a common man.'

He smiled, looking at the ground, while she chided him like a housekeeper: it was just as in the old days when there was a presbytery and meetings of the Children of Mary and all the guilds and gossip of a parish, except of course that . . . He said gently, not looking at her, with the same embarrassed smile, 'How's Brigitta?' His heart jumped at the name: a sin may have enormous consequences: it was six years since he had been—home.

'She's as well as the rest of us. What did you expect?'

He had his satisfaction, but it was connected with his crime; he had no business to feel pleasure at anything attached to that past. He said mechanically, 'That's good,' while his heart beat with its secret love. He said, 'I'm very tired. The police were about near Zapata . . .'

'Why didn't you make for Monte Cristo?'

He looked quickly up with anxiety. It wasn't the welcome that he had expected; a small knot of people had gathered between the huts and watched him from a safe distance—there was a little decaying bandstand and a single stall for gaseosas—people had brought their chairs out for the evening. Nobody came forward to kiss his hand and ask his blessing. It was as if he had descended by means of his sin into the human struggle to learn other things besides despair and love, that a man can be unwelcome even in his own home. He said, 'The Red Shirts were there.'

'Well, father,' the woman said, 'we can't turn you away. You'd better come along.' He followed her meekly, tripping once in the long peon's trousers, with the happiness wiped off his face and the smile somehow left behind like the survivor of a wreck. There were seven or eight men, two women, half a dozen children: he came among them like a beggar. He couldn't help remembering the last time . . . the excitement, the gourds of spirit brought out of holes in the ground . . . his guilt had still been fresh, yet how he had been welcomed. It was as if he had returned to them in their vicious prison as one of themselves—an émigré who comes back to his native place enriched.

'This is the father,' the woman said. Perhaps it was only that they hadn't recognised him, he thought, and waited for their greetings. They came forward one by one and kissed his hand and then stood back and watched him. He said, 'I am glad to see you . . .' he was going to say 'my children', but then it seemed to him that only the childless man has the right to call strangers his children. The real children were coming up now to kiss his hand, one by one, under the pressure of their parents. They were too young to remember the old days when the priests dressed in black and wore Roman collars and had soft superior patronising hands; he could see they were mystified at the show of respect to a peasant like their parents. He didn't look at them directly, but he was watching them closely all the same. Two were girls—a thin washed-out child—of five, six, seven? he couldn't tell, and one who had been sharpened by hunger into an appearance of devilry and malice beyond her age. A young woman stared out of the child's eyes. He watched them disperse again, saying nothing: they were strangers.

One of the men said, 'Will you be here long, father?'

He said, 'I thought, perhaps . . . I could rest . . . a few days.'

One of the other men said, 'Couldn't you go a bit farther north, father, to Pueblito?'

'We've been travelling for twelve hours, the mule and I.'

The woman suddenly spoke for him, angrily, 'Of course he'll stay here to-night. It's the least we can do.'

He said, 'I'll say Mass for you in the morning,' as if he were offering them a bribe, but it might almost have been stolen money from their expressions of shyness and unwillingness.

Somebody said, 'If you don't mind, father, very early . . . in the night perhaps.'

'What is the matter with you all?' he asked. 'Why should you be afraid?'

'Haven't you heard . . . ?'

'Heard?'

'They are taking hostages now—from all the villages where they think you've been. And if people don't tell . . . somebody is shot . . . and then they take another hostage. It happened in Concepción.'

'Concepción?' One of his lids began to twitch, up and down, up and down. He said, 'Who?' They looked at him stupidly. He said furiously, 'Who did they murder?'

'Pedro Montez.'

He gave a little yapping cry like a dog's – the absurd shorthand of grief. The old-young child laughed. He said, 'Why don't they catch me? The fools. Why don't they catch *me*?' The little girl laughed again; he stared at her sightlessly, as if he could hear the sound but couldn't see the face. Happiness was dead again before it had had time to breathe; he was like a woman with a stillborn child—bury it quickly and forget and begin again. Perhaps the next would live.

'You see, father,' one of the men said, 'why . . .'

He felt as a guilty man does before his judges. He said, 'Would you rather that I was like . . . like Padre José in the capital . . . you have heard of him . . . ?'

They said unconvincingly, 'Of course not that, father.'

He said, 'What am I saying now? It's not what you want or what I want.' He continued sharply, with authority, 'I will sleep now . . . You can wake me an hour before dawn . . . half an hour to hear your confessions . . . then Mass, and I will be gone.'

But where? There wouldn't be a village in the state to which he wouldn't be an unwelcome danger now.

The woman said, 'This way, father.'

He followed her into a small room where all the furniture had been made out of packing-cases—a chair, a bed of boards tacked together and covered with a straw mat, a crate on which a cloth had been laid and on the cloth an oil-lamp. He said, 'I don't want to turn anybody out of here.'

'It's mine.'

He looked at her doubtfully. 'Where will you sleep?' He was afraid of claims. He watched her covertly: was this all there was in marriage, this evasion and suspicion and lack of ease? When people confessed to him in terms of passion, was this all they meant—the hard bed and the busy woman and the not talking about the past?

'When you are gone.'

The light flattened out behind the forest and the long shadows of the trees pointed towards the door. He lay down upon the bed, and the woman busied herself somewhere out of sight: he could hear her scratching at the earth floor. He couldn't sleep. Had it become his duty then to run away? He had tried to escape several times, but he had always been prevented . .'. now they wanted him to go. Nobody would stop him, saying a woman was ill or a man dying. He was a sickness now.

'Maria,' he said. 'Maria, what are you doing?'

'I have saved a little brandy for you.'

He thought: if I go, I shall meet other priests: I shall go to confession: I shall feel contrition and be forgiven: eternal life will begin for me all over again. The Church taught that it was every man's first duty to save his own soul. The simple ideas of hell and heaven moved in his brain; life without books, without contact with educated men, had peeled away from his memory everything but the simplest outline of the mystery.

'There,' the woman said. She carried a small medicine bottle filled with spirit.

If he left them, they would be safe, and they would be free from his example. He was the only priest the children could remember: it was from him they would take their ideas of the faith. But it was from him too they took God—in their mouths. When he was gone it would be as if God in all this space between the sea and the mountains ceased to exist. Wasn't it his duty to stay, even if they despised him, even if they were murdered for his sake? even if they were corrupted by his example? He was shaken with the enormity of the problem. He lay with his hands over his eyes: nowhere, in all the wide flat marshy land, was there a single person he could consult. He raised the brandy to his mouth.

He said shyly, 'And Brigitta . . . is she . . . well?'

'You saw her just now.'

'No.' He couldn't believe that he hadn't recognised her. It was making light of his mortal sin: you couldn't do a thing like that and then not even recognise . . .

'Yes, she was there.' Maria went to the door and called, 'Brigitta, Brigitta,' and the priest turned on his side and watched her come in out of the outside landscape of terror and lust—that small malicious child who had laughed at him.

'Go and speak to the father,' Maria said. 'Go on.'

He made an attempt to hide the brandy bottle, but there was nowhere . . . he tried to minimise it in his hands, watching her, feeling the shock of human love.

'She knows her catechism,' Maria said, 'but she won't say it . . .'

The child stood there, watching him with acuteness and contempt. They had spent no love in her conception: just fear and despair and half a bottle of brandy and the sense of loneliness had driven him to an act which horrified him—and this scared shame-faced overpowering love was the result. He said, 'Why not? Why won't you say it?' taking quick secret glances, never meeting her gaze, feeling his heart pound in his breast unevenly, like an old donkey engine, with the baulked desire to save her from—everything.

'Why should I?'

'God wishes it.'

'How do you know?'

He was aware of an immense load of responsibility: it was indistinguishable from love. This, he thought, must be what all parents feel: ordinary men go through life like this crossing their fingers, praying against pain, afraid. . . . This is what we escape at no cost at all, sacrificing an unimportant motion of the body. For years, of course, he had been responsible for souls, but that was different . . . a lighter thing. You could trust God to make allowances, but you couldn't trust small-pox, starvation, men . . . He said, 'My dear,' tightening his grip upon the brandy bottle . . . He had baptised her at his last visit: she had been like a rag doll with a wrinkled aged face–it had seemed unlikely that she would live long . . . He had felt nothing but a regret; it was difficult even to feel shame where no one blamed him. He was the only priest most of them had ever known–they took their standard of the priesthood from him. Even the women.

'Are you the gringo?'

'What gringo?'

The woman said, 'The silly little creature. It's because the police have been looking for a man.' It seemed odd to hear of any other man they wanted but himself.

'What has he done?'

'He's a Yankee. He murdered some people in the north.'

'Why should he be here?'

'They think he's making for Quintana Roo–the chiceli plantations.' It was where many criminals in Mexico ended up: you could work on a plantation and earn good money and nobody interfered.

'Are you the gringo?' the child repeated.

'Do I look like a murderer?'

'I don't know.'

If he left the state, he would be leaving her too, abandoned. He said humbly to the woman, 'Couldn't I stay a few days here?'

'It's too dangerous, father.'

He caught the look in the child's eyes which frightened him–it was again as if a grown woman was there before her time, making her plans, aware of far too much. It was like seeing his own mortal sin look back at him, without contrition. He tried to find some contact with the child and not the woman; he said, 'My dear, tell me what games you play . . .' The child sniggered. He turned his face quickly away and stared up at the roof, where a spider moved. He remembered a proverb–it came out of the recesses of his own childhood: his father had used it–'The best smell is bread, the best savour salt, the best love that of children.' It had been a happy childhood, except that he had been afraid of too many things, and had hated poverty like a crime; he had believed that when he was a priest he would be rich and proud–that was called having a vocation. He thought of the immeasurable distance a man travels–from the first whipping-top to this bed, on which he lay clasping the brandy. And to God it was only a moment. The child's snigger and the first mortal sin lay together more closely than two blinks of the eye. He put out his hand as if he could drag her back by force from–something; but he was powerless. The man or the woman waiting to complete her corruption might not yet have been born. How could he guard her against the non-existent?

She started out of his reach and put her tongue out at him. The woman said, 'You little devil you,' and raised her hand.

'No,' the priest said. 'No.' He scrambled into a sitting position. 'Don't you dare . . .'

'I'm her mother.'

'We haven't any right.' He said to the child, 'If only I had some cards I could show you a trick or two. You could teach your friends . . .' He had never known how to talk to children except from the pulpit. She stared back at him with insolence. He asked, 'Do you know how to send messages with taps—long, short, long . . . ?'

'What on earth, father!' the woman exclaimed.

'It's a game children play. I know.' He said to the child, 'Have you any friends?' '

The child suddenly laughed again knowingly. The seven-year-old body was like a dwarf's: it disguised an ugly maturity.

'Get out of here,' the woman said. 'Get out before I teach you . . .'

She made a last impudent malicious gesture and was gone—perhaps for ever as far as he was concerned. You do not always say good-bye to those you love beside a deathbed, in an atmosphere of leisure and incense. He said, 'I wonder what *we* can teach . . .' He thought of his own death and her life going on; it might be his hell to watch her rejoining him gradually through the debasing years, sharing his weakness like tuberculosis. . . . He lay back on the bed and turned his head away from the draining light; he appeared to be sleeping, but he was wide awake. The woman busied herself with small jobs, and as the sun went down the mosquitoes came out, flashing through the air to their mark unerringly, like sailors' knives.

'Shall I put up a net, father?'

'No. It doesn't matter.' He had had more fevers in the last ten years than he could count: he had ceased to bother: they came and went and made no difference—they were part of his environment.

Presently she left the hut and he could hear her voice gossiping outside. He was astonished and a bit relieved by her resilience. Once for five minutes seven years ago they had been lovers—if you could give that name to a relationship in which she had never used his baptismal name: to her it was just an incident, a scratch which heals completely in the healthy flesh: she was even proud of having been the priest's woman. He alone carried a wound, as though a whole world had died.

*　　*　　*

It was dark: no sign as yet of the dawn. Perhaps two dozen people sat on the earth floor of the largest hut while he preached to them. He couldn't see them with any distinctness. The candles on the packing-case smoked steadily upwards—the door was shut and there was no current of air. He was talking about heaven, standing between them and the candles in the ragged peon trousers and the torn shirt. They grunted and moved restlessly. He knew they were longing for the Mass to be over: they had woken him very early, because there were rumours of police . . .

He said, 'One of the Fathers has told us that joy always depends on pain. Pain is part of joy. We are hungry and then think how we enjoy our food at last. We are thirsty . . .' He stopped suddenly, with his eyes glancing away into the shadows, expecting the cruel laugh that did not come. He said, 'We deny ourselves so that we can enjoy. You have heard of rich men in the north who eat salted foods, so that they can be thirsty—for what they call the cocktail. Before the marriage, too, there is the long betrothal . . .' Again he stopped. He felt his own unworthiness like a weight at the back of the tongue. There was a smell of hot wax from where a candle drooped in the nocturnal heat; people shifted on the hard floor in the shadows. The smell of unwashed human beings warred with the wax. He cried out stubbornly in a voice of authority, 'That is why I tell you that heaven is here: this is a part of heaven just as pain is a part of pleasure.' He said, 'Pray that you will suffer more and more and more. Never get tired of suffering. The police watching you, the soldiers gathering taxes, the beating you always get from the jefe because you are too poor to pay, smallpox and fever, hunger . . . that is all part of heaven—the preparation. Perhaps without them, who can tell, you wouldn't enjoy heaven so much. Heaven would not be complete. And heaven. What is heaven?' Literary phrases from what seemed now to be another life altogether—the strict quiet life of the seminary—became confused on his tongue: the names of precious stones: Jerusalem the Golden. But these people had never seen gold.

He went rather stumbling on, 'Heaven is where there is no jefe, no unjust laws, no taxes, no soldiers and no hunger. Your children do not die in heaven.' The door of the hut opened and a man slipped in. There was whispering out of the range of the candle-light. 'You will never be afraid there—or unsafe. There are no Red Shirts. Nobody grows old. The crops never fail. Oh, it is easy to say all the things that there will *not* be in heaven: what is there is God. That is more difficult. Our words are made to describe what we know with our senses. We say "light", but we are thinking only of the sun, "love" . . .' It was not easy to concentrate: the police were not far away. The man had probably brought news. 'That means perhaps a child . . .' The door opened again: he could see another day drawn across like a grey slate outside. A voice whispered urgently to him, 'Father.'

'Yes?'

'The police are on the way. They are only a mile off, coming through the forest.'

This was what he was used to: the words not striking home, the hurried close, the expectation of pain coming between him and his faith. He said stubbornly, 'Above all remember this—heaven is here.' Were they on horseback or on foot? If they were on foot, he had twenty minutes left to finish Mass and hide. 'Here now, at this minute, your fear and my fear are part of heaven, where there will be no fear any more for ever.' He turned his back on them and began very quickly to recite the Credo. There was a time when he had approached the Canon of the Mass with actual physical dread—the first time he had consumed the body and blood of God in a state of mortal sin. But then life bred its excuses—it hadn't after a while seemed to matter very much, whether he was damned or not, so long as these others. . . .

He kissed the top of the packing-case and turned to bless. In the inadequate light he could just see two men kneeling with their arms stretched out in the shape of a cross—they would keep that position until the consecration was over, one more mortification squeezed out of their harsh and painful lives. He felt humbled by the pain ordinary men bore voluntarily; his pain was forced on him. 'Oh Lord, I have loved the beauty of thy house . . .' The candles smoked and the people shifted on their knees—an absurd happiness bobbed up in him again before anxiety returned: it was as if he had been permitted to look in from the outside at the population of heaven. Heaven must contain just such scared and dutiful and hunger-lined faces. For a matter of seconds he felt an immense satisfaction that he could talk of suffering to them now without hypocrisy—it is hard for the sleek and well-fed priest to praise poverty. He began the prayer for the living: the long list of the Apostles and Martyrs fell like footsteps—Cornelii, Cypriani, Laurentii, Chrysogoni—soon the police would reach the clearing where his mule had sat down under him and he had washed in the pool. The Latin words ran into each other on his hasty tongue: he could feel impatience all round him. He began the Consecration of the Host (he had finished the wafers long ago—it was a piece of bread from Maria's oven); impatience abruptly died away: everything in time became a routine but this—'Who the day before he suffered took Bread into his holy and venerable hands . . .' Whoever moved outside on the forest path, there was no movement here – '*Hoc est enim Corpus Meum.*' He could hear the sigh of breaths released: God was here in the body for the first time in six years. When he raised the Host he could imagine the faces lifted like famished dogs. He began the Consecration of the Wine—in a chipped cup. That was one more surrender—for two years he had carried a chalice round with him; once it would have cost him his life, if the police officer who opened his case had not been a Catholic. It may very well have cost the officer his life, if anybody had discovered the evasion—he didn't know; you went round making God knew what martyrs—in Concepción or elsewhere—when you yourself were without grace enough to die.

The Consecration was in silence: no bell rang. He knelt by the packing-case exhausted, without a prayer. Somebody opened the door: a voice whispered urgently, 'They're here.' They couldn't have come on foot then, he thought vaguely. Somewhere in the absolute stillness of the dawn—it couldn't have been more than a quarter of a mile away—a horse whinnied.

He got to his feet—Maria stood at his elbow. She said, 'The cloth, father, give me the cloth.' He put the Host hurriedly into his mouth and drank the wine: one had to avoid profanation: the cloth was whipped away from the packing-case. She nipped the candles, so that the wick should not leave a smell . . . The room was already cleared, only the owner hung by the entrance waiting to kiss his hand. Through the door the world was faintly visible, and a cock in the village crowed.

Maria said, 'Come to the hut quickly.'

'I'd better go.' He was without a plan. 'Not be found here.'

'They are all round the village.'

Was this the end at last, he wondered? Somewhere fear waited to spring at him, he knew, but he wasn't afraid yet. He followed the woman, scurrying across the village to her hut, repeating an act of contrition mechanically as he went. He wondered when the fear would start. He had been afraid when the policeman opened his case—but that was years ago. He had been afraid hiding in the shed among the bananas, hearing the child argue with the police officer–that was only a few weeks away. Fear would undoubtedly begin again soon. There was no sign of the police–only the grey morning, and the chickens and turkeys astir, flopping down from the trees in which they had roosted during the night. Again the cock crew. If they were so careful, they must know beyond the shadow of doubt that he was here. It *was* the end.

Maria plucked at him. 'Get in. Quick. On to the bed.' Presumably she had an idea–women were appallingly practical: they built new plans at once out of the ruins of the old. But what was the good? She said, 'Let me smell your breath. O God, anyone can tell . . . wine . . . what would we be doing with wine?' She was gone again, inside, making a lot of bother in the peace and quiet of the dawn. Suddenly, out of the forest, a hundred yards away, an officer rode. In the absolute stillness you could hear the creaking of his revolver-holster as he turned and waved.

All round the little clearing the police appeared–they must have marched very quickly, for only the officer had a horse. Rifles at the trail, they approached the small group of huts–an exaggerated and rather absurd show of force. One man had a puttee trailing behind him–it had probably caught on something in the forest. He tripped on it and fell with a great clatter of cartridge-belt on gunstock: the lieutenant on the horse looked round and then turned his bitter and angry face upon the silent huts.

The woman was pulling at him from inside the hut. She said, 'Bite this. Quick. There's no time . . .' He turned his back on the advancing police and came into the dusk of the room. She had a small raw onion in her hand. 'Bite it,' she said. He bit it and began to weep. 'Is that better?' she said. He could hear the pad, pad of the cautious horse hoofs advancing between the huts.

'It's horrible,' he said with a giggle.

'Give it to me.' She made it disappear somewhere into her clothes: it was a trick all women seemed to know. He asked, 'Where's my case?'

'Never mind your case. Get on to the bed.'

But before he could move a horse blocked the doorway. They could see a leg in riding-boots piped with scarlet: brass fittings gleamed: a hand in a glove rested on the high pommel. Maria put a hand upon his arm–it was as near as she had ever come to a movement of affection: affection was taboo between them. A voice cried, 'Come on out, all of you.' The horse stamped and a little pillar of dust went up. 'Come on out, I said.' Somewhere a shot was fired. The priest left the hut.

The dawn had really broken: light feathers of colour were blown up the sky: a man still held his gun pointed upwards: a little balloon of grey smoke hung at the muzzle. Was this how the agony would start?

Out of all the huts the villagers were reluctantly emerging–the children first: they were inquisitive and unfrightened. The men and women had the air already of people condemned by authority–authority was never wrong. None of them looked at the priest. They stared at the ground and waited. Only the children watched the horse as if it were the most important thing there.

The lieutenant said, 'Search the huts.' Time passed very slowly; even the smoke of the shot seemed to remain in the air for an unnatural period. Some pigs came grunting out of a hut, and a turkey-cock paced with evil dignity into the centre of the circle, puffing out its dusty feathers and tossing the long pink membrane from its beak. A soldier came up to the lieutenant and saluted sketchily. He said, 'They're all here.'

'You've found nothing suspicious?'

'No.'

'Then look again.'

Once more time stopped like a broken clock. The lieutenant drew out a cigarette-case, hesitated and put it back again. Again the policeman approached and reported, 'Nothing.'

The lieutenant barked out, 'Attention. All of you. Listen to me.' The outer ring of police closed in, pushing the villagers together into a small group in front of the lieutenant: only the children were left free. The priest saw his own child standing close to the lieutenant's horse; she could just reach above his boot: she put up her hand and touched the leather. The lieutenant said, 'I am looking for two men—one is a gringo, a yankee, a murderer. I can see very well he is not here. There is a reward of five hundred pesos for his capture. Keep your eyes open.' He paused and ran his eye over them. The priest felt his gaze come to rest; he looked down like the others at the ground.

'The other,' the lieutenant said, 'is a priest.' He raised his voice: 'You know what that means—a traitor to the republic. Anyone who shelters him is a traitor too.' Their immobility seemed to anger him. He said, 'You're fools if you still believe what the priests tell you. All they want is your money. What has God ever done for you? Have you got enough to eat? Have your children got enough to eat? Instead of food they talk to you about heaven. Oh, everything will be fine after you are dead, they say. I tell you—everything will be fine when *they* are dead, and you must help.' The child had her hand on his boot. He looked down at her with dark affection. He said with conviction, 'This child is worth more than the Pope in Rome.' The police leant on their guns; one of them yawned; the turkey-cock went hissing back towards the hut. The lieutenant said, 'If you've seen this priest speak up. There's a reward of seven hundred pesos . . .' Nobody spoke.

The lieutenant yanked his horse's head round towards them. He said, 'We know he's in this district. Perhaps you don't know what happened to a man in Concepción.' One of the women began to weep. He said, 'Come up—one after the other—and let me have your names. No not the women, the men.'

They filed sullenly up and he questioned them, 'What's your name? What do you do? Married? Which is your wife? Have you heard of this priest?' Only one man now stood between the priest and the horse's head. He recited an act of contrition silently with only half a mind—'. . . my sins, because they have crucified my loving Saviour . . . but above all because they have offended . . .' He was alone in front of the lieutenant—'I hereby resolve never more to offend Thee . . .' It was a formal act, because a man had to be prepared: it was like making your will and might be as valueless.

'Your name?'

The name of the man in Concepción came back to him. He said, 'Montez.'

'Have you ever seen the priest?'

'No.'

'What do you do?'

'I have a little land.'

'Are you married?'

'Yes.'

'Which is your wife?'

Maria suddenly broke out, 'I'm his wife. Why do you want to ask so many questions? Do you think *he* looks like a priest?'

The lieutenant was examining something on the pommel of his saddle: it seemed to be an old photograph. 'Let me see your hands,' he said.

The priest held them up: they were as hard as a labourer's. Suddenly the lieutenant leant down from the saddle and sniffed at his breath. There was complete silence among the villagers–a dangerous silence, because it seemed to convey to the lieutenant a fear . . . He stared back at the hollow stubbled face, looked back at the photograph. 'All right,' he said, 'next,' and then as the priest stepped aside, 'Wait.' He put his hand down to Brigitta's head and gently tugged at her black stiff hair. He said, 'Look up. You know everyone in this village, don't you?'

'Yes,' she said.

'Who's that man, then? What's his name?'

'I don't know,' the child said. The lieutenant caught his breath. 'You don't know his name?' he said. 'Is he a stranger?'

Maria cried, 'Why, the child doesn't know her own name. Ask her who her father is.'

'Who's your father?'

The child stared up at the lieutenant and then turned her knowing eyes upon the priest . . . 'Sorry and beg pardon for all my sins,' he was repeating to himself with his fingers crossed for luck. The child said, 'That's him. There.'

'All right,' the lieutenant said. 'Next.' The interrogations went on: name? work? married? while the sun came up above the forest. The priest stood with his hands clasped in front of him: again death had been postponed. He felt an enormous temptation to throw himself in front of the lieutenant and declare himself–'I am the one you want.' Would they shoot him out of hand? A delusive promise of peace tempted him. Far up in the sky a vulture watched; they must appear from that height as two groups of carnivorous animals who might at any time break into conflict, and it waited there, a tiny black spot, for carrion. Death was not the end of pain–to believe in peace was a kind of heresy.

The last man gave his evidence.

The lieutenant said, 'Is no one willing to help?'

They stood silent beside the decayed bandstand. He said, 'You heard what happened at Concepción. I took a hostage there . . . and when I found that this priest had been in the neighbourhood I put the man against the nearest tree. I found out because there's always someone who changes his mind–perhaps because somebody in Concepción loved the man's wife and wanted him out of the way. It's not my business to look into reasons. I only know we found wine later in Concepción . . . Perhaps there's somebody in this village who wants your piece of land–or your cow. It's much safer to speak now. Because I'm going to take a hostage from here too.' He paused. Then he said, 'There's no need even to speak, if he's here among you. Just look at him. No one will know then that it was you who gave him away. He won't know himself if you're afraid of his curses. Now . . . This is your last chance.'

The priest looked at the ground—he wasn't going to make it difficult for the man who gave him away.

'Right,' the lieutenant said, 'then I shall choose my man. You've brought it on yourselves.'

He sat on his horse watching them—one of the policemen had leant his gun against the bandstand and was doing up a puttee. The villagers still stared at the ground; everyone was afraid to catch his eye. He broke out suddenly, 'Why won't you trust me? I don't want any of you to die. In my eyes—can't you understand—you are worth far more than he is. I want to give you'—he made a gesture with his hands which was valueless, because no one saw him—'everything.' He said in a dull voice, 'You. You there. I'll take you.'

A woman screamed. 'That's my boy. That's Miguel. You can't take my boy.'

He said dully, 'Every man here is somebody's husband or somebody's son. I know that.'

The priest stood silently with his hands clasped; his knuckles whitened as he gripped . . . He could feel all round him the beginning of hate. Because he was no one's husband or son. He said, 'Lieutenant . . .'

'What do you want?'

'I'm getting too old to be much good in the fields. Take me.'

A rout of pigs came rushing round the corner of a hut, taking no notice of anybody. The soldier finished his puttee and stood up. The sunlight coming up above the forest winked on the bottles of the gaseosa stall.

The lieutenant said, 'I'm choosing a hostage, not offering free board and lodging to the lazy. If you are no good in the fields, you are no good as a hostage.' He gave an order. 'Tie the man's hands and bring him along.'

It took no time at all for the police to be gone—they took with them two or three chickens, a turkey and the man called Miguel. The priest said aloud, 'I did my best.' He went on. 'It's *your* job—to give me up. What do you expect me to do? It's my job not to be caught.'

One of the men said, 'That's all right, father. Only will you be careful . . . to see that you don't leave any wine behind . . . like you did at Concepción?'

Another said, 'It's no good staying, father. They'll get you in the end. They won't forget your face again. Better go north, to the mountains. Over the border.'

'It's a fine state over the border,' a woman said. 'They've still got churches there. Nobody can go in them, of course—but they are there. Why, I've heard that there are priests too in the towns. A cousin of mine went over the mountains to Las Casas once and heard Mass—in a house, with a proper altar, and the priest all dressed up like in the old days. You'd be happy there, father.'

The priest followed Maria to the hut. The bottle of brandy lay on the table; he touched it with his fingers—there wasn't much left. He said, 'My case, Maria? Where's my case?'

'It's too dangerous to carry that around any more,' Maria said.

'How else can I take the wine?'

'There isn't any wine.'

'What do you mean?'

She said, 'I'm not going to bring trouble on you and everyone else. I've broken the bottle. Even if it brings a curse . . .'

He said gently and sadly, 'You mustn't be superstitious. That was simply—wine. There's nothing sacred in wine. Only it's hard to get hold of here. That's why I kept a store of it in Concepción. But they've found that.'

'Now perhaps you'll go—go away altogether. You're no good any more to anyone,' she said fiercely. 'Don't you understand, father? We don't want you any more.'

'Oh yes,' he said. 'I understand. But it's not what you want—or I want . . .'

She said savagely, 'I know about things. I went to school. I'm not like these others—ignorant. I know you're a bad priest. That time we were together—that wasn't all you've done. I've heard things, I can tell you. Do you think God wants you to stay and die—a whisky priest like you?' He stood patiently in front of her, as he had stood in front of the lieutenant, listening. He hadn't known she was capable of all this thought. She said, 'Suppose you die. You'll be a martyr, won't you? What kind of martyr do you think you'll be? It's enough to make people mock.'

That had never occurred to him—that anybody would consider him a martyr. He said, 'It's difficult. Very difficult. I'll think about it. I wouldn't want the Church to be mocked . . .'

'Think about it over the border then . . .'

'Well . . .'

She said, 'When you-know-what happened, I was proud. I thought the good days would come back. It's not everyone who's a priest's woman. And the child . . . I thought you could do a lot for her. But you might as well be a thief for all the good . . .'

He said vaguely, 'There've been a lot of good thieves.'

'For God's sake take this brandy and go.'

'There was one thing,' he said. 'In my case . . . there was something . . .'

'Go and find it yourself on the rubbish-tip then. I won't touch it again.'

'And the child,' he said, 'you're a good woman, Maria. I mean—you'll try and bring her up well . . . as a Christian.'

'She'll never be good for anything, you can see that.'

'She can't be very bad—at her age,' he implored her.

'She'll go on the way she's begun.'

He said, 'The next Mass I say will be for her.'

She wasn't even listening. She said, 'She's bad through and through.' He was aware of faith dying out between the bed and the door—the Mass would soon mean no more to anyone than a black cat crossing the path. He was risking all their lives for the sake of spilt salt or a crossed finger. He began, 'My mule . . .'

'They are giving it maize now.'

She added, 'You'd better go north. There's no chance to the south any more.'

'I thought perhaps Carmen . . .'

'They'll be watching there.'

'Oh, well . . .' He said sadly, 'Perhaps one day . . . when things are better . . .' He sketched a cross and blessed her, but she stood impatiently before him, willing him to be gone for ever.

'Well, good-bye, Maria.'

'Good-bye.'

He walked across the plaza with his shoulders hunched; he felt that there wasn't a soul in the place who wasn't watching him with satisfaction—the trouble-maker who for obscure and superstitious reasons they preferred not to betray to the police. He felt envious of the unknown gringo whom they wouldn't hesitate to trap—he at any rate had no burden of gratitude to carry round with him.

Down a slope churned up with the hoofs of mules and ragged with tree-roots there was the river—not more than two feet deep, littered with empty cans and broken bottles. A notice, which hung on a tree, read 'It is forbidden to deposit rubbish . . .' Underneath all the refuse of the village was collected and slid gradually down into the river. When the rains came it would be washed away. He put his foot among the old tins and the rotting vegetables and reached for his case. He sighed: it had been quite a good case: one more relic of the quiet past . . . Soon it would be difficult to remember that life had ever been any different. The lock had been torn off: he felt inside the silk lining . . .

The papers were there; reluctantly he let the case fall—a whole important and respected youth dropped among the cans—he had been given it by his parishioners in Concepción on the fifth anniversary of his ordination . . . Somebody moved behind a tree. He lifted his feet out of the rubbish—flies burred round his ankles. With the papers hidden in his fist he came round the trunk to see who was spying. . . . The child sat on a root, kicking her heels against the bark. Her eyes were shut tight fast. He said, 'My dear, what is the matter with you . . . ?' They came open quickly then—red-rimmed and angry, with an expression of absurd pride.

She said, 'You . . . you . . .'

'Me?'

'You are the matter.'

He moved towards her with infinite caution, as if she were an animal who distrusted him. He felt weak with longing. He said, 'My dear, why me . . . ?'

She said furiously, 'They laugh at me.'

'Because of me?'

She said, 'Everyone else has a father . . . who works.'

'I work too.'

'You're a priest, aren't you?'

'Yes.'

'Pedro says you aren't a man. You aren't any good for women.' She said, 'I don't know what he means.'

'I don't suppose he knows himself.'

'Oh, yes he does,' she said. 'He's ten. And I want to know. You're going away, aren't you?'

'Yes.'

He was appalled again by her maturity, as she whipped up a smile from a large and varied stock. She said, 'Tell me—' enticingly. She sat there on the truck of the tree by the rubbish-tip with an effect of abandonment. The world was in her heart already, like the small spot of decay in a fruit. She was without protection–she had no grace, no charm to plead for her; his heart was shaken by the conviction of loss. He said, 'My dear, be careful . . .'

'What of? Why are you going away?'

He came a little nearer; he thought–a man may kiss his own daughter, but she started away from him. 'Don't you touch me,' she screeched at him in her ancient voice and giggled. Every child was born with some kind of knowledge of love, he thought; they took it with the milk at the breast; but on parents and friends depended the kind of love they knew–the saving or the damning kind. Lust too was a kind of love. He saw her fixed in her life like a fly in amber–Maria's hand raised to strike: Pedro talking prematurely in the dusk: and the police beating the forest–violence everywhere. He prayed silently, 'O God, give me any kind of death–without contrition, in a state of sin–only save this child.'

He was a man who was supposed to save souls. It had seemed quite simple once, preaching at Benediction, organising the guilds, having coffee with elderly ladies behind barred windows, blessing new houses with a little incense, wearing black gloves . . . It was as easy as saving money: now it was a mystery. He was aware of his own desperate inadequacy.

He went down on his knees and pulled her to him, while she giggled and struggled to be free: 'I love you. I am your father and I love you. Try to understand that.' He held her tightly by the wrist and suddenly she stayed still, looking up at him. He said, 'I would give my life, that's nothing, my soul . . . my dear, my dear, try to understand that you are–so important.' That was the difference, he had always known, between his faith and theirs, the political leaders of the people who cared only for things like the state, the republic: this child was more important than a whole continent. He said, 'You must take care of yourself because you are so–necessary. The president up in the capital goes guarded by men with guns–but my child, you have all the angels of heaven—' She stared back at him out of dark and unconscious eyes; he had a sense that he had come too late. He said, 'Good-bye, my dear,' and clumsily kissed her–a silly infatuated ageing man, who as soon as he released her and started padding back to the plaza could feel behind his hunched shoulders the whole vile world coming round the child to ruin her. His mule was there, saddled, by the gaseosa stall. A man said, 'Better go north, father,' and stood waving his hand. One mustn't have human affections–or rather one must love every soul as if it were one's own child. The passion to protect must extend itself over a world–but he felt it tethered and aching like a hobbled animal to the tree trunk. He turned his mule south.

⋆   ⋆   ⋆

He was travelling in the actual track of the police. So long as he went slowly and didn't overtake any stragglers it seemed a fairly safe route. What he wanted now was wine. Without it he was useless; he might as well escape north into the mountains and the safe state beyond, where the worst that could happen to him was a fine and a few days in prison because he couldn't pay. But he wasn't ready yet for the final surrender–every small surrender had to be paid for in a further endurance, and now he felt the need of somehow ransoming his child. He would stay another month, another year . . . Jogging up and down on the mule he tried to bribe God with promises of firmness. . . . The mule suddenly dug in its hoofs and stopped dead: a tiny green snake raised itself on the path and then hissed away into the grass like a match-flame. The mule went on.

When he came near a village he would stop the mule and advance as close as he could on foot—the police might have stopped there. Then he would ride quickly through, speaking to nobody beyond a 'Buenos días', and again on the forest path he would pick up the track of the lieutenant's horse. He had no clear idea now about anything; he only wanted to put as great a distance as possible between him and the village where he had spent the night. In one hand he still carried the crumpled ball of paper. Somebody had tied a bunch of about fifty bananas to his saddle, beside the machete and the small bag, which contained his store of candles, and every now and then he ate one—ripe, brown and sodden, tasting of soap. It left a smear like a moustache over his mouth.

After six hours' travelling he came to La Candellaria, which lay, a long mean tin-roofed village, beside one of the tributaries of the Grijalva River. He came cautiously out into the dusty street—it was early afternoon. The vultures sat on the roofs with their small heads hidden from the sun, and a few men lay in hammocks in the narrow shade the houses cast. The mule plodded forward very slowly through the heavy day. The priest leant forward on his pommel.

The mule came to a stop of its own accord beside a hammock. A man lay in it, bunched diagonally, with one leg trailing to keep the hammock moving, up and down, up and down, making a tiny current of air. The priest said, 'Buenas tardes.' The man opened his eyes and watched him.

'How far is it to Carmen?'

'Three leagues.'

'Can I get a canoe across the river?'

'Yes.'

'Where?'

The man waved a languid hand—as much as to say anywhere but here. He had only two teeth left, canines which stuck yellowly out at either end of his mouth like the teeth you find enclosed in clay which have belonged to long-extinct animals.

'What were the police doing here?' the priest asked, and a cloud of flies came down, settling on the mule's neck; he poked at them with a stick and they rose heavily, leaving a small trickle of blood, and dropped again on the tough grey skin. The mule seemed to feel nothing, standing in the sun with his head drooping.

'Looking for someone,' the man said.

'I've heard,' the priest said, 'that there's a reward out—for a gringo.'

The man swung his hammock back and forth. He said, 'It's better to be alive and poor than rich and dead.'

'Can I overtake them if I go towards Carmen?'

'They aren't going to Carmen.'

'No?'

'They are making for the city.'

The priest rode on. Twenty yards farther he stopped again beside a gaseosa stall and asked the boy in charge, 'Can I get a boat across the river?'

'There isn't a boat.'

'No boat?'

'Somebody stole it.'

'Give me a sidral.' He drank down the yellow bubbly chemical liquid: it left him thirstier than before. He said, 'How do I get across?'

'Why do you want to get across?'

'I'm making for Carmen. How did the police get over?'

'They swam.'

'Mula, Mula,' the priest said, urging the mule on, past the inevitable bandstand and a statue in florid taste of a woman in a toga waving a wreath. Part of the pedestal had been broken off and lay in the middle of the road – the mule went round it. The priest looked back; far down the street the mestizo was sitting upright in the hammock watching him. The mule turned off down a steep path to the river, and again the priest looked back – the half-caste was still in the hammock, but he had both feet upon the ground. An habitual uneasiness made the priest beat at the mule – 'Mula, Mula,' but the mule took its time, sliding down the bank towards the river.

By the riverside it refused to enter the water. The priest split the end of his stick with his teeth and jabbed a sharp point into the mule's flank. It waded reluctantly in, and the water rose to the stirrups and then to the knees; the mule began to swim, splayed out flat with only the eyes and nostrils visible, like an alligator. Somebody shouted from the bank.

The priest looked round. At the river's edge the mestizo stood and called, not very loudly: his voice didn't carry. It was as if he had a secret purpose which nobody but the priest must hear. He waved his arm, summoning the priest back, but the mule lurched out of the water and up the bank beyond and the priest paid no attention – uneasiness was lodged in his brain. He urged the mule forward through the green half-light of a banana grove, not looking behind. All these years there had been two places to which he could always return and rest safely in hiding – one had been Concepción, his old parish, and that was closed to him now: the other was Carmen, where he had been born and where his parents were buried. He had imagined there might be a third, but he would never go back now. . . . He turned the mule's head towards Carmen, and the forest took them again. At this rate they would arrive in the dark, which was what he wanted. The mule unbeaten went with extreme languor, head drooping, smelling a little of blood. The priest, leaning forward on the high pommel, fell asleep. He dreamed that a small girl in stiff white muslin was reciting her Catechism – somewhere in the background, there was a bishop and a group of Children of Mary, elderly women with grey hard pious faces wearing pale blue ribbons. The bishop said, 'Excellent . . . Excellent,' and clapped his hands, plop, plop. A man in a morning coat said, 'There's a deficit of five hundred pesos on the new organ. We propose to hold a special musical performance, when it is hoped . . .' He remembered with appalling suddenness that he oughtn't to be there at all . . . he was in the wrong parish . . . he should be holding a retreat at Concepción. The man Montez appeared behind the child in white muslin, gesticulating, reminding him . . . Something had happened to Montez, he had a dry wound on his forehead. He felt with dreadful certainty a threat to the child. He said,

'My dear, my dear,' and woke to the slow rolling stride of the mule and the sound of footsteps.

He turned. It was the mestizo, padding behind him, dripping water: he must have swum the river. His two teeth stuck out over his lower lip, and he grinned ingratiatingly. 'What do you want?' the priest asked sharply.

'You didn't tell me you were going to Carmen.'

'Why should I?'

'You see, I want to go to Carmen, too. It's better to travel in company.' He was wearing a shirt, a pair of white trousers, and gym shoes through which one big toe showed–plump and yellow like something which lives underground. He scratched himself under the armpits and came chummily up to the priest's stirrup. He said 'You are not offended, señor?'

'Why do you call me señor?'

'Anyone can tell you're a man of education.'

'The forest is free to all,' the priest said.

'Do you know Carmen well?' the man asked.

'Not well. I have a few friends.'

'You're going on business, I suppose?'

The priest said nothing. He could feel the man's hand on his foot, a light and deprecating touch. The man said, 'There's a finca off the road two leagues from here. It would be as well to stay the night.'

'I am in a hurry,' the priest said.

'But what good would it be reaching Carmen at one, two in the morning? We could sleep at the finca and be there before the sun was high.'

'I do what suits me.'

'Of course, señor, of course.' The man was silent for a little while, and then said, 'It isn't wise travelling at night if the señor hasn't got a gun. It's different for a man like me . . .'

'I am a poor man,' the priest said. 'You can see for yourself. I am not worth robbing.'

'And then there's the gringo–they say he's a wild kind of a man, a real pistolero. He comes up to you and says in his own language–Stop: what is the way to–well, some place, and you do not understand what he is saying and perhaps you make a movement and he shoots you dead. But perhaps you know Americano, señor?'

'Of course I don't. How should I? I am a poor man. But I don't listen to every fairy-tale.'

'Do you come from far?'

The priest thought a moment: 'Concepción.' He could do no more harm there.

The man for the time being seemed satisfied. He walked along by the mule, a hand on the stirrup. Every now and then he spat. When the priest looked down he could see the big toe moving like a grub along the ground–he was probably harmless. It was the general condition of life that made for suspicion. The dusk fell and then almost at once the dark. The mule moved yet more slowly. Noise broke out all round them; it was like a theatre when the curtain falls and behind in the wings and passages hubbub begins. Things you couldn't put a name to–jaguars perhaps–cried in the undergrowth, monkeys moved in the upper boughs, and the mosquitoes hummed all round like sewing machines. 'It's thirsty walking,' the man said. 'Have you by chance, señor, got a little drink . . . ?'

'No.'

'If you want to reach Carmen before three, you will have to beat the mule. Shall I take the stick . . . ?'

'No, no, let the brute take its time. It doesn't matter to me . . .' he said drowsily.

'You talk like a priest.'

He came quickly awake, but under the tall dark trees he could see nothing. He said, 'What nonsense you talk.'

'I am a very good Christian,' the man said, stroking the priest's foot.

'I dare say. I wish I were.'

'Ah, you ought to be able to tell which people you can trust.' He spat in a comradely way.

'I have nothing to trust anyone with,' the priest said. 'Except these trousers—they are very torn. And this mule—it isn't a good mule; you can see for yourself.'

There was silence for a while, and then, as if he had been considering the last statement, the half-caste went on, 'It wouldn't be a bad mule if you treated it right. Nobody can teach me anything about mules. I can see for myself it's tired out.'

The priest looked down at the grey swinging stupid head. 'Do you think so?'

'How far did you travel yesterday?'

'Perhaps twelve leagues.'

'Even a mule needs rest.'

The priest took his bare feet from out of the deep leather stirrups and scrambled to the ground. The mule for less than a minute took a longer stride and then dropped to a yet slower pace. The twigs and roots of the forest path cut the priest's feet—after five minutes he was bleeding. He tried in vain not to limp. The half-caste exclaimed, 'How delicate your feet are. You should wear shoes.'

Stubbornly he reasserted, 'I am a poor man.'

'You will never get to Carmen at this rate. Be sensible, man. If you don't want to go as far off the road as the finca, I know a little hut less than half a league from here. We can sleep a few hours and still reach Carmen at daybreak.' There was a rustle in the grass beside the path—the priest thought of snakes and his unprotected feet. The mosquitoes jabbed at his wrists; they were like little surgical syringes filled with poison and aimed at the bloodstream. Sometimes a firefly held its lighted globe close to the half-caste's face, turning it on and off like a torch. He said accusingly, 'You don't trust me. Just because I am a man who likes to do a good turn to strangers, because I try to be a Christian, you don't trust me.' He seemed to be working himself into a little artificial rage. He said, 'If I wanted to rob you, couldn't I have done it already? You're an old man.'

'Not so very old,' the priest said mildly. His conscience began automatically to work: it was like a slot machine into which any coin could be fitted, even a cheater's blank disk. The words proud, lustful, envious, cowardly, ungrateful—they all worked the right springs—he was all these things. The half-caste said, 'Here I have spent many hours guiding you to Carmen—I don't want any reward because I am a good Christian. I have probably lost money by it at home—never mind that . . .'

'I thought you said you had business in Carmen?' the priest said gently.

'When did I say that?' It was true—he couldn't remember . . . perhaps he was unjust too . . . 'Why should I say a thing which isn't true? No, I give up a whole day to helping you, and you pay no attention when your guide is tired . . .'

'I didn't need a guide,' he protested mildly.

'You say that when the road is plain, but if it wasn't for me, you'd have taken the wrong path a long time ago. You said yourself you didn't know Carmen well. That was why I came.'

'But of course,' the priest said, 'if you are tired, we will rest.' He felt guilty at his own lack of trust, but all the same, it remained like a growth only a knife could rid him of.

After half an hour they came to the hut. Made of mud and twigs, it had been set up in a minute clearing by a small farmer whom the forest must have driven out, edging in on him, an unstayable natural force which he couldn't defeat with his machete and his small fires. There were still signs in the blackened ground of an attempt to clear the brushwood for some meagre and inadequate crop. The man said, 'I will see to the mule. You go in and lie down and rest.'

'But it is you who are tired.'

'Me tired?' the half-caste said. 'What makes you say that? I am never tired.'

With a heavy heart the priest took off his saddlebag, pushed at the door and went in to complete darkness. He struck a light—there was no furniture; only a raised dais of hard earth and a straw mat too torn to have been worth removing. He lit a candle and stuck it in its own wax on the dais: then sat down and waited: the man was a long time. In one fist he still carried the ball of paper salvaged from his case—a man must retain some sentimental relics if he is to live at all. The argument of danger only applies to those who live in relative safety. He wondered whether the mestizo had stolen his mule, and reproached himself for the necessary suspicion. The the door opened and the man came in—the two yellow canine teeth, the fingernails scratching in the armpit. He sat down on the earth, with his back against the door, and said, 'Go to sleep. You are tired. I'll wake you when we need to start.'

'I'm not very sleepy.'

'Blow out the candle. You'll sleep better.'

'I don't like darkness,' the priest said. He was afraid.

'Won't you say a prayer, father, before we sleep?'

'Why do you call me that?' he asked sharply, peering across the shadowy floor to where the half-caste sat against the door.

'Oh, I guessed, of course. But you needn't be afraid of me. I'm a good Christian.'

'You're wrong.'

'I could easily find out, couldn't I?' the half-caste said, 'I'd just have to say—father, hear my confession. You couldn't refuse a man in mortal sin.'

The priest said nothing, waiting for the demand to come: the hand which held the papers twitched. 'Oh, you needn't fear me,' the mestizo went carefully on. 'I wouldn't betray you. I'm a Christian. I just thought a prayer . . . would be good . . .'

'You don't need to be a priest to know a prayer.' He began, 'Pater noster qui es in coelis . . .' while the mosquitoes came droning towards the candle-flame. He was determined not to sleep–the man had some plan. His conscience ceased to accuse him of uncharity. He knew. He was in the presence of Judas.

He leant his head back against the wall and half closed his eyes–he remembered Holy Week in the old days when a stuffed Judas was hanged from the belfry and boys made a clatter with tins and rattles as he swung out over the door. Old staid members of the congregation had sometimes raised objections: it was blasphemous, they said, to make this guy out of Our Lord's betrayer; but he had said nothing and let the practice continue–it seemed to him a good thing that the world's traitor should be made a figure of fun. It was too easy otherwise to idealise him as a man who fought with God–a Prometheus, a noble victim in a hopeless war.

'Are you awake?' a voice whispered from the door. The priest suddenly giggled, as if this man, too, were absurd with stuffed straw legs and a painted face and an old straw hat who would presently be burnt in the plaza while people made political speeches and the fireworks went off.

'Can't you sleep?'

'I was dreaming,' the priest whispered. He opened his eyes and saw the man by the door was shivering–the two sharp teeth jumped up and down on the lower lip. 'Are you ill?'

'A little fever,' the man said. 'Have you any medicine?'

'No.'

The door creaked as the man's back shook. He said, 'It was getting wet in the river . . .' He slid farther down upon the floor and closed his eyes–mosquitoes with singed wings crawled over the earth bed. The priest thought: I mustn't sleep, it's dangerous, I must watch him. He opened his fist and smoothed out the paper. There were faint pencil lines visible–single words, the beginnings and ends of sentences, figures. Now that his case was gone, it was the only evidence left that life had ever been different: he carried it with him as a charm, because if life had been like that once, it might be so again. The candle-flame in the hot marshy lowland air burned to a smoky point vibrating. . . . The priest held the paper close to it and read the words Altar Society, Guild of the Blessed Sacrament, Children of Mary, and then looked up again and across the dark hut saw the yellow malarial eyes of the mestizo watching him. Christ would not have found Judas sleeping in the garden: Judas could watch more than one hour.

'What's that paper . . . father?' he said enticingly, shivering against the door.

'Don't call me father. It is a list of seeds I have to buy in Carmen.'

'Can you write?'

'I can read.'

He looked at the paper again and a little mild impious joke stared up at him in faded pencil–something about 'of one substance'. He had been referring to his corpulency and the good dinner he had just eaten: the parishioners had not much relished his humour.

*   *   *

It had been a dinner given at Concepción in honour of the tenth anniversary of his ordination. He sat in the middle of the table with—who was it on his right hand? There were twelve dishes—he had said something about the Apostles, too, which was not thought to be in the best of taste. He was quite young and he had been moved by a gentle devilry, surrounded by all the pious and middle-aged and respectable people of Concepción, wearing their guild ribbons and badges. He had drunk just a little too much; in those days he wasn't used to liquor. It came back to him now suddenly who was on his right hand—it was Montez, the father of the man they had shot.

Montez had talked at some length. He had reported the progress of the Altar Society in the last year—they had a balance in hand of twenty-two pesos. He had noted it down for comment—there is was, A.S. 22. Montez had been very anxious to start a branch of the Society of St Vincent de Paul, and some woman had complained that bad books were being sold in Concepción, fetched in from the capital by mule: her child had got hold of one called *A Husband for a Night*. In his speech he said he would write to the Governor on the subject.

The moment he had said that the local photographer had set off his flare, and so he could remember himself at that instant, just as if he had been a stranger looking in from the outside—attracted by the noise—on some happy and festal and strange occasion: noticing with envy, and perhaps a little amusement, the fat youngish priest who stood with one plump hand splayed authoritatively out while the tongue played pleasantly with the word 'Governor'. Mouths were open all round fishily, and the faces glowed magnesium-white, with the lines and individuality wiped out.

That moment of authority had jerked him back to seriousness—he had ceased to unbend and everybody was happier. He said, 'The balance of twenty-two pesos in the accounts of the Altar Society—though quite revolutionary for Concepción—is not the only cause for congratulation in the last year. The Children of Mary have increased their membership by nine—and the Guild of the Blessed Sacrament last autumn made our annual retreat more than usually successful. But we mustn't rest on our laurels, and I confess I have got plans you may find a little startling. You already think me a man, I know, of inordinate ambitions—well, I want Concepción to have a better school—and that means a better presbytery too, of course. We are a big parish and the priest has a position to keep up. I'm not thinking of myself but of the Church. And we shall not stop there—though it will take a good many years, I'm afraid, even in a place the size of Concepción, to raise the money for that.' As he talked a whole serene life lay ahead—he *had* ambition: he saw no reason why one day he might not find himself in the state capital, attached to the cathedral, leaving another man to pay off the debts in Concepción. An energetic priest was always known by his debts. He went on, waving a plump and eloquent hand, 'Of course, many dangers here in Mexico threaten our dear Church. In this state we are unusually lucky—men have lost their lives in the north and we must be prepared'—he refreshed his dry mouth with a draught of wine—'for the worst. Watch and pray,' he went vaguely on, 'watch and pray. The devil like a raging lion—' The Children of Mary stared up at him with their mouths a little open, the pale blue ribbons slanting across their dark best blouses.

He talked for a long while, enjoying the sound of his own voice: he had discouraged Montez on the subject of the St Vincent de Paul Society, because you had to be careful not to encourage a layman too far, and he had told a charming story about a child's deathbed—she was dying of consumption very firm in her faith at the age of eleven. She asked who it was standing at the end of her bed, and they had said, 'That's Father So-and-so,' and she had said, 'No, no. I know Father So-and-so. I mean the one with the golden crown.' One of the Guild of the Blessed Sacrament had wept. Everybody was very happy. It was a true story too, though he couldn't quite remember where he had heard it. Perhaps he had read it in a book once. Somebody refilled his glass. He took a long breath and said, 'My children . . .'

★   ★   ★

. . . and as the mestizo stirred and grunted by the door he opened his eyes and the old life peeled away like a label: he was lying in torn peon trousers in a dark unventilated hut with a price upon his head. The whole world had changed—no church anywhere: no brother priest, except Padre José, the outcast, in the capital. He lay listening to the heavy breathing of the half-caste and wondered why he had not gone the same road as Padre José and conformed to the laws. I was too ambitious, he thought, that was it. Perhaps Padre José was the better man—he was so humble that he was ready to accept any amount of mockery; at the best of times he had never considered himself worthy of the priesthood. There had been a conference once of the parochial clergy in the capital, in the happy days of the old governor, and he could remember Padre José slinking in at the tail of every meeting, curled up half out of sight in a back row, never opening his mouth. It was not, like some more intellectual priests, that he was over-scrupulous: he had been simply filled with an overwhelming sense of God. At the Elevation of the Host you could see his hands trembling—he was not like St Thomas who needed to put his hands into the wounds in order to believe: the wounds bled anew for him over every altar. Once Padre José had said to him in a burst of confidence, 'Every time . . . I have such fear.' His father had been a peon.

But it was different in his case—he had ambition. He was no more an intellectual than Padre José, but his father was a storekeeper, and he knew the value of a balance of twenty-two pesos and how to manage mortgages. He wasn't content to remain all his life the priest of a not very large parish. His ambitions came back to him now as something faintly comic, and he gave a little gulp of astonished laughter in the candlelight. The half-caste opened his eyes and said, 'Are you still not asleep?'

'Sleep yourself,' the priest said, wiping a little sweat off his face with his sleeve.

'I am so cold.'

'Just a fever. Would you like this shirt? It isn't much, but it might help.'

'No, no. I don't want anything of yours. You don't trust me.'

No, if he had been humble like Padre José, he might be living in the capital now with Maria on a pension. This was pride, devilish pride, lying here offering his shirt to the man who wanted to betray him. Even his attempts at escape had been half-hearted because of his pride–the sin by which the angels fell. When he was the only priest left in the state his pride had been all the greater; he thought himself the devil of a fellow carrying God around at the risk of his life; one day there would be a reward. . . . He prayed in the half-light: 'O God, forgive me–I am a proud, lustful, greedy man. I have loved authority too much. These people are martyrs–protecting me with their own lives. They deserve a martyr to care for them–not a man like me, who loves all the wrong things. Perhaps I had better escape–if I tell people how it is over here, perhaps they will send a good man with a fire of love . . .' As usual his self-confession dwindled away into the practical problem–what am I to do?

Over by the door the mestizo was uneasily asleep.

How little his pride had to feed on–he had celebrated only four Masses this year, and he had heard perhaps a hundred confessions. It seemed to him that the dunce of any seminary could have done as well . . . or better. He raised himself very carefully and began to move on his naked toes across the floor. He must get to Carmen and away again quickly before this man . . . the mouth was open, showing the pale hard toothless gums. In his sleep he was grunting and struggling; then he collapsed upon the floor and lay still.

There was a sense of abandonment, as if he had given up every struggle from now on and lay there a victim of some power. . . . The priest had only to step over his legs and push the door–it opened outwards.

He put one leg over the body and a hand gripped his ankle. The mestizo stared up at him. 'Where are you going?'

'I want to relieve myself,' the priest said.

The hand still held his ankle. 'Why can't you do it here?' the man whined at him. 'What's preventing you, father? You are a father, aren't you?'

'I have a child,' the priest said, 'if that's what you mean.'

'You know what I mean. You understand about God, don't you?' The hot hand clung. 'Perhaps you've got him there–in a pocket. You carry him around, don't you, in case there's anybody sick. . . . Well, I'm sick. Why don't you give him to me? or do you think he wouldn't have anything to do with me . . . if he knew?'

'You're feverish.'

But the man wouldn't stop. The priest was reminded of an oil-gusher which some prospectors had once struck near Concepción–it wasn't a good enough field apparently to justify further operations, but there it had stood for forty-eight hours against the sky, a black fountain spouting out of the marshy useless soil and flowing away to waste–fifty thousand gallons an hour. It was like the religious sense in man, cracking suddenly upwards, a black pillar of fumes and impurity, running to waste. 'Shall I tell you what I've done? It's your business to listen. I've taken money from women to do you know what, and I've given money to boys . . .'

'I don't want to hear.'

'It's your business.'

'You're mistaken.'

'Oh no, I'm not. You can't deceive me. Listen. I've given money to boys—you know what I mean. And I've eaten meat on Fridays.' The awful jumble of the gross, the trivial and the grotesque shot up between the two yellow fangs, and the hand on the priest's ankle shook and shook with the fever. 'I've told lies, I haven't fasted in Lent for I don't know how many years. Once I had two women—I'll tell you what I did . . .' He had an immense self-importance; he was unable to picture a world of which he was only a typical part—a world of treachery, violence and lust in which his shame was altogether insignificant. How often the priest had heard the same confession—Man was so limited he hadn't even the ingenuity to invent a new vice: the animals knew as much. It was for this world that Christ had died; the more evil you saw and heard about you, the greater glory lay around the death. It was too easy to die for what was good or beautiful, for home or children or a civilisation—it needed a God to die for the half-hearted and the corrupt. He said, 'Why do you tell me all this?'

The man lay exhausted, saying nothing; he was beginning to sweat, his hand loosed its hold on the priest's ankle. He pushed the door open and went outside—the darkness was complete. How to find the mule? He stood listening—something howled not very far away. He was frightened. Back in the hut the candle burned—there was an odd bubbling sound: the man was weeping. Again he was reminded of oil land, the little black pools and the bubbles blowing slowly up and breaking and beginning again.

The priest struck a match and walked straight forward—one, two, three paces into a tree. A match in that immense darkness was of no more value than a firefly. He whispered, 'Mula, mula,' afraid to call out in case the half-caste heard him; besides, it was unlikely that the stupid beast would make any reply. He hated it—the lurching mandarin head, the munching greedy mouth, the smell of blood and ordure. He struck another match and set off again, and again after a few paces he met a tree. Inside the hut the gaseous sound of grief went on. He had got to get to Carmen and away before that man found a means of communicating with the police. He began again, quartering the clearing—one, two, three, four—and then a tree. Something moved under his foot, and he thought of scorpions. One, two, three, and suddenly the grotesque cry of the mule came out of the dark; it was hungry, or perhaps it smelt some animal.

It was tethered a few yards behind the hut—the candle-flame swerved out of sight. His matches were running low, but after two more attempts he found the mule. The half-caste had stripped it and hidden the saddle. He couldn't waste time looking any more. He mounted, and only then realised how impossible it was to make it move without even a piece of rope round the neck; he tried twisting its ears, but they had no more sensitivity than door-handles: it stood planted there like an equestrian statue. He struck a match and held the flame against its side—it struck up suddenly with its back hooves and he dropped the match; then it was still again, with drooping sullen head and great antediluvian haunches. A voice said accusingly, 'You are leaving me here to die.'

'Nonsense,' the priest said. 'I am in a hurry. You will be all right in the morning, but I can't wait.'

There was a scuffle in the darkness and then a hand gripped his naked foot. 'Don't leave me alone,' the voice said. 'I appeal to you—as a Christian.'

'You won't come to any harm here.'

'How do you know with the gringo somewhere about?'

'I don't know anything about the gringo. I've met nobody who has seen him. Besides, he's only a man—like one of us.'

'I won't be left alone. I have an instinct . . .'

'Very well,' the priest said wearily, 'find the saddle.'

When they had saddled the mule they set off again, the mestizo holding the stirrup. They were silent—sometimes the half-caste stumbled, and the grey false dawn began; a small coal of cruel satisfaction glowed at the back of the priest's mind—this was Judas sick and unsteady and scared in the dark. He had only to beat the mule on to leave him stranded in the forest; once he dug in the point of his stick and forced it forward at a weary trot, and he could feel the pull, pull of the half-caste's arm on the stirrup holding him back. There was a groan—it sounded like 'Mother of God', and he let the mule slacken its pace. He prayed silently, 'God forgive me.' Christ had died for this man too: how could he pretend with his pride and lust and cowardice to be any more worthy of that death than the half-caste? This man intended to betray him for money which he needed, and he had betrayed God for what? Not even for real lust. He said, 'Are you sick?' and there was no reply. He dismounted and said, 'Get up. I'll walk for a while.'

'I'm all right,' the man said in a tone of hatred.

'Better get up.'

'You think you're very fine,' the man said. 'Helping your enemies. That's Christian, isn't it?'

'Are you my enemy?'

'That's what you think. You think I want seven hundred pesos—that's the reward. You think a poor man like me can't afford not to tell the police . . .'

'You're feverish.'

The man said in a sick voice of cunning, 'You're right, of course.'

'Better mount.' The man nearly fell: he had to shoulder him up. He lent hopelessly down from the mule with his mouth almost on a level with the priest's, breathing bad air into the other's face. He said, 'A poor man has no choice, father. Now if I was a rich man—only a little rich—I should be good.'

The priest suddenly—for no reason—thought of the Children of Mary eating pastries. He giggled and said, 'I doubt it.' If that were goodness . . .

'What was that you said, father? You don't trust me,' he went ambling on, 'because I'm poor, and because you don't trust me—' he collapsed over the pommel of the saddle, breathing heavily and shivering. The priest held him on with one hand and they proceeded slowly towards Carmen. It was no good; he couldn't stay there now. It would be unwise even to enter the village, for if it became known, somebody would lose his life—they would take a hostage. Somewhere a long way off a cock crew. The mist came up knee-high out of a spongy ground, and he thought of the flashlight going off in the bare church hall among the trestle tables. What hour did the cocks crow? One of the oddest things about the world these days was that there were no clocks—you could go a year without hearing one strike. They went with the churches, and you were left with the grey slow dawns and the precipitate nights as the only measurements of time.

Slowly, slumped over the pommel, the half-caste became visible, the yellow canines jutting out of the open mouth; really, the priest thought, he deserved his reward—seven hundred pesos wasn't so much, but he could probably live on it—in that dusty hopeless village—for a whole year. He giggled again; he could never take the complications of destiny quite seriously, and it was just possible, he thought, that a year without anxiety might save this man's soul. You only had to turn up the underside of any situation and out came scuttling these small absurd contradictory situations. He had given way to despair—and out of that had emerged a human soul and love—not the best love, but love all the same. The mestizo said suddenly, 'It's fate. I was told once by a fortune-teller . . . a reward . . .'

He held the half-caste firmly in the saddle and walked on. His feet were bleeding, but they would soon harden. An odd stillness dropped over the forest, and welled up in the mist from the ground. The night had been noisy, but now all was quiet. It was like an armistice with the guns silent on either side: you could imagine the whole world listening to what they had never heard before—peace.

A voice said, 'You *are* the priest, aren't you?'

'Yes.' It was as if they had climbed out of their opposing trenches and met in No Man's Land among the wires to fraternise. He remembered stories of the European war—how during the last years men had sometimes met on an impulse between the lines.

'Yes,' he said again, and the mule plodded on. Sometimes, instructing children in the old days, he had been asked by some black lozenge-eyed Indian child, 'What is God like?' and he would answer facilely with references to the father and the mother, or perhaps more ambitiously he would include brother and sister and try to give some idea of all loves and relationships combined in an immense and yet personal passion. . . . But at the centre of his own faith there always stood the convincing mystery—that we were made in God's image. God was the parent, but He was also the policeman, the criminal, the priest, the maniac and the judge. Something resembling God dangled from the gibbet or went into odd attitudes before the bullets in a prison yard or contorted itself like a camel in the attitude of sex. He would sit in the confessional and hear the complicated dirty ingenuities which God's image had thought out, and God's image shook now, up and down on the mule's back, with the yellow teeth sticking out over the lower lip, and God's image did its despairing act of rebellion with Maria in the hut among the rats. He said, 'Do you feel better now? Not so cold, eh? Or so hot?' and pressed his hand with a kind of driven tenderness upon the shoulders of God's image.

The man didn't answer, as the mule's backbone slid him first to one side, then the other.

'It isn't more than two leagues now,' the priest said encouragingly—he had to make up his mind. He carried around with him a clearer picture of Carmen than any other village or town in the state: the long slope of grass which led up from the river to the cemetery on a tiny hill where his parents were buried. The wall of the burial-ground had fallen in: one or two crosses had been smashed by enthusiasts: an angel had lost one of its stone wings, and what gravestones were left undamaged leant at an acute angle in the long

marshy grass. One image of the Mother of God had lost ears and arms and
stood like a pagan Venus over the grave of some rich forgotten timber
merchant. It was odd–this fury to deface, because, of course, you could
never deface enough. If God had been like a toad, you could have rid the
globe of toads, but when God was like yourself, it was no good being content
with stone figures–you had to kill yourself among the graves.

He said, 'Are you strong enough now to hold on?' He took away his hand.
The path divided–one way led to Carmen, the other west. He pushed the
mule on, down the Carmen path, flogging at its haunches. He said, 'You'll be
there in two hours,' and stood watching the mule go on towards his home
with the informer humped over the pommel.

The half-caste tried to sit upright. 'Where are you going?'

'You'll be my witness,' the priest said. 'I haven't been in Carmen. But if
you mention me, they'll give you food.'

'Why . . . why . . .' The half-caste tried to wrench round the mule's head,
but he hadn't enough strength: it just went on. The priest called out,
'Remember I haven't been in Carmen.' But where else now could he go? The
conviction came to him that there was only one place in the whole state
where there was no danger of an innocent man being taken as a hostage–but
he couldn't go there in these clothes. . . . The half-caste held hard on to the
pommel and swivelled his yellow eyes beseechingly, 'You wouldn't leave me
here–alone.' But it was more than the half-caste he was leaving behind on
the forest track: the mule stood sideways like a barrier, nodding a stupid
head, between him and the place where he had been born. He felt like a man
without a passport who is turned away from every harbour.

The half-caste was calling after him, 'Call yourself a Christian.' He had
somehow managed to get himself upright. He began to shout abuse–a
meaningless series of indecent words which petered out in the forest like the
weak blows of a hammer. He whispered, 'If I see you again, you can't blame
me. . .' Of course, he had every reason to be angry: he had lost seven hundred
pesos. He shrieked hopelessly, 'I don't forget a face.'

2

The young men and women walked round and round the plaza in the hot
electric night, the men one way, the girls another, never speaking to each
other. In the northern sky the lightning flapped. It was like a religious
ceremony which had lost all meaning, but at which they still wore their best
clothes. Sometimes a group of older women would join in the procession
with a little more excitement and laughter, as if they retained some memory
of how things used to go before all the books were lost. A man with a gun on
his hip watched from the Treasury steps, and a small withered soldier sat by
the prison door with a gun between his knees and the shadows of the palms
pointed at him like a zareba of sabres. Lights were burning in a dentist's
window, shining on the swivel chair and the red plush cushions and the glass

for rinsing on its little stand and the child's chest-of-drawers full of fittings. Behind the wire-netted windows of the private houses grandmothers swung back and forth in rocking-chairs, among the family photographs—nothing to do, nothing to say, with too many clothes on, sweating a little. This was the capital city of a state.

The man in the shabby drill suit watched it all from a bench. A squad of armed police went by to their quarters, walking out of step, carrying their rifles anyhow. The plaza was lit at each corner by clusters of three globes joined by ugly trailing overhead wires, and a beggar worked his way from seat to seat without success.

He sat down next the man in drill and started a long explanation. There was something confidential, and at the same time threatening, in his manner. On every side the streets ran down towards the river and the port and the marshy plain. He said that he had a wife and so many children and that during the last few weeks they had eaten so little—he broke off and fingered the cloth of the other's drill suit. 'And how much,' he said, 'did this cost?'

'You'd be surprised how little.'

Suddenly as a clock struck nine-thirty all the lights went out. The beggar said, 'It's enough to make a man desperate.' He looked this way and that as the parade drifted away down hill. The man in drill got up, and the other got up too, tagging after him towards the edge of the plaza: his flat bare feet went slap, slap on the pavement. He said, 'A few pesos wouldn't make any difference to you . . .'

'Ah, if you knew what a difference they would make.'

The beggar was put out. He said, 'A man like me sometimes feels that he would do anything for a few pesos.' Now that the lights were out all over town, they stood intimately in the shadow. He said, 'Can you blame me?'

'No, no. It would be the last thing I would do.'

Everything he said seemed to feed the beggar's irritation. 'Sometimes,' the beggar said, 'I feel as if I could kill . . .'

'That, of course, would be very wrong.'

'Would it be wrong if I got a man by the throat . . .?'

'Well, a starving man has got the right to save himself, certainly.'

The beggar watched with rage, while the other talked on as if he were considering a point of academic interest. 'In my case, of course, it would hardly be worth the risk. I possess exactly fifteen pesos seventy-five centavos in the world. I haven't eaten myself for forty-eight hours.'

'Mother of God,' the beggar said, 'you're as hard as a stone. Haven't you a heart?'

The man in the drill suit suddenly giggled. The other said, 'You're lying. Why haven't you eaten—if you've got fifteen pesos?'

'You see, I want to spend them on drink.'

'What sort of drink?'

'The kind of drink a stranger doesn't know how to get in a place like this.'

'You mean spirits?'

'Yes—and wine.'

The beggar came very close. His leg touched the leg of the other man, he put a hand upon the other's sleeve. They might have been great friends or even brothers standing intimately together in the dark. Even the lights in the houses were going out now, and the taxis, which during the day waited halfway down the hill for fares that never seemed to come, were already dispersing—a tail-lamp winked and went out past the police barracks. The beggar said, 'Man, this is your lucky day. How much would you pay me . . . ?'

'For some drink?'

'For an introduction to someone who could let you have a little brandy—real fine Vera Cruz brandy.'

'With a throat like mine,' the man in drill explained, 'it's wine I really want.'

'Pulque or mescal—he's got everything.'

'Wine?'

'Quince wine.'

'I'd give everything I've got,' the other swore solemnly and exactly, '—except the centavos, that's to say—for some real genuine grape wine.' Somewhere down the hill by the river a drum was beating, one-two, one-two, and the sound of marching feet kept a rough time: the soldiers—or the police—were going home to bed.

'How much?' the beggar repeated impatiently.

'Well, I would give you the fifteen pesos and you would get the wine for me for what you cared to spend.'

'You come with me.'

They began to go down the hill. At the corner where one street ran up past the chemist's shop towards the barracks and another ran down to the hotel, the quay, the warehouse of the United Banana Company, the man in drill stopped. The police were marching up, rifles slung at ease. 'Wait a moment.' Among them walked a half-caste with two fang-like teeth jutting out over his lip. The man in drill standing in the shadow watched him go by: once the mestizo turned his head and their eyes met. Then the police went by, up into the plaza. 'Let's go. Quickly.'

The beggar said, 'They won't interfere with us. They're after bigger game.'

'What was that man doing with them, do you think?'

'Who knows? A hostage perhaps.'

'If he had been a hostage, they would have tied his hands, wouldn't they?'

'How do I know?' he had the grudging independence you find in countries where it is the right of a poor man to beg. He said, 'Do you want the spirits or don't you?'

'I want wine.'

'I can't say he'll have this or that. You must take what comes.'

He led the way down towards the river. He said, 'I don't even know if he's in town.' The beetles were flocking out and covering the pavements; they popped under the feet like puff-balls, and a sour green smell came up from the river. The white bust of a general glimmered in a tiny public garden, all hot paving and dust, and an electric dynamo throbbed on the ground floor of the only hotel. Wide wooden stairs crawling with beetles ran up to the first floor. 'I've done my best,' the beggar said, 'a man can't do more.'

On the first floor a man dressed in formal dark trousers and a white skin-tight vest came out of a bedroom with a towel over his shoulder. He had a little grey aristocratic beard and he wore braces as well as a belt. Somewhere in the distance a pipe gurgled, and the beetles detonated against a bare globe. The beggar was talking earnestly, and once as he talked the light went off altogether and then flickered unsatisfactorily on again. The head of the stairs was littered with wicker rocking-chairs, and on a big slate were chalked the names of the guests–three only for twenty rooms.

The beggar turned back to his companion. 'The gentleman,' he said, 'is not in. The manager says so. Shall we wait for him?'

'Time to me is of no account.'

They went into a big bare bedroom with a tiled floor. The little black iron bedstead was like something somebody has left behind by accident when moving out. They sat down on it side by side and waited, and the beetles came popping in through the gaps in the mosquito wire. 'He is a very important man,' the beggar said. 'He is the cousin of the Governor–he can get anything for you, anything at all. But, of course, you must be introduced by someone he trusts.'

'And he trusts you?'

'I worked for him once.' He added frankly, 'He has to trust me.'

'Does the Governor know?'

'Of course not. The Governor is a hard man.'

Every now and then the water-pipes swallowed noisily.

'And why should he trust me?'

'Oh, anyone can tell a drinker. You'll want to come back for more. It's good stuff he sells. Better give me the fifteen pesos.' He counted them carefully twice. He said, 'I'll get you a bottle of the best Vera Cruz brandy. You see if I don't.' The light went off, and they sat in the dark; the bed creaked as one of them shifted.

'I don't want brandy,' a voice said, 'At least–not very much.'

'What do you want then?'

'I told you–wine.'

'Wine's expensive.'

'Never mind that. Wine or nothing.'

'Quince wine?'

'No, no. French wine.'

'Sometimes he has Californian wine.'

'That would do.'

'Of course himself–he gets it for nothing. From the Customs.'

The dynamo began throbbing again below and the light came dimly on. The door opened and the manager beckoned the beggar; a long conversation began. The man in the drill suit leant back on the bed. His chin was cut in several places where he had been shaving too closely; his face was hollow and ill–it gave the impression that he had once been plump and round-faced but had caved in. He had the appearance of a business man who had fallen on hard times.

The beggar came back. He said, 'The gentleman's busy, but he'll be back soon. The manager sent a boy to look for him.'

'Where is he?'

'He can't be interrupted. He's playing billiards with the Chief of Police.' He came back to the bed, squashing two beetles under his naked feet. He said, 'This is a fine hotel. Where do you stay? You're a stranger, aren't you?'

'Oh, I'm just passing through.'

'This gentleman is very influential. It would be a good thing to offer him a drink. After all, you won't want to take it all away with you. You may as well drink here as anywhere else.'

'I should like to keep a little–to take home.'

'It's all one. I say that home is where there is a chair and a glass.'

'All the same—' Then the light went out again, and on the horizon the lightning bellied out. The sound of thunder came through the mosquito-net from very far away like the noise you hear from the other end of a town when the Sunday bull-fight is on.

The beggar said confidentially, 'What's your trade?'

'Oh, I pick up what I can–where I can.'

They sat in silence together listening to the sound of feet on the wooden stairs. The door opened, but they could see nothing. A voice swore resignedly and asked, 'Who's there?' Then a match was struck and showed a large blue jaw and went out. The dynamo churned away and the light went on again. The stranger said wearily, 'Oh, it's you.'

'It's me.'

He was a small man with a too large pasty face and he was dressed in a tight grey suit. A revolver bulged under his waistcoat. He said, 'I've got nothing for you. Nothing.'

The beggar padded across the room and began to talk earnestly in a very low voice: once he gently squeezed with his bare toes the other's polished shoe. The man sighed and blew out his cheeks and watched the bed closely as if he feared they had designs on it. He said sharply to the one in the drill suit, 'So you want some Vera Cruz brandy, do you? It's against the law.'

'Not brandy. I don't want brandy.'

'Isn't beer good enough for you?'

He came fussily and authoritatively into the middle of the room, his shoes squeaking on the tiles–the Governor's cousin. 'I could have you arrested,' he threatened.

The man in the drill suit cringed formally. He said, 'Of course, your Excellency . . .'

'Do you think I've got nothing better to do than slake the thirst of every beggar who chooses . . .?

'I would never have troubled you if this man had not . . .'

The Governor's cousin spat on the tiles.

'But if your Excellency would rather I went away . . .

He said sharply, 'I'm not a hard man. I always try to oblige my fellows . . . when it's in my power and does no harm. I have a position, you understand. These drinks come to me quite legally.'

'Of course.'

'And I have to charge what they cost me.'

'Of course.'

'Otherwise I'd be a ruined man.' He walked delicately to the bed as if his shoes were cramping him and began to unmake it. 'Are you a talker?' he asked over his shoulder.

'I know how to keep a secret.'

'I don't mind you telling the right people.' There was a large rent in the mattress; he pulled out a handful of straw and put in his fingers again. The man in drill gazed out with false indifference at the public garden, the dark mud-banks and the masts of sailing-ships; the lightning flapped behind them, and the thunder came nearer.

'There,' said the Governor's cousin, 'I can spare you that. It's good stuff.'

'It wasn't really brandy I wanted.'

'You must take what comes.'

'Then I think I'd rather have my fifteen pesos back.'

The Governor's cousin exclaimed sharply, '*Fifteen* pesos.' The beggar began rapidly to explain that the gentleman wanted to buy a little wine as well as brandy: they began to argue fiercely by the bed in low voices about prices. The Governor's cousin said, 'Wine's very difficult to get. I can let you have two bottles of brandy.'

'One of brandy and one of . . .'

'It's the best Vera Cruz brandy.'

'But I am a wine drinker . . . you don't know how I long for wine . . .'

'Wine costs me a great deal of money. How much more can you pay?'

'I have only seventy-five centavos left in the world.'

'I could let you have a bottle of tequila.'

'No, no.'

'Another fifty centavos then. . . . It will be a large bottle.' He began to scrabble in the mattress again, pulling out straw. The beggar winked at the man in drill and made the motions of drawing a cork and filling a glass.

'There,' the Governor's cousin said, 'take it or leave it.'

'Oh, I will take it.'

The Governor's cousin suddenly lost his surliness. He rubbed his hands and said, 'A stuffy night. The rains are going to be early this year, I think.'

'Perhaps your Excellency would honour me by taking a glass of brandy to toast our business.'

'Well, well . . . perhaps . . .' The beggar opened the door and called briskly for glasses.

'It's a long time,' the Governor's cousin said, 'since I had a glass of wine. Perhaps it would be more suitable for a toast.'

'Of course,' the man in drill said, 'as your Excellency chooses.' He watched the cork drawn with a look of painful anxiety. He said, 'If you will excuse me, I think I will have brandy,' and smiled raggedly, with an effort, watching the wine level fall.

They toasted each other, all three sitting on the bed—the beggar drank brandy. The Governor's cousin said, 'I'm proud of this wine. It's good wine. The best Californian.' The beggar winked and motioned and the man in drill said, 'One more glass, your Excellency—or can I recommend this brandy?'

'It's good brandy—but I think another glass of wine.' They refilled their glasses. The man in drill said, 'I'm going to take some of that wine back—to my mother. She loves a glass.'

'She couldn't do better,' The Governor's cousin said, emptying his own. He said, 'So you have a mother?'

'Haven't we all?'

'Ah, you're lucky. Mine's dead.' His hand strayed towards the bottle, grasped it. 'Sometimes I miss her. I called her "my little friend".' He tilted the bottle. 'With your permission?'

'Of course, your Excellency,' the other said hopelessly taking a long draught of brandy. The beggar said, 'I too have a mother.'

'Who cares?' the Governor's cousin said sharply. He leant back and the bed creaked. He said, 'I have often thought a mother is a better friend than a father. Her influence is towards peace, goodness, charity. . . . Always on the anniversary of her death I go to her grave with flowers.'

The man in drill caught a hiccup politely. He said, 'Ah, if I could too . . .'

'But you said your mother was alive?'

'I thought you were speaking of your grandmother.'

'How could I? I can't remember my grandmother.'

'Nor can I.'

'I can,' the beggar said.

The Governor's cousin said, 'You talk too much.'

'Perhaps I could send him to have this wine wrapped up. . . . For your Excellency's sake I mustn't be seen. . . .'

'Wait, wait. There's no hurry. You are very welcome here. Anything in this room is at your disposal. Have a glass of wine.'

'I think brandy . . .'

'Then with your permission . . .' He tilted the bottle: a little of it splashed over on to the sheets. 'What were we talking about?'

'Our grandmothers.'

'I don't think it can have been that. I can't even remember mine. The earliest thing I can remember . . .'

The door opened. The manager said, 'The Chief of Police is coming up the stairs.'

'Excellent. Show him in.'

'Are you sure?'

'Of course. He's a good fellow.' He said to the others, 'But at billiards you can't trust him.'

A large stout man in a singlet, white trousers and a revolver-holster appeared in the doorway. The Governor's cousin said, 'Come in. Come in. How is your toothache? We were talking about our grandmothers.' He said sharply to the beggar, 'Make room for the jefe.'

The jefe stood in the doorway, watching them with dim embarrassment. He said, 'Well, well . . .'

'We're having a little private party. Will you join us? It would be an honour.'

The jefe's face suddenly lit up at the sight of the wine. 'Of course—a little beer never comes amiss.'

'That's right. Give the jefe a glass of beer.' The beggar filled his own glass with wine and held it out. The jefe took his place upon the bed and drained the glass: then he took the bottle himself. He said, 'It's good beer. Very good beer. Is this the only bottle?' The man in drill watched him with frigid anxiety.

'I'm afraid the only bottle.'

'Salud!'

'And what,' the Governor's cousin said, 'were we talking about?'

'About the first thing you could remember,' the beggar said.

'The first thing I can remember,' the jefe began, with deliberation, '—but this gentleman is not drinking.'

'I will have a little brandy.'

'Salud!'

'Salud!'

'The first thing I can remember with any distinctness is my first communion. Ah, the thrill of the soul, my parents round me . . .'

'How many parents then have you got?'

'Two, of course.'

'They could not have been around you—you would have needed at least four—ha, ha.'

'Salud!'

'Salud!'

'No, but as I was saying—life has such irony. It was my painful duty to watch the priest who gave me that communion shot—an old man. I am not ashamed to say that I wept. The comfort is that he is probably a saint and that he prays for us. It is not everyone who earns a saint's prayers.'

'An unusual way . . .'

'But then life is mysterious.'

'Salud!'

The man in drill said, 'A glass of brandy, jefe?'

'There is so little in this bottle that I may as well . . .'

'I was very anxious to take a little back for my mother.'

'Oh, a drop like this. It would be an insult to take it. Just the dregs.' He turned it up over his glass and chuckled, 'If you can talk of beer having dregs.' Then he stopped with the bottle held over the glass and said with astonishment, 'Why, man, you're crying.' All three watched the man in drill with their mouths a little open. He said, 'It always takes me like this—brandy. forgive me, gentlemen. I get drunk very easily and then I see . . .'

'See what?'

'Oh. I don't know, all the hope of the world draining away.'

'Man, you're a poet.'

The beggar said, 'A poet is the soul of his country.'

Lightning filled the windows like a white sheet, and thunder crashed suddenly overhead. The one globe flickered and faded up near the ceiling. 'This is bad news for my men,' the jefe said, stamping on a beetle which had crawled too near.

'Why bad news?'

'The rains coming so early. You see they are on a hunt.'

'The gringo . . . ?'

'He doesn't really matter, but the Governor's found there's still a priest, and you know what he feels about that. If it was me, I'd let the poor devil alone. He'd starve or die of fever or give up. He can't be doing any good—or any harm. Why, nobody even noticed he was about till a few months ago.'

'You'll have to hurry.'

'Oh, he hasn't any real chance. Unless he gets over the border. We've got a man who knows him. Spoke to him, spent a night with him. Let's talk of something else. Who wants to be a policeman?'

'Where do you think he is?'

'You'd be surprised.'

'Why?'

'He's here—in this town, I mean. That's deduction. You see since we started taking hostages from the villages, there's really nowhere else ... They turn him away, they won't have him. So we've set this man I told you about loose like a dog—he'll run into him one day or another—and then ...'

The man in drill said, 'Have you had to shoot many hostages?'

'Not yet. Three or four perhaps. Well, here goes the last of the beer. Salud!' He put the glass regretfully down. 'Perhaps now I could have just a drop of your—sidral, shall we say?'

'Yes. Of course.'

'Have I met you before? Your face somehow ...'

'I don't think I've had the honour.'

'That's another mystery,' the jefe said, stretching out a long fat limb and gently pushing the beggar towards the bed-knobs, 'how you think you've seen people—and places—before. Was it in a dream or in a past life? I once heard a doctor say it was something to do with the focusing of the eyes. But he was a Yankee. A materialist.'

'I remember once ...' the Governor's cousin said. The lightning shot down over the harbour and the thunder beat on the roof; this was the atmosphere of a whole state—the storm outside and the talk just going on—words like 'mystery' and 'soul' and 'the source of life' came in over and over again, as they sat on the bed talking, with nothing to do and nothing to believe and nowhere better to go.

The man in drill said, 'I think perhaps I had better be moving on.'

'Where to?'

'Oh ... friends,' he said vaguely, sketching widely with his hands a whole world of fictitious friendships.

'You'd better take your drink with you,' the Governor's cousin said. He admitted, 'After all you paid for it.'

'Thank you, Excellency.' He picked up the brandy bottle. Perhaps there were three fingers left. The bottle of wine, of course, was quite empty.

'Hide it, man, hide it,' the Governor's cousin said sharply.

'Oh, of course, Excellency, I will be careful.'

'You don't have to call him Excellency,' the jefe said. He gave a bellow of laughter and thrust the beggar right off the bed on to the floor.

'No, no, that is ...' He sidled cautiously out, with a smudge of tears under his red sore eyes and from the hall heard the conversation begin again—'mystery', 'soul'—going interminably on to no end.

*　　*　　*

The beetles had disappeared; the rain had apparently washed them away: it came perpendicularly down, with a sort of measured intensity, as if it were driving nails into a coffin lid. But the air was no clearer: sweat and rain hung together on the clothes. The priest stood for a few seconds in the doorway of the hotel, the dynamo thudding behind him, then he darted a few yards into another doorway and hesitated, staring over past the bust of the general to the tethered sailing boats and one old barge with a tin funnel. He had nowhere to go. Rain hadn't entered into his calculations: he had believed that it would be possible just to hang on somehow, sleeping on benches or by the river.

A couple of soldiers arguing furiously came down the street towards the quay—they just let the rain fall on them, as if it didn't matter, as if things were so bad anyway you couldn't notice.... The priest pushed the wooden door against which he stood, a cantina door coming down only to the knees, and went in out of the rain: stacks of gaseosa bottles and a single billiard table with the score strung on rings, three or four men—somebody had laid his holster on the bar. The priest moved too quickly and jolted the elbow of a man who was making a shot. He turned furiously: 'Mother of God!' He was a Red Shirt. Was there no safety anywhere, even for a moment?

The priest apologised humbly, edging back towards the door, but again he was too quick—his pocket caught against the wall and the brandy bottle chinked. Three or four faces looked at him with malicious amusement: he was a stranger and they were going to have fun. 'What's that you've got in your pocket?' the Red Shirt asked. He was a youth not out of his teens, with gold teeth and jesting conceited mouth.

'Lemonade,' the priest said.

'What do you want to carry lemonade with you for?'

'I take it at night—with my quinine.'

The Red Shirt swaggered up and poked the pocket with the butt of his cue. 'Lemonade, eh?'

'Yes, lemonade.'

'Let's have a look at the lemonade.' He turned proudly to the others and said, 'I can scent a smuggler at ten paces.' He thrust his hand into the priest's pocket and hauled at the brandy bottle. 'There,' he said. 'Didn't I tell you—' The priest flung himself against the swing door and burst out into the rain. A voice shouted, 'Catch him.' They were having the time of their lives.

He was off up the street towards the plaza, turned left and right again—it was lucky the streets were dark and the moon obscured. As long as he kept away from lighted windows he was almost invisible—he could hear them calling to each other. They were not giving up: it was better than billiards; somewhere a whistle blew—the police were joining in.

This was the town to which it had been his ambition to be promoted, leaving the right kind of debts behind at Concepción: he thought of the cathedral and Montez and a monsignor he once knew, as he doubled this way and that. Something buried very deep, the will to escape, cast a momentary and appalling humour over the whole situation—he giggled and panted and giggled again. He could hear them hallooing and whistling in the dark, and the rain came down; it drove and jumped upon the cement floor of the useless fronton which had once been the cathedral (it was too hot to play pelota and a few iron swings stood like gallows as its edge). He worked his way downhill again: he had an idea.

The shouts came nearer, and then up from the river a new lot of men approached; these were pursuing the hunt methodically—he could tell it by their slow pace, the police, the official hunters. He was between the two—the amateurs and the professionals. But he knew the door—he pushed it open, came quickly through into the patio and closed it behind him.

He stood in the dark and panted, hearing the steps come nearer up the street, while the rain drove down. Then he realised that somebody was watching him from the window, a small dark withered face, like one of the preserved heads tourists buy. He came up to the grill and said, 'Padre José?'

'Over there.' A second face appeared behind the other's shoulder, lit uncertainly by a candle-flame, then a third: faces sprouted like vegetables. He could feel them watching him as he splashed back across the patio and banged on a door.

He didn't for a second or two recognise Padre José in the absurd billowing nightshirt, holding a lamp. The last time he had seen him was at the conference, sitting in the back row, biting his nails, afraid to be noticed. It hadn't been necessary: none of the busy cathedral clergy even knew what he was called. It was odd to think that now he had won a kind of fame superior to theirs. He said 'José' gently, winking up at him from the splashing dark.

'Who are you?'

'Don't you remember me? Of course, it's years now ... don't you remember the conference at the cathedral ... ?'

'O God,' Padre José said.

'They are looking for me. I thought perhaps just for to-night you could perhaps ...'

'Go away,' Padre José said, 'go away.'

'They don't know who I am. They think I'm a smuggler—but up at the police station they'll know.'

'Don't talk so loud. My wife ...'

'Just show me some corner,' he whispered. He was beginning to feel fear again. Perhaps the effect of the brandy was wearing off (it was impossible in this hot damp climate to stay drunk for long: alcohol came out again under the armpits: it dripped from the forehead), or perhaps it was only that the desire of life which moves in cycles was returning—any sort of life.

In the lamplight Padre José's face wore an expression of hatred. He said, 'Why come to me? Why should you think ... ? I'll call the police if you don't go. You know what sort of a man I am.'

He pleaded gently, 'You're a good man, José. I've always known that.'

'I'll shout if you don't go.'

He tried to remember some cause of hatred. There were voices in the street—arguments, a knocking—were they searching the houses? He said, 'If I ever offended you, José, forgive me. I was conceited, proud, over-bearing—a bad priest. I always knew in my heart you were the better man.'

'Go,' José screeched at him, 'go. I don't want martyrs here. I don't belong, any more. Leave me alone. I'm all right as I am.' He tried to gather up his venom into spittle and shot it feebly at the other's face: it didn't even reach, but fell impotently through the air. He said, 'Go and die quickly. That's your job,' and slammed the door to. The door of the patio came suddenly open and the police were there. He caught a glimpse of Padre José peering through a window and then an enormous shape in a white nightshirt engulfed him and drew him away—whisked him off, like a guardian spirit, from the disastrous human struggle. A voice said, 'That's him.' It was the young Red Shirt. He let his fist open and dropped by Padre José's wall a little ball of paper: it was like the final surrender of a whole past.

He knew it was the beginning of the end—after all these years. He began to say silently an act of contrition, while they picked the brandy bottle out of his pocket, but he couldn't give his mind to it. That was the fallacy of the death-bed repentence—penitence was the fruit of long training and discipline: fear wasn't enough. He tried to think of his child with shame, but he could only think of her with a kind of famished love—what would become of her? And the sin itself was so old that like an ancient picture the deformity had faded and left a kind of grace. The Red Shirt smashed the bottle on the stone paving and the smell of spirit rose all round them—not very strongly: there hadn't been much left.

Then they took him away. Now that they had caught him they treated him in a friendly way, poking fun at his attempt to escape, except the Red Shirt whose shot he had spoiled. He couldn't find any answer to their jokes: self-preservation lay across his brain like a horrifying obsession. When would they discover who he really was? When would he meet the half-caste, or the lieutenant who had interrogated him already? They moved in a bunch slowly up the hill to the plaza. A rifle-butt grounded outside the station as they came in. A small lamp fumed against the dirty white-washed wall; in the courtyard hammocks swung, bunched around sleeping bodies like the nets in which poultry are tied. 'You can sit down,' one of the men said, and pushed him in a comradely way towards the bench. Everything now seemed irrevocable; the sentry passed back and forth outside the door, and in the courtyard among the hammocks the ceaseless murmur of sleep went on.

Somebody had spoken to him: he gaped helplessly up. 'What?' There seemed to be an argument in progress between the police and the Red Shirt as to whether somebody should be disturbed. 'But it's his duty,' the Red Shirt kept on repeating: he had rabbity front teeth. He said, 'I'll report it to the Governor.'

A policeman said, 'You plead guilty, don't you?'

'Yes,' the priest said.

'There. What more do you want? It's a fine of five pesos. Why disturb anybody?'

'And who gets the five pesos, eh?'

'That's none of your business.'

The priest said suddenly, 'No one gets them.'

'No one?'

'I have only twenty-five centavos in the world.'

The door of an inner room opened and the lieutenant came out. He said, 'What in God's name is all the noise . . . ?' The police came raggedly and unwillingly to attention.

'I've caught a man carrying spirits,' the Red Shirt said.

The priest sat with his eyes on the ground . . . 'because it has crucified . . . crucified . . . crucified . . .' contrition stuck hopelessly over the formal words. He felt no emotion but fear.

'Well,' the lieutenant said, 'what is it to do with you? We catch dozens.'

'Shall we bring him in?' one of the men asked.

The lieutenant took a look at the bowed servile figure on the bench. 'Get up,' he said. The priest rose. Now, he thought, now . . . he raised his eyes.

The lieutenant looked away, out of the door where the sentry slouched to and fro. His dark pinched face looked rattled, harassed. . . .

'He has no money,' one of the policemen said.

'Mother of God,' the lieutenant said, 'can I never teach you . . . ?' He took two steps towards the sentry and turned, 'Search him. If he has no money, put him in a cell. Give him some work. . . .' He went outside and suddenly raising his open hand he struck the sentry on the ear. He said, 'You're asleep. March as if you have some pride . . . pride,' he repeated again, while the small acetylene lamp fumed up the white-washed wall and the smell of urine came up out of the yard and the men lay in their hammocks netted and secured.

'Shall we take his name?' a sergeant asked.

'Yes, of course,' the lieutenant said, not looking at him, walking briskly and nervously back past the lamp into the courtyard; he stood there unsheltered, looking round while the rain fell on his dapper uniform. He looked like a man with something on his mind: it was as if he were under the influence of some secret passion which had broken up the routine of his life. Back he came. He couldn't keep still.

The sergeant pushed the priest ahead into the inner room. A bright commercial calendar hung on the flaking whitewash—a dark-skinned mestizo girl in a bathing-dress advertised some gaseous water; somebody had pencilled in a neat pedagogic hand a facile and over-confident statement about man having nothing to lose but his chains.

'Name?' the sergeant said. Before he could check himself he had replied, 'Montez.'

'Home?'

He named a random village: he was absorbed in his own portrait. There he sat among the white-starched dresses of the first communicants. Somebody had put a ring round his face to pick it out. There was another picture on the wall too—the gringo from San Antonio, Texas, wanted for murder and bank robbery.

'I suppose,' the sergeant said cautiously, 'that you bought the drink from a stranger . . .'

'Yes.'

'Whom you can't identify?'

'No.'

'That's the way,' the sergeant said approvingly. It was obvious he didn't want to start anything. He took the priest quite confidingly by the arm and led him out and across the courtyard; he carried a large key like the ones used in morality plays or fairy stories as a symbol. A few men moved in the hammocks—a large unshaven jaw hung over the side like something left unsold on a butcher's counter: a big torn ear: a naked black-haired thigh. He wondered when the mestizo's face would appear, elated with recognition.

The sergeant unlocked a small grated door and let out with his boot at something straddled across the entrance. He said, 'They are all good fellows, all good fellows here,' kicking his way in. A heavy smell lay on the air and somebody in the darkness wept.

The priest lingered on the threshold trying to see. He said, 'I am so dry. Could I have water?' The stench poured up his nostrils and he retched.

'In the morning,' the sergeant said, 'you've drunk enough now,' and laying a large considerate hand upon the priest's back, he pushed him in, then slammed the door to. He trod on a hand, an arm, and pressing his face against the grill, protested, 'There's no room. I can't see. Who are these people?' Outside among the hammocks the sergeant began to laugh. 'Hombre,' he said, 'hombre, have you never been in jail before?'

3

A voice near his foot said, 'Got a cigarette?'

He drew quickly back and trod on an arm. A voice said imperatively, 'Water, quick,' as if whoever it was thought he could take a stranger unawares, and make him fork out.

'Got a cigarette?'

'No.' He said weakly, 'I have nothing at all,' and imagined he could feel enmity fuming up all round him. He moved again. Somebody said, 'Look out for the bucket.' That was where the stench came from. He stood perfectly still and waited for his sight to return. Outside the rain began to stop: it dropped haphazardly and the thunder moved away. You could count forty now between the lightning flash and the roll. Halfway to the sea, or halfway to the mountains. He felt around with his foot, trying to find enough space to sit down, but there seemed to be no room at all. When the lightning went on he could see the hammocks at the edge of the courtyard.

'Got something to eat?' a voice asked, and when he didn't answer, 'Got something to eat?'

'No.'

'Got any money?' another voice said.

'No.'

Suddenly, from about five feet away, there came a tiny scream—a woman's. A tired voice said, 'Can't you be quiet?' Among the furtive movements came again the muffled cries. He realised that pleasure was going on even in this crowded darkness. Again he put out his foot and began to edge his way inch by inch away from the grill. Behind the human voices another noise went permanently on: it was like a small machine, an electric belt set at a certain tempo. It filled any silences that there were louder than human breath. It was the mosquitoes.

He had moved perhaps six feet from the grill, and his eyes began to distinguish heads—perhaps the sky was clearing: they hung around him like gourds. A voice said, 'Who are you?' He made no reply, feeling panic, edging in. Suddenly he found himself against the back wall: the stone was wet against his hand—the cell could not have been more than twelve feet deep. He found he could just sit down if he kept his feet drawn up under him. An old man lay slumped against his shoulder; he told his age from the featherweight lightness of the bones, the feeble uneven flutter of the breath. He was either somebody close to birth or death—and he could hardly be a child in this place. The old man said suddenly, 'Is that you, Catarina?' and his breath went out in a long patient sigh, as if he had been waiting a long while and could afford to wait a lot longer.

The priest said, 'No. Not Catarina.' When he spoke everybody became suddenly silent, listening, as if what he said had importance: then the voices and movements began again. But the sound of his own voice, the sense of communication with a neighbour, calmed him.

'You wouldn't be,' the old man said. 'I didn't really think you were. She'll never come.'

'Is she your wife?'

'What's that you're saying? I haven't got a wife.'

'Catarina?'

'She's my daughter.' Everybody was listening except the two invisible people who were concerned only in their cramped pleasure.

'Perhaps they won't allow her here.'

'She'll never try,' the old hopeless voice pronounced with absolute conviction. The priest's feet began to ache, drawn up under his haunches. He said, 'If she loves you . . .' Somewhere across the huddle of dark shapes the woman cried again—that finished cry of protest and abandonment and pleasure.

'It's the priests who've done it,' the old man said.

'The priests?'

'The priests.'

'Why the priests?'

'The priests.'

A low voice near his knees said, 'The old man's crazy. What's the use of asking him questions?'

'Is that you, Catarina?' He added, 'I don't really believe it, you know. It's just a question.'

'Now *I've* got something to complain about,' the voice went on. 'A man's got to defend his honour. You'll admit that, won't you?'

'I don't know anything about honour.'

'I was in the cantina and the man I'm telling you about came up to me and said, "Your mother's a whore." Well, I couldn't do anything about it: he'd got his gun on him. All I could do was wait. He drank too much beer—I knew he would—and when he was staggering I followed him out. I had a bottle and I smashed it against a wall. You see, I hadn't got my gun. His family's got influence with the jefe or I'd never be here.'

'It's a terrible thing to kill a man.'

'You talk like a priest.'

'It was the priests who did it,' the old man said. 'You're right there.'

'What does he mean?'

'What does it matter what an old man like that means? I'd like to tell you about something else . . .'

A woman's voice said, 'They took the child away from him.'

'Why?'

'It was a bastard. They acted quite correctly.'

At the word 'bastard' his heart moved painfully, as when a man in love hears a stranger name a flower which is also the name of his woman.

'Bastard!' the word filled him with miserable happiness. It brought his own child nearer: he could see her under the tree by the rubbish-dump, unguarded. He repeated 'Bastard?' as he might have repeated her name—with tenderness disguised as indifference.

'They said he was no fit father. But, of course, when the priests fled, she had to go with him. Where else could she go?' It was like a happy ending until she said, 'Of course she hated him. They'd taught her about things.' He could imagine the small set mouth of an educated woman. What was she doing here?

'Why is he in prison?'

'He had a crucifix.'

The stench from the pail got worse all the time; the night stood round them like a wall, without ventilation, and he could hear somebody making water, drumming on the tin sides. He said, 'They had no business . . .'

'They were doing what was right, of course. It was a mortal sin.'

'No right to make her hate him.'

'They knew what's right.'

He said, 'They were bad priests to do a thing like that. The sin was over. It was their duty to teach—well, love.'

'You don't know what's right. The priests know.'

He said after a moment's hesitation, very distinctly, 'I am a priest.'

It was like the end: there was no need to hope any longer. The ten years' hunt was over at last. There was silence all round him. This place was very like the world: overcrowded with lust and crime and unhappy love, it stank to heaven; but he realised that after all it was possible to find peace there, when you knew for certain that the time was short.

'A priest?' the woman said at last.

'Yes.'

'Do *they* know?'

'Not yet.'

He could feel a hand fumbling at his sleeve. A voice said, 'You shouldn't have told us. Father, there are all sorts here. Murderers . . .'

The voice which had described the crime to him said, 'You've no cause to abuse me. Because I kill a man it doesn't mean . . .' Whispering started everywhere. The voice said bitterly, 'I'm not an informer just because when a man says "Your mother was a whore . . ."'

The priest said, 'There's no need for anyone to inform on me. That would be a sin. When it's daylight they'll discover for themselves.'

'They'll shoot you, father,' the woman's voice said.

'Yes.'

'Are you afraid?'

'Yes. Of course.'

A new voice spoke, in the corner from which the sounds of pleasure had come. It said roughly and obstinately, 'A man isn't afraid of a thing like that.'

'No?' the priest asked.

'A bit of pain. What do you expect? It has to come.'

'All the same,' the priest said, 'I *am* afraid.'

'Toothache is worse.'

'We can't all be brave men.'

The voice said with contempt, 'You believers are all the same. Christianity makes you cowards.'

'Yes. Perhaps you are right. You see I am a bad priest and a bad man. To die in a state of mortal sin'—he gave an uneasy chuckle—'it makes you think.'

'There. It's as I say. Believing in God makes cowards.' The voice was triumphant, as if it had proved something.

'So then?' the priest said.

'Better not to believe—and be a brave man.'

'I see—yes. And, of course, if one believed the Governor did not exist or the jefe, if we could pretend that this prison was not a prison at all but a garden, how brave we could be then.'

'That's just foolishness.'

'But when we found that the prison was a prison, and the Governor up there in the square undoubtedly existed, well, it wouldn't much matter if we'd been brave for an hour or two.'

'Nobody could say that this prison was not a prison.'

'No? You don't think so? I can see you don't listen to the politicians.' His feet were giving him great pain: he had cramp in the soles, but he could bring no pressure on the muscles to relieve them. It was not yet midnight; the hours of darkness stretched ahead interminably.

The woman said suddenly, 'Think. We have a martyr here . . .'

The priest giggled: he couldn't stop himself. He said, 'I don't think martyrs are like this.' He became suddenly serious, remembering Maria's words—it wouldn't be a good thing to bring mockery on the Church. He said, 'Martyrs are holy men. It is wrong to think that just because one dies . . . no. I tell you I am in a state of mortal sin. I have done things I couldn't talk to you about. I could only whisper them in the confessional.' Everybody, when he spoke, listened attentively to him as if he were addressing them in church. He wondered where the inevitable Judas was sitting now, but he wasn't aware of Judas as he had been in the forest hut. He was moved by an irrational affection for the inhabitants of this prison. A phrase came to him: 'God so loved the world . . .' He said, 'My children, you must never think the holy martyrs are like me. You have a name for me. Oh, I've heard you use it before now. I am a whisky priest. I am in here now because they found a bottle of brandy in my pocket.' He tried to move his feet from under him: the cramp had passed: now they were lifeless: all feeling gone. Oh well, let them stay. He wouldn't have to use them often again.

The old man was muttering, and the priest's thoughts went back to Brigitta. The knowledge of the world lay in her like the dark explicable spot in an X-ray photograph; he longed—with a breathless feeling in the breast—to save her, but he knew the surgeon's decision—the ill was incurable.

The woman's voice said pleadingly, 'A little drink, father . . . it's not so important.' He wondered why she was here—probably for having a holy picture in her house. She had the tiresome intense note of a pious woman. They were extraordinarily foolish over pictures. Why not burn them? One didn't need a picture . . . He said sternly, 'Oh, I am not only a drunkard.' He had always been worried by the fate of pious women. As much as politicians, they fed on illusion. He was frightened for them: they came to death so often in a state of invincible complacency, full of uncharity. It was one's duty, if one could, to rob them of their sentimental notions of what was good . . . He said in hard accents, 'I have a child.'

What a worthy woman she was! Her voice pleaded in the darkness; he couldn't catch what she said, but it was something about the Good Thief. He said, 'My child, the thief repented. I haven't repented.' He remembered her coming into the hut, the dark malicious knowing look with the sunlight at her back. He said, 'I don't know how to repent.' That was true: he had lost the faculty. He couldn't say to himself that he wished his sin had never existed, because the sin seemed to him now so unimportant and he loved the fruit of it. He needed a confessor to draw his mind slowly down the drab passages which led to grief and repentance.

The woman was silent now: he wondered whether after all he had been too harsh with her. If it helped her faith to believe that he was a martyr . . . But he rejected the idea: one was pledged to truth. He shifted an inch or two on his hams and said, 'What time does it get light?'

'Four . . . five . . .' a man replied. 'How can we tell, father? We haven't clocks.'

'Have you been here long?'

'Three weeks.'

'Are you kept here all day?'

'Oh no. They let us out to clean the yard.'

He thought: that is when I shall be discovered—unless it's earlier, for surely one of these people will betray me first. A long train of thought began, which led him to announce after a while, 'They are offering a reward for me. Five hundred, six hundred pesos, I'm not sure.' Then he was silent again. He couldn't urge any man to inform against him—that would be tempting him to sin—but at the same time if there was an informer here, there was no reason why the wretched creature should be bilked of his reward. To commit so ugly a sin—it must count as murder—and to have no compensation in this world . . . He thought: it wouldn't be fair.

'Nobody here,' a voice said, 'wants their blood money.'

Again he was touched by an extraordinary affection. He was just one criminal among a herd of criminals . . . He had a sense of companionship which he had never experienced in the old days when pious people came kissing his black cotton glove.

The pious woman's voice leapt hysterically out at him, 'It is so stupid to tell them that. You don't know the sort of wretches who are here, father. Thieves, murderers . . .'

'Well,' an angry voice said, 'why are you here?'

'I had good books in my house,' she announced, with unbearable pride. He had done nothing to shake her complacency. He said, 'They are everywhere. It's no different here.'

'Good books?'

He giggled. 'No, no. Thieves, murderers . . . Oh, well, my child, if you had more experience you would know there are worse things to be.' The old man seemed to be uneasily asleep; his head lay sideways against the priest's shoulder, and he muttered angrily. God knows, it had never been easy to move in this place, but the difficulty seemed to increase as the night wore on and limbs stiffened. He couldn't twitch his shoulder now without waking the old man to another night of suffering. Well, he thought, it was my kind who robbed him: it's only fair to be made a little uncomfortable . . . He sat silent and rigid against the damp wall, with his dead feet under his haunches. The mosquitoes droned on; it was no good defending yourself by striking at the air: they pervaded the whole place like an element. Somebody as well as the old man had fallen asleep and was snoring, a curious note of satisfaction, as though he had eaten and drunk well at a good dinner and was now taking a snooze . . . The priest tried to calculate the hour: how much time had passed since he had met the beggar in the plaza? It was probably not long after midnight: there would be hours more of this.

It was, of course, the end, but at the same time you had to be prepared for everything, even escape. If God intended him to escape He could snatch him away from in front of a firing-squad. But God was merciful. There was only one reason, surely, which would make Him refuse His peace–if there was any peace–that he could still be of use in saving a soul, his own or another's. But what good could he do now? They had him on the run; he dared not enter a village in case somebody else should pay with his life–perhaps a man who was in mortal sin and unrepentant. It was impossible to say what souls might not be lost simply because he was obstinate and proud and wouldn't admit defeat. He couldn't even say Mass any longer–he had no wine. It had gone down the dry gullet of the Chief of Police. It was appallingly complicated. He was still afraid of death, he would be more afraid of death yet when the morning came, but it was beginning to attract him by its simplicity.

The pious woman was whispering to him. She must have somehow edged her way nearer. She was saying, 'Father, will you hear my confession?'

'My dear child, here! It's quite impossible. Where would be the secrecy?'

'It's been so long . . .'

'Say an Act of Contrition for your sins. You must trust God, my dear, to make allowances . . .'

'I wouldn't mind suffering . . .'

'Well, you are here.'

'That's nothing. In the morning my sister will have raised the money for my fine.'

Somewhere against the far wall pleasure began again; it was unmistakable: the movements, the breathlessness, and then the cry. The pious woman said aloud with fury, 'Why won't they stop it? The brutes, the animals!'

'What's the good of your saying an Act of Contrition now in this state of mind?'

'But the ugliness . . .'

'Don't believe that. It's dangerous. Because suddenly we discover that our sins have so much beauty.'

'Beauty,' she said with disgust. 'Here. In this cell. With strangers all round.'

'Such a lot of beauty. Saints talk about the beauty of suffering. Well, we are not saints, you and I. Suffering to us is just ugly. Stench and crowding and pain. *That* is beautiful in that corner–to them. It needs a lot of learning to see things with a saint's eye: a saint gets a subtle taste for beauty and can look down on poor ignorant palates like theirs. But we can't afford to.'

'It's mortal sin.'

'We don't know. It may be. But I'm a bad priest, you see. I know—from experience—how much beauty Satan carried down with him when he fell. Nobody ever said the fallen angels were the ugly ones. Oh no, they were just as quick and light and . . .'

Again the cry came, an expression of intolerable pleasure. The woman said, 'Stop them. It's a scandal.' He felt fingers on his knee, grasping, digging. He said, 'We're all fellow prisoners. I want drink at this moment more than anything, more than God. That's a sin too.'

'Now,' the woman said, 'I can see you're a bad priest. I wouldn't believe it before. I do now. You sympathise with these animals. If your bishop heard you . . .'

'Ah, he's a very long way off.' He thought of the old man now in Mexico City, living in one of those ugly comfortable pious houses, full of images and holy pictures, saying Mass on Sundays at one of the cathedral altars.

'When I get out of here, I shall write . . .'

He couldn't help laughing: she had no sense of how life had changed. He said, 'If he gets the letter he'll be interested to hear I'm alive.' But again he became serious. It was more difficult to feel pity for her than for the half-caste who a week ago had tagged him through the forest, but her case might be worse. The other had so much excuse—poverty and fever and innumerable humiliations. He said, 'Try not to be angry. Pray for me instead.'

'The sooner you are dead the better.'

He couldn't see her in the darkness, but there were plenty of faces he could remember from the old days which fitted the voice. When you visualised a man or woman carefully, you could always begin to feel pity—that was a quality God's image carried with it. When you saw the lines at the corners of the eyes, the shape of the mouth, how the hair grew, it was impossible to hate. Hate was just a failure of imagination. He began to feel an overwhelming responsibility for this pious woman. 'You and Father José,' she said. 'It's people like you who make people mock—at real religion.' She had, after all, as many excuses as the half-caste. He saw the kind of salon in which she spent her days, with the rocking-chair and the family photographs, meeting no one. He said gently, 'You are not married, are you?'

'Why do you want to know?'

'And you never had a vocation?'

'They wouldn't believe it,' she said bitterly.

He thought: poor woman, she's had nothing, nothing at all. If only one could find the right word . . . He leant hopelessly back, moving carefully so as not to waken the old man. But the right words never came to him. He was more out of touch with her kind than he had ever been; he would have known what to say to her in the old days, feeling no pity at all, speaking with half a mind a platitude or two. Now he felt useless: he was a criminal and ought only to talk to criminals. He had done wrong again, trying to break down her complacency. He might just as well have let her go on thinking him a martyr.

His eyes closed and immediately he began to dream. He was being pursued; he stood outside a door banging on it, begging for admission, but nobody answered–there was a word, a password, which would save him, but he had forgotten it. He tried desperately at random–cheese and child, California, excellency, milk, Vera Cruz. His feet had gone to sleep and he knelt outside the door. Then he knew why he wanted to get in: he wasn't being pursued after all: that was a mistake. His child lay beside him bleeding to death and this was a doctor's house. He banged on the door and shouted, 'Even if I can't think of the right word, haven't you a heart?' The child was dying and looked up at him with middle-aged complacent wisdom. She said, 'You animal,' and he woke again crying. He couldn't have slept for more than a few seconds because the woman was still talking about the vocation the nuns had refused to recognise. He said, 'That made you suffer, didn't it? To suffer like that–perhaps it was better than being a nun and happy,' and immediately after he had spoken he thought: a silly remark, what does it mean? Why can't I find something to say to her which she could remember?

He didn't sleep again: he was striking yet another bargain with God. This time, if he escaped from the prison, he would escape altogether. He would go north, over the border. His escape was so improbable that, if it happened, it couldn't be anything else but a sign–an indication that he was doing more harm by his example than good by his occasional confessions. The old man moved against his shoulder and the night just stayed around them. The darkness was always the same and there were no clocks–there was nothing to indicate time passing. The only punctuation of the night was the sound of urination.

★   ★   ★

Suddenly, he realised that he could see a face, and then another; he had begun to forget that it would ever be another day, just as one forgets that one will ever die. It comes suddenly on one in a screeching brake or a whistle in the air, the knowledge that time moves and comes to an end. All the voices slowly became faces–there were no surprises. The confessional teaches you to recognise the shape of a voice–the loose lip or the weak chin and the false candour of the too straightforward eyes. He saw the pious woman a few feet away, uneasily dreaming with her prim mouth open, showing strong teeth like tombs: the old man: the boaster in the corner, and his woman asleep untidily across his knees. Now that the day was at last here, he was the only one awake, except for a small Indian boy who sat cross-legged near the door with an expression of interested happiness, as if he had never known such friendly company. Over the courtyard the whitewash became visible upon the opposite wall. He began formally to pay his farewell to the world: he couldn't put any heart in it. His corruption was less evident to his senses than his death. One bullet, he thought, is almost certain to go directly through the heart–a squad must contain one accurate marksman. Life would go out in a 'fraction of a second' (that was the phrase), but all night he had been realising that time depends on clocks and the passage of light. There were no clocks and the light wouldn't change. Nobody really knew how long a second of pain could be. It might last a whole purgatory–or for ever. For some reason he thought of a man he had once shrived who was on the point of death with cancer–his relatives had had to bandage their faces, the smell of the rotting interior was so appalling He wasn't a saint. Nothing in life was as ugly as death.

A voice in the yard called 'Montez'. He sat on upon his dead feet; he thought automatically: This suit isn't good for much more. It was smeared and fouled by the cell floor and his fellow prisoners. He had obtained it at great risk in a store down by the river, pretending to be a small farmer with ideas above his station. Then he remembered he wouldn't need it much longer—it came with an odd shock, like locking the door of one's house for the last time. The voice repeated impatiently, 'Montez.'

He remembered that that, for the moment, was his name. He looked up from his ruined suit and saw the sergeant unlocking the cell door. 'Here, Montez.' He let the old man's head fall gently back against the sweating wall and tried to stand up, but his feet crumpled like pastry. 'Do you want to sleep all night?' the sergeant complained testily: something had irritated him: he wasn't as friendly as he had been the night before. He let out a kick at a sleeping man and beat on the cell door, 'Come on. Wake up all of you. Out into the yard.' Only the Indian boy obeyed, sliding unobtrusively out with his look of alien happiness. The sergeant complained, 'The dirty hounds. Do they want us to wash them? You, Montez.' Life began to return painfully to his feet. He managed to reach the door.

The yard had come sluggishly to life. A queue of men were bathing their faces at a single tap; a man in a vest and pants sat on the ground hugging a rifle. 'Get out into the yard and wash,' the sergeant yelled at them, but when the priest stepped out he snapped at him, 'Not you, Montez.'

'Not me?'

'We've got other plans for you,' the sergeant said.

The priest stood waiting while his fellow prisoners filed out into the yard. One by one they went past him; he looked at their feet and not their faces, standing like a temptation at the door. Nobody said a word: a woman's feet went draggingly by in black worn low-heeled shoes. He was shaken by the sense of his own uselessness. He whispered without looking up, 'Pray for me.'

'What's that you said, Montez?'

He couldn't think of a lie; he felt as if ten years had exhausted his whole stock of deceit.

'What's that you said?'

The shoes had stopped moving. The woman's voice said, 'He was begging.' She added mercilessly, 'He ought to have more sense. I've nothing for him.' Then she went on, flat-footed into the yard.

'Did you sleep well, Montez?' the sergeant badgered him.

'Not very well.'

'What do you expect?' the sergeant said. 'It'll teach you to like brandy too well, won't it?'

'Yes.' He wondered how much longer all these preliminaries would take.

'Well, if you spend all your money on brandy, you've got to do a bit of work in return for a night's lodging. Fetch the pails out of the cells and mind you don't spill them—this place stinks enough as it is.'

'Where do I take them to?'

The sergeant pointed to the door of the excusados beyond the tap. 'Report to me when you've finished that,' he said, and went bellowing orders back into the yard.

The priest bent down and took the pail. It was full and very heavy: he went bowed with the weight across the yard. Sweat got into his eyes. He wiped them free and saw one behind the other in the washing-queue faces he knew—the hostages. There was Miguel, whom he had seen taken away; he remembered the mother screaming out and the lieutenant's tired anger and the sun coming up. They saw him at the same time; he put down the heavy pail and looked at them. Not to recognise them would have been like a hint, a claim, a demand to them to go on suffering and let him escape. Miguel had been beaten up: there was a sore under his eye—flies buzzed round it as they buzz round a mule's raw flank. Then the queue moved on; they looked on the ground and passed him; strangers took their place. He prayed silently: Oh God, send them someone more worthwhile to suffer for. It seemed to him a damnable mockery that they should sacrifice themselves for a whisky priest with a bastard child. The soldier sat in his pants with the gun between his knees paring his nails and biting off the loose skin. In an odd way he felt abandoned because they had shown no sign of recognition.

The excusados was a cesspool with two planks across it on which a man could stand. He emptied the pail and went back across the yard to the row of cells. There were six: one by one he took the pails: once he had to stop and retch: splash, splash, to and fro across the yard. He came to the last cell. It wasn't empty; a man lay back against the wall; the early sun just reached his feet. Flies buzzed around a mound of vomit on the floor. The eyes opened and watched the priest stooping over the pail: two fangs protruded. . . .

The priest moved quickly and splashed the floor. The half-caste said in that too-familiar nagging tone, 'Wait a moment. You can't do that in here.' He explained proudly, 'I'm not a prisoner. I'm a guest.' The priest made a motion of apology (he was afraid to speak) and moved again. 'Wait a moment,' the half-caste commanded him again. 'Come here.'

The priest stood stubbornly, half-turned away, near the door.

'Come here,' the half-caste said. 'You're a prisoner, aren't you?—and I'm a guest—of the Governor. Do you want me to shout for a policeman? Then do as you're told: come here.'

It seemed as if God were deciding . . . finally. He came, pail in hand, and stood beside the large flat naked foot, and the half-caste looked up at him from the shadow of the wall, asking him sharply and anxiously, 'What are you doing here?'

'Cleaning up.'

'You know what I mean.'

'I was caught with a bottle of brandy,' the priest said, trying to roughen his voice.

'I know you,' the half-caste said. 'I couldn't believe my eyes, but when you speak . . .'

'I don't think . . .'

'That priest's voice,' the half-caste said with disgust. He was like a dog of a different breed: he couldn't help his hackles rising. The big toe moved plumply and inimically. The priest put down the pail. He argued hopelessly, 'You're drunk.'

'Beer, beer,' the half-caste said, 'nothing but beer. They promised me the best of everything, but you can't trust them. Don't I know the jefe's got his own brandy locked away?'

'I must empty the pail.'

'If you move, I'll shout. I've got so many things to think about,' the half-caste complained bitterly. The priest waited: there was nothing else to do; he was at the man's mercy–a silly phrase, for those malarial eyes had never known what mercy was. He was saved at any rate from the indignity of pleading.

'You see,' the mestizo carefully explained, 'I'm comfortable here.' His yellow toes curled luxuriously beside the vomit. 'Good food, beer, company, and this roof doesn't leak. You don't have to tell me what'll happen after–they'll kick me out like a dog, like a dog.' He became shrill and indignant. 'What have they got you here for? That's what I want to know. It looks crooked to me. It's my job, isn't it, to find you. Who's going to have the reward if they've got you already? The jefe, I shouldn't wonder, or that bastard sergeant.' He brooded unhappily. 'You can't trust a soul these days.'

'And there's a Red Shirt,' the priest said.

'A Red Shirt?'

'He really caught me.'

'Mother of God,' the mestizo said, 'and they all have the ear of the Governor.' He looked up beseechingly. He said, 'You're an educated man. Advise me.'

'It would be murder,' the priest said, 'a mortal sin.'

'I don't mean that. I mean about the reward. You see as long as they don't *know*, well, I'm comfortable here. A man deserves a few weeks' holiday. And you can't escape far, can you? It would be better, wouldn't it, to catch you out of here. In the town somewhere. I mean nobody else could claim . . .' He said furiously, 'A poor man has so much to think about.'

'I dare say,' the priest said, 'they'd give you *something* even here.'

'Something,' the mestizo said, levering himself up against the wall, 'why shouldn't I have it all?'

'What's going on in here?' the sergeant asked. He stood in the doorway, in the sunlight, looking in.

The priest said slowly, 'He wanted me to clear up his vomit. I said you hadn't told me . . .'

'Oh, he's a guest,' the sergeant said. 'He's got to be treated right. You do as he says.'

The mestizo smirked. He said, 'And another bottle of beer, sergeant?'

'Not yet,' the sergeant said. 'You've got to look round the town first.'

The priest picked up the pail and went back across the yard, leaving them arguing. He felt as if a gun were levelled at his back. He went into the excusados and emptied the pail, then came out again into the sun–the gun was levelled at his breast. The two men stood in the cell door talking. He walked across the yard: they watched him come. The sergeant said to the mestizo, 'You say you're bilious and can't see properly this morning. You clean up your own vomit then. If you don't do *your* job . . .' Behind the sergeant's back the mestizo gave him a cunning and unreassuring wink. Now that the immediate fear was over, he felt only regret. God had decided. He had to go on with life, go on making decisions, acting on his own advice, making plans . . .

It took him another half-hour to finish cleaning the cells, throwing a bucket of water over each floor; he watched the pious woman go off through the archway to where her sister waited with the fine; they were both tied up in black shawls like things bought in the market, things hard and dry and second-hand. Then he reported again to the sergeant, who inspected the cells and criticised his work and ordered him to throw more water down, and then suddenly got tired of the whole business and told him he could go to the jefe for permission to leave. So he waited another hour on the bench outside the jefe's door, watching the sentry move lackadaisically to and fro in the hot sun.

And when at last a policeman led him in, it wasn't the jefe who sat at the desk but the lieutenant. The priest stood not far from his own portrait on the wall and waited. Once he glanced quickly and nervously up at the old crumpled newspaper cutting and thought, It's not very like me now. What an unbearable creature he must have been in those days—and yet in those days he had been comparatively innocent. That was another mystery: it sometimes seemed to him that venial sins—impatience, an unimportant lie, pride, a neglected opportunity—cut you off from grace more completely than the worst sins of all. Then, in his innocence, he had felt no love for anyone; now in his corruption he had learnt . . .

'Well,' the lieutenant asked, 'has he cleaned up the cells?' He didn't take his eyes from his papers. He went on, 'Tell the sergeant I want two dozen men with properly cleaned rifles—within two minutes.' He looked abstractedly up at the priest and said, 'Well, what are you waiting for?'

'For permission, Excellency, to go away.'

'I am not an excellency. Learn to call things by their right names.' He said sharply, 'Have you been here before?'

'Never.'

'Your name is Montez. I seem to come across too many people of that name in these days. Relations of yours?' He sat watching him closely, as if memory were beginning to work.

The priest said hurriedly, 'My cousin was shot at Concepción.'

'That was not my fault.'

'I only meant—we were much alike. Our fathers were twins. Not half an hour between them. I thought your Excellency seemed to think . . .'

'As I remember him, he was quite different. A tall thin man . . . narrow shoulders . . .'

The priest said hurriedly, 'Perhaps only to the family eye . . .'

'But then I only saw him once.' It was almost as if the lieutenant had something on his conscience, as he sat with his dark Indian-blooded hands restless on the pages, brooding. . . . He asked, 'Where are you going?'

'God knows.'

'You are all alike, you people. You never learn the truth—that God knows nothing.' Some tiny scrap of life like a grain of smut went racing across the page in front of him; he pressed his finger down on it and said, 'You had no money for your fine?' and watched another smut edge out between the leaves, scurrying for refuge: in this heat there was no end to life.

'No.'

'How will you live?'

'Some work perhaps . . .'

'You are getting too old for work.' He put his hand suddenly in his pocket and pulled out a five-peso piece. 'There,' he said. 'Get out of here, and don't let me see your face again. Mind that.'

The priest held the coin in his fist—the price of a Mass. He said with astonishment, 'You're a good man.'

4

It was still very early in the morning when he crossed the river and came dripping up the other bank. He wouldn't have expected anybody to be about. The bungalow, the tin-roofed shed, the flagstaff: he had an idea that all Englishmen lowered their flag at sunset and sang 'God Save the King'. He came carefully round the corner of the shed and the door gave to his pressure. He was inside in the dark where he had been before: how many weeks ago? He had no idea. He only remembered that then the rains were a long way off: now they were beginning to break. In another week only an aeroplane would be able to cross the mountains.

He felt around him with his foot; he was so hungry that even a few bananas would be better than nothing—he had had no food for two days—but there were none here, none at all. He must have arrived on a day when the crop had gone down-river. He stood just inside the door trying to remember what the child had told him—the Morse code, her window: across the dead-white dusty yard the mosquito wire caught the sun. He was reminded suddenly of an empty larder. He began to listen anxiously. There wasn't a sound anywhere; the day here hadn't yet begun with that first sleepy slap of a shoe on a cement floor, the claws of a dog scratching as it stretched, the knock-knock of a hand on a door. There was just nothing, nothing at all.

What was the time? How many hours of light had there been? It was impossible to tell. Suppose, after all, it was not very early—it might be six, seven. . . . He realised how much he had counted on this child. She was the only person who could help him without endangering herself. Unless he got over the mountains in the next few days he was trapped—he might as well hand himself over to the police, because how could he live through the rains with nobody daring to give him food or shelter? It would have been better, quicker, if he had been recognised in the police station a week ago, so much less trouble. Then he heard a sound; it was like hope coming tentatively back: a scratching and a whining. This was what one meant by dawn—the noise of life. He waited for it—hungrily—in the doorway.

And it came: a mongrel bitch dragging herself across the yard, an ugly creature with bent ears, trailing a wounded or a broken leg, whimpering. There was something wrong with her back. She came very slowly. He could see her ribs like an exhibit in a natural history museum. It was obvious that she hadn't had food for days: she had been abandoned.

Unlike him, she retained a kind of hope. Hope is an instinct only the reasoning human mind can kill. An animal never knows despair. Watching her wounded progress he had a sense that this had happened daily–perhaps for weeks; he was watching one of the well-rehearsed effects of the new day, like bird-song in happier regions. She dragged herself up to the veranda door and began to scratch with one paw, lying oddly spreadeagled. Her nose was down to a crack: she seemed to be breathing in the unused air of empty rooms; then she whined impatiently, and once her tail beat as if she heard something move inside. At last she began to howl.

The priest could bear it no longer. He knew now what it meant: he might as well let his eyes see. He came out into the yard and the animal turned awkwardly–the parody of a watchdog–and began to bark at him. It wasn't anybody she wanted: she wanted what she was used to: she wanted the old world back.

He looked in through the window–perhaps this was the child's room. Everything had been removed from it except the useless or the broken. There was a cardboard box full of torn paper and a small chair which had lost a leg. There was a large nail in the white-washed wall where a mirror perhaps had been hung or a picture. There was a broken shoe-horn.

The bitch was dragging itself along the veranda growling: instinct is like a sense of duty–one can confuse it with loyalty very easily. He avoided the animal simply by stepping out into the sun; it couldn't turn quickly enough to follow him. He pushed at the door and it opened–nobody had bothered to lock up. An ancient alligator's skin which had been badly cut and inefficiently dried hung on the wall. There was a snuffle behind him and he turned; the bitch had two paws over the threshold, but now that he was established in the house, she didn't mind him. He was there, in possession, the master, and there were all kinds of smells to occupy her mind. She pushed herself across the floor, making a wet noise.

The priest opened a door on the left–perhaps it had been the bedroom. In a corner lay a pile of old medicine bottles. There were medicines for headaches, stomach-aches, medicines to be taken after meals and before meals. Somebody must have been very ill to need so many? There was a hair-slide, broken, and a ball of hair-combings–very fair hair turning dusty white. He thought with relief: It was her mother, only her mother.

He tried another room which faced, through the mosquito wire, the slow and empty river. This had been the living-room, for they had left behind the table, a folding card-table of plywood bought for a few shillings which hadn't been worth taking with them wherever they'd gone. Had the mother been dying, he wondered? They had cleared the crop perhaps, and gone to the capital where there was a hospital. He left that room and entered another: this was the one he had seen from the outside–the child's. He turned over the contents of the waste-paper box with sad curiosity. He felt as if he were clearing up after a death, deciding what would be too painful to keep.

He read, 'The immediate cause of the American War of Independence was what is called the Boston Tea Party.' It seemed to be part of an essay written in large firm letters, carefully. 'But the real issue' (the word was spelt wrongly, crossed out and re-written) 'was whether it was right to tax people who were not represented in Parliament.' It must have been a rough copy–there were so many corrections. He picked out another scrap at random–it was about people called Whigs and Tories–the words were incomprehensible to him. Something like a duster flopped down off the roof into the yard: it was a vulture. He read on, 'If five men took three days to mow a meadow of four acres five roods, how much would two men mow in one day?' There was a neat line ruled under the question, and then the calculations began–a hopeless muddle of figures which didn't work out. There was a hint of heat and irritation in the crumpled paper tossed aside. He could see her very clearly, dispensing with that question decisively: the neat accurately moulded face with the two pinched pigtails. He remembered her readiness to swear eternal enmity against anyone who hurt him, and he remembered his own child enticing him by the rubbish-dump.

He shut the door carefully behind him as if he were preventing an escape. He could hear the bitch–somewhere–growling, and followed her into what had once been the kitchen. She lay in a deathly attitude over a bone with her old teeth bared. An Indian's face hung outside the mosquito wire like something hooked up to dry–dark, withered and unappetising. He had his eyes on the bone as if he coveted it. He looked up as the priest came across the kitchen and immediately was gone as if he had never been there, leaving the house just as abandoned. The priest, too, looked at the bone.

There was a lot of meat on it still. A small cloud of flies hung over it a few inches from the bitch's mouth, and the bitch kept her eye fixed, now that the Indian was gone, on the priest. They were all in competition. The priest advanced a step or two and stamped twice. 'Go,' he said, 'go,' flapping his hands, but the mongrel wouldn't move, flattened above the bone, with all the resistance left in the broken body concentrated in the yellow eyes, burring between her teeth. It was like hate on a deathbed. The priest came cautiously forward; he wasn't yet used to the idea that the animal couldn't spring. One associates a dog with action, but this creature, like any crippled human being, could only think. You could see the thoughts–hunger and hope and hatred–stuck on the eyeball.

The priest put out his hand towards the bone and the flies buzzed upwards. The animal became silent, watching. 'There, there,' the priest said cajolingly; he made little enticing movements in the air and the animal stared back. Then the priest turned and moved away as if he were abandoning the bone; he droned gently to himself a phrase from the Mass, elaborately paying no attention. Then he switched quickly round again. It hadn't worked. The bitch watched him, screwing round her neck to follow his ingenious movements.

For a moment he became furious–that a mongrel bitch with a broken back should steal the only food. He swore at it–popular expressions picked up beside bandstands: he would have been surprised in other circumstances that they came so readily to his tongue. Then suddenly he laughed: this was human dignity disputing with a bitch over a bone. When he laughed the animal's ears went back, twitching at the tips, apprehensive. But he felt no pity–her life had no importance beside that of a human being. He looked round for something to throw, but the room had been cleared of nearly everything except the bone. Perhaps, who knows? it might have been left deliberately for this mongrel; he could imagine the child remembering, before she left with the sick mother and the stupid father: he had the impression that it was always she who had to think. He could find for his purpose nothing better than a broken wire rack which had been used for vegetables.

He advanced again towards the bitch and struck her lightly on the head. She snapped at the wire with her old broken teeth and wouldn't move. He beat at her again more fiercely and she caught the wire—he had to rasp it away. He struck again and again before he realised that she couldn't, except with great exertion, move at all: she was unable to escape his blows or leave the bone. She just had to endure, her eyes yellow and scared and malevolent shining back at him between the blows.

So then he changed his method; he used the vegetable rack as a kind of muzzle, holding back the teeth with it, while he bent and captured the bone. One paw tugged at it and gave way; he lowered the wire and jumped back—the animal tried without success to follow him, then lapsed upon the floor. The priest had won: he had his bone. The bitch no longer tried to growl.

The priest tore off some raw meat with his teeth and began to chew: no food had ever tasted so good, and now that for the moment he was happy he began to feel a little pity. He thought: I will eat just so much and she can have the rest. He marked mentally a point upon the bone and tore off another piece. The nausea he had felt for hours now began to die away and leave an honest hunger; he ate on and the bitch watched him. Now that the fight was over she seemed to bear no malice; her tail began to beat the floor, hopefully, questioningly. The priest reached the point he had marked, but now it seemed to him that his previous hunger had been imaginary: this was hunger, what he felt now. A man's need was greater than a dog's: he would leave that knuckle of meat at the joint. But when the moment came he ate that too—after all, the dog had teeth: it would eat the bone itself. He dropped it and left the kitchen.

He made one more progress through the empty rooms. A broken shoe-horn: medicine bottles: an essay on the American War of Independence—there was nothing to tell him why they had gone away. He came out on to the veranda and saw through a gap in the planks that a book had fallen to the ground and lay between the rough pillars of brick which raised the house out of the track of ants. It was months since he had seen a book. It was almost like a promise, mildewing there under the piles, of better things to come—life going on in private houses with wireless sets and bookshelves and beds made ready for the night and a cloth laid for food. He knelt down on the ground and reached for it. He suddenly realised that when once the long struggle was over and he had crossed the mountains and the state line, life might, after all, be enjoyed again.

It was an English book, but from his years in an American seminary he retained enough English to read it, with a little difficulty. Even if he had been unable to understand a word, it would still have been a book. It was called *Jewels Five Words Long: A Treasury of English Verse*, and on the fly-leaf was pasted a printed certificate—Awarded to . . . and then the name of Coral Fellows filled up in ink . . . for proficiency in English Composition,

Third Grade. There was an obscure coat of arms, which seemed to include a griffin and oak leaf, a Latin motto, '*Virtus Laudata Crescit*', and a signature from a rubber stamp, Henry Beckley, B.A., Principal of Private Tutorials, Ltd.

The priest sat down on the veranda steps. There was silence everywhere—no life around the abandoned banana station except the vulture which hadn't yet given up hope. The Indian might never have existed at all. After a meal, the priest thought with sad amusement, a little reading, and opened the book at random. Coral—so that was the child's name. He thought of the shops in Vera Cruz full of it—the hard brittle jewellery which was thought for some reason so suitable for young girls after their first communion.

> '*I come*' he read, '*from haunts of coot and hern,*
> *I make a sudden sally,*
> *And sparkle out among the fern,*
> *To bicker down a valley.*'

It was a very obscure poem, full of words which were like Esperanto. He thought: So this is English poetry: how odd. The little poetry he knew dealt mainly with agony, remorse and hope. These verses ended on a philosophical note—'For men may come and men may go, But I go on for ever.' The triteness and untruth of 'for ever' shocked him a little: a poem like this ought not to be in a child's hands. The vulture came picking its way across the yard, a dusty and desolate figure; every now and then it lifted sluggishly from the earth and flapped down twenty yards on. The priest read:

> '"*Come back! Come back!*" *he cried in grief*
> *Across the stormy water:*
> "*And I'll forgive your Highland chief—*
> *My daughter, O my daughter.*"'

That sounded to him more impressive—though hardly perhaps, any more than the other, stuff for children. He felt in the foreign words the ring of genuine passion and repeated to himself on his hot and lonely perch the last line—'My daughter, O my daughter.' The words seemed to contain all that he felt himself of repentance, longing and unhappy love.

★　　★　　★

It was an odd thing that ever since that hot and crowded night in the cell he had passed into a region of abandonment—almost as if he had died there with the old man's head on his shoulder and now wandered in a kind of limbo, because he wasn't good or bad enough. . . . Life didn't exist any more: it wasn't merely a matter of the banana station. Now as the storm broke and he scurried for shelter he knew quite well what he would find—nothing.

The huts leapt up in the lightning and stood there shaking, then disappeared again in the rumbling darkness. The rain hadn't come yet: it was sweeping up from Campeche Bay in great sheets, covering the whole state in its methodical advance. Between the thunder-breaks he could imagine that he heard it—a gigantic rustle moving across towards the mountains which were now so close to him—a matter of twenty miles.

He reached the first hut; the door was open, and as the lightning quivered he saw as he expected nobody at all. Just a pile of maize and the indistinct grey movement of—perhaps—a rat. He dashed for the next hut, but it was the same as ever (the maize and nothing else), just as if all human life were receding before him, as if Somebody had determined that from now on he was to be left alone—altogether alone. As he stood there the rain reached the clearing; it came out of the forest like thick white smoke and moved on. It was as if an enemy were laying a gas-cloud across a whole territory, carefully, to see that nobody escaped. The rain spread and stayed just long enough, as though the enemy had his stopwatch out and knew to a second the limit of the lungs' endurance. The roof held the rain out for awhile and then let it through—the twigs bent under the weight of water and shot apart; it came through in half a dozen places, pouring down in black funnels; then the downpour stopped and the roof dripped and the rain moved on, with the lightning quivering on its flanks like a protective barrage. In a few minutes it would reach the mountains: a few more storms like this and they would be impassable.

He had been walking all day and he was very tired; he found a dry spot and sat down. When the lightning struck he could see the clearing. All around was the gentle noise of the dripping water. It was nearly like peace, but not quite. For peace you needed human company—his aloneness was like a threat of things to come. Suddenly he remembered—for no apparent reason—a day of rain at the American seminary, the glass windows of the library steamed over with the central heating, the tall shelves of sedate books, and a young man—a stranger from Tuscon—drawing his initials on the pane with his finger—that was peace. He looked at it from the outside; he couldn't believe that he would ever again get in. He had made his own world, and this was it—the empty broken huts, the storm going by, and fear again—fear because he was not alone after all.

Somebody was moving outside, cautiously. The footsteps would come a little way and then stop. He waited apathetically, and the roof dripped behind him. He thought of the mestizo padding around the city, seeking a really cast-iron occasion for his betrayal. A face peered round the hut door at him and quickly withdrew—an old woman's face, but you could never tell with Indians—she mightn't have been more than twenty. He got up and went outside. She scampered back from before him in her heavy sack-like skirt, her black plaits swinging heavily. Apparently his loneliness was only to be broken by these evasive faces, creatures who looked as if they had come out of the Stone Age, who withdrew again quickly.

He was stirred by a sort of sullen anger—this one should not withdraw. He pursued her across the clearing, splashing in the pools, but she had a start and no sense of shame and she got into the forest before him. It was useless looking for her there, and he returned towards the nearest hut. It wasn't the hut which he had been sheltering in before, but it was just as empty. What had happened to these people? He knew well enough that these more or less savage encampments were temporary only; the Indians would cultivate a small patch of ground and when they had exhausted the soil for the time being, they would simply move away. They knew nothing about the rotation of crops, but when they moved they would take their maize with them. This was more like flight, from force or disease. He had heard of such flights in the case of sickness, and the horrible thing, of course, was that they carried the sickness with them wherever they moved; sometimes they became panicky like flies against a pane, but discreetly, letting nobody know, muting their hubbub. He turned moodily again to stare out at the clearing, and there was the Indian woman creeping back towards the hut where he had sheltered. He called out to her sharply and again she fled, shambling, towards the forest. Her clumsy progress reminded him of a bird feigning a broken wing. . . . He made no movement to follow her, and before she reached the trees she stopped and watched him; he began to move slowly back towards the other hut. Once he turned: she was following him at a distance, keeping her eyes on him. Again he was reminded of something animal or bird-like, full of anxiety. He walked on, aiming directly at the hut. Far away beyond it the lightning stabbed down, but you could hardly hear the thunder; the sky was clearing overhead and the moon came out. Suddenly he heard an odd artificial cry, and turning he saw the woman making back towards the forest; then she stumbled, flung up her arms and fell to the ground, like the bird offering herself.

He felt quite certain now that something valuable was in the hut, perhaps hidden among the maize, and he paid her no attention, going in. Now that the lightning had moved on, he couldn't see—he felt across the floor until he reached the pile of maize. Outside the padding footsteps came nearer. He began to feel all over it—perhaps food was hidden there—and the dry crackle of the leaves was added to the drip of water and the cautious footsteps, like the faint noises of people busy about their private businesses. Then he put his hand on a face.

He couldn't be frightened any more by a thing like that—it was something human he had his fingers on. They moved down the body; it was a child's which lay completely quiet under his hand. In the doorway the moonlight showed the woman's face indistinctly. She was probably convulsed with anxiety, but you couldn't tell. He thought—I must get this into the open where I can see . . .

It was a male child—perhaps three years old: a withered bullet head with a mop of black hair: unconscious, but not dead: he could feel the faintest movement in the breast. He thought of disease again until he took out his hand and found that the child was wet with blood, not sweat. Horror and disgust touched him—violence everywhere: was there no end to violence? He said to the woman sharply, 'What happened?' It was as if man in all this state had been left to man.

The woman knelt two or three feet away, watching his hands. She knew a little Spanish, because she replied, 'Americano.' The child wore a kind of brown one-piece smock. He lifted it up to the neck: the child had been shot in three places. Life was going out of him all the time: there was nothing—really—to be done, but one had to try. . . . He said 'Water' to the woman, 'Water,' but she didn't seem to understand, squatting there, watching him. It was a mistake one easily made, to think that just because the eyes expressed nothing there was no grief. When he touched the child he could see her move on her haunches—she was ready to attack him with her teeth if the child so much as moaned.

He began to speak slowly and gently (he couldn't tell how much she understood): 'We must have water. To wash him. You needn't be afraid of me. I will do him no harm.' He took off his shirt and began to tear it into strips—it was hopelessly insanitary, but what else was there to do? except pray, of course, but one didn't pray for life, this life. He repeated again, 'Water.' The woman seemed to understand—she gazed hopelessly round at where the rain stood in pools—that was all there was. Well, he thought, the earth's as clean as any vessel would have been. He soaked a piece of his shirt and leant over the child; he could hear the woman slide closer along the ground—a menacing approach. He tried to reassure her again, 'You needn't be afraid of me. I am a priest.'

The word 'priest' she understood; she leant forward and grabbed at the hand which held the wet scrap of shirt and kissed it. At that moment, while her lips were on his hand, the child's face wrinkled, the eyes opened and glared at them, the tiny body shook with a kind of fury of pain; they watched the eyeballs roll up and suddenly become fixed, like marbles in a solitaire-board, yellow and ugly with death. The woman let go his hand and scrambled to a pool of water, cupping her fingers for it. The priest said, 'We don't need that any more,' standing up with his hands full of wet shirt. The woman opened her fingers and let the water fall. She said 'Father' imploringly, and he wearily went down on his knees and began to pray.

He could feel no meaning any longer in prayers like these. The Host was different: to lay that between a dying man's lips was to lay God. That was a fact—something you could touch, but this was no more than a pious aspiration. Why should anyone listen to *his* prayers? Sin was a constriction which prevented their escape; he could feel his prayers weigh him down like undigested food.

When he had finished he lifted up the body and carried it back into the hut; it seemed a waste of time to have taken it out, like a chair you carry out into the garden and back again because the grass is wet. The woman followed him meekly; she didn't seem to want to touch the body, just watched him put it back in the dark upon the maize. He sat down on the ground and said slowly, 'It will have to be buried.'

She understood that, nodding.

He said, 'Where is your husband? Will he help you?'

She began to talk rapidly. It might have been Camacho she was speaking: he couldn't understand more than an occasional Spanish word here and there. The word 'Americano' occurred again, and he remembered the wanted man whose portrait had shared the wall with his. He asked her, 'Did *he* do this?' She shook her head. What had happened? he wondered. Had the man taken shelter here and had the soldiers fired into the huts? It was not unlikely. He suddenly had his attention caught. She had said the name of the banana station, but there had been no dying person there: no sign of violence, unless silence and desertion were signs. He had assumed the mother had been taken ill, but it might be something worse—and he imagined that stupid Captain Fellows taking down his gun, presenting himself clumsily armed to a man whose chief talent it was to draw quickly or to shoot directly from the pocket. That poor child . . . what responsibilities she had perhaps been forced to undertake.

He shook the thought away and said, 'Have you a spade?' She didn't understand that, and he had to go through the motions of digging. Another roll of thunder came between them. A second storm was coming up, as if the enemy had discovered that the first barrage after all had left a few survivors–this would flatten them. Again he could hear the enormous breathing of the rain miles away. He realised the woman had spoken the one word 'church'. Her Spanish consisted of isolated words. He wondered what she meant by that. Then the rain reached them. It came down like a wall between him and escape, fell altogether in a heap and built itself up around them. All the light went out except when the lightning flashed.

The roof couldn't keep out *this* rain. It came dripping through everywhere: the dry maize leaves where the dead child lay crackled like burning wood. He shivered with cold; he was probably on the edge of fever–he must get away before he was incapable of moving at all. The woman (he couldn't see her now) said 'Iglesia' again imploringly. It occurred to him that she wanted the child buried near a church or perhaps only taken to an altar, so that he might be touched by the feet of a Christ. It was a fantastic notion.

He took advantage of a long quivering stroke of blue light to describe with his hands his sense of the impossibility. 'The soldiers,' he said, and she replied immediately, 'Americano.' That word always came up, like one with many meanings which depends on the accent whether it is to be taken as an explanation, a warning or a threat. Perhaps she meant that the soldiers were all occupied in the chase, but even so, this rain was ruining everything. It was still twenty miles to the border, and the mountain paths after the storm were probably impassable–and a church–he hadn't the faintest idea of where there would be a church. He hadn't so much as seen such a thing for years now; it was difficult to believe that they still existed only a few days' journey off. When the lightning went on again he saw the woman watching him with stony patience.

★   ★   ★

For the last thirty hours they had only had sugar to eat–large brown lumps of it the size of a baby's skull; they had seen no one, and they had exchanged no words at all. What was the use when almost the only words they had in common were 'Iglesia' and 'Americano'? The woman followed at his heels with the dead child strapped on her back. She never seemed to tire. A day and a night brought them out of the marshes to the foot-hills; they slept fifty feet up above the slow green river, under a projecting piece of rock where the soil was dry–everywhere else was deep mud. The woman sat with her knees drawn up, and her head down. She showed no emotion, but she put the child's body behind her as if it needed protection from marauders like other possessions. They had travelled by the sun until the black wooded bar of mountain told them where to go. They might have been the only survivors of a world which was dying out; they carried the visible marks of the dying with them.

Sometimes he wondered whether he was safe, but when there are no visible boundaries between one state and another—no passport examination or customs house—danger just seems to go on, travelling with you, lifting its heavy feet in the same way as you do. There seemed to be so little progress: the path would rise steeply, perhaps five hundred feet, and fall again, clogged with mud. Once it took an enormous hairpin bend, so that after three hours they had returned to a point opposite their starting-place, less than a hundred yards away.

At sunset on the second day they came out on to a wide plateau covered with short grass. A grove of crosses stood up blackly against the sky, leaning at different angles—some as high as twenty feet, some not much more than eight. They were like trees that had been left to seed. The priest stopped and stared at them. They were the first Christian symbols he had seen for more than five years publicly exposed—if you could call this empty plateau in the mountains a public place. No priest could have been concerned in the strange rough group; it was the work of Indians and had nothing in common with the tidy vestments of the Mass and the elaborately worked out symbols of the liturgy. It was like a short cut to the dark and magical heart of the faith—to the night when the graves opened and the dead walked. There was a movement behind him and he turned.

The woman had gone down on her knees and was shuffling slowly across the cruel ground towards the group of crosses; the dead baby rocked on her back. When she reached the tallest cross she unhooked the child and held the face against the wood and afterwards the loins; then she crossed herself, not as ordinary Catholics do, but in a curious and complicated pattern which included the nose and ears. Did she expect a miracle? and if she did, why should it not be granted her, the priest wondered? Faith, one was told, could move mountains, and here was faith—faith in the spittle that healed the blind man and the voice that raised the dead. The evening star was out: it hung low down over the edge of the plateau—it looked as if it was within reach—and a small hot wind stirred. The priest found himself watching the child for some movement. When none came, it was as if God had missed an opportunity. The woman sat down, and taking a lump of sugar from her bundle began to eat, and the child lay quietly at the foot of the cross. Why, after all, should we expect God to punish the innocent with more life?

'Vamos,' the priest said, but the woman scraped the sugar with her sharp front teeth, paying no attention. He looked up at the sky and saw the evening star blotted out by black clouds. 'Vamos.' There was no shelter anywhere on this plateau.

The woman never stirred; the broken snub-nosed face between the black plaits was completely passive: it was as if she had fulfilled her duty and could now take up her everlasting rest. The priest suddenly shivered; the ache which had pressed like a stiff hat-rim across his forehead all day dug deeper in. He thought: I have to get to shelter—a man's first duty is to himself—even the Church taught that, in a way. The whole sky was blackening. The crosses stuck up like dry and ugly cacti. He made off to the edge of the plateau. Once, before the path led down, he looked back—the woman was still biting at the lump of sugar, and he remembered that it was all the food they had.

The way was very steep—so steep that he had to turn and go down backwards; on either side trees grew perpendicularly out of the grey rock, and five hundred feet below the path climbed up again. He began to sweat and he had an appalling thirst, and when the rain came it was at first a kind of relief. He stayed where he was, hunched back against a boulder. There was no shelter before he reached the bottom of the barranca, and it hardly seemed worth while to make that effort. He was shivering now more or less continuously, and the ache seemed no longer inside his head—it was something outside, almost anything, a noise, a thought, a smell. The senses were jumbled up together. At one moment the ache was like a tiresome voice explaining to him that he had taken the wrong path. He remembered a map he had once seen of the two adjoining states. The state from which he was escaping was peppered with villages—in the hot marshy land people bred as readily as mosquitoes, but in the next state—in the north-west corner—there was hardly anything but blank white paper. You're on that blank paper now, the ache told him. But there's a path, he argued wearily. Oh, a path, the ache said, a path may take you fifty miles before it reaches anywhere at all: you know you won't last that distance. There's just white paper all around.

At another time the ache was a face. He became convinced that the American was watching him—he had a skin all over spots like a newspaper photograph. Apparently he had followed them because he wanted to kill the mother as well as the child: he was sentimental in that respect. It was necessary to do something. The rain was like a curtain behind which almost anything might happen. He thought: I shouldn't have left her alone like that. God forgive me. I have no sense of responsibility: what can you expect of a whisky priest? and he struggled to his feet and began to climb back towards the plateau. He was tormented by ideas; it wasn't only the woman: he was responsible for the American as well: the two faces—his own and the gunman's—were hanging together on the police station wall, as if they were brothers in a family portrait gallery. You didn't put temptation in a brother's way.

Shivering and sweating and soaked with rain he came up over the edge of the plateau. There was nobody there—a dead child was not someone, just a useless object abandoned at the foot of one of the crosses. The mother had gone home. She had done what she wanted to do. The surprise lifted him, as it were, out of his fever before it dropped him back again. A small lump of sugar—all that was left—lay by the child's mouth—in case a miracle should happen or for the spirit to eat? The priest bent down with an obscure sense of shame and took it: the dead child couldn't growl back at him like a broken dog: but who was he to disbelieve in miracles? He hesitated, while the rain poured down; then he put the sugar in his mouth. If God chose to give back life, couldn't He give food as well?

Immediately he began to eat, the fever returned: the sugar stuck in his throat: he felt an appalling thirst. Crouching down he tried to lick some water from the uneven ground; he even sucked at his soaked trousers. The child lay under the streaming rain like a dark heap of cattle dung. The priest moved away again, back to the edge of the plateau and down the barranca side; it was loneliness he felt now—even the face had gone, he was moving alone across the blank white sheet, going deeper every moment into the abandoned land.

Somewhere, in some direction, there were towns, of course: go far enough and you reached the coast, the Pacific, the railway track to Guatemala; there were roads there and motor-cars. He hadn't seen a railway train for ten years. He could imagine the black line following the coast along the map, and he could see the fifty, hundred miles of unknown country. That was where he was: he had escaped too completely from men. Nature would kill him now.

All the same, he went on; there was no point in going back towards the deserted village, the banana station with its dying mongrel and its shoe-horn. There was nothing you could do except put one foot forward and then the other, scrambling down and then scrambling up; from the top of the barranca, when the rain passed on, there was nothing to see except a huge crumpled land, forest and mountain, with the grey wet veil moving over. He looked once and never looked again. It was too like watching despair.

It must have been hours later that he ceased to climb. It was evening and forest; monkeys crashed invisibly among the trees with an effect of clumsiness and recklessness, and what were probably snakes hissed away like match-flames through the grass. He wasn't afraid of them. They were a form of life, and he could feel life retreating from him all the time. It wasn't only people who were going, even the animals and the reptiles moved away; presently he would be left alone with nothing but his own breath. He began to recite to himself, 'O God, I have loved the beauty of Thy house,' and the smell of soaked and rotting leaves and the hot night and the darkness made him believe that he was in a mine shaft, going down into the earth to bury himself. Presently he would find his grave.

When a man came towards him carrying a gun he did nothing at all. The man approached cautiously; you didn't expect to find another person underground. He said, 'Who are you?' with his gun ready.

The priest gave his name to a stranger for the first time in ten years because he was tired and there seemed no object in going on living.

'A priest?' the man asked, with astonishment. 'Where have you come from?'

The fever lifted again: a little reality seeped back. He said, 'It is all right. I will not bring you any trouble. I am going on.' He screwed up all his remaining energy and walked on. A puzzled face penetrated his fever and receded: there were going to be no more hostages, he assured himself aloud. Footsteps followed him, he was like a dangerous man you see safely off an estate before you go home. He repeated aloud, 'It is all right. I am not staying here. I want nothing.'

'Father . . .' the voice said, humbly and anxiously.

'I will go right away.' He tried to run and came suddenly out of the forest on to a long slope of grass. There were lights and huts below, and up there at the edge of the forest a big whitewashed building–a barracks? were there soldiers? He said, 'If I have been seen I will give myself up. I assure you no one shall get into trouble because of me.'

'Father . . .' He was racked with his headache, he stumbled and put his hand against the wall for support. He felt immeasurably tired. He asked, 'The barracks?'

'Father,' the voice said, puzzled and worried, 'it is our church.'

'A church?' The priest ran his hands incredulously over the wall like a blind man trying to recognise a particular house, but he was too tired to feel anything at all. He heard the man with the gun babbling out of sight, 'Such an honour, father. The bell must be rung . . .' and he sat down suddenly on the rain-drenched grass, and leaning his head against the white wall, he fell asleep, with home behind his shoulder-blades.

His dream was full of a jangle of cheerful noise.

PART III

I

The middle-aged woman sat on the veranda darning socks; she wore pince-nez and she had kicked off her shoes for further comfort. Mr Lehr, her brother, read a New York magazine—it was three weeks old, but that didn't really matter: the whole scene was like peace.

'Just help yourself to water,' Miss Lehr said, 'when you want it.'

A huge earthenware jar stood in a cool corner with a ladle and a tumbler. 'Don't you have to boil the water?' the priest asked.

'Oh no, *our* water's fresh and clean,' Miss Lehr said primly, as if she couldn't answer for anybody else's.

'Best water in the state,' her brother said. The shiny magazine leaves crackled as they turned, covered with photographs of big clean-shaven mastiff jowls—Senators and Congressmen. Pasture stretched away beyond the garden fence, undulating gently towards the next mountain range, and a tulipan tree blossomed and faded daily at the gate.

'You certainly are looking better, father,' Miss Lehr said. They both spoke rather guttural English with slight American accents—Mr Lehr had left Germany when he was a boy to escape military service: he had a shrewd, lined and idealistic face. You needed to be shrewd in this country if you were going to retain any ideals at all and he was cunning in the defence of the good life.

'Oh,' Mr Lehr said, 'he only needed to rest up a few days.' He was quite incurious about this man whom his foreman had brought in on a mule in a state of collapse three days before. All he knew the priest had told him. That was another thing this country taught you—never to ask questions or to look ahead.

'Soon I can go on,' the priest said.

'You don't have to hurry,' said Miss Lehr, turning over her brother's sock, looking for holes.

'It's so quiet here.'

'Oh,' Mr Lehr said, 'we've had our troubles.' He turned a page and said, 'That Senator Hiram Long—they ought to control him. It doesn't do any good insulting other countries.'

'Haven't they tried to take your land?'

The idealistic face turned his way: it wore a look of innocent craft. 'Oh, I gave them as much as they asked for—five hundred acres of barren land. I saved a lot on taxes. I never could get anything to grow there.' He nodded towards the veranda posts. 'That was the last *real* trouble. See the bullet-holes. Villa's men.'

The priest got up again and drank more water. He wasn't very thirsty; he was satisfying a sense of luxury. He asked, 'How long will it take me to get to Las Casas?'

'You could do it in four days,' Mr Lehr said.

'Not in *his* condition,' Miss Lehr said. 'Six.'

'It will seem so strange,' the priest said. 'A city with churches, a university . . .'

'Of course,' Mr Lehr said, 'my sister and I are Lutherans. We don't hold with your Church, father. Too much luxury, it seems to me, while the people starve.'

Miss Lehr said, 'Now, dear, it isn't the father's fault.'

'Luxury?' the priest asked. He stood by the earthenware jar, glass in hand, trying to collect his thoughts, staring out over the long peaceful grassy slopes. 'You mean . . .' Perhaps Mr Lehr was right; he had lived very easily once and here he was, already settling down to idleness again.

'All the gold leaf in the churches.'

'It's often just paint, you know,' the priest murmured conciliatingly. He thought: yes, three days and I've done nothing, nothing, and he looked down at his feet elegantly shod in a pair of Mr Lehr's shoes, his legs in Mr Lehr's spare trousers. Mr Lehr said, 'He won't mind my speaking my mind. We're all Christians here.'

'Of course. I like to hear . . .'

'It seems to me you people make a lot of fuss about inessentials.'

'Yes? You mean . . .'

'Fasting . . . fish on Friday . . .'

Yes, he remembered like something in his childhood that there had been a time when he had observed these rules. He said, 'After all, Mr Lehr, you're a German. A great military nation.'

'I was never a soldier. I disapprove . . .'

'Yes, of course, but still you understand—discipline is necessary. Drills may be no good in battle, but they form the character. Otherwise you get—well, people like me.' He looked down with sudden hatred at the shoes—they were like the badge of a deserter. 'People like me,' he repeated with fury.

There was a good deal of embarrassment; Miss Lehr began to say something, 'Why, father . . .', but Mr Lehr forestalled her, laying down the magazine and its load of well-shaved politicians. He said in his German-American voice with its guttural precision, 'Well, I guess it's time for a bath now. Will you be coming, father?' and the priest obediently followed him into their common bedroom. He took off Mr Lehr's clothes and put on Mr Lehr's mackintosh and followed Mr Lehr barefoot across the veranda and the field beyond. The day before he had asked apprehensively, 'Are there no snakes?' and Mr Lehr had grunted contemptuously that if there were any snakes they'd pretty soon get out of the way. Mr Lehr and his sister had combined to drive out savagery by simply ignoring anything that conflicted with an ordinary German-American homestead. It was, in its way, an admirable mode of life.

At the bottom of the field there was a little shallow stream running over brown pebbles. Mr Lehr took off his dressing-gown and lay down flat on his back. There was something upright and idealistic even in the thin elderly legs with their scrawny muscles. Tiny fishes played over his chest and made little tugs at his nipples undisturbed. This was the skeleton of the youth who had disapproved of militarism to the point of flight. Presently he sat up and began carefully to soap his lean thighs. The priest afterwards took the soap and followed suit. He felt it was expected of him, though he couldn't help thinking it was a waste of time. Sweat cleaned you as effectively as water. But this was the race which had invented the proverb that cleanliness was next to godliness—cleanliness, not purity.

All the same, one did feel an enormous luxury lying there in the little cold stream while the sun sank . . . He thought of the prison cell with the old man and the pious woman, the half-caste lying across the hut door, the dead child and the abandoned station. He thought with shame of his daughter left to her knowledge and her ignorance by the rubbish-dump. He had no right to such luxury.

Mr Lehr said, 'Would you mind—the soap?'

He had heaved over on his face, and now he set to work on his back.

The priest said, 'I think perhaps I should tell you—to-morrow I am saying Mass in the village. Would you prefer me to leave your house? I do not wish to make trouble for you.'

Mr Lehr splashed seriously, cleaning himself. He said, 'Oh, they won't bother me. But you had better be careful. You know, of course, that it's against the law.'

'Yes,' the priest said. 'I know that.'

'A priest I knew was fined four hundred pesos. He couldn't pay and they sent him to prison for a week. What are you smiling at?'

'Only because it seems so—peaceful—here. Prison for a week!'

'Well, I've always heard you people get your own back when it comes to collections. Would you like the soap?'

'No, thank you. I have finished.'

'We'd better be drying ourselves then. Miss Lehr likes to have her bath before sunset.'

As they came back to the bungalow in single file they met Miss Lehr, very bulky under her dressing-gown. She asked mechanically, like a clock with a very gentle chime, 'Is the water nice to-day?' and her brother answered, as he must have answered a thousand times, 'Pleasantly cool, dear,' and she slopped down across the grass in bedroom slippers, stooping slightly with short sight.

'If you wouldn't mind,' Mr Lehr said, shutting the bedroom door, 'staying in here till Miss Lehr comes back. One can see the stream—you understand—from the front of the house.' He began to dress, tall and bony and a little stiff. Two brass bedsteads, a single chair and a wardrobe, the room was monastic, except that there was no cross—no 'inessentials' as Mr Lehr would have put it. But there was a Bible. It lay on the floor beside one of the beds in a black oilskin cover. When the priest had finished dressing he opened it.

On the fly-leaf there was a label which stated that the book was furnished by the Gideons. It went on: 'A Bible in every Hotel Guest Room. Winning Commercial Men for Christ. Good news.' There was then a list of texts. The priest read with some astonishment:

If you are in trouble read	Psalm 34.
If trade is poor	Psalm 37.
If very prosperous	I Corinthians, x, 2.
If overcome and back-sliding	James I. Hosea xiv, 4–9.
If tired of sin	Psalm 51. Luke xviii, 9–14.
If you desire peace, power and plenty	John 14.
If you are lonesome and discouraged	Psalms 23 and 27.
If you are losing confidence in men	I Corinthians, xiii.
If you desire peaceful slumbers	Psalm 121.

He couldn't help wondering how it had got here—with its ugly type and its over-simple explanations—into a hacienda in Southern Mexico. Mr Lehr turned away from his mirror with a big coarse hairbrush in his hand and explained carefully, 'My sister ran a hotel once. For drummers. She sold it to join me when my wife died, and she brought one of those from the hotel. You wouldn't understand that, father. You don't like people to read the Bible.' He was on the defensive all the time about his faith, as if he were perpetually conscious of some friction, like that of an ill-fitting shoe.

The priest asked, 'Is your wife buried here?'

'In the paddock,' Mr Lehr said bluntly. He stood listening, brush in hand, to the gentle footsteps outside. 'That's Miss Lehr,' he said, 'come up from her bath. We can go out now.'

★   ★   ★

The priest got off Mr Lehr's old horse when he reached the church and threw the rein over a bush. This was his first visit to the village since the night he collapsed beside the wall. The village ran down below him in the dusk: tin-roofed bungalows and mud huts faced each other over a single wide grass-grown street. A few lamps had been lit and fire was being carried round among the poorest huts. He walked slowly, conscious of peace and safety. The first man he saw took off his hat and knelt and kissed the priest's hand.

'What is your name?' the priest asked.

'Pedro, father.'

'Good night, Pedro.'

'Is there to be Mass in the morning, father?'

'Yes. There is to be Mass.'

He passed the rural school. The schoolmaster sat on the step: a plump young man with dark brown eyes and horn-rimmed glasses. When he saw the priest coming he looked ostentatiously away. He was the law-abiding element: he wouldn't recognise criminals. He began to talk pedantically and priggishly to someone behind him—something about the infant class. A woman kissed the priest's hand; it was odd to be wanted again, not to feel himself the carrier of death. She asked, 'Father, will you hear our confessions?'

He said, 'Yes. Yes. In Señor Lehr's barn. Before the Mass. I will be there at five. As soon as it is light.'

'There are so many of us, father . . .'

'Well to-night too then . . . At eight.'

'And, father, there are many children to be baptised. There has not been a priest for three years.'

'I am going to be here for two more days.'

'What will you charge, father?'

'Well—two pesos is the usual charge.' He thought: I must hire two mules and a guide. It will cost me fifty pesos to reach Las Casas. Five pesos for the Mass—that left forty-five.

'We are very poor here, father,' she haggled gently. 'I have four children myself. Eight pesos is a lot of money.'

'Four children are a lot of children—if the priest was here only three years ago.'

He could hear authority, the old parish intonation coming back into his voice, as if the last years had been a dream and he had never really been away from the Guilds, the Children of Mary, and the daily Mass. He asked sharply, 'How many children are there here—unbaptised?'

'Perhaps a hundred, father.'

He made calculations: there was no need to arrive in Las Casas then as a beggar; he could buy a decent suit of clothes, find a respectable lodging, settle down . . . He said, 'You must pay one peso fifty a head.'

'One peso, father. We are very poor.'

'One peso fifty.' A voice from years back said firmly into his ear: they don't value what they don't pay for. It was the old priest he had succeeded at Concepción who had explained to him: 'They will always tell you they are poor, starving, but they will always have a little store of money buried somewhere, in a pot.' The priest said, 'You must bring the money—and the children—to Señor Lehr's barn to-morrow at two in the afternoon.'

She said, 'Yes, father.' She seemed quite satisfied; she had brought him down by fifty centavos a head. The priest walked on. Say a hundred children, he was thinking, that means a hundred and sixty pesos with tomorrow's Mass. Perhaps I can get the mules and the guide for forty pesos. Señor Lehr will give me food for three days. I shall have a hundred and twenty pesos left. After all these years, it was like wealth. He felt respect all the way up the street: men took off their hats as he passed: it was as if he had got back to the days before the persecution. He could feel the old life hardening round him like a habit, a stony cast which held his head high and dictated the way he walked, and even formed his words. A voice from the cantina said, 'Father.'

The man was very fat, with three commercial chins; he wore a waistcoat in spite of the great heat, and a watch-chain. 'Yes?' the priest said. Behind the man's head stood bottles of mineral water, beer, spirits . . . The priest came in out of the dusty street to the heat of the lamp. He asked, 'What is it?' with his new-old manner of authority and impatience.

'I thought, father, you might be in need of a little sacramental wine.'

'Perhaps . . . but you will have to give me credit.'

'A priest's credit, father, is always good enough for me. I am a religious man myself. This is a religious place. No doubt you will be holding a baptism.' He leant avidly forward with a respectful and impertinent manner, as if they were two people with the same ideas, educated men.

'Perhaps . . .'

The man smiled understandingly. Between people like ourselves, he seemed to indicate, there is no need of anything explicit: we understand each other's thoughts. He said, 'In the old days, when the church was open, I was treasurer to the Guild of the Blessed Sacrament. Oh, I am a good Catholic, father. The people, of course, are very ignorant.' He asked, 'Would you perhaps honour me by taking a glass of brandy?' He was in his way quite sincere.

The priest said doubtfully, 'It is kind . . .' The two glasses were already filled. He remembered the last drink he had had, sitting on the bed in the dark, listening to the Chief of Police, and seeing, as the light went on, the last wine drain away . . . The memory was like a hand, pulling away the cast, exposing him. The smell of brandy dried his mouth. He thought: what a play-actor I am. I have no business here, among good people. He turned the glass in his hand, and all the other glasses turned too: he remembered the dentist talking of his children and Maria unearthing the bottle of spirits she had kept for him—the whisky priest.

He took a reluctant drink. 'It's good brandy, father,' the man said.

'Yes. Good brandy.'

'I could let you have a dozen bottles for sixty pesos.'

'Where would I find sixty pesos?' He thought that in some ways it was better over there, acrosss the border. Fear and death were not the worst things. It was sometimes a mistake for life to go on.

'I wouldn't make a profit out of you, father. Fifty pesos.'

'Fifty, sixty. It's all the same to me.'

'Go on. Have another glass, father. It's good brandy.' The man leant engagingly forward across the counter and said, 'Why not half a dozen, father, for twenty-four pesos?' He said slyly, 'After all, father—there are the baptisms.'

It was appalling how easily one forgot and went back; he could still hear his own voice speaking in the street with the Concepción accent—unchanged by mortal sin and unrepentance and desertion. The brandy was musty on the tongue with his own corruption. God might forgive cowardice and passion, but was it possible to forgive the habit of piety? He remembered the woman in the prison and how impossible it had been to shake her complacency. It seemed to him that he was another of the same kind. He drank the brandy down like damnation: men like the half-caste could be saved, salvation could strike like lightning at the evil heart, but the habit of piety excluded everything but the evening prayer and the Guild meeting and the feel of humble lips on your gloved hand.

'Las Casas is a fine town, father. They say you can hear Mass every day.'

This was another pious person. There were a lot of them about in the world. He was pouring a little more brandy, but going carefully—not too much. He said, 'When you get there, father, look up a compadre of mine in Guadalupe Street. He has the cantina nearest the church—a good man. Treasurer of the Guild of the Blessed Sacrament—just like I was in this place in the good days. He'll see you get what you want cheap. Now, what about some bottles for the journey?'

The priest drank. There was no point in not drinking. He had the habit now—like piety and the parish voice. He said, 'Three bottles. For eleven pesos. Keep them for me here.' He finished what was left and went back into the street; the lamps were lit in windows and the wide street stretched like a prairie in between. He stumbled in a hole and felt a hand upon his sleeve. 'Ah, Pedro. That was the name wasn't it? Thank you, Pedro.'

'At your service, father.'

The church stood in the darkness like a block of ice: it was melting away in the heat. The roof had fallen in at one place, a coign above the doorway had crumbled. The priest took a quick sideways look at Pedro, holding his breath in case it smelt of brandy, but he could see only the outlines of the face. He said—with a feeling of cunning as though he were cheating a greedy prompter inside his own heart—'Tell the people, Pedro, that I only want one peso for the baptisms . . .' There would still be enough for the brandy then, even if he arrived at Las Casas like a beggar. There was silence for as long as two seconds and then the wily village voice began to answer him, 'We are poor, father. One peso is a lot of money. I—for example—I have three children. Say seventy-five centavos, father.'

*   *   *

Miss Lehr stretched out her feet in their easy slippers and the beetles came up over the veranda from the dark outside. She said, 'In Pittsburg once . . .' Her brother was asleep with an ancient newspaper across his knee: the mail had come in. The priest gave a little sympathetic giggle as in the old days; it was a try-out which didn't come off. Miss Lehr stopped and sniffed. 'Funny. I thought I smelt—spirits.'

The priest held his breath, leaning back in the rocking-chair. He thought, how quiet it is, how safe. He remembered townspeople who couldn't sleep in country places because of the silence: silence can be like noise, dinning against the ear-drums.

'What was I saying, father?'

'In Pittsburg once . . .'

'Of course. In Pittsburg . . . I was waiting for the train. You see I had nothing to read. Books are so expensive. So I thought I'd buy a paper—any paper, the news is just the same. But when I opened it—it was called something like *Police News*. I never knew such dreadful things were printed. Of course, I didn't read more than a few lines. I think it was the most dreadful thing that's ever happened to me. It . . . well, it opened my eyes.'

'Yes.'

'I've never told Mr Lehr. He wouldn't think the same of me, I do believe, if he knew.'

'But there was nothing wrong . . .'

'It's knowing, isn't it . . . ?'

Somewhere a long way off a bird of some kind called; the lamp on the table began to smoke, and Miss Lehr leant over and turned down the wick: it was as if the only light for miles around had been lowered. The brandy returned on his palate like the smell of ether that reminds a man of a recent operation before he's used to life: it tied him to another state of being. He didn't yet belong to this deep tranquillity. He told himself: In time it will be all right, I shall pull up, I only ordered three bottles this time. They will be the last I'll ever drink, I won't need drink there–he knew he lied. Mr Lehr woke suddenly and said, 'As I was saying . . .'

'You were saying nothing, dear. You were asleep.'

'Oh no, we were talking about that scoundrel Hoover.'

'I don't think so, dear. Not for a long while.'

'Well,' Mr Lehr said, 'it's been a long day. The father will be tired too . . . after all that confessing,' he added with slight distaste.

There had been a continuous stream of penitents from eight to ten–two hours of the worst evil a small place like this could produce after three years. It hadn't amounted to very much–a city would have made a better show–or would it? There isn't much a man can do. Drunkenness, adultery, uncleanness: he sat there tasting the brandy all the while, sitting on a rocking-chair in a horse-box, not looking at the face of the one who knelt at his side. The others had waited, kneeling in an empty stall–Mr Lehr's stable had been depopulated these last few years. He had only one old horse left, which blew windily in the dark as the sins came whimpering out.

'How many times?'

'Twelve, father. Perhaps more,' and the horse blew.

It is astonishing the sense of innocence that goes with sin–only the hard and careful man and the saint are free of it. These people went out of the stable clean; he was the only one left who hadn't repented, confessed, and been absolved. He wanted to say to this man, 'Love is not wrong, but love should be happy and open–it is only wrong when it is secret, unhappy . . . It can be more unhappy than anything but the loss of God. It *is* the loss of God. You don't need a penance, my child, you have suffered quite enough,' and to this other, 'Lust is not the worst thing. It is because any day, any time, lust may turn into love that we have to avoid it. And when we love our sin then we are damned indeed.' But the habit of the confessional reasserted itself: it was as if he were back in the little stuffy wooden boxlike coffin in which men bury their uncleanness with their priest. He said, 'Mortal sin . . . danger . . . self-control,' as if those words meant anything at all. He said, 'Say three Our Fathers and three Hail Marys.'

He whispered wearily, 'Drink is only the beginning . . .' He found he had no lesson he could draw against even that common vice unless it was himself smelling of brandy in the stable. He gave out the penance, quickly, harshly, mechanically. The man would go away, saying, 'A bad priest,' feeling no encouragement, no interest . . .

He said, 'Those laws were made for man. The Church doesn't expect . . .

if you can't fast, you must eat, that's all.' The old woman prattled on and on, while the penitents stirred restlessly in the next stall and the horse whinnied, prattled of abstinence days broken, of evening prayers curtailed. Suddenly, without warning, with an odd sense of homesickness, he thought of the hostages in the prison yard, waiting at the water-tap, not looking at him—the suffering and the endurance which went on everywhere the other side of the mountains. He interrupted the woman savagely, 'Why don't you confess properly to me? I'm not interested in your fish supply or in how sleepy you are at night . . . remember your real sins.'

'But I'm a good woman, father,' she squeaked at him with astonishment.

'Then what are you doing here, keeping away the bad people?' He said, 'Have you any love for anyone but yourself?'

'I love God, father,' she said haughtily. He took a quick look at her in the light of the candle burning on the floor—the hard old raisin eyes under the black shawl—another of the pious—like himself.

'How do you know? Loving God isn't any different from loving a man—or a child. It's wanting to be with Him, to be near Him.' He made a hopeless gesture with his hands. 'It's wanting to protect Him from yourself.'

When the last penitent had gone away he walked back across the yard to the bungalow; he could see the lamp burning, and Miss Lehr knitting, and he could smell the grass in the paddock, wet with the first rains. It ought to be possible for a man to be happy here, if he were not so tied to fear and suffering—unhappiness too can become a habit like piety. Perhaps it was his duty to break it, his duty to discover peace. He felt an immense envy of all those people who had confessed to him and been absolved. In six days, he told himself, in Las Casas, I too . . . But he couldn't believe that anyone anywhere would rid him of his heavy heart. Even when he drank he felt bound to his sin by love. It was easier to get rid of hate.

Miss Lehr said, 'Sit down, father. You must be tired. I've never held, of course, with confession. Nor has Mr Lehr.'

'No?'

'I don't know how you can stand sitting there, listening to all the horrible things . . . I remember in Pittsburgh once . . .'

*   *   *

The two mules had been brought in overnight, so that he could start early immediately after Mass—the second that he had said in Mr Lehr's barn. His guide was sleeping somewhere, probably with the mules, a thin nervous creature, who had never been to Las Casas; he simply knew the route by hearsay. Miss Lehr had insisted the night before that she must call him, although he woke of his own accord before it was light. He lay in bed and heard the alarm go off in another room—dinning like a telephone—and presently he heard the slop, slop of Miss Lehr's bedroom-slippers in the passage outside and a knock-knock on the door. Mr Lehr slept on undisturbed upon his back with the thin rectitude of a bishop upon a tomb.

The priest had lain down in his clothes and he opened the door before Miss Lehr had time to get away; she gave a small squeal of dismay, a bunchy figure in a hair-net.

'Excuse me.'

'Oh, it's quite all right. How long will Mass take, father?'

'There will be a great many communicants. Perhaps three-quarters of an hour.'

'I will have some coffee ready for you—and sandwiches.'

'You must not bother.'

'Oh, we can't send you away hungry.'

She followed him to the door, standing a little behind him, so as not to be seen by anything or anybody in the wide empty early world. The grey light uncurled across the pastures; at the gate the tulipan tree bloomed for yet another day; very far off, beyond the little stream where he had bathed, the people were walking up from the village on the way to Mr Lehr's barn—they were too small at that distance to be human. He had a sense of expectant happiness all round him, waiting for him to take part, like an audience of children at a cinema or a rodeo; he was aware of how happy he might have been if he had left nothing behind him across the range except a few bad memories. A man should always prefer peace to violence, and he was going towards peace.

'You have been very good to me, Miss Lehr.'

How odd it had seemed at first to be treated as a guest, not as a criminal or a bad priest. These were heretics—it never occurred to them that he was not a good man: they hadn't the prying insight of fellow Catholics.

'We've enjoyed having you, father. But you'll be glad to be away. Las Casas is a fine city. A very moral place, as Mr Lehr always says. If you meet Father Quintana you must remember us to him—he was here three years ago.'

A bell began to ring. They had brought the church bell down from the tower and hung it outside Mr Lehr's barn; it was like any Sunday anywhere.

'I've sometimes wished,' Miss Lehr said, 'that I could go to church.'

'Why not?'

'Mr Lehr wouldn't like it. He's very strict. But it happens so seldom nowadays—I don't suppose there'll be another service now for another three years.'

'I will come back before then.'

'Oh no,' Miss Lehr said. 'You won't do that. It's a hard journey and Las Casas is a fine city. They have electric light in the streets: there are two hotels. Father Quintana promised to come back—but there are Christians everywhere, aren't there? Why should he come back here? It isn't even as if we were really badly off.'

A little group of Indians passed the gate, gnarled tiny creatures of the Stone Age. The men in short smocks walked with long poles, and the women with black plaits and knocked-about faces carried their babies on their backs. 'The Indians have heard you are here,' Miss Lehr said. 'They've walked fifty miles—I shouldn't be surprised.' They stopped at the gate and watched him; when he looked at them they went down on their knees and crossed themselves—the strange elaborate mosaic touching the nose and ears and chin. 'My brother gets so angry,' Miss Lehr said, 'if he sees somebody go on his knees to a priest, but I don't see that it does any harm.'

Round the corner of the house the mules were stamping—the guide must have brought them out to give them their maize. They were slow feeders, you had to give them a long start. It was time to begin Mass and be gone. He could smell the early morning. The world was still fresh and green, and in the village below the pastures a few dogs barked. The alarm clock tick-tocked in Miss Lehr's hand. He said, 'I must be going now.' He felt an odd reluctance to leave Miss Lehr and the house and the brother sleeping in the inside room. He was aware of a mixture of tenderness and dependence. When a man wakes after a dangerous operation he puts a special value upon the first face he sees as the anaesthetic wears away.

He had no vestments, but the Masses in this village were nearer to the old parish days than any he had known in the last eight years—there was no fear of interruption, no hurried taking of the sacraments as the police approached. There was even an altar stone brought from the locked church. But because it was so peaceful he was all the more aware of his own sin as he prepared to take the Elements—'Let not the participation of thy Body, O Lord Jesus Christ, which I, though unworthy, presume to receive, turn to my judgment and condemnation.' A virtuous man can almost cease to believe in Hell, but he carried Hell about with him. Sometimes at night he dreamed of it. *Domine, non sum dignus . . . domine, non sum dignus. . . .* Evil ran like malaria in his veins. He remembered a dream he had had of a big grassy arena lined with the statues of the saints—but the saints were alive, they turned their eyes this way and that, waiting for something. He waited, too, with an awful expectancy. Bearded Peters and Pauls, with Bibles pressed to their breasts, watched some entrance behind his back he couldn't see—it had the menace of a beast. Then a marimba began to play, tinkly and repetitive, a firework exploded, and Christ danced into the arena—danced and postured with a bleeding painted face, up and down, up and down, grimacing like a prostitute, smiling and suggestive. He woke with the sense of complete despair that a man might feel finding the only money he possessed was counterfeit.

'. . . and we saw his glory, the glory as of the only-begotten of the Father, full of grace and truth.' Mass was over.

In three days, he told himself, I shall be in Las Casas: I shall have confessed and been absolved, and the thought of the child on the rubbish-heap came automatically back to him with painful love. What was the good of confession when you loved the result of your crime?

The people knelt as he made his way down the barn. He saw the little group of Indians: women whose children he had baptised: Pedro: the man from the cantina was there too, kneeling with his face buried in his plump hands, a chain of beads falling between the fingers. He looked a good man: perhaps he was a good man. Perhaps, the priest thought, I have lost the faculty of judging—that woman in prison may have been the best person there. A horse cried in the early day, tethered to a tree, and all the freshness of the morning came in through the open door.

Two men waited beside the mules; the guide was adjusting a stirrup, and beside him, scratching under the arm-pit, awaiting his coming with a doubtful and defensive smile, stood the half-caste. He was like the small pain that reminds a man of his sickness, or perhaps like the unexpected memory which proves that love after all isn't dead. 'Well,' the priest said, 'I didn't expect you here.'

'No, father, of course not.' He scratched and smiled.

'Have you brought the soldiers with you?'

'What things you do say, father,' he protested with a callow giggle. Behind him, across the yard and through an open door, the priest could see Miss Lehr putting up his sandwiches. She had dressed, but she still wore her hair-net. She was wrapping the sandwiches carefully in grease-proof paper, and her sedate movements had a curious effect of unreality. It was the half-caste who was real. He said, 'What trick are you playing now?' Had he perhaps bribed his guide to lead him back across the border? He could believe almost anything of that man.

'You shouldn't say things like that, father.'

Miss Lehr passed out of sight, with the soundlessness of a dream.

'No?'

'I'm here, father,' the man seemed to take a long breath for his surprising stilted statement, 'on an errand of mercy.'

The guide finished with one mule and began on the next, shortening the already short Mexican stirrup; the priest giggled nervously. 'An errand of mercy?'

'Well, father, you're the only priest this side of Las Casas, and the man's dying . . .'

'What man?'

'The Yankee.'

'What are you talking about?'

'The one the police wanted. He robbed a bank. You know the one I mean.'

'He wouldn't need me,' the priest said impatiently, remembering the photograph on the peeling wall watching the first communion party.

'Oh, he's a good Catholic, father.' Scratching under his arm-pit, he didn't look at the priest. 'He's dying, and you and I wouldn't like to have on our conscience what that man . . .'

'We shall be lucky if we haven't worse.'

'What do you mean, father?'

The priest said, 'He only killed and robbed. He hasn't betrayed his friends.'

'Holy Mother of God, I've never . . .'

'We both have,' the priest said. He turned to the guide. 'Are the mules ready?'

'Yes, father.'

'We'll start then.' He had forgotten Miss Lehr completely; the other world had stretched a hand across the border, and he was again in the atmosphere of flight.

'Where are you going?' the half-caste said.

'To Las Casas.' He climbed stiffly on to his mule. The half-caste held on to his stirrup-leather, and he was reminded of their first meeting: there was the same mixture of complaint, appeal, abuse. 'You're a fine priest,' he wailed up at him. 'Your bishop ought to hear of this. A man's dying, wants to confess, and just because you want to get to the city . . .'

'Why do you think me such a fool?' the priest said. 'I know why you've come. You're the only one they've got who can recognise me, and they can't follow me into this state. Now if I ask you where this American is, you'll tell me—I know—you don't have to speak—that he's just the other side.'

'Oh no, father, you're wrong there. He's just this side.'

'A mile or two makes no difference.

'It's an awful thing, father,' the half-caste said, 'never to be believed. Just because once—well, I admit it—'

The priest kicked his mule into motion. They passed out of Mr Lehr's yard and turned south; the half-caste trotted at his stirrup.

'I remember,' the priest said, 'that you told me you'd never forget my face.'

'And I haven't,' the man put in triumphantly, 'or I wouldn't be here, would I? Listen, father, I'll admit a lot. You don't know how a reward will tempt a poor man like me. And when you wouldn't trust me, I thought, well, if that's how he feels—I'll show him. But I'm a good Catholic, father, and when a dying man wants a priest . . .'

They climbed the long slope of Mr Lehr's pastures which led to the next range of hills. The air was still fresh, at six in the morning, at three thousand feet; up there to-night it would be very cold—they had another six thousand feet to climb. The priest said uneasily, 'Why should I put my head in *your* noose?' It was too absurd.

'Look, father.' The half-caste was holding up a scrap of paper: the familiar writing caught the priest's attention—the large deliberate handwriting of a child. The paper had been used to wrap up food; it was smeared and greasy. He read, 'The Prince of Denmark is wondering whether he should kill himself or not, whether it is better to go on suffering all the doubts about his father, or by one blow . . .'

'Not that, father, on the other side. That's nothing.'

The priest turned the paper and read a single phrase written in English in blunt pencil: 'For Christ's sake, father . . .' The mule, unbeaten, lapsed into a slow heavy walk; the priest made no attempt to urge it on: this piece of paper left no doubt whatever.

He asked, 'How did this come to you?'

'It was this way, father. I was with the police when they shot him. It was in a village the other side. He picked up a child to act as a screen, but, of course, the soldiers didn't pay any attention. It was only an Indian. They were both shot, but he escaped.'

'Then how . . . ?'

'It was this way, father.' He positively prattled. It appeared that he was afraid of the lieutenant, who resented the fact that the priest had escaped, and so he planned to slip across the border, out of reach. He got his chance at night, and on the way—it was probably on this side of the state line, but who knew where one state began or another ended?—he came on the American. He had been shot in the stomach . . .

'How could he have escaped then?'

'Oh, father, he is a man of superhuman strength.' He was dying, he wanted a priest . . .

'How did he tell you that?'

'It only needed two words, father.' Then, to prove the story, the man had found enough strength to write this note, and so . . . the story had as many holes in it as a sieve. But what remained was this note, like a memorial stone you couldn't overlook.

The half-caste bridled angrily again. 'You don't trust me, father.'

'Oh no,' the priest said. 'I don't trust you.'

'You think I'm lying.'

'Most of it is lies.'

He pulled the mule up and sat thinking, facing south. He was quite certain that this was a trap—probably the half-caste had suggested it—but it was a fact that the American was there, dying. He thought of the deserted banana station where something had happened and the Indian child lay dead on the maize: there was no question at all that he was needed. A man with all that on his soul . . . The oddest thing of all was that he felt quite cheerful; he had never really believed in this peace. He had dreamed of it so often on the other side that now it meant no more to him than a dream. He began to whistle a tune—something he had heard somewhere once. 'I found a rose in my field': it was time he woke up. It wouldn't really have been a good dream—that confession in Las Casas when he would have had to admit, as well as everything else, that he had denied confession to a dying man.

He asked, 'Will the man still be alive?'

'I think so, father,' the half-caste caught him eagerly up.

'How far is it?'

'Four—five hours, father.'

'You can take it in turns to ride the other mule.'

The priest turned his mule back and called out to the guide. The man dismounted and stood inertly there, while he explained. The only remark he made was to the half-caste, motioning him into the saddle, 'Be careful of that saddle-bag. The father's brandy's there.'

They rode slowly back: Miss Lehr was at her gate. She said, 'You forgot the sandwiches, father.'

'Oh yes. Thank you.' He stole a quick look round—it didn't mean a thing to him. He said, 'Is Mr Lehr still asleep?'

'Shall I wake him?'

'No, no. But you will thank him for his hospitality?'

'Yes. And perhaps, father, in a few years we shall see you again? As you said.' She looked curiously at the half-caste, and he stared back through his yellow insulting eyes.

The priest said, 'It's possible,' glancing away with a sly secretive smile.

'Well, good-bye, father. You'd better be off, hadn't you? The sun's getting high.'

'Good-bye, my dear Miss Lehr.' The mestizo slashed impatiently at his mule and stirred it into action.

'Not that way, my man,' Miss Lehr called.

'I have to pay a visit first,' the priest explained, and breaking into an uncomfortable trot he bobbed down behind the mestizo's mule towards the village. They passed the white-washed church—that too belonged to a dream. Life didn't contain churches. The long untidy village street opened ahead of them. The schoolmaster was at his door and waved an ironic greeting, malicious and horn-rimmed. 'Well, father, off with your spoils?'

The priest stopped his mule. He said to the half-caste, 'Really . . . I had forgotten . . .'

'You did well out of the baptisms,' the schoolmaster said. 'It pays to wait a few years, doesn't it?'

'Come on, father,' the half-caste urged him. 'Don't listen to him.' He spat. 'He's a bad man.'

The priest said, 'You know the people here better than anyone. If I leave a gift, will you spend it on things that do no harm—I mean food, blankets—not books?'

'They need food more than books.'

'I have forty-five pesos here . . .'

The mestizo wailed, 'Father, what are you doing . . .?'

'Conscience money?' the schoolmaster said.

'Yes.'

'All the same, of course I thank you. It's good to see a priest with a conscience. It's a stage in evolution,' he said, his glasses flashing in the sunlight, a plump embittered figure in front of his tin-roofed shack, an exile.

They passed the last houses, the cemetery, and began to climb. 'Why, father, why?' the half-caste protested.

'He's not a bad man, he does his best, and I shan't need money again, shall I?' the priest asked, and for quite a while they rode without speaking, while the sun came blindingly out, and the mules' shoulders strained on the steep rocky paths, and the priest began to whistle again—'I have a rose'—the only tune he knew. Once the half-caste started a complaint about something, 'The trouble with you, father, is . . .' but it petered out before it was defined because there wasn't really anything to complain about as they rode steadily north towards the border.

'Hungry?' the priest asked at last.

The half-caste muttered something that sounded angry or derisive.

'Take a sandwich,' the priest said, opening Miss Lehr's packet.

2

'There,' the half-caste said, with a sort of whinny of triumph, as though he had lain innocently all these seven hours under the suspicion of lying. He pointed across the barranca to a group of Indian huts on a peninsula of rock jutting out across the chasm. They were perhaps two hundred yards away, but it would take another hour at least to reach them, winding down a thousand feet and up another thousand.

The priest sat on his mule watching intently; he could see no movement anywhere. Even the look-out, the little platform of twigs built on a mound above the huts, was empty. He said, 'There doesn't seem to be anybody about.' He was back in the atmosphere of desertion.

'Well,' the half-caste said, 'you didn't expect anybody, did you? Except him. He's there. You'll soon find that.'

'Where are the Indians?'

'There you go again,' the man complained. 'Suspicion. Always suspicion.

How should I know where the Indians are? I told you he was quite alone, didn't I?'

The priest dismounted. 'What are you doing now?' the half-caste cried despairingly.

'We shan't need the mules any more. They can be taken back.'

'Not need them? How are you going to get away from here?'

'Oh,' the priest said, 'I won't have to think about that, will I?' He counted out forty pesos and said to the muleteer, 'I hired you for Las Casas. Well, this is your good luck. Six days' pay.'

'You don't want me any more, father?'

'No, I think you'd better get away from here quickly. Leave you-know-what behind.'

The half-caste said excitedly, 'We can't walk all that way, father. Why, the man's dying.'

'We can go just as quickly on our own hooves. Now, friend, be off.' The mestizo watched the mules pick their way along the narrow stony path with a look of wistful greed; they disappeared round a shoulder of rock—crack, crack, crack, the sound of their hooves contracted into silence.

'Now,' the priest said briskly, 'we won't delay any more,' and he started down the path, with a small sack slung over his shoulder. He could hear the half-caste panting after him: his wind was bad. They had probably let him have far too much beer in the capital, and the priest thought, with an odd touch of contemptuous affection, of how much had happened to them both since that first encounter in a village of which he didn't even know the name—the half-caste lying there in the hot noonday rocking his hammock with one naked yellow foot. If he had been asleep at that moment, this wouldn't have happened. It was really shocking bad luck for the poor devil that he was to be burdened with a sin of such magnitude. The priest took a quick look back and saw the big toes protruding like slugs out of the dirty gym shoes; the man picked his way down, muttering all the time—his perpetual grievance didn't help his wind. Poor man, the priest thought, he isn't really bad enough . . .

And he wasn't strong enough either for *this* journey. By the time the priest had reached the bottom of the barranca he was fifty yards behind. The priest sat down on a boulder and mopped his forehead, and the half-caste began to complain long before he was down to his level, 'There isn't so much hurry as all that.' It was almost as though the nearer he got to his treachery the greater the grievance against his victim became.

'Didn't you say he was dying?' the priest asked.

'Oh yes, dying, of course. But that can take a long time.'

'The longer the better for all of us,' the priest said. 'Perhaps you are right. I'll take a rest here.'

But now, like a contrary child, the half-caste wanted to start again. He said, 'You do nothing in moderation. Either you run or you sit.'

'Can I do nothing right?' the priest teased him, and then put in sharply and shrewdly, 'They will let me see him, I suppose?'

'Of course,' the half-caste said and immediately checked himself. 'They, they? Who are you talking about now? First you complain that the place is empty, and then you talk of "they".' He said with tears in his voice, 'You may be a good man but why won't you talk plainly, so that a man can understand you? It's enough to make a man a bad Catholic.'

The priest said, 'You see this sack here. We don't want to carry that any farther. It's heavy. I think a little drink will do us both good. We both need courage don't we?'

'Drink, father?' the half-caste asked with excitement, and watched the priest unpack a bottle. He never took his eyes away while the priest drank. His two fangs stuck greedily out, quivering slightly on the lower lip. Then he too fastened on the mouth. 'It's illegal, I suppose,' the priest said with a giggle, 'on this side of the border—if we are on this side.' He had another draw himself and handed it back: it was soon exhausted—he took the bottle and threw it at a rock and it exploded like shrapnel. The half-caste started. He said, 'Be careful. People might think you'd got a gun.'

'As for the rest,' the priest said, 'we won't need that.'

'You mean there's more of it?'

'Two more bottles—but we can't drink any more in this heat. We'd better leave it here.'

'Why didn't you say it was heavy, father? I'll carry it for you. You've only to ask me to do a thing. I'm willing. Only you just won't ask.'

They set off again uphill, the bottles clinking gently; the sun shone vertically down on the pair of them. It took them the best part of an hour to reach the top of the barranca. Then the watch-tower gaped over their path like an upper jaw and the tops of the huts appeared over the rocks above them. Indians do not build their settlements on a mule path; they prefer to stand aside and see who comes. The priest wondered how soon the police would appear; they were keeping very carefully hidden.

'This way, father.' The half-caste took the lead, scrambling away from the path up the rocks to the little plateau. He looked anxious, almost as if he had expected something to happen before this. There were about a dozen huts; they stood quiet, like tombs against the heavy sky. A storm was coming up.

The priest felt a nervous impatience; he had walked into this trap, the least they could do was to close it quickly, finish everything off. He wondered whether they would suddenly shoot him down from one of the huts. He had come to the very edge of time: soon there would be no to-morrow and no yesterday, just existence going on for ever. He began to wish he had taken a little more brandy. His voice broke uncertainly when he said, 'Well, we are here. Where is this Yankee?'

'Oh yes, the Yankee,' the half-caste said, jumping a little. It was as if for a moment he had forgotten the pretext. He stood there, gaping at the huts, wondering too. He said, 'He was over there when I left him.'

'Well, he couldn't have moved, could he?'

If it hadn't been for that letter he would have doubted the very existence of the American—and if he hadn't seen the dead child too, of course. He began to walk across the little silent clearing towards the hut: would they shoot him before he got to the entrance? It was like walking a plank blindfold: you didn't know at what point you would step off into space for ever. He hiccuped once and knotted his hands behind his back to stop them trembling. He had been glad in a way to turn from Miss Lehr's gate—he had never really believed that he would ever get back to parish work and the daily

Mass and the careful appearances of piety, but all the same you needed to be
a little drunk to die. He got to the door—not a sound anywhere; then a voice
said, 'Father.'

He looked round. The mestizo stood in the clearing with his face
contorted: the two fangs jumped and jumped; he looked frightened.

'Yes, what is it?'

'Nothing, father.'

'Why did you call me?'

'I said nothing,' he lied.

The priest turned and went in.

The American was there all right. Whether he was alive was another
matter. He lay on a straw mat with his eyes closed and his mouth open and
his hands on his belly, like a child with stomach-ache. Pain alters a face—or
else successful crime has its own falsity like politics or piety. He was hardly
recognisable from the news picture on the police station wall; that was
tougher, arrogant, a man who had made good. This was just a tramp's face.
Pain had exposed the nerves and given the face a kind of spurious
intelligence.

The priest knelt down and put his face near the man's mouth, trying to
hear the breathing. A heavy smell came up to him—a mixture of vomit and
cigar smoke and stale drink; it would take more than a few lilies to hide this
corruption. A very faint voice close to his ear said in English, 'Beat it, father.'
Outside the door, in the stormy sunlight, the mestizo stood, staring towards
the hut, a little loose about the knees.

'So you're alive, are you?' the priest said briskly. 'Better hurry. You
haven't got long.'

'Beat it, father.'

'You wanted me, didn't you? You're a Catholic?'

'Beat it,' the voice whispered again, as if those were the only words it could
remember of a lesson learnt some while ago.

'Come now,' the priest said. 'How long is it since you went to confession?'

The eyelids rolled up and astonished eyes looked up at him. The man said
in a puzzled voice, 'Ten years, I guess. What are you doing here anyway?'

'You asked for a priest. Come now. Ten years is a long time.'

'You got to beat it, father,' the man said. He was remembering the lesson
now; lying there flat on the mat with his hands folded on his stomach, any
vitality that was left had accumulated in the brain: he was like a reptile
crushed at one end. He said in a strange voice, 'That bastard . . .' The priest
said furiously, 'What sort of a confession is this? I make a five hours'
journey . . . and all I get out of you are evil words.' It seemed to him horribly
unfair that his uselessness should return with his danger—he couldn't do
anything for a man like this.

'Listen, father . . .' the man said.

'I am listening.'

'You beat it out of here quick. I didn't know . . .'

'I haven't come all this way to talk about myself,' the priest said. 'The
sooner your confession's done, the sooner I will be gone.'

'You don't need to trouble about me. I'm through.'

'You mean damned?' the priest said angrily.

'Sure. Damned,' the man replied, licking blood away from his lips.

'You listen to me,' the priest said, leaning closer to the stale and nauseating smell, 'I have come here to listen to your confession. Do you want to confess?'

'No.'

'Did you when you wrote that note . . .?'

'Maybe.'

'I know what you want to tell me. I know it, do you understand? Let that be. Remember you are dying. Don't depend too much on God's mercy. He has given you this chance. He may not give you another. What sort of a life have you led all these years? Does it seem so grand now? You've killed a lot of people–that's about all. Anybody can do that for a while, and then he is killed too. Just as you are killed. Nothing left except pain.'

'Father.'

'Yes?' The priest gave an impatient sigh, leaning closer. He hoped for a moment that at last he had got the man started on some meagre train of sorrow.

'You take my gun, father. See what I mean? Under my arm.'

'I haven't any use for a gun.'

'Oh yes, you have.' The man detached one hand from his stomach and began to move it slowly up his body. So much effort: it was unbearable to watch. The priest said sharply, 'Lie still. It's not there.' He could see the holster empty under the arm-pit.

'Bastards,' the man said, and his hand lay wearily where it had got to, over his heart; he imitated the prudish attitude of a female statue, one hand over the breast and one upon the stomach. It was very hot in the hut; the heavy light of the storm lay over them.

'Listen, father . . .' The priest sat hopelessly at the man's side; nothing would shift that violent brain towards peace: once, hours ago perhaps, when he wrote that message–but the chance had come and gone. He was whispering now something about a knife. There was a legend believed by many criminals that dead eyes held the picture of what they had last seen–a Christian could believe that the soul did the same, held absolution and peace at the final moment, after a lifetime of the most hideous crime: or sometimes pious men died suddenly in brothels unabsolved and what had seemed a good life went out with the permanent stamp on it of impurity. He had heard men talk of the unfairness of a death-bed repentance–as if it was an easy thing to break the habit of a life whether to do good or evil. One suspected the good of the life that ended badly–or the viciousness that ended well. He made another desperate attempt. He said, 'You believed once. Try and understand–this is your chance. At the last moment. Like the thief. You have murdered men–children perhaps,' he added, remembering the little black heap under the cross. 'But that need not be so important. It only belongs to this life, a few years–it's over already. You can drop it all here, in this hut, and go on for ever . . .' He felt sadness and longing at the vaguest idea of a life he couldn't lead himself . . . words like peace, glory, love.

'Father,' the voice said urgently, 'you let me be. You look after yourself. You take my knife . . .' The hand began its weary march again–this time towards the hip. The knees crooked up in an attempt to roll over, and then the whole body gave up the effort, the ghost, everything.

The priest hurriedly whispered the words of conditional absolution, in case, for one second before it crossed the border, the spirit had repented, but it was more likely that it had gone over still seeking its knife, bent on vicarious violence. He prayed: 'O merciful God, after all he was thinking of me, it was for my sake . . .' but he prayed without conviction. At the best, it was only one criminal trying to aid the escape of another—whichever way you looked, there wasn't much merit in either of them.

<hr>

3

<hr>

A voice said, 'Well, have you finished now?'

The priest got up and made a small scared gesture of assent. He recognised the police officer who had given him money at the prison, a dark smart figure in the doorway with the stormlight glinting on his leggings. He had one hand on his revolver and he frowned sourly in at the dead gunman. 'You didn't expect to see me,' he said.

'Oh, but I did,' the priest said. 'I must thank you.'

'Thank me, what for?'

'For letting me stay alone with him.'

'I am not a barbarian,' the officer said. 'Will you come out now, please? It's no use at all your trying to escape. You can see that,' he added, as the priest emerged and looked round at the dozen armed men who surrounded the hut.

'I've had enough of escaping,' he said. The half-caste was no longer in sight; the heavy clouds were piling up the sky: they made the real mountains look like little bright toys below them. He sighed and giggled nervously. 'What a lot of trouble I had getting across those mountains, and now . . . here I am . . .'

'I never believed you would return.'

'Oh well, lieutenant, you know how it is. Even a coward has a sense of duty.' The cool fresh wind which sometimes blows across before a storm breaks touched his skin. He said with badly-affected ease, 'Are you going to shoot me now?'

The lieutenant said again sharply, 'I am not a barbarian. You will be tried . . . properly.'

'What for?'

'For treason.'

'I have to go all the way back there?'

'Yes. Unless you try to escape.' He kept his hand on his gun as if he didn't trust the priest a yard. He said, 'I could swear that somewhere . . .'

'Oh yes,' the priest said. 'You have seen me twice. When you took a hostage from my village . . . you asked my child: "Who is he?" She said: "My father," and you let me go.' Suddenly the mountains ceased to exist: it was as if somebody had dashed a handful of water into their faces.

'Quick,' the lieutenant said, 'into that hut.' He called out to one of the men. 'Bring us some boxes so that we can sit.'

The two of them joined the dead man in the hut as the storm came up all round them. A soldier dripping with rain carried in two packing-cases. 'A candle,' the lieutenant said. He sat down on one of the cases and took out his revolver. He said, 'Sit down, there, away from the door, where I can see you.' The soldier lit a candle and stuck it in its own wax on the hard earth floor, and the priest sat down, close to the American; huddled up in his attempt to get at his knife he gave an effect of wanting to reach his companion, to have a word or two in private. They looked two of a kind, dirty and unshaved: the lieutenant seemed to belong to a different class altogether. He said with contempt, 'So you have a child?'

'Yes,' the priest said.

'You—a priest?'

'You mustn't think they are all like me.' He watched the candlelight blink on the bright buttons. He said, 'There are good priests and bad priests. It is just that I am a bad priest.'

'Then perhaps we will be doing your Church a service . . .'

'Yes.'

The lieutenant looked sharply up as if he thought he was being mocked. He said, 'You told me twice. That I had seen you twice.'

'Yes, I was in prison. And you gave me money.'

'I remember.' He said furiously, 'What an appalling mockery. To have had you and then to let you go. Why, we lost two men looking for you. They'd be alive to-day . . .' The candle sizzled as the drops of rain came through the roof. 'This American wasn't worth two lives. He did no real harm.'

The rain poured ceaselessly down. They sat in silence. Suddenly the lieutenant said, 'Keep your hand away from your pocket.'

'I was only feeling for a pack of cards. I thought perhaps it would help to pass the time . . .'

'I don't play cards,' the lieutenant said harshly.

'No, no. Not a game. Just a few tricks I can show you. May I?'

'All right. If you wish to.'

Mr Lehr had given him an old pack of cards. The priest said, 'Here, you see, are three cards. The ace, the king and the jack. Now,' he spread them fanwise out on the floor, 'tell me which is the ace.'

'This, of course,' the lieutenant said grudgingly, showing no interest.

'But you are wrong,' the priest said, turning it up. 'That is the jack.'

The lieutenant said contemptuously, 'A game for gamblers—or children.'

'There is another trick,' the priest said, 'called Fly-away Jack. I cut the pack into three—so. And I take this Jack of Hearts and I put it into the centre pack—so. Now I tap the three packs.' His face lit up as he spoke—it was such a long time since he had handled cards—he forgot the storm, the dead man and the stubborn unfriendly face opposite him. 'I say Fly-away Jack'—he cut the left-hand pack in half and disclosed the jack—'and there he is.'

'Of course there are two jacks.'

'See for yourself.' Unwillingly the lieutenant leant forward and inspected the centre pack. He said, 'I suppose you tell the Indians that that is a miracle of God.'

'Oh no,' the priest giggled, 'I learnt it from an Indian. He was the richest man in the village. Do you wonder? with such a hand. No, I used to show the tricks at any entertainments we had in the parish—for the Guilds, you know.'

A look of physical disgust crossed the lieutenant's face. He said, 'I remember those Guilds.'

'When you were a boy?'

'I was old enough to know . . .'

'Yes?'

'The trickery.' He broke out furiously with one hand on his gun, as though it had crossed his mind that it would be better to eliminate this beast, now, at this instant, for ever. 'What an excuse it all was, what a fake. Sell all and give to the poor—that was the lesson, wasn't it? And Señora So-and-so, the druggist's wife, would say the family wasn't really deserving of charity, and Señor This, That and the Other would say that if they starved, what else did they deserve, they were Socialists anyway, and the priest— you—would notice who had done his Easter duty and paid his Easter offering.' His voice rose—a policeman looked into the hut anxiously and withdrew again through the lashing rain. 'The Church was poor, the priest was poor, therefore everyone should sell all and give to the Church.'

The priest said, 'You are so right.' He added quickly, 'Wrong too, of course.'

'How do you mean?' the lieutenant asked savagely. 'Right? Won't you even defend . . .?'

'I felt at once that you were a good man when you gave me money at the prison.'

The lieutenant said, 'I only listen to you because you have no hope. No hope at all. Nothing you say will make any difference.'

'No.'

He had no intention of angering the police officer, but he had had very little practice the last eight years in talking to any but a few peasants and Indians. Now something in his tone infuriated the lieutenant. He said, 'You're a danger. That's why we kill you. I have nothing against you, you understand, as a man.'

'Of course not. It's God you're against. I'm the sort of man you shut up every day—and give money to.'

'No, I don't fight against a fiction.'

'But I'm not worth fighting, am I? You've said so. A liar, a drunkard. That man's worth a bullet more than I am.'

'It's your ideas.' The lieutenant sweated a little in the hot steamy air. He said, 'You are so cunning, you people. But tell me this—what have you ever done in Mexico for *us*? Have you ever told a landlord he shouldn't beat his peon—oh yes, I know, in the confessional perhaps, and it's your duty, isn't it, to forget it at once. You come out and have dinner with him and it's your duty not to know that he has murdered a peasant. That's all finished. He's left it behind in your box.'

'Go on,' the priest said. He sat on the packing-case with his hands on his knees and his head bent; he couldn't, though he tried, keep his mind on what

the lieutenant was saying. He was thinking–forty-eight hours to the capital.
To-day is Sunday. Perhaps on Wednesday I shall be dead. He felt it as a
treachery that he was more afraid of the pain of bullets than of what came
after.

'Well, we have ideas too,' the lieutenant was saying. 'No more money for
saying prayers, no more money for building places to say prayers in. We'll
give people food instead, teach them to read, give them books. We'll see they
don't suffer.'

'But if they want to suffer . . .'

'A man may want to rape a woman. Are we to allow it because he wants to?
Suffering is wrong.'

'And you suffer all the time,' the priest commented, watching the sour
Indian face behind the candle-flame. He said, 'It sounds fine, doesn't it?
Does the jefe feel like that too?'

'Oh, we have our bad men.'

'And what happens afterwards? I mean after everybody has got enough to
eat and can read the right books–the books you let them read?'

'Nothing. Death's a fact. We don't try to alter facts.'

'We agree about a lot of things,' the priest said, idly dealing out his cards.
'We have facts, too, we don't try to alter–that the world's unhappy whether
you are rich or poor–unless you are a saint, and there aren't many of those.
It's not worth bothering too much about a little pain here. There's one belief
we both of us have–that we'll all be dead in a hundred years.' He fumbled,
trying to shuffle, and bent the cards: his hands were not steady.

'All the same, you're worried now about a little pain,' the lieutenant said
maliciously, watching his fingers.

'But I'm not a saint,' the priest said. 'I'm not even a brave man.' He looked
up apprehensively: light was coming back: the candle was no longer
necessary. It would soon be clear enough to start the long journey back. He
felt a desire to go on talking, to delay even by a few minutes the decision to
start. He said, 'That's another difference between us. It's no good your
working for your end unless you're a good man yourself. And there won't
always be good men in your party. Then you'll have all the old starvation,
beating, get-rich-anyhow. But it doesn't matter so much my being a
coward–and all the rest. I can put God into a man's mouth just the
same–and I can give him God's pardon. It wouldn't make any difference to
that if every priest in the Church was like me.'

'That's another thing I don't understand,' the lieutenant said, 'why
you–of all people–should have stayed when the others ran.'

'They didn't all run,' the priest said.

'But why did you stay?'

'Once,' the priest said, 'I asked myself that. The fact is, a man isn't
presented suddenly with two courses to follow: one good and one bad. He
gets caught up. The first year–well, I didn't believe there was really any
cause to run. Churches have been burnt before now. You know how often. It
doesn't mean much. I thought I'd stay till next month, say, and see if things
were better. Then–oh, you don't know how time can slip by.' It was quite
light again now: the afternoon rain was over: life had to go on. A policeman
passed the entrance of the hut and looked in curiously at the pair of them.

'Do you know I suddenly realised that I was the only priest left for miles around? The law which made priests marry finished them. They went: they were quite right to go. There was one priest in particular—he had always disapproved of me. I have a tongue, you know, and it used to wag. He said—quite rightly—that I wasn't a firm character. He escaped. It felt—you'll laugh at this—just as it did at school when a bully I had been afraid of—for years—got too old for any more teaching and was turned out. You see, I didn't have to think about anybody's opinion any more. The people—they didn't worry me. They liked me.' He gave a weak smile, sideways, towards the humped Yankee.

'Go on,' the lieutenant said moodily.

'You'll know all there is to know about me at this rate,' the priest said, with a nervous giggle, 'by the time I get to, well, prison.'

'It's just as well. To know an enemy, I mean.'

'That other priest was right. It was when he left I began to go to pieces. One thing went after another. I got careless about my duties. I began to drink. It would have been much better, I think, if I had gone too. Because pride was at work all the time. Not love of God.' He sat bowed on the packing-case, a small plump man in Mr Lehr's cast-off clothes. He said, 'Pride was what made the angels fall. Pride's the worst thing of all. I thought I was a fine fellow to have stayed when the others had gone. And then I thought I was so grand I could make my own rules. I gave up fasting, daily Mass. I neglected my prayers—and one day because I was drunk and lonely—well, you know how it was, I got a child. It was all pride. Just pride because I'd stayed. I wasn't any use, but I stayed. At least, not much use. I'd got so that I didn't have a hundred communicants a month. If I'd gone I'd have given God to twelve times that number. It's a mistake one makes—to think just because a thing is difficult or dangerous . . .' He made a flapping motion with his hands.

The lieutenant said in a tone of fury, 'Well, you're going to be a martyr—you've got that satisfaction.'

'Oh no. Martyrs are not like me. They don't think all the time—if I had drunk more brandy I shouldn't be so afraid.'

The lieutenant said sharply to a man in the entrance, 'Well, what is it? What are you hanging round for?'

'The storm's over, lieutenant. We wondered when we were to start?'

'We start immediately.'

He got up and put back the pistol in his holster. He said, 'Get a horse ready for the prisoner. And have some men dig a grave quickly for the Yankee.'

The priest put the cards in his pocket and stood up. He said, 'You have listened very patiently . . .'

'I am not afraid,' the lieutenant said, 'of other people's ideas.'

Outside the ground was steaming after the rain: the mist rose nearly to their knees: the horses stood ready. The priest mounted, but before they had time to move a voice made the priest turn—the same sullen whine he had heard so often. 'Father.' It was the half-caste.

'Well, well,' the priest said. 'You again.'

'Oh, I know what you're thinking,' the half-caste said. 'There's not much charity in you, father. You thought all along I was going to betray you.'

'Go,' the lieutenant said sharply. 'You've done your job.'

'May I have one word, lieutenant?' the priest asked.

'You're a good man, father,' the mestizo cut quickly in, 'but you think the worst of people. I just want your blessing, that's all.'

'What is the good? You can't sell a blessing,' the priest said.

'It's just because we won't see each other again. And I didn't want you to go off there thinking ill things . . .'

'You are so superstitious,' the priest said. 'You think my blessing will be like a blinker over God's eyes. I can't stop Him knowing all about it. Much better go home and pray. Then if He gives you grace to feel sorry, give away the money . . .'

'What money, father?' The half-caste shook his stirrup angrily. 'What money? There you go again . . .'

The priest sighed. He felt empty with the ordeal. Fear can be more tiring than a long monotonous ride. He said, 'I'll pray for you,' and beat his horse into position beside the lieutenant's.

'And I'll pray for you, father,' the half-caste announced complacently. Once the priest looked back as his horse poised for the steep descent between the rocks. The half-caste stood alone among the huts, his mouth a little open, showing the two long fangs. He might have been snapped in the act of shouting some complaint or some claim–that he was a good Catholic perhaps; one hand scratched under the arm-pit. The priest waved his hand; he bore no grudge because he expected nothing else of anything human and he had one cause at least for satisfaction–that yellow and unreliable face would be absent 'at the death'.

* * *

'You're a man of education,' the lieutenant said. He lay across the entrance of the hut with his head on his rolled cape and his revolver by his side. It was night, but neither man could sleep. The priest, when he shifted, groaned a little with stiffness and cramp. The lieutenant was in a hurry to get home, and they had ridden till midnight. They were down off the hills and in the marshy plain. Soon the whole State would be subdivided by swamp. The rains had really begun.

'I'm not that. My father was a storekeeper.'

'I mean, you've been abroad. You can talk like a Yankee. You've had schooling.'

'Yes.'

'I've had to think things out for myself. But there are some things which you don't have to learn in a school. That there are rich and poor.' He said in a low voice, 'I've shot three hostages because of you. Poor men. It made me hate you.'

'Yes,' the priest admitted, and tried to stand to ease the cramp in his right thigh. The lieutenant sat quickly up, gun in hand: 'What are you doing?'

'Nothing. Just cramp. That's all.' He lay down again with a groan.

The lieutenant said, 'Those men I shot. They were my own people. I wanted to give them the whole world.'

'Well, who knows? Perhaps that's what you did.'

The lieutenant spat suddenly, viciously, as if something unclean had got upon his tongue. He said, 'You always have answers which mean nothing.'

'I was never any good at books,' the priest said. 'I haven't any memory. But there was one thing always puzzled me about men like yourself. You hate the rich and love the poor. Isn't that right?'

'Yes.'

'Well, if I hated you, I wouldn't want to bring up my child to be like you. It's not sense.'

'That's just twisting . . .'

'Perhaps it is. I've never got your ideas straight. We've always said the poor are blessed and the rich are going to find it hard to get into heaven. Why should we make it hard for the poor man too? Oh, I know we are told to give to the poor, to see they are not hungry—hunger can make a man do evil just as much as money can. But why should we give the poor power? It's better to let him die in dirt and wake in heaven—so long as we don't push his face in the dirt.'

'I hate your reasons,' the lieutenant said. 'I don't want reasons. If you see somebody in pain, people like you reason and reason. You say—pain's a good thing, perhaps he'll be better for it one day. I want to let my heart speak.'

'At the end of a gun.'

'Yes. At the end of a gun.'

'Oh well, perhaps when you're my age you'll know the heart's an untrustworthy beast. The mind is too, but it doesn't talk about love. Love. And a girl puts her head under water or a child's strangled, and the heart all the time says love, love.'

They lay quiet for a while in the hut. The priest thought the lieutenant was asleep until he spoke again. 'You never talk straight. You say one thing to me—but to another man, or a woman, you say, "God is love." But you think that stuff won't do down with me, so you say different things. Things you think I'll agree with.'

'Oh,' the priest said, 'that's another thing altogether—God is love. I don't say the heart doesn't feel a taste of it, but what a taste. The smallest glass of love mixed with a pint pot of ditch-water. We wouldn't recognise that love. It might even look like hate. It would be enough to scare us—God's love. It set fire to a bush in the desert, didn't it, and smashed open graves and set the dead walking in the dark. Oh, a man like me would run a mile to get away if he felt that love around.'

'You don't trust him much, do you? He doesn't seem a grateful kind of God. If a man served me as well as you've served him, well, I'd recommend him for promotion, see he got a good pension . . . if he was in pain, with cancer, I'd put a bullet through his head.'

'Listen,' the priest said earnestly, leaning forward in the dark, pressing on a cramped foot, 'I'm not as dishonest as you think I am. Why do you think I tell people out of the pulpit that they're in danger of damnation if death catches them unawares? I'm not telling them fairy stories I don't believe myself. I don't know a thing about the mercy of God: I don't know how awful the human heart looks to Him. But I do know this—that if there's ever been a single man in this state damned, then I'll be damned too.' He said slowly, 'I wouldn't want it to be any different. I just want justice, that's all.'

*   *   *

'We'll be in before dark,' the lieutenant said. Six men rode in front and six behind; sometimes, in the belts of forest between the arms of the river, they had to ride in single file. The lieutenant didn't speak much, and once, when two of his men struck up a song about a fat shopkeeper and his woman, he told them savagely to be silent. It wasn't a very triumphal procession. The priest rode with a weak grin fixed on his face; it was like a mask he had stuck on, so that he could think quietly without anyone noticing. What he thought about mostly was pain.

'I suppose,' the lieutenant said, scowling ahead, 'you're hoping for a miracle.'

'Excuse me. What did you say?'

'I said I suppose you're hoping for a miracle.'

'No.'

'You believe in them, don't you?'

'Yes. But not for me. I'm no more good to anyone, so why should God keep me alive?'

'I can't think how a man like you can believe in those things. The Indians, yes. Why, the first time they see an electric light they think it's a miracle.'

'And I dare say the first time you saw a man raised from the dead you might think so too.' He giggled unconvincingly behind the smiling mask. 'Oh, it's funny, isn't it? It isn't a case of miracles not happening—it's just a case of people calling them something else. Can't you see the doctors round the dead man? He isn't breathing any more, his pulse has stopped, his heart's not beating: he's dead. Then somebody gives him back his life, and they all—what's the expression?—reserve their opinion. They won't say it's a miracle, because that's a word they don't like. Then it happens again and again perhaps—because God's about on earth—and they say: these aren't miracles, it is simply that we have enlarged our conception of what life is. Now we know you can be alive without pulse, breath, heart-beats. And they invent a new word to describe that state of life, and they say science has disproved a miracle.' He giggled again. 'You can't get round them.'

They were out of the forest track on to a hard-beaten road, and the lieutenant dug in his spur and the whole cavalcade broke into a canter. They were nearly home now. The lieutenant said grudgingly, 'You aren't a bad fellow. If there's anything I can do for you . . .'

'If you would give permission for me to confess . . .'

The first houses came into sight, little hard-baked houses of earth falling into ruin, a few classical pillars just plaster over mud, and a dirty child playing in the rubble.

The lieutenant said, 'But there's no priest.'

'Padre José.'

'Oh, Padre José,' the lieutenant said with contempt, 'he's no good for you.'

'He's good enough for me. It's not likely I'd find a saint here, is it?'

The lieutenant rode on for a little while in silence; they came to the cemetery, full of chipped angels, and passed the great portico with its black letters, 'Silencio'. He said, 'All right. You can have him.' He wouldn't look at the cemetery as they went by—there was the wall where prisoners were shot. The road went steeply downhill towards the river; on the right, where the cathedral had been, the iron swings stood empty in the hot afternoon. There was a sense of desolation everywhere, more of it than in the mountains because a lot of life had once existed here. The lieutenant thought: No pulse, no breath, no heart-beat, but it's still life—we've only got to find a name for it. A small boy watched them pass; he called out to the lieutenant, 'Lieutenant, have you got him?' and the lieutenant dimly remembered the face—one day in the plaza—a broken bottle, and he tried to smile back, an odd sour grimace, without triumph or hope. One had to begin again with that.

4

The lieutenant waited till after dark and then he went himself. It would be dangerous to send another man because the news would be around the city in no time that Padre José had been permitted to carry out a religious duty in the prison. It was wiser not to let even the jefe know. One didn't trust one's superiors when one was more successful than they were. He knew the jefe wasn't pleased that he had brought the priest in—an escape would have been better from his point of view.

In the patio he could feel himself watched by a dozen eyes. The children clustered there ready to shout at Padre José if he appeared. He wished he had promised the priest nothing, but he was going to keep his word—because it would be a triumph for that old corrupt God-ridden world if it could show itself superior on any point—whether of courage, truthfulness, justice . . .

Nobody answered his knock; he stood darkly in the patio like a petitioner. Then he knocked again, and a voice called, 'A moment. A moment.'

Padre José put his face against the bars of his window and asked, 'Who's there?' He seemed to be fumbling at something near the ground.

'Lieutenant of police.'

'Oh,' Padre José squeaked. 'Excuse me. It is my trousers. In the dark.' He seemed to heave at something and there was a sharp crack, as if his belt or braces had given way. Across the patio the children began to squeak, 'Padre José. Padre José.' When he came to the door he wouldn't look at them, muttering tenderly, 'The little devils.'

The lieutenant said, 'I want you to come to the police station.'

'But I've done nothing. Nothing. I've been so careful.'

'Padre José,' the children squeaked.

He said imploringly, 'If it's anything about a burial, you've been misinformed. I wouldn't even say a prayer.'

'Padre José. Padre José.'

The lieutenant turned and strode across the patio. He said furiously to the faces at the grid, 'Be quiet. Go to bed. At once. Do you hear me?' They dropped out of sight one by one, but immediately the lieutenant's back was turned, they were there again watching.

Padre José said, 'Nobody can do anything with those children.'

A woman's voice said, 'Where are you, José?'

'Here, my dear. It is the police.'

A huge woman in a white night-dress came billowing out at them. It wasn't much after seven; perhaps she lived, the lieutenant thought, in that dress–perhaps she lived in bed. He said, 'Your husband,' dwelling on the term with satisfaction, 'your husband is wanted at the station.'

'Who says so?'

'I do.'

'He's done nothing.'

'I was just saying, my dear . . .'

'Be quiet. Leave the talking to me.'

'You can both stop jabbering,' the lieutenant said. 'You're wanted at the station to see a man–a priest. He wants to confess.'

'To me?'

'Yes. There's no one else.'

'Poor man,' Padre José said. His little pink eyes swept the patio. 'Poor man.' He shifted uneasily, and took a quick furtive look at the sky where the constellations wheeled.

'You won't go,' the woman said.

'It's against the law, isn't it?' Padre José asked.

'You needn't trouble about that.'

'Oh, we needn't, eh?' the woman said. 'I can see through you. You don't want my husband to be let alone. You want to trick him. I know your work. You get people to ask him to say prayers–he's a kind man. But I'd have you remember this–he's a pensioner of the government.'

The lieutenant said slowly, 'This priest–he has been working for years secretly–for *your* Church. We've caught him and, of course, he'll be shot to-morrow. He's not a bad man, and I told him he could see you. He seems to think it will do him good.'

'I know him,' the woman interrupted, 'he's a drunkard. That's all he is.'

'Poor man,' Padre José said. 'He tried to hide here once.'

'I promise you,' the lieutenant said, 'nobody shall know.'

'Nobody know?' the woman cackled. 'Why, it will be all over town. Look at those children there. They never leave José alone.' She went on, 'There'll be no end to it–everybody will be wanting to confess, and the Governor will hear of it, and the pension will be stopped.'

'Perhaps, my dear,' José said, 'it's my duty . . .'

'You aren't a priest any more,' the woman said, 'you're my husband.' She used a coarse word. 'That's your duty now.'

The lieutenant listened to them with acid satisfaction. It was like rediscovering an old belief. He said, 'I can't wait here while you argue. Are you going to come with me?'

'He can't make you,' the woman said.

'My dear, it's only that . . . well . . . I *am* a priest.'

'A priest,' the woman cackled, 'you a priest.' She went off into a peal of laughter, which was taken up tentatively by the children at the window.

Padre José put his fingers up to his pink eyes as if they hurt. He said, 'My dear . . .' and the laughter went on.

'Are you coming?'

Padre José made a despairing gesture–as much as to say, what does one more failure matter in a life like this? He said, 'I don't think it's–possible.'

'Very well,' the lieutenant said. He turned abruptly–he hadn't any more time to waste on mercy, and heard Padre José's voice speak imploringly, 'Tell him I shall pray.' The children had gained confidence; one of them called out sharply, 'Come to bed, José,' and the lieutenant laughed once–a poor unconvincing addition to the general laughter which now surrounded Padre José, chiming up all round towards the disciplined constellations he had once known by name.

*   *   *

The lieutenant opened the cell door. It was very dark inside. He shut the door carefully behind him and locked it, keeping his hand on his gun. He said, 'He won't come.'

A little bunched figure in the darkness was the priest. He crouched on the floor like a child playing. He said, 'You mean–not to-night?'

'I mean he won't come at all.'

There was silence for some while, if you could talk of silence where there was always the drill-drill of mosquitoes and the little crackling explosions of beetles against the wall. At last the priest said, 'He was afraid, I suppose . . .'

'His wife wouldn't let him come.'

'Poor man.' He tried to giggle, but no sound could have been more miserable than the half-hearted attempt. His head drooped between his knees; he looked as if he had abandoned everything and been abandoned.

The lieutenant said, 'You had better know everything. You've been tried and found guilty.'

'Couldn't I have been present at my own trial?'

'It wouldn't have made any difference.'

'No.' He was silent, preparing an attitude. Then he asked with a kind of false jauntiness, 'And when, if I may ask . . . ?'

'To-morrow.' The promptness and brevity of the reply called his bluff. His head went down again and he seemed, as far as it was possible to see in the dark, to be biting his nails.

The lieutenant said, 'It's bad being alone on a night like this. If you would like to be transferred to the common cell . . .'

'No, no. I'd rather be alone. I've got plenty to do.' His voice failed, as though he had a heavy cold. He wheezed, 'So much to think about.'

'I should like to do something for you,' the lieutenant said. 'I've brought you some brandy.'

'Against the law?'

'Yes.'

'It's very good of you.' He took the small flask. 'You wouldn't need this, I dare say. But I've always been afraid of pain.'

'We have to die some time,' the lieutenant said. 'It doesn't seem to matter so much when.'

'You're a good man. You've got nothing to be afraid of.'

'You have such, odd ideas,' the lieutenant complained. He said, 'Sometimes I feel you're just trying to talk me round.'

'Round to what?'

'Oh, to letting you escape perhaps–or to believing in the Holy Catholic Church, the communion of saints . . . how does that stuff go?'

'The forgiveness of sins.'

'You don't believe much in that, do you?'

'Oh yes, I believe,' the little man said obstinately.

'Then what are you worried about?'

'I'm not ignorant, you see. I've always known what I've been doing. And I can't absolve myself.'

'Would Father José coming here have made all that difference?'

He had to wait a long while for his answer, and then he didn't understand it when it came. 'Another man . . . it makes it easier . . .'

'Is there nothing more I can do for you?'

'No. Nothing.'

The lieutenant reopened the door; mechanically putting his hand again upon his revolver he felt moody, as though now the last priest was under lock and key, there was nothing left to think about. The spring of action seemed to be broken. He looked back on the weeks of hunting as a happy time which was over now for ever. He felt without a purpose, as if life had drained out of the world. He said with bitter kindness (he couldn't summon up any hate of the small hollow man), 'Try to sleep.'

He was closing the door when a scared voice spoke. 'Lieutenant.'

'Yes.'

'You've seen people shot. People like me.'

'Yes.'

'Does the pain go on–a long time?'

'No, no. A second,' he said roughly, and closed the door, and picked his way back across the whitewashed yard. He went into the office. The pictures of the priest and the gunman were still pinned up on the wall: he tore them down–they would never be wanted again. Then he sat at his desk and put his head upon his hands and fell asleep with utter weariness. He couldn't remember afterwards anything of his dreams except laughter, laughter all the time, and a long passage in which he could find no door.

★   ★   ★

The priest sat on the floor, holding the brandy-flask. Presently he unscrewed the cap and put his mouth to it. The spirit didn't do a thing to him–it might have been water. He put it down again and began some kind of a general confession, speaking in a whisper. He said, 'I have committed fornication.' The formal phrase meant nothing at all: it was like a sentence in a newspaper: you couldn't feel repentance over a thing like that. He started again, 'I have lain with a woman,' and tried to imagine the other priest asking him, 'How many times? Was she married?' 'No.' Without thinking what he was doing, he took another drink of brandy.

As the liquid touched his tongue he remembered his child, coming in out of the glare: the sullen unhappy knowledgeable face. He said, 'Oh God, help her. Damn me, I deserve it, but let her live for ever.' This was the love he should have felt for every soul in the world: all the fear and the wish to save concentrated unjustly on the one child. He began to weep; it was as if he had to watch her from the shore drown slowly because he had forgotten how to swim. He thought: This is what I should feel all the time for everyone, and he tried to turn his brain away towards the half-caste, the lieutenant, even a dentist he had once sat with for a few minutes, the child at the banana station, calling up a long succession of faces, pushing at his attention as if it were a heavy door which wouldn't budge. For those were all in danger too. He prayed, 'God help them,' but in the moment of prayer he switched back to his child beside the rubbish-dump, and he knew it was for her only that he prayed. Another failure.

After a while he began again: 'I have been drunk – I don't know how many times; there isn't a duty I haven't neglected; I have been guilty of pride, lack of charity . . .' The words were becoming formal again, meaning nothing. He had no confessor to turn his mind away from the formula to the fact.

He took another drink of brandy, and getting up with pain because of his cramp he moved to the door and looked through the bars at the hot moony square. He could see the police asleep in their hammocks, and one man who couldn't sleep lazily rocking up and down, up and down. There was an odd silence everywhere, even in the other cells; it was as if the whole world had tactfully turned away to avoid seeing him die. He felt his way back along the wall to the farthest corner and sat down with the flask between his knees. He thought: If I hadn't been so useless, useless. . . . The eight hard hopeless years seemed to him to be only a caricature of service: a few communions, a few confessions, and an endless bad example. He thought: If I had only one soul to offer, so that I could say, Look what I've done. . . . People had died for him, they had deserved a saint, and a tinge of bitterness spread across his mind for their sake that God hadn't thought fit to send them one. Padre José and me, he thought, Padre José and me, and he took a drink again from the brandy flask. He thought of the cold faces of the saints rejecting him.

The night was slower than the last he had spent in prison because he was alone. Only the brandy, which he finished about two in the morning, gave him any sleep at all. He felt sick with fear, his stomach ached, and his mouth was dry with the drink. He began to talk aloud to himself because he couldn't stand the silence any more. He complained miserably, 'It's all very well . . . for saints,' and later, 'How does he know it only lasts a second? How long's a second?' Then he began to cry, beating his head gently against the wall. They had given a chance to Padre José, but they had never given him a chance at all. Perhaps they had got it all wrong – just because he had escaped them for such a time. Perhaps they really thought he would refuse the conditions Padre José had accepted, that he would refuse to marry, that he was proud. Perhaps if he suggested it himself, he would escape yet. The hope calmed him for a while, and he fell asleep with his head against the wall.

He had a curious dream. He dreamed he was sitting at a café table in front of the high altar of the cathedral. About six dishes were spread before him, and he was eating hungrily. There was a smell of incense and an odd sense of elation. The dishes – like all food in dreams – did not taste of much, but he had a sense that when he had finished them, he would have the best dish of all. A priest passed to and fro before the altar saying Mass, but he took no notice: the service no longer seemed to concern him. At last the six plates were empty; someone out of sight rang the sanctus bell, and the serving priest knelt before he raised the Host. But *he* sat on, just waiting, paying no attention to the God over the altar, as though that were a God for other people and not for him. Then the glass by his plate began to fill with wine, and looking up he saw that the child from the banana station was serving him. She said, 'I got it from my father's room.'

'You didn't steal it?'

'Not exactly,' she said in her careful and precise voice.

He said, 'It is very good of you. I had forgotten the code—what did you call it?'

'Morse.'

'That was it. Morse. Three long taps and one short one,' and immediately the taps began: the priest by the altar tapped, a whole invisible congregation tapped along the aisles—three long and one short. He asked, 'What is it?'

'News,' the child said, watching him with a stern, responsible and interested gaze.

When he woke up it was dawn. He woke with a huge feeling of hope which suddenly and completely left him at the first sight of the prison yard. It was the morning of his death. He crouched on the floor with the empty brandy-flask in his hand trying to remember an Act of Contrition. 'O God, I am sorry and beg pardon for all my sins . . . crucified . . . worthy of thy dreadful punishments.' He was confused, his mind was on other things: it was not the good death for which one always prayed. He caught sight of his own shadow on the cell wall; it had a look of surprise and grotesque unimportance. What a fool he had been to think that he was strong enough to stay when others fled. What an impossible fellow I am, he thought, and how useless. I have done nothing for anybody. I might just as well have never lived. His parents were dead—soon he wouldn't even be a memory—perhaps after all he wasn't really Hell-worthy. Tears poured down his face; he was not at the moment afraid of damnation—even the fear of pain was in the background. He felt only an immense disappointment because he had to go to God empty-handed, with nothing done at all. It seemed to him, at that moment, that it would have been quite easy to have been a saint. It would only have needed a little self-restraint and a little courage. He felt like someone who has missed happiness by seconds at an appointed place. He knew now that at the end there was only one thing that counted—to be a saint.

PART IV

Mrs Fellows lay in bed in the hot hotel room, listening to the siren of a boat on the river. She could see nothing because she had a handkerchief soaked in eau-de-Cologne over her eyes and forehead. She called sharply out, 'My dear. My dear,' but nobody replied. She felt that she had been prematurely buried in this big brass family tomb, all alone on two pillows, under a canopy. 'Dear,' she said again sharply, and waited.

'Yes, Trixy?' It was Captain Fellows. He said, 'I was asleep, dreaming . . .'

'Put some more Cologne on this handkerchief, dear. My head's splitting.'

'Yes, Trixy.'

He took the handkerchief away; he looked old and tired and bored – a man without a hobby, walking over to the dressing-table.

'Not too much, dear. It will be days before we can get any more.'

He didn't answer, and she said sharply, 'You heard what I said, dear, didn't you?'

'Yes.'

'You are so silent these days. You don't realise what it is to be ill and alone.'

'Well,' Captain Fellows said, 'you know how it is.'

'But we agreed, dear, didn't we, that it was better just to say nothing at all, ever. We mustn't be morbid.'

'No.'

'We've got our own life to lead.'

'Yes.'

He came across to the bed and laid the handkerchief over his wife's eyes. Then sitting down on a chair, he slipped his hand under the net and felt for her hand. They gave an odd effect of being children, lost in a strange town, without adult care.

'Have you got the tickets?' she asked.

'Yes, dear.'

'I must get up later and pack, but my head hurts so. Did you tell them to collect the boxes?'

'I forgot.'

'You really must try to think of things,' she said weakly and sullenly, 'there's no one else,' and they both sat silent at a phrase they should have avoided. He said suddenly, 'There's a lot of excitement in town.'

'Not a revolution?'

'Oh no. They caught a priest and he's being shot this morning, poor devil. I can't help wondering whether it's the man Coral—I mean the man we sheltered.'

'It's not likely.'

'No.'

'There are so many priests.'

He let go of her hand and going to the window looked out. Boats on the river, a small stony public garden with a bust, and vultures everywhere.

Mrs Fellows said, 'It will be good to be back home. I sometimes thought I should die in this place.'

'Of course not, dear.'

'Well, people do.'

'Yes, they do,' he said glumly.

'Now, dear,' Mrs Fellows said sharply, 'your promise.' She gave a long sigh, 'My poor head.'

'Would you like some aspirin?'

'I don't know where I've put it. Somehow nothing is ever in its place.'

'Shall I go out and get you some more?'

'No, dear, I can't bear to be left alone.' She went on with dramatic brightness, 'I expect I shall be all right when we get home. I'll have a proper doctor then. I sometimes think it's more than a headache. Did I tell you that I'd heard from Norah?'

'No.'

'Get me my glasses, dear, and I'll read you—what concerns us.'

'They're on your bed.'

'So they are.' One of the sailing-boats cast off and began to drift down the wide sluggish stream, going towards the sea. She read with satisfaction, 'Dear Trix: how you have suffered. That scoundrel . . .' She broke abruptly off. 'Oh yes, and then she goes on: "Of course, you and Charles must stay with us for a while until you have found somewhere to live. If you don't mind semi-detached . . ."'

Captain Fellows said suddenly and harshly, 'I'm not going back.'

'"The rent is only fifty-six pounds a year, exclusive, and there's a maid's bathroom."'

'I'm staying.'

'"A cookanheat." What on earth are you saying, dear?'

'I'm not going back.'

'We've been over that so often, dear. You know it would kill me to stay.'

'You needn't stay.'

'But I couldn't go alone,' Mrs Fellows said. 'What on earth would Norah think? Besides—oh, it's absurd.'

'A man here can do a job of work.'

'Picking bananas,' Mrs Fellows said. She gave a little cold laugh. 'And you weren't much good at that.'

He turned furiously towards the bed. 'You don't mind,' he said, 'do you—running away and leaving *her* . . .'

'It wasn't my fault. If you'd been at home . . .' She began to cry hunched up under the mosquito-net. She said, 'I'll never get home alive.'

He came wearily over to the bed and took her hand again. It was no good. They had both been deserted. They had to stick together. 'You won't leave me alone, will you, dear?' she asked. The room reeked of eau-de-Cologne.

'No, dear.'

'You do realise how absurd it is?'

'Yes.'

They sat in silence for a long while, as the morning sun climbed outside and the room got stiflingly hot. Mrs Fellows said at last, 'A penny, dear.'

'What?'

'For your thoughts.'

'I was just thinking of that priest. A queer fellow. He drank. I wonder if it's him.'

'If it is, I expect he deserves all he gets.'

'But the odd thing is—the way she went on afterwards—as if he'd told her things.'

'Darling,' Mrs Fellows repeated, with harsh weakness from the bed, 'your promise.'

'Yes, I'm sorry. I was trying, but it seems to come up all the time.'

'We've got each other, dear,' Mrs Fellows said, and the letter from Norah rustled as she turned her head, swathed in handkerchief, away from the hard outdoor light.

⋆   ⋆   ⋆

Mr Tench bent over the enamel basin washing his hands with pink soap. He said in his bad Spanish, 'You don't need to be afraid. You can tell me directly it hurts.'

The jefe's room had been fixed up as a kind of temporary dentistry—at considerable expense, for it had entailed transporting not only Mr Tench himself but Mr Tench's cabinet, chair, and all sorts of mysterious packing-cases which seemed to contain little but straw and which were unlikely to return empty.

'I've had it for months,' the jefe said. 'You can't imagine the pain . . .'

'It was foolish of you not to call me in sooner. Your mouth's in a very bad state. You are lucky to have escaped pyorrhœa.'

He finished washing and suddenly stood, towel in hand, thinking of something. 'What's the matter?' the jefe asked. Mr Tench woke with a jump, and coming forward to his cabinet, began to lay out the drill needles in a little metallic row of pain. The jefe watched with apprehension. He said, 'Your hand is very jumpy. Are you quite sure you are well enough this morning?'

'It's indigestion,' Mr Tench said. 'Sometimes I have so many spots in front of my eyes I might be wearing a veil.' He fitted a needle into the drill and bent the arm round. 'Now open your mouth very wide.' He began to stuff the jefe's mouth with plugs of cotton. He said, 'I've never seen a mouth as bad as yours—except once.'

The jefe struggled to speak. Only a dentist could have interpreted the muffled and uneasy question.

'He wasn't a patient. I expect someone cured him. You cure a lot of people in this country, don't you, with bullets?'

As he picked and picked at the tooth, he tried to keep up a running fire of conversation; that was how one did things at Southend. He said, 'An odd thing happened to me just before I came up the river. I got a letter from my wife. Hadn't so much as heard from her for—oh, twenty years. Then out of the blue she . . .' he leant closer and levered furiously with his pick: the jefe beat the air and grunted. 'Wash out your mouth,' Mr Tench said, and began grimly to fix his drill. He said, 'What was I talking about? Oh, the wife, wasn't it? Seems she had got religion of some kind. Some sort of a group—Oxford. What would she be doing in Oxford? Wrote to say that she had forgiven me and wanted to make things legal. Divorce, I mean. Forgiven *me*,' Mr Tench said, looking round the little hideous room, lost in thought, with his hand on the drill. He belched and put his other hand against his stomach, pressing, pressing, seeking an obscure pain which was nearly always there. The jefe leant back exhausted with his mouth wide open.

'It comes and goes,' Mr Tench said, losing the thread of his thought completely. 'Of course, it's nothing. Just indigestion. But it gets me locked.' He stared moodily into the mouth as though a crystal were concealed between the carious teeth. Then, as if he were exerting an awful effort of will, he leant forward, brought the arm of the drill round and began to pedal. Buzz and grate. Buzz and grate. The jefe stiffened all over and clutched the arms of the chair, and Mr Tench's foot went up and down, up and down. The jefe made odd sounds and waved his hands. 'Hold hard,' Mr Tench said, 'hold hard. There's just one tiny corner. Nearly finished. There she comes. There.' He stopped and said, 'Good God, what's that?'

He left the jefe altogether and went to the window. In the yard below a squad of police had just grounded their arms. With his hand on his stomach he protested, 'Not another revolution?'

The jefe levered himself upright and spat out a gag. 'Of course not,' he said. 'A man's being shot.'

'What for?'

'Treason.'

'I thought you generally did it,' Mr Tench said, 'up by the cemetery?' A horrid fascination kept him by the window: this was something he had never seen. He and the vultures looked down together on the little white-washed courtyard.

'It was better not to this time. There might have been a demonstration. People are so ignorant.'

A small man came out of a side door: he was held up by two policemen, but you could tell that he was doing his best—it was only that his legs were not fully under control. They paddled him across to the opposite wall; an officer tied a handkerchief round his eyes. Mr Tench thought: But I know him. Good God, one ought to do something. This was like seeing a neighbour shot.

The jefe said, 'What are you waiting for? The air gets into this tooth.'

Of course there was nothing to do. Everything went very quickly like a routine. The officer stepped aside, the rifles went up, and the little man suddenly made jerky movements with his arms. He was trying to say something: what was the phrase they were always supposed to use? That was routine too, but perhaps his mouth was too dry, because nothing came out except a word that sounded like 'Excuse'. The crash of the rifles shook Mr Tench: they seemed to vibrate inside his own guts: he felt sick and shut his eyes. Then there was a single shot, and opening them again he saw the officer stuffing his gun back into his holster, and the little man was a routine-heap beside the wall—something unimportant which had to be cleared away. Two knock-kneed men approached quickly. This was an arena, and the bull was dead, and there was nothing more to wait for any more.

'Oh,' the jefe moaned from the chair, 'the pain, the pain.' He implored Mr Tench, 'Hurry,' but Mr Tench was lost in thought beside the window, one hand automatically seeking in his stomach for the hidden uneasiness. He remembered the little man rising bitterly and hopelessly from his chair that blinding afternoon to follow the child out of town; he remembered a green watering-can, the photo of the children, that cast he was making out of sand for a split palate.

'The filling,' the jefe pleaded, and Mr Tench's eyes went to the gold on the glass dish. Currency—he would insist on foreign currency: this time he was going to clear out, clear out for good. In the yard everything had been tidied away; a man was throwing sand out of a spade, as if he were filling a grave. But there was no grave: there was nobody there: an appalling sense of loneliness came over Mr Tench, doubling him with indigestion. The little fellow had spoken English and knew about his children. He felt deserted.

*   *   *

'And now,' the woman's voice swelled triumphantly, and the two little girls with beady eyes held their breath, 'the great testing day had come.' Even the boy showed interest, standing by the window, looking out into the dark curfew-emptied street—this was the last chapter, and in the last chapter things always happened violently. Perhaps all life was like that—dull and then a heroic flurry at the end.

'When the Chief of Police came to Juan's cell he found him on his knees, praying. He had not slept at all, but had spent his last night preparing for martyrdom. He was quite calm and happy, and smiling at the Chief of Police, he asked him if he had come to lead him to the banquet. Even that evil man, who had persecuted so many innocent people, was visibly moved.'

If only it would get on towards the shooting, the boy thought: the shooting never failed to excite him, and he always waited anxiously for the *coup de grâce*.

'They led him out into the prison yard. No need to bind those hands now busy with his beads. In that short walk to the wall of execution, did young Juan look back on those few, those happy years he had so bravely spent? Did he remember days in the seminary, the kindly rebukes of his elders, the moulding discipline, days, too, of frivolity when he acted Nero before the old bishop? Nero was here beside him, and this the Roman amphitheatre.'

The mother's voice was getting a little hoarse: she fingered the remaining pages rapidly: it wasn't worth while stopping now, and she raced more and more rapidly on.

'Reaching the wall, Juan turned and began to pray—not for himself, but for his enemies, for the squad of poor innocent Indian soldiers who faced him and even for the Chief of Police himself. He raised the crucifix at the end of his beads and prayed that God would forgive them, would enlighten their ignorance, and bring them at last—as Saul the persecutor was brought—into his eternal kingdom.'

'Had they loaded?' the boy asked.

'What do you mean—"had they loaded"?'

'Why didn't they fire and stop him?'

'Because God decided otherwise.' She coughed and went on: 'The officer gave the command to present arms. In that moment a smile of complete adoration and happiness passed over Juan's face. It was as if he could see the arms of God open to receive him. He had always told his mother and sisters that he had a premonition that he would be in heaven before them. He would say with a whimsical smile to his mother, the good but over-careful housewife: "I will have tidied everything up for you." Now the moment had come, the officer gave the order to fire, and—' She had been reading too fast because it was past the little girls' bedtime and now she was thwarted by a fit of hiccups. 'Fire,' she repeated, 'and . . .'

The two little girls sat placidly side by side—they looked nearly asleep—this was the part of the book they never cared much about; they endured it for the sake of the amateur theatricals and the first communion, and of the sister who became a nun and paid a moving farewell to her family in the third chapter.

'Fire,' the mother tried again, 'and Juan, raising both arms above his head, called out in a strong brave voice to the soldiers and the levelled rifles, "Hail, Christ the King." Next moment he fell riddled with a dozen bullets and the officer, stooping over his body, put his revolver close to Juan's ear and pulled the trigger.'

A long sigh came from the window.

'No need to have fired another shot. The soul of the young hero had already left its earthly mansion, and the happy smile on the dead face told even those ignorant men where they would find Juan now. One of the men there that day was so moved by his bearing that he secretly soaked his handkerchief in the martyr's blood, and that handkerchief, cut into a hundred relics, found its way into many pious homes. And now,' the mother went rapidly on, clapping her hands, 'to bed.'

'And that one,' the boy said, 'they shot to-day. Was he a hero too?'

'Yes.'

'The one who stayed with us that time?'

'Yes. He was one of the martyrs of the Church.'

'He had a funny smell,' one of the little girls said.

'You must never say that again,' the mother said. 'He may be one of the saints.'

'Shall we pray to him then?'

The mother hesitated. 'It would do no harm. Of course, before we *know* he is a saint, there will have to be miracles . . .'

'Did he call "Viva el Cristo Rey"?' the boy asked.

'Yes. He was one of the heroes of the faith.'

'And a handkerchief soaked in blood?' the boy went on. 'Did anyone do that?'

The mother said ponderously, 'I have reason to believe . . . Señora

Jiminez told me . . . I think if your father will give me a little money, I shall be able to get a relic.'

'Does it cost money?'

'How else could it be managed? Everybody can't have a piece.'

'No.'

He squatted beside the window, staring out, and behind his back came the muffled sound of small girls going to bed. It brought it home to one–to have had a hero in the house, though it had only been for twenty-four hours. And he was the last. There were no more priests and no more heroes. He listened resentfully to the sound of booted feet coming up the pavement. Ordinary life pressed round him. He got down from the window-seat and picked up his candle–Zapata, Villa, Madero and the rest, they were all dead, and it was people like the man out there who killed them. He felt deceived.

The lieutenant came along the pavement; there was something brisk and stubborn about his walk, as if he were saying at every step, 'I have done what I have done.' He looked in at the boy holding the candle with a look of indecisive recognition. He said to himself, 'I would do much more for him and them, much more; life is never going to be again for them what it was for me,' but the dynamic love which used to move his trigger-finger felt flat and dead. Of course, he told himself, it will come back. It was like love of a woman and went in cycles: he had satisfied himself that morning, that was all. This was satiety. He smiled painfully at the child through the window and said, 'Buenas noches.' The boy was looking at his revolver-holster and he remembered an incident in the plaza when he had allowed a child to touch his gun–perhaps this boy. He smiled again and touched it too–to show he remembered, and the boy crinkled up his face and spat through the window bars, accurately, so that a little blob of spittle lay on the revolver-butt.

*   *   *

The boy went across the patio to bed. He had a little dark room with an iron bedstead that he shared with his father. He lay next the wall and his father would lie on the outside, so that he could come to bed without waking his son. He took off his shoes and undressed glumly by candlelight. He could hear the whispering of prayers in the other room; he felt cheated and disappointed because he had missed something. Lying on his back in the heat he stared up at the ceiling, and it seemed to him that there was nothing in the world but the store, his mother reading, and silly games in the plaza.

But very soon he went to sleep. He dreamed that the priest whom they had shot that morning was back in the house dressed in the clothes his father had lent him and laid out stiffly for burial. The boy sat beside the bed and his mother read out of a very long book all about how the priest had acted in front of the bishop the part of Julius Caesar: there was a fish basket at her feet, and the fish were bleeding, wrapped in her handkerchief. He was very bored and very tired and somebody was hammering nails into a coffin in the passage. Suddenly the dead priest winked at him–an unmistakable flicker of the eyelid, just like that.

He woke and there was the crack, crack on the knocker on the outer door. His father wasn't in bed and there was complete silence in the other room. Hours must have passed. He lay listening. He was frightened, but after a short interval the knocking began again, and nobody stirred anywhere in the house. Reluctantly, he put his feet on the ground – it might be only his father locked out; he lit the candle and wrapped a blanket round himself and stood listening again. His mother might hear it and go, but he knew very well that it was *his* duty. He was the only man in the house.

Slowly he made his way across the patio towards the outer door. Suppose it was the lieutenant come back to revenge himself for the spittle . . . He unlocked the heavy iron door and swung it open. A stranger stood in the street, a tall pale thin man with a rather sour mouth, who carried a small suitcase. He named the boy's mother and asked if this were the señora's house. Yes, the boy said, but she was asleep. He began to shut the door, but a pointed shoe got in the way.

The stranger said, 'I have only just landed. I came up the river to-night. I thought perhaps . . . I have an introduction for the señora from a great friend of hers.'

'She is asleep,' the boy repeated.

'If you would let me come in,' the man said with an odd frightened smile, and suddenly lowering his voice he said to the boy, 'I am a priest.'

'You?' the boy exclaimed.

'Yes,' he said gently. 'My name is Father—' But the boy had already swung the door open and put his lips to his hand before the other could give himself a name.